McDougal Littell

THE LANGUAGE OF
LITERATURE

ANNOTATED TEACHER'S EDITION

GRADE
10

 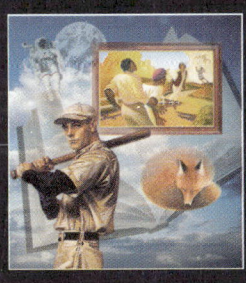    

WARNING: No part of this book may be reproduced or transmitted in any form or by any means, electronic or mechanical, including photocopying and recording, or by any information storage and retrieval system, without prior written permission of McDougal Littell Inc. unless such copying is expressly permitted by federal copyright law. Address inquiries to Manager, Rights and Permissions, McDougal Littell Inc., P.O. Box 1667, Evanston, IL 60204.

ISBN: 0-395-73712-5

Copyright © 1997 by McDougal Littell Inc.
Box 1667, Evanston, Illinois 60204

All rights reserved. Printed in the United States of America.

1 2 3 4 5 6 7 8 9 - DWO - 01 00 99 98 97 96

Table of Contents

Telling Our Story
What Is *The Language of Literature?* T4
Program Authors and Consultants. T5

Overview
Core Components T6
Resource Materials T8
Integrated Technology T8
Assessment Package T9
Access for Students Acquiring English T9

A Closer Look

TEACHING LITERATURE
The Literature Lesson: Pupil Edition T10
The Literature Lesson: Resource Materials T12

INTEGRATING LANGUAGE AND WRITING SKILLS
The Writing Workshops: Pupil Edition T14
Writing and Language: Resource Materials. T17
Special Features of the Pupil Edition T18

THE TEACHER'S EDITION
Unit Support T20
Selection and Writing Workshop Support T22

ASSESSMENT
Assessment Resources. T24

Advice from the Experts
Practical suggestions for planning your school year

Planning Your Year T26
Developing a Classroom Profile: Understanding Learning Styles T28
Developing a Classroom Profile: Students Acquiring English. T29
Planning Your Instruction T30
Setting Up Your Classroom T32
New Technology and the English Classroom T34
Preparing for Assessment T36
Making Connections T39

Annotated Student Text

Additional Unit Resources
Unit 1 Resources. 13A
Unit 2 Resources. 177A
Unit 3 Resources. 351A
Unit 4 Resources. 511A
Unit 5 Resources. 669A
Unit 6 Resources. 807A

THE LANGUAGE OF LITERATURE
Telling Our Story

What Is *The Language of Literature?*

Is it a literature anthology? an integrated language arts series? a new approach to teaching and learning? *The Language of Literature* is all of these things—and much, much more.

CLASSIC STORIES, FRESH VOICES, AND NEW PERSPECTIVES

The powerful mix of selections in *The Language of Literature* reflects the exciting nature of our own society:

- Classic and contemporary literature
- Multicultural perspectives
- A mix of genres
- Authentic readings in a variety of media.

A PROGRAM, NOT A BOOK

The Language of Literature is not simply an anthology with a collection of "extras." It is a seamlessly integrated program that links a student book to comprehensive lesson support; mini-lessons in writing, language, and communication; innovative technology; and access for students with special needs.

AN INTEGRATED APPROACH TO LANGUAGE

The selections in *The Language of Literature* become the springboard to a rich mix of language experiences:

- Writing workshops
- Grammar and vocabulary instruction
- Oral communication activities
- Critical viewing and listening
- Research skills
- Visual and media literacy

A WAY TO MAKE STUDENTS CARE

A strong student-centered approach acknowledges the differences among readers and the experiences they bring to a literary selection or writing experience. Responding options, multimodal activities, access materials for all students, and strategies for using media and technology ensure that students learn in a way that matches their individual learning styles.

A NEW WAY OF SEEING

A striking art program is only the beginning of the series' attention to visual and media literacy. Special activities and features throughout the program teach students that reading literature can be the first step toward reading the people and the world around them.

A SPRINGBOARD TO THE WORLD

Every prereading page, response section, and writing workshop provides meaningful activities and thoughtful connections that link the literature to students' own lives, to other curriculum areas, to their family and community, to other cultures, and to the situations and issues they confront every day in the "real world."

A PARTNER IN TECHNOLOGY

A rich videodisc treasury of images, audio and electronic libraries, Internet connections, and the unique Writing Coach software all support the literature and activities in this series. In addition, lessons in the pupil book model the use of technology to access information, network with others, and produce creative multimedia projects.

A WAY TO CONNECT AND REFLECT

Perhaps most importantly, *The Language of Literature* provides a way for students to connect the literature to the often confusing situations they encounter on the pathway from childhood to adulthood. The thoughtfully chosen selections, carefully crafted themes, and rich variety of learning options connect to students' lives and allow them to reflect on how universal certain experiences are.

TEACHING LITERATURE
(CONTINUED)

The Literature Lesson: Resource Materials

The literature in the Pupil Edition is reinforced and extended by the following teaching tools for students' own use.

UNIT RESOURCE BOOK
Worksheets and tests provide support for all literature selections.

- **Strategic Reading: Literature** reinforce reading strategies and extend the understanding of literary elements.

- **Vocabulary Skillbuilders** bring the teaching of vocabulary to life with motivating exercises.

- **Selection and Unit Tests** stimulate higher order thinking skills as they assess understanding of selections, literary terms, and language skills.

- **Family and Community Involvement** connects unit themes to students' world.

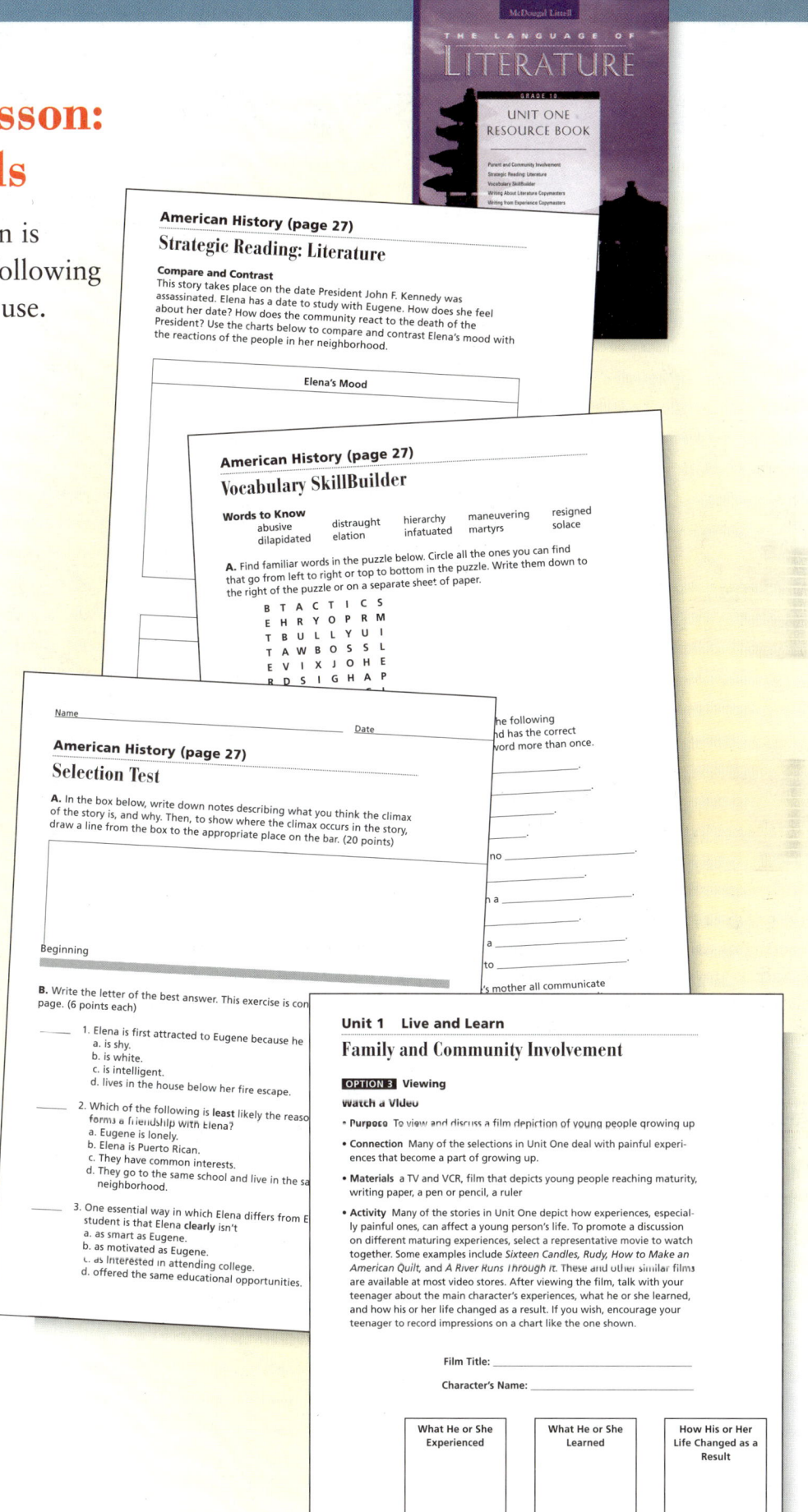

T12 THE LANGUAGE OF LITERATURE TEACHER'S EDITION

RESPONDING OPTIONS

From Personal Response to Critical Analysis Invites student-centered discussion with the response-based approach made famous by McDougal Littell. Includes questions that help students relate the literature to their own lives.

Another Pathway Offers an alternative to typical classroom discussion. Generates full exploration of major issues in the selection.

Literary Concepts Introduces or reviews major literary terms and applies them to the selection just read.

Quickwrites Give students several innovative ways of responding to what they have read through writing.

Alternative Activities Offer opportunities to respond to their reading through multimodal activities.

Words to Know Reinforces vocabulary introduced in the selection with motivating exercises.

Author Biography Makes the authors come to life with interesting, student-friendly information. Includes listings of other works by the authors.

ADDITIONAL RESPONDING OPTIONS

Critic's Corner Gives critical commentary on an author or piece of literature and asks students to respond.

Literary Links Asks students to make connection between selection just read and another selection read at an earlier point in the book.

The Writer's Style Asks students to engage in analysis of style by focusing on stylistic traits of author being studied.

Across the Curriculum Provides cross-curricular activities that invite students to go beyond the selection to investigate new areas of study.

Art Connection Asks students to reflect on a work of fine art included in the selection.

THE LANGUAGE OF LITERATURE TEACHER'S EDITION

A CLOSER LOOK
Teaching Literature

The Literature Lesson: Pupil Edition

Each literature lesson is divided into three sections: Previewing, the literature selection itself, and Responding Options. This student-centered lesson offers a wide range and choice of activities.

PREVIEWING

Personal Connection Helps students explore prior experience and knowledge about topics covered in the selection.

Historical (Biographical, Cultural, Literary, Geographical, Scientific, etc.) Connection Provides important background information relevant to the selection.

Reading Connection Presents direct instruction in a reading skill designed to improve comprehension of the selection.

Writing Connection Serves as an alternative to the Reading Connection. Allows students to explore selection-related topics through writing.

Graphic Organizer Helps students explore new topics and structure their thinking.

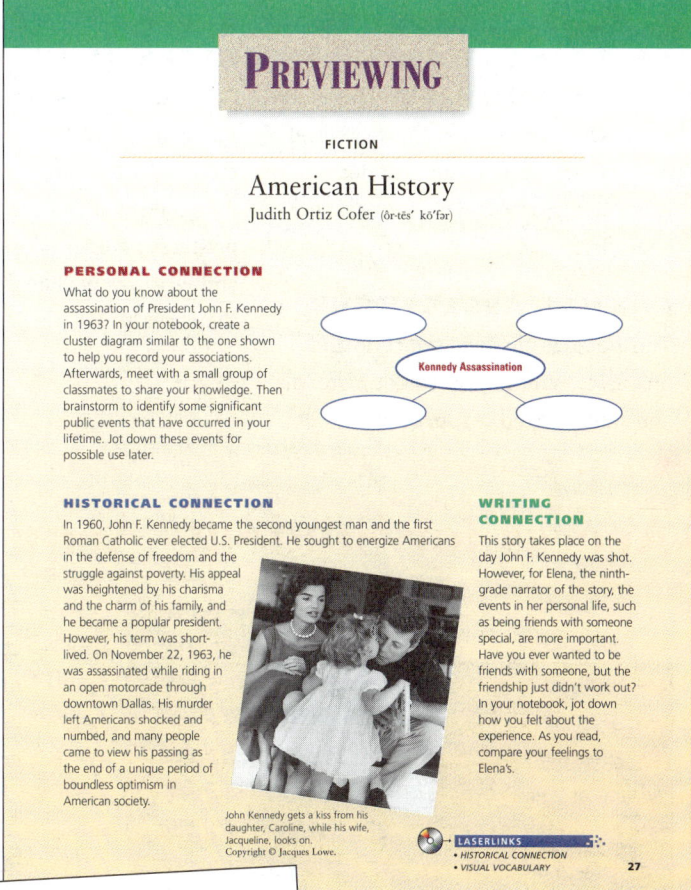

THE SELECTION

The finest literature offerings. Represented are traditional and contemporary pieces, familiar and new voices.

Natural and thematic connections. Selections are organized thematically and, where appropriate, chronologically.

Attractive, engaging design. Helps entice and motivate students.

Active reading questions. Provided as appropriate within selections to help students with comprehension of more challenging pieces.

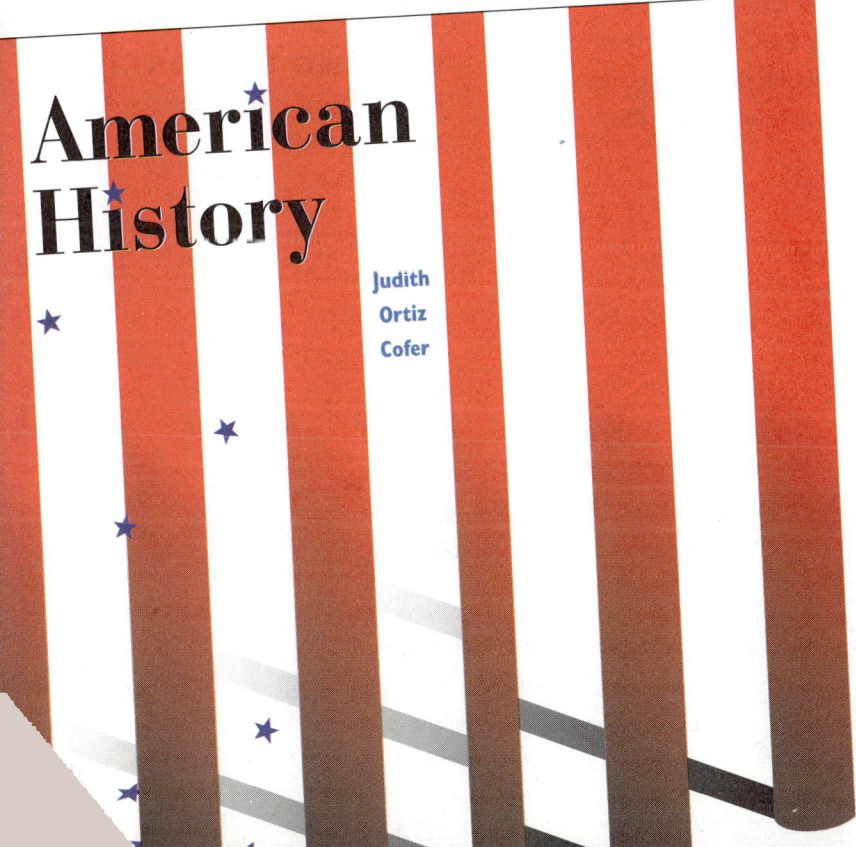

Assessment Package

TEACHER'S GUIDE TO ASSESSMENT AND PORTFOLIO USE This guide provides instruction in the types and uses of assessment and includes guidesheets, assessment forms, and checklists.

FORMAL ASSESSMENT This booklet contains selection and unit tests, writing assessment materials, and standardized test practice.

ALTERNATIVE ASSESSMENT With these materials—modeled on the authentic assessment materials used in many states and districts across the country—you can evaluate the processes students use as they read and write, as well as the products they create.

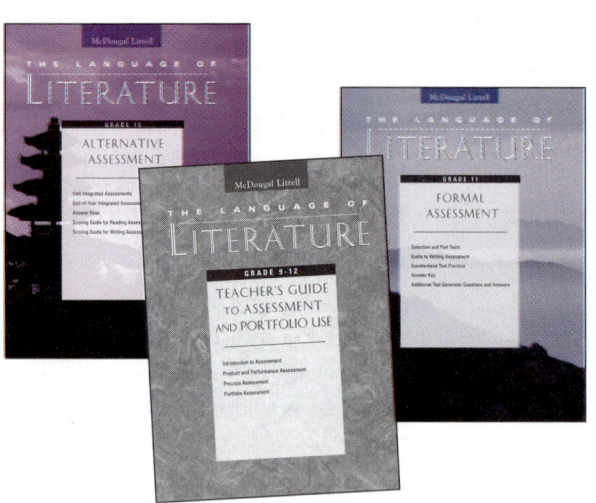

Access for Students Acquiring English

This collection of materials provides comprehensive help for students moving toward English language proficiency. The following components are included:

TEACHER'S SOURCEBOOK FOR LANGUAGE DEVELOPMENT A teacher handbook that includes teaching strategies and techniques.

SELECTION SUMMARIES Summaries of the literature in Spanish.

READING SUPPORT Practice activities that support every literature selection.

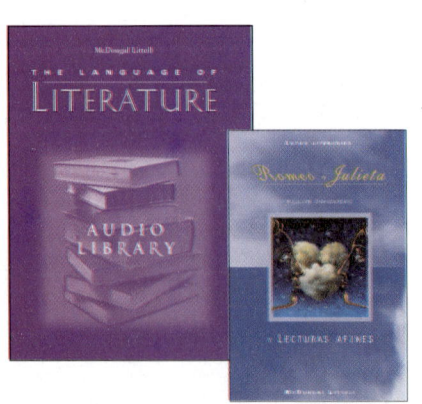

LITERATURE CONNECTIONS Spanish translations of selected titles for grades 6-12.

AUDIO LIBRARY These professional recordings may be used as support for Students Acquiring English.

OVERVIEW
(CONTINUED)

Resource Materials

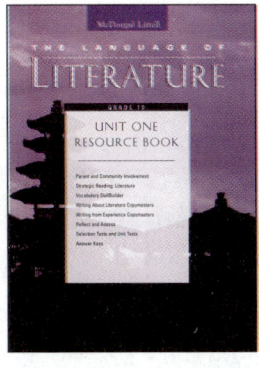

UNIT RESOURCE BOOK Organized by unit and selection, these copymasters provide you with a variety of ways to build and reinforce student skills in reading comprehension, spelling, vocabulary, and writing.

GRAMMAR MINI-LESSONS WRITING MINI-LESSONS These transparency packs allow teachers to identify areas where students need help, and to teach exactly what is needed when it is needed. Corresponding grammar sheets give students needed practice.

DAILY LANGUAGE SKILLBUILDER Through daily exercises, this product integrates grammar, usage, capitalization, proofreading, and punctuation skills with literature-based content.

Integrated Technology

 LASERLINKS
A treasury of full-motion video, photographs, and fine art, this videodisc provides the following program support:

- Selection Support: Historical and Cultural Background
- Author Interviews
- Writing Springboards
- Visual Vocabulary
- Art Galleries
- Storytelling

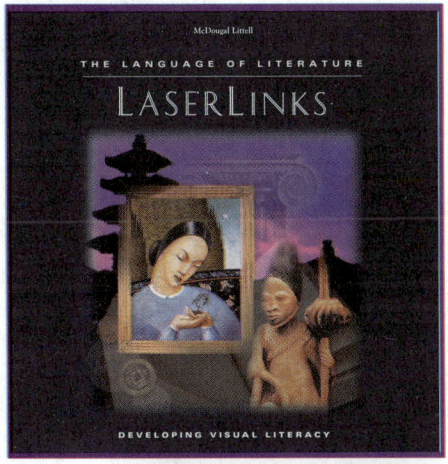

INTERNET CONNECTIONS Program-related information can be accessed through the McDougal Littell home page at http://www.hmco.com/mcdougal/lit

WRITING COACH
A comprehensive word processing program with a unique, multi-column format and on-line writing support, the Writing Coach is a powerful tool for collaborative writing, peer response, and evaluation.

AUDIO LIBRARY
These tapes contain professional recordings of nearly every selection in the anthology. The performances can be used to enhance the literature or to provide support for less proficient readers.

TEST GENERATOR
This component provides the tools for fashioning your own tests.

ELECTRONIC LIBRARY This CD-ROM allows you to easily access and print out over 50 additional pieces of classic literature from well-known authors.

LITERATURE CONNECTIONS

, Unique to *The Language of Literature,* these stand-alone books allow you to decide which plays and novels to include in your literature class. Each longer work is accompanied by several related readings that extend the subject or theme, saving you the task of searching for additional material.

SourceBook Provides you with all the information and student support materials you will need to present fresh and effective lessons.

THE LANGUAGE OF LITERATURE
Overview

Core Components

The Language of Literature is a seamlessly integrated program that provides teachers with a common-sense system for teaching literature, language, and communication skills. The components described on these pages—the core elements of the program—provide teachers and students with all of the materials they need in a flexible, customizable format. (For more information on each element, please see pages T10 to T25.)

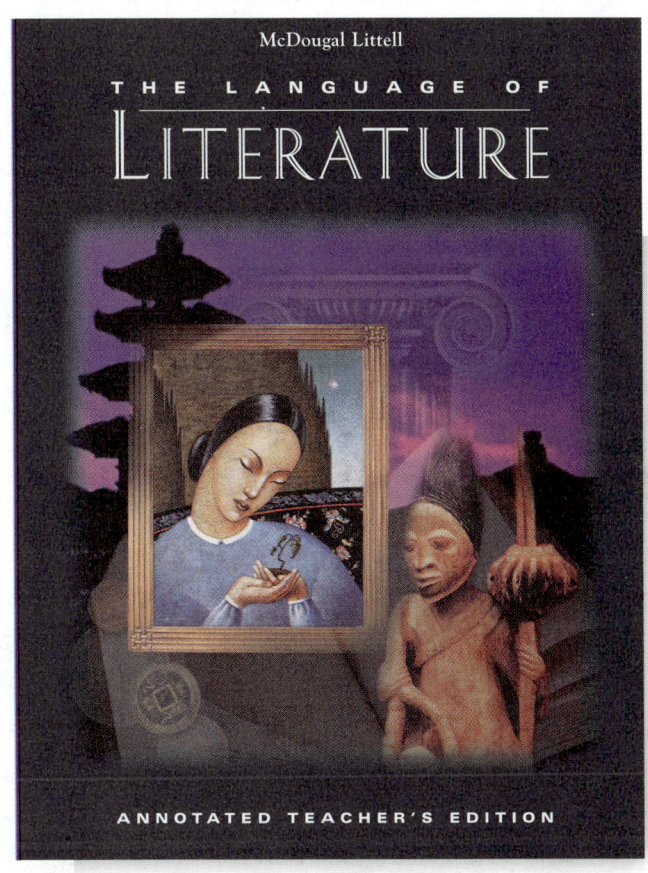

ANNOTATED TEACHER'S EDITION

This comprehensive book provides all of the material you require for a successful teaching experience.

- Unit Content Overview and Planning Charts
- Student Projects
- Professional Enrichment Pages
- Family and Community Involvement
- Annotations for Literature Selections and Writing Workshops
- Bar Codes to LaserLinks
- Recommended Resources

PUPIL EDITION

A rich mix of classic, contemporary and multicultural literature is the starting point from which your class begins its exploration of a world of ideas and experiences. Writing Workshops in each unit continue this exploration, moving students from the literature to interactions with real-world communication and technology.

Program Authors and Consultants

Arthur N. Applebee Professor of Education, State University of New York at Albany; Director, Center for the Learning and Teaching of Literature; Senior Fellow, Center for Writing and Literacy

Andrea B. Bermúdez Professor of Studies in Language and Culture; Director, Research Center for Language and Culture; Chair, Foundations and Professional Studies, University of Houston-Clear Lake

Sheridan Blau Senior Lecturer in English and Education and former Director of Composition, University of California at Santa Barbara; Director, South Coast Writing Project; Director, Literature Institute for Teachers; Vice President, National Council of Teachers of English

Rebekah Caplan Coordinator, English Language Arts K-12, Oakland Unified School District, Oakland, California; Teacher-Consultant, Bay Area Writing Project, University of California at Berkeley; served on the California State English Assessment Development Team for Language Arts

Franchelle S. Dorn Professor of Drama, Howard University, Washington, D.C.; Adjunct Professor, Graduate School of Opera, University of Maryland, College Park, Maryland; Co-founder of The Shakespeare Acting Conservatory, Washington, D.C.

Peter Elbow Professor of English, University of Massachusetts at Amherst; Fellow, Bard Center for Writing and Thinking

Susan Hynds Professor and Director of English Education, Syracuse University, Syracuse, New York

Judith A. Langer Professor of Education, State University of New York at Albany; Co-director, Center for the Learning and Teaching of Literature; Senior Fellow, Center for Writing and Literacy

James Marshall Professor of English and English Education, University of Iowa, Iowa City

LASERLINKS

A Level One videodisc program that enhances the literature curriculum, develops visual literacy, and helps students explore and interact with the literature.

- Provides historical and cultural background to strengthen interdisciplinary connections
- Helps build students' vocabulary through the Visual Vocabulary feature
- Contains author interviews
- Includes images that stimulate writing
- Presents storyteller in action

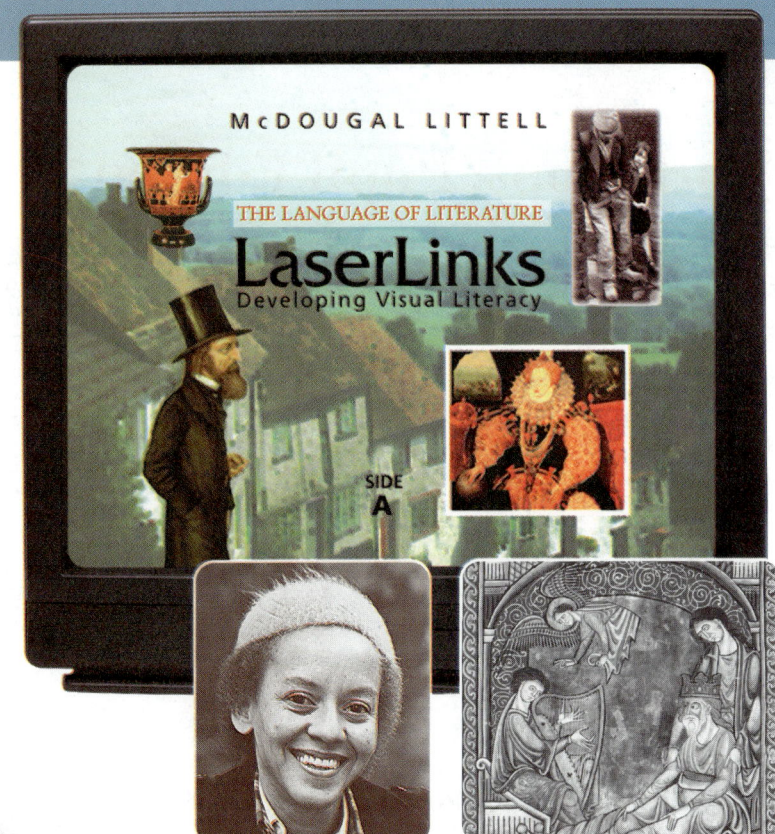

ELECTRONIC LIBRARY

A CD-ROM that provides 50 additional literature selections by classic authors. Teachers can print out copies and distribute them to students. Greatly extends the pupil edition anthology and the number of literary options available.

AUDIO LIBRARY

Recordings of almost all selections in each anthology. Provides easy listening, enhances and enriches students' literary experience, and helps students develop strategies for critical listening.

INTERNET CONNECTIONS

The following resources can be accessed through the McDougal Littell home page at http://www.hmco.com/mcdougal/lit

- Literature selection report
- Links to professional materials and organizations
- Teacher discussion groups and bulletin boards

THE LANGUAGE OF LITERATURE TEACHER'S EDITION **T13**

A CLOSER LOOK
Integrating Language and Writing Skills

The Writing Workshops: Pupil Edition

Paired writing workshops in each unit offer students two distinct ways to respond to the literature and make "real world" connections.

WRITING ABOUT LITERATURE
This workshop appears as a set of three related lessons.

- **The Writer's Style** lesson focuses on a writing skill such as sentence variety or elaboration. Literary excerpts and a real-world model show the technique in context.

- **The Guided Assignment** invites students to explore the literature through both creative and analytical writing.

- **Complete Writing Process.** Provides advice for each stage of the writing process, from prewriting to publication and reflection.

- **Student models.** Illustrate the process and choices of another student writer.

- **Peer response questions and Standards for Evaluation.** Help students assess and revise their writing.

- **Skills Instruction.** Grammar in Context and Grammar Skillbuilders teach grammar concepts that relate to the writing.

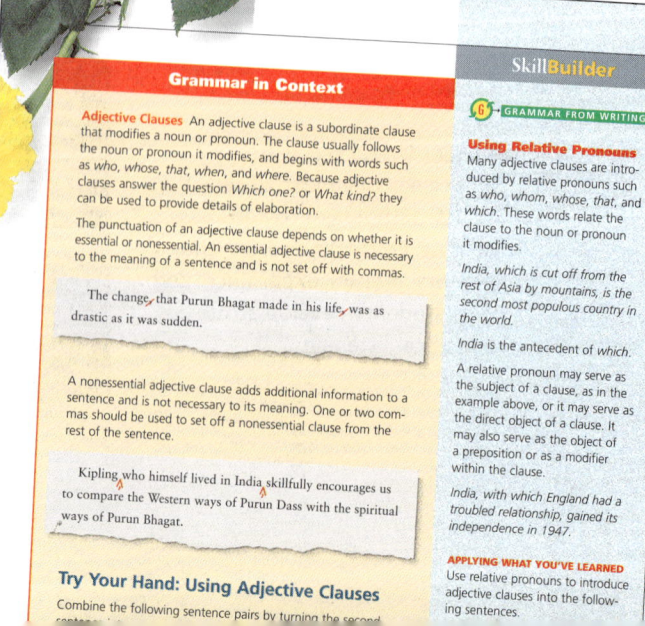

- **Reading the World** builds visual literacy and shows students how the same skills they have just used to analyze and write about literature can also be used to observe, interpret, and understand the world around them.

WRITING FROM EXPERIENCE

The second writing workshop invites students to extend the unit theme by creating products for real purposes and real audiences in situations they encounter in the world around them.

Primary source materials. Magazine and newspaper articles, photographs, charts, and graphs provide a springboard to writing while building critical thinking and media literacy skills.

Oral communication and research skills. Used during prewriting as students gather information. Students are also encouraged to use technology—from CD-ROMs to on-line services—to access information.

Alternative forms of publishing. Visual, oral, and electronic products are suggested and modeled.

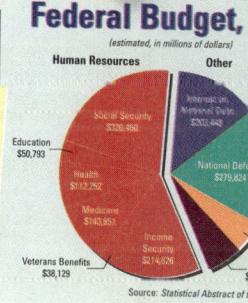

INTEGRATING LANGUAGE AND WRITING SKILLS
(CONTINUED)

SCOPE AND SEQUENCE OF WRITING INSTRUCTION

The writing workshops in *The Language of Literature* grow in sophistication as your students do, providing a rich variety of writing assignments that become more challenging in every grade. In the following chart, blue dots indicate the Writing About Literature workshops, and red dots indicate the Writing from Experience workshops. The number following each assignment represents the unit in which it appears.

Writing Strands	Grade 9	Grade 10	American Literature	British Literature
Firsthand and Expressive	• Personal Response: / 1* • First-Hand Narrative / 3	• Personal Response / 1 • First-Hand Narrative / 1	• Personal Response / 8 • Personal Essay / 3	• Process Response / 4 • Reflective Essay / 1
Narrative and Literary	• Parody / 4 • Writing in Kind: Drama / 6 • Short Story / 6	• Writing in Kind: Poetry / 3 • Change Story Element / 5 • Dramatic Scene / 5	• Speech / 2 • In Author's Style / 7 • Poetry / 6 • Short Story: Sci-Fi / 8	• Creative Response: Change Genre / 2 • Advice Essay / 3 • Poetry / 2
Expository	• Analysis: Character / 1 • Interpretive: Theme / 3 • Critical: Evaluate a Story / 5 • Investigative: Explain an Idea / 1 • Extended Definition / 4	• Analysis: Setting / 2 • Interpretive: Process / 4 • Critical: Evaluate Ideas / 6 • Compare-contrast / 3 • Cause-effect / 4	• Interpretive: Infer Ideas / 1 • Interpretive: Images/Symbols / 3 • Analysis: Story Elements / 4 • Analysis: Point of View / 5 • Critical: Compare Poets / 6 • Analytic Report / 1 • Problem-solution / 4	• Interpretive: Infer Values / 1 • Critical: Evaluate Ideas / 5 • Literary Review / 6 • Analysis: Comparative / 7 • Informative: Synthesis / 3 • Analysis / 4
Persuasion	• Persuasive Essay / 3	• Persuasive Essay / 2	• Persuasive Piece / 2 • Critical Review / 5	• Two-sided Argument / 5 • Proposal / 7
Report	• Research Paper / 5	• Research Report: Biographical / 6	• Research Report: Historical / 7	• Research Paper / 6

* Denotes unit number

Writing and Language: Resource Materials

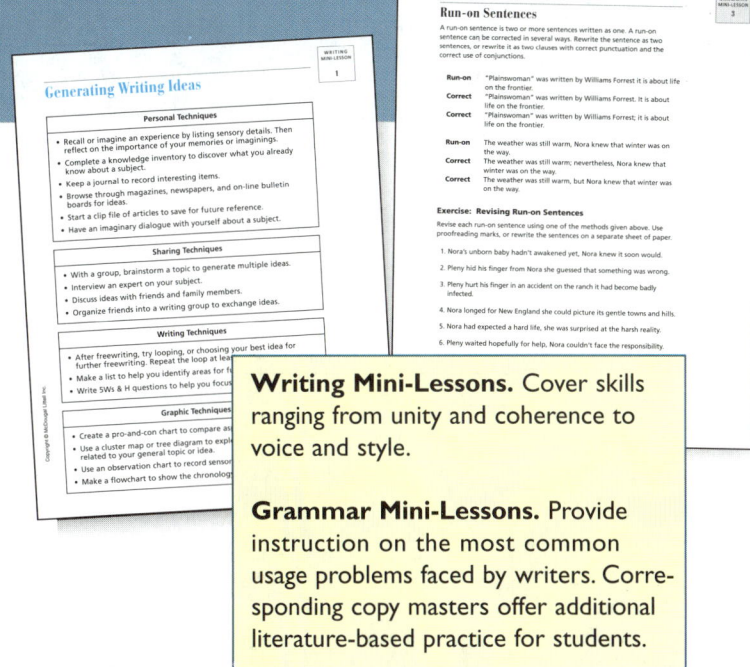

MINI-LESSONS

When do you want to teach your students about introductions and conclusions? As they write a story? Before they begin a report? The unique mini-lesson transparency packs in *The Language of Literature* allow you to decide what your students need to learn and when they need to learn it.

Writing Mini-Lessons. Cover skills ranging from unity and coherence to voice and style.

Grammar Mini-Lessons. Provide instruction on the most common usage problems faced by writers. Corresponding copy masters offer additional literature-based practice for students.

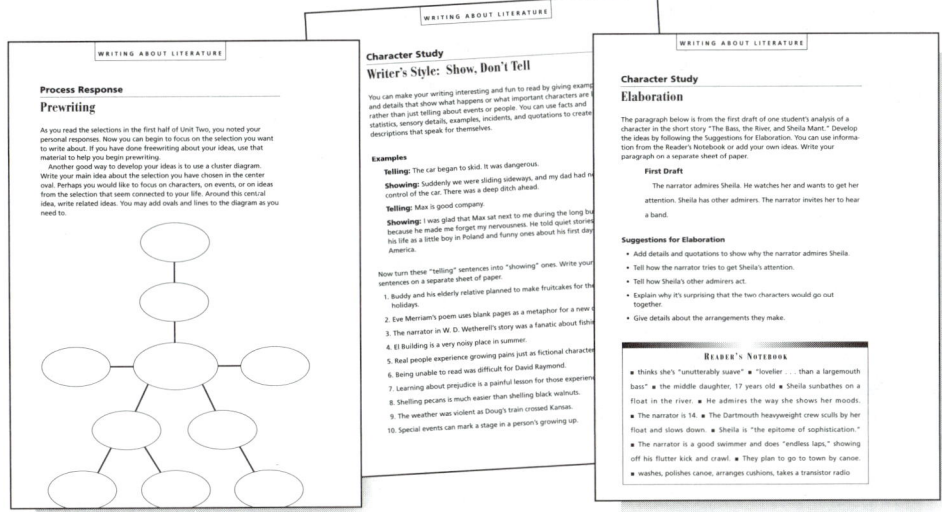

UNIT RESOURCE BOOK

In addition to support for the literature selections, the Unit Resource Book provides comprehensive practice and support for each stage of the writing process. Copymasters include the following:

Writer's Style Worksheet
Prewriting Worksheet
Elaboration Practice
Peer Response Guide
Revising and Proofreading Practice
Complete Student Model
Rubrics for Evaluation

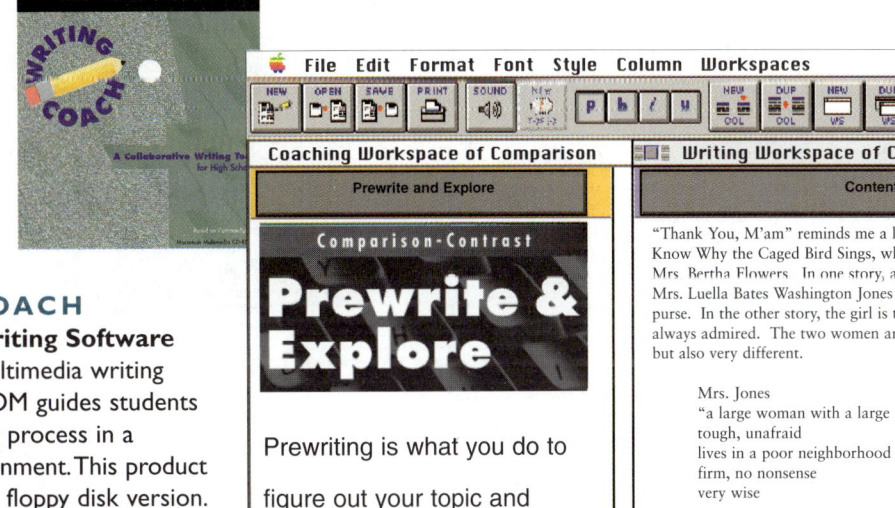

WRITING COACH

Collaborative Writing Software
This interactive, multimedia writing program on CD-ROM guides students through the writing process in a collaborative environment. This product is also available in a floppy disk version.

A CLOSER LOOK

Special Features of the Pupil Edition

This book contains a wealth of special features to help enrich each student's learning experience.

STRATEGIES FOR READING
Shows students how active readers read—what they think about as they read and how they make connections between the text and real-world experiences. Model provides thoughts and comments of two students engaged in the following active reading strategies:

- Question
- Connect
- Predict
- Clarify
- Evaluate

PART OPENER
World map showing authors' countries of origin builds awareness of geographical locations while underscoring cultural diversity. Handy "mini" table of contents for each part of a unit.

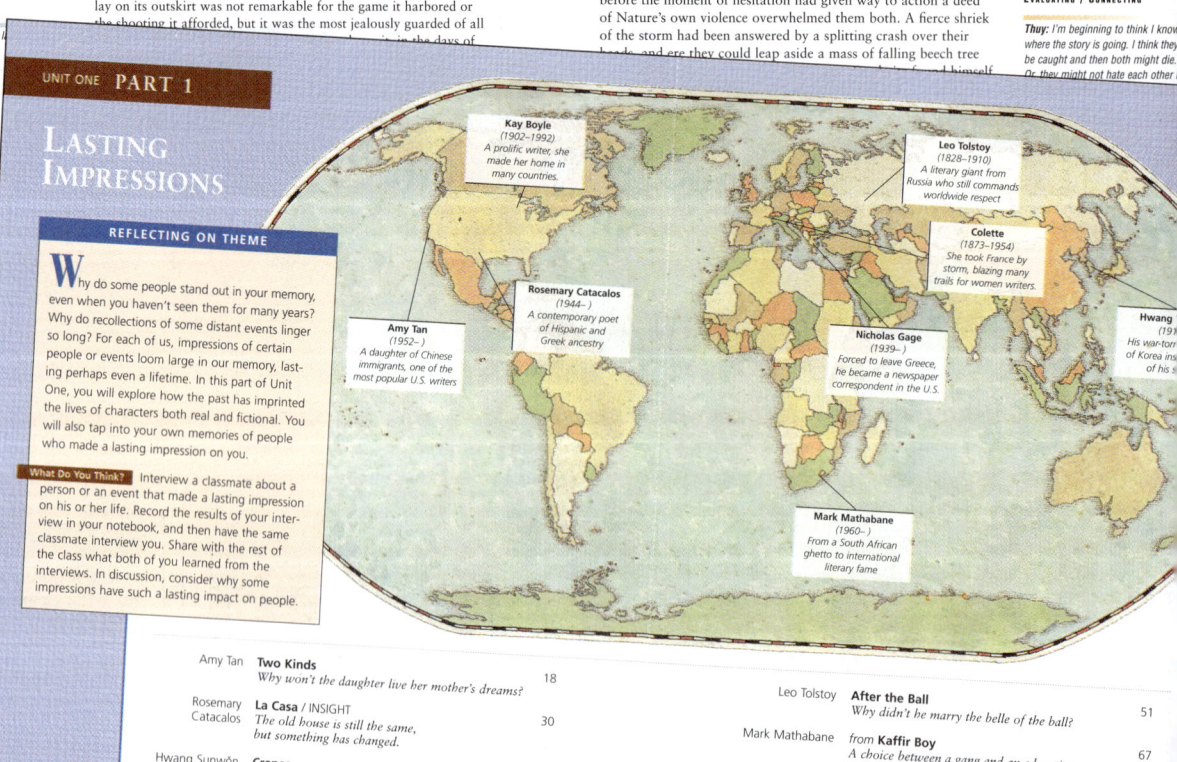

FOCUS ON FICTION/NONFICTION/POETRY/DRAMA

Helps introduce and reinforce basic knowledge of literary elements. Also includes strategies used when reading a particular genre. Feature provides students with a strong foundation for the reading of literature.

REFLECT & ASSESS

Features end-of-unit activities that help students review and reflect upon what they have learned in the course of a unit. Includes options for:

- Reflecting on Theme
- Reviewing on Literary Concepts
- Portfolio Building

STUDENT HANDBOOKS

- **Literary Terms**
- **Writing Handbook**
- **Multimedia Handbook**
- **Grammar Handbook**

Easy-to-use, comprehensive references that provide valuable information and offer practical support for the teaching of literature, writing, and grammar.

A CLOSER LOOK
The Teacher's Edition

Unit Support

Special pages in the Teacher's Edition provide professional enrichment and help you plan your lessons, organize necessary materials, and carry out unit-related projects.

SKILLS TRACE

Allows you to see at a glance the scope and sequence of reading, writing, speaking, listening, viewing, study, research, grammar, spelling, and literary skills taught within each part of a unit. Also tracks the teaching of vocabulary words and the type and frequency of multimodal activities.

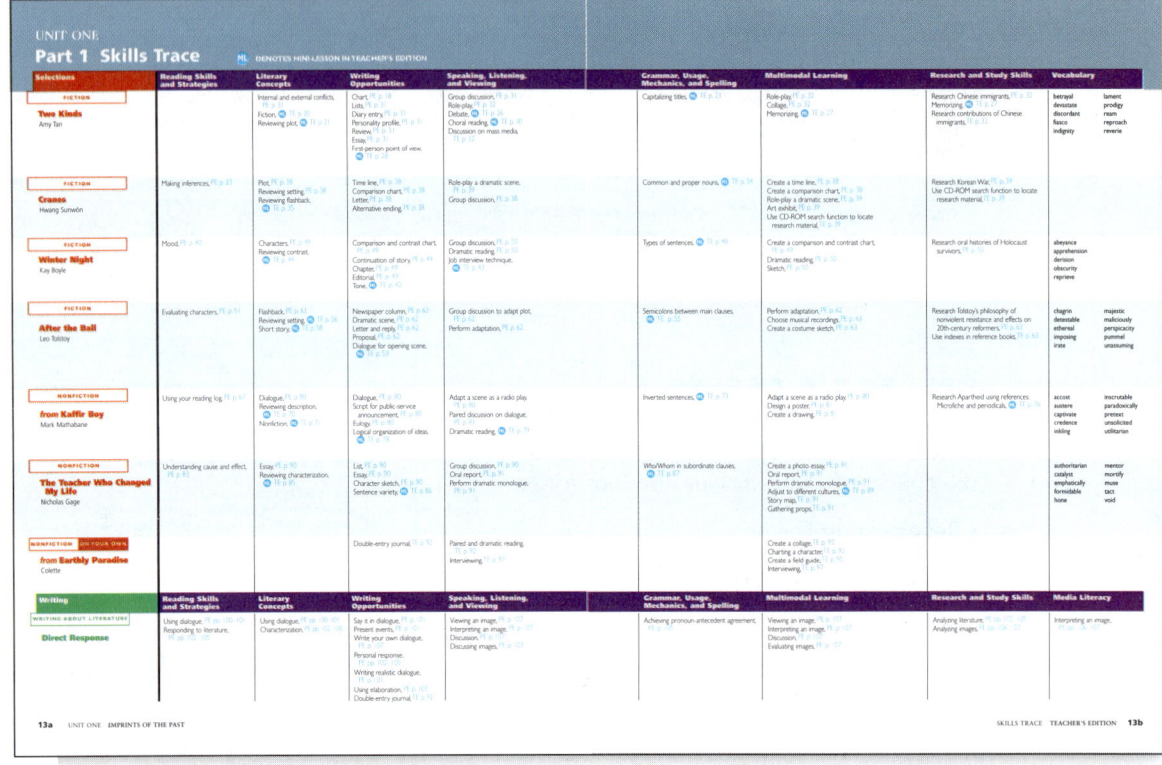

RECOMMENDED RESOURCES

Invaluable listings of unit-specific resources for both you and your students. Includes titles of novels and plays, cross-curricular readings, and media resources. Helps you extend and enrich the curriculum and enrich yourself professionally as well.

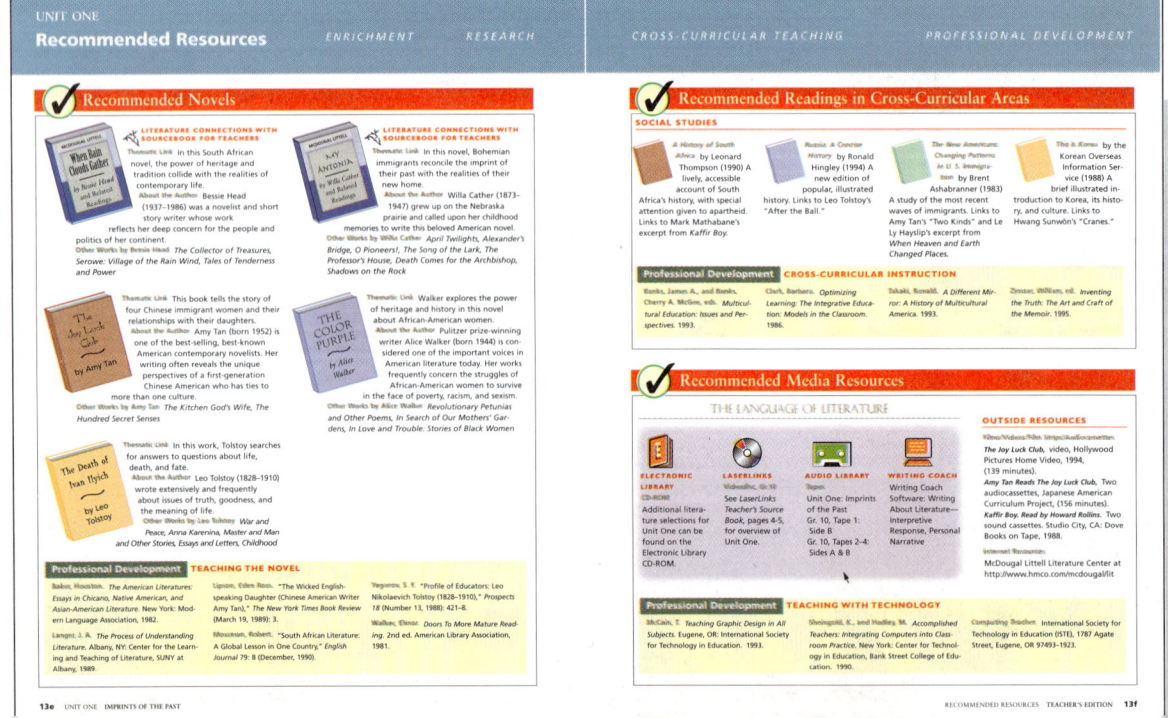

T20

PROFESSIONAL ENRICHMENT

Articles written by teachers, authors, and other noted authorities. Offers insights and practical strategies for teaching literature and writing.

STARTING POINTS FOR UNIT PROJECTS

Ideas for helping you initiate content-related projects during the course of the unit. Includes ideas for both individual and group projects.

FAMILY AND COMMUNITY INVOLVEMENT

Activities designed to involve parents and other family members and to foster students' interaction with other people in their communities. Corresponding worksheets are provided.

LESSON PLANNER

Helps you plan your lessons by indicating approximate length of time for each task. Allows you to accommodate a variety of classroom situations and needs.

T21

TEACHERS EDITION
(CONTINUED)

Selection and Writing Workshop Support

The Annotated Teacher's Edition of *The Language of Literature* is a professional sourcebook designed to promote effective and efficient teaching. Each page contains features that allow you take students into, through, and beyond the literature.

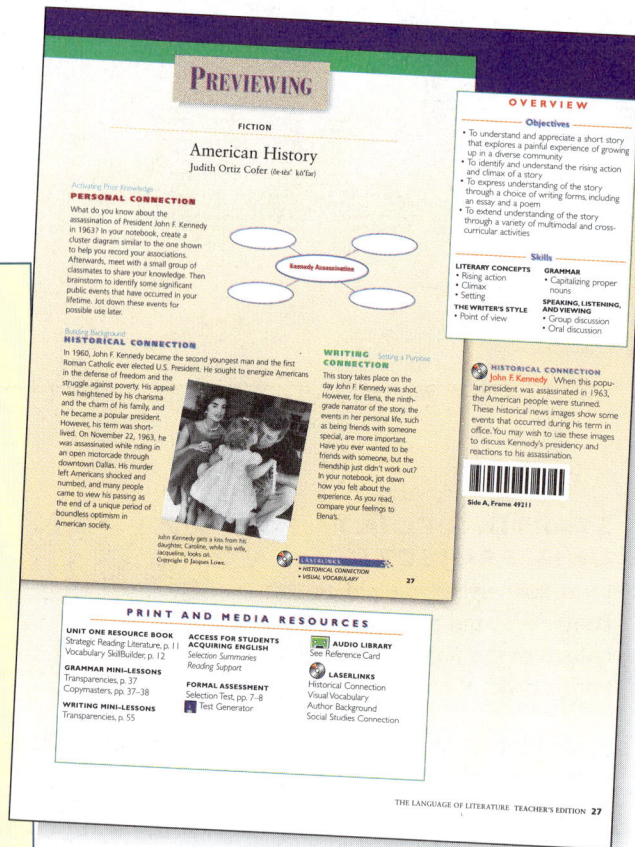

SELECTION ANNOTATIONS

Notes on literary concepts and critical thinking skills appear with each selection and its corresponding activity pages. Also included are the following features.

- **Overview** Lists objectives, key skills, and cross-curricular connections
- **Print and Media Resources**
- **Selection Summary**
- **LaserLinks bar codes**
- **Words To Know**
- **Art Notes**
- **Customizing for**
  - multiple learning styles
  - students acquiring English
  - gifted and talented students
  - less-proficient readers

- **Activities** Suggestions for whole class, small group, and individual activities
- **Mini-Lessons** Provided for grammar, spelling, reading, genre, writing, and a number of other subjects.
- **Active Reading Questions**
- **Comprehension Check**
- **Assessment Options**
- **Links Across the Curriculum**
- **Links to *The Writer's Craft***
- **Activity Support and Answer Keys**

T22

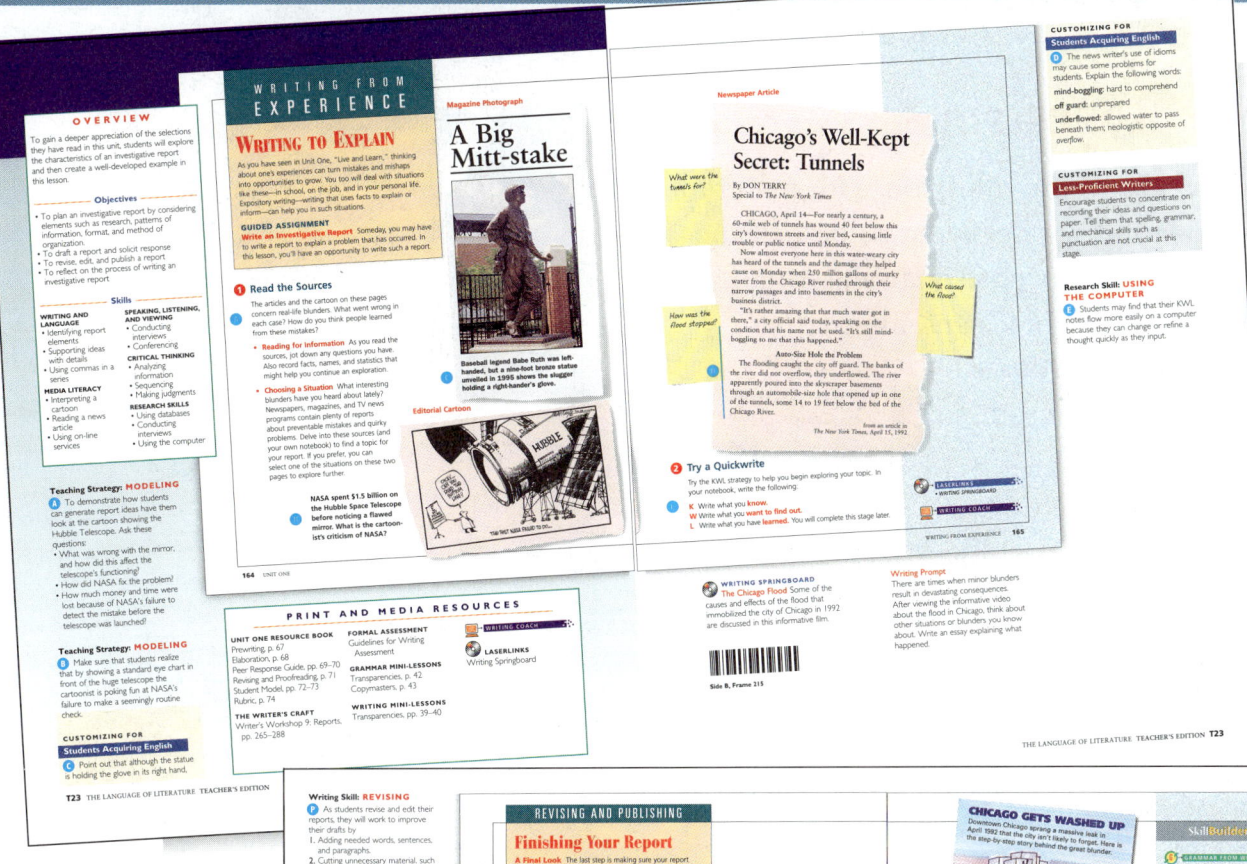

WORKSHOP ANNOTATIONS

The Teacher's Edition notes for the Writing Workshops provide support similar to that provided for each literary selection. In addition, Writing Workshops contain the following:

- **Writing Springboards** Provides writing ideas from LaserLinks.
- **Modeling** Gives suggestions for using both literary models and student writing models.
- **SkillBuilder Mini-Lesson Support**
- **Visual and Media Literacy Features**
- **Research Skills**
- **Oral Communication**
- **Rubrics**
- **Standards for Evaluation**

T23

A CLOSER LOOK

Assessment

Assessment Resources

The Language of Literature provides you with material that allows you to customize assessment to best fit the activities and structure of your particular classroom. With options for formal, informal, and alternative assessment, these resources provide you with all the support you need.

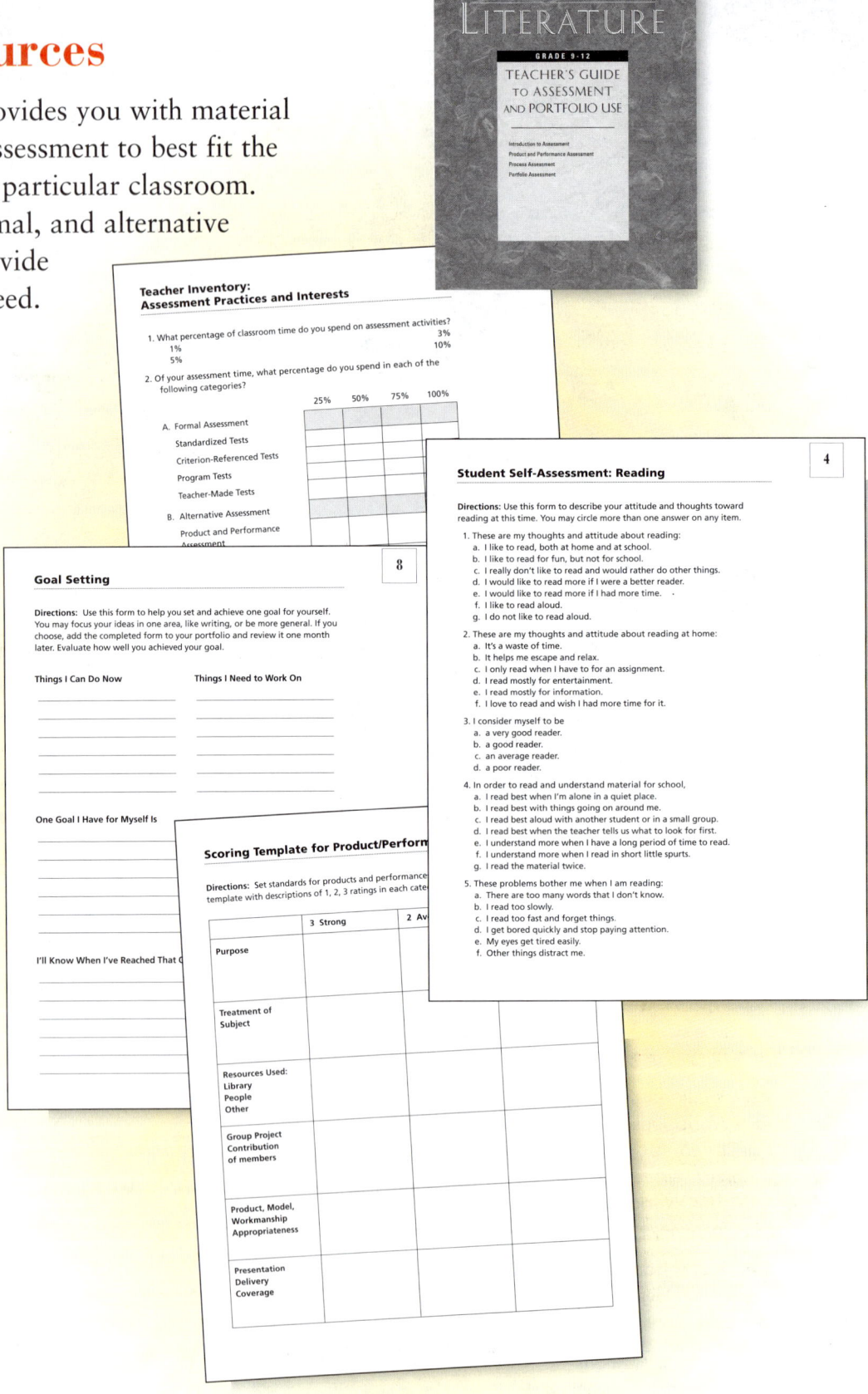

GUIDE TO ASSESSMENT AND PORTFOLIO USE

This Teacher's Guide

- provides information on different types and forms of assessment: formal selection and unit tests, portfolio building, authentic assessment, reading notebooks, self-assessment, group and project assessment, and more.

- helps you decide which assessment types you wish to use and explains how to implement those approaches.

- provides forms and checklists that can be used to give shape to assessment choices.

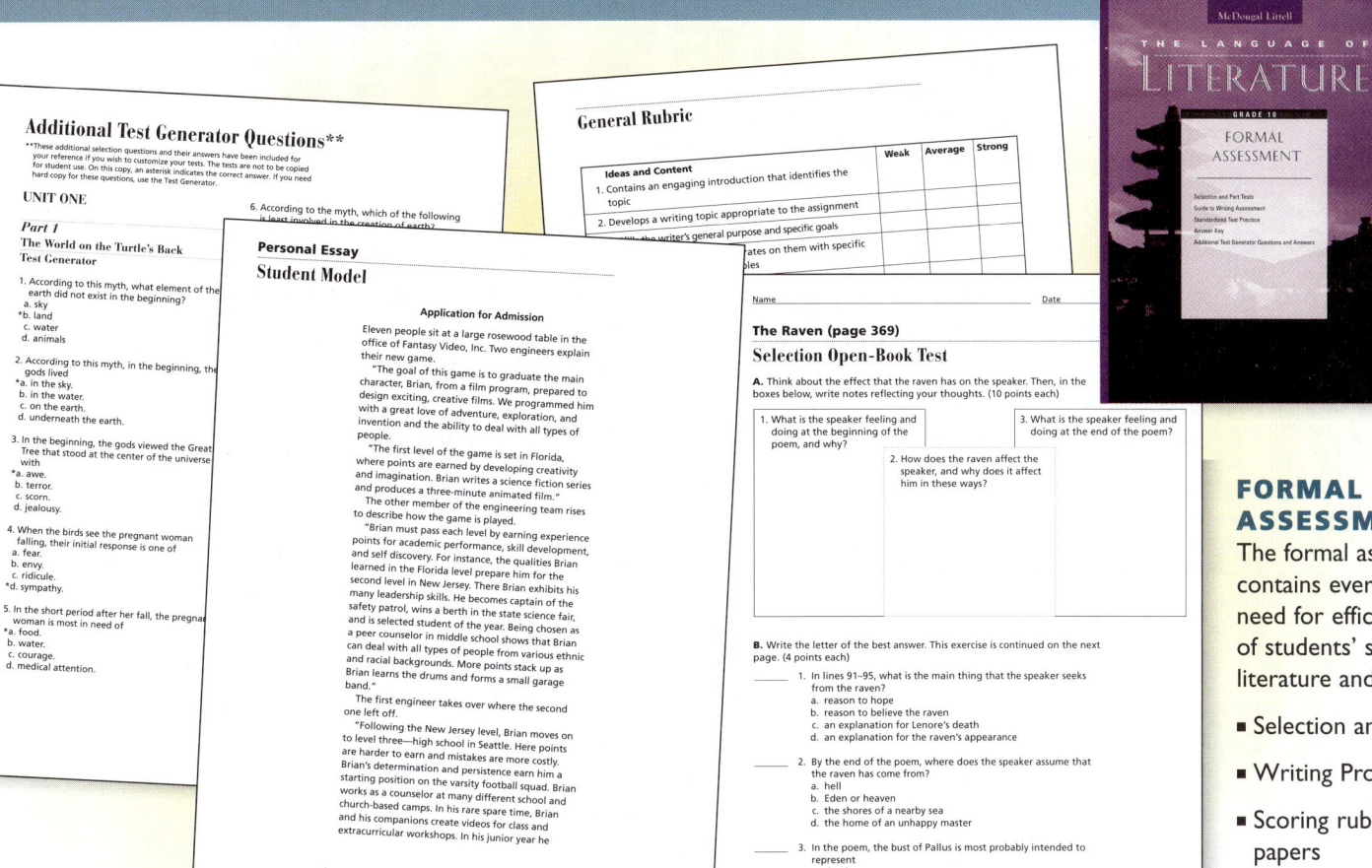

FORMAL ASSESSMENT

The formal assessment booklet contains everything you will need for efficient assessment of students' skills in reading literature and in writing.

- Selection and Unit Tests
- Writing Prompts
- Scoring rubrics and sample papers
- Standardized Test Practice

Also, a test generator is available to help you customize assessment.

ALTERNATIVE ASSESSMENT

These assessments integrate all of the language arts processes and are modeled on authentic assessment materials used in many states across the country.

- **Unit Integrated Assessments** are completed over two days and are based on the On Your Own selections in the student book. Prereading activities and post-reading response and discussion lead to in-depth writing options.

- The **End-of-Year Integrated Assessment** includes a reader and a Student Response Booklet. It is completed over several days and requires students to respond to three or more related selections.

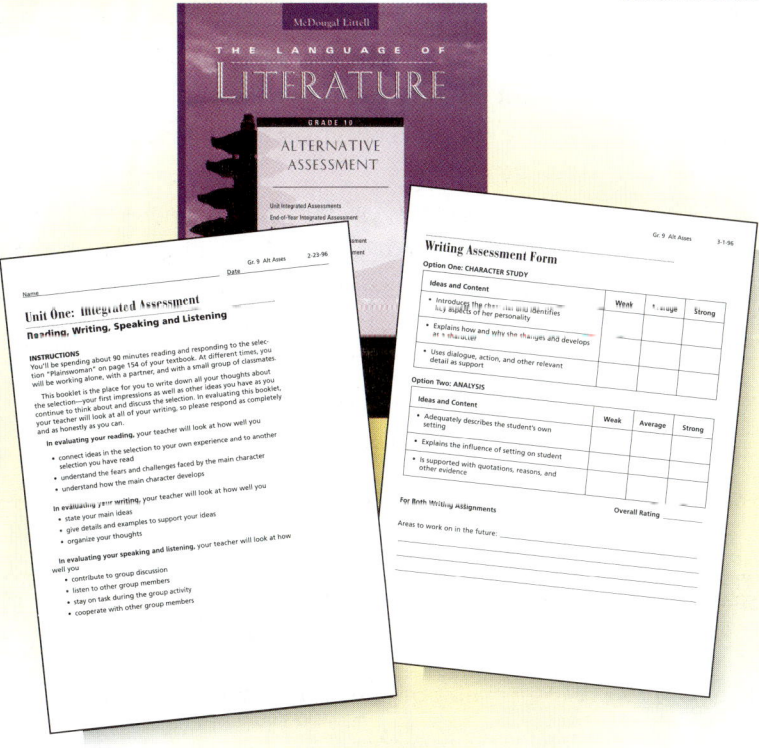

THE LANGUAGE OF LITERATURE TEACHER'S EDITION **T25**

GETTING STARTED...
Advice from the Experts

Planning YOUR YEAR

Every new school year requires much planning. The information and advice on these pages comes from the consultants on *The Language of Literature* and is designed to help you bring some of your plans into focus. (You may want to copy the pages and keep them in your lesson planner for easy reference.) As you begin your planning, here's a list of questions to consider. Their answers and some additional information can be found on the pages cited.

Developing a Classroom Profile   See pages T28–T29.

✔ **Who are my students?**

- ☐ What can I learn about my students from previous teachers, students, records, and portfolios—and how can I best use this information?
- ☐ What are my students' preferred learning styles, and how can I best accommodate them?
- ☐ If I have students who are not proficient in English, what will their needs be?
- ☐ Are there any other special needs represented in my class?
- ☐ What adjustments do I need to make due to tracking, mainstreaming, and other situations?

Planning My Instruction   See pages T30–T31.

✔ **What do I want to teach?**

- ☐ What are the requirements of my school, district, and state?
- ☐ What are my personal preferences?
- ☐ What are my students' preferences?
- ☐ How can I use both classic literature and young-adult literature to reflect the needs and interests of my students?
- ☐ What mix of stories, poetry, essays, and novels do I want to teach?
- ☐ How can I effectively combine writing, language, and communication skills?
- ☐ Do I want to teach a research paper and/or other longer projects?

✔ **How much collaborating do I want to do with other teachers?**

- ☐ To plan thematic units and/or projects
- ☐ To coordinate instruction

✔ **What mix of instructional styles do I want to use?**

- ☐ Lectures
- ☐ Cooperative/collaborative work
- ☐ Writing workshops/peer response groups

✔ **How will I organize the content?**

- ☐ By genre or mode
- ☐ By theme

Setting Up My Classroom
See pages T32–T33.

✔ **How will I organize my classroom?**

- ☐ In rows of desks
- ☐ With tables and chairs
- ☐ In paired-seating arrangements
- ☐ In cooperative learning groups
- ☐ In stations or centers

Taking Advantage of Technology
See pages T34–T35.

✔ **How large a role will technology play in my classroom?**

- ☐ What technological resources do I have at my disposal?
- ☐ For what purpose or purposes do I want to use them?
- ☐ How can I best set up my classroom or use a lab to take advantage of these resources?

Preparing for Assessment
See pages T36–T38.

✔ **What types of assessment do I want to use or prepare for?**

Do I want to use one or more of the following:

- ☐ Portfolios, journals, and/or logs
- ☐ Process assessment
- ☐ Product assessment
- ☐ Peer and self-assessment
- ☐ My own observations
- ☐ Tests from *The Language of Literature*
- ☐ District- or state-mandated tests
- ☐ Standardized tests

Planning Connections
See pages T39–T40.

✔ **What kinds of connections do I want to make outside the classroom?**

- ☐ To other curriculum areas
- ☐ To other classrooms or schools
- ☐ To my students' parents
- ☐ To the community
- ☐ To the world

DEVELOPING A Classroom PROFILE

> *To avoid misunderstanding, it is critical that teachers disregard the assumption that all students have the same, or similar, frames of reference or perceptions about the world.*
>
> *Andrea Bermúdez*
> *Professor of Studies in Language and Culture, University of Houston-Clear Lake*

UNDERSTANDING LEARNING STYLES

Your students are all unique. They have different sets of characteristics, abilities, and needs. It should not be surprising, therefore, to learn that they have different learning styles as well. This theory gained acceptance in the early 1980s, due in large part to the research of Harvard psychologist Howard Gardner. Gardner recognizes seven types of intelligences: linguistic, logical-mathematical, spatial, musical, bodily-kinesthetic, interpersonal, and intrapersonal. He claims that everyone has all seven of these intelligences, but in different proportions.

Understanding your students' intelligences, or learning styles, will help you teach them more effectively. How can you tell which learning style or styles your students favor? As you consider each of your students, asking yourself these questions will help.

Does the student . . .	Then he or she is mostly a . . .	So try these activities and assignments:
☐ Have good verbal skills? think in words? have highly developed auditory skills? like to read and write?	**Linguistic Learner**	Creative writing; essays; debates and speeches; oral reports; dramatic readings and performances; storytelling; joke, pun, and riddle telling
☐ Think conceptually? think and reason in a highly abstract and logical way?	**Logical-Mathematical Learner**	Graphic organizers; charts, graphs, and time lines; coded messages; prediction exercises; models; computer projects; science experiments
☐ Think in visual images and pictures? enjoy drawing, designing, building, daydreaming, inventing?	**Spatial Learner**	Drawings and paintings; comic strips; maps and flow charts; dioramas, displays, and murals; collages; drawing games; photography activities
☐ Have a sensitivity to music, nonverbal sounds, and rhythm? enjoy singing, playing, and listening to and moving to music?	**Musical Learner**	Interpretive dances; musical plays and compositions; rap songs, jingles, and melodies; rhyming games; playing a musical instrument
☐ Process knowledge through bodily sensations? have exceptional fine-motor coordination? communicate through body language?	**Bodily-Kinesthetic Learner**	Demonstration speeches; experiments; using gestures, facial expressions, and pantomime; impersonations; role-playing
☐ Understand other people? organize, communicate, and socialize well?	**Interpersonal Learner**	Discussions; cooperative and collaborative projects; peer coaching; conducting interviews; simulation activities; human graphs
☐ Prefer working alone? seem intuitive, independent, private, and self-motivated?	**Intrapersonal Learner**	Response journals, dialogue journals, learning logs; observations; photo essays; autobiographical stories; written reports

A PROFILE OF THE STUDENT ACQUIRING ENGLISH

Culturally and linguistically diverse students bring to the classroom a wealth of experiences that can enrich the learning environment of all your students. Developing multicultural sensitivity involves (a) acceptance of each student's circumstances, (b) a genuine search for information about his or her background and prior knowledge, (c) an updated bank of teaching strategies, and (d) a desire to find the best options for each student.

The Student Acquiring English

- generally focuses attention on style, not content
- is often unaware of learning strategies that could facilitate comprehension
- may become disorderly and disobedient due to an inability to relate to the learning environment
- often does not make eye contact when addressing others
- may seem to have difficulty meeting deadlines
- may not seem to understand classroom "rules"
- generally shows a different speaking and listening style
- may organize thoughts in a pattern that does not correspond to the expected linear-sequential pattern characteristic of standard English communication
- may exhibit an external locus of control, seeming overly dependent on teachers or peers for validation of responses

Common Problem Areas

The following problem areas pose special challenges to students acquiring English as they try to read and understand information.

Vocabulary Difficulty
If the student has no prior experience with the words appearing in a selection, the normal links between certain concepts and their labels will not occur. Problems often arise when a selection contains the following:

- low frequency words
- idiomatic or dialectal expressions
- jargon

Unfamiliar Content
The student may misunderstand the message in what he or she is reading if not given the proper context. This often happens as a result of the following:

- a lack of prior experience with the context
- ideas expressed in an unfamiliar or abstract way
- ideas expressed being of an unfamiliar culture

Grammatical Features of the Selection
Comprehension problems arise when the student encounters the following:

- dialectal forms
- outdated grammatical forms
- unusual word order

Effective Teaching and Learning Strategies

These instructional strategies have been shown to be successful when used with students acquiring English.

Cognitive Mapping
- Many SAE students, however, may organize and categorize information differently than English speakers would. Instruction in cognitive mapping can enable students to integrate previous experience with new knowledge.

An Integrated Approach
- The integrated approach to learning is particularly successful with students acquiring English. Students learn about reading and writing while listening, they learn about writing from reading, and they gain insights into reading from writing. Any strategy or approach based on dissecting language and mutually exclusive components jeopardizes second-language acquisition by not drawing on the prior knowledge and strengths of the learner.

Cooperative Learning
- Cooperative learning is a generic term that refers to a variety of approaches to integrating students into group activities where each participant is responsible for contributing to group outcomes and products. Cooperative learning strategies significantly improve students' achievement and productivity for a wide range of subjects and grade levels. This approach also improves self-esteem and respect for others. For more detailed information, see the *Teacher's SourceBook for Language Development*.

Planning YOUR INSTRUCTION

Just as your students all have their own preferred learning styles, you have your own preferred teaching styles. Understanding when and where your most comfortable style really works—and when another method would reach your goals and the goals of your students more effectively—will help you plan just the right type of instruction for every situation.

Here are some questions to ask yourself as you make decisions about your instruction:

- ☐ What is my objective for the lesson . . . today, this week, this month, this term?
- ☐ What is my time frame . . . 45 minutes, 90 minutes, three class periods, longer?
- ☐ Who are my students (refer to your classroom profiles, pages T28 and T29)?
- ☐ What teaching styles am I most comfortable with?
- ☐ What additional teaching techniques would be effective with these students and this material?

Consider these options . . .

WHOLE-CLASS INSTRUCTION

Lecture
EXAMPLES:
- ☐ Introducing a new unit of study
- ☐ Providing instruction for a project
- ☐ Introducing grammatical principles or definitions of literary elements

Teacher-led Discussion
EXAMPLES:
- ☐ Exploring students' ideas about and responses to literature selections and themes
- ☐ Examining complex issues and problems

Viewing
EXAMPLES:
- ☐ Viewing a filmstrip or a videotape
- ☐ Watching demonstrations, performances, and project presentations

COLLABORATIVE LEARNING

Pairs or Partners
EXAMPLES:
- ☐ Sharing responses to literature
- ☐ Interviewing and reciprocal questioning
- ☐ Brainstorming for project or writing ideas
- ☐ Peer tutoring
- ☐ Writing workshops

Small Groups (3-8 students)
EXAMPLES:
- ☐ Discussing literature or other topics
- ☐ Planning and problem-solving activities
- ☐ Writing workshops
- ☐ Cooperative work on reports, projects, and presentations
- ☐ Cooperative planning and producing of larger projects such as plays, panel discussions or debates, and videotapes

INDEPENDENT LEARNING

Students Working Individually
EXAMPLES:
- ☐ Independent reading and writing
- ☐ Drawing, painting, and collages
- ☐ Listening to audiotapes

... for meeting these instructional goals ...	... with these guidelines and cautions:
☐ Developing critical listening and note-taking skills ☐ Providing unknown historical or cultural background ☐ Introducing new concepts or skills	☐ Lectures appeal to linguistic learners with highly developed auditory skills. Other students may tune you out because this style lacks interactivity. ☐ Lectures are most effective if no longer than 20 minutes. Research shows that immediately after a 10-minute presentation, average adult listeners retain less than 50% of what they hear—and 48 hours later, they only recall 25%.
☐ Developing critical listening, responding, and conversational skills ☐ Introducing or reviewing skills	☐ Not all students are comfortable speaking in front of their peers. Highly verbal students can drown out students who favor other learning styles. ☐ When you lead the discussion, students may tend to direct their comments to you rather than to other students. Encourage students to speak directly to one another as well as to you.
☐ Supporting and improving visual literacy ☐ Developing evaluative skills ☐ Encouraging appreciation for music, art, and various kinds of performances	☐ Although viewing is a comfortable activity for most students, it's essentially passive. You'll want to choose occasions carefully. ☐ To help students remain focused, agree on goals ahead of time and provide standards and forms for evaluating what students are watching.
☐ Reinforcing cooperative learning skills ☐ Providing support for students acquiring English ☐ Encouraging peer feedback for writing	☐ It's important to cultivate a classroom atmosphere of support and trust so that pair interactions are effective and productive. ☐ You may want to pair students differently for different purposes. Strong students may be paired with weaker students, native English speakers with students acquiring English, talkative students with more reserved students, and so on.
☐ Developing problem solving skills ☐ Encouraging peer feedback for writing ☐ Reinforcing cooperative learning skills ☐ Providing opportunities for students to explore various points of view ☐ Improving social skills and promoting self-esteem in students of all abilities	☐ Some students will lean too hard on other members of the group. Both groups and individual students need to be accountable. ☐ Some students can get lost in the shuffle of a larger group. Individual students should have specific responsibilities. ☐ Group size can be determined by the task. Small groups are appropriate for sharing personal writing and receiving individual attention; larger groups are effective when the task is large or complex. ☐ The "jigsaw" method may be useful for groups working on complex tasks. The group divides the assignment into pieces and assigns each student a piece. Then students work together to meld the pieces into a coherent whole.
☐ Providing opportunities for reflection and self-assessment ☐ Providing support for students acquiring English	☐ Individual learning tasks require a quiet classroom atmosphere. Highly developed interpersonal learners may distract other students. ☐ Using independent learning too frequently can hinder students' development of collaborative and cooperative skills.

Setting Up YOUR CLASSROOM

Are you planning to try some new instructional approaches this year? If so, you also may want to consider some new classroom setups. Moving away from the traditional arrangement of desks in rows will provide you and your students a welcome change—and will be more conducive to different teaching and learning situations. Here are a few pointers:

> The ideal literature classroom is a literary community where students... have room to respond, interpret, think critically, and contrast their ideas with those of other readers.
>
> Judith Langer and Arthur Applebee
> Professors of Education, State University of New York at Albany

If you teach in the same room all day, the ideas on these pages will provide ways to set up your room for a variety of purposes.

If you switch rooms, team teach, or share your room, you can find an arrangement that best meets everyone's needs. Some options:

- One arrangement that works for everyone
- Different classrooms for different purposes
- A resource room or common area that could be used for specific types of activities

Before you arrange your classroom, draw a scale floor plan of it. Then add furniture and design a setting that will best accommodate your instructional plans.

When you have your floor plan firmed up, post lists of procedures in the different areas of your classroom. Encourage students to add new procedures as needs arise in the future.

Don't be afraid to experiment with different arrangements throughout the year. You may find that some arrangements work better than others for specific projects or assignments.

A LOOK AT THREE CLASSROOM SETUPS
Lectures and Demonstrations

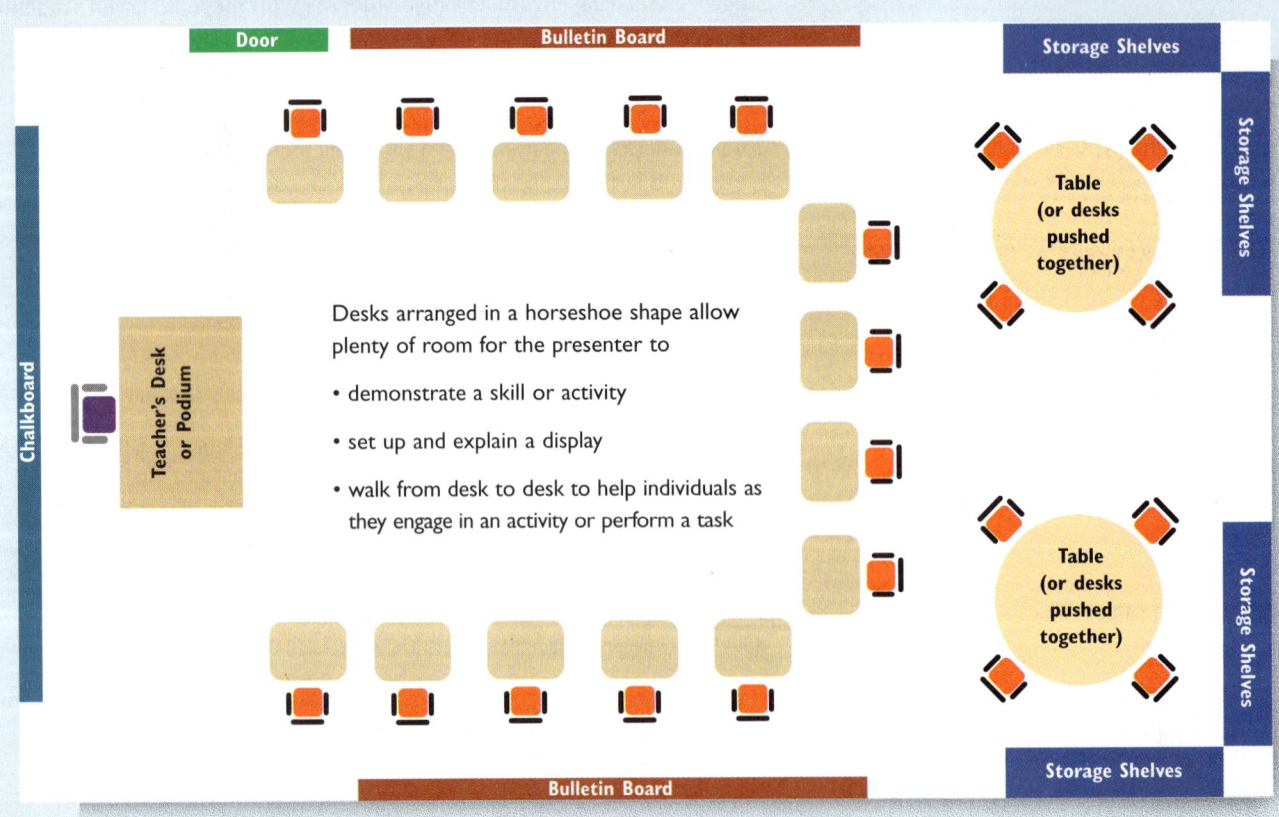

Desks arranged in a horseshoe shape allow plenty of room for the presenter to

- demonstrate a skill or activity
- set up and explain a display
- walk from desk to desk to help individuals as they engage in an activity or perform a task

T32 THE LANGUAGE OF LITERATURE TEACHER'S EDITION

Peer Tutoring & Cooperative Learning

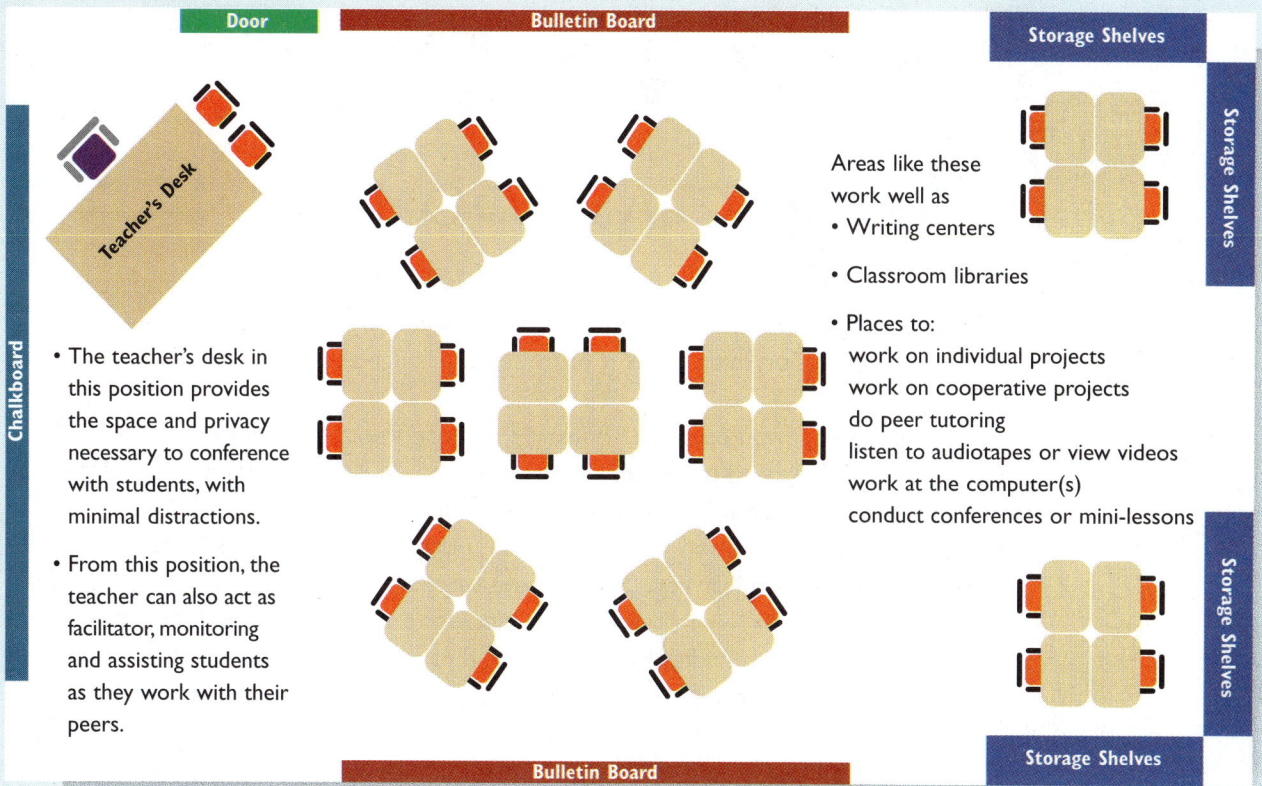

Work Stations

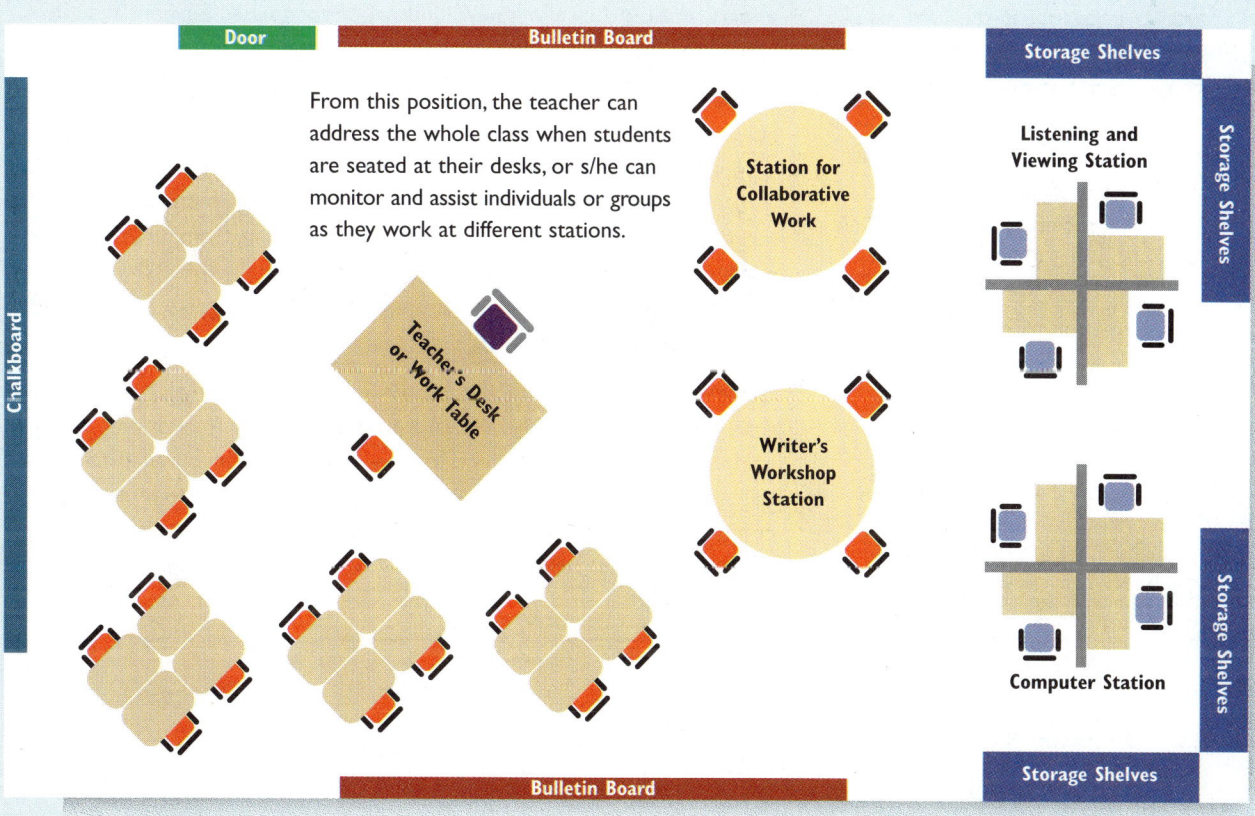

THE LANGUAGE OF LITERATURE TEACHER'S EDITION **T33**

NEW Technology AND THE ENGLISH CLASSROOM

> Technology enables students to become active participants in their own learning.
> — Jeffrey N. Golub
> Assistant Professor of English Education, University of South Florida, Tampa

The idea of using technology as part of your instructional plan is not simply the latest passing fad. Instead, it reflects continuing revelations about what is worth knowing and how students learn. For this reason, it promises to change the nature of classroom instruction.

Why is technology so important? Primarily because the use of computers is not a "spectator sport." Rather, computers require users to do the work themselves instead of passively sitting back and watching or listening to someone else—typically a teacher—dispense information. Thus, using technology enables students to become active participants in their own learning. Similarly, the teacher's role changes to that of a "designer" and "director"—one who *designs* innovative and worthwhile instructional activities and then *directs* students as they work through these activities.

Let's look for a moment at how technology is being used in English classrooms across the country.

Bringing Literature to Life

Teachers are always striving to make connections between literature and students' lives by providing "real-world" relevance in the form of historical and biographical information, cross-curricular ties, and connections to current issues. Recordings and films have always been the primary resources used to achieve this goal, but more recent technology—such as laser discs and CD-ROMs—is providing teachers with new worlds of information to draw from.

Taking the Fear Out of Writing

In probably their most familiar function, computers offer terrific opportunities for writing because (1) they provide students with more efficient and effective means of drafting, revising, editing, and publishing their writing efforts, and (2) they allow new kinds of opportunities for peer response, collaboration, and sharing.

More Enthusiastic Writers   Research has shown repeatedly that students tend to be more fluent and less inhibited when they work at computers: the many editing features and on-line resources make revision easy. In addition, publishing programs allow students to create products far more exciting than words on paper have ever been. Computers can also make portfolio building simpler and cleaner: journal entries, drafts and revisions, and finished products are easy to store, categorize, and retrieve on computers or disks.

Easier Collaboration.   If you have access to a writing lab, you will find that, with readily available software programs and by networking, or linking, the computers, students can be more easily encouraged to collaborate on their planning and writing efforts. When students can compose and comment on-screen they often become much more articulate and less reserved.

Making Connections

One of the most commonly heard complaints among teachers is that they seldom have a chance to network with each other and share ideas. Through the wonders of the Internet, this problem has all but disappeared. Education sites exist where teachers can find information ranging from developments in state assessments to projects that have worked well in other classrooms. Through the Internet, teachers can also set up classroom exchanges with other schools across the country, allow their students to go on electronic field trips, and plan interactions between the class and famous authors, scientists, and other professionals.

Developing Information Literacy

The use of technology in the English classroom enables teachers to help their students develop what will become one of the most basic skills needed for the 21st-century—media and information literacy. Students need to learn how to access information from a wide variety of both print and electronic sources; how to select appropriate information from the vast array of available resources; how to analyze and evaluate information that they read, see, and hear daily; and how to communicate their conclusions and insights clearly, completely, ethically, and persuasively. In particular, the growth of telecommunications opportunities in the form of information webs presents students with the opportunity to actively seek pertinent information and to engage in the processes of selection, analysis, and evaluation.

Conclusion These are just some of the ways in which technology can make learning happen for your students. But they help demonstrate that, if used creatively, technology can bring new excitement and levels of success to any English classroom—even while helping us achieve the same goals we have always had: to make our students solid readers, thinkers, and communicators.

Technology	Uses in the English Classroom	*The Language of Literature*
Laser Disc A 12-inch disc, used with a laser disc player, that can store thousands of still images as well as full-motion video. Images can be accessed immediately through the use of bar codes.	• To provide background information and cross-curricular connections for selection enrichment • For presenting real-world situations and images that can be used as writing springboards • To bring movies, archival material, and recordings of live performances into the classroom • To teach visual literacy	**LASERLINKS** Support for lessons in the student book, including • Author and Selection Background • Visual Vocabulary • Professional Storyteller • Writing Springboards
Floppy Discs and CD-ROMS Both are information storage devices that can hold text, still images, and full-motion video. Compact discs, however, are able to store encyclopedic amounts of information.	• As sources of additional or enhanced selections • As a reference tool: encyclopedias, atlases, and almanacs are all available in CD-ROM form • For writing: publishing software, image banks, and word processing programs all enhance student writing	**THE ELECTRONIC LIBRARY** Additional classic selections to expand program options **WRITING COACH** Special word processing program with on-line writing tips and handbooks, multiple text columns for revision and peer response, and a multimedia Idea Generator
Internet/ World Wide Web/ On-line Services A connected system of on-line computer networks through which mail and data can be transferred.	• To obtain additional information on a selection, author, or topic • To teach information-access skills • To gather professional materials, project ideas, research articles • To network with other teachers and set up classroom exchanges • To interact with authors, public figures, scientists, and other professionals	**THE MCDOUGAL LITTELL HOME PAGE** Can be accessed on World Wide Web at http://www.hmco.com/mcdougal and contains the following resources: • Internet links for specific selections in *The Language of Literature* • Teacher discussion groups/ bulletin boards • Links to professional organizations

PREPARING FOR Assessment

The word *assessment* conjures up many different images and raises just as many questions in teachers' minds. Although assessment options are often categorized as either formal or alternative, assessment activities usually embrace qualities of both kinds. Most teachers use a combination of many types of assessment in determining what a student knows or is able to do. The overview on these three pages will introduce you to the types of assessment used in *The Language of Literature* and will help you decide which ones you might want to try with your students this year. (For teacher resources and information on implementing these types of assessment, see the following three booklets: *Teacher's Guide to Assessment and Portfolio Use, Formal Assessment,* and *Alternative Assessment.*)

WHAT TYPES OF ASSESSMENT ARE THERE?

TYPES OF ASSESSMENT

FORMAL
Asks "What do you know?"

PURPOSES
Usually paper-and-pencil tests; helps teachers
- measure students' achievement against students in their own class, district, state, or country
- report students' achievement to parents and administrators
- make appropriate instructional and grouping decisions

FORMATS
Test formats are commonly
- true-false
- multiple choice
- matching
- essay
- standardized
- norm-referenced
- criterion-referenced
- objective

ALTERNATIVE
Asks "What can you do?"

PURPOSES
Usually tasks that emulate real-life situations; helps teachers
- get a broad picture of each student as a problem solver, critical thinker, and acquirer of knowledge
- measure student growth over time

TASKS
Tasks are commonly
- authentic
- products or performances
- processes

WHAT FORMS CAN ALTERNATIVE ASSESSMENT TAKE?

For more information on implementing these types of assessment, see the *Teacher's Guide to Assessment and Portfolio Use*.

> Portfolios offer one of the best vehicles for classroom-based assessment because they typically contain a variety of student work and they make it easy to separate evaluation from the process of instruction.
>
> Judith Langer and Arthur Applebee
> Professors of Education, State University of New York at Albany

✓ Product and Performance Assessment

- Requires students to produce tangible products or create performances that demonstrate their understanding of skills and concepts
- Focuses teacher's attention on the end product rather than the processes, behaviors, or strategies students used to create them
- Is based on judgment and observation guided by criteria

TYPES OF EVALUATION CRITERIA USED
Can include rubrics, formal scales and checklists, and peer and self-evaluations

POSSIBLE PRODUCTS
- scripts, dialogues
- audiotapes, videotapes
- charts, maps, graphs
- games, puzzles
- puppet shows
- plays, skits, talent shows
- interviews, debates
- role-playing
- dances
- mock trials
- cooking or sports demonstrations
- recipes, menus
- children's books
- museum exhibits
- research papers
- inventions
- book or movie reviews
- questionnaires, surveys
- print or TV ads
- poems, riddles, jokes
- time capsules
- awards
- oral histories
- murals, collages
- computer programs
- scale models, dioramas
- essays, editorials
- family trees

✓ Process Assessment

- Requires students to demonstrate or share their processes, behaviors, strategies, and critical thinking abilities as they work to understand skills and concepts
- Focuses teacher's attention on student processes, behaviors, and strategies rather than the final results
- Is based on judgment and observation guided by criteria

TYPES OF EVALUATION CRITERIA USED
Can include rubrics, formal scales and checklists, anecdotal records, observations, and self- and peer evaluations

POSSIBLE PROCESSES
While the evaluator observes students' abilities to apply higher-order thinking skills during certain processes, he or she focuses on the following:

- the use of reading strategies to develop interpretations of a text
- behavior during peer review
- evidence of investment in a task
- the ability to work in a collaborative group
- drafts created while writing an essay
- the ability to participate in class discussions
- the use of conferences to refine work
- evolving personal criteria and standards

✓ Portfolio Assessment

- Is a purposeful collection of student work that exhibits overall efforts, progress, and achievement over time in one or more areas of the curriculum
- Is a combination of process and product assessment, with a strong measure of self-evaluation and self-reflection

TYPES OF EVALUATION CRITERIA USED
Can include inventories, conference notes, rubrics, formal scales and checklists, anecdotal records, observations, and peer evaluations

POSSIBLE PRODUCTS TO INCLUDE IN THE PORTFOLIO
- interest inventories
- outlines
- written assignments
- videotapes
- reading records
- audiotapes
- performance plans
- photographs
- logs
- sketches or drawings
- journal entries
- works in progress
- textbook tasks
- research findings
- reports
- book reports or reviews
- project evaluations
- standardized tests

> If criteria for evaluation are consistent with those stressed during instruction, and if response is shared between student and teacher, assessment can become an effective complement to any learning situation.
>
> Judith Langer and Arthur Applebee
> Professors of Education, State University of New York at Albany

HOW CAN I PREPARE MY STUDENTS FOR THESE TYPES OF ASSESSMENT?

A major difference between formal assessment and alternative assessment is what you choose to assess and how you choose to assess it. Alternative assessment is a natural outgrowth and extension of classroom practices. Therefore, it is important to establish an effective learning—and testing—environment right away. Following are a few pointers to help you get started.

✔ Establish an environment based on trust.

Because alternative assessment makes students much more in charge of their own learning, and much more responsible for demonstrating their learning in a variety of ways, it is important to establish a classroom environment that is based on trust. Many of the activities students will be engaging in will be unfamiliar to them—and to you. Let them see that you are right in there with them, taking risks and trying new experiences. Help them understand that it's all right to try and fail—even seemingly unsuccessful experiences bring about growth and learning.

✔ Establish a tone of reflection and self-evaluation.

At the beginning of the year, ask your students to write letters describing themselves as readers, writers, and classroom participants. Also have them describe what they hope to accomplish during the coming year. Have them keep their letters in their notebooks, journals, or portfolios; encourage them to reread the letters regularly. Reflecting on their performance will help them acknowledge and evaluate their growth over the year. It will also help them see that learning and evaluating are ongoing and ever-changing processes.

✔ Help your students set goals and make commitments.

In order to grow as learners, your students must become actively involved in setting goals and making commitments. Their goals can be for a day, a week, a project, or the year; but whatever their duration, encourage students to consider their strengths and limitations so that the goals they set will be realistic.

✔ Help students view assessment in a new light.

One of the best things you can do for your students is help them break away from the notion that a "test" is something to study for the night before and then to forget. Help them see that alternative assessment involves a demonstration of what they know at a particular moment, but that what they know is bound to keep changing as new knowledge builds on old.

✔ Help your students discover their individual learning styles and preferences.

Chances are, most of your students are not fully aware of their own learning styles and preferences. Why not help them recognize which tasks and situations suit them best and help them learn more effectively? (See page T28.) After all, the better your students understand themselves, the better you'll understand how to teach and assess them.

✔ Encourage peer review as a regular part of the assessment process.

Sometimes it's easier for students to "get inside the minds" of their peers. And sometimes it's easier for them to take instruction or criticism from their peers. This is an excellent strategy, as long as growth and learning are taking place.

✔ Help your students learn to operate independently of you.

As students get comfortable with their learning environment, they'll probably want to do more and more without your help. Try to provide as many opportunities as possible for them to develop into independent learners— you'll be doing one of the best things you can do to prepare them for life in the real world!

✔ Improve and increase your own assessment tools.

As an evaluator, your goal should be to get as broad a view as possible of each of your students. Increasing your ability to provide situations in which you can observe your students will help you get more complete pictures of them. It will also help you learn more about yourself!

MAKING Connections

The Language of Literature bases all of its instruction on a "connected" approach to learning. On every page—from the Previewing pages to the Writing Workshops and Reading the World feature— students are encouraged to find the links between the literature, other subject areas, their own lives, and the world around them.

Of course, there are always more connections to be made, and certain themes and selections are particularly rich with possibilities. When you identify a selection or idea that you feel might have particular interest for your students, you may want to involve the class, as well as other teachers, in expanding the lesson into a more customized exploration. The following chart describes one way to accomplish this.

STEP 1 What Will We Explore?

As a class, or in small groups, have students ask questions such as the following:

- What really excited me or fascinated me about this selection?
- What questions did I have as I read this?
- What didn't I understand?
- What would I like to find out more about?
- What people, experiences, issues, or situations did this remind me of that might be interesting to explore?

TIP: Clustering, discussion, brainstorming, freewriting, and notebooks and logs are among the methods that can be used to generate ideas.

STEP 2 What Skills or Information Will We Need?

Once the questions are in place, have students identify the skills needed to find the answers. For example, the story "The Circuit" might prompt questions about the lives of the migrant worker. Will students need certain map-reading or geographical skills to learn the answers? Would information about farming or economics be important?

STEP 3 What Resources Will We Use?

At this point, students can be encouraged to plan the kinds of resources they might use to continue their exploration. Remind them of the following possibilities:

- Print resources
- Interviews
- Surveys and Questionnaires
- CD-ROM
- The Internet and other on-line resources

TIP: This is also the point at which you might collaborate with other teachers to take advantage of team teaching and block scheduling to coordinate overlapping topics. Classroom exchanges within or between schools may also be useful to arrange at this point. Technology can provide exciting options for networking as well.

STEP 4 How Will the Results Be Shared?

The methods for sharing information will be as varied as the projects themselves. Following are just a few of the possibilities students might consider:

- essays
- photo journals
- dramas
- videos
- speeches
- oral histories
- paintings
- music
- multimedia
- panel
- fairs
- community program

See page T40 for an example of the explorations generated from the selection "The Moustache."

> Teachers need to help their students feel integral and involved in their community and the larger world.
>
> Susan Hynds
> Professor of English Education,
> Syracuse University, Syracuse, New York

A SAMPLE PLANNING MAP

Below is an example of the different explorations that were generated from one story by a teacher following the approach outlined on page T39.

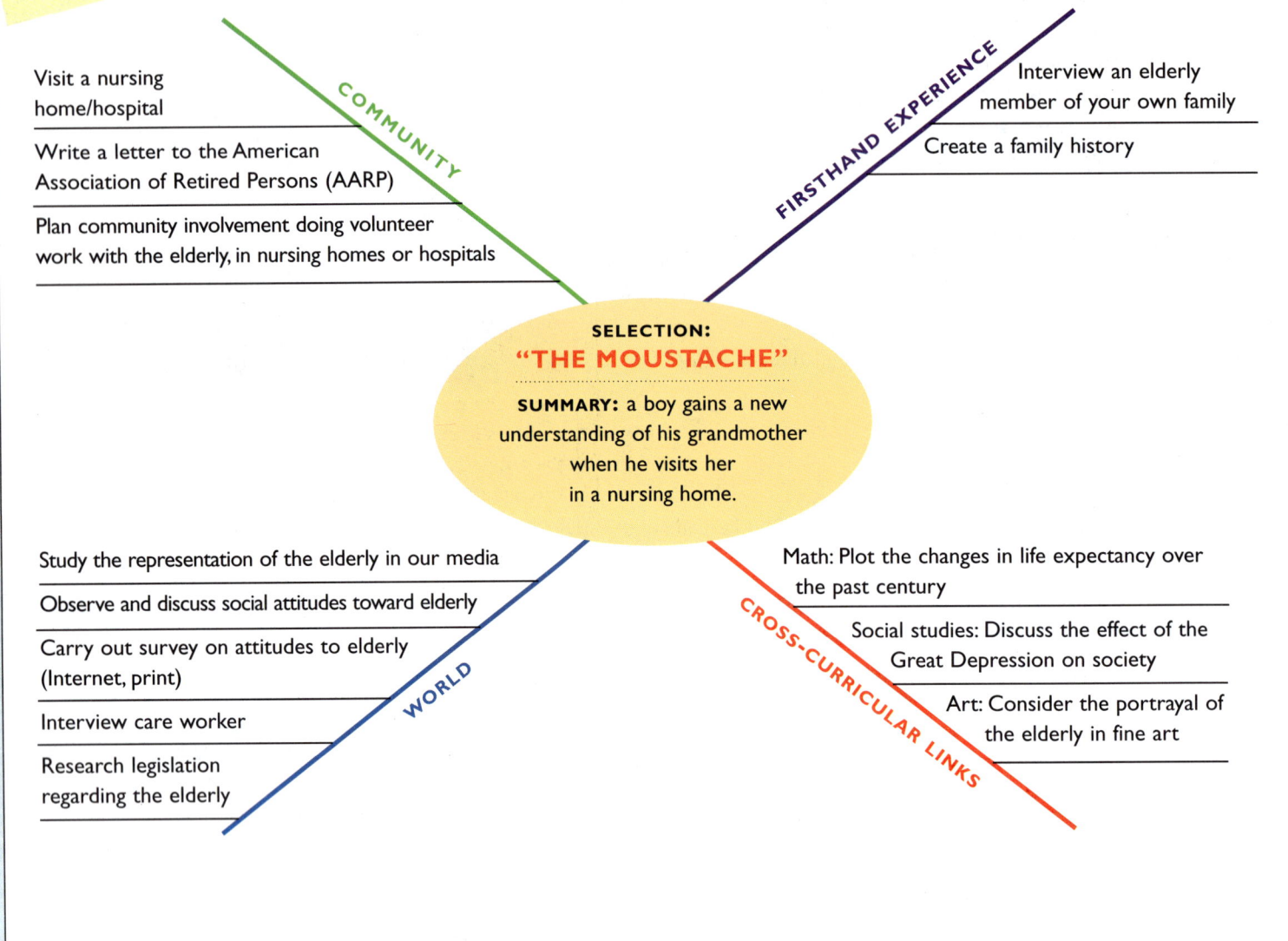

COMMUNITY
- Visit a nursing home/hospital
- Write a letter to the American Association of Retired Persons (AARP)
- Plan community involvement doing volunteer work with the elderly, in nursing homes or hospitals

FIRSTHAND EXPERIENCE
- Interview an elderly member of your own family
- Create a family history

SELECTION: "THE MOUSTACHE"
SUMMARY: a boy gains a new understanding of his grandmother when he visits her in a nursing home.

WORLD
- Study the representation of the elderly in our media
- Observe and discuss social attitudes toward elderly
- Carry out survey on attitudes to elderly (Internet, print)
- Interview care worker
- Research legislation regarding the elderly

CROSS-CURRICULAR LINKS
- Math: Plot the changes in life expectancy over the past century
- Social studies: Discuss the effect of the Great Depression on society
- Art: Consider the portrayal of the elderly in fine art

T40 THE LANGUAGE OF LITERATURE TEACHER'S EDITION

McDougal Littell

THE LANGUAGE OF
LITERATURE

McDougal Littell

THE LANGUAGE OF
LITERATURE

Arthur N. Applebee

Andrea B. Bermúdez

Sheridan Blau

Rebekah Caplan

Franchelle Dorn

Peter Elbow

Susan Hynds

Judith A. Langer

James Marshall

McDougal Littell
A HOUGHTON MIFFLIN COMPANY

Evanston, Illinois ▪ Boston ▪ Dallas

Acknowledgments

Unit One

Putnam Publishing Group: "Two Kinds" from *The Joy Luck Club* by Amy Tan; Copyright © 1989 by Amy Tan. By permission of G. P. Putnam's Sons, a division of Putnam Publishing Group.

Rosemary Catacalos: "La Casa," from *Again for the First Time* by Rosemary Catacalos; Copyright © 1984. By permission of the author.

University of Hawaii Press: "Cranes" by Hwang Sunwŏn, from *Flowers of Fire: Twentieth-Century Korean Stories,* edited and translated by Peter H. Lee; Copyright © 1974, 1986 by the University of Hawaii Press. By permission of the University of Hawaii Press.

New Directions Publishing Corp. and Watkins/Loomis Agency, Inc.: "Winter Night," from *Fifty Stories* by Kay Boyle; Copyright © 1980 by Kay Boyle. Reprinted by permission of New Directions Publishing Corp. and the estate of Kay Boyle.

Simon & Schuster, Inc.: Excerpt from *Kaffir Boy* by Mark Mathabane; Copyright © 1986 by Mark Mathabane. Reprinted by permission of Simon & Schuster.

Continued on page 1122

Cover Art

Background photo: Bali, Indonesia, Copyright © Ian Lloyd / Black Star. **Painting:** *Forbidden Fruit*, Simon Ng. Reprinted with the permission of Simon & Schuster Books for Young Readers, an imprint of Simon & Schuster Children's Publishing Division. From *Tales from Gold Mountain: Stories of the Chinese in the New World*, a Groundwood Book / Douglas & McIntyre. Text Copyright © by Paul Yee, illustrations Copyright © 1989 by Simon Ng. **Statue:** Ere alaafin Shangó [Shangó, Oyo-Ilé warrior-king] (early 19th century), Oyo-Shangó artist. Collection of the Nigerian Museum, Lagos. Photo by Robert Farris Thompson, 1962. **Book:** Photo by Alan Shortall. **Coins and frame:** Photos by Sharon Hoogstraten.

Warning: No part of this work may be reproduced or transmitted in any form or by any means, electronic or mechanical, including photocopying and recording, or by any information storage or retrieval system without prior written permission of McDougal Littell Inc. unless such copying is expressly permitted by federal copyright law. Address inquiries to Manager, Rights and Permissions, McDougal Littell Inc., P.O. Box 1667, Evanston, IL 60204

ISBN 0-395-73705-2

Copyright © 1997 by McDougal Littell Inc. All rights reserved.
Printed in the United States of America.

1 2 3 4 5 6 7 8 9 – RRD – 02 01 00 99 98 97 96

Senior Consultants

The senior consultants guided the conceptual development for *The Language of Literature* series. They participated actively in shaping prototype materials for major components, and they reviewed completed prototypes and/or completed units to ensure consistency with current research and the philosophy of the series.

Arthur N. Applebee Professor of Education, State University of New York at Albany; Director, Center for the Learning and Teaching of Literature; Senior Fellow, Center for Writing and Literacy

Andrea B. Bermúdez Professor of Studies in Language and Culture; Director, Research Center for Language and Culture; Chair, Foundations and Professional Studies, University of Houston-Clear Lake

Sheridan Blau Senior Lecturer in English and Education and former Director of Composition, University of California at Santa Barbara; Director, South Coast Writing Project; Director, Literature Institute for Teachers; Vice President, National Council of Teachers of English

Rebekah Caplan Coordinator, English Language Arts K-12, Oakland Unified School District, Oakland, California; Teacher-Consultant, Bay Area Writing Project, University of California at Berkeley; served on the California State English Assessment Development Team for Language Arts

Franchelle Dorn Professor Drama, Howard University, Washington, D.C.; Adjunct Professor, Graduate School of Opera, University of Maryland, College Park, Maryland; Co-founder of The Shakespeare Acting Conservatory, Washington, D.C.

Peter Elbow Professor of English, University of Massachusetts at Amherst; Fellow, Bard Center for Writing and Thinking

Susan Hynds Professor and Director of English Education, Syracuse University, Syracuse, New York

Judith A. Langer Professor of Education, State University of New York at Albany; Co-director, Center for the Learning and Teaching of Literature; Senior Fellow, Center for Writing and Literacy

James Marshall Professor of English and English Education, University of Iowa, Iowa City

Contributing Consultants

Tommy Boley Associate Professor of English, University of Texas at El Paso

Jeffrey N. Golub Assistant Professor of English Education, University of South Florida, Tampa

William L. McBride, Ph.D. Reading and Curriculum Specialist; former middle and high school English instructor

Multicultural Advisory Board

The multicultural advisors reviewed literature selections for appropriate content and made suggestions for teaching lessons in a multicultural classroom.

Dr. Joyce M. Bell, Chairperson, English Department, Townview Magnet Center, Dallas, Texas

Dr. Eugenia W. Collier, author; lecturer; Chairperson, Department of English and Language Arts; teacher of Creative Writing and American Literature, Morgan State University, Maryland

Kathleen S. Fowler, President, Palm Beach County Council of Teachers of English, Boca Raton Middle School, Boca Raton, Florida

Noreen M. Rodriguez, Trainer for Hillsborough County School District's Staff Development Division, independent consultant, Gaither High School, Tampa, Florida

Michelle Dixon Thompson, Seabreeze High School, Daytona Beach, Florida

Teacher Review Panels

The following educators provided ongoing review during the development of the tables of contents, lesson design, and key components of the program.

FLORIDA

Judi Briant, English Department Chairperson, Armwood High School, Hillsborough County School District

Beth Johnson, Polk County English Supervisor, Polk County School District

Sharon Johnston, Learning Resource Specialist, Evans High School, Orange County School District

Continued on page 1131

Manuscript Reviewers

The following educators reviewed prototype lessons and tables of contents during the development of *The Language of Literature* program.

Carol Alves, English Department Chairperson, Apopka High School, Apopka, Florida

Jacqueline Anderson, James A. Foshay Learning Center, Los Angeles, California

Kathleen M. Anderson-Knight, United Township High School, East Moline, Illinois

Anita Arnold, Thomas Jefferson High School, San Antonio, Texas

Cassandra L. Asberry, Justin F. Kimball High School, Dallas, Texas

Don Baker, English Department Chairperson, Peoria High School, Peoria, Illinois

Continued on page 1133

Student Board

The student board members read and evaluated selections to assess their appeal for tenth-grade students.

Jayme Charak, Niles North High School, Skokie, Illinois

Amy Dobelstein, Shades Valley Resource Learning Center, Birmingham, Alabama

Quoleshna Z. Elbert, Lincoln College Preparatory Academy, Kansas City, Missouri

Katrina Gorski, Loudon County High School, Leesburg, Virginia

Geoffrey L. Harvey, Phineas Banning High School, Wilmington, California

Katherine McGuire, Lyons Township High School, Western Springs, Illinois

Emily Myers, Union High School, Grand Rapids, Michigan

Ronnie G. Pigao, Phineas Banning High School, Wilmington, California

Josh Raub, Lakeview High School, Lakeville, Minnesota

Kevin Schatzman, Miami Killian Sr. High School, Miami, Florida

Stephanie Stone, John Marshall High School, San Antonio, Texas

Cynthia Villicana, Phineas Banning High School, Wilmington, California

Adriana M. Zuñiga, San Marcos High School, San Marcos, Texas

THE LANGUAGE OF LITERATURE
Overview

Student Anthology
Learning the Language of Literature

Strategies for Reading 5
Reading Model: The Interlopers by Saki 6

UNIT ONE — ***Imprints of the Past*** 12
    PART 1: Lasting Impressions / 14   **PART 2:** The Power of Heritage / 108
        WRITING ABOUT LITERATURE: WRITING FROM EXPERIENCE:
        Direct Response / 100   Firsthand and Expressive Writing / 166

UNIT TWO — ***Reflecting on Society*** 176
    PART 1: Challenging the System / 178   **PART 2:** Prisoners of Circumstance / 264
        WRITING ABOUT LITERATURE: WRITING FROM EXPERIENCE:
        Analysis / 256   Persuasion / 340

UNIT THREE — ***In the Name of Love*** 350
    PART 1: The Ties That Bind / 352   **PART 2:** Mysteries of the Heart / 428
        WRITING ABOUT LITERATURE: WRITING FROM EXPERIENCE:
        Creative Response / 420   Informative Exposition / 500

UNIT FOUR — ***Moments of Truth*** 510
    PART 1: Unexpected Realizations / 512   **PART 2:** What Matters Most / 592
        WRITING ABOUT LITERATURE: WRITING FROM EXPERIENCE:
        Interpretation / 584   Informative Exposition / 658

UNIT FIVE — ***Nothing Stays the Same*** 668
    PART 1: Progress and its Price / 670   **PART 2:** Cultural Crossroads / 742
        WRITING ABOUT LITERATURE: WRITING FROM EXPERIENCE:
        Creative Response / 734   Narrative and Literary Writing / 796

UNIT SIX — ***The Making of Heroes*** 806
    PART 1: A Strength from Within / 808   **PART 2:** The Heroic Tradition / 902
        WRITING ABOUT LITERATURE: WRITING FROM EXPERIENCE:
        Criticism / 894   Report / 984

Words to Know: Access Guide 996
Handbook of Literary Terms 1000
Writing Handbook 1018
Multimedia Handbook 1048
Grammar Handbook 1058
Index of Fine Art 1104
Index of Skills 1108
Index of Titles and Authors 1119

Literature Connections

Each book in the Literature Connections series combines a novel or play with related readings—poems, stories, plays, essays, articles—that provide new perspectives on the theme or subject matter of the longer work. For example, Nathaniel Hawthorne's *The Scarlet Letter* is combined with the following readings, which focus on modern applications and humorous retellings of the novel and on such topics as the Puritans, scapegoating, sin, and temptation.

John Dunton	**Muddy Brains**
Richard Armour	*from* **The Classics Reclassified**
Kate Chopin	**A Respectable Woman**
Emily Dickinson	**For Each Ecstatic Instant**
Emily Dickinson	**Mine Enemy Is Growing Old**
Bible	**Psalm 32**
Shirley Jackson	**The Lottery**
Toni Locy	**Concerns Raised on "Scarlet Letter" for Drunk Drivers**

The Adventures of Huckleberry Finn*
Mark Twain

. . . And the Earth Did Not Devour Him
Tomás Rivera

Animal Farm
George Orwell

The Crucible
Arthur Miller

Ethan Frome
Edith Wharton

Fallen Angels
Walter Dean Myers

The Friends
Rosa Guy

Hamlet
William Shakespeare

Jane Eyre*
Charlotte Brontë

Julius Caesar
William Shakespeare

Macbeth
William Shakespeare

A Midsummer Night's Dream
William Shakespeare

My Ántonia
Willa Cather

Nervous Conditions
Tsitsi Dangarembga

Picture Bride
Yoshiko Uchida

A Place Where the Sea Remembers
Sandra Benítez

Pygmalion
George Bernard Shaw

A Raisin in the Sun
Lorraine Hansberry

The Scarlet Letter
Nathaniel Hawthorne

A Tale of Two Cities*
Charles Dickens

Things Fall Apart
Chinua Achebe

To Kill a Mockingbird: The Screenplay
Horton Foote

The Tragedy of Romeo and Juliet*
William Shakespeare

The Underdogs
Mariano Azuela

West with the Night
Beryl Markham

When Rain Clouds Gather
Bessie Head

*McDougal Littell offers a Spanish version.

UNIT ONE *Imprints of the Past* 12

Part 1 Lasting Impressions

WHAT DO YOU THINK? Reflecting on Theme 14

▸ **FOCUS ON FICTION** 16

Amy Tan ■ United States	**Two Kinds** . . . . FICTION 18	
Rosemary Catacalos ■ United States	**La Casa** / INSIGHT . . . . POETRY 30	
Hwang Sunwŏn ■ Korea	**Cranes** . . . . FICTION 33	
Kay Boyle ■ United States	**Winter Night** . . . . FICTION 40	
Leo Tolstoy ■ Russia	**After the Ball** . . . . FICTION 51	

▸ **FOCUS ON NONFICTION** 65

Mark Mathabane ■ South Africa / United States   *from* **Kaffir Boy** . . . . NONFICTION 67

Nicholas Gage ■ Greece / United States   **The Teacher Who Changed My Life** . . . . NONFICTION 83

Colette ■ France   *from* **Earthly Paradise**
ON YOUR OWN / ASSESSMENT OPTION . . . . NONFICTION 92

✏ **WRITING ABOUT LITERATURE**   **Direct Response**

Writer's Style: Creating Dialogue 100
Guided Assignment: Write a Personal Response 102
Grammar in Context: Pronouns and Their Antecedents 105
   SKILLBUILDERS: Writing Realistic Dialogue, Using Elaboration,
                          Achieving Pronoun-Antecedent Agreement

READING THE WORLD: VISUAL LITERACY 106
Portrayal of a Group 107
   SKILLBUILDER: Evaluating Images

x

x THE LANGUAGE OF LITERATURE TEACHER'S EDITION

Part 2 The Power of Heritage

WHAT DO YOU THINK? Reflecting on Theme 108

Alice Walker ▪ United States	**Everyday Use**	FICTION	110
Teresa Paloma Acosta ▪ United States	**My Mother Pieced Quilts** / INSIGHT	POETRY	120
Tom Whitecloud ▪ United States	**Blue Winds Dancing**	NONFICTION	124
	▶FOCUS ON POETRY		133
D. H. Lawrence ▪ England	**Piano**	POETRY	135
Robert Hayden ▪ United States	**Those Winter Sundays**	POETRY	135
Le Ly Hayslip ▪ Vietnam	*from* **When Heaven and Earth Changed Places**	NONFICTION	140
Frank O'Connor ▪ Ireland	**The Study of History**	FICTION	151
Langston Hughes ▪ United States	**Afro-American Fragment**	POETRY	164

ON YOUR OWN / ASSESSMENT OPTION

WRITING FROM EXPERIENCE   Firsthand and Expressive Writing

Guided Assignment: Write about an Autobiographical Incident............ 166
  Prewriting: Exploring Experiences
  Drafting: Getting Your Ideas Down
  Revising and Publishing: Finishing Your Story
  SKILLBUILDERS: Locating Information, Using Levels of
       Language Appropriately, Using
       Quotation Marks in Dialogue

UNIT REVIEW: Reflect & Assess 174

UNIT TWO Reflecting on Society

Part 1 Challenging the System

WHAT DO YOU THINK?	Reflecting on Theme		178
	▶ FOCUS ON DRAMA		180
Josephine Tey ▪ Great Britain	**The Pen of My Aunt**	DRAMA	182
W. P. Kinsella ▪ Canada	**The Thrill of the Grass**	FICTION	198
Heinrich Böll ▪ Germany	**The Balek Scales**	FICTION	211
Coretta Scott King ▪ United States	from **Montgomery Boycott**	NONFICTION	221
Margaret Walker ▪ United States	**Sit-Ins** / INSIGHT	POETRY	229
Bessie Head ▪ South Africa / Botswana	**The Prisoner Who Wore Glasses**	FICTION	232
Armando Valladares ▪ Cuba	**They Have Not Been Able /** **No Han Podido** / INSIGHT	POETRY	239
Luisa Valenzuela ▪ Argentina	**The Censors**	FICTION	242
E. M. Forster ▪ Great Britain	from **Tolerance**	NONFICTION	248
Li Bo ▪ China	**Fighting South of the Ramparts** ON YOUR OWN / ASSESSMENT OPTION	POETRY	254

WRITING ABOUT LITERATURE — Analysis

Writer's Style: Paragraph Coherence 256
Guided Assignment: Analyze a Setting 258
Grammar in Context: Prepositional Phrases 261
   SKILLBUILDERS: Using Transition Words and Phrases, Creating a Mood, Achieving Subject-Verb Agreement with Prepositional Phrases

READING THE WORLD: VISUAL LITERACY 262
Impact of Setting 262
   SKILLBUILDER: Analyzing Components of Setting

Part 2 Prisoners of Circumstance

WHAT DO YOU THINK? Reflecting on Theme 264

Tim O'Brien ▪ United States	**On the Rainy River**	FICTION	266
Yukio Mishima ▪ Japan	**The Pearl**	FICTION	284
Brent Staples ▪ United States	**Black Men and Public Space**	NONFICTION	297
Lucille Clifton ▪ United States	**Miss Rosie**	POETRY	303
Gwendolyn Brooks ▪ United States	**Kitchenette Building**	POETRY	303
Elie Wiesel ▪ Romania / United States	from **Night**	NONFICTION	308
	from **Nobel Prize Acceptance Speech** / INSIGHT	NONFICTION	314
Blaga Dimitrova ▪ Bulgaria	**The Women Who Are Poets in My Land**	POETRY	317
Julio Cortázar ▪ Argentina	**House Taken Over**	FICTION	321
Jeanne Wakatsuki Houston and James D. Houston ▪ United States	from **Farewell to Manzanar** ON YOUR OWN / ASSESSMENT OPTION	NONFICTION	330

✏️ **WRITING FROM EXPERIENCE**   Persuasion

Guided Assignment: Write a Persuasive Essay 340
    Prewriting: Investigating the Issue
    Drafting: Getting Your Ideas Down
    Revising and Publishing: Fine-Tuning Your Essay
    SKILLBUILDERS: Evaluating Sources, Creating Emphasis, Using Pronouns

UNIT REVIEW: Reflect & Assess 348

xiii

THE LANGUAGE OF LITERATURE **TEACHER'S EDITION** **xiii**

UNIT THREE *In the Name of Love* — 350

Part 1 The Ties That Bind

WHAT DO YOU THINK? Reflecting on Theme 352

Rosamunde Pilcher ▪ Great Britain	**Lalla**	FICTION	354
Luis Lloréns Torres ▪ Puerto Rico	**Love Without Love**	POETRY	370
Amy Lowell ▪ United States	**The Taxi**	POETRY	370
William Shakespeare ▪ Great Britain	**Sonnet 18**	POETRY	376
Edna St. Vincent Millay ▪ United States	**Sonnet 30**	POETRY	376
James Herriot ▪ Great Britain	**A Case of Cruelty**	NONFICTION	381
Gabriela Mistral ▪ Chile	**Eight Puppies / Ocho Perritos** / INSIGHT	POETRY	392
Zhang Jie ▪ China	**Love Must Not Be Forgotten**	FICTION	396
Mary Lavin ▪ Ireland	**Brigid**	FICTION	411

ON YOUR OWN / ASSESSMENT OPTION

WRITING ABOUT LITERATURE   Creative Response

Writer's Style: Figurative Language 420
Guided Assignment: Write a Poem 422
Grammar in Context: Participial Phrases 425
   SKILLBUILDERS: Avoiding Clichés, Using Sound Devices,
      Using Punctuation in Poetry

READING THE WORLD: VISUAL LITERACY 426
Seeing Metaphor 427
   SKILLBUILDER: Making Observations

Part 2 Mysteries of the Heart

WHAT DO YOU THINK? Reflecting on Theme 428

Mark Twain ▪ United States	**The Californian's Tale**	FICTION	430
Su Dong Po ▪ China	**To a Traveler** / INSIGHT	POETRY	438
N. Scott Momaday ▪ United States	**Simile**	POETRY	441
Pablo Neruda ▪ Chile)	**Tonight I Can Write . . . / Puedo Escribir Los Versos . . .**	POETRY	441
Aleksandr Pushkin ▪ Russia	**To . . .**	POETRY	448
Rachel de Queiroz ▪ Brazil	**Metonymy, or The Husband's Revenge**	FICTION	452
Bernard Malamud ▪ United States	**The First Seven Years**	FICTION	460
Anton Chekhov ▪ Russia	**The Bear**	DRAMA	473
Anonymous ▪ China	**The Lady Who Was a Beggar**	FOLK TALE	488

ON YOUR OWN / ASSESSMENT OPTION

✏️ **WRITING FROM EXPERIENCE**   Informative Exposition

Guided Assignment: Write a Compare-and-Contrast Essay 500
    Prewriting: Exploring Information
    Drafting: Getting Your Ideas Down
    Revising and Publishing: Finishing Your Essay
    SKILLBUILDERS: Using Library Resources, Using Parallel
        Structure, Avoiding Double Comparisons

UNIT REVIEW: Reflect & Assess 508

UNIT FOUR Moments of Truth — 510

Part 1 Unexpected Realizations

WHAT DO YOU THINK? Reflecting on Theme 512

Jorge Luis Borges ▪ Argentina	**The Meeting**	FICTION	514
Agatha Christie ▪ Great Britain	**The Witness for the Prosecution**	FICTION	523
Anita Desai ▪ India	**Games at Twilight**	FICTION	545
Octavio Paz ▪ Mexico	**The Street / La Calle**	POETRY	556
Juan Ramón Jiménez ▪ Spain	**I Am Not I / Yo No Soy Yo**	POETRY	556
Loren Eiseley ▪ United States	from **The Unexpected Universe**	NONFICTION	562
Guy de Maupassant ▪ France	**Two Friends**	FICTION	567
José Martí ▪ Cuba	from **Simple Poetry / Versos Sencillos** / INSIGHT	POETRY	577
Samuel Selvon ▪ Trinidad	**When Greek Meets Greek** ON YOUR OWN / ASSESSMENT OPTION	FICTION	580

✏️ WRITING ABOUT LITERATURE Interpretation

Writer's Style: Using Tone 584
Guided Assignment: Interpret a Poem 586
Grammar in Context: Quoting from Poetry 589
   SKILLBUILDERS: Recognizing Connotation, Writing a Thesis Statement, Styling Titles of Literary Texts

READING THE WORLD: VISUAL LITERACY 590
Look Again 591
   SKILLBUILDER: Making Careful Observations

xvi THE LANGUAGE OF LITERATURE TEACHER'S EDITION

Part 2 What Matters Most

WHAT DO YOU THINK? Reflecting on Theme...................................... 592

Sarah Orne Jewett ▪ United States	**A White Heron**.................................	FICTION	594
R. K. Narayan ▪ India	**Like the Sun**...................................	FICTION	608
Emily Dickinson ▪ United States	**Tell all the Truth but tell it slant—** / INSIGHT	POETRY	612
Gabriel Okara ▪ Nigeria	**Once upon a Time**............................	POETRY	615
Maxine Kumin ▪ United States	**Making the Jam Without You**..............	POETRY	615
Rabindranath Tagore ▪ India	**The Cabuliwallah**.............................	FICTION	622
Denise Levertov ▪ Great Britain / United States	**For the New Year, 1981**.....................	POETRY	632
Dahlia Ravikovitch ▪ Israel	**Pride**..	POETRY	632
Abioseh Nicol ▪ Sierra Leone	**As the Night the Day**.......................	FICTION	638
Yevgeny Yevtushenko ▪ Russia	from **A Precocious Autobiography**........	NONFICTION	652

ON YOUR OWN / ASSESSMENT OPTION

✏️ **WRITING FROM EXPERIENCE** **Informative Exposition**

Guided Assignment: Write a Cause-and-Effect Essay............ 658
  Prewriting: Answering Questions
  Drafting: Making Connections
  Revising and Publishing: Clarifying Connections
  SKILLBUILDERS: Avoiding Logical Fallacies, Creating Coherence in Paragraphs, Avoiding Sentence Fragments

UNIT REVIEW: Reflect & Assess............................... 666

UNIT FIVE *Nothing Stays the Same*   668

Part 1 Progress and Its Price

WHAT DO YOU THINK? Reflecting on Theme 670

Joan Aiken ▪ Great Britain	**Searching for Summer**	FICTION	672
Ray Bradbury ▪ United States	**A Sound of Thunder**	FICTION	682
Tao Qian ▪ China	**Poem on Returning to Dwell in the Country**	POETRY	696
Mary Oliver ▪ United States	**The Sun**	POETRY	696
E. B. White ▪ United States	**Once More to the Lake**	NONFICTION	702
Stephen Vincent Benét ▪ United States	**By the Waters of Babylon**	FICTION	713
Sara Teasdale ▪ United States	**There Will Come Soft Rains** / INSIGHT	POETRY	723
Stanislaw Lem ▪ Poland	**Trurl's Machine**	FICTION	727

ON YOUR OWN / ASSESSMENT OPTION

✏️ **WRITING ABOUT LITERATURE**   Creative Response

Writer's Style: Paragraph Unity 734
Guided Assignment: Change a Story Element 736
Grammar in Context: Past Perfect Tense 739
  SKILLBUILDERS: Using Compound Subjects and Predicates, Using Graphic Organizers, Past Participles of Irregular Verbs

READING THE WORLD: VISUAL LITERACY 740
New and Improved? 740
  SKILLBUILDER: Comparing and Contrasting Products

Part 2 Cultural Crossroads

WHAT DO YOU THINK? Reflecting on Theme 742

Doris Lessing ▪ Southern Rhodesia / Great Britain	**No Witchcraft for Sale** .... FICTION 744
Nguyen Thi Vinh ▪ Vietnam	**Thoughts of Hanoi** .... POETRY 754
Isaac Bashevis Singer ▪ Poland / United States	**The Son from America** .... FICTION 761
Linda Pastan ▪ United States	**Grudnow** / INSIGHT .... POETRY 768
Santha Rama Rau ▪ India	**By Any Other Name** .... NONFICTION 772
Chinua Achebe ▪ Nigeria	**Marriage Is a Private Affair** .... FICTION 780
Cathy Song ▪ United States	**Lost Sister** .... POETRY 789
Judith Wright ▪ Australia	**Bora Ring** .... POETRY 794

ON YOUR OWN / ASSESSMENT OPTION

✏ WRITING FROM EXPERIENCE   Narrative and Literary Writing

Guided Assignment: Write a Scene for a Play 796
    Prewriting: Setting the Stage
    Drafting: Developing Your Script
    Revising and Publishing: Staging Your Scene
    SKILLBUILDERS: Writing Stage Directions, Writing Dialogue, Formatting Your Script

UNIT REVIEW: Reflect & Assess 804

UNIT SIX The Making of Heroes   806

Part 1 A Strength from Within

WHAT DO YOU THINK? Reflecting on Theme 808

Nadine Gordimer ▪ South Africa	**A Chip of Glass Ruby**	FICTION	810
Roger Rosenblatt ▪ United States	**The Man in the Water**	NONFICTION	823
Isabel Allende ▪ Chile / United States	**And of Clay Are We Created**	FICTION	829
Rosario Castellanos ▪ Mexico	**Nocturne / Nocturno** / INSIGHT	POETRY	840
Louise Erdrich ▪ United States	**The Leap**	FICTION	844
Yossi Ghinsberg ▪ Israel	from **Back from Tuichi**	NONFICTION	855
Josephina Niggli ▪ Mexico / United States	**The Ring of General Macías**	DRAMA	869
Doris Herold Lund ▪ United States	**Gift from a Son Who Died**	NONFICTION	886

ON YOUR OWN / ASSESSMENT OPTION

✏️ WRITING ABOUT LITERATURE   Criticism

Writer's Style: Elaboration 894
Guided Assignment: Write a Critical Essay 896
Grammar in Context: Using Adverbs 899
   SKILLBUILDERS: Using Adjective Clauses, Types of Peer
               Responses, Positioning Adverbs Correctly

READING THE WORLD: VISUAL LITERACY 900
Focus on Ideas 900
   SKILLBUILDER: Interpreting a Situation

Part 2   The Heroic Tradition

WHAT DO YOU THINK? Reflecting on Theme 902

Sir Thomas Malory ▪ Great Britain	*from* **Le Morte d'Arthur** .... ROMANCE .... 904 **The Crowning of Arthur** **Sir Launcelot du Lake**	
John Steinbeck ▪ United States	*from* **The Acts of King Arthur** .... ROMANCE .... 923 **and His Noble Knights**	
Adrienne Rich ▪ United States	**The Knight** / INSIGHT .... POETRY 932	
Sophocles ▪ Ancient Greece translated by Dudley Fitts and Robert Fitzgerald	**Antigone** .... DRAMA 936	
Traditonal ▪ West Africa	**Old Song** .... POETRY 982	

WRITING FROM EXPERIENCE   Report

Guided Assignment: Write a Biographical Research Paper 984
   Prewriting: Researching Your Hero
   Drafting: Drafting Your Report
   Revising and Publishing: The Finishing Touches
   SKILLBUILDERS: Finding Reference Sources, Evaluating
         Sources, Using Ellipses and Brackets

UNIT REVIEW: Reflect & Assess 992

xxi

Electronic Library

The *Electronic Library* is a CD-ROM that contains additional fiction, nonfiction, poetry, and drama for each unit in *The Language of Literature*.

Preliminary List of Titles

Unit 1

Pat Mora	**The Border**
Tacitus	**The Burning of Rome**
Lu Xün	**My Old Home**
Léon Damas	**Hiccups**
Anatole France	**Putois**
Sophocles	**Oedipus Rex**
Tru Vu	**Who Am I?**
Czeslaw Milosz	**My Faithful Mother Tongue**
Minfong Ho	**The Winter Hibiscus**

Unit 2

Italo Calvino	**Santa's Children**
Henrik Ibsen	**A Doll's House**
Bertolt Brecht	**To Posterity**
Mikhail Zoshchenko	**Bees and People**
Ilse Aichinger	**The Bound Man**
Franz Kafka	**A Hunger Artist**
Miguel Hernández	**War**
Ben Okri	**In the Shadow of War**

Unit 3

Karel Čapek	**The Stamp Collection**
Tu Fu	**The Return**
Alfonsina Storni	**One More Time**
Petrarch	**The Spring Returns**
Sappho	**Leaving Crete**
Ovid	**The Story of Pyramus and Thisbe**
Colette	**The Other Wife**
Isak Dinesen	**The Ring**
Luigi Pirandello	**War**

Note: A complete list of literature available for all grade levels accompanies each CD-ROM.

Gabriela Mistral	**Intimate**
Serafín and Joaquín Alvarez Quintero	**A Sunny Morning**
Horacio Quiroga	**Three Letters . . . and a Footnote**

Unit 4

Selma Lagerlöf	**The Rat Trap** **The Silver Mine**
Junichiro Tanizaki	**The Thief**
Woody Allen	**Death Knocks**
Marguerite Yourcenar	**How Wang-Fo Was Saved**
Molière	**Tartuffe**
Nicholasa Mohr	**A Thanksgiving Celebration**
Nathaniel Hawthorne	**The Birthmark**
Elizabeth Jolley	**Mr. Parker's Valentine**
Emily Brontë	**To Imagination**
Jesus del Corral	**Cross Over, Sawyer!**
E.T.A. Hoffmann	**The Sandman**

Unit 5

Yehuda Amichai	**The Diameter of the Bomb**
Walter Van Tilburg Clark	**The Portable Phonograph**
H.G. Wells	**The Stolen Bacillus**
Naguib Mahfouz	**Half a Day**
Witi Ihimaera	**His First Ball**
Alphonse Daudet	**The Last Lesson**

Unit 6

Isaac Bashevis Singer	**The Washwoman**
Stephen Crane	**A Mystery of Heroism**
Albert Camus	**The Myth of Sisyphus**
Willa Cather	**Neighbor Rosicky**
Émile Zola	**The Attack on the Mill**
Virgil	***from* the Aeneid**
Plato	***from* The Apology**
Ursula Le Guin	**The Lady of Moge**
Edgar Allan Poe	**Eldorado**
Johann Wolfgang von Goethe	**Prometheus**

Selections by Genre, Writing Workshops

Fiction

The Interlopers	6
Two Kinds	18
Cranes	33
Winter Night	40
After the Ball	51
Everyday Use	110
The Study of History	151
The Thrill of the Grass	198
The Balek Scales	211
The Prisoner Who Wore Glasses	232
The Censors	242
On the Rainy River	266
The Pearl	284
House Taken Over	321
Lalla	354
Love Must Not Be Forgotten	396
Brigid	411
The Californian's Tale	430
Metonymy, or The Husband's Revenge	452
The First Seven Years	460
The Lady Who Was a Beggar	488
The Meeting	514
The Witness for the Prosecution	523
Games at Twilight	545
Two Friends	567
When Greek Meets Greek	580
A White Heron	594
Like the Sun	608
The Cabuliwallah	622
As the Night the Day	638
Searching for Summer	672
A Sound of Thunder	682
By the Waters of Babylon	713
Trurl's Machine	727
No Witchcraft for Sale	744
The Son from America	761
Marriage Is a Private Affair	780
A Chip of Glass Ruby	810
And of Clay Are We Created	829
The Leap	844
from Le Morte d'Arthur	904
The Acts of King Arthur and His Noble Knights	923

Nonfiction

from Kaffir Boy	67
The Teacher Who Changed My Life	83
from Earthly Paradise	92
Blue Winds Dancing	124
from When Heaven and Earth Changed Places	140
from Montgomery Boycott	221
from Tolerance	248
Black Men and Public Space	297
from Night	308
from Elie Wiesel's Nobel Prize Acceptance Speech	314
from Farewell to Manzanar	330
A Case of Cruelty	381
from The Unexpected Universe	562
from A Precocious Autobiography	652
Once More to the Lake	702
By Any Other Name	772
The Man in the Water	823
from Back from Tuichi	855
Gift from a Son Who Died	886

Drama

The Pen of My Aunt	182

The Bear	473
The Ring of General Macías	869
Antigone	936

Poetry

La Casa	30
My Mother Pieced Quilts	120
Piano	135
Those Winter Sundays	135
Afro-American Fragment	164
Sit-Ins	229
They Have Not Been Able / No Han Podido	239
Fighting South of the Ramparts	254
Miss Rosie	303
Kitchenette Building	303
The Women Who Are Poets in My Land	317
Love Without Love	370
The Taxi	370
Sonnet 18, Shakespeare	375
Sonnet 30, St. Vincent Millay	375
Eight Puppies / Ocho Perritos	392
To a Traveler	438
Simile	441
Tonight I Can Write . . . / Puedo Escribir Los Versos	441
To . . .	448
The Street / La Calle	556
I Am Not I / Yo No Soy Yo	556
from Simple Poetry / Versos Sencillos	577
Tell all the Truth but tell it slant—	612
Once upon a Time	615
Making the Jam Without You	615
For the New Year, 1981	632
Pride	632
Poem on Returning to Dwell in the Country	696
The Sun	696
There Will Come Soft Rains	723
Thoughts of Hanoi	754
Grudnow	768
Lost Sister	789
Bora Ring	794
Nocturne / Nocturno	840
The Knight	932
Old Song	982

Writing About Literature

Direct Response	100
Analysis	256
Creative Response	420
Interpretation	584
Creative Response	734
Criticism	894

Reading the World: Visual Literacy

Portrayal of a Group	106
The Impact of Setting	262
Seeing Metaphor	426
Look Again	590
New and Improved?	740
Focus on Ideas	900

Writing from Experience

Firsthand and Expressive Writing	166
Report	340
Persuasion	500
Informative Exposition	658
Informative Exposition	796
Narrative and Literary Writing	984

LEARNING THE LANGUAGE OF LITERATURE

Designed to help students realize that their encounters with the literature in this book will challenge them to discover new ways of reading, learning, and understanding, this section has the following purposes:
- To involve students in an activity that will help them perceive the study of literature in a new way
- To help students discover how literature connects to their own lives and the world around them
- To introduce students to the parts of the book
- To familiarize students with the tools necessary for learning, such as a reading log, a notebook, and strategies for reading
- To provide a model of real students using reading strategies to become involved with literature

xxvi THE LANGUAGE OF LITERATURE TEACHER'S EDITION

Do You See What I See?

This painting is radiant with striking colors, shapes, and brush strokes. Why do you think the artist composed the painting in this way? The answer lies in the subject matter of the painting. Can you guess what it is?

LOOK AGAIN

In small groups, try to make sense of the painting. Here are some ideas about how to proceed.

1. Have group members take turns holding the book and looking carefully at the image.
2. Try holding the image very close to your face and then moving it farther and farther away.
3. Guess the subject of the painting, and jot down your guess on a small piece of paper.
4. Share guesses as a group. Can the group agree on an answer?
5. When your group is satisfied, compare your answer with the answers arrived at by other groups.
6. If other groups came up with different answers than your group did, describe to them how you got your answer.
7. Can your class agree on what the painting portrays?

CONNECT TO LITERATURE

Just as this painting mixes different colors and shapes to create an image, literature pieces together bits of reality and imagination to create experiences in readers' minds. Once you figure out how the parts work together to create a whole, you can fully enjoy the experience of reading. For a look at what you might encounter, turn the page.

Look Again

It may be necessary for students to view this picture from a distance in order to discern the image. Most students will see the right side of a pair of glasses and one greatly magnified eye peering through it at them. You may wish to have students draw or sketch what they see and compare their perceptions with those of others in the class. If any students are having difficulty finding the hidden picture, encourage volunteers to help them "see" it by tracing with a finger the outline of the glasses and the eye itself. Students may also find it helpful to place a sheet of clear plastic over the picture.

Connect to Literature

Encourage students to understand the reason for this activity by stressing the idea that reading literature is similar to looking at this picture. In other words, understanding and appreciating literature involves looking beyond the obvious, or "reading between the lines," to make new discoveries.

What Can Literature Reveal?

These two pages are designed both to extend the explanation of literature that was introduced in the opening activity and to provide an overview of the book for students.

You can help students work through this page by first generating a class discussion. Invite students to describe how literature currently affects their lives by asking questions such as the following:

- *What does the word* literature *mean to you?*
- *What kinds of literature do you like to read?*
- *Do you think studying literature is important? Why or why not?*
- *Do you think literature, or the study of literature, can affect people's lives? How?*
- *Have you ever read something that helped you to see things in a new way or that strongly affected your emotions?*

What Can Literature Reveal?

Literature can be an eye-opening experience, as you are sure to discover in this book. Hundreds of destinations and stunning sights await you. What do you think literature might reveal?

WORLDS OF WONDER

Literature can show you the way to Africa, the Americas, Europe, India, China, Japan—the whole world! You can even zoom backward or forward in time. As you journey through the **literature selections** in this book, you'll encounter history and heroes, truth and change, love, and much more. To see how a story can reflect society, take a look through Yukio Mishima's "The Pearl" on page 284.

CLOSE-UPS OF YOU

Literature can give you insights into yourself. Most of the selections begin with a **Previewing** page that taps into your knowledge of a subject and gives you background information as well. On page 51, for example, you'll explore qualities both good and evil before reading a story by Leo Tolstoy. The **Responding** pages after a selection give you opportunities to build on what you have learned from the literature. For a glimpse at some of those opportunities, see the activities on page 62.

2

2 THE LANGUAGE OF LITERATURE TEACHER'S EDITION

HIDDEN LINKS

The people and cultures you read about may seem worlds away, but eventually you'll begin to notice certain links between yourself and the world. When you're ready to share your many discoveries with others, the **Writing About Literature** workshops can show you how. For example, the workshop on page 420 invites you to respond to Shakespeare and other poets. For opportunities to connect unit themes to real life, turn to the **Writing from Experience** workshops. Unit 3, for example, explores how family life varies among cultures. Then in the workshop on page 500, you'll compare two or more cultures.

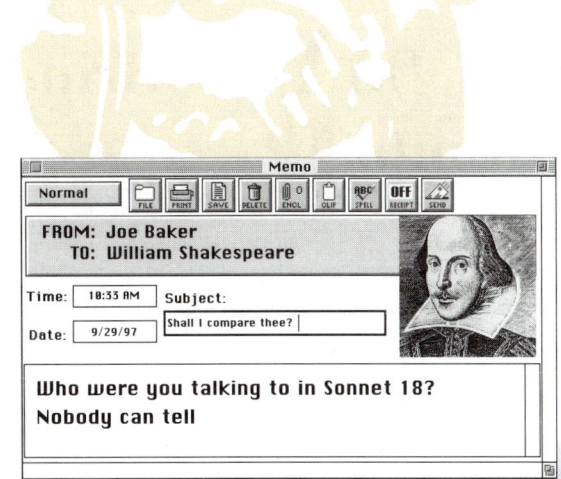

NEW PERSPECTIVES

Sometimes it seems that life is a little too pressing. Literature lets you step back and take stock of your experiences. In the **Reading the World** features, you will see how strategies that help you clarify your understanding of literature can also help you make sense of the world around you. For an exercise in observation, see page 426.

Chuck Close, Self Portrait, 1986 (Detail shown on page 1)

You may wish to have students read these two pages on their own, with a partner, or as a class. Encourage students to turn to the specific pages and examples suggested. Also suggest that they write down any comments or questions they think of while reading these two pages. Then discuss the questions students have recorded and ask them if their expectations about the book or the study of literature have changed. (For further information about each of the book sections that are mentioned, please turn to pages T10–T11 and T14–T15 at the front of this Teacher's Edition.)

MULTIPLE PATHWAYS
Help students to understand the concept of multiple pathways by engaging them in the following activity. Have students imagine that they are going to take a trip across the country, from the East Coast to the West Coast. Ask them to identify as many forms of transportation as possible that they could use and to identify the differences among the forms of transportation. Make sure students understand that the end result with each form of transportation is the same—it's the means by which they get to their destination that differs. Tell students that learning is similar to traveling. There are many ways to learn, all of which involve different strategies and experiences.

PORTFOLIO
Students will use their portfolios to file the work that they will carry out in the projects and activities throughout the book. You can determine the way in which students use their portfolios. For instance, you may wish to have students include not only their completed work, but also outlines, drafts, and revisions. These portfolios can also be used to help students reflect on and assess what they learned from these projects.

NOTEBOOK
Students will use their notebooks to record their responses to some items on the Previewing and Responding pages. At various times, you may wish to have students use their notes to help them participate in paired or group discussions. You may also wish to return to these previewing notes after students have finished reading a selection to allow them to reflect and assess whether any of their thoughts have changed.

READING LOG
Students will use their reading logs to record their thoughts and responses while reading. At times, students will be responding to questions incorporated in the selections, but they should also be encouraged to record their ideas and questions whenever they read independently.

You can use these three tools in any number of ways that best suit the needs of your class. Refer to the *Teacher's Guide to Assessment and Portfolio Use* for more information on using these tools and to the *Unit One Resource Book* for copymasters of different examples of reading logs.

How Do You Bring It into Focus?

You're beginning to see that you can look at literature from a variety of perspectives. Now it is time to learn techniques that can help you get clearer pictures and develop your own unique views.

MULTIPLE PATHWAYS
How do you learn best? Do you prefer to work alone or with the help of a friend? In this book, you are presented with a variety of learning opportunities that allow you to chart the course to your own success, whether your strengths lie mainly in written, oral, dramatic, or artistic activities. In addition, you will collaborate with classmates to share ideas, improve your writing, and make connections to other subject areas. You may even use technological tools such as the Laserlinks and the Writing Coach software program to further personalize your learning.

Portfolio

PORTFOLIO
Many artists, photographers, designers, and writers keep samples of their work in a portfolio to show to others. Like them, you will be collecting your work—writing samples, records of activities, artwork—in a portfolio throughout the year. You probably won't want to put all your work in your portfolio, just carefully chosen pieces. Discuss with your teacher portfolio plans for this year. Suggestions for how to use your portfolio occur throughout this book.

Reading Log

Notebook

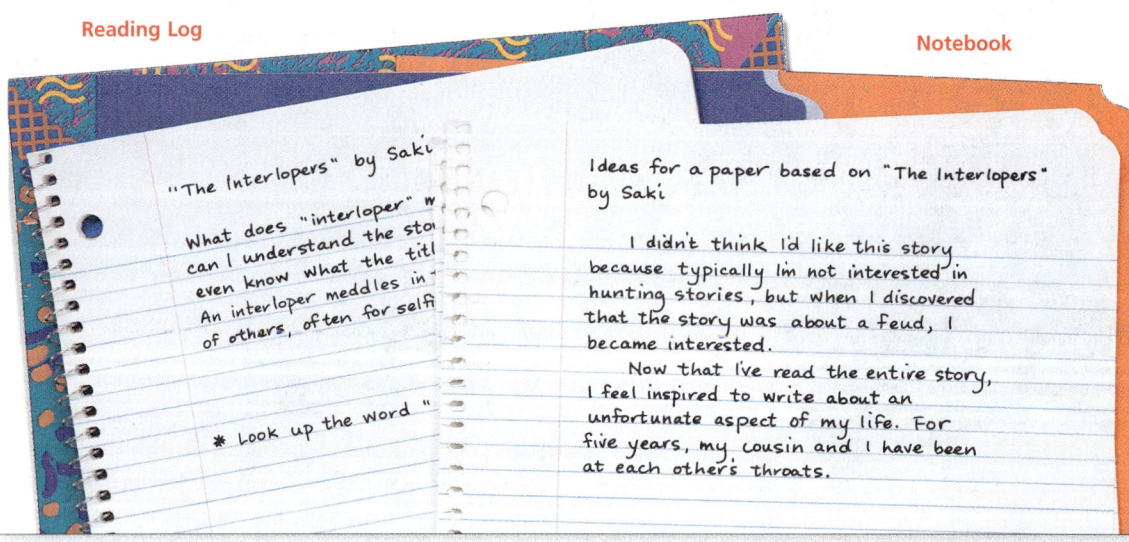

...in the kitchen learning to cook or in the living room learning to embroider. She often says she wants me to be strong and independent. I think she feels strongly about this because she wasn't raised that way herself.

Sometimes, however, she forgets that she wants me to be independent. Sometimes she complains that I care more about my friends and activities than I do about her. She'd say that American girls have too much freedom and that in Argentina a daughter would stay home and keep her mother company.

It is true that I haven't stayed home much on the weekends this year. I'm a sophomore now, and there are parties and dances to go to. My friends expect me to come, and I want to be with them. Sometimes I change my plans when my Mom complains, but this Friday, I wasn't going to let her grumbling upset me. I was a flag girl in the band and had to perform at half-time.

"Sorry, Mom," I answered. "You know there's a football game tonight. I have to be there in a half hour."

NOTEBOOK

Choose any type of notebook, and dedicate it to your study of literature. Divide the notebook into three sections. Use the first section to jot down ideas, describe personal experiences, take notes, and express your thoughts before, while, and after you read a selection. Also include any charts, diagrams, and drawings that help you connect your reading to your life. The second section will be for your reading log, described below. Use the third section as a writer's notebook to record ideas and inspirations that may prove useful in your writing.

READING LOG

Your reading log is for a special kind of response to literature—the comments you make as you read a selection. The reading strategies detailed at the right will help you think through what you read. In your reading log experiment with recording your own comments as you read. Specific opportunities to use your reading log appear throughout this book.

Strategies for Reading

To get the most out of literature, you must think about what you read. The strategies below describe the kinds of thinking that active readers do as they read. When you study these strategies, you will see that you, too, can put them to use.

QUESTION

Question what's happening while you read. Searching for reasons behind events and characters' feelings can help you feel more involved in what you're reading. Note confusing words or statements. Don't worry if you don't understand everything; further reading will probably make things clear.

CONNECT

Connect personally with what you're reading. Think of similarities between the descriptions in the selection and what you have personally experienced, heard about, or read about.

PREDICT

Try to figure out what will happen next and how the selection might end. Then read on to see if you made good guesses.

CLARIFY

Stop occasionally to review what you understand so far. But get ready to have your understanding change and develop as you read on. Also, watch for answers to questions you had earlier.

EVALUATE

Form opinions while you're reading and after you've finished. Develop your own mental images of characters and your own ideas about events.

Now turn the page to see how two student readers put these strategies to work.

Strategies for Reading

Ask volunteers to talk about a time they read a very exciting story. Ask students to describe their reading experiences of being actively involved in the story. Tell students that when they are involved in reading they are probably using some of the strategies described on this page. Explain that these strategies are ways that active readers get more pleasure and understanding from what they read and that using these strategies can make reading easier and more enjoyable.

Invite students to read aloud and to discuss the descriptions of the strategies for reading on this page. Ask students to share occasions when they have used these strategies. Explain that the model they are about to read shows what two readers thought as they were reading the story. Suggest that they cover the remarks in the margin while they read each page; then they can go back and compare their thoughts with the printed ones. Stress that these readers' thoughts are not "right" answers but rather a set of possible active responses.

READING MODEL

This model can be used in several ways:

- You may wish to have students cover the sidebar notes and read "The Interlopers" as they practice recording their thoughts in a reading log. Afterwards, students can compare their responses to those of other classmates and to the student readers to illustrate how different readers respond to the same selection.

- You might read the selection aloud, pausing to have students record their ideas and reactions. You may wish to read aloud and have students take turns role-playing Robert and Thuy's questions.

A For now, this is a passing thought, but Robert may later want to verify where the Carpathians are. Readers who make such connections broaden their general knowledge and increase their pleasure.

B Thuy is using the opening paragraph to establish what's going on, but she is also opening the door to wider speculation. Sometimes a single word can spark something in a reader's mind; perhaps Thuy's mind is playing with two meanings of the word *game*.

C The author announces that the land is jealously guarded, but Robert wants to know why. Such questions can lead to clarification of plot elements or understanding of characters.

READING MODEL

Alongside "The Interlopers" are the spoken comments made by two tenth-grade students, Robert Wingader and Thanh-Thuy Nguyen (tăn tōō ē wĭn), while they were reading the story. Their comments provide a glimpse into the minds of readers actively engaged in the process of reading. You'll notice that in the course of reading, Robert and Thuy (tōō ē) quite naturally used the Strategies for Reading that were introduced on page 5. You'll also note that these readers responded differently to the story—no two readers think the same way.

To benefit most from this model of active reading, read the story first, jotting down your own responses in your reading log. Then read Robert's and Thuy's comments and compare their processes of reading with your own.

THE INTERLOPERS

Saki

A **Robert:** *I've heard of the Carpathians, but I don't know where they are.*
CONNECTING / QUESTIONING

B **Thuy:** *At first I thought he was hunting, but now I think it's like a game to him. He's hunting another man.*
CLARIFYING

C **Robert:** *Why is the land so jealously guarded?*
QUESTIONING

In a forest of mixed growth somewhere on the eastern spurs of the Carpathians, a man stood one winter night watching and listening, as though he waited for some beast of the woods to come within the range of his vision, and, later, of his rifle. But the game for whose presence he kept so keen an outlook was none that figured in the sportman's calendar as lawful and proper for the chase; Ulrich von Gradwitz patrolled the dark forest in quest of a human enemy.

The forest lands of Gradwitz were of wide extent and well stocked with game; the narrow strip of precipitous woodland that lay on its outskirt was not remarkable for the game it harbored or the shooting it afforded, but it was the most jealously guarded of all its owner's territorial possessions. A famous lawsuit, in the days of his grandfather, had wrested it from the illegal possession of a neighboring family of petty landowners; the dispossessed party had never acquiesced in the judgment of the Courts, and a long series of poaching affrays and similar scandals had embittered the relationships between the families for three generations. The neighbor feud had grown into a personal one since Ulrich had come to be head of his family; if there was a man in the world whom he detested and wished ill to it was Georg Znaeym, the inheritor of the quarrel and the tireless game-snatcher and raider of the disputed border-forest. The feud might, perhaps, have died down or been compromised if the personal ill-will of the two men had not stood in the way; as boys they had thirsted for one another's blood, as men each prayed that misfortune might fall on the other, and this wind-scourged winter night Ulrich had banded together his foresters to watch the dark forest, not in quest of four-footed quarry, but to keep a lookout for the prowling thieves whom he suspected of being afoot from across the land boundary. The roebuck, which usually kept in the sheltered hollows during a storm wind, were running like driven things tonight, and there was movement and unrest among the creatures that were wont to sleep through the dark hours. Assuredly there was a disturbing element in the forest, and Ulrich could guess the quarter from whence it came.

He strayed away by himself from the watchers whom he had placed in ambush on the crest of the hill, and wandered far down the steep slopes amid the wild tangle of undergrowth, peering through the tree trunks and listening through the whistling and skirling of the wind and the restless beating of the branches for sight or sound of the marauders. If only on this wild night, in this dark, lone spot, he might come across Georg Znaeym, man to man, with none to witness—that was the wish that was uppermost in his thoughts. And as he stepped around the trunk of a huge beech, he came face to face with the man he sought.

The two enemies stood glaring at one another for a long silent moment.

Each had a rifle in his hand, each had hate in his heart and murder uppermost in his mind. The chance had come to give full play to the passions of a lifetime. But a man who has been brought up under the code of a restraining civilization cannot easily nerve himself to shoot down his neighbor in cold blood and without word spoken, except for an offense against his hearth and honor. And before the moment of hesitation had given way to action a deed of Nature's own violence overwhelmed them both. A fierce shriek of the storm had been answered by a splitting crash over their heads, and ere they could leap aside a mass of falling beech tree had thundered down on them. Ulrich von Gradwitz found himself stretched on the ground, one arm numb beneath him and the other held almost as helplessly in a tight tangle of forked branches, while both legs were pinned beneath the fallen mass. His heavy shooting

---

Thuy: I picture Ulrich and Georg as having rocky childhoods. These two guys hated each other and were very competitive.
EVALUATING — D

Thuy: Ulrich is hunting not for animals but for people who are trespassing. That's the game for him.
CLARIFYING — E

Thuy: He's got vengeance in his eyes; he wants to murder Georg. He's bloodthirsty!
CLARIFYING — F

Robert: It's ironic that Ulrich found Georg just as he had hoped. Seems unrealistic. I'm reminded that so many wars are just about land. Murder seems too harsh a penalty for a land dispute.
EVALUATING / CONNECTING — G

Thuy: I'm beginning to think I know where the story is going. I think they'll be caught and then both might die. Or, they might not hate each other in the end and have to work together to save their lives.
PREDICTING — H

THE INTERLOPERS 7

D Thuy is probably basing her evaluation on prior experience of competitive young people, or perhaps of adults who bear grudges. Readers who apply their knowledge of people to characters in stories often become more fully engaged in their reading.

E Thuy confirms her earlier reaction and may still be playing with the double meaning of the word game.

F Thuy seems to be visualizing the scene and reaching inside the mind of Georg; both strategies help readers clarify a story.

G Here a number of thoughts are tumbling through Robert's head, a frequent experience for readers. First Robert forms the basis for a possible critical evaluation of the story; then he ranges far beyond the story into thoughts about war. His final comment may reflect a return to the story or a connection between war and murder. In any event, Robert is obviously an active participant in the story.

H Thuy's thoughts, too, are exploring a number of avenues. Using either her knowledge of people or of other stories—or both—she is leaping ahead in imagination to what comes next. Far from spoiling any coming surprise, this strategy allows readers to be part of the creative process.

I Thuy is again envisioning the scene, which is a tribute to both the author's descriptive skills and to Thuy's reading strategies.

J Both Thuy and Robert are identifying links with other stories, links which not only enrich their experience of this story but also provide a jumping-off point for later comparison and contrast. Robert is also collecting more potential evidence for later critical evaluation of the story, but he'll have to wait to the end to determine if his preliminary evaluation is valid.

K Thuy is again putting herself inside a character's head. This strategy of allowing oneself to think as another thinks helps a reader gain understanding of the characters and of human nature. Notice, too, that in doing so, Thuy provides a rational basis for her judgment of Georg.

L Robert is apparently using his own common sense to evaluate the characters' discussion at this point. While passive readers might simply observe such a scene, active readers are critical or approving, amazed or furious, as the case may dictate—but they also remain open to future modification of their current judgments.

M Thuy is connecting with another piece of literature. Her interpretation at this point could well become part of a character study of Georg.

I **Thuy:** This is a bloody scene. It's like you're watching a movie when the tree falls. It reminds me of Jurassic Park.
CONNECTING

J **Robert:** This reminds me of another story that I read in which a character is trapped by circumstances in nature. The tree falling seems unlikely but convenient for the author.
CONNECTING / EVALUATING

K **Thuy:** Georg's laughing at the guy he hates. He's thinking "you're getting what you deserve. Even if you're not dying, at least you're in pain." It seems like he's taking some joy in that—I really don't like this guy.
CLARIFYING / EVALUATING

L **Robert:** All the bickering about whose men are going to find them seems pointless and feeble.
EVALUATING

M **Thuy:** This reminds me of The Inferno by Dante and how only God can damn you and cause your death. Georg is thinking he's God—or at least as powerful as God—by damning Ulrich.
CONNECTING / CLARIFYING

---

boots had saved his feet from being crushed to pieces, but if his fractures were not as serious as they might have been, at least it was evident that he could not move from his present position till someone came to release him. The descending twigs had slashed the skin of his face, and he had to wink away some drops of blood from his eyelashes before he could take in a general view of the disaster. At his side, so near that under ordinary circumstances he could almost have touched him, lay Georg Znaeym, alive and struggling, but obviously as helplessly pinioned down as himself. All around them lay a thick-strewn wreckage of splintered branches and broken twigs.

Relief at being alive and exasperation at his captive plight brought a strange medley of pious thank offerings and sharp curses to Ulrich's lips. Georg, who was nearly blinded with the blood which trickled across his eyes, stopped his struggling for a moment to listen, and then gave a short, snarling laugh.

"So you're not killed, as you ought to be, but you're caught, anyway," he cried; "caught fast. Ho, what a jest, Ulrich von Gradwitz snared in his stolen forest. There's real justice for you!"

And he laughed again, mockingly and savagely.

"I'm caught in my own forest land," retorted Ulrich. "When my men come to release us, you will wish, perhaps, that you were in a better plight than caught poaching on a neighbor's land, shame on you."

Georg was silent for a moment; then he answered quietly.

"Are you sure that your men will find much to release? I have men, too, in the forest tonight, close behind me, and they will be here first and do the releasing. When they drag me out from under these damned branches, it won't need much clumsiness on their part to roll this mass of trunk right over on the top of you. Your men will find you dead under a fallen beech tree. For form's sake I shall send my condolences to your family."

"It is a useful hint," said Ulrich fiercely. "My men had orders to follow in ten minutes' time, seven of which must have gone by already, and when they get me out—I will remember the hint. Only as you will have met your death poaching on my lands, I don't think I can decently send any message of condolence to your family."

"Good," snarled Georg, "good. We fight this quarrel out to the death, you and I and our foresters, with no cursed interlopers to come between us. Death and damnation to you, Ulrich von Gradwitz."

"The same to you, Georg Znaeym, forest thief, game snatcher."

Both men spoke with the bitterness of possible defeat before them, for each knew that it might be long before his men would seek him out or find him; it was a bare matter of chance which party would arrive first on the scene.

Both had now given up the useless struggle to free themselves from the mass of wood that held them down; Ulrich limited his endeavors to an effort to bring his one partially free arm near enough to his outer coat pocket to draw out his wine flask. Even when he had accomplished that operation, it was long before he could manage the unscrewing of the stopper or get any of the liquid down his throat. But what a heaven-sent draft it seemed! It was an open winter, and little snow had fallen as yet, hence the captives suffered less from the cold than might have been the case at that season of the year; nevertheless, the wine was warming and reviving to the wounded man, and he looked across with something like a throb of pity to where his enemy lay, just keeping the groans of pain and weariness from crossing his lips.

"Could you reach this flask if I threw it over to you?" asked Ulrich suddenly; "there is good wine in it, and one may as well be as comfortable as one can. Let us drink, even if tonight one of us dies."

"No, I can scarcely see anything; there is so much blood caked around my eyes," said Georg, "and in any case I don't drink wine with an enemy."

Ulrich was silent for a few minutes and lay listening to the weary screeching of the wind. An idea was slowly forming and growing in his brain, an idea that gained strength every time that he looked across at the man who was fighting so grimly against pain and exhaustion. In the pain and languor that Ulrich himself was feeling the old fierce hatred seemed to be dying down.

"Neighbor," he said presently, "do as you please if your men come first. It was a fair compact. But as for me, I've changed my mind. If my men are the first to come, you shall be the first to be helped, as though you were my guest. We have quarreled like devils all our lives over this stupid strip of forest, where the trees can't even stand upright in a breath of wind. Lying here tonight, thinking, I've come to think we've been rather fools; there are better things in life than getting the better of a boundary dispute. Neighbor, if you will help me to bury the old quarrel I—I will ask you to be my friend."

Georg Znaeym was silent for so long that Ulrich thought, perhaps, he had fainted with the pain of his injuries. Then he spoke slowly and in jerks.

Robert: It's a good thing that Ulrich finally saw past the feud.
EVALUATING **N**

Thuy: When Ulrich drinks the wine he feels warm and some relief from his suffering. It's the first time he feels pity toward his enemy.
CLARIFYING **O**

Thuy: Ulrich does have some human characteristics, I don't hate him as much as I used to.
EVALUATING **P**

Robert: It's pitiful that Georg wouldn't accept Ulrich's offer. It's hard to believe that he's that uneasy about drinking wine with his enemy.
EVALUATING **Q**

Thuy: Ulrich calls Georg "neighbor," which contradicts "enemy." He's almost like a friend now.
CLARIFYING **R**

Thuy: Now I know why they hate each other and have been quarreling all this time—it's because of the forest. They see now that they have been fools in the past because of this.
CLARIFYING / EVALUATING **S**

N Note how Robert uses his own sense of what is reasonable and fair to judge the actions of Georg. His evaluation here could prompt a wider discussion of morality and conflict resolution.

O Sometimes readers know more than they put into words. Thuy's own comments or outside questioning or discussion could lead her to see a connection between Ulrich's physical warmth and a broader thawing.

P Thuy has not simply written Ulrich off; she is open to this new evaluation of Ulrich's character. In later discussion or writing, students can be asked to trace the evolution of their judgments of characters or situations.

Q Robert is apparently again using common sense in his evaluation and understanding of Georg's rigid nature.

R Again, Thuy notes the significance of a single word, neighbor. When Thuy says Ulrich is like a friend, she is probably relying not just on that word, but on all Ulrich's recent thought, words, and deeds. One of the advantages of active reading is that it gives readers a starting point for further discussion and writing.

S Thuy has apparently been unclear about the basis of the dispute between the two men. If she returns to the second paragraph now or after she completes the story, it will probably make more sense. Readers must learn to judge when they should reread to clarify confusion and when they should read on. In any event, Thuy is using the text and her own values as the basis for evaluation.

T The notoriety of the feud was at least implied at the beginning of the story, but Thuy apparently didn't pick that up. Nevertheless, at this point she clearly understands the momentousness of what has happened between the two men. Thuy's experience emphasizes the fact that readers need not—indeed, cannot—catch everything in a story on a first reading.

U Given this and earlier reactions, Robert apparently has some strong opinions and feelings about social conflicts and their resolution.

V Robert's question probably links his previous reaction (see annotation U) and the story. He was considering gangs, but Georg and Ulrich are also vivid in his mind, and his train of thought leads naturally to these men's "gangs," their foresters, even though there is no text reference at this point. We are all familiar with the phenomenon of one thought leading to another; readers who encourage this process can make important discoveries.

W Thuy again seems struck by the momentousness of the change in the men's attitudes.

X There is a note of satisfaction in Robert's comment that ties in with his earlier criticism of the men. As readers proceed through a story, new events will clarify and modify their attitudes toward the characters and situations.

Y Sometimes readers raise questions about points they don't understand; at other times, their questions reflect the suspense in the story, and can lead to a discussion of how an author achieves suspense.

T *Thuy:* The whole village knows about the feud. It would be a big surprise if they came back to the village as friends.
CLARIFYING / PREDICTING

U *Robert:* All feuds should be settled like this; gangs, for instance, could make peace and avoid futile battles.
EVALUATING / CONNECTING

V *Robert:* I wonder how Georg's and Ulrich's men will react to the ending of the feud.
QUESTIONING

W *Thuy:* At first, each man wanted his own people to come first so the other would be killed, but now, each wants to be first to save the other's life. They both want to be first to show their friendship.
CLARIFYING

X *Robert:* They're finally working together to save themselves.
CLARIFYING

Y *Robert:* I wonder whose men these are.
QUESTIONING

"How the whole region would stare and gabble if we rode into the market square together. No one living can remember seeing a Znaeym and a von Gradwitz talking to one another in friendship. And what peace there would be among the forester folk if we ended our feud tonight. And if we choose to make peace among our people, there is none other to interfere, no interlopers from outside. . . . You would come and keep the Sylvester night beneath my roof, and I would come and feast on some high day at your castle. . . . I would never fire a shot on your land, save when you invited me as a guest; and you should come and shoot with me down in the marshes where the wildfowl are. In all the countryside there are none that could hinder if we willed to make peace. I never thought to have wanted to do other than hate you all my life, but I think I have changed my mind about things too, this last half-hour. And you offered me your wine flask. . . . Ulrich von Gradwitz, I will be your friend."

For a space both men were silent, turning over in their minds the wonderful changes that this dramatic reconciliation would bring about. In the cold, gloomy forest, with the wind tearing in fitful gusts through the naked branches and whistling around the tree trunks, they lay and waited for the help that would now bring release and succor to both parties. And each prayed a private prayer that his men might be the first to arrive, so that he might be the first to show honorable attention to the enemy that had become a friend.

Presently, as the wind dropped for a moment, Ulrich broke silence.

"Let's shout for help," he said; "in this lull our voices may carry a little way."

"They won't carry far through the trees and undergrowth," said Georg, "but we can try. Together, then."

The two raised their voices in a prolonged hunting call.

"Together again," said Ulrich a few minutes later, after listening in vain for an answer halloo.

"I heard something that time, I think" said Ulrich.

"I heard nothing but the pestilential wind," said Georg hoarsely.

There was silence again for some minutes, and then Ulrich gave a joyful cry.

"I can see figures coming through the wood. They are following in the way I came down the hillside."

Both men raised their voices in as loud a shout as they could muster.

10 READING MODEL

Border Patrol (1951), Andrew Wyeth. Private collection.

"They hear us! They've stopped. Now they see us. They're running down the hill towards us," cried Ulrich.

"How many of them are there?" asked Georg.

"I can't see distinctly," said Ulrich; "nine or ten."

"Then they are yours," said Georg; "I had only seven out with me."

"They are making all the speed they can, brave lads," said Ulrich gladly.

"Are they your men?" asked Georg. "Are they your men?"

"No," said Ulrich with a laugh, the idiotic chattering laugh of a man unstrung with hideous fear.

"Who are they?" asked Georg quickly, straining his eyes to see what the other would gladly not have seen.

"Wolves." ❖

UNIT ONE

UNIT THEMES

Unit One

Imprints of the Past In Unit One, students will read selections which explore ways in which the past affects people in the present. This unit contains two parts: Part 1, "Lasting Impressions," and Part 2, "The Power of Heritage." Selections in both Parts 1 and 2 contribute to the unit theme by recounting the lasting effects of memory and heritage on a variety of characters.

Part 1

Lasting Impressions Selections in Part 1 emphasize the power of memories. For example, in "Winter Night," a woman's memories of another child shape her response to a child temporarily in her care.

Part 2

The Power of Heritage Selections in Part 2 emphasize the power that family, culture, and tradition exercise over characters. For example, in "Everyday Use," a woman realizes which of her two daughters truly understands, shares, and will perpetuate family traditions.

UNIT ONE

IMPRINTS of the PAST

One's past is what one is.

OSCAR WILDE
Irish-born poet, playwright, and novelist
1854–1900

Discussion Questions

To help students explore the connections among the art, the quotation, and the unit theme, have them consider the following questions:

1. Define "imprint" for students, and ask them what an "imprint of the past" might mean. *(Possible response: the phrase "imprint of the past" refers to the lasting effect on people of the events, the circumstances, and the traditions of their past.)*

2. Do you agree with Oscar Wilde's statement? Why? *(Possible responses: Yes, because one is unavoidably affected by the events, circumstances, and experiences of one's past; no, because one has it in one's power to make choices without the past having predetermined those choices.)*

3. What can you infer about the subjects of this photograph? What details in the photograph support your inferences? *(Responses will vary. Accept all well-supported responses.)*

4. What kinds of stories and experiences might you expect to read about in this unit? *(Possible responses: These selections may deal with themes of memory, of family relationships across generations, or of cultural heritage.)*

5. Discuss one way an event in your past, or an aspect of your cultural heritage, affects you in your everyday life. *(Responses will vary.)*

DESIGN NOTE

This photograph shows a family of Italian immigrants at Ellis Island in New York Harbor. From 1892 to 1924 the immigration station at Ellis Island was the main entry point for immigrants to the United States. New arrivals had to pass health and other tests given by immigration inspectors. Those who failed to pass the tests were sent back to their homeland.

Reading the Photograph *Where do you think the people in this photograph are going? What do you think they have left behind?*

THE LANGUAGE OF LITERATURE **TEACHER'S EDITION** **13**

UNIT ONE
Part 1 Skills Trace

ML DENOTES MINI-LESSON IN TEACHER'S EDITION

Selections	Reading Skills and Strategies	Literary Concepts	Writing Opportunities	Speaking, Listening, and Viewing
FICTION **Two Kinds** Amy Tan		Internal and external conflicts, PE p. 31 Fiction, ML TE p. 20 Reviewing plot, ML TE p. 21	Chart, PE p. 18 Lists, PE p. 31 Diary entry, PE p. 31 Personality profile, PE p. 31 Review, PE p. 31 Essay, PE p. 31 First-person point of view, ML TE p. 28	Group discussion, PE p. 31 Role-play, PE p. 32 Debate, ML TE p. 26 Choral reading, ML TE p. 30 Discussion on mass media, TE p. 32
FICTION **Cranes** Hwang Sunwŏn	Making inferences, PE p. 33	Plot, PE p. 38 Reviewing setting, PE p. 38 Reviewing flashback, ML TE p. 35	Time line, PE p. 38 Comparison chart, PE p. 38 Letter, PE p. 38 Alternative ending, PE p. 38	Role-play a dramatic scene, PE p. 39 Group discussion, PE p. 38
FICTION **Winter Night** Kay Boyle	Mood, PE p. 40	Characters, PE p. 49 Reviewing contrast, ML TE p. 44	Comparison and contrast chart, PE p. 49 Continuation of story, PE p. 49 Chapter, PE p. 49 Editorial, PE p. 49 Tone, ML TE p. 42	Group discussion, PE p. 50 Dramatic reading, PE p. 50 Job interview technique, ML TE p. 43
FICTION **After the Ball** Leo Tolstoy	Evaluating characters, PE p. 51	Flashback, PE p. 63 Reviewing setting, ML TE p. 56 Short story, ML TE p. 58	Newspaper column, PE p. 62 Dramatic scene, PE p. 62 Letter and reply, PE p. 62 Proposal, PE p. 62 Dialogue for opening scene, ML TE p. 53	Group discussion to adapt plot, PE p. 62 Perform adaptation, PE p. 62
NONFICTION *from* **Kaffir Boy** Mark Mathabane	Using your reading log, PE p. 67	Dialogue, PE p. 80 Reviewing description, ML TE p. 70 Nonfiction, ML TE p. 71	Dialogue, PE p. 80 Script for public-service announcement, PE p. 80 Eulogy, PE p. 80 Logical organization of ideas, ML TE p. 78	Adapt a scene as a radio play, PE p. 80 Paired discussion on dialogue, PE p. 81 Dramatic reading, ML TE p. 79
NONFICTION **The Teacher Who Changed My Life** Nicholas Gage	Understanding cause and effect, PE p. 83	Essay, PE p. 90 Reviewing characterization, ML TE p. 85	List, PE p. 90 Essay, PE p. 90 Character sketch, PE p. 90 Sentence variety, ML TE p. 86	Group discussion, PE p. 90 Oral report, PE p. 91 Perform dramatic monologue, PE p. 91
NONFICTION ON YOUR OWN *from* **Earthly Paradise** Colette			Double-entry journal, TE p. 92	Paired and dramatic reading, TE p. 92 Interviewing, TE p. 97
Writing **WRITING ABOUT LITERATURE** **Direct Response**	Reading Skills and Strategies Using dialogue, PE pp. 100–101 Responding to literature, PE pp. 102–105	Literary Concepts Using dialogue, PE pp. 100–101 Characterization, PE pp. 102–105	Writing Opportunities Say it in dialogue, PE p. 101 Present events, PE p. 101 Write your own dialogue, PE p. 107 Personal response, PE pp. 102–105 Writing realistic dialogue, PE p. 101 Using elaboration, PE p. 103 Double-entry journal, TE p. 92	Speaking, Listening, and Viewing Viewing an image, PE p. 107 Interpreting an image, PE p. 107 Discussion, PE p. 107 Discussing images, PE p. 107

Grammar, Usage, Mechanics, and Spelling	Multimodal Learning	Research and Study Skills	Vocabulary
Capitalizing titles, (ML) TE p. 23	Role-play, PE p. 32 Collage, PE p. 32 Memorizing, (ML) TE p. 27	Research Chinese immigrants, PE p. 32 Memorizing, (ML) TE p. 27 Research contributions of Chinese immigrants, TE p. 32	betrayal lament devastate prodigy discordant ream fiasco reproach indignity reverie
Common and proper nouns, (ML) TE p. 34	Create a time line, PE p. 38 Create a comparison chart, PE p. 38 Role-play a dramatic scene, PE p. 39 Art exhibit, PE p. 39 Use CD-ROM search function to locate research material, TE p. 39	Research Korean War, PE p. 39 Use CD-ROM search function to locate research material, TE p. 39	
Types of sentences, (ML) TE p. 48	Create a comparison and contrast chart, PE p. 49 Dramatic reading, PE p. 50 Sketch, PE p. 50	Research oral histories of Holocaust survivors, PE p. 50	abeyance apprehension derision obscurity reprieve
Semicolons between main clauses, (ML) TE p. 55	Perform adaptation, PE p. 62 Choose musical recordings, PE p. 63 Create a costume sketch, PE p. 63	Research Tolstoy's philosophy of nonviolent resistance and effects on 20th-century reformers, PE p. 63 Use indexes in reference books, TE p. 63	chagrin majestic detestable maliciously ethereal perspicacity imposing pummel irate unassuming
Inverted sentences, (ML) TE p. 73	Adapt a scene as a radio play, PE p. 80 Design a poster, PE p. 81 Create a drawing, PE p. 81	Research Apartheid using references: Microfiche and periodicals, (ML) TE p. 76	accost inscrutable austere paradoxically captivate pretext credence unsolicited inkling utilitarian
Who/Whom in subordinate clauses, (ML) TE p. 87	Create a photo essay, PE p. 91 Oral report, PE p. 91 Perform dramatic monologue, PE p. 91 Adjust to different cultures, (ML) TE p. 89 Story map, TE p. 91 Gathering props, TE p. 91		authoritarian mentor catalyst mortify emphatically muse formidable tact hone void
	Create a collage, TE p. 92 Charting a character, TE p. 92 Create a field guide, TE p. 95 Interviewing, TE p. 97		

Grammar, Usage, Mechanics, and Spelling	Multimodal Learning	Research and Study Skills	Media Literacy
Achieving pronoun-antecedent agreement, PE p. 105	Viewing an image, PE p. 107 Interpreting an image, PE p. 107 Discussion, PE p. 107 Evaluating images, PE p. 107	Analyzing literature, PE pp. 102–105 Analyzing images, PE pp. 106–107	Interpreting an image, PE pp. 106–107

UNIT ONE
Part 2 Skills Trace

ML DENOTES MINI-LESSON IN TEACHER'S EDITION

Selections	Reading Skills and Strategies	Literary Concepts	Writing Opportunities	Speaking, Listening, and Viewing
FICTION **Everyday Use** Alice Walker	Drawing conclusions, PE p. 110 Using your reading log, PE p. 110	Figurative language, PE p. 122 Reviewing characterization, ML TE p. 112	Write a description, PE p. 121 Draft an essay, PE p. 121 Write a memo, PE p. 121 Write a sequel, PE p. 121 Sensory details, ML TE p. 115 Essay tests, ML TE p. 118	Group discussion, PE p. 121 Role-play a scenario, PE p. 121 Oral report, PE p. 122 Interviewing, ML TE p. 118
NONFICTION **Blue Winds Dancing** Tom Whitecloud		Description, PE p. 131 Reviewing conflict, ML TE p. 126	Write a paragraph or two on meaning of outsider, PE p. 124 Write a speech, PE p. 131 Create a legend, PE p. 131 Write a skit, PE p. 131 Word chains: repeated words and sentence fragments, ML TE p. 127	Small group discussion, PE p. 141 Perform a skit, PE p. 131 Oral report, TE p. 132
POETRY **Piano** D.H. Lawrence **Those Winter Sundays** Robert Hayden	Visualizing images, PE p. 135	Imagery, PE p. 138 Reviewing rhyme, ML TE p. 136 Lyric poetry, ML TE p. 137	Write a poem, PE p. 138 Write a eulogy, PE p. 138 Write a dictionary of sensory images, PE p. 139	Choral reading, PE p. 138 Listen to music, PE p. 139
NONFICTION **from When Heaven and Earth Changed Places** Le Ly Hayslip	Evaluating, PE p. 140	Autobiography, PE p. 149 Reviewing theme, ML TE p. 145	Autobiographical essay, PE p. 149 Write a magazine advice column, PE p. 149 Create song lyrics, PE p. 149 Create a chart, PE p. 149 Cause and effect, ML TE p. 146	Discussion, PE p. 149 Conduct a debate, PE p. 150 Prepare a skit, PE p. 150 Oral report, PE p. 150
FICTION **The Study of History** Frank O'Connor	Analyzing details, PE p. 151	Characterization, PE p. 162 Short story, ML TE p. 153 Reviewing setting, ML TE p. 158	Write an autobiographical incident, PE p. 162 Write love letters, PE p. 162 Dialects, ML TE p. 154	Interview family members, TE p. 163 Finish story "Larry Reads," TE p. 163
POETRY ON YOUR OWN **Afro-American Fragment** Langston Hughes			Writing a poem, TE p. 165	Choral reading, TE p. 164

Writing	Reading Skills and Strategies	Literary Concepts	Writing Opportunities	Speaking, Listening, and Viewing
WRITING FROM EXPERIENCE **Firsthand and Expressive Writing**			Writing an autobiographical account, PE pp. 166–173 Drafting, PE pp. 170–171 Using levels of language appropriately, PE p. 171 Revising and publishing, PE pp. 172–173	Tables, PE p. 166 Cartoons, PE p. 167 Telling a story, PE p. 169 Interviewing, PE p. 169 Radio broadcast, PE p. 173

Grammar, Usage, Mechanics, and Spelling	Multimodal Learning	Research and Study Skills	Vocabulary
Compound subjects and predicates, ML TE p. 116	Group discussion, PE p. 121 Role-play a scenario, PE p. 121 Design a story quilt, PE p. 122 Create a collage, mobile, or sculpture, PE p. 122 Oral report, PE p. 122 Interviewing, ML TE p. 118 Create a visual aid, TE p. 122	Research sharecropping system of rural South, PE p. 122 Research Black Muslim movement of 1960s and 1970s, PE p. 122 Taking essay tests, ML TE p. 119	deliberately doctrine furtive oppress sidle
Forming adverbs with -ly, ML TE p. 128	Small-group discussion, PE p. 131 Perform a skit, PE p. 131 Trace a map and indicate route, PE p. 132 Create a landscape painting, PE p. 132 Oral report, TE p. 132	Research history, culture, and traditions of one Native American group Whitehead mentions, TE p. 132	imperceptibly rabid maelstrom rapt mirage serene petrified silhouetted pulsate vice
	Choral reading, PE p. 138 Choose music, PE p. 139	Research musicals, square dancing, and singalongs, TE p. 139	
Unusually-placed subjects, ML TE p. 142	Discussion, PE p. 149 Conduct a debate, PE p. 150 Prepare a skit, PE p. 150 Oral report, PE p. 150 Teaching others, ML TE p. 144 Acting a role, TE p. 150	Research modern Vietnamese culture, PE p. 149 Research U.S. involvement in Vietnam War, PE p. 150	abstain diligent empathy lenient supple
Possessive pronouns, ML TE p. 157	Design and draw a storyboard, PE p. 162 Diagram family tree, PE p. 163 Interview family members, TE p. 163 Draw family portraits of Delanys and O'Briens, TE p. 163 Sketching images, TE p. 164	Research your family tree, PE p. 163 Taking objective tests: Analogies, ML TE p. 156	biased impertinent brooding incredulously complacently ordained contemptuously saucy exasperated uncanny

Grammar, Usage, Mechanics, and Spelling	Multimodal Learning	Research and Study Skills	Media Literacy
Using levels of language appropriately, PE p. 171 Using quotation marks in dialogue, PE p. 173	Interviewing, PE p. 169 Reading tables, PE p. 166 Analyzing cartoons, PE p. 167 Analyzing family heirlooms, PE p. 167	Locating sources, PE p. 169 Analyzing family heirlooms, PE p. 167	Analyzing cartoons, PE p. 167

UNIT ONE
Recommended Resources

ENRICHMENT   RESEARCH

✓ Recommended Novels

LITERATURE CONNECTIONS WITH SOURCEBOOK FOR TEACHERS
Thematic Link In this South African novel, the power of heritage and tradition collide with the realities of contemporary life.
About the Author Bessie Head (1937–1986) was a novelist and short story writer whose work reflects her deep concern for the people and politics of her continent.
Other Works by Bessie Head *The Collector of Treasures, Serowe: Village of the Rain Wind, Tales of Tenderness and Power*

LITERATURE CONNECTIONS WITH SOURCEBOOK FOR TEACHERS
Thematic Link In this novel, Bohemian immigrants reconcile the imprint of their past with the realities of their new home.
About the Author Willa Cather (1873–1947) grew up on the Nebraska prairie and called upon her childhood memories to write this beloved American novel.
Other Works by Willa Cather *April Twilights, Alexander's Bridge, O Pioneers!, The Song of the Lark, The Professor's House, Death Comes for the Archbishop, Shadows on the Rock*

Thematic Link This book tells the story of four Chinese immigrant women and their relationships with their daughters.
About the Author Amy Tan (born 1952) is one of the best-selling, best-known American contemporary novelists. Her writing often reveals the unique perspectives of a first-generation Chinese American who has ties to more than one culture.
Other Works by Amy Tan *The Kitchen God's Wife, The Hundred Secret Senses*

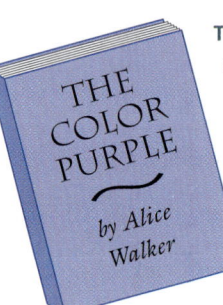

Thematic Link Walker explores the power of heritage and history in this novel about African-American women.
About the Author Pulitzer prize-winning writer Alice Walker (born 1944) is considered one of the important voices in American literature today. Her works frequently concern the struggles of African-American women to survive in the face of poverty, racism, and sexism.
Other Works by Alice Walker *Revolutionary Petunias and Other Poems, In Search of Our Mothers' Gardens, In Love and Trouble: Stories of Black Women*

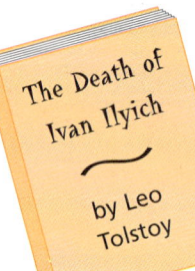

Thematic Link In this work, Tolstoy searches for answers to questions about life, death, and fate.
About the Author Leo Tolstoy (1828–1910) wrote extensively and frequently about issues of truth, goodness, and the meaning of life.
Other Works by Leo Tolstoy *War and Peace, Anna Karenina, Master and Man and Other Stories, Essays and Letters, Childhood*

Professional Development   TEACHING THE NOVEL

Baker, Houston. *The American Literatures: Essays in Chicano, Native American, and Asian-American Literature.* New York: Modern Language Association, 1982.

Langer, J. A. *The Process of Understanding Literature.* Albany, NY: Center for the Learning and Teaching of Literature, SUNY at Albany, 1989.

Lipson, Eden Ross. "The Wicked English-speaking Daughter (Chinese American Writer Amy Tan)," *The New York Times Book Review* (March 19, 1989): 3.

Mossman, Robert. "South African Literature: A Global Lesson in One Country," *English Journal* 79: 8 (December, 1990).

Yegorov, S. F. "Profile of Educators: Leo Nikolaevich Tolstoy (1828–1910)," *Prospects* 18 (Number 13, 1988): 421–8.

Walker, Elinor. *Doors To More Mature Reading.* 2nd ed. American Library Association, 1981.

CROSS-CURRICULAR TEACHING   PROFESSIONAL DEVELOPMENT

✓ Recommended Readings in Cross-Curricular Areas

SOCIAL STUDIES

 *A History of South Africa* by Leonard Thompson (1990) A lively, accessible account of South Africa's history, with special attention given to apartheid. Links to Mark Mathabane's excerpt from *Kaffir Boy*.

 *Russia: A Concise History* by Ronald Hingley (1994) A new edition of popular, illustrated history. Links to Leo Tolstoy's "After the Ball."

 *The New Americans: Changing Patterns in U.S. Immigration* by Brent Ashabranner (1983) A study of the most recent waves of immigrants. Links to Amy Tan's "Two Kinds" and Le Ly Hayslip's excerpt from *When Heaven and Earth Changed Places*.

This Is Korea by the Korean Overseas Information Service (1988) A brief illustrated introduction to Korea, its history, and culture. Links to Hwang Sunwŏn's "Cranes."

Professional Development — CROSS-CURRICULAR INSTRUCTION

Banks, James A., and Banks, Cherry A. McGee, eds. *Multicultural Education: Issues and Perspectives.* 1993.

Clark, Barbara. *Optimizing Learning: The Integrative Education: Models in the Classroom.* 1986.

Takaki, Ronald. *A Different Mirror: A History of Multicultural America.* 1993.

Zinsser, William, ed. *Inventing the Truth: The Art and Craft of the Memoir.* 1995.

✓ Recommended Media Resources

THE LANGUAGE OF LITERATURE

ELECTRONIC LIBRARY
CD-ROM
Additional literature selections for Unit One can be found on the Electronic Library CD-ROM.

LASERLINKS
Videodisc, Gr. 10
See *LaserLinks Teacher's Source Book*, pages 4–5, for overview of Unit One.

AUDIO LIBRARY
Tapes
Unit One: Imprints of the Past
Gr. 10, Tape 1: Side B
Gr. 10, Tapes 2–4: Sides A & B

WRITING COACH
Writing Coach Software: Writing About Literature—Interpretive Response, Personal Narrative

OUTSIDE RESOURCES

Films/Videos/Film Strips/Audiocassettes
The Joy Luck Club, video, Hollywood Pictures Home Video, 1994, (139 minutes).
Amy Tan Reads The Joy Luck Club, Two audiocassettes, Japanese American Curriculum Project, (156 minutes).
Kaffir Boy. Read by Howard Rollins. Two sound cassettes. Studio City, CA: Dove Books on Tape, 1988.

Internet Resources
McDougal Littell Literature Center at http://www.hmco.com/mcdougal/lit

Professional Development — TEACHING WITH TECHNOLOGY

McCain, T. *Teaching Graphic Design in All Subjects.* Eugene, OR: International Society for Technology in Education. 1993.

Sheingold, K., and Hadley, M. *Accomplished Teachers: Integrating Computers into Classroom Practice.* New York: Center for Technology in Education, Bank Street College of Education. 1990.

Computing Teacher. International Society for Technology in Education (ISTE), 1787 Agate Street, Eugene, OR 97493–1923.

UNIT ONE
Professional Enrichment

Twenty (Better) Questions
Kris L. Myers

The following article proposes a strategy for the study of literature that has wide-reaching application.

Maybe you don't struggle getting your students to read literature assignments, but I do. Getting an edge on MTV, mall-walking, and girl- or boy-watching is difficult, but I am competing better since I've changed my tack in evaluating students' knowledge of literature and my view of what that knowledge should be.

Most of us have used the "pop quiz" as a quick check to see who has read last night's assignment. We rationalize that it is positive motivation—a reward for those who have read, rather than punishment for those who have not. We make quizzes "simple" so any fool who has skimmed the assignment can pass.

But do you remember *taking* one of those quizzes? I do. I remember heart palpitations, silent prayers that the teacher would ask what I'd remembered of the details (and they were always about details), and brain freeze. I couldn't remember the name of the main character, the author of the story, or even the setting. And I'd read it; I had!

Well, I'm guilty of having given those infernal quizzes, too. Why don't I give them any more? The influence of two people changed my approach to quizzing and my whole outlook on what is important to know about literature.

The first influence was a wide-eyed high achiever in my first period class three years ago. Heidi was an eager student, willing to participate in all class activities. She went beyond what most students did. Needless to say, she always read her assignments, often more than once. Yet she would come in panic-stricken the day after a reading assignment, begging to know if we were having a pop quiz.

On the day we quizzed Thurber's *The Dog That Bit People,* Heidi froze. It was a true/false quiz with "simple" questions, but Heidi missed them all. She left her paper totally blank; she didn't even record her name. But the agony for me was watching her face as I read each question. I saw various stages of panic, fear, agitation, and resignation, ending finally in silent tears.

She was silent the entire class period. As the classroom cleared at the bell, she came to my desk and stood for several moments. Then she apologized. She had read the story twice, she said, but didn't know the "important" parts; she would work harder, read again, do whatever I could suggest. But she didn't know how to figure out what I thought was important. That gave me pause. What *I* thought? Is this what I wanted her to do: psych out what *I* felt was important about Thurber's story? Is that what teaching literature should be?

The second influence was Maia Pank Mertz at The Ohio State University. She introduced me to reader-response criticism by opening to me the worlds of Louise Rosenblatt, David Bleich, Norman Holland, and Alan Purves. But, more importantly, her classroom procedures were response-centered theories in action.

So, do I still struggle to get my students to read their assignments? Well, yes, but less so. Do I still give pop quizzes? Not exactly. Instead, I have students keep response journals. I use David Bleich's response heuristic to help students define and refine their responses. In *Reading and Feelings* (Urbana: NCTE, 1975), Bleich suggests that readers respond first to their perception of the work (what it means), then to the connections and associations within them that caused the affective response.

Students are used to looking to teachers for answers. They are seldom asked to reflect on what they think about what they read, or even less so, why they think what they think. Bloom's Taxonomy levels of application, analysis, synthesis, and evaluation are still largely ignored in most classrooms. But my students are responding to literature on all of these levels. I give students the following list of questions at the beginning of the school year and ask them to keep the list in their response journals to use all year:

1. What character(s) was your favorite? Why?
2. What character(s) did you dislike? Why?
3. Does anyone in this work remind you of anyone you know? Explain.
4. Are you like any character in this work? Explain.
5. If you could be any character in this work, who would you be? Explain.
6. What quality(ies) of which character strikes you as a good characteristic to develop within yourself over the years? Why? How does the character demonstrate this quality?
7. Overall, what kind of a feeling did you have after reading a few paragraphs of this work? Midway? After finishing the work?
8. Do any incidents, ideas, or actions in this work remind you of your own life or something that happened to you? Explain.
9. Are you like this piece of work? Why or why not?
10. Are there any parts of this work that were confusing to you? Which parts? Why do you think you got confused?
11. Do you feel there is an opinion expressed by the author through this work? What is it? How do you know this? Do you agree? Why or why not?
12. Do you think the title of this work is appropriate? Is it significant? Explain. What do you think the title means?
13. Would you change the ending of this story in any way? Tell your ending. Why would you change it?

14. What kind of person do you feel the author is? What makes you feel this way?
15. How did this work make you feel? Explain.
16. Do you share any of the feelings of the characters in this work? Explain.
17. Sometimes works leave you with the feeling that there is more to tell. Did this work do this? What do you think might happen?
18. Would you like to read something else by this author? Why or why not?
19. What do you feel is the most important word, phrase, passage, or paragraph in this work? Explain why it is important.
20. If you were an English teacher, would you want to share this work with your students? Why or why not?

I am constantly revising this list, and students may use any of the questions when writing their responses, providing they answer all of the question fully. What is important about this list is not the specific questions on it, but the nature of the questions, the attitude about literature that is fostered by the questions. The focus is constantly *on the students* and their perceptions, feelings, and associations which result from the work.

I still "check up" on my students' reading by randomly grading written responses, but students know what will be asked of them. Usually I require a minimum of a half a page of writing but nearly always get more. Sometimes I ask students to include in their response a reaction to a specific question on the list, but most students tend to drop the crutch the list provides.

How do I grade responses? I use Bleich's suggestions again and grade on seriousness of intent and obvious knowledge of the story. Unlike answers on the objective pop quiz, responses are impossible to fake; the reader knows immediately whether the student has read and thought about the work. Also, I do not grade every response. I try to include my own written response to their writing occasionally as well.

I encourage students to take their journals with them and respond to the work while it is fresh in their minds. I am available to read and respond to their writing upon request. Sometimes they write, discuss the work, then write again. Or we discuss and then write. And the work doesn't end when the students leave the classroom. It becomes something they "own" and is forever a part of them.

Yes, more of my students are reading their assignments more of the time. They *do* see response writings as a positive reward. But more than that, they see themselves as critics and meaning-carriers. They are less intimidated by and more intimate with the printed work. The mystery in the text has become the mystery in them. And that is a mystery they want to solve.

Copyrighted material reprinted with permission.

UNIT ONE
Starting Points for Unit Projects

The following suggestions will help you initiate individual and group projects during the course of the unit.

Creating a Map

GROUP ART PROJECT Have the class create a large world map like the one in the Unit Opener to show the national and cultural heritages of all the students in your class. Some students may be able to trace their heritage to several different countries. Under the map, have students write a summary that shows how many students trace their origins to each country.

Presenting a Monologue

LITERATURE/DRAMA PROJECT Have students research the childhood of one of the authors in this unit and then present a monologue in which they assume the identity of the author and share memories of his or her youth and of how those years affected his or her later life.

Presenting an International Music Festival

GROUP MUSIC PROJECT Divide the class into groups and have each group research the traditional music of one of the cultures featured in this unit or of one of their own ethnic backgrounds. Have them locate recordings of the music or invite local performers to play. Groups can take turns presenting the music of each culture and discussing its importance in shaping cultural identity.

Creating a Class "Heritage Quilt"

ART PROJECT Have each student design a five-inch square representing something important from his or her ethnic, religious, or family heritage. Students may design fabric squares and then stitch them together, or you can simply divide up a large sheet of paper into as many squares as you need.

Creating a Cultural Diorama

RESEARCH/ART PROJECT Have students research one of the cultures represented in this unit and create a diorama showing a typical scene from family or community life in that culture.

Collecting Oral Histories

ORAL HISTORY PROJECT Have students interview several adults to find out the one person who has influenced them most in their lives. Have students tape-record the adults describing the impact of their special person. With the adults' permission, students can then play back the best responses for the class.

Family and Community Involvement

Family

The selections in Unit One explore the various effects of the past on people's lives. The following activities will help students, their families, and other community members to share their own experiences of the past and to reflect upon the lasting imprints of such experiences.

OPTION 1 STUDY PHOTO ALBUMS
- **Connection** All of the selections in Unit One explore the imprints of the past on the present.
- **Activity** *Copymaster 4* Students and family members can look through family photo albums, asking themselves which people or experiences had a lasting imprint on their lives. Each family member can share memories and reflect upon how various people and experiences influenced him or her.

OPTION 2 WATCH A VIDEO
- **Connection** "Two Kinds" and "The Teacher Who Changed My Life" both deal with the experiences of immigrants.
- **Activity** *Copymaster 5* Students and family members may watch a movie about immigrant families, such as the film version of Amy Tan's *The Joy Luck Club*. After viewing the film, the family can discuss what they learned about the lives of immigrants and the problems they encountered in the United States.

OPTION 3 WRITE AN ANECDOTE
- **Connection** "Earthly Paradise" and "Everyday Use" are first-person narratives that explore memorable experiences.
- **Activity** *Copymaster 6* Students and family members should trade anecdotes about especially memorable experiences. They may write, tape-record, or videotape the one they think the class would most enjoy.

Community

OPTION 1
- **Connection** All of the selections in Unit One explore a character's memories of the past.
- **Activity** Invite older alumni of your school to visit your class to share their experiences of what school was like when they were students.

OPTION 2
- **Connection** "Cranes" explores the effects of the past on the present.
- **Activity** Invite a member of the local historical society to give a talk about the various groups of people who have settled over the years in your geographic vicinity.

OPTION 3
- **Connection** "Winter Night" deals with one immigrant's experiences before and after leaving Europe.
- **Activity** Have the class interview someone who has emigrated to the United States to find out why he or she made the journey and about his or her experiences in adjusting to life in a new land.

UNIT ONE
Part 1 Lesson Planner

TIME ALLOTMENTS SHOWN ARE APPROXIMATE. DEPENDING ON YOUR GOALS AND THE NEEDS OF YOUR STUDENTS, YOU MAY WISH TO ALLOW MORE OR LESS TIME FOR CERTAIN PORTIONS OF THE LESSON.

Table of Contents	Discussion	Previewing the Selection	Reading the Selection
PART OPENER **Lasting Impressions** page 12	**20 MINUTES** • Reflect on the part theme		
GENRE LESSON **Focus on Fiction** page 16	**20 MINUTES** • Discuss concepts of fiction • Discuss strategies for reading fiction		
SELECTION **Two Kinds** page 19 AVERAGE		**20 MINUTES** • PERSONAL CONNECTION • CULTURAL CONNECTION • WRITING CONNECTION	**40 MINUTES** • Introduce vocabulary • Read pp. 19–29 (11 pp.)
SELECTION **Cranes** page 34 AVERAGE		**20 MINUTES** • PERSONAL CONNECTION • HISTORICAL CONNECTION • READING CONNECTION: Making inferences	**15 MINUTES** • Read pp. 34–37 (4 pp.)
SELECTION **Winter Night** page 41 AVERAGE		**20 MINUTES** • PERSONAL CONNECTION • HISTORICAL CONNECTION • READING CONNECTION: Identifying mood	**30 MINUTES** • Introduce vocabulary • Read pp. 41–48 (8 pp.)
SELECTION **After the Ball** page 52 CHALLENGING		**20 MINUTES** • PERSONAL CONNECTION • HISTORICAL CONNECTION • READING CONNECTION: Evaluating characters	**40 MINUTES** • Introduce vocabulary • Read pp. 52–61 (10 pp.)
GENRE LESSON **Focus on Nonfiction** page 65	**20 MINUTES** • Discuss concepts of nonfiction • Discuss strategies for reading nonfiction		
SELECTION **from Kaffir Boy** page 68 AVERAGE		**20 MINUTES** • PERSONAL CONNECTION • HISTORICAL CONNECTION • READING CONNECTION: Using a reading log	**60 MINUTES** • Introduce vocabulary • Read pp. 68–79 (12 pp.)
SELECTION **The Teacher Who Changed My Life** page 84 EASY		**20 MINUTES** • PERSONAL CONNECTION • BIOGRAPHICAL CONNECTION • READING CONNECTION: Understanding cause and effect	**40 MINUTES** • Introduce vocabulary • Read pp. 84–89 (6 pp.)
NONFICTION ON YOUR OWN **from Earthly Paradise** page 92 AVERAGE			**40 MINUTES** • Read pp. 92–99 (8 pp.)

Writing	Writer's Style	Prewriting	Drafting and Revising
WRITING ABOUT LITERATURE **Direct Response**	**20 MINUTES**	**20 MINUTES**	**50 MINUTES**

Time estimates assume in-class work. You may wish to assign some of these stages as homework.

Responding to the Selection

FROM PERSONAL RESPONSE TO CRITICAL ANALYSIS	OR	ANOTHER PATHWAY	LITERARY CONCEPTS	QUICKWRITES
		50 MINUTES		
• Discussion questions	OR	• Character comparison	• Internal/external conflicts	• Diary entry • Personality profile • Review • Essay
		40 MINUTES		
• Discussion questions	OR	• Time line	• Plot	• Comparison chart • Letter • Alternative ending
		40 MINUTES		
• Discussion questions	OR	• Compare/contrast	• Characters	• Continuation • Chapter • Editorial
		50 MINUTES		
• Discussion questions	OR	• Plot adaptation	• Flashback	• Newspaper column • Dramatic scene • Letter • Proposal
		50 MINUTES		
• Discussion questions	OR	• Radio play	• Dialogue	• Dialogue • Public-service announcement • Eulogy
		40 MINUTES		
• Discussion questions	OR	• Character evaluation	• Essay	• Essay • Character sketch

Extension Activities

• ALTERNATIVE ACTIVITIES • LITERARY LINKS • CRITIC'S CORNER • THE WRITER'S STYLE • ACROSS THE CURRICULUM • ART CONNECTION • WORDS TO KNOW • BIOGRAPHY

	ALTERNATIVE ACTIVITIES	LITERARY LINKS	CRITIC'S CORNER	THE WRITER'S STYLE	ACROSS THE CURRICULUM	ART CONNECTION	WORDS TO KNOW	BIOGRAPHY
40 MINUTES	✓			✓	HISTORY		✓	✓
20 MINUTES	✓				HISTORY			✓
40 MINUTES	✓		✓		HISTORY		✓	✓
40 MINUTES	✓		✓		HISTORY	✓	✓	✓
50 MINUTES	✓	✓	✓		HISTORY		✓	✓
30 MINUTES	✓	✓					✓	✓

Publishing and Reflecting	Grammar in Context	Reading the World
25 MINUTES	**15 MINUTES**	**30 MINUTES**

LESSON PLANNER TEACHER'S EDITION

PART 1

REFLECTING ON THEME

Suggest that students each list three or four strong memories and jot down a phrase or a sentence to describe each one. Then have them assign each memory a category: People, Places, Events, and Images (or a combination of one or more of these). Take a class poll to discover which category of memories is most prevalent, and discuss why the memories in that particular category might seem so strong.

What Do You Think?

Remind students that certain skills are helpful in conducting a successful interview and advise them to keep in mind the following points:
- Be prepared with a list of questions.
- Listen carefully to the subject's answers.
- Be ready to think of new questions that may motivate the subject to elaborate on certain ideas or to pursue a more productive line of thought.

Students will return to this activity on pages 39, 64, and 82.

UNIT ONE **PART 1**

LASTING IMPRESSIONS

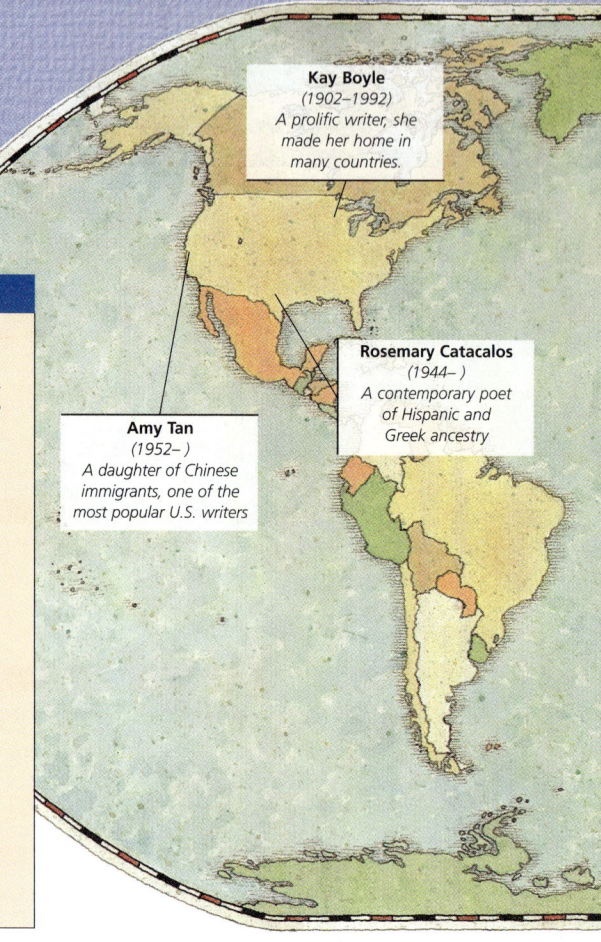

Kay Boyle (1902–1992) A prolific writer, she made her home in many countries.

Rosemary Catacalos (1944–) A contemporary poet of Hispanic and Greek ancestry

Amy Tan (1952–) A daughter of Chinese immigrants, one of the most popular U.S. writers

REFLECTING ON THEME

Why do some people stand out in your memory, even when you haven't seen them for many years? Why do recollections of some distant events linger so long? For each of us, impressions of certain people or events loom large in our memory, lasting perhaps even a lifetime. In this part of Unit One, you will explore how the past has imprinted the lives of characters both real and fictional. You will also tap into your own memories of people who made a lasting impression on you.

What Do You Think? Interview a classmate about a person or an event that made a lasting impression on his or her life. Record the results of your interview in your notebook, and then have the same classmate interview you. Share with the rest of the class what both of you learned from the interviews. In discussion, consider why some impressions have such a lasting impact on people.

Amy Tan	**Two Kinds** *Why won't the daughter live her mother's dreams?*	18
Rosemary Catacalos	**La Casa** / INSIGHT *The old house is still the same, but something has changed.*	30
Hwang Sunwŏn	**Cranes** *Two friends now on opposite sides in war*	33
Kay Boyle	**Winter Night** *A mysterious woman shares her past.*	40

Map Note

This map shows the diverse backgrounds of the authors featured in this part of Unit One. Point out that some of the authors listed on the map could call more than one country home or could claim more than one heritage. You might want to ask students the following questions:

- What might cause someone to move from one country to another?
- How might a mixed heritage influence an author's writing?

Leo Tolstoy	**After the Ball** *Why didn't he marry the belle of the ball?*	51
Mark Mathabane	from **Kaffir Boy** *A choice between a gang and an education*	67
Nicholas Gage	**The Teacher Who Changed My Life** *A wartime refugee and his incredible teacher*	83
Colette	from **Earthly Paradise** *A loving portrait of her mother*	92

THE LANGUAGE OF LITERATURE TEACHER'S EDITION

FOCUS ON FICTION

This feature defines *fiction* and provides an explanation of the terms used to discuss it. It also introduces students to the conventions of the genre and suggests strategies for reading fiction. The terms introduced here are covered in depth in the fiction selections that follow in the textbook.

Objectives
- To understand and appreciate fiction
- To understand some major elements of fiction: character, setting, plot, and theme
- To learn effective strategies for reading fiction

Teaching Strategies:
ELEMENTS OF FICTION

Character Ask students to identify main and minor characters from novels or short stories they have read recently. Choose a few of these and ask students which are fairly two-dimensional and which fully developed. Ask which are dynamic and which static and, in the case of dynamic characters, what changes they undergo.

Setting Ask students to identify some stories in which setting is very important and some in which it is less important. Explore with students what made the setting important in those stories.

Plot Ask students to identify the conflict in some of the stories they have already mentioned. Choose a story that many or all of the students are familiar with and have the class identify events that make up the rising action, the moment of climax, and the events of the falling action. Since some students have difficulty identifying the climax, you might engage the class in a discussion of a number of stories. At this point, correct answers are not as important as getting students to focus on the turning point—a point of decision or discovery.

Theme Ask students if any of the stories they have identified so far are purely entertaining stories. Of those that are not, challenge students to state the theme. If students use character names or overly specific events in their theme statements, guide them to a more general wording.

FOCUS ON FICTION

The origins of the word *fiction* can be traced to the Latin verb *fingere* (fĭng′gĕ-rĕ), which had two meanings: "to make up or invent" and "to make by shaping." Both meanings are relevant to fiction. A work of **fiction** is a narrative that springs from the imagination of a writer, though it may be based on actual events and real people. The writer shapes his or her narrative to capture the reader's interest and to achieve desired effects.

The two major types of fiction are **novels** and **short stories**. A novel is a fictional prose narrative of considerable length, usually taking several days or even weeks to read. Typically, a novel has a complex plot that unfolds though the actions, speech, and thoughts of the characters. A short story, on the other hand, is a brief work of fiction that can be read at one sitting. Generally, it develops one primary conflict and produces a single effect. Despite these differences in length and complexity, short stories and novels share the elements of **character, setting, plot,** and **theme**.

CHARACTER Characters are the individuals who take part in the action of a story. The events of the story center on the most important characters—the **main characters.** Less prominent characters are known as **minor characters.** Whereas some characters are two-dimensional, with only one or two dominant traits, a fully developed character possesses many traits, mirroring the psychological complexity of a real person. In longer works of fiction, main characters often undergo change as the plot unfolds. Such characters are called **dynamic characters,** as opposed to **static characters,** who remain the same.

SETTING The events of a story occur in a particular time and place, or setting. The setting is very important in some stories but no more than a backdrop in others. A story can be set in a realistic or an imaginary place, and its events can occur in the past, the present, or the future.

PLOT The word *plot* refers to the chain of related events that take place in a story. The plot is the writer's blueprint for what happens, when it happens, and to whom it happens. Usually, the events of a plot progress because of a **conflict,** or struggle between opposing forces.

Although there are many types of plots, most include the following stages:

Exposition The exposition lays the groundwork for the plot and provides the reader with essential background information. Characters are

16   UNIT ONE   PART 1: LASTING IMPRESSIONS

introduced, the setting is described, and the plot begins to unfold. Although the exposition generally appears at the opening of a story, it may also occur later in the narrative.

Rising Action As the story progresses, **complications** usually arise, causing difficulties for the main characters and making the conflict more difficult to resolve. As the characters struggle to find solutions to the conflict, suspense builds.

Climax The climax is the turning point of the action, the moment when interest and intensity reach their peak. The climax of a story usually involves an important event, decision, or discovery that affects the final outcome.

Falling Action The falling action consists of the events that occur after the climax. Often, the conflict is resolved, and the intensity of the action subsides. Sometimes this phase of the plot is called the **denouement** (dā′nōō-män′), from a French word that means "untying." In the denouement, the tangles of the plot are untied and mysteries are solved.

THEME A theme is an important idea or message conveyed by a work of fiction. It is a perception about life or human nature that the writer shares with the reader. Some pieces of fiction are intended only for entertainment and, as such, have no underlying themes. Most serious writing, however, comments on life or the human condition. Themes are seldom stated directly; often they can be uncovered only by means of careful reading and thought.

The following suggestions will help you unlock the theme or themes of a work:

- Review what happened to the main character. Did he or she change during the story? What did he or she learn about life?
- Skim the selection for key phrases and sentences—statements that move beyond the action of the story to say something important about life or people.
- Think about the title of the selection. Does it have a special meaning that could lead you to discover a major theme?

STRATEGIES FOR READING FICTION

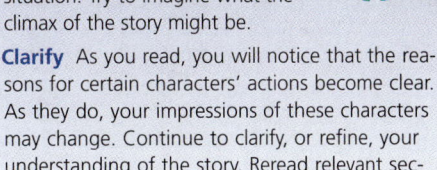

- **Preview** Before you begin a work of fiction, look ahead to see what the title, the art, or other noticeable features tell you about the story.
- **Visualize and Connect** As you read the exposition, picture in your mind the characters and setting described. Look for specific adjectives that can help you imagine how the opening scene might look. Try connecting what you read with people, places, and situations that you know from personal experience.
- **Observe and Question** Be an active reader by making observations and asking questions about the story. Note whether the narrator is a character within the story or is watching the action from outside. Ask yourself what the central problem, or conflict, seems to be. Ask why the characters behave as they do.
- **Predict** Once you begin to understand the problems the characters face, predict what will happen next. Think about what the characters might do or say in their situation. Try to imagine what the climax of the story might be.
- **Clarify** As you read, you will notice that the reasons for certain characters' actions become clear. As they do, your impressions of these characters may change. Continue to clarify, or refine, your understanding of the story. Reread relevant sections of the selection to help you understand fully what has happened or why it has happened.
- **Reflect** Don't forget to make judgments about what you read. Draw your own conclusions about the characters and their actions, just as you would about people you know in real life.
- **Evaluate** When you finish reading, take a few minutes to think about your impressions. How do you feel about the story's events and main characters? What did you enjoy about the story?

OVERVIEW

Objectives

- To understand and appreciate a fictional story about how a mother's dreams for her daughter influence their relationship
- To identify and understand internal and external conflicts
- To recognize and appreciate the role of humor in a work of fiction
- To express understanding of the selection through a choice of writing forms, including a diary entry, a personality profile, a review, and an essay
- To extend understanding of the selection through a variety of multimodal and cross-curricular activities
- To provide an opportunity to assess students' performance through an alternative assessment instrument

Skills

LITERARY CONCEPTS
- Conflict
- Plot
- Irony

THE WRITER'S STYLE
- First-person point of view

GRAMMAR
- Capitalizing titles

GENRE STUDY
- Fiction

SPEAKING, LISTENING, AND VIEWING
- Group discussion
- Debate
- Choral reading

CULTURAL CONNECTION

America's Chinatowns Historically, many Chinese people who immigrated to the United States congregated in Chinatowns in San Francisco, New York City, and other major cities. These photographs show scenes from American Chinatowns. The pictures suggest the setting of "Two Kinds."

Side A, Frame 49291

PREVIEWING

FICTION

Two Kinds
Amy Tan United States

Activating Prior Knowledge
PERSONAL CONNECTION

Think of a time when someone in authority had high expectations of you—expectations that you were not sure you could meet. Perhaps a parent expected straight A's, a bandleader gave you a difficult solo, or a coach put you in a game at a critical moment. Share your experience with your classmates.

Building Background
CULTURAL CONNECTION

During the 1930s and 1940s, China was invaded by Japan and racked by political upheavals that led to a bitter civil war. Some Chinese citizens escaped these dangers by emigrating to the United States. To many Chinese immigrants, life in the United States was so different from life in war-torn China that anything seemed possible, especially for their children. The children were expected to pursue the American dream of material success, but without sacrificing the traditional Chinese values of obedience and respect for one's elders. "Two Kinds" is narrated by a young woman who, like Amy Tan herself, is the daughter of Chinese immigrants.

Setting a Purpose
WRITING CONNECTION

Why do you think many parents have high expectations of their children? To help you sort out your thoughts on this issue, create a chart similar to the one shown here. Then write a brief explanation of why parents sometimes have high expectations. As you read this story, keep in mind your thoughts on this subject.

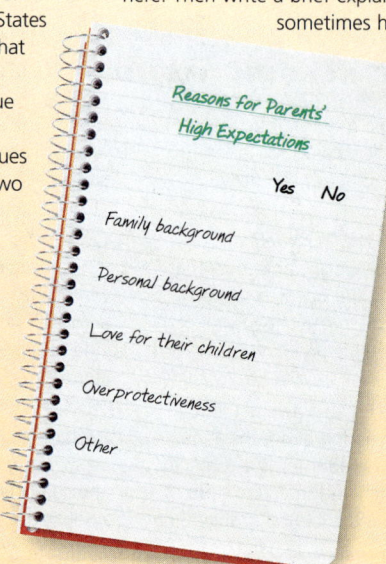

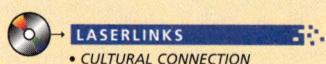
• CULTURAL CONNECTION

18 UNIT ONE PART 1: LASTING IMPRESSIONS

PRINT AND MEDIA RESOURCES

UNIT ONE RESOURCE BOOK
Strategic Reading: Literature, p. 7
Vocabulary SkillBuilder, p. 8

GRAMMAR MINI-LESSONS
Transparencies, p. 38
Copymasters, p. 39

ACCESS FOR STUDENTS ACQUIRING ENGLISH
Selection Summaries
Reading Support

TEACHER'S GUIDE TO ASSESSMENT AND PORTFOLIO USE

FORMAL ASSESSMENT
Selection Test, pp. 5–6
 Test Generator

 AUDIO LIBRARY
See Reference Card

 **LASERLINKS**
Cultural Connection

18 THE LANGUAGE OF LITERATURE TEACHER'S EDITION

TWO KINDS

AMY TAN

My mother believed you could be anything you wanted to be in America. You could open a restaurant. You could work for the government and get good retirement. You could buy a house with almost no money down. You could become rich. You could become instantly famous.

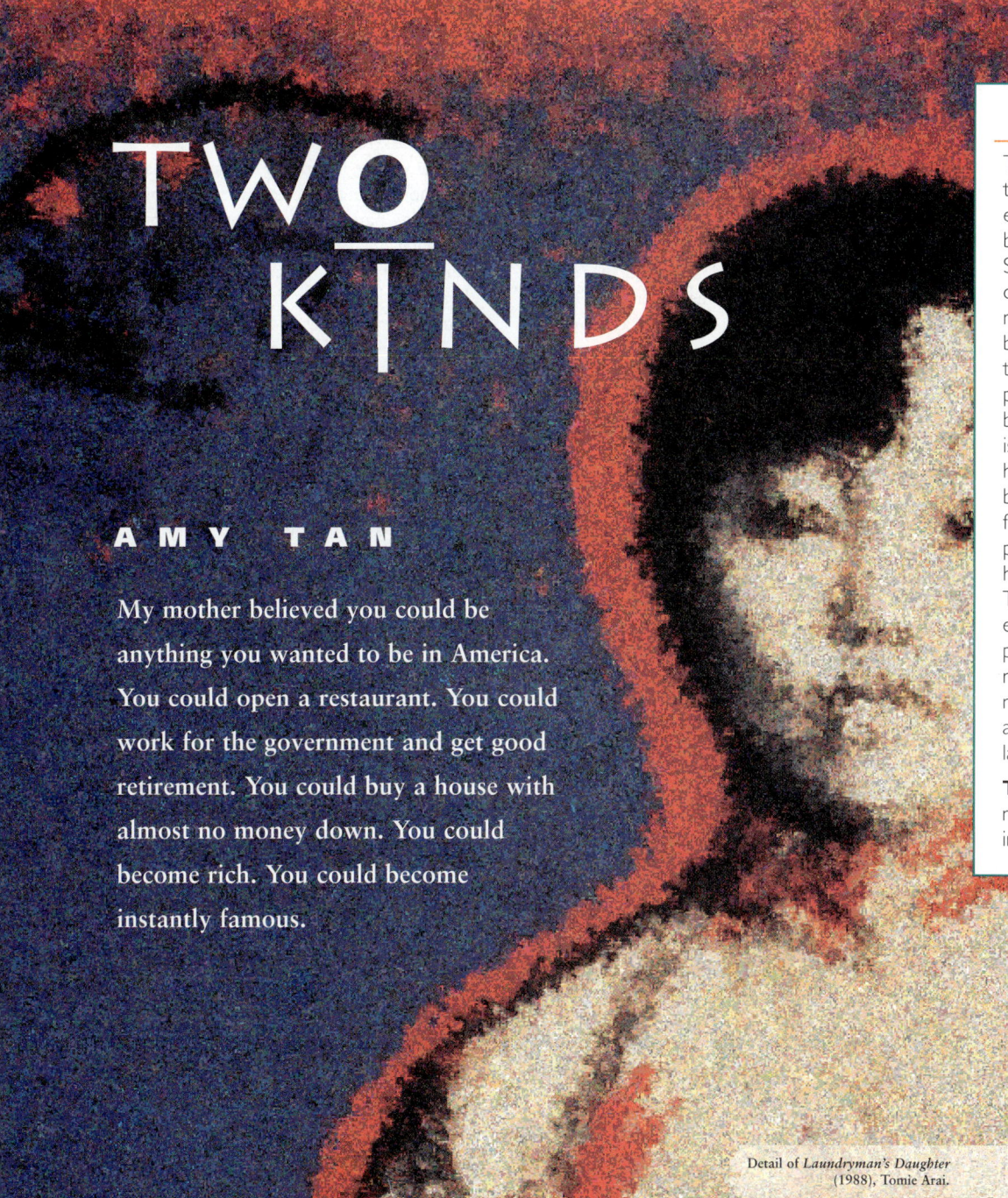

Detail of *Laundryman's Daughter* (1988), Tomie Arai.

SUMMARY

The narrator's mother emigrated from China to the United States in 1949 after losing everything—mother, father, home, first husband, and twin baby daughters. In the United States, she has high hopes that her nine-year-old daughter will be a prodigy. Eventually, the mother decides that the narrator will become a great pianist. Despite the narrator's protests, her mother forces her to take piano lessons from their downstairs neighbor, Mr. Chong, a retired piano teacher who is now deaf. Knowing that Mr. Chong cannot hear her playing, the narrator tricks him into believing that she is trying her best when, in fact, she does not. At a piano recital, she plays miserably, surprising and humiliating herself and her family, especially her mother. The mother never mentions the failure and expects her daughter to continue playing piano, causing an argument that leaves the narrator with a terrible burden of guilt. Her mother never asks her to play piano again, and the narrator never does—until years later, after her mother's death.

Thematic Link: *Lasting Impressions* A mother's high expectations make a lasting impression on her daughter.

CUSTOMIZING FOR
Students Acquiring English

- Use **ACCESS FOR STUDENTS ACQUIRING ENGLISH**, *Reading Support*.
- The mother's dialect may confuse students. You may also want to preteach the following musical terms: *treble, half time, scale, sharp, flat, chord*.
- As you guide students through the selection, you may also want to use the suggestions under Strategic Reading for Less-Proficient Readers.

WORDS TO KNOW

betrayal (bē-trā′əl) *n.* an act of disloyalty or treachery (p. 28)
devastate (dĕv′ə-stāt′) *v.* to destroy or overwhelm (p. 26)
discordant (dĭ-skôr′dnt) *adj.* having a disagreeable or clashing sound; not in harmony (p. 24)
fiasco (fē-ăs′kō) *n.* a complete failure (p. 26)
indignity (ĭn-dĭg′nĭ-tē) *n.* a loss of dignity or honor; a source of such loss (p. 20)
lament (lə-mĕnt′) *v.* to express grief or deep regret (p. 25)
prodigy (prŏd′ə-jē) *n.* a young person who is exceptionally talented or intelligent (p. 20)
ream (rēm) *n.* a unit used to measure quantities of paper, usually equal to 500 sheets; hence, a large amount of something (p. 23)
reproach (rĭ-prōch′) *n.* blame; criticism (p. 20)
reverie (rĕv′ə-rē) *n.* a daydream (p. 24)

STRATEGIC READING FOR
Less-Proficient Readers

Set a Purpose To help students become immersed in the story, stop after reading the first four paragraphs and ask students to list areas in which a child might be a prodigy. Then ask them to read on to find out in which areas the narrator's mother harbors high hopes for her daughter.

Use **UNIT ONE RESOURCE BOOK**, p. 7, for guidance in reading the selection.

CUSTOMIZING FOR
Gifted and Talented Students

Have students consider, as they read, why the mother is so eager to have her daughter be a prodigy. Have students cite details from the text to support their views.

Possible responses:

Some students may say the mother is trying to make up for the losses she suffered in China.

- *Page 20—"But she never looked back . . ."*
- *Page 26—"But my mother's expression was what devastated me . . ."*

Other students may say that because the mother sees remarkable children everywhere, she assumes her daughter can be successful too.

- *Page 20—"Of course you can be prodigy, too, . . ."*
- *Page 20—"She would present new tests, taking her examples from stories of amazing children she had read . . ."*

Some students might point to the competition between the mother and her friends.

- *Pages 24–25—"And then one day I heard my mother and her friend Lindo Jong both talking . . ."*

Literary Concept: DIALOGUE

A Ask students to note the techniques Amy Tan uses to make the mother's dialogue sound realistic. *(Possible responses: She includes an occasional Chinese phrase; she has the mother speak a nonstandard English typical of someone learning the language.)*

CUSTOMIZING FOR
Students Acquiring English

I Some students may not be familiar with the story of Cinderella. Ask a volunteer to recite the fairy tale for the class.

Critical Thinking: SPECULATING

B Ask students to suggest who the "prodigy" in the narrator might be. *(Possible responses: the narrator's real and hitherto undiscovered talent; the narrator's real self.)*

"Of course you can be <u>prodigy</u>, too," my mother told me when I was nine. "You can be best anything. What does Auntie Lindo know? Her daughter, she is only best tricky."

America was where all my mother's hopes lay. She had come here in 1949 after losing everything in China: her mother and father, her family home, her first husband, and two daughters, twin baby girls. But she never looked back with regret. There were so many ways for things to get better.

We didn't immediately pick the right kind of prodigy. At first my mother thought I could be a Chinese Shirley Temple.[1] We'd watch Shirley's old movies on TV as though they were training films. My mother would poke my arm and say, *"Ni kan"*—You watch. And I would see Shirley tapping her feet, or singing a sailor song, or pursing her lips into a very round O while saying, "Oh my goodness."

A *"Ni kan,"* said my mother as Shirley's eyes flooded with tears. "You already know how. Don't need talent for crying!"

Soon after my mother got this idea about Shirley Temple, she took me to a beauty training school in the Mission district[2] and put me in the hands of a student who could barely hold the scissors without shaking. Instead of getting big fat curls, I emerged with an uneven mass of crinkly black fuzz. My mother dragged me off to the bathroom and tried to wet down my hair.

"You look like Negro Chinese," she lamented, as if I had done this on purpose.

The instructor of the beauty training school had to lop off these soggy clumps to make my hair even again. "Peter Pan is very popular these days," the instructor assured my mother. I now had hair the length of a boy's, with straight-across bangs that hung at a slant two inches above my eyebrows. I liked the haircut, and it made me actually look forward to my future fame.

In fact, in the beginning, I was just as excited as my mother, maybe even more so. I pictured this prodigy part of me as many different images, trying each one on for size. I was a dainty ballerina girl standing by the curtains, waiting to hear the right music that would send me floating on my tiptoes. I was like the Christ child lifted out of the straw manger, crying with holy <u>indignity</u>. I was Cinderella stepping from her pumpkin carriage with sparkly cartoon music filling the air.

In all of my imaginings, I was filled with a sense that I would soon become *perfect*. My mother and father would adore me. I would be beyond <u>reproach</u>. I would never feel the need to sulk for anything.

But sometimes the prodigy in me became impatient. "If you don't hurry up and get me out of here, I'm disappearing for good," it warned. "And then you'll always be nothing."

Every night after dinner, my mother and I would sit at the Formica[3] kitchen table. She would present new tests, taking her examples from stories of amazing children she had read in *Ripley's Believe It or Not,* or *Good Housekeeping, Reader's Digest,* and a dozen other magazines she kept in a pile in our bathroom. My mother got these magazines from people whose houses she cleaned. And since she cleaned many houses each week, we had a great assortment. She would look through them all,

---

1. **Shirley Temple:** a popular child movie star of the 1930s.
2. **Mission district:** a residential neighborhood in San Francisco.
3. **Formica** (fôr-mī′kə): a heat-resistant plastic used on tops of kitchen counters, tables, and the like.

| WORDS TO KNOW | **prodigy** (prŏd′ə-jē) *n.* a young person who is exceptionally talented or intelligent
 indignity (ĭn-dĭg′nĭ-tē) *n.* a loss of dignity or honor; a source of such loss
 reproach (rĭ-prōch′) *n.* blame; criticism |

20

Mini-Lesson   Genre Study

FICTION Draw on the chalkboard the diagram shown here, and use it to explain the typical structure of a work of **fiction**. Mention these points:
- Fiction comes from the imagination of the author.
- Fiction includes novels and short stories.
- Fiction may be based on actual events and real people.
- The main purpose of fiction is to entertain, although it can serve to inform or enlighten.

Application Have students copy the web into their notebooks. Ask them to refer to it as they look for the characteristics of fiction in "Two Kinds."

20 THE LANGUAGE OF LITERATURE **TEACHER'S EDITION**

searching for stories about remarkable children.

The first night she brought out a story about a three-year-old boy who knew the capitals of all the states and even most of the European countries. A teacher was quoted as saying the little boy could also pronounce the names of the foreign cities correctly.

"What's the capital of Finland?" my mother asked me, looking at the magazine story.

All I knew was the capital of California, because Sacramento was the name of the street we lived on in Chinatown. "Nairobi!"[4] I guessed, saying the most foreign word I could think of. She checked to see if that was possibly one way to pronounce "Helsinki" before showing me the answer.

The tests got harder—multiplying numbers in my head, finding the queen of hearts in a deck of cards, trying to stand on my head without using my hands, predicting the daily temperatures in Los Angeles, New York, and London.

One night I had to look at a page from the Bible for three minutes and then report everything I could remember. "Now Jehoshaphat[5] had riches and honor in abundance and . . . that's all I remember, Ma," I said.

And after seeing my mother's disappointed face once again, something inside of me began to die. I hated the tests, the raised hopes and failed expectations. Before going to bed that night, I looked in the mirror above the bathroom sink and when I saw only my face staring back—and that it would always be this ordinary face—I began to cry. Such a sad, ugly girl! I made high-pitched noises like a crazed animal, trying to scratch out the face in the mirror.

And then I saw what seemed to be the prodigy side of me—because I had never seen that face before. I looked at my reflection, blinking so I could see more clearly. The girl staring back at me was angry, powerful. This girl and I were the same. I had new thoughts, willful thoughts, or rather thoughts filled with lots of won'ts. I won't let her change me, I promised myself. I won't be what I'm not.

> I won't let her change me, I promised myself. I won't be what I'm not.

So now on nights when my mother presented her tests, I performed listlessly, my head propped on one arm. I pretended to be bored. And I was. I got so bored I started counting the bellows of the foghorns out on the bay while my mother drilled me in other areas. The sound was comforting and reminded me of the cow jumping over the moon. And the next day, I played a game with myself, seeing if my mother would give up on me before eight bellows. After a while I usually counted only one, maybe two bellows at most. At last she was beginning to give up hope.

Two or three months had gone by without any mention of my being a prodigy again. And then one day my mother was watching *The Ed Sullivan Show*[6] on TV. The TV was old and the sound kept shorting out. Every time my mother got halfway up from the sofa to adjust the set, the sound would go back on and Ed would be talking. As soon as she sat down, Ed would go silent again. She got up, the TV broke into loud

---

4. **Nairobi** (nī-rō′bē): the capital of the African nation of Kenya.
5. **Jehoshaphat** (jə-hŏsh′ə-făt′): a king of Judah in the ninth century B.C.
6. *The Ed Sullivan Show*: a popular weekly variety show on television from 1948 to 1971.

Mini-Lesson Literary Concepts

REVIEWING PLOT Remind students that plot is the sequence of actions and events in a literary work. Explain that most plots center on a conflict, which the characters struggle to resolve. Also point out that plots usually follow a specific pattern: exposition, rising action, climax, and falling action. You might want to represent the typical plot graphically, as shown here.

Application Have students record in their notebooks the four stages of a plot. Then ask students to go back through the story and write down the page numbers that correspond (approximately) to each stage. Encourage them to discuss their conclusions with a partner, to see whether they agree on the four stages.

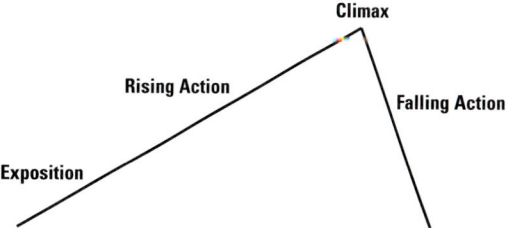

Literary Concept: IRONY

C Remind students that irony is a contrast between what is expected and what actually exists or happens. Have students suggest why it is ironic that the narrator's mother is trying to turn her daughter into a prodigy by giving her tests. (*A child prodigy is, by definition, born with special abilities.*)

STRATEGIC READING FOR
Less-Proficient Readers

D Use the following prompts to make sure students understand the mother's dreams for her daughter:

- What talents has the narrator's mother tried to develop in her daughter? (*She has tried to develop the talents of a child star, a mathematical whiz, a geography whiz, a magician, a gymnast, a weather forecaster, and someone with a photographic memory.*)
Summarizing

- How do you react to the mother's efforts? (*Possible responses: Some students might be angry with her; others may argue that mothers should have high expectations of their children.*)
Connecting

Set a Purpose Ask students to read on to find out what the mother finally decides will be her daughter's true talent.

Literary Concept:
INTERNAL CONFLICT

E Discuss how the mother's attempts to make her daughter a prodigy have upset the daughter's peace of mind. (*She is unhappy with herself because she has disappointed her mother so many times.*)

DESIGN NOTE

The Chinese character used as a background for the quotation means "peace."

Literary Concept: EXPOSITION

F Remind students that exposition is the part of the plot that provides background information and introduces the characters, setting, and conflict in a story. Point out that the exposition of this plot ends here. Ask students to summarize the exposition. (*The author has introduced the narrator and her mother and has shown that the mother has high expectations for her daughter but that the daughter shows no promise of, or interest in, being a prodigy.*)

Laundryman's Daughter (1988), Tomie Arai. Silkscreen print, 22″ × 30″ unframed, printed in an edition of 35 by Avocet Editions.

piano music. She sat down. Silence. Up and down, back and forth, quiet and loud. It was like a stiff, embraceless dance between her and the TV set. Finally she stood by the set with her hand on the sound dial.

She seemed entranced by the music, a little frenzied piano piece with this mesmerizing quality, sort of quick passages and then teasing lilting ones before it returned to the quick playful parts.

"*Ni kan,*" my mother said, calling me over with hurried hand gestures, "Look here."

I could see why my mother was fascinated by the music. It was being pounded out by a little Chinese girl, about nine years old, with a Peter Pan haircut. The girl had the sauciness of a Shirley Temple. She was proudly modest like a proper Chinese child. And she also did this fancy sweep of a curtsy, so that the fluffy skirt of her white dress cascaded slowly to the floor like the petals of a large carnation.

In spite of these warning signs, I wasn't worried. Our family had no piano and we couldn't afford to buy one, let alone <u>reams</u> of sheet music and piano lessons. So I could be generous in my comments when my mother bad-mouthed the little girl on TV.

"Play note right, but doesn't sound good! No singing sound," complained my mother.

"What are you picking on her for?" I said carelessly. "She's pretty good. Maybe she's not the best, but she's trying hard." I knew almost immediately I would be sorry I said that.

"Just like you," she said. "Not the best. Because you not trying." She gave a little huff as she let go of the sound dial and sat down on the sofa.

The little Chinese girl sat down also to play an encore of "Anitra's Dance" by Grieg.[7] I remember the song, because later on I had to learn how to play it.

Three days after watching *The Ed Sullivan Show*, my mother told me what my schedule would be for piano lessons and piano practice. She had talked to Mr. Chong, who lived on the first floor of our apartment building. Mr. Chong was a retired piano teacher and my mother had traded housecleaning services for weekly lessons and a piano for me to practice on every day, two hours a day, from four until six.

When my mother told me this, I felt as though I had been sent to hell. I whined and then kicked my foot a little when I couldn't stand it anymore.

"Why don't you like me the way I am? I'm *not* a genius! I can't play the piano. And even if I could, I wouldn't go on TV if you paid me a million dollars!" I cried.

My mother slapped me. "Who ask you be genius?" she shouted. "Only ask you be your best. For you sake. You think I want you be genius? Hnnh! What for! Who ask you!"

"So ungrateful," I heard her mutter in Chinese. "If she had as much talent as she has temper, she would be famous now."

Mr. Chong, whom I secretly nicknamed Old Chong, was very strange, always tapping his fingers to the silent music of an invisible orchestra. He looked ancient in my eyes. He had lost most of the hair on top of his head and he wore thick glasses and had eyes that always looked tired and sleepy. But he must have been younger than I thought, since he lived with his mother and was not yet married.

I met Old Lady Chong once and that was enough. She had this peculiar smell like a baby that had done something in its pants. And her fingers felt like a dead person's, like an old peach I once found in the back of the refrigerator; the

---

7. **Grieg** (grēg): the Norwegian composer Edvard Grieg (1843–1907).

WORDS TO KNOW

ream (rēm) *n.* a unit used to measure quantities of paper, usually equal to 500 sheets; hence, a large amount of something

23

Mini-Lesson  Grammar

CAPITALIZING TITLES Point out the titles on page 23 ("Anitra's Dance" and *The Ed Sullivan Show*), and elicit that one is the title of a short musical piece and the other the title of a TV show. Remind students that they must capitalize the first and last words and all other important words in titles. Also remind them that conjunctions, articles, and prepositions with fewer than five letters are not capitalized.

Application Ask students to use the rules for capitalizing words in titles to correct the following items:
1. *Ripley's Believe It Or Not*
2. *Classical music Digest*
3. *star search*
4. *Immortal beloved*

Reteaching/Reinforcement
- *Grammar Handbook*, anthology p. 1088
- *Grammar Mini-Lessons* copymasters, p. 39, transparencies, p. 38

The Writer's Craft
Titles, pp. 774–775

Literary Concept: STYLE

G Invite students to describe the author's writing style in this paragraph and to tell why the style is appropriate for the content. (*Possible response: The style mimics the up-and-down, back-and-forth movements of the "dance" that the narrator's mother is having with her TV set.*)

Literary Concept: CONFLICT

H Ask students what the mother's response reveals about the conflict brewing between the narrator and her mother. (*Possible response: The mother is angry at her daughter because she thinks the daughter is not trying to do her best.*)

STRATEGIC READING FOR
Less-Proficient Readers

I Have students tell what area the narrator's mother has staked out for her daughter's genius. (*piano playing*) Noting Relevant Details

- Ask students to speculate whether the narrator is likely to become a prodigy at the keyboard. (*Given the narrator's attitudes, it isn't likely that she will become an outstanding pianist.*) Making Predictions

Set a Purpose Have students read on to find out whether the narrator becomes an outstanding pianist.

Literary Concept: RISING ACTION

J Ask students to explain how the conflict between the mother and daughter is causing the tension in the story to rise. (*As the daughter begins to rebel against her mother's dreams for her, their relationship becomes more tense.*)

Literary Concept: DESCRIPTION

K Invite students to share their reactions to the description of Old Lady Chong and to tell which of their senses the details appeal to. (*smell and touch*)

THE LANGUAGE OF LITERATURE TEACHER'S EDITION 23

skin just slid off the meat when I picked it up.

I soon found out why Old Chong had retired from teaching piano. He was deaf. "Like Beethoven!"[8] he shouted to me. "We're both listening only in our head!" And he would start to conduct his frantic silent sonatas.

Our lessons went like this. He would open the book and point to different things, explaining their purpose: "Key! Treble! Bass! No sharps or flats! So this is C major! Listen now and play after me!"

And then he would play the C scale a few times, a simple chord, and then, as if inspired by an old, unreachable itch, he gradually added more notes and running trills and a pounding bass until the music was really something quite grand.

I would play after him, the simple scale, the simple chord, and then I just played some nonsense that sounded like a cat running up and down on top of garbage cans. Old Chong smiled and applauded and then said, "Very good! But now you must learn to keep time!"

So that's how I discovered that Old Chong's eyes were too slow to keep up with the wrong notes I was playing. He went through the motions in half-time. To help me keep rhythm, he stood behind me, pushing down on my right shoulder for every beat. He balanced pennies on top of my wrists so I would keep them still as I slowly played scales and arpeggios.[9] He had me curve my hand around an apple and keep that shape when playing chords. He marched stiffly to show me how to make each finger dance up and down, staccato[10] like an obedient little soldier.

He taught me all these things, and that was how I also learned I could be lazy and get away with mistakes, lots of mistakes. If I hit the wrong notes because I hadn't practiced enough, I never corrected myself. I just kept playing in rhythm. And Old Chong kept conducting his own private reverie.

So maybe I never really gave myself a fair chance. I did pick up the basics pretty quickly, and I might have become a good pianist at that young age. But I was so determined not to try, not to be anybody different, that I learned to play only the most ear-splitting preludes,[11] the most discordant hymns.

Over the next year, I practiced like this, dutifully in my own way. And then one day I heard my mother and her friend Lindo Jong both talking in a loud, bragging tone of voice so others could hear. It was after church, and I was leaning against the brick wall wearing a dress with stiff white petticoats. Auntie Lindo's daughter, Waverly, who was about my age, was standing farther down the wall about five feet away. We had grown up together and shared all the closeness of two sisters squabbling over crayons and dolls. In

> ... I also learned I could get away with mistakes, lots of mistakes.

---

8. **Beethoven** (bā′tō′vən): the German composer Ludwig van Beethoven (1770–1827), who began losing his hearing in 1801 and was deaf by 1819.
9. **arpeggios** (är-pěj′ē-ōz′): chords in which the notes are played separately in quick sequence rather than at the same time.
10. **staccato** (stə-kä′tō): producing distinct, abrupt breaks between successive tones.
11. **preludes** (prĕl′yo͞odz′): short piano compositions, each usually based on a single musical theme.

WORDS TO KNOW
reverie (rĕv′ə-rē) *n.* a daydream
discordant (dĭ-skôr′dnt) *adj.* having a disagreeable or clashing sound; not in harmony

---

Critic's Corner

"These moving and powerful stories share the irony, pain, and sorrow of the imperfect ways in which mothers and daughters love each other. Tan's vision is courageous and insightful."

Denise Chong, critic
From a review of Amy Tan's
The Joy Luck Club in *Quill and Quire*

O other words, for the most part, we hated each other. I thought she was snotty. Waverly Jong had gained a certain amount of fame as "Chinatown's Littlest Chinese Chess Champion."

"She bring home too many trophy," lamented Auntie Lindo that Sunday. "All day she play chess. All day I have no time do nothing but dust off her winnings." She threw a scolding look at Waverly, who pretended not to see her.

"You lucky you don't have this problem," said Auntie Lindo with a sigh to my mother.

And my mother squared her shoulders and bragged: "Our problem worser than yours. If we ask Jing-mei[12] wash dish, she hear nothing but music. It's like you can't stop this natural talent."

P And right then, I was determined to put a stop to her foolish pride.

A few weeks later, Old Chong and my mother conspired to have me play in a talent show which would be held in the church hall. By then, my parents had saved up enough to buy me a secondhand piano, a black Wurlitzer spinet[13] with a scarred bench. It was the showpiece of our living room.

Q For the talent show, I was to play a piece called "Pleading Child" from Schumann's[14] *Scenes from Childhood*. It was a simple, moody piece that sounded more difficult than it was. I was supposed to memorize the whole thing, playing the repeat parts twice to make the piece sound longer. But I dawdled over it, playing a few bars and then cheating, looking up to see what notes followed. I never really listened to what I was playing. I daydreamed about being somewhere else, about being someone else.

The part I liked to practice best was the fancy curtsy: right foot out, touch the rose on the carpet with a pointed foot, sweep to the side, left leg bends, look up and smile.

My parents invited all the couples from the Joy Luck Club to witness my debut.[15] Auntie Lindo and Uncle Tin were there. Waverly and her two older brothers had also come. The first two rows were filled with children both younger and older than I was. The littlest ones got to go first. They recited simple nursery rhymes, squawked out tunes on miniature violins, twirled Hula-Hoops,[16] pranced in pink ballet tutus,[17] and when they bowed or curtsied, the audience would sigh in unison, "Awww," and then clap enthusiastically.

When my turn came, I was very confident. I remember my childish excitement. It was as if I knew, without a doubt, that the prodigy side of me really did exist. I had no fear whatsoever, no nervousness. I remember thinking to myself, This is it! This is it! I looked out over the audience, at my mother's blank face, my father's yawn, Auntie Lindo's stiff-lipped smile, Waverly's sulky expression. I had on a white dress layered with sheets of lace, and a pink bow in my Peter Pan haircut. As I sat down I envisioned people jumping to their feet and Ed Sullivan rushing up to introduce me to everyone on TV.

R And I started to play. It was so beautiful. I was so caught up in how lovely I looked that at first I didn't worry how I would sound. So it was a surprise to me when I hit the first wrong note and I realized something didn't sound

---

12. **Jing-mei** (jǐng'mā').
13. **spinet** (spǐn'ǐt): a small upright piano.
14. **Schumann's** (shoō'mänz'): of Robert Schumann (1810–1856), a German composer famous for his piano works.
15. **debut** (dā-byoō'): first public performance.
16. **Hula-Hoops:** plastic hoops that are whirled around the body by means of hip movements similar to those of the hula, a Hawaiian dance.
17. **tutus** (toō'toōz): short layered skirts worn by ballerinas.

WORDS TO KNOW
lament (lə-měnt') v. to express grief or deep regret

Literary Concept: IRONY

O Have students discuss why this sentence is ironic: "In other words, for the most part, we hated each other." (The narrator has just said that she and Waverly had "shared all the closeness of two sisters." Therefore, we would expect her to be close to Waverly.)

Critical Thinking: ANALYZING

P Ask students if they agree with the narrator, Jing-mei, that it is "foolish pride" that motivates her mother to want her to be a pianist. (Possible responses: Some students may say that the mother's pride is foolish; others may say that the mother believes in her daughter.)

Literary Concept: SYMBOL

Q Ask students to think about "Pleading Child," the title of the piece Jing-mei is to play, and to suggest how this title might be symbolic of the narrator. (Possible response: The title suggests the narrator herself; by playing this piece, the narrator will be pleading with her mother to be given the freedom to develop her own talents in her own ways.)

Critical Thinking: ANALYZING

R Ask students what aspects of her performance Jing-mei is most concerned with and what aspect is less important to her. (Possible responses: Some students might say that Jing-mei is excited that her "prodigy side" will finally appear. Others might say she's much more concerned with her appearance, her curtsy, and the impact her debut will make than with the actual quality of her playing.)

Multicultural Perspectives

IMMIGRANT SOCIAL CLUBS Students may be interested to know that it was common for immigrants such as Jing-mei's mother to form social clubs with close friends and neighbors from the same culture. Organizations like the Joy Luck Club provided a sort of support group that helped newcomers to the United States adjust to the challenges of a new culture while maintaining certain traditions of the old culture. Often, the members of a social club helped one another in emergencies, sponsored relatives who wanted to join them in the new country, and lent money to newcomers to find housing or jobs or to start businesses.

quite right. And then I hit another and another followed that. A chill started at the top of my head and began to trickle down. Yet I couldn't stop playing, as though my hands were bewitched. I kept thinking my fingers would adjust themselves back, like a train switching to the right track. I played this strange jumble through two repeats, the sour notes staying with me all the way to the end.

When I stood up, I discovered my legs were shaking. Maybe I had just been nervous and the audience, like Old Chong, had seen me go through the right motions and had not heard anything wrong at all. I swept my right foot out, went down on my knee, looked up and smiled. The room was quiet, except for Old Chong, who was beaming and shouting, "Bravo! Bravo! Well done!" But then I saw my mother's face, her stricken face. The audience clapped weakly, and as I walked back to my chair, with my whole face quivering as I tried not to cry, I heard a little boy whisper loudly to his mother, "That was awful," and the mother whispered back, "Well, she certainly tried."

And now I realized how many people were in the audience, the whole world it seemed. I was aware of eyes burning into my back. I felt the shame of my mother and father as they sat stiffly throughout the rest of the show.

We could have escaped during intermission. Pride and some strange sense of honor must have anchored my parents to their chairs. And so we watched it all: the eighteen-year-old boy with a fake mustache who did a magic show and juggled flaming hoops while riding a unicycle. The breasted girl with white makeup who sang from *Madama Butterfly*[18] and got honorable mention. And the eleven-year-old boy who won first prize playing a tricky violin song that sounded like a busy bee.

After the show, the Hsus,[19] the Jongs, and the St. Clairs from the Joy Luck Club came up to my mother and father.

"Lots of talented kids," Auntie Lindo said vaguely, smiling broadly.

"That was somethin' else," said my father, and I wondered if he was referring to me in a humorous way, or whether he even remembered what I had done.

Waverly looked at me and shrugged her shoulders. "You aren't a genius like me," she said matter-of-factly. And if I hadn't felt so bad, I would have pulled her braids and punched her stomach.

But my mother's expression was what devastated me: a quiet, blank look that said she had lost everything. I felt the same way, and it seemed as if everybody were now coming up, like gawkers at the scene of an accident, to see what parts were actually missing. When we got on the bus to go home, my father was humming the busy-bee tune and my mother was silent. I kept thinking she wanted to wait until we got home before shouting at me. But when my father unlocked the door to our apartment, my mother walked in and then went to the back, into the bedroom. No accusations. No blame. And in a way, I felt disappointed. I had been waiting for her to start shouting, so I could shout back and cry and blame her for all my misery.

assumed my talent-show fiasco meant I never had to play the piano again. But two days later, after school, my mother came out of the kitchen and saw me watching TV.

"Four clock," she reminded me as if it were any other day. I was stunned, as though she were asking me to go through the talent-show

---

18. **Madama** (mä-dä′mä) **Butterfly**: a famous opera by the Italian composer Giacomo Puccini.
19. **Hsus** (shüz).

WORDS TO KNOW

devastate (dĕv′ə-stāt′) *v.* to destroy or overwhelm
fiasco (fē-ăs′kō) *n.* a complete failure

26

Mini-Lesson: Speaking, Listening, and Viewing

DEBATE Explain to students that debate offers them an opportunity to explore opposing sides of important issues and to practice speaking logically and persuasively. Ask students to debate whether Jing-mei was right to rebel against her mother's dreams for her or whether she should have been obedient and tried to become a top-flight pianist.

To help students prepare for the debate, ask them to form small groups and to list arguments for both sides of the issue. Have them take into consideration the mother's requests, Jing-mei's personality, and the final outcome of the story. Students may use experiences from real life to bolster their arguments.

Application Randomly assign different groups to debate each other. Do not tell the groups which side of the issue they will be arguing until the very last minute. Allow each student on each team to present a short argument. Ask students to listen carefully to the debate and to decide afterward which team has been more persuasive.

The Stairway (1970), Will Barnet. Photo courtesy of Terry Dintenfass Gallery, New York. © 1995 Will Barnet/Licensed by VAGA, New York, NY.

torture again. I wedged myself more tightly in front of the TV.

"Turn off TV," she called from the kitchen five minutes later.

I didn't budge. And then I decided. I didn't have to do what my mother said anymore. I wasn't her slave. This wasn't China. I had listened to her before and look what happened. She was the stupid one.

She came out from the kitchen and stood in the arched entryway of the living room. "Four clock," she said once again, louder.

"I'm not going to play anymore," I said nonchalantly. "Why should I? I'm not a genius."

She walked over and stood in front of the TV. I saw her chest was heaving up and down in an angry way.

"No!" I said, and I now felt stronger, as if my true self had finally emerged. So this was what had been inside me all along.

"No! I won't!" I screamed.

She yanked me by the arm, pulled me off the

TWO KINDS 27

Art Note

The Stairway by Will Barnet Will Barnet's work has a distinct character and is instantly recognizable. His paintings have been described as serene and poetic. Common themes are enigmatic women, cats, stairways, and the faraway seas.

Reading the Art How might the figure of the girl slowly descending the staircase call to mind Jing-mei's slow movement toward knowing her true self?

Literary Concept: MOTIVE

U Ask students to describe Jing-mei's reasons for finally standing up to her mother and saying "No!" *(Possible response: The fiasco at the talent show has persuaded her not to continue pretending that she is a pianist; her true self is finally emerging.)*

Literary Concept: CLIMAX

V How does the intense scene that begins at this point mark the climax, or turning point, in the long conflict between Jing-mei and her mother? *(Possible response: The narrator finally stands up to her mother and refuses to go along with her dreams; the narrator deflates her mother's optimism and puts an end to her unrealistic demands.)*

Mini-Lesson Study Skills

MEMORIZING Have students recall the disappointing results, noted on page 21, of Jing-mei's attempt to memorize a page from the Bible. Suggest that if they, too, have trouble memorizing material, they can practice techniques that will improve their ability to remember new information.

Have students suggest techniques that have helped them memorize material, and record their suggestions on a web such as the one shown.

Application Ask students to use one of the strategies on the web to memorize important facts or ideas on a page of their science or social studies textbook.

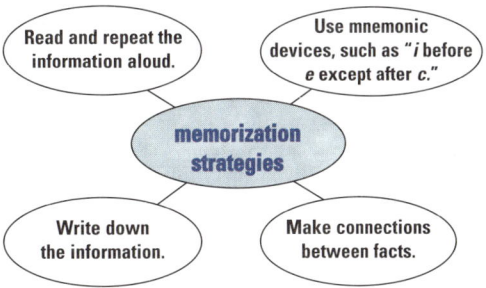

THE LANGUAGE OF LITERATURE TEACHER'S EDITION 27

Literary Concept: THEME

W Invite students to suggest how the phrase "two kinds" helps express the main message of the story. *(Possible responses: The "two kinds" of daughters symbolize the two conflicting sides of the narrator; the phrase also suggests the clash between a traditional culture and modern American values.)*

Cultural Note

X In China, obedience to one's elders, called filial obedience, is highly valued. This tradition dates back to the philosopher Confucius (551?–479 B.C.), who said: "Filial sons nowadays are people who see to it that their parents get enough to eat. But even dogs and horses are cared for to that extent. If there is no feeling of respect, wherein lies the difference?"

CUSTOMIZING FOR
Students Acquiring English

3 Explain to students that *Alakazam* is a nonsensical magic word. Students may be more familiar with *abracadabra*.

Critical Thinking: SPECULATING

Y If the narrator had asked these questions, how might her mother have responded? *(Possible response: She might have said that she hoped to compensate for all the losses she had suffered earlier and that she had given up hope of her daughter's becoming a prodigy because she was afraid of losing her too.)*

Literary Concept: FALLING ACTION

Z Remind students that after the climax in a story, the action begins to fall, as it does here. Have students list questions they still want answered about the results of the narrator's fight with her mother. *(Possible responses: What type of relationship do the two have after their falling out? Does the mother ever acknowledge that her dreams for Jing-mei were unrealistic?)*

---

floor, snapped off the TV. She was frighteningly strong, half pulling, half carrying me toward the piano as I kicked the throw rugs under my feet. She lifted me up and onto the hard bench. I was sobbing by now, looking at her bitterly. Her chest was heaving even more and her mouth was open, smiling crazily as if she were pleased I was crying.

"You want me to be someone that I'm not!" I sobbed. "I'll never be the kind of daughter you want me to be!"

"Only two kinds of daughters," she shouted in Chinese. "Those who are obedient and those who follow their own mind! Only one kind of daughter can live in this house. Obedient daughter!"

"Then I wish I wasn't your daughter. I wish you weren't my mother," I shouted. As I said these things I got scared. It felt like worms and toads and slimy things crawling out of my chest, but it also felt good, as if this awful side of me had surfaced, at last.

"Too late change this," said my mother shrilly.

And I could sense her anger rising to its breaking point. I wanted to see it spill over. And that's when I remembered the babies she had lost in China, the ones we never talked about. "Then I wish I'd never been born!" I shouted. "I wish I were dead! Like them."

It was as if I had said the magic words. Alakazam!—and her face went blank, her mouth closed, her arms went slack, and she backed out of the room, stunned, as if she were blowing away like a small brown leaf, thin, brittle, lifeless.

> "Only two kinds of daughters," she shouted in Chinese. "Those who are obedient and those who follow their own mind!"

It was not the only disappointment my mother felt in me. In the years that followed, I failed her so many times, each time asserting my own will, my right to fall short of expectations. I didn't get straight A's. I didn't become class president. I didn't get into Stanford. I dropped out of college.

For unlike my mother, I did not believe I could be anything I wanted to be. I could only be me.

And for all those years, we never talked about the disaster at the recital or my terrible accusations afterward at the piano bench. All that remained unchecked, like a **betrayal** that was now unspeakable. So I never found a way to ask her why she had hoped for something so large that failure was inevitable.

And even worse, I never asked her what frightened me the most: Why had she given up hope?

For after our struggle at the piano, she never mentioned my playing again. The lessons stopped. The lid to the piano was closed, shutting out the dust, my misery, and her dreams.

So she surprised me. A few years ago, she offered to give me the piano, for my thirtieth birthday. I had not played in all those years. I saw the offer as a sign of forgiveness, a tremendous burden removed.

"Are you sure?" I asked shyly. "I mean, won't you and Dad miss it?"

"No, this your piano," she said firmly. "Always your piano. You only one can play."

WORDS TO KNOW
betrayal (bĭ-trā′əl) *n.* an act of disloyalty or treachery

 Mini-Lesson — The Writer's Style

FIRST–PERSON POINT OF VIEW Point out that this story is narrated by Jing-mei, who is also a character in the story and who tells everything in her own words. Have students find the first-person pronouns (*I, me, my*) that indicate point of view. Explain that this point of view enables readers to know the narrator's own experiences, attitudes, and opinions. Finally, ask students how the highlighted passage above affects their understanding of the narrator. *(Discovering that the narrator is in her 30s when she relates this story puts the story in a new light; we realize she is looking back at events that happened long ago and trying to put them into perspective.)*

Application Invite students to rewrite one short scene from the story from the point of view of the mother, using first-person pronouns.

Reteaching/Reinforcement

 The Writer's Craft

Point of View, pp. 447–451

"Well, I probably can't play anymore," I said. "It's been years."

"You pick up fast," said my mother, as if she knew this was certain. "You have natural talent. You could been genius if you want to."

"No I couldn't."

"You just not trying," said my mother. And she was neither angry nor sad. She said it as if to announce a fact that could never be disproved. "Take it," she said.

But I didn't at first. It was enough that she had offered it to me. And after that, every time I saw it in my parents' living room, standing in front of the bay windows, it made me feel proud, as if it were a shiny trophy I had won back.

Last week I sent a tuner over to my parents' apartment and had the piano reconditioned, for purely sentimental reasons. My mother had died a few months before and I had been getting things in order for my father, a little bit at a time. I put the jewelry in special silk pouches. The sweaters she had knitted in yellow, pink, bright orange—all the colors I hated—I put those in mothproof boxes. I found some old Chinese silk dresses, the kind with little slits up the sides. I rubbed the old silk against my skin, then wrapped them in tissue and decided to take them home with me.

After I had the piano tuned, I opened the lid and touched the keys. It sounded even richer than I remembered. Really, it was a very good piano. Inside the bench were the same exercise notes with handwritten scales, the same second-hand music books with their covers held together with yellow tape.

I opened up the Schumann book to the dark little piece I had played at the recital. It was on the left-hand side of the page, "Pleading Child." It looked more difficult than I remembered. I played a few bars, surprised at how easily the notes came back to me.

And for the first time, or so it seemed, I noticed the piece on the right-hand side. It was called "Perfectly Contented." I tried to play this one as well. It had a lighter melody but the same flowing rhythm and turned out to be quite easy. "Pleading Child" was shorter but slower; "Perfectly Contented" was longer, but faster. And after I played them both a few times, I realized they were two halves of the same song. ❖

Art Note

***Comadre Rafaelita* by Emil J. Bisttram**
Point out to students the drooped shoulders and lined face of this elderly woman.

Reading the Art What do you think her life has been like?

INSIGHT

1. How do the mothers in the poem seem to differ from their children? *(Possible response: The mothers are more traditional, relying on religious and cultural beliefs; the children seem more modern, going beyond the traditional in their life journeys.)*
2. What do you think the speaker means when she says the mothers have "reeled" their children out "on such very weak string"? *(Possible response: In this fishing (or kite-flying) metaphor, the speaker suggests that the string or line may break and the children will get away or be lost.)*
3. Do you think it is ever possible to become "simple again?" *(Possible responses: Some students may say no—that once one breaks out of a traditional role or lifestyle, it's impossible to return. Others may say that it is possible but that doing so could mean giving up many things.)*

ROSEMARY CATACALOS

Poet Rosemary Catacalos was born in 1944 to Greek-Mexican parents and grew up in a barrio in San Antonio, Texas. For many years, she conducted bilingual poetry workshops in Texas and Arizona. She also has taught at the University of Texas at Austin, at Stanford University, and at San Francisco State University. Catacalos's poetry, which strongly reflects her Greek and Mexican heritage, has been published in two collections—*As Long as It Takes* and *Again for the First Time*.

INSIGHT

LA CASA[1]
Rosemary Catacalos

Comadre Rafaelita (1934), Emil J. Bisttram. Courtesy of The Anschutz Collection, Denver. Photo courtesy of James O. Milmoe.

The house by the *acequia*,[2]
its front porch dark and
cool with begonias,
an old house, always there,
5   always of the same adobe,[3]
always full of the same lessons.
We would like to stop.
We know we belonged there once.
Our mothers are inside.
10 All the mothers are inside,
lighting candles, swaying
back and forth on their knees,
begging The Virgin's forgiveness
for having reeled us out
15 on such very weak string.
They are afraid for us.
They know we will not stop.
We will only wave as we pass by.
They will go on praying
20 that we might be simple again.

---
1. **La Casa** (lä kä′sä) *Spanish:* "The House."
2. **acequia** (ä-sě′kyä) *Spanish:* an irrigation ditch or canal.
3. **adobe** (ə-dō′bē): a building material consisting of mud or clay mixed with straw and dried in the sun.

30   UNIT ONE   PART 1: LASTING IMPRESSIONS

Another Pathway

Cooperative Learning Suggest that students work in pairs, with each pair identifying either the mother's or the daughter's complaints. Then ask the groups to reconvene, to compare lists and discuss whether the complaints are justified and how they might be resolved. Suggest that one student record the decisions of the group and that two others share the group's findings with the class.

Rubric
3 Full Accomplishment Lists are comprehensive. Explanations about which complaints are justified are reasonable. Possible resolutions are realistic.
2 Substantial Accomplishment Lists are fairly complete, but the explanations may not be complete. Possible resolutions are adequate.
1 Little or Partial Accomplishment Few complaints are listed, and justifications are not supported. Possible resolutions are questionable.

RESPONDING OPTIONS

FROM PERSONAL RESPONSE TO CRITICAL ANALYSIS

REFLECT
1. In your notebook, describe your impressions of the two main characters.

RETHINK
2. What might the narrator mean by saying that "Pleading Child" and "Perfectly Contented" are "two halves of the same song"?
   Consider
   - her behavior as a young girl
   - why she takes up playing the piano again
   - what the names of the pieces reveal about her relationship with her mother

Close Textual Reading

3. Why do you think the narrator's feelings about being a prodigy change during the story?
   Consider
   - her daydreams at the beginning of the story
   - her response to her mother's expectations
   - her opinions about herself

4. Why do you think the mother had such unrealistic expectations for her daughter? Use evidence from the story to support your ideas. You might also review the explanation you wrote for the Writing Connection on page 18.

RELATE
5. How does the mother-child relationship presented in the Insight poem "La Casa" compare with the mother-child relationship depicted in "Two Kinds"?

Literary Link

6. In this story, the mother's high expectations have a negative effect on the narrator. When can high expectations have a positive effect? Explain, drawing on your experience.

LITERARY CONCEPTS

The events of a story almost always involve one or more **conflicts**, or struggles between opposing forces. A conflict may be **external**, pitting a character against an outside force—such as another character, a physical obstacle, or an aspect of nature or society—or it may be **internal**, occurring within a character. What are the external and internal conflicts in "Two Kinds"?

Multimodal Learning
ANOTHER PATHWAY
Cooperative Learning

In a small group, make two lists, one of the mother's complaints about her daughter and one of the daughter's complaints. Use story details to complete each list. With the other members of your group, decide which complaints are justified and how they might be effectively resolved. Explain your findings to the class.

QUICKWRITES

1. Write a **diary entry** in which the mother explains her hopes, dreams, and expectations for her daughter, as well as her sense of frustration.

2. Write a **personality profile** of either the mother or the daughter. Describe your subject's distinctive traits.

3. Write a **review** of the talent show for a Chinatown newspaper. Discuss all the performances described in the story.

4. Find out more about Waverly and Auntie Lindo by reading the chapter "Rules of the Game" in Amy Tan's *The Joy Luck Club*. Write an **essay** comparing the mother-daughter relationship in that story with the one in "Two Kinds."

📁 **PORTFOLIO** Save your writing. You may want to use it later as a springboard to a piece for your portfolio.

TWO KINDS **31**

From Personal Response to Critical Analysis

1. Accept all reasonable responses.
2. Some students may speculate that these pieces characterize the mother-daughter relationship. At first, the mother and daughter fight over the daughter's lack of accomplishments; later, they seem to forgive each other. Other students might say that the pieces reflect two sides of the daughter. As a child, she pleads that her mother let her be herself; as an adult, she comes to terms with her mother.
3. Students may suggest that at first, the idea of being a prodigy is appealing to the narrator, but as she comes to realize that she is not a genius, she begins to revolt. Students may say that the narrator is beginning to understand who and what she really is and wants to be.
4. Some students may suggest that the mother tried to compensate for the loss of her twins by pinning all her hopes on the narrator. Others might point out that the mother felt that all things were possible in America or that she was in competition with her friends to have the most brilliant daughter.
5. Both the narrator's mother and the mothers in "La Casa" are concerned about their children. However, the mothers in the poem are not as actively involved in their children's lives. Instead of persuading their children to act a certain way, the mothers pray for them.
6. Accept all reasonable responses. Some students may say that high expectations can motivate them to try harder, especially if the expectations are held by someone they respect. Others might say that such expectations might give them self-confidence or a sense of pride because someone else appreciates and has faith in them.

Literary Concepts

Have students work in small groups. When the groups are finished, they should compare their answers to see whether they agree. Groups should understand that the external conflict in the story occurs between Jing-mei and her mother and that the internal conflict occurs within the narrator's mind. Groups might also point out that the narrator's mother had conflicts in her mind (internal) and that there was some conflict between Jing-mei and Old Chong (external).

QuickWrites

1. Suggest that students have the mother write about Jing-mei's recital and her attitude toward her daughter in later years.
2. Remind students that a personality profile should be a formal, objective report.
3. Suggest that Jing-mei's poor performance would probably get only a brief mention.
4. Students may want to use a comparison chart to organize their thoughts.

The Writer's Craft

Character Sketch, pp. 78–82
Observing Situations and Settings, pp. 58–71
Comparison and Contrast, pp. 118–132

THE LANGUAGE OF LITERATURE TEACHER'S EDITION **31**

The Writer's Style

Invite volunteers to read aloud selected passages and tell why they find them humorous. Students might identify instances in which the humor is based on irony, exaggeration, or the writer's tone. Some students might suggest that the humorous tone makes the problems seem less serious. Others might see the narrator's humor as a cover-up of her true feelings.

Across the Curriculum

History Encourage students to research the contributions of Chinese immigrants in exploring the gold fields of California in the 1850s and in building the transcontinental railroad. Students can also look into the causes and effects of the Chinese Exclusion Act of 1882.

Words to Know

1. c
2. f
3. g
4. j
5. a
6. i
7. h
8. d
9. b
10. e

Reteaching/Reinforcement
- *Unit One Resource Book*, p. 8

AMY TAN

Amy Tan never planned a literary career. She began taking fiction-writing lessons as a hobby, to relax from her full-time job. Although Tan once tried to distance herself from her background, writing helped her to discover "how very Chinese I was." Today Ms. Tan likes to relax by playing the piano.

Multimodal Learning

ALTERNATIVE ACTIVITIES

1. With a classmate, **role-play** a **conversation** between the narrator's mother and Auntie Lindo, in which the narrator's mother describes her daughter's talent-show performance.
2. Many of the mother's ideas about the United States come from television and popular magazines. Collect pictures from various magazines and create a **collage** showing the misleading impression of American life that an immigrant might derive from these publications.

THE WRITER'S STYLE

Although Amy Tan's story deals with the serious problem of a parent's unrealistic expectations, **humor** plays an important role in it. Go through the story again and identify places where events or descriptions add a humorous tone to the story. What effect does the humor have on your view of the narrator's problem?

Multimodal Learning

ACROSS THE CURRICULUM

History The 1930s and 1940s were not the only period of time when large numbers of people emigrated from China to the United States. Find out about the influx of Chinese immigrants during the mid-1800s. Present your findings in an oral report to the class.

WORDS TO KNOW

Review the Words to Know at the bottom of the selection pages. On your paper, match each word on the left with a synonym on the right.

1. prodigy
2. indignity
3. reproach
4. discordant
5. lament
6. ream
7. reverie
8. devastate
9. fiasco
10. betrayal

a. mourn
b. disaster
c. genius
d. ruin
e. disloyalty
f. humiliation
g. condemnation
h. daydream
i. heap
j. inharmonious

AMY TAN

1952 –

Amy Tan, the daughter of Chinese immigrants, was born in Oakland, California. She earned a bachelor's degree in linguistics and English and a master's degree in linguistics at San Jose State University, then went on to become a successful business writer before turning her talents to fiction. "Two Kinds" is part of her popular work *The Joy Luck Club*, a book that weaves together separate stories about four Chinese mothers and their American-born daughters. After its release in 1989, the book spent eight months on the New York Times bestseller list; in 1993, it was made into a movie. *The Joy Luck Club* was a finalist for the National Book Award and the National Book Critics Circle Award, and it received the 1990 Bay Area Book Reviewers Award for Fiction. It has been translated into more than 15 languages, including Chinese.

OTHER WORKS "Mother Tongue" in *The Best American Essays 1991*, *The Kitchen God's Wife*

Extended Reading

32   UNIT ONE   PART 1: LASTING IMPRESSIONS

Alternative Activities

1. Remind students that the narrator's mother and Auntie Lindo have a rivalry over the relative talents of their daughters. Therefore, the narrator's mother will attempt to minimize the problem of Jing-mei's discordant playing.
2. Begin by having students discuss whether they think TV and popular magazines reflect an accurate image of life in the United States. Ask them to list some of the values that mass media seem to advance and to speculate on how these values might influence a recent immigrant from a more traditional society.

PREVIEWING

FICTION

Cranes
Hwang Sunwŏn (hwäng sŏŏn'wən') Korea

Activating Prior Knowledge
PERSONAL CONNECTION
Have you ever been in a situation in which your friend became your opponent? Perhaps you were pitted against each other in a competition or found yourselves on opposite sides of an important issue. In your notebook, describe the situation and the feelings that it evoked.

Building Background
HISTORICAL CONNECTION
This story takes place during the Korean War, a conflict that often pitted friend against friend and even brother against brother. In 1948, shortly after World War II, the nation of Korea, which occupies a peninsula on the eastern shore of Asia, became officially divided. Two separate governments were established: a Communist government in the north and a non-Communist government in the south. In 1950, North Korea invaded South Korea, beginning a civil war in which other nations, including the United States and China, soon became involved. A truce was signed in 1953, but tension between the two Koreas has continued for decades.

Much of the war took place near the 38th parallel of north latitude, the dividing line between the two countries. This area was the scene of hotly contested battles in which thousands died and the control of villages often shifted back and forth between the North Koreans and the South Koreans. One of these villages is the setting of "Cranes."

Activating Prior Knowledge/Setting a Purpose
READING CONNECTION
Making Inferences In a work of fiction, a character's **motives,** or reasons for behaving a certain way, may be implied rather than stated directly. In such a case, the reader must make inferences, based on evidence in the story, about what motivates the character. As you read "Cranes," pay attention to the main character's behavior toward his friend, and try to determine the motives behind that behavior.

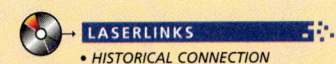
• HISTORICAL CONNECTION

OVERVIEW
Objectives
- To understand and appreciate a short story about the conflict between loyalty to a friend and loyalty to a political cause
- To identify and understand plot and setting
- To express understanding of the selection through a choice of writing forms, including a comparison chart, a letter, and a revised ending for the story
- To extend understanding of the selection through a variety of multimodal and cross-curricular activities

Skills

LITERARY CONCEPTS
- Plot and setting
- Flashback

READING SKILLS/ STRATEGIES
- Making inferences

GENRE STUDY
- Fiction: short story

GRAMMAR
- Common and proper nouns

SPEAKING, LISTENING, AND VIEWING
- Role-playing
- Group discussion
- Oral presentation

HISTORICAL CONNECTION
The Korean War, 1950–1953
Approximately 3 million people were killed in the Korean War. Cities were leveled, industries destroyed, and farms ruined. These photographs show some of the devastation of that war.

Side A, Frame 49297

PRINT AND MEDIA RESOURCES

UNIT ONE RESOURCE BOOK
Strategic Reading: Literature, p. 11

GRAMMAR MINI–LESSONS
Transparencies, p. 37
Copymasters, pp. 37–39

ACCESS FOR STUDENTS ACQUIRING ENGLISH
Selection Summaries
Reading Support

FORMAL ASSESSMENT
Selection Test, pp. 7–8
 Test Generator

 AUDIO LIBRARY
See Reference Card

 **LASERLINKS**
Historical Connection
Cultural Connection

 INTERNET RESOURCES
McDougal Littell Literature Center at http://www.hmco.com/mcdougal/lit

THE LANGUAGE OF LITERATURE TEACHER'S EDITION

CRANES

Hwang Sunwŏn

SUMMARY

Sŏngsam returns to his Korean village, which shows little damage from the war but is much changed. When he reaches a farmhouse that has been turned into a Public Peace Police office, he is stunned to find his boyhood friend Tŏkchae under arrest for communist activity. Sŏngsam offers to take the prisoner to a place where Tŏkchae is to be questioned and shot. He leads Tŏkchae away, outraged that his old friend has become an enemy. As the two men walk, Sŏngsam learns that Tŏkchae, now married, decided to stay on the farm with his ailing father rather than to escape from the enemy army. The two men reflect upon old times, especially on the time they captured a crane and then freed it when its life was endangered. Finally, Sŏngsam tells Tŏkchae to help him hunt a crane by flushing it out. Tŏkchae stares in confusion, then finally understands. He crawls through the weeds to freedom, as nearby cranes soar into the sky.

Thematic Link: Lasting Impressions For two friends, the memories of a shared childhood overcome political pressures.

CUSTOMIZING FOR
Students Acquiring English
- Use **ACCESS FOR STUDENTS ACQUIRING ENGLISH**, *Reading Support*.

STRATEGIC READING FOR
Less-Proficient Readers

Set a Purpose Suggest that students write the names of the two main characters on a sheet of paper, with a dividing line between them. Then have students read to find out what has come between the two characters.

Use **UNIT ONE RESOURCE BOOK**, p. 11, for guidance in reading the selection.

Literary Concept:
PLOT AND SETTING

Ⓐ Ask how the location of the village—on the Thirty-eighth Parallel—might affect the events in the story. *(Possible response: Because the Thirty-eighth Parallel was the hotly contested dividing line between North and South Korea, the events in the story might involve some kind of political conflict.)*

The northern village lay snug beneath the high, bright autumn sky, near the border at the Thirty-eighth Parallel. **Ⓐ**

White gourds lay one against the other on the dirt floor of an empty farmhouse. Any village elders who passed by extinguished their bamboo pipes first, and the children, too, turned back some distance off. Their faces were marked with fear.

As a whole, the village showed little damage from the war, but it still did not seem like the same village Sŏngsam[1] had known as a boy.

At the foot of a chestnut grove on the hill behind the village he stopped and climbed a chestnut tree. Somewhere far back in his mind he heard the old man with a wen[2] shout, "You bad boy, climbing up my chestnut tree again!"

The old man must have passed away, for he was not among the few village elders Sŏngsam had met. Holding on to the trunk of the tree, Sŏngsam gazed up at the blue sky for a time. Some chestnuts fell to the ground as the dry clusters opened of their own accord.

A young man stood, his hands bound, before a farmhouse that had been converted into a Public Peace Police office. He seemed to be a stranger, so Sŏngsam went up for a closer look. He was stunned: this young man was none other than his boyhood playmate, Tŏkchae.[3]

Sŏngsam asked the police officer who had come with him from Ch'ŏnt'ae[4] for an explanation. The prisoner was the vice-chairman of the Farmers' Communist League and had just been flushed[5] out of hiding in his own house, Sŏngsam learned.

Sŏngsam sat down on the dirt floor and lit a cigaret.

---

1. Sŏngsam (sŏng′säm′).
2. **wen:** a harmless skin tumor.
3. Tŏkchae (tŏk′jä′).
4. Ch'ŏnt'ae (chŏn′tä′).
5. **flushed:** driven from hiding.

34

Mini-Lesson   Grammar

COMMON AND PROPER NOUNS Review the definitions of common and proper nouns. Elicit that proper nouns always begin with a capital letter. Ask students to identify some common and proper nouns on page 34.

Common Nouns	Proper Nouns
village	Ch'ŏnt'ae
border	Thirty-eighth Parallel
farmhouse	Public Peace Police
boy	Tŏkchae

Application Have students write down these sentences, capitalizing proper nouns:
1. The vice-chairman of the communist league was a man named tŏkchae.
2. His wife was shorty, a small woman.
3. An official from seoul wanted to catch cranes.

Reteaching/Reinforcement
- *Grammar Handbook*, anthology pp. 1085–1088
- *Grammar Mini-Lessons* copymasters pp. 37–39, transparencies, p. 37

Capitalization, pp. 762–780

34 THE LANGUAGE OF LITERATURE TEACHER'S EDITION

Tŏkchae was to be escorted to Ch'ŏngdan[6] by one of the peace police.

After a time, Sŏngsam lit a new cigaret from the first and stood up.

"I'll take him with me."

Tŏkchae averted his face and refused to look at Sŏngsam. The two left the village.

Sŏngsam went on smoking, but the tobacco had no flavor. He just kept drawing the smoke in and blowing it out. Then suddenly he thought that Tŏkchae, too, must want a puff. He thought of the days when they had shared dried gourd leaves behind sheltering walls, hidden from the adults' view. But today, how could he offer a cigaret to a fellow like this?

B Once, when they were small, he went with Tŏkchae to steal some chestnuts from the old man with the wen. It was Sŏngsam's turn to climb the tree. Suddenly the old man began shouting. Sŏngsam slipped and fell to the ground. He got chestnut burrs all over his bottom, but he kept on running. Only when the two had reached a safe place where the old man could not overtake them did Sŏngsam turn his bottom to Tŏkchae. The burrs hurt so much as they were plucked out that Sŏngsam could not keep tears from welling up in his eyes. Tŏkchae produced a fistful of chestnuts from his pocket and thrust them into Sŏngsam's . . . Sŏngsam threw away the cigaret he had just lit, and then made up his mind not to light another while he was escorting Tŏkchae.

They reached the pass at the hill where he and Tŏkchae had cut fodder[7] for the cows until Sŏngsam had to move to a spot near Ch'ŏnt'ae, south of the Thirty-eighth Parallel, two years before the liberation.

Sŏngsam felt a sudden surge of anger in spite of himself and shouted, "So how many have you killed?"

For the first time, Tŏkchae cast a quick glance at him and then looked away.

"You! How many have you killed?" he asked again.

Tŏkchae looked at him again and glared. The glare grew intense, and his mouth twitched.

"So you managed to kill quite a few, eh?" Sŏngsam felt his mind becoming clear of itself, as if some obstruction had been removed. "If you were vice-chairman of the Communist League, why didn't you run? You must have been lying low with a secret mission."

Tŏkchae did not reply.

"Speak up. What was your mission?"

Tŏkchae kept walking. Tŏkchae was hiding something, Sŏngsam thought. He wanted to take a good look at him, but Tŏkchae kept his face averted.

Fingering the revolver at his side, Sŏngsam went on: "There's no need to make excuses. You're going to be shot anyway. Why don't you tell the truth here and now?"

"I'm not going to make any excuses. They made me vice-chairman of the League because I was a hardworking farmer and one of the poorest. If that's a capital offense,[8] so be it. I'm still what I used to be—the only thing I'm good at is tilling the soil." After a short pause, he added, "My old man is bedridden at home. He's been ill almost half a year." Tŏkchae's father was a widower, a poor, hardworking farmer who lived only for his son. Seven years before his back had given out, and he had contracted a skin disease.

"Are you married?"

"Yes," Tŏkchae replied after a time.

"To whom?"

"Shorty."

"To Shorty?" How interesting! A woman so small and plump that she knew the earth's

---

6. **Ch'ŏngdan** (chəng′dän′).
7. **fodder:** coarsely chopped hay or straw used as food for farm animals.
8. **capital offense:** a crime calling for the death penalty.

CRANES **35**

Mini-Lesson  Literary Concepts

REVIEWING FLASHBACK Remind students that a flashback is a conversation or an event that happened before the beginning of the story. Point out that a flashback interrupts the chronological order of events in a story and helps readers understand the present actions or attitudes of a character.

Application Ask students to think about the flashback highlighted above in the story and to suggest what it reveals about Tŏkchae and his boyhood friendship with Sŏngsam.

CUSTOMIZING FOR
Students Acquiring English

I Tell students that "a cold fish" is a metaphor for someone who is distant and not very friendly or warm.

Cultural Note

D Until recently, Korea was an agricultural society in which the interests of the family were more important than those of the individual or the nation. Grandparents, parents, unmarried daughters, sons, and sons' wives and children lived together in extended families. All persons were expected to obey the head of the family—the oldest male—without question.

Literary Concept: PLOT AND SETTING

E Have students consider, as they read the next four paragraphs, how the setting reminds Sŏngsam of his friendship with Tŏkchae. (*Sŏngsam keeps coming across places where he and Tŏkchae had worked and played together as boys; this landscape triggers warm memories.*)

Literary Concept: SYMBOL

F Have students discuss why the crane symbolizes Tŏkchae in his present situation. (*Possible response: He is tied up and in danger of being shot by officials.*)

Linking to Science

G As a group, cranes are best known for their interesting courtship dances. In these dances, the cranes circle one another and leap into the air, sometimes whooping in unison.

Literary Concept: FLASHBACK

H Ask students what the flashback with the pet crane reveals about the two boys. (*Possible responses: The two boys loved their pet; they were not afraid to defy authority to save it.*)

---

vastness, but not the sky's height. Such a cold fish! He and Tŏkchae had teased her and made her cry. And Tŏkchae had married her!

"How many kids?"

"The first is arriving this fall, she says."

Sŏngsam had difficulty swallowing a laugh that he was about to let burst forth in spite of himself. Although he had asked how many children Tŏkchae had, he could not help wanting to break out laughing at the thought of the wife sitting there with her huge stomach, one span around. But he realized that this was no time for joking.

"Anyway, it's strange you didn't run away."

"I tried to escape. They said that once the South invaded, not a man would be spared. So all of us between seventeen and forty were taken to the North. I thought of evacuating, even if I had to carry my father on my back. But Father said no. How could we farmers leave the land behind when the crops were ready for harvesting? He grew old on that farm depending on me as the prop and the mainstay of the family. I wanted to be with him in his last moments so I could close his eyes with my own hand. Besides, where can farmers like us go, when all we know how to do is live on the land?"

Sŏngsam had had to flee the previous June. At night he had broken the news privately to his father. But his father had said the same thing: Where could a farmer go, leaving all the chores behind? So Sŏngsam had left alone. Roaming about the strange streets and villages in the South, Sŏngsam had been haunted by thoughts of his old parents and the young children, who had been left with all the chores. Fortunately, his family had been safe then, as it was now.

They had crossed over a hill. This time Sŏngsam walked with his face averted. The autumn sun was hot on his forehead. This was an ideal day for the harvest, he thought.

When they reached the foot of the hill, Sŏngsam gradually came to a halt. In the middle of a field he espied a group of cranes that resembled men in white, all bent over. This had been the demilitarized zone[9] along the Thirty-eighth Parallel. The cranes were still living here, as before, though the people were all gone.

Once, when Sŏngsam and Tŏkchae were about twelve, they had set a trap here, unbeknown to the adults, and caught a crane, a Tanjŏng crane.[10] They had tied the crane up, even binding its wings, and paid it daily visits, patting its neck and riding on its back. Then one day they overheard the neighbors whispering: someone had come from Seoul[11] with a permit from the governor-general's office to catch cranes as some kind of specimens. Then and there the two boys had dashed off to the field. That they would be found out and punished had no longer mattered; all they cared about was the fate of their crane. Without a moment's delay, still out of breath from running, they untied the crane's feet and wings, but the bird could hardly walk. It must have been weak from having been bound.

The two held the crane up. Then, suddenly, they heard a gunshot. The crane fluttered its wings once or twice and then sank back to the ground.

The boys thought their crane had been shot. But the next moment, as another crane from a nearby bush fluttered its wings, the boys' crane stretched its long neck, gave out a whoop, and disappeared into the sky. For a long while the two boys could not tear their eyes away from the blue sky up into which their crane had soared.

"Hey, why don't we stop here for a crane hunt?" Sŏngsam said suddenly.

---

9. **demilitarized zone**: an area—generally one separating two hostile nations or armies—from which military forces are prohibited.
10. **Tanjŏng** (tän′jŏng′) **crane**: a type of crane found in Asia.
11. **Seoul** (sōl): the capital and largest city of South Korea.

36 UNIT ONE PART 1: LASTING IMPRESSIONS

Multicultural Perspectives

The crane is an important symbol in many cultures. In China, it is a symbol of happiness and longevity. In Greco-Roman mythology, cranes are sacred to Apollo, the sun god, as heralds of spring and light. The people of eastern Asia also view the return of the crane as a symbol of spring. In fact, the Ainu of Japan have a crane dance in honor of "Honorable Lord Crane."

Cranes are often depicted as flying toward the sun, an image symbolizing an ascent to a higher level of being. Some students may be interested in exploring this motif in Korean ceramic art, brush painting, and tapestries.

36 THE LANGUAGE OF LITERATURE TEACHER'S EDITION

Yi Dynasty rank badge (about 1600–1700). Colored silk and gold paper, thread on figured silk, Victoria & Albert Museum, London / Art Resource, New York.

Tŏkchae was dumbfounded.

"I'll make a trap with this rope; you flush a crane over here."

Sŏngsam had untied Tŏkchae's hands and was already crawling through the weeds.

Tŏkchae's face whitened. "You're sure to be shot anyway"—these words flashed through his mind. Any instant a bullet would come flying from Sŏngsam's direction, Tŏkchae thought.

Some paces away, Sŏngsam quickly turned toward him.

"Hey, how come you're standing there like a dummy? Go flush a crane!"

Only then did Tŏkchae understand. He began crawling through the weeds.

A pair of Tanjŏng cranes soared high into the clear blue autumn sky, flapping their huge wings. ❖

Translated by Peter H. Lee

COMPREHENSION CHECK
1. Who is the prisoner at the police office? *(The prisoner is Sŏngsam's boyhood playmate, Tŏkchae.)*
2. What is likely to happen to Tŏkchae? Why? *(Tŏkchae will be shot for being an official of the Farmers' Communist League.)*
3. When Sŏngsam and Tŏkchae were boys, why did they release the crane they had caught? *(They didn't want a government official to catch it.)*
4. What does Sŏngsam do with Tŏkchae at the end of the story? *(Sŏngsam lets his old friend go.)*

Art Note

The crane depicted on this rank badge is done by an anonymous artist. Like the cranes in the story, this one soars skyward.

Reading the Art *What emotions do you feel when you look at the badge?*

CUSTOMIZING FOR
Students Acquiring English

2 Tell students that *was dumbfounded* means "was made speechless with surprise or amazement."

STRATEGIC READING FOR
Less-Proficient Readers

I Use the following prompts to make sure students understand the choice Sŏngsam made between his friend and his politics:
- Why does Tŏkchae think he will be shot? *(because Sŏngsam released him for no apparent reason and could shoot him, claiming Tŏkchae was trying to escape)* **Making Inferences**
- What does Tŏkchae finally understand? *(that his friend is letting him escape)* **Noting Sequence of Events**

Critical Thinking: SPECULATING

J What price, if any, do you think Sŏngsam will have to pay for releasing Tŏkchae? What will he tell the authorities when they realize the prisoner is gone? *(Possible response: Sŏngsam might claim that Tŏkchae escaped; if the authorities learn that the prisoner was deliberately released, Sŏngsam himself might be imprisoned or shot.)*

CUSTOMIZING FOR
Gifted and Talented Students

Have students discuss why people at war dehumanize and demonize their enemies. Point out that this process occurs even among people who have much in common—North and South Koreans, Protestants and Catholics in Northern Ireland, Christians and Muslims in Bosnia. How can people with such historical and geographical ties become such fierce enemies?

From Personal Response to Critical Analysis

1. Student responses will vary.
2. Possible responses: Some students may say that Sŏngsam's childhood memories reminded him of his friendship with Tŏkchae. Others may say Sŏngsam realizes that Tŏkchae hasn't really done anything wrong—that he was simply following his father's wishes.
3. Possible responses: Students who say yes may note that Tŏkchae is not Sŏngsam's enemy or even very politically inclined and that factors beyond their control have come between them. Those who say no may note that Sŏngsam is betraying his country by releasing an enemy.
4. Possible responses: Some students might note that the bound crane symbolizes Tŏkchae as he faces execution and that the freed crane symbolizes the friends after they break free of the politics that divide them. Other students might say that the cranes serve as a reminder of Sŏngsam's friendship with Tŏkchae and symbolize peacetime.
5. Possible response: The author might argue that the bonds of friendship are stronger than duty to country.
6. Student responses will vary. All thoughtful responses are valid.

Another Pathway
Cooperative Learning Suggest that students divide the tasks so that one or two group members search through the selection for relevant events and another actually records the events on the time line. Then students, as a group, could discuss how Sŏngsam's attitude toward Tŏkchae changes.

Help students plan their time lines by pointing out that the main action takes place about 1952, at the height of the Korean War, when the two main characters are about 20 years old. The action described in the flashback on page 35 occurs when the characters were about 5 or 6 years old, and that on page 36 occurs when they were 12.

Rubric
3 Full Accomplishment The time line shows the events in the friends' lives and their changing relationship.
2 Substantial Accomplishment The time line shows events and changes in the relationship in proper sequence but may be missing some information.
1 Little or Partial Accomplishment The time line conveys no sense of the sequence and misinterprets Sŏngsam's feelings for Tŏkchae.

RESPONDING OPTIONS

FROM PERSONAL RESPONSE TO CRITICAL ANALYSIS

REFLECT
1. What went through your mind at the end of the story? Describe your reaction in your notebook.

RETHINK
2. What is Sŏngsam's motivation for letting Tŏkchae go free?
   Consider
   - what Sŏngsam says will happen to Tŏkchae
   - what Sŏngsam learns about Tŏkchae during their walk
   - Sŏngsam's memories of their childhood friendship

   Close Textual Reading

3. Do you think Sŏngsam makes the right decision at the end? Give reasons for your answer.

4. What do you think is the significance of the cranes in the story?
   Consider
   - the cranes still living in the demilitarized zone
   - the crane that the boys caught and then freed
   - the last sentence of the story

   Close Textual Reading

5. What conclusions can you reach about the author's views on war and friendship?

RELATE
6. Think of situations when loyalty to friends comes into conflict with duty. In such cases, which do you think should take priority—loyalty or duty? Share your thoughts.

Multimodal Learning
ANOTHER PATHWAY

Cooperative Learning
With a small group of classmates, create a time line to show the different phases of the relationship between Sŏngsam and his childhood friend. List major events in the relationship and describe the changes in Sŏngsam's attitude toward Tŏkchae.

QUICKWRITES

1. Create a **comparison chart** showing the similarities and differences between the lives of Sŏngsam and Tŏkchae. Remember to review the observations that you made about the characters' motives while you were reading.

2. Assume the identity of Sŏngsam and write a **letter** to Tŏkchae's father, in which you explain what has happened to his son.

3. Imagine that Sŏngsam chose duty over friendship in the end. Create an **alternative ending;** rewrite the last few paragraphs of the story, changing Sŏngsam's and Tŏkchae's thoughts and actions and the final image of the cranes.

📁 **PORTFOLIO** Save your writing. You may want to use it later as a springboard to a piece for your portfolio.

LITERARY CONCEPTS

Plot refers to the actions and events presented in a literary work. The plot of a work is often influenced by the work's **setting,** the time and place in which the events unfold. With a partner, make a list of details from "Cranes" that establish the story's setting. Then compare your list with those made by other students. Discuss how the setting influences the plot of the story.

38 UNIT ONE PART 1: LASTING IMPRESSIONS

Literary Concepts
Students' lists might include the following: "The northern village lay snug beneath the high, bright autumn sky, near the border at the Thirty-eighth Parallel" (page 34); "They reached the pass at the hill where he and Tŏkchae had cut fodder for the cows until Sŏngsam had to move to a spot near Ch'ŏnt'ae, south of the Thirty-eighth Parallel, two years before the liberation" (page 35); "In the middle of a field he espied a group of cranes that resembled men in white, all bent over. This had been the demilitarized zone along the Thirty-eighth Parallel" (page 36).

QuickWrites
1. Suggest that students use a two-column chart with the heads "Similarities" and "Differences."
2. Suggest that Sŏngsam may not want to incriminate himself and thus may only hint at what happened.
3. Make sure students understand that if Sŏngsam had chosen duty over friendship, Tŏkchae would have been shot.

Comparison, p. 334
Conclusions for Narratives, pp. 388–389

Multimodal Learning

ALTERNATIVE ACTIVITIES

1. Role-play a **dramatic scene** in which Sŏngsam explains Tŏkchae's escape to a superior.
2. Photocopy pictures of Korean and other Asian art depicting cranes, and use the pictures to create an **art exhibit**. In a brief presentation, discuss the feelings that the artwork evokes and compare these feelings to those evoked by the cranes in the story.

ACROSS THE CURRICULUM

History Find out more about the events that led to the outbreak of the Korean War. Present your findings in a pictorial essay.

HWANG SUNWŎN

1915 –

For Korea's Hwang Sunwŏn, becoming a published writer in his native tongue was no easy matter. For the first three decades of Hwang's life, Korea was ruled by Japan. The Japanese tried to stamp out Korean nationalism by setting up Japanese-language schools, arresting Korean scholars, and at one point even forcing Koreans to adopt Japanese names. Hwang had to travel to Japan to receive his higher education. However, his years at Waseda University proved stimulating, and he returned to his homeland to publish his first story collection in 1940.

Two years later, his career plans were temporarily blocked when, at the height of World War II, the Japanese banned all Korean-language publications.

After the Japanese departed at the war's end, Hwang and his family still faced hardships in the Communist-dominated north where they lived. Luckily, they were able to flee to the south, but invasion by the North Korean forces at the start of the Korean War soon made them refugees once again. Only after the signing of the truce in 1953 was Hwang able to return full-time to his writing.

Over the years, Hwang has produced 7 novels and over 100 short stories, which have won him several prestigious awards in his homeland. "Cranes," written in 1953, was the title story of a 1956 collection.
OTHER WORKS *Trees on the Cliff, The Book of Masks, Shadows of a Sound*
Extended Reading

• CULTURAL CONNECTION

CRANES **39**

REFLECTING ON THEME
What Do You Think?

Have students think about the interviews that they conducted before reading the selections in Part One. Ask them how Sŏngsam's recollection of his childhood friendship compares with the lasting impressions that were shared during the interviews. Also ask them whether, as a result of reading this story, they would like to change the questions that they asked during the interviews.

Across the Curriculum

History Suggest that students with access to a CD-ROM encyclopedia use the Search function to locate material about the Korean War. Students also might refer to magazine and newspaper articles from the 1940s and 1950s. They can make copies of pictures from these sources for their pictorial essays. Some students might try creating their own drawings or paintings, based on their research.

HWANG SUNWŎN

Hwang Sunwŏn, a master of the short story form, writes about the peasants he knew as a child, concentrating on children and older people. In particular, he explores the innocence of childhood and the loneliness of old age. Childhood memories fortify many of Hwang's characters as they wander through a solitary existence, only occasionally making contact with an old friend or acquaintance.

Alternative Activities

1. Remind students that Sŏngsam, by releasing Tŏkchae, has placed himself in jeopardy. Have students decide, before they role-play, whether Sŏngsam will admit his act or attempt to lie about it. Instruct students to make up a list of questions that the police will be likely to ask Sŏngsam during an interrogation.
2. Make books of Asian art available to students so that they may peruse them for pictures of cranes. Suggest that students also include in their exhibits portions of folklore about cranes or their own original artwork. Students might be able to conclude that in Asia, cranes traditionally represent longevity and wisdom.

CULTURAL CONNECTION
South Korea Today More than 40 years after the Korean War, Korea remains divided. North Korea and South Korea have rebuilt their economies in much different ways. Following the Communist model, North Korean industry is nationally controlled. South Korea has prospered with a capitalistic economy. The photographs in this set show modern-day scenes from South Korea.

Side A, Frame 49303

THE LANGUAGE OF LITERATURE TEACHER'S EDITION **39**

OVERVIEW

Objectives

- To comprehend a short story that explores the emotional impact of war
- To identify and understand major and minor characters
- To appreciate images that establish mood
- To express understanding of the selection through a choice of writing forms, including a continuation of the story, an autobiographical sketch, and an editorial
- To extend understanding of the selection through a variety of multimodal and cross-curricular activities

Skills

LITERARY CONCEPTS
- Character
- Contrast

READING SKILLS/STRATEGIES
- Identifying mood

THE WRITER'S STYLE
- Tone

GRAMMAR
- Types of sentences

SPEAKING, LISTENING, AND VIEWING
- Group discussion
- Dramatic reading

PREVIEWING

FICTION

Winter Night

Kay Boyle United States

Activating Prior Knowledge
PERSONAL CONNECTION

Throughout history, war has had a profound effect on the lives of people—both soldiers and civilians. In the story "Cranes," for example, war tests a relationship between old friends. With a group of classmates, create a list of other ways in which war can impact human lives. As you make your list, be sure to consider both the physical and the emotional effects that war can have.

Building Background
HISTORICAL CONNECTION

After the German dictator Adolf Hitler took power in 1933, he ordered the construction of concentration camps for the imprisonment of minority groups and people who opposed his Nazi party. Over time, more than 20 such camps were built, not only in Germany but also in Poland and other German-occupied countries in Europe. During World War II many of the camps became extermination centers where prisoners were murdered in gas chambers. Most of the 6 million Jews who were killed during the war perished in these concentration camps; Hitler's forces were also responsible for the deaths of more than 5 million others.

   Although people living in the United States during World War II did not experience the physical presence of the war, its impact was still felt across the country. The main character in this story is a little girl living in New York whose once-secure life has been changed by the eruption of the war. Her father has left to serve in the armed forces. Her mother works in an office and frequently goes out in the evenings, leaving her with "sitting parents," or baby sitters. On the winter night when the story takes place, the girl's sitting parent is a mysterious woman whose life has also been affected by the war. This woman tells her a story she does not fully understand. You, however, will be able to see meanings that the little girl cannot.

Active Reading/Setting a Purpose
READING CONNECTION

Identifying Mood Mood is the feeling, or atmosphere, that a writer creates for the reader. Descriptive words, setting, dialogue, and figurative language contribute to the mood of a work, as do the sound and rhythm of the language. As you read "Winter Night," think about the story's mood. Does it change as the story progresses? What does the mood reveal about the effects of war?

40 UNIT ONE PART 1: LASTING IMPRESSIONS

PRINT AND MEDIA RESOURCES

UNIT ONE RESOURCE BOOK
Strategic Reading: Literature, p. 15
Vocabulary SkillBuilder, p. 16

GRAMMAR MINI–LESSONS
Transparencies, p. 48

WRITING MINI–LESSONS
Transparencies, p. 44

ACCESS FOR STUDENTS ACQUIRING ENGLISH
Selection Summaries
Reading Support

FORMAL ASSESSMENT
Selection Test, pp. 9–10
🖬 Test Generator

AUDIO LIBRARY
See Reference Card

INTERNET RESOURCES
McDougal Littell Literature Center at http://www.hmco.com/mcdougal/lit

Winter Night
Kay Boyle

There is a time of apprehension that begins with the beginning of darkness and to which only the speech of love can lend security. It is there, in abeyance, at the end of every day, not urgent enough to be given the name of fear but rather of concern for how the hours are to be reprieved from fear, and those who have forgotten how it was when they were children can remember nothing of this. It may begin around five o'clock on a winter afternoon, when the light outside is dying in the windows. At that hour, the New York apartment in which Felicia lived was filled with shadows, and the little girl would wait alone in the living room, looking out at the winter-stripped trees which stood black in the Park against the isolated ovals of unclean snow. Now it was January, and the day had been a cold one; the water of the artificial lake was frozen fast, but because of the cold and the coming darkness, the skaters had ceased to move across its surface. The street that lay between the Park and the apartment house was wide, and the two-way streams of cars and buses, some with their headlamps already shining, advanced and halted, halted and poured swiftly on, to the tempo of the traffic signals' altering lights. The time of apprehension had set in, and Felicia, who was seven, stood at the window in the evening and waited before she asked the questions. When the signals below changed from red to green again, or when the double-decker bus turned the corner below, she would ask it. The words of it were already there, tentative in her mouth, when the answer came from the far end of the hall.

"Your mother," said the voice among the sound of kitchen things, "she telephoned up before you came in from school. She won't be back in time for supper. I was to tell you a sitter was coming in from the sitting parents' place."

Felicia turned back from the window into the obscurity of the living room, and she looked toward the open door and into the hall beyond it, where the light from the kitchen fell in a clear, yellow angle across the wall and onto the strip of carpet. Her hands were cold, and she put them in her jacket pockets as she walked carefully across the living-room rug and stopped at the edge of light.

"Will she be home late?" she said.

For a moment there was the sound of water running in the kitchen, a long way away, and then the sound of the water ceased, and the high, Southern voice went on, "She'll come home when she gets ready to come home. That's all I have to say. If she wants to spend two dollars and fifty cents and ten cents carfare on top of that three or four nights out of the week for a sitting parent to come in here and sit, it's her own business. It certainly ain't nothing to do

---

WORDS TO KNOW
apprehension (ăp'rĭ-hĕn'shən) *n.* a feeling of anxiety or dread
abeyance (ə-bā'əns) *n.* a temporary suspension
reprieve (rĭ-prēv') *v.* to bring relief to; deliver from
obscurity (ŏb-skyŏor'ĭ-tē) *n.* indistinctness; darkness

41

CUSTOMIZING FOR
Gifted and Talented Students

Have students look, as they read, for details that show the probable effects of the camp on the woman's mental and emotional health.

Possible responses:

- Page 44—The woman seems to be in a constant state of grief: "and now the mask of grief had come back upon her face."
- Page 44—Little things trigger the woman's suppressed rage: "When I see milk like that . . . I want to cry out loud, I want to beat my hands on the table."
- Page 46—At times the woman is unable to control her emotions: "Why am I saying all this to you, why am I doing it?"

Literary Concept: DIALOGUE

A Ask students what they can infer about the housekeeper from her answers to Felicia's questions. *(Possible response: The housekeeper is insensitive to Felicia; she may feel overwhelmed by her own hard life, leading her to lash out at Felicia.)*

Literary Concept: CHARACTER

B Invite students to suggest why the author doesn't tell us the name of this "voice" or anything about her. *(Possible response: Calling her a voice emphasizes that she is just one of many caretakers and is not emotionally attached to Felicia.)*

Literary Concept: CONTRAST

C Have students discuss Felicia's fascination with shadows and light and what they might mean to her. *(Possible response: Perhaps the light represents security, for Felicia finally steps out of the shadows and into the light when she thinks about life after the war, with a father who returns each evening.)*

---

with you or me. She makes her money, just like the rest of us does. She works all day down there in the office, or whatever it is, just like the rest of us works, and she's entitled to spend her money like she wants to spend it. There's no law in the world against buying your own freedom. Your mother and me, we're just buying our own freedom, that's all we're doing. And we're not doing nobody no harm."

> *The voice from the kitchen had no name. It was as variable as the faces and figures of the women who came and sat in the evenings.*

"Do you know who she's having supper with?" said Felicia from the edge of dark. There was one more step to take and then she would be standing in the light that fell on the strip of carpet, but she did not take the step.

"Do I know who she's having supper with?" the voice cried out in what might have been <u>derision</u>, and there was the sound of dishes striking the metal ribs of the drainboard by the sink. "Maybe it's Mr. Van Johnson[1] or Mr. Frank Sinatra,[2] or maybe it's just the Duke of Wincers[3] for the evening. All I know is you're having soft-boiled egg and spinach and applesauce for supper, and you're going to have it quick now because the time is getting away."

The voice from the kitchen had no name. It was as variable as the faces and figures of the women who came and sat in the evenings. Month by month the voice in the kitchen altered to another voice, and the sitting parents were no more than lonely aunts of an evening or two, who sometimes returned and sometimes did not to this apartment in which they had sat

before. Nobody stayed anywhere very long any more, Felicia's mother told her. It was part of the time in which you lived, and part of the life of the city, but when the fathers came back, all this would be miraculously changed. Perhaps you would live in a house again, a small one, with fir trees on either side of the short brick walk, and Father would drive up every night from the station just after darkness set in. When Felicia thought of this, she stepped quickly into the clear angle of light, and she left the dark of the living room behind her and ran softly down the hall.

The drop-leaf table stood in the kitchen between the refrigerator and the sink, and Felicia sat down at the place that was set. The voice at the sink was speaking still, and while Felicia ate it did not cease to speak until the bell of the front door rang abruptly. The girl walked around the table and went down the hall, wiping her dark palms in her apron, and, from the drop-leaf table, Felicia watched her step from the angle of light into darkness and open the door.

"You put in an early appearance," the girl said, and the woman who had rung the bell came into the hall. The door closed behind her, and the girl showed her into the living room and lit the lamp on the bookcase, and the shadows were suddenly bleached away. But when the girl turned, the woman turned from the living room, too, and followed her, humbly and in silence, to the threshold of the kitchen. "Sometimes they keep me standing around

---

1. **Van Johnson:** an American film actor popular in the 1940s.
2. **Frank Sinatra:** a famous American singer and movie star.
3. **Duke of Wincers:** a mispronunciation of "Duke of Windsor," the title given King Edward VIII of Great Britain after he gave up the throne to marry the woman he loved in 1937.

WORDS TO KNOW
derision (dĭ-rĭzh′ən) *n.* contempt or ridicule

42

Mini-Lesson The Writer's Style

TONE Point out the highlighted opening sentences on page 41, and ask students to note Kay Boyle's use of long sentences and formal words, such as *apprehension, abeyance,* and *reprieved.* Ask students how the sentence structure and the word choice create the author's tone. *(Possible response: The sentence structure and the word choice help create a tone of seriousness and concern, suggesting that the writer is probing an important, somber subject.)*

Application Write a paragraph describing a situation that makes you apprehensive or nervous. Give your writing a serious and concerned tone by using formal words and complex sentences.

Reteaching/Reinforcement
- *Writing Mini-Lessons* transparencies, p. 44

 **The Writer's Craft**

Ways to Develop Your Voice, pp. 422–428

waiting after it's time for me to be getting on home, the sitting parents do," the girl said, and she picked up the last two dishes from the table and put them in the sink. The woman who stood in the doorway was small, and when she undid the white silk scarf from around her head, Felicia saw that her hair was black. She wore it parted in the middle, and it had not been cut but was drawn back loosely into a knot behind her head. She had very clean white gloves on, and her face was pale, and there was a look of sorrow in her soft black eyes. "Sometimes I have to stand out there in the hall with my hat and coat on, waiting for the sitting parents to turn up," the girl said, and as she turned on the water in the sink, the contempt she had for them hung on the kitchen air. "But you're ahead of time," she said, and she held the dishes, first one and then the other, under the flow of steaming water.

The woman in the doorway wore a neat black coat, not a new-looking coat, and it had no fur on it, but it had a smooth velvet collar and velvet lapels. She did not move or smile, and she gave no sign that she had heard the girl speaking above the sound of water at the sink. She simply stood looking at Felicia, who sat at the table with the milk in her glass not finished yet. "Are you the child?" she said at last, and her voice was low and the pronunciation of the words a little strange.

"Yes, this here's Felicia," the girl said, and the dark hands dried the dishes and put them away. "You drink up your milk quick, now, Felicia, so's I can rinse your glass."

"I will wash the glass," said the woman. "I would like to wash the glass for her," and Felicia sat looking across the table at the face in the doorway that was filled with such unspoken grief. "I will wash the glass for her and clean off the table," the woman was saying quietly. "When the child is finished, she will show me where her night things are."

"The others, they wouldn't do anything like that," the girl said, and she hung the dishcloth over the rack. "They wouldn't put their hand to housework, the sitting parents. That's where they got the name for them," she said.

Whenever the front door closed behind the girl in the evening, it would usually be that the sitting parent who was there would take up a book of fairy stories and read aloud for a while to Felicia, or else would settle herself in the big chair in the living room and begin to tell the words of a story in drowsiness to her, while Felicia took off her clothes in the bedroom, and folded them, and put her pajamas on, and brushed her teeth, and did her hair. But this time that was not the way it happened. Instead, the woman sat down on the other chair at the kitchen table, and she began at once to speak, not of good fairies or bad, or of animals endowed with human speech, but to speak quietly, in spite of the eagerness behind her words, of a thing that seemed of singular importance to her.

"It is strange that I should have been sent here tonight," she said, her eyes moving slowly from feature to feature of Felicia's face, "for you look like a child that I knew once, and this is the anniversary of that child."

"Did she have hair like mine?" Felicia asked quickly, and she did not keep her eyes fixed on the unfinished glass of milk in shyness any more.

"Yes, she did. She had hair like yours," said the woman, and her glance paused for a moment on the locks which fell straight and thick on the shoulders of Felicia's dress. It may have been that she thought to stretch out her hand and touch the ends of Felicia's hair, for her fingers stirred as they lay clasped together on the table, and then they relapsed into passivity again. "But it is not the hair alone, it is the delicacy of your face, too, and your eyes the same, filled with the

WINTER NIGHT 43

Literary Concept: IRONY

G Explain that dramatic irony occurs when the reader knows information that a character in the story does not know. Ask how knowing that the "camp" is a concentration camp allows readers to see the little girl's situation in ways that Felicia cannot. *(Possible response: Readers realize the little girl suffered terribly and is probably dead, whereas Felicia thinks she was on a vacation or an outing.)*

Linking to History

H Explain to students that Jews were often tricked into believing they would be resettled in Eastern Europe. The Nazis gave them specific instructions about what possessions to bring for their new lives. These Jews were deported from Germany and Western Europe, and many were taken to the Auschwitz-Birkenau extermination camp in Poland. In some cases, the Nazis furthered their deception by forcing families to send postcards back home to friends, telling happy stories of their new homes.

Literary Concept: IRONY

I Ask the group why this detail—the young girl's taking her ballet slippers to a concentration camp—is ironic. *(Possible response: The beauty and grace of ballet contrast sharply with the horrors of the camp; the contrast emphasizes the gap between the girl's expectations and the hopelessness of her situation.)*

CUSTOMIZING FOR Students Acquiring English

 Define *stuttered* as "spoke with stops and starts and repetition of sounds."

Critical Thinking: ANALYZING

J Why is Felicia suddenly "alone again in the time of apprehension"? *(Possible response: Felicia had been drawn to the woman's emotional warmth, but the woman's sudden outburst about the milk frightens the girl.)*

---

same spring-lilac color," the woman said, pronouncing the words carefully. "She had little coats of golden fur on her arms and legs," she said, "and when we were closed up there, the lot of us in the cold, I used to make her laugh when I told her that the fur that was so pretty, like a little fawn's skin on her arms, would always help to keep her warm."

> *"It was not a school, but still there were a lot of children there. It was a camp—that was the name the place had."*

"And did it keep her warm?" asked Felicia, and she gave a little jerk of laughter as she looked down at her own legs hanging under the table, with the bare calves thin and covered with a down of hair.

"It did not keep her warm enough," the woman said, and now the mask of grief had come back upon her face. "So we used to take everything we could spare from ourselves, and we would sew them into cloaks and other kinds of garments for her and for the other children."

"Was it a school?" said Felicia when the woman's voice had ceased to speak.

"No," said the woman softly, "it was not a school, but still there were a lot of children there. It was a camp—that was the name the place had; it was a camp. It was a place where they put people until they could decide what was to be done with them." She sat with her hands clasped, silent a moment, looking at Felicia. "That little dress you have on," she said, not saying the words to anybody, scarcely saying them aloud. "Oh, she would have liked that little dress, the little buttons shaped like hearts, and the white collar—"

"I have four school dresses," Felicia said.

"I'll show them to you. How many dresses did she have?"

"Well, there, you see, there in the camp," said the woman, "she did not have any dresses except the little skirt and the pullover. That was all she had. She had brought just a handkerchief of her belongings with her, like everybody else—just enough for three days away from home was what they told us, so she did not have enough to last the winter. But she had her ballet slippers," the woman said, and her clasped fingers did not move. "She had brought them because she thought during her three days away from home she would have the time to practice her ballet."

"I've been to the ballet," Felicia said suddenly, and she said it so eagerly that she stuttered a little as the words came out of her mouth. She slipped quickly down from the chair and went around the table to where the woman sat. Then she took one of the woman's hands away from the other that held it fast, and she pulled her toward the door. "Come into the living room and I'll do a pirouette⁴ for you," she said, and then she stopped speaking, her eyes halted on the woman's face. "Did she—did the little girl—could she do a pirouette very well?" she said.

"Yes, she could. At first she could," said the woman, and Felicia felt uneasy now at the sound of sorrow in her words. "But after that she was hungry. She was hungry all winter," she said in a low voice. "We were all hungry, but the children were the hungriest. Even now," she said, and her voice went suddenly savage, "when I see milk like that, clean, fresh milk standing in a glass, I want to cry out loud, I want to beat my hands on the table, because it did not have to be!" She had drawn her fingers abruptly away from Felicia now, and Felicia stood before her, cast off, forlorn, alone again in the time of apprehension. "That was three years ago," the

---

4. **pirouette** (pĭr′ōō-ĕt′): in ballet, a full turn of the body on the point of the toe or the ball of the foot.

44 UNIT ONE PART 1: LASTING IMPRESSIONS

Mini-Lesson · Literary Concepts

REVIEWING CONTRAST Remind students that contrast is a stylistic technique in which one element is shown in opposition to another. These elements may be contrasting ideas or contrasting images. Contrasts in literature often contribute to an understanding of character.

Application Have students identify some contrasts in the story. For example:
- darkness and light—pp. 41–42
- the cook and the sitting parent—p. 43
- the girl in the camp and Felicia—pp. 44–48

Ask students to explain, for each example, how the juxtaposition of the two elements contributes to their understanding of the main characters.

Elizabeth in a Red Chair (1961), Fairfield Porter. Oil on canvas, 44¼″ × 39¾″, Collection of the Heckscher Museum, Huntington, New York, gift of the family of Fairfield Porter (1982.3).

WINTER NIGHT   **45**

Art Note

Elizabeth in a Red Chair by Fairfield Porter American figurative painter Fairfield Porter was born in 1907. From 1930 until his death in 1975, Porter produced a body of work noted for its rich use of light and its classic American subject matter. This portrait of a child shows the postimpressionists' influence on Porter and Porter's interest in the abstract.

Reading the Art *How would you describe the expression on the girl's face?*

CUSTOMIZING FOR
Multiple Learning Styles

K **Spatial or Graphic Learners** Have students suggest ways in which this painting echoes the mood of "Winter Night."

THE LANGUAGE OF LITERATURE TEACHER'S EDITION **45**

STRATEGIC READING FOR
Less-Proficient Readers

L Ask students whether they think Felicia is getting along well with her new baby sitter, and if so, why. *(Yes; the new sitter is clearly drawn to Felicia and relates to her in a personal and caring way.)* **Summarizing**

Ask them to list some ways in which the girl in the camp is like Felicia. *(The girls look alike; both like ballet; both have mothers who are absent.)* **Noting Relevant Details**

Set a Purpose Have students read on to find other ways in which the two girls are alike.

Literary Concept:
POINT OF VIEW

M Point out to students that the story is narrated by a third-person omniscient, or all-knowing, narrator. Have students discuss why this narrative point of view is appropriate for the story. *(Possible response: The narrator can describe the feelings of both the woman and the girl and the way in which they meet each other's needs.)*

CUSTOMIZING FOR
Students Acquiring English

3 Define *reverence* as "a deep feeling of awe and respect."

Critical Thinking: ANALYZING

N How would you describe the woman's state of mind in general? *(Possible response: The woman was badly scarred emotionally by her experiences in the camp, yet her ability to show affection to Felicia suggests she will recover her emotional health.)*

---

woman was saying, and one hand was lifted, as if in weariness, to shade her face. "It was somewhere else, it was in another country," she said, and behind her hand her eyes were turned upon the substance of a world in which Felicia had played no part.

"Did—did the little girl cry when she was hungry?" Felicia asked, and the woman shook her head.

"Sometimes she cried," she said, "but not very much. She was very quiet. One night, when she heard the other children crying, she said to me, 'You know, they are not crying because they want something to eat. They are crying because their mothers have gone away.'"

"Did the mothers have to go out to supper?" Felicia asked, and she watched the woman's face for the answer.

"No," said the woman. She stood up from her chair, and now that she put her hand on the little girl's shoulder, Felicia was taken into the sphere of love and intimacy again. "Shall we go into the other room, and you will do your pirouette for me?" the woman said, and they went from the kitchen and down the strip of carpet on which the clear light fell. In the front room, they paused, hand in hand, in the glow of the shaded lamp, and the woman looked about her, at the books, the low tables with the magazines and ashtrays on them, the vase of roses on the piano, looking with dark, scarcely seeing eyes at these things that had no reality at all. It was only when she saw the little white clock on the mantelpiece that she gave any sign, and then she said quickly, "What time does your mother put you to bed?"

Felicia waited a moment, and in the interval of waiting, the woman lifted one hand and, as if in reverence, touched Felicia's hair.

"What time did the little girl you knew in the other place go to bed?" Felicia asked.

"Ah, God, I do not know, I do not remember," the woman said.

"Was she your little girl?" said Felicia softly, stubbornly.

"No," said the woman. "She was not mine. At least, at first she was not mine. She had a mother, a real mother, but the mother had to go away."

> *"They are not crying because they want something to eat. They are crying because their mothers have gone away."*

"Did she come back late?" asked Felicia.

"No, ah, no, she could not come back, she never came back," the woman said, and now she turned, her arm around Felicia's shoulders, and she sat down in the low, soft chair. "Why am I saying all this to you, why am I doing it?" she cried out in grief, and she held Felicia close against her. "I had thought to speak of the anniversary to you, and that was all, and now I am saying these other things to you. Three years ago today, exactly, the little girl became my little girl because her mother went away. That is all there is to it. There is nothing more."

Felicia waited another moment, held close against the woman, and listening to the swift, strong heartbeats in the woman's breast.

"But the mother," she said then, in the small, persistent voice, "did she take a taxi when she went?"

"This is the way it used to happen," said the woman, speaking in hopelessness and bitterness in the softly lighted room. "Every week they used to come into the place where we were and they would read a list of names out. Sometimes it would be the names of children they would read out, and then a little later they would have to go away. And sometimes it would be the grown people's names, the names of the mothers

46 UNIT ONE PART 1: LASTING IMPRESSIONS

Critic's  Corner

"A steady passionate concern for social justice and an equally unswerving compassion for the poignancies of human suffering are powerful and noble weapons in any artist's arsenal—and to these Kay Boyle can justly lay claim."

Earl Rovit
The *Nation*

Invite students to discuss how "Winter Night" shows Boyle's concern for justice and compassion for suffering.

or big sisters, or other women's names. The men were not with us. The fathers were somewhere else, in another place."

"Yes," Felicia said. "I know."

"We had been there only a little while, maybe ten days or maybe not so long," the woman went on, holding Felicia against her still, "when they read the name of the little girl's mother out, and that afternoon they took her away."

"What did the little girl do?" Felicia said.

"She wanted to think up the best way of getting out, so that she could go find her mother," said the woman, "but she could not think of anything good enough until the third or fourth day. And then she tied her ballet slippers up in the handkerchief again, and she went up to the guard standing at the door." The woman's voice was gentle, controlled now. "She asked the guard please to open the door so that she could go out. 'This is Thursday,' she said, 'and every Tuesday and Thursday I have my ballet lessons. If I miss a ballet lesson, they do not count the money off, so my mother would be just paying for nothing, and she cannot afford to pay for nothing. I missed my ballet lesson on Tuesday,' she said to the guard, 'and I must not miss it again today.'"

Felicia lifted her head from the woman's shoulder, and she shook her hair back and looked in question and wonder at the woman's face.

"And did the man let her go?" she said.

"No, he did not. He could not do that," said the woman. "He was a soldier and he had to do what he was told. So every evening after her mother went, I used to brush the little girl's hair for her," the woman went on saying. "And while I brushed it, I used to tell her the stories of the ballets. Sometimes I would begin with *Narcissus*,"⁵ the woman said, and she parted Felicia's locks with her fingers, "so if you will go and get your brush now, I will tell it while I brush your hair."

"Oh, yes," said Felicia, and she made two whirls as she went quickly to her bedroom. On the way back, she stopped and held onto the piano with the fingers of one hand while she went up on her toes. "Did you see me? Did you see me standing on my toes?" she called to the woman, and the woman sat smiling in love and contentment at her.

"Yes, wonderful, really wonderful," she said. "I am sure I have never seen anyone do it so well." Felicia came spinning toward her, whirling in pirouette after pirouette, and she flung herself down in the chair close to her, with her thin bones pressed against the woman's soft, wide hip. The woman took the silver-backed, monogrammed brush and the tortoise-shell comb in her hands, and now she began to brush Felicia's hair. "We did not have any soap at all and not very much water to wash in, so I never could fix her as nicely and prettily as I wanted to," she said, and the brush stroked regularly, carefully down, caressing the shape of Felicia's head.

"If there wasn't very much water, then how did she do her teeth?" Felicia said.

"She did not do her teeth," said the woman, and she drew the comb through Felicia's hair. "There were not any toothbrushes or toothpaste, or anything like that."

Felicia waited a moment, constructing the unfamiliar scene of it in silence, and then she asked the tentative question.

"Do I have to do my teeth tonight?" she said.

"No," said the woman, and she was thinking of something else, "you do not have to do your teeth."

"If I am your little girl tonight, can I pretend there isn't enough water to wash?" said Felicia.

"Yes," said the woman, "you can pretend that if you like. You do not have to wash," she said, and the comb passed lightly through Felicia's hair.

---

5. **Narcissus** (när-sĭs′əs): a ballet based on the myth of Narcissus, a handsome youth who pined away for love of his own reflection in a pool of water.

WINTER NIGHT 47

Critical Thinking: ANALYZING

O Ask why Felicia says, "I know." *(Felicia's own father, and perhaps her friends' fathers, are in the armed services; because of the wartime setting, Felicia assumes that all fathers are somewhere else.)*

Literary Concept: CHARACTER

P Invite students to describe the effect the woman is having on Felicia. *(Possible response: Felicia enjoys the woman's presence so much that she dances with happiness.)*

CUSTOMIZING FOR
Students Acquiring English

4 Explain to students that *monogrammed* means "marked with initials."

STRATEGIC READING FOR
Less-Proficient Readers

Q Ask students to suggest how the war may have affected the girls in similar ways. *(The war has separated both girls from their fathers; like the girl in the camp, Felicia misses her mother; the sitter has been acting like a mother for both girls.)* Summarizing

Set a Purpose Have the students finish reading the story to see how the evening ends for Felicia.

Assessment Option

INFORMAL ASSESSMENT You can assess students' understanding of the selection and of the main characters' feelings and motivations by setting up the following role-playing scenarios:
- Felicia's mother wakes up the sitting parent and asks her why Felicia is asleep in her clothes in the living room.
- In the morning, the mother asks Felicia about the new sitting parent and what they did together the previous evening.

Rubric

3 Full Accomplishment The role-playing accurately reflects the events of the story and fully reveals the emotional connection between Felicia and the sitter.

2 Substantial Accomplishment The role-playing reflects the events of the story fairly accurately and reveals that the sitter showed Felicia emotional warmth.

1 Little or Partial Accomplishment Students have difficulty role-playing since they do not understand the events and show little grasp of the emotional bond between the two main characters.

Literary Concept: CONTRAST

R Ask students how the story of the ballet contrasts with the story of the girl in the camp. *(The story of the ballet is set in a forest glade, not a prison camp; it is springtime, not winter.)*

Critical Thinking: ANALYZING

S Ask why the woman says, "They must be quietly asleep somewhere." *(Possible responses: Perhaps she cannot admit that the people in the camp are dead; she is trying to find comfort.)*

STRATEGIC READING FOR
Less-Proficient Readers

T Use the following prompts to check students' understanding:

- How does the story end? *(Felicia's mother returns to find Felicia and the sitter asleep in each other's arms.)*
  Summarizing

- Why is this sight so startling to the mother? *(She is shocked by the sight of Felicia in another woman's arms.)*
  Making Inferences

CUSTOMIZING FOR
Gifted and Talented Students

How do people attempt to resolve the loss of a loved one?

COMPREHENSION CHECK

1. Who takes care of Felicia? *(housekeepers and sitting parents)*
2. How are the little girl and Felicia alike? *(They look alike; they enjoy ballet; they miss their mothers.)*
3. Why is the sitting parent so upset by her memories of the little girl? *(The girl died in a concentration camp after being left in the woman's care.)*
4. How do Felicia and the sitting parent fill each other's emotional needs? *(Felicia receives affection, and the sitting parent experiences again the love she felt for a girl she lost.)*

"Will you tell me the story of the ballet?" said Felicia, and the rhythm of the brushing was like the soft, slow rocking of sleep.

"Yes," said the woman. "In the first one, the place is a forest glade with little, pale birches growing in it, and they have green veils over their faces and green veils drifting from their fingers, because it is the springtime. There is the music of a flute," said the woman's voice softly, softly, "and creatures of the wood are dancing—"

"But the mother," Felicia said, as suddenly as if she had been awaked from sleep. "What did the little girl's mother say when she didn't do her teeth and didn't wash at night?"

"The mother was not there, you remember," said the woman, and the brush moved steadily in her hand. "But she did send one little letter back. Sometimes the people who went away were able to do that. The mother wrote it in a train, standing up in a car that had no seats," she said, and she might have been telling the story of the ballet still, for her voice was gentle and the brush did not falter on Felicia's hair. "There were perhaps a great many other people standing up in the train with her, perhaps all trying to write their little letters on the bits of paper they had managed to hide on them, or that they had found in forgotten corners as they travelled. When they had written their letters, then they must try to slip them out through the boards of the car in which they journeyed, standing up," said the woman, "and these letters fell down on the tracks under the train, or they were blown into the fields or onto the country roads, and if it was a kind person who picked them up, he would seal them in envelopes and send them to where they were addressed to go. So a letter came back like this from the little girl's mother," the woman said, and the brush followed the comb, the comb the brush, in steady pursuit through Felicia's hair. "It said goodbye to the little girl, and it said please to take care of her. It said, 'Whoever reads this letter in the camp, please take good care of my little girl for me, and please have her tonsils looked at by a doctor if this is possible to do.'"

"And then," said Felicia softly, persistently, "what happened to the little girl?"

"I do not know. I cannot say," the woman said. But now the brush and comb had ceased to move, and in the silence Felicia turned her thin, small body on the chair, and she and the woman suddenly put their arms around each other. "They must all be asleep now, all of them," the woman said, and in the silence that fell on them again, they held each other closer. "They must be quietly asleep somewhere and not crying all night because they are hungry and because they are cold. For three years I have been saying 'They must all be asleep, and the cold and the hunger and the seasons or night or day or nothing matters to them.'"

It was after midnight when Felicia's mother put her key in the lock of the front door, and pushed it open, and stepped into the hallway. She walked quickly to the living room, and just across the threshold she slipped the three blue-fox skins from her shoulders and dropped them, with her little velvet bag, upon the chair. The room was quiet, so quiet that she could hear the sound of breathing in it, and no one spoke to her in greeting as she crossed toward the bedroom door. And then, as startling as a slap across her delicately tinted face, she saw the woman lying sleeping on the divan, and Felicia, in her school dress still, asleep within the woman's arms. ❖

Mini-Lesson Grammar

TYPES OF SENTENCES Explain the four different types of sentences: declarative, interrogative, imperative, and exclamatory. Then share with students the material on the chart shown.

Application Have students identify each of the following sentences by type. Then ask students to write four sentences, one of each type, that express their reactions to the story.

1. Felicia missed her mother on winter evenings. *(declarative)*
2. What was the new sitting parent like? *(interrogative)*
3. What a terrible experience she has had! *(exclamatory)*
4. What happened to the little girl at the camp? *(interrogative)*
5. Never forget the horrors of the Holocaust. *(imperative)*

Reteaching/Reinforcement
- *Grammar Handbook*, anthology p. 1103
- *Grammar Mini-Lessons* transparencies, p. 48

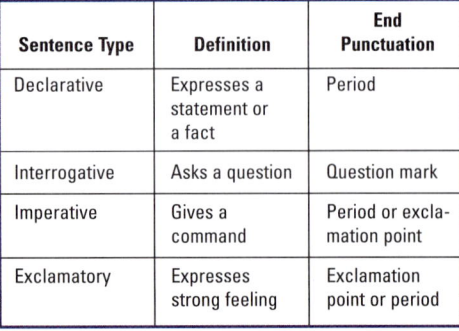

Sentence Type	Definition	End Punctuation
Declarative	Expresses a statement or a fact	Period
Interrogative	Asks a question	Question mark
Imperative	Gives a command	Period or exclamation point
Exclamatory	Expresses strong feeling	Exclamation point or period

RESPONDING OPTIONS

FROM PERSONAL RESPONSE TO CRITICAL ANALYSIS

REFLECT
1. In your notebook, jot down some words and phrases that express the mood of this story. Then, jot down anything you have questions about.

RETHINK
2. How would you describe Felicia's life?
   Consider
   - Felicia's "time of apprehension" at the beginning of the story
   - the description of the apartment in which she lives
   - how the war has affected her life
   - her curiosity about the little girl in the sitting parent's story

   Close Textual Reading

3. What kind of person is the sitting parent?
   Consider
   - the way she treats Felicia
   - how she has been affected by the war
   - her relationship with the little girl in the camp

4. How do you account for the immediate bond that forms between Felicia and the sitting parent? Use details from the story to support your response.

   Thematic Link
5. Imagine both Felicia and the sitting parent ten years after their encounter. What impact, if any, might the war still have on each of them?

RELATE
6. What lessons can others learn from the experiences of survivors of war?

ANOTHER PATHWAY
Cooperative Learning
Work with a small group to create a chart that compares and contrasts Felicia and the girl in the camp. If you have a graphics program on your computer, use it to help you construct the chart.

QUICKWRITES

1. Write a **continuation** of the story, starting where Kay Boyle left off. Try to maintain the mood of the selection and to include dialogue and descriptive images characteristic of Boyle's style.

2. Imagine that you are Felicia, as an adult, writing her autobiography. Write a **chapter** titled "The Mysterious Sitter," in which she focuses on her encounter with the sitting parent.

3. Write an **editorial** explaining what you think are the universal needs of children, no matter what their life circumstances. Use examples and quotations from the story to support your views.

 PORTFOLIO Save your writing. You may want to use it later as a springboard to a piece for your portfolio.

LITERARY CONCEPTS

Characters are the people (and occasionally animals or fantasy creatures) who participate in the action of literary works. A character may be considered either main or minor, depending on the extent of the character's development and on his or her importance in a work. Like "Winter Night," a piece of literature may include a story within a story, complete with main and minor characters of its own. Make a list of the main and minor characters in "Winter Night," and tell what they add to the story.

WINTER NIGHT **49**

From Personal Response to Critical Analysis

1. Accept all reasonable responses. Encourage students to share their questions in small groups.
2. Possible responses: Felicia's life is materially secure, but her parents' absence has left her lonely; her sitters do not meet her emotional needs.
3. Possible responses: The sitting parent is intelligent and is loving with Felicia; she is a kind woman attempting to cope with the trauma of seeing so many people die in the camp.
4. Possible responses: The woman and Felicia both greatly miss people whom the war has taken away from them; Felicia sees the woman as a substitute mother; Felicia reminds the woman of a girl in the concentration camp.
5. Possible responses: As a Holocaust survivor, the woman may suffer painful memories all her life; Felicia's sense of isolation may ease if her family life becomes more stable after the war.
6. Answers will vary.

Another Pathway

Cooperative Learning Students may work in groups of three. One student can go through the story to find ways in which the girls are similar (for example, they miss their mothers; their fathers are away; they like ballet; they look alike). Another student can search for differences (for example, Felicia has pretty clothes; she has plenty to eat; she is in no danger). The third student can construct the chart that presents their findings.

Rubric
- **3 Full Accomplishment** Students' charts clearly show the similarities and differences between the two girls and are exhaustive.
- **2 Substantial Accomplishment** Students' charts show many of the similarities and differences between the two girls but do not contain all possible findings.
- **1 Little or Partial Accomplishment** Students' charts do not differentiate between the girls' similarities and differences, and few findings are given.

Literary Concepts

If students have problems listing the characters or discussing their roles, use these prompts:
1. Who are the main characters in "Winter Night"? *(Felicia and the sitting parent)* What do they add to the story? *(Both of them feel a sense of loss; they are lonely and in need of companionship.)*
2. Who are the minor characters in the story? *(the housekeeper and Felicia's mother)* What do they add to the story? *(They typify the lack of love in Felicia's life.)*
3. Who is the main character in the story within "Winter Night"? *(the little girl who looks like Felicia)* Why is she so important? *(Her story helps us to understand the grief of the sitting parent, while bringing out Felicia's own emotional needs.)*

QuickWrites

1. Students can list the unanswered questions they have about the story and then use the continuation as a way to answer them.
2. Remind students that autobiographies are written from a first-person point of view. This chapter should focus on Felicia's feelings about the sitter.
3. Suggest that students choose words with powerful connotations to make their editorials persuasive.

The Writer's Craft
Dialogue, pp. 452–455
Writing Autobiography, pp. 26–40
Editorial Writing, pp. 228–232

THE LANGUAGE OF LITERATURE TEACHER'S EDITION **49**

Across the Curriculum

History Students' findings should note that during the regime of Adolf Hitler, the German Nazis imprisoned Jews, other minorities, and political opponents. The Nazis seized their property and stripped them of their citizenship. Most were sent to concentration camps, where they were enslaved, starved, and exterminated. By the end of 1945, the Nazi campaign of mass murder had resulted in the deaths of about 12 million people.

Words to Know

1. before going on stage
2. later
3. no
4. in a dense forest
5. an annoying fool

Reteaching/Reinforcement
- *Unit One Resource Book,* p. 16

KAY BOYLE

During the 1920s, Kay Boyle was part of the "lost generation" literary set that flourished in Paris. Always active in politics, she spoke out against Senator Joseph McCarthy's Communist-hunting tactics in the 1950s, the Vietnam War in the 1960s, and the bombing of Libya in the 1980s.

ALTERNATIVE ACTIVITIES

1. Get together with classmates and prepare a **dramatic reading** of "Winter Night." Three people can read the dialogue; a fourth can be the narrator. As a group, decide which paragraphs the narrator needs to read and which parts of the narration can be communicated through the actions of the characters.
2. Make a charcoal or pencil **sketch** of a scene from "Winter Night." Try to use light and dark images the way Kay Boyle does in her writing.

ACROSS THE CURRICULUM

History Study oral histories of Holocaust survivors—either in print or on film—to see if their memories are similar to the ones shared by the sitting parent in "Winter Night." Present your findings to the class.

WORDS TO KNOW

Answer each of the questions below.

1. Is a performer in a school play more likely to feel **apprehension** before going on stage or after the play is over?
2. If debate on an issue is in **abeyance**, is the issue debated now or later?
3. If a queen **reprieves** a prisoner, will the prisoner be executed immediately?
4. Is a person in **obscurity** more likely to be standing in a dense forest or in an open field?
5. Who is a more likely object of **derision**—a wise counselor or an annoying fool?

THE WRITER'S STYLE

Throughout "Winter Night," Kay Boyle uses images of light and dark to add meaning and to establish mood. Look for these images as you carefully review the story, keeping a list of the examples you find. Then get together with classmates and discuss how these images affect your reading of the story.

KAY BOYLE

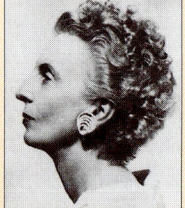

1902–1992

Kay Boyle began writing stories when she was a young child, making books for family members as birthday and Christmas presents. She went on to become a prolific writer of short stories, as well as novels, poetry, and essays. Among the many honors and literary awards she received in her lifetime were two Guggenheim fellowships and two O. Henry awards for best short story of the year.

Boyle was born in St. Paul, Minnesota, but she spent her early childhood and much of her adulthood in Europe. She was living in France with her husband and children when the country was invaded by Nazi Germany in 1940, and she was unable to move back to the United States until the summer of 1941. Several of her novels concern this period of the war in France. Boyle returned to Europe after the war; she lived in France and West Germany from 1946 to 1953 while serving as a foreign correspondent for *The New Yorker* magazine. Later, she taught at several colleges and universities in the United States.

The human need for love is an underlying theme in much of Boyle's writing, but her work also focuses on moral responsibility and social justice. In an interview with the *Los Angeles Times,* Boyle once said, "The older I grow, the more I feel that all writers should be more committed to their times and write of their times and of the issues of their times."

OTHER WORKS *The White Horses of Vienna and Other Stories, The Smoking Mountain: Stories of Post-War Germany, Fifty Stories, Life Being the Best and Other Stories*

50 UNIT ONE PART 1: LASTING IMPRESSIONS

The Writer's Style

Help students find and discuss these and other images of light and dark:
- Page 41, paragraph 1: The dying of the day's light and the beginning of darkness is the time of apprehension; darkness is equated with fear.
- Page 41, paragraph 3: Lonely Felicia stands in the dark living room; the light and human companionship is in the kitchen.
- Page 42, paragraph 3: Felicia identifies the return of her father with passage into the light.

Alternative Activities

1. Remind students that the most important part of their dramatic reading will be the tone of their voices. Ask them to think about how to project the fearfulness and innocence of Felicia's voice, the melancholy and sometimes bitter tone of the sitting parent, and the insensitive, offhand tone of the cook.
2. Suggest possibilities for sketches, including the opening scene of the park, the angle of light just outside the kitchen, or the sitter's black-and-white appearance.

PREVIEWING

FICTION

After the Ball
Leo Tolstoy Russia

Activating Prior Knowledge
PERSONAL CONNECTION

In your notebook, list the qualities and behaviors that you associate with a good person, and then list those that you associate with an evil person. Now think of several famous people you have heard of, and try to classify each as good or evil. Can you always tell whether a person is good or evil?

Building Background
HISTORICAL CONNECTION

Leo Tolstoy was an important Russian writer, reformer, and moral thinker of the 19th century. For much of his life he was preoccupied with questions of good and evil, the meaning of life, and the structure of society. The major events in "After the Ball" take place in the 1840s. The characters belong to the polite society of the time, where lavish dances, or balls, were major social events.

Active Reading/Setting a Purpose
READING CONNECTION

Evaluating Characters As you read this story, use a chart like the one below to keep track of the personal qualities and behaviors of the main characters. Then decide whether you think each one is good or evil or a mixture of the two, and record your evaluation in the right-hand column.

Qualities and Behaviors		
Character	**Good**	**Evil**
Ivan Vassilievich		
Varenka		
Varenka's father, the colonel		

A court ball at the Winter Palace, St. Petersburg, Russia, 1888. Culver Pictures.

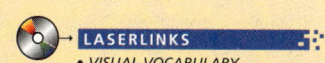
• VISUAL VOCABULARY

OVERVIEW

Objectives

- To understand and appreciate a short story that explores how one chance incident changes the course of a young man's life
- To identify and understand flashbacks
- To express understanding of the selection through a choice of writing forms, including a newspaper column, a dramatic scene, a letter, and a proposal
- To extend understanding of the selection through a variety of multimodal and cross-curricular activities

Skills

LITERARY CONCEPTS
- Flashback
- Setting

READING SKILLS/ STRATEGIES
- Evaluating characters

THE WRITER'S STYLE
- Catching the reader's attention
- Using dialogue as an opener

GENRE STUDY
- Fiction: short story

GRAMMAR
- Semicolons between main clauses

SPEAKING, LISTENING, AND VIEWING
- Improvisation
- Oral presentation

PRINT AND MEDIA RESOURCES

UNIT ONE RESOURCE BOOK
Strategic Reading: Literature, p. 19
Vocabulary SkillBuilder, p. 20

GRAMMAR MINI-LESSONS
Transparencies, p. 39
Copymasters, p. 41

WRITING MINI-LESSONS
Transparencies, p. 56

ACCESS FOR STUDENTS ACQUIRING ENGLISH
Selection Summaries
Reading Support

FORMAL ASSESSMENT
Selection Test, pp. 11–12
 Test Generator

 AUDIO LIBRARY
See Reference Card

LASERLINKS
Historical Connection
Visual Vocabulary

INTERNET RESOURCES
McDougal Littell Literature Center at http://www.hmco.com /mcdougal/lit

THE LANGUAGE OF LITERATURE TEACHER'S EDITION

SUMMARY

Ivan Vassilievich claims that everything in life depends on chance, as he recalls how the direction of his own life changed one night after a ball. He was in love with the beautiful Varenka, daughter of a colonel, and left the ball early in the morning, intoxicated with love after dancing with Varenka most of the night. Unable to sleep, Ivan wandered toward Varenka's home. In the field near her house, he saw a military procession and heard the sounds of a fife and drum, evil and ominous. A runaway Tartar was being mercilessly whipped and pummeled under the cruel supervision of Varenka's father. Filled with anguish at what he had witnessed, Ivan questioned what the colonel knew that he did not. Ivan decided not to do any of the things that he had planned to do in the future. His love for Varenka subsided and ultimately came to nothing.

CUSTOMIZING FOR
Students Acquiring English

- Use **ACCESS FOR STUDENTS ACQUIRING ENGLISH,** *Reading Support.*
- This selection may challenge some students because of its complex sentence structure. You may want to read page 53 aloud to get students into the story.
- As you guide students through the selection, you may want to use the suggestions under Strategic Reading for Less-Proficient Readers as well as the suggestions in these boxes.

STRATEGIC READING FOR
Less-Proficient Readers

Set a Purpose Read the display type on page 53 and elicit that "circumstances" may include such things as where we live, who our parents are, and how much money we have. Then elicit that "chance," on the other hand, includes those unpredictable events that affect us deeply. Ask students to read to find out about the circumstances and chance events in the life of young Ivan Vassilievich.

Use **UNIT ONE RESOURCE BOOK,** p. 19, for guidance in reading the selection.

The Reception (about 1883–1885), James Tissot. Oil on canvas, 56″ × 40″, Albright-Knox Art Gallery, Buffalo, New York, gift of William M. Chase, 1909.

WORDS TO KNOW

chagrin (shə-grĭn′) *n.* a feeling of humiliation or embarrassment (p. 61)

detestable (dĭ-těs′tə-bəl) *adj.* worthy of scorn; hateful (p. 55)

ethereal (ĭ-thîr′ē-əl) *adj.* not earthly; heavenly (p. 55)

imposing (ĭm-pō′zĭng) *adj.* impressive (p. 56)

irate (ī-rāt′) *adj.* extremely angry; enraged (p. 61)

majestic (mə-jĕs′tĭk) *adj.* showing lofty dignity or nobility; stately (p. 54)

maliciously (mə-lĭsh′əs-lē) *adv.* with ill will; spitefully (p. 61)

perspicacity (pûr′spĭ-kăs′ĭ-tē) *n.* keen perception or understanding (p. 55)

pummel (pŭm′əl) *v.* to hit repeatedly; beat (p. 60)

unassuming (ŭn′ə-soō′mĭng) *adj.* not pretentious; modest (p. 56)

 VISUAL VOCABULARY

- **mazurka** (mə-zûr′kə)
- **quadrille** (kwŏ-drĭl′)

Side A, Frame 49310

52 THE LANGUAGE OF LITERATURE TEACHER'S EDITION

After the Ball

Leo Tolstoy

"You say a man can't tell good from evil, that everything depends on circumstances, that circumstances determine everything. While I think everything depends on chance. I speak from my own experience."

These were the much-respected Ivan Vassilievich's[1] introductory words following a discussion we had had about the necessity of changing living conditions before people could improve themselves. Strictly speaking, no one had said it was impossible to tell good from evil, but Ivan Vassilievich had a way of answering the thoughts a discussion provoked in his own mind, and then recounting episodes of his own life related to these thoughts. He was often so transported by his story, particularly since he told stories earnestly and honestly, that he completely forgot his reason for telling it. That is what happened this time, too.

"I speak from my own experience. My whole life took one direction instead of another, not because of circumstances, but something completely different."

---
1. Ivan Vassilievich (ĭ-vän′ və-syĭl′yə-vĭch′).

Literary Concept: FORESHADOWING

C Invite students to suggest how this hint of things to come builds readers' interest in the story. *(Possible response: It makes readers curious to find out about this one chance event that had such an impact on Ivan.)*

Literary Concept: FICTION

D Remind students that the story and the characters in it are fictional. Then ask why Tolstoy doesn't give Varenka's surname. *(Possible response: The use of "B——" creates the illusion that the story is about a real person; this helps readers get involved in the plot.)*

Literary Note

E The biographical details of Ivan's life are very similar to those of Tolstoy's. A wealthy, aristocratic youth, Tolstoy attended a provincial university in the 1840s and enjoyed carousing and gambling. In fact, it was largely to escape the lure of Moscow's gaming tables that Tolstoy joined the army in the Crimea, where he witnessed an event similar to that described later in this story.

Literary Concept: CHARACTER

F Invite students to tell what they know so far about Ivan from the comments of his friends and listeners. *(Possible responses: He is modest; he describes situations well; he is "much respected"; he tells stories "earnestly and honestly.")*

CUSTOMIZING FOR
Students Acquiring English

1 Define *puce* as "a dark red" and *coronet* as "a small crown."

2 Define *serfs* as "peasants who were owned by a lord and bound to the land."

"What was it then?" we asked.

"Well, that's a long story. To make you understand, I'd have to explain it at length."

"Well, tell us."

Ivan Vassilievich became thoughtful, nodded his head.

"Yes," he said. "My whole life was changed by one night, or rather by one morning."

"But what happened?"

"It happened that I was greatly in love. I had been in love many times, but this was my greatest love. It's past: she has married daughters by now. It was B——, yes, Varenka B—— (Ivan Vassilievich mentioned her surname). At the age of fifteen, she was already a remarkable beauty. As a young girl of eighteen, she was enchanting: tall, well-formed, graceful, <u>majestic</u>—most of all, majestic. She carried herself unusually erect as though she were unable to do otherwise, tipping her head slightly back. Despite her slenderness, even boniness, this posture gave her, with her beauty and her height, a sort of queenly aspect which would have frightened people away from her had it not been for her tenderness, the merry smile on her lips, her enchanting, sparkling eyes, and her whole sweet young self."

"How well Ivan Vassilievich describes her!"

"No matter how much I described her, I could never make you realize what she was like. But that's beside the point; what I wanted to tell about happened in the forties. I was then a student in a provincial university. Whether it was good or bad I don't know, but at that time we had no clubs or theories in our universities; and we were simply young men, living as young men do: studying and being merry. I was a very gay and venturesome boy, and rich as well. I had a fast trotter and used to take sleigh rides in the hills with the ladies (skates were not yet in fashion) and carouse with my comrades (at that time we drank nothing but champagne; if we had no money, we didn't drink, but we never drank vodka as we do now). Parties and balls were my greatest pleasures. I was a good dancer and not ugly."

"No need to be modest," interrupted one of the ladies. "After all, we've seen your daguerreotype.[2] You weren't just not ugly; you were handsome."

"Handsome or not, that's beside the point. The point is that at the time of my greatest love for her, I was at a ball given the last day of Shrovetide[3] by the provincial governor, an affable old man, rich, a generous host, and a nobleman. His wife received equally graciously in a puce velvet dress with her diamond coronet on her head, and her bare, old, plump, white shoulders and throat like the portrait of Elizabeth Petrovna.[4] The ball was marvelous: an excellent ballroom, singers, and musicians—the serfs of a music-loving landowner who were then famous, a magnificent buffet, and a sea of champagne. Although I loved champagne, I did not drink because I was drunk with love without wine, but

> "At the age of fifteen, she was already a remarkable beauty. As a young girl of eighteen, she was enchanting: tall, well formed, graceful, majestic—most of all, majestic."

---

2. **daguerreotype** (də-gâr′ə-tīp′): an early type of photograph.
3. **the last day of Shrovetide**: Mardi Gras, a day of festivity preceding the fasting and penance of the Christian season of Lent.
4. **Elizabeth Petrovna** (pə-trôv′nə): empress of Russia from 1741 to 1762.

WORDS TO KNOW
majestic (mə-jĕs′tĭk) *adj.* showing lofty dignity or nobility; stately

I danced until exhausted; I danced quadrilles[5] and waltzes and polkas; everything I could, of course, with Varenka. She wore a white dress, a pink sash, and white kid gloves just short of her thin, sharp elbows, and white satin slippers. The detestable Engineer Anisimov[6] beat me to the mazurkas[7]—to this day I haven't forgiven him for that. He had invited her just as she arrived, while I had had to go to the hairdresser's and to fetch a pair of gloves, and was late. So it happened that I danced the mazurka not with her, but with a German girl I had courted a bit before. But I'm afraid I was not very polite to her; I didn't talk to her, didn't look at her; I saw only the tall, well-formed figure in the white dress with the pink sash, her radiant, pink-cheeked, dimpled face and her gentle, kind eyes. I was not alone; everyone looked at her and loved her; men and women loved her, in spite of the fact that she eclipsed them all. It was impossible not to love her.

According to the rules, so to speak, I was not her partner for the mazurkas; but in reality, I danced with her almost all the time. In cotillions,[8] she would cross the whole ballroom straight to me without embarrassment, and I would jump up without waiting for her invitation, and she would thank me for my perspicacity with a smile. When she failed to guess what character trait I had chosen to represent, she would give her hand to someone other than me with a shrug of her thin shoulders and would smile at me as a sign of regret and consolation. When the mazurka featured a waltz, I would waltz with her for a long time, and she, often out of breath, would smile and say 'Encore'[9] to me. And I would waltz again, feeling completely bodiless."

"Come, how could you feel bodiless! I should think you would feel quite the opposite when you took her by the waist; not only your own body, but hers," said one of the guests.

Ivan Vassilievich suddenly blushed and almost shouted in his anger:

"Yes, that's like you, indeed, today's youth. You see nothing but bodies. In our day it wasn't like that. The more I loved her, the more ethereal she became for me. Now you can see feet, ankles, and still more; you denude the women you love; for me, as Alphonse Karr said—now there was a good writer—the object of my love always wore clothes of bronze. We not only did not denude them but tried to cover up their nakedness, like the good son of Noah. But you wouldn't understand . . ."

"Don't listen to him. What happened next?" said one of us.

"Yes. So I danced some more with her not noticing how time was passing. The musicians had already reached a sort of desperate stage of tiredness, you know, as often happens at the end of a ball; they kept repeating the same mazurka; the papas and mamas had already gotten up from the card tables in the salons and were waiting for supper; the lackeys[10] ran back and forth more and more frequently. It was after two. I had to make use of the last remaining minutes. I chose her once more, and we went across the ballroom for the hundredth time.

"'Then, after supper, the quadrille is mine?' I asked her, escorting her back to her place.

---

5. **quadrilles** (kwŏ-drĭlz'): dances performed by groups of four couples.
6. **Anisimov** (ə-nyĭs'ĭ-môv').
7. **mazurkas** (mə-zûr'kəz): lively Polish dances similar to the polka.
8. **cotillions** (kō-tĭl'yənz): ballroom dances for couples.
9. **encore** (äN-kôr') *French:* again; once more.
10. **lackeys:** servants.

WORDS TO KNOW	**detestable** (dĭ-tĕs'tə-bəl) *adj.* worthy of scorn; hateful **perspicacity** (pûr'spĭ-kăs'ĭ-tē) *n.* keen perception or understanding **ethereal** (ĭ-thîr'ē-əl) *adj.* not earthly; heavenly

---

Mini-Lesson Grammar

SEMICOLONS BETWEEN MAIN CLAUSES
Show students that semicolons often join the main clauses of a compound sentence, as in this quotation from the story: "No, I was too happy; I could not sleep." A main clause contains a subject and a verb and can stand alone as a sentence. Invite students to find the main clauses and the three semicolons in the  passage above. Explain that the semicolons show the close relationship of the clauses they join.

Application Invite students to tell where the semicolons belong in these sentences from the story.

1. I was not alone everyone looked at her and loved her her men and women loved her.
2. I was happy, blessed I was pure I was not I, but a kind of unearthly being.

Reteaching/Reinforcement
- *Grammar Handbook,* anthology p. 1089
- *Grammar Mini-Lessons* copymasters p. 41, transparencies p. 39

The Writer's Craft

The Semicolon, pp. 804–805
Compound Sentences, pp. 619–620

CUSTOMIZING FOR
Students Acquiring English

④ "I was not I . . . only of good." Ask students to paraphrase this statement of Ivan's, using context clues. *(Possible responses: I did not feel like myself anymore; I was so happy I felt as if I were in heaven.)*

Linking to History

L Czar Nicholas I, ruler of Russia at the time of this story, was noted both for his stylish good looks and for his harshness. He refused to allow any moves toward political reform and avidly supported serfdom—a form of slavery in which peasants toiled for the owners of large estates. Nicholas's rule was profoundly corrupt. He created a powerful and cruel police system, banned all political organizations, introduced censorship, and exiled writers with liberal views.

STRATEGIC READING FOR
Less-Proficient Readers

M Ask students to give their impressions of Varenka's father. *(He is a handsome army colonel who seems to be friendly, kind, and a loving parent.)* **Evaluating**

Ask them how Ivan feels about the colonel. *(Ivan admires him; watching him dance with his daughter fills Ivan with "intense emotion.")* **Summarizing**

Set a Purpose Have students read on to find out where Ivan next sees the colonel.

"'Of course; if they don't take me home,' she said, smiling.

"'I won't give you up,' I said.

"'Give me back my fan, anyway,' she said.

"'It's hard to give it back,' I said, handing back her <u>unassuming</u>, white fan.

"'Then I'll give you something so you won't be sad,' she said and tore off a feather from the fan to give me.

"I took the feather and could only express all my enthusiasm and gratitude with a look. I was not only merry and content, I was happy, blessed; I was pure; I was not I, but a kind of unearthly being, knowing no evil and capable only of good. I hid the feather in my glove and stood there, powerless to leave her.

④

"'Look, Papa is asking someone to dance,' she said to me, pointing out the tall, dignified figure of her father, a colonel with silver epaulettes,[11] standing at the entrance with the hostess and other ladies.

"'Varenka, come here,' we heard the deep voice of the hostess with her diamond coronet and Elizabethan shoulders say.

"Varenka went to the entrance, and I followed her.

"'Come, *ma chère*,[12] your father will dance with you. Please, now, Piotr Vladislavich.' The hostess turned toward the colonel.

"Varenka's father was a very handsome, <u>imposing</u>, and well-preserved old man. His face was rosy with curled, white mustaches *à la* Nikolai I[13] joining his equally white sideburns with their curls combed forward at the temples. His eyes and lips wore the same gentle, joyous smile as his daughter's. He had a handsome build: long, well-formed legs, strong shoulders,

L

> "The entire ballroom followed the couple's every movement. As for me, I was not just admiring, but was watching them with intense emotion."

and a military chest bearing large, unornate decorations. He was a military commander in the tradition of Nikolai I.

"When we reached the entrance, the colonel was protesting, saying he had forgotten how to dance, but just the same, smiling, bending his left hand behind him, he unbuckled his sword, handed it to an obliging young man, and pulling his chamois[14] glove on his right hand—'Must observe the rules,' he said, smiling—he took his daughter's hand and stood in the third row, waiting for the beat.

"At the beginning of the mazurka theme, he nimbly tapped one leg, bent the other, and his tall, robust figure moved around the ballroom, now quietly and smoothly, now noisily and energetically, clicking his feet together. The graceful figure of Varenka swam around him, from time to time imperceptibly shortening or lengthening the steps of her tiny, white satin shoes. The entire ballroom followed the couple's every movement. As for me, I was not just admiring, but was watching them with intense emotion. I was particularly impressed by his boots, drawn tight with straps—fine, calf boots, but unfashionable, ancient ones with square toes and no heels. They were obviously designed as battle boots. 'So his beloved daughter can be well dressed and go out, he wears

---

11. **epaulettes** (ĕp′ə-lĕts′): ornamental fringed shoulder pads on a military uniform.
12. *ma chère* (mä shĕr) *French:* my dear.
13. *à la* **Nikolai** (nyĭk-ə-lī′) **I:** in the style of Nicholas I, czar of Russia from 1825 to 1855.
14. **chamois** (shăm′ē): a soft leather made from the skin of an antelope.

| WORDS TO KNOW | **unassuming** (ŭn′ə-sōō′mĭng) *adj.* not pretentious; modest |
| | **imposing** (ĭm-pō′zĭng) *adj.* impressive |

56

Mini-Lesson — Literary Concepts

REVIEWING SETTING Remind students that details of setting are often used to create a particular mood. In the ballroom scene, Tolstoy describes the colonel's dancing, the mazurka melody, the card tables in the salon, and the servants. He also describes Varenka's tiny white satin shoes and her white feathered fan. Such details create a festive, romantic mood and help the reader to appreciate the grace, beauty, and joy of the party.

Application Have students think about how these details of the ballroom setting contrast sharply with the foggy, dreary field by Varenka's house (described on page 59). Ask students to write a few adjectives describing the field and the feeling it evokes.

Self-Portrait (about 1865), James Tissot. The Fine Arts Museums of San Francisco, Mildred Anna Williams Collection (1961.16).

Art Note

Self-Portrait by James Tissot In his day, Tissot was considered to be a highly successful gentleman-painter, a position much more admired then than now. He was thought to be well-groomed and to carry himself with reserved elegance. His success, however, caused critics to make jealous and often sarcastic comments about his work. His reputation later came under attack for a variety of reasons. He lost the admiration of French friends and patrons when he joined the Paris Commune; later, he was discredited in England as a result of a scandal in his private life.

Reading the Art *What do you think the artist in the portrait is thinking?*

Literary Concept:
DESCRIPTION

N Ask students why they think Tolstoy describes the details of the colonel's "primitive" square-toed "battle boots." *(Possible response: The boots seem out of place when compared to the rest of the colonel's elegant clothing; perhaps the battlefield, not the ballroom, is the true domain of the colonel.)*

Literary Concept: SIMILE

O How does this simile help you appreciate Ivan's feelings of love? *(Possible response: It helps us visualize Ivan as being swept away by a love that he cannot contain.)*

Critical Thinking: SPECULATING

P Remind students that Ivan is telling about a chance event that changed his life forever. Elicit that he hasn't yet described this event. Then, after pointing out this bit of foreshadowing, have volunteers speculate on what might happen in the second half of the story.

Literary Concept: SYMBOL

Q Have students suggest how the white feather from the fan can be interpreted as a symbol of Ivan's love for Varenka. *(Possible response: The white color suggests purity, and the bird's feather symbolizes Ivan's high-soaring feelings while dancing with Varenka.)*

Critical Thinking: DRAWING CONCLUSIONS

R How has Ivan's love for Varenka affected his feelings for the people and things around him? *(Possible response: He views his brother, his servant, and aspects of everyday life with the deepest affection.)*

---

primitive shoes instead of buying fashionable new ones,' I thought, and those square toes on his boots particularly affected me. It was evident that he had once danced beautifully, but now he was heavy, and his legs were not sufficiently limber for all the elegant, rapid steps he tried to execute. But he completed two turns of the room skillfully, just the same. Everyone burst into loud applause when, quickly spreading his legs apart then joining them together again, he dropped, although somewhat heavily, on one knee, while she, smiling and straightening her skirt, which he had ruffled, turned smoothly around him. Raising himself with some effort, he tenderly and gently placed his hands on his daughter's ears and, kissing her on the forehead, led her back to me on the assumption that I had the next dance. I said that I was not her partner.

"'Well, it doesn't matter; go with her now,' he said, smiling kindly and replacing his sword.

"It was as though a huge stream had been poured into a bottle which was only one drop short of full—that was how my love for Varenka released all the hidden capacities for love in my heart. I embraced the whole world with my love then. I loved the hostess in her coronet with her Elizabethan bust, and her husband, and her guests, and her lackeys, and even the sulking Engineer Anisimov. Toward her father, with his clumsy boots and his gentle smile so like hers, I felt an intense, tender emotion.

"The mazurka came to an end, and the hostess asked the guests to come to supper, but Colonel B. declined, saying he had to get up early the following day, and he bid the hosts good-by. I was afraid he would take her away, but she stayed with her mother.

"After supper I danced the promised quadrille with her, and although it seemed to me I was already infinitely happy, my happiness kept growing and growing. We never spoke of love. I never even asked either her or myself whether she loved me. It was sufficient for me that I loved her. The only thing I feared was that something might spoil my happiness.

"When I reached home, undressed and thought of sleep, I realized that sleeping was out of the question. In my hand lay the feather from her fan and the glove she had given me when she got into her carriage, and I had helped seat first her mother, then her. I looked at these things and without closing my eyes saw her before me when, choosing between two partners, she guessed the character trait I was representing; I could hear her sweet voice as she said: 'It's pride. Right?'—and gladly gave me her hand. I saw her, as she sipped a glass of champagne at supper and looked up at me with her tender eyes. But I saw her most clearly as she danced with her father, glided smoothly around him, and glanced with pride and joy at the admiring spectators. And I unconsciously included them both in the same gentle, tender emotion.

"At that time, my late brother and I lived alone. My brother did not like society at all and did not go to balls; he was preparing himself for his baccalaureate[15] at that time and led a particularly regulated life. He was asleep. I looked at his head buried in his pillow and half-covered with a flannel blanket, and I felt an affectionate pity for him; pity because he did not know or share my happiness. Our servant, Petrusha, met me with a candle and wanted to help me undress, but I let him go. The sight of his sleepy face and disheveled hair seemed very touching to me. Trying to make no noise, I went to my own room on tiptoe and sat down on the bed. No, I was too happy; I could not sleep. Then I began to feel too hot in the heated rooms, and, still dressed, I went quietly out to

---

15. **baccalaureate** (băk′ə-lôr′ē-ĭt): bachelor's degree.

58 UNIT ONE PART 1: LASTING IMPRESSIONS

Mini-Lesson Genre Study

FICTION Explain that "After the Ball" is the type of fiction known as a **short story**. Have students identify features of this genre, and list them on the board on a word web, such as the one shown.

Application Have students discuss how "After the Ball" contains each of the features on the web.

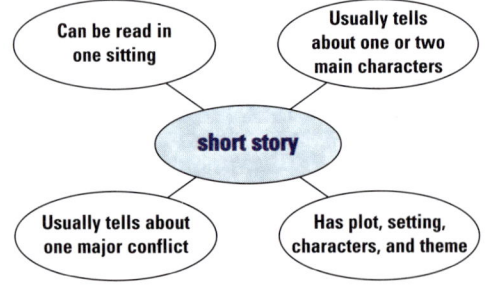

the entry, put on my overcoat, opened the outer door and went into the street.

"I had left the ball at five o'clock, then gone home and sat there a bit; two hours had gone by, and when I went out it was already light. It was typical Shrovetide weather: fog, water-soaked snow melting on the roads, and water dripping from all the roofs. The B——s then lived at the edge of town, next to a big field with a promenade[16] at one end and a girl's school at the other. I went through our deserted side street and came out onto a big road, where I began to encounter people on foot and others carting firewood on sleds, whose runners scraped the pavement. The horses, rhythmically swinging their wet heads under the glistening shaft bows, and the drivers covered with sacking, splashing in huge boots near their wagons, and the houses looking very tall in the fog—all seemed particularly dear and meaningful to me.

"When I came to the field where her house stood, I saw at the end of it, in the direction of the promenade, something large and black, and I heard the sounds of a fife and drum coming from there. All this time I had continued humming and hearing the theme of the mazurka intermittently. But this was a different, cruel, evil music.

"'What can it be?' I thought, and crossing the middle of the field over a slippery path, I walked in the direction of the sound. After covering a hundred paces, I began to discern a number of black forms through the fog. Soldiers, obviously. 'It must be a drill,' I thought, and along with a blacksmith in his greasy coat and apron, carrying something and walking in front of me, I went closer. Soldiers in dark uniforms were drawn up in two ranks facing each other, standing motionless, holding their rifles at their sides. Behind them stood the drummer and the fifer, repeating the same unpleasant, shrill melody without stopping.

"'What are they doing?' I asked the blacksmith, who had stopped next to me.

"'They're whipping a Tartar[17] for running off,' the blacksmith said angrily, glancing at the farthest end of the ranks.

"I looked in that direction and between the ranks caught sight of something dreadful moving toward me. It was a man stripped to the waist, tied to the rifles of two soldiers, who led him. Next to him walked a tall officer in an overcoat and forage cap whose face seemed familiar to me. Resisting with his whole body, his feet splashing in the melting snow, the victim was lurching toward me under the blows falling on him from both sides; now he keeled over backward—and the sergeants who were dragging him by their rifles shoved him forward; then he fell forward—and the sergeants, preventing him from falling, pulled him back. And never leaving the victim's side, halting and advancing with a firm tread, was the tall officer. It was her father, with his rosy face and white mustache and sideburns.

"At each blow, the victim, as if surprised, turned his pain-distorted face to the side from which it fell and, disclosing his white teeth, repeated the same words over and over. It was only when he was very close that I heard these words clearly. He sobbed rather than said: 'Brothers, have mercy. Brothers, have mercy.' But his brothers did not have mercy, and when the procession was even with me, I saw how the soldier standing opposite me stepped forward

> "I looked in that direction and between the ranks caught sight of something dreadful moving toward me."

---

16. **promenade:** a public walkway.
17. **Tartar:** a member of a Turkic people of southern Russia.

Art Note

The Monument to Peter I on Senate Square in Petersburg by Vasilii Ivanovich Surikov Descended from a long line of Siberian Cossacks, Surikov (1848–1916) often took trips to Siberia and Crimea. He is best known for his monuments—in this case, a beautiful historic site on the bank of the Neva River. In the background looms St. Isaac's Cathedral.

Reading the Art What mood does this fog-shrouded scene of sleds in a snowy square evoke in you?

Literary Concept: MOOD

U Have students identify words and phrases in this scene that establish a mood of horror and helplessness. *(Possible responses: "pain-distorted"; "sobbed"; "swinging his stick"; "striped, wet, red")*

STRATEGIC READING FOR
Less-Proficient Readers

V Ask students what Ivan has just learned about Varenka's father. *(Possible responses: He is a brutal disciplinarian; he is inhumane.)* **Drawing Conclusions**

Ask students if they can think of other characters in literature or history with two sides to their personality. *(Possible response: Dr. Jekyll and Mr. Hyde)* **Connecting**

Set a Purpose Have students complete the story to see how learning about this side of the colonel affects Ivan.

The Monument to Peter I on Senate Square in Petersburg (1870), Vasilii Ivanovich Surikov. The State Russian Museum, St. Petersburg, Russia.

decisively and, swinging his stick through the air with a swish, brought it down hard on the Tartar's back. The Tartar pulled forward, but the sergeants held him back, and an identical blow fell on him from the other side, and then again from this side, and again from the other side. The colonel walked on, looking now at the victim, now at his own feet, drawing in his breath, blowing out his cheeks, and letting the air out slowly through his puckered mouth. When the procession had passed the spot where I stood, I caught a glimpse of the victim's back between the ranks. It was striped, wet, red; unrecognizable to the point that I could not believe it was the body of a man.

"'Oh, God,' murmured the blacksmith beside me.

"The procession was moving on, and the blows continued to fall from both sides just as before on the stumbling, shrinking man, and the drum beat as before, and the fife played, and, as before, the tall, dignified figure of the colonel moved with a firm tread next to the victim. Suddenly the colonel stopped and approached one of the soldiers abruptly.

"'I'll trounce you,' I heard his <u>irate</u> voice say. 'Will you beat now? Will you?'

"And I saw him <u>pummel</u> the frightened, under-

WORDS TO KNOW
irate (ī-rāt′) *adj.* extremely angry; enraged
pummel (pŭm′əl) *v.* to hit repeatedly; beat

Critic's Corner

"Even if no other literature survived from Russia in the first decade of this century except this one, extremely short story ["After the Ball"], we should be able to predict the Revolution, and the subsequent character of Russian life in the twentieth century. It contains all the horrible paradox that a nation which can feel so tenderly has somehow been condemned to policemen and armies and governors of the most ruthless severity."

A. N. Wilson
From his biography of Leo Tolstoy

How might this story "predict" the Communist Revolution of 1917 and the cruelty of subsequent Russian leaders such as Joseph Stalin?

sized, frail soldier with his strong, chamois-gloved hand for not having brought his stick down hard enough on the Tartar's red back.

"'Form fresh gauntlets!'[18] he cried and, glancing around, caught sight of me. He pretended he did not know me; he frowned threateningly and maliciously, hurriedly turned around. All the way home I kept hearing first the roll of the drum beating and the whistle of the fife, and then the self-assured, irate voice of the colonel shouting: 'Will you beat now? Will you?' And in my heart there was an almost physical anguish approaching nausea, so strong that I stopped several times, and I felt as though I were about to vomit all the horror with which the spectacle had filled me. I don't remember how I got home and into bed. But as soon as I started to fall asleep, I heard and saw everything again and jumped up.

"'Obviously, he knows something I don't know,' I thought in reference to the colonel. 'If I knew what he knows, I would understand what I saw, and it would not disturb me.' But no matter how much I thought about it, I couldn't figure out what it was the colonel knew, and I went to sleep only toward evening, and then only after visiting a friend and drinking with him until I was completely drunk.

"I suppose you think that I decided then that what I had seen was an evil thing? Not at all. 'If this was done with such conviction and recognized as necessary by all, then it must be that they knew something that I didn't know,' I thought, and I tried to find out what. But no matter how I tried, I could not find out. And not having found out, I could not go into military service, as I had previously wanted to, and not only did I not go into service, but I never served anywhere and, as you see, was never fit for anything."

"Come, we know how you were never fit for anything," said one of us. "But tell us: how many people are really fit for anything, if you're not?"

"Come, that's complete nonsense," Ivan Vassilievich said with sincere chagrin.

"But what about love?" we asked.

"Love? From that day, love went into a decline. When, as frequently happened, she became thoughtful, although still smiling, I would immediately remember the colonel on the field; it became somehow awkward and unpleasant for me, and I began seeing her less frequently. And so love came to nothing. That's how these things happen, and that's what changes and determines a man's whole life. And you say . . . ," and thus he finished. ❖

Translated by Arthur Mendel and Barbara Makanowitzky

---

18. **gauntlets** (gônt′lĭts): two parallel lines of people who deliver punishment by striking with clubs or other weapons a person forced to run between them.

WORDS TO KNOW
maliciously (mə-lĭsh′əs-lē) *adv.* with ill will; spitefully
chagrin (shə-grĭn′) *n.* a feeling of humiliation or embarrassment

From Personal Response to Critical Analysis

1. Responses will vary.
2. Possible responses: Ivan's love for Varenka fades because he cannot forget her father's cruelty; perhaps Ivan feels that Varenka herself is contaminated by her father's actions; Ivan has lost his innocence and can no longer believe in love.
3. Possible responses: Tolstoy may have wanted to show that the colonel was cruel to anyone who got in his way; Tolstoy may have wanted to show that Ivan represented a threat to the colonel's unchecked power.
4. Possible responses: Some students may feel that Ivan is better off for having learned about the colonel's cruelty before becoming his son-in-law and joining the army; other students may feel that witnessing such cruelty destroyed Ivan's ideals and high spirits.
5. Some students may agree, pointing out that two major decisions in Ivan's life—his marriage and his career—were changed by one chance event; others may disagree, saying that Ivan's story is just as much about circumstances as about chance.
6. Accept all reasonable responses.
7. Some students may feel that corporal punishment is unjustified because it is cruel or unlikely to change behavior; others may feel that corporal punishment is an effective deterrent for some offenses.

Literary Link

Like Ivan Vassilievich, Sŏngsam in "Cranes" refuses to accept the harsh cruelty of the military. Ask students how the two men's responses differ. *(Sŏngsam takes a more active stance against the military, freeing a prisoner who is to be shot; Ivan decides to take no part in the system.)*

Another Pathway

Cooperative Learning Students may divide their work within the group as follows: One or two students may review the events leading up to Ivan's witnessing the colonel's brutality. One or two students may review the course of Ivan's life after he sees that brutal scene. Another student might be responsible for retelling the narrative in a straightforward chronology.

RESPONDING
OPTIONS

FROM PERSONAL RESPONSE TO CRITICAL ANALYSIS

REFLECT
1. What images and ideas from the story linger in your mind? Record them in your notebook and share them with a partner.

RETHINK
2. Why do you think the colonel's actions lead to a change in Ivan Vassilievich's feelings for Varenka?

3. Ivan reveals that when the colonel caught sight of him the morning after the ball, "he pretended he did not know me; he frowned threateningly and maliciously, hurriedly turned around." Why do you think Tolstoy includes this detail in his story?

4. Do you think Ivan is better off because of what he saw after the ball?
   Consider
   Close Textual Reading
   - how his friends describe him
   - how the course of his life was changed
   - how he views his life

5. Ivan tells his story to illustrate that everything depends on "chance" rather than "circumstances." Do you think he succeeds? Explain your answer.

6. Compare the chart you made for the Reading Connection on page 51 with those of your classmates, giving reasons for your assessment of each character as good or evil.

RELATE
7. In American society, corporal (bodily) punishment is less common than it once was, but it still exists. Drawing on your own ideas and observations and on the depiction of corporal punishment in "After the Ball," comment on whether you think its use is ever justified.

ANOTHER PATHWAY

Cooperative Learning
Work with a small group to adapt the plot of "After the Ball" to a contemporary American setting. For example, you might have the events take place at a high school prom, or you might have Varenka's father be a police officer. Perform your adaptation as an improvisation for the class.

QUICKWRITES

1. Imagine that you are a gossip columnist for a Russian newspaper. Write a **newspaper column** about the ball. Include descriptions of Varenka, her father, and Ivan, as well as details about romance in the making.

2. Write a **dramatic scene** in which the colonel explains to his daughter the beating of the Tartar.

3. Varenka may know nothing of the event that turns Ivan's love away from her. Create a **letter** that Varenka writes to an advice column, explaining her situation and feelings. Also provide a reply.

4. With a partner, devise an alternative to the gauntlet as a means of punishing deserters. Write a **proposal** to the czar in which you explain your idea.

📁 **PORTFOLIO** Save your writing. You may want to use it later as a springboard to a piece for your portfolio.

62 UNIT ONE PART 1: LASTING IMPRESSIONS

QuickWrites

1. Discuss the breezy, coy tone typical of a gossip columnist. If possible, read a sample column from a local newspaper.
2. You might suggest that students begin their scenes by having Varenka confront her father about the beating, linking it to Ivan's sudden coolness toward her.
3. Have students work in pairs to brainstorm possible advice the columnist might give.
4. Have students begin their proposals by outlining the reasons why running the gauntlet is a cruel and ineffective punishment.

📄 The Writer's Craft

Tone, p. 422
Using Dialogue in Plays, pp. 453–454

LITERARY CONCEPTS

A **flashback** is an account of a conversation, an episode, or an event that happened before the beginning of a story. Often a flashback interrupts the chronological flow of a story to give information that can help readers to understand a character's present situation. "After the Ball" is a story told almost entirely in flashback. The events that happened to Ivan as a young man help readers to understand why he now believes that chance is more important than circumstances in determining the course of a person's life.

With four or five classmates, re-create the chronology of events in this story. Then have one person retell the story in strict chronological order, without the use of a flashback. As a whole group, compare the retelling with the original. What does Tolstoy gain or lose by using a flashback?

CRITIC'S CORNER

The Russian critic Leo Shestov said: "In his youth Tolstoy described life as a fascinating ball; and later, when he was old, it was like the running of the gauntlet." How does this comment apply to "After the Ball" (which, by the way, was written when Tolstoy was in his 70s)?

ART CONNECTION

How does the portrait on page 57 compare to your own mental image of the young Ivan?

Detail of *Self-Portrait* (about 1865), James Tissot. The Fine Arts Museums of San Francisco, Mildred Anna Williams Collection (1961.16).

Multimodal Learning

ALTERNATIVE ACTIVITIES

1. Put together a series of **musical recordings** that represent the different parts of the story. For example, you might choose a waltz or mazurka to represent the ball; a darker, more serious piece of music might represent Ivan's witnessing the beating. Share your recordings with the class.

2. Create a **costume sketch** of the clothing of one or more of the characters. Use details from the story as well as books about the fashions of 19th-century Russian society for ideas.

Russian gown

ACROSS THE CURRICULUM

History Find out more about Tolstoy's philosophy of nonviolent resistance and its effects on such 20th-century reformers as Martin Luther King, Jr., and Mohandas K. Gandhi. Present your findings in the form of a magazine article.

AFTER THE BALL **63**

Critic's Corner

You might share with students that Tolstoy, like Ivan in the story, was a wealthy young nobleman. Tolstoy had a 22-room mansion and a large estate called Yasnaya Polyana. After finishing his university education, Tolstoy enjoyed the typical idle life of an aristocrat, gambling away about a quarter of his inheritance. Also explain that Tolstoy's relentless search for truth in his later years led him to iconoclastic and controversial views that put him at odds with the Russian government, the Russian Orthodox Church, and his own wife and children.

Across the Curriculum

History Encourage students to make use of indexes in reference books and in biographies of King and Gandhi. Students may find it helpful to search through computerized indexes, using *nonviolence*, *Tolstoy*, *Martin Luther King, Jr.*, and *Gandhi* as search words.

Art Connection

Students might point out that the figure shown on page 57 is young and handsome, like Ivan. Moreover, the expression on his face suggests someone who is sensitive and thoughtful, much like young Ivan.

Literary Concepts

The following questions may help students put together a chronology of the story:
- How old is Varenka at the ball? How old is she when Ivan recalls the events years later?
- Where in the story do old Ivan's friends interrupt his storytelling with comments and questions?

Alternative Activities

1. Interested students might record a soundtrack that could accompany an oral reading of the story. Point out that the music needs to convey an appropriate mood but that it does not necessarily have to reflect the time period of the selection.

2. In addition to drawing the elaborate mid-19th-century ball gowns worn by Varenka and the hostess, students might research uniforms worn by Russian army officers in the 1840s. Students might also contrast these styles with those worn at the turn of the century, when old Ivan tells his story.

Words to Know

Exercise A
1. d
2. e
3. c
4. d
5. a

Exercise B
1. b
2. b
3. a
4. a
5. c

Reteaching/Reinforcement
• *Unit One Resource Book*, p. 20

LEO TOLSTOY

After serving in the army, Leo Tolstoy opened his own elementary school and taught the children of serfs. Much ahead of his time, he successfully showed that teaching should be adapted to the individual needs of the pupil. Tolstoy believed that everyone had the power to understand what is good and that striving to do good was a way for people to justify themselves.

AUTHOR BACKGROUND
Leo Tolstoy Tolstoy is considered by many to be the greatest Russian novelist. This film clip highlights his life and work.

Side A, Frame 422

WORDS TO KNOW

EXERCISE A Determine the relationship between each pair of capitalized words below. On your paper, write the letter of the choice that shows the most similar relationship.

1. QUEEN : MAJESTIC :: (a) comedy : tragic (b) sky : dark (c) recreation : sports (d) monster : gruesome (e) education : elementary
2. CHAGRIN : EMBARRASSMENT :: (a) ability : musical (b) expense : tax (c) misery : joy (d) sleep : death (e) worry : anxiety
3. BOXERS : PUMMEL :: (a) teachers : punish (b) lawyers : win (c) detectives : investigate (d) scholars : cheat (e) collectors : lose
4. HEAVEN : ETHEREAL :: (a) grass : dried (b) water : muddy (c) baseball : athletic (d) desert : arid (e) soup : cold
5. PERSPICACITY : SHARP :: (a) intelligence : clever (b) fool : wise (c) courage : stupid (d) shyness : sociable (e) sense : visual

EXERCISE B Using your understanding of the boldfaced word, write on your paper the letter of the word or phrase that best completes each sentence below.

1. Tolstoy talked **maliciously** about his wife Sonya because he (a) admired her, (b) fought bitterly with her, (c) enjoyed her wit.
2. She became **irate** when he (a) showed her kindness, (b) wanted to give away their wealth, (c) managed their estate wisely.
3. The pilgrims to Tolstoy's estate found him **imposing** because of his (a) reputation, (b) forgetfulness, (c) unruly hair.
4. Sonya thought the visitors were **detestable** because they (a) lacked refinement, (b) enjoyed her company, (c) earned her respect.
5. In old age, Tolstoy was **unassuming** about his earlier works; he judged them (a) boldly original, (b) perfect, (c) flawed.

LEO TOLSTOY

1828–1910

When the 82-year-old Tolstoy died at a small railroad station just days after running away from his wife and family, the event became front-page news around the world. Nothing about Tolstoy's life, or death, was small.

Born into a wealthy, aristocratic family, Tolstoy was orphaned by the age of nine and, along with his three brothers, was raised by aunts. As a young man dissatisfied with his life, he volunteered in the Russian army. Tolstoy led an unsettled life, with periodic bouts of excess. His experience as a soldier in the Crimean War (a war between Russia and British, French, and Turkish troops) provided material for *Sevastopol Sketches* (1855), a collection of stories that won him literary fame. The next 25 years saw the publication of his two greatest novels, *War and Peace* (1869) and *Anna Karenina* (1877).

At the height of his creativity, Tolstoy underwent a spiritual crisis that led him to reexamine his life and works. In the last 30 years of his life, he became a kind of prophet, preaching his own gospel for the world's salvation. Though Tolstoy continued literary work, he now believed that literature must teach moral truths. He wrote many books and essays about his beliefs, which included love for humanity, rejection of private property, and suspicion of all forms of government.

Tolstoy's efforts to free himself from the burdens of property led to bitter quarrels with his wife, Sonya, the mother of his 13 children. He eventually decided to leave her, fleeing in the company of his youngest daughter and his doctor. He became ill on a train journey and died days later.

OTHER WORKS *The Death of Ivan Ilych and Other Stories, Master and Man and Other Stories, Essays and Letters, Childhood*

 LASERLINKS
• AUTHOR BACKGROUND

64 UNIT ONE PART 1: LASTING IMPRESSIONS

REFLECTING ON THEME
What Do You Think?

Have students recall the interviews that they conducted before reading the selections in Part One. Ask them how Ivan's lasting impression compares with the impressions that were shared during the interviews. Then ask them how reading this story has affected their understanding of the power of a lasting impression.

FOCUS ON NONFICTION

Nonfiction is prose writing about real people, places, and events. Unlike fiction, nonfiction is largely concerned with factual information, although the writer shapes the information according to his or her purpose and viewpoint. Nonfiction includes an amazingly diverse range of writing; newspaper articles, cookbooks, letters, movie reviews, editorials, speeches, true-life adventure stories—all are considered nonfiction. Some of the major types of nonfiction that are represented in this book are described below.

AUTOBIOGRAPHY An **autobiography** is a writer's account of his or her own life and is almost always told in the first person—that is, with the writer using the pronoun *I* to refer to himself or herself. In an autobiography, the writer focuses on the most significant events and people in his or her life. In this book, the selections by Mark Mathabane, Le Ly Hayslip, and Yevgeny Yevtushenko are drawn from their autobiographies.

An autobiography is usually book length because it covers a long span of years. Shorter types of autobiographical narratives include **journals, diaries,** and **letters,** which often originate as private writing. Some types of autobiographical writing, such as the **autobiographical essay,** focus on single persons or events in the authors' lives—for example, Nicholas Gage's "The Teacher Who Changed My Life" and Santha Rama Rau's "By Any Other Name." Other types—such as *Night* by Elie Wiesel and *Farewell to Manzanar* by Jeanne Wakatsuki Houston and her husband, James—focus on important periods in the authors' lives.

BIOGRAPHY A **biography** is an account of a person's life, written by another person. The writer of a biography, or biographer, often researches his or her subject in order to present accurate information. A biographer may also draw upon personal knowledge of his or her subject. For example, Corettta Scott King's *My Life with Martin Luther King, Jr.* (from which "Montgomery Boycott" is drawn) is based on the author's intimate knowledge of her subject. Although biographies are usually book length, there are also shorter forms of biographical writing, such as the excerpt from Colette's *Earthly Paradise,* which is a biographical sketch of the writer's mother, and Doris Herold Lund's "Gift from a Son Who Died," which focuses on the life of Lund's son.

FOCUS ON NONFICTION 65

FOCUS ON NONFICTION

This feature defines *nonfiction* and provides students with a common vocabulary to use in describing it. Strategies for reading fiction are also introduced. The terms introduced on these pages are covered in depth in the nonfiction selections that follow in the textbook.

— **Objectives** —

- To understand and appreciate nonfiction
- To understand some major categories of nonfiction: autobiography, biography, essay, true-life adventure, and the speech
- To learn strategies for reading nonfiction

Teaching Strategies:
CATEGORIES OF NONFICTION

Autobiography Have students read the description of autobiography, and then draw the following word web on the board, filling in the center with *autobiography.* Elicit from students the characteristics of autobiography as shown on the word web.

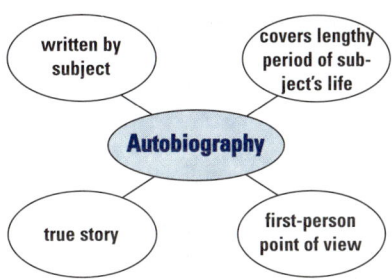

Ask students to name some advantages an autobiographical or eyewitness account of an event has over a third-person account of the same event. *(Possible responses: It is more immediate; the author has experienced the event and can describe it vividly.)* What are some disadvantages? *(Possible responses: The author may be biased; the author may know only part of the story.)*

Biography After students read the description of biography, ask why they think some historical figures have had numerous biographies written about them. *(Possible responses: Different biographers have different perspectives on the individual; as time passes, more information about the individual becomes available; some historical people are exceptionally interesting and capture the imagination of biographers.)* Have volunteers discuss some biographies they have read and what they find most interesting about the subject of the biography.

THE LANGUAGE OF LITERATURE **TEACHER'S EDITION** 65

Essay Ask volunteers to describe the topics of essays they have written. Elicit discussion of the range of essay types. Ask students to describe some memorable essays they have read. Then point out that well-written essays can be as interesting and entertaining as stories.

Reading Strategies: MODELING

Tell students they will be using the following strategies for reading as they read the excerpt from *Kaffir Boy* on page 67 and other nonfiction selections that follow. Model the following strategies for reading as students read the excerpt.

- **Preview.** *"From the title, the pictures, and the opening paragraph, I think this excerpt will be about a South African boy whose mother wants him to go to school."*
- **Think about what you already know.** *"I know that in the past people of color in South Africa were segregated from whites under a system called apartheid. Black South Africans were often very poor and suffered under harsh laws."*
- **Set purposes.** *"I would like to know what schools were like for black children in South Africa."*
- **Identify organization.** *"This is an autobiographical narrative, and it is ordered chronologically around the event of beginning school."*
- **Separate facts from opinions.** *"The author presents some facts about life in the South African township and about the marriage customs of South African tribes. In the beginning, he offers a positive opinion about the lifestyle of gangs of boys who roamed the streets and didn't go to school, but he seems to change his opinion in the end."*
- **Consider the writer's tone.** *"The writer takes a personal, emotional tone in the narrative. He lets the reader know his anger and frustration at being forced to school. When his father abuses his mother, he is enraged. In the end, he is grateful that his mother forced him to school even when he hated it."*
- **Summarize.** *"The boy was initially attracted to life in the streets, but his mother forced him to school. When his father, who never went to school, abuses his mother for sending him to school, he realizes what she has sacrificed for him, and he decides to choose education over ignorance."*

ESSAY An **essay** is a brief composition on a single subject, usually presenting the personal views of the writer. Because essays can be put to so many different uses, they are difficult to classify. An essay may seek to persuade, as does E. M. Forster's "Tolerance." An essay may offer a reflection on an episode in the writer's life, in the manner of E. B. White's "Once More to the Lake." Other essays, such as Roger Rosenblatt's "The Man in the Water" and Brent Staples's "Black Men and Public Space," are reflections on current events or social problems. Of course, there are many types of essays other than those included in this book, ranging from political and historical analysis to humorous commentary.

Other forms of nonfiction represented in this book are the **true-life adventure** (the excerpt from Yossi Ghinsberg's *Back from Tuichi*) and the **speech** (Elie Wiesel's Nobel Prize acceptance speech).

Keep in mind that many works of nonfiction fit into more than one category. For example, Nicholas Gage's "The Teacher Who Changed My Life" is an autobiographical essay. It has the brevity and single focus of an essay; at the same time, it is autobiographical.

STRATEGIES FOR READING NONFICTION

When reading narrative types of nonfiction—such as autobiographies, biographies, true-life adventures, and some essays—you can apply the same strategies that you use in reading fiction. When reading informative types of nonfiction, you can apply the strategies described below.

- **Preview.** For clues to what a nonfiction selection is about, look first at the title and at any headings, pictures, graphs, charts, and other noticeable features. If you are looking for specific information, previewing will help you decide whether a particular piece addresses your needs.
- **Think about what you already know.** Once you know the topic of a selection, take a moment to think about what you might already know about that topic. Activating your prior knowledge helps you understand what you read.
- **Set purposes.** As you begin to read, focus your thinking by setting purposes to guide your reading. Ask yourself what information you want or expect to find.
- **Identify the method of organization.** Writers of informative nonfiction organize their works according to their purpose for writing. In a selection meant to inform or persuade, the writer may organize the material around main ideas. In a selection meant to explain a process or a subject, the writer may use a step-by-step organization or a chronological presentation of facts. Some nonfiction, especially in history and science textbooks, includes headings that state the topics of individual sections.
- **Separate facts from opinions.** It is important to weigh and evaluate the facts that a writer presents. **Facts** are statements that can be proved. **Opinions** are unprovable statements that express a writer's beliefs. Sometimes, however, a writer presents an opinion as if it were a fact. Be sure to recognize which statements are facts and which are opinions.
- **Consider the writer's tone.** The attitude a writer takes toward a subject is called his or her tone. A writer's tone may, for example, be critical, amused, cynical, or nostalgic. To identify a writer's tone, look closely at the writer's choice of words and the kinds of statements he or she makes.
- **Summarize.** When you have finished reading a selection, take a few moments to summarize or restate the main points. Reread anything that is still unclear. If the selection has headings, use them as guidelines for your review of the text. For longer works, you may wish to summarize at the end of each chapter and take notes in the form of an outline. Summarizing shows you what you have learned and what you might still want to find out.

PREVIEWING

NONFICTION

from Kaffir Boy
Mark Mathabane (mä′tä-bä′nə) South Africa / United States

Activating Prior Knowledge
PERSONAL CONNECTION

Think back to your earliest memories of school. What was your attitude toward school and education then? Use a word web like the one shown to explore your early attitude.

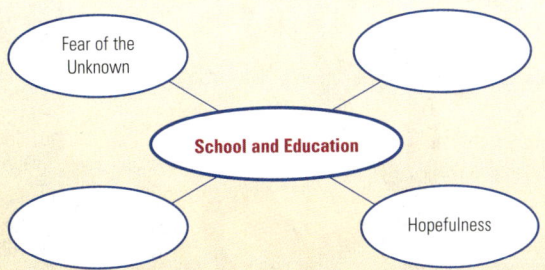

Building Background
HISTORICAL CONNECTION

For black South Africans who lived under apartheid (ə-pärt′hīt′), education was difficult to attain. Apartheid laws—in effect from 1948 to 1991—prescribed a rigid separation of races. Black South Africans were forced to reside in overcrowded, disease-ridden areas, such as Alexandra—a township just outside Johannesburg (jō-hăn′ĭs-bûrg)—where Mark Mathabane and his family lived. Apartheid laws also severely limited blacks' job opportunities and forced black children to attend separate, inferior schools.

In his autobiography *Kaffir Boy,* Mathabane describes what it was like to grow up under these conditions. The word *Kaffir* (kăf′ər), an insulting term that many white South Africans applied to blacks, reflects the racism he experienced.

Active Reading/Setting a Purpose
READING CONNECTION

Using a Reading Log The reading strategies introduced on page 5 showed the kinds of connections active readers make when they read. To help you practice some of those strategies, questions have been inserted periodically throughout *Kaffir Boy.* Record your responses to each of the questions in your reading log. Also record other thoughts and feelings that come to you. After you have finished reading, discuss some of your responses with your classmates.

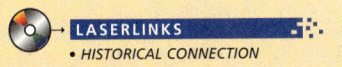
LASERLINKS
• HISTORICAL CONNECTION

OVERVIEW

Objectives
- To understand and appreciate an autobiography that tells about the experiences of a young black African boy about to begin school in South Africa
- To enrich reading by using active reading strategies
- To identify and understand dialogue
- To express understanding of the selection through a choice of writing forms, including a dialogue, a public-service announcement, and a eulogy
- To extend understanding of the selection through a variety of multimodal and cross-curricular activities

Skills

LITERARY CONCEPTS
- Dialogue
- Description

READING SKILLS/STRATEGIES
- Using a reading log
- Predicting
- Evaluating
- Clarifying

THE WRITER'S STYLE
- Logical presentation of ideas

GRAMMAR
- Inverted sentences

GENRE STUDY
- Nonfiction: autobiography

SPEAKING, LISTENING, AND VIEWING
- Group discussion

ALTERNATIVE
Previewing

Ask students to recall how they felt when they were first starting to go to school. Use the following prompts:

Personal Connection

Discussion Prompts
- *How did you view school—as an opportunity or a punishment?*
- *Who made the biggest impression on you—the principal, your teacher, a classmate?*

HISTORICAL CONNECTION
Apartheid in South Africa, 1948–1991 For 43 years South African laws enforced a strict separation of racial groups in the country. These photographs depict the lives of black South Africans living under apartheid rule. Exclusion, poverty, and protest characterized the lives of many. These photographs offer students a visual context for the setting of "Kaffir Boy."

Side A, Frame 49313

PRINT AND MEDIA RESOURCES

UNIT ONE RESOURCE BOOK
Strategic Reading: Literature, p. 23
Vocabulary SkillBuilder, p. 24

GRAMMAR MINI-LESSONS
Transparencies, p. 7
Copymasters, p. 9

WRITING MINI-LESSONS
Transparencies, p. 56

ACCESS FOR STUDENTS ACQUIRING ENGLISH
Selection Summaries
Reading Support

FORMAL ASSESSMENT
Selection Test, pp. 13–14
 Test Generator

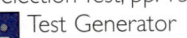 **AUDIO LIBRARY**
See Reference Card

 **LASERLINKS**
Historical Connection

INTERNET RESOURCES
McDougal Littell Literature Center at http://www.hmco.com/mcdougal/lit

THE LANGUAGE OF LITERATURE **TEACHER'S EDITION** 67

SUMMARY

Mark Mathabane describes what it was like growing up black under the system of apartheid in Johannesburg, South Africa, in the 1960s. At age seven, Mark enjoyed the adventurous life of a gang member and vowed never to attend school. One morning, however, his mother took him to a tribal school to register him as a student, and he learned how difficult it was for her to do so. He weighed the reasons for going to school or not. Later that evening, Mark's parents argued about his education, his father physically abusing his mother. Mark learned that his mother wanted him to attend school to avoid the difficulties that she and his father had faced. He began to appreciate her struggle to give him a better future, and he committed himself to knowledge rather than ignorance.

Thematic Link: *Lasting Impressions* A mother's fierce determination that her son, a young African, overcome ignorance and poverty through education makes a lasting impression on the boy.

CUSTOMIZING FOR
Students Acquiring English

- Use **ACCESS FOR STUDENTS ACQUIRING ENGLISH,** *Reading Support.*
- This selection may be difficult for some students because in the dialogue, speakers are not always identified and because some South African words are used. You may want to read the story aloud to students acquiring English and have them stop you when they hear something they don't understand.
- As you guide students through the selection, you may want to use the suggestions under Strategic Reading for Less-Proficient Readers as well as the suggestions in these boxes.

from Kaffir Boy
Mark Mathabane

When my mother began dropping hints that I would soon be going to school, I vowed never to go because school was a waste of time. She laughed and said, "We'll see. You don't know what you're talking about." My philosophy on school was that of a gang of ten-, eleven- and twelve-year-olds whom I so revered that their every word seemed that of an oracle.

68 UNIT ONE PART 1: LASTING IMPRESSIONS

WORDS TO KNOW

accost (ə-kôst′) *v.* to approach and speak to, especially in a pushy way (p. 75)
austere (ô-stîr′) *adj.* stern; strict; severely self-disciplined (p. 73)
captivate (kăp′tə-vāt′) *v.* to attract and hold; fascinate (p. 69)
credence (krēd′ns) *n.* belief or believability (p. 75)
inkling (ĭng′klĭng) *n.* a vague idea or notion (p. 74)

inscrutable (ĭn-skrōō′tə-bəl) *adj.* hard to understand or interpret; mysterious (p. 73)
paradoxically (păr′ə-dŏk′sĭ-klē) *adv.* in a seemingly contradictory way (p. 74)
pretext (prē′tĕkst′) *n.* a pretended reason; excuse (p. 78)
unsolicited (ŭn′sə-lĭs′ĭ-tĭd) *adj.* not requested (p. 72)
utilitarian (yōō-tĭl′ĭ-târ′ē-ən) *adj.* useful (p. 73)

A boy peeks around a wall in a South African village. South Light / Gamma Liaison Network.

These boys had long left their homes and were now living in various neighborhood junkyards, making it on their own. They slept in abandoned cars, smoked glue and benzene,[1] ate pilchards[2] and brown bread, sneaked into the white world to caddy and, if unsuccessful, came back to the township to steal beer and soda bottles from shebeens,[3] or goods from the Indian traders on First Avenue. Their life-style was exciting, adventurous and full of surprises; and I was attracted to it. My mother told me that they were no-gooders, that they would amount to nothing, that I should not associate with them, but I paid no heed. What does she know? I used to tell myself. One thing she did not know was that the gang's way of life had <u>captivated</u> me wholly, particularly their philosophy on school: they hated it and considered an education a waste of time.

They, like myself, had grown up in an environment where the value of an education was never

---

1. **benzene:** a clear, poisonous liquid derived from petroleum, used in cleaning and as a motor fuel.
2. **pilchards** (pĭl′chərdz): sardines.
3. **shebeens** (shə-bēnz′): unlicensed taverns.

WORDS TO KNOW
captivate (kăp′tə-vāt′) v. to attract and hold; fascinate

69

Active Reading: PREDICT

B Discuss the students' predictions about the mother's actions. You may wish to use the following model to help them predict.

Think-Aloud Model *Mark says his mother has been dropping hints about his starting school. Parents want their kids to be clean for school, so it seems likely that she's getting him ready to go.*

Literary Note

C The police raided the neighborhood of Alexandra regularly, and both Mr. and Mrs. Mathabane had been arrested several times in the past for not having their passes, or official paperwork, in order. They live in constant fear that the police will deport them to a tribal homeland.

Literary Concept: DIALOGUE

D Ask students what impressions they have of Mark's mother in light of the conversation she has with Mark while he is putting on the old clothes. *(She is tough and determined, refusing to listen to Mark's protests.)*

---

emphasized, where the first thing a child learned was not how to read and write and spell, but how to fight and steal and rebel; where the money to send children to school was grossly lacking, for survival was first priority. I kept my membership in the gang, knowing that for as long as I was under its influence, I would never go to school.

One day my mother woke me up at four in the morning.

"Are they here? I didn't hear any noises," I asked in the usual way.

"No," my mother said. "I want you to get into that washtub over there."

"What!" I balked, upon hearing the word *washtub*. I feared taking baths like one feared the plague. Throughout seven years of hectic living the number of baths I had taken could be counted on one hand with several fingers missing. I simply had no natural inclination for water; cleanliness was a trait I still had to acquire. Besides, we had only one bathtub in the house, and it constantly sprung a leak.

B **PREDICT**
What do the mother's actions seem to be leading to?

"I said get into that tub!" My mother shook a finger in my face.

Reluctantly, I obeyed, yet wondered why all of a sudden I had to take a bath. My mother, armed with a scrobbrush and a piece of Lifebuoy soap, purged me of years and years of grime till I ached and bled. As I howled, feeling pain shoot through my limbs as the thistles of the brush encountered stubborn calluses, there was a loud knock at the door.

C Instantly my mother leaped away from the tub and headed, on tiptoe, toward the bedroom. Fear seized me as I, too, thought of the police. I sat frozen in the bathtub, not knowing what to do.

"Open up, Mujaji⁴ [my mother's maiden name]," Granny's voice came shrilling through the door. "It's me."

My mother heaved a sigh of relief; her tense limbs relaxed. She turned and headed to the kitchen door, unlatched it, and in came Granny and Aunt Bushy.

"You scared me half to death," my mother said to Granny. "I had forgotten all about your coming."

What's going on? What's Granny doing at our house this ungodly hour of the morning?

"Are you ready?" Granny asked my mother.

"Yes—just about," my mother said, beckoning me to get out of the washtub.

She handed me a piece of cloth to dry myself. As I dried myself, questions raced through my mind: What's going on? What's Granny doing at our house this ungodly hour of the morning? And why did she ask my mother, "Are you ready?" While I stood debating, my mother went into the bedroom and came out with a stained white shirt and a pair of faded black shorts.

"Here," she said, handing me the togs, "put these on."

"Why?" I asked.

"Put them on I said!"

I put the shirt on; it was grossly loose fitting. It reached all the way down to my ankles. Then I saw the reason why: it was my father's shirt!

"But this is Papa's shirt," I complained. "It don't fit me."

"Put it on," my mother insisted. "I'll make it fit."

"The pants don't fit me either," I said. "Whose are they anyway?"

---
4. Mujaji (mōō-jä′jē).

70 UNIT ONE PART 1: LASTING IMPRESSIONS

Mini-Lesson  Literary Concepts

REVIEWING DESCRIPTION Description is writing that helps a reader picture scenes, events, or characters. To create descriptions, writers often use sensory images—words that appeal to the reader's senses.

Application Have students find details in the description of Alexandra at the bottom of page 71 that appeal to their sense of sight. Ask them what details appeal to their sense of hearing. Then ask them to find details elsewhere in the selection that appeal to other senses. Use a table, like the one shown, to record students' responses.

Sense	Sensory Details
Sight	wizened old men and women
Hearing	bawling infants
Taste	beer drinking
Smell	dusty streets
Touch	piggybacking

70 THE LANGUAGE OF LITERATURE TEACHER'S EDITION

"Put them on," my mother said. "I'll make them fit."

Moments later I had the garments on; I looked ridiculous. My mother started working on the pants and shirt to make them fit. She folded the shirt in so many intricate ways and stashed it inside the pants, they too having been folded several times at the waist. She then choked the pants at the waist with a piece of sisal rope to hold them up. She then lavishly smeared my face, arms and legs with a mixture of pig's fat and vaseline. "This will insulate you from the cold," she said. My skin gleamed like the morning star, and I felt as hot as the center of the sun, and I smelled God knows like what. After embalming me, she headed to the bedroom.

"Where are we going, Gran'ma?" I said, hoping that she would tell me what my mother refused to tell me. I still had no idea I was about to be taken to school.

"Didn't your mother tell you?" Granny said with a smile. "You're going to start school."

"What!" I gasped, leaping from the chair where I was sitting as if it were made of hot lead. "I am not going to school!" I blurted out and raced toward the kitchen door.

My mother had just reappeared from the bedroom, and guessing what I was up to, she yelled, "Someone get the door!"

Aunt Bushy immediately barred the door. I turned and headed for the window. As I leaped for the windowsill, my mother lunged at me and brought me down. I tussled, "Let go of me! I don't want to go to school! Let me go!" but my mother held fast onto me.

"It's no use now," she said, grinning triumphantly as she pinned me down. Turning her head in Granny's direction, she shouted, "Granny! Get a rope quickly!"

Granny grabbed a piece of rope nearby and came to my mother's aid. I bit and clawed every hand that grabbed me, and howled protestations against going to school; however, I was no match for the two determined matriarchs.[5] In a jiffy they had me bound, hands and feet.

"What's the matter with him?" Granny, bewildered, asked my mother. "Why did he suddenly turn into an imp when I told him you're taking him to school?"

"You shouldn't have told him that he's being taken to school," my mother said. "He doesn't want to go there. That's why I requested you come today, to help me take him there. Those boys in the streets have been a bad influence on him."

As the two matriarchs hauled me through the door, they told Aunt Bushy not to go to school but stay behind and mind the house and the children.

The sun was beginning to rise from beyond the veld[6] when Granny and my mother dragged me to school. The streets were beginning to fill with their everyday traffic: old men and women, wizened, bent and ragged, were beginning their rambling; workless men and women were beginning to assemble in their usual coteries[7] and head for shebeens in the backyards where they discussed how they escaped the morning pass raids[8] and contemplated the conditions of life amidst intense beer drinking and vacant, uneasy laughter; young boys and girls, some as young as myself, were beginning their aimless wanderings along the narrow, dusty streets in search of food, carrying bawling infants piggyback.

As we went along some of the streets, boys and girls who shared the same fears about school as I were making their feelings known

---

5. **matriarchs** (mā′trē-ärks′): female rulers of families, clans, or tribes.
6. **veld** (vĕlt): in South Africa, an area of grassland.
7. **coteries** (kō′tə-rēz): close circles of friends, usually with common interests.
8. **pass raids:** police raids regularly conducted under apartheid to check that black South Africans had the papers authorizing them to be in particular areas.

KAFFIR BOY 71

Mini-Lesson Genre Study

NONFICTION Draw on the board the web shown here, and use it to explain that an **autobiography** is a kind of nonfiction with these characteristics:

- It is a factual account of a person's life written by that person.
- It is usually written from the first-person point of view.
- It is intended to give readers insight into the person's character, feelings, and attitudes.
- It reflects on how events in the author's life affected him or her.

Application Have students copy the web into their notebooks. Ask them to refer to it as they look for the characteristics of an autobiography in the excerpt from *Kaffir Boy*.

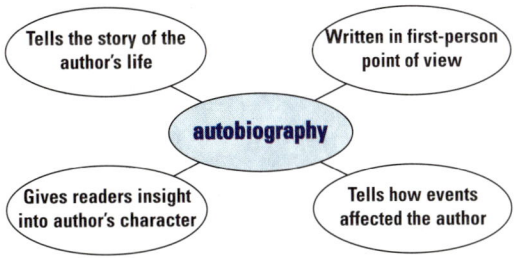

Critical Thinking: SPECULATING

E Have students speculate why Mark is wearing his father's clothes, which are far too big for him. (*Possible responses: Mark has no good clothes of his own; his family is too poor to buy him new clothes for school.*)

Literary Concept: SIMILE

F Ask students what colorful similes Mark Mathabane uses to describe himself after his mother coats his skin with fat. (*"My skin gleamed like the morning star, and I felt as hot as the center of the sun."*)

CUSTOMIZING FOR
Students Acquiring English

I Define *imp* as "a little demon or mischievous child." Ask students what actions caused his grandmother to call him an imp. (*Possible responses: He tried to escape; he fought going to school; he bit and clawed at his mother and grandmother.*)

STRATEGIC READING FOR
Less-Proficient Readers

G Make sure that students understand who the main characters are and what conflicts they have. Ask them the following questions:

- Who are the main characters so far in the story? (*young Mark Mathabane, his mother, and his Granny*) Noting Relevant Details
- What do Mark and his mother and grandmother disagree about? (*Mark's relatives want him to go to school, but Mark wants to hang out with his gang.*) Finding the Main Idea

Set a Purpose Have students read on to discover who and what influence Mark's thinking about school.

Literary Concept:
DESCRIPTION

H Ask students what the description of the Alexandra street scene tells them about life in Mark's community. (*Possible response: Unemployment, poverty, and alcoholism are serious problems. People scrounge to get by and find amusement where they can.*)

THE LANGUAGE OF LITERATURE TEACHER'S EDITION 71

Children play among the roughly built shacks, or shanties, in Khayelitsha, South Africa, a settlement near Cape Town. Copyright © Louise Gubb / JB Pictures Ltd.

in a variety of ways. They were howling their protests and trying to escape. A few managed to break loose and make a mad dash for freedom, only to be recaptured in no time, admonished or whipped, or both, and ordered to march again.

As we made a turn into Sixteenth Avenue, the street leading to the tribal school I was being taken to, a short, chubby black woman came along from the opposite direction. She had a scuttle[9] overflowing with coal on her *doek*-covered (cloth-covered) head. An infant, bawling deafeningly, was loosely swathed with a piece of sheepskin onto her back. Following closely behind the woman, and picking up pieces of coal as they fell from the scuttle and placing them in a small plastic bag, was a half-naked, potbellied and thumb-sucking boy of about four. The woman stopped abreast. For some reason we stopped too.

"I wish I had done the same to my oldest son," the strange woman said in a regretful voice, gazing at me. I was confounded by her stopping and offering her unsolicited opinion.

"I wish I had done that to my oldest son," she repeated and suddenly burst into tears; amidst sobs, she continued, "before . . . the street claimed him . . . and . . . turned him into a *tsotsi*."[10]

---

9. **scuttle:** a metal pail for carrying coal.
10. ***tsotsi*** (tsŏt′sē): a street hoodlum armed with a knife or some other weapon.

WORDS TO KNOW

unsolicited (ŭn′sə-lĭs′ĭ-tĭd) *adj.* not requested

Granny and my mother offered consolatory remarks to the strange woman.

"But it's too late now," the strange woman continued, tears now streaming freely down her puffy cheeks. She made no attempt to dry them. "It's too late now," she said for the second time, "he's beyond any help. I can't help him even if I wanted to. *Uswile*[11] [He is dead]."

"How did he die?" my mother asked in a sympathetic voice.

"He shunned school and, instead, grew up to live by the knife. And the same knife he lived by ended his life. That's why whenever I see a boy child refuse to go to school, I stop and tell the story of my dear little *mbitsini*[12] [heartbreak]."

Having said that, the strange woman left as mysteriously as she had arrived.

"Did you hear what that woman said!" my mother screamed into my ears. "Do you want the same to happen to you?"

I dropped my eyes. I was confused.

"Poor woman," Granny said ruefully. "She must have truly loved her son."

Finally, we reached the school, and I was ushered into the principal's office, a tiny cubicle facing a row of privies[13] and a patch of yellowed grass.

"So this is the rascal we'd been talking about," the principal, a tall, wiry man, foppishly[14] dressed in a black pinstriped suit, said to my mother as we entered. His <u>austere</u>, shiny face, <u>inscrutable</u> and imposing, reminded me of my father. He was sitting behind a brown table upon which stood piles of dust and cobweb-covered books and papers. In one upper pocket of his jacket was arrayed a variety of pens and pencils; in the other nestled a lily-white handkerchief whose presence was more decorative than <u>utilitarian</u>. Alongside him stood a disproportionately portly black woman, fashionably dressed in a black skirt and a white blouse. She had but one pen, and this she held in her hand. The room was hot and stuffy and buzzing with flies.

"Yes, Principal," my mother answered, "this is he."

"He's just like the rest of them . . . Once they get out into the streets, they become wild."

"I see he's living up to his notoriety," remarked the principal, noticing that I had been bound. "Did he give you too much trouble?"

"Trouble, Principal," my mother sighed. "He was like an imp."

"He's just like the rest of them, Principal," Granny sighed. "Once they get out into the streets, they become wild. They take to the many vices of the streets like an infant takes to its mother's milk. They begin to think that there's no other life but the one shown them by the *tsotsis*. They come to hate school and forget about the future."

"Well," the principal said. "We'll soon remedy all that. Untie him."

"He'll run away," my mother cried.

---

11. *Uswile* (ōō-swē′lā).
12. *mbitsini* (əm-bĭt-sē′nē).
13. privies (prĭv′ēz): outhouses.
14. foppishly: with great attention to niceties of clothing; in the manner of a fop, a vain man who pays too much attention to his clothes.

WORDS TO KNOW
austere (ô-stîr′) *adj.* stern; strict; severely self-disciplined
inscrutable (ĭn-skrōō′tə-bəl) *adj.* hard to understand or interpret; mysterious
utilitarian (yōō-tĭl′ĭ-târ′ē-ən) *adj.* useful

Literary Concept: DIALOGUE

J Have students discuss why the author might have included an occasional African word in the dialogue—*tsotsi, uswile, mbitsini*. (Possible responses: The African words lend authenticity to the autobiography and make it more interesting; they help readers imagine the scene better; the woman may actually be mixing an African language with English.)

STRATEGIC READING FOR Less-Proficient Readers

K To help students understand the events that influence Mark, suggest that they reread the dialogue of the stranger who stops Mark and his mother, beginning on page 72.

- Ask students how the woman's moving words might affect Mark. (Her story might give Mark "food for thought" and soften his determination not to go to school.) Making Inferences

Set a Purpose Have students read on to find out about the problems involved in enrolling Mark in school.

Literary Concept: DESCRIPTION

L Invite students to note sensory details about the school. (Possible responses: the office facing the row of privies; the yellow grass; the dusty, cobweb-covered books; the buzzing flies) Ask them what type of school these details describe. (Possible response: a rather poor and run-down school)

Mini-Lesson Grammar

INVERTED SENTENCES Point out to students that an inverted sentence is one in which the verb is positioned before the subject. Explain that this often occurs in questions or in sentences beginning with the words *there* and *here*. Less often, writers place the verb before the subject for emphasis.

Application Ask students to identify the subject in each clause of this sentence from page 73: "In one upper pocket of his jacket was arrayed a variety of pens and pencils; in the other nestled a lily-white handkerchief." *(variety; handkerchief)* Then have students reword the clauses so they are not in inverted order. Discuss how the inverted order adds dramatic emphasis to the sentence.

Reteaching/Reinforcement
- *Grammar Mini-Lessons* copymasters p. 9, transparencies p. 7

The Writer's Craft

Subjects in Inverted Sentences, pp. 573–575

Cultural Note

M Canes are flexible wooden rods that are used to whip misbehaving students. Once common around the world, this type of corporal punishment is less popular today. Mark, however, was caned regularly by his teachers when his parents failed to pay his school fees on time or to provide him with the proper uniform.

Active Reading: EVALUATE

N Encourage students to evaluate Mrs. Mathabane's actions—spending a year collecting the necessary papers, tying Mark up and dragging him to school, and finding money for tuition.

Literary Concept: DIALOGUE

O Have students carefully read the principal's conversation with Mark's grandmother and tell what they can infer about the principal from his words. (*Possible response: He is formal and well-spoken; he takes his responsibilities very seriously; although he hates apartheid, he obeys the rules of Pretoria exactly, perhaps because he is afraid the white authorities will shut his school if he does not.*)

Critical Thinking: ANALYZING

P Have students analyze Granny's comment "I understand, Principal, but I don't understand" and tell what they think she means. (*Possible response: Granny understands that the principal needs the papers to admit Mark, but she doesn't understand why the papers are so important or why it takes so long to get them from the government.*)

Linking to Social Studies

Q The white national government regarded South Africa's black population as ten separate nations. These nations were assigned reserves, called homelands, in eastern South Africa. The two largest ethnic groups in South Africa are the Zulu and the Xhosa.

"I don't think he's that foolish to attempt that with all of us here."

"He *is* that foolish, Principal," my mother said as she and Granny began untying me. "He's tried it before. Getting him here was an ordeal in itself."

The principal rose from his seat, took two steps to the door and closed it. As the door swung closed, I spotted a row of canes of different lengths and thicknesses hanging behind it. The principal, seeing me staring at the canes, grinned and said, in a manner suggesting that he had wanted me to see them, "As long as you behave, I won't have to use any of those on you."

Use those canes on me? I gasped. I stared at my mother—she smiled; at Granny—she smiled too. That made me abandon any <u>inkling</u> of escaping.

"So they finally gave you the birth certificate and the papers," the principal addressed my mother as he returned to his chair.

"Yes, Principal," my mother said, "they finally did. But what a battle it was. It took me nearly a year to get all them papers together."

EVALUATE

N What conclusions can you draw about the mother's attitude toward education?

She took out of her handbag a neatly wrapped package and handed it to the principal. "They've been running us around for so long that there were times when I thought he would never attend school, Principal," she said.

"That's pretty much standard procedure, Mrs. Mathabane," the principal said, unwrapping the package. "But you now have the papers, and that's what's important."

"As long as we have the papers," he continued, minutely perusing the contents of the package, "we won't be breaking the law in admitting your son to this school, for we'll be in full compliance with the requirements set by the authorities in Pretoria."[15]

"Sometimes I don't understand the laws from Pitori,"[16] Granny said. "They did the same to me with my Piet[17] and Bushy. Why, Principal, should our children not be allowed to learn because of some piece of paper?"

"The piece of paper you're referring to, Mrs. Mabaso [Granny's maiden name]," the principal said to Granny, "is as important to our children as a pass is to us adults. We all hate passes; therefore, it's only natural we should hate the regulations our children are subjected to. But as we have to live with passes, so our children have to live with the regulations, Mrs. Mabaso. I hope you understand; that is the law of the country. We would have admitted your grandson a long time ago, as you well know, had it not been for the papers. I hope you understand."

"I understand, Principal," Granny said, "but I don't understand," she added <u>paradoxically</u>.

One of the papers caught the principal's eye, and he turned to my mother and asked, "Is your husband a Shangaan,[18] Mrs. Mathabane?"

"No, he's not, Principal," my mother said. "Is there anything wrong? He's Venda,[19] and I'm Shangaan."

The principal reflected for a moment or so and then said, concernedly, "No, there's nothing seriously wrong. Nothing that we can't take care of. You see, Mrs. Mathabane, technically,

---

15. **Pretoria** (prĭ-tôr′ē-ə): a city north of Johannesburg that serves as the administrative capital of South Africa.
16. **Pitori** (pĭ-tôr′ē): a mispronunciation of "Pretoria."
17. **Piet** (pēt).
18. **Shangaan** (shäng-gän′): a member of an ethnic group of northeastern South Africa.
19. **Venda** (věn′də): a member of another ethnic group of northeastern South Africa.

WORDS TO KNOW

inkling (ĭng′klĭng) *n.* a vague idea or notion
paradoxically (păr′ə-dŏk′sĭ-klē) *adv.* in a seemingly contradictory way

74

Critic's  Corner

"What television newscasts did to expose the horrors of the Vietnam War in the 1960s, books like *Kaffir Boy* may well do for the horrors of apartheid in the '80s."

Diane Manuel
Chicago Tribune reviewer

Have students discuss the horrors they think were exposed in this excerpt from Mathabane's book.

the fact that your child's father is a Venda makes him ineligible to attend this tribal school because it is only for children whose parents are of the Shangaan tribe. May I ask what language the children speak at home?"

"Both languages," my mother said worriedly, "Venda and Shangaan. Is there anything wrong?"

The principal coughed, clearing his throat, then said, "I mean which language do they speak more?"

"It depends, Principal," my mother said, swallowing hard. "When their father is around, he wants them to speak only Venda. And when he's not, they speak Shangaan. And when they are out at play, they speak Zulu and Sisotho."[20]

"Well," the principal said, heaving a sigh of relief. "In that case, I think an exception can be made. The reason for such an exception is that there's currently no school for Vendas in Alexandra. And should the authorities come asking why we took in your son, we can tell them that. Anyway, your child is half-half."

Everyone broke into a nervous laugh, except me. I was bewildered by the whole thing. I looked at my mother, and she seemed greatly relieved as she watched the principal register me; a broad smile broke across her face. It was as if some enormously heavy burden had finally been lifted from her shoulders and her conscience.

"Bring him back two weeks from today," the principal said as he saw us to the door. "There're so many children registering today that classes won't begin until two weeks hence. Also, the school needs repair and cleaning up after the holidays. If he refuses to come, simply notify us, and we'll send a couple of big boys to come fetch him, and he'll be very sorry if it ever comes to that."

As we left the principal's office and headed home, my mind was still against going to school. I was thinking of running away from home and joining my friends in the junkyard.

I didn't want to go to school for three reasons: I was reluctant to surrender my freedom and independence over to what I heard every school-going child call "tyrannous discipline." I had heard many bad things about life in tribal school—from daily beatings by teachers and mistresses who worked you like a mule to long school hours—and the sight of those canes in the principal's office gave ample credence to rumors that school was nothing but a torture chamber. And there was my allegiance to the gang.

But the thought of the strange woman's lamentations over her dead son presented a somewhat strong case for going to school: I didn't want to end up dead in the streets. A more compelling argument for going to school, however, was the vivid recollection of all that humiliation and pain my mother had gone through to get me the papers and the birth certificate so I could enroll in school. What should I do? I was torn between two worlds.

But later that evening something happened to force me to go to school.

I was returning home from playing soccer when a neighbor accosted me by the gate and told me that there had been a bloody fight at my home.

"Your mother and father have been at it again," the neighbor, a woman, said.

"And your mother left."

I was stunned.

"Was she hurt badly?"

"A little bit," the woman said. "But she'll be all right. We took her to your grandma's place."

I became hot with anger.

---

20. **Zulu** (zōō'lōō) and **Sisotho** (sĭ-sō'tō): languages spoken by two peoples of eastern South Africa.

WORDS TO KNOW
credence (krēd'ns) *n.* belief or believability
accost (ə-kôst') *v.* to approach and speak to, especially in a pushy way

"Is anyone in the house?" I stammered, trying to control my rage.

"Yes, your father is. But I don't think you should go near the house. He's raving mad. He's armed with a meat cleaver. He's chased out your brother and sisters, also. And some of the neighbors who tried to intervene he's threatened to carve them to pieces. I have never seen him this mad before."

I brushed aside the woman's warnings and went. Shattered windows convinced me that there had indeed been a skirmish of some sort. Several pieces of broken bricks, evidently broken after being thrown at the door, were lying about the door. I tried opening the door; it was locked from the inside. I knocked. No one answered. I knocked again. Still no one answered, until, as I turned to leave:

"Who's out there?" my father's voice came growling from inside.

"It's me, Johannes,"[21] I said.

"Go away, . . . !" he bellowed. "I don't want you or that . . . mother of yours setting foot in this house. Go away before I come out there and kill you!"

"Let me in!" I cried. "Dammit, let me in! I want my things!"

"What things? Go away, you black swine!"

I went to the broken window and screamed obscenities at my father, daring him to come out, hoping that if he as much as ever stuck his black face out, I would pelt him with the half-a-loaf brick in my hand. He didn't come out. He continued launching a tirade of obscenities at my mother and her mother. . . . He was drunk, but I wondered where he had gotten the money to buy beer because it was still the middle of the week and he was dead broke. He had lost his entire wage for the past week in dice and had had to borrow bus fare.

"I'll kill you someday for all you're doing to my mother," I threatened him, overwhelmed with rage. Several nosey neighbors were beginning to congregate by open windows and doors. Not wanting to make a spectacle of myself, which was something many of our neighbors seemed to always expect from our family, I backtracked away from the door and vanished into the dark street. I ran, without stopping, all the way to the other end of the township where Granny lived. There I found my mother, her face swollen and bruised and her eyes puffed up to the point where she could scarcely see.

"What happened, Mama?" I asked, fighting to hold back the tears at the sight of her disfigured face.

Most children in South Africa dress in Western-style clothing.

---

21. **Johannes** (yō-hän′əs): the author's original name, which he later changed to Mark.

"Nothing, child, nothing," she mumbled, almost apologetically, between swollen lips. "Your papa simply lost his temper, that's all."

"But why did he beat you up like this, Mama?" Tears came down my face. "He's never beaten you like this before."

My mother appeared reluctant to answer me. She looked searchingly at Granny, who was pounding millet with pestle and mortar and mixing it with sorghum and nuts for an African delicacy. Granny said, "Tell him, child, tell him. He's got a right to know. Anyway, he's the cause of it all."

"Your father and I fought because I took you to school this morning," my mother began. "He had told me not to, and when I told him that I had, he became very upset. He was drunk. We started arguing, and one thing led to another."

"Why doesn't he want me to go to school?"

"He says he doesn't have money to waste paying for you to get what he calls a useless white man's education," my mother replied. "But I told him that if he won't pay for your schooling, I would try and look for a job and pay, but he didn't want to hear that, also. 'There are better things for you to work for,' he said. 'Besides, I don't want you to work. How would I look to other men if you, a woman I owned, were to start working?' When I asked him why shouldn't I take you to school, seeing that you were now of age, he replied that he doesn't believe in schools. I told him that school would keep you off the streets and out of trouble, but still he was belligerent."

"Is that why he beat you up?"

"Yes, he said I disobeyed his orders."

"He's right, child," Granny interjected. "He paid *lobola* [bride price] for you. And your father ate it all up before he left me."

To which my mother replied, "But I desperately want to leave this beast of a man. But with his *lobola* gone I can't do it. That worthless thing you call your husband shouldn't have sold Jackson's scrawny cattle and left you penniless."

"Don't talk like that about your father, child," Granny said. "Despite all, he's still your father, you know. Anyway, he asked for *lobola* only because he had to get back what he spent raising you. And you know it would have been taboo for him to let you or any of your sisters go without asking for *lobola*."

"You and Papa seemed to forget that my sisters and I have minds of our own," my mother said. "We didn't need you to tell us whom to marry, and why, and how. If it hadn't been for your interference, I could have married that schoolteacher."

Granny did not reply; she knew well not to. When it came to the act of "selling" women as marriage partners, my mother was vehemently opposed to it. Not only was she opposed to this one aspect of tribal culture, but to others as well, particularly those involving relations between men and women and the upbringing of children. But my mother's sharply differing opinion was an exception rather than the rule among tribal women. Most times, many tribal women questioned her sanity in daring to question well-established mores.²² But my mother did not seem to care; she would always scoff at her opponents and call them fools in letting their husbands enslave them completely.

Though I disliked school, largely because I knew nothing about what actually went on there, and the little I knew had painted a dreadful picture, the fact that a father would not want his son to go to school, especially a father who didn't go to school, seemed hard to understand.

"Why do you want me to go to school, Mama?" I asked, hoping that she might, some-

---

22. **mores** (môr′āz′): traditional customs of a social group.

KAFFIR BOY 77

Multicultural Perspectives

ARRANGED MARRIAGES Explain to the class that being the first wife and having wealth and children were important considerations in Granny's Shangaan homeland. Most Shangaan girls married when they were 15 or 16, accepting the husbands that their parents had chosen for them. (According to custom, parents had more experience and judgment on which to base this important decision.)

In Granny's case, the arranged marriage proved disastrous. Her new husband worked in far-off Johannesburg, rarely saw Granny, and deserted her at a young age. That is why Granny forced her own daughter to marry an older man—Mark's father—since he would be less likely to desert a young wife.

THE LANGUAGE OF LITERATURE TEACHER'S EDITION 77

**Critical Thinking:
MAKING JUDGMENTS**

Z Invite students to consider whether they agree with Mrs. Mathabane's main point here. *(Possible responses: Most students will agree with her; some might argue that Mark's personality differs from his father's anyway.)*

Literary Concept: CHARACTER

AA Ask students to consider what Mrs. Mathabane's arguments for going to school reveal about her. *(Possible response: She is logical and intelligent; she is also compassionate in that she attempts to understand her husband's cruel behavior in the light of the societal forces that have shaped him.)*

Literary Concept: REPETITION

BB Have students discuss the effect of Mrs. Mathabane's repeating the sentence opener "It [Education] will . . ." or "It'll" so many times in this paragraph. *(Possible response: Repeating this phrase with each benefit of education that she names helps to emphasize the major importance of education in one's life.)*

EDITOR'S NOTE With the permission of the author or copyright holder, potentially offensive material has been deleted from the selection.

---

how, clear up some of the confusion that was building in my mind.

"I want you to have a future, child," my mother said. "And, contrary to what your father says, school is the only means to a future. I don't want you growing up to be like your father."

The latter statement hit me like a bolt of lightning. It just about shattered every defense mechanism and every <u>pretext</u> I had against going to school.

"Your father didn't go to school," she continued, dabbing her puffed eyes to reduce the swelling with a piece of cloth dipped in warm water; "that's why he's doing some of the bad things he's doing. Things like drinking, gambling and neglecting his family. He didn't learn how to read and write; therefore, he can't find a decent job. Lack of any education has narrowly focused his life. He sees nothing beyond himself. He still thinks in the old, tribal way and still believes that things should be as they were back in the old days when he was growing up as a tribal boy in Louis Trichardt.²³ Though he's my husband, and your father, he doesn't see any of that."

"Why didn't he go to school, Mama?"

"He refused to go to school because his father led him to believe that an education was a tool through which white people were going to take things away from him, like they did black people in the old days. And that a white man's education was worthless insofar as black people were concerned because it prepared them for jobs they can't have. But I know it isn't totally so, child, because times have changed somewhat. Though our lot isn't any better today, an education will get you a decent job. If you can read or write, you'll be better off than those of us who can't. Take my situation: I can't find a job because I don't have papers, and I can't get papers because white people mainly want to register people who can read and write. But I want things to be different for you, child. For you and your brother and sisters. I want you to go to school, because I believe that an education is the key you need to open up a new world and a new life for yourself, a world and life different from that of

> *"I want you to go to school, because I believe that an education is the key you need to open up a new world . . ."*

either your father's or mine. It is the only key that can do that, and only those who seek it earnestly and perseveringly will get anywhere in the white man's world. Education will open doors where none seem to exist. It'll make people talk to you, listen to you and help you; people who otherwise wouldn't bother. It will make you soar, like a bird lifting up into the endless blue sky, and leave poverty, hunger and suffering behind. It'll teach you to learn to embrace what's good and shun what's bad and evil. Above all, it'll make you a somebody in this world. It'll make you grow up to be a good and proud person. That's why I want you to go to school, child, so that education can do all that, and more, for you."

A long, awkward silence followed, during which I reflected upon the significance of my

---

23. **Louis Trichardt** (loo´ĭs trĭch´ərt): a town in northern South Africa.

WORDS TO KNOW
pretext (prē´tĕkst´) *n.* a pretended reason; excuse

78

Mini-Lesson — The Writer's Style

LOGICAL ORGANIZATION OF IDEAS Ask students to look again at Mrs. Mathabane's reasons for getting an education and to think about how she has presented these ideas logically. Point out that she begins by describing Mark's father, showing how his lack of an education has caused both poverty and suffering. Next, she turns to herself and explains that her own illiteracy has prevented her from finding a job. Finally, she discusses her children, describing education as the key that will open up a new world for them and bring a brighter future.

Application Ask students to imagine they are talking to a friend who is considering dropping out of school. Have them write a dialogue offering reasons why that friend should stay in school.

Reteaching/Reinforcement
• *Writing Mini-Lessons* transparencies, p. 56

The Writer's Craft

Types of Organization, pp. 342–347
Writing Dialogue, pp. 452–455

---

78 THE LANGUAGE OF LITERATURE **TEACHER'S EDITION**

mother's lengthy speech. I looked at my mother; she looked at me.

Finally, I asked, "How come you know so much about school, Mama? You didn't go to school, did you?"

"No, child," my mother replied. "Just like your father, I never went to school." For the second time that evening, a mere statement of fact had a thunderous impact on me. All the confusion I had about school seemed to leave my mind, like darkness giving way to light. And what had previously been a dark, yawning void in my mind was suddenly transformed into a beacon of light that began to grow larger and larger, until it had swallowed up, blotted out, all the blackness. That beacon of light seemed to reveal things and facts, which, though they must have always existed in me, I hadn't been aware of up until now.

"But unlike your father," my mother went on, "I've always wanted to go to school but couldn't because my father, under the sway of tribal traditions, thought it unnecessary to educate females. That's why I so much want you to go, child, for if you do, I know that someday I too would come to go, old as I would be then. Promise me, therefore, that no matter what, you'll go back to school. And I, in turn, promise that I'll do everything in my power to keep you there."

With tears streaming down my cheeks and falling upon my mother's bosom, I promised her that I would go to school "forever." That night, at seven and a half years of my life, the battle lines in the family were drawn. My mother on the one side, illiterate but determined to have me drink, for better or for worse, from the well of knowledge. On the other side, my father, he too illiterate, yet determined to have me drink from the well of ignorance. Scarcely aware of the magnitude of the decision I was making or, rather, the decision which was being emotionally thrust upon me, I chose to fight on my mother's side, and thus my destiny was forever altered.

KAFFIR BOY **79**

Mini-Lesson: Speaking, Listening, and Viewing

DRAMATIC READING Tell students that Mrs. Mathabane's powerful monologue on page 78 provides a good opportunity for them to practice a dramatic reading in which they interpret and express the feelings of a main character.

In preparation for the reading, students should consider the emotions that Mrs. Mathabane is experiencing—fear that her son will turn to gangs and ignorance, physical and emotional pain over her situation, sorrow about her family's current condition, and hope for a better tomorrow. Have them consider ways to use their voices, their faces, and gestures to express these feelings.

Application Have students work in small groups, with one or more volunteers reading the dialogue while the others listen and offer constructive criticism. Have the students list what makes each reading most dramatic.

Literary Concept: SYMBOL

CC Have students explain what the "dark, yawning void" and "beacon of light" stand for. *(Possible responses: Some students may say the void is Mark's confusion about school; others may say it's his fear of the unknown. Students might say the beacon is his newfound understanding of the importance of education; some might say it is the promise of a bright future.)* Ask students what mood this figurative language creates. *(Possible response: a hopeful mood)*

STRATEGIC READING FOR Less-Proficient Readers

DD Have students explain Mark's decision about school at the end of the selection. Ask them why they think he made this decision. *(Possible response: Some students may say that Mark decides to go to school mainly because he is shocked by his mother's statement that she doesn't want him to grow up to be uneducated like his father. Others might say Mark is impressed by the strength of his mother's concerns, hopes, and dreams for him.)* **Drawing Conclusions**

CUSTOMIZING FOR Gifted and Talented Students

Have students discuss the concept of destiny. Can our life decisions really alter our destinies forever? Or are our lives and futures laid out for us by a fate over which we have little or no control? Ask students to support their views with specifics from the selection.

COMPREHENSION CHECK

1. Why doesn't Mark want to go to school? *(He wants to run wild with his gang; he thinks school will be torture.)*
2. How does Mrs. Mathabane get Mark to register at school? *(She and her mother tie him up and drag him there.)*
3. Why has it taken Mrs. Mathabane a year to enroll Mark? *(The government in Pretoria would not send the necessary papers.)*
4. What does Mark's father do when he hears Mark has been to school? *(He beats up Mark's mother and throws the other children out of the house; he threatens to kill Mark.)*
5. What does Mark do at the end of the story? *(He decides to become educated.)*

From Personal Response to Critical Analysis

1. Accept all reasonable responses. Encourage students to offer reasons why the incident stands out so vividly.
2. Possible responses: her husband's attitude toward education; overcoming the government's paperwork regulations; convincing Mark of the value of an education
3. Accept all reasonable, well-supported responses.
4. Possible responses: Some students may say that tribal traditions, such as the subservience of women in marriage, are more ingrained in the grandmother, who has lived her whole life by them. Mark's mother has suffered under the tribal traditions, being given as a bride to a man she detests, and thus opposes them openly. Other students might point out that times had changed and generally women were exposed to more options than their mothers had been.
5. Accept all reasonable, well-supported responses. Some students might say the value of education; others might say the importance of courage in standing up for what you believe in, even against government oppression and physical abuse.
6. Accept all reasonable responses.

Another Pathway

Cooperative Learning Students should collaborate to make sure their radio plays are a success. One student can be responsible for adapting the scene as dialogue. Another student can acquire and perform the necessary sound effects, while a third, serving as narrator, can prepare the necessary narrative lead-in and sequence.

Rubric

3 Full Accomplishment The radio play contains gripping dialogue that reveals the characters and the plot. Sound effects enhance the atmosphere of the scene.

2 Substantial Accomplishment The radio play contains some gripping dialogue, but it misrepresents one or more of the characters and confuses events.

1 Substantial Accomplishment The dialogue fails to convey what happens in the scene, and the characterizations are weak.

RESPONDING OPTIONS

FROM PERSONAL RESPONSE TO CRITICAL ANALYSIS

REFLECT
1. What incident in the selection stands out most vividly in your mind? Why?

RETHINK
2. What do you think is Mrs. Mathabane's greatest challenge in getting her son an education?

   Close Textual Reading

   Consider
   - the regulations that discourage black education
   - her husband's attitude toward education
   - tribal traditions about a woman's status
   - the influence of the gang on her son

3. What is your opinion of Mathabane's father? Support your opinion with details from the selection.

4. Why do you think the mother and the grandmother have such different opinions about a woman's role in marriage?

RELATE
5. What do you think is the most important message that Mathabane conveys in this selection?

   Consider
   - how apartheid affects the lives of blacks
   - the effect of tribal marriage traditions on women's lives
   - the doors that may or may not be opened by education

6. For Mathabane, the prediction "Education will open doors where none seem to exist" came true. Do you think this statement is generally true in our society? Why or why not?

Multimodal Learning
ANOTHER PATHWAY

Cooperative Learning
With a few classmates, adapt a scene from the selection as a radio play. Your adaptation should consist mainly of dialogue, with some sound effects and perhaps a narrator's remarks. Try to capture the personalities of the characters.

QUICKWRITES

1. Imagine that you are young Mark Mathabane and that a gang member confronts you about your decision to attend school. Using dialogue in the selection as a model, write a **dialogue** in which you defend your decision to the gang member.

2. Write a script for a **public-service announcement** on South African television, in which the adult Mark Mathabane advises young South African blacks to go to school.

3. Write a **eulogy,** or memorial speech, that the woman on Sixteenth Avenue might have delivered at her son's funeral. Use details from her conversation with the Mathabanes for ideas about what she might say.

📁 **PORTFOLIO** *Save your writing. You may want to use it later as a springboard to a piece for your portfolio.*

80   UNIT ONE   PART 1: LASTING IMPRESSIONS

QuickWrites

1. Encourage students to have Mark use some of the same arguments with the gang member that his mother used with him. Students might have the gang member use dialogue that attempts to embarrass or threaten Mark for his decision to go to school.
2. Suggest that students discuss public-service announcements they have seen on television before beginning the assignment.
3. You might ask a volunteer to read the strange woman's dialogue aloud so that students can get a sense of her voice.

📘 The Writer's Craft

Writing Dialogue, pp. 452–453
Persuasive Speech, pp. 222–227

LITERARY CONCEPTS

Dialogue is conversation between two or more characters. The use of dialogue in writing brings characters to life and gives the reader insights into the characters' personality traits. For example, consider the dialogue between the strange woman and Mathabane's mother. This conversation between a mother who has lost her son and a mother fighting to keep hers dramatizes the regret and sorrow of the one and the sympathy and determination of the other. With a partner, examine another passage of dialogue in the selection. What does the dialogue reveal about the characters who participate in it? Share your ideas with your classmates.

LITERARY LINKS

Compare and contrast Mark Mathabane's childhood rebelliousness with that of the narrator of "Two Kinds."

Multimodal Learning

ALTERNATIVE ACTIVITIES

1. Design a **poster** in which art or photos are used to encourage students from Mark Mathabane's township to stay in school.
2. Create a **drawing** that illustrates two different ways of viewing school. One way should be that of Mathabane's mother; the other should be that of the gang's.

CRITIC'S CORNER

One newspaper review praised *Kaffir Boy* as an autobiography "told with relentless honesty." What details in the selection support this evaluation? Do you agree that "relentless honesty" is praiseworthy in an autobiography? Explain your opinion.

ACROSS THE CURRICULUM

History Find out more about apartheid. How did this system originate? What were its effects on people's lives? What brought an end to apartheid? Present your findings in a research paper.

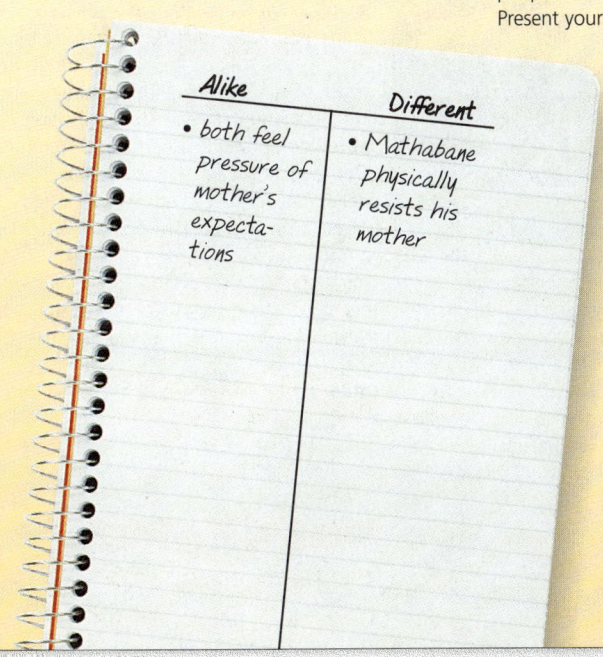

Across the Curriculum

History Encourage students to focus their research as much as possible. Be sure they discover that the word *apartheid* means "separateness" in Afrikaans, the language spoken by South Africa's Dutch settlers.

Critic's Corner

As examples of Mark Mathabane's relentless honesty, students might point to the dreary description of Alexandra's poor people, the lawbreaking of the young boys in Mark's gang, and the brutal way in which Mr. Mathabane batters his wife and talks to his son.

Students might suggest that "relentless honesty" is praiseworthy in an autobiography like this because one of its purposes is to fight apartheid. Others might say that relentless honesty in autobiographies hurts people, such as Mark's father, who are portrayed negatively.

Literary Links

Possible responses:

Similarity

- Both Mark and the narrator of "Two Kinds" rebel against goals that their mothers have set for them.

Differences

- Mark rebelled against his mother strongly and openly from the outset; eventually, though, he came to accept her viewpoint.
- The narrator of "Two Kinds" went along with her mother at first, but gradually she grew discouraged and rebelled.

Alternative Activities

1. Remind students that to be effective, a poster must make a strong visual impact while keeping the amount of type to a minimum. Also remind them that a catchy or a stark heading for the poster will grab the viewer's attention. If possible, have them check the school bulletin board and discuss what makes some of the posters there effective.
2. Encourage students to review the attitudes that the members of Mark's gang had toward school. Remind students that the gang saw school as a prison in which youngsters were tortured. Have students discuss ways in which they might illustrate Mark's new attitude toward school—a beacon of light leading away from ignorance.

Literary Concepts

Suggest that students analyze the dialogue between Mark's mother and the principal on page 74, the dialogue between Mark and his father on page 76, or that between Mark and his mother on page 78. Suggest that they ask themselves these questions as they examine a passage of dialogue:

- How would you describe the tone of each speaker's voice?
- Why do you think the speaker is saying these things?
- What do the speaker's words reveal about his or her character?

When students have finished, have them compare their interpretations.

Words to Know

1. pretext
2. austere
3. captivated
4. Paradoxically
5. inscrutable
6. inkling

Reteaching/Reinforcement
• *Unit One Resource Book*, p.24

MARK MATHABANE

Although Mark Mathabane was unable to afford the necessary primers and other textbooks during his few years in school, he always managed to finish at the top of his class. His father was never willing to pay his school tuition, so his mother found a job as a cleaner to pay the fees for Mark and his sisters. Later, Mark won a full scholarship to a high school that admitted boys from all the black ethnic groups. Mark was especially happy to go to this school because most classes were taught in English, a language he was "in love with."

WORDS TO KNOW

EXERCISE A On your paper write the word that best completes each sentence below.

1. Apartheid laws set up separate black schools on the (pretext, credence) that such schools would preserve tribal traditions.
2. The schools for blacks were underfunded and had (austere, unsolicited) budgets.
3. The dream of educating her son had (accosted, captivated) Mrs. Mathabane for years.
4. (Paradoxically, Unsolicited), Mark's father limited his own future by refusing to cooperate with the white-controlled schools.
5. Books and documents seem (utilitarian, inscrutable) to those who cannot read.
6. When Mark entered school, he had no (inkling, pretext) of the fame that he would eventually achieve.

EXERCISE B Find an object or a picture of an object that can be described with one of the four adjectives among the Words to Know.

MARK MATHABANE

1960–

Inspired by his mother's sacrifices, young Mark Mathabane became a top student at his school and began learning English—his fifth language—when he was about ten. To help with his family's meager finances, he also started doing odd jobs at the home of the white family for whom his grandmother worked. From that family, who did not believe in apartheid, Mathabane received copies of classic novels like *Treasure Island* and *David Copperfield;* he also received an old tennis racket. His interest in tennis skyrocketed when, a year later, the African-American tennis star Arthur Ashe—an outspoken critic of apartheid—was allowed to play in South Africa for the first time.

In 1977 Mathabane met another American tennis champion, Stan Smith, who helped him win a tennis scholarship to an American college. Once there, however, Mathabane realized that his tennis skills would never be of Smith's and Ashe's caliber. He began to devote most of his attention to his studies and, during his junior year, started writing his autobiography. Published in 1986, *Kaffir Boy* quickly became an international bestseller. Nevertheless, it was banned in South Africa until the political situation there began to change in the early 1990s.

Mathabane hopes that the story of his life will inspire "other boys and girls into believing that you can still grow up to be as much of an individual as you have the capacity to be."

OTHER WORKS *Kaffir Boy in America, Love in Black and White* Extended Reading

82 UNIT ONE PART 1: LASTING IMPRESSIONS

REFLECTING ON THEME
What Do You Think?

Have students review the interviews that they conducted before reading the selections in Part One. Ask them whether any of the interviews focused on memories of school, and if so, how those memories compare with Mathabane's experience. Ask students whether their own appreciation of lasting impressions has grown as a result of reading this selection.

PREVIEWING

NONFICTION

The Teacher Who Changed My Life
Nicholas Gage Greece / United States

Activating Prior Knowledge
PERSONAL CONNECTION

Think of the various people who have influenced the course of your life. When you look back, 10 or 20 years from now, which of these people do you think will have made a lasting impression on you? In your notebook, jot down your thoughts about one of these people.

Building Background
BIOGRAPHICAL CONNECTION

Nicholas Gage was born in 1939 in Lia, a mountain village in northwestern Greece. Nicholas lived his early years with his mother, Eleni, and four older sisters. His father, Christos, had left his impoverished village to find work in the United States, eventually settling in Worcester, Massachusetts. Before World War II began, his father had been able to return home for extended visits, but the war and the German occupation of Greece made such travel impossible.

After World War II, Eleni and her five children found themselves caught in Greece's bitter civil war between the Communists and the royalists, those who supported rule by the king. In 1947 the Communists took control of Lia, blocking all exit opportunities. In the spring of 1948, the Communists began retreating into nearby Albania, taking the village children with them. Eleni made secret arrangements for the family to flee, but her plan was only partially successful. Though Nicholas and three sisters escaped, one daughter and the mother were left behind. Eventually, Nicholas and his three sisters were able to join their father in the United States.

Active Reading/Setting a Purpose
READING CONNECTION

Understanding Cause and Effect
As you read this selection, focus on the changes in the author's life that were brought about by his teacher's influence. Use a diagram like the one below to record the effects of her influence.

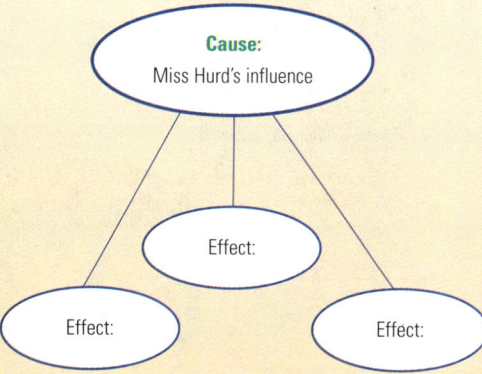

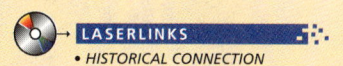
• HISTORICAL CONNECTION

OVERVIEW
Objectives
- To understand and appreciate an autobiographical essay that explores the lasting impression a teacher makes on a young boy
- To identify and understand an essay
- To express understanding of the essay through a choice of writing forms, including an essay and a character sketch
- To extend understanding of the essay through a variety of multimodal and cross-curricular activities

Skills

LITERARY CONCEPTS
- Essay
- Characterization

GRAMMAR
- *Who/whom* in subordinate clauses

READING SKILLS/ STRATEGIES
- Understanding cause and effect

SPEAKING, LISTENING, AND VIEWING
- Group discussion
- Dramatic monologue
- Oral report

THE WRITER'S STYLE
- Sentence variety

ALTERNATIVE
Previewing

Students can work in groups and use the following prompts to prepare for their reading of the selection.

Personal Connection

Discussion Prompts
- *To whom do you turn when you're upset or discouraged?*
- *Who has taught you a skill or hobby you enjoy?*
- *Who most influenced the development of your own goals and beliefs?*

As you read, look for ways in which the author's life was changed by someone special.

HISTORICAL CONNECTION
The Greek Civil War, 1947–1949
The bitter Greek civil war between the communists and the royalists in the late 1940s forced many Greek people to flee their homes. Like Nicholas Gage's mother, many Greeks fought to survive and risked everything to ensure the safety of their families. The following photographs reflect the struggles of the civilians and the soldiers.

Side A, Frame 49319

PRINT AND MEDIA RESOURCES

UNIT ONE RESOURCE BOOK
Strategic Reading: Literature, p. 27
Vocabulary SkillBuilder, p. 28

GRAMMAR MINI-LESSONS
Transparencies, p. 19
Copymasters, p. 21

WRITING MINI-LESSONS
Transparencies, p. 53

ACCESS FOR STUDENTS ACQUIRING ENGLISH
Selection Summaries
Reading Support

FORMAL ASSESSMENT
Selection Test, pp. 15–16
Test Generator

 **AUDIO LIBRARY**
See Reference Card

 **LASERLINKS**
Historical Connection

THE LANGUAGE OF LITERATURE TEACHER'S EDITION **83**

SUMMARY

Nicholas Gage describes how the power of the written word transformed a meek immigrant boy into a prize-winning writer. Gage recalls how he came to the United States as a nine-year-old refugee. Unable to speak English, Gage was placed in a class for the mentally retarded. By the time he met his teacher and mentor four years later, Miss Marjorie Hurd, he had learned English and had advanced to the college-preparatory track in the public school. Miss Hurd drilled the class in grammar, assigned reading, and asked young Nick to write about his past. Nick's account of his nighttime escape from his village, the death of his mother, and his stay in a refugee camp earned him a medal. Nick went on to study journalism, and he won the Hearst Award for College Journalism. He also turned his mother's story into a book that later inspired President Ronald Reagan to seek an arms agreement with the Soviet Union. Gage notes that none of these honors would have been his had it not been for the efforts of Miss Hurd, who remains important in his life.

Thematic Link: *Lasting Impressions* The lasting impression of a memorable teacher led the author to become an award-winning reporter and writer.

CUSTOMIZING FOR
Students Acquiring English

- Use **ACCESS FOR STUDENTS ACQUIRING ENGLISH,** *Reading Support.*
- Be sensitive to the fact that some students, like the author, may have become separated from family members in leaving their native countries.
- As you guide students through the selection, you may want to use the suggestions under Strategic Reading for Less-Proficient Readers, as well as the suggestions in these boxes.

STRATEGIC READING FOR
Less-Proficient Readers

Set a Purpose Have students read ahead to find out the immediate effects of becoming Miss Hurd's student.

Use **UNIT ONE RESOURCE BOOK,** p. 28, for guidance in reading the selection.

A portion of the author's third-grade class. Nicholas Gage is circled; his sister Fotini is on the left in the second row from the bottom. Courtesy of Nicholas Gage.

84

WORDS TO KNOW

authoritarian (ə-thôr′ĭ-târ′ē-ən) *adj.* expecting or demanding absolute obedience (p. 85)

catalyst (kăt′l-ĭst) *n.* something that causes change or action (p. 89)

emphatically (ĕm-făt′ĭ-klē) *adv.* forcefully; strongly (p. 89)

formidable (fôr′mĭ-də-bəl) *adj.* inspiring awe, fear, or wonder (p. 85)

hone (hōn) *v.* to sharpen (p. 86)

mentor (mĕn′tôr) *n.* a wise and trusted teacher (p. 85)

mortify (môr′tə-fī′) *v.* to cause to feel shame or humiliation (p. 87)

muse (myōoz) *n.* a guiding spirit or source of inspiration (p. 85)

tact (tăkt) *n.* the sensitivity to say and do what is appropriate when dealing with other people (p. 87)

void (void) *n.* a feeling of loss; emptiness (p. 88)

84 THE LANGUAGE OF LITERATURE TEACHER'S EDITION

The person who set the course of my life in the new land I entered as a young war refugee—who, in fact, nearly dragged me onto the path that would bring all the blessings I've received in America—was a salty-tongued, no-nonsense schoolteacher named Marjorie Hurd. When I entered her classroom in 1953, I had been to six schools in five years, starting in the Greek village where I was born in 1939.

When I stepped off a ship in New York Harbor on a gray March day in 1949, I was an undersized 9-year-old in short pants who had lost his mother and was coming to live with the father he didn't know. My mother, Eleni Gatzoyiannis,[1] had been imprisoned, tortured and shot by Communist guerrillas for sending me and three of my four sisters to freedom. She died so that her children could go to their father in the United States.

The portly, bald, well-dressed man who met me and my sisters seemed a foreign, authoritarian figure. I secretly resented him for not getting the whole family out of Greece early enough to save my mother. Ultimately, I would grow to love him and appreciate how he dealt with becoming a single parent at the age of 56, but at first our relationship was prickly, full of hostility.

As Father drove us to our new home—a tenement in Worcester, Mass.—and pointed out the huge brick building that would be our first school in America, I clutched my Greek notebooks from the refugee camp, hoping that my few years of schooling would impress my teachers in this cold, crowded country. They didn't. When my father led me and my 11-year-old sister to Greendale Elementary School, the grim-faced Yankee principal put the two of us in a class for the mentally retarded. There was no facility in those days for non-English-speaking children.

By the time I met Marjorie Hurd four years later, I had learned English, been placed in a normal, graded class and had even been chosen for the college preparatory track in the Worcester public school system. I was 13 years old when our father moved us yet again, and I entered Chandler Junior High shortly after the beginning of seventh grade. I found myself surrounded by richer, smarter and better-dressed classmates, who looked askance at my strange clothes and heavy accent. Shortly after I arrived, we were told to select a hobby to pursue during "club hour" on Fridays. The idea of hobbies and clubs made no sense to my immigrant ears, but I decided to follow the prettiest girl in my class—the blue-eyed daughter of the local Lutheran minister. She led me through the door marked "Newspaper Club" and into the presence of Miss Hurd, the newspaper adviser and English teacher who would become my mentor and my muse.

A formidable, solidly built woman with salt-and-pepper hair, a steely eye and a flat Boston accent, Miss Hurd had no patience with layabouts. "What are all you goof-offs doing here?" she bellowed at the would-be journalists. "This is the Newspaper Club! We're going to put out a *newspaper*. So if there's anybody in this room who doesn't like work, I suggest you go across to the Glee Club now, because you're going to work your tails off here!"

I was soon under Miss Hurd's spell. She did indeed teach us to put out a newspaper, skills I

---

1. Eleni Gatzoyiannis (ĕ-lĕ′nē gät′zô-yän′ĭs).

WORDS TO KNOW	**authoritarian** (ə-thôr′ĭ-târ′ē-ən) *adj.* expecting or demanding absolute obedience **mentor** (mĕn′tôr) *n.* a wise and trusted teacher **muse** (myo͞oz) *n.* a guiding spirit or source of inspiration **formidable** (fôr′mĭ-də-bəl) *adj.* inspiring awe, fear, or wonder

Passport photo of Nicholas Gage and three of his sisters. Courtesy of Nicholas Gage.

honed during my next 25 years as a journalist. Soon I asked the principal to transfer me to her English class as well. There, she drilled us on grammar until I finally began to understand the logic and structure of the English language. She assigned stories for us to read and discuss; not tales of heroes, like the Greek myths I knew, but stories of underdogs—poor people, even immigrants, who seemed ordinary until a crisis drove them to do something extraordinary. She also introduced us to the literary wealth of Greece—giving me a new perspective on my war-ravaged, impoverished homeland. I began to be proud of my origins.

One day, after discussing how writers should write about what they know, she assigned us to compose an essay from our own experience. Fixing me with a stern look, she added, "Nick, I want you to write about what happened to your family in Greece." I had been trying to put those painful memories behind me and left the assignment until the last moment. Then, on a warm spring afternoon, I sat in my room with a yellow pad and pencil and stared out the window at the buds on the trees. I wrote that the coming of spring always reminded me of the last time I said goodbye to my mother on a green and gold day in 1948.

I kept writing, one line after another, telling how the Communist guerrillas occupied our village, took our home and food, how my mother started planning our escape when she learned that the children were to be sent to re-education camps[2] behind the Iron Curtain[3] and

---

2. **re-education camps:** camps where people were forced to go to be indoctrinated with Communist ideas and beliefs.
3. **behind the Iron Curtain:** on the Communist side of the imaginary divide between the democracies of Western Europe and the Communist dictatorships of Eastern Europe; in this case, the camps were in Albania.

WORDS TO KNOW

hone (hōn) *v.* to sharpen

how, at the last moment, she couldn't escape with us because the guerrillas sent her with a group of women to thresh wheat in a distant village. She promised she would try to get away on her own, she told me to be brave and hung a silver cross around my neck, and then she kissed me. I watched the line of women being led down into the ravine and up the other side, until they disappeared around the bend—my mother a tiny brown figure at the end who stopped for an instant to raise her hand in one last farewell.

I wrote about our nighttime escape down the mountain, across the minefields and into the lines of the Nationalist soldiers, who sent us to a refugee camp. It was there that we learned of our mother's execution. I felt very lucky to have come to America, I concluded, but every year, the coming of spring made me feel sad because it reminded me of the last time I saw my mother.

For the first time I began to understand the power of the written word. A secret ambition took root in me.

I handed in the essay, hoping never to see it again, but Miss Hurd had it published in the school paper. This mortified me at first, until I saw that my classmates reacted with sympathy and tact to my family's story. Without telling me, Miss Hurd also submitted the essay to a contest sponsored by the Freedoms Foundation at Valley Forge, Pa., and it won a medal. The Worcester paper wrote about the award and quoted my essay at length. My father, by then a "five-and-dime-store chef," as the paper described him, was ecstatic with pride, and the Worcester Greek community celebrated the honor to one of its own.

For the first time I began to understand the power of the written word. A secret ambition took root in me. One day, I vowed, I would go back to Greece, find out the details of my mother's death and write about her life, so her grandchildren would know of her courage. Perhaps I would even track down the men who killed her and write of their crimes. Fulfilling that ambition would take me 30 years.

Meanwhile, I followed the literary path that Miss Hurd had so forcefully set me on. After junior high, I became the editor of my school paper at Classical High School and got a part-time job at the Worcester *Telegram and Gazette.* Although my father could only give me $50 and encouragement toward a college education, I managed to finance four years at Boston University with scholarships and part-time jobs in journalism. During my last year of college, an article I wrote about a friend who had died in the Philippines—the first person to lose his life working for the Peace Corps—led to my winning the Hearst Award for College Journalism. And the plaque was given to me in the White House by President John F. Kennedy.

For a refugee who had never seen a motorized vehicle or indoor plumbing until he was 9, this was an unimaginable honor. When the Worcester paper ran a picture of me standing next to President Kennedy, my father rushed out to buy a new suit in order to be properly dressed to receive the congratulations of the Worcester Greeks. He clipped out the photograph, had it laminated in plastic and carried it in his breast pocket for the rest of his life to show everyone he met. I found the much-worn photo in his pocket on the day he died 20 years later.

WORDS TO KNOW
mortify (môr′tə-fī) *v.* to cause to feel shame or humiliation
tact (tăkt) *n.* the sensitivity to say and do what is appropriate when dealing with other people

87

Mini-Lesson Grammar

WHO/WHOM IN SUBORDINATE CLAUSES
Tell students that when the relative pronoun *who* or *whom* begins an adjective clause, it relates the clause to the word it modifies. Explain that *who* is used to modify the subject of a sentence and that *whom* is used to modify a direct object or an object of a preposition.

For instance, in the first sentence of the selection, *who* appears twice, each time relating back to the subject of the sentence. In the sentence beginning "She taught for a total of 41 years," which appears in the second paragraph on page 88, *whom* is the object of the preposition *in.*

Application Invite students to suggest original sentences about the selection in which they correctly use *who* or *whom* to introduce a subordinate clause.

Reteaching/Reinforcement
• *Grammar Handbook,* anthology pp. 1073–1074
• *Grammar Mini-Lessons* copymasters p. 21, transparencies p. 19

The Writer's Craft

Kinds of Subordinate Clauses, pp. 607–609
Who and *Whom,* pp. 720–721

Linking to History

The civil war in Greece between Communists and Nationalists broke out in 1944 as soon as the Nazi German occupiers left. At first, the British fought the Communists to prevent them from taking over Greece. Then, under the Truman Doctrine of 1947, which guaranteed American aid to any free nation trying to combat Communist forces, the United States replaced the British in supporting the Nationalists. By late 1949, the Communist rebels had been defeated.

Critical Thinking: SYNTHESIZING

Invite students to express their personal understanding of "the power of the written word." Ask students to draw upon their own experience as writers and readers to describe this power.

CUSTOMIZING FOR Students Acquiring English

To help students understand the strength of Gage's ambition as indicated by the phrase "took root in me," encourage them to visualize a tree's roots—how solidly they are lodged in the ground, and how much strength it takes to pull them out.

Literary Concept: CHARACTERIZATION

Ask students what the simple detail that the author provides about his father—that his father kept the laminated picture of his son and President Kennedy in his breast pocket all his life—tells us about the man. *(Possible response: He is intensely proud of his son.)*

THE LANGUAGE OF LITERATURE TEACHER'S EDITION **87**

Literary Concept: CHARACTERIZATION

J Have students note that the author sums up the teaching style of Miss Hurd in this paragraph. In light of these details, how would students describe her? *(Possible responses: She is concerned, insightful, and determined.)*

Critical Thinking: ANALYZING

K Ask students why President Reagan's decision to seek an arms agreement was a fitting monument to the author's mother. *(Possible response: The author's mother died crying out for her children. The arms agreement was intended to ensure that wars would never again separate children from their parents.)*

In our isolated Greek village, my mother had bribed a cousin to teach her to read, for girls were not supposed to attend school beyond a certain age. She had always dreamed of her children receiving an education. She couldn't be there when I graduated from Boston University, but the person who came with my father and shared our joy was my former teacher, Marjorie Hurd. We celebrated not only my bachelor's degree but also the scholarships that paid my way to Columbia's Graduate School of Journalism. There, I met the woman who would eventually become my wife. At our wedding and at the baptisms of our three children, Marjorie Hurd was always there, dancing alongside the Greeks.

> **She would alternately bully and charm each one with her own special brand of tough love until the spark caught fire.**

By then, she was Mrs. Rabidou, for she had married a widower when she was in her early 40s. That didn't distract her from her vocation of introducing young minds to English literature, however. She taught for a total of 41 years and continually would make a "project" of some balky student in whom she spied a spark of potential. Often these were students from the most troubled homes, yet she would alternately bully and charm each one with her own special brand of tough love until the spark caught fire. She retired in 1981 at the age of 62 but still avidly follows the lives and careers of former students while overseeing her adult stepchildren and driving her husband on camping trips to New Hampshire.

Miss Hurd was one of the first to call me on Dec. 10, 1987, when President Reagan, in his television address after the summit meeting with Gorbachev,[4] told the nation that Eleni Gatzoyiannis's dying cry, "My children!" had helped inspire him to seek an arms agreement "for all the children of the world."

"I can't imagine a better monument for your mother," Miss Hurd said with an uncharacteristic catch in her voice.

Although a bad hip makes it impossible for her to join in the Greek dancing, Marjorie Hurd Rabidou is still an honored and enthusiastic guest at all our family celebrations, including my 50th birthday picnic last summer, where the shish kebab was cooked on spits, clarinets and *bouzoukis*[5] wailed, and costumed dancers led the guests in a serpentine line around our Colonial farmhouse, only 20 minutes from my first home in Worcester.

My sisters and I felt an aching <u>void</u> because my father was not there to lead the line, balancing a glass of wine on his head while he danced, the way he did at every celebration during his 92 years. But Miss Hurd was there, surveying the scene with quiet satisfaction. Although my parents are gone, her presence was a consolation, because I owe her so much.

This is truly the land of opportunity, and I would have enjoyed its bounty even if I hadn't walked into Miss Hurd's classroom in 1953. But she was the one who directed my grief and pain into writing, and if it weren't for her, I wouldn't have become an investigative reporter and foreign correspondent, recorded the story of my mother's life and death in *Eleni* and now my father's story in *A Place for Us*, which is

---

4. **summit meeting with Gorbachev** (gôr′bə-chôf′): a high-level meeting between U.S. president Ronald Reagan and Mikhail Gorbachev, the last premier of the Soviet Union.
5. ***bouzoukis*** (boo-zoo′kēz): traditional Greek stringed instruments resembling mandolins.

WORDS TO KNOW
void *n.* a feeling of loss; emptiness

Assessment Option

INFORMAL ASSESSMENT You can informally assess your students' understanding of the selection by having pairs of students act out the following scenario using what they know from the essay:

Imagine that Miss Hurd and Nicholas Gage are talking at Gage's 50th birthday party. The conversation turns to Gage's experiences in Miss Hurd's classroom and how they affected him later.

Rubric

3 Full Accomplishment Students accurately and concisely bring out specific details from the essay that show the influence of Miss Hurd on the author.

2 Substantial Accomplishment Students describe events from the essay, but they do not clearly express the influence Miss Hurd had on the author.

1 Little or Partial Accomplishment Students have difficulty expressing events from the essay; the students' conversation does not reveal the nature of the relationship that existed between Miss Hurd and Gage.

Pictured at left, Marjorie Hurd Rabidou and Nicholas Gage. Copyright © Eddie Adams / SYGMA. At right, Nicholas Gage and his family at the harbor in Piraeus, Greece, ready to set out for the United States. Courtesy of Nicholas Gage.

also a testament to the country that took us in. She was the catalyst that sent me into journalism and indirectly caused all the good things that came after. But Miss Hurd would probably deny this emphatically.

A few years ago, I answered the telephone and heard my former teacher's voice telling me, in that won't-take-no-for-an-answer tone of hers, that she had decided I was to write and deliver the eulogy at her funeral. I agreed (she didn't leave me any choice), but that's one assignment I never want to do. I hope, Miss Hurd, that you'll accept this remembrance instead.

> WORDS TO KNOW
> **catalyst** (kăt′l-ĭst) *n.* something that causes change or action
> **emphatically** (ĕm-făt′ĭ-klē) *adv.* forcefully; strongly

From Personal Response to Critical Analysis

1. Accept all reasonable responses.
2. Possible responses: Miss Hurd helped Gage come to terms with the hardships of his life; she encouraged him to take pride in his past; she helped him to develop his own talent and to take pride in his work.
3. Possible responses: Miss Hurd's tough, no-nonsense style might make it difficult for her to accept Gage's praise. She might also feel that Gage was downplaying his own talent.
4. Responses will vary. Students answering yes might point out that she tried to bring out the best in her students. Those answering no might find Miss Hurd's teaching style to be too intimidating and her demands too exacting.
5. Possible responses: Students might say that Gage succeeded because he valued education and because he set goals for himself. Some students will agree that these qualities are helpful to everyone. Others may note that prejudice against immigrants may prevent them from achieving their full potential.

Another Pathway

Cooperative Learning Students should recall the best teachers they have had and the characteristics they liked most about them. One group member can list the three or four criteria that seem most important, based on the group's discussion. A pair of students can peruse the selection for details about Miss Hurd. A fourth student can decide which criteria these examples illustrate.

Rubric

3 Full Accomplishment Students show good judgment in establishing criteria, and they support their opinions about Miss Hurd with evidence from the selection.

2 Substantial Accomplishment Students establish criteria for a good teacher, but they are not always able to support their evaluations of Miss Hurd with appropriate evidence.

1 Little or Partial Accomplishment Students fail to establish appropriate criteria and are unable to evaluate Miss Hurd in a systematic fashion.

RESPONDING OPTIONS

FROM PERSONAL RESPONSE TO CRITICAL ANALYSIS

REFLECT 1. What words and phrases sum up your response to this selection? Write them in your notebook.

RETHINK 2. Review the cause-and-effect diagram that you made about Miss Hurd's influence on the author. What do you think were the most important effects that she had on his life?

Thematic Link

Consider
- the hardships of Nicholas Gage's childhood
- Miss Hurd's essay assignment
- their friendship

3. Gage says that Miss Hurd would probably deny that she "was the catalyst that sent [him] into journalism and indirectly caused all the good things that came after." Why do you think he says this?

Close Textual Reading

Consider
- what you learned about her personality and teaching style
- how she might view his tribute to her influence

RELATE 4. Would you want Miss Hurd for your teacher? Give reasons for your answer.

5. In your opinion, what personal qualities helped Nicholas Gage to succeed in his adopted homeland? Do you think these same qualities would prove helpful to immigrants today?

ANOTHER PATHWAY

Cooperative Learning
Work with a small group to list the characteristics you think are necessary in a good teacher. Then evaluate Miss Hurd in terms of those characteristics, citing evidence from the selection to support your evaluation. Share your findings with the rest of the class.

QUICKWRITES

1. Write an **essay** about someone who has made a lasting impression on your life. You may want to use what you jotted down for the Personal Connection on page 83 as a starting point.

2. Describe either Nicholas Gage or Miss Hurd in a **character sketch**. Include details from the selection.

📁 **PORTFOLIO** Save your writing. You may want to use it later as a springboard to a piece for your portfolio.

LITERARY CONCEPTS

An **essay** is a brief nonfiction work, usually offering an opinion on a subject. Its main purpose may be to express ideas and feelings, to analyze, to inform, to entertain, or to persuade. Work with a partner to identify Gage's purpose for writing. Make a list of the statements in his essay that helped you to identify that purpose.

Purposes of Essays
- to express ideas and feelings
- to analyze
- to entertain
- to inform
- to persuade

90 UNIT ONE PART 1: LASTING IMPRESSIONS

Literary Concepts

The following questions may help students identify Gage's purpose for writing.
- What are the main ideas in the essay? What feelings does Gage express?
- What did you find entertaining about the essay?
- Did the essay persuade you to think about or do something?
- What information is in the essay? Why is that information important?

QuickWrites

1. Have them recall specific details and events that show the person's lasting impression and that reflect their purposes.
2. Students may wish to use dialogue or a telling anecdote to profile their character.

Autobiographical Incident, pp. 26–40
Character Sketch, pp. 78–82

Multimodal Learning

ALTERNATIVE ACTIVITIES

1. Create a **photo essay** about someone who has influenced your life. Include captions that explain what the photographs depict.
2. Read *Eleni*, Nicholas Gage's 1983 book about his mother, or view the 1985 movie adaptation of it on videocassette. Then summarize the book or film in an **oral report** to classmates.
3. Imagine that you are the author's father. Perform a **dramatic monologue** in which you tell the story of your son's life and explain your feelings about him.

LITERARY LINKS

Compare and contrast Miss Hurd with Mark Mathabane's mother in *Kaffir Boy*. What similarities and differences do you see in the women's personalities, their values, and their effects on the lives of others?

WORDS TO KNOW

On your own paper match each word on the left with the word on the right that is most nearly *opposite* in meaning. Use each word only once.

1. authoritarian
2. mentor
3. muse
4. formidable
5. hone
6. mortify
7. tact
8. void
9. catalyst
10. emphatically

a. fullness
b. opponent
c. flatter
d. weakly
e. awkwardness
f. lenient
g. result
h. unimpressive
i. pupil
j. dull

NICHOLAS GAGE

1939–

Miss Hurd's influence helped launch Nicholas Gage (originally Nikola Gatzoyiannis) on a remarkable career as an investigative reporter. For the *Boston Herald Traveler* he exposed shocking conditions at a school for the mentally retarded; for the *Wall Street Journal* he reported on organized crime in both the United States and Great Britain. In 1970 Gage was recruited by the *New York Times*. While there, he wrote news stories on a number of controversial issues, including drug trafficking and government corruption in Latin America and an attempt to sell New York's Metropolitan Museum of Art a fake vase for a million dollars. During this time he also wrote two novels, as well as nonfiction about his native Greece.

In 1980 Gage retired from journalism to devote all his time to researching a book about his mother. His investigations led him to the man responsible for his mother's death, whom he considered killing. In the end, however, he refused to exact vengeance, realizing that to do so would be to "become like him, purging myself as he did of all humanity or compassion."

OTHER WORKS *Eleni, Hellas: A Portrait of Greece, A Place for Us*

THE TEACHER WHO CHANGED MY LIFE

OBJECTIVES

- To promote independent active reading
- To practice and apply skills learned in previous selections

Reading Pathways

- Suggest that students choose partners and do a paired reading of the excerpt, alternating paragraph by paragraph.
- Encourage trios of students to try a dramatic reading. One student can read the paragraphs that include Sido's dialogue, one can read the paragraphs that include Colette's dialogue, and the third can read paragraphs that are straight narration.
- Suggest that students keep a sketch pad handy as they read, in order to create a collage of images that reflect Sido's "earthly paradise."
- Invite students to keep a double-entry journal as they read. The headings for the two columns might be "What Sido Does" and "My Reaction."
- Evaluate how well students can read, interpret, discuss, and write about the selection on their own by using the Integrated Assessment for Unit One, located in the Alternative Assessment booklet. Administer the assessment at the end of the unit after students have read all the selections and completed all the writing that they have been assigned. Allow two class periods, or about two hours, for the assessment.

EDITOR'S NOTE *With the permission of the author or copyright holder, the following selection was excerpted from a longer work. Material was deleted to focus the selection.*

ON YOUR OWN
REFLECT & ASSESS

from Earthly Paradise

Colette ❧ France

The French writer Colette lovingly remembers her mother, Sido (sē-dō'), in these three excerpts from a collection of her autobiographical writings. The first excerpt, beginning "I could live in Paris . . . ," describes Colette's memories of her childhood with Sido, when they lived together in a French country village. The second excerpt, beginning "The time came . . . ," presents Sido many years later, when she was an old woman living alone. The third excerpt, beginning "Sir, You ask me . . . ," is a reflection on a letter that Sido wrote to Colette's second husband and captures Sido's remarkable spirit.

"I could live in Paris . . ."

"I could live in Paris only if I had a beautiful garden," she would confess to me. "And even then! I can't imagine a Parisian garden where I could pick those big bearded oats I sew on a bit of cardboard for you because they make such sensitive barometers." I chide myself for having lost the very last of those rustic barometers made of oat grains whose two awns,[1] as long as a shrimp's feelers, crucified on a card, would turn to the left or the right according to whether it was going to be fine or wet.

No one could equal Sido, either, at separating and counting the talc-like skins of onions. "One—two—three coats; three coats on the onions!" And letting her spectacles or her lorgnette[2] fall on her lap, she would add pensively: "That means a hard winter. I must have the pump wrapped in straw. Besides, the tortoise has dug itself in already, and the squirrels round about Guillemette[3] have stolen quantities of walnuts and cobnuts for their stores. Squirrels always know everything."

If the newspapers foretold a thaw, my mother would shrug her shoulders and laugh scornfully. "A thaw? Those Paris meteorologists can't teach me anything about that! Look at the cat's paws!" Feeling chilly, the cat had indeed folded her paws out of sight beneath her, and shut her eyes tight. "When there's only going to be a short spell of cold," went on Sido, "the cat rolls herself into a turban with her nose against the

---

1. **awns:** slender bristles on the ears of certain grasses.
2. **lorgnette** (lôrn-yĕt'): a pair of eyeglasses attached to a handle.
3. **Guillemette** (gē-mĕt').

92 UNIT ONE PART 1: LASTING IMPRESSIONS

PRINT AND MEDIA RESOURCES

UNIT ONE RESOURCE BOOK
Strategic Reading: Literature, p. 31

FORMAL ASSESSMENT
Selection Test, pp. 17–18
Part Test, pp. 19–20
Test Generator

ALTERNATIVE ASSESSMENT
Unit One Integrated Assessment, pp. 1–6

ACCESS FOR STUDENTS ACQUIRING ENGLISH
Selection Summaries

Old House and Garden, East Hampton, Long Island (1898), Frederick Childe Hassam. Oil on canvas, 24 1/16" × 20", Henry Art Gallery, University of Washington, Seattle, Horace C. Henry Collection (26.70).

SUMMARY

Colette lovingly recalls her mother, Sido, by focusing on Sido's keen observation of nature, her ecstatic love of flowers, her willfulness, and her vigorous independence. In the first excerpt, Colette celebrates the apparent contradiction of Sido's refusal to part with her flowers for a funeral in contrast to her joy in handing a blossom to a ten-month-old. She also contrasts Sido's placing a scarecrow in a cherry tree with her delight in observing a blackbird feeding on the same tree. In the second excerpt, Colette reflects on her mother as a woman whose health had declined but whose spirit remains undaunted, despite falls, burns, and other setbacks. Beset with illness, Sido nevertheless enjoys such forbidden pleasures as the thrill of sawing logs in the crisp, early morning air. The final excerpt begins with a letter Sido wrote to Colette's second husband. Colette reflects that she was proud to be the daughter of the letter's author: a woman full of life, love, and energy; a woman who was, like the blooms she loved, continually flowering.

Thematic Link: *Lasting Impressions* A mother's willpower and aesthetic sensibilities make a lasting impression on her daughter.

Art Note

Old House and Garden, East Hampton, Long Island **by Frederick Childe Hassam** Frederick Childe Hassam (1859–1935), an American painter influenced by French impressionism, used patchy brush strokes to capture the effects of sunlight and shade. In general, Hassam's work has more details, more realistic colors, and a greater use of perspective than does the work of the French impressionists.

Reading the Art *How does this painting help you appreciate the setting that Sido has created for herself?*

OPTION 1

Individual Activity
CHARTING A CHARACTER

Ask students to think about how details in the selection lead them to form conclusions about Sido's character traits and personal qualities. Have students list on a chart, like the one shown, details about Sido and the conclusions they draw about her character.

What Sido Says or Does	What This Tells Me About Her
"I could live in Paris only if I had a beautiful garden."	She loves nature most of all.
She saws logs when she is over 70.	She is stubborn and energetic and likes hard work.

Teacher's Role On the board, set up a sample chart, like the one shown above, for students to copy. After students have completed their own charts, call on volunteers to share some of the details and conclusions they listed.

Rubric

3 Full Accomplishment Student lists a wide range of telling details and conclusions that follow logically from the details; conclusions accurately reveal Sido's traits and qualities.

2 Substantial Accomplishment Student lists some details and conclusions; conclusions may not all follow logically from the details.

1 Little or Partial Accomplishment Student lists few details; conclusions may not follow logically from the details or show insight into Sido's character.

---

root of her tail. But when it's going to be really bitter, she tucks in the pads of her front paws and rolls them up like a muff."

All the year round she kept racks full of plants in pots standing on green-painted wooden steps. There were rare geraniums, dwarf rose bushes, spiraeas with misty white and pink plumes, a few "succulents," hairy and squat as crabs, and murderous cacti. Two warm walls formed an angle which kept the harsh winds from her trial ground, which consisted of some red earthenware bowls in which I could see nothing but loose, dormant earth.

"Don't touch!"

"But nothing's coming up!"

"And what do you know about it? Is it for you to decide? Read what's written on the labels stuck in the pots! These are seeds of blue lupin; that's a narcissus bulb from Holland; those are seeds of winter cherry; that's a cutting of hibiscus—no, of course it isn't a dead twig!—and those are some seeds of sweet peas whose flowers have ears like little hares. And that . . . and that . . ."

"Yes, and that?"

My mother pushed her hat back, nibbled the chain of her lorgnette, and put the problem frankly to me:

"I'm really very worried. I can't remember whether it was a family of crocus bulbs I planted there, or the chrysalis of an emperor moth."

"We've only got to scratch to find out."

A swift hand stopped mine. Why did no one ever model or paint or carve that hand of Sido's, tanned and wrinkled early by household tasks, gardening, cold water, and the sun, with its long, finely tapering fingers and its beautiful, convex,[4] oval nails?

"Not on your life! If it's the chrysalis, it'll die as soon as the air touches it, and if it's the crocus, the light will shrivel its little white shoot and we'll have to begin all over again. Are you taking in what I say? You won't touch it?"

"No, Mother."

As she spoke, her face, alight with faith and an all-embracing curiosity, was hidden by another, older face, resigned and gentle. She knew that I should not be able to resist, any more than she could, the desire to know, and that like herself I should ferret in the earth of that flowerpot until it had given up its secret. I never thought of our resemblance, but she knew I was her own daughter and that, child though I was, I was already seeking for that sense of shock, the quickened heartbeat, and the sudden stoppage of the breath—symptoms of the private ecstasy of the treasure seeker. A treasure is not merely something hidden under the earth or the rocks or the sea. The vision of gold and gems is but a blurred mirage. To me the important thing is to lay bare and bring to light something that no human eye before mine has gazed upon.

She knew then that I was going to scratch on the sly in her trial ground until I came upon the upward-climbing claw of the cotyledon, the sturdy sprout urged out of its sheath by the spring. I thwarted the blind purpose of the bilious-looking, black-brown chrysalis, and hurled it from its temporary death into a final nothingness.

"You don't understand . . . you can't understand. You're nothing but a little eight-year-old murderess—or is it ten? You just can't understand something that wants to live." That was the only punishment I got for my misdeeds; but that was hard enough for me to bear.

Sido loathed flowers to be sacrificed. Although her one idea was to give, I have seen her refuse a request for flowers to adorn a hearse or a grave. She would harden her heart, frown, and answer "No" with a vindictive[5] look.

"But it's for poor Monsieur Enfert,[6] who died

---

4. **convex:** having a surface that curves outward.
5. **vindictive** (vĭn-dĭk′tĭv): spiteful; vengeful.
6. **Monsieur Enfert** (mə-syœ′ än-fĕr′).

94 UNIT ONE PART 1: LASTING IMPRESSIONS

Critic's Corner

"[Sido's] superior understanding of nature and people does not come from some mysterious or magical power, but from her instincts, her intuitive participation in nature, her reverent respect towards the holiness of all life."

Sylvie Romanowski, describing Sido
in an essay on Colette

Invite students to cite details in the selection that support or refute the critic's opinion.

last night! Poor Madame Enfert's so pathetic, she says if she could see her husband depart covered with flowers, it would console her! And you've got such lovely moss roses, Madame Colette."

"My moss roses on a corpse! What an outrage!"

It was an involuntary cry, but even after she had pulled herself together she still said: "No. My roses have not been condemned to die at the same time as Monsieur Enfert."

But she gladly sacrificed a very beautiful flower to a very small child, a child not yet able to speak, like the little boy whom a neighbor to the east proudly brought into the garden one day, to show him off to her. My mother found fault with the infant's swaddling clothes, for being too tight, untied his three-piece bonnet and his unnecessary woolen shawl, and then gazed to her heart's content on his bronze ringlets, his cheeks, and the enormous, stern black eyes of a ten months' old baby boy, really so much more beautiful than any other boy of ten months! She gave him a *cuisse-de-nymphe-émue*[7] rose, and he accepted it with delight, put it in his mouth, and sucked it; then he kneaded it with his powerful little hands and tore off the petals, as curved and carmine[8] as his own lips.

"Stop it, you naughty boy!" cried his young mother.

But mine, with looks and words, applauded his massacre of the rose, and in my jealousy I said nothing.

She also regularly refused to lend double geraniums, pelargoniums, lobelias, dwarf rose bushes and spiraea for the wayside altars on Corpus Christi day, for although she was baptized and married in church, she always held aloof from Catholic trivialities and pageantries. But she gave me permission, when I was between eleven and twelve, to attend catechism classes and to join in the hymns at the evening service.

On the first of May, with my comrades of the catechism class, I laid lilac, camomile, and roses before the altar of the Virgin, and returned full of pride to show my "blessed posy." My mother laughed her irreverent laugh and, looking at my bunch of flowers, which was bringing the May bugs into the sitting room right under the lamp, she said: "Do you suppose it wasn't already blessed before?"

I do not know where she got her aloofness from any form of worship. I ought to have tried to find out. My biographers, who get little information from me, sometimes depict her as a simple farmer's wife and sometimes make her out to be a "whimsical bohemian."[9] One of them, to my astonishment, goes so far as to accuse her of having written short literary works for young persons!

In reality, this Frenchwoman spent her childhood in the Yonne,[10] her adolescence among painters, journalists, and musicians in Belgium, where her two elder brothers had settled, and

---

7. *cuisse-de-nymphe-émue* (kwēs′də-nănf′ ā-mü′): the French name of a variety of rose.
8. **carmine** (kär′mīn): red or purplish-red.
9. **bohemian** (bō-hē′mē-ən): an artistic person who lives in a free, unconventional way.
10. **Yonne** (yän): a rural region in central France, named for the Yonne River.

then returned to the Yonne, where she married twice. But whence, or from whom, she got her sensitive understanding of country matters and her discriminating appreciation of the provinces, I am unable to say. I sing her praises as best I may, and celebrate the native lucidity[11] which, in her, dimmed and often extinguished the lesser lights painfully lit through the contact of what she called "the common run of mankind."

I once saw her hang up a scarecrow in a cherry tree to frighten the blackbirds, because our kindly neighbor of the west, who always had a cold and was shaken with bouts of sneezing, never failed to disguise his cherry trees as old tramps and crown his currant bushes with battered opera hats. A few days later I found my mother beneath the tree, motionless with excitement, her head turned toward the heavens in which she would allow human religions no place.

"Sssh! Look!"

A blackbird, with a green and violent sheen on his dark plumage, was pecking at the cherries, drinking their juice and lacerating their rosy pulp.

"How beautiful he is!" whispered my mother. "Do you see how he uses his claw? And the movements of his head and that arrogance of his? See how he twists his beak to dig out the stone! And you notice that he only goes for the ripest ones."

"But, mother, the scarecrow!"

"Sssh! The scarecrow doesn't worry him!"

"But, mother, the cherries!"

My mother brought the glance of her rain-colored eyes back to earth: "The cherries? Yes, of course, the cherries."

In those eyes there flickered a sort of wild gaiety, a contempt for the whole world, a lighthearted disdain which cheerfully spurned me along with everything else. It was only momentary, and it was not the first time I had seen it. Now that I know her better, I can interpret those sudden gleams in her face. They were, I feel, kindled by an urge to escape from everyone and everything, to soar to some high place where only her own writ ran.[12] If I am mistaken, leave me to my delusion.

But there, under the cherry tree, she returned to earth once more among us, weighed down with anxieties, and love, and a husband and children who clung to her. Faced with the common round of life, she became good and comforting and humble again.

"Yes, of course, the cherries . . . you must have cherries too."

The blackbird, gorged, had flown off, and the scarecrow waggled his empty opera hat in the breeze. . . .

The time came . . .

The time came when all her strength left her. She was amazed beyond measure and would not believe it. Whenever I arrived from Paris to see her, as soon as we were alone in the afternoon in her little house, she had always some sin to confess to me. On one occasion she turned up the hem of her dress, rolled her stocking down over her shin, and displayed a

---

11. **lucidity** (lōō-sĭd′ĭ-tē): a state of being clear-headed or rational.
12. **writ ran:** law was enforced.

purple bruise, the skin nearly broken.

"Just look at that!"

"What on earth have you done to yourself this time, Mother?"

She opened wide eyes, full of innocence and embarrassment.

"You wouldn't believe it, but I fell downstairs!"

"How do you mean—'fell'?"

"Just what I said. I fell, for no reason. I was going downstairs and I fell. I can't understand it."

"Were you going down too quickly?"

"Too quickly? What do you call too quickly? I was going down quickly. Have I time to go downstairs majestically like the Sun King? And if that were all . . . But look at this!"

On her pretty arm, still so young above the faded hand, was a scald forming a large blister.

"Oh goodness! Whatever's that!"

"My footwarmer."

"The old copper footwarmer? The one that holds five quarts?"

"That's the one. Can I trust anything, when that footwarmer has known me for forty years? I can't imagine what possessed it, it was boiling fast, I went to take it off the fire, and crack, something gave in my wrist. I was lucky to get nothing worse than the blister. But what a thing to happen! After that I let the cupboard alone. . . ."

She broke off, blushing furiously.

"What cupboard?" I demanded severely.

My mother fenced, tossing her head as though I were trying to put her on a lead.

"Oh, nothing! No cupboard at all!"

"Mother! I shall get cross!"

"Since I've said, 'I let the cupboard alone,' can't you do the same for my sake? The cupboard hasn't moved from its place, has it? So, shut up about it!"

The cupboard was a massive object of old walnut, almost as broad as it was high, with no carving save the circular hole made by a Prussian bullet that had entered by the right-hand door and passed out through the back panel.

"Do you want it moved from the landing, Mother?"

An expression like that of a young she-cat, false and glittery, appeared on her wrinkled face.

"I? No, it seems to me all right there—let it stay where it is!"

All the same, my doctor brother and I agreed that we must be on the watch. He saw my mother every day, since she had followed him and lived in the same village, and he looked after her with a passionate devotion which he hid. She fought against all her ills with amazing elasticity, forgot them, baffled them, inflicted on them signal if temporary defeats, recovered, during entire days, her vanished strength; and the sound of her battles, whenever I spent a few days with her, could be heard all over the house till I was irresistibly reminded of a terrier tackling a rat.

At five o'clock in the morning I would be awakened by the clank of a full bucket being set down in the kitchen sink immediately opposite my room.

"What are you doing with that bucket, Mother? Couldn't you wait until Josephine arrives?"

And out I hurried. But the fire was already blazing, fed with dry wood. The milk was boiling on the blue-tiled charcoal stove. Nearby, a bar of chocolate was melting in a little water for my breakfast, and, seated squarely in her cane armchair, my mother was grinding the fragrant coffee which she roasted herself. The morning hours were always kind to her. She wore their rosy colors in her cheeks. Flushed with a brief return to health, she would gaze at the rising sun, while the church bell rang for

EARTHLY PARADISE **97**

OPTION 4

Class Discussion
SHARING IDEAS

After students have read the selection, engage them in a class discussion, using the questions below:

Teacher's Role Ensure that all students have an opportunity to participate in the discussion. Have students support their answers and opinions with specific details from the selection.

1. What is it about Sido that leads her to see her surroundings as an "earthly paradise"? *(Possible responses: Some students may say that Sido loves the world of nature and has a close affinity for all living things. Others might point out that she is a happy, observant person who takes great pleasure in the simple things of life or that she is always aware of the natural world around her.)*

2. What types of attitudes and outlooks does Sido foster in her daughter? *(Responses will vary. Some students may point out that Sido gives her daughter an independent view of life and the will to express personal convictions. Others may say she encourages knowledge and love of the natural world.)*

3. What problems does Sido face with the onset of old age, and how well do you think she copes with them? *(Possible response: In old age, Sido suffers from physical frailty and a loss of independence; nevertheless, she battles these problems, maintaining her vitality, sense of humor, and clarity of mind, and she continues to enjoy simple pleasures.)*

4. Does Sido remind you of anyone you know? If so, what things do they have in common? If not, what do you think makes Sido unique? *(Accept all reasonable responses.)*

5. Usually we think of paradise as a perfect place, yet the title of this book contains the word *Earthly*. What do you think is significant about this word in relation to *Paradise*? *(Possible response: Some students may say that earth, like paradise, is filled with countless wonders and pleasures that we can enjoy. Others may say that even though earth can seem like paradise, life on earth is filled with problems, such as the inevitable onset of old age and death.)*

---

early Mass, and rejoice at having tasted, while we still slept, so many forbidden fruits.

The forbidden fruits were the overheavy bucket drawn up from the well, the firewood split with a billhook on an oaken block, the spade, the mattock, and above all the double steps propped against the gable window of the woodhouse. There were the climbing vine whose shoots she trained up to the gable windows of the attic, the flowery spikes of the too-tall lilacs, the dizzy cat that had to be rescued from the ridge of the roof. All the accomplices of her old existence as a plump and sturdy little woman, all the minor rustic divinities who once obeyed her and made her so proud of doing without servants, now assumed the appearance and position of adversaries. But they reckoned without that love of combat which my mother was to keep till the end of her life. At seventy-one, dawn still found her undaunted, if not always undamaged. Burnt by the fire, cut with the pruning knife, soaked by melting snow or spilled water, she had always managed to enjoy her best moments of independence before the earliest risers had opened their shutters. She was able to tell us of the cats' awakening, of what was going on in the nests, of news gleaned, together with the morning's milk and the warm loaf, from the milkmaid and the baker's girl, the record in fact of the birth of a new day.

It was not until one morning when I found the kitchen unwarmed, and the blue enamel saucepan hanging on the wall, that I felt my mother's end to be near. Her illness knew many respites, during which the fire flared up again on the hearth, and the smell of fresh bread and melting chocolate stole under the door together with the cat's impatient paw. These respites were periods of unexpected alarms. My mother and the big walnut cupboard were discovered together in a heap at the foot of the stairs, she having determined to transport it in secret from the upper landing to the ground floor. Whereupon my elder brother insisted that my mother should keep still and that an old servant should sleep in the little house. But how could an old servant prevail against a vital energy so youthful and mischievous that it contrived to tempt and lead astray a body already half fettered by death? My brother, returning before sunrise from attending a distant patient, one day caught my mother red-handed in the most wanton of crimes. Dressed in her nightgown, but wearing heavy gardening sabots, her little gray septuagenarian's plait of hair turning up like a scorpion's tail on the nape of her neck, one foot firmly planted on the crosspiece of the beech trestle, her back bent in the attitude of the expert jobber, my mother, rejuvenated by an indescribable expression of guilty enjoyment, in defiance of all her promises and of the freezing morning dew, was sawing logs in her own yard.

"Sir, You ask me . . ."

"Sir,

"You ask me to come and spend a week with you, which means I would be near my daughter, whom I adore. You who live with her know how rarely I see her, how much her presence delights me, and I'm touched that you should ask me to come and see her. All the same I'm not going to accept your kind invitation, for the time being at any rate. The reason is that my pink cactus is probably going to flower. It's a very rare plant I've been given, and I'm told that in our climate it flowers only once every four years. Now, I am already a very old woman, and if I went away when my pink cactus is about to flower, I am certain I shouldn't see it flower again.

"So I beg you, sir, to accept my sincere thanks and my regrets, together with my kind regards."

COLETTE

Colette was among the first feminist writers who questioned what it means to be male or female, how one can love yet not be enslaved, and why there is a frightening connection between love and jealousy. The book *Earthly Paradise*, from which this selection comes, consists of material drawn from nearly 40 volumes of her nonfiction. "I could live in Paris . . ." comes from *Sido* (1930), Colette's full-length portrait of her parents. "The time came . . ." comes from *La Maison de Claudine* (1922), stories about Colette's childhood. The last piece, "Sir, you ask me . . ." is from *La Naissance du jour* (1928), which recalls her house in Provence.

This note, signed *"Sidonie Colette, née Landoy,"* was written by my mother to one of my husbands, the second. A year later she died, at the age of seventy-seven.

Whenever I feel myself inferior to everything about me, threatened by my own mediocrity, frightened by the discovery that a muscle is losing its strength, a desire its power, or a pain the keen edge of its bite, I can still hold up my head and say to myself: "I am the daughter of the woman who wrote that letter—that letter and so many more that I have kept. This one tells me in ten lines that at the age of seventy-six she was planning journeys and undertaking them, but that waiting for the possible bursting into bloom of a tropical flower held everything up and silenced even her heart, made for love. I am the daughter of a woman who, in a mean, close-fisted, confined little place, opened her village home to stray cats, tramps, and pregnant servant girls. I am the daughter of a woman who many a time, when she was in despair at not having enough money for others, ran through the wind-whipped snow to cry from door to door, at the houses of the rich, that a child had just been born in a poverty-stricken home to parents whose feeble, empty hands had no swaddling clothes for it. Let me not forget that I am the daughter of a woman who bent her head, trembling, between the blades of a cactus, her wrinkled face full of ecstasy over the promise of a flower, a woman who herself never ceased to flower, untiringly, during three quarters of a century." ❖

Translated by Enid McCleod and Una Vincenzo Troubridge

COLETTE

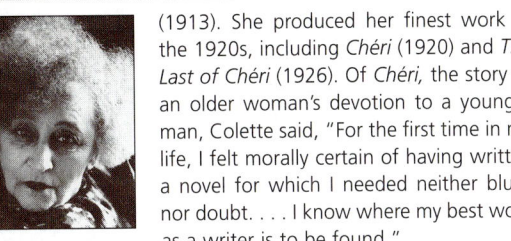
1873–1954

Sidonie-Gabrielle Colette (sē-dô-nē′ gä-brē-ĕl′ kô-lĕt′), known simply as Colette, was a major French writer. Her novels, short stories, and autobiographical writings are marked by a fine attention to sensory detail and a sensitivity to the complexities of human desire.

Colette's first husband, Henri Gauthier-Villars (äN-rē′ gō-tyä′vē-lär′), was a hack writer who discovered Colette's talent and encouraged her to publish her "Claudine" novels under his pen name, Willy, in the years 1900–1903. These novels tell about the escapades of a young, mischievous woman as she learns about life and love.

After a divorce in 1906, Colette pursued an independent career for several years both as a writer and as a music-hall performer. She wrote about this period of her life in *The Vagabond* (1910) and *Recaptured* (1913). She produced her finest work in the 1920s, including *Chéri* (1920) and *The Last of Chéri* (1926). Of *Chéri,* the story of an older woman's devotion to a younger man, Colette said, "For the first time in my life, I felt morally certain of having written a novel for which I needed neither blush nor doubt. . . . I know where my best work as a writer is to be found."

By then a legendary figure, Colette spent her final years confined to her Paris apartment, crippled by arthritis and surrounded by her beloved cats. When she died in 1954, she had produced an impressive variety of works and had received a number of distinguished literary honors. Her funeral was the first state funeral ever given to a woman in France.

OTHER WORKS *Creatures Great and Small, Journey for Myself: Selfish Memories, Gigi, Sido*

OVERVIEW

In the Guided Assignment for this section, students will write an essay responding to the portrayal of an event, a group, or an individual in a story. Writing a personal response will enable students to better understand how good writers use dialogue and description to create strong images of events and characters. As preparation for this assignment, students will use The Writer's Style to help them understand the importance of dialogue in literature. In Reading the World, students will explore the media's portrayal of a group in real life.

Objectives

- To recognize how authors use dialogue effectively
- To write dialogue that sounds like real speech
- To use elaboration techniques
- To write dialogue that reveals character or provides important information
- To write a personal response to a portrayal of an event, a group, or an individual
- To analyze a real-world image of a group

Skills

LITERATURE
- Identifying and analyzing uses of dialogue

GRAMMAR AND USAGE
- Achieving pronoun-antecedent agreement

MEDIA LITERACY
- Analyzing a magazine cover

SPEAKING, LISTENING, AND VIEWING
- Discussing the evaluation of an image
- Group conferencing

CRITICAL THINKING
- Evaluating images
- Synthesizing

Teaching Strategy: MODELING
In the following models, dialogue is used to provide background information and to show what characters are like. This technique is useful in fiction, drama, nonfiction, and poetry.

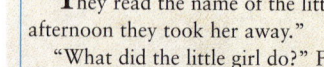 **Boyle** Possible response: The dialogue reveals that after the little girl and her mother were separated, the girl spent three or four days devising a plan to fool the guard and rejoin her mother.

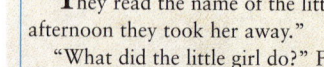 **Tan** Possible response: The dialogue reveals a tense, combative relationship between mother and daughter. The mother demands obedience from her child; the daughter insists that the mother recognize her right to be herself.

WRITING ABOUT LITERATURE

DISCUSSING A PORTRAYAL

What does the conversation between Felicia and the woman in "Winter Night" tell you about their past? How does dialogue show character in "Two Kinds"? On the following pages, you will see and hear how dialogue gives you a better understanding of events and characters. You will also

- study how writers use dialogue
- write your response to the portrayal of a group or event
- think about how media shapes your impressions

The Writer's Style: Creating Dialogue Writers use the words of a character to show what the character is like, to show what is going on, and to add interest.

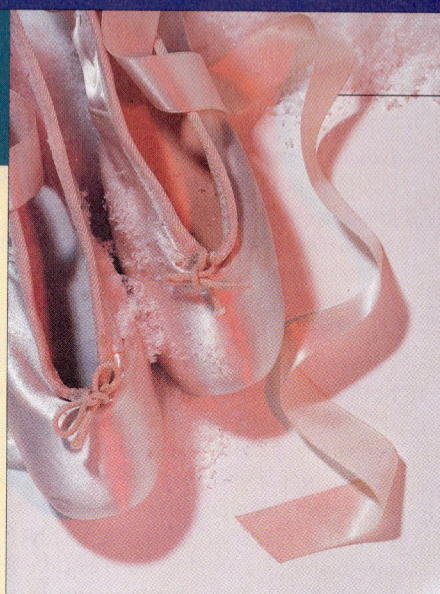

Read the Literature
Notice how writers use dialogue in these excerpts.

Literature Models

Dialogue Reveals Background Information
What background information does this dialogue provide?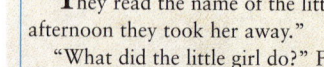

> "They read the name of the little girl's mother out, and that afternoon they took her away."
> "What did the little girl do?" Felicia said.
> "She wanted to think up the best way of getting out, so that she could go find her mother," said the woman, "but she could not think of anything good enough until the third or fourth day. And then she tied her ballet slippers up in the handkerchief again, and she went up to the guard standing at the door."
>
> Kay Boyle, from "Winter Night"

Dialogue Reveals Conflict
What does this dialogue reveal about the relationship between these characters?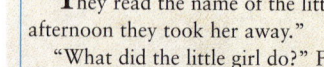

> "You want me to be someone I'm not!" I sobbed. "I'll never be the kind of daughter you want me to be!"
> "Only two kinds of daughters," she shouted in Chinese. "Those who are obedient and those who follow their own mind! Only one kind of daughter can live in this house. Obedient daughter!"
> "Then I wish I wasn't your daughter. I wish you weren't my mother," I shouted.
>
> Amy Tan, from "Two Kinds"

PRINT AND MEDIA RESOURCES

UNIT ONE RESOURCE BOOK
Prewriting, p. 36
Elaboration, p. 37
Peer Response Guide, pp. 38–39
Revising and Proofreading, p. 40
Student Model, pp. 41–42
Rubric, p. 43

GRAMMAR MINI-LESSONS
Transparencies, pp. 6, 44
Copymasters, pp. 8, 45–46

WRITING MINI-LESSONS
Transparencies, pp. 42, 56

FORMAL ASSESSMENT
Guidelines for Writing Assessment

 **WRITING COACH**

 **The Writer's Craft**
Elaboration, pp. 364–369
Pronoun-Antecedent Agreement, pp. 727–729

Connect to Life

You read dialogue in books, magazines, and newspapers, and you listen to dialogue whenever people talk to one another on TV or in movies. Of course, you engage in dialogue each time you talk to someone. Read the dialogue between the cartoon characters below.

Cartoon

Dialogue Reveals Character
What does this dialogue reveal about the differences between these two characters?

Try Your Hand: Writing Dialogue

1. **Say It in Dialogue** Revise the following paragraph to include dialogue that reveals character:

   Jake and I are best friends, but we disagree about everything. Our personalities, at times, are exact opposites. The argument over the way he treats Randy really shows how differently we view our world!

2. **Present Events** Choose one of the following topics and write a dialogue that provides important information:
   - two old friends recall a practical joke they once played
   - a newcomer learns why nobody goes near the old house

3. **Write Your Own Dialogue** Write a dialogue between you and someone you'd like to have a conversation with.

SkillBuilder

WRITER'S CRAFT

Writing Realistic Dialogue

When you write dialogue, try to make the conversation of your characters sound like real speech. You might select interesting language, such as dialect or slang. You can also use contractions or incomplete sentences. Just remember that formal and informal situations call for different language.

Notice the realistic dialogue in this passage from "Everyday Use":

"I reckon she would," I said. "God knows I been saving 'em for long enough with nobody using 'em. I hope she will!"

APPLYING WHAT YOU'VE LEARNED

Use informal language to revise the following dialogue:

"I do not wish to go to school," I said.

My mother replied, "Please do not be difficult. You will go to school."

"I really have no desire to go," I said, as she and Granny dragged me out the door.

WRITING ABOUT LITERATURE 101

Teaching Strategy: MODELING

C Possible response: The dialogue reveals that one character is serious-minded, whereas the other has an offbeat, wacky sense of humor.

Try Your Hand

1. Responses will vary. Passages should contain telling dialogue that reveals character. For example:
   - "Why don't we pitch the tent down by the river, Jake? That way we'll have a great view of the water birds early tomorrow morning."
   - "Are you kiddin'? We gotta be near the other campers! We've got some serious partyin' to do tonight, old buddy."
2. Passages of dialogue should use specific details to describe the situation that students choose. For example:
   - "You remember how we spooked Doyle that time in physics class, Herb?"
   - "I sure do, Tim. I don't think Doyle ever suspected that when he opened the desk drawer to get a piece of chalk, he'd find a baby iguana instead. He sure defied gravity for a few moments that day!"
3. Make sure that students' dialogues reveal character and are true to life.

SkillBuilder WRITER'S CRAFT

WRITING REALISTIC DIALOGUE Point out that informal language encompasses a broad range of forms and structures. Sentence fragments, contractions, abbreviations, nicknames, slang, and dialect are only some of the possibilities.

Applying What You've Learned Possible responses:
- "I don't <u>wanna</u> go to school," I whined.
- Mama shot back, "What you want isn't what you need! You're going to school."
- "Lemme go!" I shrieked, as she and Granny dragged me out the door.

Additional Suggestions Encourage students to use informal language in a revision of this dialogue.
- "I do not understand your behavior, Gina. I thought you enjoyed having Harold as a friend."
- "You are not mistaken, Shirl. I consider Harold to be both talented and attractive."
- "Why, then, did you decline to speak to him when he telephoned last Friday evening?"

Reteaching/Reinforcement
- *Writing Mini-Lessons*, transparencies, p. 56
- *Grammar Mini-Lessons* copymasters, pp. 45–46, transparencies p. 44

 **The Writer's Craft**

Writing Dialogue, pp. 452–455

THE LANGUAGE OF LITERATURE TEACHER'S EDITION 101

Critical Thinking:
SYNTHESIZING

D Point out that a personal response to a literary portrayal involves synthesizing, or combining creatively, a writer's ideas and images with a reader's own ideas, images, and reactions. If necessary, model the process by using the sample notes shown on this page. Point out that the notes contain information, examples, and quotations from the story as well as impressions of the reader's thoughts and feelings.

Teaching Strategy: USING THE SKILLBUILDER

E You can help students gather specific details from the story by teaching the SkillBuilder on Using Elaboration. Your discussion will help students to focus on how to use examples and quotations as support for their ideas in writing about literature.

WRITING ABOUT LITERATURE

Personal Response

D Well-written dialogue and description can help create a strong image of a particular event, group, or individual. The image created by the writer may or may not match an image or idea you already have in your head. Personally responding to a portrayal helps you sort out these ideas or images.

GUIDED ASSIGNMENT

Write a Personal Response The following pages will help you write a personal response to the portrayal of an event, a group, or an individual in a selection from this unit.

Student's Prewriting List

The Portrayal of the Holocaust

Notes and my reactions

Felicia reminds the woman of a little girl at the concentration camp.
Story reminds me of movies and books I have read about the Holocaust
— reminds me to value my personal freedom
— need for hope in the world
— universal idea of love

Examples and Quotes

"We were all hungry, but the children were the hungriest."
"That afternoon they took her away."
"They must be quietly asleep somewhere and not crying all night because they are hungry and because they are cold."
— the first quote in the story about love

1 Prewrite and Explore

Think about the selections in this unit. Did one of the authors portray an event, a group, or a person in a way that seemed to match your ideas?

EXAMINING THE SELECTION

As you review each of the selections, jot down your responses to the portrayal of a group or event. Reflect on these questions:

- What did I think about this group or an event before I read the selection?
- What was my initial reaction to the author's portrayal?
- Do I agree with the author's ideas? Why or why not?
- How does the portrayal make me feel?
- How does the dialogue contribute to my reaction?

GATHERING INFORMATION

Your personal response should include an explanation of your own impression of what is portrayed, as well as details and examples from the selection to explain the reasons for your feelings, opinions, and insights. You can use a simple list like the one at the left to help you gather examples. This sample shows one student's reaction to the portrayal of the Holocaust in "Winter Night." **E**

102 UNIT ONE: IMPRINTS OF THE PAST

Assessment Option

SELF-ASSESSMENT After students have completed the list described under Gathering Information, ask them to assess the entries by answering the following questions:
- Have I focused on the writer's portrayal of a person, a group, or an event?

- Have I noted my initial reaction to the portrayal?
- Did I convey my thoughts and feelings as I compared my reactions with the author's images and ideas?
- Do the examples and quotes that I collected from the story explain or support my opinions and insights?

② Write and Analyze a Discovery Draft

 Begin drafting by writing freely about ideas on your prewriting list. Remember that you'll eventually want to organize your draft to help your reader understand your response.

The discovery draft below includes the student's analysis on yellow notes.

Student's Discovery Draft

What other specific descriptions of the event can I include?

This story was about the Holocaust. I felt sorry for the woman and angry at injustice. Felicia's mother acting selfishly angered me too. I can't forget the mother standing on the train scratching a note on a piece of paper, hoping that it would reach the hands of someone who cares.

I feel sadness, but I feel hopeful too. The woman is a strong individual and a loving person. She sees beyond injustice and loss. In this story, the Holocaust is portrayed as a horrifying, senseless event. It's also portrayed as a stern lesson in love. I agree with both of these ideas.

Which ideas should I expand? I want to use this idea in my conclusion.

③ Draft and Share

 Now you are ready to write a rough draft with an introduction that gives your readers enough information about the work. Your draft should also contain an explanation of why you feel as you do and a conclusion that sums up your overall reaction. The SkillBuilder on using elaboration will help you to include support. Consider the following questions:

- Does my response clearly explain my feelings?
- Have I included enough specific examples and quotations?

When you are finished, invite a peer to read your rough draft.

PEER RESPONSE

- Do I explore my reactions to the selection in depth? How?
- Which quotes and details clearly support my response?

SkillBuilder

WRITER'S CRAFT

Using Elaboration

Elaboration is the technique of using incidents, evidence, and other details to support your ideas. It is an important tool that enables your readers to understand more clearly the events, characters, and ideas about which you are writing.

Below are two types of elaboration that are useful for writing about literature.

Quotations Quotations allow you to reveal more about particular characters and their situations through their own words.

Examples Specific examples are another way to elaborate on an idea. By using examples, you can support and expand upon your main ideas.

Refer to the student's prewriting list on the opposite page. How might the notes help the student to elaborate on a personal response?

APPLYING WHAT YOU'VE LEARNED
Refer to your discovery draft. Check to see that you have used elaboration techniques to develop your ideas. If you haven't, take time to skim the text and revise.

 WRITING HANDBOOK

For more information on elaboration, see page 1029 of the Writing Handbook.

WRITING ABOUT LITERATURE 103

Writing Skill: USING RELEVANT DETAILS

 The Discovery Draft provides an opportunity for students to sort through the information they have gathered and to explore ideas. Suggest that they focus on evaluating the relevance of the details. Each detail they select—such as a quotation or an example from the story—should support one of the main ideas in their response. Guide them to think about a logical way of organizing the details.

Teaching Strategy: HELPING STUDENTS ORGANIZE INFORMATION

 Point out that the introduction in a personal response to a portrayal has to "set the scene" by giving readers an adequate amount of background about the selection. For example, the fourth and fifth sentences in the first sample passage on page 104 provide basic information about the situation and the main characters in "Winter Night."

SkillBuilder — WRITER'S CRAFT

USING ELABORATION Guide students to realize that the notes in the prewriting list on page 102 furnish examples and quotations for elaborating ideas in an essay about the story.

Applying What You've Learned Ask students how the sample passages on this page can be improved by using elaboration. For example, in the first passage, the writer might quote from the story to show the selfish action of Felicia's mother. In the second passage, the writer might mention a concrete example to illustrate the woman's strength and loving nature or to show how she sees beyond injustice and loss.

Additional Suggestions Ask students to discuss other kinds of elaboration: for example, anecdotes and arguments. Challenge the class to suggest why those kinds of elaboration would provide support for a writer's personal opinions.

Reteaching/Reinforcement
- *Writing Handbook,* anthology pp. 1029–1030
- *Writing Mini-Lessons* transparencies, p. 42

The Writer's Craft
Elaboration, pp. 364–368

THE LANGUAGE OF LITERATURE TEACHER'S EDITION 103

Critical Thinking: ANALYZING

H Point out to students that before they revise their drafts they should determine how well they have addressed their audience and achieved their purpose. Students should also:
- check to see that they have clearly stated a main idea
- make sure that the details they have included support their response
- check that they have used a logical order to present their details and reactions

Teaching Strategy: MODELING

I Discuss how this sample meets the Standards for Evaluation on this page. Point out that by quoting the story's opening sentence, the writer gives us a specific feeling for Kay Boyle's narrative, for one of the story's major themes, and for the tone of the tale. In the second and third sentences, the writer not only identifies the author and title but also begins to develop personal response to the story.

Standards for Evaluation

Ideas and Content
- Identifies the work by title and author.
- Gives a brief summary of the work.
- Uses details and quotations from the work as well as the writer's personal experience to support the writer's response.
- Ends with a summary of the response and a conclusion.

Structure and Form
- Demonstrates proper paragraphing.
- Includes transitional words to show relationships among ideas.
- Uses a variety of sentence structures.

Grammar, Usage, and Mechanics
- Contains no more than two or three minor errors in grammar and usage.
- Contains no more than two or three minor errors in spelling, capitalization, and punctuation.

WRITING ABOUT LITERATURE

4 Revise and Edit

H Check the Standards for Evaluation below as you revise your draft. Look back at your prewriting list to make sure you supported your response. Reread your draft. Does it reflect your thoughts and feelings about the points that are most important to you?

I Student's Final Draft

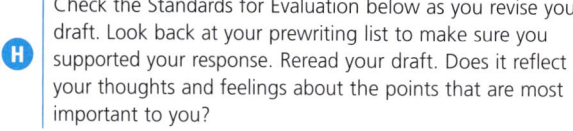

Response to the Portrayal of the Holocaust in "Winter Night"

"There is a time of apprehension that begins with the beginning of darkness and to which only the speech of love can lend security." This opening sentence of "Winter Night" by Kay Boyle sets the tone for me. It makes me feel as if the darkness is the Holocaust and only love can begin to help heal. The story of the Holocaust is told through the dialogue of a sad woman and an innocent little girl. Even though she has survived a terrible experience, the woman speaks of love. The content of this conversation fascinates me and makes me angry too.

Notice how the student uses a quotation from the story to provide an interesting introduction.

How does the student use personal knowledge and experience to support ideas?

As the woman puts her arms around Felicia and gives her love, I feel hope and am reminded of a book. This book, by a hopeful survivor of the Holocaust, is about the power of love in the face of injustice. The woman speaks of this injustice when she says, "I want to beat my hands on the table, because it did not have to be!" I agree with the sad woman, but I also believe in the security that love can provide.

Standards for Evaluation

A personal response
- identifies the author and title of the story and introduces an overall response in the first paragraph
- provides readers with enough information about the story for them to understand the response
- clearly supports your ideas with quotations or other details

104 UNIT ONE: IMPRINTS OF THE PAST

Assessment Option

SELF-ASSESSMENT To help students assess their own writing, have them ask themselves the following questions:
- What is my overall response to the event, group, or individual that I have chosen from the selection?
- Have I told my readers what they need to know to understand my personal response?
- Would more examples and quotations help me make my point of view more convincing?

Grammar in Context

Pronouns and Their Antecedents In any writing you do, including responding to literature, all pronouns should have clear antecedents—words naming the persons or things to which the pronouns refer.

> As the woman puts her arms around Felicia and gives her love, I feel hope and am reminded of a book. This book, by a hopeful survivor of the Holocaust, is about the power of love in the face of injustice. S~~he~~ [The woman] speaks of this injustice when she says, "I want to beat my hands on the table, because it did not have to be!" I agree with h~~er~~ [the sad woman], but I also believe in the security that love can lend.

If you use *she, he, it,* or other pronouns without clear antecedents, you'll confuse your readers. Look at the third sentence in the model. Two antecedents, *the woman* and *Felicia*, are possible for the word *she*. Before the edit, the reference was not clear.

Try Your Hand: Pronouns and Antecedents

On a separate sheet of paper, revise the following paragraph so that each pronoun has a clear antecedent:

> The little girl was thrilled that the sad woman was listening to her. She twirled around and around, pretending to be a ballerina. Then she nestled in her lap and listened to her tell a story about the past. The story was about a little girl who liked the ballet, just like her. She continued to talk about her mother and the strange cold camp where she could not brush her teeth. Finally, she yawned and snuggled closer to her. Her dreams were filled with a little girl practicing her ballet.

SkillBuilder

GRAMMAR FROM WRITING

Achieving Pronoun-Antecedent Agreement

A pronoun must agree with its antecedent in number, gender, and person. Some examples follow:

Some indefinite antecedents such as *all, some, any,* and *none* may require either a singular or a plural pronoun, depending on the meaning of the sentence.

Singular Antecedent	Pronoun
anybody, no one, somebody, everyone	his or her

Plural Antecedent	Pronoun
both, few, many, several	our, your, their

APPLYING WHAT YOU'VE LEARNED

On a separate sheet of paper, correct the sentences below.

1. Everyone brought their belongings to the camp.
2. None of them had his winter clothes.
3. Few of the people remained with his or her family.

GRAMMAR HANDBOOK

For more information on pronoun–antecedent agreement, see page 1071 of the Grammar Handbook.

WRITING ABOUT LITERATURE **105**

PORTFOLIO

Ask students to explain whether the act of writing helped them to clarify or expand their own responses to the literature. Those students who answer affirmatively should use examples to illustrate how writing affected their understanding. Students may wish to include their essays in their portfolio, along with their reflections about the relationship between writing and understanding.

CUSTOMIZING FOR

Students Acquiring English

Before you begin this page, be sure that students understand that a pronoun is a word used in place of a noun, another pronoun, or a verbal. Write the following examples on the chalkboard:
1. The woman shows that she understands that injustice and love are opposing forces.
2. Several recommended this book to me, and I am grateful to them.
3. The little girl loved dancing and storytelling; in fact, they were her favorite pastimes.

Try Your Hand

Possible response: The little girl was thrilled that the sad woman was listening to her. The girl twirled around and around, pretending to be a ballerina. Then she nestled in the woman's lap and listened to her tell a story about the past. The story was about a little girl who liked the ballet, just like the young listener. The woman continued to talk about the mother of the girl in the story and the strange cold camp where the girl could not brush her teeth. Finally, the young listener yawned and snuggled closer to the sad woman. The sleeping child's dreams were filled with a little girl practicing her ballet.

SkillBuilder — GRAMMAR FROM WRITING

ACHIEVING PRONOUN-ANTECEDENT AGREEMENT Tell students that the object in the prepositional phrase following an indefinite pronoun can help them determine whether the pronoun is singular or plural. For example:

Some of the stew had lost its flavor.

Most of the students boosted their scores.

Applying What You've Learned Answers:
1. Everyone brought his or her belongings to the camp.
2. None of them had their winter clothes.
3. Few of the people remained with their families.

Additional Suggestions You may wish to add these sentences as further practice in achieving pronoun-antecedent agreement.
1. Anyone who needs their story graded should place it in this folder. (his or her)
2. All of the exercises seemed awesome in its complexity. (their)

Reteaching/Reinforcement
- Grammar Handbook, anthology pp. 1071–1073
- *Grammar Mini-Lessons* copymasters p. 8, transparencies p. 6

The Writer's Craft

Indefinite Pronouns as Subjects, pp. 692–693

READING THE WORLD

On pages 102–105, students wrote a personal response to a literary portrayal. They should also be aware that selected images are used by media professionals to portray events, individuals, and groups in real life. In this lesson, students will examine how women as a group are portrayed.

Critical Thinking: OBSERVING

N Few students will know women who are as glamorously beautiful as the model on the magazine cover. Students may mention that besides featuring the young woman's image, the magazine cover gives the titles of articles in the issue. The subjects include romance, dating, the mysteries of men, personal appearance, and the risks of a serious disease.

Media Literacy: INTERPRETING AN IMAGE

O Students may point out that this image portrays women as being preoccupied with surface appearances. They may suggest that the photograph of the glamorous young model, reclining in a seductive way, presents women as objects of attraction who are concerned with making themselves glamorous. Students may also say that the headlines portray women as interested in taking risks to win at the game of love.

Speaking and Listening: GROUP DISCUSSION

P Have students work in groups to identify their overall responses. Recommend that students take turns explaining any changes that occurred in their responses to the image after they have taken a second look at the cover and have thought about the titles.

READING THE WORLD

PORTRAYAL OF A GROUP

You've explored how writers create a particular image of a group or event. In our everyday world, advertisers, TV directors, and other media professionals are busy doing the same thing. How do these images affect your attitudes and beliefs? Take a closer look at how women are portrayed in the world around you.

View As you look at the image, jot down your thoughts. Do you know many people who look like this? What other information appears on this cover?

Interpret How would you summarize the portrayal of women in this image? How do the headlines contribute to the overall impression?

Discuss In a group, discuss various responses to the image. What key ideas influence the reactions that your classmates have? You might list them on a separate sheet or in your notebook. Now use the SkillBuilder on evaluating images to reinforce your understanding.

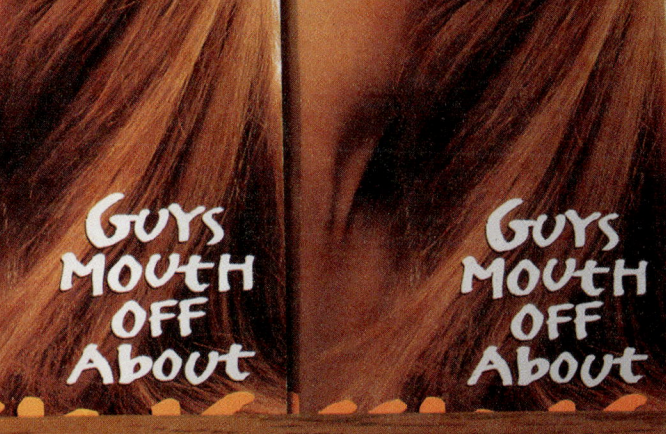

SkillBuilder

CRITICAL THINKING

Evaluating Images

"Consider the source!" You've probably heard this warning before. Each time you view or read advertisements, magazines, newspapers, and television, you should consider why that source has chosen to portray a group or an event in a specific way. What image is being conveyed?

Why does the editor of a magazine choose to portray a group in a certain light? Who will be receiving the message a magazine conveys? What does that fact tell you about the message?

The next time you notice that a group or an event is portrayed by the media in a certain way, decide for yourself whether you agree with that portrayal.

APPLYING WHAT YOU'VE LEARNED

Use the image on this page as a starting point. Create a list of phrases that describe women as they are portrayed in the media.

In a group, evaluate other portrayals in the media such as

- the portrayal of traditional families
- the portrayal of the elderly
- the portrayal of teenagers

READING THE WORLD   107

SkillBuilder — CRITICAL THINKING

EVALUATING IMAGES One way to focus on "considering the source" is to ask students to examine a range of images in specialty magazines: for example, the portrayal of an exciting contest or a handsome athlete in a sports magazine or the portrayal of a group of senior citizens in a magazine designed for retired persons.

Applying What You've Learned
- In a discussion of the media's portrayal of traditional families, students may mention phrases such as "healthy-looking," "well-dressed," "carefree," "conventional," "family of four—with Dad, Mom, son, and daughter."
- Students may say that elderly people are often portrayed as wrinkled, infirm, kindly, fragile, and non-threatening.
- Students might point out that teenagers in the media are frequently portrayed as rebellious, quirky, self-centered, love-struck, moody, trendy, disrespectful, confused, unreliable, or unpredictable.

THE LANGUAGE OF LITERATURE TEACHER'S EDITION   107

UNIT ONE
Part 2 Lesson Planner

TIME ALLOTMENTS SHOWN ARE APPROXIMATE. DEPENDING ON YOUR GOALS AND THE NEEDS OF YOUR STUDENTS, YOU MAY WISH TO ALLOW MORE OR LESS TIME FOR CERTAIN PORTIONS OF THE LESSON.

Table of Contents	Discussion	Previewing the Selection	Reading the Selection
PART OPENER The Power of Heritage page 108	**20 MINUTES** • Reflect on the part theme		
SELECTION Everyday Use page 111 EASY		**20 MINUTES** • PERSONAL CONNECTION • HISTORICAL CONNECTION • READING CONNECTION: Drawing conclusions/Using your reading log	**40 MINUTES** • Introduce vocabulary • Read pp. 111–119 (9 pp.)
SELECTION Blue Winds Dancing page 125 EASY		**20 MINUTES** • PERSONAL CONNECTION • CULTURAL CONNECTION • WRITING CONNECTION	**30 MINUTES** • Introduce vocabulary • Read pp. 125–130 (6 pp.)
GENRE LESSON Focus on Poetry page 133	**20 MINUTES** • Discuss concepts of poetry • Discuss strategies for reading poetry		
SELECTIONS Piano/ Those Winter Sundays page 136 AVERAGE		**20 MINUTES** • PERSONAL CONNECTION • BIOGRAPHICAL CONNECTION • READING CONNECTION: Visualizing images	**15 MINUTES** • Read pp. 136–137 (2 pp.)
SELECTION *from* When Heaven and Earth Changed Places page 141 AVERAGE		**20 MINUTES** • PERSONAL CONNECTION • BIOGRAPHICAL CONNECTION • READING CONNECTION: Evaluating	**40 MINUTES** • Introduce vocabulary • Read pp. 141–148 (8 pp.)
SELECTION The Study of History page 152 CHALLENGING		**20 MINUTES** • PERSONAL CONNECTION • BIOGRAPHICAL CONNECTION • READING CONNECTION: Analyzing details	**40 MINUTES** • Introduce vocabulary • Read pp. 152–161 (10 pp.)
POETRY ON YOUR OWN Afro-American Fragment page 164 AVERAGE			**20 MINUTES** • Read pp. 164–165 (2 pp.)

Writing	Exploring Topics	Prewriting	Drafting and Revising
WRITING FROM EXPERIENCE Firsthand and Expressive Writing	**25 MINUTES**	**30 MINUTES**	**70 MINUTES**

Time estimates assume in-class work. You may wish to assign some of these stages as homework.

Responding to the Selection

FROM PERSONAL RESPONSE TO CRITICAL ANALYSIS	OR	ANOTHER PATHWAY	LITERARY CONCEPTS	QUICKWRITES
50 MINUTES				
• Discussion questions	OR	• Role-play	• Figurative language	• Description • Essay • Memo • Sequel
40 MINUTES				
• Discussion questions	OR	• Skit	• Description	• Speech • Legend
40 MINUTES				
• Discussion questions	OR	• Choral reading	• Imagery	• Poem • Eulogy
60 MINUTES				
• Discussion questions	OR	• Statement review	• Autobiography	• Autobiography • Advice column • Song lyrics • Chart
50 MINUTES				
• Discussion questions	OR	• Storyboard	• Characterization	• Autobiographical incident • Love letters

Extension Activities

	ALTERNATIVE ACTIVITIES	LITERARY LINKS	CRITIC'S CORNER	THE WRITER'S STYLE	ACROSS THE CURRICULUM	ART CONNECTION	WORDS TO KNOW	BIOGRAPHY
60 MINUTES	✔	✔	✔		HISTORY	✔	✔	✔
30 MINUTES	✔		✔	✔			✔	✔
20 MINUTES	✔	✔						✔
40 MINUTES	✔				HISTORY		✔	✔
30 MINUTES		✔			SCIENCE		✔	✔

Publishing and Reflecting

25 MINUTES

PART 2

REFLECTING ON THEME

Point out to students the variety of heritages represented by the authors named on these pages. Have students think about their own heritage by writing down the answers to the following questions: Have they lived in more than one country, like some of the authors in the first part of this unit? Where were their parents born and brought up? Do students speak more than one language? If they were to add their own names to the literary map, where would they place them?

What Do You Think?

Review with students the concept of percentages: the pieces of the pie graph each represent a percentage of the whole, so in a pie graph divided into four equal parts, for example, each piece would represent 25%. Elicit that assigning percentages to an abstract concept such as heritage must be somewhat subjective. Students will return to this activity on pages 123 and 163.

UNIT ONE **PART 2**

THE POWER OF HERITAGE

REFLECTING ON THEME

How would you define heritage? Would you describe it in terms of ethnic or racial background? Is it shaped by family, religious, or cultural traditions? In this part of Unit One, you will read about characters and real people who come to important realizations about their heritage and its power. You will also be asked to explore your own heritage.

What Do You Think? Create a pie graph showing the different aspects of your own heritage. Use separate labels, such as "Family," "Religion," "Social Groups," and "Ethnic Background" to identify each piece of your heritage pie. The sizes of the pieces should reflect the relative importance of each aspect of your heritage. The largest piece should represent the most important aspect; the smallest should represent the least important.

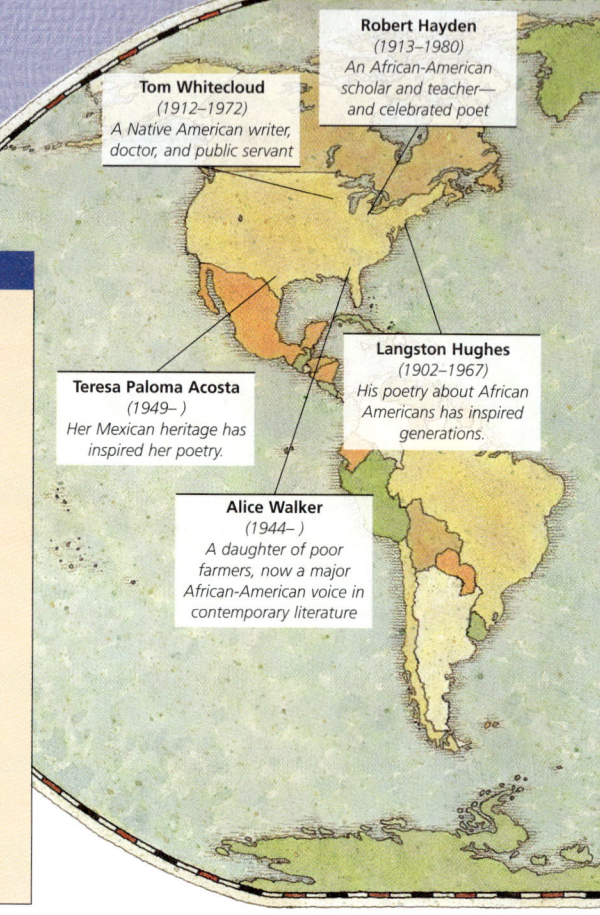

Robert Hayden (1913–1980)
An African-American scholar and teacher—and celebrated poet

Tom Whitecloud (1912–1972)
A Native American writer, doctor, and public servant

Langston Hughes (1902–1967)
His poetry about African Americans has inspired generations.

Teresa Paloma Acosta (1949–)
Her Mexican heritage has inspired her poetry.

Alice Walker (1944–)
A daughter of poor farmers, now a major African-American voice in contemporary literature

Alice Walker	**Everyday Use** *Which daughter will inherit Grandma's quilts?*	110
Teresa Paloma Acosta	**My Mother Pieced Quilts** / INSIGHT *The fabric of memory*	120
Tom Whitecloud	**Blue Winds Dancing** *A long journey home*	124
D. H. Lawrence	**Piano** *The music stirs his memory.*	135
Robert Hayden	**Those Winter Sundays** *Remembering a father's sacrifice*	135

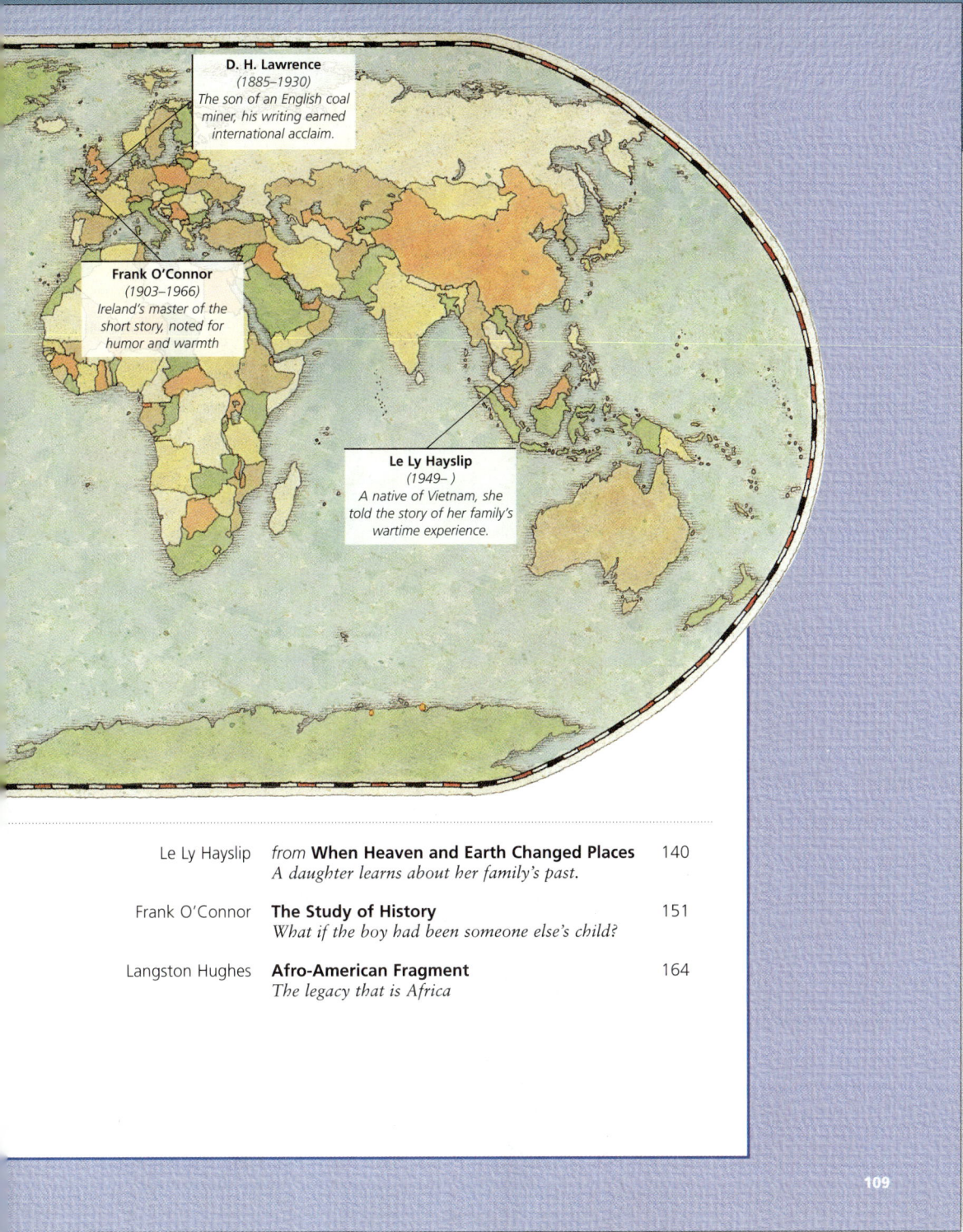

Map Note

The purpose of the map is to show the diverse backgrounds of the authors in this section. Ask a class, go over the information about each of the authors, then ask students to speculate about how each author's heritage might influence his or her writing.

Le Ly Hayslip	from **When Heaven and Earth Changed Places** *A daughter learns about her family's past.*	140
Frank O'Connor	**The Study of History** *What if the boy had been someone else's child?*	151
Langston Hughes	**Afro-American Fragment** *The legacy that is Africa*	164

OVERVIEW

Objectives

- To understand and appreciate a short story that explores the meaning and importance of heritage
- To enrich reading by using active reading strategies
- To recognize and understand the author's use of figurative language
- To express understanding of the story through a choice of writing forms, including a description, an essay, a memo, and a sequel
- To extend understanding of the story through a variety of multimodal and cross-curricular activities

Skills

LITERARY CONCEPTS
- Figurative language
- Characterization

READING SKILLS/ STRATEGIES
- Drawing conclusions
- Evaluating

THE WRITER'S STYLE
- Sensory details

GRAMMAR
- Compound subjects and predicates

SPEAKING, LISTENING, AND VIEWING
- Interviewing
- Role-playing
- Art
- Group discussion
- Oral presentation

HISTORICAL CONNECTION
The Black Pride Movement

Starting in the late 1960s, the black pride movement promoted racial unity and economic independence among African Americans. "Black is beautiful" and "black power" were two of the movement's catch phrases. These photographs reflect the movement's celebration of ethnic pride.

Side A, Frames 49327

PREVIEWING

FICTION

Everyday Use
Alice Walker United States

Activating Prior Knowledge
PERSONAL CONNECTION

What aspects of your family's heritage are especially important to you? In your notebook, make a chart similar to the one shown. Under each heading in the chart, record one or more examples drawn from your heritage. For example, under "Language" you might write expressions that you have heard your parents or grandparents use. Then share your heritage chart with a small group of classmates. Be sure to save your work for use after you read the selection.

Heritage	
Family Treasures	Traditional Foods
Holidays	Language

Building Background
HISTORICAL CONNECTION

This story is set in the rural South of the 1960s, a time when many African Americans sought to learn more about their heritage. The "black pride" movement, which grew out of the civil rights campaigns of that era, called upon African Americans to appreciate their African roots and to affirm all aspects of their cultural identity. The advocates of black pride were often young and rebellious; they were impatient with their elders, who they believed were too fearful of offending or displeasing whites. The movement helped to spur interest in black history, literature, art, and fashion.

As an expression of black pride, young people sometimes adopted African names and styles of dress. Others even changed their religious affiliations and practices. During this time, the Black Muslims gained national prominence. This group combined aspects of the Islamic religion (based on the teachings of Mohammed) with political activism. The Black Muslims encouraged blacks to separate from whites and to achieve economic independence.

Active Reading/Setting a Purpose
READING CONNECTION

Drawing Conclusions In reading "Everyday Use," you will be using clues, facts, or other evidence to draw important conclusions about three women. As you read, jot down in your notebook what you conclude about each of the three women and her sense of heritage.

Using Your Reading Log Use your reading log to record your responses to the questions inserted at various points in this selection.

• HISTORICAL CONNECTION

110

PRINT AND MEDIA RESOURCES

UNIT ONE RESOURCE BOOK
Strategic Reading: Literature, p. 47
Vocabulary SkillBuilder, p. 48

GRAMMAR MINI–LESSONS
Transparencies, p. 5
Copymasters, p. 7

WRITING MINI–LESSONS
Transparencies, p. 46

ACCESS FOR STUDENTS ACQUIRING ENGLISH
Selection Summaries
Reading Support

FORMAL ASSESSMENT
Selection Test, p. 21
 Test Generator

LASERLINKS
Historical Connection
Cultural Connection

Everyday Use

Alice Walker

Working Woman (1947), Elizabeth Catlett. Oil on canvas, courtesy of the Barnett-Aden Collection, Museum of African American Art, Tampa, Florida.

I will wait for her in the yard that Maggie and I made so clean and wavy yesterday afternoon. A yard like this is more comfortable than most people know. It is not just a yard. It is like an extended living room.

SUMMARY

A mother and her younger daughter, Maggie, anxiously await the visit of Dee, the sophisticated older daughter. Dee arrives, dressed in trendy African-inspired styles in stark contrast to her mother's and sister's simple dress. During her visit, Dee shows an interest in household items that reflect African-American heritage, and she decides to take two special family quilts. The mother hesitates, saying that the quilts are for Maggie. Dee retorts that Maggie will subject the quilts to "everyday use" rather than treat them as art objects. The mother realizes that Maggie values the quilts more than Dee does and decides to give them to her younger daughter.

Thematic Link: *The Power of Heritage*
A mother realizes that her two daughters have very different ideas about their heritage.

CUSTOMIZING FOR
Students Acquiring English

- Use **ACCESS FOR STUDENTS ACQUIRING ENGLISH.**
- Students may have difficulty with this story because of the characters' dialect, the gradually revealed narrator, and the use of African proper names. You may wish to read certain passages aloud.

STRATEGIC READING FOR
Less-Proficient Readers

Set a Purpose Ask students to discuss people they admire. How do students feel when these people visit? Then have them read to find out how Maggie reacts when her sister Dee arrives.

Use **UNIT ONE RESOURCE BOOK**, p. 47, for guidance in reading the selection.

Art Note

Working Woman **by Elizabeth Catlett**
In this painting, Catlett emphasizes the strength of an African-American woman. Point out her muscular forearms and large hands.

Reading the Art How is the woman's body framed? What impression does this create?

WORDS TO KNOW

deliberately (dĭ-lĭb′ər-ĭt-lē) *adv.* as a result of careful thought (p. 113)

doctrine (dŏk′trĭn) *n.* a principle or rule taught by a religious, political, or philosophical group (p. 117)

furtive (fûr′tĭv) *adj.* sneaky, shifty, or secretive (p. 115)

oppress (ə-prĕs′) *v.* to keep down by the cruel or unjust use of power or authority (p. 116)

sidle (sīd′l) *v.* to move sideways, especially in a shy or sneaky way (p. 113)

CUSTOMIZING FOR
Gifted and Talented Students

Mother-daughter relationships are complex. As students read, have them think about the evolution of the relationship between Dee and her mother as the story progresses. *(Possible response: Some students may say that when Dee was living at home, she despised her surroundings and her mother's way of life, but now she looks on them, and her mother, as picturesque symbols of her heritage. Others might point out that the mother is aware of Dee's ambition and self-centeredness, but she admires her drive. By the end of the story, she denies Dee the quilts because she feels that Dee doesn't appreciate her simple, everyday way of life.)*

Active Reading: EVALUATE

A Have students consider Maggie's reaction to Dee's impending visit, and the mother's dream about herself and Dee on television.

Literary Concept: CHARACTERIZATION

B Ask students what they can infer about the narrator at this point in their reading. *(Possible response: She has two daughters, Maggie and Dee. She has a realistic view of her own strengths and those of Dee. She is tough and strong, but realizes Dee wishes she were more polished.)*

When the hard clay is swept clean as a floor and the fine sand around the edges lined with tiny, irregular grooves, anyone can come and sit and look up into the elm tree and wait for the breezes that never come inside the house.

Maggie will be nervous until after her sister goes: she will stand hopelessly in corners, homely and ashamed of the burn scars down her arms and legs, eying her sister with a mixture of envy and awe. She thinks her sister has held life always in the palm of one hand, that "no" is a word the world never learned to say to her. **A**

You've no doubt seen those TV shows where the child who has "made it" is confronted, as a surprise, by her own mother and father, tottering in weakly from backstage. (A pleasant surprise, of course: What would they do if parent and child came on the show only to curse out and insult each other?) On TV mother and child embrace and smile into each other's faces. Sometimes the mother and father weep, the child wraps them in her arms and leans across the table to tell how she would not have made it without their help. I have seen these programs. Sometimes I dream a dream in which Dee and I are suddenly brought together on a TV program of this sort. Out of a dark and soft-seated limousine I am ushered into a bright room filled with many people. There I meet a smiling, gray, sporty man like Johnny Carson who shakes my hand and tells me what a fine girl I have. Then we are on the stage and Dee is embracing me with tears in her eyes. She pins on my dress a large orchid, even though she has told me once that she thinks orchids are tacky flowers.

EVALUATE
What impression have you formed of Dee so far?
Using a Reading Log

In real life I am a large, big-boned woman with rough, man-working hands. In the winter I wear flannel nightgowns to bed and overalls during the day. I can kill and clean a hog as mercilessly as a man. My fat keeps me hot in zero weather. I can work outside all day, breaking ice to get water for washing; I can eat pork liver cooked over the open fire minutes after it comes steaming from the hog. One winter I knocked a bull calf straight in the brain between the eyes with a sledge hammer and had the meat hung up to chill before nightfall. But of course all this does not show on television. I am the way my daughter would want me to be: a hundred pounds lighter, my skin like an uncooked barley pancake. My hair glistens in the hot bright lights. Johnny Carson has much to do to keep up with my quick and witty tongue.

But that is a mistake. I know even before I wake up. Who ever knew a Johnson with a quick tongue? Who can even imagine me looking a strange white man in the eye? It seems to me I have talked to them always with one foot raised in flight, with my head turned in whichever way is farthest from them. Dee, though. She would always look anyone in the eye. Hesitation was no part of her nature. **B**

112 UNIT ONE PART 2: THE POWER OF HERITAGE

Mini-Lesson Literary Concepts

REVIEWING CHARACTERIZATION

Remind students that characterization refers to the techniques a writer uses to develop characters. A writer can reveal a character: through physical description; through the character's words, thoughts, feelings, and actions; through the narrator's direct comments about a character; and through the words, thoughts, feelings and actions of other characters.

Application Have groups create character webs for each of the three women in "Everyday Use," supporting their ideas with examples from the story. After each example, groups should identify which method of characterization the writer used.

Uneducated
"I never had an education myself."
character's own words

Fat
"large, big-boned woman," "My fat keeps me hot in zero weather."
physical description

Narrator

Loving
"hugged Maggie to me"
character's action

Hard-working
"I can work outside all day," "rough, man-working hands"
character's own words

112 THE LANGUAGE OF LITERATURE TEACHER'S EDITION

"How do I look, Mama?" Maggie says, showing just enough of her thin body enveloped in pink skirt and red blouse for me to know she's there, almost hidden by the door.

"Come out into the yard," I say.

Have you ever seen a lame animal, perhaps a dog run over by some careless person rich enough to own a car, sidle up to someone who is ignorant enough to be kind to him? That is the way my Maggie walks. She has been like this, chin on chest, eyes on ground, feet in shuffle, ever since the fire that burned the other house to the ground.

Dee is lighter than Maggie, with nicer hair and a fuller figure. She's a woman now, though sometimes I forget. How long ago was it that the other house burned? Ten, twelve years? Sometimes I can still hear the flames and feel Maggie's arms sticking to me, her hair smoking and her dress falling off her in little black papery flakes. Her eyes seemed stretched open, blazed open by the flames reflected in them. And Dee. I see her standing off under the sweet gum tree she used to dig gum out of; a look of concentration on her face as she watched the last dingy gray board of the house fall in toward the red-hot brick chimney. Why don't you do a dance around the ashes? I'd wanted to ask her. She had hated the house that much.

I used to think she hated Maggie, too. But that was before we raised the money, the church and me, to send her to Augusta[1] to school. She used to read to us without pity; forcing words, lies, other folks' habits, whole lives upon us two, sitting trapped and ignorant underneath her voice. She washed us in a river of make-believe, burned us with a lot of knowledge we didn't necessarily need to know. Pressed us to her with the serious way she read, to shove us away at just the moment, like dimwits, we seemed about to understand.

Dee wanted nice things. A yellow organdy dress to wear to her graduation from high school; black pumps to match a green suit she'd made from an old suit somebody gave me. She was determined to stare down any disaster in her efforts. Her eyelids would not flicker for minutes at a time. Often I fought off the temptation to shake her. At sixteen she had a style of her own: and knew what style was.

I never had an education myself. After second grade the school was closed down. Don't ask me why: in 1927 colored asked fewer questions than they do now. Sometimes Maggie reads to me. She stumbles along good-naturedly but can't see well. She knows she is not bright. Like good looks and money, quickness passed her by. She will marry John Thomas (who has mossy teeth in an earnest face) and then I'll be free to sit here and I guess just sing church songs to myself. Although I never was a good singer. Never could carry a tune. I was always better at a man's job. I used to love to milk till I was hooked in the side in '49. Cows are soothing and slow and don't bother you, unless you try to milk them the wrong way.

EVALUATE
What conclusions have you drawn so far about the narrator and Maggie?
Using a Reading Log

I have deliberately turned my back on the house. It is three rooms, just like the one that burned, except the roof is tin; they don't make shingle roofs any more. There are no real windows, just some holes cut in the sides, like the portholes in a ship, but not round and not square, with rawhide holding the shutters up on the outside. This house is in a pasture, too, like the other one. No doubt when

---
1. **Augusta:** a city in Georgia.

WORDS TO KNOW
sidle (sīd′l) v. to move sideways, especially in a shy or sneaky way
deliberately (dĭ-lĭb′ər-ĭt-lē) adv. as a result of careful thought

Art Note

Nia: Purpose by Varnette P. Honeywood This monoprint, completed in 1991 by an African-American artist, Varnette Honeywood, includes many traditionally African designs and symbols. The blue and white background pattern is representative of African cloth patterns, which the artist collects. The figure in the middle represents a helmet mask, or *chi wara*, used by the Bambara peoples of Mali. The four symbols in the corners are often used in patterns on cloth from Ghana. *Nia: Purpose* is part of Honeywood's Kwanzaa series, in which she commemorates the African-American holiday of thanksgiving.

Reading the Art *What do you find most interesting about this monoprint? What do you think is the overall mood of the piece?*

Nia: Purpose (1991), Varnette Honeywood. Monoprint, collection of Karen Kennedy. Copyright © Varnette P. Honeywood, 1991.

Dee sees it she will want to tear it down. She wrote me once that no matter where we "choose" to live, she will manage to come see us. But she will never bring her friends. Maggie and I thought about this and Maggie asked me, "Mama, when did Dee ever *have* any friends?"

She had a few. Furtive boys in pink shirts hanging about on wash-day after school. Nervous girls who never laughed. Impressed with her they worshiped the well-turned phrase, the cute shape, the scalding humor that erupted like bubbles in lye. She read to them.

When she was courting Jimmy T she didn't have much time to pay to us, but turned all her faultfinding power on him. He *flew* to marry a cheap city girl from a family of ignorant flashy people. She hardly had time to recompose herself.

When she comes I will meet—but there they are!

Maggie attempts to make a dash for the house, in her shuffling way, but I stay her with my hand. "Come back here," I say. And she stops and tries to dig a well in the sand with her toe.

It is hard to see them clearly through the strong sun. But even the first glimpse of leg out of the car tells me it is Dee. Her feet were always neat-looking, as if God himself had shaped them with a certain style. From the other side of the car comes a short, stocky man. Hair is all over his head a foot long and hanging from his chin like a kinky mule tail. I hear Maggie suck in her breath. "Uhnnnh," is what it sounds like. Like when you see the wriggling end of a snake just in front of your foot on the road. "Uhnnnh."

Dee next. A dress down to the ground, in this hot weather. A dress so loud it hurts my eyes. There are yellows and oranges enough to throw back the light of the sun. I feel my whole face warming from the heat waves it throws out. Earrings gold, too, and hanging down to her shoulders. Bracelets dangling and making noises when she moves her arm up to shake the folds of the dress out of her armpits. The dress is loose and flows, and as she walks closer, I like it. I hear Maggie go "Uhnnnh" again. It is her sister's hair. It stands straight up like the wool on a sheep. It is black as night and around the edges are two long pigtails that rope about like small lizards disappearing behind her ears.

"Wa-su-zo-Tean-o!" she says, coming on in that gliding way the dress makes her move. The short stocky fellow with the hair to his navel is all grinning and he follows up with "Asalamalakim, my mother and sister!" He moves to hug Maggie but she falls back, right up against the back of my chair. I feel her trembling there and when I look up I see the perspiration falling off her chin.

"Don't get up," says Dee. Since I am stout it takes something of a push. You can see me trying to move a second or two before I make it. She turns, showing white heels through her sandals, and goes back to the car. Out she peeks next with a Polaroid. She stoops down quickly and lines up picture after picture of me sitting

> **HER FEET WERE ALWAYS NEAT-LOOKING, AS IF GOD HIMSELF HAD SHAPED THEM**

2. **Wa-su-zo-Tean-o!** (wä-sōō′zō-tē′nō) . . . **Asalamalakim!** (ə-sǎl′ə-mə-lăk′əm): greetings used by members of the Black Muslims.

WORDS TO KNOW

furtive (fûr′tĭv) *adj.* sneaky, shifty, or secretive

Mini-Lesson The Writer's Style

DESCRIPTION: SENSORY DETAILS Point out that Walker describes characters, places, and things by using details that appeal to the five senses: hearing, sight, smell, taste, and touch. These are called sensory details. For example, the detail about Dee's bracelets dangling and making noise appeals to the senses of sight and hearing. Have students point out other sensory details in the highlighted area above.

Application Invite each student to write a description of an object. The descriptions should include sensory details appealing to at least three of the five senses. Suggest that students trade descriptions with a partner and identify to which senses the details appeal.

Reteaching/Reinforcement
- *Writing Handbook,* anthology p. 1030–1031
- *Writing Mini-Lessons* transparencies, p. 46

 The Writer's Craft

Sensory Details, p. 366

CUSTOMIZING FOR
Students Acquiring English

I Explain that the narrator refers to the man as *Asalamalakim* (the Black Muslim greeting wishing peace onto a person) until she learns his actual name, Hakim-a-barber, later in the story.

STRATEGIC READING FOR
Less-Proficient Readers

M Ask students to summarize Maggie's actions since Dee and her friend have arrived. *(She utters a frightened noise, cowers behind her mother, and tries to pull her hand away when Dee's friend wants to shake it.)*
Summarizing

Set a Purpose As students finish reading the story, ask them to pay special attention to Maggie's reaction to the events that unfold.

Critical Thinking:
MAKING INFERENCES

N Ask students what point they think the narrator is trying to make by listing all her relatives named Dicie. *(Possible responses: That Dee's name has been a proud tradition in the family for generations; that the name came from loved ones, not oppressors.)*

---

there in front of the house with Maggie cowering behind me. She never takes a shot without making sure the house is included. When a cow comes nibbling around the edge of the yard she snaps it and me and Maggie *and* the house. Then she puts the Polaroid in the back seat of the car, and comes up and kisses me on the forehead.

Meanwhile Asalamalakim is going through motions with Maggie's hand. Maggie's hand is as limp as a fish, and probably as cold, despite the sweat, and she keeps trying to pull it back. It looks like Asalamalakim wants to shake hands but wants to do it fancy. Or maybe he don't know how people shake hands. Anyhow, he soon gives up on Maggie.

"Well," I say. "Dee."

"No, Mama," she says. "Not 'Dee,' Wangero Leewanika Kemanjo!"[3]

"What happened to 'Dee'?" I wanted to know.

"She's dead," Wangero said. "I couldn't bear it any longer, being named after the people who oppress me."

"You know as well as me you was named after your aunt Dicie," I said. Dicie is my sister. She named Dee. We called her "Big Dee" after Dee was born.

"But who was *she* named after?" asked Wangero.

"I guess after Grandma Dee," I said.

"And who was she named after?" asked Wangero.

"Her mother," I said, and saw Wangero was getting tired. "That's about as far back as I can trace it," I said. Though, in fact, I probably could have carried it back beyond the Civil War through the branches.

> "I COULDN'T BEAR IT ANY LONGER, BEING NAMED AFTER THE PEOPLE WHO OPPRESS ME."

"Well," said Asalamalakim, "there you are."

"Uhnnnh," I heard Maggie say.

"There I was not," I said, "before 'Dicie' cropped up in our family, so why should I try to trace it that far back?"

He just stood there grinning, looking down on me like somebody inspecting a Model A[4] car. Every once in a while he and Wangero sent eye signals over my head.

"How do you pronounce this name?" I asked.

"You don't have to call me by it if you don't want to," said Wangero.

"Why shouldn't I?" I asked. "If that's what you want us to call you, we'll call you."

"I know it might sound awkward at first," said Wangero.

"I'll get used to it," I said. "Ream it out again."

Well, soon we got the name out of the way. Asalamalakim had a name twice as long and three times as hard. After I tripped over it two or three times he told me to just call him Hakim-a-barber.[5] I wanted to ask him was he a barber, but I didn't really think he was, so I didn't ask.

"You must belong to those beef-cattle peoples down the road," I said. They said "Asalamalakim" when they met you, too, but they didn't shake hands. Always too busy: feeding the cattle, fixing the fences, putting up salt-lick shelters, throwing down hay. When the white folks poisoned some of the herd the men

---

3. **Wangero Leewanika Kemanjo** (wän-gâr′ō lē-wä-nē′kə kĕ-män′jō).
4. **Model A:** an automobile manufactured by Ford from 1927 to 1931.
5. **Hakim-a-barber** (hä-kē′mə-bär′bər).

WORDS TO KNOW
oppress (ə-prĕs′) *v.* to keep down by the cruel or unjust use of power or authority

116

Mini-Lesson Grammar

COMPOUND SUBJECTS AND PREDICATES Remind students that a compound subject is made up of two or more nouns. A compound predicate is made up of two or more verbs.

Compound Subject: *Maggie* and her *mother* wait for Dee.

Compound Predicate: Dee *hugs* and *kisses* me.

Application Invite students to find an example of a compound subject and an example of a compound predicate on page 116. Then have partners make up four sentences about the story, two using compound subjects and two using compound predicates.

Reteaching/Reinforcement
- *Grammar Handbook,* anthology pp. 1061–1062
- *Grammar Mini-Lessons* copymasters p. 7, transparencies p. 5

 **The Writer's Craft**

Subject and Verb Agreement, pp. 689–691

stayed up all night with rifles in their hands. I walked a mile and a half just to see the sight.

Hakim-a-barber said, "I accept some of their <u>doctrines</u>, but farming and raising cattle is not my style." (They didn't tell me, and I didn't ask, whether Wangero (Dee) had really gone and married him.)

We sat down to eat and right away he said he didn't eat collards and pork was unclean. Wangero, though, went on through the chitlins and corn bread, the greens and everything else. She talked a blue streak over the sweet potatoes. Everything delighted her. Even the fact that we still used the benches her daddy made for the table when we couldn't afford to buy chairs.

"Oh, Mama!" she cried. Then turned to Hakim-a-barber. "I never knew how lovely these benches are. You can feel the rump prints," she said, running her hands underneath her and along the bench. Then she gave a sigh and her hand closed over Grandma Dee's butter dish. "That's it!" she said. "I knew there was something I wanted to ask you if I could have." She jumped up from the table and went over in the corner where the churn stood, the milk in it clabber[6] by now. She looked at the churn and looked at it.

"This churn top is what I need," she said. "Didn't Uncle Buddy whittle it out of a tree you all used to have?"

"Yes," I said.

"Uh huh," she said happily. "And I want the dasher,[7] too."

"Uncle Buddy whittle that, too?" asked the barber.

Dee (Wangero) looked up at me.

"Aunt Dee's first husband whittled the dash," said Maggie so low you almost couldn't hear her. "His name was Henry, but they called him Stash."

"Maggie's brain is like an elephant's," Wangero said, laughing. "I can use the churn top as a centerpiece for the alcove table," she said, sliding a plate over the churn, "and I'll think of something artistic to do with the dasher."

When she finished wrapping the dasher the handle stuck out. I took it for a moment in my hands. You didn't even have to look close to see where hands pushing the dasher up and down to make butter had left a kind of sink in the wood. In fact, there were a lot of small sinks; you could see where thumbs and fingers had sunk into the wood. It was beautiful light yellow wood, from a tree that grew in the yard where Big Dee and Stash had lived.

After dinner Dee (Wangero) went to the trunk at the foot of my bed and started rifling through it. Maggie hung back in the kitchen over the dishpan. Out came Wangero with two quilts. They had been pieced by Grandma Dee and then Big Dee and me had hung them on the quilt frames on the front porch and quilted them. One was in the Lone Star pattern. The other was Walk Around the Mountain. In both of them were scraps of dresses Grandma Dee had worn fifty and more years ago. Bits and pieces of Grandpa Jarrell's Paisley shirts. And one teeny faded blue piece, about the size of a penny matchbox, that was from Great Grandpa Ezra's uniform that he wore in the Civil War.

---

6. **clabber:** curdled milk.
7. **dasher:** the plunger of a churn, a device formerly used to stir cream or milk to produce butter.

| WORDS TO KNOW | **doctrine** (dŏk′trĭn) *n.* a principle or rule taught by a religious, political, or philosophic group |

**Literary Concept:
CHARACTERIZATION**

R Ask students why they think Dee refuses the quilts with machine-sewn borders. *(Possible responses: Some students may say those quilts aren't as valuable or fashionable. Others may say the quilts have less sentimental value.)*

Critical Thinking: ANALYZING

S Ask students how this insertion of the phrase "everyday use" helps to explain the story's title. Through this phrase, what is Alice Walker trying to say about heritage? *(Possible response: For Walker, heritage and daily life are intertwined. Maggie carries on her heritage by using the quilts in the way their makers intended them to be used. For Dee, heritage is something that is not lived and used, but displayed.)*

**Critical Thinking:
MAKING JUDGMENTS**

T Ask students if they think Dee has a right to be so angry about the quilts. Why or why not? *(Accept any reasonable responses.)*

"Mama," Wangero said sweet as a bird. "Can I have these old quilts?"

I heard something fall in the kitchen, and a minute later the kitchen door slammed.

"Why don't you take one or two of the others?" I asked. "These old things was just done by me and Big Dee from some tops your grandma pieced before she died."

"No," said Wangero. "I don't want those. They are stitched around the borders by machine."

"That'll make them last better," I said.

"That's not the point," said Wangero. "These are all pieces of dresses Grandma used to wear. She did all this stitching by hand. Imagine!" She held the quilts securely in her arms, stroking them.

"Some of the pieces, like those lavender ones, come from old clothes her mother handed down to her," I said, moving up to touch the quilts. Dee (Wangero) moved back just enough so that I couldn't reach the quilts. They already belonged to her.

"Imagine!" she breathed again, clutching them closely to her bosom.

"The truth is," I said, "I promised to give them quilts to Maggie, for when she marries John Thomas."

She gasped like a bee had stung her.

"Maggie can't appreciate these quilts!" she said. "She'd probably be backward enough to put them to everyday use."

"I reckon she would," I said. "God knows I been saving 'em for long enough with nobody using 'em. I hope she will!" I didn't want to bring up how I had offered Dee (Wangero) a quilt when she went away to college. Then she had told me they were old-fashioned, out of style.

"But they're *priceless!*" she was saying now, furiously; for she has a temper. "Maggie would put them on the bed and in five years they'd be in rags. Less than that!"

"She can always make some more," I said. "Maggie knows how to quilt."

Dee (Wangero) looked at me with hatred. "You just will not understand. The point is *these* quilts, these quilts!"

"Well," I said, stumped. "What would *you* do with them?"

"Hang them," she said. As if that was the only thing you *could* do with quilts.

Maggie by now was standing in the door. I could almost hear the sound her feet made as they scraped over each other.

"She can have them, Mama," she said, like somebody used to never winning anything, or having anything reserved for her. "I can 'member Grandma Dee without the quilts."

I looked at her hard. She had filled her bottom lip with checkerberry snuff and it gave her face a kind of dopey, hangdog look. It was Grandma Dee and Big Dee who taught her how to quilt herself. She stood there with her scarred hands hidden in the folds of her skirt. She looked at her sister with something like fear but she wasn't mad at her. This was Maggie's portion. This was the way she knew God to work.

When I looked at her like that something hit me in the top of my head and ran down to the soles of my feet. Just like when I'm in church and the spirit of God touches me and I get happy and shout. I did something I never had done before: hugged Maggie to me, then dragged her on into the room, snatched the quilts out of Miss Wangero's hands and dumped them into Maggie's lap. Maggie just sat there on my bed with her mouth open.

"Take one or two of the others," I said to Dee.

But she turned without a word and went out to Hakim-a-barber.

118

Mini-Lesson: Speaking, Listening, and Viewing

INTERVIEWING Explain that interviews are a good way to find out about someone's opinions, beliefs, history, and heritage. Interviews provide personal insights and original ideas that books cannot provide.

Discuss effective interviewing techniques. Point out that interviewers should be relaxed and friendly, have thoughtful questions prepared, and be flexible.

Application Invite students to interview friends or family members about what they value most about their heritage. Suggest they create a list of who, what, where, when, why and how questions beforehand. Students can share their findings with the class. Some interviewers may want to use tape recorders, after they have the subject's permission to do so.

"You just don't understand," she said, as Maggie and I came out to the car.

"What don't I understand?" I wanted to know.

"Your heritage," she said. And then she turned to Maggie, kissed her, and said, "You ought to try to make something of yourself, too, Maggie. It's really a new day for us. But from the way you and Mama still live you'd never know it."

She put on some sunglasses that hid everything above the tip of her nose and her chin. Maggie smiled; maybe at the sunglasses. But a real smile, not scared. After we watched the car dust settle I asked Maggie to bring me a dip of snuff. And then the two of us sat there just enjoying, until it was time to go in the house and go to bed. ❖

QUESTION
What does Dee mean when she says that her mother doesn't understand her heritage?
Using a Reading Log

Active Reading: QUESTION
 Have students consider Dee's change of name and her mother's reaction. Also have them consider Dee's and her mother's contrasting opinions about the quilts.

STRATEGIC READING FOR
Less-Proficient Readers

V Have students explain how Maggie has changed by the end of the story. *(Possible responses: Some students may say that, as her smile shows, Maggie is more self-confident. Others might say she feels more secure in her mother's love.)*
Drawing Conclusions

CUSTOMIZING FOR
Gifted and Talented Students

Have students go back through the selection looking for examples of the narrator's wry humor.

Possible responses:

- Page 116—"I wanted to ask him was he a barber, but I didn't really think he was, so I didn't ask."
- Page 119—"She put on some sunglasses that hid everything above the tip of her nose and her chin."

COMPREHENSION CHECK

1. Who are the three main characters? How are they related? *(the narrator, Maggie, and Dee; they are a mother and two daughters)*
2. When Dee first arrives for her visit, why does her mother think she has changed? *(Dee has changed her name and her dress and hairstyle; she seems happy to be home and is interested in the house instead of ashamed of it.)*
3. Why does Dee want the churn top and the dasher? *(She thinks these things, handmade by her relatives, are valuable products of her heritage.)*
4. Why does the mother give the quilts to Maggie? *(The mother realizes that Maggie cares more deeply about the quilts and about the family they represent than Dee does.)*

Mini-Lesson — Study Skills

TAKING ESSAY TESTS: PLANNING YOUR ANSWER Explain to students that they will often have to respond to a prompt like the following: *How are the three women in "Everyday Use" alike and different?* Explain that before students begin writing, they should analyze the question and plan their response. Suggest they rephrase the question as a statement, which can then become the topic sentence of their response.

Application Ask students to analyze the essay prompt given above and then create a topic sentence and an outline for it. Students' topic sentences and outlines might resemble the model shown.

Topic Sentence: Although the mother and daughters in "Everyday Use" appear very different, they are alike in several ways.

I. How they are different
   A. Maggie—meek
   B. Dee—bold, self-confident
   C. Mother—uneducated but wise
II. How they are alike
   A. Dee and mother—both strong-willed
   B. Maggie and mother—both simple country folk
   C. Maggie and Dee—both value heritage, though in different ways

INSIGHT

My Mother Pieced Quilts
Teresa Paloma Acosta

they were just meant as covers
in winters
as weapons
against pounding january winds
5 but it was just that every morning I awoke to
       these
october ripened canvases
passed my hand across their cloth faces
and began to wonder how you pieced
all these together
10 these strips of gentle communion cotton and
       flannel nightgowns
wedding organdies
dime store velvets

how you shaped patterns square and oblong
       and round
positioned
15 balanced
then cemented them
with your thread
a steel needle
a thimble
20 how the thread darted in and out
galloping along the frayed edges, tucking
       them in
as you did us at night
oh how you stretched and turned and re-
       arranged
your michigan spring faded curtain pieces
25 my father's santa fe work shirt[1]
the summer denims, the tweeds of fall
in the evening you sat at your canvas
—our cracked linoleum floor the drawing
       board
me lounging on your arm
30 and you staking out the plan
whether to put the lilac purple of easter
       against the red plaid of winter-going-
into-spring
whether to mix a yellow with blue and white
       and paint the
corpus christi[2] noon when my father held
       your hand
35 whether to shape a five-point star from the
somber black silk you wore to grandmother's
       funeral

you were the river current
carrying the roaring notes
forming them into pictures of a little boy
       reclining
40 a swallow flying
you were the caravan master at the reins
driving your threaded needle artillery across
       the mosaic cloth bridges
delivering yourself in separate testimonies.

oh mother you plunged me sobbing and
       laughing
45 into our past
into the river crossing at five
into the spinach fields
into the plainview[3] cotton rows
into tuberculosis wards
50 into braids and muslin dresses
sewn hard and taut to withstand the
       thrashings of twenty-five years

stretched out they lay
armed/ready/shouting/celebrating

knotted with love
55 the quilts sing on

---

1. **santa fe work shirt:** work shirt bearing the insignia of the Santa Fe Railroad.
2. **corpus christi:** of Corpus Christi, a port city in southern Texas.
3. **plainview:** of Plainview, a city in northwestern Texas.

Multicultural Perspectives

QUILTING Students may find it interesting to know that quilting and the related crafts of embroidery and appliqué are popular all over the world. Even within the United States, particular groups of people have developed their own distinctive styles of quilting.

African Americans have a long quilting history in the United States. During the antebellum period, many of the quilts used on Southern plantations were stitched by slaves. The quilting tradition was carried on after the Civil War.

One type of quilt thought to be unique to Southern African-American women is the Bible quilt. These quilts tell stories by depicting biblical scenes. Like the African tradition of oral storytelling, these quilts seek to record history, instruct, and entertain. African Americans have also influenced quilt-making traditions abroad. Slaves who escaped to Canada through the underground railroad took their Southern quilting designs and ideas with them. Former slaves are also responsible for the introduction of American quilting designs into Liberia.

RESPONDING OPTIONS

FROM PERSONAL RESPONSE TO CRITICAL ANALYSIS

REFLECT
1. How did you react to the characters in this story? Briefly describe your reactions in your notebook.

RETHINK
2. Which character in this story do you like best, and which do you like least? Review the notes you jotted down about the three women characters.

3. Do you agree with the narrator's decision to give the quilts to Maggie rather than to Dee? Explain your answer.

Thematic Link
4. Who do you think better appreciates her heritage, Dee or Maggie?
   Consider
Close Textual Reading
   - why Dee takes photographs of her family and their house
   - which sister knows more about the family's history
   - Dee's African clothing, name, hairstyle, and greeting
   - why Dee now wants the churn and the quilts
   - Maggie's own ability to quilt

5. In your opinion, what is Alice Walker's ultimate judgment of Dee? In supporting your opinion, cite examples of what Walker might admire in Dee and what she might dislike about Dee.

RELATE
6. Which of the characters in "Everyday Use" do you think would most appreciate the quilts described in the Insight poem "My Mother Pieced Quilts"?

Literary Link
7. In recent years, many people have come to take an interest in their heritage—both family traditions and cultural past. What do you think accounts for this interest?

Multimodal Learning
ANOTHER PATHWAY
Cooperative Learning
Imagine a scenario in which the narrator and Dee are reunited on a television show after a long separation. With three of your classmates, decide who should play the parts of the narrator, Dee, Maggie, and the television host, then role-play the scenario.

QUICKWRITES

1. Review Walker's vivid and imaginative descriptions of her characters. Then write a **description** of the physical appearance of someone in your family.

2. Maggie and Dee are obviously very different. Draft an **essay** describing how you are different from one of your brothers, sisters, or best friends.

3. If you were going to direct a film based on this short story, what actors would you choose to play the narrator, Maggie, Dee, and "Hakim-a-barber"? Write a **memo** to the producer of the film, explaining your choices.

4. Write a **sequel** showing what might happen at a Johnson family reunion held ten years after the events of this story.

PORTFOLIO Save your writing. You may want to use it later as a springboard to a piece for your portfolio.

From Personal Response to Critical Analysis

1. Accept all reasonable responses.
2. Accept all reasonable responses. Make sure students give reasons for their preferences.
3. Possible responses: Yes, because Maggie values the quilts and the people who made them more than Dee does; no, because what Dee says is true, these priceless heirlooms may be damaged by everyday use.
4. Possible responses: Maggie, because she knows more about her family and can quilt; Dee, because she is aware of her African ancestry and prizes her family's things.
5. Possible responses: Some students might think Walker dislikes Dee's trendy interest in her heritage but admires the fact that she has made something of herself. Others might suggest that Walker dislikes Dee's attitude but is pleased with her discovery of her African roots.
6. Possible responses: Maggie, because she knows how to quilt, and her own quilts remind her of the loved ones who made them; Dee, because she knows how much handmade quilts are worth; the narrator, because, like Teresa Paloma Acosta, her mother was the one who made quilts.
7. Accept all reasonable responses.

Another Pathway
Cooperative Learning Students should work together in groups of four to plan what will happen on the television show.

Rubric
3 Full Accomplishment Students' characterizations and the events of the reunion are consistent with the story.
2 Substantial Accomplishment Students enact the characters adequately, but occasionally the dialogue or action seems inappropriate.
1 Little or Partial Accomplishment Students' characterizations are unrecognizable.

QuickWrites

1. Suggest that students use sensory details to make their descriptions come alive.
2. Remind students to use signal words and phrases that show contrast, such as "different from," "in contrast to," and "unlike."
3. Go over the memo format with students. Remind them to include the headings *date:; to:; from:;* and *re:;* which should state the subject of the memo. They should include reasons for their choice of actors.
4. Suggest that students make a list of questions that their sequels can answer, such as *How does the appearance of everyone change? Where do they live? What would they say to one another?* and *Have they resolved their conflicts over heirlooms and heritage?*

The Writer's Craft

Description, pp. 58–71
Comparison and Contrast, pp. 118–132
Short Story, pp. 102–107

Literary Links

Possible responses:

- The daughter in "Two Kinds" and Dee in "Everyday Use" are both in conflict with their mothers.
- Unlike the daughter in "Two Kinds," Maggie reflects her mother's values and heritage.

Critic's Corner

Possible response: The mother, Dee, and Maggie might all represent disparate strands of Walker's existence. Dee could represent her African ancestry, Maggie the oppression of African Americans, and the mother the value of hard work, faith, and common sense.

Across the Curriculum

History Students might use encyclopedias or books on economic development in the South after the Civil War for information. Encourage students to create a visual aid, such as a chart, to illustrate the system of sharecropping for their oral report.

Economics Suggest that students use magazine and newspaper articles from the 1960s and 1970s for their research.

LITERARY CONCEPTS

Figurative language is language that communicates ideas other than the literal meanings of the words. Although what is said is not literally true, it stimulates vivid pictures or concepts in the mind of the reader. An example in this selection is the passage in which Dee's pigtails are said to "rope about like small lizards disappearing behind her ears." Look through the story for three other examples of figurative language, and compare your findings with those of another student.

Multimodal Learning

ALTERNATIVE ACTIVITIES

1. Design a **story quilt** that depicts important characters, objects, and events in "Everyday Use." Be sure to use colors that help convey the mood of the story.
2. Create a **collage, mobile,** or **sculpture,** using objects that you associate with your family. For example, you might include photographs, pieces of cloth, toys, household objects, recipe cards, invitations, and graduation programs. Drawings or magazine photographs of these objects can also be included. You might find it useful to refer to the heritage chart you created for the Personal Connection on page 110.

122 UNIT ONE PART 2: THE POWER OF HERITAGE

LITERARY LINKS

Compare and contrast the parent-child relationships portrayed in this story with those portrayed in Amy Tan's "Two Kinds."

CRITIC'S CORNER *Thematic Link*

A critic has written that Walker's poetry "reveals a sensitive African-American intellectual coming to terms with disparate strands of her own existence." How might this statement be applied to her writing of this story?

Multimodal Learning

ACROSS THE CURRICULUM

History With a partner, research the sharecropping system of the rural South. Find out how sharecropping developed as an economic system and how it operated in the 20th century. Then review the story to find details that suggest the Johnson family's participation in this system. Present your findings in an oral report.

Economics Research the activities of the Black Muslim movement in the 1960s and 1970s. Find out about their ideas for encouraging the economic independence of African Americans. Where possible, describe economic enterprises that were established by the Black Muslims. Present your findings in a written report.

Literary Concepts

Students may find the following examples, among others:

Page 112—"skin like an uncooked barley pancake"

Page 113—"washed us in a river of make-believe," "holes . . . like the portholes in a ship"

Page 115—"hanging from his chin like a kinky mule tail"

Page 116— "Maggie's hand is as limp as a fish," "grinning, looking down on me like somebody inspecting a Model A car"

Alternative Activities

1. Remind students that the representations in their story quilts do not have to be literal. Suggest they look back at the monoprint on page 114 for inspiration. Before students begin, initiate a class discussion about which colors evoke which moods in most viewers.
2. Encourage students to be as creative as possible when planning and making their collages, sculptures, or mobiles. Point out that the art form they choose in itself conveys a message. Students can turn the classroom into an art gallery and display their work for other classes.

ART CONNECTION

Look again at the painting *Working Woman* on page 111. What qualities of this painting are also present in "Everyday Use"?

Detail of *Working Woman* (1947), Elizabeth Catlett. Oil on canvas, courtesy of the Barnett-Aden Collection, Museum of African American Art, Tampa, Florida.

WORDS TO KNOW

Review the Words to Know at the bottom of the selection pages. Then, on your paper, write the word that best completes each sentence.

1. The presence of Dee seemed to _____ Maggie, making it difficult for her to feel comfortable.
2. Dee _____ dressed in clothing that expressed her African heritage.
3. Maggie's _____ expression showed her lack of self-confidence.
4. Maggie would often _____ up to her mother for protection and comfort.
5. The narrator of the story believes in the _____ of hard work and simple living.

ALICE WALKER

In the poems, short stories, and novels of the Pulitzer Prize–winning writer Alice Walker, African-American women struggle to survive in the face of poverty, alienation, racism, and sexism. These issues are quite familiar to Walker, who, like Dee and Maggie in "Everyday Use," was a daughter of poor Georgia sharecroppers.

Although neither of her parents made it past the fifth grade and she was nearly blinded by a shot from her brother's BB gun when she was eight, Walker was determined to succeed in

1944–

school. She started school early and graduated at the top of her high school class. After college, she worked for the civil rights movement in Mississippi, traveled, and taught at a number of universities. Today, she is considered an important voice in American literature.

OTHER WORKS *Revolutionary Petunias and Other Poems*, *In Love and Trouble: Stories of Black Women*, *The Color Purple*, *In Search of Our Mothers' Gardens*, *Horses Make a Landscape Look More Beautiful* Extended Reading

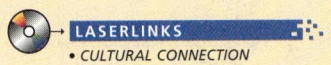
- CULTURAL CONNECTION

EVERYDAY USE **123**

Words to Know

1. oppress
2. deliberately
3. furtive
4. sidle
5. doctrine

Reteaching/Reinforcement
- *Unit One Resource Book*, p. 48

Art Connection

Possible response: sadness, hard work, awkwardness, despair

CULTURAL CONNECTION
Quilt Patterns The patchwork quilt is a popular form of American folk art. The top layer of a quilt is pieced together with scraps of fabric to create a decorative pattern. The following pictures demonstrate some of the patterns and artistry found in American quilts.

Side A, Frame 49333

ALICE WALKER

Walker's own mother was an enormous influence on her life. In a book called *In Search of Our Mother's Gardens*, Walker writes:

"So many of the stories that I write, that we all write, are my mother's stories." Walker feels her mother "handed on the creative spark" that enables her to live as an artist.

REFLECTING ON THEME
What Do You Think?

Ask students to review the heritage pie graphs they made for themselves at the beginning of this part of Unit 1. Then have them make a similar pie graph for one of the women in this selection and compare their personal graph to that of the character. What similarities or differences do they find? What new insights about themselves and the power of their own heritage do they gain from this comparison?

OVERVIEW

Objectives

- To understand and appreciate an autobiographical essay
- To recognize and appreciate descriptive language
- To express understanding of the selection through a choice of writing forms, including a speech and a legend
- To extend understanding of the story through a variety of multimodal and cross-curricular activities

Skills

LITERARY CONCEPTS
- Description
- Conflict

SPEAKING LISTENING, AND VIEWING
- Drama performance
- Art
- Group discussion
- Oral presentation

THE WRITER'S STYLE
- Word chains

GRAMMAR
- Forming adverbs with -ly

HISTORICAL CONNECTION
The Chippewa Chippewa tribes have a rich cultural heritage. These videodisc photographs show tribal activities and crafts from Chippewa village life as it was 50 to 100 years ago.

Side A, Frame 49342

PREVIEWING

NONFICTION

Blue Winds Dancing
Tom Whitecloud United States

PERSONAL CONNECTION *Activating Prior Knowledge*

When and where do you feel most comfortable or accepted? Who or what makes you feel as if you really belong? Discuss with classmates the different people, places, and situations that give you a sense of belonging.

Building Background
CULTURAL CONNECTION

Tom Whitecloud's sense of belonging came from a place called home, a Chippewa (chĭp′ə-wô′) village in Wisconsin where he spent much of his youth. The Chippewa, also called Ojibwa (ō-jĭb′wā′), are a Native American people of the Great Lakes region. They traditionally lived in small villages on the edge of the area's vast forests, where birch trees provided bark used for shelters, canoes, arts and crafts, and the sacred scrolls on which Chippewa medicine men scratched symbols recording important events and rituals. Chippewa customs have also been preserved orally; even today, some Chippewa gather at the local medicine lodge, celebrating their traditions and perpetuating their culture in song, dance, and storytelling.

In "Blue Winds Dancing," Tom Whitecloud reflects on his heritage as he makes a Christmastime journey home from college in California. His journey took place during the Great Depression of the 1930s, when travelers too poor to pay train fare often hid themselves on freight trains to get a free ride.

Setting a Purpose
WRITING CONNECTION

What comes to mind when you hear the word *outsider*? What does a person who is an outsider look like? Why might a person feel like an outsider? In your notebook, write a paragraph or two about someone who is an outsider, and tell what the person might do to satisfy his or her need for a sense of belonging. Keep these issues in mind as you read about Tom Whitecloud's journey.

Chippewa settlement in Wisconsin (about 1939).
Courtesy of Milwaukee (Wisconsin) Public Museum.

124 UNIT ONE PART 2: THE POWER OF HERITAGE

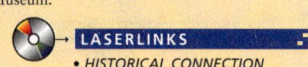 **LASERLINKS**
- HISTORICAL CONNECTION

PRINT AND MEDIA RESOURCES

UNIT ONE RESOURCE BOOK
Strategic Reading: Literature, p. 51
Vocabulary SkillBuilder, p. 52

GRAMMAR MINI-LESSONS
Transparencies, p. 22
Copymasters, p. 24

ACCESS FOR STUDENTS ACQUIRING ENGLISH
Selection Summaries
Reading Support

FORMAL ASSESSMENT
Selection Test, p. 23
Test Generator

 **AUDIO LIBRARY**
See Reference Card

 **LASERLINKS**
Historical Connection

124 THE LANGUAGE OF LITERATURE TEACHER'S EDITION

Blue Winds Dancing

Tom Whitecloud

There is a moon out tonight. Moon and stars and clouds tipped with moonlight. And there is a fall wind blowing in my heart. Ever since this evening, when against a fading sky I saw geese wedge southward. They were going home.... Now I try to study, but against the pages I see them again, driving southward. Going home.

Across the valley there are heavy mountains holding up the night sky, and beyond the mountains there is home. Home, and peace, and the beat of drums, and blue winds dancing over snow fields. The Indian lodge will fill with my people, and our gods will come and sit among them. I should be there then. I should be at home.

But home is beyond the mountains, and I am here. Here where fall hides in the valleys, and winter never comes down from the mountains. Here where all the trees grow in rows; the palms stand stiffly by the roadsides, and in the groves the orange trees line in military rows and endlessly bear fruit. Beautiful, yes; there is always beauty in order, in rows of growing things! But it is the beauty of captivity. A pine fighting for existence on a windy knoll[1] is much more beautiful.

In my Wisconsin, the leaves change before the snows come. In the air there is the smell of wild rice and venison cooking; and when the winds come whispering through the forests, they carry the smell of rotting leaves. In the evenings, the loon calls, lonely; and birds sing their last songs before leaving. Bears dig roots and eat late fall berries, fattening for their long winter sleep. Later, when the first snows fall, one awakens in the morning to find the world white and beautiful and clean. Then one can look back over his trail and see the tracks following. In the woods there are tracks of deer and snowshoe rabbits, and long streaks where partridges slide to alight. Chipmunks make tiny footprints on the limbs; and one can hear squirrels busy in hollow trees, sorting acorns. Soft lake waves wash the shores, and sunsets burst each evening over the lakes and make them look as if they were afire.

That land which is my home! Beautiful, calm—where there is no hurry to get anywhere, no driving to keep up in a race that knows no ending and no goal. No classes where men talk and talk and then stop now and then to hear their own words come back to them from the students. No constant peering into the maelstrom of one's mind; no worries about grades and honors; no hysterical preparing for life until that life is half over; no anxiety about one's place in the thing they call Society.

I hear again the ring of axes in deep woods, the crunch of snow beneath my feet. I feel again

---

1. **knoll** (nōl): a small, rounded hill.

WORDS TO KNOW
maelstrom (māl′strəm) *n.* a violent turbulence; whirlpool

WORDS TO KNOW

imperceptibly (ĭm′pər-sĕp′tə-blē) *adv.* so slightly or gradually as to be barely noticeable (p. 130)
maelstrom (māl′strəm) *n.* a violent turbulence; whirlpool (p. 125)
mirage (mĭ-räzh′) *n.* an optical illusion producing the appearance of water where none exists (p. 127)
petrified (pĕt′rə-fīd′) *adj.* having been turned to stone **petrify** *v.* (p. 127)
pulsate (pŭl′sāt′) *v.* to expand and contract rhythmically; beat (p. 130)

rabid (răb′ĭd) *adj.* extremely enthusiastic; fanatical (p. 126)
rapt (răpt) *adj.* deeply absorbed; engrossed (p. 130)
serene (sə-rēn′) *adj.* calm; undisturbed (p. 130)
silhouetted (sĭl′ōō-ĕt′ĭd) *adj.* seen as a dark outline against a light background **silhouette** *v.* (p. 129)
vice (vīs) *n.* a degrading, immoral, or evil practice or habit (p. 129)

SUMMARY

During the winter holiday at school, a Native American college student in California longs for his home on a reservation in Wisconsin. He daydreams about the beauty and calm of the northern woods, and he muses about the talents of his people—talents he feels civilization has taken away from the whites. He thinks about how terrible it is to have to feel inferior and to have his culture misunderstood. The young man hops a freight train for home. On the train, he watches the landscape change and wonders if he will fit in at home. His fears are allayed, when he reaches his poor but serene people. He finds that they know how to dance, how to share a mood without using words, and how to welcome him home.

Thematic Link: *The Power of Heritage* A lonely Chippewa college student pining for his own culture makes a daring cross-country trek.

CUSTOMIZING FOR
Students Acquiring English

- Use **ACCESS FOR STUDENTS ACQUIRING ENGLISH.**
- Point out that parts of the piece are written in the style of an internal monologue; students should watch for potentially confusing sentence fragments.

STRATEGIC READING FOR
Less-Proficient Readers

Set a Purpose Ask students if they have ever been homesick. If so, have them tell what they missed most about their homes.

Have students read on to find out what Tom Whitecloud misses about his home.

Use **UNIT ONE RESOURCE BOOK,** p. 51, for guidance in reading the selection.

CUSTOMIZING FOR
Gifted and Talented Students

As students read, ask them to consider the different things that the word "home" might symbolize in this essay. (*Possible responses: the reservation, Tom's family, the natural beauty of Wisconsin, the traditions of the Chippewa*)

Literary Concept: CONFLICT

A Invite students to analyze the conflict Whitecloud faces. *(Possible response: Whitecloud is caught between his Chippewa heritage and the values of mainstream white culture; he is trying to adjust to non-Chippewa society, yet he doesn't want to abandon the values of his own culture.)*

CUSTOMIZING FOR
Students Acquiring English

1 Explain that the expression *I'm licked* means "I'm defeated." Present other idiomatic synonyms, such as *I'm whipped* and *I'm beaten*. Have students present similar idioms in their native languages.

Literary Concept: SENSORY DETAILS

B Ask students to which senses the details in this paragraph appeal. How does this description help readers to visualize Whitecloud's home? *(Possible response: the details appeal to sight, touch, and hearing; they help readers to form concrete images of the reservation.)*

STRATEGIC READING FOR
Less-Proficient Readers

C Ask the following questions to make sure students understand that Whitecloud makes his journey out of homesickness and alienation.

- What does Whitecloud dislike about California? *(It is very unlike his home; the seasons change very little; the landscape is ordered and groomed, not wild and free.)* **Summarizing**

- Why does Whitecloud want to go home? *(He misses the Wisconsin landscape, the lodges, and the ceremonies of his people.)* **Making Inferences**

Set a Purpose As students continue reading, ask them to look for experiences and thoughts Whitecloud has on his journey home.

CUSTOMIZING FOR
Students Acquiring English

2 Tell students that *a place to hang his hat* means "a home." Students might discuss how this idiom captures the idea of *home*.

---

the smooth velvet of ghost-birch bark. I hear the rhythm of the drums. . . . I am tired. I am weary of trying to keep up this bluff of being civilized. Being civilized means trying to do everything you don't want to, never doing anything you want to. It means dancing to the strings of custom and tradition; it means living in houses and never knowing or caring who is next door. These civilized white men want us to be like them—always dissatisfied—getting a hill and wanting a mountain.

Then again, maybe I am not tired. Maybe I'm licked. Maybe I am just not smart enough to grasp these things that go to make up civilization. Maybe I am just too lazy to think hard enough to keep up.

Still, I know my people have many things that civilization has taken from the whites. They know how to give; how to tear one's piece of meat in two and share it with one's brother. They know how to sing—how to make each man his own songs and sing them; for their music they do not have to listen to other men singing over a radio. They know how to make things with their hands, how to shape beads into designs and make a thing of beauty from a piece of birch bark.

But we are inferior. It is terrible to have to feel inferior; to have to read reports of intelligence tests and learn that one's race is behind. It is terrible to sit in classes and hear men tell you that your people worship sticks of wood—that your gods are all false, that the Manitou[2] forgot your people and did not write them a book.

I am tired. I want to walk again among the ghost-birches. I want to see the leaves turn in autumn, the smoke rise from the lodgehouses, and to feel the blue winds. I want to hear the drums; I want to hear the drums and feel the blue whispering winds.

There is a train wailing into the night. The trains go across the mountains. It would be easy to catch a freight. They will say he has gone back to the blanket;[3] I don't care. The dance at Christmas. . . .

A bunch of bums warming at a tiny fire talk politics and women and joke about the Relief and the WPA[4] and smoke cigarettes. These men in caps and overcoats and dirty overalls living on the outskirts of civilization are free, but they pay the price of being free in civilization. They are outcasts. I remember a sociology professor lecturing on adjustment to society; hobos and prostitutes and criminals are individuals who never adjusted, he said. He could learn a lot if he came and listened to a bunch of bums talk. He would learn that work and a woman and a place to hang his hat are all the ordinary man wants. These are all he wants, but other men are not content to let him want only these. He must be taught to want radios and automobiles and a new suit every spring. Progress would stop if he did not want these things. I listen to hear if there is any talk of communism or socialism in the hobo jungles. There is none. At best there is a sort of disgusted philosophy about life. They seem to think there should be a better distribution of wealth, or more work, or something. But they are not <u>rabid</u> about it. The radicals live in the cities.

I find a fellow headed for Albuquerque and talk road-talk with him. "It is hard to ride fruit cars. Bums break in. Better to wait for a cattle

---

2. **Manitou** (măn′ĭ-tōō′): in the traditional religious beliefs of the Chippewa and many other Native Americans, the deity or spiritual force that permeates the world and is possessed to some degree by every being.
3. **gone back to the blanket:** returned to the Native American tribal way of life.
4. **the Relief and the WPA:** public assistance and the Works Progress Administration—programs set up by the federal government during the Great Depression of the 1930s to combat unemployment and poverty.

WORDS TO KNOW

rabid (răb′ĭd) *adj.* extremely enthusiastic; fanatical

126

Mini-Lesson  Literary Concepts

REVIEWING CONFLICT Remind students that conflict is the struggle between two opposing forces that forms the basis of a narrative or a drama. External conflict occurs between a character and an outside force, such as nature or society. Internal conflict refers to a character's inner struggle over important decisions or conflicting emotions.

Application Have student groups get together and analyze the internal and external conflicts in this autobiographical essay. Suggest that groups turn their analyses into a graphic like the one shown here.

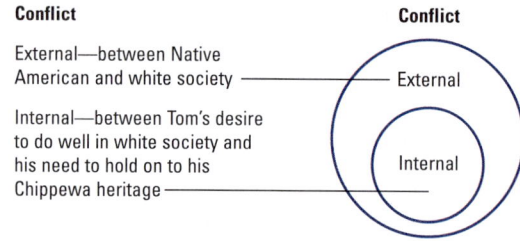

Conflict

External—between Native American and white society

Internal—between Tom's desire to do well in white society and his need to hold on to his Chippewa heritage

Descending Stars, Zoltan Szabo. 9″ × 10½″.

car going back to the Middle West and ride that." We catch the next eastbound and walk the tops until we find a cattle car. Inside, we crouch near the forward wall, huddle, and try to sleep. I feel peaceful and content at last. I am going home. The cattle car rocks. I sleep.

Morning and the desert. Noon and the Salton Sea, lying more lifeless than a mirage under a somber sun in a pale sky. Skeleton mountains rearing on the skyline, thrusting out of the desert floor, all rock and shadow and edges. Desert. Good country for an Indian reservation. . . .

Yuma[5] and the muddy Colorado. Night again, and I wait shivering for the dawn.

Phoenix. Pima[6] country. Mountains that look like cardboard sets on a forgotten stage. Tucson. Papago[7] country. Giant cacti that look like petrified hitchhikers along the highways. Apache[8] country. At El Paso my road-buddy decides to

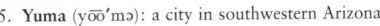

5. **Yuma** (yōō′mə): a city in southwestern Arizona.
6. **Pima** (pē′mə): a Native American people of south central Arizona.
7. **Papago** (păp′ə-gō′): a Native American people of southern Arizona and northwestern Mexico.
8. **Apache** (ə-păch′ē): a Native American people of southeastern Arizona, southwestern New Mexico, and nearby areas.

WORDS TO KNOW
mirage (mĭ-räzh′) *n.* an optical illusion producing the appearance of water where none exists
petrified (pĕt′rə-fīd) *adj.* having been turned to stone **petrify** *v.*

127

Art Note

Descending Stars by Zoltan Szabo
This watercolor by Zoltan Szabo captures the mood of winter through subtle uses of color and brush stroke. The artist uses a variety of brush strokes to create blurred edges and undefined shapes. He uses different concentrations of blue paint to achieve various shades, giving the painting dimension.

Reading the Art *What mood does the artist evoke by using only blue in this winter scene?*

Linking to History

D Point out that the bitterly ironic statement, "Good country for an Indian reservation," refers to the fact that much of the land the United States government set aside for Indian reservations in the West was desert, useless for cultivation or ranching and unwanted by settlers.

**Literary Concept:
DESCRIPTION**

E Ask students to point out the descriptions of mountains and cacti on this page. What figurative device does the author use to describe these things? *(He uses similes, comparing the mountains to cardboard sets on a forgotten stage and the cacti to petrified hitchhikers.)* What impression do these images create? *(Possible responses: stillness; emptiness; desolation)*

Mini-Lesson The Writer's Style

WORD CHAINS: REPEATED WORDS AND SENTENCE FRAGMENTS Point out that throughout "Blue Winds Dancing" the author repeats certain words and phrases, such as "Good country," "Pima country," "Papago country," "Apache country," and strings together sentence fragments with related images. This strategy helps to give the essay a poetic feel and rhythm. It also emphasizes the mood of the piece. Have students look at the highlighted passage on this page. The short descriptive phrases and times of day noted here evoke the rhythm of a passing train and the landscape as seen from it. In another example of repetition, the phrase "blue winds dancing" is used to evoke an image of the narrator's home and the joy he associates with it.

Application Invite students to write paragraphs that use sentence fragments and repeated words and phrases to describe a scene and set a mood.

Reteaching/Reinforcement
• Writing Handbook, anthology pp. 1026–1027

The Writer's Craft
Word Chains, pp. 382–383

Literary Concept: CHARACTERIZATION

F Tom Whitecloud does risky things in order to get back to Wisconsin. Invite students to discuss what this reveals about him. *(Possible responses: He is very homesick; he is brave and determined; he is foolhardy.)*

STRATEGIC READING FOR
Less-Proficient Readers

G Have students review Whitecloud's journey by answering the following questions:

- What does Whitecloud learn from the people he meets on his journey? *(He learns that most just want the basics in life and that their society teaches people to want more.)*
  Summarizing

- What impressions does Whitecloud have of the land he travels through? *(Much of it is lifeless and empty.)*
  Making Inferences

Set a Purpose Ask students to finish reading the essay to find out Whitecloud's feelings as he nears home and to discover what he finally finds there.

Literary Concept: CONFLICT

H Have students discuss what Whitecloud is afraid of. How is this fear related to the conflict described earlier? *(Possible response: Tom is afraid of how his family and community will view him. Also, he worries about Native Americans of his generation, because they have to find a place for themselves that encompasses both life outside the reservation and their Native American heritage.)*

---

go on to Houston. I leave him and head north to the mesa⁹ country. Las Cruces and the terrible Organ Mountains, jagged peaks that instill fear and wondering. Albuquerque. Pueblos along the Rio Grande. On the boardwalk there are some Indian women in colored sashes selling bits of pottery. The stone age offering its art to the twentieth century. They hold up a piece and fix the tourist with black eyes until, embarrassed, he buys or turns away. I feel suddenly angry that my people should have to do such things for a living. . . .

> *So many things seem to be clear now that I am away from school and do not have to worry about some man's opinion of my ideas.*

F Santa Fe trains are fast, and they keep them pretty clean of bums. I decide to hurry and ride passenger coal tenders.¹⁰ Hide in the dark, judge the speed of the train as it leaves, and then dash out and catch it. I hug the cold steel wall of the tender and think of the roaring fire in the engine ahead and of the passengers back in the dining car reading their papers over hot coffee. Beneath me there is a blur of rails. Death would come quick if my hands should freeze and I fall. Up over the Sangre De Cristo range, around cliffs and through canyons to Denver. Bitter cold here, and I must watch out for Denver Bob. He is a railroad bull¹¹ who has thrown bums from fast freights. I miss him. It is too cold, I suppose. On north to the Sioux¹² country.

Small towns lit for the coming Christmas. On the streets of one I see a beam-shouldered young farmer gazing into a window filled with shining silver toasters. He is tall and wears a blue shirt buttoned, with no tie. His young wife by his side looks at him hopefully. He wants decorations for his place to hang his hat to please his woman. . . .

Northward again. Minnesota, and great white fields of snow; frozen lakes, and dawn running into dusk without noon. Long forests wearing white. Bitter cold, and one night the northern lights. I am nearing home.

G I reach Woodruff¹³ at midnight. Suddenly I am afraid, now that I am but twenty miles from home. Afraid of what my father will say, afraid of being looked on as a stranger by my own people. I sit by a fire and think about myself and all other young Indians. We just don't seem to fit in anywhere—certainly not among the whites and not among the older people. I think again about the learned sociology professor and his professing. So many things seem to be clear now that I am away from school and do not have to worry about some man's opinion of my ideas. It is easy to think while looking at dancing flames.

H Morning. I spend the day cleaning up and buying some presents for my family with what is left of my money. Nothing much, but a gift is a gift, if a man buys it with his last quarter. I wait until evening, then start up the track toward home.

Christmas Eve comes in on a north wind. Snow clouds hang over the pines, and the night

---

9. **mesa** (mā´sə): a broad, flat-topped hill with clifflike sides, common in the southwestern United States.
10. **ride passenger coal tenders:** illegally hitch rides on the railroad cars that carry coal as fuel for the passenger trains' steam locomotives.
11. **railroad bull:** a guard employed by a railway to eject nonpaying passengers.
12. **Sioux** (sōō): a group of Native American peoples of northern Nebraska, North and South Dakota, and nearby areas.
13. **Woodruff:** a town in northern Wisconsin.

128   UNIT ONE PART 2: THE POWER OF HERITAGE

Mini-Lesson   Grammar

FORMING ADVERBS WITH -LY Remind students that adverbs are most often used to modify verbs, and that a great many adverbs are formed by adding the suffix -ly to the adjective form of a word. Point out that spelling changes may result.

Adjectives	Adverbs
cold snow	snow crunches *coldly*
lazy smoke	smoke that rises *lazily*

Also remind students that some modifiers that end in –ly, such as *friendly* and *lonely*, are adjectives.

Application Ask students to list at least five other adjectives in "Blue Winds Dancing" that can be made into adverbs by adding -ly. Examples of words students might list are *heavy, beautiful* (p. 125); *peaceful* (p. 127); *bitter, clear* (p. 128); *faint, soft* (p. 129); *rapt, happy* (p. 130).

Reteaching/Reinforcement
- *Grammar Handbook,* anthology pp. 1076–1080
- *Grammar Mini-Lessons* copymasters p. 24, transparencies p. 22

Using Modifiers pp. 737–739

128 THE LANGUAGE OF LITERATURE TEACHER'S EDITION

comes early. Walking along the railroad bed, I feel the calm peace of snowbound forests on either side of me. I take my time; I am back in a world where time does not mean so much now. I am alone; alone but not nearly so lonely as I was back on the campus at school. Those are never lonely who love the snow and the pines; never lonely when the pines are wearing white shawls and snow crunches coldly underfoot. In the woods I know there are the tracks of deer and rabbit; I know that if I leave the rails and go into the woods, I shall find them. I walk along feeling glad because my legs are light and my feet seem to know that they are home. A deer comes out of the woods just ahead of me and stands <u>silhouetted</u> on the rails. The North, I feel, has welcomed me home. I watch him and am glad that I do not wish for a gun. He goes into the woods quietly, leaving only the design of his tracks in the snow. I walk on. Now and then I pass a field, white under the night sky, with houses at the far end. Smoke comes from the chimneys of the houses, and I try to tell what sort of wood each is burning by the smoke; some burn pine, others aspen, others tamarack. There is one from which comes black coal smoke that rises lazily and drifts out over the tops of the trees. I like to watch houses and try to imagine what might be happening in them.

Just as a light snow begins to fall, I cross the reservation boundary; somehow it seems as though I have stepped into another world. Deep woods in a white-and-black winter night. A faint trail leading to the village.

The railroad on which I stand comes from a city sprawled by a lake—a city with a million people who walk around without seeing one another; a city sucking the life from all the country around; a city with stores and police and intellectuals and criminals and movies and apartment houses; a city with its politics and libraries and zoos.

Laughing, I go into the woods. As I cross a frozen lake, I begin to hear the drums. Soft in the night the drums beat. It is like the pulse beat of the world. The white line of the lake ends at a black forest, and above the trees the blue winds are dancing.

I come to the outlying houses of the village. Simple box houses, etched black in the night. From one or two windows soft lamplight falls on the snow. Christmas here, too, but it does not mean much; not much in the way of parties and presents. Joe Sky will get drunk. Alex Bodidash will buy his children red mittens and a new sled. Alex is a Carlisle man[14] and tries to keep his home up to white standards. White standards. Funny that my people should be ever falling farther behind. The more they try to imitate whites, the more tragic the result. Yet they want us to be imitation white men. About all we imitate well are their <u>vices</u>.

The village is not a sight to instill pride, yet I am not ashamed; one can never be ashamed of his own people when he knows they have dreams as beautiful as white snow on a tall pine.

Father and my brother and sister are seated around the table as I walk in. Father stares at me for a moment, then I am in his arms, crying on his shoulder. I give them the presents I have brought, and my throat tightens as I watch my sister save carefully bits of red string from the packages. I hide my feelings by wrestling with my brother when he strikes my shoulder in token of affection. Father looks at me, and I know he

---

14. **Carlisle** (kär-lĭl´) **man:** a graduate of the Carlisle Indian School in Pennsylvania, which stressed assimilation into white society.

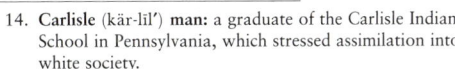

| WORDS TO KNOW | **silhouetted** (sĭl´ōō-ĕt´ĭd) *adj.* seen as a dark outline against a light background **silhouette** *v.* |
| | **vice** (vīs) *n.* a degrading, immoral, or evil practice or habit |

129

Multicultural Perspectives

SWEET DREAMS Tom Whitecloud says his people have "dreams as beautiful as white snow on a tall pine." According to the Chippewa, the night is filled with good and bad dreams. These dreams are caught by dream catchers, loops of willow with a woven web over the loop and a feather and beads attached at the center. The catcher is placed by people's beds—the good dreams slip through the web and slide down the feather to the sleeper, while the bad dreams become tangled in the web.

CUSTOMIZING FOR
Multiple Learning Styles

M **Musical Learners** Ask students to point out details that appeal to their sense of sound in this passage. Perhaps a volunteer might tap out the pulsating drumbeat Whitecloud feels.

Literary Concept: CONFLICT

N Invite students to think about the problem Whitecloud is struggling with in this passage. How does he resolve it? *(Struggle: Does he belong in the Chippewa world or the outside world? Resolution: He belongs with his people, because he still believes their legends.)*

STRATEGIC READING FOR
Less-Proficient Readers

O Ask students what Whitecloud finds out at the lodge. *(Possible responses: Some students might say he finds a warm welcome. Others may say he finds his cultural and spiritual identity or a sense of belonging and being at home.)*
Drawing Conclusions

CUSTOMIZING FOR
Gifted and Talented Students

Have students go back through the essay looking for passages that express traditional Native American values that Whitecloud feels the outsiders lack. *(Possible responses: a sense of community; an appreciation of the wilderness; generosity; a love of singing; respect for making things with one's own hands)*

COMPREHENSION CHECK

1. Why is Whitecloud unhappy at college? *(He misses his home surroundings; he feels out of place.)*
2. How does he return to Wisconsin? *(by way of freight trains)*
3. What strikes Whitecloud as strange when he first enters the lodge? *(No one is talking.)* What does he then remember? *(His people can share a mood and be happy in silence.)*

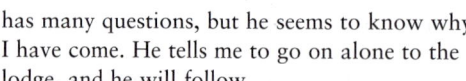

has many questions, but he seems to know why I have come. He tells me to go on alone to the lodge, and he will follow.

I walk along the trail to the lodge, watching the northern lights forming in the heavens. White waving ribbons that seem to <u>pulsate</u> with the rhythm of the drums. Clean snow creaks beneath my feet, and a soft wind sighs through the trees, singing to me. Everything seems to say, "Be happy! You are home now—you are free. You are among friends—we are your friends; we, the trees, and the snow, and the lights." I follow the trail to the lodge. My feet are light, my heart seems to sing to the music, and I hold my head high. Across white snow fields blue winds are dancing.

Before the lodge door I stop, afraid. I wonder if my people will remember me. I wonder—"Am I Indian, or am I white?" I stand before the door a long time. I hear the ice groan on the lake and remember the story of the old woman who is under the ice, trying to get out, so she can punish some runaway lovers. I think to myself, "If I am white, I will not believe that story; if I am Indian, I will know that there is an old woman under the ice." I listen for a while, and I know that there is an old woman under the ice. I look again at the lights and go in.

Inside the lodge there are many Indians. Some sit on benches around the walls, others dance in the center of the floor around a drum. Nobody seems to notice me. It seems as though I were among a people I have never seen before. Heavy women with long black hair. Women with children on their knees—small children that watch with intent black eyes the movements of the dancers, whose small faces are solemn and <u>serene</u>. The faces of the old people are serene,

too, and their eyes are merry and bright. I look at the old men. Straight, dressed in dark trousers and beaded velvet vests, wearing soft moccasins. Dark, lined faces intent on the music. I wonder if I am at all like them. They dance on, lifting their feet to the rhythm of the drums, swaying lightly, looking upward. I look at their eyes and am startled at the <u>rapt</u> attention to the rhythm of the music.

The dance stops. The men walk back to the walls and talk in low tones or with their hands. There is little conversation, yet everyone seems to be sharing some secret. A woman looks at a small boy wandering away, and he comes back to her.

Strange, I think, and then remember. These people are not sharing words—they are sharing a mood. Everyone is happy. I am so used to white people that it seems strange so many people could be together without someone talking. These Indians are happy because they are together, and because the night is beautiful outside, and the music is beautiful. I try hard to forget school and white people, and be one of these—my people. I try to forget everything but the night, and it is a part of me; that I am one with my people and we are all a part of something universal. I watch eyes and see now that the old people are speaking to me. They nod slightly, <u>imperceptibly</u>, and their eyes laugh into mine. I look around the room. All the eyes are friendly; they all laugh. No one questions my being here. The drums begin to beat again, and I catch the invitation in the eyes of the old men. My feet begin to lift to the rhythm, and I look out beyond the walls into the night and see the lights. I am happy. It is beautiful. I am home. ❖

WORDS TO KNOW
pulsate (pŭl′sāt′) *v.* to expand and contract rhythmically; beat
serene (sə-rēn′) *adj.* calm; undisturbed
rapt (răpt) *adj.* deeply absorbed; engrossed
imperceptibly (ĭm′pər-sĕp′tə-blē) *adv.* so slightly or gradually as to be barely noticeable

RESPONDING OPTIONS

FROM PERSONAL RESPONSE TO CRITICAL ANALYSIS

REFLECT
1. What went through your mind as you finished this essay? Respond in your notebook, and then share your thoughts with a partner.

RETHINK
2. Why do you think Whitecloud called this essay "Blue Winds Dancing"?
3. Reread the third paragraph. Do you agree with Whitecloud's definition of beauty in the natural world? Explain your answer.
4. How would you describe the author's attitude toward "Society"?
   Consider
   - what he says about his school and his teachers
   - what "being civilized" means to him
   - how he says his people are treated by whites
   - his opinions about the people in the hobo jungles

Close Textual Reading

RELATE
5. This essay was written more than half a century ago. Do you think people today still experience conflicts between their own cultural heritages and mainstream American society? Are there strong pressures to assimilate or to act like other people in order to fit in? Give reasons for your opinions.

Thematic Link

Multimodal Learning
ANOTHER PATHWAY
Cooperative Learning
Imagine that while Tom Whitecloud is home for Christmas, he talks to his family about whether he should return to college in California. Working with a small group of classmates, write and perform a skit that realistically captures the scene.

QUICKWRITES

1. Imagine that 30 years after graduating from college, Tom Whitecloud returns to campus to give a commencement speech. Write the **speech** Whitecloud might give to the graduating class, focusing on the meaning and importance of cultural heritage.

2. Whitecloud mentions a story about "the old woman who is under the ice." Supplying details from your imagination, create a **legend** about the old woman that could be included in a book of folklore.

📁 **PORTFOLIO** Save your writing. You may want to use it later as a springboard to a piece for your portfolio.

LITERARY CONCEPTS

Description is writing that helps a reader to picture scenes, events, and characters. Effective description enables a reader to see, hear, smell, taste, or feel the subject that is described. Notice the effect of Whitecloud's descriptive language: "Clean snow creaks beneath my feet, and a soft wind sighs through the trees, singing to me." Rewrite two of the following sentences, adding descriptive details so that the style resembles Tom Whitecloud's.
- The train went through the town.
- Those mountaintops are covered with snow.
- I could tell that leaves were burning.

BLUE WINDS DANCING 131

From Personal Response to Critical Analysis
1. Accept all reasonable responses.
2. Possible responses: Some students might say the image reminds him of home. Others might suggest it's an image of happiness or freedom.
3. Possible responses: Yes, because nature is most beautiful before humans touch it; no, because lush, orderly things are pleasing to the eye.
4. Accept all reasonable responses. Encourage students to support their ideas with specific references to the selection.
5. Accept all reasonable, well-supported responses.

Another Pathway
Cooperative Learning Students should work in groups of six to collaborate on the script. Have one student act as a recorder. Assign another to be the director and the rest to take the roles of different family members.

Rubric
3 Full Accomplishment The dialogue reflects the cultural values expressed in the selection, and the family members are plausibly presented.
2 Substantial Accomplishment The dialogue occasionally wanders off the topic, but the family members seem believable.
1 Little or Partial Accomplishment The characters are unrecognizable, and the dialogue includes little about the conflict of cultures discussed in the essay.

Literary Concepts
Have students identify the senses to which descriptive words in the quoted sentence appeal (*clean*—sight; *creaks*—hearing; *soft*—touch; *sighs, singing*—hearing). The class might then work together to amplify the first sentence in the exercise.

Example: *The dark, rumbling train sped through the quiet of the sleepy town, cracking its silence.*

Students can then work in groups of two or three to rewrite the other two sentences.

QuickWrites
1. Suggest that students try to capture the rhythm of this essay in their speeches. Remind them of the narrative power of repeating key words and phrases.
2. Remind students that a legend is a traditional tale that has been passed down through many generations. Most legends are full of mystery and magic. Encourage students to include as much sensory detail as possible in their legends.

📖 **The Writer's Craft**
Speech, pp. 222–227
Myth, pp. 162–167

THE LANGUAGE OF LITERATURE TEACHER'S EDITION 131

Across the Curriculum

Social Studies Have students research the history, culture, and traditions of one of the Native American groups Tom Whitecloud mentions. Students can present their information orally or in writing. Encourage them to use graphics.

Alternative Activities

1. Suggest that students list all the places mentioned in the essay before marking the map.
2. Have students first review the various scenes Whitecloud describes, discuss his mood as he views each, then think about what colors are best suited to the different landscapes and moods. You may wish to display landscape paintings or color photos of Wisconsin and the Southwest to inspire ideas.

Critic's Corner

Responses will vary. Make sure students give reasons for their opinions.

Words to Know

1. maelstrom
2. serene
3. rabid
4. rapt
5. vices
6. pulsate
7. mirage
8. silhouetted
9. petrified
10. imperceptibly

Reteaching/Reinforcement
- *Unit One Resource Book*, p. 52

The Writer's Style

In their analyses help students find the connections between *place* and *feeling*.

The Writer's Craft

Setting, p. 32
Mood, p. 94

Multimodal Learning

ALTERNATIVE ACTIVITIES

1. Trace a **map** of the United States and label all the bodies of water, mountain ranges, cities, and states mentioned in the essay. Then draw a line on the map to indicate the route Tom Whitecloud may have taken on his journey.
2. Create a **landscape painting** of one of the scenes described in "Blue Winds Dancing." Try to capture the mood of the scene.

CRITIC'S CORNER

When asked to comment on this story, student reviewer Amy Dobelstein remarked: "The imagery made you feel you were with the narrator, walking through snow, smelling pine, etc." Do you agree? Explain your answer.

THE WRITER'S STYLE

Analyze the relationship between the setting and the mood of "Blue Winds Dancing."

WORDS TO KNOW

Review the Words to Know at the bottom of the selection pages. Then choose the word that could be substituted for the italicized word or phrase in each sentence below.

1. The author found it difficult to adjust to the *hectic swirl* of life in college.
2. He longed for his *peaceful* Chippewa home.
3. He criticized society, but he was not *fanatical* about his opinions.
4. When the hoboes told their stories, he was a *completely attentive* audience.
5. The hoboes displayed many *wicked habits,* yet he enjoyed their straightforward talk.
6. As the train shook from side to side, the sound of the wheels on the tracks seemed to *beat a rhythm* in the passenger's ears.
7. Staring out the window at the desert sands, he saw a *false vision of water.*
8. A mountain was *outlined* against the morning sky.
9. A deer stood *like stone* in the middle of the road.
10. The old woman smiled *so slightly that it was difficult to observe.*

TOM WHITECLOUD

Born in New York City, Tom Whitecloud (1912–1972) spent part of his youth on the Lac du Flambeau (läk′ də flăm′bō) Chippewa reservation in Wisconsin, where his father's family had its roots. As a young man, Whitecloud worked at various jobs—from boxer to farm hand—before deciding to pursue a career in medicine. He studied at the University of New Mexico and at the University of Redlands in California, where he earned his undergraduate degree, and went on to study medicine at Tulane University in New Orleans. Dr. Whitecloud devoted himself to improving the health of Native Americans, and he helped found the American Association of Indian Physicians.

Because writing was not his primary career, most of Whitecloud's essays, poems, and stories remained unpublished during his lifetime. An exception is "Blue Winds Dancing," which appeared as a prize-winning essay in *Scribner's Magazine* in 1938, when Whitecloud was a senior in college.

OTHER WORKS "An Indian Prayer," in *Return of the Indian Spirit* (ed. Vinson Brown); "Thief," in *American Indian Prose and Poetry* (ed. Gloria Levitas et al.)

Extended Reading

132 UNIT ONE PART 2: THE POWER OF HERITAGE

REFLECTING ON THEME
What Do You Think?

Ask students to look back at the pie graphs they developed at the beginning of this part of Unit One showing the relative importance they assigned to different aspects of their heritage. Ask them if they still agree with the proportions of their graphs, or if their views have been changed by reading the selection.

Focus on Poetry

Of the four major genres, poetry may be the most difficult to define because of its wide-ranging variety. Yet most people can recognize poetry immediately by the arrangement of lines on the page. In poetry, the physical aspects of language—the look and sound of it—are inseparable from meaning. Like a sculptor, a poet pays close attention to all the aspects of the materials (that is, words) used in his or her creation. The word *poet* comes from the Greek *poietes,* meaning "one who makes or fashions." Indeed, writing poetry involves the careful crafting of words.

The language of poetry is more compressed than that of prose and often more musical, designed to stir the imagination and the emotions. Samuel Taylor Coleridge, a famous British poet, once described poetry as "the best words in the best order." To the French poet Paul Valéry, "prose was walking, poetry dancing."

FORM At its simplest, the form of a poem is the physical arrangement of words on the page, including the length and placement of the lines and the grouping of lines into stanzas. The term *form* can also refer to other types of patterning in a poem, including rhythm and other sound patterns.

SOUND Because poetry depends so much upon sound, it should be read aloud. Here are some techniques that poets use to create sound effects:

Alliteration is a repetition of initial consonant sounds.
So long lives this, and this gives life to thee.
(Shakespeare)

Assonance is a repetition of a vowel sound within nonrhyming words.
from labor in the weekday weather made / banked fires blaze . . . (Robert Hayden)

Consonance is a repetition of consonant sounds within and at the ends of words.
I call out for you against the jutted stars
(Amy Lowell)

Onomatopoeia is the use of words—like *creak, whir,* and *clunk*—whose pronunciations suggest their meanings.
. . . with cracked hands that ached
(Robert Hayden)

Rhyme is a repetition of the sound of the stressed vowels and all succeeding sounds in two or more words. Note the two rhymes in the following example:
I recollect that wondrous meeting,
That instant I encountered you,

FOCUS ON POETRY **133**

FOCUS ON POETRY

This feature defines *poetry* and provides students with a common vocabulary to use in describing it. It also introduces students to the conventions of the genre and suggests strategies for reading poetry. The terms introduced on these pages are covered in depth in the poetry selections that follow in the textbook.

Objectives

- To understand and appreciate poetry
- To understand some major elements of poetry: form, sound, imagery, and figurative language
- To develop effective strategies for reading poetry

Teaching Strategies:
ELEMENTS OF POETRY

Form Have students browse the textbook to view the variety of possible forms. Then have them compare the form of "Piano" with "Those Winter Sundays" on pages 136 and 137.

Sound Invite students to read aloud the examples of each of the sound devices described on this page. You may wish to offer other examples of the sound devices. Then initiate discussion of how each sound device affects the reader.

Imagery Encourage students to identify to which sense each image in the sample appeals. Have students browse in the textbook to find other images they find interesting, startling, or appealing. Initiate discussion of how these images add to the meaning of the poem.

Figurative Language Have students skim through the textbook to locate similes, metaphors, and personification. Or suggest that they create their own examples of each. Ask students why they think poets use figurative language. (*Possible responses: to make their ideas vivid to the reader; to condense their ideas; to add color and interest to the poem*)

Reading Strategies: MODELING

Invite volunteers to read aloud the Strategies for Reading Poetry. Tell students they will be using these strategies as they read the poems on pages 136 and 137. Model the following strategies for reading as students read the excerpt.

- **Read a poem at least three times.** Emphasize the importance of reading the poems aloud. Point out that the rhythm and sound devices of a poem can only be appreciated when read aloud.
- **Pay close attention to the title** *"Both 'Piano' and 'Those Winter Sundays' are things intimately tied to the poets' memories of a parent."*
- **Identify the speaker.** *"In both poems the speaker is an adult recalling a childhood memory of a parent. Both speakers seem to be male."*
- **Visualize the setting and situation.** *"In 'Piano' I can see a small boy crouching under a piano as his mother plays hymns. In 'Those Winter Sundays' I can see a father getting up early to start a fire in a cold house, polish a boy's shoes, and then wake the boy when the house is warm."*
- **Reflect upon the parts that puzzle or confuse you.** *"In 'Piano' lines 11 and 12 seem confusing at first. After rereading, I see that the poet is saying that the piano music has called up a flood of memories from childhood, making him feel again like that child crouching under the piano. In 'Those Winter Sundays' line 9 is puzzling. By 'chronic angers of that house' the poet may mean cold drafts that blew through the house despite the warm fire, or he may mean creaks and groans of the old house."*
- **Determine the theme.** *"Both poems are about a childhood memory of a loving parent. In the first poem, the speaker remembers with nostalgia a happy time when he felt safe beneath his mother's piano. In the second poem, the speaker remembers how his father quietly performed an act of love for him on winter mornings; the speaker regrets that he did not realize or appreciate his father's love at the time."*

When like an apparition fleeting
Like beauty's spirit, past you flew.
(Aleksandr Pushkin)

Repetition is the repeating of a sound, word, phrase, line, or unit for the purpose of emphasis.

So long,
So far away
Is Africa. (Langston Hughes)

Rhythm is a pattern or flow of sound created by the arrangement of stressed and unstressed syllables in a line of poetry. Some poems contain a regular pattern, or **meter**, of stressed and unstressed syllables. In the following example, stressed syllables are marked with a ´ and unstressed or lightly stressed syllables are marked with a ˇ.

Nǒr yét ǎ flóatǐng spár tǒ mén thǎt sínk
Aňd rǐse aňd sínk aňd rǐse aňd sínk ǎgáin
(Edna St. Vincent Millay)

Other poems do not have strict meters, making use of rhythm in less formal ways.

IMAGERY Poets choose words that help readers see, hear, feel, taste, and smell the things being described. This kind of description is called imagery. Note the senses being appealed to.

There will come soft rains and the smell of the ground,
And swallows circling with their shimmering sound;
And frogs in the pools singing at night,
And wild plum-trees in tremulous white . . .
(Sara Teasdale)

FIGURATIVE LANGUAGE Figurative language is language that communicates ideas beyond the ordinary, literal meanings of the words.

Similes are comparisons of two dissimilar things by means of the word *like* or *as*. N. Scott Momaday uses a simile to draw a comparison between people in a damaged relationship and deer: ". . . now we are as the deer / who walk in single file."

Metaphors are direct comparisons of unlike things, as when the main character in Lucille Clifton's "Miss Rosie" is described as a "wet brown bag of a woman."

Personification is the giving of human qualities to an object, animal, or idea. In Dahlia Ravikovitch's "Pride," human physical attributes are given to rocks in the phrases "they lie on their backs."

STRATEGIES FOR READING POETRY

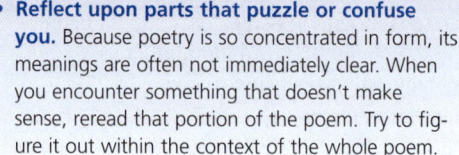

- **Read a poem at least three times.** First, read through it quickly to get a general idea of the meaning. Then read it slowly and carefully, stopping to look up any unfamiliar words. Finally, read the poem aloud.
- **Pay close attention to the poem's title,** which often supplies key information.
- **Identify the speaker.** Often, a poet creates a speaker with a distinctive identity. The speaker in Gwendolyn Brooks's "Kitchenette Building" is a poor resident of substandard housing.
- **Visualize the setting and situation.** Use details and your imagination to help you envision the poem's setting. Where and when does it take place? Are there people portrayed? If so, who are they?
- **Reflect upon parts that puzzle or confuse you.** Because poetry is so concentrated in form, its meanings are often not immediately clear. When you encounter something that doesn't make sense, reread that portion of the poem. Try to figure it out within the context of the whole poem.
- **Determine the theme.** What important ideas about life or human nature does the poem convey? If the poem is humorous, is there a deeper meaning beneath the humor?

134 UNIT ONE PART 2: THE POWER OF HERITAGE

PREVIEWING

POETRY

Piano
D. H. Lawrence England

Those Winter Sundays
Robert Hayden United States

Activating Prior Knowledge
PERSONAL CONNECTION
Recall a routine household activity from your childhood that now evokes strong feelings in you. Perhaps your mother read to you at night, your father patiently helped you with homework, or your grandmother baked a weekly pie. In your notebook, create a simple chart, like the one shown here, to record sensations that you associate with that memory. Fill in all applicable boxes.

Building Background
BIOGRAPHICAL CONNECTION
The two poems that you are about to read draw upon the poets' memories of their own childhood. D. H. Lawrence, the son of a coal miner and his cultured wife, grew up in the late 19th century near Nottingham, England. Robert Hayden, born in 1913, was raised by poor, hard-working foster parents in Detroit, Michigan. Each poet, coincidentally, examines a parent's legacy by recalling activities of long-ago winter Sundays.

Setting a Purpose
READING CONNECTION
Visualizing Images As you read these two poems, develop your own mental pictures of the characters and scenes that are described. Pay close attention to the details that convey memories in the poems.

PIANO / THOSE WINTER SUNDAYS **135**

OVERVIEW

Objectives
- To understand and appreciate poetry that explores childhood memories
- To identify and examine imagery in poems
- To express understanding of the selection through a choice of writing forms, including a poem and a eulogy
- To extend understanding of the poems through a variety of multimodal and cross-curricular activities

Skills

LITERARY CONCEPTS
- Imagery
- Rhyme

SPEAKING, LISTENING, AND VIEWING
- Choral reading
- Music
- Art
- Group discussion
- Oral presentation

READING SKILLS/ STRATEGIES
- Visualizing

GENRE STUDY
- Poetry: lyric poetry

ALTERNATIVE
Previewing
Students who prefer to brainstorm without using their notebooks can respond to the following prompts by speaking into a tape recorder.

Personal Connection
Think of a household activity from your childhood that has left a lasting impression on you. Record your memories of that activity on a tape recorder. The following questions might help you get started:

- *What was the activity?*
- *Why is this memory such a strong one for you?*
- *What sensations do you associate with the activity?*

As you read these poems, compare your memories and feelings with those of the speakers.

PRINT AND MEDIA RESOURCES

UNIT ONE RESOURCE BOOK
Strategic Reading: Literature, p. 55

ACCESS FOR STUDENTS ACQUIRING ENGLISH
Reading Support

FORMAL ASSESSMENT
Selection Test, p. 25
 Test Generator

AUDIO LIBRARY
See Reference Card

THE LANGUAGE OF LITERATURE TEACHER'S EDITION **135**

Thematic Link: *The Power of Heritage*
Childhood memories have a powerful effect on the speakers of these two poems.

CUSTOMIZING FOR
Students Acquiring English

- Use **ACCESS FOR STUDENTS ACQUIRING ENGLISH.**
- To help students use punctuation marks as a guide to comprehension, model how to read these poems aloud, accenting the pauses and run-on lines.

Literary Concept: RHYME

A Have a volunteer read the poem aloud while the class listens for the rhymes. Then ask students to suggest why Lawrence chose to use rhyme in this poem. *(Possible response: Perhaps Lawrence made the poem rhyme to strengthen its connection to music.)*

Literary Concept: IMAGERY

B Ask students to relate how they envision the room described in lines 7–8. *(Answers will vary. Possible response: An old-fashioned living room with a fire blazing in the hearth and lamps glowing in the frosty windows.)*

Literary Note

C Lawrence revised this poem substantially before publishing it. In an earlier draft, the conclusion describes Lawrence's musical memories as being "devoured" by the "glamour" of the music he is presently hearing.

From Personal Response to Critical Analysis

1. All responses are valid.
2. Possible responses: He misses the sense of well being of Sunday evenings at the piano; he misses the love of his mother.
3. Possible responses: Some students might suggest that this singer's passionate singing can't erase his memories of childhood music. Others might say the past is stronger than the present.

Piano
D. H. Lawrence

  Softly, in the dusk, a woman is singing to me;
Taking me back down the vista of years, till I see
A child sitting under the piano, in the boom of the tingling strings
And pressing the small, poised feet of a mother who smiles as she sings.

5 In spite of myself, the insidious mastery of song
Betrays me back, till the heart of me weeps to belong
To the old Sunday evenings at home, with winter outside
And hymns in the cozy parlour, the tinkling piano our guide.

  So now it is vain for the singer to burst into clamour
10 With the great black piano appassionato. The glamour
Of childish days is upon me, my manhood is cast
Down in the flood of remembrance, I weep like a child for the past.

2 vista (vĭs´tə): a passage affording a distant view.

5 insidious (ĭn-sĭd´ē-əs): working subtly and gradually; treacherous.

9 vain: useless.
10 appassionato (ə-pä´sē-ə-nä´tō): an Italian word meaning "with deep emotion," used as a musical direction.

FROM PERSONAL RESPONSE TO CRITICAL ANALYSIS

REFLECT 1. When you finished this poem, what picture lingered in your mind? In your notebook, draw a quick sketch of that mental image or describe it in words.

RETHINK 2. Why does the speaker "weep like a child for the past"?
Consider
Close Textual Reading
- what he means by "the glamour of childish days"
- what he values about "the old Sunday evenings at home"

3. Why does the speaker say that "now it is vain for the singer to burst into clamour"?
Consider
Close Textual Reading
- why the woman might be singing to him
- the difference between his situations now and in the past

136   UNIT ONE   PART 2: THE POWER OF HERITAGE

Mini-Lesson  **Literary Concepts**

REVIEWING RHYME Remind students that rhyme is the occurrence of similar or identical sounds at the ends of words. A poem can contain rhyme at the beginning, the middle, or the end of lines. Rhymes at the end of lines, known as end rhymes, are most common. Most rhyming poems follow a rhyme scheme, or pattern of end rhymes. The rhyme scheme can be charted by assigning a letter of the alphabet to each line. Lines that rhyme are given the same letter. For instance, if every other line of a poem rhymes, then the poem has a rhyme scheme of *abab*.

Application Ask students to figure out the rhyme scheme of this poem. If they need help, suggest that they assign a letter to each rhyming sound. *(The poem has a rhyme scheme of* aabb ccdd eeff.*)*

Sunday Morning Breakfast (1943), Horace Pippin. Private collection, courtesy of Galerie St. Etienne, New York.

Those Winter Sundays

Robert Hayden

Sundays too my father got up early
and put his clothes on in the blueblack cold,
then with cracked hands that ached
from labor in the weekday weather made
5 banked fires blaze. No one ever thanked him.

I'd wake and hear the cold splintering, breaking.
When the rooms were warm, he'd call,
and slowly I would rise and dress,
fearing the chronic angers of that house,

10 Speaking indifferently to him,
who had driven out the cold
and polished my good shoes as well.
What did I know, what did I know
of love's austere and lonely offices?

9 **chronic** (krŏn´ĭk): lasting or recurring for a long time.

14 **austere** (ô-stîr´): stern; severe; **offices**: duties; ceremonies.

Mini-Lesson   Genre Study

POETRY Explain that "Piano" and "Those Winter Sundays" are examples of **lyric poetry**. Then write the characteristics of lyric poetry shown at the right on the chalkboard.

Application Have students choose one of the poems and explain how the characteristics of lyric poetry apply to it.

Lyric Poetry
- presents thoughts and feelings
- uses a single speaker to communicate these thoughts and feelings
- usually is fairly short
- usually explores a single subject
- often is musical

Art Note

Sunday Morning Breakfast **by Horace Pippin** In this oil painting, the chipped walls, the plain furnishings, and the torn curtain and shirt hint at the poverty of the people portrayed. The sparkle of the yellows and whites and the burning stove, however, add a touch of brightness to the morning scene.

Reading the Art What is the mood of this painting?

CUSTOMIZING FOR
Multiple Learning Styles

D **Bodily-Kinesthetic Learners** Ask four students to assume the poses of the people in the painting. Then ask: "Who is separate?" *(the father)* "Who is together?" *(the mother and children)* Discuss how this relates to the two poems.

Literary Concept: IMAGERY

E Ask students to discuss what the phrase "blueblack cold" brings to mind.

Critical Thinking: MAKING INFERENCES

F Ask students what the father's actions of rising early, building a fire, and polishing his son's shoes show about him. *(Possible responses: He loves his son; he is a hard worker; he is self-sacrificing.)*

Critical Thinking: ANALYZING

G Have students discuss why the speaker repeats the phrase "what did I know." *(Possible responses: To emphasize his regret at not being kinder to his father; to emphasize the fact a child doesn't always recognize signs of love.)*

From Personal Response to Critical Analysis

1. Accept all reasonable responses.
2. Accept all reasonable responses. Many students will identify with the regret of the speaker.
3. Possible responses: Some students may say people can show love through actions instead of words. Others may point out that people often don't appreciate their parents' efforts until long after childhood.
4. Possible responses: Both speakers remember their childhood with nostalgia; the speaker in "Piano" remembers the happiness of his childhood and mourns that he can't recapture it; the speaker in "Those Winter Sundays" regrets that he didn't recognize or appreciate his father's love until it was too late.
5. Possible responses: Childhood experiences are an important part of our heritage; family customs and attitudes pass through the generations from parent to child.
6. Accept all reasonable responses.

Another Pathway

Cooperative Learning Students should work in groups of four or five to prepare their choral reading. Groups should decide which lines (if any) should be read by individuals and which lines should be read by the ensemble. One student might serve as a rehearsal director, providing cues for individual and group entrances.

Rubric

3 Full Accomplishment Choral readings are clearly spoken and well paced. Pauses occur at appropriate times, as indicated by punctuation. Important ideas are emphasized.

2 Substantial Accomplishment Important lines are emphasized but readers sometimes fail to stay together. Readers occasionally base pauses on line breaks regardless of punctuation.

1 Little or Partial Accomplishment Readings are out of sync and show little understanding of the poem.

RESPONDING
OPTIONS

FROM PERSONAL RESPONSE TO CRITICAL ANALYSIS

REFLECT 1. In your notebook, jot down three words or phrases that explain the sensations you experienced while reading "Those Winter Sundays."

RETHINK 2. What is your opinion of the speaker?
Consider
- the speaker's observations in lines 5 and 10
- the question that ends the poem
- the possible reason that the speaker recalls this memory

Close Textual Reading

3. What lessons might be learned from this poem? Explain your answer.

RELATE 4. Compare and contrast the speakers' attitudes toward their childhood in "Piano" and "Those Winter Sundays."

Literary Link

5. In what way does each of these two poems relate to the theme of this part of Unit One, "The Power of Heritage"?

Thematic Link

6. What feelings or memories from your own life did these poems awaken?

Multimodal Learning
ANOTHER PATHWAY

Working with a small group of classmates, prepare a choral reading of one of these poems. Discuss what emotions should be communicated, where pauses should fall, and which words or phrases should be given emphasis. Then practice your reading aloud, perfecting your timing and enunciation. Perform your reading for the class.

LITERARY CONCEPTS

Imagery involves the use of words and phrases to create sensory experiences for readers. Each such experience, or **image**, appeals to one or more of the five senses: sight, hearing, taste, smell, and touch. For example, "A child sitting under the piano" appeals to the sense of sight, "the boom of the tingling strings" appeals to the senses of hearing and touch, and "pressing the small, poised feet" appeals to the senses of sight and touch. List three more images from "Piano" and three images from "Those Winter Sundays," naming the sense or senses to which each appeals. Then decide which poem, in your opinion, uses sensory images more effectively.

QUICKWRITES

1. Use the chart you created for the Personal Connection on page 135 as the starting point for a **poem** about your childhood memory. Include vivid imagery that appeals to different senses.

2. Write a **eulogy** that the speaker of "Piano" might deliver for his mother or one that the speaker of "Those Winter Sundays" might deliver for his father.

📁 **PORTFOLIO** Save your writing. You may want to use it later as a springboard to a piece for your portfolio.

138 UNIT ONE PART 2: THE POWER OF HERITAGE

QuickWrites

1. Suggest that students might like to try using poetic devices such as rhythm, rhyme, repetition, and alliteration in their poems.
2. Remind students that a eulogy is a speech based on personal memories of an admired person. Suggest that they analyze the details in these poems to see which ones might be appropriate for a eulogy.

The Writer's Craft
Poem, pp. 88–100
Character Sketch, pp. 78–82

Literary Concepts

Students might make lists in chart form to record sensory details they find. Remind them that many sensory details appeal to more than one sense. Examples: "Those Winter Sundays"—cracked hands (sight and touch); banked fires blaze (sight and touch); the cold splintering and breaking (hearing and touch). "Piano"—in the dusk (sight); winter outside (sight and touch); tinkling piano (hearing).

Opinions will vary about which poem uses sensory detail more effectively. Urge students to use their charts to support their opinions.

Multimodal Learning

ALTERNATIVE ACTIVITIES

1. For an audience of your classmates, play live or recorded **music** that you think captures the mood of one of these poems.
2. Begin a **dictionary** of sensory images. Under the headings "Sight," "Hearing," "Touch," "Taste," and "Smell," record words and phrases from your reading, including those encountered in "Piano" and "Those Winter Sundays." Refer to the dictionary when completing future writing assignments.

LITERARY LINKS

Compare the speaker in "Piano" with the narrator of "Two Kinds." How does each feel about his or her experience with music?

D. H. Lawrence

1885–1930

David Herbert Lawrence grew up in poverty in the coal-mining district of Nottinghamshire, England. His father was a hardworking, hard-drinking coal miner; his mother, to whom he was deeply attached, was a former schoolteacher who instilled in her son a love of learning and culture. A sickly but intellectually gifted child, Lawrence attended school on scholarships and after graduation became a schoolteacher himself, writing fiction and poetry in his spare time.

Lawrence's first poems were published when a girlfriend submitted them to a magazine whose editor was impressed with Lawrence's efforts. With the editor's help, Lawrence was able to publish his first novel, *The White Peacock,* in 1911. He went on to produce a string of critically acclaimed novels, many of which focus on male-female relationships with a frankness that shocked the public of his day.

Lawrence has for decades been recognized as a first-rate poet. "Piano," a famous example of his poetic craftsmanship, was written in 1918, seven years after his mother died.

OTHER WORKS *Sons and Lovers, The Complete Short Stories of D. H. Lawrence, The Complete Poems of D. H. Lawrence* Extended Reading

Robert Hayden

1913–1980

Robert Hayden grew up in Detroit, Michigan, where he was raised by foster parents who made great sacrifices to insure his education. Their efforts were also encouraged by Hayden's natural mother, who occasionally sent him books to read. Hayden began writing poems in elementary school, although for years he doubted that he could make a career of it. In 1938 he was employed by the Federal Writers' Project to research African-American history and folklore. Soon afterward, he began working part-time for an African-American weekly paper whose editor helped him publish his first book of poetry, *Heart-Shape in the Dust* (1940).

In 1941, Hayden enrolled in graduate school at the University of Michigan, where one of his most inspiring professors was the British poet W. H. Auden. Eventually becoming a professor himself, Hayden taught for over 20 years at Fisk University in Nashville, Tennessee. As his reputation as a scholar grew, so did his fame as a poet. "Those Winter Sundays," one of his best-known shorter poems, was first collected in the volume *A Ballad of Remembrance,* published in 1962.

OTHER WORKS *Angle of Ascent: New and Selected Poems, Collected Prose, Robert Hayden: Collected Poems* Extended Reading

Literary Links

Possible response: In "Piano" music is central to some of the happy times the narrator shared with his mother, while in "Two Kinds" music is something that comes between the narrator and her mother.

Across the Curriculum

Social Studies *Cooperative Learning* Suggest that groups of three or four students work together. Three students can research topics like *musicals, square dancing,* and *sing-alongs*. One student can coordinate the research. All group members can then cooperate in drawing a conclusion about family "togetherness"—today and yesterday—as seen in shared music.

D. H. Lawrence

D. H. Lawrence was a rebel who felt that modern industrial society and conventional Anglo-Saxon Puritanism were destroying England. Persecuted during World War I for his alleged pro-German leanings, Lawrence left his home and traveled the world looking for a new place to settle, a place with a healthful climate that would ease his tuberculosis. He died in the south of France on March 2, 1930, at the age of 45.

Robert Hayden

While in high school, Hayden's favorite books were George Eliot's novel *Romola* (1863), Nathaniel Hawthorne's *The Marble Faun* (1860), and Edward George Earle Lytton Bulwer-Lytton's *The Last Days of Pompeii* (1834). He wrote, "I loved those books, partly because they took me completely out of the environment I lived in … because they were full of strange and wonderful things."

Alternative Activities

1. To help students, invite a class member with musical knowledge to demonstrate the different moods of songs in major and minor keys.
2. For help with beginning their dictionaries students might refer to the sensory detail charts they made for the Literary Concepts activity on page 138. One good way to organize the dictionary is to use divider tabs labeled with the five senses.

OVERVIEW

Objectives

- To understand and appreciate an excerpt from an autobiography that explores the importance of culture and heritage
- To identify and understand the elements of an autobiography
- To express understanding of the selection through a choice of writing forms, including an autobiographical essay, an advice column, song lyrics, and a chart
- To extend understanding of the selection through a variety of multimodal and cross-curricular activities

Skills

LITERARY CONCEPTS
- Autobiography
- Theme

READING SKILLS/ STRATEGIES
- Evaluating

THE WRITER'S STYLE
- Cause and effect

GRAMMAR
- Unusually placed subjects

SPEAKING, LISTENING, AND VIEWING
- Debate
- Drama
- Group discussion
- Oral presentation

HISTORICAL CONNECTION

Vietnam in Wartime What was the Vietnam War like for the Vietnamese people? In this selection, Le Ly Hayslip describes the war's impact on her family. These photographs reveal some of the hardships of life in a war zone.

Side A, Frame 49351

PREVIEWING

NONFICTION

from When Heaven and Earth Changed Places

Le Ly Hayslip (lā′ lē′ hā′slĭp) Vietnam

Activating Prior Knowledge
PERSONAL CONNECTION

With another student, create a list of words and phrases that come to mind when you hear the word *Vietnam*. Compare your list with those of other classmates.

The author's parents.
Courtesy of Le Ly Hayslip.

Building Background
BIOGRAPHICAL CONNECTION

Vietnam has had a long history of war. For centuries, the Vietnamese fought against Chinese domination. In the late 1800s, the French invaded Vietnam and began to rule it as a colony. After World War II, the Vietnamese—led by Ho Chi Minh (hō′ chē′ mĭn′) and his Communist organization, the Vietminh (vē-ĕt′mĭn′)—fought a long war of independence against the French (1946–1954). Following France's defeat, the country was divided into Communist North Vietnam and the non-Communist Republic of South Vietnam.

Another war broke out in South Vietnam in 1955, when the Vietcong—Communist rebels backed by North Vietnam—began to fight against the republican forces, who were supported by the United States. The Vietcong sought to unite both parts of the country under Communist leadership, whereas the republican forces wanted to keep out the Communists and preserve their capitalistic way of life. During this time, the writer of this selection was growing up in the village of Ky La (kē′ lä′) in central Vietnam. In this excerpt from her autobiography, she shares childhood memories of her father and reveals the war's impact on her family.

READING CONNECTION Setting a Purpose

Evaluating As you read about the writer's recollections of Vietnam, identify the statements that seem to you to be most important. After your reading, reevaluate your choices. List your final choices on a sheet of paper or in your notebook.

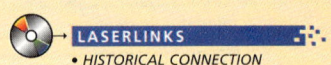
• HISTORICAL CONNECTION

140 UNIT ONE PART 2: THE POWER OF HERITAGE

PRINT AND MEDIA RESOURCES

UNIT ONE RESOURCE BOOK
Strategic Reading: Literature, p. 59
Vocabulary SkillBuilder, p. 60

GRAMMAR MINI-LESSONS
Transparencies, p. 7
Copymasters, p. 9

WRITING MINI-LESSONS
Transparencies, pp. 18–19

ACCESS FOR STUDENTS ACQUIRING ENGLISH
Selection Summaries
Reading Support

FORMAL ASSESSMENT
Selection Test, p. 27
 Test Generator

AUDIO LIBRARY
See Reference Card

 LASERLINKS
Historical Connection
Geographical Connection

140 THE LANGUAGE OF LITERATURE TEACHER'S EDITION

from When Heaven and Earth Changed Places

Le Ly Hayslip

After my brother Bon went North, I began to pay more attention to my father.

He was built solidly—big boned—for a Vietnamese man, which meant he probably had well-fed, noble ancestors. People said he had the body of a natural-born warrior.

SUMMARY

In this excerpt from her autobiography, Le Ly Hayslip describes her childhood in wartime Vietnam, remembering how unusual and understanding her father was. She recalls a time when he cared for her during her mother's trip to Danang and shared stories with her about getting his land and hiding from enemy soldiers. Her father told her to honor her ancestors and to tell what she has seen to the next generation so that her family's tradition of survival and love of their land can continue.

Thematic Link: *The Power of Heritage*
Le Ly Hayslip remembers and cherishes both her father and the Vietnamese heritage that he instilled in her.

CUSTOMIZING FOR
Students Acquiring English

- Use ACCESS FOR STUDENTS ACQUIRING ENGLISH.
- Some students may have difficulty with the non-linear style of the selection. Explain that the writer is not telling a story with a plot but rather is providing "snapshot" images of her childhood and her father.

STRATEGIC READING FOR
Less-Proficient Readers

Set a Purpose To help students understand where the story takes place, help them find Vietnam on a globe or world map.

Have students read on to find out what happens to the author and her family in Vietnam.

Use UNIT ONE RESOURCE BOOK, p. 59, for guidance in reading the selection.

WORDS TO KNOW

abstain (ăb-stān′) *v.* to deliberately refrain from an activity (p. 142)
diligent (dĭl′ə-jənt) *adj.* marked by persistent effort; painstaking (p. 142)
empathy (ĕm′pə-thē) *n.* an identification with the situation, feelings, and motives of another person; understanding (p. 142)
lenient (lē′nē-ənt) *adj.* tolerant or merciful in disposition (p. 143)
supple (sŭp′əl) *adj.* easily bent; pliant (p. 143)

CUSTOMIZING FOR
Gifted and Talented Students

Although Hayslip focuses on her father, she also reveals her mother's character. Have students look for details about Hayslip's mother and use them to make inferences about her character.

Possible responses:

- *Page 143*—The mother is less lenient than the father; she spanks her children.
- *Page 143*—The mother can't appreciate her husband's songs. She doesn't have a sense of humor about serious situations.
- *Page 143*—The mother argues with her husband but then feels ashamed. She is strong willed but holds traditional beliefs.
- *Page 146*—The mother passes her mother-in-law's tests. She is a diligent worker.

Literary Concept:
CHARACTERIZATION

A Have students summarize this description of the author's father. *(Possible response: He is handsome, easygoing, hard working, kind, and honest.)*

CUSTOMIZING FOR
Students Acquiring English

I Explain that in this context *soy* refers to the dark sauce used to flavor Asian foods.

CUSTOMIZING FOR
Multiple Learning Styles

B **Musical Learners** Invite students to sing the father's songs. Suggest that they vary their tone of voice and facial expressions to help convey the humor and message of the songs.

A He was a year younger and an inch shorter than my mother, but just as good-looking. His face was round, like a Khmer or Thai,[1] and his **I** complexion was brown as soy from working all his life in the sun. He was very easygoing about everything and seldom in a hurry. Seldom, too, did he say no to a request—from his children or his neighbors. Although he took everything in stride, he was a hard and <u>diligent</u> worker. Even on holidays, he was always mending things or tending to our house and animals. He would not wait to be asked for help if he saw someone in trouble. Similarly, he always said what he thought, although he knew, like most honest men, when to keep silent. Because of his honesty, his <u>empathy</u>, and his openness to people, he understood life deeply. Perhaps that is why he was so easygoing. Only a half-trained mechanic thinks everything needs fixing.

He loved to smoke cigars and grew a little tobacco in our yard. My mother always wanted him to sell it, but there was hardly ever enough to take to market. I think for her it was the principle of the thing: smoking cigars was like burning money. Naturally, she had a song for such gentle vices—her own habit of chewing betel[2] nuts included:

*Get rid of your tobacco,
And you will get a water buffalo.
Give away your betel,
And you will get more paddy land.*[3]

Despite her own good advice, she never <u>abstained</u> from chewing betel, nor my father from smoking cigars. They were rare luxuries that life and the war allowed them.

My father also liked rice wine, which we made, and enjoyed an occasional beer, which he purchased when there was nothing else we needed. After he'd had a few sips, he would tell jokes and happy stories, and the village kids would flock around. Because I was his youngest daughter, I was entitled to listen from his knee—the place of honor. Sometimes he would sing funny songs about whoever threatened the village, and we would feel better. For example, when the French or Moroccan[4] soldiers were near, he would sing:

There are many kinds of vegetables;
*Why do you like spinach?
There are many kinds of wealth;
Why do you use Minh money?
There are many kinds of people;
Why do you love terrorists?*

We laughed because these were all the things the French told us about the Viet Minh fighters whom we favored in the war. Years later, when the Viet Cong were near, he would sing:

*There are many kinds of vegetables;
Why do you like spinach?
There are many kinds of money;
Why do you use Yankee dollars?
There are many kinds of people;
Why do you disobey your ancestors?*

This was funny because the words were taken from the speeches the North Vietnamese cadres[5] delivered to shame us for helping the Republic. He used to have a song for when the Viet Minh were near too, which asked in the same way,

---

1. **Khmer** (kmâr) or **Thai** (tī): a member of the Khmer people of Cambodia or the Thai people of Thailand.
2. **betel** (bēt′l) **nuts**: seeds of the betel palm, chewed as a mild stimulant.
3. **paddy land**: fields for growing rice.
4. **Moroccan** (mə-rŏk′ən): from the North African nation of Morocco, then a French colony.
5. **cadres** (kăd′rēz): tightly knit groups of revolutionaries.

WORDS TO KNOW
diligent (dĭl′ə-jənt) *adj.* marked by persistent effort; painstaking
empathy (ĕm′pə-thē) *n.* an identification with the situation, feelings, and motives of another person; understanding
abstain (ăb-stān′) *v.* to deliberately refrain from an activity

142

Mini-Lesson Grammar

UNUSUALLY PLACED SUBJECTS Review with students that in statements beginning with *here* or *there*, the subject comes after the verb. *There were soldiers in the field.* Then point out the position of the subject in the sentence highlighted on this page. Point out that this kind of construction is used to emphasize particularly important ideas.

Application Invite students to find two statements on page 145 of the selection in which the subject falls between two parts of the verb, as marked by the highlighting. Then ask students to complete the following statements using the construction discussed above.

1. Just for a moment could _____ _____ _____.

2. Not until years later did _____ _____ _____.

Reteaching/Reinforcement
- *Grammar Handbook,* anthology p. 1065
- *Grammar Mini-Lessons* copymasters p. 9, transparencies p. 7

Unusually Placed Subjects, pp. 573–575

142 THE LANGUAGE OF LITERATURE TEACHER'S EDITION

"Why do you use francs?"[6] and "Why do you love French traitors?" Because he sang these songs with a comical voice, my mother never appreciated them. She couldn't see the absurdity of our situation as clearly as we children. To her, war and real life were different. To us, they were all the same.

Even as a parent, my father was more lenient than our mother, and we sometimes ran to him for help when she was angry. Most of the time it didn't work, and he would lovingly rub our heads as we were dragged off to be spanked. The village saying went: "A naughty child learns more from a whipping stick than a sweet stick." We children were never quite sure about that but agreed the whipping stick was an eloquent teacher. When he absolutely had to punish us himself, he didn't waste time. Wordlessly, he would find a long, supple bamboo stick and let us have it behind our thighs. It stung, but he could have whipped us harder. I think seeing the pain in his face hurt more than receiving his halfhearted blows. Because of that, we seldom did anything to merit a father's spanking—the highest penalty in our family. Violence in any form offended him. For this reason, I think, he grew old before his time.

One of the few times my father ever touched my mother in a way not consistent with love was during one of the yearly floods, when people came to our village for safety from the lower ground. We sheltered many in our house, which was nothing more than a two-room hut with woven mats for a floor. I came home one day in winter rain to see refugees and Republican soldiers milling around outside. They did not know I lived there, so I had to elbow my way inside. It was nearly suppertime, and I knew my mother would be fixing as much food as we could spare.

In the part of the house we used as our kitchen, I discovered my mother crying. She and my father had gotten into an argument outside a few minutes before. He had assured the refugees he would find something to eat for everyone, and she insisted there would not be enough for her children if everyone was fed. He repeated his order to her, this time loud enough for all to hear. Naturally, he thought this would end the argument. She persisted in contradicting him, so he had slapped her.

> *Even as a parent, my father was more lenient than our mother, and we sometimes ran to him for help when she was angry.*

This show of male power—we called it *do danh vo*[7]—was usual behavior for Vietnamese husbands but unusual for my father. My mother could be as strict as she wished with his children, and he would seldom interfere. Now, I discovered there were limits even to his great patience. I saw the glowing red mark on her cheek and asked if she was crying because it hurt. She said no. She said she was crying because her action had caused my father to lose face in front of strangers. She promised that if I ever did what she had done to a husband, I would have both cheeks glowing: one from his blow and one from hers.

Once, when I was the only child at home, my

---

6. **francs:** French money.
7. ***do danh vo*** (dô zän′yɔ vô).

WORDS TO KNOW
lenient (lē′nē-ənt) *adj.* tolerant or merciful in disposition
supple (sŭp′əl) *adj.* easily bent; pliant

Linking to Science

G Rice is the staple food and crop of Vietnam. Grown in flooded fields called paddies, rice plants are hardy and yield a bigger harvest per acre than most other foods. Rice contains carbohydrates and many essential vitamins and minerals. Some foods made from rice—called *com* in Vietnamese—include noodles, desserts, rice cookies, and wine.

Images for this selection are from the movie *Heaven and Earth*, directed by Oliver Stone. Copyright © Warner Bros./Regency Enterprises/Le Studio Canal.

144 UNIT ONE PART 2: THE POWER OF HERITAGE

Mini-Lesson Workplace Literacy

SCANS GOAL: Teaches Others

Teaching Others Tell students that teaching people how to do a task is an important job skill. Just as Le Ly's father shows her how to make things, workers are often required to demonstrate how to perform certain tasks. Helping others learn requires both patience and good communication skills.

Application Ask students to choose a piece of school equipment and to give oral instructions to a group of classmates on how to operate the equipment. Choices could include computers, VCRs, television sets, cameras, or tape recorders. Have the other students in the group give feedback on the instructions.

mother went to Danang[8] to visit Uncle Nhu, and my father had to take care of me. I woke up from my nap in the empty house and cried for my mother. My father came in from the yard and reassured me, but I was still cranky and continued crying. Finally, he gave me a rice cookie to shut me up. Needless to say, this was a tactic my mother never used.

The next afternoon I woke up, and although I was not feeling cranky, I thought a rice cookie might be nice. I cried a fake cry, and my father came running in.

"What's this?" he asked, making a worried face. "Little Bay Ly[9] doesn't want a cookie?"

I was confused again.

"Look under your pillow," he said with a smile.

I twisted around and saw that, while I was sleeping, he had placed a rice cookie under my pillow. We both laughed, and he picked me up like a sack of rice and carried me outside while I gobbled the cookie.

In the yard, he plunked me down under a tree and told me some stories. After that, he got some scraps of wood and showed me how to make things: a doorstop for my mother and a toy duck for me. This was unheard of—a father doing these things with a child that was not a son! Where my mother would instruct me on cooking and cleaning and tell stories about brides, my father showed me the mystery of hammers and explained the customs of our people.

His knowledge of the Vietnamese went back to the Chinese Wars in ancient times. I learned how one of my distant ancestors, a woman named Phung Thi Chinh,[10] led Vietnamese fighters against the Han.[11] In one battle, even though she was pregnant and surrounded by Chinese, she delivered the baby, tied it to her back, and cut her way to safety wielding a sword in each hand. I was amazed at this warrior's bravery and impressed that I was her descendant. Even more, I was amazed and impressed by my father's pride in her accomplishments (she was, after all, a humble female), and his belief that I was worthy of her example. "*Con phai theo got chan co ta*"[12] (Follow in her footsteps), he said. Only later would I learn what he truly meant.

Never again did I cry after my nap. Phung Thi women were too strong for that. Besides, I was my father's daughter, and we had many things to do together.

On the eve of my mother's return, my father cooked a feast of roast duck. When we sat down to eat it, I felt guilty, and my feelings showed on my face. He asked why I acted so sad.

"You've killed one of mother's ducks," I said. "One of the fat kind she sells at the market. She says the money buys gold which she saves for her daughters' weddings. Without gold for a dowry—*con o gia*[13]—I will be an old maid!"

My father looked suitably concerned, then brightened and said, "Well, Bay Ly, if you can't get married, you will just have to live at home forever with me!"

I clapped my hands at the happy prospect.

My father cut into the rich, juicy bird and said, "Even so, we won't tell your mother about the duck, okay?"

I giggled and swore myself to secrecy.

The next day, I took some water out to him in the fields. My mother was due home any time, and I used every opportunity to step outside and watch for her. My father stopped working, drank gratefully, then took my hand and led me to the top of a nearby hill. It had a

---

8. **Danang** (də-năng′): a seaport in central Vietnam.
9. **Bay Ly** (bī′ lē′): the author's childhood nickname, indicating that she was the sixth child of her parents.
10. **Phung Thi Chinh** (po̅o̅ng′ tē′ jĭn′yə).
11. **Han:** the principal ethnic group of China.
12. **Con phai theo got chan co ta** (kôn pī tĕ-ô′ gô jän kô tä).
13. **con o gia** (kôn ŭ jē-ä′).

WHEN HEAVEN AND EARTH CHANGED PLACES **145**

Literary Concept: AUTOBIOGRAPHY

H Ask students how these sentences show that Hayslip is looking back on this incident from a later time. *(Possible responses: Some students might point out that they are written in the past tense. Others might say that as a child, she wouldn't have realized that her father gave her the cookie to quiet her.)*

Literary Concept: CHARACTERIZATION

I Ask students what they can conclude about Le Ly's father from the actions described in the next two paragraphs. *(Possible responses: He is fun and kind; he loves his daughter; he doesn't believe in traditional Vietnamese notions about how to treat daughters; he is educated and a good storyteller.)*

Cultural Note

J Hayslip uses the word *dowry* to mean the money and other goods that a bride brings to her husband in marriage. Dowries are a tradition in many cultures. Besides money, the dowry of a Vietnamese village bride in the 1950s might have included water buffaloes, other farm animals, and household items.

Critical Thinking: SYNTHESIZING

K Ask students if this scene confirms or contradicts what they have already learned about Le Ly's father. *(Possible responses: Confirms, because he is empathetic and loving and takes young Le Ly's concerns seriously; contradicts, because he was described as honest and yet he is asking Le Ly to do something dishonest)*

Mini-Lesson   Literary Concepts

REVIEWING THEME Remind students that the theme of a literary work is the message or insight about life or human nature that the writer presents to the reader through the characters, setting, plot, and narration. Point out that some works may have more than one theme, and that sometimes a theme is stated directly, but often it is not.

Application Ask students how Hayslip views the role of heritage in a person's life. Have them consider the following:
- her statement that "After all, we had learned in school that one's country is as sacred as a father's grave." (p. 146)
- her parents' respect for Vietnamese traditions
- her father's teaching her Vietnamese customs and history

THE LANGUAGE OF LITERATURE **TEACHER'S EDITION** **145**

Linking to Geography

L Like much of Southeast Asia, Vietnam contains varied types of land forms, such as the Mekong Delta, an agricultural flood plain in the south. In the north are mountains covered with a subtropical jungle. Le Ly's family lived in central Vietnam, which occupies a narrow strip of land along the South China Sea.

Literary Concept: THEME

M Ask students what Le Ly's father means by "a country is more than a lot of dirt, rivers, and forests." (*Possible responses: Some students may say he means that a person's country also includes its people. Others may say a country also includes its culture and history, and he wants Le Ly to value her country's past.*)

Critical Thinking: MAKING JUDGMENTS

N Ask students if they agree with Le Ly's father's statement that "Freedom is never a gift . . . It must be won and won again." (*Possible responses: Agree, because people have always had to fight for freedom; disagree, because people born into a free country sometimes do not appreciate their freedoms*)

Cultural Note

O In traditional Vietnamese society, marriages are arranged by the parents with the help of a matchmaker. The Vietnamese emphasize harmony in a marriage, so parents seek a match in which the boy and the girl are similar in character and in economic background.

---

good view of the village and the land beyond it, almost to the ocean. I thought he was going to show me my mother coming back, but he had something else in mind.

He said, "Bay Ly, you see all this here? This is the Vietnam we have been talking about. You understand that a country is more than a lot of dirt, rivers, and forests, don't you?"

I said, "Yes, I understand." After all, we had learned in school that one's country is as sacred as a father's grave.

"Good. You know, some of these lands are battlefields where your brothers and cousins are fighting. They may never come back. Even your sisters have all left home in search of a better life. You are the only one left in my house. If the enemy comes back, you must be both a daughter and a son. I told you how the Chinese used to rule our land. People in this village had to risk their lives diving in the ocean just to find pearls for the Chinese emperor's gown. They had to risk tigers and snakes in the jungle just to find herbs for his table. Their payment for this hardship was a bowl of rice and another day of life. That is why Le Loi, Gia Long,[14] the Trung sisters, and Phung Thi Chinh fought so hard to expel the Chinese. When the French came, it was the same old story. Your mother and I were taken to Danang to build a runway for their airplanes. We labored from sunup to sundown and well after dark. If we stopped to rest or have a smoke, a Moroccan would come up and whip our behinds. Our reward was a bowl of rice and another day of life. Freedom is never a gift, Bay Ly. It must be won and won again. Do you understand?"

I said that I did.

"Good." He moved his finger from the patchwork of brown dikes, silver water, and rippling stalks to our house at the edge of the village. "This land here belongs to me. Do you know how I got it?"

I thought a moment, trying to remember my mother's stories, then said honestly, "I can't remember."

He squeezed me lovingly. "I got it from your mother."

"What? That can't be true!" I said. Everyone in the family knew my mother was poor and my father's family was wealthy. Her parents were dead, and she had to work like a slave for her mother-in-law to prove herself worthy. Such women don't have land to give away!

"It's true." My father's smile widened. "When I was a young man, my parents needed someone to look after their lands. They had to be very careful about who they chose as wives for their three sons. In the village, your mother had a reputation as the hardest worker of all. She raised herself and her brothers without parents. At the same time, I noticed a beautiful woman working in the fields. When my mother said she was going to talk to the matchmaker about this hard-working village girl she'd heard about, my heart sank. I was too attracted to this mysterious tall woman I had seen in the rice paddies. You can imagine my surprise when I found out the girl my mother heard about and the woman I admired were the same.

"Well, we were married, and my mother tested your mother severely. She not only had to cook and clean and know everything about children, but she had to be able to manage several farms and know when and how to take the extra produce to the market. Of course, she was testing her other daughters-in-law as well. When my parents died, they divided their several farms among their sons, but you know what? They gave your mother and me the biggest share because they knew we would take care of it best. That's why I say the land came from her, because it did."

I suddenly missed my mother very much and looked down the road to the south, hoping to

---

14. Le Loi (lā′ loi′), Gia Long (jē-ä′ lông′).

146 UNIT ONE PART 2: THE POWER OF HERITAGE

Mini-Lesson • The Writer's Style

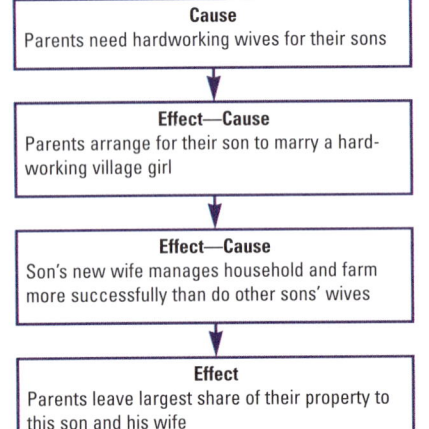

CAUSE AND EFFECT Point out that most actions arise from earlier causes and give rise to later effects. The effect of one action will become the cause of another, creating a chain of causes and effects. In recreating a chain of causes and effects, a writer must show how each event leads to the next. For example, in the passage highlighted above, a chain of causes and effects culminates in Le Ly's father inheriting the largest share of his parents' land.

Application Invite students to write a description of an event in their own lives that involved a series of causes and effects. Before beginning to write, students may wish to organize their ideas into a chart like the one shown.

Reteaching/Reinforcement
- Writer's Handbook, anthology p. 1038
- *Writing Mini-Lessons* transparencies, pp. 18–19

 **The Writer's Craft**

Cause-effect, p. 346

see her. My father noticed my sad expression.

"Hey." He poked me in the ribs. "Are you getting hungry for lunch?"

"No. I want to learn how to take care of the farm. What happens if the soldiers come back? What did you and Mother do when the soldiers came?"

My father squatted on the dusty hilltop and wiped the sweat from his forehead. "The first thing I did was to tell myself that it was my duty to survive—to take care of my family and my farm. That is a tricky job in wartime. It's as hard as being a soldier. The Moroccans were very savage. One day the rumor passed that they were coming to destroy the village. You may remember the night I sent you and your brothers and sisters away with your mother to Danang."

"You didn't go with us!" My voice still held the horror of the night I thought I had lost my father.

"Right! I stayed near the village—right on this hill—to keep an eye on the enemy and on our house. If they really wanted to destroy the village, I would save some of our things so that we could start over. Sure enough, that was their plan.

"The real problem was to keep things safe and avoid being captured. Their patrols were everywhere. Sometimes I went so deep in the forest that I worried about getting lost, but all I had to do was follow the smoke from the burning huts and I could find my way back.

"Once, I was trapped between two patrols that had camped on both sides of a river. I had to wait in the water for two days before one of them moved on. When I got out, my skin was shriveled like an old melon. I was so cold I could hardly move. From the waist down, my body was black with leeches.[15] But it was worth all the pain. When your mother came back, we still had some furniture and tools to cultivate the earth. Many people lost everything. Yes, we were very lucky."

My father put his arms around me. "My

> "The first thing I did was to tell myself that it was my duty to survive—to take care of my family."

brother Huong[16]—your uncle Huong—had three sons and four daughters. Of his four daughters, only one is still alive. Of his three sons, two went north to Hanoi,[17] and one went south to Saigon.[18] Huong's house is very empty. My other brother, your uncle Luc, had only two sons. One went north to Hanoi; the other was killed in the fields. His daughter is deaf and dumb. No wonder he has taken to drink, eh? Who does he have to sing in his house and tend his shrine when he is gone? My sister Lien[19] had three daughters and four sons. Three of the four sons went to Hanoi, and the fourth went to Saigon to find his fortune. The girls all tend their in-laws and mourn slain husbands. Who will care for Lien when she is too feeble to care for herself? Finally, my baby sister Nhien[20] lost her husband to French bombers. Of her two sons, one went to Hanoi, and the other joined the Republic, then defected, then was murdered in his house. Nobody knows which side killed him. It doesn't really matter."

My father drew me out to arm's length and

---

15. **leeches:** bloodsucking worms that live in water.
16. **Huong** (hŏŏ-ông').
17. **Hanoi** (hă-noi'): the capital of North Vietnam from 1954 until 1976; now the capital of the unified country of Vietnam.
18. **Saigon** (sī-gŏn'): the capital of South Vietnam from 1954 until 1976; now called Ho Chi Minh City.
19. **Lien** (lē-ĕn').
20. **Nhien** (nē-ĕn').

WHEN HEAVEN AND EARTH CHANGED PLACES 147

Multicultural Perspectives

BROTHER AGAINST BROTHER Vietnamese civilians faced conflicting demands during the Indochina War. Many in Hayslip's village supported the Vietminh, while their southern relatives fought on the French side. Americans faced similar conflicts of loyalty in both the Revolutionary War and the Civil War. Many colonists remained loyal to England, while their neighbors clamored for independence. Neighbor was set against neighbor, and Tories were forced to conceal their desire for reconciliation with England. The secession of the southern states in the U.S. Civil War forced family members against one another. Relatives who had been citizens of one united country suddenly found themselves on opposite sides of the Mason-Dixon Line. Many families had sons in each army.

Literary Concept: THEME

 Ask students what they think the father meant by saying Le Ly would "be worth more than any soldier who ever took up a sword" by staying alive and teaching her children what her father taught her. *(Possible responses: Some students might say she would be doing something positive to keep her culture alive. Others might say her father values peaceful actions more than violent ones.)*

STRATEGIC READING FOR
Less-Proficient Readers

 Have students review the various stories Le Ly's father has told her. Ask them what they think of the relationship she has with her father. *(Some may say they have a good relationship; they love each other very much. Others might say that their relationship is somewhat different from traditional Vietnamese father/daughter relationships. He entertains and instructs her and respects her potential as a person.)* **Evaluating**

CUSTOMIZING FOR
Gifted and Talented Students

Have students discuss why they think Hayslip titled her autobiography *When Heaven and Earth Changed Places.* What do they think represents "Heaven"?

COMPREHENSION CHECK

Ask students to decide if the following statements are true or false:
1. Le Ly's father was stricter and more traditional than her mother. *(false)*
2. Le Ly grew up in an area consistently opposed to the Viet Cong. *(false)*
3. Le Ly's father urged her to fight and, if necessary, to die for her country. *(false)*
4. Le Ly and her father had a very close relationship. *(true)*

looked me squarely in the eye. "Now, Bay Ly, do you understand what your job is?"

I squared my shoulders and put on a soldier's face. "My job is to avenge my family. To protect my farm by killing the enemy. I must become a woman warrior like Phung Thi Chinh!"

My father laughed and pulled me close. "No, little peach blossom. Your job is to stay alive— to keep an eye on things and keep the village safe. To find a husband and have babies and tell the story of what you've seen to your children and anyone else who'll listen. Most of all, it is to live in peace and tend the shrine of our ancestors. Do these things well, Bay Ly, and you will be worth more than any soldier who ever took up a sword." ❖

148 UNIT ONE PART 2: THE POWER OF HERITAGE

Assessment Option

SELF-ASSESSMENT Have students write a letter from Le Ly to her mother in Danang, describing her time at home with her father. Suggest that students use the following rubric to assess their own work.

Rubric

3 Full Accomplishment The voice and tone of the letter are consistent and sound like a younger version of the speaker. The letter covers the main things her father did and said, and it is written in proper letter form.

2 Substantial Accomplishment The voice and tone of the letter are fairly consistent, but may not sound like a younger version of the speaker. Most of the important points are covered, but proper letter format is not strictly followed.

1 Little or Partial Accomplishment The voice and tone of the letter have little similarity to the speaker's. There are few specific references to Le Ly's time with her father and proper letter format is not followed.

RESPONDING OPTIONS

FROM PERSONAL RESPONSE TO CRITICAL ANALYSIS

REFLECT
1. What is your impression of the writer's life during the Vietnam War? Write your thoughts in your notebook.

RETHINK
2. What qualities of the writer's father emerge in this portrayal of him?

   Consider
   - the songs he sang before the soldiers
   - his treatment of the refugees
   - his relationship with his family
   - what he did to save the family's property

   Close Textual Reading

3. The writer's father tells his daughter that her job is not to fight but to stay alive and raise a family. What do you think of his advice?

4. If the writer had not been the youngest daughter and the only child left at home, how do you think her relationship with her father might have been different?

5. What have you learned about Vietnam from this selection? Compare your insights with the list you made for the Personal Connection on page 140.

RELATE
6. What lessons have you learned from this selection that can be applied to your own life?

Multimodal Learning
ANOTHER PATHWAY
Cooperative Learning
Working with a small group of classmates, review the lists of important statements you made for the Reading Connection on page 140. Then choose one statement that you think best represents the spirit of the selection. Share your results with the rest of the class, explaining why you chose that statement.

QUICKWRITES

1. Write an **autobiographical essay** in which you describe the impact that a particular event has had on your family.
2. Write a magazine **advice column** on child rearing that Hayslip's father might have written.
3. Create **song lyrics** that convey your own attitude toward war.
4. Do research to find out more about modern Vietnamese culture. Present your information in a **chart** that compares the Vietnamese and American cultures in terms of values, family unity, types of work, economy, and social customs.

📁 **PORTFOLIO** Save your writing. You may want to use it later as a springboard to a piece for your portfolio.

LITERARY CONCEPTS

An **autobiography** is a person's account of his or her own life. Often, a person writing an autobiography—an autobiographer—looks back on his or her past in an effort to understand it better. The autobiographer can then make judgments about people or events of the past in a way that might not have been possible earlier. For example, Hayslip looks back on her father's dread of violence and concludes, "For this reason, I think, he grew old before his time."

Working with a partner, look through the selection to find at least two more instances in which Hayslip makes judgments about events that took place in her girlhood. Share your examples with your classmates.

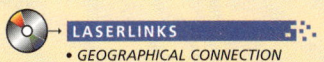
- GEOGRAPHICAL CONNECTION

WHEN HEAVEN AND EARTH CHANGED PLACES **149**

From Personal Response to Critical Analysis

1. Accept all reasonable responses.
2. Possible responses: his sense of humor, his love, his generosity, his courage
3. Accept all reasonable, well-supported responses.
4. Possible responses: Some students might say the father and daughter may not have spent so much time together. Others might suggest that he may not have taught her things that are usually taught to boys.
5. Accept all reasonable responses.
6. Accept all reasonable, well-supported responses.

Literary Links
Ask students to compare Le Ly Hayslip's attitude toward her family and culture with Tom Whitecloud's in "Blue Winds Dancing." *(Possible responses: They both have close, loving family relationships; they both cherish their way of life and are sad to see that it is threatened.)*

Another Pathway
Cooperative Learning Suggest that groups create a master list of choices by having one student record suggestions from other students in the group. Another student might act as a moderator to facilitate the group discussion and voting on a statement, and a third student might write an explanation of the group's choice.

Rubric
3 Full Accomplishment Students work together well, choose a statement that accurately represents the spirit of the selection, and explain their choice clearly.
2 Substantial Accomplishment Students work together well and choose an appropriate statement, but they have some trouble explaining their choice.
1 Little or Partial Accomplishment Students choose an inappropriate statement and cannot explain their choice.

Literary Concepts

Students might use the annotations on pages 143 and 145 to focus attention on personal judgments about past events. To help students understand the importance of this characteristic of autobiography, draw the web shown on the board. Then discuss how the shaded areas of the web set autobiographies apart from historical writing or journalism.

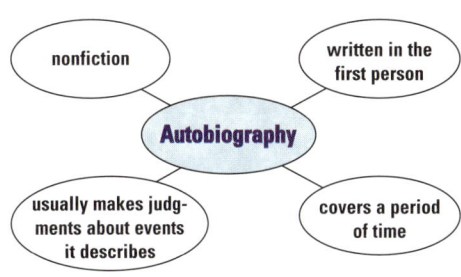

QuickWrites

1. Encourage students to make judgments about the event they are describing.
2. Students may want to look at newspaper advice columns for ideas about format.
3. Remind students that song lyrics use devices such as rhyme, rhythm, and repetition to help create meaning.
4. Students could present their information in a Venn diagram.

Autobiographical Essay, pp. 28–40
Advice Column, pp. 190–94
Comparison-and-Contrast Chart, p. 334

THE LANGUAGE OF LITERATURE TEACHER'S EDITION **149**

Words To Know

1. a
2. c
3. a
4. b
5. b

Reteaching/Reinforcement
- *Unit One Resource Book*, p. 60

Across the Curriculum

History *Cooperative Learning*
Encourage students to form research teams to find out about the Indochina War in Vietnam. Some students could be researchers, others could be recorders and organizers, and others could present the oral report to the class. Suggest that teams create graphics to accompany their reports.

LE LY HAYSLIP

Hayslip has been praised for her contributions to immigrant literature, for her unique perspective on the events she documents, and for her incorporation of Eastern and Western values.

GEOGRAPHICAL CONNECTION
Vietnam Today More than two decades after the war, Vietnam continues to rebuild its society and economy. These photographs show typical scenes of urban and rural areas in Vietnam today.

Side A, Frame 49357

Multimodal Learning

ALTERNATIVE ACTIVITIES

1. Conduct a **debate** on whether women can better serve their country by fighting alongside men or by remaining at home to care for their families. Organize the class into two groups, each arguing a different side of the issue.
2. Read the rest of *When Heaven and Earth Changed Places*. With other students, prepare a **skit** that depicts another event in Le Ly Hayslip's life.

ACROSS THE CURRICULUM

History Find out more about the involvement of the United States in the Vietnam War. How did it begin? What did the United States hope to accomplish in Vietnam? What were the effects of our nation's participation in the war? Share the results in an oral report.

WORDS TO KNOW

Write the letter of the word or phrase that best completes each sentence below.

1. You would know that a farmer was **diligent** if he or she (a) took on extra responsibilities, (b) composed humorous songs, (c) enjoyed a good meal.
2. Hayslip's father showed **empathy** when he (a) slapped his wife, (b) hid from soldiers, (c) showed awareness of his daughter's feelings.
3. The author's parents would **abstain** from physical punishment if they (a) no longer spanked their children, (b) spanked their children only for serious offenses, (c) explained their reasoning to their children.
4. If Hayslip's mother were more **lenient**, she would (a) punish her daughter more often, (b) overlook some of her daughter's misdeeds, (c) show more affection for her husband.
5. A bamboo stick is **supple** because it is (a) hard, (b) flexible, (c) long.

LE LY HAYSLIP

Le Ly Hayslip grew up in a traditional Buddhist family in the rural village of Ky La in central Vietnam. When she was 12, the Vietnam War turned her life into a nightmare of imprisonments, torture, and threats of execution. Her father, who refused to leave the family's home, did not survive the war. Separated from his wife and children, harassed by both the Vietcong and the American forces, and saddened by the destruction of his village, he eventually committed suicide.

Hayslip married an American serviceman and left Vietnam in 1970, settling in California. After the Vietnam War ended, she helped to found the East

1949–

Meets West Foundation, a nonprofit organization that builds clinics and schools in Vietnam. In 1986, Hayslip returned to Vietnam for a reunion with remaining family members. She realized one of her fondest dreams three years later, when the East Meets West Foundation opened a clinic in her childhood home of Ky La.

Published in 1989, Hayslip's book *When Heaven and Earth Changed Places* is one of the few autobiographical accounts of the Vietnam War from a Vietnamese point of view. It was used as the basis of the film *Heaven and Earth* by the director Oliver Stone.

OTHER WORKS *Child of War, Woman of Peace* Extended Reading

150 UNIT ONE PART 2: THE POWER OF HERITAGE

Alternative Activities

1. Help students craft a debate question, then write it on the chalkboard. Suggest that they follow proper debate procedure, in which one side makes a presentation and the second side rebuts it. Then the second side makes a presentation and the first side gets a rebuttal. Caution each side not to interrupt while the other one is presenting. You may wish to create a panel of judges, made up of students from other classes, to vote on the debate.
2. Remind students that acting a role involves more than repeating lines accurately. Playing a character well means using appropriate facial expressions, gestures, and physical actions, as well as varying voice pitch and tone. Suggest that students look through *When Heaven and Earth Changed Places* and make a list of details that they can use to help them portray their characters.

PREVIEWING

FICTION

The Study of History
Frank O'Connor Ireland

The author's parents. Courtesy of Harriet O'Donovan.

Activating Prior Knowledge
PERSONAL CONNECTION
What would your life have been like if your ancestors had made different decisions before you were born? For example, what if your family had decided to settle in a different country? What if your mother had chosen a different mate, so that you had a different father? Imagine a different set of circumstances in your family background. Then freewrite in your notebook for five minutes about who you might be or what your life might be like.

BIOGRAPHICAL CONNECTION
Building Background
The boy who would come to be known as Frank O'Connor often daydreamed about who he might have been if his family background had been different. Born Michael Francis O'Donovan in 1903, O'Connor grew up in Barrackton, a slum on the outskirts of Cork in southwestern Ireland. He shared a close bond with his mother, and he adopted her maiden name when he decided to write under a pseudonym.

Not only did O'Connor write two autobiographies; he also wrote autobiographical fiction about a boy named Laurence ("Larry") Delaney. Larry appears in a number of O'Connor's short stories, and like the author himself, he is an only child who is sometimes frustrated by the sharp contrasts between the rich and the poor in Cork. Naive and full of insecurities, he is often embarrassed by the commonness of his parents. Larry Delaney is the main character in the story you are about to read.

Setting a Purpose
READING CONNECTION
Analyzing Details As you read "The Study of History," pay attention to the details that O'Connor uses in describing his characters. What do these details tell you about the characters' personalities, attitudes, and family backgrounds?

• HISTORICAL CONNECTION

OVERVIEW
Objectives
- To understand and appreciate a short story that explores a child's view of how his family has shaped his life
- To notice and appreciate characterization
- To express understanding of the story through a choice of writing forms, including an autobiographical incident and love letters
- To extend understanding of the story through a variety of multimodal and cross-curricular activities

Skills
LITERARY CONCEPTS
- Characterization
- Setting

GENRE STUDY
- Fiction: short story

THE WRITER'S STYLE
- Varieties of language

GRAMMAR
- Possessive pronouns

CUSTOMIZING FOR
Students Acquiring English
- Use **ACCESS FOR STUDENTS ACQUIRING ENGLISH**.
- To help make the humor of this story accessible to students, explain that the ideas and events are presented from a young child's viewpoint.
- As you guide students through the selection, you may want to use the suggestions in these boxes as well as the suggestions under Strategic Reading for Less-Proficient Readers.

HISTORICAL CONNECTION
The Ireland of Frank O'Connor
These pohtographs show scenes in and around Cork, Ireland, where Frank O'Connor grew up and where many of his stories are set.

Side A, Frame 49370

PRINT AND MEDIA RESOURCES

UNIT ONE RESOURCE BOOK
Strategic Reading: Literature, p. 63
Vocabulary SkillBuilder, p. 64

GRAMMAR MINI-LESSONS
Transparencies, p. 15
Copymasters, p. 18

WRITING MINI-LESSONS
Transparencies, p. 56

ACCESS FOR STUDENTS ACQUIRING ENGLISH
Selection Summaries
Reading Support

FORMAL ASSESSMENT
Selection Test, pp. 29–30
 Test Generator

 **AUDIO LIBRARY**
See Reference Card

 **LASERLINKS**
Historical Connection

THE STUDY OF HISTORY

Frank O'Connor

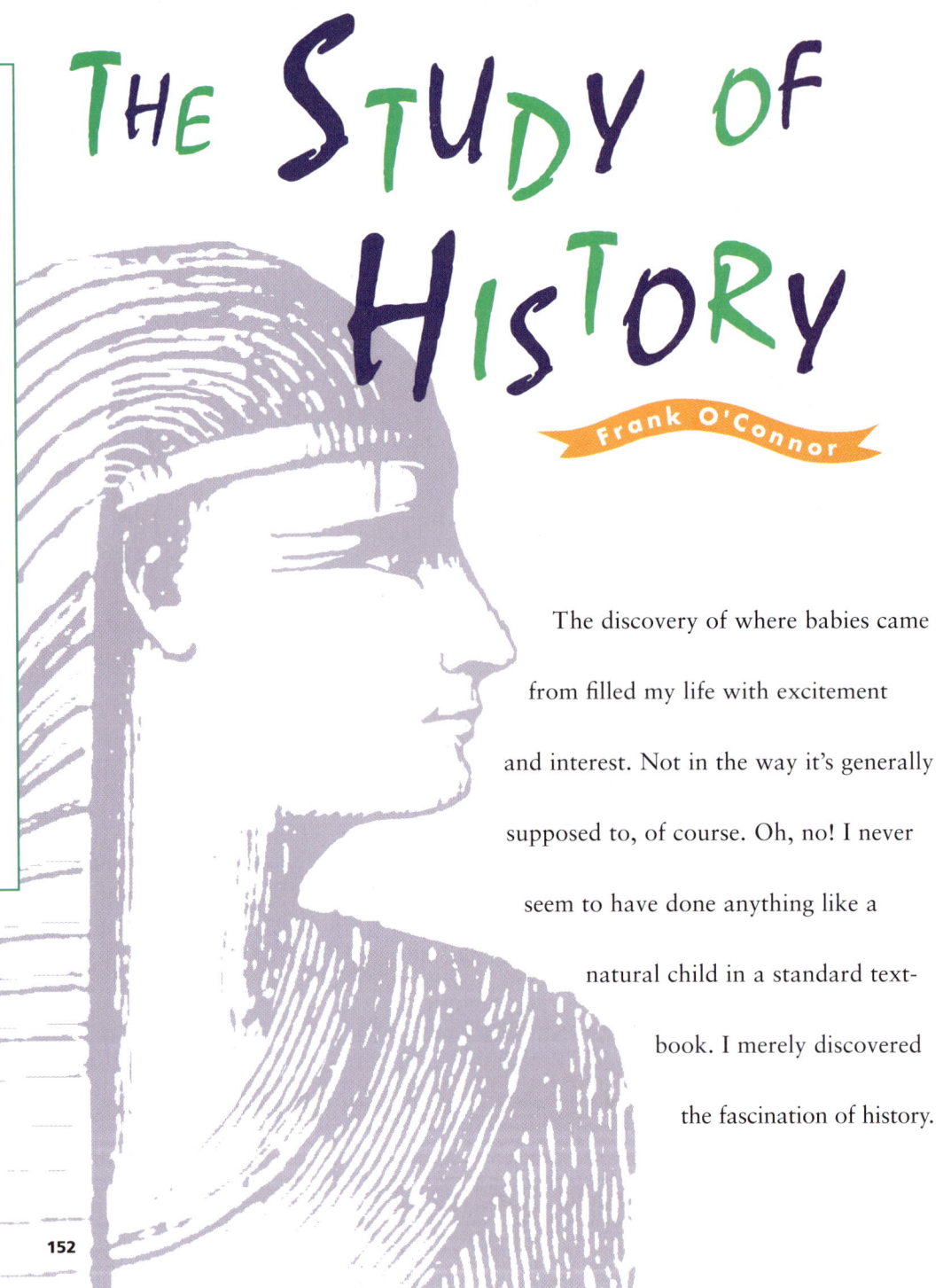

SUMMARY

Laurence Delaney is fascinated by the variety of people his mother and father might have married—and the different possibilities of whom he might have become. His questions amuse his father, whose teasing upsets his mother. Laurence visits the place where one of his mother's suitors had lived and often visits the place where his father's old sweetheart still lives. One day, after inquiring about the woman, he meets her son, who is just his age. The boy introduces Laurence to his mother. Laurence impresses Mrs. O'Brien, and, in turn, is fascinated by her flirting manner, and colorful household, but he returns home with a new appreciation for his own family. When he recounts his adventures, his father is delighted, but his mother is disturbed by his experiment, causing Laurence to feel guilty. Later that night, he becomes disoriented by the alternative identities he might have had and he cannot find comfort again until he takes his mother's hand and shrinks back into his own familiar identity.

Thematic Link: *The Power of Heritage*
Confronting what he might have been if his father had married someone else, a young boy realizes the vital role that his parents have played in his life.

STRATEGIC READING FOR
Less-Proficient Readers

Set a Purpose Invite students to discuss what children learn or inherit from their families. Ask them how these traits have shaped their characters. Have students read on to learn what Larry finds interesting about the past.

Use **UNIT ONE RESOURCE BOOK**, p. 63, for guidance in reading the selection.

DESIGN NOTE

Cleopatra has often been considered one of history's most fascinating women. The first footnote explains the narrator's allusion to her.

The discovery of where babies came from filled my life with excitement and interest. Not in the way it's generally supposed to, of course. Oh, no! I never seem to have done anything like a natural child in a standard textbook. I merely discovered the fascination of history.

WORDS TO KNOW

biased (bī′əst) *adj.* marked by an unfair preference; prejudiced (p. 156)
brooding (brōō′dĭng) *adj.* having a moody or depressed disposition **brood** *v.* (p. 153)
complacently (kəm-plā′sənt-lē) *adv.* in a contented, unconcerned manner (p. 157)
contemptuously (kən-tĕmp′chōō-ə-slē) *adv.* in a way that shows one's low opinion of someone or something; scornfully (p. 159)
exasperated (ĭg-zăs′pə-rā′-tĭd) *adj.* made impatient or angry; annoyed **exasperate** *v.* (p. 154)

impertinent (ĭm-pûr′tn-ənt) *adj.* rude, insolent (p. 161)
incredulously (ĭn-krĕj′ə-lə-slē) *adv.* in a manner expressing skepticism or disbelief (p. 156)
ordained (ôr-dānd′) *adj.* established by authority or fate **ordain** *v.* (p. 153)
saucy (sô′sē) *adj.* disrespectful in a bold or high-spirited way; pert (p. 157)
uncanny (ŭn-kăn′ē) *adj.* strange; eerie; weird (p. 154)

Up to this, I had lived in a country of my own that had no history, and accepted my parents' marriage as an event <u>ordained</u> from the creation; now, when I considered it in this new, scientific way, I began to see it merely as one of the turning points of history, one of those apparently trivial events that are little more than accidents but have the effect of changing the destiny of humanity. I had not heard of Pascal, but I would have approved his remark about what would have happened if Cleopatra's nose had been a bit longer.[1]

It immediately changed my view of my parents. Up to this, they had been principles, not characters, like a chain of mountains guarding a green horizon. Suddenly a little shaft of light, emerging from behind a cloud, struck them, and the whole mass broke up into peaks, valleys, and foothills; you could even see whitewashed farmhouses and fields where people worked in the evening light, a whole world of interior perspective. Mother's past was the richer subject for study. It was extraordinary the variety of people and settings that woman had had in her background. She had been an orphan, a parlor-maid, a companion, a traveler; and had been proposed to by a plasterer's apprentice, a French chef who had taught her to make superb coffee, and a rich and elderly shopkeeper in Sunday's Well.[2] Because I liked to feel myself different, I thought a great deal about the chef and the advantages of being a Frenchman, but the shopkeeper was an even more vivid figure in my imagination because he had married someone else and died soon after—of disappointment, I had no doubt—leaving a large fortune. The fortune was to me what Cleopatra's nose was to Pascal: the ultimate proof that things might have been different.

"How much was Mr. Riordan's fortune, Mummy?" I asked thoughtfully.

"Ah, they said he left eleven thousand," Mother replied doubtfully, "but you couldn't believe everything people say."

That was exactly what I could do. I was not prepared to minimize a fortune that I might so easily have inherited.

"And weren't you ever sorry for poor Mr. Riordan?" I asked severely.

"Ah, why would I be sorry, child?" she asked with a shrug. "Sure, what use would money be where there was no liking?"

That, of course, was not what I meant at all. My heart was full of pity for poor Mr. Riordan who had tried to be my father; but, even on the low level at which Mother discussed it, money would have been of great use to me. I was not so fond of Father as to think he was worth eleven thousand pounds, a hard sum to visualize but more than twenty-seven times greater than the largest salary I had ever heard of—that of a Member of Parliament. One of the discoveries I was making at the time was that Mother was not only rather hard-hearted but very impractical as well.

But Father was the real surprise. He was a <u>brooding</u>, worried man who seemed to have no proper appreciation of me and was always wanting me to go out and play or go upstairs and read, but the historical approach changed him like a character in a fairy tale. "Now let's talk about the ladies Daddy nearly married," I would say; and he would stop whatever he was doing

---

1. **Pascal** (pă-skăl′) . . . **longer:** The 17th-century French philosopher and mathematician Blaise Pascal wrote that if Cleopatra's nose had been shorter (not longer, as the narrator says), "the whole face of the world would have been changed." Cleopatra (69–30 B.C.), a queen of Egypt famous for her beauty, affected history through her romances with the Roman leaders Julius Caesar and Mark Antony.
2. **in Sunday's Well:** on Sunday's Well Road, a street in the wealthier part of the city of Cork.

WORDS TO KNOW
ordained (ôr-dānd′) *adj.* established by authority or fate **ordain** *v.*
brooding (brōō′dĭng) *adj.* having a moody or depressed disposition **brood** *v.*

Literary Concept: TONE

C Invite students to discuss the adult narrator's attitude toward his younger self. *(Possible responses: Some students may say his attitude is humorous and sometimes a little self-mocking. Others might say the narrator is amused by his childish judgments and confusion but sympathetic to his emotions and fantasies.)*

CUSTOMIZING FOR
Students Acquiring English

I Explain the image conveyed by "carroty." *(bright orange, like a carrot)* Explain also that Larry's mother's description of Miss Cadogan's hair as "carroty" is meant to be unflattering.

Literary Concept:
CHARACTERIZATION

D Ask students what conclusions they can draw about Larry's mother from her reaction to her husband's teasing. *(Possible responses: She is sensitive; she has a temper; she gets jealous easily.)*

---

and give a great guffaw. "Oh, ho, ho!" he would say, slapping his knee and looking slyly at Mother, "you could write a book about them." Even his face changed at such moments. He would look young and extraordinarily mischievous. Mother, on the other hand, would grow black.

"You could," she would say, looking into the fire. "Daisies!"

"'The handsomest man that walks Cork!'" Father would quote with a wink at me. "That's what one of them called me."

"Yes," Mother would say, scowling. "May Cadogan!"

"The very girl!" Father would cry in astonishment. "How did I forget her name? A beautiful girl! 'Pon my word, a most remarkable girl! And still is, I hear."

"She should be," Mother would say in disgust. "With six of them!"

"Oh, now, she'd be the one that could look after them! A fine head that girl had."

"She had. I suppose she ties them to a lamp-post while she goes in to drink and gossip."

That was one of the peculiar things about history. Father and Mother both loved to talk about it but in different ways. She would only talk about it when we were together somewhere, in the Park or down the Glen, and even then it was very hard to make her stick to the facts, because her whole face would light up and she would begin to talk about donkey carriages, or concerts in the kitchen, or oil lamps, and though nowadays I would probably value it for atmosphere, in those days it sometimes drove me mad with impatience. Father, on the other hand, never minded talking about it in front of her, and it made her angry—particularly when he mentioned May Cadogan. He knew this perfectly well, and he would wink at me and make me laugh outright, though I had no idea of why I laughed, and, anyway, my sympathy was all with her.

"But, Daddy," I would say, presuming on his high spirits, "if you liked Miss Cadogan so much, why didn't you marry her?"

At this, to my great delight, he would let on to be filled with doubt and distress. He would put his hands in his trousers pockets and stride to the door leading into the hallway.

"That was a delicate matter," he would say, without looking at me. "You see, I had your poor mother to think of."

"I was a great trouble to you," Mother would say, in a blaze.

"Poor May said it to me herself," he would go on as though he had not heard her, "and the tears pouring down her cheeks. 'Mick,' she said, 'that girl with the brown hair will bring me to an untimely grave.'"

"She could talk of hair!" Mother would hiss. "With her carroty mop!"

"Never did I suffer the way I suffered then, between the two of them," Father would say with deep emotion as he returned to his chair by the window.

"Oh, 'tis a pity about ye!" Mother would cry in an <u>exasperated</u> tone and suddenly get up and go into the front room with her book to escape his teasing. Every word that man said she took literally. Father would give a great guffaw of delight, his hands on his knees and his eyes on the ceiling, and wink at me again. I would laugh with him, of course, and then grow wretched because I hated Mother's sitting alone in the front room. I would go in and find her in her wicker chair by the window in the dusk, the book open on her knee, looking out at the Square. She would always have regained her composure when she spoke to me, but I would have an <u>uncanny</u> feeling of unrest in her and stroke her and talk to her soothingly as if we had changed places and I were the adult and she the child.

C

I

D

| WORDS TO KNOW | **exasperated** (ĭg-zăs′pə-rā′tĭd) *adj.* made impatient or angry; annoyed **exasperate** *v.*
uncanny (ŭn-kăn′ē) *adj.* strange; eerie; weird |

154

Mini-Lesson   The Writer's Style

VARIETIES OF LANGUAGE: DIALECTS
Remind students that a dialect is a form of a language that is different from the standard language in its grammar and pronunciation. Point out that writers often use dialect to make their stories more realistic, to bring characters to life, and to help convey a story's setting. O'Connor's use of the dialect of Cork, Ireland in "The Study of History" accomplishes all these things. Sentence constructions such as "Sure, what use would money be where there was no liking?" and expressive words and phrases such as "Oh, 'tis a pity about ye!" help to capture both the language and the lilt of the Cork dialect.

Application Have students write an anecdote told by someone using a regional dialect.

Reteaching/Reinforcement
• Grammar Handbook, anthology pp. 1096–1097
• *Writing Mini-Lessons* transparencies, p. 56

The Writer's Craft
Dialects, p. 431

---

154 THE LANGUAGE OF LITERATURE TEACHER'S EDITION

Jimmy O'D (about 1925), Robert Henri. Oil on canvas, 24″ × 20″, Collection of the Montclair (New Jersey) Art Museum, museum purchase, Picture Buying Fund (26.1).

But if I was excited by what history meant to them, I was even more excited by what it meant to me. My potentialities were double theirs. Through Mother I might have been a French boy called Laurence Armady or a rich boy from Sunday's Well called Laurence Riordan. Through Father I might, while still remaining a Delaney, have been one of the six children of the mysterious and beautiful Miss Cadogan. I was fascinated by the problem of who I would have been if I hadn't been me, and, even more, by the problem of whether or not I would have known that there was anything wrong with the arrangement. Naturally, I tended to regard Laurence Delaney as the person I was intended to be, and so I could not help wondering whether as Laurence Riordan I would not have been aware of Laurence Delaney as a real gap in my make-up.

I remember that one afternoon after school I walked by myself all the way up to Sunday's Well, which I now regarded as something like a second home. I stood for a while at the garden gate of the house where Mother had been working when she was proposed to by Mr. Riordan, and then went and studied the shop itself. It had clearly seen better days, and the cartons and advertisements in the window were dusty

THE STUDY OF HISTORY **155**

Art Note

***Jimmy O'D* by Robert Henri** Robert Henri was born Robert Henry Cozad in Cincinnati in 1865. He was strongly influenced by Thomas Eakins, an American painter of the previous generation. Henri first went to Ireland in 1913. He spent every summer there, from 1923 until his death in 1929, painting many portraits of Irish children. *Jimmy O'D* dates from about 1925. It was painted with broad, fast brush strokes, a technique Henri used because he felt that portraits must be painted quickly in order to capture the subject's personality.

Reading the Art *Does your image of Larry Delaney resemble the boy in this portrait? Why or why not?*

CUSTOMIZING FOR
Multiple Learning Styles

E **Spatial or Graphic Learners** Invite students to create portraits of all the different possible Larrys as the narrator might imagine them: the real Laurence Delaney, Laurence Riordan, Laurence Armady, and Laurence Delaney.

CUSTOMIZING FOR
Students Acquiring English

2 For students less familiar with the custom of using a first name followed by the father's last name, explain what the narrator means by "trying on" these different last names. Ask students to explain the traditional naming practices of their original cultures.

THE LANGUAGE OF LITERATURE TEACHER'S EDITION **155**

Literary Concept: SETTING

F Invite students to identify details of the setting that show a change in the characters' social status. *(Possible responses: The mother relaxing in the parlor, instead of working; the boy attending a private school instead of a public one and carrying an expensive book bag.)* Ask students how Larry's daydream about living in this setting made him feel. *(Possible response: Some students might suggest he feels sad that a rich "Laurence Riordan" wouldn't even notice someone like Larry Delaney.)*

Critical Thinking: COMPARE AND CONTRAST

G Ask students to contrast Larry's "solemn and unnatural politeness" with the behavior of the other boy. *(Possible response: The other boy is blunt and informal, much rougher than Larry.)*

STRATEGIC READING FOR
Less-Proficient Readers

H Ask students the following questions to make sure they understand why Larry is intrigued by the past:

- What fact about his parents most interests Larry? *(He is fascinated by the fact that they might have married other people.)* **Summarizing**

- Why is Larry interested in Mrs. O'Brien? *(She is an old sweetheart of Larry's father, and Larry wonders what he would have been like if she had been his mother.)* **Clarifying**

Set a Purpose Have students read on to find out what happens when Larry meets Mrs. O'Brien.

---

and sagging. It wasn't like one of the big stores in Patrick Street, but at the same time, in size and fittings, it was well above the level of a village shop. I regretted that Mr. Riordan was dead, because I would have liked to see him for myself instead of relying on Mother's impressions, which seemed to me to be biased. Since he had, more or less, died of grief on Mother's account, I conceived of him as a really nice man; lent him the countenance and manner of an old gentleman who always spoke to me when he met me on the road; and felt I could have become really attached to him as a father. I could imagine it all: Mother reading in the parlor while she waited for me to come home up Sunday's Well in a school-cap and blazer, like the boys from the Grammar School,[3] and with an expensive leather satchel instead of the old cloth school bag I carried over my shoulder. I could see myself walking slowly and with a certain distinction, lingering at gateways and looking down at the river; and later I would go out to tea in one of the big houses with long gardens sloping to the water, and maybe row a boat on the river along with a girl in a pink frock. I wondered only whether I would have any awareness of the National School[4] boy with the cloth school bag who jammed his head between the bars of a gate and thought of me. It was a queer, lonesome feeling that all but reduced me to tears.

But the place that had the greatest attraction of all for me was the Douglas Road, where Father's friend Miss Cadogan lived, only now she wasn't Miss Cadogan but Mrs. O'Brien. Naturally, nobody called Mrs. O'Brien could be as attractive to the imagination as a French chef or an elderly shopkeeper with eleven thousand pounds, but she had a physical reality that the other pair lacked. As I went regularly to the library at Parnell Bridge, I frequently found myself wandering up the road in the direction of Douglas and always stopped in front of the long row of houses where she lived. There were high steps up to them, and in the evening the sunlight fell brightly on the house fronts till they looked like a screen. One evening as I watched a gang of boys playing ball in the street outside, curiosity overcame me. I spoke to one of them. Having been always a child of solemn and unnatural politeness, I probably scared the wits out of them.

"I wonder if you could tell me which house Mrs. O'Brien lives in, please?" I asked.

"Hi, Gussie!" he yelled to another boy. "This fellow wants to know where your old one lives."

This was more than I had bargained for. Then a thin, good-looking boy of about my own age detached himself from the group and came up to me with his fists clenched. I was feeling distinctly panicky, but all the same I studied him closely. After all, he was the boy I might have been.

"What do you want to know for?" he asked suspiciously.

Again, this was something I had not anticipated.

"My father was a great friend of your mother," I explained carefully, but, so far as he was concerned, I might as well have been talking a foreign language. It was clear that Gussie O'Brien had no sense of history.

"What's that?" he asked incredulously.

At this point we were interrupted by a woman I had noticed earlier, talking to another over the railing between the two steep gardens. She was small and untidy looking and occasionally rocked

---

3. **Grammar School:** a private school.
4. **National School:** a public school funded by the government.

WORDS TO KNOW
biased (bī′əst) *adj.* marked by an unfair preference; prejudiced
incredulously (ĭn-krĕj′ə-ləs-lē) *adv.* in a manner expressing skepticism or disbelief

156

Mini-Lesson — Study Skills

TAKING OBJECTIVE TESTS: ANALOGIES
Explain that analogies are often used on standardized tests as a way of testing vocabulary comprehension. The key to understanding analogies is to figure out the relationship between the first pair of words presented, and then to apply that relationship to a second pair of words. For example, the analogy ceiling: up :: floor: ____ is completed by the word down, because the relationship in each pair in the analogy is one of location.

Application Ask students to complete these analogies by analyzing the relationship between the first pair of words of each one.

1. pram: baby carriage :: _____: elevator *(lift; British synonyms for American terms)*
2. Mr. Delaney: Mrs. O'Brien :: Mrs. Delaney: _____ *(Mr. Riordan; people Larry's parents might have married)*
3. public school: private school :: National School: _____ *(Grammar School; opposites)*

156 THE LANGUAGE OF LITERATURE TEACHER'S EDITION

the pram⁵ in an absent-minded way as though she only remembered it at intervals.

"What is it, Gussie?" she cried, raising herself on tiptoe to see us better.

"I don't really want to disturb your mother, thank you," I said, in something like hysterics, but Gussie anticipated me, actually pointing me out to her in a manner I had been brought up to regard as rude.

"This fellow wants you," he bawled.

"I don't really," I murmured, feeling that now I was in for it. She skipped down the high flight of steps to the gate with a laughing, puzzled air, her eyes in slits and her right hand arranging her hair at the back. It was not carroty as Mother described it, though it had red lights when the sun caught it.

"What is it, little boy?" she asked coaxingly, bending forward.

"I didn't really want anything, thank you," I said in terror. "It was just that my daddy said you lived up here, and, as I was changing my book at the library, I thought I'd come up and inquire. You can see," I added, showing her the book as proof, "that I've only just been to the library."

"But who is your daddy, little boy?" she asked, her gray eyes still in long, laughing slits. "What's your name?"

"My name is Delaney," I said. "Larry Delaney."

"Not *Mike* Delaney's boy?" she exclaimed wonderingly. "Well, for God's sake! Sure, I should have known it from that big head of yours." She passed her hand down the back of my head and laughed. "If you'd only get your hair cut, I wouldn't be long recognizing you. You wouldn't think I'd know the feel of your old fellow's head, would you?" she added roguishly.

"No, Mrs. O'Brien," I replied meekly.

"Why, then indeed I do, and more along with it," she added in the same saucy tone, though the meaning of what she said was not clear to me. "Ah, come in and give us a good look at you! That's my eldest, Gussie, you were talking to," she added, taking my hand. Gussie trailed behind us for a purpose I only recognized later.

"Ma-a-a-a, who's dat fella with you?" yelled a fat little girl who had been playing hopscotch on the pavement.

"That's Larry Delaney," her mother sang over her shoulder. I don't know what it was about that woman but there was something about her high spirits that made her more like a regiment than a woman. You felt that everyone should fall into step behind her. "Mick Delaney's son from Barrackton. I nearly married his old fellow once. Did he ever tell you that, Larry?" she added slyly. She made sudden swift transitions from brilliance to intimacy that I found attractive.

"Yes, Mrs. O'Brien, he did," I replied, trying to sound as roguish as she, and she went off into a delighted laugh, tossing her red head.

"Ah, look at that now! How well the old divil didn't forget me! You can tell him I didn't forget him either. And if I married him, I'd be your mother now. Wouldn't that be a queer old three and fourpence?⁶ How would you like me for a mother, Larry?"

"Very much, thank you," I said complacently.

"Ah, go on with you, you would not," she exclaimed, but she was pleased all the same. She struck me as the sort of woman it would be easy enough to please. "Your old fellow always said it: your mother was a *most* superior woman, and you're a *most* superior child. Ah, and I'm not

---

5. **pram:** a baby carriage.
6. **a queer old three and fourpence:** slang expression meaning "an odd thing."

WORDS TO KNOW

saucy (sô′sē) *adj.* disrespectful in a bold or high-spirited way; pert
complacently (kəm-plā′sənt-lē) *adv.* in a contented, unconcerned manner

157

Mini-Lesson Grammar

POSSESSIVE PRONOUNS Remind students that although certain possessive pronouns and contractions sound the same, they are spelled differently and have different uses. Have students find the highlighted contraction *who's* on this page. Point out that this contraction is made up of the two words *who* and *is;* however, the possessive pronoun *whose* is spelled differently and is used to show ownership. Remind students that possessive pronouns never use apostrophes, whereas contractions always do.

Application Write the following sentences on the chalkboard and have students choose the correct words:

1. Larry thinks about Mr. Riordan, (who's/whose) shop this was. *whose*
2. (It's/Its) hard not to like Larry. *It's*
3. (Who's/Whose) having bread and jam? *Who's*
4. The sixpence had lost (it's/its) shine. *its*

Reteaching/Reinforcement
• *Grammar Handbook,* anthology p. 1070
• *Grammar Mini-Lessons* copymasters p. 18, transparencies p. 15

Possessive Pronouns, p. 528

THE LANGUAGE OF LITERATURE **Teacher's Edition** 157

Art Note

***Spring in St. John's Wood* by Laura Knight** The British artist Laura Knight (1877–1970) was well-known during her lifetime and became the first artist to be made a Dame of the British Empire. A realistic painter, Knight painted such diverse subjects as landscapes and villages; scenes from the ballet, theater, and circus; and the trials of Nazi war criminals at Nuremberg. This outdoor scene, painted in 1933, uses subdued colors and shadowing to evoke a sense of calm.

Reading the Art What time of day is it in this painting? What makes you think so?

Linking to Geography

St. John's Wood is a residential neighborhood in the northwestern part of London. Like many London neighborhoods, St. John's Wood was originally a village of its own until it was absorbed into an expanding London. Today St. John's Wood is more urban than this 1933 painting shows; however, it still retains a quiet air and neighborhood feeling.

Spring in St. John's Wood (1933), Dame Laura Knight. Oil on canvas, 51¼″ × 45½″, Board of Trustees of the National Museums and Galleries on Merseyside, Walker Art Gallery, Liverpool, Great Britain.

Mini-Lesson  Literary Concepts

REVIEWING SETTING Remind students that the setting of a short story is the time and place in which the action occurs. Stories can be set in the present, past, or future, at any time of the day or night, and in any real or imaginary place. In some short stories the setting plays an important role and is clearly defined. In others it is left more to the reader's imagination.

Application Have students look for the ways in which Frank O'Connor creates the setting of this story. Suggest that they look for such details as characters' names, the words the characters use, and specific place names and sensory details that describe physical surroundings. Have students turn their findings into a chart like the one shown.

Details of Setting	
Names of characters:	May Cadogan,
Words characters use:	tanner,
Place names:	Cork,
Details of surroundings:	"scribbles on the walls"

too bad myself either," she added with a laugh and a shrug, wrinkling up her merry little face.

In the kitchen she cut me a slice of bread, smothered it with jam, and gave me a big mug of milk. "Will you have some, Gussie?" she asked in a sharp voice as if she knew only too well what the answer would be. "Aideen," she said to the horrible little girl who had followed us in, "aren't you fat and ugly enough without making a pig of yourself? Murder the Loaf we call her," she added smilingly to me. "You're a polite little boy, Larry, but damn the politeness you'd have if you had to deal with them. Is the book for your mother?"

"Oh, no, Mrs. O'Brien," I replied. "It's my own."

"You mean you can read a big book like that?" she asked incredulously, taking it from my hands and measuring the length of it with a puzzled air.

"Oh, yes, I can."

"I don't believe you," she said mockingly. "Go on and prove it!"

There was nothing I asked better than to prove it. I felt that as a performer I had never got my due, so I stood in the middle of the kitchen, cleared my throat, and began with great feeling to enunciate one of those horribly involved opening paragraphs you found in children's books of the time. "On a fine evening in Spring, as the setting sun was beginning to gild the blue peaks with its lambent[7] rays, a rider, recognizable as a student by certain niceties[8] of attire, was slowly, and perhaps regretfully, making his way . . ." It was the sort of opening sentence I loved.

"I declare to God!" Mrs. O'Brien interrupted in astonishment. "And that fellow there is one age with you, and he can't spell *house*. How well you wouldn't be down at the library, you caubogue,[9] you! . . . That's enough now, Larry," she added hastily as I made ready to entertain them further.

"Who wants to read that blooming[10] old stuff?" Gussie said contemptuously.

Later, he took me upstairs to show me his air rifle and model airplanes. Every detail of the room is still clear to me: the view into the back garden with its jungle of wild plants where Gussie had pitched his tent (a bad site for a tent as I patiently explained to him, owing to the danger from wild beasts); the three cots still unmade; the scribbles on the walls; and Mrs. O'Brien's voice from the kitchen telling Aideen to see what was wrong with the baby, who was screaming his head off from the pram outside the front door. Gussie, in particular, fascinated me. He was spoiled, clever, casual; good-looking, with his mother's small clean features; gay and calculating. I saw that when I left and his mother gave me a sixpence.[11] Naturally I refused it politely, but she thrust it into my trousers pocket, and Gussie dragged at her skirt, noisily demanding something for himself.

"If you give him a tanner,[12] you ought to give me a tanner," he yelled.

"I'll tan you," she said laughingly.

"Well, give up a lop[13] anyway," he begged, and she did give him a penny to take his face off her, as she said herself, and after that he followed me down the street and suggested we should go to the shop and buy sweets. I was

---

7. **lambent:** flickering lightly on a surface.
8. **niceties:** fine points or details.
9. **caubogue** (kô-bōg′): simpleton; bumpkin (from the Irish *cábóg*).
10. **blooming:** in Ireland and Britain, a slang word used to add intensity to a statement.
11. **sixpence:** a coin worth six British pennies.
12. **tanner:** another term for a sixpence.
13. **lop:** chunk; piece.

WORDS TO KNOW

contemptuously (kən-tĕmp′chōō-əs-lē) *adv.* in a way that shows one's low opinion of someone or something; scornfully

159

STRATEGIC READING FOR
Less-Proficient Readers

P Ask the following questions to make sure students understand what happens when Larry meets Mrs. O'Brien:

- What does Larry do at Mrs. O'Brien's house? *(He eats bread and jam, impresses Mrs. O'Brien with his reading skills, and looks at Gussie's room.)* **Summarizing**

- Ask students how Mrs. O'Brien feels about Larry and how she demonstrates these feelings. *(She likes him and is impressed by him, because she says so and offers him money.)* **Making Inferences**

Set a Purpose Have students read on to find out how Larry and his parents react to his visit.

CUSTOMIZING FOR
Students Acquiring English

3 Explain that *with a real flourish* means "with a showy gesture that reflects delight and pride," that *blowed* means "astonished," and that a *guffaw* is a huge laugh.

Critical Thinking: SPECULATING

Q Ask students what the narrator might mean when he says that "This was an aspect of history I only studied later." *(Possible responses: Some students may say it was only when he was older that he understood that married couples often don't like to hear about their partner's past loves. Others might say that he learned that bringing up the past can hurt people by triggering painful or unpleasant memories.)*

---

simple-minded, but I wasn't an out-and-out fool, and I knew that if I went to a sweetshop with Gussie, I should end up with no sixpence and very few sweets. So I told him I could not buy sweets without Mother's permission, at which he gave me up altogether as a sissy or worse.

It had been an exhausting afternoon but a very instructive one. In the twilight I went back slowly over the bridges, a little regretful for that fast-moving, colorful household, but with a new appreciation of my own home. When I went in, the lamp was lit over the fireplace and Father was at his tea.

"What kept you, child?" Mother asked with an anxious air, and suddenly I felt slightly guilty, and I played it as I usually did whenever I was at fault—in a loud, demonstrative, grown-up way. I stood in the middle of the kitchen with my cap in my hand and pointed it first at one, then at the other.

"You wouldn't believe who I met!" I said dramatically.

"Wisha,[14] who, child?" Mother asked.

"Miss Cadogan," I said, placing my cap squarely on a chair and turning on them both again. "Miss May Cadogan. Mrs. O'Brien as she is now."

"Mrs. O'Brien?" Father exclaimed, putting down his cup. "But where did you meet Mrs. O'Brien?"

"I said you wouldn't believe it. It was near the library. I was talking to some fellows, and what do you think but one of them was Gussie O'Brien, Mrs. O'Brien's son. And he took me home with him, and his mother gave me bread and jam, and she gave me *this*." I produced the sixpence with a real flourish.

"Well, I'm blowed!" Father gasped, and first he looked at me, and then he looked at Mother and burst into a loud guffaw.

"And she said to tell you she remembers you too, and that she sent her love."

"Oh, by the jumping bell of Athlone!"[15] Father crowed and clapped his hands on his knees. I could see he believed the story I had told and was delighted with it, and I could see, too, that Mother did not believe it and that she was not in the least delighted. That, of course, was the trouble with Mother. Though she would do anything to help me with an intellectual problem, she never seemed to understand the need for experiment. She never opened her mouth while Father cross-questioned me, shaking his head in wonder and storing it up to tell the men in the factory. What pleased him most was Mrs. O'Brien's remembering the shape of his head, and later, while Mother was out of the kitchen, I caught him looking in the mirror and stroking the back of his head.

But I knew too that for the first time I had managed to produce in Mother the unrest that Father could produce, and I felt wretched and guilty and didn't know why. This was an aspect of history I only studied later.

That night I was really able to indulge my passion. At last I had the material to work with. I saw myself as Gussie O'Brien, standing in the bedroom, looking down at my tent in the garden, and Aideen as my sister, and Mrs. O'Brien as my mother, and, like Pascal, I re-created history. I remembered Mrs. O'Brien's laughter, her scolding, and the way she stroked my head. I knew she was kind—casually kind—and hot-tempered, and recognized that in dealing with her I must somehow be a different sort of person. Being good at reading would never satisfy her. She would almost compel you to be as Gussie

---

14. **wisha:** in Ireland, an introductory interjection meaning "Well!" or "Indeed!"
15. **by the jumping bell of Athlone** (ăth-lōn′): a humorous exclamation. Athlone is a town in central Ireland.

was: flattering, impertinent, and exacting. Though I couldn't have expressed it in those terms, she was the sort of woman who would compel you to flirt with her.

Then, when I had had enough, I deliberately soothed myself as I did whenever I had scared myself by pretending that there was a burglar in the house or a wild animal trying to get in the attic window. I just crossed my hands on my chest, looked up at the window, and said to myself: "It is not like that. I am not Gussie O'Brien. I am Larry Delaney, and my mother is Mary Delaney, and we live in Number 8, Wellington Square. Tomorrow I'll go to school at the Cross, and first there will be prayers, and then arithmetic, and after that composition."

For the first time the charm did not work. I had ceased to be Gussie, all right, but somehow I had not become myself again, not any self that I knew. It was as though my own identity was a sort of sack I had to live in, and I had deliberately worked my way out of it, and now I couldn't get back again because I had grown too big for it. I practiced every trick I knew to reassure myself. I tried to play a counting game; then I prayed, but even the prayer seemed different, as though it didn't belong to me at all. I was away in the middle of empty space, divorced from mother and home and everything permanent and familiar. Suddenly I found myself sobbing. The door opened, and Mother came in in her nightdress, shivering, her hair over her face.

"You're not sleeping, child," she said in a wan and complaining voice.

I snivelled, and she put her hand on my forehead.

"You're hot," she said. "What ails you?"

I could not tell her of the nightmare in which I was lost. Instead, I took her hand, and gradually the terror retreated, and I became myself again, shrank into my little skin of identity, and left infinity and all its anguish behind.

"Mummy," I said, "I promise I never wanted anyone but you." ❖

WORDS TO KNOW

impertinent (ĭm-pûr′tn-ənt) *adj.* rude; insolent

Assessment Option

INFORMAL ASSESSMENT To assess students' understanding of the selection, ask them to create a time line that tracks the events of the story in chronological order and also indicates important events that take place before the story, such as the parents' prior romances.

Rubric

3 Full Accomplishment Students include all the major events, including those predating the story's action, in the correct order.

2 Substantial Accomplishment Students include many of the major events. One or two may not be in correct order.

1 Little or Partial Accomplishment Students leave out important events and present several events out of sequence.

STRATEGIC READING FOR Less-Proficient Readers

R Have students discuss the parents' reactions to the news of Larry's visit to Mrs. O'Brien's. *(His father finds the details of the visit amusing and flattering, but his mother becomes upset.)* **Compare and Contrast**

Ask students how Larry feels after he tells his parents about his visit. *(For a while he feels separated from his real life, as if everything is changed and he's unable to go back to being his old self.)* **Summarizing**

CUSTOMIZING FOR Gifted and Talented Students

Have students discuss the concepts of "self" or "identity." Ask how someone might grow "too big" for his or her identity, as Larry says he does. What makes Larry feel finally that he has resumed his real identity?

COMPREHENSION CHECK

1. About which of his mother's old suitors does Larry daydream? *(a French chef and a rich elderly shopkeeper)*
2. How does Larry's mother react when his father starts talking about old sweethearts? *(She gets upset and leaves the room.)*
3. Why does Larry go to Mrs. O'Brien's house? *(She used to be a sweetheart of his father's; he is curious about her and about how his life might have been if she had been his mother.)*
4. What happens to Larry the night of his visit to Mrs. O'Brien? *(He imagines he's Gussie O'Brien, and then he gets scared because he can't go back to being himself until his mother comes in to reassure him.)*

From Personal Response to Critical Analysis

1. Accept all reasonable responses. Be sure that students give details in their descriptions.
2. Possible responses: He is intelligent; he has a vivid imagination; he is curious; he loves his mother and is in awe of his father; he is quick to judge other people; he is slightly egotistical and proud of his accomplishments.
3. Possible responses: Yes, because Mrs. O'Brien would spoil him and amuse him; no, because he needs a more sensitive and intellectual environment than she could give him.
4. Possible responses: The narrator is amused yet nostalgic when he describes his parents' relationship; he seems to miss the naïveté and nerve he had as a child; he seems happy that he finally realized how fortunate he is to have his parents.
5. Possible responses: Many facets of our lives are dependent on accidental factors; every experience has a good and a bad side; our parents are an important part of who we are.
6. Accept all reasonable responses. Be sure that students explain their opinions.

Another Pathway

Cooperative Learning Groups of students can collaborate on their storyboards. One student may record the group's ideas, while another organizes the ideas to make sure they show the plot of the story. A third student can assign drawing tasks and monitor the group to make sure everyone is working towards the same goal.

Rubric

3 Full Accomplishment Students accurately sketch out the scene or scenes they choose, with appropriate characters and settings.

2 Substantial Accomplishment Students include most of the relevant features of their chosen scenes, but may leave out a character or get the setting wrong.

1 Little or Partial Accomplishment Students have trouble sketching scenes or get the characters and settings wrong.

RESPONDING OPTIONS

FROM PERSONAL RESPONSE TO CRITICAL ANALYSIS

REFLECT
1. Did you find this story humorous? serious? both? Describe your impressions.

RETHINK
2. How would you describe young Larry Delaney?
   Consider
   - how he spends his free time
   - his relationship with each of his parents
   - *Thematic Link* why he fantasizes about a different family background
   - his encounter with Gussie and Mrs. O'Brien

3. Do you think Larry would be happy as Mrs. O'Brien's son? Why or why not?

4. What seems to be the narrator's attitude toward his own childhood? Support your response with details from the story.

5. Frank O'Connor once said that storytelling "doesn't deal with problems; it doesn't have any solutions to offer; it just states the human conditions." What do you think the writer is trying to say about the human condition in this story?

RELATE
6. Which do you feel is more influential in determining what kind of person a child becomes—biological factors (inherited genes) or environmental factors (culture, friendships, economic status, and so forth)? Explain your opinion.

ANOTHER PATHWAY
Plan a film version of "The Study of History" by designing and drawing a storyboard—a series of sketches showing the sets and the positions of the actors in one or more scenes of the story.

LITERARY CONCEPTS

Characterization consists of the techniques that a writer uses to develop characters. There are four basic methods of characterization: **1.** through physical description; **2.** through a character's speech, thoughts, feelings, and actions; **3.** through the speech, thoughts, feelings, and actions of other characters; and **4.** through the narrator's direct comments about the character's nature. O'Connor uses all four techniques to bring the characters in "The Study of History" to life. Choose one of the characters in the story and find passages that illustrate each different method of characterization.

QUICKWRITES

1. Write an **autobiographical incident** that, like Larry Delaney's story, deals with a turning point in your life. If you prefer, write from the point of view of the person you might have become if the circumstances of your birth had been different, using as a springboard the freewriting you did for the Personal Connection on page 151.

2. Write several **love letters** that Michael Delaney and May Cadogan might have exchanged. Alternatively, write a love letter in which Mr. Riordan proposes marriage to Larry's mother, then write her "Dear John" response.

📁 **PORTFOLIO** Save your writing. You may want to use it later as a springboard to a piece for your portfolio.

162 UNIT ONE PART 2: THE POWER OF HERITAGE

Literary Concepts

Students can make charts like the one shown here for Mrs. O'Brien for the character they choose.

Physical description	Her hair "had red lights when the sun caught it."
Character's own speech, thoughts, feelings, and actions	She gives Larry a mug of milk and a slice of bread smothered with jam
Other characters' speech, thoughts, feelings, and actions	Larry's mother: "I suppose she ties (her children) to a lamppost while she goes in to drink and gossip."
Narrator's direct statements	" . . . her high spirits . . ."

QuickWrites

1. Encourage students to use at least one of the methods of characterization to develop the characters in their incidents.
2. Suggest students make a list of details from the story for each character. Then they can use their lists to help them decide how a letter from a particular character should sound.

The Writer's Craft

Autobiographical Incident, pp. 26–40
Punctuating Letters, p. 797

ACROSS THE CURRICULUM

Science Prepare a diagram of your family tree as far back as you can research it. Try to include information about genetic traits that are passed along from generation to generation, such as eye color and hair color.

WORDS TO KNOW

On a separate piece of paper, write the letter of the antonym of each boldfaced word below.

1. **brooding:** (a) reserved, (b) moody, (c) lighthearted
2. **uncanny:** (a) artificial, (b) familiar, (c) mysterious
3. **exasperated:** (a) calm, (b) confused, (c) disturbed
4. **impertinent:** (a) polite, (b) minor, (c) fearful
5. **incredulously:** (a) surprisingly, (b) densely, (c) trustfully
6. **ordain:** (a) explain, (b) prohibit, (c) decree
7. **biased:** (a) stubborn, (b) crooked, (c) fair
8. **contemptuously:** (a) cruelly, (b) respectfully, (c) disgustingly
9. **complacently:** (a) argumentatively, (b) falsely, (c) dishonestly
10. **saucy:** (a) tasteless, (b) wishful, (c) shy

LITERARY LINKS

Compare and contrast Larry's attitude toward his parents with that of another character in a fiction or

FRANK O'CONNOR

1903–1966

Frank O'Connor grew up in a troubled, impoverished home, but he found refuge in the imaginary world of literature. He was an avid reader as a young boy and by the time he was 12 had already begun to pursue his life's work as a writer, creating an anthology of his own biographies, poems, and essays on Irish history.

For many years, O'Connor worked as a librarian in Cork and in Dublin, his occupation being one that gave him time to write. Eventually he became one of Ireland's most influential literary figures, producing everything from poetry to novels, travel books to literary criticism. O'Connor is best known for his intimate and realistic short stories, however. According to James Matthews, O'Connor's biographer, "Only when he had a story banging around in the echo chamber of his mind was Frank O'Connor really alive." His passion for writing is evident not only in his work but also in his writing habits: he was known to revise his stories over and over again, even after they were published.

OTHER WORKS *Domestic Relations, An Only Child, Collected Stories*

THE STUDY OF HISTORY   163

Across The Curriculum

Science Students can study family photos and conduct interviews to gather the information for their family trees. Students who don't live with their birth parents may choose to include information about personality traits rather than genetic traits.

Literary Links

Possible responses:

Like Mark Mathabane in *Kaffir Boy*, Larry feels closer to his mother than to his father.

Like Le Ly Hayslip in *When Heaven and Earth Changed Places*, Larry delights in the stories his parents tell.

Like Ivan Vassilievich in "After the Ball," Larry is interested in the idea that people's lives are determined by chance.

Words To Know

1. c	6. b
2. b	7. c
3. a	8. b
4. a	9. a
5. c	10. c

Reteaching/Reinforcement
- *Unit One Resource Book*, p. 64

FRANK O'CONNOR

As a teenager, O'Connor joined the Irish Republican Army and fought in the Irish Civil War from 1919 to 1921. After the war's end, he continued the fight to include Northern Ireland in the Irish Republic. As a result of this activity, he was arrested and sent to prison. After he had served his jail sentence, O'Connor began to publish the stories that would make him one of Ireland's best-known literary figures.

Alternative Activities

1. Invite students to draw family portraits of the Delaneys and the O'Briens. Suggest that they look back through the story for descriptive details about the characters. They can use their imaginations and what they know about characters' personalities to create the characters who aren't described physically.
2. Invite students to complete the children's story that Larry begins reading on page 159. Suggest that they might keep the old-fashioned tone and narrative voice of the first sentence.

REFLECTING ON THEME
What Do You Think?

In this selection, Larry likes to imagine what his life might have been like if he had different parents and, thus, a different heritage. Ask students to review the heritage pie graphs they made at the beginning of this part of Unit One and any changes they have made as a result of reading these selections. Then ask them to imagine how their own lives might be different if one aspect of their heritage were changed. How might the pieces of their heritage pie graphs change in size?

OBJECTIVES

- To promote independent active reading
- To practice and apply skills learned in previous selections

Reading Pathways

- Invite students to choose partners and do a choral reading. Partners should decide which lines they will read together and which lines will be read solo. Suggest that they pay special attention to the repetition and the rhythm in the poem. After some rehearsal, partners may wish to present their choral reading for a group of classmates.
- Have students read the poem twice, once for content and once for form. Suggest that they note the poetic devices they find and analyze how these contribute to the meaning.
- Invite students to read the poem and sketch the images it brings to mind.

Art Note

Haitian Drum, artist unknown
Although this drum was made in Haiti, its design is clearly African. Unlike in the United States, where drumming was forbidden on southern plantations, the African drumming tradition was well preserved in Caribbean slave communities. This drum, called the *Maman* (which means "mother" in French), is used in the Haitian *Vodun* ceremony of *Rada*, a ritual that originated in Africa. The serpent around the base of the drum represents Damballah, the Haitian god of life. The patterns on the drum are similar to patterns found in central African textiles.

Reading the Art *How does the existence of this drum reinforce what Hughes is saying in "Afro-American Fragment"?*

ON YOUR OWN

AFRO-AMERICAN FRAGMENT
LANGSTON HUGHES UNITED STATES

So long,
So far away
Is Africa.
Not even memories alive
5 Save those that history books create,
Save those that songs
Beat back into the blood—
Beat out of blood with words sad-sung
In strange un-Negro tongue—
10 So long,
So far away
Is Africa.

Subdued and time-lost
Are the drums—and yet
15 Through some vast mist of race
There comes this song
I do not understand,
This song of atavistic[1] land,
Of bitter yearnings lost
20 Without a place—
So long,
So far away
Is Africa's
Dark face.

---

1. **atavistic** (ăt′ə-vĭs′tĭk): showing a recurrence of characteristics possessed by remote ancestors.

Haitian drum (1940s), artist unknown. Wood and goat skin, 43 × 24 × 24 inches. Collection of Virgil Young.

164 UNIT ONE PART 2: THE POWER OF HERITAGE

PRINT AND MEDIA RESOURCES

UNIT ONE RESOURCE BOOK
Strategic Reading: Literature, p. 67

FORMAL ASSESSMENT
Selection Test, p. 31
Part Test, pp. 33–34
Test Generator

AUDIO LIBRARY
See Reference Card

INTERNET RESOURCES
McDougal Littell Literature Center at http://www.hmco.com/mcdougal/lit

LANGSTON HUGHES

1902–1967

Langston Hughes was among the foremost figures in 20th-century African-American literature. Born in Joplin, Missouri, James Langston Hughes was the son of a schoolteacher mother and a shopkeeper father who separated soon after his birth. Until he was 12, he was raised principally by his grandmother. After her death, he lived with his mother and stepfather, eventually settling in Cleveland, Ohio. At the age of 19, Hughes published the poem "The Negro Speaks of Rivers" in a prestigious magazine. During the same year, he moved to New York City, where he briefly attended Columbia University. Hughes next held a series of varied jobs that took him to Africa and Europe as a sailor and to Paris, where he worked as a cook. On returning to the United States, he took a job as a busboy at a Washington, D.C., hotel, where one night he served the famous American poet Vachel Lindsay. Hughes daringly dropped a few of his poems beside Lindsay's plate; Lindsay was so impressed that he read them aloud at a poetry recital he attended that very night. Soon afterward, Hughes had his poetry published in the African-American journal *Opportunity* and in a now-famous volume, *The Weary Blues* (1926).

Settling in Harlem, the New York City neighborhood that was a mecca for African-American artists in the 1920s, Hughes began a long and influential career marked by achievements in virtually every form of literature—plays, novels, short stories, essays, biographies, and, of course, poetry. He also championed the careers of younger black writers and edited several anthologies of African and African-American literature.

OTHER WORKS *The Big Sea, The Dream Keeper and Other Poems, I Wonder As I Wander, Selected Poems*

AFRO-AMERICAN FRAGMENT **165**

LANGSTON HUGHES

Langston Hughes was one of the most prolific writers of the twentieth century and was the first African American to earn his living solely from writing. In much of his poetry, Hughes used the strong jazz rhythms of African-American music and drew on the dialect of the people of Harlem to help reflect their lives. Hughes' poetry has been translated into at least six languages, and some of his poems have been set to music.

Thematic Link: *The Power of Heritage*
In this poem, Langston Hughes reflects upon the continuing power of an African heritage from which he is far removed.

 OPTION 1

Individual Activity:
WRITING A POEM

Invite students to write their own poems in response to "Afro-American Fragment." Suggest that they begin by analyzing the poem for themes and poetic devices they would like to use.

Teacher's Role Before students begin writing, you can facilitate their analyses of "Afro-American Fragment" through a group discussion of students' responses to the poem.

Rubric

3 Full Accomplishment Students' poems address themes and use poetic devices appropriately.

2 Substantial Accomplishment Students' poems do not fully use themes or poetic devices.

1 Little or Partial Accomplishment Students' poems show little or no use of theme or poetic devices.

 **OPTION 2**

Class Discussion:
SHARING IDEAS

After students have read the selection, engage the class in a discussion by using the following questions. Encourage students to support their answers by quoting appropriate lines from the poem.

Teacher's Role You can facilitate class discussion by asking students to share their responses to each question.

1. Why do you think Hughes uses repetition in the poem? *(Possible responses: to create rhythm; to emphasize certain ideas; to enhance the drum imagery)*
2. What is the mood, or predominant emotion, of this poem? Why? *(Possible responses: Sad, because slavery made it difficult for African Americans to keep their heritage; bittersweet, because Hughes feels much of his African heritage is lost to him)*

THE LANGUAGE OF LITERATURE TEACHER'S EDITION **165**

OVERVIEW

To gain a deeper appreciation of the selections they have read in this unit, students will explore the characteristics of a firsthand narrative and then create a well-developed example in this lesson.

Objectives

- To plan a firsthand narrative about an autobiographical incident by considering elements such as vivid images, dialogue, and the significance of an experience
- To draft a firsthand narrative and solicit response
- To revise, edit, and publish a firsthand narrative
- To reflect on the process of writing a firsthand narrative

Skills

WRITING AND LANGUAGE
- Writing dialogue
- Using levels of language appropriately

GRAMMAR AND USAGE
- Using quotation marks in dialogue

MEDIA LITERACY
- Analyzing a statistical table
- Interpreting a cartoon
- Reading a novel excerpt

SPEAKING, LISTENING, AND VIEWING
- Conducting interviews
- Conferencing

CRITICAL THINKING
- Classifying/categorizing
- Making judgments
- Drawing conclusions

RESEARCH SKILLS
- Locating sources
- Conducting interviews
- Using the computer

Teaching Strategy: MODELING

A The table gives the United States population for 27 selected ancestry groups in 1990. After checking students' understanding of the statistical table, ask students to suggest what the table's footnote reveals about American culture.

Critical Thinking: CLASSIFYING/CATEGORIZING

B Suggest that students create a chart with columns headed as follows: "Family Culture," "Social/Ethnic/Religious Culture," "American Culture," "Regional Culture." Under each heading students can list significant people, events, values, or associations.

WRITING FROM EXPERIENCE

WRITING A FIRSTHAND NARRATIVE

As you have seen in Unit One, "Imprints of the Past," the families and cultures in which people grow up help mold them into the people they become. Having an awareness of your heritage can help you better understand yourself and others.

GUIDED ASSIGNMENT
Write About an Autobiographical Incident Many people have stories about times they suddenly understood the value of their heritage or times they rebelled against their heritage, perhaps in order to grow. Writing about an autobiographical incident can help you recognize and understand the significance of such an experience and share that discovery with others.

❶ Analyze What You Read

A In a small group, discuss the items on these pages. What information do you get from the table of statistics and its footnote? What ideas about heritage do the cartoon and the novel excerpt show? Make notes of your ideas.

❷ Examine Your Heritage

B Think of ways you experience your heritage or culture. Remember that you are the product of several cultures—a family culture, an American culture, and perhaps a regional, religious, social, or ethnic culture. Think about any conflicts that you have experienced among these cultures, beliefs, or customs. Then write a paragraph about your culture or heritage.

❸ Collect Your Ideas

C Look over your notes. List several autobiographical incidents you could write about that would tell something about your culture, heritage, beliefs, customs, or family history.

166 UNIT ONE: IMPRINTS OF THE PAST

Statistical Table

U.S. Population by Selected Ancestry Group: 1990

Race*	Number
African-American	23,777,000
American Indian	8,708,000
Asian Indian	570,000
Chinese	1,505,000
Cuban	860,000
Czech	1,296,000
Dutch	6,227,000
English	32,652,000
Filipino	1,451,000
French	10,321,000
French Canadian	2,167,000
German	57,947,000
Greek	1,110,000
Irish	38,736,000
Italian	14,665,000
Japanese	1,005,000
Korean	837,000
Mexican	11,587,000
Norwegian	3,869,000
Polish	9,366,000
Puerto Rican	1,955,000
Russian	2,953,000
Scottish	5,394,000
Slovak	1,883,000
Spanish	2,024,000
Swedish	4,681,000
Vietnamese	536,000

*The concept of race as used by the U.S. Census Bureau reflects self-identification; it does not denote any scientific classification based on biological stock. Persons who reported one or more ancestry groups may be included in more than one category.

Source: U.S. Bureau of the Census, 1990 Census of Population.

PRINT AND MEDIA RESOURCES

UNIT ONE RESOURCE BOOK
Prewriting, p. 71
Elaboration, p. 72
Peer Response Guide, pp. 73–74
Revising and Proofreading, p. 75
Student Model, pp. 76–77
Rubric, p. 78

GRAMMAR MINI-LESSONS
Transparencies, p. 44
Copymasters, pp. 45–46

WRITING MINI-LESSONS
Transparencies, p. 56, p. 59

FORMAL ASSESSMENT
Guidelines for Writing Assessment

LASERLINKS
Writing Springboard

Personal and Expressive Writing, pp. 26–40

166 THE LANGUAGE OF LITERATURE

CUSTOMIZING FOR
Students Acquiring English

C Point out that students' cultural backgrounds will probably interest their classmates. Encourage students to think of holiday customs, ceremonies, music, or sports that have particular cultural significance to them.

Media Literacy:
READING A CARTOON

D In the cartoon, two rattlesnakes are watching their child attempt to rattle its head rather than its tail. One parent blames the other's family lineage for their offspring's peculiar behavior. Explain to students that the cartoonist is poking fun at the way in which some people may jump to conclusions about heritage.

Teaching Strategy:
STUMBLING BLOCK

E Some of the vocabulary in the novel excerpt may cause problems for readers. You may wish to explain the following:

mutant tag of DNA: an altered particle of deoxyribonucleic acid, which contains a cell's genetic code
replicating: copying, reproducing
syndrome: used here in its technical, medical sense of a number of disease symptoms occurring together

---

Novel Excerpt

The narrator is starting to feel her Chinese heritage in her blood.

Cartoon

THE FAR SIDE By GARY LARSON

"This is your side of the family, you realize."

The narrator thought being Chinese meant acting weird.

I felt different about being Argentinean after I spent a week in Argentina.

Family Heirloom

A PAIR OF TICKETS

The minute our train leaves the Hong Kong border and enters Shenzhen, China, I feel different. I can feel the skin on my forehead tingling, my blood rushing through a new course, my bones aching with a familiar old pain. And I think, My mother was right. I am becoming Chinese.

"Cannot be helped," my mother said when I was fifteen and had vigorously denied that I had any Chinese whatsoever below my skin. I was a sophomore at Galileo High in San Francisco, and all my Caucasian friends agreed: I was about as Chinese as they were. But my mother had studied at a famous nursing school in Shanghai, and she said she knew all about genetics. So there was no doubt in her mind, whether I agreed or not: Once you are born Chinese, you cannot help but feel and think Chinese.

"Someday you will see," said my mother. "It is in your blood, waiting to be let go."

And when she said this, I saw myself transforming like a werewolf, a mutant tag of DNA suddenly triggered, replicating itself insidiously into a *syndrome*, a cluster of telltale Chinese behaviors, all those things my mother did to embarrass me—haggling with store owners, pecking her mouth with a toothpick in public, being color-blind to the fact that lemon yellow and pale pink are not good combinations for winter clothes.

But today I realize that I've never really known what it means to be Chinese. I am thirty-six years old. My mother is dead and I am on a train, carrying with me her dreams of coming home. I am going to China.

306

THE JOY LUCK CLUB AMY TAN

LASERLINKS
• WRITING SPRINGBOARD

WRITING COACH

WRITING FROM EXPERIENCE **167**

WRITING SPRINGBOARD

The Influence of a Mentor Donald Taylor is a high school student who has found a mentor. Karl Malone, a star professional basketball player, spoke at Donald's school. They became friends, and Malone invited Donald to attend Malone's basketball camp. In this film interview, Donald talks about Malone's influence and the importance of helping others.

Writing Prompt Write about an incident in which someone helped to change your life in a positive way.

Side B, Frame 215

THE LANGUAGE OF LITERATURE **TEACHER'S EDITION** **167**

Teaching Strategy:
STUMBLING BLOCK

F If students have trouble generating webs about abstractions like values, suggest that they "warm up" using more concrete topics like food, music, or clothing. Encourage them to consider how these prompts relate to their everyday experiences and family history, and what the prompts illustrate about their cultures.

Critical Thinking:
MAKING JUDGMENTS

G In addition to answering the questions listed in the text, students can use these criteria for assessing their story ideas:
- Does the story idea contain a clear conflict between people or a struggle in my own mind?
- Do I remember specific, vivid details about the experience?
- Did I change or grow significantly because of the experience?

PREWRITING

Exploring Experiences

A Closer Look Now that you've thought about what makes up your heritage and culture, you're ready to decide on a story to tell about it. The ideas on these pages will help you choose an autobiographical incident and begin writing about it.

① Brainstorm Further

F Take several sheets of paper. On each page, write a word or phrase that has to do with heritage or culture, such as *values* or *traditions*. On each page, complete a web with examples from your experience or family history. Think of autobiographical incidents you could relate about these that would say something about your heritage or culture.

Student's Brainstorming Web

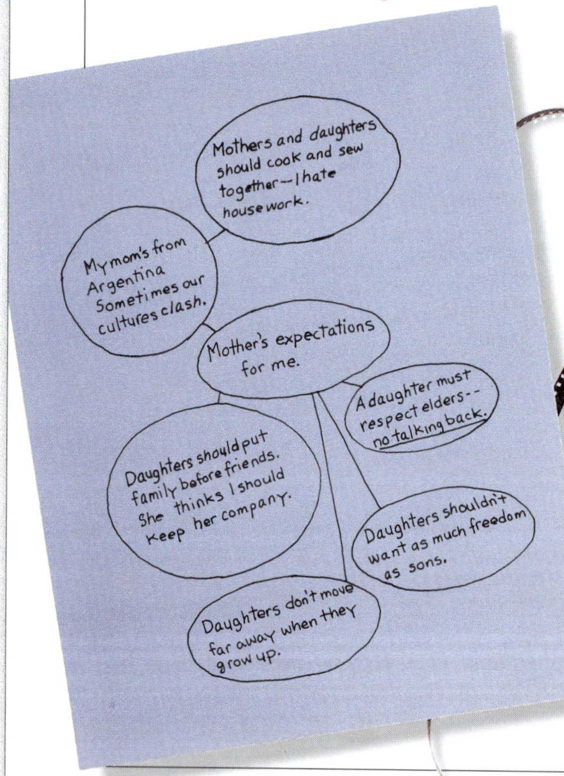

- Mothers and daughters should cook and sew together—I hate housework.
- My mom's from Argentina. Sometimes our cultures clash.
- Mother's expectations for me.
- A daughter must respect elders—no talking back.
- Daughters should put family before friends. She thinks I should keep her company.
- Daughters shouldn't want as much freedom as sons.
- Daughters don't move far away when they grow up.

② Choose Your Topic

You may have several ideas for a story. Asking yourself questions like the following will help you choose one idea.

- Which idea interests me the most?
- Which memory brings up strong emotions? **G**
- Which incident would make the best story?
- Am I comfortable sharing this story?
- Will this story say something significant about my heritage?

168 UNIT ONE: IMPRINTS OF THE PAST

Mini-Lesson — The Writer's Style

Reteaching/Reinforcement
- *Writing Mini-Lessons*, transparencies, p. 56
- *Grammar Mini-Lessons* copymasters, pp. 45–46, transparencies p. 44

DIALOGUE IN NARRATIVES Remind students that dialogue can be an effective way to show, rather than tell about, events in a narrative. In addition to showing events, dialogue can reveal character and contribute to atmosphere or mood. Suggest the following guidelines for writing dialogue:
- Make the words sound natural, the way people really speak in everyday conversation. Use sentence fragments, dialect, or slang when appropriate, but don't overuse those devices.
- Make the words reveal something about their speaker's personality.

Application Have students work with partners to convert one of the situations featured in the web to a brief passage of dialogue. You can use the following example to model the activity:
- "Well, Mom, how come Tommy gets to go with his friends to the movies every Friday night?"
- "That's not your business, Nina," snapped Mom. "A good daughter stays home with her family."

Additional Suggestions Extend the activity by having each set of partners read their dialogues aloud and then listen to other students' suggestions.

168 THE LANGUAGE OF LITERATURE TEACHER'S EDITION

3 Talk Over Your Ideas

Share your story idea with your classmates.

- Pay attention to your classmates' reactions to your story idea. This will help you know what you need to explain about your heritage or about a family custom if you write this story.
- Listen carefully to your classmates' story ideas. Learning about other people's backgrounds can help you to see your own more clearly.

4 Get the Facts Straight

Do you have the information you need to begin writing?

- If you are telling a story from your past, do you remember everything clearly? List your questions and consult with others who shared the experience.
- If you are telling about a family tradition or holiday celebration, is the history or meaning of the tradition or celebration clear to you? The SkillBuilder at the right can help you do some research to find out more about the custom.

5 Think About Audience and Purpose

Consider your audience as you think about what form your story might take. If you intend to share your story at a school or neighborhood festival celebrating heritage, you may tell if differently than if you intend to share it with friends. Whatever your audience, remember that if you can make clear why an incident from your past or a part of your heritage is important to you, your story will hold their interest.

To focus on your audience and purpose, jot down the answers to some of these questions:

- What information do your readers need about the characters or setting of your story?
- What other background information do they need?
- What dialogue or description will help to tell your story?
- What point do you want to make with your story?

SkillBuilder

RESEARCH SKILLS

Locating Information

If you are telling about your family history or about a tradition or custom, there may be some questions that you want to have answered before you write. You may want to

- talk to an expert on your heritage—someone connected with a church or cultural center, perhaps
- look for information in a library or museum
- interview a grandparent or an older relative or friend

APPLYING WHAT YOU'VE LEARNED
Decide what sources you will use to find answers for a question you have about your heritage. If one of your sources is a family member or expert, contact this person. Be sure to take notes or record interviews electronically.

THINK & PLAN

Reflecting on Your Ideas

1. How did you decide what story to tell? How do you think you will share your story?
2. How did sharing your ideas with your classmates help you plan your story?
3. Which of the methods you used to gather ideas were particularly helpful? Which will you want to try again?

Speaking and Listening: COLLABORATIVE OPPORTUNITY

H If possible, have students work in small groups with classmates of different cultural backgrounds. Guide students to see that listening to others' responses to their own story ideas can help them understand what their audience will need to know about characters, setting, and other background information.

Critical Thinking: DRAWING CONCLUSIONS

I Tell students that answering the following questions will help them identify the central meaning of the autobiographical incident:
- What did I learn about myself and others as a result of this experience?
- How did this incident change my thoughts or feelings?

SkillBuilder RESEARCH SKILLS

J **INTERVIEWING** Remind students that conducting a successful interview requires both preparation and follow-up. Offer them these guidelines:
- To prepare for an interview, draw up a list of questions or topics and organize the list in a sequence that makes sense.
- If possible, arrange to tape record the interview. Because the main purpose of an interview is to acquire information or gain perspectives from another person, make a conscious effort to listen more than speak during the interview.
- As soon as possible after the interview, use a modified outline form to make written notes on the main points of the conversation.

Applying What You've Learned Ask students to write a list of five questions to ask a grandparent or an older relative.

Reteaching/Reinforcement
- *Writing Mini-Lessons*, transparencies, p. 59

Interview, pp. 72–76

CUSTOMIZING FOR
Less-Proficient Writers

K Encourage students to structure their narratives chronologically. You may wish to pair students acquiring English with more proficient partners who can help them use sensory language and make vivid word choices as they write their descriptions.

Teaching Strategy: MANAGING THE PAPER LOAD

As you read the drafts, concentrate on the single element that each student finds most troublesome, such as creating a vivid setting or writing natural, conversational dialogue. Students can work out less serious story problems in a peer review setting.

DRAFTING

Getting Your Ideas Down

The Story Begins Once you have thought about your story, you can begin writing it. Some people dive in and write a story from beginning to end. Others start in the middle of an important scene and fill in the background later. Begin in the way that seems best for getting the significance of your story across to your audience.

❶ Write a Rough Draft
Write your story down as it comes to you. Don't worry yet about how it sounds.

Student's Rough Draft

I guess I want to show how I resented Mom's demands on my time.

It was Friday night and my mother had just asked me to stay home and read romance novels with her.

"Sorry, Mom," I answered. "You know there's a football game tonight. I have to be there in a half hour." I was a flag girl in the band and had to perform at halftime.

Add dialogue to help show Mom's disappointment?

Mom looked hurt. She had often accused me of caring more about my friends and activities than her. In Argentina, ~~where she's from,~~ daughters stay home and keep their mothers company.

Check with Mom to see how she remembers this incident.

This year, I hadn't stayed home much on the weekends. I was a sophomore now, and there were parties and dances to go to. My friends expected me to come, and I wanted to be with them.

We ~~Mom and I~~ often read books together, comparing plots in Agatha Christie stories or making fun of bookcovers that showed overly dramatic characters in flowing costumes. We would also have serious talks. Mom said she *grew up in Argentina, and* wanted me to be strong and independent because she hadn't been raised that way. Sometimes, however, she said I was "too modern."

170 UNIT ONE: IMPRINTS OF THE PAST

WRITING SPRINGBOARD
Caught Between Cultures Amin is a 17-year-old student who came to the United States from Armenia with her parents in 1988. In this film interview, Amin tells how she wants to enjoy the freedoms that she feels other American teenagers have, despite her parents' desire to maintain their protective "old ways."

Side B, Frames 3976

Writing Prompt Write about an autobiographical incident describing a struggle that is as important to you as Amin's is for her.

170 THE LANGUAGE OF LITERATURE TEACHER'S EDITION

2 Evaluate Your Rough Draft

Asking yourself questions like these may help you decide whether you've told the incident the way you wanted to.

- Does the story make the point I want to make?
- What actions, descriptions, or dialogue could I add to help make my point?
- Do I need to explain any terms or ideas that my readers might not know?
- Do I need to insert a flashback, add background information, or reorganize my story to make it clear?

The example at the left shows the changes one student considered making to her rough draft.

3 Rework and Share

The guidelines below can help you revise your rough draft and make your story clearer and more interesting to your readers.

LET YOUR STORY FLOW

- Begin your story in a way that makes the significance of the event you describe clear to your readers.
- Use transitions such as *before, next, after, meanwhile,* and *finally* to make the sequence of events clear to your reader.

CREATE VIVID IMAGES

- Use sensory details to describe important characters or settings in your story.
- Add details and dialogue that will help to make the incident real to your readers.
- Use vivid action verbs to tell what characters do.

PEER RESPONSE

A peer reviewer can help you identify the strengths and weaknesses of your draft. Ask questions like the following:

- What was unclear about my story?
- What more do you need to know about the characters, setting, events, or background of my story?
- Why do you think I chose to tell this incident?

SkillBuilder

WRITER'S CRAFT

Using Levels of Language Appropriately

A speech or a report uses formal language. A personal narrative, however, uses more informal, natural-sounding language. Informal language includes contractions such as *can't* or *we're,* idioms such as *crack down* or *pushing his luck,* shorter words and sentences, even slang. Using an informal, conversational tone draws your readers into your story and helps them identify with your feelings and experiences.

APPLYING WHAT YOU'VE LEARNED
Rewrite the following sentence, using informal language:

It was Friday; therefore, my mother requested that I remain at home in order to provide companionship for her.

If your draft sounds too formal, write your story again as if you were writing to a friend.

RETHINK & EVALUATE

Preparing to Revise

1. How have you organized your story to be sure that readers can clearly follow the events?
2. How have you used informal language to create a conversational tone in your story?
3. In what parts of the story might you want to add dialogue, description, or action?

WRITING FROM EXPERIENCE 171

Teaching Strategy: MODELING

Make sure that students understand why the writer made the revisions shown in the draft on page 170. For example, invite volunteers to explain why the final six lines were transposed to the first paragraph. (*They give helpful background information and set the scene for the conflict.*)

Writing Skill: USING THE COMPUTER

Point out that if students use a computer to write their narratives, they can use The Writing Coach, which provides columns for peer response and revision ideas, as well as pre-programmed tips. Also, remind students to save their drafts as separate electronic files. Before students begin, show them how to title a file for each draft so that nothing will be lost or written over in successive drafts. For example, students can choose a key title word and number each draft consecutively—MOM 1, MOM 2, and so on.

Teaching Strategy: COLLABORATIVE OPPORTUNITY

Remind students that creating vivid dialogue tags for the direct quotations in their story can help to reveal characters' feelings and states of mind. For example, instead of the relatively neutral or unemotional words *said, asked,* and *answered,* writers can use more colorful verbs such as *whispered, probed,* or *retorted.* Form students into small groups, and have them reread one of the short stories in this unit. Encourage them to make a list of vivid dialogue tags that the writer uses. Then have groups share their lists.

Teaching Strategy: COLLABORATIVE OPPORTUNITY

Ask peer reviewers to read the entire story before they make their comments. During a second reading, they should jot down brief suggestions. Remind students to include specific ideas for revision. "You should tell the audience precisely how this experience made you feel."

SkillBuilder

WRITER'S CRAFT

USING LEVELS OF LANGUAGE APPROPRIATELY Evaluating levels of language inevitably involves subjective elements, but you can help students appreciate some of the basic distinctions by having them compare the style of a formal speech as transcribed in a newspaper or a science report in a newspaper with a personal essay or op-ed column.

Applying What You've Learned *Possible response: It was Friday and my mom wanted me to stay home to be with her.*

Additional Suggestions Remind students that while informal diction and idioms are appropriate for the narrative portions of their story, dialect, slang, and sentence fragments should be reserved for the dialogue and used judiciously.

Reteaching/Reinforcement
- *Writing Mini-Lessons* transparencies, p. 44

The Writer's Craft

Varieties of Language, pp. 428–432

THE LANGUAGE OF LITERATURE TEACHER'S EDITION 171

Writing Skill: REVISING

P Students may wish to approach the revision process as four tasks:
1. adding needed words, sentences, and paragraphs
2. cutting unnecessary material by targeting repetitive or unrelated details for deletion
3. substituting other words, sentences, and paragraphs for deleted material if necessary
4. rearranging parts of the text to create coherence and unity

Teaching Strategy: MODELING

Q Discuss how this model meets the standards for evaluation on page 173. For example, details in the first paragraph that help set the scene include "small apartment," "a few minutes after 7 P.M.," "her old canvas bag," "curl up on the couch," "a juicy book and a cup of coffee," "slipped off her shoes," "rubbed her feet."

Teaching Strategy: MODELING

R Transitional words and phrases that keep the sequence of events clear include the following: *sometimes, other times, when usually, this time, ever since.*

Standards for Evaluation

Ideas and Content
- Focuses on a clear, well-defined incident or experience.
- Includes details that develop settings, characters, and events.
- Uses description and dialogue as appropriate to develop setting and character.
- Shows why the event is important to the writer.

Structure and Form
- Uses a logical and effective pattern of organization.
- Uses transitional words and phrases to maintain coherence and establish sequence within and between paragraphs.
- Includes sentences with a variety of structures.

Grammar, Usage, and Mechanics
- Contains no more than two or three minor errors in grammar and usage.
- Contains no more than two or three minor errors in spelling, capitalization, and punctuation.

REVISING AND PUBLISHING

Finishing Your Story

The Final Touch To create a strong impression in your readers' minds, your narrative should be free of distracting errors in spelling, grammar, and punctuation. Follow the steps on these pages to put the finishing touches on your story.

P **1** Revise and Edit

Read your draft aloud slowly. Look for awkward phrasings and places where you can remove unnecessary description, dialogue, or explanation that gets in the way of your story. Look for errors. Underline words, sentences, or sections you want to revise, and write notes or questions to yourself in the margins.

- Use peer comments and the Standards for Evaluation to decide which terms or ideas need more explanation.
- Use the Editing Checklist in the SkillBuilder on the next page to help you use dialogue effectively.
- The model shows how one student revised and edited her draft, using details to develop the setting and characters.

R **What transitional words keep the sequence of events clear?**

Student's Revised Draft

What details help set the scene?

Mom walked through the door of our small apartment at a few minutes after 7 P.M., her old canvas bag in hand. After work she had stopped at the library for a few mysteries and romance novels. It was Mom's Friday-night ritual: curl up on the couch with a juicy book and a cup of coffee. She plopped onto the couch, slipped off her shoes, and rubbed her feet. "Want to do some light reading tonight?" she asked.

I knew I wasn't living up to her expectations, and sometimes I felt guilty about that. Other times I just felt resentful. How could I be the strong, independent American daughter she wanted and the dutiful Argentinean one too?

When I told Mom I wasn't staying home, I thought she'd get mad. Usually, she does. This time, she didn't say anything. She just looked lonely. I thought about how I sometimes missed her too. I remembered how much my friends liked her.

"Mom, why don't you come with me?" I asked her. "In fact, I'd really like it if you would."

Mom liked the idea. She has been coming to all of the home football games ever since.

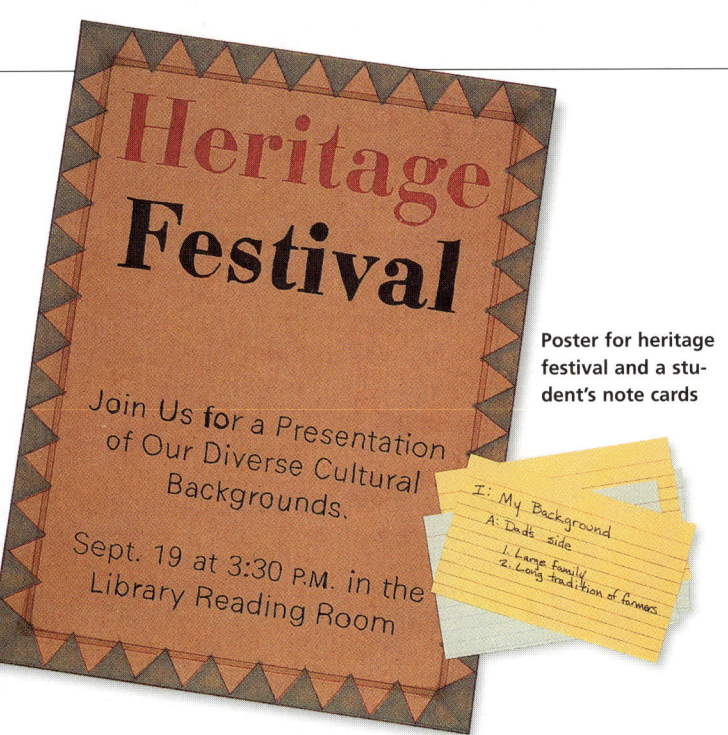

Poster for heritage festival and a student's note cards

2 Share Your Work

Are you craving a wider audience? You may want to share your story at a school or neighborhood festival celebrating heritage. Think about photographs and other visual aids that could accompany your story.

PUBLISHING IDEAS

- Your class could collect stories about heritage and publish them in an illustrated booklet.
- Stories could be part of a radio broadcast about heritage.
- Your story could be published in a family newsletter.
- You could save your story in a family memory album.

Standards for Evaluation
A firsthand narrative
• includes details that develop settings, characters, and events
• has dialogue that makes characters seem real
• reveals why the incident was significant

SkillBuilder

 GRAMMAR FROM WRITING

Using Quotation Marks in Dialogue
Dialogue can make characters seem real or help move a story along. For direct quotations, use quotation marks.

"If we don't leave now," Pam said, "we're going to be late."

Do not use quotation marks with indirect quotations.

Pam said that if we didn't leave immediately we would be late.

 GRAMMAR HANDBOOK

For more information on using quotation marks, see page 1096 of the Grammar Handbook.

Editing Checklist Use the following editing tips as you revise:
- Are words spelled correctly?
- Are sentences, including dialogue, punctuated correctly?

REFLECT & ASSESS

Evaluating the Experience

1. What method of generating writing ideas worked for you?
2. Which of the stories shared in class did you like best? Why?
3. What did you learn about heritage from this assignment?

 PORTFOLIO You may want to add your story and your evaluation to your portfolio.

WRITING FROM EXPERIENCE 173

 SkillBuilder — WRITER'S CRAFT

USING QUOTATION MARKS IN DIALOGUE
For some students, especially those acquiring English, additional practice in distinguishing direct from indirect quotations may be desirable. Remind students that the material within quotation marks consists of a speaker's exact words.

Applying What You've Learned Have students work in groups of three. Two students should engage in role-play, exchanging one line of dialogue each. The third student should then rephrase the exchange as an indirect quotation. Every student should have a turn at rephrasing the dialogues.

Additional Suggestions Remind students that question marks and exclamation points are placed inside quotation marks only if they belong to the direct quotation.

Reteaching/Reinforcement
Grammar Handbook, anthology pp. 1096–1097
Grammar Mini-Lessons copymasters pp. 45–47, transparencies, p. 44

 **The Writer's Craft**

Writing Dialogue, pp. 452–453

UNIT REVIEW

This page has been designed to help students reflect on what they have learned in Unit One. It also provides opportunities for them to evaluate the theme and to test their understanding of specific literary concepts. Challenge students to choose more than one option for each section. You may wish to participate in the activities by informally assessing students' speaking and listening skills and their ability to engage in cooperative work.

Objectives

- To allow students to reflect on and assess their understanding of theme
- To allow students to reflect on and assess their understanding of literary concepts, such as conflict and plot
- To give students the opportunity to assess and build their portfolios

REFLECTING ON THEME

OPTION 1

Before students compare their lists, you may want to appoint a recorder to put together a master list of all the students' perceptions of the characters and real people in the unit.

OPTION 2

Remind students that their speeches should contain factual information about the people's achievements, not just subjective impressions of their personality traits. Help students consider the ways in which education, reputation, and life experience make their candidates good choices.

OPTION 3

Consider appointing a monitor in each group to facilitate this activity. This student could allot a specific amount of time for each member of the group to give his or her character's point of view and could make sure that all members get a chance to share their personal opinions.

Self-Assessment Encourage students to spend some time rereading key passages from the selections before they create their charts. Ask them to be as specific as possible about the positive and negative influences they identify and to specify how each one affects the person's life.

REFLECT & ASSESS

UNIT ONE: IMPRINTS OF THE PAST

How have your own views about the past been affected by the selections in this unit? How have you developed or improved your skills? Explore these questions by completing one or more of the options in each of the following sections.

REFLECTING ON THEME

OPTION 1 **Classifying Imprints of the Past** Draw a horizontal line in the middle of a sheet of paper. On the top half, list characters or real people from this unit who you think have been positively affected by the past. On the bottom half, list characters who you think have been negatively affected. Add yourself or people you know to either category. Then, with a small group compare your lists.

OPTION 2 **Nominating a Guest Speaker** Imagine that your school's administration has asked for suggestions on how to improve the annual Heritage Day assembly. In past years, the speakers at this assembly have been known to cause drowsiness and boredom. Choose from this unit a character or writer who might breathe new life into the event. The person you choose should be not only interesting but also capable of communicating valuable insights about the importance of heritage. Write a nominating speech in which you explain your choice.

OPTION 3 **Role-Playing** This unit begins with a quotation from Oscar Wilde: "One's past is what one is." (See page 12.) How do you think the various characters, real people, and writers in this unit would respond to that quotation? Would they agree with it or disagree with it? Work with a small group of classmates to conduct a role-playing activity, with each member of the group assuming the identity of a character, real person, or writer in the unit. Then share your own views about the quotation.

Self-Assessment: Now that you have considered how your views about the past have been affected by the selections in this unit, make a chart. In the first column, record insights about how the past influences people's lives; in the second, list selections that prompted the insights.

REVIEWING LITERARY CONCEPTS

OPTION 1 **Understanding Conflict** In the selections in this unit, individuals become involved in a variety of external and internal conflicts. In a chart similar to the one shown, name at least six characters or real people in the unit and describe an important conflict that each one faces. Then rate the difficulty of resolving each conflict, from 1 (somewhat difficult) to 5 (extremely difficult). Compare your chart with those of your classmates and discuss the differences.

Character or Person/Selection	Type of Conflict	Description of Conflict	Difficulty of Resolving Conflict
Mark Mathabane/ *Kaffir Boy*	External	Mark resists his mother's plans to enroll him in school.	4

174 UNIT ONE: IMPRINTS OF THE PAST

OPTION 2 **Examining Plot** Review the selections that you have read in this unit. In which does the narrative proceed in chronological order? In which does the narrative not follow a strict chronological sequence? Discuss the advantages and the disadvantages of both types of narration with a small group of classmates, drawing on the selections for examples. Then share your group's conclusions with the rest of the class.

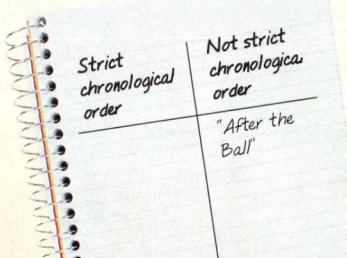

Self-Assessment: On a sheet of paper, copy the following list of literary terms introduced in this unit. Underline the terms that you feel you understand completely. Put question marks next to any terms that you do not understand fully. You may want to review the terms you marked with question marks.

conflict	essay
plot	figurative language
setting	description
characters	imagery
flashback	autobiography
dialogue	characterization

PORTFOLIO BUILDING

- **QuickWrites** For some of the QuickWrites activities in this unit, you assumed the identities of characters or real people depicted in selections. Review your writing for those activities, and pick out one or two pieces that you feel are particularly successful in portraying a character's personality or views. In a cover note, explain what makes the piece or pieces that you selected effective. Add the pieces and the note to your portfolio.

- **Writing About Literature** In this unit you responded personally to a writer's portrayal of a group or an event. Write a note to accompany your response. Briefly tell what a personal response is, what the subject of your response was, and whether you feel that the response was successful. Then tell what you learned about the importance of portraying a subject fairly and accurately.

- **Writing from Experience** By now you've written a firsthand narrative about your cultural heritage. How would you describe that writing experience? List two or three things that you discovered about yourself and your cultural heritage from your research and writing. Decide whether to include your note in your portfolio.

- **Personal Choice** Reflect upon all the activities and writing that you have completed for this unit, including any work that you may have done on your own. Also look over the evaluations and responses that you have received from peers. Which of the activities or writing projects proved the most rewarding? Write a note that explains your choice, and add it to your portfolio.

Self-Assessment: At this point, you may just be beginning your portfolio. Review the pieces that you have chosen for your portfolio. Do they have anything in common? What do they suggest about your strengths and interests as a writer?

SETTING GOALS

As you worked through the activities in this unit, you probably became more aware of your strengths and weaknesses in reading and writing skills. After reviewing the work that you did for this unit, create a list of skills that you would like to work on in the next unit.

REFLECT & ASSESS **175**

REVIEWING LITERARY CONCEPTS

OPTION 1
Some students may note that some characters experience both internal and external conflicts at the same time. For example, in "Two Kinds," the narrator's mother tries to turn her daughter into a child prodigy (external conflict) and the child rebels because she has doubts about her own talent and wants to be herself (internal conflict).

OPTION 2
Remind students that a narrative can begin at the beginning, in the middle, or at the end of the events, depending on the author's purpose. For example, we need to know something about Nicholas Gage's life in the United States before we can understand how it has been affected by the painful events in his past.

Self-Assessment Ask students who have placed a question mark next to a specific term to form a group. Then select or invite a student who understands the term to work with them. Suggest that students use the explanation in the book as a starting point for their discussion.

PORTFOLIO BUILDING

Review the main elements in the portfolio system that students are using. Ask them to choose from the options suggested in the book, or help them work out an alternative that meets the needs of the class. Encourage students to include as many personal statements as possible, since they provide valuable insights into the learning process of each individual. Remind them that the portfolios are kept confidential and that only you and the writer have access to them.

Self-Assessment You may wish to suggest general assessment guidelines to use with all portfolio work. For example, students can rate each piece of work on a three-point scale: (1) This one was easy for me. (2) I had some problems with this one. (3) This one was difficult for me.

SETTING GOALS

Encourage students to set their own goals. Remind them that they can focus on any aspects of reading or writing that they choose. They can work on a general area, such as increasing reading comprehension, or develop a specific focus, such as improving spelling by using a dictionary to check their work. Whatever they choose, they should set realistic goals and state them in clear, simple sentences. For example:

- *As I read, I will stop at the end of each page and try to identify the main ideas on that page.*
- *I will use the dictionary to be sure I have spelled unfamiliar words correctly.*

THE LANGUAGE OF LITERATURE TEACHER'S EDITION **175**

UNIT TWO

UNIT THEMES

Unit Two

Reflecting on Society In Unit Two, students will read selections which explore the individual's place in society. This unit contains two parts: Part 1, "Challenging the System," and Part 2, "Prisoners of Circumstance." Selections in both parts contribute to the unit theme by recounting various characters' struggles with the societies of which they are members.

Part 1

Challenging the System Selections in Part 1 examine a number of ways in which individuals challenge the laws, government, and social contracts under which they live. For example, in "The Pen of My Aunt," three people use their wits to defy and manipulate a soldier of the enemy army.

Part 2

Prisoners of Circumstance Part 2 recounts the stories of individuals who must learn to live within repressive systems. For example, in "The Women Who Are Poets in My Land," women who are forced to keep silent in deference to their husbands and their mothers-in-law express themselves by writing poetry.

UNIT TWO

Reflecting on Society

Literature is one of a society's instruments of self-awareness.

ITALO CALVINO
Italian novelist and short story writer
1923-1985

Central America: Children in Transition (1982), Betty LaDuke. From *Multi-Cultural Celebrations, the Paintings of Betty LaDuke 1972–1992*.

Discussion Questions

To help students explore the connections between the art, the quotation, and the unit theme, have them consider the following questions:

1. Do you believe it is important to reflect on the society in which you live? Why? *(Possible responses: Some students may say yes, reflection will help one understand why society has particular rules, whether one approves of those rules, and how one might go about changing them. Other students might say no, that what is important is how an individual acts, regardless of the society.)*

2. Do you agree with Italo Calvino's assessment of the role of literature in society? Explain. *(Possible responses: Some students might agree, pointing out that most writers, in one way or another, write about their society. Others may disagree, saying literature, especially fiction, is unreal and therefore doesn't give a true picture of society.)*

3. How would you describe the kind of society in which the characters pictured here live? *(Possible responses: a hostile one, since they seem to be huddling together for protection; a supportive one, since they stand so close together and touch one another)*

4. What kinds of characters might you expect to encounter in this unit? *(Possible responses: characters evaluating their place in society; characters trying to change society)*

5. Discuss various societies of which you are members. (clubs, families, classes, teams) Are you satisfied with your places in these societies? Why? *(Responses will vary.)*

Art Note

Central America: Children in Transition by Betty LaDuke
LaDuke, an American of Eastern European ancestry, was born in 1930. Her early art teachers were Elizabeth Catlett and Charles White. Later, she moved to Mexico and her work began to reflect the influence of the Mexican muralist movement. In addition to painting, she has written several books about art and artists.

Reading the Art *Why do you think the subjects of the painting are all looking outward in different directions?*

UNIT TWO
Part 1 Skills Trace

ML DENOTES MINI-LESSON IN TEACHER'S EDITION

Selections	Reading Skills and Strategies	Literary Concepts	Writing Opportunities	Speaking, Listening, and Viewing
DRAMA **The Pen of My Aunt** Josephine Tey		Stage directions, PE p. 196 Reviewing plot, PE p. 196 Drama, ML TE p. 187 Reviewing dialogue, ML TE p. 188	List qualities, PE p. 182 Write a scene, PE p. 195 Write a review, PE p. 195 Write a monologue, PE p. 195 Write a log entry, PE p. 195 Denotation and connotation, ML TE p. 185	Reader's theater performance, PE p. 195 Negotiating, ML TE p. 193
FICTION **The Thrill of the Grass** W.P. Kinsella		Simile, PE p. 209 Reviewing imagery, ML TE p. 204	Write about an experience, PE p. 198 Write a description, PE p. 209 Television commercial, PE p. 209 Newspaper article, PE p. 209 Verb tense, ML TE p. 203 Write survey questions, TE p. 210	Conduct a mock trial, PE p. 209 Conduct a survey, PE p. 210 Present oral movie review, PE p. 210 Play-by-play sportscast, ML TE p. 200
FICTION **The Balek Scales** Heinrich Böll	Making predictions, PE p. 211 Using your reading log, PE p. 211	Tone, PE p. 220 Reviewing setting, ML TE p. 214	Write a sermon, PE p. 219 Write an editorial, PE p. 219 Write a journal entry, PE p. 219 Sentence length and structure, ML TE p. 216	
NONFICTION *from* **Montgomery Boycott** Coretta Scott King	Identifying multiple effects, PE p. 221	Author's purpose, PE p. 230 Reviewing autobiography, ML TE p. 226	Write editorials, PE p. 230 Write a diary entry, PE p. 230 Write an analysis, PE p. 230 Create protest signs, PE p. 230 Coherence in longer pieces of writing, ML TE p. 225	Retell story, PE p. 231 Play recording of Martin Luther King Jr's speech, PE p. 231 Discuss speech, PE p. 231 Speeches, ML TE p. 228 View PBS series "Eyes on the Prize," TE p. 231
FICTION **The Prisoner Who Wore Glasses** Bessie Head		First-person point of view, PE p. 240 Third-person point of view, PE p. 240 Reviewing setting, PE p. 240 Reviewing conflict, ML TE p. 235	Assertiveness scale, PE p. 232 Write a letter, PE p. 240 Draft a personal essay, PE p. 240 Write a plot summary, PE p. 240 Create a chart, PE p. 240 Make a list of steps, PE p. 241 Transitions, ML TE p. 236	Deliver a speech, PE p. 241 With partner, resolve a conflict, PE p. 241 View satirical political cartoons, TE p. 241
FICTION **The Censors** Luisa Valenzuela		Irony, PE p. 246	Life under censorship, PE p. 242 List of criteria, PE p. 246 Dramatic scene, PE p. 246 Letter, PE p. 246 List of rules, PE p. 246 Transitions that show contrast, ML TE p. 244	Class discussion, PE p. 246 Conduct interviews, PE p. 247 Class discussion, PE p. 247
NONFICTION *from* **Tolerance** E. M. Forster	Clarifying concepts, PE p. 248	Theme, PE p. 252 Reviewing tone, PE p. 252 Reviewing nonfiction, ML TE p. 250	Write an essay, PE p. 252 Critical analysis, PE p. 252 Fable or parable, PE p. 252 List specific steps, PE p. 252	Discussing conflict, PE p. 252 Deliver speech, PE p. 253
POETRY ON YOUR OWN **Fighting South of the Ramparts** Li Bo				Paired reading, TE p. 254
Writing **WRITING ABOUT LITERATURE** **Analysis**	Analyzing organization, PE pp. 256–257 Responding to literature, PE pp. 258–261	Analyzing organization, PE pp. 256–257 Setting, PE pp. 258–261	Use spatial order, PE p. 257 Describe a place, PE p. 257 Double description, PE p. 257 Analyze setting, PE pp. 258–261 Creating mood, PE p. 259	Viewing a scene, PE p. 262 Interpreting a scene, PE p. 262 Discussion, PE p. 262 Discussing setting, PE p. 263

Grammar, Usage, Mechanics, and Spelling	Multimodal Learning	Research and Study Skills	Vocabulary	
The dash, ML TE p. 189	Reader's theater performance, PE p. 195 Draw a set design, PE p. 196 Create a map, PE p. 196	Research French translations, PE p. 196 Memorizing, ML TE p. 190	acclimatized anathema caliber deduce implement	inexplicable miscreant repressive speculation testify
Hyphens in compound adjectives, ML TE p. 202	Conduct a mock trial, PE p. 209 Conduct a survey, PE p. 210 Present oral movie review, PE p. 210 Conduct math workshop, PE p. 210		affable cohort contemplate divulge immaculate	imminent methodically rampant skulk surreptitious
Colons, ML TE p. 215	Create a pie graph, PE p. 219 Math questions, TE p. 220		antiquated flout forlorn meager preside	
Infinitives and infinitive phrases, ML TE p. 224	Retell story, PE p. 231 Play recording of Martin Luther King Jr's speech, PE p. 231 Bulletin board display or exhibit, PE p. 231 Discuss speech, PE p. 231 Leading a meeting, ML TE p. 227	Research and prepare a time line on civil rights movement, PE p. 231 Use Reader's Guide to Periodical Literature, TE p. 231	coercion coherently degrading devoid exaltation	exposé militant oppression perpetuation radiant
	Deliver a speech, PE p. 241 With partner, resolve a conflict, PE p. 241 Create a chart, PE p. 240 Create a narrative cartoon, PE p. 241 View satirical political cartoons, TE p. 241		acute bedlam chaos commodity conviction	cower irrelevant perpetrate ruefully tirade
Complements, ML TE p. 245	Class discussion, PE p. 246 Create a poster, PE p. 247 Conduct interviews, PE p. 247 Class discussion, PE p. 247	Research the Bill of Rights, PE p. 247	conniving irreproachable staidness subtle subversive	
	Deliver essay as speech, PE p. 253 Design a poster, PE p. 253 Give a multimedia presentation, PE p. 253	Research role of radio during WWII, PE p. 253 Researching Chinese history, TE p. 255	appallingly conversely diplomacy entail maim	makeshift perilous proclaiming purge secular

Grammar, Usage, Mechanics, and Spelling	Multimodal Learning	Research and Study Skills	Media Literacy
Using transition words and phrases, PE p. 257 Prepositional phrases, PE p. 261 Subject-verb agreement with prepositional phrases, PE p. 261	Viewing a scene, PE p. 262 Interpreting a scene, PE p. 262 Discussion, PE p. 262 Discussing setting, PE p. 263	Analyzing literature, PE pp. 258–261 Analyzing components of setting, PE p. 263	Interpreting a scene, PE pp. 262–263

UNIT TWO
Part 2 Skills Trace

ML DENOTES MINI-LESSON IN TEACHER'S EDITION

Selections	Reading Skills and Strategies	Literary Concepts	Writing Opportunities	Speaking, Listening, and Viewing
FICTION **On the Rainy River** Tim O'Brien	Drawing conclusions, PE p. 266	First-person point of view, PE p. 282 Reviewing description, **ML** TE p. 271 Reviewing symbolism, **ML** TE p. 272	Letter, PE p. 281 Definition essay, PE p. 281 Alternative ending, PE p. 281 Personal essay, PE p. 281 Feature story for school newspaper, PE p. 282 Address the reader directly, **ML** TE p. 277	Conduct a point/counterpoint discussion, PE p. 281 Listen to protest songs from Vietnam War, PE p. 282 Discussion on Vietnam War, PE p. 282 Interviews, PE p. 282 Drama performance, **ML** TE p. 279
FICTION **The Pearl** Yukio Mishima	Understanding problems and solutions, PE p. 284 Using your reading log, PE p. 284	Satire, PE p. 295 Reviewing tone, PE p. 295 Reviewing characterization, **ML** TE p. 291	Time line, PE p. 295 Dialogue, PE p. 295 Character sketch, PE p. 295 Satiric story, PE p. 295 Skit, PE p. 296 Spatial relationships, **ML** TE p. 287	Small group organization and discussion, PE p. 295 Rehearse and perform skit, PE p. 296
NONFICTION **Black Men and Public Space** Brent Staples		Structure, PE p. 301 Nonfiction, **ML** TE p. 300	Paragraph, PE p. 297 Review, PE p. 301 Descriptive paragraph, PE p. 301 Dramatic scene, PE p. 301 Editorial, PE p. 301 Personal narrative, PE p. 301	Interview police officer, PE p. 302 Create a skit, TE p. 302
POETRY **Miss Rosie** Lucille Clifton **Kitchenette Building** Gwendolyn Brooks	Making inferences in poetry, PE p. 303	Speaker in a poem, PE p. 306 Reviewing theme, PE p. 306	Adapt poem into new poem, PE p. 306 Prepare a report card, PE p. 306 Sound devices, **ML** TE p. 305 Create a poem, **ML** TE p. 305	Prepare dramatic reading, PE p. 306 Oral reading, PE p. 307 Choral reading, **ML** TE p. 304 Oral report, TE p. 307
NONFICTION *from* **Night** Elie Wiesel		Style, PE p. 315 Reviewing setting, **ML** TE p. 312	Describe thoughts and feelings, PE p. 308 Generalizations, PE p. 315 Rewrite the excerpt, PE p. 315 Eyewitness account, PE p. 315 Questions, PE p. 315 Consider your audience, **ML** TE p. 311	Discuss generalizations, PE p. 315 Dramatic reading, PE p. 315 Oral report, PE p. 315 View *Schindler's List*, PE p. 316 Oral review, PE p. 316 View videotape of "Playing for Time," TE p. 316
POETRY **The Women Who Are Poets in My Land** Blaga Dimitrova		Stanzas, PE p. 319 Reviewing imagery, PE p. 319	Write a description, PE p. 317 Write a speech, PE p. 319 Write a poem, PE p. 319 Write a letter, PE p. 319 Translate a poem, **ML** TE p. 318	Read poem aloud, PE p. 319 Dramatization, PE p. 320 Listen to Bulgarian folk music, PE p. 320 Translations, **ML** TE p. 318
FICTION **House Taken Over** Julio Cortázar	Recognizing fantasy, PE p. 321	Magical realism, PE p. 328 Reviewing setting, PE p. 328 Reviewing description, **ML** TE p. 324 Fiction, **ML** TE p. 325	Chart, PE p. 328 Draft an essay, PE p. 328 Write a story, PE p. 328 Purpose, **ML** TE p. 326 Write brief narrative, **ML** TE p. 326	Dramatize "House Taken Over," TE p. 329 Music in suspense and mystery films, TE p. 329
NONFICTION ON YOUR OWN *from* **Farewell to Manzanar** Jeanne Wakatsuki Houston and James D. Houston			Write a list of questions, TE p. 329 Writing a letter, TE p. 331	Grouped reading, TE p. 329

Writing	Reading Skills and Strategies	Literary Concepts	Writing Opportunities	Speaking, Listening, and Viewing
WRITING FROM EXPERIENCE **Persuasion**			Writing a persuasive essay, PE pp. 340–347 Drafting, PE pp. 344–345 Creating emphasis, PE p. 345 Publishing, PE pp. 346–347	Graphs, PE p. 341 Visual aids, PE p. 347 Conducting a poll, PE p. 342 Persuasive speech, PE p. 347 Interviewing, PE p. 342

Grammar, Usage, Mechanics, and Spelling	Multimodal Learning	Research and Study Skills	Vocabulary
Subordinating conjunctions, ML TE p. 276	Conduct a point/counterpoint discussion, PE p. 281 Listen to protest songs from Vietnam War, PE p. 282 Compare painting and story, PE p. 282 Create a collage, PE p. 282 Discussion on Vietnam War, PE p. 282 Interviews, PE p. 282 Reading maps, ML TE p. 274	Research Vietnam War, PE p. 282	acquiescence platitude consensus preoccupied fathom pretense impassive reticence imperative vigil
Adverb clauses, ML TE p. 288	Prepare time line, PE p. 295 Draw caricatures, PE p. 296 Rehearse and perform skit, PE p. 296	Research Japanese culture from 1920–1960, TE p. 296 Research the current pearl market, TE p. 296	ambiguous incensed fastidious infamy impetuous malicious implicitly prudence inauspicious scruple
Noun clauses, ML TE p. 299	Interview police officer, PE p. 302 Make a collage, TE p. 302 Create a skit, TE p. 302		affluent errant avid retrospect congenial solace cursory taut elicit unwieldy
	Prepare dramatic reading, PE p. 306 Oral reading, PE p. 307 Paint or sketch two portraits, PE p. 307 Choral reading, ML TE p. 304 Oral report, TE p. 307	Research Alzheimer's disease, TE p. 307	
Auxiliary verbs, ML TE p. 310	Small group discussion, PE p. 315 Dramatic reading, PE p. 315 Oral report, PE p. 315 View *Schindler's List*, PE p. 316 Oral review, PE p. 316 View videotape of "Playing for Time," TE p. 316	Summarizing, ML TE p. 313 Read *Schindler's List*, TE p. 316 Research the Auschwitz Orchestra, TE p. 316	din emaciated interminable notorious stature
	Create a bulletin board display, PE p. 320 Dramatization using pantomime and facial expressions, PE p. 320 Listen to Bulgarian folk music, PE p. 320		
Semicolons, ML TE p. 323	Dramatize "House Taken Over," TE p. 329 Listen and identify music used in suspense and mystery films, TE p. 329 Create a painting, PE p. 329 Compile recordings, PE p. 329		brusquely commune dexterity obscure replete
	Sketch impressions, TE p. 329 Create a display, TE p. 335		

Grammar, Usage, Mechanics, and Spelling	Multimodal Learning	Research and Study Skills	Media Literacy
Creating emphasis, PE p. 345 Using pronouns, PE p. 347	Analyzing news reports, PE pp. 340–342 Analyzing graphs, PE p. 341	Searching indexes, PE p. 342 Designing opinion polls, ML TE p. 342	Using on-line sources, PE p. 342 Analyzing news reports, PE pp. 340–342 Analyzing graphs, PE p. 341

UNIT TWO
Recommended Resources ENRICHMENT RESEARCH

✓ Recommended Novels and Play

LITERATURE CONNECTIONS WITH SOURCEBOOK FOR TEACHERS

Thematic Link This historical melodrama, set during the Reign of Terror after the French Revolution, tells of the redemption of a wasted life.

About the Author Since the publication of his first novel, Charles Dickens (1812–1870) has continued to have an enormous popular and critical following. Because of this, he accomplished a great deal towards social reform by making the public aware of the plight of the Victorian poor and dispossessed.

Other Works by Charles Dickens *The Pickwick Papers, Oliver Twist, Bleak House, David Copperfield, Nicholas Nickleby, Hard Times, Great Expectations*

LITERATURE CONNECTIONS WITH SOURCEBOOK FOR TEACHERS

Thematic Link In ancient Rome, tragic heroes—good and noble characters—make fatal errors in judgment that lead to their downfall.

About the Author William Shakespeare (1524–1616), the gifted playwright and poet, probed the mysteries of human nature, creating memorable characters whose experiences transcend time and place.

Other Works by William Shakespeare *Hamlet, Macbeth, A Midsummer Night's Dream, Romeo and Juliet, Antony and Cleopatra*

LITERATURE CONNECTIONS WITH SOURCEBOOK FOR TEACHERS

Thematic Link Set during the Mexican Revolution of 1910, this powerful novel exposes the chaos and corruption of the revolutionary struggle.

About the Author Born in Jalisco, Mexico, Azuela (1873–1952), a physician and novelist, is best-known for his stirring chronicles of the Mexican Revolution.

Other Works by Mariano Azuela *The Flies, The Bosses, The Trials of a Respectable Family, The Firefly*

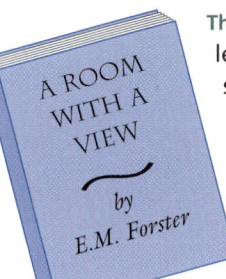

Thematic Link An engaging heroine challenges the narrow minds of her Victorian society by falling in love during a holiday in Italy.

About the Author E.M. Forster (1879–1970) used Italy as the setting for most of his novels. It symbolized freedom to him, in contrast with the restrictions of English society.

Other Works by E.M. Forster *Where Angels Fear to Tread, Howard's End, A Passage to India, Maurice*

Thematic Link This work tells of a personal war against the Nazis that ends with the affirmation of the human spirit.

About the Author While working as a chemist, Primo Levi (1919–1987) was deported to Auschwitz. As a writer, Levi's realistic approach and clear style offered direction to many future writers.

Other Works by Primo Levi *The Monkey's Wrench, Survival in Auschwitz*

Professional Development TEACHING THE NOVEL

Boldy, Stephen. *The Novels of Julio Cortázar.* Cambridge, England: Cambridge University Press, 1980.

Forster, E. M. *Aspects of the Novel.* NY: Harcourt Brace Jovanovich, 1927.

Levi, Primo. *Moments of Reprieve.* NY: Penguin, 1981.

Maltz, Carole. "Brutus—Guilty or Not Guilty?" *Ideas Plus.* Urbana, IL: NCTE, 1986.

Marrus, Michael R. *The Holocaust in History.* NY: Penguin, 1987.

Robinson, Randal. *Unlocking Shakespeare's Language.* Urbana, IL. NCTE, 1988.

CROSS-CURRICULAR TEACHING   PROFESSIONAL DEVELOPMENT

Recommended Readings in Cross-Curricular Areas

SOCIAL STUDIES

Parting the Waters: America in the King Years 1954–1963 by Taylor Branch (1989) A documentation of America during the Civil Rights Movement. Links to Coretta Scott King's excerpt from *Montgomery Boycott*.

No Bland Facility: Selected Writings on Literature, Religion and Censorship by Peter Connolly (1991) Engaging essays on censorship that raise provocative issues. Links to Luisa Valenzuela's "The Censors."

The Vietnam War edited by Bruce H. Franklin (1996) Remarkably broad and prismatic selection of writings by survivors of the Vietnam War. Links to Tom O'Brien's "On the Rainy River."

Holocaust Poetry edited by Hilda Schiff (1995) An extensive collection of poetry about the war experience by some of this century's greatest writers. Links to Elie Wiesel's excerpt from *Night*.

Professional Development — CROSS-CURRICULAR INSTRUCTION

Hawkins, Mary Louise, and Graham, Dolores M. *Curriculum Architecture*. Columbus, OH: NMSA, 1994.

Tchudi, Stephen, ed. *The Astonishing Curriculum: Integrating Science and Humanities Through Language.* Urbana, IL: NCTE, 1993.

Stinson, Joseph. "Reinventing High Schools," *Electronic Learning*. 13:4, 20.

Xiao-Ming, Li. *Good Writing in Cross-Cultural Context.* Albany, NY: State University of New York Press, 1996.

Recommended Media Resources

THE LANGUAGE OF LITERATURE

ELECTRONIC LIBRARY
CD-ROM
Additional literature selections for Unit Two can be found on the Electronic Library CD-ROM.

LASERLINKS
Videodisc, Gr. 10
See *LaserLinks Teacher's Source Book,* pages 18–19, for overview of Unit Two.

AUDIO LIBRARY
Tapes
Gr. 10, Tapes 5–8: Sides A & B

Novel in Spanish
Historia de dos ciudades (A Tale of Two Cities)

WRITING COACH
Writing Coach Software: Writing About Literature—Critical Response, Persuasive Essay

OUTSIDE RESOURCES

Films/Videos/Film Strips/Audiocassettes
Field of Dreams, video, MCA/Universal Home Video, 1989, (106 minutes).
Gwendolyn Brooks, filmstrip, Educational Directions, 1975.
My Life with Martin Luther King by Coretta Scott King, audiocassette, Caedmon.
Margaret Walker Reads, audiocassette, American Audio Prose Library, (108 minutes).

Internet Resources
McDougal Littell Literature Center at http://www.hmco.com/mcdougal/lit

Professional Development — TEACHING WITH TECHNOLOGY

Collins, Allan. "Goal-Based Scenarios and the Problem of Situated Learning," *Educational Technology*. 34:9 (November/December 1994) 30.

Electronic Learning. Scholastic, Inc., 555 Broadway, New York, NY 10012.

Zabinsky, Toby. "Cybersteps: Students Use Gopher to Research and Discover the Holocaust," *Electronic Learning*. 15:1 (September 1995) 18.

UNIT TWO
Professional Enrichment

Performing Literature
Franchelle S. Dorn, Howard University, Washington D.C.

The following essay gives a strong argument for including dramatic performance in the English classroom and offers tips on how to make it happen.

Acting is something everyone can do, as you can see from watching preschoolers at play. Anyone who has ever played make-believe (playing Barbie or Mortal Kombat) knows the process of suspension of disbelief. However, problems arise when we get older and the conventions of our society start to shut down our creative juices. Parents know how cute a two-year-old can be who turns a somersault in the middle of a department store yet how embarrassing it can be to watch a seven-year-old perform the same feat! In many ways we start to sacrifice creativity in the name of decorum and conformity. Those who do not conform become ostracized.

Dramatic literature is an area of study in which nonconformity can be a virtue, creativity can be rewarded, and the class cutup may be the star of the show—if we can channel that energy into the basic act of telling a moving story. Exploring another time, another place, or another world should be fun and exciting for students and teachers alike. Escaping one's own environment and examining someone else's can be an enlightening experience. People don't have to be good at it; they simply have to give it a try! If students give it their best shot, they may learn something about themselves, or better yet, teach others something about themselves and about the world we live in.

GETTING READY TO PERFORM
There are several ways to begin exploring the art of dramatic performance. Reading a play, novel, or short story in class as an acting assignment can often get people interested. However, if it is possible to actually see a theatrical production and talk to the performers afterward, by all means do it! The immediacy of live theater cannot be duplicated in film and television because of the effect that the audience has on the performance. (A stand-up comic will succeed far better in his or her act if the audience is laughing than if it is not.) It is important for students to understand their contribution as an audience whether they are in a theater or in a classroom. Most Americans would rather die than speak in front of a group. Anyone who stands up to do anything creative in front of a class should be greatly supported!

If a play is not something students can see, then try starting a discussion on acting using the media they know: film, television, and radio. Ask your students the following:
- Who are your favorite performers and why?
- How do they make you feel?
- What are they trying to say to you?
- How do they use their voices, bodies, emotions, and imaginations to get the "acting" job done?
- How do their clothes (costumes) influence their performance and help them tell the story?
- Do you remember them as themselves or as the characters they portray? Is that desirable or not?
- How have the director and sound and lighting designers helped to evoke a mood and to tell the story?
- What has the pace of the performance to do with what we see and feel?
- What would you do differently if you had a chance to be a performer or the director?

COOPERATIVE PERFORMANCE
After discussing the above questions on performances that students are acquainted with, they should then be able to make some choices about how they want to approach their own performance of the literature at hand. The delegation of tasks should then be the next order of business. Let people volunteer as much as possible. Someone will have to do props, design the set (even if it is just rearranging chairs), provide sound, find costumes (funny paper hats? masks?), stage manage, direct, act, and so on. Whether this is a closed, in-class project with limited time or a major project for schoolwide viewing, try to get students involved with something other than the usual assignment of simply reading the work of literature.

Make the process of exploring drama something that students can do on their own level. Regardless of the period of the piece, find the link to contemporary life—whether it be the world of politics, social justice, interpersonal relationships, entertainment, or whatever immediate interests that students have. The style of the performance you choose can reflect most contemporary notions.

The following are some suggested ideas for turning a work of literature into a one-day performance assignment:
- Change the gender of the characters. (Have girls read boys' parts and vice versa.)
- Do a round robin read-aloud. (Change the order of who reads next.)
- Turn the work into a "rap" performance. (All characters read in rhythm.)
- Make some characters arbitrarily slow or fast speakers. (How does that change what we think of them?)

With slightly more time, you might try these assignments:
- Divide a long play into acts and/or scenes and assign an entire cast and crew for each division.
- Give the same major roles to a variety of people and let them put their own spin on the characters. Then, as the work is read aloud, change actors mid-sentence from time to time to bring fresh interpretations to the roles.

HELPFUL HINTS FOR STUDENT ACTORS

The following categories of questions are those that every actor must ask him- or herself about the character being portrayed. Be sure to share these questions with your students. Many of the answers will be provided by the playwright or author of the work being performed, but remind students that they have the opportunity to invent answers when the playwright or author has left gaps.

- *Who am I?* What's my name and age? Where was I born and into what environment? Am I from a different country? Do I have an accent? What is my psychological profile—friendly, shy, angry, strong, and so on? What do I wear?
- *Where am I?* Is this environment new of familiar? How does it make me feel? (Be specific; you know your behavior changes depending on your surroundings. For example, you behave one way at home, another way at school, and still another way when out on your own with friends.)
- *When does the action take place?* This can vary over the course of the play. What year? month? Is it day or night? What's the weather like? What has occurred before the action takes place to bring you to this specific moment in time? (For example, before the play starts, we know that Hamlet's father has died and he's pretty upset over his mother marrying his uncle.)
- *What do I want?* This is the big question at the center of the dramatic action. Without a specific goal, the actor really has no reason for being.
- *Why do I want this?* For revenge? adventure? escape? peace of mind? sense of decency?
- *How will I get what I want?* These are the actions you perform on other characters in order to reach your goal—to frighten, to comfort, to befriend, to browbeat. In a sense, these actions happen underneath the words in the script. Don't confuse them with activities, such as sweeping the floor or pouring tea. Don't forget that the actions will not necessarily lead immediately to your goal, because that will usually signify the end of the performance. The dramatic interest is in watching how characters continue to pursue their goals in spite of the obstacles placed in their way.

CONCLUSION

The famous actor and acting teacher Uta Hagen says that actors must know more about their characters than they could ever conceivably know about themselves. I suggest that you invite your students to learn more about themselves by exploring the world of literature through performance.

UNIT TWO
Starting Points for Unit Projects

The following suggestions will help you initiate individual and group projects during the course of the unit.

Having a Small-Group Discussion

GROUP SOCIAL STUDIES PROJECT Have students work in groups of three to research a current social issue and then have a serious small-group discussion on that issue.

Creating a Work of Fiction or Drama

LITERATURE/DRAMA PROJECT Have students imagine what would happen if two or three characters in the unit were to face a challenge together. Would they find a solution to their common problem, or would they have difficulty working together? Have students write a short story or a one-act play that shows what would happen. If students write a play, invite them to perform it or read it aloud for the rest of the class.

Comparing and Contrasting Responses to War

HISTORY PROJECT Have students research how American citizens responded to World War II and the Vietnam War. Students can use books, magazine articles from the 1940s and 1960s, and interviews with older friends and relatives who either served in one of the wars or protested it. Students can present their findings in oral reports. If students audiotaped or videotaped any of the interviews, encourage them to incorporate the tapes into their reports.

Delivering a Speech

HISTORY PROJECT Have students research audio and video recordings of speeches against war and injustice. Possibilities include the speeches of Dr. Martin Luther King, Jr., Franklin D. Roosevelt, Nelson Mandela, Robert Kennedy, and Winston Churchill. Have students listen to the speeches and then memorize part or all of one to deliver to the class.

Recording a Soundtrack

MUSIC PROJECT Have students research songs used during the Civil Rights movement, the antiwar movement, the struggle to end apartheid, and other recent social struggles. Then have them record parts of the songs they consider most effective to make a soundtrack for Unit Two.

Creating a Photo Montage

ART PROJECT Have students create a photo montage depicting examples of social injustice, including those described in this unit. Students can photocopy images from books and magazines, or they may be able to copy photographs from their own or their parents' personal collections. Have students come up with a stirring headline or quotation to sum up the message the images convey.

Family and Community Involvement

Family

The following Copymasters provide activities that students can take home and complete with a parent or other family member.

OPTION 1 RESEARCH FAMILY ACTIVISTS
- **Connection** All of the selections in Unit Two describe characters' struggles within their societies.
- **Activity** *Copymaster 1* Students and family members can research their own family history to find members who have been involved in actions to change their world. These can include activities in civil rights and human rights movements, protection of the environment, the improvement of schools or communities, and so on.

OPTION 2 WATCH A VIDEO
- **Connection** *Farewell to Manzanar* explores one family's reaction to sudden oppression.
- **Activity** *Copymaster 2* Students and family members may watch a video about people living through wartime or other social upheavals. Suggestions include *Come See the Paradise*, about the internment of Japanese-Americans during World War II, or *The Long Walk Home*, set during the American Civil Rights movement.

OPTION 3 WRITE A PERSONAL ACCOUNT
- **Connection** "On the Rainy River" features a main character dealing with fear and uncertainty about an action he is about to take.
- **Activity** *Copymaster 3* Students and family members may discuss events and situations in their lives that have caused them to be fearful. How has each person handled the fear? Has he or she gone ahead with the action anyway?

Community

OPTION 1
- **Connection** All of the selections in Unit Two describe characters' struggles within their societies.
- **Activity** Contact a historical society in your area to find some local townspeople who have been involved in reform movements. This can include activities ranging from the Underground Railroad Movement of the 19th century to recent projects for the homeless.

OPTION 2
- **Connection** The excerpt from *Montgomery Boycott* tells about a group's struggle to bring about needed change in society.
- **Activity** Have the class find one or more activist groups in their community with which they can be involved during after-school hours. For example, students can seek out environmental activities, projects to assist people who are homeless or without food, or organizations that work with abused children.

OPTION 3
- **Connection** "The Balek Scales" focuses on one family's struggle to overcome societal oppression.
- **Activity** Seek out one or more of the following to speak to the class about his or her experiences: a Vietnam veteran, a concentration camp survivor, a union organizer, an environmental activist.

UNIT TWO
Part 1 Lesson Planner

TIME ALLOTMENTS SHOWN ARE APPROXIMATE. DEPENDING ON YOUR GOALS AND THE NEEDS OF YOUR STUDENTS, YOU MAY WISH TO ALLOW MORE OR LESS TIME FOR CERTAIN PORTIONS OF THE LESSON.

Table of Contents	Discussion	Previewing the Selection	Reading the Selection
PART OPENER Challenging the System page 178	**20 MINUTES** • Reflect on the part theme		
GENRE LESSON Focus on Drama page 180	**20 MINUTES** • Discuss concepts of drama • Discuss strategies for reading drama		
SELECTION The Pen of My Aunt page 183 AVERAGE		**20 MINUTES** • PERSONAL CONNECTION • HISTORICAL CONNECTION • WRITING CONNECTION	**60 MINUTES** • Introduce vocabulary • Read pp. 183–194 (12 pp.)
SELECTION The Thrill of the Grass page 199 EASY		**20 MINUTES** • PERSONAL CONNECTION • CULTURAL CONNECTION • WRITING CONNECTION	**50 MINUTES** • Introduce vocabulary • Read pp. 199–208 (10 pp.)
SELECTION The Balek Scales page 212 AVERAGE		**20 MINUTES** • PERSONAL CONNECTION • HISTORICAL CONNECTION • READING CONNECTION: Making predictions/Using your reading log	**40 MINUTES** • Introduce vocabulary • Read pp. 212–218 (7 pp.)
SELECTION from Montgomery Boycott page 222 EASY		**20 MINUTES** • PERSONAL CONNECTION • HISTORICAL CONNECTION • READING CONNECTION: Identifying multiple effects	**40 MINUTES** • Introduce vocabulary • Read pp. 222–228 (7 pp.)
SELECTION The Prisoner Who Wore Glasses page 233 CHALLENGING		**20 MINUTES** • PERSONAL CONNECTION • HISTORICAL CONNECTION • WRITING CONNECTION	**30 MINUTES** • Introduce vocabulary • Read pp. 233–238 (6 pp.)
SELECTION The Censors page 243 CHALLENGING		**20 MINUTES** • PERSONAL CONNECTION • HISTORICAL CONNECTION • WRITING CONNECTION	**20 MINUTES** • Introduce vocabulary • Read pp. 243–245 (3 pp.)
SELECTION from Tolerance page 249 CHALLENGING		**20 MINUTES** • PERSONAL CONNECTION • HISTORICAL CONNECTION • READING CONNECTION: Clarifying concepts	**20 MINUTES** • Introduce vocabulary • Read pp. 249–251 (3 pp.)
POETRY ON YOUR OWN Fighting South of the Ramparts page 254 AVERAGE			**15 MINUTES** • Read pp. 254–255 (2 pp.)
Writing WRITING ABOUT LITERATURE Analysis	Writer's Style **20 MINUTES**	Prewriting **25 MINUTES**	Drafting and Revising **60 MINUTES**

Time estimates assume in-class work. You may wish to assign some of these stages as homework.

Responding to the Selection

Extension Activities

FROM PERSONAL RESPONSE TO CRITICAL ANALYSIS	OR	ANOTHER PATHWAY	LITERARY CONCEPTS	QUICKWRITES	ALTERNATIVE ACTIVITIES	LITERARY LINKS	CRITIC'S CORNER	THE WRITER'S STYLE	ACROSS THE CURRICULUM	ART CONNECTION	WORDS TO KNOW	BIOGRAPHY
50 MINUTES					*40 MINUTES*							
• Discussion questions	OR	• Readers theater performance	• Stage directions • Plot	• Scene • Review • Monologue • Log entry				✓	WORLD LAN-GUAGES		✓	✓
60 MINUTES					*40 MINUTES*							
• Discussion questions	OR	• Mock trial	• Simile	• Description • Television commercial • Newspaper article	✓	✓			MATH		✓	✓
40 MINUTES					*20 MINUTES*							
• Discussion questions	OR	• Pie graph	• Tone	• Sermon • Editorial • Journal entry		✓	✓				✓	✓
60 MINUTES					*30 MINUTES*							
• Discussion questions	OR	• Newspaper editorials	• Author's purpose	• Diary entry • Analysis • Protest	✓	✓			HISTORY		✓	✓
50 MINUTES					*30 MINUTES*							
• Discussion questions	OR	• Character conflicts	• First/third-person points of view • Setting	• Letter • Personal essay • Plot	✓	✓			PSY-CHOLOGY		✓	✓
50 MINUTES					*30 MINUTES*							
• Discussion questions	OR	• Character evaluation	• Situational/verbal/dramatic irony	• Dramatic scene • Letter • List of rules	✓				HISTORY		✓	✓
50 MINUTES					*60 MINUTES*							
• Discussion questions	OR	• News article on conflict	• Theme • Tone	• Essay • Critical analysis • Fable/parable	✓		✓		MEDIA	✓	✓	✓

Publishing and Reflecting — 25 MINUTES

Grammar in Context — 15 MINUTES

Reading the World — 30 MINUTES

PART 1

REFLECTING ON THEME

Give students the following hypothetical situation: "Suppose you have a job at a large, prestigious company. One day you discover by accident that a co-worker who was hired at the same time and has the same qualifications is paid more than you. What would you do?" Ask students to pair up to list some questions they might need answered before taking a course of action. They should then each explain to their partners what they think they would do and why.

What Do You Think?

Encourage students to use available resources, such as the local library, the internet, or CD-ROMS. Many libraries have computer access to national newspapers. Students might want to browse through topics and read summaries of articles on those topics that particularly interest them. Students can also locate news on current events and issues via the internet. Students will return to this activity on page 197.

UNIT TWO **PART 1**

CHALLENGING THE SYSTEM

REFLECTING ON THEME

How do you respond to problems or injustices in society—or in your own immediate surroundings? Do you take action, even if it means going against the crowd? Or do you stand by and watch, perhaps feeling powerless? This part of Unit Two focuses on people who take a stand. You'll encounter a woman who deceives Nazi officers, a young boy who exposes corruption, and others who challenge the system—sometimes with surprising results.

What Do You Think? Skim a daily newspaper or weekly newsmagazine to find articles related to social issues. Based on what you find, jot down a list of those issues that you care about—the ones that touch your heart, raise your temper, or maybe even spur you to action. Then share your list with a partner and discuss how it reflects your values and concerns.

W. P. Kinsella (1935–)
This Canadian writer turned a baseball diamond into a field of dreams.

Margaret Walker (1915–)
A prominent African-American poet, a chronicler of her times

Corretta Scott King (1927–)
Prominent civil rights activist—and widow of Dr. Martin Luther King, Jr.

Armando Valladares (1937–)
Twenty-two years in a Cuban prison; his poetry is a cry for freedom

Luisa Valenzuela (1944–)
A native of Argentina, today a major voice in Latin American writing

---

Josephine Tey	**The Pen of My Aunt** *A Nazi soldier at her door, a stranger's life in her hands*	182
W. P. Kinsella	**The Thrill of the Grass** *What turns these men into conspirators?*	198
Heinrich Böll	**The Balek Scales** *A boy uncovers the truth.*	211
Coretta Scott King	**Montgomery Boycott** *An episode in civil rights history remembered*	221
Margaret Walker	**Sit-Ins** / INSIGHT *An act of civil disobedience*	229

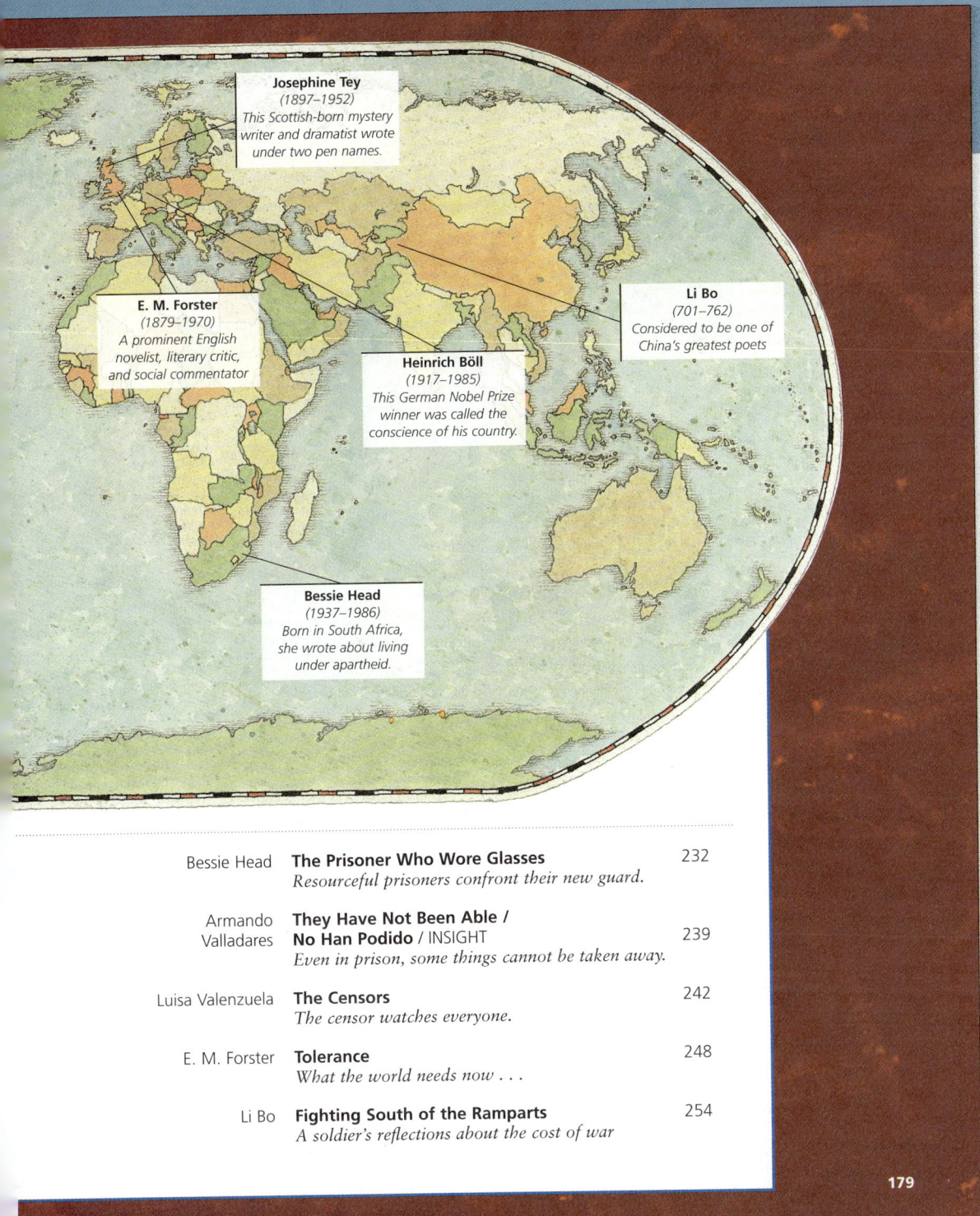

Josephine Tey (1897–1952)
This Scottish-born mystery writer and dramatist wrote under two pen names.

E. M. Forster (1879–1970)
A prominent English novelist, literary critic, and social commentator

Heinrich Böll (1917–1985)
This German Nobel Prize winner was called the conscience of his country.

Li Bo (701–762)
Considered to be one of China's greatest poets

Bessie Head (1937–1986)
Born in South Africa, she wrote about living under apartheid.

Map Note

The purpose of the map is to show the diversity of the authors in this section. Have students study the map, then ask them the following questions:

- What injustices might these authors have had to fight against?
- What do you know about apartheid, the official policy of racial segregation that was practiced in South Africa, Bessie Head's homeland?

Bessie Head	**The Prisoner Who Wore Glasses** *Resourceful prisoners confront their new guard.*	232
Armando Valladares	**They Have Not Been Able / No Han Podido** / INSIGHT *Even in prison, some things cannot be taken away.*	239
Luisa Valenzuela	**The Censors** *The censor watches everyone.*	242
E. M. Forster	**Tolerance** *What the world needs now . . .*	248
Li Bo	**Fighting South of the Ramparts** *A soldier's reflections about the cost of war*	254

THE LANGUAGE OF LITERATURE TEACHER'S EDITION

Focus on Drama

What comes to mind when you hear the word *drama*? Do you see a troupe of actors on a stage beneath the glaring lights, with an audience in rapt attention? Or perhaps you recall a spellbinding movie. Broadly defined, drama is any story in dialogue that is performed by actors before an audience. A Broadway play, a television comedy, a Hollywood movie—all can be defined as drama.

The origin of the word *drama,* from the Greek word *dran,* meaning "to do" or "to act," reminds us that all dramas portray human actions. Unlike other forms of literature, such as fiction and poetry, a work of drama requires the collaboration of many people in order to come to life. In an important sense, a drama in printed form is an incomplete work of art. It is a skeleton that must be fleshed out by a director, actors, set designers, and others who interpret the work and stage a performance, whether before cameras or a live audience. From ancient times to the present, drama has always been a communal activity.

Most forms of drama share certain elements, described below.

PLOT As in fiction, the plot in drama is a series of interrelated actions. Typically, a drama opens with a problem or conflict, which then intensifies, reaches a peak, and is eventually resolved. The elements of plot—**exposition, rising action, climax, falling action,** and **dénouement**—are described in detail on page 16–17.

Dramatic plots are often divided into **scenes.** Each scene establishes a different time or place. Long plays, such as Shakespeare's *Julius Caesar,* are divided into **acts,** with each act comprising related scenes.

CHARACTERS Many of the same types of characters that populate fiction can be found in drama. A **round character** (also known as a **dynamic character**), for example, is one that goes through a change or development in the course of the drama, while a **flat character** (or **static character**) is one that remains the same throughout. A **protagonist** is usually the central character, often the one that the audience most closely identifies with. The **antagonist** opposes the protagonist, which results in the central conflict. In Sophocles' *Antigone,* the protagonist is Antigone; she seeks to bury her brother, who has been killed in a civil war. Creon, the **antagonist,** has forbidden burial rites for those who rebelled, which leads to a series of confrontations between him and Antigone.

180   UNIT TWO   PART 1: CHALLENGING THE SYSTEM

DIALOGUE Dialogue, or conversation between characters, is the lifeblood of drama. Virtually everything of consequence, from plot details to character revelations, flows from the dialogue. Of course, dialogue plays an important role in fiction and sometimes in poetry, but usually such dialogue is framed by the commentary of a narrator or speaker. In drama, dialogue is seldom filtered through a controlling viewpoint (though some dramas do make use of narrators). As a result, the director, the performers, and the audience have more freedom to form their own interpretations.

In addition to speech between two or more characters, drama may make use of **monologue**, a long speech spoken by a single character to himself or herself or to the audience. Drama may also make use of an **aside**, a short speech delivered to the audience, beyond the hearing of the remaining characters.

STAGE DIRECTIONS In the history of drama, stage directions are relatively new; they did not become common until the 19th century, which explains why Chekhov used them but Sophocles did not. The stage directions in a script serve as a kind of instructional manual for the director, actors, and stage crew as well as the general reader. Often the stage directions are printed in italic type, and they may be enclosed in parentheses or brackets. Directions may describe the **scenery**, or **setting**, the environment created on stage or on film that produces the illusion of a specific time or place. Directions may also describe the **props**—objects, furniture, and the like—that are used during a performance. Stage directions may describe lighting, costumes, music, sound effects, or, in the case of film productions, camera angles and shots. Most important, the stage directions usually provide hints to the performers on how the characters look, move, and speak.

STRATEGIES FOR READING DRAMA

- **Pay close attention to the beginning.** Much important information is revealed at the very beginning of a play. Before you begin reading, review the cast of characters and familiarize yourself with the names. Read the opening stage directions carefully to learn about the characters and the setting. Likewise, go slowly through the opening scene, which usually reveals crucial background information and introduces the main conflict or problem.

- **Search for the conflicts.** As you read, always be on the lookout for any signs of tension, turmoil, or unresolved problems. Watch for both **external conflict**, that is, conflict between characters, and internal conflict, the struggle between opposing tendencies within a single character.

- **Stage the play in your mind.** It is not enough just to read the words; you need to visualize the action. Imagine the feelings behind the dialogue and the stage directions that accompany the dialogue. Form an image of each major character and try to hear the words as he or she speaks. To read a drama successfully, you need to be a director as well as a reader.

- **Take sides with the characters.** Drama is always more enjoyable if you look for a character you can identify with, one who can engage your interest and sympathies. As you read, decide where the characters stand in relation to your own values and beliefs. Taking sides with the characters will help you to become more involved.

- **Read the play aloud with others.** After you have read a play silently, read it aloud with others. When possible, get together with friends or classmates to stage a "read through," with each person reading a different character's lines. Better yet, stage a production of a scene or of the entire play.

FOCUS ON DRAMA 181

OVERVIEW

Objectives

- To understand and appreciate a one-act play that explores a challenge to an army of occupation
- To identify and understand stage directions
- To appreciate humor as a way of developing dramatic characters
- To express understanding of a selection through a choice of writing forms, including an original scene, a review, a monologue, and a log entry
- To extend understanding of the selection though a variety of multimodal and cross-curricular activities

Skills

THE WRITER'S STYLE
- Denotation and connotation

GRAMMAR
- The dash

LITERARY CONCEPTS
- Stage directions
- Plot
- Dialogue

GENRE STUDY
- Drama: one-act play

SPEAKING, LISTENING, AND VIEWING
- Dramatic reading
- Group discussion
- Oral presentation

HISTORICAL CONNECTION
The Rise and Fall of the Nazis In World War II, France was occupied by Germany's military forces from 1940 to 1944. Photographs from this period show Nazi occupation troops, members of the French resistance, and French collaborators.

Side A, Frame 49376

PREVIEWING

DRAMA

The Pen of My Aunt
Josephine Tey Great Britain

Activating Prior Knowledge
PERSONAL CONNECTION

Imagine that you live in a country occupied by a foreign military power that uses terror and brutality to maintain control. How do you think you would respond to such a situation? Would you resist? Share your ideas with your classmates.

Building Background
HISTORICAL CONNECTION

The Pen of My Aunt is set in Nazi-occupied France during World War II. On June 22, 1940, France surrendered to the invading forces of Germany, who occupied first part and then all of the nation. Some French soldiers escaped to England and established the Free French forces, who joined in the Allied fight against the Nazis. In France itself, many people also fought the Nazis, banding together in a resistance movement that practiced a kind of underground warfare. The French resistance conducted raids, bombings, ambushes, and other missions designed to weaken the Nazis. The resistance also organized an escape network for downed Allied pilots and resistance fighters who needed to flee the country. For anyone caught working with the resistance, the usual punishment was execution.

Some French citizens, however, fully cooperated with the forces of the German occupation. These people, who were called collaborators, often helped the Nazi cause, even to the point of betraying their fellow citizens. Aided by collaborators, the Nazis exerted strict control over the everyday lives of French citizens. At all times, people needed to carry identification papers, which helped the police to monitor their activities and travels.

Setting a Purpose
WRITING CONNECTION

In your notebook, list the qualities that you think someone who participates in a resistance movement would need to have. As you read, determine whether the main character, Madame, exhibits those qualities.

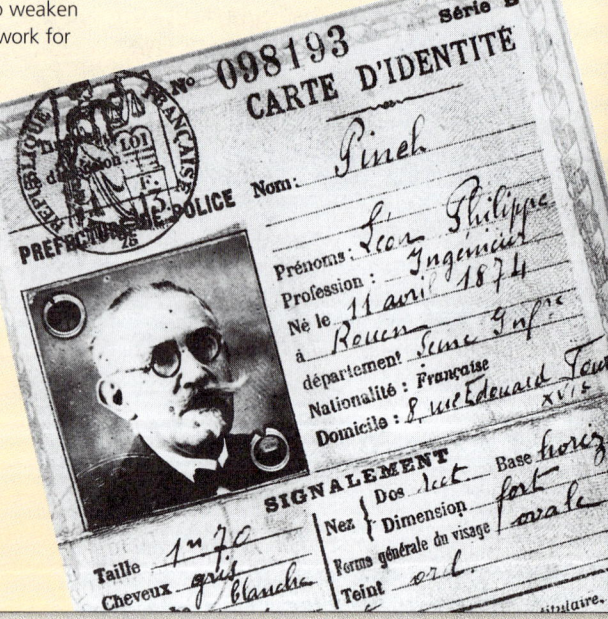

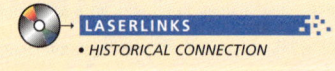
LASERLINKS
• HISTORICAL CONNECTION

PRINT AND MEDIA RESOURCES

UNIT TWO RESOURCE BOOK
Strategic Reading: Literature, p. 4
Vocabulary SkillBuilder, p. 5

WRITING MINI–LESSONS
Transparencies, p. 45

ACCESS FOR STUDENTS ACQUIRING ENGLISH
Selection Summaries
Reading Support

TEACHER'S GUIDE TO ASSESSMENT AND PORTFOLIO USE

FORMAL ASSESSMENT
Selection Test, pp. 35–36
 Test Generator

 **AUDIO LIBRARY**
See Reference Card

 **LASERLINKS**
Historical Connection

 **INTERNET RESOURCES**
McDougal Littell Literature Center at http://www.hmco.com/mcdougal/lit

The Pen of My Aunt

Josephine Tey

Characters

Madame Stranger
Simone Corporal

The scene is a French country house during the Occupation. The lady of the house is seated in her drawing room.[1]

Simone (*approaching*). Madame! Oh, madame! Madame, have you—

Madame. Simone.

Simone. Madame, have you seen what—

Madame. Simone!

Simone. But madame—

Madame. Simone, this may be an age of barbarism, but I will have none of it inside the walls of this house.

Simone. But madame, there is a—there is a—

Madame (*silencing her*). Simone. France may be an occupied country, a ruined nation, and a conquered race, but we will keep, if you please, the usages of civilization.

Simone. Yes, madame.

Madame. One thing we still possess, thank God; and that is good manners. The enemy never had it; and it is not something they can take from *us*.

Simone. No, madame.

---

1. **drawing room:** a large, often elegant room where guests are entertained.

WORDS TO KNOW

acclimatized (ə-klī'mə-tīzd) *adj.* accustomed to something, especially an area or an environment **acclimatize** *v.* (p. 190)

anathema (ə-năth'ə-mə) *n.* something or someone to be shunned or despised; a curse (p. 185)

caliber (kăl'ə-bər) *n.* degree of worth; quality (p. 194)

deduce (dĭ-dōōs') *v.* to reach a conclusion by reasoning; to figure out (p. 192)

implement (ĭm'plə-mənt) *n.* an instrument used to perform a task; a tool (p. 193)

inexplicable (ĭn'ĭk-splĭk'ə-bəl) *adj.* difficult or impossible to explain (p. 184)

miscreant (mĭs'krē-ənt) *n.* one who does evil; a villain (p. 193)

repressive (rĭ-prĕs'ĭv) *adj.* causing or inclined to put down by force or hold back (p. 185)

speculation (spĕk'yə-lā'shən) *n.* consideration of a subject, especially based on incomplete or unclear evidence; guesswork (p. 185)

testily (tĕs'tĭ-lē) *adv.* in an irritated or impatient manner (p. 192)

CUSTOMIZING FOR
Gifted and Talented Students

Have students look, as they read, for details that reveal how class divisions in French society affect the play. *(Possible responses: Madame's upper-class status enables her to appeal to Nazi prejudices concerning dress and discipline. She can also pretend to be offended by the corporal's bad manners and put him on the defensive. Simone, a member of the working class, might be expected by upper-class society to be coarse and argumentative. She can use this prejudice to stage a convincingly raucous argument with the "nephew" to hoodwink the Nazi.)*

Literary Concept: PLOT

A Invite students to discuss how Simone's opening dialogue advances the plot. *(Possible responses: Tey creates suspense by having Simone describe alarming events which are happening offstage. Simone's step-by-step account of the approach of the soldiers and an unknown man piques readers' curiosity.)*

Literary Concept: STAGE DIRECTIONS

B Invite the group to discuss how these stage directions help reveal Madame's character traits. *(Possible responses: They show her to be firm, yet kind; they portray her sympathetically.)*

Madame. Go out of the room again. Open the door—

A **Simone.** Oh, *madame!* I wanted to tell you—

Madame. —open the door, shut it behind you—quietly—take two paces into the room, and say what you came to say. (*Simone goes hastily out, shutting the door. She reappears, shuts the door behind her, takes two paces into the room, and waits.*) Yes, Simone?

Simone. I expect it is too late now; they will be here.

Madame. Who will?

Simone. The soldiers who were coming up the avenue.

Madame. After the last few months I should not have thought that soldiers coming up the avenue was a remarkable fact. It is no doubt a party with a billeting order.[2]

Simone (*crossing to the window*). No, madame, it is two soldiers in one of their little cars, with a civilian between them.

Madame. Which civilian?

Simone. A stranger, madame.

Madame. A stranger? Are the soldiers from the combatant branch?

Simone. No, they are those beasts of administration.[3] Look, they have stopped. They are getting out.

Madame (*at the window*). Yes, it is a stranger. Do you know him, Simone?

Simone. I have never set eyes on him before, madame.

Madame. You would know if he belonged to the district?

Simone. Oh, madame, I know every man between here and St. Estèphe.[4]

Madame (*dryly*). No doubt.

Simone. Oh, merciful God, they are coming up the steps.

Madame. My good Simone, that is what the steps were put there for.

Simone. But they will ring the bell and I shall have to—

Madame. And you will answer it and behave as if you had been trained by a butler and ten upper servants instead of being the charcoal-burner's daughter from over at Les Chênes.[5] (*This is said encouragingly, not in unkindness.*) You will be very calm and correct— **B**

Simone. Calm! Madame! With my inside turning over and over like a wheel at a fair!

Madame. A good servant does not have an inside, merely an exterior. (*comforting*) Be assured, my child. You have your place here; that is more than those creatures on our doorstep have. Let that hearten you—

Simone. Madame! They are not going to ring. They are coming straight in.

Madame (*bitterly*). Yes. They have forgotten long ago what bells are for. (*Door opens.*)

Stranger (*in a bright, confident, casual tone*). Ah, there you are, my dear aunt. I am so glad. Come in, my friend, come in. My dear aunt, this gentleman wants you to identify me.

Madame. Identify you?

Corporal. We found this man wandering in the woods—

Stranger. The corporal found it <u>inexplicable</u> that anyone should wander in a wood.

Corporal. And he had no papers on him—

---

2. **billeting order:** a written order demanding that troops be lodged in a private home or another location.
3. **combatant branch . . . beasts of administration:** The German occupying force included both combat troops fighting the war and officials who administered and controlled the occupied territory.
4. **St. Estèphe** (săⁿ′tĕs-tĕf′).
5. **Les Chênes** (lā-shĕn′).

WORDS TO KNOW
inexplicable (ĭn′ĭk-splĭk′ə-bəl) *adj.* difficult or impossible to explain

184

Stranger. And I rightly pointed out that if I carry all the papers one is supposed to these days, I am no good to God or man. If I put them in a hip pocket, I can't bend forward; if I put them in a front pocket, I can't bend at all.

Corporal. He said that he was your nephew, madame, but that did not seem to us very likely, so we brought him here.

(*There is the slightest pause; just one moment of silence.*)

Madame. But of course this is my nephew.

Corporal. He is?

Madame. Certainly.

Corporal. He lives here?

Madame (*assenting*). My nephew lives here.

Corporal. So! (*recovering*) My apologies, madame. But you will admit that appearances were against the young gentleman.

Madame. Alas, Corporal, my nephew belongs to a generation who delight in flouting appearances. It is what they call "expressing their personality," I understand.

Corporal (*with contempt*). No doubt, madame.

Madame. Convention is anathema to them, and there is no sin like conformity. Even a collar is an offense against their liberty, and a discipline not to be borne by free necks.

Corporal. Ah yes, madame. A little more discipline among your nephew's generation, and we might not be occupying your country today.

Stranger. You think it was that collar of yours that conquered my country? You flatter yourself, Corporal. The only result of wearing a collar like that is varicose veins in the head.

Madame (*repressive*). Please! My dear boy. Let us not descend to personalities.

Stranger. The matter is not personal, my good aunt, but scientific. Wearing a collar like that retards the flow of fresh blood to the head, with the most disastrous consequences to the grey matter of the brain. The hypothetical grey matter. In fact, I have a theory—

Corporal. Monsieur,[6] your theories do not interest me.

Stranger. No? You do not find speculation interesting?

Corporal. In this world one judges by results.

Stranger (*after a slight pause of reflection*). I see. The collared conqueror sits in the high places, while the collarless conquered lies about in the woods. And who comes best out of that, would you say? Tell me, Corporal, as man to man, do you never have a mad, secret desire to lie unbuttoned in a wood?

Corporal. I have only one desire, monsieur, and that is to see your papers.

Stranger (*taken off guard and filling in time*). My papers?

Madame. But is that necessary, Corporal? I have already told you that—

Corporal. I know that madame is a very good collaborator and in good standing—

Madame. In that case—

Corporal. But when we begin an affair we like to finish it. I have asked to see monsieur's papers, and the matter will not be finished until I have seen them.

Madame. You acknowledge that I am in "good standing," Corporal?

Corporal. So I have heard, madame.

---

6. **monsieur** (mə-syœ′): A French form of address, corresponding to "sir" or "mister."

WORDS TO KNOW
anathema (ə-năth′ə-mə) *n.* something or someone to be shunned or despised; a curse
repressive (rĭ-prĕs′ĭv) *adj.* causing or inclined to put down by force or hold back
speculation (spĕk′yə-lā′shən) *n.* consideration of a subject, especially based on incomplete or unclear evidence; guesswork

185

Mini-Lesson — The Writer's Style

DENOTATION AND CONNOTATION
Remind students that the denotation of a word is its dictionary meaning while its connotation is the attitudes and feelings people associate with the word. Point out that Madame's very formal language on page 185—using terms such as *anathema, flouting appearances,* and *offense against liberty*—connotes a philosophical stance and is meant to convince the Corporal that she is making fun of her nephew and the fact that he dresses poorly due to his personal beliefs.

Application Have students discuss the connotations of the terms the Stranger uses in the highlighted dialogue on this page to characterize the Corporal—*varicose veins in the head, retards the flow of fresh blood,* and *hypothetical gray matter.* Then ask them to write additional dialogue in which the Stranger continues to use language with connotations that insult the Corporal's intelligence.

Reteaching/Reinforcement
- *Writing Mini-Lessons* transparencies, p. 45

Denotation and Connotation, p. 424

Art Note

The Suitor by Edouard Vuillard French artist Edouard Vuillard (1868–1940) portrayed the private world of his family and friends in their homes at the end of the 1800s. Vuillard gave this familiar subject matter a subtle, dreamlike quality through a pastiche of brush strokes. The brilliantly colored, flat patterns of Vuillard's painting were strongly influenced by Japanese art.

Reading the Art *How does this interior scene of a French country house help you better appreciate the setting of* The Pen of My Aunt?

The Suitor (1893), Edouard Vuillard. Oil on millboard panel, Smith College Museum of Art, Northampton, Massachusetts. Purchased, Drayton Hillyer Fund, 1938.

Madame. Then I must consider it a discourtesy on your part to demand my nephew's credentials.

Corporal. It is no reflection on madame. It is a matter of routine, nothing more.

Stranger (*murmuring*). The great god Routine.

Madame. To ask for his papers was routine; to insist on their production is discourtesy. I shall say so to your commanding officer.

Corporal. Very good, madame. In the meantime, I shall inspect your nephew's papers.

Madame. And what if I—

Stranger (*quietly*). You may as well give it up, my dear. You could as easily turn a steamroller. They have only one idea at a time. If the corporal's heart is set on seeing my papers, he shall see them. (*moving towards the door*) I left them in the pocket of my coat.

Simone (*unexpectedly, from the background*). Not in your *linen* coat?

Stranger (*pausing*). Yes. Why?

Simone (*with apparently growing anxiety*). Your *cream* linen coat? The one you were wearing yesterday?

Stranger. Certainly.

Simone. Merciful Heaven! I sent it to the laundry!

Stranger. To the laundry!

Simone. Yes, monsieur; this morning; in the basket.

Stranger (*in incredulous anger*). You sent my coat, *with my papers in the pocket*, to the laundry!

Simone (*defensive and combatant*). I didn't know monsieur's papers were in the pocket.

Stranger. You didn't know! You didn't know that a packet of documents weighing half a ton were in the pocket. An identity card, a *laisser passer*,[7] a food card, a drink card, an army discharge, a permission to wear civilian clothes, a permission to go farther than ten miles to the east, a permission to go more than ten miles to the west, a permission to—

Simone (*breaking in with spirit*). How was I to know the coat was heavy! I picked it up with the rest of the bundle that was lying on the floor.

Stranger (*snapping her head off*). My coat was on the back of the chair.

Simone. It was on the floor.

Stranger. On the back of the chair!

Simone. It was on the floor with your dirty shirt and your pajamas, and a towel and what not. I put my arms round the whole thing and then—woof! into the basket with them.

Stranger. I tell you that coat was on the back of the chair. It was quite clean and was not going to the laundry for two weeks yet—if then. I hung it there myself, and—

Madame. My dear boy, what does it matter? The damage is done now. In any case, they will find the papers when they unpack the basket, and return them tomorrow.

Stranger. If someone doesn't steal them. There are a lot of people who would like to lay hold of a complete set of papers, believe me.

Madame (*reassuring*). Oh, no. Old Fleureau[8] is the soul of honesty. You have no need to worry about them. They will be back first thing tomorrow, you shall see; and then we shall have much pleasure in sending them to the administration office for the corporal's inspection. Unless, of course, the corporal insists on your personal appearance at the office.

Corporal (*cold and indignant*). I have seen monsieur. All that I want now is to see his papers.

Stranger. You shall see them, Corporal, you shall see them. The whole half-ton of them. You may inspect them at your leisure. Provided,

---

7. *laisser passer* (lĕs′ā pä-sā′) *French:* a travel pass.
8. Fleureau (flœ-rō′).

STRATEGIC READING FOR
Less-Proficient Readers

I Have students discuss how Simone and Madame help the Stranger when the Corporal asks for his papers. *(Simone quickly makes up a story about sending the papers to the laundry in a linen coat; Madame assures the Corporal the papers will be back the next day.)*
Summarizing

Set a Purpose Ask students to read on to discover the new problem that confronts the Stranger.

CUSTOMIZING FOR
Students Acquiring English

3 To help students understand and remember the term *collaborator*, point out that the prefix *co-* means "together" and the root word *labor* means "work" to arrive at a definition, "people who work together."

Critical Thinking:
MAKING INFERENCES

J Ask volunteers to explain why "after the last six months" the French might be less likely to believe in "the brotherhood of man." *(Some students might point out that France has just been invaded by its neighbor Germany. Others might suggest this is a reference to the way the Nazis have been treating French citizens.)*

Literary Concept:
FIGURATIVE LANGUAGE

K Have students discuss what Madame means when she says she borrows her nephew's cloak. *(Since her nephew is a well-known collaborator, Madame wraps herself in his politics, as if it were a cloak, and so hides her own work for the Resistance.)*

Critical Thinking:
MAKING INFERENCES

L Have students explain how Madame might persuade her collaborator nephew to lend her his papers. *(She might threaten to disinherit him.)*

---

that is, that they come back from the laundry to which this idiot has consigned them.

Madame (*again reassuring*). They will come back, never fear. And you must not blame Simone. She is a good child, and does her best.

Simone (*with an air of belated virtue*). I am not one to pry into pockets.

Madame. Simone, show the corporal out, if you please.

Simone (*natural feeling overcoming her for a moment*). He knows the way out. (*recovering*) Yes, madame.

Madame. And Corporal, try to take your duties a little less literally in future. My countrymen appreciate the spirit rather than the letter.

Corporal. I have my instructions, madame, and I obey them. Good day, madame. Monsieur.

(*He goes, followed by* Simone—*door closes. There is a moment of silence.*)

Stranger. For a good collaborator, that was a remarkably quick adoption.

Madame. Sit down, young man. I will give you something to drink. I expect your knees are none too well.

Stranger. My knees, madame, are pure gelatine. As for my stomach, it seems to have disappeared.

Madame (*offering him the drink she has poured out*). This will recall it, I hope.

Stranger. You are not drinking, madame?

Madame. Thank you, no.

Stranger. Not with strangers. It is certainly no time to drink with strangers. Nevertheless, I drink the health of a collaborator. (*He drinks.*) Tell me, madame, what will happen tomorrow when they find that you have no nephew?

Madame (*surprised*). But of course I have a nephew. I tell lies, my friend; but not *silly* lies. My charming nephew has gone to Bonneval[9] for the day. He finds country life dull.

Stranger. Dull? This—this heaven?

Madame (*dryly*). He likes to talk and here there is no audience. At headquarters in Bonneval he finds the audience sympathetic.

Stranger (*understanding the implication*). Ah.

Madame. He believes in the brotherhood of man—if you can credit it.

Stranger. After the last six months?

Madame. His mother was American, so he has half the Balkans[10] in his blood. To say nothing of Italy, Russia, and the Levant.[11]

Stranger (*half-amused*). I see.

Madame. A silly and worthless creature, but useful.

Stranger. Useful?

Madame. I—borrow his cloak.

Stranger. I see.

Madame. Tonight I shall borrow his identity papers, and tomorrow they will go to the office in St. Estèphe.

Stranger. But—he will have to know.

Madame (*placidly*). Oh, yes, he will know, of course.

Stranger. And how will you persuade such an enthusiastic collaborator to deceive his friends?

Madame. Oh, that is easy. He is my heir.

Stranger (*amused*). Ah.

Madame. He is, also, by the mercy of God, not too unlike you, so that his photograph will not startle the corporal too much tomorrow. Now tell me what you were doing in my wood.

---

9. **Bonneval** (bôn-väl′).
10. **Balkans** (bôl′kənz): the Balkan Peninsula of southeastern Europe. Madame is insulting her nephew, suggesting that his collaboration with the Nazis can be blamed on his mixed ancestry.
11. **Levant** (lə-vănt′): the countries bordering the eastern Mediterranean Sea, today including Turkey, Syria, Lebanon, Israel, and Egypt.

188 UNIT TWO PART 1: CHALLENGING THE SYSTEM

Mini-Lesson  Literary Concepts

REVIEWING DIALOGUE Remind students that dialogue is conversation between two or more characters and that it brings characters to life and gives the reader insights into the characters' personality traits. In drama especially, dialogue is also instrumental in advancing the plot. Have students look again at the dialogue highlighted on this page between Madame and the Stranger, and discuss what this exchange reveals about the characters. What predictions might students make about the future course of the plot based on this dialogue?

Application Have students work with a partner to find and examine another example of dialogue that is especially revealing of the characters' personalities or that is instrumental in advancing the plot. Then ask students to share their ideas with the class.

Stranger. Resting my feet—I am practically walking on my bones. And waiting for tonight.

Madame. Where are you making for? (*as he does not answer immediately*) The coast? (*He nods.*) That is four days away—five if your feet are bad.

Stranger. I know it.

Madame. Have you friends on the way?

Stranger. I have friends at the coast, who will get me a boat. But no one between here and the sea.

Madame (*rising*). I must consult my list of addresses. (*pausing*) What was your service?

Stranger. Army.

Madame. Which regiment?

Stranger. The 79th.

Madame (*after the faintest pause*). And your colonel's name?

Stranger. Delavault[12] was killed in the first week, and Martin[13] took over.

Madame (*going to her desk*). A "good collaborator" cannot be too careful. Now I can consult my notebook. A charming color, is it not? A lovely shade of red.

Stranger. Yes—but what has a red quill pen to do with your notebook?—Ah, you write with it of course—stupid of me.

Madame. Certainly I write with it—but it is also my notebook—look—I only need a hairpin—and then—so—out of my quill pen comes my notebook—a tiny piece of paper—but enough for a list of names.

Stranger. You mean that you keep that list on your desk? (*He sounds disapproving.*)

Madame. Where did you expect me to keep it, young man? In my corset?[14] Did you ever try to get something out of your corset in a hurry? What would you advise as the ideal quality in a hiding place for a list of names?

Stranger. That the thing should be difficult to find, of course.

Madame. Not at all. That it should be easily destroyed in emergency. It is too big for me to swallow—I suspect they do that only in books—and we have no fires to consume it, so I had to think of some other way. I did try to memorize the list, but what I could not be sure of remembering were those that—that had to be scored off. It would be fatal to send someone to an address that—that was no longer available. So I had to keep a written record.

Stranger. And if you neither eat it nor burn it when the moment comes, how do you get rid of it?

Madame. I could, of course, put a match to it, but scraps of freshly-burned paper on a desk take a great deal of explaining. If I ceased to be looked on with approval, my usefulness would end. It is important therefore that there should be no sign of anxiety on my part: no burned paper, no excuses to leave the room, no nods and becks[15] and winks. I just sit here at my desk and go on with my letters. I tilt my nice big inkwell sideways for a moment and dip the pen into the deep ink at the side. The ink flows into the hollow of the quill, and all is blotted out. (*consulting the list*) Let me see. It would be good if you could rest your feet for a day or so.

Stranger (*ruefully*). It would.

Madame. There is a farm just beyond the Marnay[16] crossroads on the way to St. Estèphe— (*She pauses to consider.*)

Stranger. St. Estèphe is the home of the single-minded corporal. I don't want to run into him again.

---

12. **Delavault** (də-lä-vō′).
13. **Martin** (mär-tăɴ′).
14. **corset** (kôr′sĭt): a close-fitting, reinforced undergarment worn to give shape or support to the figure.
15. **becks**: summoning gestures.
16. **Marnay** (mär-nĕ′).

THE PEN OF MY AUNT **189**

Literary Concept: DIALOGUE

P Ask students what this dialogue reveals to them about Madame and her real nephew. *(Possible responses: His talk about brotherhood is insincere; he scorns low-ranking Germans and curries favor among the powerful officers. She does not admire his attitudes.)*

Literary Concept: CHARACTERIZATION

Q Have students discuss how Simone has demonstrated that she has "a great heart." *(Possible response: She is courageous enough to risk her life for the unknown Stranger.)*

Literary Concept: PLOT

R Point out that since the Corporal has left the room, the suspense level has fallen; the playwright is likely to introduce a new complication soon. Have students predict what suspense-building event might be interrupting Madame's last line of their discussion, as indicated by the dash. *(Accept all reasonable responses.)*

Madame. No, that might be awkward; but that farm of the Cherfils[17] would be ideal. A good hiding place, and food to spare, and fine people—

Stranger. If your nephew is so friendly with the invader, how is it that the corporal doesn't know him by sight?

Madame (*absently*). The unit at St. Estèphe is a noncommissioned one.

Stranger. Does the brotherhood of man exclude sergeants, then?

Madame. Oh, definitely. Brotherhood does not really begin under field rank, I understand.

Stranger. But the corporal may still meet your nephew somewhere.

Madame. That is a risk one must take. It is not a very grave one. They change the personnel every few weeks, to prevent them becoming too <u>acclimatized</u>. And even if he met my nephew, he is unlikely to ask for the papers of so obviously well-to-do a citizen. If you could bear to go *back* a little—

Stranger. Not a step! It would be like—like denying God. I have got so far, against all the odds, and I am not going a yard back. Not even to rest my feet!

Madame. I understand; but it is a pity. It is a long way to the Cherfils farm—two miles east of the Marnay crossroads it is, on a little hill.

Stranger. I'll get there; don't worry. If not tonight then tomorrow night. I am used to sleeping in the open by now.

Madame. I wish we could have you here, but it is too dangerous. We are liable to be billeted on at any moment, without notice. However, we can give you a good meal, and a bath. We have no coal, so it will be one of those flat-tin-saucer baths.[18] And if you want to be very kind to Simone, you might have it somewhere in the kitchen regions and so save her carrying water upstairs.

Stranger. But of course.

Madame. Before the war I had a staff of twelve. Now I have Simone. I dust and Simone sweeps, and between us we keep the dirt at bay. She has no manners but a great heart, the child.

Stranger. The heart of a lion.

Madame. Before I put this back you might memorize these: Forty Avenue Foch,[19] in Crest,[20] the back entrance.

Stranger. Forty Avenue Foch, the back entrance.

Madame. You may find it difficult to get into Crest, by the way. It is a closed area. The pot boy[21] at the Red Lion in Mans.[22]

Stranger. The pot boy.

Madame. Denis[23] the blacksmith at Laloupe.[24] And the next night should take you to the sea and your friends. Are they safely in your mind?

Stranger. Forty Avenue Foch in Crest: the pot boy at the Red Lion in Mans: and Denis the blacksmith at Laloupe. And to be careful getting into Crest.

Madame. Good. Then I can close my notebook—or roll it up, I should say—then—it fits neatly, does it not? Now let us see about some food for you. Perhaps I could find you other clothes. Are these all you—

---

17. **Cherfils** (shĕr-fēs′).
18. **flat-tin-saucer baths:** sponge baths.
19. **Foch** (fôsh).
20. **Crest** (krĕst).
21. **pot boy:** a boy or man who serves customers and does chores at a public inn.
22. **Mans** (mäⁿ).
23. **Denis** (də-nē′).
24. **Laloupe** (lä-lo͞op′): a town in northwestern France; also spelled *La Loupe*.

WORDS TO KNOW

acclimatized (ə-klī′mə-tīzd′) *adj.* accustomed to something, especially an area or an environment **acclimatize** *v.*

190

Mini-Lesson Study Skills

MEMORIZING The ability to memorize information was a matter of life and death for French Resistance fighters. Actors too rely heavily on their ability to memorize. Discuss with students some of the techniques actors use to remember lines. For example, for long sections of dialogue, an actor may memorize the first sentence, say it, memorize the next sentence, say the two together, memorize the next, and so on until the entire section is memorized. On his or her copy of the script, the actor might highlight the lines to memorize in one color, and then use another color to highlight the cue words—the last line or phrase said by the preceding character.

Application Invite students to use some of these memorization techniques as they work with a partner to memorize a small section of this play. You may wish to make copies of the pages so students can highlight their parts.

190 THE LANGUAGE OF LITERATURE **TEACHER'S EDITION**

L'Arlésienne: Madame Joseph-Michel Ginoux (Marie Julien, 1848–1911) (1888), Vincent van Gogh. Oil on canvas, 36″ × 29″, The Metropolitan Museum of Art, bequest of Sam A. Lewisohn, 1951 (51.112.3).

Art Note

***L'Arlesienne: Madame Joseph-Michel Ginoux [Marie Julien]* by Vincent van Gogh** Vincent van Gogh (1853–1890) is considered one of the most influential painters of the 19th century. Although his work is now highly sought after by collectors, Van Gogh sold only one painting during his lifetime. He died in poverty.

Reading the Art *How would you describe the mood of this painting? How do your impressions of the subject compare with your impressions of Tey's Madame?*

THE LANGUAGE OF LITERATURE **TEACHER'S EDITION**

Literary Concept:
STAGE DIRECTIONS

S Ask students what these stage directions reveal to them about the Corporal. *(Possible responses: Some students may say that although he is part of the conquering army, he is a low-ranking officer unaccustomed to questioning an order. Others may mention that he displays the unquestioning discipline demanded of German soldiers.)*

Literary Concept:
DIALOGUE

T Ask students how this dialogue between Madame and the Corporal adds to the play. *(Possible responses: Many students will say the witty wordplay and a fast comeback add to the play's humor. Others will say this reinforces the idea that Madame is quick-witted, or that it shows the Corporal isn't as smart as he thinks he is.)*

Cultural Note

U Explain that Madame's explanation is not so far-fetched. In French, Simone would have used the subjunctive mood to express the idea of wishing something that was contrary to fact. The subjunctive verb endings, which would be less familiar to the Corporal, are quite similar to the regular indicative verb endings.

STRATEGIC READING FOR
Less-Proficient Readers

V Have students explain the new complication that arises and how Madame manages to resolve this difficulty. *(The Corporal overhears Simone say she had never seen the Stranger before. Madame persuades the Corporal that Simone said she wished she had never seen the Stranger.)* **Summarizing**

Set a Purpose Ask students to find out what happens to the Stranger by the end of the play.

(The Corporal's voice is heard mingled in fury with the still more furious tones of Simone. She is yelling: "Nothing of the sort, I tell you, nothing of the sort," but no words are clearly distinguishable in the angry row.

The door is flung open, and the Corporal bursts in dragging a struggling Simone by the arm.)

Simone (*screaming with rage and terror*). Let me go, you foul fiend, you murdering foreigner, let me go. (*She tries to kick him.*)

Corporal (*at the same time*). Stop struggling, you lying deceitful little bit of no-good.

Madame. Will someone explain this extraordinary—

Corporal. This creature—

Madame. Take your hand from my servant's arm, Corporal. She is not going to run away.

Corporal (*reacting to the voice of authority and automatically complying*). Your precious servant was overheard telling the gardener that she had never set eyes on this man.

Simone. I did not! Why should I say anything like that?

Corporal. With my own ears I heard her, my own two ears. Will you kindly explain that to me if you can.

Madame. You speak our language very well, Corporal, but perhaps you are not so quick to understand.

Corporal. I understand perfectly.

Madame. What Simone was saying to the gardener was no doubt what she was announcing to all and sundry at the pitch of her voice this morning.

Corporal (*unbelieving*). And what was that?

Madame. That she *wished* she had never set eyes on my nephew.

Corporal. And why should she say that?

Madame. My nephew, Corporal, has many charms, but tidiness is not one of them. As you may have <u>deduced</u> from the episode of the coat. He is apt to leave his room—

Simone (*on her cue; in a burst of scornful rage*). Cigarette ends, pajamas, towels, bedclothes, books, papers—all over the floor like a *flood*. Every morning I tidy up, and in two hours it is as if a bomb had burst in the room.

Stranger (*testily*). I told you already that I was sor—

Simone (*interrupting*). As if I had nothing else to do in this enormous house but wait on you.

Stranger. Haven't I said that I—

Simone. And when I have climbed all the way up from the kitchen with your shaving water, you let it get cold; but will you shave in cold? Oh, no! I have to bring up another—

Stranger. I didn't ask you to climb the damned stairs, did I?

Simone. And do I get a word of thanks for bringing it? Do I indeed? You say: "*Must* you bring it in that hideous jug; it offends my eyes."

Stranger. So it does offend my eyes!

Madame. Enough, enough! We had enough of that this morning. You see, Corporal?

Corporal. I could have sworn—

Madame. A natural mistake, perhaps. But I think you might have used a little more common sense in the matter. (*coldly*) And a great deal more dignity. I don't like having my servants manhandled.

Corporal. She refused to come.

Simone. Accusing me of things I never said!

Madame. However, now that you are here again you can make yourself useful. My nephew wants to go into Crest the day after tomorrow, and that requires a special pass. Perhaps you would make one out for him.

WORDS TO KNOW
deduce (dĭ-dōōs´) *v.* to reach a conclusion by reasoning; to figure out
testily (tĕs´tĭ-lē) *adv.* in an irritated or impatient manner

192

Assessment ✓ Option

INFORMAL ASSESSMENT You can informally assess your students' understanding of the selection by describing the following scenario to students:

A TV company is mounting a production of The Pen of My Aunt *and you are its casting director. For each character in the play, write a description summing up the various traits and attributes that an actor would need to portray in that role.*

Rubric

3 Full Accomplishment Students show a clear and full awareness of the main traits of each of the four characters.

2 Substantial Accomplishment Students show a fair understanding of the general traits of the characters, but do not develop their descriptions fully.

1 Little or Partial Accomplishment Students are unable to describe the characters accurately.

Corporal. But I—

Madame. You have a little book of permits in your pocket, haven't you?

Corporal. Yes. I—

Madame. Very well. Better make it valid for two days. He is always changing his mind.

Corporal. But it is not for me to grant a pass.

Madame. You sign them, don't you?

Corporal. Yes, but only when someone tells me to.

Madame. Very well, if it will help you, I tell you to.

Corporal. I mean, permission must be granted before a pass is issued.

Madame. And have you any doubt that a permission will be granted to my nephew?

Corporal. No, of course not, madame.

Madame. Then don't be absurd, Corporal. To be absurd twice in five minutes is too often. You may use my desk—and my own special pen. Isn't it a beautiful quill, Corporal?

Corporal. Thank you, madame, no. We Germans have come a long way from the geese.

Madame. Yes?

Corporal. I prefer my fountain pen. It is a more efficient <u>implement</u>. (*He writes.*) For the 15th and the 16th. "Holder of identity card number"—What is the number of your identity, monsieur?

Stranger. I have not the faintest idea.

Corporal. You do not know?

Stranger. No. The only numbers I take an interest in are lottery numbers.

Simone. I know the number of monsieur's card.

Madame (*afraid that she is going to invent one*). I don't think that likely, Simone.

Simone (*aware of what is in her mistress's mind, and reassuring her*). But I really *do* know, madame. It is the year I was born, with two ones after it. Many a time I have seen it on the outside of the card.

Corporal. It is good that someone knows.

Simone. It is—192411.

Corporal. 192411. (*He fills in the dates.*)

Madame (*as he nears the end*). Are you going back to St. Estèphe now, Corporal?

Corporal. Yes, madame.

Madame. Then perhaps you will give my nephew a lift as far as the Marnay crossroads.

Corporal. It is not permitted to take civilians as passengers.

Stranger. But you took me here as a passenger.

Corporal. That was different.

Madame. You mean that when you thought he was a <u>miscreant</u> you took him in your car, but now that you know he is my nephew you refuse?

Corporal. When I brought him here it was on service business.

Madame (*gently reasonable*). Corporal, I think you owe me something for your general lack of tact this afternoon. Would it be too much to ask you to consider my nephew a miscreant for the next hour while you drive him as far as the Marnay crossroads?

Corporal. But—

Madame. Take him to the crossroads with you and I shall agree to forget your—your lack of efficiency. I am sure you are actually a very efficient person, and likely to be a sergeant any day now. We won't let a blunder or two stand in your way.

Corporal. If I am caught giving a lift to a civilian, I shall *never* be a sergeant.

Madame (*still gentle*). If I report on your conduct this afternoon, tomorrow you will be a private.

WORDS TO KNOW
implement (ĭm′plə-mənt) *n.* an instrument used to perform a task; a tool
miscreant (mĭs′krē-ənt) *n.* one who does evil; a villain

Literary Concept: IRONY

AA Ask students why they think the audience might laugh as the Corporal prepares to give the Stranger a ride. *(Possible responses: This is an unexpected and ironic twist; for the third time, Madame has tricked the Corporal.)*

STRATEGIC READING FOR
Less-Proficient Readers

BB Have students explain what happens to the Stranger at the end of the play. *(The Corporal drives the Stranger to the Marnay crossroads, unwittingly helping him escape.)* Summarizing

CUSTOMIZING FOR
Gifted and Talented Students

Ask students if they think this play accurately reflects conditions during the German occupation of France, or whether it tends to romanticize them? Encourage students to support their opinions with details from the play as well as with what they know from history.

EDITOR'S NOTE *With the permission of the copyright holder, potentially offensive material has been deleted from the selection.*

Corporal (*after a long pause*). Is monsieur ready to come now?

Stranger. Quite ready.

Corporal. You will need a coat.

Madame. Simone, get monsieur's coat from the cupboard in the hall. And when you have seen him off, come back here.

Simone. Yes, madame. (*Exit* Simone.)

Corporal. Madame.

Madame. Good day to you, Corporal. (*Exit* Corporal.)

Stranger. Your talent for blackmail is remarkable.

Madame. The place has a yellow barn. You had better wait somewhere till evening, when the dogs are chained up.

Stranger. I wish I had an aunt of your caliber. All mine are authorities on crochet.

Madame. I could wish you were my nephew. Good luck, and be careful. Perhaps one day you will come back, and dine with me, and tell me the rest of the tale.

(*The sound of a running engine comes from outside.*)

Stranger. Two years today, perhaps?

Madame. One year today.

Stranger (*softly*). Who knows? (*He lifts her hand to his lips.*) Thank you, and *au revoir.*²⁵ (*turning at the door*) Being sped on my way by the enemy is a happiness I had not anticipated. I shall never be able to repay you for that. (*He goes out.*) (*off*) Ah, my coat—thank you, Simone.

(*Sound of car driving off.* Madame *pours out two glasses. As she finishes,* Simone *comes in, shutting the door correctly behind her and taking two paces into the room.*)

Simone. You wanted me, madame?

Madame. You will drink a glass of wine with me, Simone.

Simone. With you, madame!

Madame. You are a good daughter of France and a good servant to me. We shall drink a toast together.

Simone. Yes, madame.

Madame (*quietly*). To Freedom.

Simone (*repeating*). To Freedom. May I add a bit of my own, madame?

Madame. Certainly.

Simone (*with immense satisfaction*). And a very bad end to that corporal!

Curtain

---

25. *au revoir* (ō′rə-vwär′) *French:* good-bye.

WORDS TO KNOW
caliber (kăl′ə-bər) *n.* degree of worth; quality

COMPREHENSION CHECK

1. Why does Madame say the Stranger is her nephew? *(Madame wants to help the Stranger since, like her, he is part of the Resistance.)*
2. Why does Simone say she has sent the Stranger's coat to the laundry? *(This lie explains why the nephew's papers aren't in the house.)*
3. What is the Stranger's goal? *(to reach the sea so he can get a boat out of France)*
4. What information does Madame keep in her pen? *(the names and locations of people who will help Resistance fighters)*
5. How does the Stranger get to the Marnay crossroads? *(Madame tricks the German corporal into taking him there.)*

RESPONDING OPTIONS

FROM PERSONAL RESPONSE TO CRITICAL ANALYSIS

REFLECT
1. As you read the play, what images of the set and characters came to mind? Sketch one of those images in your notebook.

RETHINK
2. What is your opinion of each of the characters in the play? Give your reasoning.
3. Do you think that the way Madame, the Stranger, and Simone succeed in fooling the Corporal is believable?
   Consider
   Close Textual Reading
   - the explanations offered for the Stranger's unkempt appearance, his wandering in the woods, and his missing papers
   - the explanation for Simone's comment that she "had never set eyes" on the Stranger
   - the improvised roles adopted by Madame, the Stranger, and Simone
4. Does Madame exhibit the qualities that you associate with a resistance fighter, as you described for the Writing Connection? Explain, using examples from the play to support your opinion.
5. In your judgment, what is the theme of the play?
   Consider
   Close Textual Reading
   - the personal qualities exhibited by the French characters
   - the contrast between Madame's real nephew and the Stranger
   - what the French hope to achieve by their resistance

RELATE
6. Though Madame plays the role of a collaborator, she actually works for the resistance. Under what circumstances, if any, would you consider playing a double role in order to serve a worthy cause?

Multimodal Learning
ANOTHER PATHWAY
Cooperative Learning
Stage a Readers Theater performance of the play. In Readers Theater, performers read their lines from the text, paying close attention to how the lines should be interpreted. They rely on the oral reading alone to convey their characters' thoughts and feelings.

QUICKWRITES

1. Write an additional **scene** for this play, showing, perhaps, the return of the real nephew or the Stranger's return to thank Madame after France is liberated. Include both dialogue and stage directions.
2. Write a **review** of the play, based either on the text or on an imagined performance.
3. Write a **monologue** in which Madame offers her reflections on the war and on the differences between her nephew and the Stranger.
4. Write the **log entry** that the Corporal might have written on the day of the play's events. Think about what he would have deliberately included or omitted.

📁 **PORTFOLIO** Save your writing. You may want to use it later as a springboard to a piece for your portfolio.

THE PEN OF MY AUNT   195

From Personal Response to Critical Analysis

1. Accept all reasonable responses.
2. Accept all well-supported responses. Possible responses: Madame is brave and quick-thinking to acknowledge the Stranger as her nephew; she outwits the Corporal with her intelligence and authority. Simone is brave and a clever actress, yet perhaps a bit foolish to let the Corporal overhear her. The Stranger shows himself to be imaginative by pretending to be Madame's nephew and later arguing with Simone; the Corporal is stubborn, unimaginative, and easily cowed by authority.
3. Possible responses: Some students may respond that the protagonists are unusually skilled improvisers; others might suggest that an actual German corporal would have been more ruthless.
4. Accept all reasonable, well-supported responses.
5. Possible responses: Some students might mention patriotism or suggest that love of freedom leads many people to challenge a conquering invader. Others may say intelligence is a powerful weapon.
6. Accept all reasonable responses.

Another Pathway
Cooperative Learning Suggest that students work together in groups of five, with four reading the parts of the players and the fifth serving as director. Be sure that students pay attention to the dashes and other marks of punctuation that signal one character is interrupting another or that a character is hesitant or angry.

Rubric
3 Full Accomplishment Students' performance shows deep insight into the characters; delivery is natural and engaging.
2 Substantial Accomplishment Students' delivery of the text is fairly engaging, revealing adequate understanding of characters and their motivations.
1 Little or Partial Accomplishment Students' delivery is awkward and unnatural, revealing a lack of understanding of the characters and their motivations.

QuickWrites
1. If students choose to portray the return of the real nephew in their scenes, they might focus on Madame's reaction to him and his views after spending time with the Stranger, then explore the tension that results from Madame's and her nephew's political differences.
2. Remind students that a review gives an overview of the dramatic situation without revealing the ending, comments on the believability of the action, and critiques the performance of the actors or the writing of the playwright.
3. Suggest that a simple prop or two—a pack of official papers, a quill pen—might be effective tools for illustrating Madame's feelings.
4. Remind students that a log entry is an official document and might be read by the Corporal's superior officers, so the Corporal would in all likelihood omit any mention of his deviations from official policy.

📄 The Writer's Craft
Dialogue in Plays, pp. 453–454
Writing About Literature, pp. 238–253
Monologue, pp. 108–112

THE LANGUAGE OF LITERATURE TEACHER'S EDITION   195

Alternative Activities

1. Ask students to note that the set descriptions and the actions of the characters call for an entrance door, a window, and a desk and chair. Suggest that students look at page 186 for ideas about the furnishings of a French country house. Among the necessary props are a plume pen, an inkwell, decanters and glasses, and a coat.
2. The place names *Marnay, Crest, Mans,* and *Laloupe* are on page 190. Have students determine how far the Stranger must travel to reach the sea.

Across the Curriculum

World Languages Suggest that students use English-French dictionaries or travelers' phrase books to find the translations: *le collaborateur* (collaborator), *le bourgeois* or *le civil* (civilian), *le carnet* (notebook), *l'occupation* (occupation). Students might also suggest other French phrases that are used by English speakers, such as *a la carte, bon voyage, touché, c'est la vie, cul-de-sac,* and *cuisine.*

The Writer's Style

Students might cite as humorous and character-revealing the Stranger's daring suggestion that the Corporal has no brain (page 185), the quick-witted arguments between Simone and the Stranger (pages 187 and 192), Madame's fast cover-up of Simone's comment (page 192), and Madame's clever manipulation of the Corporal at the end of the play.

 The Writer's Craft

Development of Characters, pp. 80–82

LITERARY CONCEPTS

As you know, **stage directions** are the notes included in a play to help actors and directors put on the play and to help readers picture the action. The stage directions may describe setting, lighting, sound effects, the gestures and movements of the actors, or the way in which dialogue is to be spoken. With a small group of classmates, choose a section of the play, such as the first confrontation with the Corporal, and add more stage directions, focusing on how the performers should act. Rehearse your section, making sure that you follow the stage directions, and then perform it for the rest of the class. When you have finished, discuss whether the additional stage directions enhanced your performance.

CONCEPT REVIEW: Plot On the horizontal axis of a line graph like the one started below, list in sequence the plot events of the play. On the vertical axis, rank the events according to the suspense that they generate. The highest point of your graph should be the event that creates the most suspense.

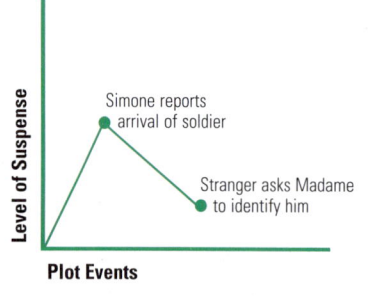

Multimodal Learning

ALTERNATIVE ACTIVITIES

1. Draw a **set design** for a production of this play. Be sure to include the furniture and props mentioned in the dialogue and stage directions.
2. On a detailed map of France, locate some of the place names mentioned in the play. Then create a **map** of the Stranger's likely escape route.

THE WRITER'S STYLE

Besides being suspenseful, this play employs wit and humor. With a partner, examine the section where Madame describes her nephew to the Stranger (page 185), or a section of your choice. In your opinion, what lines would make the audience laugh? How does the use of humor contribute to the development of the characters? Share your observations with your classmates.

ACROSS THE CURRICULUM

World Languages The title *The Pen of My Aunt* is the literal translation of the French expression *la plume de ma tante* (lä-plōōm′də-mä-tänt′). Find the French translations of several words or phrases that you think are important in the play, such as *collaborator, civilian, notebook,* and *occupation.* Read aloud the French words to your classmates, and have them guess the meanings.

---

196 UNIT TWO PART 1: CHALLENGING THE SYSTEM

Literary Concepts

Stage Directions To help students write additional stage directions, suggest that groups use the following questions to analyze any section of the play that seemed unclear to them at first.

- What additional stage directions might help clarify this section of the play?
- What additional stage directions might bring out the traits of the characters better?

During rehearsals, actors should consider if any new stage directions might help them speak or move more effectively on stage.

Plot Have students identify and plot two additional events in the play that generate significant suspense. (Examples are the demand for the "nephew's" papers and the Corporal's overhearing Simone say she had never seen the Stranger.) The final scene, in which Madame persuades the Corporal to give the Stranger a ride, also generates interest and serves as an amusingly ironic climax.

WORDS TO KNOW

EXERCISE A Write the letter of the word pair that expresses the relationship that is most similar to the relationship of the word pair in capital letters.

1. MISCREANT : WRONGDOING :: (a) hero : cowardice, (b) traitor : treason, (c) collaborator : resistance
2. DICTATORSHIP : REPRESSIVE :: (a) tyranny : democratic, (b) war : peaceful, (c) injury: painful
3. ANATHEMA : BLESSING :: (a) sin : virtue, (b) crime : punishment, (c) preacher : prayer
4. CALIBER : QUALITY :: (a) frankness : sincerity, (b) courage : cowardice, (c) inch : foot
5. PENCIL : IMPLEMENT :: (a) thermometer : heat, (b) hammer : tool, (c) plume : quill
6. EXPLAIN : INEXPLICABLE :: (a) change : variable, (b) rely : reliable, (c) dispute : indisputable
7. SPECULATION : CERTAINTY :: (a) science : experiment, (b) practicality : usefulness, (c) danger : safety
8. ANNOYED : TESTILY :: (a) worried : nervously, (b) insulted : politely, (c) overjoyed : calmly
9. DEDUCE : CONCLUSION :: (a) deceive : truth, (b) judge : objectivity, (c) search : discovery
10. CLIMATE : ACCLIMATIZED :: (a) circle : circular, (b) custom : accustomed, (c) mortality : immortal

EXERCISE B Choose one of the Words to Know to act out in front of a small group of classmates. Feel free to use props if appropriate. See whether the others can guess your word.

Words to Know
1. b   6. c
2. c   7. c
3. a   8. a
4. a   9. c
5. b   10. b

Reteaching/Reinforcement
- *Unit Two Resource Book*, p. 5

JOSEPHINE TEY (GORDON DAVIOT)

Mackintosh published her first book by entering and winning a 1929 contest for mystery writers. At the time, she was working as a physical education teacher. Three years later, her passion for history and theater came together in the London hit *Richard of Bordeaux*. While shedding new light on Richard II, who ruled England from 1377 to 1399, the play also spoke to the contemporary situation in Europe, where Hitler had come to power and fears of war were mounting.

JOSEPHINE TEY (GORDON DAVIOT)

1897–1952

Josephine Tey and Gordon Daviot were the two pen names of Elizabeth Mackintosh, a Scottish-born writer who first went to England to study and teach physical education. Literary success came in 1929, with the publication of a novel called *The Man in the Queue*. Thereafter, Mackintosh devoted herself to writing, with literary achievements as divergent as the two pen names she adopted. Writing as Josephine Tey, she produced well-crafted detective novels that won the praise of critics and mystery fans alike. Using the pen name of Gordon Daviot, she created several hit plays for the London stage; the most famous of these, *Richard of Bordeaux* (1933), starred the famous British actor Sir John Gielgud and was successful enough to be brought overseas for a run in New York City.

Many of Tey's mysteries feature Alan Grant, an inspector with Scotland Yard. In *The Daughter of Time* (1951), Grant investigates one of English history's most brutal crimes, the murder of two young princes in the Tower of London, which most historians—and playwright William Shakespeare—lay at the feet of King Richard III. This book has been widely praised as one of the best mysteries of all time.

OTHER WORKS *Leith Sands and Other Short Plays, Miss Pym Disposes, The Singing Sands, Plays by Gordon Daviot*

Extended Reading

REFLECTING ON THEME
What Do You Think?

Ask students to look back at the list they wrote at the beginning of this part of Unit Two showing issues they care about. Suggest that they make similar lists for Madame and one other character in this play. How do the characters' lists compare with their own? After reading this play, do they want to change or add to their lists in any way?

OVERVIEW

Objectives

- To understand and appreciate a short story that explores a baseball fan's protest against changes in the game
- To identify and understand similes
- To express understanding of the story through a choice of writing forms, including a description, a TV commercial, and a newspaper article
- To extend understanding of the selection though a variety of multimodal and cross-curricular activities

Skills

THE WRITER'S STYLE
- Verb Tense

GRAMMAR
- Hyphens in compound adjectives

LITERARY CONCEPTS
- Simile
- Imagery

SPEAKING, LISTENING, AND VIEWING
- Play-by-play sportscast
- Film
- Group discussion
- Oral presentation

ALTERNATIVE

Previewing

Instead of writing about a time when they were motivated to take drastic action, students can choose partners and discuss their experiences.

Writing Connection

Discussion Prompts *Think of times when your strong feelings on a particular issue compelled you to take action. Describe your feelings and actions to your partner. Then listen as your partner describes his or her experience. If you need help getting started, use the following questions:*

- *What was the issue?*
- *What were your feelings?*
- *What did you do?*

As you read "The Thrill of the Grass," notice the issue that moved the narrator to uncharacteristic action.

PREVIEWING

FICTION

The Thrill of the Grass

W. P. Kinsella   Canada

Activating Prior Knowledge
PERSONAL CONNECTION

Baseball is often called America's national pastime. Why do you think so many people have such strong feelings about the game? Discuss your opinions with classmates.

Building Background
CULTURAL CONNECTION

Like other sports, the game of baseball has changed over the years. A major change occurred in 1965 when the city of Houston built its Astrodome, the first indoor baseball stadium. This stadium featured a nylon, grasslike carpet called AstroTurf® that served as a substitute for natural grass. Over the next few decades, variations of this artificial turf, which is padded and covers an asphalt surface, came to be used in other stadiums. People who support the use of artificial turf note that it holds up well in any weather and requires little maintenance. Critics, however, point out that its hard surface causes injuries and makes the ball bounce in unusual ways. They also regret the loss of natural grass, which they associate with pleasant memories of baseball in years past.

"The Thrill of the Grass" deals with the issue of artificial turf and the strong feelings that it elicits from fans. The story is set during the baseball strike of 1981, when, for 49 days, major-league players refused to play while they awaited a new contract.

Setting a Purpose
WRITING CONNECTION

In your notebook, write about a time when your strong feelings for a person or an issue motivated you to take drastic action, perhaps to do something that you would never have imagined yourself doing. As you read the story, compare your experience with that of the narrator.

AstroTurf® is a registered trademark of Southwest Recreational Industries, Inc.

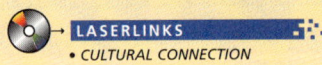
• CULTURAL CONNECTION

198   UNIT TWO   PART 1: CHALLENGING THE SYSTEM

PRINT AND MEDIA RESOURCES

UNIT TWO RESOURCE BOOK
Strategic Reading: Literature, p. 9
Vocabulary SkillBuilder, p. 10

GRAMMAR MINI-LESSONS
Transparencies, p. 31
Copymasters, p. 29

ACCESS FOR STUDENTS ACQUIRING ENGLISH
Selection Summaries
Reading Support

FORMAL ASSESSMENT
Selection Test, pp. 37–38
 Test Generator

 **AUDIO LIBRARY**
See Reference Card

 **LASERLINKS**
Cultural Connection

---

198   THE LANGUAGE OF LITERATURE   **TEACHER'S EDITION**

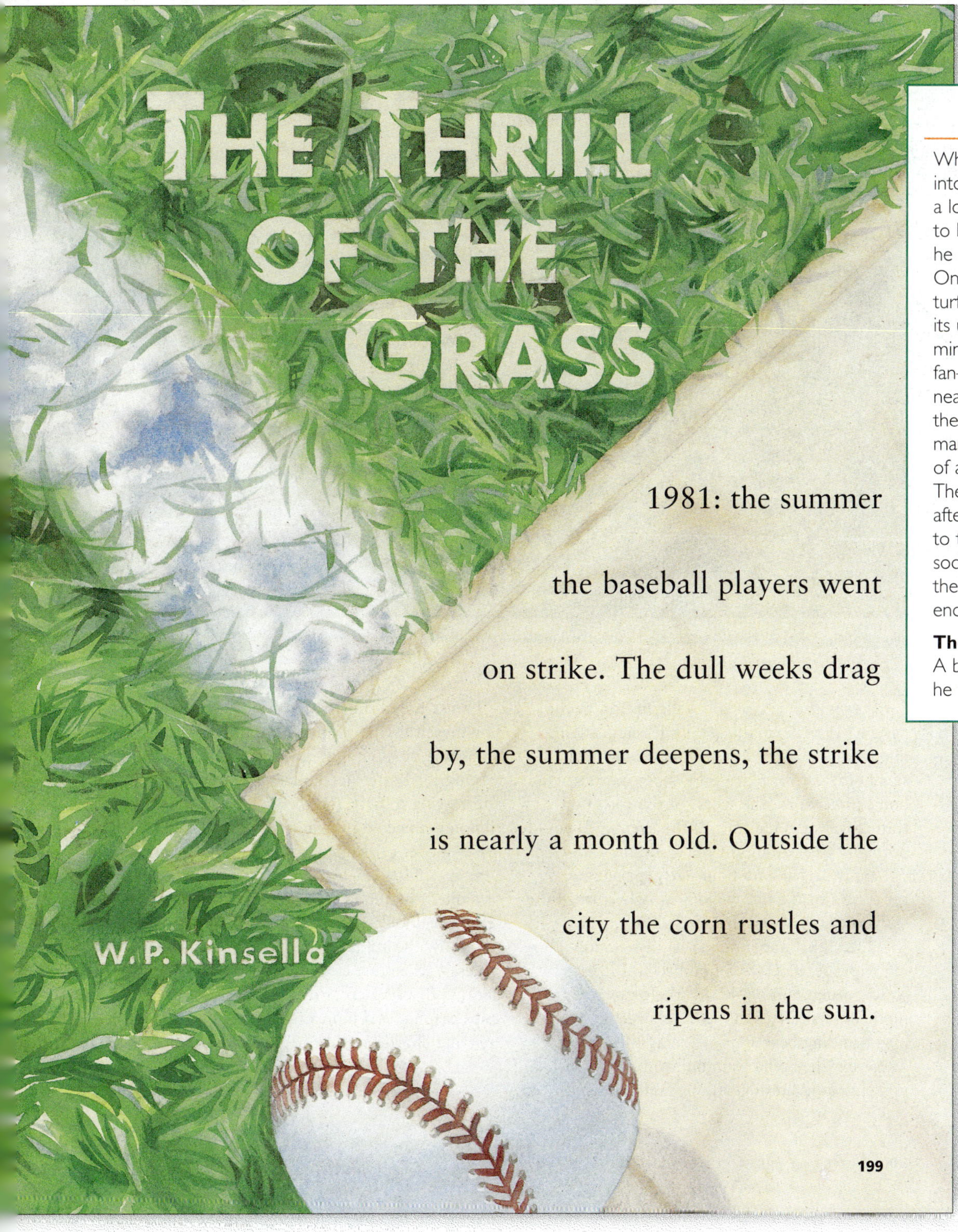

The Thrill of the Grass

W. P. Kinsella

1981: the summer the baseball players went on strike. The dull weeks drag by, the summer deepens, the strike is nearly a month old. Outside the city the corn rustles and ripens in the sun.

SUMMARY

When a strike turns the summer of 1981 into a season without major-league baseball, a lone fan visits an empty stadium. He longs to be inside, and as he walks along the fence, he discovers a door he is able to unlock. Once inside, he gazes at the prickly artificial turf that covers the field. As he muses about its ugliness, an idea forms and ripens in his mind. The man visits another avid baseball fan—a prominent man he has seen in a seat near his. He invites the man to meet him at the empty ballpark. That night, the businessman watches his new friend cut out a square of artificial turf and replace it with real sod. Then the two men plan a return trip. Night after night, they bring more friends, returning to the stadium with rakes, hoes, hoses, and sod. In this way, the fans rebuild the park of their dreams, just in time for the strike to end.

Thematic Link: *Challenging the System*
A baseball fan passionately protests changes he feels have marred the game.

CUSTOMIZING FOR
Students Acquiring English

- Use **ACCESS FOR STUDENTS ACQUIRING ENGLISH,** *Reading Support.*
- This selection includes dozens of technical baseball terms and challenging metaphorical language. Words and phrases such as *inning, mound, shortstop,* and *recalcitrant joints crackling like twigs* may pose problems for students. Have a baseball fan in your class explain the technical baseball terms in the story.

CULTURAL CONNECTION
The Old Ball Game Starting in the mid-1960s, many of the great old major league baseball parks were torn down and replaced with modern structures. This film shows these changes in baseball stadiums and helps students understand the feeling of loss many fans have about the way the game used to be.

Side A, Frame 4401

WORDS TO KNOW

affable (ăf'ə-bəl) *adj.* pleasant; easy to talk to (p. 206)
cohort (kō'hôrt') *n.* a member of the same group; a companion or an associate (p. 204)
contemplate (kŏn'təm-plāt') *v.* to look at attentively and thoughtfully; to consider carefully (p. 202)
divulge (dĭ-vŭlj') *v.* to make known (p. 206)
immaculate (ĭ-măk'yə-lĭt) *adj.* without stain; perfectly clean (p. 206)
imminent (ĭm'ə-nənt) *adj.* likely to happen soon (p. 207)
methodically (mə-thŏd'ĭ-kə-lē) *adv.* in a regular, systematic way (p. 206)
rampant (răm'pənt) *adj.* unchecked; unrestrained; out of control (p. 204)
skulk (skŭlk) *v.* to move in a way that is an attempt to escape notice (p. 206)
surreptitious (sûr'əp-tĭsh'əs) *adj.* done or made by secretive means; stealthy (p. 201)

STRATEGIC READING FOR
Less-Proficient Readers

To help students become immersed in the selection, ask them if they feel baseball has changed over the years. Do they think the sport is as popular as it used to be?

Set a Purpose Have students read to find where the narrator goes after work.

Use **UNIT TWO RESOURCE BOOK**, p. 9, for guidance in reading the selection.

CUSTOMIZING FOR
Gifted and Talented Students

Suggest to students that as they read the selection they note ways in which the author portrays the love of traditional baseball as a sort of religion for a select group of true-believing fans.

Possible responses:

Page 200 —"*Summer without baseball; a disruption to the psyche*"/ Baseball plays an important role in the narrator's psyche, or soul.

Page 203 —"*. . . holding it on the upturned palms of my hand like an offering*"/ Bringing real grass to the stadium is like making an offering.

Page 206 —"*. . . like marrying outside the faith, she has been converted to the third-base side*"/ Different sects within the baseball religion prefer different parts of the stands.

Page 206 —"*. . . my compatriots and I are involved in a* ritual *for* true believers"/ The words *ritual* and *true believers* suggest a religion.

Page 207 —"*. . . Our secret* rites *have been performed with love*"/ The word *rites* again suggests the work has religious significance.

Linking to History

Ⓐ Since its inception, major league baseball has endured about half a dozen strikes. The most serious of these was the 1994 strike, which lasted so long that, for the first time since 1904, no World Series was played. The 1994 strike was especially damaging because the season had been a thrilling one. Tony Gwynn might have been the first man since 1941 to bat .400, and Ken Griffey, Jr., and Matt Williams each might have broken Roger Maris's record of 61 home runs in a season.

Busch Stadium (1982), Jim Dow. Three-panel panorama from 8″ × 10″ color negatives.

Ⓐ Summer without baseball: a disruption to the psyche.[1] An unexplainable aimlessness engulfs me. I stay later and later each evening in the small office at the rear of my shop. Now, driving home after work, the worst of the rush hour traffic over, it is the time of the evening I would normally be heading for the stadium.

I enjoy arriving an hour early, parking in a far corner of the lot, walking slowly toward the stadium, rays of sun dropping softly over my shoulders like tangerine ropes, my shadow gliding with me, black as an umbrella. I like to watch young families beside their campers, the mothers in shorts, grilling hamburgers, their men drinking beer. I enjoy seeing little boys dressed in the home team uniform, barely toddling, clutching hotdogs in upraised hands.

I am a failed shortstop. As a young man, I saw myself diving to my left, graceful as a toppling tree, fielding high grounders like a cat leaping for butterflies, bracing my right foot and tossing to first, the throw true as if a steel ribbon connected my hand and the first baseman's glove. I dreamed of leading the American League in hitting—being inducted into the Hall of Fame. I batted .217 in my senior year of high school and averaged 1.3 errors per nine innings.

I know the stadium will be deserted; nevertheless I wheel my car down off the freeway, park, and walk across the silent lot, my footsteps rasping and mournful. Strangle-grass and creeping charlie are already inching up through

---

1. **psyche** (sī′kē): the human spirit or soul.

200   UNIT TWO   PART 1: CHALLENGING THE SYSTEM

Mini-Lesson: Speaking, Listening, and Viewing

PLAY-BY-PLAY SPORTSCAST Discuss with students how radio sportscasters have to meet a challenge not posed by television: they must describe the action on the field so vividly that listeners can envision it in their mind's eye. Vivid descriptions, plus voice tones that rise and fall, express emotions and keep listeners informed and interested. Have students recall dramatic techniques radio sportscasters use to keep the attention of the listening audience: for example, holding occasional interviews with retired players; providing brief biographies of the players on the field; and relating statistics and personal recollections of past games.

Application Have students work in pairs to play the roles of radio sportscasters reporting on the unusual activities of the baseball fans in "The Thrill of the Grass." Suggest that partners first skim the story and note major actions they will report. Invite partners to present their broadcasts to classmates.

200 THE LANGUAGE OF LITERATURE **TEACHER'S EDITION**

the gravel, surreptitious, surprised at their own ease. Faded bottle caps, rusted bits of chrome, an occasional paper clip, recede into the earth. I circle a ticket booth, sun-faded, empty, the door closed by an oversized padlock. I walk beside the tall, machinery-green, board fence. A half mile away a few cars hiss along the freeway; overhead a single-engine plane fizzes lazily. The whole place is silent as an empty classroom, like a house suddenly without children.

It is then that I spot the door-shape. I have to check twice to be sure it is there: a door cut in the deep green boards of the fence, more the promise of a door than the real thing, the kind of door, as children, we cut in the sides of cardboard boxes with our mother's paring knives. As I move closer, a golden circle of lock, like an acrimonious² eye, establishes its certainty.

I stand, my nose so close to the door I can smell the faint odour of paint, the golden eye of a lock inches from my own eyes. My desire to be inside the ballpark is so great that for the first time in my life I commit a criminal act. I have been a locksmith for over forty years. I take the small tools from the pocket of my jacket, and in less time than it would take a speedy runner to circle the bases I am inside the stadium. Though the ballpark is open-air, it smells

---

2. **acrimonious** (ăk´rə-mō´nē-əs): harsh; bitter.

WORDS TO KNOW

surreptitious (sûr´əp-tĭsh´əs) *adj.* done or made by secretive means; stealthy

CUSTOMIZING FOR
Students Acquiring English

I Ask students to use context clues to guess the meaning of *laid off*. *(forced to leave a job)*

STRATEGIC READING FOR
Less-Proficient Readers

E Have students explain where the narrator is and how he got there. *(He is inside the deserted baseball stadium; to get in, he picked a lock.)* Summarizing

• Ask what the narrator dislikes about the field, and why. *(the artificial turf, because it injures the players and alters the natural bounce of ground balls)* Noting Relevant Details

Set a Purpose Have students read to see what the narrator will do in the stadium.

Critical Thinking: SPECULATING

F Have students speculate about what the narrator's idea is. *(Possible response: to get rid of the artificial turf.)*

Literary Note

G The word *fan* is derived from the word *fanatic*, meaning "marked by excessive enthusiasm and often intense, uncritical devotion." Ask students to consider whether or not they think the narrator is fanatic toward baseball.

Literary Concept: POINT OF VIEW

H Ask students to identify the point of view in the story and tell how it has affected their feelings about the main character so far. *(The story is in the first-person point of view; this perspective allows us to share the narrator's innermost feelings about baseball.)*

---

of abandonment; the walkways and seating areas are cold as basements. I breathe the odours of rancid popcorn and wilted cardboard.

I The maintenance staff were laid off when the strike began. Synthetic grass does not need to be cut or watered. I stare down at the ball diamond, where just to the right of the pitcher's mound, a single weed, perhaps two inches high, stands defiant in the rain-pocked dirt.

The field sits breathless in the orangy glow of the evening sun. I stare at the potato-coloured earth of the infield, that wide, dun³ arc, surrounded by plastic grass. As I contemplate the prickly turf, which scorches the thighs and buttocks of a sliding player as if he were being seared by hot steel, it stares back in its uniform ugliness. The seams that send routinely hit ground balls veering at tortuous angles, are vivid, grey as scars.

E I remember the ballfields of my childhood, the outfields full of soft hummocks⁴ and brown-eyed gopher holes.

I stride down from the stands and walk out to the middle of the field. I touch the stubble that is called grass, take off my shoes, but find it is like walking on a row of toothbrushes. It was an evil day when they stripped the sod from this ballpark, cut it into yard-wide swathes,⁵ rolled it, memories and all, into great green-and-black cinnamon-roll shapes, trucked it away. Nature temporarily defeated. But Nature is patient.

F Over the next few days an idea forms within me, ripening, swelling, pushing everything else into a corner. It is like knowing a new, wonderful joke and not being able to share. I need an accomplice.

> BASEBALL IS MEANT TO BE PLAYED ON SUMMER EVENINGS AND SUNDAY AFTERNOONS, ON GRASS JUST CUT BY A HORSE-DRAWN MOWER.

I go to see a man I don't know personally, though I have seen his face peering at me from the financial pages of the local newspaper, and the *Wall Street Journal*, and I have been watching his profile at the baseball stadium, two boxes to the right of me, for several years.

He is a fan. Really a fan. When the weather is intemperate, or the game not close, the people around us disappear like flowers closing at sunset, but we are always there until the last pitch. I know he is a man who attends because of the beauty and mystery of the game, a man who can sit during the last of the ninth with the game decided innings ago, and draw joy from watching the first baseman adjust the angle of his glove as the pitcher goes into his windup.

G He, like me, is a first-base-side fan. I've always watched baseball from behind first base. The positions fans choose at sporting events are like politics, religion, or philosophy: a view of the world, a way of seeing the universe. They make no sense to anyone, have no basis in anything but stubbornness.

H I brought up my daughters to watch baseball from the first-base side. One lives in Japan and sends me box scores from Japanese newspapers, and Japanese baseball magazines with pictures of superstars politely bowing to one another. She has a season ticket in Yokohama;⁶ on the first-base side.

---

3. **dun:** brownish gray.
4. **hummocks:** low, rounded hills.
5. **swathes** (swŏths): strips as wide as the blade of a mowing machine.
6. **Yokohama** (yō′kə-ha′mə): a large city in Japan.

WORDS TO KNOW
contemplate (kŏn′təm-plāt′) *v.* to look at attentively and thoughtfully; to consider carefully

202

Mini-Lesson  Grammar

HYPHENS IN COMPOUND ADJECTIVES
Point out to students that Kinsella frequently forms compound adjectives to describe things and people in colorful detail. On the chalkboard, copy the highlighted passages from this page. Show students that hyphens are placed between the words that make up each compound adjective used before a noun.

Application Have students identify the compound adjective in each sentence and hyphenate it correctly.
1. I walk beside the tall, machinery green, board fence. *(machinery-green)*
2. I take from my belt a sickle shaped blade, the kind used for cutting carpet. *(sickle-shaped)*
3. Two men pass me, each carrying a grasshopper legged sprinkler. *(grasshopper-legged)*

The Writer's Craft
The Hyphen, pp. 812–813

"Tell him a baseball fan is here to see him," is all I will say to his secretary. His office is in a skyscraper, from which he can look out over the city to where the prairie rolls green as mountain water to the limits of the eye. I wait all afternoon in the artificially cool, glassy reception area with its yellow and mauve chairs, chrome and glass coffee tables. Finally, in the late afternoon, my message is passed along.

"I've seen you at the baseball stadium," I say, not introducing myself.

"Yes," he says. "I recognize you. Three rows back, about eight seats to my left. You have a red scorebook and you often bring your daughter . . ."

"Granddaughter. Yes, she goes to sleep in my lap in the late innings, but she knows how to calculate an ERA[7] and she's only in Grade 2."

"One of my greatest regrets," says this tall man, whose moustache and carefully styled hair are polar-bear white, "is that my grandchildren all live over a thousand miles away. You're very lucky. Now, what can I do for you?"

"I have an idea," I say. "One that's been creeping toward me like a first baseman when the bunt sign is on.[8] What do you think about artificial turf?"

"Hmmmf," he snorts, "that's what the strike should be about. Baseball is meant to be played on summer evenings and Sunday afternoons, on grass just cut by a horse-drawn mower," and we smile as our eyes meet.

"I've discovered the ballpark is open, to me anyway," I go on. "There's no one there while the strike is on. The wind blows through the high top of the grandstand, whining until the pigeons in the rafters flutter. It's lonely as a ghost town."

"And what is it you do there, alone with the pigeons?"

"I dream."

"And where do I come in?"

"You've always struck me as a man who dreams. I think we have things in common. I think you might like to come with me. I could show you what I dream, paint you pictures, suggest what might happen . . ."

He studies me carefully for a moment, like a pitcher trying to decide if he can trust the sign his catcher has just given him.

"Tonight?" he says. "Would tonight be too soon?"

"Park in the northwest corner of the lot about 1:00 a.m. There is a door about fifty yards to the right of the main gate. I'll open it when I hear you."

He nods.

I turn and leave.

he night is clear and cotton warm when he arrives. "Oh, my," he says, staring at the stadium turned chrome-blue by a full moon. "Oh, my," he says again, breathing in the faint odours of baseball, the reminder of fans and players not long gone.

"Let's go down to the field," I say. I am carrying a cardboard pizza box, holding it on the upturned palms of my hands, like an offering.

When we reach the field, he first stands on the mound, makes an awkward attempt at a windup, then does a little sprint from first to about half-way to second. "I think I know what you've brought," he says, gesturing toward the box, "but let me see anyway."

I open the box, in which rests a square foot of sod, the grass smooth and pure, cool as a swatch of satin, fragile as baby's hair.

"Ohhh," the man says, reaching out a finger to test the moistness of it. "Oh, I see."

---

7. **ERA:** earned run average for a baseball pitcher; that is, the average number of earned runs—runs scored without the aid of an error—a pitcher allows every nine innings.
8. **when the bunt sign is on:** when the coach has signaled the batter to tap at the pitched ball instead of swinging at it.

THE THRILL OF THE GRASS 203

 Mini-Lesson   The Writer's Style

VERB TENSE Point out that although the events of this story took place in the past, Kinsella has the narrator use verbs in the present tense to relate the tale. Tell students that, when used in this way, the verb tense is called the historical present tense. Ask students how Kinsella's use of the historical present tense affects their reactions to the story. *(Possible responses: Some students may say the historical present tense makes them feel like they are witnessing the events as they take place. Others might say it gives the story the feel of an oral tale, or that it helps communicate the narrator's involvement in the events.)*

Application Have students use the historical present tense to write a paragraph describing an event from their past.

Reteaching/Reinforcement
- *Grammar Handbook,* anthology pp. 1081–1083
- *Grammar Mini-Lessons* copymasters p. 29, transparencies p. 31

 The Writer's Craft

Verb Tenses, pp. 660–664

Critical Thinking:
MAKING INFERENCES

I Ask students why they think the narrator doesn't give his name to the secretary or to the businessman. *(Possible responses: Some students may say the businessman doesn't know him by name, but will recognize him by sight. Others may say he's sure the businessman is such a baseball fan that mentioning baseball will be enough.)*

Literary Concept: SIMILE

J Have students find the simile used to describe the development of the narrator's idea and tell why it is appropriate for the story. *(The idea is likened to a first baseman creeping forward. Students who know baseball may point out that when the first baseman thinks the batter will bunt, he or she moves slowly toward the plate, preparing to make a play on the ball.)*

Literary Concept:
CHARACTERIZATION

K Ask students to discuss what the businessman's reaction here reveals about him. *(Possible responses: He holds very traditional views about baseball; he loves the game and doesn't want it changed.)*

Critical Thinking:
MAKING JUDGMENTS

L Ask students to consider whether or not it's realistic that unauthorized people could enter the stadium undetected two nights in a row. *(Possible responses: yes, because the maintenance personnel have been let go; no, because a guard would probably be on duty)* Ask students if they think elements of fantasy are beginning to enter the story? *(Accept all reasonable responses.)*

STRATEGIC READING FOR
Less-Proficient Readers

M Have students discuss what the narrator does in the stadium.

- Why did the narrator decide to replace the artificial turf? *(because it was a concrete symbol of what had gone wrong with the game)* **Drawing Conclusions**

- What do the narrator and the businessman plan to do? *(They plan to bring many others to help replace the artificial turf.)* **Summarizing**

Set a Purpose Invite students to read on to find out whether the plan works out.

CUSTOMIZING FOR
Multiple Learning Styles

N **Logical-Mathematical Learners** Explain to students that each major league baseball diamond is a square of 90 feet per side. Most of the infield, or the area inside the diamond, is covered with grass or artificial turf. A typical field has a dirt path that extends for three feet on either side of each baseline. Near the center of the infield, the pitcher's mound, which is a circle measuring 18 feet in diameter, is also covered with dirt. Have students draw plans of a baseball infield and work out how long it is likely to take Kinsella's characters to re-sod the infield alone. *(Students' responses will vary depending on how many people they estimate will participate. In general, the area to be covered with sod would be about 6,800 square feet.)*

Literary Concept: IMAGERY

O Ask students to name the senses to which the descriptions in this passage appeal. Then have them cite specific images for each sense. *(hearing—"snug thud"; "sizzle like frying onions"; "silent as a snake"; touch—"open the door"; sight—"grasshopper-legged sprinkler"; "silver sparkler in the moonlight")*

We walk across the field, the harsh, prickly turf making the bottoms of my feet tingle, to the left-field corner where, in the angle formed by the foul line and the warning track, I lay down the square foot of sod. "That's beautiful," my friend says, kneeling beside me, placing his hand, fingers spread wide, on the verdant[9] square, leaving a print faint as a veronica.[10]

I take from my belt a sickle-shaped blade, the kind used for cutting carpet. I measure along the edge of the sod, dig the point in and pull carefully toward me. There is a ripping sound, like tearing an old bed sheet. I hold up the square of artificial turf like something freshly killed, while all the time digging the sharp point into the packed earth I have exposed. I replace the sod lovingly, covering the newly bared surface.

"A protest," I say.

"But it could be more," the man replies.

"I hoped you'd say that. It could be. If you'd like to come back . . ."

"Tomorrow night?"

"Tomorrow night would be fine. But there will be an admission charge . . ."

"A square of sod?"

"A square of sod two inches thick . . ."

"Of the same grass?"

"Of the same grass. But there's more."

"I suspected as much."

"You must have a friend . . ."

"Who would join us?"

"Yes."

"I have two. Would that be all right?"

"I trust your judgment."

"My father. He's over eighty," my friend says. "You might have seen him with me once or twice. He lives over fifty miles from here, but if I call him, he'll come. And my friend . . ."

"If they pay their admission, they'll be welcome . . ."

M "And *they* may have friends . . ."

"Indeed they may. But what will we do with this?" I say, holding up the sticky-backed square of turf, which smells of glue and fabric.

"We could mail them anonymously to baseball executives, politicians, clergymen."

"Gentle reminders not to tamper with Nature."

We dance toward the exit, <u>rampant</u> with excitement.

"You will come back? You'll bring others?"

"Count on it," says my friend.

They do come, those trusted friends, and friends of friends, each making a live, green deposit. At first, a tiny row of sod squares begins to inch along toward left-centre field. The next night even more people arrive, the following night more again, and the night after there is positively a crowd. Those who come once seem always to return accompanied by friends, occasionally a son or young brother, but mostly men my age or older, for we are the ones who remember the grass.

Night after night the pilgrimage continues. The first night I stand inside the deep green door, listening. I hear a vehicle stop; hear a car door close with a snug thud. I open the door when the sound of soft-soled shoes on gravel tells me it is time. The door swings silent as a snake. We nod curt greetings to each other. Two men pass me, each carrying a grasshopper-legged sprinkler. Later, each sprinkler will sizzle like frying onions as it wheels, a silver sparkler in the moonlight.

During the nights that follow, I stand sentinel-like at the top of the grandstand, watching as my <u>cohorts</u> arrive. Old men walking across a parking lot in a row, in the dark, carrying

---

9. **verdant** (vûr′dnt): covered with green growth.
10. **a print faint as a veronica** (və-rŏn′ĭ-kə): a simile referring to the image of Jesus' face supposedly left on the handkerchief offered to him by Saint Veronica for wiping away his blood on the way to the crucifixion.

WORDS TO KNOW
rampant (răm′pənt) *adj.* unchecked; unrestrained; out of control
cohort (kō′hôrt′) *n.* a member of the same group; a companion or an associate

204

Mini-Lesson · Literary Concepts

REVIEWING IMAGERY Remind students that imagery refers to words and phrases that appeal to the reader's senses, often in a startling way.

Application Have students think about the sense that each of these images appeals to.

1. . . . her toast-warm hand on my cold thigh. *(touch)*
2. Occasionally the moon finds a knife blade . . . *(sight)*
3. Everyone should be humming "Take Me Out to the Ball Game." *(hearing)*
4. . . . the smell of water, of sod, of sweat, small perfumes in the air. *(smell)*

Ask students to find and discuss other examples of vivid imagery in the story.

---

204 THE LANGUAGE OF LITERATURE TEACHER'S EDITION

Michael W. Straus (1961), Fairfield Porter. Oil on canvas, 45 3/16" × 39 1/2".

Art Note

Michael W. Straus by Fairfield Porter
The artist Fairfield Porter (1907–), who was a cousin of the writer T. S. Eliot and brother of the nature photographer Eliot Porter, spent much of his life in the company of writers, artists, and critics in New York City, Southampton, Long Island, and Great Spruce Head Island, Maine. The artist's subjects were always himself, his friends and family, and the landscapes he loved. He painted these quintessentially American subjects in rich, luminous colors. In his art, he followed the credo "Make everything more beautiful."

Reading the Art *How does this figure compare to your mental image of the narrator?*

Multicultural Perspectives

THE NATIONAL PASTIME Just as baseball is something between a sport and a religion to Kinsella's characters, cricket is the national game and the national passion of the English. Although cricket dates back to the Middle Ages, it achieved its current preeminence during the 18th century. English soldiers and others took cricket with them to South Africa, India, Australia, and the Caribbean, where it has remained popular. Some elements of cricket are familiar to baseball fans; cricket has its equivalents of baseball's pitchers, batters, and bases (called bowlers, batsmen, and wickets), and one team fields while the other bats. However, cricket uses a different ball and differently shaped bats from those used in baseball, and the rules are so different that baseball fans can find their first cricket match bewildering.

Literary Concept: MOOD

P Have students discuss the mood Kinsella creates in describing the workers' nightly ritual. *(Possible responses: Words such as* slipped away *and* skulked *evoke a mood of stealth. Comparing the arriving men to locomotive wheels makes the workers seem like a machine. The mood is one of hushed mystery and otherworldliness.)*

Literary Concept: SIMILE

Q Have students discuss the similes that compare the stadium to a mountain and the light standards to sunflowers. How do these similes reflect the narrator's feelings about baseball? *(The similes suggest that, to the narrator, baseball is just as natural as parts of the landscape.)*

Critical Thinking: MAKING INFERENCES

R Ask students to explain what problem the narrator and the other men are having. *(Possible response: Their wives and families are growing suspicious of them since they are leaving their houses late every night without explanation.)*

STRATEGIC READING FOR
Less-Proficient Readers

S Have students discuss whether they think the narrator's original plan is likely to become a reality.

- Why might the narrator's plan succeed? *(He has gotten help from many other fans.)* Making Inferences

- Why might the plan fail? *(The strike might be settled before the grass is all planted; stadium guards might catch the fans in the act.)* Making Inferences

Set a Purpose Have students complete the story to find out whether the narrator and his friends are able to keep their work a secret.

P coiled hoses, looking like the many wheels of a locomotive, old men who have slipped away from their homes, skulked down their sturdy sidewalks, breathing the cool, grassy, after-midnight air. They have left behind their sleeping, grey-haired women, their immaculate bungalows, their manicured lawns. They continue to walk across the parking lot, while occasionally a soft wheeze, a nibbling, breathy sound like an old horse might make, divulges their humanity. They move methodically toward the baseball stadium which hulks against the moon-blue sky like a small mountain. Beneath the tint of starlight, the tall light standards which rise above the fences and grandstand glow purple, necks bent forward, like sunflowers heavy with seed.

Q

My other daughter lives in this city, is married to a fan, but one who watches baseball from behind third base. And like marrying outside the faith, she has been converted to the third-base side. They have their own season tickets, twelve rows up just to the outfield side of third base. I love her, but I don't trust her enough to let her in on my secret.

I could trust my granddaughter, but she is too young. At her age she shouldn't have to face such responsibility. I remember my own daughter, the one who lives in Japan, remember her at nine, all knees, elbows and missing teeth—remember peering in her room, seeing her asleep, a shower of well-thumbed baseball cards scattered over her chest and pillow.

I haven't been able to tell my wife—it is like

IT IS LIKE MY COMPATRIOTS AND I ARE INVOLVED IN A RITUAL FOR TRUE BELIEVERS ONLY.

my compatriots and I are involved in a ritual for true believers only. Maggie, who knew me when I still dreamed of playing professionally myself—Maggie, after over half a lifetime together, comes and sits in my lap in the comfortable easy chair which has adjusted through the years to my thickening shape, just as she has. I love to hold the lightness of her, her tongue exploring my mouth, gently as a baby's finger.

"Where do you go?" she asks sleepily when I crawl into bed at dawn.

I mumble a reply. I know she doesn't sleep well when I'm gone. I can feel her body rhythms change as I slip out of bed after midnight.

"Aren't you too old to be having a change of life," she says, placing her toast-warm hand on my cold thigh.

I am not the only one with this problem.

"I'm developing a reputation," whispers an affable man at the ballpark. "I imagine any number of private investigators following any number of cars across the city. I imagine them creeping about the parking lot, shining penlights on licence plates, trying to guess what we're up to. Think of the reports they must prepare. I wonder if our wives are disappointed that we're not out discoing with frizzy-haired teenagers?"

Night after night, virtually no words are spoken. Each man seems to know his assignment. Not all bring sod. Some carry rakes, some hoes, some hoses, which, when joined together,

R

S

WORDS TO KNOW	**skulk** (skŭlk) *v.* to move in a way that is an attempt to escape notice
	immaculate (ĭ-măk′yə-lĭt) *adj.* without stain; perfectly clean
	divulge (dĭ-vŭlj′) *v.* to make known
	methodically (mə-thŏd′ĭ-kə-lē) *adv.* in a regular, systematic way
	affable (ăf′ə-bəl) *adj.* pleasant; easy to talk to

snake across the infield and outfield, dispensing the blessing of water. Others cradle in their arms bags of earth for building up the infield to meet the thick, living sod.

I often remain high in the stadium, looking down on the men moving over the earth, dark as ants, each sodding, cutting, watering, shaping. Occasionally the moon finds a knife blade as it trims the sod or slices away a chunk of artificial turf, and tosses the reflection skyward like a bright ball. My body tingles. There should be symphony music playing. Everyone should be humming "America the Beautiful."

Toward dawn, I watch the men walking away in groups, like small patrols of soldiers, carrying instead of arms, the tools and utensils which breathe life back into the arid ballfield.

Row by row, night by night, we lay the little squares of sod, moist as chocolate cake with green icing. Where did all the sod come from? I picture many men, in many parts of the city, surreptitiously cutting chunks out of their own lawns in the leafy midnight darkness, listening to the uncomprehending protests of their wives the next day—pretending to know nothing of it—pretending to have called the police to investigate.

When the strike is over, I know we will all be here to watch the workouts, to hear the recalcitrant[11] joints crackling like twigs after the forced inactivity. We will sit in our regular seats, scattered like popcorn throughout the stadium, and we'll nod as we pass on the way to the exits, exchange secret smiles, proud as new fathers.

For me, the best part of all will be the surprise. I feel like a magician who has gestured hypnotically and produced an elephant from thin air. I know that I am not alone in my wonder. I know that rockets shoot off in half-a-hundred chests—the excitement of birthday mornings, Christmas eves, and hometown doubleheaders, boils within each of my conspirators. Our secret rites[12] have been performed with love, like delivering a valentine to a sweetheart's door in that blue-steel span of morning just before dawn.

Players and management are meeting around the clock. A settlement is <u>imminent</u>. I have watched the stadium covered square foot by square foot until it looks like green graph paper. I have stood and felt the cool odours of the grass rise up and touch my face. I have studied the lines between each small square, watched those lines fade until they were visible to my eyes alone, then not even to them.

What will the players think, as they straggle into the stadium and find the miracle we have created? The old-timers will raise their heads like ponies, as far away as the parking lot, when the thrill of the grass reaches their nostrils. And, as they dress, they'll recall sprawling in the lush fields of childhood, the grass as cool as a mother's hand on a forehead.

---

11. **recalcitrant** (rĭ-kăl´sĭ-trənt): showing stubborn resistance.
12. **rites:** ceremonies.

WORDS TO KNOW
imminent (ĭm´ə-nənt) *adj.* likely to happen soon

Critic's ★ Corner

The critic William French makes the following comment about Kinsella's baseball novels.

> His novels are animated by a light-hearted wit and bubbling imagination. . . . To be obsessed with baseball is to be touched by grace in Kinsella's universe.

Ask students how this comment might apply to "The Thrill of the Grass," and whether they agree with French's assessment of Kinsella's writing.

Stretching at First (about 1976), John Dobbs. Oil on canvas, 36″ × 40″, collection of Gilbert Kinney, Washington, D.C.

"Goodbye, goodbye," we say at the gate, the smell of water, of sod, of sweat, small perfumes in the air. Our secrets are safe with each other. We go our separate ways.

Alone in the stadium in the last chill darkness before dawn, I drop to my hands and knees in the centre of the outfield. My palms are sodden. Water touches the skin between my spread fingers. I lower my face to the silvered grass, which, wonder of wonders, already has the ephemeral[13] odours of baseball about it. ❖

---

13. **ephemeral** (ĭ-fĕm′ər-əl): short-lived; passing quickly.

208 UNIT TWO PART 1: CHALLENGING THE SYSTEM

COMPREHENSION CHECK

1. How does the narrator get into the stadium? *(He picks a lock.)*
2. Why is the stadium deserted? *(The players are on strike and the maintenance people have been laid off.)*
3. What do the narrator and the others do at the stadium? *(rip up the artificial turf and plant real grass)*
4. What does the narrator finally accomplish? *(With the help of others, he restores beauty, in the form of natural sod, to the field.)*

RESPONDING OPTIONS

FROM PERSONAL RESPONSE TO CRITICAL ANALYSIS

REFLECT
1. Do you approve of the action taken by the narrator and his friends? Explain your opinion in your notebook.

RETHINK
2. Why do you think the narrator and his friends take such drastic action?
   Consider
   Close Textual Reading
   - your discussion for the Personal Connection on page 198 about the feelings associated with baseball
   - how the narrator describes his feelings
   - the memories that the men associate with natural grass
   - what the men might hope to accomplish

3. When the narrator chooses his first accomplice, how does he know this man will share his dream?

Thematic Link
4. Do you agree with the story's message about the value of challenging the system? Cite details to support your opinion.

RELATE
5. Do you think what happens in this story could really happen? Explain your position.

6. Do you think that such spectator sports as baseball, basketball, and football play a positive role in the lives of their fans? Explain your opinion.

Multimodal Learning
ANOTHER PATHWAY

Cooperative Learning
Conduct a mock trial of the lawbreakers in this story. Assign the roles of prosecutor, defense attorney, judge, defendants, and witnesses such as police, stadium staff, turf company officials, and the team owner. The rest of the class can serve as the jury.

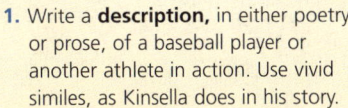

QUICKWRITES

1. Write a **description**, in either poetry or prose, of a baseball player or another athlete in action. Use vivid similes, as Kinsella does in his story.

2. Write a **television commercial** to promote the game of baseball. Try to convey "the beauty and mystery of the game" that so captivated the narrator and his fellow conspirators.

3. Write a **newspaper article** reporting the discovery of real grass at the ballpark. Include the reactions of players, fans, and others.

 **PORTFOLIO** Save your writing. You may want to use it later as a springboard to a piece for your portfolio.

LITERARY CONCEPTS

A **simile** is a figure of speech, usually containing the word *like* or *as*, that makes a comparison between two unlike things that nevertheless have something in common. In "The Thrill of the Grass," for example, the narrator describes his shadow as being "black as an umbrella."

Divide into teams to find other similes in the story. List the similes on the board, then discuss why Kinsella might have chosen to use so many similes in the story.

THE THRILL OF THE GRASS 209

From Personal Response to Critical Analysis

1. Accept all reasonable responses. Some students may approve the actions as showing the courage to do what one believes is right; others may disapprove because the actions are illegal.
2. Possible responses: Their love for baseball is like a religion; every detail of the game has special significance. They may be taking things into their own hands because they are frustrated by the strike. They want baseball to be like it was.
3. The narrator recognizes that the businessman is a long-time fan who probably loves the game "the way it used to be."
4. Accept all reasonable, well supported responses.
5. Many students will say that the story events are unlikely, since most stadiums take security precautions, and baseball fields in major league ballparks are too large for a few men to re-sod within a few weeks.
6. Accept all reasonable responses.

Literary Links

Have students discuss who took greater personal risks in challenging the system—Kinsella's narrator, or Madame in *The Pen of My Aunt*?

Another Pathway

Cooperative Learning Students should engage in collaborative planning to assign the various roles.

Rubric
3 Full Accomplishment Students grasp the core issues and work as a group to present and resolve them.
2 Substantial Accomplishment Students seem to grasp the core issues but have some difficulty making them clear.
1 Little or Partial Accomplishment Students display little understanding of the issues and are unable to define and resolve them.

Literary Concepts

Similes in this story include the following examples from page 207:
- men ... dark as ants
- sod ... moist as chocolate cake
- joints crackling like twigs
- we will sit ... scattered like popcorn
- stadium looks like green graph paper
- grass as cool as a mother's hand

Some students might say that likening baseball to so many other aspects of life shows how interwoven baseball is in the narrator's own life, or how integral a part of society baseball is.

QuickWrites

1. Remind students to write similes that appeal to the various senses.
2. Point out that the video footage that makes up the TV commercial should work in conjunction with the accompanying text.
3. Encourage students to make up quotes that reveal the likely reactions of fans and players.

The Writer's Craft
Character Sketch, pp. 78–82
Advertising, pp. 511–516
Elaboration, pp. 364–368

THE LANGUAGE OF LITERATURE Teacher's Edition 209

Words to Know

1. c	6. b
2. b	7. d
3. a	8. b
4. a	9. b
5. c	10. c

Reteaching/Reinforcement
- *Unit Two Resource Book*, p. 10

W. P. KINSELLA

Of all the traits needed to write fiction—passion, ability, imagination, and stamina—W. P. Kinsella considers the last most important. "Ninety-eight percent of writing is accomplished by perspiration," he notes. This echoes Thomas Edison's remark that genius is 1 percent inspiration and 99 percent perspiration. Kinsella published his first story at age 42 and has written 200 short stories and more than 15 books, including *Box Socials* (1991). He makes his home in White Rock, British Columbia.

Across the Curriculum

Mathematics For students who may not know, point out that a batter's average is found by dividing the total number of hits by the number of times at bat minus walks. For example, if a batter batted 30 times and got seven hits and four walks, his or her batting average would be 7 divided by 26 (30 minus 4), which works out to be .269. A pitcher's earned run average is generally determined by dividing the total number of earned runs scored against him or her by the total number of innings pitched and multiplying that number by nine. (An earned run is made without the benefit of an error.)

Multimodal Learning

ALTERNATIVE ACTIVITIES

1. Conduct a **survey,** asking people whether they think baseball deserves to be known as our national pastime. Tabulate the results of your survey on a bar graph or a circle graph.

2. View the film *Field of Dreams,* based on Kinsella's novel *Shoeless Joe.* Then present an **oral movie review** similar to those provided by television movie critics. In your review, include comparisons with "The Thrill of the Grass."

CRITIC'S CORNER

One reviewer described W. P. Kinsella's novel *Shoeless Joe* as "not so much about baseball as . . . about dreams, magic, life." How might this quote apply to "The Thrill of the Grass"?

WORDS TO KNOW

Write the letter of the word that is not similar in meaning to the other words in each numbered set.

1. (a) sneaky, (b) **surreptitious,** (c) candid, (d) secret
2. (a) **contemplate,** (b) ignore, (c) examine, (d) observe
3. (a) restrained, (b) **rampant,** (c) uncontrollable, (d) wild
4. (a) outsider, (b) colleague, (c) **cohort,** (d) companion
5. (a) **skulk,** (b) slink, (c) stoop, (d) prowl
6. (a) spotless, (b) smeared, (c) stainless, (d) **immaculate**
7. (a) tell, (b) reveal, (c) **divulge,** (d) disguise
8. (a) **methodically,** (b) carelessly, (c) systematically, (d) deliberately
9. (a) friendly, (b) distant, (c) **affable,** (d) pleasant
10. (a) probable, (b) **imminent,** (c) delayed, (d) approaching

Multimodal Learning

ACROSS THE CURRICULUM

Mathematics Conduct a math workshop, showing how math applies to baseball. For example, you might explain the narrator's .217 batting average, a pitcher's ERA, and other statistics. Define the baseball terms so that classmates who are not fans will understand.

W. P. KINSELLA

1935–

Success did not come easily to William Patrick Kinsella. Born in Edmonton, Alberta, Canada, Kinsella says that he always thought of himself as a writer, though he wrote more than 50 stories before getting published. He also worked at various odd jobs, such as running his own pizza restaurant, managing a credit agency, and driving a taxicab. Kinsella did not begin college until he was in his 30s.

Kinsella grew up loving the game of baseball, though he was a poor player himself. He penned his first baseball story, a murder mystery called "Diamond Doom," when he was in the eighth grade. Kinsella published his first collection of baseball stories, *Shoeless Joe Jackson Comes to Iowa,* in 1980. He expanded the title story into his award-winning novel *Shoeless Joe* (1982), which garnered much attention when it was adapted and produced as the 1989 Hollywood movie *Field of Dreams.*

OTHER WORKS *Dance Me Outside, The Alligator Report, The Iowa Baseball Confederacy, The Further Adventures of Slugger McBatt*   Extended Reading

210   UNIT TWO   PART 1: CHALLENGING THE SYSTEM

Alternative Activities

1. Remind students to write survey questions that are as objective as possible to avoid influencing responses in any one way.

   Provide the following examples:

   Influencing responses: Do you agree that baseball deserves to be known as our national pastime?

   Leaving responses open: Does baseball deserve to be called our national pastime?

2. Ask students to think of an opening for their review that will grab their listeners' attention. Remind them to include some information about the plot without giving the ending away. Also urge them to include examples and details that support their opinions about the movie.

PREVIEWING

FICTION

The Balek Scales
Heinrich Böll   (hĭn′rĭk bœl)   Germany

Activating Prior Knowledge
PERSONAL CONNECTION

What does the word *justice* mean to you? Explore the meaning of the word and its associations by filling out a diagram like the one shown. Then compare your ideas with those of your classmates.

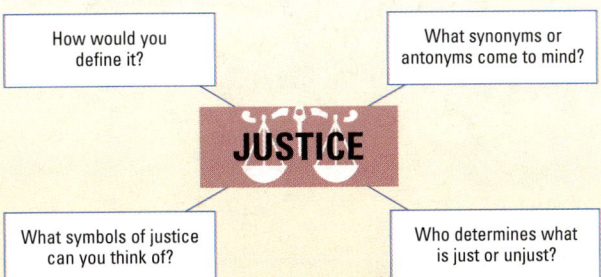

- How would you define it?
- What synonyms or antonyms come to mind?
- What symbols of justice can you think of?
- Who determines what is just or unjust?

JUSTICE

Building Background
HISTORICAL CONNECTION

This story takes place in central Europe around 1900. In that era, much of Europe was characterized by a strict social hierarchy in which a person's social position was largely determined by birth. At the top of the social ladder were such royal figures as kings or emperors, followed by counts and barons and other members of the aristocracy who passed their titles down to their children. Ranking below the aristocracy were wealthy landowners who had no titles but who often hoped to acquire them as a reward for service or influence. At the bottom of the social ladder were the common people, the vast bulk of the population.

In the story you are about to read, the Baleks, a wealthy family, have controlled the lives of the common people for five generations, even to the point of creating laws to control the system of justice. The Baleks live in an elegant chateau (shă-tō′), or country house, and own much of the land in the area. Most of the common people work on Balek land, crushing and drying flax plants used to make fabric.

A European chateau. Copyright © Charlie Waite / Tony Stone Images

Active Reading/Setting a Purpose
READING CONNECTION

Making Predictions Predicting is a useful reading strategy because it helps you to focus your attention and to sharpen your perceptiveness. Based on the title, "The Balek Scales," and on the information provided on this page, what do you predict about the role of justice in this story? As you read, compare your prediction with what actually happens.

Using Your Reading Log Use your reading log to record your responses to the questions inserted throughout the selection. Also jot down other thoughts and feelings that come to you as you read.

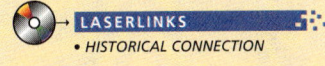
LASERLINKS
• HISTORICAL CONNECTION

211

OVERVIEW

Objectives

- To understand and appreciate a short story that explores what happens when a young boy protests an injustice
- To enrich reading by using active reading strategies
- To identify and understand tone
- To express understanding of the selection through a choice of writing forms, including a sermon, an editorial, and a journal entry
- To extend understanding of the selection through a variety of multimodal and cross-curricular activities

Skills

READING SKILLS/ STRATEGIES
- Predicting
- Clarifying

THE WRITER'S STYLE
- Sentence length and structure

GRAMMAR
- Colons

LITERARY CONCEPTS
- Tone
- Setting

SPEAKING, LISTENING, AND VIEWING
- Dramatic reading
- Group discussion
- Oral presentation

HISTORICAL CONNECTION
Rich and Poor in Europe, Around 1900 A strict social hierarchy existed in central Europe at the turn of the 20th century. These photographs show the two ends of the social spectrum—the aristocrats and the fieldworkers.

Side A, Frame 49387

PRINT AND MEDIA RESOURCES

UNIT TWO RESOURCE BOOK
Strategic Reading: Literature, p. 13
Vocabulary SkillBuilder, p. 14

WRITING MINI-LESSONS
Transparencies, p. 50

ACCESS FOR STUDENTS ACQUIRING ENGLISH
Selection Summaries
Reading Support

FORMAL ASSESSMENT
Selection Test, pp. 00–00
 Test Generator

 AUDIO LIBRARY
See Reference Card

 **LASERLINKS**
Historical Connection

THE LANGUAGE OF LITERATURE TEACHER'S EDITION **211**

SUMMARY

The narrator recalls the small village where his grandfather and most everyone else worked in flax sheds. When the children were not in school, they picked mushrooms, herbs, and hayflowers, which they sold to the Balek family, who owned the surrounding woods. The narrator notes that only the Baleks were allowed to own a scale. Raised to the aristocracy, the Baleks showed their graciousness by giving a quarter pound of coffee to each family at Christmastime. But one year, when the grandfather was still a boy, he learned that the scales were off by 55 grams, in favor of the Baleks. He shared the news with his neighbors, who rebelled, even stealing the scales and logbook. Gendarmes appeared, shooting and stabbing those in their way and threatening the people with prison. The grandfather's family was forced to leave the village. They became basket weavers, traveling the country roads and telling their tale of injustice to the few who would listen.

Thematic Link: Challenging the System
A child learns that challenging the system can have dire consequences.

CUSTOMIZING FOR
Students Acquiring English

- Use **ACCESS FOR STUDENTS ACQUIRING ENGLISH,** *Reading Support.*
- This selection contains many long, compound and complex sentences which may prove difficult to students. Suggest that students view each long sentence as a series of short ones, joined together by a comma and the word *and* or by semicolons or colons. You may want to read certain sentences aloud to help students work their way through them.

STRATEGIC READING FOR
Less-Proficient Readers

Set a Purpose Have students read to discover how the Baleks administer their land and their tenants.

Use **UNIT TWO RESOURCE BOOK,** p. 13, for guidance in reading the selection.

The Balek Scales

Heinrich Böll

Where my grandfather came from, most of the people lived by working in the flax sheds. For five generations they had been breathing in the dust which rose from the crushed flax stalks, letting themselves be killed off by slow degrees, a race of long-suffering, cheerful people who ate goat cheese, potatoes, and now and then a rabbit; in the evening they would sit at home spinning and knitting; they sang, drank mint tea and were happy.

WORDS TO KNOW

antiquated (ăn′tĭ-kwā′tĭd) *adj.* old-fashioned; outmoded (p. 213)
flout (flout) *v.* to show contempt for; to scorn (p. 214)
forlorn (fər-lôrn′) *adj.* appearing sad or lonely because one has been left alone (p. 218)

meager (mē′gər) *adj.* lacking quantity, fullness, strength, or fertility; feeble; scanty (p. 213)
preside (prĭ-zīd′) *v.* to hold the chief position of authority or control (p. 213)

212 THE LANGUAGE OF LITERATURE TEACHER'S EDITION

During the day they would carry the flax stalks to the antiquated machines, with no protection from the dust and at the mercy of the heat which came pouring out of the drying kilns.¹ Each cottage contained only one bed, standing against the wall like a closet and reserved for the parents, while the children slept all around the room on benches. In the morning the room would be filled with the odor of thin soup; on Sundays there was stew, and on feast days² the children's faces would light up with pleasure as they watched the black acorn coffee turning paler and paler from the milk their smiling mother poured into their coffee mugs.

The parents went off early to the flax sheds, the housework was left to the children: they would sweep the room, tidy up, wash the dishes and peel the potatoes, precious pale-yellow fruit whose thin peel had to be produced afterwards to dispel any suspicion of extravagance or carelessness.

As soon as the children were out of school, they had to go off into the woods and, depending on the season, gather mushrooms and herbs: woodruff and thyme, caraway, mint and foxglove, and in summer, when they had brought in the hay from their meager fields, they gathered hayflowers. A kilo³ of hayflowers was worth one pfennig,⁴ and they were sold by the apothecaries⁵ in town for twenty pfennigs a kilo to highly strung ladies. The mushrooms were highly prized: they fetched twenty pfennigs a kilo and were sold in the shops in town for one mark twenty.⁶ The children would crawl deep into the green darkness of the forest during the autumn when dampness drove the mushrooms out of the soil, and almost every family had its own places where it gathered mushrooms, places which were handed down in whispers from generation to generation.

The woods belonged to the Baleks, as well as the flax sheds, and in my grandfather's village the Baleks had a chateau, and the wife of the head of the family had a little room next to the dairy where mushrooms, herbs and hayflowers were weighed and paid for. There on the table stood the great Balek scales, an old-fashioned, ornate bronze-gilt⁷ contraption, which my grandfather's grandparents had already faced when they were children, their grubby hands holding their little baskets of mushrooms, their paper bags of hayflowers, breathlessly watching the number of weights Frau⁸ Balek had to throw on the scale before the swinging pointer came to rest exactly over the black line, that thin line of justice which had to be redrawn every year. Then Frau Balek would take the big book covered in brown leather, write down the weight, and pay out the money, pfennigs or ten-pfennig pieces and very, very occasionally, a mark. And when my grandfather was a child, there was a big glass jar of lemon drops standing there, the kind that cost one mark a kilo, and when Frau Balek—whichever one happened to be presiding over the little room—was in a good mood, she would put her hand into this jar and give each

---

1. **kilns** (kĭlnz): ovens, used here to dry the flax.
2. **feast days**: holidays, especially religious holidays honoring saints.
3. **kilo** (kē′lō): short for *kilogram*, a metric measure equal to 1,000 grams, or about 2.2 pounds.
4. **pfennig** (fĕn′ĭg): a coin equal to a hundredth of a deutsche mark, the basic unit of German currency. The word *pfennig* is related to the English *penny*.
5. **apothecaries** (ə-pŏth′ĭ-kĕr′ēz): pharmacists; druggists.
6. **one mark twenty**: one mark and twenty pfennigs.
7. **bronze-gilt**: covered with a thin layer of bronze.
8. **Frau** (frou): a German title indicating a married woman.

WORDS TO KNOW
antiquated (ăn′tĭ-kwā′tĭd) *adj.* old-fashioned; outmoded
meager (mē′gər) *adj.* lacking quantity, fullness, strength, or fertility; feeble; scanty
preside (prĭ-zīd′) *v.* to hold the chief position of authority or control

213

Critic's Corner

The critic Robert Conrad makes the following point about the symbolism associated with Böll's story.

> The word *Brücher* is from *brechen* ("to break") and from *Bruch* ("breach"). Hence the grandfather is a person who breaks with the past at the dawn of a new era by trying to enlighten the people about a social injustice.... Young Brücher, besides being a harbinger of political change, is also a David figure who carries a sling and attempts to slay the mythical giant Bilgan, whom the Baleks have chosen as the emblem on their coat-of-arms.

Ask students to explain in their own words what points Conrad is making here about the story. Encourage students to evaluate whether or not Conrad's comments contribute to their understanding of the story.

CUSTOMIZING FOR Gifted and Talented Students

Have students identify details that can be used to make generalizations about Böll's social and political views.

Possible responses:
- Page 212: "For five generations... killed off by slow degrees"/ Workers are exploited by their employers.
- Page 213: "Each cottage ... the odor of thin soup ..."/ Workers live in dire poverty.
- Page 216: "It is the amount that is short of justice."/ The rich often cheat the poor.
- Page 218: "The reeve's gendarmes arrived ...."/ Owners use force to maintain the status quo.

Literary Concept: TONE

A Ask students to discuss the narrator's tone as the story opens. (*Possible responses: The tone is matter-of-fact; it is sympathetic to the people's simple pleasures and stoic suffering.*)

Literary Concept: NARRATOR

B Point out that the story is narrated by someone who presumably heard it many times from his grandfather. Ask students why Böll might have chosen this narrative device. (*Possible response: This device gives the story the authenticity of oral family history.*)

CUSTOMIZING FOR Students Acquiring English

Explain that *highly strung* means "nervous."

DESIGN NOTE

The balance scale pictured on page 212 would be impossible to use as shown. The base of the pivot is resting on one of the pans, holding it down.

Active Reading: PREDICT

C Invite students to share their predictions

Think-Aloud Model I think the Baleks must have had a selfish reason for this rule. Maybe they wanted a monopoly on the buying of mushrooms and flowers. Or maybe their scales were rigged in order to cheat people.

STRATEGIC READING FOR
Less-Proficient Readers

D Use these questions to check students' grasp of the system in place on the Baleks' land.

- Who are the Baleks? *(a wealthy family that owns the land and the flax sheds where people work)* **Summarizing**

- How do the Baleks use their scales? *(to weigh flowers, herbs, and mushrooms that children gather and sell to them)* **Summarizing**

- What is special about the Balek scales? *(They are the only scales in the village; no one else can own scales.)* **Noting Relevant Details**

Set a Purpose Have the students read on to find out what the narrator's grandfather discovers about the Balek scales.

Literary Concept:
FORESHADOWING

E Ask students to predict how they think the narrator's grandfather will "test the justice of the Baleks." *(Possible response: He will test their scales to see if they are accurate.)*

Literary Concept:
CHARACTERIZATION

F Have students suggest what the details in this passage reveal to them about the boy. *(Possible responses: He is hardworking, determined, patient, and unafraid; he is careful and scrupulous.)*

---

child a lemon drop, and the children's faces would light up with pleasure, the way they used to when on feast days their mother poured milk into their coffee mugs, milk that made the coffee turn paler and paler until it was as pale as the flaxen pigtails of the little girls.

One of the laws imposed by the Baleks on the village was: no one was permitted to have any scales in the house. The law was so ancient that nobody gave a thought as to when and how it had arisen, and it had to be obeyed, for anyone who broke it was dismissed from the flax sheds, he could not sell his mushrooms or his thyme or his hayflowers, and the power of the Baleks was so far-reaching that no one in the neighboring villages would give him work either or buy his forest herbs. But since the days when my grandfather's parents had gone out as small children to gather mushrooms and sell them in order that they might season the meat of the rich people of Prague[9] or be baked into game pies, it had never occurred to anyone to break this law: flour could be measured in cups, eggs could be counted, what they had spun could be measured by the yard, and besides, the old-fashioned bronze-gilt, ornate Balek scales did not look as if there was anything wrong with them, and five generations had entrusted the swinging black pointer with what they had gone out as eager children to gather from the woods.

True, there were some among those quiet people who flouted the law, poachers bent on making more money in one night than they could earn in a whole month in the flax sheds, but even these people apparently never thought of buying scales or making their own. My grandfather was the first person bold enough to test the justice of the Baleks, the family who lived in the chateau and drove two carriages, who always maintained one boy from the village while he studied theology at the seminary[10] in Prague, the family with whom the priest played taroc[11] every Wednesday, on whom the local reeve,[12] in his carriage emblazoned with the Imperial coat of arms, made an annual New Year's Day call and on whom the Emperor conferred a title on the first day of the year 1900.

My grandfather was hardworking and smart: he crawled further into the woods than the children of his clan had crawled before him, he penetrated as far as the thicket where, according to legend, Bilgan the Giant was supposed to dwell, guarding a treasure. But my grandfather was not afraid of Bilgan: he worked his way deep into the thicket, even when he was quite little, and brought out great quantities of mushrooms; he even found truffles,[13] for which Frau Balek paid thirty

PREDICT

C Why do you think the Baleks outlawed the ownership of scales?

Using a Reading Log

---

9. **Prague** (präg): the capital of the present-day Czech (chĕk) Republic, which borders southeastern Germany. At the time of the story, Prague was ruled by German-speaking Austria and was home to many German merchants as well as native Czechs.

10. **studied theology at the seminary:** studied religious philosophy at the school for training members of the clergy.

11. **taroc** (tăr′ək): a European card game played with a 78-card pack; also spelled *tarok*.

12. **reeve** (rēv): a local authority, here representing the emperor's government.

13. **truffles** (trŭf′əlz): edible fungi that resemble mushrooms but are far rarer and are considered a great delicacy.

WORDS TO KNOW
flout (flout) *v.* to show contempt for; to scorn

214

Mini-Lesson — Literary Concepts

REVIEWING SETTING Remind students that the setting of a work of fiction is the time and place in which the action occurs. A work may be set in the past, the present, or the future; during the day or at night; during a particular time of year or in a certain historical period.

Application Have students think about the role that setting plays in "The Balek Scales." For example, what qualities of the small, turn-of-the-century agricultural village allow the Baleks to get away with their injustice? How do the rigid class structure and wide disparities in wealth of this period affect the villagers? Students might also discuss the symbolic significance of the time setting—New Year's Day of 1900.

214 THE LANGUAGE OF LITERATURE TEACHER'S EDITION

pfennigs a pound. Everything my grandfather took to the Baleks he entered on the back of a torn-off calendar page: every pound of mushrooms, every gram of thyme, and on the right-hand side, in his childish handwriting, he entered the amount he received for each item; he scrawled in every pfennig, from the age of seven to the age of twelve, and by the time he was twelve the year 1900 had arrived, and because the Baleks had been raised to the aristocracy by the Emperor, they gave every family in the village a quarter of a pound of real coffee, the Brazilian kind; there was also free beer and tobacco for the men, and at the chateau there was a great banquet; many carriages stood in the avenue of poplars leading from the entrance gates to the chateau.

But the day before the banquet the coffee was distributed in the little room which had housed the Balek scales for almost a hundred years, and the Balek family was now called Balek von Bilgan because, according to legend, Bilgan the Giant used to have a great castle on the site of the present Balek estate.

My grandfather often used to tell me how he went there after school to fetch the coffee for four families: the Cechs, the Weidlers, the Vohlas[14] and his own, the Brüchers.[15] It was the afternoon of New Year's Eve: there were the front rooms to be decorated, the baking to be done, and the families did not want to spare four boys and have each of them go all the way to the chateau to bring back a quarter of a pound of coffee.

And so my grandfather sat on the narrow wooden bench in the little room while Gertrud the maid counted out the wrapped four-ounce packages of coffee, four of them, and he looked at the scales and saw that the pound weight was still lying on the left-hand scale; Frau Balek von Bilgan was busy with preparations for the banquet. And when Gertrud was about to put her hand into the jar with the lemon drops to give my grandfather one, she discovered it was empty: it was refilled once a year and held one kilo of the kind that cost a mark.

Gertrud laughed and said: "Wait here while I get the new lot," and my grandfather waited with the four four-ounce packages which had been wrapped and sealed in the factory, facing the scales on which someone had left the pound weight, and my grandfather took the four packages of coffee, put them on the empty scale, and his heart thudded as he watched the black finger of justice come to rest on the left of the black line: the scale with the pound weight stayed down, and the pound of coffee remained up in the air; his heart thudded more than if he had been lying behind a bush in the forest waiting for Bilgan the Giant, and he felt in his pocket for the pebbles he always carried with him so he could use his catapult[16] to shoot the sparrows which pecked away at his mother's cabbage plants—he had to put three, four, five pebbles beside the packages of coffee before the scale with the pound weight rose and the pointer at last came to rest over the black line. My grandfather took the coffee from the scale, wrapped the five pebbles in his kerchief,

---

14. **the Cechs** (chĕks), **the Weidlers** (vīd′lərz), **the Vohlas** (vō′läz).
15. **Brüchers** (brü′ᴋʜərz): The name *Brücher* derives from the German words for "to break" and "to breach."
16. **catapult** (kăt′ə-pŭlt′): here, a slingshot.

THE BALEK SCALES 215

Mini-Lesson Grammar

COLONS Review the uses of colons illustrated by the highlighted sentences on this page and on page 214.
- Use a colon to introduce a list of items.
  . . . to fetch the coffee for four families: the Cechs, the Weidlers, the Vohlas, and . . .
- Use a colon to set off a quotation, especially if it lacks explanatory words.
  Gertrud laughed and said: "Wait here while I get the new lot. . . ."
- Use a colon between two independent clauses when the second explains the first.
  My grandfather was hard-working and smart: he crawled further. . . .

Application Invite students to find at least five other colons in the story and to explain the purpose that each colon serves.

Reteaching/Reinforcement
- Grammar Handbook, anthology p. 1092

The Writer's Craft
The Colon, pp. 806–808

Active Reading: CLARIFY

L The narrator's grandfather has discovered that the Balek scales are inaccurate. By using scales weighted in their favor, the Baleks have been cheating the villagers.

Linking to Science

M The dust in the flax sheds contains tiny plant particles. When breathed in, these cause brown lung, or *byssinosis*, a disease marked by tightness in the chest, coughing, and shortness of breath. The only way to cure the disease is to cease exposure to the dust.

STRATEGIC READING FOR Less-Proficient Readers

N Use these questions to check students' understanding of what the boy discovered.

- How did the boy test the scales? *(He weighed a pound of coffee on the scale, then used five pebbles to gauge by how much the scales were off.)* Noting Relevant Details

- Why is the boy so upset? *(The Baleks have been cheating his people for generations.)* Noting Relevant Details

Set a Purpose Have students read to see what the villagers do when they learn about the fraud.

Literary Concept: SETTING

O Have students discuss why they think the author sets events on the first day of a new century. *(Possible responses: Some students may say this momentous date adds importance to the boy's discovery; others may say the new century suggests the possibility of a new beginning.)*

---

and when Gertrud came back with the big kilo bag of lemon drops which had to last for another whole year in order to make the children's faces light up with pleasure, when Gertrud let the lemon drops rattle into the glass jar, the pale little fellow was still standing there, and nothing seemed to have changed. My grandfather only took three of the packages, then Gertrud looked in startled surprise at the white-faced child who threw the lemon drop onto the floor, ground it under his heel, and said: "I want to see Frau Balek."

"Balek von Bilgan, if you please," said Gertrud.

"All right, Frau Balek von Bilgan," but Gertrud only laughed at him, and he walked back to the village in the dark, took the Cechs, the Weidlers and the Vohlas their coffee, and said he had to go and see the priest.

CLARIFY
What has the grandfather discovered?
Using a Reading Log

Instead he went out into the dark night with his five pebbles in his kerchief. He had to walk a long way before he found someone who had scales, who was permitted to have them; no one in the villages of Blaugau and Bernau[17] had any, he knew that, and he went straight through them till, after two hours' walking, he reached the little town of Dielheim[18] where Honig[19] the apothecary lived. From Honig's house came the smell of fresh pancakes, and Honig's breath, when he opened the door to the half-frozen boy, already smelled of punch, there was a moist cigar between his narrow lips, and he clasped the boy's cold hands firmly for a moment, saying: "What's the matter, has your father's lung got worse?"

"No, I haven't come for medicine, I wanted . . ." My grandfather undid his kerchief, took out the five pebbles, held them out to Honig and said: "I wanted to have these weighed." He glanced anxiously into Honig's face, but when Honig said nothing and did not get angry, or even ask him anything, my grandfather said: "It is the amount that is short of justice," and now, as he went into the warm room, my grandfather realized how wet his feet were. The snow had soaked through his cheap shoes, and in the forest the branches had showered him with snow which was now melting, and he was tired and hungry and suddenly began to cry because he thought of the quantities of mushrooms, the herbs, the flowers, which had been weighed on the scales which were short five pebbles' worth of justice. And when Honig, shaking his head and holding the five pebbles, called his wife, my grandfather thought of the generations of his parents, his grandparents, who had all had to have their mushrooms, their flowers, weighed on the scales, and he was overwhelmed by a great wave of injustice and began to sob louder than ever, and, without waiting to be asked, he sat down on a chair, ignoring the pancakes, the cup of hot coffee which nice plump Frau Honig put in front of him, and did not stop crying till Honig himself came out from the shop at the back and, rattling the pebbles in his hand, said in a low voice to his wife: "Fifty-five grams, exactly."

My grandfather walked the two hours home through the forest, got a beating at home, said nothing, not a single word, when he was asked about the coffee, spent the whole evening doing sums on the piece of paper on which he had written down everything he had sold to Frau Balek, and when midnight struck, and the cannon could be heard from the chateau, and the whole village rang with shouting and laughter and the noise of rattles, when the family kissed and embraced all

---

17. **Blaugau** (blou′gou′) and **Bernau** (bĕr′nou).
18. **Dielheim** (dēl′him′).
19. **Honig** (hô′nĭкн).

216 UNIT TWO PART 1: CHALLENGING THE SYSTEM

Mini-Lesson  The Writer's Style

SENTENCE LENGTH AND STRUCTURE
Have students count the number of complete sentences in the highlighted passage above *(three)* and generalize about the sentence structure of the story. *(Böll uses long, compound and complex sentences.)* Point out that the brief final phrase, "Fifty-five grams, exactly," has a dramatic impact because of its contrasting abruptness.

Application Challenge students to write an original sentence with the exact structure of one of Böll's longer sentences. Suggest that the sentence tell about an injustice the student or a family member has experienced.

Reteaching/Reinforcement
- *Writing Mini-Lessons* transparencies, p. 50

The Writer's Craft
Creating Sentence Variety, pp. 434–435

216 THE LANGUAGE OF LITERATURE TEACHER'S EDITION

Une Battue en Campine [Beating the bushes in Campine] (about 1882–1885), Théodor Verstraete. Oil on canvas, 41 ¼" × 71", collection of Crédit Communal, Brussels, Belgium.

around, he said into the New Year silence: "The Baleks owe me eighteen marks and thirty-two pfennigs." And again he thought of all the children there were in the village, of his brother Fritz who had gathered so many mushrooms, of his sister Ludmilla; he thought of the many hundreds of children who had all gathered mushrooms for the Baleks, and herbs and flowers, and this time he did not cry but told his parents and brothers and sisters of his discovery.

When the Baleks von Bilgan went to High Mass on New Year's Day, their new coat of arms—a giant crouching under a fir tree—already emblazoned in blue and gold on their carriage, they saw the hard, pale faces of the people all staring at them. They had expected garlands in the village, a song in their honor, cheers and hurrahs, but the village was completely deserted as they drove through it, and in church the pale faces of the people were turned toward them, mute and hostile, and when the priest mounted the pulpit to deliver his New Year's sermon, he sensed the chill in those otherwise quiet and peaceful faces, and he stumbled painfully through his sermon and went back to the altar drenched in sweat. And as the Baleks von Bilgan left the church after Mass, they walked through a lane of mute, pale faces. But young Frau Balek von Bilgan stopped in front of the children's pews, sought out my grandfather's face, pale little Franz Brücher, and asked him, right there in the church: "Why didn't you take the coffee for your mother?" And my grandfather stood up and said: "Because you owe me as much money as five kilos of coffee would cost." And he pulled the five

THE BALEK SCALES 217

Cultural Note

R The hymn refers to the trial of Jesus before Pontius Pilate. According to the hymn, Jesus was put to death even though he was innocent of wrongdoing. The singers liken this Roman "justice" to that of the Baleks.

STRATEGIC READING FOR
Less-Proficient Readers

S Have students sum up what happens when the villagers learn they have been cheated. *(They steal the record book to find out what they are owed, but then they are threatened by gendarmes, and eventually they go back to work.)*
Summarizing

Active Reading: EVALUATE

T Possible responses: Some students may say that in addition to having the Emperor's gendarmes at their disposal, the Baleks control the land and flax trade, so they can make people do as they wish. Others may point out that the villagers were simply continuing their long history of submitting to the Baleks.

CUSTOMIZING FOR
Gifted and Talented Students

Have students find and research the meanings behind various symbols of justice, including that of Athena holding a balance scale. Ask students to work in groups to create an original symbol for either justice or injustice. Invite a volunteer from each group to explain their symbol to the class.

---

pebbles from his pocket, held them out to the young woman and said: "This much, fifty-five grams, is short in every pound of your justice"; and before the woman could say anything the men and women in the church lifted up their voices and sang: "The justice of this earth, O Lord, hath put Thee to death. . . ."

While the Baleks were at church, Wilhelm Vohla, the poacher, had broken into the little room, stolen the scales and the big fat leather-bound book in which had been entered every kilo of mushrooms, every kilo of hayflowers, everything bought by the Baleks in the village, and all afternoon of that New Year's Day the men of the village sat in my great-grandparents' front room and calculated, calculated one tenth of everything that had been bought—but when they had calculated many thousands of talers[20] and had still not come to an end, the reeve's gendarmes[21] arrived, made their way into my great-grandfather's front room, shooting and stabbing as they came, and removed the scales and the book by force. My grandfather's little sister Ludmilla lost her life, a few men were wounded, and one of the gendarmes was stabbed to death by Wilhelm Vohla the poacher.

Our village was not the only one to rebel: Blaugau and Bernau did too, and for almost a week no work was done in the flax sheds. But a great many gendarmes appeared, and the men and women were threatened with prison, and the Baleks forced the priest to display the scales publicly in the school and demonstrate that the finger of justice swung to and fro accurately. And the men and women went back to the flax sheds—but no one went to the school to watch the priest: he stood there all alone, helpless and forlorn with his weights, scales, and packages of coffee.

And the children went back to gathering mushrooms, to gathering thyme, flowers and foxglove, but every Sunday, as soon as the Baleks entered the church, the hymn was struck up: "The justice of this earth, O Lord, hath put Thee to death," until the reeve ordered it proclaimed in every village that the singing of this hymn was forbidden.

My grandfather's parents had to leave the village and the new grave of their little daughter; they became basket weavers but did not stay long anywhere because it pained them to see how everywhere the finger of justice swung falsely. They walked along behind their cart, which crept slowly over the country roads, taking their thin goat with them, and passers-by could sometimes hear a voice from the cart singing: "The justice of this earth, O Lord, hath put Thee to death." And those who wanted to listen could hear the tale of the Baleks von Bilgan, whose justice lacked a tenth part. But there were few who listened. ❖

Translated by Leila Vennewitz

EVALUATE
Why do you think the Baleks were able to return to business as usual?
Using a Reading Log

---

20. **talers** (tä′lərz): silver coins used in central Europe until around the turn of the century.
21. **gendarmes** (zhän′därmz′): police officers.

WORDS TO KNOW
forlorn (fər-lôrn′) *adj.* appearing sad or lonely because one has been left alone

---

COMPREHENSION CHECK

1. Who are the Baleks? *(a powerful family that controls the local land and economy)*
2. What does the main character learn about the Baleks from their scale? *(They have been cheating the people for generations.)*
3. What happens when the people rebel? *(Gendarmes put down the rebellion.)*

RESPONDING OPTIONS

FROM PERSONAL RESPONSE TO CRITICAL ANALYSIS

REFLECT
1. What were your reactions to the final outcome of the villagers' protests? Record your thoughts in your notebook.

RETHINK
2. How would you describe the narrator's grandfather as a boy? Support your answer with details from the story.

3. Consider the thoughts about justice that you explored for the Personal Connection on page 211. In your opinion, what is the worst injustice in the story? Explain your position.

4. How would you explain the main message about justice that is communicated in this story?
Consider

Close Textual Reading
- the hymn sung by villagers when the Baleks enter church
- why it took so long for the inaccuracy of the scales to be discovered
- what the Balek scales symbolize
- why the narrator's grandfather and his family found that "the finger of justice swung falsely" everywhere they went

5. How does the prediction you made in the Reading Connection on page 211 compare with what actually happens in the story?

RELATE
6. The Baleks seem to control nearly every aspect of life in the village, from the weighing of mushrooms to the activities of the police and clergy. Do you think wealthy people in the United States today exert a similar kind of power? Explain your reasoning.

LITERARY LINKS

Thematic Link Compare the outcome of challenging the system in this story with the outcomes in *The Pen of My Aunt* and "The Thrill of the Grass."

Multimodal Learning
ANOTHER PATHWAY
Cooperative Learning
Create a pie graph that shows who may be held responsible for injustices in the story. Each segment should represent a different person or group and should be proportional to the degree of responsibility.

QUICKWRITES

1. Imagine that a new priest is assigned to the village and learns about the events related to the scales. Write a **sermon** in which the priest offers his moral judgment of these events.

2. Write a guest **editorial** that the Balek family might have placed in the local paper in which they attempt to win back the favor of the villagers.

3. Write a **journal entry** in which the grandfather, as an adult, reflects upon the lessons about justice that he learned as a result of discovering the scales' false measure.

 **PORTFOLIO** Save your writing. You may want to use it later as a springboard to a piece for your portfolio.

THE BALEK SCALES 219

From Personal Response to Critical Analysis
1. Accept all reasonable responses.
2. Accept all well-supported responses. Possible responses: He was intelligent in finding a way to test the scales; he was brave in confronting the Baleks.
3. Accept all reasonable, well-supported responses.
4. Possible responses: There is no real justice anywhere; wealthy people with power use the system only to further their own ends.
5. Accept all reasonable responses.
6. Accept all reasonable responses. Possible responses: Some students may reason that wealthy people have great control over today's society. Others may argue that a free press, public investigations, and the legal system curb abuses of power.

Literary Links
In the first two stories, the main characters successfully challenge the system. In "The Balek Scales," the villagers' challenge is repressed.

Another Pathway
Cooperative Learning With one group member acting as recorder, students can work together to list unjust persons or groups in the story, such as the Baleks, the priest, the gendarmes, and the Emperor. Individuals can then present evidence from the story of the injustices of each person or group. On the basis of these presentations, the group can decide upon degrees of guilt, then create a pie graph.

Rubric
3 Full Accomplishment Students work well together, back up their opinions with story data, and create a graph that clearly reflects their conclusions.
2 Substantial Accomplishment Students reach agreement and illustrate it on the graph, but do not sufficiently back up their opinions.
1 Little or Partial Accomplishment Students have difficulty reaching agreement, backing up opinions, and creating a coherent graph.

QuickWrites
1. Remind students that a sermon, in addition to making moral judgments about events that have already happened, prescribes guidelines for appropriate conduct in similar situations in the future.
2. Before students write the Balek editorial, review some techniques of persuasive writing. Also have students imagine and describe a bold and generous gesture that the Baleks might make to prove that they have learned from the experience.
3. Suggest that the grandfather's journal might voice regrets that no restitution was made to the people. He also might take pride in knowing that in revealing the truth he had made the people more wary in their future business dealings.

The Writer's Craft
Advice Essay, pp. 190–194
Persuasive Writing, pp. 213–218
Autobiographical Incident, pp. 26–40

Words to Know

1. antiquated
2. meager
3. flout
4. preside
5. forlorn

Reteaching/Reinforcement
• Unit Two Resource Book, p. 14

Across the Curriculum

Math Ask students to assume that one child had sold the Baleks 20 pounds of mushrooms according to the Balek's logbook. What was the actual weight of the mushrooms the child had sold and how much did the Baleks owe the child? *(22.4 pounds; 22 pfennigs)*

HEINRICH BÖLL

"The Balek Scales" illustrates Böll's disgust with people's greed and his anger that the poor cannot control their own destinies. His open criticism of the negative effects of prosperity made him a controversial figure in post–World War II Germany. Böll was critical of the church and state, and he held on to his idealism and religious convictions throughout his life.

LITERARY CONCEPTS

Tone is the attitude a writer or narrator takes toward a subject. The language and details a writer chooses help to create the tone, which might be playful, serious, bitter, angry, or detached, among other possibilities. To identify the tone of a work, you might find it helpful to read the work aloud, as if giving a dramatic reading. The emotions that you convey in reading should give you hints as to the tone of the work. With a small group of classmates, read aloud the opening and closing paragraphs of "The Balek Scales." Then come up with the words or phrases that describe the tone of these paragraphs. Compare your descriptions with those of other groups.

CRITIC'S CORNER

Editor Ralph Ley described Böll as "the humane and incorruptible conscience of his country." What does this story reveal about Böll's conscience?

WORDS TO KNOW

Review the Words to Know at the bottom of the selection pages. Then, on your paper, match each example below with the appropriate vocabulary word.

1. The machines used for drying the flax were so old that no one could remember when they had first been used.
2. Most of the people had very little to eat; even milk was considered a treat.
3. By refusing the coffee, the grandfather ridiculed the authority of the Baleks.
4. In the next generation, another Frau Balek would be in control of the room with the scales.
5. The grandfather and his family must have felt lonely as they moved from town to town.

HEINRICH BÖLL

1917–1985

Heinrich Böll grew up in Cologne (kə-lōn′), Germany, the descendant of English Catholics who centuries before had fled to the Continent to escape religious persecution. Raised in a tolerant household at a time when many Germans were embracing intolerance, Böll watched in growing horror as the Nazis rose to power. During World War II, he was forced to join the German army; he was wounded four times and was captured and imprisoned by American forces. After the war, he began to publish novels and short stories. His early novels were harshly critical of warfare, which the Nazis had glorified. In *The Train Was on Time* (1949), he traced the despair of a sensitive young German soldier, not unlike himself; in *Adam, Where Art Thou?* (1951), he compared warfare to a contagious and deadly disease.

With time, Böll broadened his themes, though he remained a social critic. The corruption of power, the victimization of the innocent by those in power, and the dehumanizing effects of modern life are often treated in his novels and short stories. Böll also championed the rights of oppressed fellow writers, providing lodgings for Russian author Aleksandr Solzhenitsyn (ăl′ĭk-săn′dər sōl′zhə-nēt′sĭn) when he was forced to leave his then-Communist homeland. Over the years, Böll produced nearly 40 books and was honored with a Nobel Prize. "The Balek Scales," one of his most widely read stories, was first published in German in 1955.

OTHER WORKS *Eighteen Stories, The Stories of Heinrich Böll, What's to Become of the Boy?*

Extended Reading

220 UNIT TWO PART 1: CHALLENGING THE SYSTEM

Literary Concepts

Groups' impressions of the tone may vary. Accept all reasonable, well-supported responses. Possible responses include the following:

• The tone of the opening paragraph is somewhat mixed, as if the author has two competing attitudes toward his subject. On the one hand, the tone is bitter because the people were so poor and suffered so much in their work. However, there are also details that suggest a more upbeat tone: the people are cheerful and find joy in the simple things of life.

• The tone of the last paragraph is pessimistic, hopeless, or bitter. The family must leave their village and their daughter's grave; they wander from place to place; they find false justice everywhere and little interest in their story.

PREVIEWING

NONFICTION

from Montgomery Boycott
Coretta Scott King United States

Activating Prior Knowledge
PERSONAL CONNECTION
What do you know about the civil rights movement and two of its key participants, Rosa Parks and Martin Luther King, Jr.? Share your knowledge with your classmates in a class discussion.

Rosa Parks being fingerprinted. AP/Wide World Photos.

Dr. Martin Luther King, Jr., leading a protest march. UPI/Bettmann.

Building Background
HISTORICAL CONNECTION
In the 1890s and early decades of the 20th century, many states, especially in the South, passed laws to ensure segregation, the complete separation of the races in public places. These so-called Jim Crow laws—named after a character in an old song—discriminated against African Americans. After World War II, opponents of these laws challenged their legality. In 1954 the Supreme Court, reversing an earlier decision, declared that it was unconstitutional to force whites and blacks to attend separate schools. Soon afterward, African Americans in Montgomery, Alabama, began the bus boycott that is the subject of the following selection.

A pivotal event in the civil rights movement, the Montgomery boycott first brought to national attention the Reverend Martin Luther King, Jr., the writer's husband. King's eye-opening efforts of nonviolent protest helped inspire many others in the struggle for civil rights. In 1960, for example, African-American students in Greensboro, North Carolina, initiated a new protest strategy, the sit-in, when they risked arrest for insisting on being served at a local segregated lunch counter.

READING CONNECTION
Active Reading/Setting a Purpose
Identifying Multiple Effects "Montgomery Boycott" reports a now-famous incident from the civil rights movement in which one woman's refusal to give up her seat on a bus had significant effects. As you read the selection, identify the multiple effects of her decision. Jot them down on a diagram like this one.

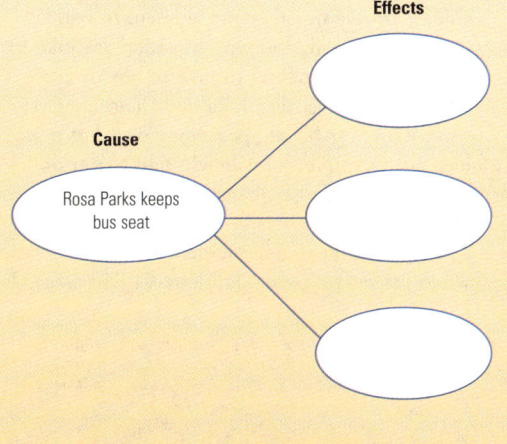

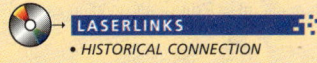
LASERLINKS
• HISTORICAL CONNECTION

OVERVIEW

Objectives
- To understand and appreciate an autobiography that explores how nonviolent protests can affect an unjust system
- To identify and understand an author's purpose
- To express understanding of a selection through a choice of writing forms, including a diary entry, a written analysis, and protest signs
- To extend understanding of the selection through a variety of multimodal and cross-curricular activities

Skills

LITERARY CONCEPTS
- Author's purpose
- Autobiography

READING SKILLS/STRATEGIES
- Identifying multiple effects

THE WRITER'S STYLE
- Coherence in longer pieces of writing

GRAMMAR
- Infinitives and infinitive phrases

SPEAKING, LISTENING AND VIEWING
- Retelling a story
- Group discussion

HISTORICAL CONNECTION
The Montgomery Bus Boycott In December 1955, in Montgomery, Alabama, Mrs. Rosa Parks refused a bus driver's command to give up her seat to a white man. She was arrested and fined $14. This incident touched off a 381-day boycott of buses in Montgomery. This film shows rare footage of the boycott and helps students visualize this key event in the civil rights movement.

Side A, Frame 7002

PRINT AND MEDIA RESOURCES

UNIT TWO RESOURCE BOOK
Strategic Reading: Literature, p. 17
Vocabulary SkillBuilder, p. 18

WRITING MINI-LESSONS
Transparencies, p. 8, p. 40

ACCESS FOR STUDENTS ACQUIRING ENGLISH
Selection Summaries
Reading Support

FORMAL ASSESSMENT
Selection Test, pp. 41–42
 Test Generator

 **AUDIO LIBRARY**
See Reference Card

 LASERLINKS
Historical Connection

 INTERNET RESOURCES
McDougal Littell Literature Center at http://www.hmco.com/mcdougal/lit

MONTGOMERY BOYCOTT

CORETTA SCOTT KING

Of all the facets of segregation in Montgomery, the most degrading were the rules of the Montgomery City Bus Lines. This northern-owned corporation outdid the South itself. Although seventy percent of its passengers were black, it treated them like cattle—worse than that, for nobody insults a cow. The first seats on all buses were reserved for whites. Even if they were unoccupied and the rear seats crowded, blacks would have to stand at the back in case some whites might get aboard; and if the front seats happened to be occupied and more white people boarded the bus, black people seated in the rear were forced to get up and give them their seats. Furthermore—and I don't think northerners ever realized this—blacks had to pay their fares at the front of the bus, get off, and walk to the rear door to board again. Sometimes the bus would drive off without them after they had paid their fare. This would happen to elderly people or pregnant women, in bad weather or good, and was considered a joke by the drivers. Frequently the white bus drivers abused their passengers, calling them niggers, black cows, or black apes. Imagine what it was like, for example, for a black man to get on a bus with his son and be subjected to such treatment.

There had been one incident in March 1955, when fifteen-year-old Claudette Colvin refused

At one time, signs ordering the segregation of black and white passengers were posted on buses and trains in the South. This photograph was taken the day the Supreme Court banned segregation on public transportation. UPI/Bettmann Newsphotos.

WORDS TO KNOW

degrading (dĭ-grā′dĭng) *adj.* tending to lower one's dignity; insulting **degrade** *v.*

WORDS TO KNOW

coercion (kō-ûr′zhən) *n.* the use of power or threats to force someone to do something (p. 228)

coherently (kō-hîr′ənt-lē) *adv.* in a manner that shows clear thinking and makes sense (p. 226)

degrading (dĭ-grā′dĭng) *adj.* tending to lower one's dignity; insulting **degrade** *v.* (p. 222)

devoid (dĭ-void′) *adj.* completely lacking; empty (p. 228)

exaltation (ĕg′zôl-tā′shən) *n.* the act of glorifying, praising, or honoring (p. 229)

exposé (ĕk′spō-zā′) *n.* an account that reveals something negative to the public (p. 225)

militant (mĭl′ĭ-tənt) *adj.* showing a fighting spirit; aggressive (p. 228)

oppression (ə-prĕsh′ən) *n.* unjust or cruel exercise of power or authority (p. 228)

perpetuation (pər-pĕch′ōō-ā′shən) *n.* a long-lasting continuation (p. 228)

radiant (rā′dē-ənt) *adj.* bright; glowing (p. 224)

NOTICE
IT IS REQUIRED BY LAW UNDER
PENALTY OF FINE OF $5.00 TO $25.00
THAT WHITE AND NEGRO PASSENGERS MUST
OCCUPY THE RESPECTIVE SPACE OR SEATS
INDICATED BY SIGNS IN THIS VEHICLE
TEXAS PENAL CODE ARTICLE 1659 SEC 4
DALLAS CITY ORDINANCE NO 2904

COLORED →

STRATEGIC READING FOR
Less-Proficient Readers

Set a Purpose To prepare students for reading "Montgomery Boycott," ask them to consider different ways of responding to an injustice. Have students read on to find out what African Americans did in 1955 to put an end to segregated buses.

Use **UNIT TWO RESOURCE BOOK**, p. 17, for guidance in reading the selection.

CUSTOMIZING FOR
Gifted and Talented Students

Have students find and explain details that show the conflicts Dr. King experienced during the boycott.

Possible responses:

- Page 225—"...whether the boycott method was basically unchristian."/ As a minister, Dr. King struggled to live by high religious ideals; he measured the boycott by those ideals.

- Page 227—"...he was nervous about telling me he had accepted the presidency of the protest movement..."/ Dr. King feared the protest would affect his young family's security.

- Page 227—"...thinking about the responsibility and the reporters and television cameras, he almost panicked."/ Dr. King feared he might not be up to the task; he might disappoint everyone.

Critical Thinking: SPECULATING

A Invite students to speculate on how the scenario Mrs. King describes here might affect a black man and his son. *(Possible responses: A child might lose respect for his parent; the father might feel ashamed of his powerlessness.)*

CUSTOMIZING FOR
Multiple Learning Styles

B **Spatial or graphic learners** Have the students speculate on the contrast between the mood of the women in the photograph with the opening description of stark conditions on the buses. Make sure that they read the caption, which identifies the timing of the paragraph.

Multicultural Perspectives

Explain to students that the tactic of staging a boycott is an old one. The first victim of this practice was Captain Charles Cunningham Boycott, a rent collector for the Earl of Erne in County Mayo, Ireland. When he raised the rents too high after two years of bad potato crops in the 1880s, the tenant farmers ostracized Boycott, refusing to talk to him or sell him goods. In the end, Boycott was forced to flee to England.

Similarly, in India beginning in 1917, Mohandas Gandhi organized a series of boycotts in which the Indian people refused to buy cloth from their British rulers. Gandhi encouraged Indians to spin their own material. In fact, he himself practiced spinning a half-hour every day and made the spinning wheel a symbol of his National Congress Party. In 1930 Gandhi led another boycott against the British-controlled salt mines and ocean salt fields. Although it was against British law, he encouraged thousands to gather their own salt from the sea.

Literary Concept:
FIGURATIVE LANGUAGE

C Ask students to explain the comparison King is making here. *(Possible response: She likens the anger of African Americans to a slow-burning fire that blazes up when fuel is thrown on it.)*

Literary Note

D Point out that the sentence "Her cup had run over" is an allusion to the 23rd Psalm of the Bible. The allusion is ironic because in the psalm the psalmist's cup runs over with blessings, but in Rosa Park's case it runs over with indignities.

Linking to History

E Founded in 1925 by A. Philip Randolph, the Brotherhood of Sleeping Car Porters (now part of the Brotherhood of Railway and Airline Clerks) was one of the first unions to organize African-American workers. By threatening a march on Washington, D.C., in 1941, Randolph opened defense industry jobs to blacks.

Literary Concept:
FIGURATIVE LANGUAGE

F Have students note how King continues using fire as a metaphor in this paragraph. *(E. D. Nixon is "fiery"; the sudden civil rights activity is "spontaneous combustion.")*

Literary Concept:
AUTHOR'S PURPOSE

G Have students suggest what this comment reveals about King's purpose for writing. *(Possible response: She wishes to inform readers about the Christian origins of the civil rights movement.)*

---

to give up her seat to a white passenger. The high school girl was handcuffed and carted off to the police station. At that time Martin served on a committee to protest to the city and bus-company officials. The committee was received politely—and nothing was done.

C The fuel that finally made that slow-burning fire blaze up was an almost routine incident. On December 1, 1955, Mrs. Rosa Parks, a forty-two-year-old seamstress whom my husband aptly described as "a charming person with a radiant personality," boarded a bus to go home after a long day working and shopping. The bus was crowded, and Mrs. Parks found a seat at the beginning of the black section. At the next stop more whites got on. The driver ordered Mrs. Parks to give her seat to a white man who boarded; this meant that she would have to stand all the way home. Rosa Parks was not in a revolutionary frame of mind. She had not planned to do what she did. Her cup had run over. As she said later, "I was just plain tired, and my feet hurt." So she sat there, refusing to get up. The driver called a policeman, who arrested her and took her to the courthouse. From there Mrs. Parks called E. D. Nixon, who came down and signed a bail bond for her.

E Mr. Nixon was a fiery Alabamian. He was a Pullman porter[1] who had been active in A. Philip Randolph's Brotherhood of Sleeping Car Porters, and in civil rights activities. Suddenly he also had had enough; suddenly, it seemed, almost every African American in Montgomery had had enough. It was spontaneous combustion.[2] **F** Phones began ringing all over the black section of the city. The Women's Political Council suggested a one-day boycott of the buses as a protest. E. D. Nixon courageously agreed to organize it.

The first we knew about it was when Mr. Nixon called my husband early in the morning of Friday, December 2. He had already talked to Ralph Abernathy.[3] After describing the incident, Mr. Nixon said, "We have taken this type of thing too long. I feel the time has come to boycott the buses. It's the only way to make the white folks see that we will not take this sort of thing any longer."

Martin agreed with him and offered the Dexter Avenue Church as a meeting place. After much telephoning, a meeting of black ministers and civic leaders was arranged for that evening. Martin said later that as he approached his church Friday evening, he was nervously wondering how many leaders would really turn up. To his delight, Martin found over forty people, representing every segment of African-American life, crowded into the large meeting room at Dexter. There were doctors, lawyers, businessmen, federal-government employees, union leaders, and a great many ministers. The latter were particularly welcome, not only because of their influence, but because it meant that they were beginning to accept Martin's view that "religion deals with both heaven and earth.... Any religion that professes to be concerned with the souls of men and is not concerned with the slums that doom them, the economic conditions that strangle them, and the social conditions that cripple them, is dry-as-dust religion." From that very first step, the Christian ministry provided the leadership of our struggle, as Christian ideals were its source. **G**

---

1. **Pullman porter:** a railroad employee who serves people in a Pullman car; that is, a passenger car with seats that can be converted into beds.
2. **spontaneous combustion** (spŏn-tā′nē-əs kəm-bŭs′chən): literally, the situation that occurs when something bursts into flames on its own, without the addition of heat from an outside source.
3. **Ralph Abernathy** (1926–1990): a minister who became a close colleague of Martin Luther King, Jr., and an important civil rights leader.

radiant (rā′dē-ənt) *adj.* bright; glowing

224

INFINITIVES AND INFINITIVE PHRASES
Tell students that an infinitive is a verb form that begins with *to* and functions as a noun, an adjective, or an adverb. Place these examples on the board:

Everyone wants *to sit*. [*The infinitive functions as a noun and direct object.*]

Rosa Parks is a person *to admire*. [*The infinitive functions as an adjective, modifying* person.]

She boarded a bus *to go*. [*The infinitive functions as an adverb, modifying the verb* boarded.]

Explain that an infinitive phrase includes the infinitive and any modifiers and complements.

Application Have students identify the infinitives and infinitive phrases highlighted in the first paragraph on page 224. Discuss the role each plays.

Reteaching/Reinforcement

The Writer's Craft

Infinitives and Infinitive Phrases, pp. 592–593

Everyone wants to sit.

Rosa Parks is a person to admire.

She boarded a bus to go.

Martin told me after he got home that the meeting was almost wrecked because questions or suggestions from the floor were cut off. However, after a stormy session, one thing was clear: however much they differed on details, everyone was unanimously for a boycott. It was set for Monday, December 5. Committees were organized; all the ministers present promised to urge their congregations to take part. Several thousand leaflets were printed on the church mimeograph machine, describing the reasons for the boycott and urging all blacks not to ride buses "to work, to town, to school, or anyplace on Monday, December 5." Everyone was asked to come to a mass meeting at the Holt Street Baptist Church on Monday evening for further instructions. The Reverend A. W. Wilson had offered his church because it was larger than Dexter and more convenient, being in the center of the black district.

Saturday was a busy day for Martin and the other members of the committee. They hustled around town talking with other leaders, arranging with the black-owned taxi companies for special bulk fares and with the owners of private automobiles to get the people to and from work. I could do little to help because Yoki[4] was only two weeks old, and my physician, Dr. W. D. Pettus, who was very careful, advised me to stay in for a month. However, I was kept busy answering the telephone, which rang continuously, and coordinating from that central point the many messages and arrangements.

Our greatest concern was how we were going to reach the fifty thousand black people of Montgomery, no matter how hard we worked. The white press, in an outraged exposé, spread the word for us in a way that would have been impossible with only our own resources.

As it happened, a white woman found one of our leaflets, which her black maid had left in the kitchen. The irate woman immediately telephoned the newspapers to let the white community know what the blacks were up to.

BOYCOTT

Our greatest concern was how we were going to reach the fifty thousand black people of Montgomery.

We laughed a lot about this, and Martin later said that we owed them a great debt.

On Sunday morning, from their pulpits, almost every African-American minister in town urged people to honor the boycott.

Martin came home late Sunday night and began to read the morning paper. The long articles about the proposed boycott accused the NAACP[5] of planting Mrs. Parks on the bus—she had been a volunteer secretary for the Montgomery chapter—and likened the boycott to the tactics of the White Citizens Councils.[6] This upset Martin. That awesome conscience of his began to gnaw at him, and he wondered if he was doing the right thing. Alone in his study, he struggled with the question of whether the boycott method was basically unchristian. Certainly it could be used for unethical ends. But, as he said, "We were using it to give birth to freedom . . . and to urge men to comply with the law of the land. Our concern was not to put

---

4. **Yoki:** nickname of the Kings' daughter Yolanda.
5. **NAACP:** the National Association for the Advancement of Colored People, a prominent civil rights organization.
6. **White Citizens Councils:** groups that formed, first in Mississippi and then throughout the South, to resist the 1954 Supreme Court decision to desegregate the schools.

WORDS TO KNOW
exposé (ĕk′spō-zā′) *n.* an account that reveals something negative to the public

225

Literary Concept: AUTOBIOGRAPHY

H Invite students to point out details in the text that indicate that the selection is autobiographical. *(Possible response: Details about King's health and her baby Yoki indicate that the selection is a first-person account of the writer's life during a momentous historical event.)*

Literary Concept: IRONY

I Ask a volunteer to explain the irony of the newspaper exposé. *(Possible response: In attempting to condemn and perhaps stop the boycott, the newspaper unwittingly publicized it and contributed to its success.)*

Linking to History

J The NAACP was founded in 1909, when concerned blacks and whites united to fight discrimination and segregation. Every year since 1914, the organization has awarded the Spingarn Medal for the highest achievement of a black American. Winners include Dr. Martin Luther King, Jr., Langston Hughes, and Colin Powell.

Literary Concept: CHARACTERIZATION

K Have students discuss what this incident reveals about Dr. King. *(Possible responses: He is very conscientious about his religious convictions; he is thoughtful and concerned with questions of ethics.)*

Mini-Lesson — The Writer's Style

COHERENCE IN LONGER PIECES OF WRITING Explain that this account of the boycott is coherent, or easy to follow, because it focuses on a major topic and moves quickly and sequentially. King achieves this coherence with a tight chronology of events, beginning on Friday, December 2, and continuing through Monday, December 5, 1955. Note that King helps us to focus on the fast-moving events of this period by referring to specific days and times of day, such as the following examples:

- "Saturday was a busy day for Martin"
- "Martin came home late Sunday night"

Application Ask students to review narratives in their portfolios and to evaluate their own use of chronology. They may wish to underline words and phrases that help establish chronological sequences.

Reteaching/Reinforcement
- *Writer's Handbook,* anthology pp. 1027, 1035
- *Writing Mini-Lessons* transparencies, pp. 8, 40

The Writer's Craft
Chronological Order, pp. 343–344

THE LANGUAGE OF LITERATURE **Teacher's Edition** 225

Literary Note

L In his essay "Civil Disobedience," Henry David Thoreau (1817–1862) claimed that people need not obey unjust laws. His ideas inspired the Indian leader Mohandas Gandhi, who in turn inspired Dr. King to promote non-violent resistance (civil disobedience) to fight injustice.

Critical Thinking: ANALYZING

M Have students discuss the different connotations of the terms *boycott* and *massive noncooperation*. (Possible responses: *Boycott* suggests economic coercion; *massive noncooperation* suggests a nonviolent philosophical stance.)

Literary Concept: SYMBOL

N Ask students to visualize the brightly lit, empty bus racing through the morning darkness and then suggest what it might symbolize. (Possible responses: Like a light in the darkness, the bus symbolizes hope; it symbolizes the dawning of a new day without the evils of segregation.)

STRATEGIC READING FOR
Less-Proficient Readers

O Make sure students understand the events that have occurred so far.

- What happened to Rosa Parks? (*She was arrested for not giving up her bus seat to a white.*) **Reviewing**

- As a result of Rosa Parks's arrest, what did the African Americans of Montgomery decide to do? (*boycott the buses*) **Noting Cause and Effect**

Set a Purpose Have students read on to find out what further role Dr. King plays in the boycott.

---

the bus company out of business, but to put justice in business." He recalled Thoreau's[7] words, "We can no longer lend our cooperation to an evil system," and he thought, "He who accepts evil without protesting against it is really cooperating with it." Later Martin wrote, "From this moment on I conceived of our movement as an act of massive noncooperation. From then on I rarely used the word 'boycott.'"

Serene after his inner struggle, Martin joined me in our sitting room. We wanted to get to bed early, but Yoki began crying and the telephone kept ringing. Between interruptions we sat together talking about the prospects for the success of the protest. We were both filled with doubt. Attempted boycotts had failed in Montgomery and other cities. Because of changing times and tempers, this one seemed to have a better chance, but it was still a slender hope. We finally decided that if the boycott was sixty percent effective we would be doing all right, and we would be satisfied to have made a good start.

A little after midnight we finally went to bed, but at five-thirty the next morning we were up and dressed again. The first bus was due at six o'clock at the bus stop just outside our house. We had coffee and toast in the kitchen; then I went into the living room to watch. Right on time, the bus came, headlights blazing through the December darkness, all lit up inside. I shouted, "Martin! Martin, come quickly!" He ran in and stood beside me, his face lit with excitement. There was not one person on that usually crowded bus!

We stood together waiting for the next bus. It was empty too, and this was the most heavily traveled line in the whole city. Bus after empty bus paused at the stop and moved on. We were so excited we could hardly speak coherently. Finally Martin said, "I'm going to take the car and see what's happening other places in the city."

He picked up Ralph Abernathy and they cruised together around the city. Martin told me about it when he got home. Everywhere it was the same—a few white people and maybe one or two blacks in otherwise empty buses. Martin and Ralph saw extraordinary sights—the sidewalks crowded with men and women trudging to work; the students of Alabama State College walking or thumbing rides; taxicabs with people clustered in them. Some of our people rode mules; others went in horse-drawn buggies. But most of them were walking, some making a round-trip of as much as twelve miles. Martin later wrote, "As I watched them I knew that there is nothing more majestic than the determined courage of individuals willing to suffer and sacrifice for their freedom and dignity."

Martin rushed off again at nine o'clock that morning to attend the trial of Mrs. Parks. She was convicted of disobeying the city's segregation ordinance and fined ten dollars and costs. Her young attorney, Fred D. Gray, filed an appeal. It was one of the first clear-cut cases of an African American being convicted of disobeying the segregation laws—usually the charge was disorderly conduct or some such thing.

The leaders of the Movement called a meeting for three o'clock in the afternoon to organize the mass meeting to be held that night. Martin was a bit late, and as he entered the hall, people said to him, "Martin, we have elected you to be our president. Will you accept?"

Fear was an invisible presence at the meeting, along with courage and hope. Proposals were voiced to make the organization, which the

---

7. **Thoreau** (thə-rō′): Henry David Thoreau (1817–1862), American writer whose famous essay "Civil Disobedience" helped inspire the ideas of nonviolent resistance used in the civil rights movement.

WORDS TO KNOW

coherently (kō-hîr′ənt-lē) *adv.* in a manner that shows clear thinking and makes sense

---

Mini-Lesson Literary Concept

REVIEWING AUTOBIOGRAPHY Remind students that an autobiography is a factual account of a person's life written by that person. It is usually written from the first-person point of view and is intended to give the reader insight into the person's character, feelings, and attitudes.

Application Have students think about how Coretta Scott King's autobiography, *My Life with Martin Luther King, Jr.*, is special in that the author, while telling about her own experiences, also gives insight into her husband's character, feelings, and attitudes. Ask students to find passages in the text where Mrs. King's unique role as wife gives us a behind-the-scenes, personal view of Dr. King. These include his struggling with his conscience about the boycott, his joy at seeing the first empty buses, his nervousness about accepting the leadership of the boycott, and so on.

Dr. Martin Luther King, Jr. (*left*), and Coretta Scott King in their early days as civil rights activists. Culver Pictures.

leaders decided to call the Montgomery Improvement Association, or MIA, a sort of secret society, because if no names were mentioned it would be safer for the leaders. E. D. Nixon opposed that idea. "We're acting like little boys," he said. "Somebody's name will be known, and if we're afraid, we might just as well fold up right now. The white folks are eventually going to find out anyway. We'd better decide now if we are going to be fearless men or scared little boys."

That settled that question. It was also decided that the protest would continue until certain demands were met. Ralph Abernathy was made chairman of the committee to draw up the demands.

Martin came home at six o'clock. He said later that he was nervous about telling me he had accepted the presidency of the protest movement, but he need not have worried, because I sincerely meant what I said when I told him that night: "You know that whatever you do, you have my backing."

Reassured, Martin went to his study. He was to make the main speech at the mass meeting that night. It was now six-thirty and—this was the way it was usually to be—he had only twenty minutes to prepare what he thought might be the most decisive speech of his life. He said afterward that thinking about the responsibility and the reporters and television cameras, he almost panicked. Five minutes wasted and only fifteen minutes left. At that moment he

MONTGOMERY BOYCOTT 227

Linking to History

P Students may not realize how much the protesters had to fear. Civil rights demonstrators in the South often faced police brutality. Their churches and homes were bombed, and some organizers, such as Medgar Evers, were murdered by angry whites. The Kings' own home was bombed in 1956 by racists. Finally, Dr. King himself was assassinated in 1968.

Literary Concept:
AUTOBIOGRAPHY

Q Ask students to discuss why King is able to be so precise about time in her autobiography. *(Possible responses: She may have kept a journal during that time and referred to it as she wrote; she may have very clear memories of the crucial events.)*

Critical Thinking:
MAKING INFERENCES

R Ask students why Dr. King might have hesitated to tell his wife about his new position. *(Possible responses: He knew she would be worried about him; he feared she might ask him not to accept for the sake of the safety of his family.)*

Literary Concept:
INTERNAL CONFLICT

S Have students suggest what internal conflict King must have been experiencing. *(Possible responses: He was afraid of failure; he feared his speech might incite a riot or cause the protesters to lose heart.)*

Mini-Lesson  Workplace Literacy

SCANS GOAL: Exercises Leadership

LEADING A MEETING Meetings play an important role in community and business organizations. The leader of a meeting is responsible for keeping order and focusing attention on major goals. Have students discuss how Dr. King might have conducted the meeting of Movement workers on the day the boycott began. Explain that the basic steps of running a meeting include:

- Making sure a quorum, or majority of members, is present
- Calling the meeting to order
- Reading the minutes of the last meeting
- Taking up unfinished business from the last meeting
- Introducing new business
- Adjourning or closing the meeting

Application Invite students to use the basic steps to role-play the meeting that was held on the day of the boycott.

Literary Concept: MOOD

T Have students note the mood these details convey. *(Possible response: The traffic jam, the 5,000 people singing, and the crowd passing Martin over their heads suggest a mood of excitement and anticipation.)*

CUSTOMIZING FOR
Gifted and Talented Students

U In the context of Dr. King's comment, "Open your mouth and God will speak for you," have students discuss possible sources of inspiration for King's eloquence.

Literary Concept: AUTHOR'S PURPOSE

V Invite students to suggest why King quotes her husband's speech at length. *(Possible response: Her husband's own words are the best way to present the philosophy of the civil rights movement.)*

Literary Concept: CONTRAST

W Ask students to explain how Dr. King uses contrast to organize this portion of his speech. *(He contrasts point by point the negative tactics of the White Citizens Council with the positive goals and tactics of the civil rights movement.)*

STRATEGIC READING FOR
Less-Proficient Readers

X Ask students to identify the main message of Dr. King's speech. *(Possible response: Dr. King protested the injustice segregating busing; he mapped out a strategy of protest based upon love, not hate, and founded on Christian principles.)*

---

turned to prayer. He asked God "to restore my balance and be with me in a time when I need Your guidance more than ever."

How could he make his speech <u>militant</u> enough to rouse people to action and yet <u>devoid</u> of hate and resentment? He was determined to do both.

Martin and Ralph went together to the meeting. When they got within four blocks of the Holt Street Baptist Church, there was an enormous traffic jam. Five thousand people stood outside the church listening to loudspeakers and singing hymns. Inside it was so crowded, Martin told me, the people had to lift Ralph and him above the crowd and pass them from hand to hand over their heads to the platform. The crowd and the singing inspired Martin, and God answered his prayer. Later Martin said, "That night I understood what the older preachers meant when they said, 'Open your mouth and God will speak for you.'"

First the people sang "Onward, Christian Soldiers" in a tremendous wave of five thousand voices. This was followed by a prayer and a reading of the Scriptures. Martin was introduced. People applauded; television lights beat upon him. Without any notes at all he began to speak. Once again he told the story of Mrs. Parks, and rehearsed some of the wrongs black people were suffering. Then he said,

But there comes a time when people get tired. We are here this evening to say to those who have mistreated us so long, that we are tired. Tired of being segregated and humiliated; tired of being kicked about by the brutal feet of <u>oppression</u>.

The audience cheered wildly, and Martin said,

We have no alternative but to protest. We have been amazingly patient . . . but we come here tonight to be saved from that patience that makes us patient with anything less than freedom and justice.

Taking up the challenging newspaper comparison with the White Citizens Councils and the Klan,[8] Martin said,

They are protesting for the <u>perpetuation</u> of injustice in the community; we're protesting for the birth of justice . . . their methods lead to violence and lawlessness. But in our protest there will be no cross-burnings, no white person will be taken from his home by a hooded Negro mob and brutally murdered . . . We will be guided by the highest principles of law and order.

Having roused the audience for militant action, Martin now set limits upon it. His study of nonviolence and his love of Christ informed his words. He said,

No one must be intimidated to keep them from riding the buses. Our method must be persuasion, not <u>coercion</u>. We will only say to the people, "Let your conscience be your guide." . . . Our actions must be guided by the deepest principles of the Christian faith. . . . Once again we must hear the words of Jesus, "Love your enemies. Bless them that curse you. Pray for them that despitefully use you." If we fail to do this, our protest will end up as a meaningless drama on the stage of history

---

8. **Klan:** the Ku Klux Klan, a secret society trying to establish white power and authority by unlawful and violent methods directed against African Americans and other minority groups.

WORDS TO KNOW
militant (mĭl´ĭ-tənt) *adj.* showing a fighting spirit; aggressive
devoid (dĭ-void´) *adj.* completely lacking; empty
oppression (ə-prĕsh´ən) *n.* unjust or cruel exercise of power or authority
perpetuation (pər-pĕch´ōō-ā´shən) *n.* a long-lasting continuation
coercion (kō-ûr´zhən) *n.* the use of power or threats to force someone to do something

228

Mini-Lesson: Speaking, Listening, and Viewing

SPEECHES Explain to students that giving a powerful speech is an effective way to inform and persuade an audience. Point out that nervousness before speaking, such as Dr. King experienced, is normal and can even gear up a speaker for a better delivery. Tell them that while few speakers are as eloquent as Dr. King, all good speakers can do as he did in carefully choosing a topic and sticking to it; organizing ideas coherently; and understanding the audience.

Application A few students might like to deliver the segments of Dr. King's speeches given on pages 228 and 229, or practice and deliver longer portions of other speeches by Dr. King. (To help students get started, you may wish to play tape recordings of Dr. King's speeches.) Alternatively, students might choose to write a speech that informs their classmates about a problem in their own community and persuades them to take some action.

---

228 THE LANGUAGE OF LITERATURE TEACHER'S EDITION

and its memory will be shrouded in the ugly garments of shame. . . . We must not become bitter and end up by hating our white brothers. As Booker T. Washington[9] said, "Let no man pull you so low as to make you hate him."

Finally, Martin said,

If you will protest courageously, and yet with dignity and Christian love, future historians will say, "There lived a great people—a black people—who injected new meaning and dignity into the veins of civilization." This is our challenge and our overwhelming responsibility.

As Martin finished speaking, the audience rose cheering in <u>exaltation</u>. And in that speech my husband set the keynote and the tempo of the Movement he was to lead, from Montgomery onward. ❖

---
9. **Booker T. Washington** (1856–1915): African-American educator and writer.

INSIGHT

SIT-INS
Margaret Walker

Greensboro, North Carolina, in the Spring of 1960

You were our first brave ones to defy their
   dissonance of hate
With your silence
With your willingness to suffer
Without violence
5 Those first bright young to fling names across pages
Of new southern history
With courage and faith, convictions, and intelligence
The first to blaze a flaming path for justice
And awaken consciences
10 Of these stony ones.

Come, Lord Jesus, Bold Young Galilean[1]
Sit Beside this Counter, Lord, with Me!

---
1. **Galilean** (găl′ə-lē′ən): a term used as a synonym for Jesus, because Galilee was the center of Jesus' ministry.

WORDS TO KNOW

exaltation (ĕg′zôl-tā′shən) *n.* the act of glorifying, praising, or honoring

From Personal Response to Critical Analysis

1. Accept all reasonable responses.
2. Possible responses: Mrs. Parks's decision resulted in integrated buses; it started the civil rights movement; it launched the civil rights career of Martin Luther King, Jr.
3. Possible responses: yes, because the flare-up of indignation and protest was unplanned and spread quickly throughout the community; no, because resentment had been simmering for years and organizers carefully planned the boycott
4. Possible responses: Dr. King shows himself to be compassionate, courageous, and deeply religious; his goal was to win freedom and justice for his fellow African Americans; his principles included nonviolence, compassion, and Christian love.
5. Possible response: Through her courage and dignity, she inspired the civil rights movement.
6. Possible responses: nonviolence; justice; bravery; love
7. Accept all reasonable responses. Make sure that students address the issues of effectiveness and fairness in the examples they give.

Another Pathway

Cooperative Learning Groups should first discuss the main ideas each editorial will express. One student can draft one editorial, a second student can draft the other editorial, and the third and fourth students can each edit a draft.

Rubric

3 Full Accomplishment Each editorial argues persuasively either from the black or white perspectives; the main point is clearly communicated in terms appropriate to the audience.

2 Substantial Accomplishment The editorials have substance but may sometimes confuse the two perspectives or argue illogically.

1 Little or Partial Accomplishment Editorials do not distinguish between the two points of view and fail to present logical arguments.

RESPONDING OPTIONS

FROM PERSONAL RESPONSE TO CRITICAL ANALYSIS

REFLECT
1. What feelings did you experience while reading the selection? Describe them in your notebook.

RETHINK
2. Review the cause-and-effect diagram that you completed for the Reading Connection on page 221. What do you think were the most important effects of Rosa Parks's decision not to give up her bus seat?

3. Do you think the phrase "spontaneous combustion" is a good description of the events leading up to the boycott?
Close Textual Reading
Consider
  - Rosa Parks's motivation for challenging the system
Thematic Link
  - how segregation had affected the African-American community

4. What does the selection suggest about the character, goals, and principles of Martin Luther King, Jr.?

5. What is your opinion of Rosa Parks and her accomplishments? Explain your opinion.
Thematic Link

RELATE
6. Based on your understanding of "Montgomery Boycott" and the Insight poem "Sit-Ins," what qualities do you think were valued by the early participants in the civil rights movement?

7. Do you think a boycott is an effective and fair means of protest? Use examples to explain your reasoning.

LITERARY CONCEPTS

Author's purpose refers to a writer's main reason for writing. Writers of nonfiction usually write for one or more of the following purposes: to inform, to give an opinion, to entertain, or to persuade. For example, the purpose of a news report is to inform readers about events; the purpose of an editorial may be to persuade readers to do or believe something. What would you identify as Coretta Scott King's main purpose in writing this selection? Cite details to support your response.

230   UNIT TWO   PART 1: CHALLENGING THE SYSTEM

Multimodal Learning
ANOTHER PATHWAY
Cooperative Learning

Work together in a small group to write two newspaper editorials on the Montgomery boycott that might have appeared the day after it began. Write one from the perspective of a paper aimed primarily at African-American readers and the second from the perspective of a paper that serves a mostly white readership.

QUICKWRITES

1. Write the diary entry Rosa Parks might have written just after her famous bus ride and arrest. Expand on ideas touched upon in the selection and in your prereading discussion.

2. In describing the boycott, Rosa Parks reported, "Many whites, even white Southerners, told me that even though it may have seemed like the blacks were being freed, they felt more free and at ease themselves." Write an analysis of what you think she meant.

3. Create several protest signs that demonstrators might have carried on the first day of the bus boycott.

📁 **PORTFOLIO** Save your writing. You may want to use it later as a springboard to a piece for your portfolio.

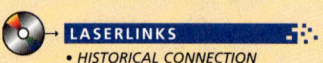
- HISTORICAL CONNECTION

QuickWrites

1. In writing the entries, ask students to try to capture Mrs. Parks's down-to-earth tone ("I was just plain tired, and my feet hurt.").
2. To help students explore Parks's comment, ask them why whites might have felt uncomfortable on segregated buses.
3. If students research the early civil rights era, they will find photographs of signs actually carried by protesters.

Hypothesis (exposition: analysis), pp. 168–172

Literary Concepts

Some students may believe that Coretta Scott King's main purpose is to inform readers about the events leading up to the Montgomery bus boycott and to show her husband's emergence as the defining influence in the civil rights movement. Others may view her purpose as a persuasive one, intended to convince readers of the rightness of her husband's cause and to urge them to support that cause. Encourage all students to support their answers with details from the text.

Multimodal Learning

ALTERNATIVE ACTIVITIES

1. Retell the **story** of the boycott as if you were presenting it to an audience of young children celebrating Martin Luther King Day. If possible, present your story to an audience of children.

2. Find and photocopy news stories and magazine articles that reported the Montgomery boycott when it happened. Use them in a "Moments in History" **bulletin-board display** or **exhibit**.

3. Bring to class and play a recording of a **speech** by Martin Luther King, Jr. Explain when and where he made the speech and why it is significant.

ACROSS THE CURRICULUM

History Research and prepare a time line that identifies and briefly describes events in the civil rights movement. You might begin with the Montgomery boycott or with the 1954 Supreme Court decision in *Brown v. Board of Education of Topeka, Kansas.*

LITERARY LINKS

What person, real or fictional, that you have read about in this book do you think is most like Rosa Parks? Explain your answer.

WORDS TO KNOW

Review the Words to Know at the bottom of the selection pages. Then, on a separate sheet, indicate whether the following pairs of words are synonyms or antonyms.

1. degrading—humiliating
2. radiant—dim
3. exposé—tribute
4. oppression—injustice
5. coherently—sensibly
6. militant—meek
7. devoid—full
8. perpetuation—halt
9. coercion—intimidation
10. exaltation—glorification

CORETTA SCOTT KING

As a child in Heiberger, Alabama, Coretta Scott had to walk five miles a day to a one-room schoolhouse while white children rode past her on a school bus. That experience and others made her determined to struggle for racial equality. Recognizing education as the key to winning that struggle, she studied hard and eventually won a scholarship to Antioch College in Ohio, where her sister Edythe had been the first African-American student on campus. After graduation, she moved to Boston to study music and there met Martin Luther King, Jr., then a graduate student at Boston University, whose dreams of fighting for racial equality coincided with her own. The two were married in 1953, two years before the Montgomery boycott.

1927–

Over the years, Coretta Scott King has shown great determination and courage in her fight for civil rights. In 1956 her home was bombed; in 1968 her husband was assassinated in Memphis, Tennessee. Nevertheless, on the day before her husband's funeral, she led a march of striking Memphis garbage collectors, and the next year she published *My Life with Martin Luther King, Jr.,* the book from which "Montgomery Boycott" is taken. Since then, she has remained a tireless champion in the struggle for racial justice, most notably as founder and chief executive officer of the Martin Luther King, Jr., Center for Nonviolent Social Change in Atlanta, Georgia.

OTHER WORKS *The Words of Martin Luther King, Jr.*

Extended Reading
MONTGOMERY BOYCOTT **231**

Words to Know

1. synonyms	6. antonyms
2. antonyms	7. antonyms
3. antonyms	8. antonyms
4. synonyms	9. synonyms
5. synonyms	10. synonyms

Reteaching/Reinforcement
• *Unit Two Resource Book,* p. 18

Literary Links

Possible response: Students might suggest that Rosa Parks reminds them of Mrs. Mathabane in *Kaffir Boy* in that both women in racially charged situations risk personal injury to do what they believe is right.

Across the Curriculum

Students might include these events:

The Civil Rights Act of 1957, which created the Civil Rights Division in the Department of Justice to enforce civil rights laws.

The 24th Amendment, ratified in 1964, barred poll taxes in federal elections.

The Civil Rights Act of 1964 ordered businesses to serve the public without regard to race, color, religion, or national origin; and established the Equal Employment Opportunity Commission.

The Voting Rights Act, passed in 1965, outlawed literacy tests for voting.

The Civil Rights Act of 1968 barred discrimination in housing.

CORETTA SCOTT KING

Today King heads the Martin Luther King, Jr., Center for Nonviolent Social Change in Atlanta, Georgia. She is known for her composure in times of crisis. "It seems that when there's a crisis, I call upon all my energy, my resources," she once remarked. "There is no problem that we can't solve if we can corral our resources."

HISTORICAL CONNECTION
The Civil Rights Movement

Protests, confrontations, and conflict characterized the struggle for civil rights in the 1950s and 1960s. A lunch counter sit-in and an armed escort for black students are among the photographs giving a human face to the civil rights movement.

Side A, Frame 49393

Alternative Activities

1. Suggest to students that in retelling the story for young children, they might dramatize key events—Rosa Parks saying "no," the Kings joyfully seeing the first empty bus, the crowd in the church handing Dr. King over their heads.

2. Suggest that students use the *Readers' Guide to Periodical Literature* to locate back issues of *Ebony, Life, Look, Time,* and *Newsweek* from late 1955 and 1956 that covered the events in the selection. The Time-Life photo books on this period will also be a good source.

3. If your library has the tapes of the PBS series *Eyes on the Prize,* suggest that students review it to find excerpts of Dr. King's key speeches. Another book by Coretta Scott King, *The Words of Martin Luther King, Jr.,* is a good source for copies of his speeches.

THE LANGUAGE OF LITERATURE **TEACHER'S EDITION** 231

OVERVIEW

Objectives

- To understand and appreciate a short story that explores the use of assertiveness to challenge an inhumane system
- To identify and understand point of view
- To express understanding of a selection through a choice of writing forms, including a letter, a personal essay, and a plot summary
- To extend understanding of the selection though a variety of multimodal and cross-curricular activities

Skills

LITERARY CONCEPTS
- Point of view
- Conflict

THE WRITER'S STYLE
- Transitional devices

SPEAKING, LISTENING, AND VIEWING
- Group discussion
- Speech

CUSTOMIZING FOR Students Acquiring English

- Use **ACCESS FOR STUDENTS ACQUIRING ENGLISH,** *Reading Support.*
- Students may have trouble understanding the dialect spoken by the warder. Suggest that students read aloud his dialogue. When necessary, clarify the warder's words, such as *tink* for *think,* and *'ere* for *here.*

CUSTOMIZING FOR Gifted and Talented Students

Have students look for textual evidence that shows how Brille's opinion of Hannetjie gradually changes.

Possible responses:

Page 234 —"Because he's not human." / At first, Brille is frightened by the warder's brutality.

Page 237 —"I saw today that Hannetjie is just a child and stupidly truthful." / After Brille discovers Hannetjie's vulnerability, he no longer sees him as a threat; he realizes that he can control the warder.

Page 238 —"...his [Hannetjie's] interpretation of what was good and human often left the prisoners of Span One speechless with surprise." / Because Hannetjie is so conscientious in meeting the prisoners' needs, Brille begins to see the warder as a decent person.

PREVIEWING

FICTION

The Prisoner Who Wore Glasses

Bessie Head South Africa / Botswana

PERSONAL CONNECTION

In a class discussion, tell what you think it means to be assertive. Then discuss the possible advantages and disadvantages of acting assertively. Use examples from various social situations—at home, at school, in your community, and so on.

HISTORICAL CONNECTION

From the late 1940s to the early 1990s, black South Africans who tried to be assertive frequently became political prisoners. Some people were imprisoned, for example, simply for speaking out against the government or publicly protesting government policies. South Africa was then ruled by a white minority government whose official policy of apartheid (ə-pärt'hīt') kept the races separate and legally discriminated against the nation's black majority and other people of color. "The Prisoner Who Wore Glasses" is set on a South African prison farm in the years when apartheid was still the law of the land. The two main characters in the story are a black political prisoner and a white prison guard, or warder. The warder is an Afrikaner (ăf'rĭ-kä'nər), a white South African of Dutch descent, who speaks English with a heavy accent.

Riot in Durban, South Africa, 1959. Archive Photos.

WRITING CONNECTION

Do you find it easy to voice your own needs and wants, or are you reluctant to speak up for yourself? In your notebook, rate your own assertiveness on a scale of 0 to 10, like the one to the right, and then explain your reasoning. As you read, notice how assertive the main characters are.

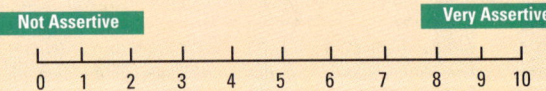

232 UNIT TWO PART 1: CHALLENGING THE SYSTEM

PRINT AND MEDIA RESOURCES

UNIT TWO RESOURCE BOOK
Strategic Reading: Literature, p. 21
Vocabulary SkillBuilder, p. 22

WRITING MINI-LESSONS
Transparencies, p. 41

ACCESS FOR STUDENTS ACQUIRING ENGLISH
Selection Summaries
Reading Support

FORMAL ASSESSMENT
Selection Test, pp. 43–44
 Test Generator

AUDIO LIBRARY
See Reference Card

INTERNET RESOURCES
McDougal Littell Literature Center at http://www.hmco.com/mcdougal/lit

The Prisoner Who Wore Glasses
Bessie Head

Chain Gang (1939–1940), William H. Johnson. National Museum of American Art, Washington, D.C./Art Resource, New York.

Scarcely a breath of wind disturbed the stillness of the day, and the long rows of cabbages were bright green in the sunlight. Large white clouds drifted slowly across the deep blue sky. Now and then they obscured the sun and caused a chill on the backs of the prisoners who had to work all day long in the cabbage field.

SUMMARY

Hannetjie, a tough new prison guard, or warder, takes charge of Span One, a closely knit group of black political prisoners in a South African work camp. Unlike earlier warders, Hannetjie punishes Brille, the prisoner with glasses, severely for stealing and talking back to him. Brille, a father of 12, is philosophical about prison violence and wise about human brutality and the politics of coexistence. Eventually, Brille catches Hannetjie stealing fertilizer and uses this as leverage to strike a bargain with him. In time, Span One and the new warder work out a relationship of cooperation: the prisoners enjoy privileges that enable them to endure their long, hard confinement and, in turn, they become the hardest workers in the camp, helping Hannetjie steal fertilizer and other items he can use on his farm.

Thematic Link: **Challenging the System** Prisoners and warder alike challenge a rigid prison system, remaking it to suit everyone's needs.

STRATEGIC READING FOR
Less-Proficient Readers

Set a Purpose Have students read the first three paragraphs aloud and then describe the main character. *(He is thin, little, comic-looking, and has fanciful ideas.)*

Then ask students to read on to find out more about the main character, Brille, and what happens to him.

Use **UNIT TWO RESOURCE BOOK**, p. 21, for guidance in reading the selection.

Art Note

Chain Gang by William Henry Johnson William Henry Johnson (1902–1970) sought to express his African-American roots through the artistic vehicle of primitivism, a style of art marked by simple shapes and strong colors.

Reading the Art *What emotions are suggested by the figures in the painting? What details from the painting suggest those emotions?*

WORDS TO KNOW

acute (ə-kyōōt′) *adj.* very sharp or severe (p. 237)
bedlam (bĕd′ləm) *n.* a place or situation of great noise and confusion (p. 235)
chaos (kā′ŏs′) *n.* total disorder (p. 235)
commodity (kə-mŏd′ĭ-tē) *n.* an item—especially a farming or mining product—that can be turned to commercial use or that can provide another advantage (p. 238)

conviction (kən-vĭk′shən) *n.* certainty; a strong belief (p. 237)
cower (kou′ər) *v.* to cringe in fear (p. 234)
irrelevant (ĭ-rĕl′ə-vənt) *adj.* not related to the matter at hand (p. 237)
perpetrate (pûr′pĭ-trāt′) *v.* to commit (p. 235)
ruefully (rōō′fə-lē) *adv.* with regret (p. 235)
tirade (tī′rād′) *n.* a long, angry speech (p. 237)

CUSTOMIZING FOR

Students Acquiring English

I Clarify what a *political prisoner* is. Ask students what kinds of crimes these ten men probably committed.

Literary Concept: POINT OF VIEW

A Ask students to identify who is telling the story. *(a person who is not part of the action, a narrator who knows about the prisoners and the prison authorities)* How does the reader know the narrator is not Brille? *(The narrator uses third-person pronouns, such as* he *and* they; *if Brille were narrating, he'd rely on first-person pronouns.)*

Literary Concept: CONFLICT

B Ask students to explain why the conflict between the Span One prisoners and their warders is unusual. *(Possible responses: Unlike common criminals, the men in Span One do not feel guilt because they have done nothing but protest a political situation; the prisoners are assertive, and warders don't know how to cope with assertive prisoners.)*

Literary Concept: SYMBOL

C Point out that both the title of the story and Brille's nickname highlight his eyeglasses. Have students suggest what the glasses might symbolize. *(Possible responses: The glasses might symbolize Brille's unique viewpoint; they might also symbolize his wisdom or knowledge.)*

This trick the clouds were playing with the sun eventually caused one of the prisoners who wore glasses to stop work, straighten up and peer short-sightedly at them. He was a thin little fellow with a hollowed-out chest and comic knobbly knees. He also had a lot of fanciful ideas because he smiled at the clouds.

"Perhaps they want me to send a message to the children," he thought tenderly, noting that the clouds were drifting in the direction of his home some hundred miles away. But before he could frame the message, the warder in charge of his work span[1] shouted:

"Hey, what you tink you're doing, Brille?"[2]

The prisoner swung round, blinking rapidly, yet at the same time sizing up the enemy. He was a new warder, named Jacobus Stephanus Hannetjie.[3] His eyes were the color of the sky but they were frightening. A simple, primitive, brutal soul gazed out of them. The prisoner bent down quickly and a message was quietly passed down the line:

"We're in for trouble this time, comrades."

"Why?" rippled back up the line.

"Because he's not human," the reply rippled down, and yet only the crunching of the spades as they turned over the earth disturbed the stillness.

This particular work span was known as Span One. It was composed of ten men, and they were all political prisoners. They were grouped together for convenience, as it was one of the prison regulations that no black warder should be in charge of a political prisoner lest this prisoner convert him to his views. It never seemed to occur to the authorities that this very reasoning was the strength of Span One and a clue to the strange terror they aroused in the warders. As political prisoners they were unlike the other prisoners in the sense that they felt no guilt nor were they outcasts of society. All guilty men instinctively <u>cower</u>, which was why it was the kind of prison where men got knocked out cold with a blow at the back of the head from an iron bar. Up until the arrival of Warder Hannetjie, no warder had dared beat any member of Span One and no warder had lasted more than a week with them. The battle was entirely psychological. Span One was assertive and it was beyond the scope of white warders to handle assertive black men. Thus, Span One had got out of control. They were the best thieves and liars in the camp. They lived all day on raw cabbages. They chatted and smoked tobacco. And since they moved, thought and acted as one, they had perfected every technique of group concealment.

Trouble began that very day between Span One and Warder Hannetjie. It was because of the shortsightedness of Brille. That was the nickname he was given in prison and is the Afrikaans[4] word for someone who wears glasses. Brille could never judge the approach of the prison gates, and on several previous occasions he had munched on cabbages and dropped them almost at the feet of the warder, and all previous warders had overlooked this. Not so Warder Hannetjie.

"Who dropped that cabbage?" he thundered.

Brille stepped out of line.

"I did," he said meekly.

"All right," said Hannetjie. "The whole span goes three meals off."

"But I told you I did it," Brille protested.

The blood rushed to Warder Hannetjie's face.

---

1. **work span:** a work group in the prison.
2. **Brille** (brĭl′ə).
3. **Jacobus Stephanus Hannetjie** (yä-kō′büs stä-fän′üs hä′nĕt-yē).
4. **Afrikaans** (ăf′rĭ-käns′): a language closely related to Dutch and spoken by South Africans of Dutch descent.

WORDS TO KNOW

cower (kou′ər) *v.* to cringe in fear

"Look 'ere," he said. "I don't take orders from a kaffir.[5] I don't know what kind of kaffir you tink you are. Why don't you say Baas.[6] I'm your Baas. Why don't you say Baas, hey?"

Brille blinked his eyes rapidly but by contrast his voice was strangely calm.

"I'm twenty years older than you," he said. It was the first thing that came to mind, but the comrades seemed to think it a huge joke. A titter swept up the line. The next thing Warder Hannetjie whipped out a knobkerrie[7] and gave Brille several blows about the head. What surprised his comrades was the speed with which Brille had removed his glasses or else they would have been smashed to pieces on the ground.

That evening in the cell Brille was very apologetic.

"I'm sorry, comrades," he said. "I've put you into a hell of a mess."

"Never mind, brother," they said. "What happens to one of us, happens to all."

"I'll try to make up for it, comrades," he said. "I'll steal something so that you don't go hungry."

Privately, Brille was very philosophical about his head wounds. It was the first time an act of violence had been perpetrated against him, but he had long been a witness of extreme, almost unbelievable human brutality. He had twelve children and his mind traveled back that evening through the sixteen years of bedlam in which he had lived. It had all happened in a small drab little three-bedroomed house in a small drab little street in the Eastern Cape,[8] and the children kept coming year after year because neither he nor Martha managed the contraceptives the right way and a teacher's salary never allowed moving to a bigger house and he was always taking exams to improve this salary only to have it all eaten up by hungry mouths. Everything was pretty horrible, especially the way the children fought. They'd get hold of each other's heads and give them a good bashing against the wall. Martha gave up somewhere along the line, so they worked out a thing between them. The bashings, biting and blood were to operate in full swing until he came home. He was to be the bogeyman,[9] and when it worked he never failed to have a sense of godhead[10] at the way in which his presence could change savages into fairly reasonable human beings.

Yet somehow it was this chaos and mismanagement at the center of his life that drove him into politics. It was really an ordered beautiful world with just a few basic slogans to learn along with the rights of mankind. At one stage, before things became very bad, there were conferences to attend, all very far away from home.

"Let's face it," he thought ruefully. "I'm only learning right now what it means to be a politician.

> "But I told you I did it," Brille protested. The blood rushed to Warder Hannetjie's face.

---

5. **kaffir** (kăf′ər): in South Africa, an insulting term for a black.
6. **Baas** (bäs): Afrikaans for *master*. The word has the same Dutch origins as the English *boss*.
7. **knobkerrie** (nŏb′kĕr′ē): a short club with a knobbed end.
8. **the Eastern Cape:** the eastern part of the Cape Province in southern South Africa.
9. **bogeyman** (boŏg′ē-măn′): a terrifying figure of fear, dread, or harassment.
10. **godhead:** divinity; the quality or state of being a god.

WORDS TO KNOW
perpetrate (pûr′pĭ-trāt′) *v.* to commit
bedlam (bĕd′ləm) *n.* a place or situation of great noise and confusion
chaos (kā′ŏs) *n.* total disorder
ruefully (rōō′fə-lē) *adv.* with regret

235

Art Note

Le negre Scipion by Paul Cézanne
Known for his use of color, French painter Paul Cézanne (1839–1906) has had a significant impact on artists of this century. Cézanne may be most famous for his colorful landscapes of the French countryside, but his early paintings expressed a darker side of life. Like the painting here, they employed somber colors, heavy paint, and brush strokes that gave a textural, almost sculptured appearance.

Reading the Art How does Cézanne's use of bright and dark colors contribute to the overall effect of the painting?

STRATEGIC READING FOR Less-Proficient Readers

F Ask students what they know about Brille and why he is in prison. *(He worked as a teacher, is the father of twelve children, and went into politics; he is a political prisoner, probably because he opposed South Africa's apartheid laws.)* Noting Relevant Details

- How do Brille's political views affect his relations with the warder? *(He refuses to call Hannetjie "Baas"; he risks punishment by speaking openly.)* Noting Relevant Details

Set a Purpose Have students read on to find out how the relationship between Brille and the warder develops.

Critical Thinking: MAKING INFERENCES

G What does the narrator mean by "the pain in his head brought a hard lump to his [Brille's] throat"? *(Possible responses: Brille chokes up with tears; the warder's brutality makes Brille realize that he was wrong to let his children hit each other; he should have fostered a caring, cooperative attitude among his many children.)*

Literary Concept: THEME

H Have students discuss whether Brille's "message" might be the theme of the story. *(Possible responses: Yes, Span One is a model of cooperation in prison; Brille seems to be seeking a way to get Hannetjie's cooperation, which suggests that such cooperation should be extended throughout South African society. No, Span One consists of prisoners who refuse to cooperate with apartheid; the story suggests the necessity of not cooperating with an evil system.)*

Le nègre Scipion [Black Scipio] (about 1866–1868), Paul Cézanne. Museu de Arte de São Paulo (Brazil) Assis Chateaubriand. Photo by Luiz Hossaka.

F All this while I've been running away from Martha and the kids."

G And the pain in his head brought a hard lump to his throat. That was what the children did to each other daily and Martha wasn't managing, and if Warder Hannetjie had not interrupted him that morning, he would have sent the following message:

"Be good comrades, my children. Cooperate, then life will run smoothly." **H**

The next day Warder Hannetjie caught this old man with twelve children stealing grapes from the farm shed. They were an enormous quantity of grapes in a ten-gallon tin,[11] and for this misdeed the old man spent a week in the

---
11. **tin**: the British word for a can, used in South Africa and many other former British colonies.

236   UNIT TWO   PART 1: CHALLENGING THE SYSTEM

Mini-Lesson ✒ The Writer's Style

TRANSITIONAL DEVICES Point out that Bessie Head has organized her story chronologically around a series of events that occur over the course of a month or more. Explain that Head uses transitional devices from paragraph to paragraph to show the exact time relationships. Have students note the following time transitions at the beginnings of paragraphs on pages 236 and 237: "The next day," "For about two weeks," "The following day," and "On another occasion."

Application Invite students to review pieces of original fiction in their portfolios that are organized chronologically. Ask them to revise the work for greater clarity, adding transitional words and phrases that denote time.

Reteaching/Reinforcement
- *Writer's Handbook*, anthology pp. 1027–1029
- *Writing Mini-Lessons* transparencies, p. 41

📘 **The Writer's Craft**
Transition Devices, pp. 376–382

236 THE LANGUAGE OF LITERATURE   TEACHER'S EDITION

isolation cell. In fact, Span One as a whole was in constant trouble. Warder Hannetjie seemed to have eyes at the back of his head. He uncovered the trick about the cabbages, how they were split in two with the spade and immediately covered with earth and then unearthed again and eaten with split-second timing. He found out how tobacco smoke was beaten into the ground, and he found out how conversations were whispered down the wind.

For about two weeks Span One lived in acute misery. The cabbages, tobacco and conversations had been the pivot of jail life to them. Then one evening they noticed that their good old comrade who wore the glasses was looking rather pleased with himself. He pulled out a four-ounce packet of tobacco by way of explanation, and the comrades fell upon it with great greed. Brille merely smiled. After all, he was the father of many children. But when the last shred had disappeared, it occurred to the comrades that they ought to be puzzled. Someone said:

"I say, brother. We're watched like hawks these days. Where did you get the tobacco?"

"Hannetjie gave it to me," said Brille.

There was a long silence. Into it dropped a quiet bombshell.

"I saw Hannetjie in the shed today," and the failing eyesight blinked rapidly. "I caught him in the act of stealing five bags of fertilizer, and he bribed me to keep my mouth shut."

There was another long silence.

"Prison is an evil life," Brille continued, apparently discussing some irrelevant matter. "It makes a man contemplate all kinds of evil deeds."

He held out his hand and closed it.

"You know, comrades," he said. "I've got Hannetjie. I'll betray him tomorrow."

Everyone began talking at once.

"Forget it, brother. You'll get shot."

Brille laughed.

"I won't," he said. "That is what I mean about evil. I am a father of children, and I saw today that Hannetjie is just a child and stupidly truthful. I'm going to punish him severely because we need a good warder."

The following day, with Brille as witness, Hannetjie confessed to the theft of the fertilizer and was fined a large sum of money. From then on Span One did very much as they pleased while Warder Hannetjie stood by and said nothing. But it was Brille who carried this to extremes. One day, at the close of work Warder Hannetjie said:

"Brille, pick up my jacket and carry it back to the camp."

"But nothing in the regulations says I'm your servant, Hannetjie," Brille replied coolly.

"I've told you not to call me Hannetjie. You must say Baas," but Warder Hannetjie's voice lacked conviction. In turn, Brille squinted up at him.

"I'll tell you something about this Baas business, Hannetjie," he said. "One of these days we are going to run the country. You are going to clean my car. Now, I have a fifteen-year-old son, and I'd die of shame if you had to tell him that I ever called you Baas."

Warder Hannetjie went red in the face and picked up his coat.

On another occasion Brille was seen to be walking about the prison yard, openly smoking tobacco. On being taken before the prison commander he claimed to have received the tobacco from Warder Hannetjie. All throughout the tirade from his chief, Warder Hannetjie failed to defend himself, but his nerve broke completely. He called Brille to one side.

"Brille," he said. "This thing between you and me must end. You may not know it, but I

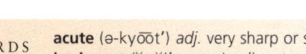

WORDS TO KNOW	**acute** (ə-kyōōt′) *adj.* very sharp or severe
	irrelevant (ĭ-rĕl′ə-vənt) *adj.* not related to the matter at hand
	conviction (kən-vĭk′shən) *n.* certainty; a strong belief
	tirade (tī′rād) *n.* a long, angry speech

237

have a wife and children, and you're driving me to suicide."

"Why don't you like your own medicine, Hannetjie?" Brille asked quietly.

"I can give you anything you want," Warder Hannetjie said in desperation.

"It's not only me but the whole of Span One," said Brille cunningly. "The whole of Span One wants something from you."

Warder Hannetjie brightened with relief.

"I tink I can manage if it's tobacco you want," he said.

Brille looked at him, for the first time struck with pity and guilt. He wondered if he had carried the whole business too far. The man was really a child.

"It's not tobacco we want, but you," he said. "We want you on our side. We want a good warder because without a good warder we won't be able to manage the long stretch ahead."

Warder Hannetjie interpreted this request in his own fashion, and his interpretation of what was good and human often left the prisoners of Span One speechless with surprise. He had a way of slipping off his revolver and picking up a spade and digging alongside Span One. He had a way of producing unheard-of luxuries like boiled eggs from his farm nearby and things like cigarettes, and Span One responded nobly and got the reputation of being the best work span in the camp.

And it wasn't only taken from their side. They were awfully good at stealing commodities like fertilizer which were needed on the farm of Warder Hannetjie. ❖

> "You may not know it, but I have a wife and children, and you're driving me to suicide."

WORDS TO KNOW

commodity (kə-mŏd′ĭ-tē) *n.* an item—especially a farming or mining product—that can be turned to commercial use or that can provide another advantage

---

Critic's Corner

"'Prison'... suggests a willed control over a naturally outgoing personality, an imprisonment not for stagnation but for recollection and renewal—a severely practical self-imposed isolation which is part of natural growth... Like the silkworm's cocoon, it is made for shelter, while strengths are gathered for outbreak and a fresh continuance."

Arthur Ravenscroft
The Novels of Bessie Head

Have students relate this comment to Brille, noting how his prison experience was an opportunity to collect and renew himself. Discuss what Brille may be like when he emerges from prison.

INSIGHT

THEY HAVE NOT BEEN ABLE

NO HAN PODIDO

ARMANDO VALLADARES
(är-män'dô bä-yä-dä'rĕs)

They have not been able to take away
the rain's song
not yet
not even in this cell
but perhaps they'll do it tomorrow
that's why I want to enjoy it now,
to listen to the drops
drumming against
the boarded windows.
And suddenly it comes
through I don't know what crack
through I don't know what opening
that pungent odor
of wet earth
and I inhale deeply
filling myself to the brim
because perhaps they will also
prohibit that tomorrow.

*Translated by
Marguerite Guzman Bouvard*

No han podido quitarme
todavía
en este encierro
el canto de la lluvia
pero quizás lo hagan mañana
por eso quiero ahora disfrutarlo
escuchar las gotas
más allá de mis ojos
y los esperos muros
golpear con insistencia
las ventanas tapiadas.
Y de pronto me llega
no sé por qué ranura
no sé por qué intersticio
ese olor agradable
de la tierra mojada
y la aspiro muy hondo
para llenarme bien
porque quizás también
lo prohiban mañana.

Hombre y su sombra [Man and his shadow] (1971), Rufino Tamayo. Oil on canvas, 50 cm × 40 cm, collection of INBA-Museo de Arte Moderno, Mexico City.

INSIGHT

Ask students the following questions:
1. Do you think the speaker in this poem is anything like Brille? *(Possible responses: yes, because they are prisoners who appreciate life's daily occurrences: no, because he seems pessimistic about what tomorrow may bring)*
2. The poem reflects the experience of the poet, who, like Brille, was a political prisoner. Do you feel taking political prisoners is ever justified? Why or why not? *(Answers will vary. Encourage students who want to help free political prisoners or improve their living conditions to write to Amnesty International, Box 1270, Mederland, CO 80466.)*

ARMANDO VALLADARES

Poet Armando Valladares (1937–) was imprisoned by the Castro regime in 1960 for alleged subversive activities. In an attempt to force him to recant his beliefs, prison officials tortured Valladares and paralyzed him. The poet was finally set free in 1982 after European intellectuals campaigned for his release.

Art Note

Man and His Shadow **by Rufino Tamayo**
The paintings of Mexico's Rufino Tamayo are a synthesis of modern influences, such as Surrealism and Expressionism, and ancient, pre-Columbian styles. Using a limited range of colors designed to bring out the interplay of tones, Tamayo paints figures of people and animals that are full of profound meaning.

Reading the Art How do the stark figures and limited colors of *Man and His Shadow* suggest the situation of the speaker in "They Have Not Been Able"?

From Personal Response to Critical Analysis

1. Accept all reasonable, well-supported responses.
2. Possible responses: Hannetjie learns to bend prison rules in order to get the cooperation of the prisoners; Hannetjie discovers that Brille is more clever than he is, and that he would thus be better off cooperating with him. Perhaps Hannetjie has come to respect the prisoners and to understand their needs.
3. Possible responses: Brille's message to his children, "Be good comrades.... Cooperate, then life will run smooth," also applies to Hannetjie; Brille intimidates his children just as he does the warder; Brille comes to realize the violence needs to be replaced with cooperation, whether in the family or in prison.
4. Possible responses: The story suggests the importance of knowing when to cooperate and when to assert yourself; assertiveness means stating your position rather than using brute force; cooperation brings benefits to all parties; sometimes assertiveness is necessary before there can be cooperation.
5. Possible responses: The speaker in "They Have Not Been Able" has a passive, almost fatalistic, attitude toward prison life; Brille has an active, positive attitude, believing he can better the prison environment; both the speaker and Brille make the best of the present moment and enjoy what they can.
6. Accept all reasonable, well-supported responses.

Another Pathway

Cooperative Learning Students should identify each conflict and then discuss it, concentrating on its relevance to South Africa at large.

Rubric

3 Full Accomplishment Students accurately chart major conflicts, articulate the motivations behind each character's actions, and clearly appreciate the significance of the incident as a reflection of race relations in South Africa.

2 Substantial Accomplishment Students chart incidents but do not fully detail the characters' motivations or the connections to South Africa.

1 Little or Partial Accomplishment Students have difficulty identifying conflicts, motivations, and relationships.

RESPONDING OPTIONS

FROM PERSONAL RESPONSE TO CRITICAL ANALYSIS

REFLECT
1. What are your thoughts and feelings about the relationship between Brille and Hannetjie? Describe your response in your notebook.

RETHINK
2. Why do you think Hannetjie becomes such a "good warder" at the end of the story?
3. How does Brille's relationship with his children compare with his relationship with Hannetjie?
4. In your opinion, what is this story saying about assertiveness and cooperation?
   Consider
   Close Textual Reading
   - how the different characters assert themselves
   - the effectiveness of assertive acts in the story
   - how the men cooperate at the end of the story

RELATE
5. Compare Brille's attitude with that of the speaker in the Insight poem "They Have Not Been Able."
6. Consider the hardships endured by Brille and the other prisoners of Span One. What do you think would be the most difficult aspect of life in prison?

LITERARY CONCEPTS

Point of view refers to the narrative method used in a literary work. In **first-person point of view,** the narrator is a character in the story who describes the action in his or her own words, referring to himself or herself with first-person pronouns such as *I, me,* and *us.* In **third-person point of view,** the narrator is not a character but instead stands outside the action, referring to all characters with third-person pronouns such as *he, she,* and *they.* "The Prisoner Who Wore Glasses" uses third-person point of view. Why do you think Bessie Head chose *not* to have Brille tell the story himself?

CONCEPT REVIEW: Setting The story is set in South Africa at a time when apartheid was still in effect. Why do you think Head set the story in a prison instead of a factory, a slum, or some other place?

240   UNIT TWO   PART 1: CHALLENGING THE SYSTEM

ANOTHER PATHWAY

Cooperative Learning
In a small group, identify the incidents involving conflict between Brille and Hannetjie. Then create a chart in which you describe each incident, note the beliefs that motivate Brille and Hannetjie, and explain how the incident reflects the larger conflict between whites and blacks in South Africa.

QUICKWRITES

1. Assume Brille's identity and write a **letter** to his children. In it, reveal what you have learned as a result of your experience in prison. Include some advice about assertiveness and cooperation.
2. Draft a **personal essay** in which you compare Brille's response to his warder with your likely response to such a situation.
3. If Brille had not caught Hannetjie stealing fertilizer, how might the outcome of the story be different? Write a **plot summary** of the events that might have happened.

📁 **PORTFOLIO** Save your writing. You may want to use it later as a springboard to a piece for your portfolio.

QuickWrites

1. Help students recall that Brille felt remorse for allowing his children to fight and then acting "the bogeyman" when he returned home. In prison Brille learned to cooperate to gain peace.
2. Suggest that they recall interactions between Hannetjie and Brille and imagine how their responses might have differed from Brille's.
3. Encourage students to make a list of events that might have happened if Hannetjie was not caught, from which they can create a plot summary.

📁 The Writer's Craft

Advice Essay, pp. 190–194
Comparison and Contrast, pp. 118–132

Literary Concepts

To clarify issues of point of view, ask students what Head would gain by having Brille narrate his own story. *(The reader would have direct access to his thoughts and feelings.)* Then draw attention to places in the story that include details and events that Brille would not necessarily know or see, such as the paragraph on page 234 which begins, "This particular work span."

Setting Discuss which of the three settings mentioned—a prison, a factory, and a slum—would most forcefully present the power structure of apartheid.

240   THE LANGUAGE OF LITERATURE TEACHER'S EDITION

Multimodal Learning

ALTERNATIVE ACTIVITIES

1. Create a **narrative cartoon** based on this story. Try to capture the personalities of the characters in your illustrations.
2. Deliver a **speech** that Brille might have made to political supporters on the day of his release from prison.

ACROSS THE CURRICULUM

Psychology Work with a partner to make a list of steps that might help to resolve a conflict, based on the resolution of the conflict between Brille and Hannetjie in the story.

LITERARY LINKS

Compare Brille's means of challenging the system with that of the narrator in "The Thrill of the Grass" by W. P. Kinsella. Which character did you find cleverer? Why?

WORDS TO KNOW

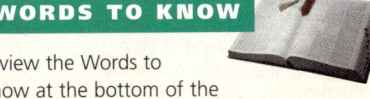

Review the Words to Know at the bottom of the selection pages. Then, for each word, complete a pyramid like the one shown below for the word *assertive*. Use a dictionary or thesaurus if you need help.

Word: assertive

Definition: inclined to bold expression or action

Synonyms: forceful, confident, outspoken, insistent, aggressive

Sentence: The prisoner was assertive when he defied the warder.

BESSIE HEAD

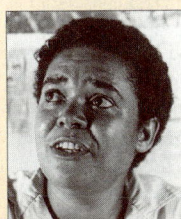

1937–1986

Born in South Africa, Bessie Head experienced firsthand the effects of apartheid. Designated as a "colored" person (part black and part white) under apartheid's rigid classification system, she was denied the full privileges of citizenship in her homeland. Head never knew her parents; she was raised from birth by a child welfare agency and was later placed with foster parents. After training in a missionary school, she worked for several years as a teacher and journalist before immigrating to a small village in Botswana, a neighboring country that was then under British control. Head taught for a few more years, then led a quiet life of writing and farming.

Though Head left South Africa physically, its problems were rarely far from her thoughts. While some of her novels and stories explore village life in Botswana, many writings reveal the tragedies and injustices of the land where she was born. Her attitude toward South Africa blended realism and idealism. "It is to be hoped," she once said, "that great leaders will arise there who remember the suffering of racial hatred and out of it formulate a common language of human love for all people." Though she died of hepatitis before reaching her 50th birthday, she left behind an impressive body of work, remarkable for its attentiveness to the lives of ordinary people.

OTHER WORKS *When Rain Clouds Gather, The Collector of Treasures, Serowe: Village of the Rain Wind, Tales of Tenderness and Power*

Extended Reading

THE PRISONER WHO WORE GLASSES 241

Words to Know

Synonyms for Words to Know include:

acute sharp, severe

bedlam pandemonium, madness, confusion

chaos disorder, upheaval

commodity goods, wares, merchandise

conviction certainty, certitude, creed

cower cringe, crouch, recoil

irrelevant unrelated, immaterial, extraneous

perpetrate commit, enact, mastermind

ruefully regretfully, remorsefully, sorrowfully

tirade harangue, diatribe, outburst

Reteaching/Reinforcement
• *Unit Two Resource Book*, p. 22

Literary Links

Possible responses: Brille was more clever because he subverted the prison system in a way that benefited everyone; the narrator in the "Thrill of the Grass" was more clever because he carried out his challenge to a successful conclusion.

Across the Curriculum

Psychology Suggest that partners select a conflict they're familiar with, such as dating, or dealing with troublesome classmates, friends, or neighbors. Students might then consider Brille's steps toward conflict resolution and apply them to the conflict they're considering. Steps might be (1) identify the conflict; (2) identify the different viewpoints of the conflicting parties; (3) identify the benefits of compromise to both parties; (4) suggest areas of compromise in which each party gives up something in return for gaining something.

BESSIE HEAD

Bessie Head's first novel, *When Rain Clouds Gather* (1968), tells of South Africans who, like Head, fled apartheid and settled in Botswana. Her second novel, *Maru* (1971), explores questions of identity among Botswanan villagers. Describing how she writes, Head says, "Every story or book starts with something just for myself. Then from that small me it becomes a panorama—the big view that has something for everyone."

Alternative Activities

1. If possible, bring in examples of political cartoons from newspapers and periodicals to point out the serious concerns cartoonists often satirically address. Suggest that students work with a partner to identify three or four incidents to portray in panels of the cartoon.
2. Suggest that Brille's release might coincide with the ending of apartheid and that Brille might recount his experiences with Hannetjie to suggest a way in which black and white South Africans can resolve their differences. If available, have students research Nelson Mandela's speech upon his release from prison in 1990 for more information.

THE LANGUAGE OF LITERATURE TEACHER'S EDITION 241

OVERVIEW

Objectives

- To understand and appreciate a short story that explores how a system can defeat a challenger
- To identify and understand irony
- To express understanding of the story through a choice of writing forms, including a dramatic scene, a letter, and a list of rules
- To extend understanding of the selection though a variety of multimodal and cross-curricular activities

Skills

THE WRITER'S STYLE
- Transitions that show contrast

GRAMMAR
- Complements

LITERARY CONCEPTS
- Irony

SPEAKING, LISTENING, AND VIEWING
- Interviews
- Group discussion
- Oral presentation

ALTERNATIVE
Previewing

Have students choose partners and use the following prompts to preview "The Censors" orally.

Writing Connection

Discussion Prompts *Think about the ways in which you give and receive news and information. Discuss with your partner how you think your life might change if these avenues of communication were monitored or heavily censored. Then listen as your partner describes his or her ideas. If you need help getting started, the following questions might help:*

- *How often do you discuss issues with friends—either by telephone, letter, fax, or e-mail?*
- *When was the last time you spoke out about a school, community, or national policy that you thought was misguided?*
- *What information have you gotten recently that throws light on the actions of government officials? How did this information affect your ideas about government?*

As you read "The Censors," notice how the main character changes as a result of government censorship.

PREVIEWING

FICTION

The Censors
Luisa Valenzuela (lōō-ē′sä vä-lĕn-swä′lä) Argentina

Activating Prior Knowledge
PERSONAL CONNECTION

What does the word *censorship* mean to you? With your class, create a word web, like the one shown, to explore the meaning of *censorship* and to give examples of different types of censorship.

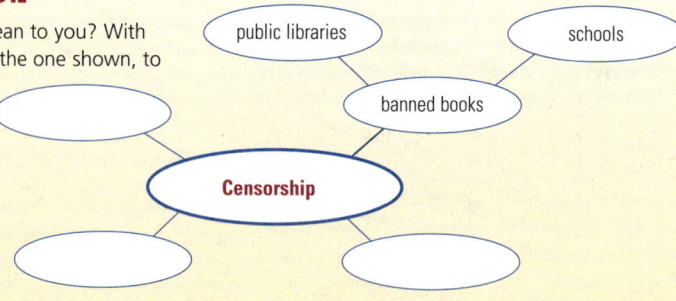

Building Background
HISTORICAL CONNECTION

Although every form of government has employed censorship to some degree, especially in times of war, the strictest censorship is most often found in dictatorships. In the 1960s and 1970s, a number of Latin American countries, including Luisa Valenzuela's native Argentina, were governed by military dictators. These leaders often employed censorship to control their opponents and limit the free expression of ideas. Their measures included the closing of newspapers and magazines, the suppression of public meetings, and censorship of the arts, especially literature. "The Censors" focuses on a common type of censorship—the reading of personal letters in order to control the flow of information and guard against acts of rebellion. The story, inspired by the political situation in Argentina, takes place in a fictional Latin American setting.

Setting a Purpose
WRITING CONNECTION

Imagine living in a dictatorship where the government censors all writing and people can be arrested for what they write. In your notebook, describe how you might feel about living under such conditions.

242 UNIT TWO PART 1: CHALLENGING THE SYSTEM

PRINT AND MEDIA RESOURCES

UNIT TWO RESOURCE BOOK
Strategic Reading: Literature, p. 25
Vocabulary SkillBuilder, p. 26

WRITING MINI–LESSONS
Transparencies, p. 41

ACCESS FOR STUDENTS ACQUIRING ENGLISH
Selection Summaries
Reading Support

FORMAL ASSESSMENT
Selection Test, pp. 45–46
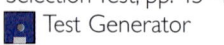 Test Generator

AUDIO LIBRARY
See Reference Card

INTERNET RESOURCES
McDougal Littell Literature Center at http://www.hmco.com/mcdougal/lit

242 THE LANGUAGE OF LITERATURE TEACHER'S EDITION

The Censors

Luisa Valenzuela

Poor Juan![1] One day they caught him with his guard down before he could even realize that what he had taken as a stroke of luck was really one of fate's dirty tricks. These things happen the minute you're careless, as one often is. Juancito[2] let happiness—a feeling you can't trust—get the better of him when he received from a confidential source Mariana's new address in Paris and knew that she hadn't forgotten him. Without thinking twice, he sat down at his table and wrote her a letter. *The* letter that now keeps his mind off his job during the day and won't let him sleep at night (what had he scrawled, what had he put on that sheet of paper he sent to Mariana?).

Juan knows there won't be a problem with the letter's contents, that it's irreproachable, harmless. But what about the rest? He knows that they examine, sniff, feel, and read between the lines of each and every letter, and check its tiniest comma and most accidental stain. He knows that all letters pass from hand to hand and go through all sorts of tests in the huge censorship offices and that, in the end, very few continue on their way. Usually it takes months, even years, if there aren't any snags; all this time the freedom, maybe even the life, of both sender and receiver is in jeopardy. And that's why Juan's so troubled: thinking that something might happen to Mariana because of

---

1. **Juan** (hwän).
2. **Juancito** (hwän-sē′tô): an affectionate nickname for Juan.

WORDS TO KNOW
irreproachable (ĭr′ĭ-prō′chə-bəl) *adj.* perfect or blameless in every respect; faultless

---

WORDS TO KNOW

conniving (kə-nī′vĭng) *adj.* scheming **connive** *v.* (p. 245)
irreproachable (ĭr′ĭ-prō′chə-bəl) *adj.* perfect or blameless in every respect; faultless (p. 243)
staidness (stād′nĭs) *n.* a quiet, often strait-laced dignity (p. 244)
subtle (sŭt′l) *adj.* difficult to detect, usually because of the clever means employed; not obvious (p. 245)
subversive (səb-vûr′sĭv) *adj.* intended or serving to overthrow established authority (p. 245)

CUSTOMIZING FOR
Gifted and Talented Students

Ask students to note the author's tone toward Juan as they read. (*Some students might say that at first, Valenzuela adopts a pitying tone. Others might suggest that her initial tone is mocking, but sympathetic. Students might say that as the story progresses, the narrator becomes more mocking, and by the end, she scorns Juan completely.*)

CUSTOMIZING FOR
Students Acquiring English

I Explain that *machinery* here means "the government." Be sure students realize that Juan plans to defy the system.

Critical Thinking: ANALYZING

A Ask students why they think Valenzuela's narration changes verb tense here? (*Some students may say the present tense in the opening makes readers feel as if they are looking in on Juan. Others may say it adds to her condescending, mocking tone. The past-tense portion has a more distant tone, and the events become increasingly absurd.*)

Literary Concept: IRONY

B Ask students why it is ironic that Juan reports the strike organizers to his superiors. (*He became a censor to sabotage the system; now he's cooperating with it.*)

Literary Note

C Valenzuela's fiction is influenced by absurdists, such as Edward Albee and Eugene Ionesco. Their works use irony, exaggeration, and satire to mock conformity, as does "The Censors."

---

his letters. Of all people, Mariana, who must finally feel safe there where she always dreamt she'd live. But he knows that the Censor's Secret Command operates all over the world and cashes in on the discount in air fares; there's nothing to stop them from going as far as that hidden Paris neighborhood, kidnapping Mariana, and returning to their cozy homes, certain of having fulfilled their noble mission.

> Well, you've got to ~~beat them to the punch,~~ do what everyone tries to do: ~~sabotage the machinery,~~ throw sand ~~in its gears,~~ get to the bottom of the problem ~~so as to stop it.~~

I Well, you've got to beat them to the punch, do what everyone tries to do: sabotage the machinery, throw sand in its gears, get to the bottom of the problem so as to stop it.

A This was Juan's sound plan when he, like many others, applied for a censor's job—not because he had a calling³ or needed a job: no, he applied simply to intercept his own letter, a consoling albeit unoriginal idea. He was hired immediately, for each day more and more censors are needed and no one would bother to check on his references.

Ulterior motives⁴ couldn't be overlooked by the Censorship Division, but they needn't be too strict with those who applied. They knew how hard it would be for the poor guys to find the letter they wanted and even if they did, what's a letter or two when the new censor would snap up so many others? That's how Juan managed to join the Post Office's Censorship Division, with a certain goal in mind.

The building had a festive air on the outside that contrasted with its inner **staidness**. Little by little, Juan was absorbed by his job, and he felt at peace since he was doing everything he could to get his letter for Mariana. He didn't even worry when, in his first month, he was sent to Section K where envelopes are very carefully screened for explosives.

It's true that on the third day, a fellow worker had his right hand blown off by a letter, but the division chief claimed it was sheer negligence on the victim's part. Juan and the other employees were allowed to go back to their work, though feeling less secure. After work, one of them tried to organize a strike to demand higher wages for unhealthy work, but Juan didn't join in; after thinking it over, he reported the man to his superiors and thus got promoted. **B**

You don't form a habit by doing something once, he told himself as he left his boss's office. And when he was transferred to Section F, where letters are carefully checked for poison dust, he felt he had climbed a rung in the ladder. **C**

By working hard, he quickly reached Section E, where the job became more interesting, for he could now read and analyze the letters'

---

3. **had a calling:** had an inner urge to go into a particular occupation or career.
4. **ulterior motives:** reasons for doing something that are concealed in order to deceive.

WORDS TO KNOW
staidness (stād´nĭs) *n.* a quiet, often strait-laced dignity

244

Mini-Lesson The Writer's Style

TRANSITIONS THAT SHOW CONTRAST
Tell students that Luisa Valenzuela develops a distinctive rhythm in this story by pairing contrasting ideas. To do this, she uses transitions that show contrast, such as *but*, *though*, and *yet*. Have students read aloud the highlighted sentences on page 244, noting the contrast in each and the transition word that signals the contrast. Have students discuss what this back-and-forth rhythm reflects about Juan's own convictions.

Application Invite students to elaborate on one of the scenes in the story, such as Juan's work with explosive letters in Section K. Have them write four or more sentences of contrast, each using a word of contrast such as *but*, *though*, or *however*.

Reteaching/Reinforcement
- *Writer's Handbook*, anthology p. 1028
- *Writing Mini-Lessons* transparencies, p. 41

Transitions That Show Contrast, pp. 379–380

contents. Here he could even hope to get hold of his letter, which, judging by the time that had elapsed, had gone through the other sections and was probably floating around in this one.

Soon his work became so absorbing that his noble mission blurred in his mind. Day after day he crossed out whole paragraphs in red ink, pitilessly chucking many letters into the censored basket. These were horrible days when he was shocked by the subtle and conniving ways employed by people to pass on subversive messages; his instincts were so sharp that he found behind a simple "the weather's unsettled" or "prices continue to soar" the wavering hand of someone secretly scheming to overthrow the Government.

His zeal brought him swift promotion. We don't know if this made him happy. Very few letters reached him in Section B—only a handful passed the other hurdles—so he read them over and over again, passed them under a magnifying glass, searched for microprint with an electronic microscope, and tuned his sense of smell so that he was beat by the time he made it home. He'd barely manage to warm up his soup, eat some fruit, and fall into bed, satisfied with having done his duty. Only his darling mother worried, but she couldn't get him back on the right track. She'd say, though it wasn't always true: Lola called, she's at the bar with the girls, they miss you, they're waiting for you. Or else she'd leave a bottle of red wine on the table. But Juan wouldn't overdo it: any distraction could make him lose his edge, and the perfect censor had to be alert, keen, attentive, and sharp to nab cheats. He had a truly patriotic task, both self-denying and uplifting.

His basket for censored letters became the best fed as well as the most cunning basket in the whole Censorship Division. He was about to congratulate himself for having finally discovered his true mission, when his letter to Mariana reached his hands. Naturally, he censored it without regret. And just as naturally, he couldn't stop them from executing him the following morning, another victim of his devotion to his work. ❖

Translated by David Unger

WORDS TO KNOW	**subtle** (sŭt′l) *adj.* difficult to detect, usually because of the clever means employed; not obvious **conniving** (kə-nī′vĭng) *adj.* scheming **connive** *v.* **subversive** (səb-vûr′sĭv) *adj.* intended or serving to overthrow established authority

245

Mini-Lesson  Grammar

COMPLEMENTS Explain that a complement is the word or group of words that completes the meaning of the verb. A direct object receives the action of an active verb and answers the question *what?* or *whom?* about the verb. An indirect object tells to whom or for whom the action of the verb is performed. Have students study the highlighted sentence: *His zeal brought him swift promotion.* Show that *promotion* is the direct object because it tells what was brought, and *him* is the indirect object since it tells to whom the promotion was brought.

Application Have students identify the direct and indirect object in each sentence.
1. Juan sent Mariana the letter without thinking. *(letter, Mariana)*
2. The Post Office gave Juan the job. *(job, Juan)*
3. Eventually, the censors handed him his letter. *(letter, him)*

Reteaching/Reinforcement

 The Writer's Craft

Complements, pp. 577–578

From Personal Response to Critical Analysis

1. Accept all reasonable responses.
2. Accept all well-supported opinions. Some students may think Juan deserves his fate for joining a corrupt system; others may see him as a victim of the system.
3. Possible responses: more and more censors are needed every day; Juan's fanaticism as a censor, his self-censorship, and his execution.
4. Accept all reasonable responses.
5. Possible responses: Some students may say dictators seek to maintain their power by stifling the ideas of their opponents. Others may suggest that censorship is a way for dictators to learn what people are thinking.
6. Accept all reasonable responses. Some students might say it is acceptable in wartime.

Another Pathway

You may suggest the following criteria for students to use to evaluate Juan: obeying the laws of the land, performing useful work, taking an active role in community life, respecting the privacy of others, showing respect to co-workers.

Rubric

3 Full Accomplishment Student lists include a variety of valid criteria for defining a good citizen. Students grade Juan accurately based on the story.

2 Substantial Accomplishment Criteria lists are fairly complete, but may lack some important criteria for judging a person's citizenship. Grading is fairly accurate.

1 Little or Partial Accomplishment Lists are incomplete. Grading does not accurately reflect the facts of the story.

Literary Links

Compare and contrast the ways Juan and the young boy in "The Balek Scales" seek to challenge the system. Are the results the same or different? *(the same, because the systems remain intact)*

RESPONDING OPTIONS

FROM PERSONAL RESPONSE TO CRITICAL ANALYSIS

REFLECT
1. What is your reaction to the ending of the story? Record your reaction in your notebook.

RETHINK
2. What is your opinion of Juan? Support your opinion with examples from the story.
3. *Absurd* means "ridiculously incongruous or unreasonable." What parts of the story would you describe as absurd?
4. How has the story influenced your understanding of censorship? Explain your views.

RELATE
5. Why do you think censorship is more severe in dictatorships than in democracies?
6. Do you think that censorship is necessary in certain circumstances? Use examples to explain your views.

Multimodal Learning
ANOTHER PATHWAY

With a partner, evaluate Juan as a citizen. Create a list of criteria by which to judge him, and then give him a grade for each of the criteria. Share your results with your classmates.

LITERARY CONCEPTS

Irony is a contrast between what is expected and what actually exists or happens. Three types of irony follow:

Situational irony is the contrast between what a character or reader expects and what actually happens. For example, when Juan begins his job, the reader may expect that he will find a way to interfere with the censors. However, Juan becomes an enthusiastic censor himself.

Verbal irony occurs when a character or narrator says one thing and means another. For instance, the narrator tells the reader that Juan "had a truly patriotic task." The narrator really means that Juan's work was harmful.

Dramatic irony refers to the contrast between what a character knows and what the reader or audience knows. For example, Juan believes that the phrase "the weather's unsettled" really means that someone is scheming to overthrow the government. The reader knows, however, that the letter writer was only describing the weather.

With a partner, list three or four other examples of irony in this story. Determine why each example is ironic, and identify the type of irony it represents.

QUICKWRITES

1. Expand the writing you did for the Writing Connection on page 242 into a **dramatic scene** about life in a dictatorship with strict censorship.
2. Write Juan's **letter** to Mariana. Then censor it as you think Juan might have. Explain to the class how you decided to censor it.
3. Create a **list of rules** for the workers in the Post Office's Censorship Division. Include at least five do's and five don'ts.

 PORTFOLIO Save your writing. You may want to use it later as a springboard to a piece for your portfolio.

246 UNIT TWO PART 1: CHALLENGING THE SYSTEM

Literary Concepts

Examples of irony in the story include:
- page 244—"The Censor's Secret Command . . . cashes in on the discount in air fares . . ." /Situational irony—we wouldn't expect a powerful government agency to shop for discount air fares.
- page 244—". . . having fulfilled their noble mission." /Verbal irony—kidnapping innocent people is evil, not noble.
- page 245—"Naturally, he censored it without regret." /Situational irony—Juan became a censor to intercept his letter, not censor it.

QuickWrites

1. In their dramatic scenes, students might have two censors discussing the ethics of their work.
2. Suggest that in their letters students include a few ambiguous details or phrases that an overly dedicated censor like Juan might misinterpret.
3. Students might like to include in their lists absurd rules such as *Be on the lookout for exploding stamps* or *Watch out for envelopes with poison dust*.

The Writer's Craft

Using Dialogue in Plays and Skits, pp. 453–454
Denotation and Connotation, p. 424

Multimodal Learning

ALTERNATIVE ACTIVITIES

1. Create a **poster** that might be used to recruit new employees for the Post Office's Censorship Division.
2. Conduct **interviews** with administrators or teachers to learn if there are any official policies about censorship that apply to the school library, the school newspaper, or the classroom.

Multimodal Learning

ACROSS THE CURRICULUM

History Read the Bill of Rights to find the amendments guaranteeing freedoms that limit the power of government to impose censorship. Then hold a class discussion on how these freedoms affect the everyday lives of citizens.

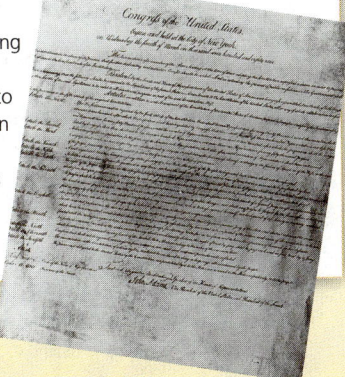

WORDS TO KNOW

Use your understanding of the boldfaced words below to complete each of the sentences.

1. An **irreproachable** censor would (a) never work, (b) always do his job well, (c) whine about the demands of the job.
2. A **subtle** message in a letter would (a) be easy to understand, (b) reveal the ignorance of the writer, (c) not be immediately obvious.
3. **Conniving** citizens might be expected to (a) try to fool the authorities, (b) follow all the rules, (c) be reluctant to take action of any kind.
4. A government agency characterized by **staidness** would (a) have a festive air, (b) be noted for its efficiency, (c) be a sober place to work.
5. A **subversive** employee might (a) dutifully attend to details, (b) work to topple the government, (c) look for ways to advance his or her career.

LUISA VALENZUELA

When Luisa Valenzuela was very young, her older sister used to read her horror stories to make her eat. "I would open my mouth in fright and she would stuff it," Valenzuela reports. "I swallowed my fear and my fascination along with the food." Literature continued to play a role in Valenzuela's life. Her mother was a well-known writer, and their home in Buenos Aires, Argentina, was often visited by literary figures. When Valenzuela took an interest in writing, her career moved quickly: at age 17 she published her first short story.

Feeling stifled by Argentina's political situation, the adult Valenzuela lived abroad when she could, work-

1944–

ing in Paris for the French broadcasting agency, attending the International Writers' Program at the University of Iowa, and becoming a writer-in-residence at Columbia University in New York City. She published her first novel, *Something to Smile About*, in 1966 and her first story collection, *The Heretics*, a year later. Valenzuela once said that she writes to shake people up. Much of her best work communicates her ideas about power, politics, and human relationships.

OTHER WORKS *He Who Searches, The Lizard's Tail, Open Door, Strange Things Happen Here*

Extended Reading

THE CENSORS 247

Words to Know

1. b
2. c
3. a
4. c
5. b

Reteaching/Reinforcement
- Unit Two Resource Book, p. 26

Across the Curriculum

History Since 1791, the First Amendment to the United States Constitution has protected the individual's freedom of speech. Since 1925, the Supreme Court has used the due process clause of the 14th Amendment to protect free speech from interference by state and local governments. Due process of law is a basic principle in the American legal system requiring fairness in the government's dealing with persons.

LUISA VALENZUELA

Luisa Valenzuela's fiction is highly experimental, with shifting points of view, far-ranging use of metaphors, and frequent word play. In her work, the laws of logic and reason are commonly replaced by those of magic and surrealism. The surreal, illogical quality of Argentine politics is a recurring theme. The author sees her most popular novel, *The Lizard's Tail*, as an attempt to understand how the Argentine people could allow themselves to be victimized by harsh military regimes for so long.

Alternative Activities

1. Explain that most recruitment posters stress how employees will learn new skills and contribute to some grand and important goal through their work. Remind students that posters of most kinds feature some catchy slogan or motto, and include a symbol that stands for the organization doing the recruitment.
2. Suggest that students collaborate, with each student conducting one interview. Beforehand, students can work up a list of sample questions to pose to subjects. After students have conducted their interviews, they can hold a class discussion to come up with some conclusions on the issue of censorship.

OVERVIEW

Objectives

- To understand and appreciate an essay that expresses the need for tolerance of other people
- To identify and understand theme
- To appreciate and write brief sentences
- To express understanding of the selection through a choice of writing forms, including an essay, a critical analysis, and a fable or parable
- To extend understanding of the essay through a variety of multimodal and cross-curricular activities

Skills

READING SKILLS/STRATEGIES
- Clarifying

LITERARY CONCEPTS
- Theme

GENRE STUDY
- Nonfiction: essay

SPEAKING, LISTENING, AND VIEWING
- Speech
- Group discussion
- Oral presentation

CUSTOMIZING FOR Students Acquiring English

- Use ACCESS FOR STUDENTS ACQUIRING ENGLISH, *Reading Support.*
- Students may have difficulty with some of the British words and spellings and the formal tone in this selection. You may want to restate certain sentences in a manner that is more familiar to students.

PREVIEWING

NONFICTION

from Tolerance
E. M. Forster Great Britain

Activating Prior Knowledge
PERSONAL CONNECTION

Complete the statement shown on the right with one word that best represents your thinking about what the world needs. You may pick one of the words in the brackets or another word of your choice. In your notebook, explain your reasons for your choice. Then share your ideas with your classmates.

> In the world today, people need to treat one another with _____ [compassion, respect, love, tolerance, kindness, generosity].

Building Background
HISTORICAL CONNECTION

As the title of the following essay suggests, Great Britain's E. M. Forster ranked tolerance high among the qualities necessary for the world at large. The essay is one of several that Forster broadcast over the radio during or just after World War II (1939–1945) and later collected in his volume *Two Cheers for Democracy* (1951). In these essays, Forster often explores the means by which citizens of democracies can counter the spread of the kind of thinking that leads to brutal dictatorships—dictatorships like that of Nazi Germany, Britain's foe during the war. With their claims of racial superiority, their attempts to conquer neighboring nations that they labeled as inferior, and their mass murder of ethnic groups that they branded as undesirable, the Nazis were the supreme example of *in*tolerance.

READING CONNECTION
Active Reading/Setting a Purpose

Clarifying Concepts As you read this excerpt from Forster's essay, try to pin down exactly what Forster means by his use of the word *tolerance*. Create a chart like the one below, and record on it brief notes about Forster's intent.

Tolerance
Words and phrases that describe or define tolerance:
Benefits of tolerance:
Why tolerance is needed:

248 UNIT TWO PART 1: CHALLENGING THE SYSTEM

PRINT AND MEDIA RESOURCES

UNIT TWO RESOURCE BOOK
Strategic Reading: Literature, p. 29
Vocabulary SkillBuilder, p. 30

ACCESS FOR STUDENTS ACQUIRING ENGLISH
Selection Summaries
Reading Support

FORMAL ASSESSMENT
Selection Test, pp. 47–48
 Test Generator

AUDIO LIBRARY
See Reference Card

248 THE LANGUAGE OF LITERATURE TEACHER'S EDITION

Italian Landscape II: Europa (1944), Ben Shahn. Copyright © 1995 Estate of Ben Shahn / Licensed by VAGA, New York.

from
TOLERANCE
E. M. Forster

Surely the only sound foundation for a civilisation is a sound state of mind. Architects, contractors, international commissioners, marketing boards, broadcasting corporations will never, by themselves, build a new world.

WORDS TO KNOW

appallingly (ə-pô′lĭng-lē) *adv.* in an upsetting manner; shockingly; dreadfully (p. 250)
conversely (kən-vûrs′lē) *adv.* in reverse; on the other hand (p. 251)
diplomacy (dĭ-plō′mə-sē) *n.* the art or practice of conducting international relations and discussing and resolving differences among nations (p. 250)
entail (ĕn-tāl′) *v.* to have or need as a necessary accompaniment (p. 251)
maim (mām) *v.* to injure in a way that leaves permanent damage (p. 251)
makeshift (māk′shĭft′) *n.* a temporary or useful substitute when other means fail or are unavailable (p. 251)
perilous (pĕr′ə-ləs) *adj.* dangerous (p. 250)
proclaiming (prō-klā′mĭng) *adj.* announcing officially and publicly **proclaim** *v.* (p. 251)
purge (pûrj) *v.* to get rid of people considered undesirable; to purify (p. 251)
secular (sĕk′yə-lər) *adj.* worldly rather than spiritual; not specifically related to religion (p. 250)

Linking to History

A The "series of cataclysms" Forster refers to include World War I, the Great Depression, the Stalinist purges, World War II, and the Holocaust. These events had undermined people's faith in human decency.

Literary Concept: AUTHOR'S PURPOSE

B Ask why Forster bothers to mention love, since he doesn't believe it will work as a guiding principle for rebuilding society. (*Forster is anticipating a strong counterargument that he expects readers to make.*)

Literary Concept: THEME

C Invite students to express what Forster's main purpose is in writing this essay. (*To convince his audience that tolerance is a substantial cornerstone for a peaceful society.*)

Literary Concept: TONE

D Point out that Forster deals with a serious topic here in a tongue-in-cheek way. Invite students to cite humorous passages in this paragraph. (*Possible responses: the Nazis' claiming to be the salt of the earth; criticizing people for insignificant things*)

They must be inspired by the proper spirit, and there must be the proper spirit in the people for whom they are working. . . .

What though is the proper spirit? . . . There must be a sound state of mind before <u>diplomacy</u> or economics or trade conferences can function. But what state of mind is sound? Here we may differ. Most people, when asked what spiritual quality is needed to rebuild civilisation, will reply "Love." Men must love one another, they say; nations must do likewise, and then the series of cataclysms[1] which is threatening to destroy us will be checked.

B Respectfully but firmly, I disagree. Love is a great force in private life; it is indeed the greatest of all things: but love in public affairs does not work. It has been tried again and again: by the Christian civilisations of the Middle Ages, and also by the French Revolution, a <u>secular</u> movement which reasserted the brotherhood of man.[2] And it has always failed. The idea that nations should love one another, or that business concerns or marketing boards should love one another, or that a man in Portugal should love a man in Peru of whom he has never heard—it is absurd, unreal, dangerous. It leads us into <u>perilous</u> and vague sentimentalism.[3] "Love is what is needed," we chant and then sit back, and the world goes on as before. The fact is we can only love what we know personally. And we cannot know much. In public affairs, in the rebuilding of civilisation, something much

> NO ONE HAS EVER WRITTEN AN ODE TO TOLERANCE OR RAISED A STATUE TO HER. YET THIS IS THE QUALITY WHICH WILL BE MOST NEEDED AFTER THE WAR.

less dramatic and emotional is needed, namely, tolerance. Tolerance is a very dull virtue. It is boring. Unlike love, it has always had a bad press. It is negative. It merely means putting up with people, being able to stand things. No one has ever written an ode[4] to tolerance or raised a statue to her. Yet this is the quality which will be most needed after the war. This is the sound state of mind which we are looking for. This is the only force which will enable different races and classes and interests to settle down together to the work of reconstruction.

The world is very full of people—<u>appallingly</u> full; it has never been so full before, and they are all tumbling over each other. Most of these people one doesn't know, and some of them one doesn't like; doesn't like the colour of their skins, say, or the shapes of their noses, or the way they blow them or don't blow them, or the way they talk, or their smell, or their clothes, or their fondness for jazz or their dislike of jazz, and so on. Well, what is one to do? There are two solutions. One of them is the Nazi solution. If you don't like people, kill them, banish them, segregate them, and then strut up and down

---

1. **cataclysms** (kăt′ə-klĭz′əmz): violent upheavals causing great change and destruction.
2. **French Revolution . . . brotherhood of man:** the French Revolution, which lasted from 1789 to 1799, had the motto "Liberty! Equality! Brotherhood!"
3. **sentimentalism** (sĕn′tə-mĕn′tl-ĭz′əm): a tendency toward too much tender, often shallow emotion.
4. **ode** (ōd): a usually formal poem on a serious subject.

WORDS TO KNOW
diplomacy (dĭ-plō′mə-sē) *n.* the art or practice of conducting international relations and discussing and resolving differences among nations
secular (sĕk′yə-lər) *adj.* worldly rather than spiritual; not specifically related to religion
perilous (pĕr′ə-ləs) *adj.* dangerous
appallingly (ə-pô′lĭng-lē) *adv.* in an upsetting manner; shockingly; dreadfully

---

Mini-Lesson — Genre Study

NONFICTION Review with students that an **essay** is a short nonfiction work that deals with one subject and usually presents the personal views of the writer. Point out that this selection is excerpted from a persuasive essay. In a persuasive essay, the writer argues a particular point.

Application Ask students to look at Forster's conclusion to note what he has done to bolster his essay's persuasive appeal. (*He has restated his thesis, asserting that tolerance is more effective than love since the latter "gives out." Then he gives the idea new life by suggesting everyday situations in which we must practice it. He anticipates objections to his claims for tolerance, readily agreeing that, "It is dull," yet also suggesting that it entails imagination.*)

proclaiming that you are the salt of the earth.[5] The other way is much less thrilling, but it is on the whole the way of the democracies, and I prefer it. If you don't like people, put up with them as well as you can. Don't try to love them: you can't; you'll only strain yourself. But try to tolerate them. On the basis of that tolerance a civilised future may be built. Certainly I can see no other foundation for the postwar world.

For what it will most need is the negative virtues: not being huffy, touchy, irritable, revengeful. I have lost all faith in positive militant ideals; they can so seldom be carried out without thousands of human beings getting maimed or imprisoned. Phrases like "I will purge this nation," "I will clean up this city," terrify and disgust me. They might not have mattered when the world was emptier: they are horrifying now, when one nation is mixed up with another, when one city cannot be organically separated from its neighbours. . . .

I don't then regard tolerance as a great eternally established divine principle, though I might perhaps quote "In my Father's house are many mansions"[6] in support of such a view. It is just a makeshift, suitable for an overcrowded and overheated planet. It carries on when love gives out, and love generally gives out as soon as we move away from our home and our friends and stand among strangers in a queue[7] for potatoes. Tolerance is wanted in the queue; otherwise we think, "Why will people be so slow?"; it is wanted in the tube,[8] or "Why will people be so fat?"; it is wanted at the telephone, or "Why are they so deaf?" or conversely, "Why do they mumble?" It is wanted in the street, in the office, at the factory, and it is wanted above all between classes, races, and nations. It's dull. And yet it entails imagination. For you have all the time to be putting yourself in someone else's place. Which is a desirable spiritual exercise. ❖

---

5. **salt of the earth:** the finest or noblest people. The expression derives from a statement in the New Testament of the Bible (Matthew 5:13).
6. **"In my Father's house are many mansions":** a quotation from the New Testament (John 14:2).
7. **queue** (kyōō): a chiefly British expression for a line of people.
8. **tube:** British term for the Underground, or London subway.

WORDS TO KNOW
proclaiming (prō-klā'mĭng) *adj.* announcing officially and publicly **proclaim** *v.*
maim (mām) *v.* to injure in a way that leaves permanent damage
purge (pûrj) *v.* to get rid of people considered undesirable; to purify
makeshift (māk'shĭft') *n.* a temporary or useful substitute when other means fail or are unavailable
conversely (kən-vûrs'lē) *adv.* in reverse; on the other hand
entail (ĕn-tāl') *v.* to have or need as a necessary accompaniment

From Personal Response to Critical Analysis

1. Accept all reasonable responses.
2. Possible responses: Yes; tolerance is negative because it means *not* behaving in certain ways. No; tolerance is positive because it involves actively building an acceptance of ways that are different from one's own.
3. Some students will agree that tolerance is more realistic. Others may feel that love establishes a deeper and longer-lasting basis for a peaceful civilization.
4. Possible response: Some students may say that Forster believes people must be practical and choose an attainable virtue in desperate times. Others might say that if people can't have love and compassion, at least they can tolerate each other.
5. Accept all reasonable, well-supported responses.

Another Pathway

Cooperative Learning Have students work in groups of four or five. Two or three students can find and present articles about conflicts. The group as a whole can select the article to focus on. One group member can guide the discussion of how the conflict relates to Forster's essay; another can take notes. Group members can work together to develop steps for promoting tolerance.

Rubric

3 Full Accomplishment The group chooses a recognizable conflict, analyzes the opposing viewpoints, and suggests sensible steps for promoting tolerance.

2 Substantial Accomplishment The group identifies a conflict, but has difficulty developing a plan to promote tolerance between the two sides in conflict.

1 Little or Partial Accomplishment The conflict identified by the group may be specious; the steps the group suggests are not realistic and do not relate to tolerance.

RESPONDING OPTIONS

FROM PERSONAL RESPONSE TO CRITICAL ANALYSIS

REFLECT
1. Did you find Forster's arguments convincing? Describe your reaction in your notebook.

RETHINK
2. Do you agree with Forster's view that tolerance is a negative virtue?
   Consider
   Close Textual Reading
   - how Forster defines "negative virtue"
   - the chart that you completed for the Reading Connection on page 248
   - his contrast between "negative virtues," and "positive militant ideals"

3. Do you agree with Forster that tolerance is more useful than love as a foundation of civilization?
   Consider
   Close Textual Reading
   - why he thinks "love in public affairs does not work"
   - his belief that "we can only love what we know personally"
   - your own views about love and tolerance

4. Why do you think Forster describes tolerance as a "makeshift, suitable for an overcrowded and overheated planet"?

RELATE
5. Do you think that the world is becoming a more tolerant place in which to live? Use examples from current affairs to support your opinion.

Multimodal Learning
ANOTHER PATHWAY
Cooperative Learning
In a small group, review a newspaper or newsmagazine to find an article about a conflict between two groups of people in your community or in the world. Analyze the conflict in light of Forster's essay, then list specific steps that might be taken to promote tolerance between the two groups.

LITERARY CONCEPTS

Theme is the central idea or message in a work of literature. Theme should not be confused with subject, or what the work is about. Rather, theme is a perception about life or human nature. Sometimes the theme is directly stated within the work; at other times it is implied, and the reader must infer the theme. In one sentence, state what you feel is the theme of the excerpt from "Tolerance." Then compare your statement of the theme with the statements of your classmates. Discuss whether the theme is stated directly or implied.

CONCEPT REVIEW: Tone In your opinion, is the tone of the excerpt formal or informal?

QUICKWRITES

1. Expand your ideas from the Personal Connection on page 248 into an **essay** about a quality that you believe is needed in the world today. Directly state your theme, and support it with details and logical arguments.

2. Write a **critical analysis** in which you explain the meaning of the biblical quotation "In my Father's house are many mansions" and its relevance to Forster's theme.

3. Write a **fable** or **parable** that illustrates Forster's theme about tolerance.

📁 **PORTFOLIO** *Save your writing. You may want to use it later as a springboard to a piece for your portfolio.*

252 UNIT TWO PART 1: CHALLENGING THE SYSTEM

Literary Concept

Theme Accept all reasonable, well-supported statements. Most responses will reflect Forster's belief that tolerance of other people is the "proper spirit" on which to build a peaceful civilization.

Concept Review
Tone Review how Forster uses short sentences, examples from everyday life, and idioms to create a conversational tone.

QuickWrites

1. Encourage students to pattern their essays after Forster's, beginning by explaining why the quality is necessary, countering opposing arguments, stating the main ideas, and concluding with a recap of the main points.

2. Discuss what *mansions* may mean in this quotation. (*Possible responses: ways of thinking or believing; places where people are accepted and welcomed*)

3. Remind students that fables teach a lesson and often use animal characters to symbolize human points of view.

The Writer's Craft

Persuasive Essay, pp. 206–221
Interpretive Essay, pp. 238–253
Myth, pp. 162–167

Multimodal Learning

ALTERNATIVE ACTIVITIES

1. Rehearse and deliver Forster's essay as a **speech** to be broadcast on the radio.
2. Design a **poster** for an ad campaign promoting tolerance. If you have access to a computer with graphic applications, you may wish to design the poster electronically.

Multimodal Learning

ACROSS THE CURRICULUM

Media Find out more about the role of radio during World War II, especially how it affected public information and morale. Report your findings in a multimedia presentation that includes original recordings or your own simulations of actual broadcasts.

WRITER'S STYLE

With a partner, review Forster's essay and list all the sentences that have six or fewer words. What effects do you think Forster is trying to achieve by using such brief sentences?

ART CONNECTION

Why do you think the painting on page 249, *Italian Landscape II: Europa*, was chosen to illustrate Forster's essay?

Detail of *Italian Landscape II: Europa* (1944), Ben Shahn. Copyright © 1995 Estate of Ben Shahn/Licensed by VAGA, New York.

WORDS TO KNOW

Match each numbered word with its synonym.

1. makeshift   a. risky
2. maim   b. cleanse
3. proclaiming   c. negotiation
4. secular   d. worldly
5. perilous   e. stand-in
6. conversely   f. disable
7. entail   g. require
8. purge   h. oppositely
9. diplomacy   i. disturbingly
10. appallingly   j. broadcasting

E. M. FORSTER

1879–1970

Edward Morgan Forster, who was born in Coventry, England, spent the early part of his life hating the private boys' school that he attended, where he was subject to the taunts of classmates and the severity of teachers. He felt liberated by his subsequent years of study at Cambridge University, which enabled him to expand his intellectual horizons, make close friends, and dedicate himself to the literary life. Forster began publishing stories soon after graduation and published his first novel in 1905. There followed a number of acclaimed novels; the best known of these—*A Room with a View* (1908), *Howards End* (1910), and *A Passage to India* (1924)—have recently enjoyed a resurgence of popularity sparked by successful film adaptations.

During the 1920s, Forster achieved prominence as a literary critic, but in the next two decades he turned increasingly to social criticism and virtually gave up writing fiction. Horrified by events in Germany and elsewhere, Forster reacted with lectures and radio broadcasts that stressed the value of goodwill and reason in combating totalitarian thinking.

OTHER WORKS *Abinger Harvest, The Collected Tales of E. M. Forster, Two Cheers for Democracy*

Extended Reading
TOLERANCE **253**

Words to Know

1. e	6. h
2. f	7. g
3. j	8. b
4. d	9. c
5. a	10. i

Reteaching/Reinforcement
• *Unit Two Resource Book*, p. 30

The Writer's Style

Sentences with six or fewer words include:

• What though is the proper spirit? (p. 250)
• Tolerance is a very dull virtue. (p. 250)
• There are two solutions. (p. 250)
• But try to tolerate them. (p. 251)

Students might point out that the short sentences add to the conversational tone of the essay. More importantly, they emphasize critical points.

The Writer's Craft

Sentence Length, pp. 434–435

Art Connections

Students might say the painting depicts the situation that Forster addresses: in 1944, Europe was in ruins and in desperate need of rebuilding.

Across the Curriculum

Media Suggest that students find out about the use of radio for informing people, bolstering morale, and spreading propaganda. Encourage students to look for information about Winston Churchill's speeches, Franklin Roosevelt's "fireside chats," and the broadcasts of Edward R. Murrow and George Orwell during this period. Also suggest they research the Voice of America and "Tokyo Rose."

E. M. FORSTER

As a young man, Forster lived in Greece, Italy, Egypt, and India. His widespread travel helped shape his writing. In general, Forster's novels show the social, psychological, and racial obstacles that can stand in the way of personal relationships. A recurring theme in his books is the importance of following generous impulses.

Alternative Activities

1. Suggest that students listen to tapes of their rehearsals to check the pace and tone. Students may wish to tape other persuasive essays and arrange a series of radio addresses.
2. Invite students to work together to come up with some symbols for tolerance with which they are familiar. Also, students' posters might make use of news photos that portray the tragic results of intolerance.

THE LANGUAGE OF LITERATURE TEACHER'S EDITION **253**

Objectives

- To promote independent active reading
- To practice and apply skills learned in previous selections
- To provide an opprtunity to assess students' performance through an alternative assessment instrument

Reading Pathways

- Suggest that students choose partners and do a paired oral reading, imagining the poem as a conversation between two soldiers. Partners can alternate the reading sentence by sentence.

- Invite students to reread the poem, looking for ideas that might apply to modern society and warfare. Ask students to share their discoveries with the class.

- After students have read through the poem once, suggest that they reread the poem and write down all the phrases that suggest strong visual images to them. Encourage students to use their lists of phrases to design a monument for the dead soldiers.

- Evaluate how well students can read, interpret, discuss, and write about the selection on their own by using the Integrated Assessment for Unit Two, located in the Alternative Assessment booklet. Set aside two class periods, or about two hours, to administer the assessment after students have completed the final writing assignment for the unit.

Art Note

Bronze horseman armed with spear

Reading the Art What aspects of the horseman and his horse do you think the artist was trying to emphasize?

ON YOUR OWN

Fighting South of the Ramparts

Li Bo   China

In the past, China was ruled by dynasties, successions of rulers from the same family or line. Under the Han dynasty (206 B.C. to A.D. 220)—one of the most famous in Chinese history—the country more than doubled in size through warfare against such peoples as the Huns in the north, the Vietnamese in the south, and the central Asians and the Tartars in the west.

Li Bo wrote the following poem around the year 751, basing it on an earlier folk song about the border wars during the Han dynasty. To fight those wars, the Han government raised taxes and forced the Chinese peasants to leave their lands and join the army, causing popular unrest. In describing these events from China's past, Li Bo was actually criticizing similar policies of the Tang dynasty, the dynasty in power during Bo's lifetime. In the early 700s, the Tang dynasty extended China's borders even farther than the Han dynasty had done. Once again, however, the warfare was proving expensive, and peasants were being forced from their lands to fight in remote border areas.

PRINT AND MEDIA RESOURCES

UNIT TWO RESOURCE BOOK
Strategic Reading: Literature, p. 33

FORMAL ASSESSMENT
Selection Test, p. 49
Part Test, pp. 51–52
 Test Generator

ALTERNATIVE ASSESSMENT
Unit One Integrated Assessment, pp. 7–12

ACCESS FOR STUDENTS ACQUIRING ENGLISH
Selection Summaries

AUDIO LIBRARY
See Reference Card

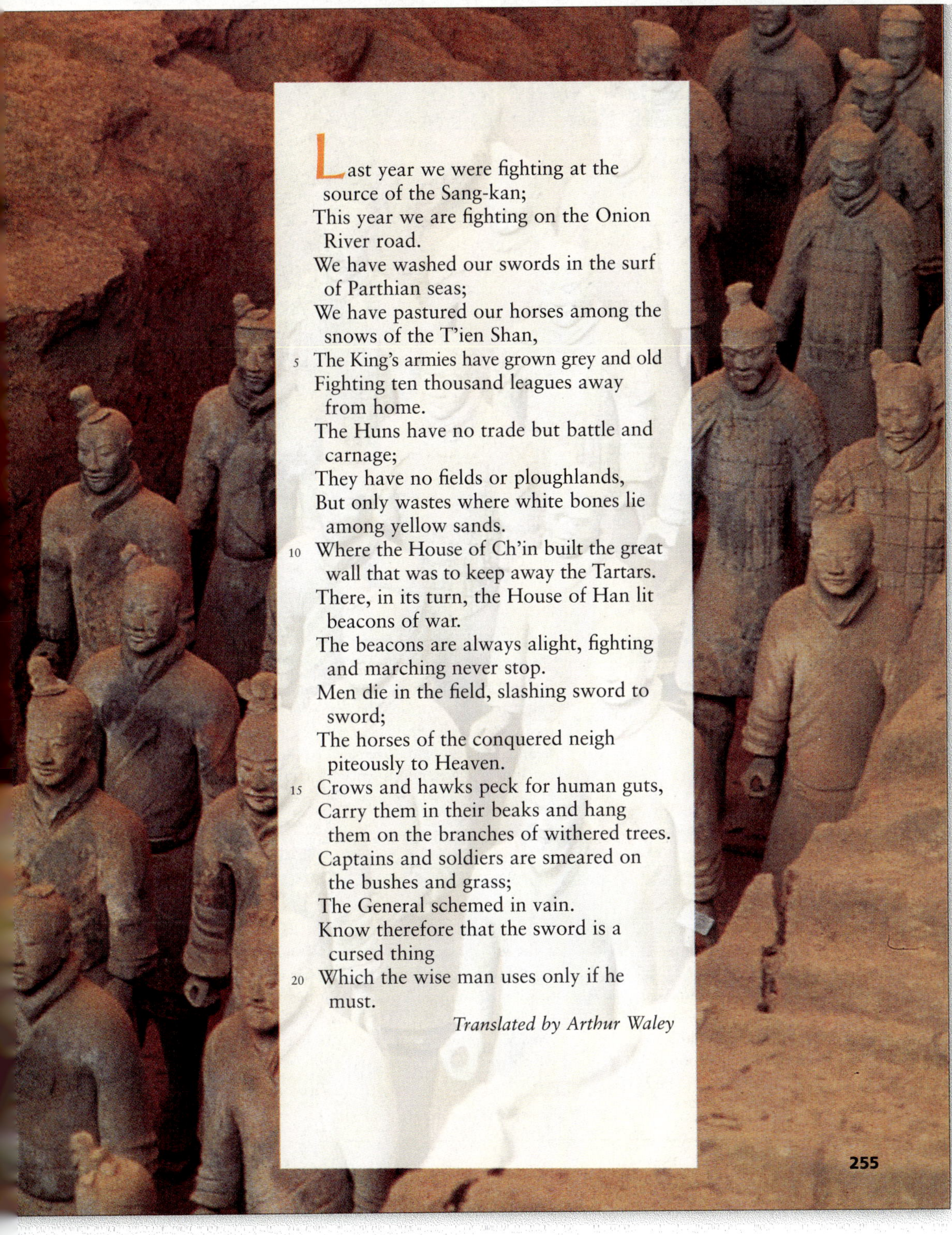

Last year we were fighting at the
   source of the Sang-kan;
This year we are fighting on the Onion
   River road.
We have washed our swords in the surf
   of Parthian seas;
We have pastured our horses among the
   snows of the T'ien Shan,
5 The King's armies have grown grey and old
Fighting ten thousand leagues away
   from home.
The Huns have no trade but battle and
   carnage;
They have no fields or ploughlands,
But only wastes where white bones lie
   among yellow sands.
10 Where the House of Ch'in built the great
   wall that was to keep away the Tartars,
There, in its turn, the House of Han lit
   beacons of war.
The beacons are always alight, fighting
   and marching never stop.
Men die in the field, slashing sword to
   sword;
The horses of the conquered neigh
   piteously to Heaven.
15 Crows and hawks peck for human guts,
Carry them in their beaks and hang
   them on the branches of withered trees.
Captains and soldiers are smeared on
   the bushes and grass;
The General schemed in vain.
Know therefore that the sword is a
   cursed thing
20 Which the wise man uses only if he
   must.

Translated by Arthur Waley

Thematic Link: *Challenging the System*
Li Bo challenges the emperor's militarism and expansionist policies by citing the enormous human costs of warfare.

OPTION 1

Cooperative Learning
RESEARCHING CHINESE HISTORY

Assign groups of five students to research China's dynastic history. Each member can choose one of the dynasties named below, create a map that indicates the area of the dynasty's reign, and list five important facts about the dynasty on a time line.

Han Dynasty (202 B.C.–A.D. 220); Tang Dynasty (A.D. 618–907); Song Dynasty (960–1279); Mongol Rule (1279–1368); Ming Dynasty (1368–1644).

Teacher's Role Suggest the group create one map, with overlays to show the area for each dynasty.

Rubric
3 **Full Accomplishment** Students show a good grasp of chronology, of important facts, and of the dynastic territories.
2 **Substantial Accomplishment** Students show a fair grasp of important facts, chronology, and the dynastic territories.
1 **Little or Partial Accomplishment** Students cite irrelevant facts; the time line is not chronological; maps are inaccurate.

OPTION 2

Class Discussion
SHARING IDEAS

Teacher's Role After students have read the selection, engage them in a class discussion using the following questions:

1. How would you describe the speaker's tone, or attitude, toward warfare? Cite specific lines from the poem to support your opinion. *(Accept all well-supported and reasonable responses. Possible responses: disenchanted; bitter)*
2. Why do you think the poet uses such graphic images of death? *(He wants to impress upon readers the horrors of war.)*
3. Why might Li Bo have chosen to write about a war that took place hundreds of years earlier rather than about the one China was waging during his lifetime? *(Possible responses: to avoid being punished for criticizing the government; to emphasize how long China had been at war)*

OVERVIEW

In the Guided Assignment for this section, students will write an essay analyzing the setting of a selection. By analyzing setting, students will gain insight into how much the physical environment of a story can affect their impressions of the story. As preparation for this assignment, they will use The Writer's Style to help them understand the importance of developing coherence in a description. In Reading the World, students will explore the setting of a real-world image.

Objectives

- To recognize how writers arrange details in a coherent order
- To use transition words and phrases effectively
- To write an essay analyzing the role of setting in a literary selection
- To analyze components of setting in a real-world image.

Skills

LITERATURE
- Identifying and analyzing methods of organizing details

GRAMMAR AND USAGE
- Achieving subject-verb agreement with prepositional phrases

MEDIA LITERACY
- Analyzing setting in a photograph

SPEAKING, LISTENING, AND VIEWING
- Group conferencing
- Group discussion

CRITICAL THINKING
- Analyzing
- Analyzing components of setting

Teaching Strategy: MODELING

In the following models, the writers organize details of setting to convey an overall impression as well as impressions of certain relationships. This technique is useful in fiction, drama, and nonfiction.

Ⓐ Kinsella Possible response: The narrator first notices the condition of the ground; then he describes the ticket booth, the fence, sounds from the freeway, and overhead sounds.

Ⓑ Cortázar Possible response: Showing details in the order of their physical position helps readers to see the setting as they might see it in a photograph. Readers can also imagine that they are walking in a linear progression from the entrance of the house to its back section. Words that show relationships include *through, onto, into, either side of, opposite, back section, down the passage, beyond which.*

WRITING ABOUT LITERATURE

SETTING THE SCENE

Could you picture the stadium in "The Thrill of the Grass"? Did the description in "House Taken Over" seem to put you in the scene? Understanding setting, in stories and in real life, helps you see how much your own surroundings affect you and others. On the next pages you will

- explore the ways writers organize the details of a setting
- write about the relation of setting to events in a story
- examine how real-world settings affect you

The Writer's Style: Paragraph Coherence When writing a description, writers arrange details in an order that helps readers imagine the subject and understand its impression.

Read the Literature

Note how writers organize the details in the following excerpts.

Literature Models

Order of Impression
Notice how the writer presents details in the order the narrator perceives them.

Ⓐ Strangle-grass and creeping charlie are already inching up through the gravel, surreptitious, surprised at their own ease. Faded bottle caps, rusted bits of chrome, an occasional paper clip, recede into the earth. I circle a ticket booth, sun-faded, empty, the door closed by an oversized padlock. I walk beside the tall, machinery-green, board fence. A half mile away a few cars hiss along the freeway; overhead a single-engine plane fizzes lazily.

W. P. Kinsella, from "The Thrill of the Grass"

Spatial Order
How does presenting the details in order of their physical position help you to picture the setting? Which words help to show relationships among the details?

Ⓑ One entered the house through a vestibule with enameled tiles, and a wrought-iron grated door opened onto the living room. You had to come in through the vestibule and open the gate to go into the living room; the doors to our bedrooms were on either side of this, and opposite it was the corridor leading to the back section; going down the passage, one swung open the oak door beyond which was the other part of the house.

Julio Cortázar, from "House Taken Over"

256 UNIT TWO: REFLECTING ON SOCIETY

PRINT AND MEDIA RESOURCES

UNIT TWO RESOURCE BOOK
Writer's Style, p. 37
Prewriting, p. 38
Elaboration, p. 39
Peer Response Guide, pp. 40–41
Revising and Proofreading, p. 42
Student Model, pp. 43–44
Rubric, p. 45

GRAMMAR MINI-LESSONS
Transparencies, p. 4
Copymasters, p. 5

WRITING MINI-LESSONS
Transparencies, pp. 41, 45

FORMAL ASSESSMENT
Guidelines for Writing Assessment

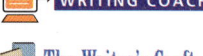
WRITING COACH

The Writer's Craft

Observation and Description, pp. 58–71
Coherence Within Paragraphs, pp. 376–383

Connect to Life

Travel books and articles often organize details of a setting by describing the manner in which items are positioned or seen. Sometimes, though, a writer uses both spatial order and order of impression to create a picture in the reader's mind. Using both techniques helps the reader imagine the setting.

Travel Article

Just north of the little town of Wickenburg, Arizona, I turned off U.S. Highway 89 and headed slowly down a narrow country road. At once everything seemed to signal a return to the storybook West. Whiteface cattle ambled across my path, rolling their eyes. Beyond a barbed wire fence a massive Brahman bull grazed. In the next field a handsome, high-strung yearling colt reared, wheeled, and galloped away. A snake at least four feet long wriggled across the road just ahead of my car. I rattled over the cattle guard at the portal to the Kay El Bar Guest Ranch and thought to myself: The rough, tough frontier is alive and well.

Merrill Windsor, from "Welcome to Wickenburg," *National Geographic Traveler*, Winter 1984/85

Combined Order Which details are presented in spatial order? How does the writer also use order of impression for details?

Try Your Hand: Ordering the Details

1. **Use Spatial Order** Choose one of the following topics, and write a descriptive paragraph using spatial order.
   - your hangout
   - the scene from a rooftop
   - the scene surrounding you at a sporting event

2. **Describe a Place** In a paragraph, describe a place that's special to you. Organize details to emphasize spatial order.

3. **Double Description** Describe your classroom during the last period of the day in two ways—first using order of impression and then spatial order.

SkillBuilder

WRITER'S CRAFT

Using Transition Words and Phrases

To relate details and show connections between ideas, writers use transition words and phrases. The list below shows some words that can be used to present ideas in the order of physical position, or spatial order.

Words and Phrases Used to Show Spatial Relationships

behind	in front of
around	over
here	through
inside	on the right of
beneath	down
there	above

APPLYING WHAT YOU'VE LEARNED
Locate words or phrases showing spatial relationships in the following paragraph:

The men walked through the parking lot in anticipation. Inside the ballpark, they gazed at the spectacle—empty seats above them and cold plastic grass beneath them. After placing squares of sod on top of the packed earth, they looked down from the seats behind home plate and smiled.

 WRITING HANDBOOK

For more information on transition words, see page 1027 of the Writing Handbook. For more information on organizing details, see page 1031 of the Writing Handbook.

WRITING ABOUT LITERATURE **257**

Teaching Strategy: MODELING

C Windsor Possible responses: Spatial order from near to far is shown in the details about the whiteface cattle, the barbed wire fence, the Brahman bull, and the yearling colt. A chronological order of impression is apparent in details about turning off the highway, heading slowly down the narrow country road, spotting the snake, and rattling over the cattle guard.

Try Your Hand

1. Responses will vary. Suggest that certain methods of ordering details are more appropriate than others for particular subjects. For example, a paragraph about a student's hangout might suitably use spatial order shown by the arrangement of details from front to back, while a paragraph about the view from a rooftop might move logically and naturally from near to far or from top to bottom. The surroundings of a sporting event might be described from left to right or from right to left.
2. Remind students to signal the use of spatial order in their paragraphs by using appropriate transition words and phrases.
3. Students might use order of impression to organize details that the writer has noticed within a chronological framework: for example, with twenty minutes to go till the end of the school day, with five minutes to go, and with one minute to go. Spatial order might be appropriate for details that the writer has observed, starting with the teacher's desk at the front of the classroom and ending with the last row of students' desks at the back of the room.

 **WRITER'S CRAFT**

USING TRANSITION WORDS AND PHRASES Have students describe their surroundings in the classroom or at a location on the school grounds, using five transition words and phrases. Students' descriptions should be in complete sentences.

Applying What You've Learned Answers: *through the parking lot, inside the ballpark, above them, beneath them, on top of the packed earth, down from the seats, behind home plate.*

Additional Suggestions Challenge students to use transition words to revise brief descriptive passages such as the following:

1. The sky darkened. The stadium lights came on. The infield blazed with a white-orange intensity.
2. The dog growled menacingly. The child stood frightened. The mother raced to the scene.

Reteaching/Reinforcement
- *Writing Handbook*, anthology, pp. 1027–1029
- *Writing Mini-Lessons*, transparencies, p. 41

The Writer's Craft
Transitional Devices, pp. 376–382

Critical Thinking: ANALYZING

D Be sure the students understand that analyzing involves breaking a whole topic into its parts to study its nature and identify its essential features. Remind students that components of setting which they may want to analyze include facts such as physical location, time of day, and time of year, as well as sensory images and word choices that affect mood.

Teaching Strategy: USING THE SKILLBUILDER

E Help students answer the prewriting questions by teaching the SkillBuilder on Creating Mood. It will help students recognize how writers' word choices can generate a range of moods.

WRITING ABOUT LITERATURE

Analysis

When writers describe a setting, they are doing more than simply presenting a place. They may use setting to create a mood or as a driving force in a story. You can analyze how a writer uses setting to create a particular impression. Closely analyzing information about setting helps you make connections—in stories and in everyday life.

GUIDED ASSIGNMENT

Analyze a Setting The following pages will help you think about the setting from a selection and analyze how it plays an important role in your impression of the story.

1 Prewrite and Explore

Begin thinking about two or three selections in which setting seems to play a key role. Why is the setting significant? Perhaps it creates a mood, affects a character's actions and feelings, provides details, or makes the story convincing.

Student's Prewriting Chart

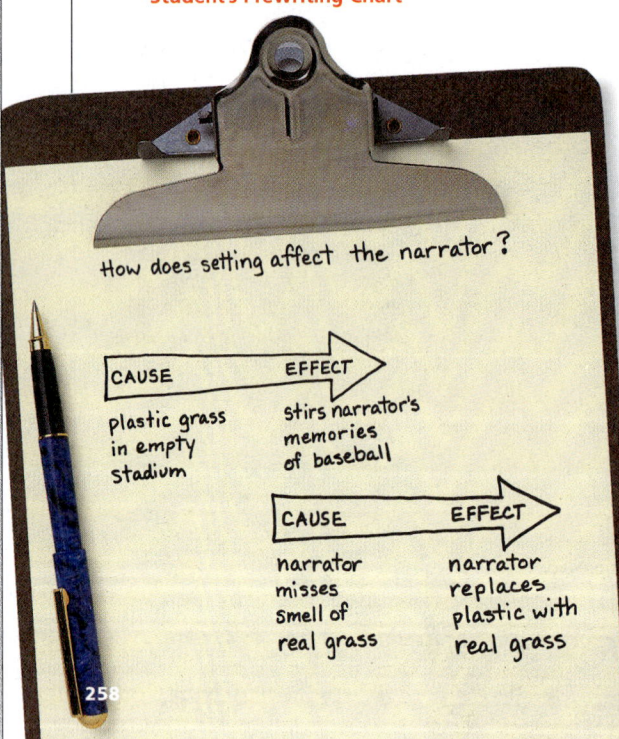

How does setting affect the narrator?

CAUSE	EFFECT
plastic grass in empty stadium	stirs narrator's memories of baseball
narrator misses smell of real grass	narrator replaces plastic with real grass

EXAMINING SETTINGS

The following questions might help you explore why a particular setting seems important to a story.

- Where and when does the story take place?
- How does the setting affect events?
- How does it affect how characters act or feel?
- How would a change in setting affect the story?
- What mood is created by descriptions of the setting?

Decision Point Based on your responses, which setting would you most like to explore?

LOOK FOR CONNECTIONS

Creating a cause-and-effect chart can help you visualize the connections between the setting, mood, events, and characters. Remember that a chart does not need to be all facts. Feel free to include your feelings and reactions.

Assessment Option

SELF-ASSESSMENT After students have explored the connections between the setting, mood, events, and characters, they should assess the details listed on their cause and effect charts by answering the following questions:

- Have I listed details that show how the setting affects the events in the plot?
- Have I shown how the setting affects the characters' emotions and motivations?
- Have I explained any important connections between the author's descriptions of the setting and the mood of the story?

---

258 THE LANGUAGE OF LITERATURE TEACHER'S EDITION

❷ Write and Analyze a Discovery Draft

F With so many possibilities, how can you choose a focus for your writing about setting? Begin freewriting using the topics from your cause-and-effect chart.

Student's Discovery Draft

> When I think about the setting in "The Thrill of the Grass," I picture the empty stadium. It's so lonely and artificial—it doesn't even have real grass. That's it! Without the setting, there would be no story. The narrator is deeply affected by its emptiness and lack of green grass. It stirs his emotions.

I think I'll include how he feels before and after he changes the setting.

The setting is the cause for the narrator's action—main point.

> The narrator physically changes the setting by removing squares of the plastic grass and adding sod. I see that as the setting changes, his feelings about the stadium and baseball change too. The grass smells like baseball and he feels at home.

Following are some questions that you can ask yourself when you finish your writing.

- What main point about the setting seems to surface?
- Do I want to focus on a specific aspect of the setting or the overall role of the setting in the story?
- What examples from the selection can I use for support?

❸ Draft and Share

G Now it's time to write a focused draft. Analysis, on page 1040 of the Writing Handbook, will help you to write an analysis about setting. If you will be discussing how the setting creates a mood, consult the SkillBuilder on creating mood. Trade your paper with a writing partner and ask for a response.

PEER RESPONSE

- What is my main point about the setting?
- Is there anything in my paper that confuses you or seems beside the point?

SkillBuilder
WRITER'S CRAFT

Creating Mood

Good writers carefully select words to describe a setting. Those words, though, do more than describe. They can actually create a feeling or mood in the reader. Different word choices can inspire moods such as peaceful, cheerful, or fearful.

What moods do the words and phrases below create?

- brightly colored streamers, lively music, laughing children
- dimly lit passages, creaking of a door, cobwebs, dampness
- scratching of pencils on paper, a clock ticking, sighs of frustration

APPLYING WHAT YOU'VE LEARNED

Check your draft. Do you analyze the words a writer uses to create a mood in the setting? Check the selection for mood-creating words. Can you effectively discuss the writer's word choices in your draft?

WRITING HANDBOOK

For more information on descriptive writing, see page 1030 of the Writing Handbook.

Writing Skill: USING SENSORY LANGUAGE

F The Discovery Draft provides an opportunity for students to sort through the information that they have gathered and to explore ideas. Suggest that they focus on sensory images as they freewrite. Help them notice how the author of a selection creates vivid descriptions by appealing to sight, hearing, touch, taste, and smell. Suggest that students fill in observation charts that show to which sense each image appeals.

Teaching Strategy: CUSTOMIZING FOR LESS-PROFICIENT WRITERS

G Point out that the introduction to the essay should present the student's idea about the setting. The body of the essay should present supporting details in a coherent order. The conclusion should restate and reinforce the main idea.

WRITING ABOUT LITERATURE **259**

SkillBuilder — WRITER'S CRAFT

CREATING MOOD Remind students that words contribute to certain moods through their connotations, or emotional overtones, as well as through their denotations, or literal (dictionary) meanings. Ask how the mood of the first example would have been affected if it had read "garish streamers, frantic music, tittering children."

Applying What You've Learned Discuss how the details in the sample discovery draft might be revised to convey the precise mood of a setting. For example, the phrases *empty stadium* and *green grass* in the first passage might be made more graphic. In the second passage, the writer might add sensory language to help the readers sense that the smell of the grass is more pungent or earthy.

Additional Suggestions Ask students to comment on the mood created by the following groups of words and phrases:

1. fluffy white clouds, gentle breeze, soft drone of dragonflies
2. bright flashing lights, screeching siren, crackle of flames, sulfurous odor of smoke

Reteaching/Reinforcement
- *Writing Mini-Lessons* transparencies, p. 45

The Writer's Craft
Denotation and Connotation, p. 424

THE LANGUAGE OF LITERATURE TEACHER'S EDITION **259**

Critical Thinking: ANALYZING

H To evaluate and revise their analyses of setting, students should check that they have given the audience adequate description and needed background information and that they have stated and supported their idea.

Teaching Strategy: USING THE SKILLBUILDER

I You can help students achieve subject-verb agreement with prepositional phrases by teaching the SkillBuilder on page 261 before students make their final revisions.

Teaching Strategy: MODELING

J Discuss how this sample meets the Standards for Evaluation on this page. The essay will be about the setting of the baseball stadium. The main point is that the narrator's motivation leads him to recreate the setting and to change the story's atmosphere. Details showing the effect of the setting include the change in his feelings and the way in which he bends down to pay respect to the natural, wonderful grass. The quotation reveals the narrator's joyful appreciation of the fresh grass.

Standards for Evaluation

Have students review their setting analysis for the following:

Ideas and Content
- Gives the author, title, and a brief summary.
- States the writer's point in a clear manner.
- Analyzes the setting of the story.
- Supports analysis with evidence from the story.
- Ending summarizes the analysis and draws an overall conclusion.

Structure and Form
- Uses well-organized paragraphs and a clear organization.
- Uses a variety of sentence structures.

Grammar, Usage, and Mechanics
- Contains only a few minor errors in grammar, usage, spelling, capitalization, and punctuation.

PORTFOLIO

Ask students to review their analysis papers to identify the strongest sections. Invite students to read aloud excerpts from those sections and to discuss the elements of an effective analysis. Students may wish to include their papers in their portfolios.

WRITING ABOUT LITERATURE

4 Revise and Edit

H
I
Review your thoughts and the responses of your peers. How have you made your ideas clear? Do you include enough support? Did you use good quotes or comment on the writer's word choice if these support your main point? After you make your final copy, reflect on how your thoughts have changed.

Student's Final Draft

What will this essay be about? What is the student's main point?

J

The Thrill of the Grass

Sometimes the scent of a certain place or setting can stir a memory or feeling from long ago. In "The Thrill of the Grass" by W. P. Kinsella, scents of a baseball stadium—particularly fresh grass—remind the narrator of days in the outfield as a child and the pure pleasure of a baseball game. However, the lonely stadium in his town, whose outfield is plastic grass, lacks the scent of baseball. The setting itself, a silent stadium, causes the narrator to take action during the summer of a baseball strike.

How do the details and quotations show that setting affects the narrator's actions?

As the narrator and his accomplices change the setting—the outfield—his feelings change too. He used to feel mournful; now he feels full of wonder. The scent of the grass stirs something within him. Alone in the newly sodded setting, he bows in the center of the outfield to pay respect. He says, "I lower my face to the silvered grass, which, wonder of wonders, already has the ephemeral odours of baseball about it."

Standards for Evaluation

The setting analysis
- identifies the selection by author and title and briefly describes it
- clearly describes the point the writer wants to make
- presents an organized analysis of the setting or a specific aspect of it
- offers support for the writer's points by using details and quotations

260 UNIT TWO: REFLECTING ON SOCIETY

Assessment Option

SELF-ASSESSMENT To help students assess their own writing, they can ask themselves the following questions:
- *Have I identified and briefly described the literary selection?*
- *Have I clearly stated my major idea about the setting?*
- *Have I analyzed details of setting and given examples of the author's choice of words to support my main idea?*
- *Have I restated my main idea in an effective conclusion?*

Grammar in Context

Prepositional Phrases When creating descriptions, writers often use spatial order to organize the details. Prepositional phrases show spatial order, or the physical position of objects or people in a description. As a review, examine the following excerpt from the student's draft and note the prepositional phrases that show spatial relationships.

> The narrator parks his car ^at the far end of the lot ^across the lot toward the stadium. As he walks slowly, he dreams about his childhood baseball days. When he arrives ^at the deserted stadium ^within inches of the door, he stands and contemplates breaking in. As he thinks about what lies on the other side ^of the door, he skillfully picks the padlock ^under the latch. He enters and feels rejuvenated.

Prepositional phrases can add richness to a piece of writing. In the example above, the inserted prepositional phrases show how elements in the story are physically related. For more information about prepositional phrases, see page 1064 of the Grammar Handbook.

Try Your Hand: Using Prepositional Phrases

Revise the following paragraph to include prepositional phrases that describe spatial relationships.

> After walking through the door, the narrator saw the ballpark. It felt cold and desolate. The plastic grass shimmered. Seams stood out. Rows of bleachers loomed. The dugouts looked lonely. Even the pressbox wasn't impressive.

SkillBuilder

GRAMMAR FROM WRITING

Achieving Subject-Verb Agreement with Prepositional Phrases

Making sure your subjects and verbs agree when you use prepositional phrases can be challenging. Try not to mistake a word in a prepositional phrase for the subject of a sentence.

*The **narrator**, with his accomplices, **decides** to plant sod in the outfield.*

(The subject, *narrator*, is singular; *with his accomplices* is a prepositional phrase; therefore, the verb, *decides*, is singular.)

***Scents** of a baseball stadium **remind** the narrator of days in the outfield.*

(The subject, *scents*, is plural; *of a baseball stadium* is a prepositional phrase; the verb, *remind*, is plural.)

APPLYING WHAT YOU'VE LEARNED

Choose the verb that agrees with its subject.

1. The stadium in the shadows (stand/stands) mournfully.
2. The men with their boxes of sod (arrive/arrives) after midnight.

GRAMMAR HANDBOOK

Consult page 1064 in the Grammar Handbook to review subject-verb agreement with prepositional phrases.

WRITING ABOUT LITERATURE 261

Teaching Strategy: STUMBLING BLOCK

Remind students that a prepositional phrase consists of a preposition plus the nouns or pronouns that are its object, together with their modifiers. Point out that although prepositional phrases add richness and detail by specifying relationships, overusing them can produce a wordy, awkward style. For example, ask students to critique the following variation of the opening sentence of the model: *At this point in the tale, the narrator of the story parks his car in a space at the far end of the stadium lot opposite the main entrance to the ballpark.* Most students will note the wordiness of this example. Point out that several prepositional phrases can be omitted with no loss of clarity.

Try Your Hand

Possible response: After walking through the stadium door and down the gently sloping ramp, the narrator saw the ballpark spread out before him. In its emptiness, it felt cold and desolate. The plastic grass shimmered on the field. Seams stood out down the right and left foul lines. Rows of bleachers loomed beyond the end of the outfield. On both sides of home plate, the dugouts looked lonely. Even the press box above the box seats wasn't impressive.

SkillBuilder — GRAMMAR FROM WRITING

ACHIEVING SUBJECT-VERB AGREEMENT WITH PREPOSITIONAL PHRASES If students have difficulty making subject and verb agree, recommend that, when proofreading, they mentally "block out" any phrases or clauses intervening between the subject and the main verb of each sentence. Encourage students to say the subject and verb aloud in order to check agreement.

Applying What You've Learned
1. stands
2. arrive

Additional Suggestions You may wish to add the following exercise items so that students can practice subject-verb agreement in sentences that contain intervening phrases:
1. Something about the scent of the sod, in its lush emerald squares, (is/are) profoundly satisfying.
2. The narrator, along with his friends, (feel/feels) rejuvenated.

Reteaching/Reinforcement
- Grammar Handbook, anthology pp. 1061–1065
- *Grammar Mini-Lessons* copymasters p. 5, transparencies p. 4

The Writer's Craft
Words Between Subject and Verb, p. 687

READING THE WORLD

On pages 258–261, students analyzed a setting in a literary work and its effect on the story. Students should also be aware that settings in real life affect people's reactions to other people and events. In this lesson, students will examine their responses to the impact of a real-life setting.

Critical Thinking: OBSERVING

L Students should include factual details such as the crumbling buildings and the debris of the urban neighborhood, the white formal clothing of the bride and groom, the way in which the bride lifts her dress as she attempts to pick her way through the rubble, and so forth. Students' reactions to the bride and groom will vary. Some students might suggest that their presence is incongruous, or even comic, in this setting. Other students may express admiration and sympathy, inferring from the shattered surroundings that although they appear to be intrepid, the newlyweds face difficult challenges at the beginning of their married life.

Media Literacy: INTERPRETING A PHOTOGRAPH

M Students' answers will vary. Some may suggest that the setting causes them to question the young couple's longevity because they appear to be living in a war zone. Others might say the couple seems hopeful because they are beginning a new life together amidst the ruins of war.

Speaking and Listening: GROUP DISCUSSION

N Discuss what qualities make an event newsworthy. Encourage students to support their answers with examples from news media. Then have students work in small groups to compare their comments on why this image is newsworthy. Encourage them to compare this image to one of a bride and groom in a conventional context: for example, on the steps outside a church or synagogue or dancing together at a sumptuous wedding reception.

READING THE WORLD

THE IMPACT OF SETTING

Just as setting in literature affects characters and events, so setting in your life affects your reaction to events. How do you respond to the settings in your world?

View Examine the situation shown in this photo. Describe what you see. What is your reaction to the bride and groom in this setting?

Interpret Think about why the setting is important. How might the setting affect your assumptions about the couple?

Discuss In a group, discuss why this image is newsworthy. What is important about this photo? With your group, share ideas on how setting affects your understanding of events. Now use the SkillBuilder on the next page to help you analyze the components of setting.

262 THE LANGUAGE OF LITERATURE TEACHER'S EDITION

SkillBuilder

 CRITICAL THINKING

Analyzing Components of Setting

Have you ever seen a movie or play in which the setting played a starring role? What made it memorable? Setting can create a mood, affect a person's feelings or actions, or even portray symbols.

When you analyze, you take apart, examine, and explain an idea or a subject. Think about how you might use these skills to analyze the importance of settings in your life. How is the backdrop of an urban school meant to affect people's perceptions of a politician's speech on the importance of education for all young people? How might your response change if the same speech were given in front of a video arcade or outside a mansion? Can you think of other examples?

APPLYING WHAT YOU'VE LEARNED
In a small group, discuss the memorable settings of books, television shows, plays, or movies. Talk about real-life settings too. In your discussion, analyze how setting plays an important role. Consider differences in group members' analyses of the settings.

READING THE WORLD 263

SkillBuilder CRITICAL THINKING

ANALYZING COMPONENTS OF SETTING
Lead a discussion of the specific examples in the text. For example, suggest that the backdrop of an urban school for a politician's speech on education is meant to reinforce the seriousness of his or her message. Point out that the setting of a video arcade or a mansion may run the risk of trivializing the speech or of alienating an audience with middle- or lower- class incomes.

Applying What You've Learned You may wish to appoint one member of each group as the moderator and another student as the recorder. You might suggest that students consider real-life events that have been dramatized by the media. Ask students how the setting of the dramatization compares to the real-life setting.

THE LANGUAGE OF LITERATURE TEACHER'S EDITION 263

UNIT TWO
Part 2 Lesson Planner

TIME ALLOTMENTS SHOWN ARE APPROXIMATE. DEPENDING ON YOUR GOALS AND THE NEEDS OF YOUR STUDENTS, YOU MAY WISH TO ALLOW MORE OR LESS TIME FOR CERTAIN PORTIONS OF THE LESSON.

Table of Contents	Discussion	Previewing the Selection	Reading the Selection
PART OPENER **Prisoners of Circumstance** page 264	**20 MINUTES** • Reflect on the part theme		
SELECTION **On the Rainy River** page 267 AVERAGE		**20 MINUTES** • PERSONAL CONNECTION • HISTORICAL CONNECTION • READING CONNECTION: Drawing conclusions	**90 MINUTES** • Introduce vocabulary • Read pp. 267–280 (14 pp.)
SELECTION **The Pearl** page 285 CHALLENGING		**20 MINUTES** • PERSONAL CONNECTION • CULTURAL CONNECTION • READING CONNECTION: Problems and solutions/Reading log	**50 MINUTES** • Introduce vocabulary • Read pp. 285–294 (10 pp.)
SELECTION **Black Men and Public Space** page 298 EASY		**20 MINUTES** • PERSONAL CONNECTION • CULTURAL CONNECTION • WRITING CONNECTION	**15 MINUTES** • Introduce vocabulary • Read pp. 298–300 (3 pp.)
SELECTIONS **Miss Rosie/ Kitchenette Building** page 304 CHALLENGING		**20 MINUTES** • PERSONAL CONNECTION • BIOGRAPHICAL CONNECTION • READING CONNECTION: Making inferences in poetry	**30 MINUTES** • Read pp. 304–305 (2 pp.)
SELECTION *from* **Night** page 309 CHALLENGING		**20 MINUTES** • PERSONAL CONNECTION • HISTORICAL CONNECTION • WRITING CONNECTION	**30 MINUTES** • Introduce vocabulary • Read pp. 309–313 (5 pp.)
SELECTION **The Women Who Are Poets in My Land** page 318 CHALLENGING		**20 MINUTES** • PERSONAL CONNECTION • HISTORICAL/CULTURAL CONNECTION • WRITING CONNECTION	**10 MINUTES** • Introduce vocabulary • Read p. 318 (1 p.)
SELECTION **House Taken Over** page 322 AVERAGE		**20 MINUTES** • PERSONAL CONNECTION • BIOGRAPHICAL CONNECTION • READING CONNECTION: Recognizing fantasy	**40 MINUTES** • Introduce vocabulary • Read pp. 322–327 (6 pp.)
NONFICTION ON YOUR OWN *from* **Farewell to Manzanar** page 330 AVERAGE			**50 MINUTES** • Read pp. 330–339 (10 pp.)
Writing WRITING FROM EXPERIENCE **Persuasion**	**Exploring Topics** **30 MINUTES**	**Prewriting** **30 MINUTES**	**Drafting and Revising** **70 MINUTES**

Time estimates assume in-class work. You may wish to assign some of these stages as homework.

Responding to the Selection

FROM PERSONAL RESPONSE TO CRITICAL ANALYSIS	OR	ANOTHER PATHWAY	LITERARY CONCEPTS	QUICKWRITES
		60 MINUTES		
• Discussion questions	OR	• Point/counterpoint discussion	• Point of view	• Letter • Definition essay • Alternative ending • Personal essay
		30 MINUTES		
• Discussion questions	OR	• Time line	• Satire • Tone	• Dialogue • Character sketch • Satiric story
		50 MINUTES		
• Discussion questions	OR	• Review	• Structure	• Description • Dramatic scene • Editorial • Personal narrative
		30 MINUTES		
• Discussion questions	OR	• Dramatic reading	• Speaker • Theme	• Poem • Report card
		30 MINUTES		
• Discussion questions	OR	• Reading a poem aloud	• Stanzas • Imagery	• Speech • Poem • Letter
		30 MINUTES		
• Discussion questions	OR	• List of generalizations	• Style	• Excerpt • Eyewitness account • List of questions
		40 MINUTES		
• Discussion questions	OR	• Realistic/fantastic chart	• Magical realism • Setting	• Essay • Story

Extension Activities

ALTERNATIVE ACTIVITIES	LITERARY LINKS	CRITIC'S CORNER	THE WRITER'S STYLE	ACROSS THE CURRICULUM	ART CONNECTION	WORDS TO KNOW	BIOGRAPHY
40 MINUTES							
✔	✔			HISTORY JOURNALISM	✔	✔	✔
30 MINUTES							
✔			✔			✔	✔
40 MINUTES							
	✔			PSYCHOLOGY	✔	✔	✔
30 MINUTES							
✔		✔	✔				✔
20 MINUTES							
✔	✔	✔		MUSIC			✔
20 MINUTES							
✔				MEDIA		✔	✔
30 MINUTES							
✔		✔			✔	✔	✔

Publishing and Reflecting

20 MINUTES

LESSON PLANNER TEACHER'S EDITION **263b**

PART 2

REFLECTING ON THEME

Have students discuss the idea that it is possible to achieve anything, provided one really wants it. Remind them that Wilma Rudolph, crippled by polio as a child, became an Olympic track athlete, and that Beethoven composed music despite being deaf. Have students provide examples of other people who have broken out of a "prison of circumstances."

What Do You Think?

Students may wish to include literary figures in their charts. When charts are completed, you might have a whole-class discussion of the results. Ask students to identify which kinds of obstacles seem most prevalent on their lists. Then have students suggest ways in which the individuals and groups on their lists might overcome the obstacles. Students will return to this activity on page 283.

UNIT TWO **PART 2**

PRISONERS OF CIRCUMSTANCE

REFLECTING ON THEME

Do you ever feel trapped by society? Do you ever worry that your dreams may be blocked by forces beyond your control? As you will see in this part of Unit Two, individuals can be trapped or imprisoned by many circumstances. War, poverty, prejudice, injustice, pressures to conform—such forces can cast a net around an individual. People respond to such restrictions in different ways. Some manage to fight their way free.

What Do You Think? With several classmates, create a two-column chart. In the left column, list individuals or groups of people who seem to be prisoners of circumstance. In the right column, list the factors—such as poverty, ignorance, and so on—that restrict each individual or group. Present your chart to the rest of the class.

Tim O'Brien (1946–) His fiction about the Vietnam War has won him fame.

Lucille Clifton (1936–) Another major voice in African-American poetry

Jeanne Wakatsuki Houston (1934–) and **James D. Houston** (1933–) This husband and wife wrote about her experience in a Japanese-American detention camp.

Brent Staples (1951–) A leading African-American journalist and author

Gwendolyn Brooks (1917–) The first African-American poet to win a Pulitzer Prize

Julio Cortázar (1914–1984) A leading Argentinean writer, noted for experimentation

Tim O'Brien	**On the Rainy River** *Will he fight in Vietnam or flee to Canada?*	266
Yukio Mishima	**The Pearl** *A social gathering gets out of hand.*	284
Brent Staples	**Black Men and Public Space** *Put yourself in his place.*	297
Lucille Clifton	**Miss Rosie** *How did she get like this?*	303
Gwendolyn Brooks	**Kitchenette Building** *Can dreams survive?*	303

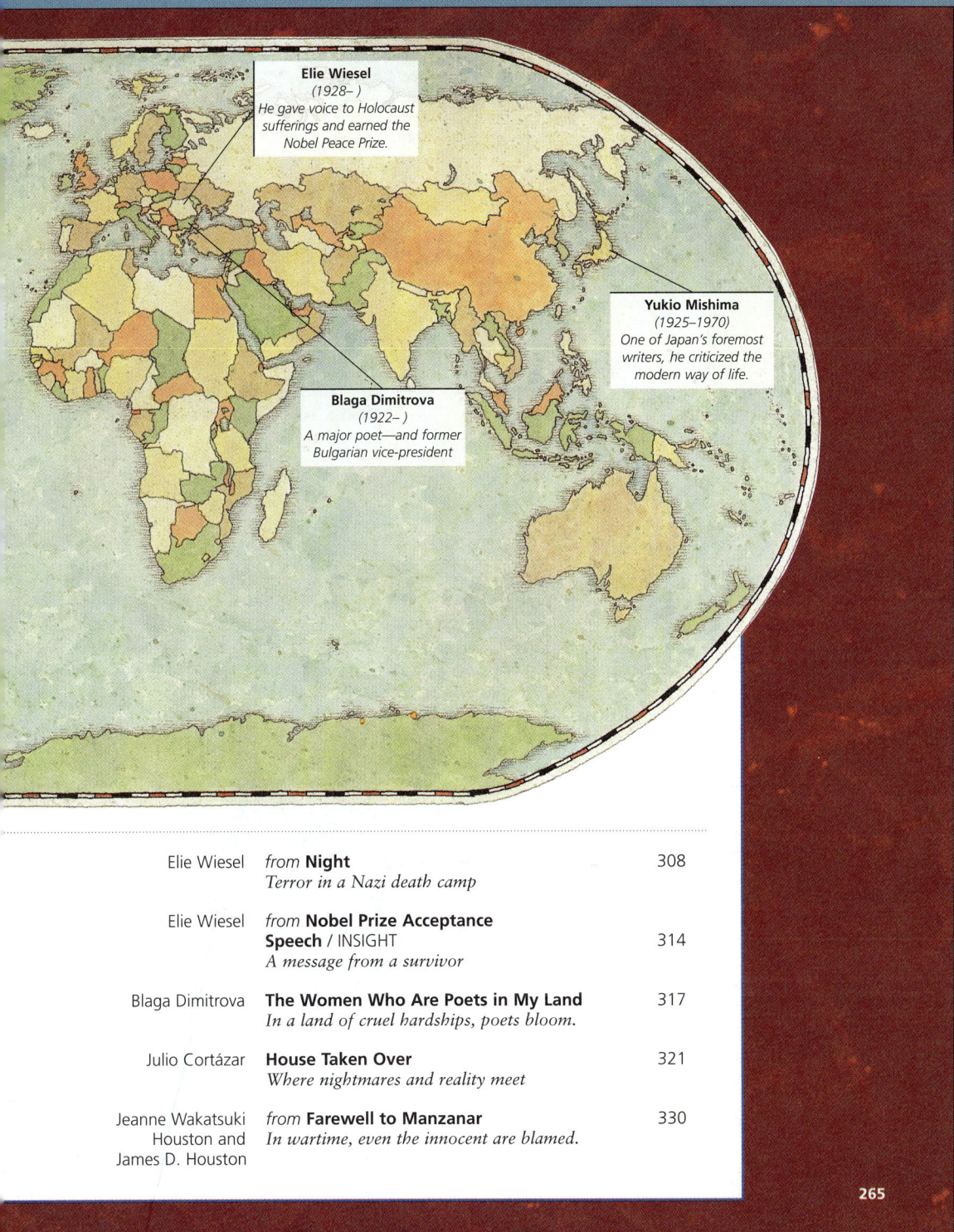

Map Note

This map shows the diversity of the authors represented by the selections in this part of the unit. Encourage students to think about circumstances that might restrict people by asking questions like these:

- What do you know about the experiences of Japanese-Americans in the United States during World War II?
- What kinds of restrictive circumstances might a poet from Bulgaria write about?

Elie Wiesel	from **Night** *Terror in a Nazi death camp*	308
Elie Wiesel	from **Nobel Prize Acceptance Speech** / INSIGHT *A message from a survivor*	314
Blaga Dimitrova	**The Women Who Are Poets in My Land** *In a land of cruel hardships, poets bloom.*	317
Julio Cortázar	**House Taken Over** *Where nightmares and reality meet*	321
Jeanne Wakatsuki Houston and James D. Houston	from **Farewell to Manzanar** *In wartime, even the innocent are blamed.*	330

OVERVIEW

Objectives

- To understand and appreciate a short story that explores a difficult choice thrust upon a young man by war
- To identify and understand point of view
- To express understanding of the story through a choice of writing forms, including a letter, a definition essay, an alternative ending, and a personal essay
- To extend understanding of the story through a variety of multimodal and cross-curricular activities

Skills

READING SKILLS/STRATEGIES
- Drawing conclusions

THE WRITER'S STYLE
- Addressing the reader directly

GRAMMAR
- Subordinating conjunctions

LITERARY CONCEPTS
- Point of view
- Description
- Symbolism

SPEAKING, LISTENING, AND VIEWING
- Drama performance
- Music
- Group discussion
- Oral presentation

HISTORICAL CONNECTION
Going to Vietnam The Vietnam War was the most unpopular war in United States history. This film provides historical background for understanding the narrator's dilemma in O'Brien's story.

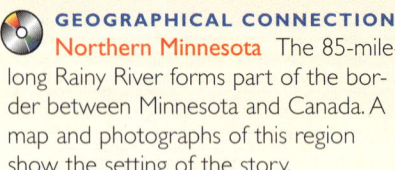

Side A, Frame 12923

GEOGRAPHICAL CONNECTION
Northern Minnesota The 85-mile-long Rainy River forms part of the border between Minnesota and Canada. A map and photographs of this region show the setting of the story.

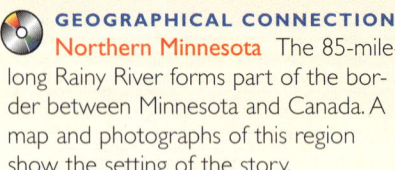

Side A, Frame 49402

PREVIEWING

FICTION

On the Rainy River
Tim O'Brien United States

Activating Prior Knowledge
PERSONAL CONNECTION

In this story, a young man must decide whether to fight in a war he opposes. Under what conditions would you be willing to fight in a war? Under what conditions would you be unwilling to fight? Respond in your notebook by listing your ideas in a chart like the one to the right.

I would fight if . . .	I would not fight if . . .

Building Background
HISTORICAL CONNECTION

The Vietnam War (1957–1975), a war between South and North Vietnam, was the longest and one of the most controversial military conflicts in which the United States has been involved. The United States entered the war in 1964 in hopes of preventing the spread of communism throughout Southeast Asia. During the course of the war, nearly 3 million Americans were sent overseas to defend the South Vietnamese government against a takeover by Communist North Vietnam and the Viet Cong, a South Vietnamese Communist rebel force. The last American troops were pulled out of Vietnam in 1973, and two years later the South Vietnamese government surrendered to North Vietnam.

During the war, nearly 2 million men were drafted into the military, first by a system that allowed college students and others to defer their service and later by a lottery that allowed fewer exemptions. Those who were drafted but who opposed the war faced a difficult decision: whether to risk their lives in a foreign war they couldn't justify or risk imprisonment at home by refusing to serve. Some burned their draft cards as a form of protest; others fled the country, most often by crossing the border into Canada.

Vietnam War protest march in the late 1960s. Copyright © Peter de Krassel / Photo Researchers, Inc.

Active Reading/Setting a Purpose
READING CONNECTION

Drawing Conclusions As you read "On the Rainy River," pay particular attention to the narrator's judgments. Decide whether you agree with his views about war and with his ultimate decision.

▶ **LASERLINKS**
- GEOGRAPHICAL CONNECTION
- HISTORICAL CONNECTION

266 UNIT TWO PART 2: PRISONERS OF CIRCUMSTANCE

PRINT AND MEDIA RESOURCES

UNIT TWO RESOURCE BOOK
Strategic Reading: Literature, p. 49
Vocabulary SkillBuilder, p. 50

GRAMMAR MINI–LESSONS
Transparencies, p. 50
Copymasters, p. 3

ACCESS FOR STUDENTS ACQUIRING ENGLISH
Selection Summaries
Reading Support

FORMAL ASSESSMENT
Selection Test, p. 53
 Test Generator

 AUDIO LIBRARY
See Reference Card

 LASERLINKS
Historical Connection
Geographical Connection

 INTERNET RESOURCES
McDougal Littell Literature Center at http://www.hmco.com/mcdougal/lit

On the Rainy River

Tim O'Brien

Portrait of Donald Schrader (1962), Fairfield Porter. The Metropolitan Museum of Art, bequest of Arthur M. Bullowa, 1993 (1993.406.12). Copyright © 1995 The Metropolitan Museum of Art.

This is one story I've never told before. Not to anyone. Not to my parents, not to my brother or sister, not even to my wife. To go into it, I've always thought, would only cause embarrassment for all of us, a sudden need to be elsewhere, which is the natural response to a confession. Even now, I'll admit, the story makes me squirm. For more than twenty years I've had to live with it, feeling the shame, trying to push it away, and so by this act of remembrance, by putting the facts down on paper, I'm hoping to relieve at least some of the pressure on my dreams.

SUMMARY

Although the narrator has taken a modest stand against the Vietnam War, he does not feel personally involved in or threatened by it until he is drafted during the summer of 1968. He opens the draft notice in disbelief, which turns to rage, then self-pity, then numbness. He feels that he should flee to Canada to avoid killing and being killed, but he fears exile just as he has feared and hated the war. One morning, he walks away from his factory job and drives north. He stops at the rundown Tip Top Lodge to struggle with his conscience and his fate. On the sixth day of his visit, Elroy Berdahl, the owner of the lodge and a hero to O'Brien, takes the narrator fishing on the Rainy River. As they pull up near the Canadian border, the narrator sees his past and future and begins to cry. He realizes that he does not have the courage to run away and knows that he will kill and maybe die—because he is embarrassed not to go to war.

Thematic Link: *Prisoners of Circumstance*
In this story, the narrator is a prisoner of two circumstances: his community's belief in the rightness of the Vietnam War and his own belief that the war is wrong.

CUSTOMIZING FOR
Students Acquiring English

- Use **ACCESS FOR STUDENTS ACQUIRING ENGLISH,** *Reading Support.*
- Review the facts in the Historical Connection on page 266 with students. Ask volunteers to describe any similar experiences that young people in other countries have had.

STRATEGIC READING FOR
Less-Proficient Readers

Set a Purpose Ask students to discuss occasions when their views on important issues have differed from those of their families and friends. Suggest that students read to see how the narrator's view of the Vietnam War differs from the views of others in his hometown.

Use **UNIT TWO RESOURCE BOOK,** p. 49, for guidance in reading the selection.

WORDS TO KNOW

acquiescence (ăk′wē-ĕs′əns) *n.* passive agreement; agreement without protest (p. 271)
consensus (kən-sĕn′səs) *n.* general agreement by a group (p. 268)
fathom (făth′əm) *v.* to penetrate the meaning or understand the nature of (p. 269)
impassive (ĭm-păs′ĭv) *adj.* revealing no emotion; expressionless (p. 280)
imperative (ĭm-pĕr′ə-tĭv) *n.* urgent necessity or duty (p. 268)
platitude (plăt′ĭ-tōōd′) *n.* a trite or unoriginal statement, especially one expressed as if it were original or significant; a cliché (p. 271)
preoccupied (prē-ŏk′yə-pīd′) *adj.* absorbed in one's thoughts; distracted **preoccupy** *v.* (p. 273)
pretense (prē′tĕns′) *n.* a false outward appearance (p. 277)
reticence (rĕt′ĭ-səns) *n.* the state or quality of being reserved and keeping one's thoughts to oneself (p. 274)
vigil (vĭj′əl) *n.* a watch kept by a person, especially during normal sleeping hours or to show devotion (p. 277)

CUSTOMIZING FOR
Gifted and Talented Students

Suggest that as they read the story, students think about the narrator's relationship with his parents. What details give insight into this relationship? *(Possible responses: The fact that he can't share his dilemma with his parents shows that their relationship is not completely open; the fact that he lives at home shows that they get along reasonably well; the fact that he doesn't want to shame them by dodging the draft shows that he loves and respects them.)*

CUSTOMIZING FOR
Students Acquiring English

1 Explain that the Lone Ranger was a cowboy hero who appeared in radio, television, and movie dramas for many years. Many people saw this brave masked man as the quintessential American hero.

Literary Concept: SIMILE

A Ask students to identify the extended simile in this paragraph. *(comparison of courage to inherited money)* Ask whether they feel the comparison is valid. *(Accept all reasonable responses.)*

Literary Concept: TONE

B Discuss why the narrator uses a series of questions here. What attitude toward the Vietnam War is he expressing? *(Possible responses: confusion; uncertainty; frustration)*

CUSTOMIZING FOR
Students Acquiring English

2 Explain that *men in pinstripes* refers to businessmen, politicians, and other executives. The business suits such men wear to work are often made of dark fabric with narrow stripes.

Still, it's a hard story to tell. All of us, I suppose, like to believe that in a moral emergency we will behave like the heroes of our youth, bravely and forthrightly, without thought of personal loss or discredit. Certainly that was my conviction back in the summer of 1968. Tim O'Brien: a secret hero. The Lone Ranger. If the stakes ever became high enough—if the evil were evil enough, if the good were good enough—I would simply tap a secret reservoir of courage that had been accumulating inside me over the years. Courage, I seemed to think, comes to us in finite quantities, like an inheritance, and by being frugal and stashing it away, and letting it earn interest, we steadily increase our moral capital in preparation for that day when the account must be drawn down. It was a comforting theory. It dispensed with all those bothersome little acts of daily courage; it offered hope and grace to the repetitive coward; it justified the past while amortizing the future.

In June of 1968, a month after graduating from Macalester College, I was drafted to fight a war I hated. I was twenty-one years old. Young, yes, and politically naive, but even so the American war in Vietnam seemed to me wrong. Certain blood was being shed for uncertain reasons. I saw no unity of purpose, no consensus on matters of philosophy or history or law. The very facts were shrouded in uncertainty: Was it a civil war? A war of national liberation or simple aggression? Who started it, and when, and why? What really happened to the U.S.S. *Maddox* on that dark night in the Gulf of Tonkin?[1] Was Ho Chi Minh[2] a Communist stooge, or a nationalist savior, or both, or neither? What about the Geneva Accords?[3] What about SEATO[4] and the Cold War?[5] What about dominoes?[6] America was divided on these and a thousand other issues, and the debate had spilled out across the floor of the United States Senate and into the streets,

> **I was too *good* for this war. Too smart, too compassionate, too everything.**

and smart men in pinstripes could not agree on even the most fundamental matters of public policy. The only certainty that summer was moral confusion. It was my view then, and still is, that you don't make war without knowing why. Knowledge, of course, is always imperfect, but it seemed to me that when a nation goes to war it must have reasonable confidence in the justice and imperative of its cause. You can't fix your mistakes. Once people are dead, you can't make them undead.

In any case those were my convictions, and back in college I had taken a modest stand against the war. Nothing radical, no hothead

---

1. **U.S.S. *Maddox* . . . Gulf of Tonkin:** an alleged attack on the U.S. destroyer *Maddox* in the Gulf of Tonkin, off the coast of North Vietnam, in 1964, which provided a basis for expanding U.S. involvement in the Vietnam conflict.
2. **Ho Chi Minh** (hō' chē' mĭn'): a political leader who waged a successful fight against French colonial rule and established a Communist government in North Vietnam.
3. **Geneva Accords:** a 1954 peace agreement providing for the temporary division of Vietnam into North and South Vietnam and calling for national elections.
4. **SEATO:** the Southeast Asia Treaty Organization, an alliance of seven nations, including the United States, formed to halt Communist expansion in Southeast Asia after Communist forces defeated France in Indochina.
5. **Cold War:** a term for the post–World War II struggle for influence between Communist and democratic nations.
6. **dominoes:** refers to the domino theory, which holds that if a nation becomes a Communist state, neighboring nations will also become Communist.

WORDS TO KNOW
consensus (kən-sĕn'səs) *n.* general agreement by a group
imperative (ĭm-pĕr'ə-tĭv) *n.* urgent necessity or duty

stuff, just ringing a few doorbells for Gene McCarthy,[7] composing a few tedious, uninspired editorials for the campus newspaper. Oddly, though, it was almost entirely an intellectual activity. I brought some energy to it, of course, but it was the energy that accompanies almost any abstract endeavor; I felt no personal danger; I felt no sense of an impending crisis in my life. Stupidly, with a kind of smug removal that I can't begin to fathom, I assumed that the problems of killing and dying did not fall within my special province.

The draft notice arrived on June 17, 1968. It was a humid afternoon, I remember, cloudy and very quiet, and I'd just come in from a round of golf. My mother and father were having lunch out in the kitchen. I remember opening up the letter, scanning the first few lines, feeling the blood go thick behind my eyes. I remember a sound in my head. It wasn't thinking, it was just a silent howl. A million things all at once—I was too *good* for this war. Too smart, too compassionate, too everything. It couldn't happen. I was above it. I had the world—Phi Beta Kappa and summa cum laude and president of the student body and a full-ride scholarship for grad studies at Harvard. A mistake, maybe—a foul-up in the paperwork. I was no soldier. I hated Boy Scouts. I hated camping out. I hated dirt and tents and mosquitoes. The sight of blood made me queasy, and I couldn't tolerate authority, and I didn't know a rifle from a slingshot. I was a *liberal*: If they needed fresh bodies, why not draft some back-to-the-stone-age hawk? Or some dumb jingo[8] in his hardhat and Bomb Hanoi button? Or one of LBJ's[9] pretty daughters? Or Westmoreland's[10] whole family—nephews and nieces and baby grandson? There should be a law, I thought. If you support a war, if you think it's worth the price, that's fine, but you have to put your own life on the line. You have to head for the front and hook up with an infantry unit and help spill the blood. And you have to bring along your wife, or your kids, or your lover. A *law*, I thought.

I remember the rage in my stomach. Later it burned down to a smoldering self-pity, then to numbness. At dinner that night my father asked what my plans were.

"Nothing," I said. "Wait."

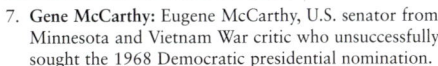 spent the summer of 1968 working in an Armour meat-packing plant in my hometown of Worthington, Minnesota. The plant specialized in pork products, and for eight hours a day I stood on a quarter-mile assembly line—more properly, a disassembly line—removing blood clots from the necks of dead pigs. My job title, I believe, was Declotter. After slaughter, the hogs were decapitated, split down the length of the belly, pried open, eviscerated, and strung up by the hind hocks on a high conveyer belt. Then gravity took over. By the time a carcass reached my spot on the line, the fluids had mostly drained out, everything except for thick clots of blood in the neck and upper chest cavity. To remove the stuff, I used a kind of water gun. The machine was heavy, maybe eighty pounds, and was suspended from the ceiling by a heavy rubber cord. There was some bounce to it, an

---

7. **Gene McCarthy:** Eugene McCarthy, U.S. senator from Minnesota and Vietnam War critic who unsuccessfully sought the 1968 Democratic presidential nomination.
8. **jingo** (jĭng′gō): one who aggressively supports his or her country and favors war as a means of settling political disputes.
9. **LBJ:** Lyndon B. Johnson, U.S. president from 1963 to 1969.
10. **Westmoreland's:** referring to William Westmoreland, American general and the senior commander of U.S. forces in Vietnam from 1964 to 1968.

WORDS TO KNOW

fathom (făth′əm) *v.* to penetrate the meaning or understand the nature of

elastic up-and-down give, and the trick was to maneuver the gun with your whole body, not lifting with the arms, just letting the rubber cord do the work for you. At one end was a trigger; at the muzzle end was a small nozzle and a steel roller brush. As a carcass passed by, you'd lean forward and swing the gun up against the clots and squeeze the trigger, all in one motion, and the brush would whirl and water would come shooting out and you'd hear a quick splattering sound as the clots dissolved into a fine red mist. It was not pleasant work. Goggles were a necessity, and a rubber apron, but even so it was like standing for eight hours a day under a lukewarm blood-shower. At night I'd go home smelling of pig. I couldn't wash it out. Even after a hot bath, scrubbing hard, the stink was always there—like old bacon, or sausage, a dense greasy pig-stink that soaked deep into my skin and hair. Among other things, I remember, it was tough getting dates that summer. I felt isolated; I spent a lot of time alone. And there was also that draft notice tucked away in my wallet.

In the evenings I'd sometimes borrow my father's car and drive aimlessly around town, feeling sorry for myself, thinking about the war and the pig factory and how my life seemed to be collapsing toward slaughter. I felt paralyzed. All around me the options seemed to be narrowing, as if I were hurtling down a huge black funnel, the whole world squeezing in tight. There was no happy way out. The government had ended most graduate school deferments; the waiting lists for the National Guard and Reserves[11] were impossibly long; my health was solid; I didn't qualify for CO[12] status—no religious grounds, no history as a pacifist.[13] Moreover, I could not claim to be opposed to war as a matter of general principle. There were occasions, I believed, when a nation was justified in using military force to achieve its ends, to stop a Hitler or some comparable evil, and I told myself that in such circumstances I would've willingly marched off to the battle. The problem, though, was that a draft board did not let you choose your war.

Beyond all this, or at the very center, was the raw fact of terror. I did not want to die. Not ever. But certainly not then, not there, not in a wrong war. Driving up Main Street, past the courthouse and the Ben Franklin store, I sometimes felt the fear spreading inside me like weeds. I imagined myself dead. I imagined myself doing things I could not do—charging an enemy position, taking aim at another human being.

At some point in mid-July I began thinking seriously about Canada. The border lay a few hundred miles north, an eight-hour drive. Both my conscience and my instincts were telling me to make a break for it, just take off and run like hell and never stop. In the beginning the idea seemed purely abstract, the word Canada printing itself out in my head; but after a time I could see particular shapes and images, the sorry details of my own future—a hotel room in Winnipeg, a battered old suitcase, my father's eyes as I tried to explain myself over the telephone. I could almost hear his voice, and my mother's. Run, I'd think. Then I'd think, Impossible. Then a second later I'd think, *Run.*

---

11. **National Guard and Reserves:** military reserve units run by each state in the United States. Some men joined these units to avoid service in Vietnam.
12. **CO:** conscientious objector, a person exempted from military service because of strongly held moral or religious beliefs that do not permit participation in war.
13. **pacifist** (păs′ə-fĭst): one who opposes war or other violence as a means of settling disputes.

It was a kind of schizophrenia.[14] A moral split. I couldn't make up my mind. I feared the war, yes, but I also feared exile. I was afraid of walking away from my own life, my friends and my family, my whole history, everything that mattered to me. I feared losing the respect of my parents. I feared the law. I feared ridicule and censure.[15] My hometown was a conservative little spot on the prairie, a place where tradition counted, and it was easy to imagine people sitting around a table at the old Gobbler Café on Main Street, coffee cups poised, the conversation slowly zeroing in on the young O'Brien kid, how the damned sissy had taken off for Canada. At night, when I couldn't sleep, I'd sometimes carry on fierce arguments with those people. I'd be screaming at them, telling them how much I detested their blind, thoughtless, automatic acquiescence to it all, their simple-minded patriotism, their prideful ignorance, their love-it-or-leave-it platitudes, how they were sending me off to fight a war they didn't understand and didn't want to understand. I held them responsible. By God, yes I *did*. All of them—I held them personally and individually responsible—the polyestered Kiwanis boys, the merchants and farmers, the pious churchgoers, the chatty housewives, the PTA and the Lions club and the Veterans of Foreign Wars and the fine upstanding gentry out at the country club. They didn't know Bao Dai[16] from the man in the moon. They didn't know history. They didn't know the first thing about Diem's[17] tyranny, or the nature of Vietnamese nationalism, or the long colonialism of the French—this was all too damned complicated, it required some reading—but no matter, it was a war to stop the Communists, plain and simple, which was how they liked things, and you were treasonous if you had second thoughts about killing or dying for plain and simple reasons.

I was bitter, sure. But it was so much more than that. The emotions went from outrage to terror to bewilderment to guilt to sorrow and then back again to outrage. I felt a sickness inside me. Real disease.

Most of this I've told before, or at least hinted at, but what I have never told is the full truth. How I cracked. How at work one morning, standing on the pig line, I felt something break open in my chest. I don't know what it was. I'll never know. But it was real. I know that much, it was a physical rupture—a cracking-leaking-popping feeling. I remember dropping my water gun. Quickly, almost without thought, I took off my apron and walked out of the plant and drove home. It was midmorning, I remember, and the house was empty. Down in my chest there was still that leaking sensation, something very warm and precious spilling out, and I was covered with blood and hog-stink, and for a long while I just concentrated on holding myself together. I remember taking a hot shower. I remember packing a suitcase and carrying it out to the kitchen, standing very still for a few minutes, looking carefully at the familiar objects all around me. The old chrome toaster, the telephone, the pink and white Formica on the kitchen counters. The room was full of bright sunshine.

14. **schizophrenia** (skĭt′sə-frē′nē-ə): a mental disorder. Here, the narrator refers to a split personality.
15. **censure** (sĕn′shər): an expression of strong disapproval or harsh criticism.
16. **Bao Dai** (bou′dī′): the last emperor of Vietnam (1926–1945) and chief of state from 1949 to 1955.
17. **Diem:** Ngo Dinh Diem (nō′ dĭn′ dē-ĕm′), the first president of South Vietnam, who led his country like a brutal dictator. He was murdered by his own generals in 1963.

WORDS TO KNOW
acquiescence (ăk′wē-ĕs′əns) *n.* passive agreement; agreement without protest
platitude (plăt′ĭ-tōōd) *n.* a trite or unoriginal statement, especially one expressed as if it were original or significant; a cliché

271

Mini-Lesson Literary Concepts

REVIEWING DESCRIPTION Remind students that descriptive writing creates a picture of a scene, an event, or a character. Sometimes descriptions can also reveal things about a character's attitude. To create a description, writers often use sensory details and figurative language.

Application Have students think about the various descriptions given in "On the Rainy River." Have them find sensory details in the description of the narrator's job (page 270), and details on page 271 about the people in the narrator's hometown. What do these descriptions reveal about the narrator's community? What do they reveal about the narrator's attitude?

Literary Concept: CONFLICT

H Invite students to discuss the many concerns involved in the narrator's internal conflict. (*Possible responses: He's afraid of war and doesn't believe in it, but he also doesn't want to give up his life as he knows it. He's doesn't want to break the law or lose other people's love and respect.*)

CUSTOMIZING FOR
Students Acquiring English

4 Explain that Kiwanis and Lions clubs are organizations made up of community leaders and business people. You might also explain the membership of PTAs and the Veterans of Foreign Wars. Point out that all these organizations represent "community opinion and values."

STRATEGIC READING FOR
Less-Proficient Readers

I Make sure students understand what the narrator's conflict is about.

- Compare and contrast the narrator's feelings about the war with the feelings of others in his hometown. (*He thinks the war is wrong, but other people support the war.*) **Compare and Contrast**

- Why is this a problem for him? (*He knows if he goes to Canada his neighbors and family will condemn him.*) **Clarifying**

Set a Purpose Have students read to find out what the narrator does to try to resolve his conflict.

Literary Concept: SYMBOLISM

J Ask students to speculate about what the narrator's feelings and action here might symbolize. (*Possible responses: Some students might point out that his feelings reflect what happens to the hogs at the plant, and he feels he's going to be slaughtered. Others might suggest that by throwing down his water gun and tearing off his uniform he's renouncing military service.*)

Critical Thinking: ANALYZING

K Ask students how the Rainy River separates "one life from another" for the narrator. *(Possible response: The river, because it forms the border between Minnesota and Canada, separates the narrator's life in the United States from the one he would have in Canada as a draft dodger.)*

Linking to Geography

L In this story the narrator drives the length of Minnesota, starting in Worthington in the southwestern corner of the state, and ending up at the Rainy River on the northern border. Invite students to identify the places the narrator mentions and trace his route on a map of Minnesota. If they have trouble locating places on the map, suggest they use an index or start at the Rainy River and trace his route backwards.

CUSTOMIZING FOR
Students Acquiring English

5 Explain that sap is the sticky, sweet liquid found in trees—forming, for instance, the basis of maple syrup. Ask students to guess what the word *sappy* means. *(overly sentimental)*

Literary Concept: DESCRIPTION

M Call attention to the physical description of Elroy Berdahl, including the images of sharpness and cutting. On the basis of this description, what kind of person is Elroy? *(Possible responses: a straightforward man; a man who sees through outward appearances; a man who works hard and leads a simple life.)*

J Everything sparkled. My house, I thought. My life. I'm not sure how long I stood there, but later I scribbled out a short note to my parents.

What it said exactly, I don't recall now. Something vague. Taking off, will call, love Tim.

I drove north.

It's a blur now, as it was then, and all I remember is a sense of high velocity and the feel of the steering wheel in my hands. I was riding on adrenaline.[18] A giddy feeling, in a way, except there was the dreamy edge of impossibility to it—like running a dead-end maze—no way out—it couldn't come to a happy conclusion and yet I was doing it anyway because it was all I could think to do. It was pure flight, fast and mindless. I had no plan. Just hit the border at high speed and crash through and keep on running. Near dusk I passed through Bemidji, then turned northeast toward International Falls. I spent the night in the car behind a closed-down gas station a half mile from the border. In the morning, after gassing up, I headed straight west along the **K** Rainy River, which separates Minnesota from Canada, and which for me separated one life from another. The land was mostly wilderness. Here and there I passed a motel or bait shop, but otherwise the country unfolded in great sweeps of pine and birch and sumac. Though it was still August, the air already had the smell of October, football season, piles of yellow-red leaves, everything crisp and clean. I remember a huge blue sky. Off to my right was the Rainy **L** River, wide as a lake in places, and beyond the Rainy River was Canada.

For a while I just drove, not aiming at anything, then in the late morning I began looking for a place to lie low for a day or two. I was exhausted, and scared sick, and around noon I pulled into an old fishing resort called the Tip Top Lodge. Actually, it was not a lodge at all, just eight or nine tiny yellow cabins clustered on a peninsula that jutted northward into the Rainy River. The place was in sorry shape. There was a dangerous wooden dock, an old minnow tank, a flimsy tar paper boathouse along the shore. The main building, which stood in a

> **It was pure flight, fast and mindless. I had no plan. Just hit the border at high speed . . . and keep on running.**

cluster of pines on high ground, seemed to lean heavily to one side, like a cripple, the roof sagging toward Canada. Briefly, I thought about turning around, just giving up, but then I got out of the car and walked up to the front porch.

The man who opened the door that day is the hero of my life. How do I say this without sounding sappy? Blurt it out—the man saved me. He offered exactly what I needed, without questions, without any words at all. He took me in. He was there at the critical time—a silent, watchful presence. Six days later, when it ended, I was unable to find a proper way to thank him, and I never have, and so, if nothing else, this story represents a small gesture of gratitude twenty years overdue.

Even after two decades I can close my eyes and return to that porch at the Tip Top Lodge. I can see the old guy staring at me. Elroy Berdahl: eighty-one years old, skinny and shrunken and mostly bald. He wore a flannel shirt and brown work pants. In one hand, I remember, he carried a green apple, a small paring knife in the other. His eyes had the bluish gray color of a razor

---

18. **adrenaline** (ə-drĕn′ə-lĭn): a hormone that is released into the bloodstream in response to physical or mental stress, such as fear, and that initiates or heightens several physical responses, including an increase in heart rate.

272 UNIT TWO PART 2: PRISONERS OF CIRCUMSTANCE

Mini-Lesson  Literary Concepts

REVIEWING SYMBOLISM Remind students that a symbol is a person, place, or thing that represents something beyond itself. In "On the Rainy River," many things in the narrator's life are used as symbols for other, more important things. For instance, the Rainy River, which is literally the border between the United States and Canada, also represents the division between one way of life and another for the narrator—and between two entirely different futures.

Application Invite students to complete this symbolism chart for "On the Rainy River," and encourage them to add any other symbols they notice. Then have the class discuss how O'Brien's use of symbolism contributes to their understanding of the story.

Symbol	What it stands for
Rainy River	division between two futures
narrator's house	
pork smell	
draft notice	

blade, the same polished shine, and as he peered up at me I felt a strange sharpness, almost painful, a cutting sensation, as if his gaze were somehow slicing me open. In part, no doubt, it was my own sense of guilt, but even so I'm absolutely certain that the old man took one look and went right to the heart of things—a kid in trouble. When I asked for a room, Elroy made a little clicking sound with his tongue. He nodded, led me out to one of the cabins, and dropped a key in my hand. I remember smiling at him. I also remember wishing I hadn't. The old man shook his head as if to tell me it wasn't worth the bother.

"Dinner at five-thirty," he said. "You eat fish?"

"Anything," I said.

Elroy grunted and said, "I'll bet."

We spent six days together at the Tip Top Lodge. Just the two of us. Tourist season was over, and there were no boats on the river, and the wilderness seemed to withdraw into a great permanent stillness. Over those six days Elroy Berdahl and I took most of our meals together. In the mornings we sometimes went out on long hikes into the woods, and at night we played Scrabble or listened to records or sat reading in front of his big stone fireplace. At times I felt the awkwardness of an intruder, but Elroy accepted me into his quiet routine without fuss or ceremony. He took my presence for granted, the same way he might've sheltered a stray cat—no wasted sighs or pity—and there was never any talk about it. Just the opposite. What I remember more than anything is the man's willful, almost ferocious silence. In all that time together, all those hours, he never asked the obvious questions: Why was I there? Why alone? Why so preoccupied? If Elroy was curious about any of this, he was careful never to put it into words.

My hunch, though, is that he already knew. At least the basics. After all, it was 1968, and guys were burning draft cards, and Canada was just a boat ride away. Elroy Berdahl was no hick. His bedroom, I remember, was cluttered with books and newspapers. He killed me at the Scrabble board, barely concentrating, and on those occasions when speech was necessary, he had a way of compressing large thoughts into small, cryptic[19] packets of language. One evening, just at sunset, he pointed up at an owl circling over the violet-lighted forest to the west.

"Hey, O'Brien," he said. "There's Jesus."

The man was sharp—he didn't miss much. Those razor eyes. Now and then he'd catch me staring out at the river, at the far shore, and I could almost hear the tumblers clicking in his head. Maybe I'm wrong, but I doubt it.

One thing for certain, he knew I was in desperate trouble. And he knew I couldn't talk about it. The wrong word—or even the right word—and I would've disappeared. I was wired and jittery. My skin felt too tight. After supper one evening I vomited and went back to my cabin and lay down for a few moments and then vomited again; another time, in the middle of the afternoon, I began sweating and couldn't shut it off. I went through whole days feeling dizzy with sorrow. I couldn't sleep; I couldn't lie still. At night I'd toss around in bed, half awake, half dreaming, imagining how I'd sneak down to the beach and quietly push one of the old man's boats out into the river and start paddling my way toward Canada. There were times when I thought I'd gone off the psychic edge. I

---

19. **cryptic** (krĭp′tĭk): having a hidden or mysterious meaning; mystifying.

WORDS TO KNOW
preoccupied (prē-ŏk′yə-pīd′) *adj.* absorbed in one's thoughts; distracted **preoccupy** *v.*

Multicultural Perspectives

CROSSING THE BORDER Canada did not refuse entry to those young Americans who evaded the U.S. draft or deserted the military. In fact, Canada had long opposed the concept of military conscription and regarded United States involvement in Vietnam as a terrible mistake. From 1964 to 1973 approximately 10,000 men of draft age fled the country to avoid serving in Vietnam. In 1977, President Carter pardoned most of those who had violated draft laws during that era. The pardon did not extend to some 100,000 military deserters.

Linking to History

N During the Vietnam War, thousands of young men refused to register for the draft; many more burned their draft cards in public protests. The late 1960s saw the peak of antiwar demonstrations, climaxed by a huge march on Washington. On college campuses and city streets, protesters chanted antiwar slogans, including, "Hell no, we won't go!"

Critical Thinking: ANALYZING

O Ask students what they think Elroy means when he identifies the owl as Jesus. *(Possible responses: God can be found in nature; the answers to big problems are often simple and obvious.)*

Literary Concept: POINT OF VIEW

P Ask students to discuss how the story might be different if Elroy Berdahl were telling it. What insights would readers lose? What insights might be added? *(Possible responses: Some students may point out that readers might not appreciate the intensity of the young man's feelings, if the story were narrated by Elroy. Others might say readers would gain a more rational, less emotional telling of the young man's story, as seen through the eyes of someone who was older and not immediately involved.)*

Literary Concept: SYMBOLISM

Q Note that the narrator sees baseball, hamburgers, and cherry Cokes as symbols of mainstream American life. Ask students what things represent the United States to them. *(Possible responses: the flag; apple pie; rap music; the Constitution; money; hot dogs; the Fourth of July; shopping malls)*

Literary Concept: CHARACTERIZATION

R Ask students to summarize the traits of Elroy Berdahl they have observed up to this point in the story. *(Possible response: He is quiet and still like the wilderness, perceptive, well-read, intelligent, insightful, and respectful of others' privacy.)*

Literary Concept: CONFLICT

S Have students identify the internal conflict and discuss their opinions of it. *(intellect vs. emotion; conscience vs. shame. Accept all reasonable responses.)*

---

couldn't tell up from down, I was just falling, and late in the night I'd lie there watching weird pictures spin through my head. Getting chased by the Border Patrol—helicopters and searchlights and barking dogs—I'd be crashing through the woods, I'd be down on my hands and knees—people shouting out my name—the law closing in on all sides—my hometown draft board and the FBI and the Royal Canadian Mounted Police. It all seemed crazy and impossible. Twenty-one years old, an ordinary kid with all the ordinary dreams and ambitions, and all I wanted was to live the life I was born to—a mainstream life—I loved baseball and hamburgers and cherry Cokes—and now I was off on the margins of exile, leaving my country forever, and it seemed so impossible and terrible and sad.

I'm not sure how I made it through those six days. Most of it I can't remember. On two or three afternoons, to pass some time, I helped Elroy get the place ready for winter, sweeping down the cabins and hauling in the boats, little chores that kept my body moving. The days were cool and bright. The nights were very dark. One morning the old man showed me how to split and stack firewood, and for several hours we just worked in silence out behind his house. At one point, I remember, Elroy put down his maul[20] and looked at me for a long time, his lips drawn as if framing a difficult question, but then he shook his head and went back to work. The man's self-control was amazing. He never pried. He never put me in a position that required lies or denials. To an extent, I supposed, his reticence was typical of that part of Minnesota, where privacy still held value, and even if I'd been walking around with some horrible deformity—four arms and three heads—I'm sure the old man would've talked about everything except those extra arms and heads. Simple politeness was part of it. But even more than that, I think, the man understood that words were insufficient. The problem had gone beyond discussion. During that long summer I'd been over and over the various arguments, all the pros and cons, and it was no longer a question that could be decided by an act of pure reason. Intellect had come up against emotion. My conscience told me to run, but some irrational and powerful force was resisting, like a weight pushing me toward the war. What it came down to, stupidly, was a sense of shame. Hot, stupid shame. I did not want people to think badly of me. Not my parents, not my brother and sister, not even the folks down at the Gobbler Café. I was ashamed to be there at the Tip Top Lodge. I was ashamed of my conscience, ashamed to be doing the right thing.

Some of this Elroy must've understood. Not the details, of course, but the plain fact of crisis.

Although the old man never confronted me about it, there was one occasion when he came close to forcing the whole thing out into the open. It was early evening, and we'd just finished supper, and over coffee and dessert I asked him about my bill, how much I owed so far. For a long while the old man squinted down at the tablecloth.

"Well, the basic rate," he said, "is fifty bucks a night. Not counting meals. This makes four nights, right?"

I nodded. I had three hundred and twelve dollars in my wallet.

Elroy kept his eyes on the tablecloth. "Now that's an on-season price. To be fair, I suppose we should knock it down a peg or two." He leaned back in his chair. "What's a reasonable number, you figure?"

"I don't know," I said. "Forty?"

"Forty's good. Forty a night. Then we tack

---

20. **maul** (môl): heavy, long-handled hammer.

WORDS TO KNOW
reticence (rĕt′ĭ-səns) *n.* the state or quality of being reserved and keeping one's thoughts to oneself

274

Mini-Lesson — Workplace Literacy

SCANS Goal: Interprets and Communicates Information

READING MAPS Point out that in order to drive from Worthington to the Canadian border, the narrator had to be able to understand a road map. Explain that reading a road map is useful both on the job and in everyday life. Tell students that to interpret a map, they should first look at the key to find out what each symbol represents. Then they can locate their destinations and plan their routes. Remind students that being able to look at a map and communicate directions orally to another person is also a useful skill.

Application Have students pair up and practice reading a road map and giving directions. One partner should ask how to get to a destination, and the other should read the road map and give directions. Students should practice both roles.

274 THE LANGUAGE OF LITERATURE TEACHER'S EDITION

Sea Air (1987), Douglas Brega. Dry brush on paper, 14″ × 21″, courtesy of the artist.

on food—say another hundred? Two hundred sixty total?"

"I guess."

He raised his eyebrows. "Too much?"

"No, that's fair. It's fine. Tomorrow, though . . . I think I'd better take off tomorrow."

Elroy shrugged and began clearing the table. For a time he fussed with the dishes, whistling to himself as if the subject had been settled. After a second he slapped his hands together.

"You know what we forgot?" he said. "We forgot wages. Those odd jobs you done. What we have to do, we have to figure out what your time's worth. Your last job—how much did you pull in an hour?"

"Not enough," I said.

"A bad one?"

"Yes. Pretty bad."

Slowly then, without intending any long sermon, I told him about my days at the pig plant. It began as a straight recitation of the facts, but before I could stop myself I was talking about the blood clots and the water gun and how the smell had soaked into my skin and how I couldn't wash it away. I went on for a long time. I told him about wild hogs squealing in my dreams, the sounds of butchery, slaughterhouse sounds, and how I'd sometimes wake up with that greasy pig-stink in my throat.

When I was finished, Elroy nodded at me.

"Well, to be honest," he said, "when you first showed up here, I wondered about that. The aroma, I mean. Smelled like you was awful damned fond of pork chops." The old man

ON THE RAINY RIVER 275

STRATEGIC READING FOR
Less-Proficient Readers

V Have students explain why the narrator is staying at the Tip Top Lodge. *(He drove to the U.S.-Canadian border to get away from his hometown and found the lodge along the river. He doesn't know what to do about his draft notice and was thinking about fleeing to Canada.)* **Clarifying**

- What does the narrator do while he is there? *(He hikes, does work for Elroy, hangs out with him, and thinks about his situation.)* **Summarizing**

Set a Purpose Have students read to find out what decision the narrator finally makes.

Critical Thinking:
HYPOTHESIZING

W Have students discuss why the experience at the Tip Top Lodge seems unreal to the narrator, as if "in some other dimension." *(Possible responses: because he is so emotionally distressed; because the experience is so intense he distances himself from it)*

Critical Thinking: SPECULATING

X Ask students what they think the narrator might be like now, twenty years later, based on the details in this passage. *(Possible responses: thinning hair, out of shape, a smoker and a drinker, cynical)*

---

almost smiled. He made a snuffling sound, then sat down with a pencil and a piece of paper. "So what'd this crud job pay? Ten bucks an hour? Fifteen?"

"Less."

Elroy shook his head. "Let's make it fifteen. You put in twenty-five hours here, easy. That's three hundred seventy-five bucks total wages. We subtract the two hundred sixty for food and lodging. I still owe you a hundred and fifteen."

He took four fifties out of his shirt pocket and laid them on the table.

"Call it even," he said.

"No."

"Pick it up. Get yourself a haircut."

The money lay on the table for the rest of the evening. It was still there when I went back to my cabin. In the morning though, I found an envelope tacked to my door. Inside were the four fifties and a two-word note that said EMERGENCY FUND.

The man knew.

Looking back after twenty years, I sometimes wonder if the events of that summer didn't happen in some other dimension, a place where your life exists before you've lived it, and where it goes afterward. None of it ever seemed real. During my time at the Tip Top Lodge I had the feeling that I'd slipped out of my own skin, hovering a few feet away while some poor yo-yo with my name and face tried to make his way toward a future he didn't understand and didn't want. Even now I can see myself as I was then. It's like watching an old home movie: I'm young and tan and fit. I've got hair—lots of it. I don't smoke or drink. I'm wearing faded blue jeans and a white polo shirt. I can see myself sitting on Elroy Berdahl's dock near dusk one evening, the sky a bright shimmering pink, and I'm finishing up a letter to my parents that tells what I'm about to do and why I'm doing it and how sorry I am that I've never found the courage to talk to them about it. I ask them not to be angry. I try to explain some of my feelings, but there aren't enough words, and so I just say that it's a thing that has to be done. At the end of the letter I talk about the vacations we used to take up in this north country, at a place called Whitefish Lake, and how the scenery here reminds me of those good times. I tell them I'm fine. I tell them I'll write again from Winnipeg or Montreal or wherever I end up.

On my last full day, the sixth day, the old man took me out fishing on the Rainy River. The afternoon was sunny and cold. A stiff breeze came in from the north, and I remember how the little fourteen-foot boat made sharp rocking motions as we pushed off from the dock. The current was fast. All around us, I remember, there was a vastness to the world, an unpeopled rawness, just the trees and the sky and the water reaching out toward nowhere. The air had the brittle scent of October.

For ten or fifteen minutes Elroy held a course upstream, the river choppy and silver-gray, then he turned straight north and put the engine on full throttle. I felt the bow lift beneath me. I remember the wind in my ears, the sound of the old outboard Evinrude. For a time I didn't pay attention to anything, just feeling the cold spray against my face, but then it occurred to me that at some point we must've passed into Canadian waters, across that dotted line between two different worlds, and I remember a sudden tightness in my chest as I looked up and watched the far shore come at me. This wasn't a daydream. It was tangible and real. As we came in toward land, Elroy cut the engine, letting the boat fishtail lightly about twenty yards off shore. The old man didn't look at me or speak. Bending down, he opened up his tackle box and busied himself with a bobber and a piece of wire leader,

276 UNIT TWO PART 2: PRISONERS OF CIRCUMSTANCE

Mini-Lesson / Grammar

Subordinating Conjunctions

Time:	after, as, as long as, as soon as, before, since, until, when
Manner:	as, as if
Place:	where, wherever
Cause or Reason:	because, since
Comparison:	as, as much as, than
Condition:	although, as long as, even if, even though, if, provided that, though, unless, while
Purpose:	in order that, so that, that

SUBORDINATING CONJUNCTIONS
Direct students' attention to the sentences highlighted on this page and point out that each sentence contains an independent and a subordinate clause. Remind students that a subordinating conjunction introduces a subordinate clause and joins a subordinate clause to an independent clause. Subordinating conjunctions show relationships, as shown on this chart.

Application Have students join each pair of sentences using a subordinating conjunction that shows the relationship noted in parentheses.

1. Elroy took me fishing. I was confused and scared. *(time)*
2. We headed toward shore. The Canadian border beckoned me. *(place)*
3. The Vietnam War continued. I couldn't go home. *(condition)*

Reteaching/Reinforcement
- *Grammar Mini-Lessons* copymasters p. 3, transparencies p. 50

The Writer's Craft
Subordinating Conjunctions, p. 555

humming to himself, his eyes down.

It struck me then that he must've planned it. I'll never be certain, of course, but I think he meant to bring me up against the realities, to guide me across the river and to take me to the edge and to stand a kind of vigil as I chose a life for myself.

I remember staring at the old man, then at my hands, then at Canada. The shoreline was dense with brush and timber. I could see tiny red berries on the bushes. I could see a squirrel up in one of the birch trees, a big crow looking at me from a boulder along the river. That close— twenty yards—and I could see the delicate latticework of the leaves, the texture of the soil, the browned needles beneath the pines, the configurations of geology and human history. Twenty yards. I could've done it. I could've jumped and started swimming for my life. Inside me, in my chest, I felt a terrible squeezing pressure. Even now, as I write this, I can still feel that tightness. And I want you to feel it—the wind coming off the river, the waves, the silence, the wooded frontier. You're at the bow of a boat on the Rainy River. You're twenty-one years old, you're scared, and there's a hard squeezing pressure in your chest.

What would you do?

Would you jump? Would you feel pity for yourself? Would you think about the family and your childhood and your dreams and all you're leaving behind? Would it hurt? Would it feel like dying? Would you cry, as I did?

I tried to swallow it back. I tried to smile, except I was crying.

Now, perhaps, you can understand why I've never told this story before. It's not just the embarrassment of tears. That's part of it, no doubt, but what embarrasses me much more, and always will, is the paralysis that took my heart. A moral freeze: I couldn't decide, I couldn't act, I couldn't comport myself with even a pretense of modest human dignity.

All I could do was cry. Quietly, not bawling, just the chest-chokes.

At the rear of the boat Elroy Berdahl pretended not to notice. He held a fishing rod in his hands, his head bowed to hide his eyes. He kept humming a soft, monotonous little tune. Everywhere, it seemed, in the trees and water and sky, a great worldwide sadness came pressing down on me, a crushing sorrow, sorrow like I had never known before. And what was so sad, I realized, was that Canada had become a pitiful fantasy. Silly and hopeless. It was no longer a possibility. Right then, with the shore so close, I understood that I would not do what I should do. I would not swim away from my hometown and my country and my life. I would not be brave. That old image of myself as a hero, as a man of conscience and courage, all that was just a threadbare pipe dream.[21] Bobbing there on the Rainy River, looking back at the Minnesota shore, I felt a sudden swell of helplessness come over me, a drowning sensation, as if I had toppled overboard and was being swept away by the silver waves. Chunks of my own history flashed by. I saw a seven-year-old boy in a white cowboy

> I think he meant to bring me up against the realities . . . to stand a kind of vigil as I chose a life for myself.

---

21. **pipe dream:** daydream or fantasy that will never happen; vain hope.

WORDS TO KNOW	**vigil** (vĭj′əl) *n.* a watch kept by a person, especially during normal sleeping hours or to show devotion
	pretense (prē′tĕns′) *n.* a false outward appearance

Art Note

Atascadero Dusk by Robert Reynolds
In this painting, Reynolds, a well-known watercolor artist, repeats the colors and shadings of the sky and trees in the water reflections. This helps give the painting unity and draws the viewer's eye beyond the boat to the water and the shore behind it.

Reading the Art *Do you think the mood of this painting matches the mood of the story? Why or why not?*

Linking to Geography

Minnesota, known as the land of ten thousand lakes, also contains many rivers and other bodies of water. The Rainy River runs for more than 100 miles along the Minnesota-Canada border. Most of the rest of the border is lined with lakes and wilderness.

Atascadero Dusk (about 1990), Robert Reynolds. Watercolor, 22″ × 15″. From *Painting Nature's Beautiful Places*, published by North Light Books.

Critic's ★ Corner

"... at crucial points in our lives I think it is helpful to have witnesses—not advisers, not counselors, not people urging us one way or the other. Rather, the witness is simply there, mute and watchful and supportive.... I suppose Elroy may be an analog for conscience. Or for God. Or for the feeling you get that a dead father might still be looking on as you ... make moral choices...."

Tim O'Brien
discussing Elroy Berdahl in an interview

Have students discuss O'Brien's explanation of Elroy.

hat and a Lone Ranger mask and a pair of holstered six-shooters; I saw a twelve-year-old Little League shortstop pivoting to turn a double play; I saw a sixteen-year-old kid decked out for his first prom, looking spiffy in a white tux and a black bow tie, his hair cut short and flat, his shoes freshly polished. My whole life seemed to spill out into the river, swirling away from me, everything I had ever been or ever wanted to be. I couldn't get my breath; I couldn't stay afloat; I couldn't tell which way to swim. A hallucination, I suppose, but it was as real as anything I would ever feel. I saw my parents calling to me from the far shoreline. I saw my brother and sister, all the townsfolk, the mayor and the entire Chamber of Commerce and all my old teachers and girlfriends and high school buddies. Like some weird sporting event: everybody screaming from the sidelines, rooting me on—a loud stadium roar. Hotdogs and popcorn—stadium smells, stadium heat. A squad of cheerleaders did cartwheels along the banks of the Rainy River; they had megaphones and pompoms and smooth brown thighs. The crowd swayed left and right. A marching band played fight songs. All my aunts and uncles were there, and Abraham Lincoln and Saint George,22 and a nine-year-old girl named Linda who had died of a brain tumor back in fifth grade, and several members of the United States Senate, and a blind poet scribbling notes, and LBJ, and Huck Finn, and Abbie Hoffman,23 and all the dead soldiers back from the grave, and the many thousands who were later to die—villagers with terrible burns, little kids without arms or legs—yes, and the Joint Chiefs of Staff24 were there, and a couple of popes, and a first lieutenant named Jimmy Cross, and the last surviving veteran of the American Civil War, and Jane Fonda dressed up as Barbarella,25 and an old man sprawled beside a pigpen, and my grandfather, and Gary Cooper,26 and a kind-faced woman carrying an umbrella and a copy of Plato's *Republic*,27 and a million ferocious citizens waving flags of all shapes and colors—people in hardhats, people in headbands—they were all whooping and chanting and urging me toward one shore or the other. I saw faces from my distant past and distant future. My wife was there. My unborn daughter waved at me, and my two sons hopped up and down, and a drill sergeant named Blyton sneered and shot up a finger and shook his head. There was a choir in bright purple robes. There was a cabbie from the Bronx. There was a slim young man I would one day kill with a hand grenade along a red clay trail outside the village of My Khe.28

The little aluminum boat rocked softly beneath me. There was the wind and the sky.

I tried to will myself overboard.

I gripped the edge of the boat and leaned forward and thought, *Now*.

I did try. It just wasn't possible.

All those eyes on me—the town, the whole universe—and I couldn't risk the embarrassment. It was as if there were an audience to my life, that swirl of faces along the river, and in my head I could hear people screaming at me. Traitor! they yelled. Turncoat! I felt myself

---

22. **Saint George:** Christian martyr (killed about A.D. 303) and patron saint of England who, according to legend, slew a frightening dragon.
23. **Abbie Hoffman:** social organizer and radical anti–Vietnam War activist known for his humor and politically inspired pranks.
24. **Joint Chiefs of Staff:** the principal military advisors of the U.S. president, including the chiefs of the army, navy, and air force and the commandant of the marines.
25. **Jane Fonda dressed up as Barbarella:** anti–Vietnam War activist and actress Jane Fonda (1937–), dressed as Barbarella, the title character she played in a 1968 science fiction film.
26. **Gary Cooper:** American actor famous for playing strong, quiet heroes.
27. **Plato's *Republic*:** a famous work in which the ancient Greek philosopher Plato describes the ideal state or society.
28. **My Khe** (mē′ kē′).

ON THE RAINY RIVER   279

STRATEGIC READING FOR
Less-Proficient Readers

DD Have students explain the reason for the narrator's decision. *(He decides to go to war because he is too embarrassed not to. He doesn't want his family and members of his community to be angry with or ashamed of him.)*
Summarizing

Critical Thinking:
SYNTHESIZING

EE Ask students to recall how the narrator, on page 272, calls Elroy Berdahl "the hero of my life." What qualities does the narrator consider "heroic?" *(Possible responses: Students may note the following heroic aspects of Elroy's character: living according to what you believe and letting other people make up their own minds; being empathetic to the problems other people face; being nonjudgmental; presenting alternatives.)*

CUSTOMIZING FOR
Gifted and Talented Students

Invite students to analyze the water imagery in this story. *(the connection between the river's name and the narrator's tears, or the juxtaposition between the usual image of water as a cleansing, purifying, life-giving force, and its use here as an agent of destruction, in the meat-packing plant, and as a sign of shame, when the narrator cries over his cowardice.)*

EDITOR'S NOTE *With the permission of the author or copyright holder, potentially offensive material has been deleted from the selection.*

COMPREHENSION CHECK

1. When did the events recalled by the narrator take place? *(in 1968, during the Vietnam War)*
2. What does the narrator receive that upsets him? *(his draft notice)*
3. Whom does the narrator consider the hero of his life? *(Elroy Berdahl)*
4. What does Elroy Berdahl do to help the narrator make up his mind about the draft notice? *(He takes him fishing to a place where he can easily escape to Canada.)*
5. What does the narrator do that he thinks is cowardly? *(He goes to war rather than to Canada.)*

---

blush. I couldn't tolerate it. I couldn't endure the mockery, or the disgrace, or the patriotic ridicule. Even in my imagination, the shore just twenty yards away, I couldn't make myself be brave. It had nothing to do with morality. Embarrassment, that's all it was.

And right then I submitted.

I would go to the war—I would kill and maybe die—because I was embarrassed not to.

That was the sad thing. And so I sat in the bow of the boat and cried.

It was loud now. Loud, hard crying.

Elroy Berdahl remained quiet. He kept fishing. He worked his line with the tips of his fingers, patiently, squinting out at his red and white bobber on the Rainy River. His eyes were flat and impassive. He didn't speak. He was simply there, like the river and the late-summer sun. And yet by his presence, his mute watchfulness, he made it real. He was the true audience. He was a witness, like God, or like the gods, who look on in absolute silence as we live our lives, as we make our choices or fail to make them.

"Ain't biting," he said.

Then after a time the old man pulled in his line and turned the boat back toward Minnesota.

I don't remember saying goodbye. That last night we had dinner together, and I went to bed early, and in the morning Elroy fixed breakfast for me. When I told him I'd be leaving, the old man nodded as if he already knew. He looked down at the table and smiled.

At some point later in the morning it's possible that we shook hands—I just don't remember—but I do know that by the time I'd finished packing the old man had disappeared. Around noon, when I took my suitcase out to the car, I noticed that his old black pickup truck was no longer parked in front of the house. I went inside and waited for a while, but I felt a bone certainty that he wouldn't be back. In a way, I thought, it was appropriate. I washed up the breakfast dishes, left his two hundred dollars on the kitchen counter, got into the car, and drove south toward home.

The day was cloudy. I passed through towns with familiar names, through the pine forests and down to the prairie, and then to Vietnam, where I was a soldier, and then home again. I survived, but it's not a happy ending. I was a coward. I went to the war. ❖

WORDS TO KNOW
impassive (ĭm-păs′ĭv) *adj.* revealing no emotion; expressionless

RESPONDING OPTIONS

FROM PERSONAL RESPONSE TO CRITICAL ANALYSIS

REFLECT
1. In your notebook, write your reaction to the narrator's final decision.

RETHINK
2. The narrator feels he was a coward for fighting in the Vietnam War. Do you share his opinion? Why or why not?

3. What do you think the narrator means when he says that Elroy Berdahl "saved" him?

Close Textual Reading

Consider
- the effect of Elroy's silence
- his offer of money to the narrator
- why he takes the narrator fishing

4. The narrator gives a detailed description of his summer job in a meat-packing plant. Why do you think this description is included?

5. If you had been in the narrator's position, would you have chosen to fight in the war or to flee to Canada? Consider the chart you created for the Personal Connection on page 266.

Thematic Link
6. "Prisoners of Circumstance" is the title given to this part of Unit Two. In what sense is the narrator a prisoner of circumstance?

RELATE
7. Should a government be able to compel citizens to fight in wars? Why or why not?

Multimodal Learning
ANOTHER PATHWAY
Cooperative Learning

With your entire class, conduct a point/counterpoint discussion that explores both sides of the narrator's conscience. One side of the class should argue in favor of military service; the other side should argue in favor of fleeing to Canada. Use evidence from the story to support your views.

QUICKWRITES

1. Assume the identity of Elroy in "On the Rainy River" and write a **letter** to a relative, telling about your unusual week with the boy from Minnesota.

2. Draft a **definition essay** about courage, showing how your personal definition is similar to or different from the narrator's. If you are using a computer, don't forget to use the spelling checker before you print your essay.

3. Imagine that when the narrator feels the impulse to jump from the boat and swim toward Canada, he actually does so. Write an **alternative ending** to the story from this point on.

4. Recall a time when you wrestled with your conscience about the right thing to do. Write a **personal essay** about the experience.

PORTFOLIO *Save your writing. You may want to use it later as a springboard to a piece for your portfolio.*

United States Marines in Vietnam, 1965. Copyright © Larry Burrows Collection.

From Personal Response to Critical Analysis

1. Accept all reasonable responses.
2. Some students may agree with the narrator's view, because he cared more for the opinions of others than for his own beliefs. Other students may think that the narrator is being hard on himself and that either decision—avoiding war or going to war—required courage.
3. Possible responses: Some students may say Elroy provides the narrator with a quiet, supportive place in which to work through his conflicting feelings. Others may point out that by giving the narrator a chance to flee to Canada, Elroy helps him confront his decision; he respects the fact that the narrator has to make his own decision, rather than trying to influence the narrator one way or the other.
4. Possible responses: because the plant reflects the narrator's dislike of killing and blood; because the job reflects the working-class community in which the narrator lives; to show that the narrator is responsible enough to stick to an unpleasant job
5. Accept all reasonable, well-supported responses.
6. Possible responses: he is a prisoner of the circumstance of the Vietnam War; he is a prisoner of the values of his society, which makes it hard for him to follow his conscience; he is a prisoner of a particular time, when draft deferments were difficult to obtain.
7. Some students may say that a government should have this power because otherwise a country would not be able to pull together a large enough army to defend itself or its allies against attack. Other students may believe that citizens should have the freedom to choose the causes for which they will fight.

Another Pathway
Cooperative Learning Encourage teams to anticipate, and plan to counter, the arguments their opponents might use.

Rubric
- **3 Full Accomplishment** Students give valid reasons for their points of view, cite story details, and reply precisely to counterpoints.
- **2 Substantial Accomplishment** present a good argument but don't support it with story details. Responses to challenges are vague.
- **1 Little or Partial Accomplishment** Students have trouble articulating a point of view or relating it to the story. Their responses to their opponents are weak.

QuickWrites
1. Encourage students to recall Elroy's manner in the story before trying to write in his style.
2. Remind students to define courage first for themselves and then for the narrator.
3. Suggest that students use techniques from the story to maintain a similar narrative voice.
4. Point out that students' essays should examine both the causes and effects of a particular decision.

The Writer's Craft
Voice, pp. 420–423
Definition Essay, pp. 134–137
Autobiographical Incident, pp. 26–40

Literary Links

Possible responses: For Hayslip's father, it means the chance to live in peace, without foreign and local soldiers endangering one's family and land. To the narrator, it means being able to choose your own future without interference from the government. For both, it's something difficult to attain. If the two had met, they might have both expressed regret at the narrator's inability to follow his conscience.

Art Connection

The painting shows a young man who seems to be in a state of indecision and deep thought. This is the status of the narrator as the story begins.

Across the Curriculum

History *Cooperative Learning* Each group should have a coordinator who arranges research times and organizes group attendance, a recorder who keeps track of the information the group finds, a moderator to control the debate proceedings, and several debaters for each side who can take turns presenting valid arguments.

Journalism Suggest that students write down a list of questions they might want to ask their subjects. Remind them, however, that good interviewers are flexible and can add or subtract questions as the situation demands. Caution them not to interrupt when the subject is speaking. Encourage them to think of catchy headlines and good leads for their articles.

LITERARY CONCEPTS

Point of view refers to the narrative method, or the kind of narrator, used in a literary work. In the **first-person point of view,** the narrator is a character in the story who tells everything in his or her own words. The first-person point of view can sometimes make a fictional story seem more true to life, particularly when the writer gives the narrator his or her own name, as Tim O'Brien did. How does O'Brien's use of the first-person point of view affect how you feel about the narrator? How does it affect your understanding of Elroy Berdahl?

LITERARY LINKS

In the excerpt from *When Heaven and Earth Changed Places* in Unit One, Le Ly Hayslip's father says, "Freedom is never a gift. . . . It must be won and won again." What do you think freedom means to this Vietnamese father? What do you think it means to the American narrator of "On the Rainy River"? If the two men had met in Vietnam, what might they have said to each other?

Multimodal Learning

ALTERNATIVE ACTIVITIES

1. Create a **collage** based on the vision the narrator has while he's on the Rainy River (pages 277–279). You may include photos, clippings from newspapers and magazines, and your own drawings of the images that the narrator thinks he sees.

2. Bring in recordings of folk and rock **protest songs** from the Vietnam War era and play them for your class. Discuss how these songs express moral and political objections to the conflict.

282   UNIT TWO   PART 2: PRISONERS OF CIRCUMSTANCE

ART CONNECTION

What do you think is the connection between the painting *Portrait of Donald Schrader* on page 267 and the first part of the story?

Multimodal Learning

ACROSS THE CURRICULUM

History *Cooperative Learning* Working with a group of classmates, conduct research on the Vietnam War. What was the United States trying to achieve by participating in the conflict? Why did some people support our role in the war, and why did others oppose it? Divide your group in two and hold a debate that might have taken place between hawks and doves in 1968.

Journalism Tape-record or videotape interviews with people who lived through the Vietnam War era. Have them describe their feelings about the war and their experiences with the draft, the fighting itself, and the rallies or protests on the home front. Then write a feature story for the school newspaper.

Literary Concepts

Students might feel that, because they are privy to O'Brien's thoughts and feelings through the first-person point of view, they have a better understanding of him and are therefore more sympathetic to his plight. They may also feel that this point of view limits their understanding of Elroy Berdahl. However, some students may feel that it deepens their understanding of Berdahl because they are allowed to see the kindness and sympathy which is not outwardly apparent.

Alternative Activities

1. Suggest that students refer not only to library sources, but also to friends and family who may have kept magazines and newspapers from the Vietnam War era. Students can photocopy these visuals for use in their collages.

2. Point out that many of these songs were sung not only by professional musicians, but also by groups of protesters during antiwar demonstrations. Then discuss how singing can be a powerful form of protest.

WORDS TO KNOW

Review the Words to Know at the bottom of the selection pages. Then choose the word that best completes each of the following sentences.

1. Grandma says that long before Dad was drafted, he was so _____ with the Vietnam War that he couldn't focus on his schoolwork and his grades were falling.
2. Dad believed in the _____ of defending one's country, but he didn't understand how the Vietnam War was connected to freedom at home.
3. He found the tangled web of Vietnamese politics difficult to _____.
4. In the United States, there was no _____ about the war; hawks said one thing, and doves said another.
5. My grandfather understood Dad's reluctance to fight in that war; he used to say "War is hell," but that was only a _____.
6. After receiving his draft notice, Dad stayed up all night holding a lonely _____.
7. Since Dad was usually so cheerful and talkative in the morning, his _____ at the breakfast table the next day made my grandfather feel sad.
8. To Grandma he seemed calm, but that was merely _____, for deep down he was troubled.
9. He kept his face _____ so that Grandma could not observe his feelings.
10. When Grandma asked if he would soon be going overseas to fight, he nodded in _____.

Words to Know

1. preoccupied
2. imperative
3. fathom
4. consensus
5. platitude
6. vigil
7. reticence
8. pretense
9. impassive
10. acquiescence

Reteaching/Reinforcement
- *Unit Two Resource Book*, p. 50

TIM O'BRIEN

1946–

Though the events depicted in "On the Rainy River" are fictional, many details in the story match the writer's own experiences. Like the narrator, the real Tim O'Brien grew up in Minnesota and was an exceptional student at Macalester College. He also was drafted into the U.S. Army immediately after graduation, and he was later admitted to graduate school at Harvard. An opponent of the Vietnam War, O'Brien, like the narrator, debated fleeing the country (his choice of destination was Sweden, not Canada), but ultimately he decided to serve. "I did not want to be a soldier, not even an observer to war," he later wrote. "But neither did I want to upset a peculiar balance between the order I knew, the people I knew, and my own private world."

During the Vietnam War, O'Brien was promoted to the rank of sergeant; he also was wounded in combat and awarded the Purple Heart. His experiences in the army affected him profoundly and have inspired much of his writing. His first book, *If I Die in a Combat Zone, Box Me Up and Ship Me Home* (1973), is a nonfiction memoir of his tour of duty. O'Brien's popular second novel about Vietnam, *Going After Cacciato,* won two O. Henry Memorial Awards and the 1978 National Book Award. "On the Rainy River" appeared in *The Things They Carried* (1990), a collection of interrelated stories about the Vietnam War and its victims. Despite the presence of a narrator named Tim O'Brien, the stories in the collection are fictional. For O'Brien, whether a story is literally true is less important than the truths it conveys. "I want you to feel what I felt," he once explained. "I want you to know why story truth is truer sometimes than happening truth."

OTHER WORKS *Northern Lights, In the Lake of the Woods*

Extended Reading

TIM O'BRIEN

In 1990, O'Brien visited Vietnam for the first time in 20 years. He was there to attend a writer's conference in Hanoi. Whether in Vietnam or the United States, the war is never far from O'Brien's thoughts or writing. He remarks: "After each of my books about the war has appeared, I thought it might be the last, but I've stopped saying that to myself. There are just too many stories left to tell.... more war stories will come out. They have to."

ON THE RAINY RIVER **283**

REFLECTING ON THEME
What Do You Think?

Ask students to look back at the chart they made at the beginning of this part of Unit Two showing factors that restrict the lives of various people. Have students add the narrator of "On the Rainy River" to their chart and compare the factors that restrict his life to those of other prisoners of circumstance. Ask students if they would like to revise their charts in any way after reading this story.

OVERVIEW

Objectives

- To understand and appreciate a short story that explores the deceptions and hypocrisies motivated by social customs and the standards of polite behavior
- To enrich reading by using active reading strategies
- To identify and understand satire
- To appreciate a writer's formal style
- To express understanding of the story through a choice of writing forms, including a dialogue, a character sketch, and a satiric story
- To extend understanding of the story through a variety of multimodal and cross-curricular activities

Skills

LITERARY CONCEPTS
- Satire
- Characterization

READING SKILLS/STRATEGIES
- Questioning

THE WRITER'S STYLE
- Showing spatial relationships

GRAMMAR
- Adverb clauses

SPEAKING, LISTENING, AND WRITING
- Group discussion
- Oral presentation
- Skit

ALTERNATIVE
Previewing

Instead of writing about a memory of an awkward social situation, students can choose partners and discuss their experiences.

Personal Connection

Discussion Prompts Share your memory of an awkward moment with your partner. Use the following prompts:

- What was the situation?
- How did you handle it?

As you read "The Pearl," watch to see how the four ladies cope with their hostess's awkward loss.

PREVIEWING

FICTION

The Pearl
Yukio Mishima (yōō′kē-ō mĭ-shē′mä) Japan

Activating Prior Knowledge
PERSONAL CONNECTION

Have you ever been caught in an awkward or embarrassing moment at a party or social event? What did you do? In your notebook, describe a time when you felt you needed to "save face," or keep your standing in the eyes of others.

Building Background *read*
CULTURAL CONNECTION

Polite behavior is important in Japanese society, as it is in American society, but the customs and the rules of etiquette in the two cultures are often quite different. In Japan it is considered rude to sneeze or blow your nose in public, for example, and you must be careful not to accidentally bump someone with your foot because feet are considered unclean. Japanese society places great value on self-restraint and duty, and the need to maintain dignity in embarrassing or awkward situations often motivates personal behavior. This was particularly true three or four decades ago, when the following story takes place. Set in Tokyo, the capital of Japan, "The Pearl" portrays five friends from middle-class Japanese society who become entangled in an awkward social situation.

Two businessmen in Osaka, Japan.
Copyright © Will and Deni McIntyre / Tony Stone Images.

Active Reading/Setting a Purpose
READING CONNECTION

Understanding Problems and Solutions "The Pearl" takes several twists and turns as each character independently tries to resolve the awkward situation that has affected the entire group. To keep track of the action in the story, copy this problem-and-solution chart into your notebook and fill it out as you read.

Character	Problem(s)	Solution(s)
Mrs. Sasaki		
Mrs. Yamamoto		
Mrs. Matsumura		
Mrs. Azuma		
Mrs. Kasuga		

Using Your Reading Log Use your reading log to record your responses to the questions inserted throughout the selection. Also, jot down other thoughts and feelings that come to you as you read.

284 UNIT TWO PART 2: PRISONERS OF CIRCUMSTANCE

PRINT AND MEDIA RESOURCES

UNIT TWO RESOURCE BOOK
Strategic Reading: Literature, p. 53
Vocabulary SkillBuilder, p. 54

GRAMMAR MINI-LESSONS
Transparencies, p. 22
Copymasters, p. 24

WRITING MINI-LESSONS
Transparencies, p. 40

ACCESS FOR STUDENTS ACQUIRING ENGLISH
Selection Summaries
Reading Support

FORMAL ASSESSMENT
Selection Test, p. 55
 Test Generator

AUDIO LIBRARY
See Reference Card

The Pearl

Yukio Mishima

December 10 was Mrs. Sasaki's[1] birthday, but since it was Mrs. Sasaki's wish to celebrate the occasion with the minimum of fuss, she had invited to her house for afternoon tea only her closest friends. Assembled were Mesdames Yamamoto, Matsumura, Azuma, and Kasuga[2]—all four being forty-three years of age, exact contemporaries of their hostess.

These ladies were thus members, as it were, of a Keep-Our-Ages-Secret Society and could be trusted implicitly not to divulge to outsiders the number of candles on today's cake. In inviting to her birthday party only guests of this nature, Mrs. Sasaki was showing her customary prudence.

On this occasion Mrs. Sasaki wore a pearl ring. Diamonds at an all-female gathering had not seemed in the best of taste. Furthermore, pearls better matched the color of the dress she was wearing on this particular day.

Shortly after the party had begun, Mrs. Sasaki was moving across for one last inspection of the cake when the pearl in her ring, already a little loose, finally fell from its socket. It seemed a most inauspicious event for this happy occasion, but it would have been no less embarrassing to have everyone aware of the misfortune, so Mrs. Sasaki simply left the pearl close by the rim of the large cake dish and resolved to do something about it later. Around the cake were set out the plates, forks, and paper napkins for herself and the four guests. It now occurred to Mrs. Sasaki that she had no wish to be seen wearing a ring with no stone while cutting this cake, and accordingly she removed the ring from her finger and very deftly,

---

1. **Sasaki** (sä-sä′kē).
2. **Mesdames Yamamoto** (mā-däm′ ya′mə-mō′tō), **Matsumura** (mät′sōō-mōō′rə), **Azuma** (ə-zōō′mä), **and Kasuga** (kə-sōō′gä): *Mesdames* is the plural form of the French title for a married woman, *Madame*, which is equivalent to the English title *Mrs.*

WORDS TO KNOW
implicitly (ĭm-plĭs′ĭt-lē) *adv.* absolutely; without doubt or question
prudence (prōōd′ns) *n.* good judgment; caution in regard to one's conduct
inauspicious (ĭn′ô-spĭsh′əs) *adj.* unfavorable; unlucky

285

WORDS TO KNOW

ambiguous (ăm-bĭg′yōō-əs) *adj.* open to more than one interpretation (p. 287)
fastidious (fă-stĭd′ē-əs) *adj.* showing meticulous attention to detail; excessively careful in matters of taste or manners (p. 288)
impetuous (ĭm-pĕch′ōō-əs) *adj.* abrupt or impulsive; spontaneous (p. 290)
implicitly (ĭm-plĭs′ĭt-lē) *adv.* absolutely, without doubt or question (p. 285)
inauspicious (ĭn′ô-spĭsh′əs) *adj.* unfavorable, unlucky (p. 285)

incensed (ĭn-sĕnst′) *adj.* extremely angered
incense *v.* (p. 287)
infamy (ĭn′fə-mē) *n.* evil fame or reputation (p. 290)
malicious (mə-lĭsh′əs) *adj.* deliberately harmful; spiteful (p. 289)
prudence (prōōd′ns) *n.* good judgment; caution in regard to one's conduct (p. 285)
scruple (skrōō′pəl) *n.* an ethical principle that inhibits action (p. 294)

SUMMARY

At Mrs. Sasaki's birthday party, a pearl that resembles one of the small, round, silvery cake decorations falls out of Mrs. Sasaki's ring. Her four friends then begin a round of trickery, deceit, suspicion, accusations, innuendo, and cover-ups to save their own reputations. One friend takes the blame for accidentally eating the pearl; another hides the pearl in the purse of a woman she dislikes; two friends, in an effort to save face when they look guilty, purchase pearls that do not fit the ring. In the end two close friends have their friendship destroyed by the incident, two enemies have become close friends, and Mrs. Sasaki has a new ring crafted from the two pearls returned to her, neither of which is the one she lost.

Thematic Link: *Prisoners of Circumstance*
Five women are "prisoners" of both social mores and their own rules.

CUSTOMIZING FOR
Students Acquiring English

- Use **ACCESS FOR STUDENTS ACQUIRING ENGLISH,** *Reading Support.*
- Many of the sentences in this story are long, and the diction is formal. The language reflects the air of propriety that governs the behavior of the five ladies. You may find it helpful to have students pause frequently while reading to discuss the ruses each lady devises. Help students to see that many of Mishima's ornate phrasings are satirical.
- As you guide students through the selection, you may want to use the suggestions under Strategic Reading for Less-Proficient Readers, as well as the suggestions in these boxes.

STRATEGIC READING FOR
Less-Proficient Readers

Set a Purpose Invite students to brainstorm a list of embarrassing things that might happen at a birthday party. Then have students read to find out what awkward incident occurs at the birthday party in this story.

Use **UNIT TWO RESOURCE BOOK,** p. 53, for guidance in reading the selection.

CUSTOMIZING FOR
Gifted and Talented Students

Ask students to identify some of Mishima's satirical descriptions and explain what is being satirized.

Possible responses:

- Page 285—"These ladies were thus members, as it were, of a Keep-Our-Ages-Secret Society" (Mishima is poking fun at the ladies' vanity.)
- Page 290—"Mrs. Matsumura proposed to escape forever the infamy of suspicion and equally—by a small outlay of cash—the pricks of an uneasy conscience." (Mishima is pointing out Mrs. Matsumura's ridiculous need to save face; she's buying a pearl to protect her good name.)

Art Note

Firescreen by Vanessa Bell English painter Vanessa Bell shows the influence of the Post-Impressionists in her work, especially Gaugin's decorative patterns and Cézanne's preoccupation with spatial forms. Bell, the sister of the English novelist Virginia Woolf, also drew inspiration from Japanese art and subject matter.

Reading the Art How does the mood of this painting compare with the mood of the birthday party described on this page?

Literary Concept: TONE

A Ask students how the author feels about these women and their attitudes toward age. *(Possible responses: contemptuous, amused)*

Firescreen (1935), Vanessa Bell. Gouache on board, 104 × 107 cm, The Charleston Trust, East Sussex. Photo by Susanna Price.

without turning around, slipped it into a recess in the wall behind her back.

Amid the general excitement of the exchange of gossip, and Mrs. Sasaki's surprise and pleasure at the thoughtful presents brought by her guests, the matter of the pearl was very quickly forgotten. Before long it was time for the customary ceremony of lighting and extinguishing the candles on the cake. Everyone crowded excitedly about the table, lending a hand in the not untroublesome task of lighting forty-three candles.

Mrs. Sasaki, with her limited lung capacity, could hardly be expected to blow out all that number at one puff, and her appearance of utter helplessness gave rise to a great deal of hilarious comment.

The procedure followed in serving the cake was that, after the first bold cut, Mrs. Sasaki carved for each guest individually a slice of whatever thickness was requested and transferred this to a small plate, which the guest then carried back with her to her own seat. With everyone stretching out hands at the same time, the crush and confusion around the table was considerable.

On top of the cake was a floral design executed in pink icing and liberally interspersed with small silver balls. These were silver-painted crystals of sugar—a common enough decoration

286 UNIT TWO PART 2: PRISONERS OF CIRCUMSTANCE

286 THE LANGUAGE OF LITERATURE TEACHER'S EDITION

on birthday cakes. In the struggle to secure helpings, moreover, flakes of icing, crumbs of cake, and a number of these silver balls came to be scattered all over the white tablecloth. Some of the guests gathered these stray particles between their fingers and put them on their plates. Others popped them straight into their mouths.

In time all returned to their seats and ate their portions of cake at their leisure, laughing. It was not a homemade cake, having been ordered by Mrs. Sasaki from a certain high-class confectioner's,[3] but the guests were unanimous in praising its excellence.

Mrs. Sasaki was bathed in happiness. But suddenly, with a tinge of anxiety, she recalled the pearl she had abandoned on the table, and, rising from her chair as casually as she could, she moved across to look for it. At the spot where she was sure she had left it, the pearl was no longer to be seen.

Mrs. Sasaki abhorred losing things. At once and without thinking, right in the middle of the party, she became wholly engrossed in her search, and the tension in her manner was so obvious that it attracted everyone's attention.

"Is there something the matter?" someone asked.

"No, not at all, just a moment. . . ."

Mrs. Sasaki's reply was ambiguous, but before she had time to decide to return to her chair, first one, then another, and finally every one of her guests had risen and was turning back the tablecloth or groping about on the floor.

Mrs. Azuma, seeing this commotion, felt that the whole thing was just too deplorable for words. She was incensed at a hostess who could create such an impossible situation over the loss of a solitary pearl.

Mrs. Azuma resolved to offer herself as a sacrifice and to save the day. With a heroic smile she declared: "That's it then! It must have been a pearl I ate just now! A silver ball dropped on the tablecloth when I was given my cake, and I just picked it up and swallowed it without thinking. It *did* seem to stick in my throat a little. Had it been a diamond, now, I would naturally return it—by an operation, if necessary—but as it's a pearl, I must simply beg your forgiveness."

This announcement at once resolved the company's anxieties, and it was felt, above all, that it had saved the hostess from an embarrassing predicament. No one made any attempt to investigate the truth or falsity of Mrs. Azuma's confession. Mrs. Sasaki took one of the remaining silver balls and put it in her mouth.

"Mm," she said. "Certainly tastes like a pearl, this one!"

Thus, this small incident, too, was cast into the crucible[4] of good-humored teasing, and there—amid general laughter—it melted away.

When the party was over, Mrs. Azuma drove off in her two-seater sportscar, taking with her in the other seat her close friend and neighbor Mrs. Kasuga. Before two minutes had passed, Mrs. Azuma said, "Own up! It was you who swallowed the pearl, wasn't it? I covered up for you and took the blame on myself."

This unceremonious manner of speaking concealed deep affection, but, however friendly the intention may have been, to Mrs. Kasuga a wrongful accusation was a wrongful accusation. She had no recollection whatsoever of having swallowed a pearl in mistake for a sugar ball. She was—as Mrs. Azuma too must surely

QUESTION
Why are Mrs. Sasaki and her guests laughing?
Using a Reading Log

---

3. **confectioner's** (kən-fĕk′shə-nərz): a shop or caterer specializing in candies, cakes, and other sweets.
4. **crucible** (krōō′sə-bəl): test or trial.

WORDS TO KNOW
ambiguous (ăm-bĭg′yōō-əs) *adj.* open to more than one interpretation
incensed (ĭn-sĕnst′) *adj.* extremely angered **incense** *v.*

287

Literary Concept:
CHARACTERIZATION

D Ask students to discuss Mishima's use of details to characterize Mrs. Azuma and Mrs. Kasuga in this scene. *(Possible responses: Mrs. Azuma's continued teasing of her friend is insensitive; Mrs. Kasuga's "small voice," mild protest, and embarrassment show that she is gentle and not strong.)*

STRATEGIC READING FOR
Less-Proficient Readers

E Make sure students understand the incident that arose at the birthday party, the action that Mrs. Azuma took to resolve it, and the conflict that arose between Mrs. Azuma and Mrs. Kasuga.

- What happens at Mrs. Sasaki's birthday party? *(Mrs. Sasaki loses a pearl and Mrs. Azuma claims that she accidentally swallowed it.)* **Summarizing**

- Why does a conflict arise between Mrs. Azuma and Mrs. Kasuga? *(Possible response: Mrs. Azuma teasingly accuses her friend of swallowing the pearl, which causes Mrs. Kasuga to become worried about the possibility of having done so; then Mrs. Kasuga begins to mistrust her friend.)* **Analyzing**

Set a Purpose Have students read to find out what further complications arise.

Critical Thinking: ANALYZING

F Ask students what conclusions they can draw about Mrs. Matsumura from this detail. *(Possible responses: She is vain; she was very shaken up by the incident at the party.)*

CUSTOMIZING FOR
Students Acquiring English

3 Explain that in a boarding school, a *school-captain* is a senior student who has been given a measure of responsibility for keeping order among other students.

---

know—<u>fastidious</u> in her eating habits, and, if she so much as detected a single hair in her food, whatever she happened to be eating at the time immediately stuck in her gullet.

"Oh, really now!" protested the timid Mrs. Kasuga in a small voice, her eyes studying Mrs. Azuma's face in some puzzlement. "I just couldn't do a thing like that!"

"It's no good pretending. The moment I saw that green look on your face, I knew."

The little disturbance at the party had seemed closed by Mrs. Azuma's frank confession, but even now it had left behind it this strange awkwardness. Mrs. Kasuga, wondering how best to demonstrate her innocence, was at the same time seized by the fantasy that a solitary pearl was lodged somewhere in her intestines. It was unlikely, of course, that she should mistakenly swallow a pearl for a sugar ball, but in all that confusion of talk and laughter, one had to admit that it was at least a possibility. Though she thought back over the events of the party again and again, no moment in which she might have inserted a pearl into her mouth came to mind—but, after all, if it was an unconscious act, one would not expect to remember it.

Mrs. Kasuga blushed deeply as her imagination chanced upon one further aspect of the matter. It had occurred to her that when one accepted a pearl into one's system, it almost certainly—its luster a trifle dimmed, perhaps, by gastric juices[5]—reemerged intact within a day or two.

And with this thought the design of Mrs. Azuma, too, seemed to have become transparently clear. Undoubtedly Mrs. Azuma had viewed this same prospect with embarrassment and shame and had therefore cast her responsibility onto another, making it appear that she had considerately taken the blame to protect a friend.

Meanwhile Mrs. Yamamoto and Mrs. Matsumura, whose homes lay in a similar direction, were returning together in a taxi. Soon after the taxi had started, Mrs. Matsumura opened her handbag to make a few adjustments to her make-up. She remembered that she had done nothing to her face since all that commotion at the party.

As she was removing the powder compact, her attention was caught by a sudden dull gleam as something tumbled to the bottom of the bag. Groping about with the tips of her fingers, Mrs. Matsumura retrieved the object and saw to her amazement that it was a pearl.

Mrs. Matsumura stifled an exclamation of surprise. Recently her relationship with Mrs. Yamamoto had been far from cordial, and she had no wish to share with that lady a discovery with such awkward implications for herself.

Fortunately Mrs. Yamamoto was gazing out of the window and did not appear to have noticed her companion's momentary start of surprise.

Caught off balance by this sudden turn of events, Mrs. Matsumura did not pause to consider how the pearl had found its way into her bag but immediately became a prisoner of her own private brand of school-captain morality. It was unlikely—she thought—that she would do a thing like this, even in a moment of abstraction. But since, by some chance, the object had found its way into her handbag, the proper course was to return it at once. If she failed to do so, it would weigh heavily upon her conscience. The fact that it was a pearl, too—an article you could call neither all that expensive nor yet all

---

5. **gastric juices:** fluids used by the stomach during digestion.

WORDS TO KNOW

fastidious (fă-stĭd′ē-əs) *adj.* showing meticulous attention to detail; excessively careful in matters of taste or manners

288

Mini-Lesson ✏ Grammar

ADVERB CLAUSES Remind students that an adverb clause is a subordinate clause that is used to modify a verb, an adjective, or another adverb. Like adverbs, adverb clauses can tell *where, when, how,* or *to what extent.* They can also explain *why* or *under what circumstances.* For example, in "The Pearl," Mishima uses the adverb clause "as she was removing the powder compact" to describe when and how Mrs. Matsumura discovered the lost pearl.

Application Invite students to use these adverb clauses to create sentences about "The Pearl."

1. As soon as she got home
2. While Mrs. Matsumura was eating cake
3. Wherever the pearl had gone
4. As if she didn't believe the story
5. Although she knew she was innocent

Reteaching/Reinforcement
- *Grammar Handbook,* anthology p. 1076
- *Grammar Mini-Lessons* copymasters p. 24, transparencies p. 22

Adverb Clauses, pp. 612–613

that cheap—only made her position more ambiguous.

At any rate, she was determined that her companion, Mrs. Yamamoto, should know nothing of this incomprehensible development—especially when the affair had been so nicely rounded off, thanks to the selflessness of Mrs. Azuma. Mrs. Matsumura felt she could remain in the taxi not a moment longer, and on the pretext of remembering a promise to visit a sick relative on her way back, she made the driver set her down at once, in the middle of a quiet residential district.

Mrs. Yamamoto, left alone in the taxi, was a little surprised that her practical joke should have moved Mrs. Matsumura to such abrupt action. Having watched Mrs. Matsumura's reflection in the window just now, she had clearly seen her draw the pearl from her bag.

> *Mrs. Yamamoto . . . was a little surprised that her practical joke should have moved Mrs. Matsumura to such abrupt action.*

At the party Mrs. Yamamoto had been the very first to receive a slice of cake. Adding to her plate a silver ball which had spilled onto the table, she had returned to her seat—again before any of the others—and there had noticed that the silver ball was a pearl. At this discovery she had at once conceived a <u>malicious</u> plan. While all the others were preoccupied with the cake, she had quickly slipped the pearl into the handbag left on the next chair by that insufferable hypocrite Mrs. Matsumura.

Stranded in the middle of a residential district where there was little prospect of a taxi, Mrs. Matsumura fretfully gave her mind to a number of reflections on her position.

First, no matter how necessary it might be for the relief of her own conscience, it would be a shame indeed, when people had gone to such lengths to settle the affair satisfactorily, to go and stir up things all over again; and it would be even worse if in the process—because of the inexplicable nature of the circumstances—she were to direct unjust suspicions upon herself.

Secondly—notwithstanding these considerations—if she did not make haste to return the pearl now, she would forfeit her opportunity forever. Left till tomorrow (at the thought Mrs. Matsumura blushed), the returned pearl would be an object of rather disgusting speculation and doubt. Concerning this possibility, Mrs. Azuma herself had dropped a hint.

It was at this point that there occurred to Mrs. Matsumura, greatly to her joy, a master scheme which would both salve[6] her conscience and at the same time involve no risk of exposing her character to any unjust suspicion. Quickening her step, she emerged at length onto a comparatively busy thoroughfare, where she hailed a taxi and told the driver to take her quickly to a certain celebrated pearl shop on the Ginza.[7] There she took the pearl from her bag and showed it to the attendant, asking to see a pearl of slightly larger size and clearly superior quality. Having made her purchase, she proceeded once more, by taxi, to Mrs. Sasaki's house.

Mrs. Matsumura's plan was to present this newly purchased pearl to Mrs. Sasaki, saying she had found it in her jacket pocket. Mrs. Sasaki would accept it and later attempt to fit it into the ring. However, being a pearl of a different size, it would not fit into the ring, and Mrs. Sasaki—puzzled—would try to return it to Mrs.

---

6. **salve** (săv): soothe, heal, or ease.
7. **Ginza** (gĭn′zə): an elegant shopping district in Tokyo.

WORDS TO KNOW
malicious (mə-lĭsh′əs) *adj.* deliberately harmful; spiteful

289

Active Reading: CLARIFY

J Suggest that students summarize the train of thought that leads Mrs. Matsumura to her decision. Stress that her main motive is to avoid suspicion.

CUSTOMIZING FOR
Students Acquiring English

4 You may wish to discuss the meaning of these two phrases: "her innocence on the gastronomic count" and "the shameful and hardly mentionable suspicion would inevitably have intervened." Make sure that students understand that Mishima is mocking this elaborate way of avoiding the mention of bodily functions.

Literary Concept: HUMOR

K Ask students if they find this chain of events humorous. Have them give reasons for their opinions. *(Possible responses: yes, the absurdity of the two women buying and returning the wrong size pearls is funny; no, it's sad and pathetic that people are so bound by social appearances that they act in such ridiculous ways.)*

Matsumura, but Mrs. Matsumura would refuse to have it returned. Thereupon Mrs. Sasaki would have no choice but to reflect as follows: The woman has behaved in this way in order to protect someone else. Such being the case, it is perhaps safest simply to accept the pearl and forget the matter. Mrs. Matsumura has doubtless observed one of the three ladies in the act of stealing the pearl. But at least, of my four guests, I can now be sure that Mrs. Matsumura, if no one else, is completely without guilt. Whoever heard of a thief stealing something and then replacing it with a similar article of greater value?

By this device Mrs. Matsumura proposed to escape forever the infamy of suspicion and equally—by a small outlay of cash—the pricks of an uneasy conscience.

CLARIFY
Why does Mrs. Matsumura purchase a new pearl for Mrs. Sasaki instead of returning the original one that was lost?

J

Using a Reading Log

To return to the other ladies. After reaching home, Mrs. Kasuga continued to feel painfully upset by Mrs. Azuma's cruel teasing. To clear herself of even a ridiculous charge like this—she knew—she must act before tomorrow or it would be too late. That is to say, in order to offer positive proof that she had not eaten the pearl, it was above all necessary for the pearl itself to be somehow produced. And, briefly, if she could show the pearl to Mrs. Azuma immediately, her innocence on the gastronomic count (if not on any other) would be firmly established. But if she waited until tomorrow, even though she managed to produce the pearl, the shameful and hardly mentionable suspicion would inevitably have intervened.

4

The normally timid Mrs. Kasuga, inspired with the courage of impetuous action, burst from the house to which she had so recently returned, sped to a pearl shop in the Ginza, and selected and bought a pearl which, to her eye, seemed of roughly the same size as those silver balls on the cake. She then telephoned Mrs. Azuma. On returning home, she explained, she had discovered in the folds of the bow of her sash the pearl which Mrs. Sasaki had lost, but, since she felt too ashamed to return it by herself, she wondered if Mrs. Azuma would be so kind as to go with her, as soon as possible. Inwardly Mrs. Azuma considered the story a little unlikely, but since it was the request of a good friend, she agreed to go.

Mrs. Sasaki accepted the pearl brought to her by Mrs. Matsumura and, puzzled at its failure to fit the ring, fell obligingly into that very train of thought for which Mrs. Matsumura had prayed; but it was a surprise to her when Mrs. Kasuga arrived about an hour later, accompanied by Mrs. Azuma, and returned another pearl.

Mrs. Sasaki hovered perilously on the brink of discussing Mrs. Matsumura's prior visit but checked herself at the last moment and accepted the second pearl as unconcernedly as she could. She felt sure that this one at any rate would fit, and as soon as the two visitors had taken their leave, she hurried to try it in the ring. But it was too small and wobbled loosely in the socket. At this discovery Mrs. Sasaki was not so much surprised as dumbfounded.

K

On the way back in the car both ladies found it impossible to guess what the other might be thinking, and, though normally relaxed and loquacious[8] in each other's company, they now lapsed into a long silence.

Mrs. Azuma, who believed she could do nothing without her own full knowledge, knew

---

8. **loquacious** (lō-kwā′shəs): very talkative.

WORDS TO KNOW
infamy (ĭn′fə-mē) *n.* evil fame or reputation
impetuous (ĭm-pĕch′ōō-əs) *adj.* abrupt or impulsive; spontaneous

290 THE LANGUAGE OF LITERATURE TEACHER'S EDITION

Illustration by Leslie Wu.

for certain that she had not swallowed the pearl herself. It was simply to save everyone from embarrassment that she had cast shame aside and made that declaration at the party—more particularly, it was to save the situation for her friend, who had been fidgeting about and looking conspicuously guilty. But what was she to think now? Beneath the peculiarity of Mrs. Kasuga's whole attitude, and beneath this elaborate procedure of having herself accompany her as she returned the pearl, she sensed that there lay something much deeper. Could it be that Mrs. Azuma's intuition had touched upon a weakness in her friend's make-up which it was forbidden to touch upon and that by thus driving her friend into a corner she had transformed an unconscious, impulsive kleptomania[9] into a deep mental derangement beyond all cure?

---

9. **kleptomania** (klĕp′tə-mā′nē-ə): obsessive impulse to steal, regardless of economic need.

Literary Concept: SATIRE

L What character trait do you think Mishima is ridiculing in this passage? *(Possible responses: the tendency to assume the worst about others; the tendency to speculate wildly about other people's actions)*

THE PEARL **291**

Mini-Lesson Literary Concepts

REVIEWING CHARACTERIZATION
Remind students that writers show characterization in four different ways: through physical description; through a character's actions, thoughts, feelings, and words; through a narrator's direct comments about a character; and through the actions, words, and feelings of other characters.

Application Divide the class into five groups and assign each group a character from the selection. Have each group compile quotations about the assigned character that illustrate each of the four types of characterization. For instance, the reference to Mrs. Matsumura's "school-captain morality" is a narrator's comment, while another character in the story, Mrs. Yamamoto, describes Mrs. Matsumura as an "insufferable hypocrite." Students can conclude the activity by making webs on the chalkboard, similar to the one shown here, to identify the most important traits revealed by the quotations.

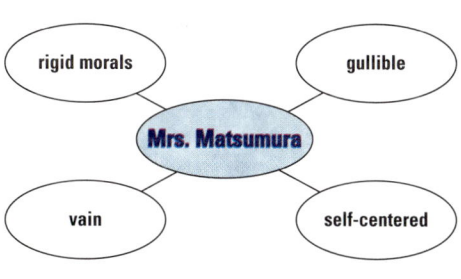

THE LANGUAGE OF LITERATURE TEACHER'S EDITION **291**

Active Reading: PREDICT

M Encourage students to base their predictions on what they already know about the characters. You may wish to share the following model of the thought process involved in making such predictions.

Think-Aloud Model: *Based on what I've read, none of the women seem particularly interested in telling or finding out the truth. In fact, some of them, such as Mrs. Matsumura, actually try to hide the truth, so I doubt that the group will learn what really happened to the pearl.*

STRATEGIC READING FOR
Less-Proficient Readers

N Ask students how each of Mrs. Sasaki's four friends responds to the problem of the missing pearl. *(Possible responses: Mrs. Azuma publicly takes responsibility but privately blames someone else; Mrs. Kasuga and Mrs. Matsumura try to replace the missing pearl with new ones; Mrs. Yamamoto, the real culprit, plays a practical joke to make Mrs. Matsumura think she has taken the pearl. Following the party, the women all blame one another for the events.)*

Summarizing

Set a Purpose Have students read to find out if Mrs. Yamamoto will confess to her deed.

CUSTOMIZING FOR
Students Acquiring English

5 Explain to students that *weak-kneed* is an idiom meaning "cowardly."

Linking to Geography

O Ceylon tea comes from the island nation of Sri Lanka, located at the southeastern tip of India. The island was ruled as a British colony under the name of Ceylon from 1802 until 1948, when it achieved its independence. In 1972, Ceylon changed its name to Sri Lanka, which means "Resplendent Land." Tea is Sri Lanka's primary industry, comprising about two-thirds of the nation's total exports.

Mrs. Kasuga, for her part, still retained the suspicion that Mrs. Azuma had genuinely swallowed the pearl and that her confession at the party had been the truth. If that was so, it had been unforgivable of Mrs. Azuma, when everything was smoothly settled, to tease her so cruelly on the way back from the party, shifting the guilt onto herself. As a result, timid creature that she was, she had been panic-stricken and, besides spending good money, had felt obliged to act out that little play—and was it not exceedingly ill-natured of Mrs. Azuma that, even after all this, she still refused to confess it was she who had eaten the pearl? And if Mrs. Azuma's innocence was all pretense, she herself—acting her part so painstakingly—must appear in Mrs. Azuma's eyes as the most ridiculous of third-rate comedians.

> **PREDICT**
>
> Do you think that, by the end of the story, Mrs. Sasaki and the other women will learn the truth about what happened to the pearl?
>
> *Using a Reading Log*

To return to Mrs. Matsumura. That lady, on her way back from obliging Mrs. Sasaki to accept the pearl, was feeling now more at ease in her mind and had the notion to make a leisurely reinvestigation, detail by detail, of the events of the recent incident. When going to collect her portion of the cake, she had most certainly left her handbag on the chair. Then, while eating the cake, she had made liberal use of the paper napkin—so there could have been no necessity to take a handkerchief from her bag. The more she thought about it, the less she could remember having opened her bag until she touched up her face in the taxi on the way home. How was it, then, that a pearl had rolled into a handbag which was always shut?

She realized now how stupid she had been not to have remarked this simple fact before, instead of flying into a panic at the mere sight of the pearl. Having progressed this far, Mrs. Matsumura was struck by an amazing thought. Someone must purposely have placed the pearl in her bag in order to incriminate her. And of the four guests at the party the only one who would do such a thing was, without doubt, the detestable Mrs. Yamamoto. Her eyes glinting with rage, Mrs. Matsumura hurried toward the house of Mrs. Yamamoto.

From her first glimpse of Mrs. Matsumura standing in the doorway, Mrs. Yamamoto knew at once what had brought her. She had already prepared her line of defense.

However, Mrs. Matsumura's cross-examination was unexpectedly severe, and from the start it was clear that she would accept no evasions.

"It was you, I know. No one but you could do such a thing," began Mrs. Matsumura, deductively.

"Why choose me? What proof have you? If you can say a thing like that to my face, I suppose you've come with pretty conclusive proof, have you?" Mrs. Yamamoto was at first icily composed.

To this Mrs. Matsumura replied that Mrs. Azuma, having so nobly taken the blame on herself, clearly stood in an incompatible relationship with mean and despicable behavior of this nature; and as for Mrs. Kasuga, she was much too weak-kneed for such dangerous work; and that left only one person—yourself.

Mrs. Yamamoto kept silent, her mouth shut tight like a clamshell. On the table before her gleamed the pearl which Mrs. Matsumura had set there. In the excitement she had not even had time to raise a teaspoon, and the Ceylon tea she had so thoughtfully provided was beginning to get cold.

"I had no idea that you hated me so." As she said this, Mrs. Yamamoto dabbed at the corners of her eyes, but it was plain that Mrs. Matsumura's resolve not to be deceived by tears was as firm as ever.

"Well, then," Mrs. Yamamoto continued,

292 UNIT TWO PART 2: PRISONERS OF CIRCUMSTANCE

Multicultural Perspectives

TEA Although most Americans prefer coffee, tea is the world's most popular hot beverage. Its cultivation and use go back over 4,000 years to ancient China. Today, tea is prized and enjoyed in such diverse places as Great Britain, Japan, and Morocco. In many cultures, the making and drinking of tea is a ritual, with its own set of social rules. In Britain, for example, the ritual of afternoon tea developed in the mid-1800s during the era when the British East India Company had a monopoly on trade with India and East Asia, the world's top tea-growing regions. Traditionally, the British take their tea with milk and sugar, accompanied by cookies, cake, or biscuit-like cakes called scones. Japan's very formalized tea ceremony is probably the oldest of all tea rituals. It originated in the 12th century and became such an important part of Japanese life that in the 16th century the tea master Senno Rikyu created strict rules for it.

"I shall say what I had thought I must never say. I shall mention no names, but one of the guests . . ."

"By that, I suppose, you can only mean Mrs. Azuma or Mrs. Kasuga?"

"Please, I beg at least that you allow me to omit the name. As I say, one of the guests had just opened your bag and was dropping something inside when I happened to glance in her direction. You can imagine my amazement! Even if I had felt *able* to warn you, there would have been no chance. My heart just throbbed and throbbed, and on the way back in the taxi—oh, how awful not to be able to speak even then! If we had been good friends, of course, I could have told you quite frankly, but since I knew of your apparent dislike for me . . ."

"I see. You have been very considerate, I'm sure. Which means, doesn't it, that you have now cleverly shifted the blame onto Mrs. Azuma and Mrs. Kasuga?"

"Shifted the blame! Oh, how can I get you to understand my feelings? I only wanted to avoid hurting anyone."

"Quite. But you didn't mind hurting me, did you? You might at least have mentioned this in the taxi."

"And if you had been frank with me when you found the pearl in your bag, I would probably have told you, at that moment, everything I had seen—but no, you chose to leave the taxi at once, without saying a word!"

For the first time, as she listened to this, Mrs. Matsumura was at a loss for a reply.

"Well, then. Can I get you to understand? I wanted no one to be hurt."

Mrs. Matsumura was filled with an even more intense rage.

"If you are going to tell a string of lies like that," she said, "I must ask you to repeat them, tonight if you wish, in my presence, before Mrs. Azuma and Mrs. Kasuga."

At this Mrs. Yamamoto started to weep.

"And thanks to you," she sobbed reprovingly,[10] "all my efforts to avoid hurting anyone will have come to nothing."

It was a new experience for Mrs. Matsumura to see Mrs. Yamamoto crying, and, though she kept reminding herself not to be taken in by tears, she could not altogether dismiss the feeling that perhaps somewhere, since nothing in this affair could be proved, there might be a modicum[11] of truth even in the assertions of Mrs. Yamamoto.

"One of the guests had just opened your bag and was dropping something inside when I happened to glance in her direction."

In the first place—to be a little more objective—if one accepted Mrs. Yamamoto's story as true, then her reluctance to disclose the name of the guilty party, whom she had observed in the very act, argued some refinement of character. And just as one could not say for sure that the gentle and seemingly timid Mrs. Kasuga would never be moved to an act of malice, so even the undoubtedly bad feeling between Mrs. Yamamoto and herself could, by one way of looking at things, be taken as actually lessening the likelihood of Mrs. Yamamoto's guilt. For if she were to do a thing like this, with their relationship as it was, Mrs. Yamamoto would be the first to come under suspicion.

"We have differences in our natures," Mrs. Yamamoto continued tearfully, "and I cannot deny that there are things about yourself which

---

10. **reprovingly** (rĭ-prōō′vĭng-lē): in a manner that finds fault or conveys disappointment.
11. **modicum** (mŏd′ĭ-kəm): a small amount.

Literary Concept: CHARACTERIZATION

P Ask students to discuss the lie that Mrs. Yamamoto tells here. What does this lie reveal about her character? (Possible responses: It confirms that she is not an honest person; it shows that she likes to amuse herself at the expense of others.)

Critical Thinking: SYNTHESIZING

Q Ask students to use what they know about Mrs. Matsumura to explain why she is willing to believe Mrs. Yamamoto's lies. (Possible responses: Her "school-captain morality" makes it impossible for her to believe that anyone would be so malicious; she doesn't realize how much Mrs. Yamamoto dislikes her; she is gullible and taken in by Mrs. Yamamoto's tears.)

Literary Concept: SATIRE

R Point out that although Mrs. Matsumura is upset and surprised by Mrs. Yamamoto's tears, she does not express these feelings, but instead goes through a laborious period of logical thinking. Ask students what the author may be mocking here. (Possible responses: Like the other women, Mrs. Matsumura seems incapable of a direct response to anything. The author is mocking the insincerity and needlessly complex rationalizations that characterize these social relationships.)

Critic's Corner

"[In Mishima's fiction,] however ugly the businessmen, the politicians, the housewives, the lovers, the priests . . . there is beauty—to be glimpsed but never grasped."

Gwenn Boardman Petersen,
The Moon in the Water: Understanding Tanizaki, Kawabata, and Mishima

Ask students if they think Petersen's comment applies to "The Pearl." They should support their opinions with details from the story.

STRATEGIC READING FOR
Less-Proficient Readers

Ask students to retell how Mrs. Azuma and Mrs. Kasuga have a falling out, and how Mrs. Yamamoto and Mrs. Matsumura become close friends. *(Mrs. Azuma and Mrs. Kasuga both suspect each other of being responsible for the disappearance of the pearl, while Mrs. Matsumura, deceived into believing that Mrs. Yamamoto's behavior is honorable, decides that she has misjudged Mrs. Yamamoto.)* **Reviewing**

CUSTOMIZING FOR
Gifted and Talented Students

Ask students to suggest situations in which the formality and good manners which Mishima derides might actually serve a good or worthy purpose, or be useful in solving a problem.

COMPREHENSION CHECK

1. Who attends Mrs. Sasaki's birthday party? *(Mrs. Azuma, Mrs. Kasuga, Mrs. Yamamoto, and Mrs. Matsumura)*
2. What happens at the party? *(A pearl that falls out of Mrs. Sasaki's ring disappears, and Mrs. Azuma falsely admits to having swallowed it.)*
3. Who really took the pearl, and why? *(Mrs. Yamamoto took the pearl and placed it in Mrs. Matsumura's purse as a practical joke.)*
4. What is wrong with the pearls that Mrs. Kasuga and Mrs. Matsumura buy to replace the lost one? *(One is too big and the other is too small.)*
5. What does Mrs. Sasaki do with the two new pearls? *(She has them made into a new ring.)*

I dislike. But, for all that, it is really too bad that you should suspect me of such a petty trick to get the better of you. . . . Still, on thinking it over, to submit quietly to your accusations might well be the course most consistent with what I have felt in this matter all along. In this way I alone shall bear the guilt, and no other will be hurt."

After this pathetic pronouncement Mrs. Yamamoto lowered her face to the table and abandoned herself to uncontrolled weeping.

Watching her, Mrs. Matsumura came, by degrees, to reflect upon the impulsiveness of her own behavior. Detesting Mrs. Yamamoto as she had, there had been times in her castigation¹² of that lady when she had allowed herself to be blinded by emotion.

When Mrs. Yamamoto raised her head again after this prolonged bout of weeping, the look of resolution on her face, somehow remote and pure, was apparent even to her visitor. Mrs. Matsumura, a little frightened, drew herself upright in her chair.

"This thing should never have been. When it is gone, everything will be as before." Speaking in riddles, Mrs. Yamamoto pushed back her disheveled hair and fixed a terrible, yet hauntingly beautiful, gaze upon the top of the table. In an instant she had snatched up the pearl from before her, and, with a gesture of no ordinary resolve, tossed it into her mouth. Raising her cup by the handle, her little finger elegantly extended, she washed the pearl down her throat with one gulp of cold Ceylon tea.

Mrs. Matsumura watched in horrified fascination. The affair was over before she had time to protest. This was the first time in her life she had seen a person swallow a pearl, and there was in Mrs. Yamamoto's manner something of that desperate finality one might expect to see in a person who had just drunk poison.

However, heroic though the action was, it was above all a touching incident, and not only did Mrs. Matsumura find her anger vanished into thin air, but so impressed was she by Mrs. Yamamoto's simplicity and purity that she could only think of that lady as a saint. And now Mrs. Matsumura's eyes too began to fill with tears, and she took Mrs. Yamamoto by the hand.

"Please forgive me, please forgive me," she said. "It was wrong of me."

For a while they wept together, holding each other's hands and vowing to each other that henceforth they would be the firmest of friends.

When Mrs. Sasaki heard rumors that the relationship between Mrs. Yamamoto and Mrs. Matsumura, which had been so strained, had suddenly improved, and that Mrs. Azuma and Mrs. Kasuga, who had been such good friends, had suddenly fallen out, she was at a loss to understand the reasons and contented herself with the reflection that nothing was impossible in this world.

However, being a woman of no strong <u>scruples</u>, Mrs. Sasaki requested a jeweler to refashion her ring and to produce a design into which two new pearls could be set, one large and one small, and this she wore quite openly, without further mishap.

Soon she had completely forgotten the small commotion on her birthday, and when anyone asked her age, she would give the same untruthful answers as ever. ❖

Translated by Geoffrey W. Sargent

---

12. **castigation** (kăs′tĭ-gā′shən): the act of punishing or criticizing severely.

WORDS TO KNOW
scruple (skrōō′pəl) *n.* an ethical principle that inhibits action

294

Assessment Option

INFORMAL ASSESSMENT You can informally assess your students' understanding of the selection's theme and satirical aspects by inviting them to update the story so that it takes place in the United States today. Explain that the only things that have to be the same about the story are the number of friends, the effect the incident has on the friendships, and the satire, or social criticism, in the story. Students can write or tell their updated versions.

Rubric
- **3 Full Accomplishment** Students update the setting, plot, and characters while accurately reflecting the relationships and social criticism of Mishima's story.
- **2 Substantial Accomplishment** Students update the story but omit its satirical edge.
- **1 Little or Partial Accomplishment** Students have trouble updating the story and show little understanding of the social criticism it contains.

RESPONDING OPTIONS

FROM PERSONAL RESPONSE TO CRITICAL ANALYSIS

REFLECT 1. In your notebook, jot down your impressions of the five women and their problems.

RETHINK 2. Who do you think is most responsible for the confusion resulting from the loss of the pearl? Explain your opinion.

3. Why do you think these women behave as they do?
Consider
- how the women relate to one another
Close Textual Reading
- the positions in which the women are placed when the pearl is lost
- the ways in which they try to save face
- the mores of their culture

4. Explain whether you think Mrs. Yamamoto's swallowing of the pearl is a good resolution to the situation. What do you think you would have done?

5. If the story had been told by one of the women rather than by a narrator outside the story, how might "The Pearl" have been different?

RELATE 6. Do you think the incidents described in the story could happen in American society today? Why or why not?

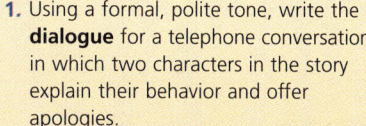

Multimodal Learning
ANOTHER PATHWAY
Cooperative Learning
Working in a small group, organize information from "The Pearl" in a time line. For each scene in the story, indicate the location and the events and characters involved. Share your time line with other groups of classmates. Then discuss what you learned about the story by doing this activity.

QUICKWRITES

1. Using a formal, polite tone, write the **dialogue** for a telephone conversation in which two characters in the story explain their behavior and offer apologies.

2. Imagine that you are directing an adaptation of "The Pearl" for the stage. To help your actresses prepare for their roles, write a brief **character sketch** of each of the five women.

3. Write a draft of a **satiric story** based on an awkward situation you've experienced. The writing you did for the Personal Connection on page 284 can help get you started.

 PORTFOLIO Save your writing. You may want to use it later as a springboard to a piece for your portfolio.

THE PEARL **295**

LITERARY CONCEPTS

Satire is a literary technique in which ideas, customs, behaviors, or institutions are ridiculed for the purpose of improving society. Satire may be gently witty, mildly abrasive, or bitterly critical, and it often uses exaggeration to force readers to see something in a more critical light. What aspects of society would you say "The Pearl" is ridiculing? What improvements to society might Mishima be trying to promote?

CONCEPT REVIEW: Tone In a small group, discuss Mishima's tone, or the attitude he takes toward his subject. List phrases or sentences from the story that support your group's opinions. Then, for each quotation, jot down what you think is being satirized.

From Personal Response to Critical Analysis

1. Accept all reasonable responses.
2. Possible responses: Mrs. Sasaki, because she overreacts to the loss of the pearl; Mrs. Yamamoto, because she began the chain of events with her cruel trick; Mrs. Azuma, because she falsely takes the blame; Mrs. Matsumura, because even when she discovers the pearl she doesn't return it.
3. Possible response: They are concerned with maintaining their reputations and will go to any lengths to keep their good names; the women reflect their society's excessive preoccupation with appearances and politeness.
4. Accept all reasonable, well-supported responses.
5. Possible responses: the reader would not know the other characters' motivations and unspoken feelings; the characters might have been portrayed differently, with the narrator making herself out to be the most dignified and most honest.
6. Possible responses: Yes, because Americans get very upset if they are unjustly accused of something; no, because saving face and maintaining dignity are not as important in American society today.

Another Pathway
Cooperative Learning A group of four might divide the responsibilities as follows: two researchers, one person to draft the timeline, and one person to do a final version.

Rubric
3 Full Accomplishment The timeline contains the correct sequence of events, locations, and characters.
2 Substantial Accomplishment The sequence is generally correct, but some events, locations, or characters are missing.
1 Little or Partial Accomplishment The sequence is incorrect and a substantial number of items have been omitted.

Literary Concepts
Possible responses: Mishima's witty story makes fun of the hypocrisy and deception that people practice to protect their own and others' reputations. He may be trying to promote more honest and open communication in Japanese society.

Tone Possible responses: Some groups may find Mishima's tone to be one of amused contempt, illustrated by such phrases as "being a woman of no strong scruples" and "she could only think of that lady as a saint." Other groups may find his tone to be detached and ironic, illustrated by such phrases as "became a prisoner of her private brand of school-captain morality."

QuickWrites
1. Remind students that it is important that each woman's statements be in character and believable. The dialogue should be formal and indirect, in keeping with their style of speaking.
2. Students can use the webs they created for the mini-lesson on characterization to help them write their character sketches.
3. Suggest that students review satire and keep its elements in mind as they write.

The Writer's Craft
Dialogue, pp. 452–455
Character Sketch, pp. 78–82
Story, pp. 102–107

THE LANGUAGE OF LITERATURE **Teacher's Edition** **295**

Words To Know

1. synonyms
2. synonyms
3. antonyms
4. antonyms
5. antonyms
6. antonyms
7. synonyms
8. synonyms
9. synonyms
10. synonyms

Reteaching/Reinforcement
- *Unit Two Resource Book*, p. 54

Across the Curriculum

History Ask students to research Japanese culture from 1920 to 1960, roughly the span of Mishima's life. Special attention should be paid to changes in Japanese society occurring after 1945. How might these changes be reflected in "The Pearl"?

Science Mrs. Matsumura thinks of the pearl as "an article you could call neither all that expensive nor yet all that cheap." Is that still true about pearls today? Have students research the current pearl market. Which countries produce or harvest pearls? Which countries buy them?

Yukio Mishima

Born to a noble family of the samurai warrior class, Mishima observed the samurai tenets of excellence in the martial arts, indifference to pain, and unquestioning loyalty to the emperor. After World War II ended, Japan adopted a constitution which stripped the emperor of power, and began a process of Westernization. In 1968 Mishima formed a "shield society" whose 83 members were intent on restoring the samurai tradition. In 1970, upon realizing that Japan would never return to its traditional ways, Mishima committed suicide.

Multimodal Learning

ALTERNATIVE ACTIVITIES

1. Draw **caricatures** of the women in "The Pearl" using the medium of your choice. To visualize the characters, review the story, looking for descriptive details and mannerisms that help to portray both the action of the story and the emotional state of each woman. Then choose one line from the story as a caption for each drawing.

2. **Cooperative Learning** In a small group, create and rehearse a satirical **skit** that is a sequel to "The Pearl," a skit in which the five women meet again, at another social gathering. Then perform the skit for your classmates.

THE WRITER'S STYLE

Yukio Mishima wrote "The Pearl" in a formal style that the translator has tried to preserve. The phrasing is often elaborate and indirect. For example, in the fourth paragraph, Mishima wrote, "It now occurred to Mrs. Sasaki that she had no wish to be seen" instead of simply "Mrs. Sasaki did not want to be seen." Find three more examples of formal word choice or indirect phrasing. Why do you think Mishima used such a formal style for this particular story?

WORDS TO KNOW

On your paper, indicate whether the words in each numbered pair below are synonyms or antonyms.

1. infamy—notoriety
2. malicious—wicked
3. prudence—foolishness
4. fastidious—sloppy
5. impetuous—cautious
6. inauspicious—promising
7. incensed—infuriated
8. ambiguous—unclear
9. implicitly—unquestioningly
10. scruple—qualm

YUKIO MISHIMA

Born Kimitake Hiraoka (kē'mĭ-tä'kē hĭ'rä-ō'kä) in Tokyo, Japan, Yukio Mishima adopted his pen name in 1941 when he published his first long work, "The Forest in Full Bloom," in a school magazine. Three years later, as his school's star pupil, Mishima received a special graduation prize from the emperor of Japan. Mishima went on to study law at Tokyo University. He worked for several years in the Ministry of Public Finance before devoting himself to writing.

1925–1970

Mishima's first novel, the semiautobiographical *Confessions of a Mask*, became an instant popular and critical success when it was published in 1949. His writing career then flourished, and he became famous for his many novels, short stories, and essays, as well as for his film writing, acting, and directing. Throughout his lifetime, Mishima was devoted to Japanese culture, values, and history, and his fascination with the Japanese past led him to adapt many traditional plays for the modern stage. Shortly before his premature death by *seppuku*, a ritual form of suicide, Mishima wrote, "I came to wish to sacrifice myself for the old, beautiful tradition of Japan, which is disappearing very quickly day by day."

OTHER WORKS *The Sound of Waves, The Temple of the Golden Pavilion, The Sailor Who Fell from Grace with the Sea, Death in Midsummer and Other Stories, Five Modern No Plays* Extended Reading

296 UNIT TWO PART 2: PRISONERS OF CIRCUMSTANCE

The Writer's Style

Help students understand that Mishima's formal style only serves to emphasize the satirical and humorous qualities of the story.

The Writer's Craft
The Components of Voice, pp. 420–422

Alternative Activities

1. Remind students that caricatures exaggerate one or more of a person's distinctive physical features as well as facial expressions.

2. In preparation for a skit, each group member should review the selection for information about his or her chosen character. The group should exchange different ideas about the best setting for a sequel.

PREVIEWING

NONFICTION

Black Men and Public Space
Brent Staples United States

Activating Prior Knowledge
PERSONAL CONNECTION
Consider the types of people you encounter on the street that make you fearful or uneasy. Why do you think you feel uncomfortable around these people? Are your fears reasonable, or do you think they might be exaggerated? In a group discussion, share your experiences and opinions with your classmates.

Outdoor mall in Manhattan, New York City.
Copyright © Rafael Macia/Photo Researchers, Inc.

Building Background
CULTURAL CONNECTION
Much of the news we are exposed to on television, on the radio, and in newspapers concerns crime; the number of reported car jackings, drive-by shootings, robberies, assaults, and even murders seems to be ever on the rise. Crime rates increase for a variety of reasons, including population growth, drug use, inadequate education, and lack of economic opportunities, especially for the urban poor. Because crime has become widespread, people are often fearful or suspicious of strangers—particularly those that are different from themselves—even when the strangers mean no harm. In the essay you are about to read, writer Brent Staples shows that while crime itself is a problem, the fear in which people sometimes live creates another set of problems.

Setting a Purpose
WRITING CONNECTION
If you were walking down the street late at night, do you think other people on the street might feel afraid of you? Explore your thoughts in a paragraph or two in your notebook. Then put yourself in Brent Staples's shoes as you read his essay.

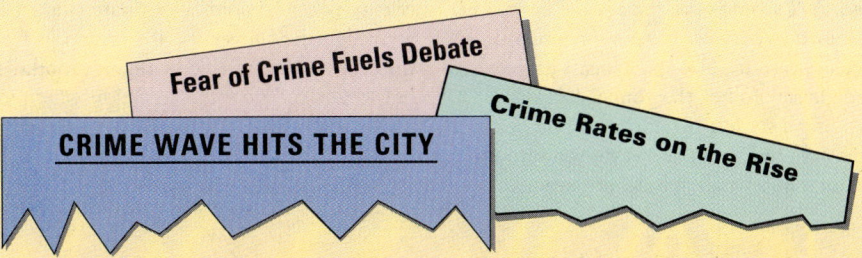

BLACK MEN AND PUBLIC SPACE   **297**

OVERVIEW

Objectives
- To understand and appreciate an essay that explores one man's experience of racial prejudice
- To identify and understand structure
- To express understanding of the selection through a choice of writing forms, including a descriptive paragraph, a dramatic scene, an editorial, and a personal narrative
- To extend understanding of the selection through a variety of multimodal and cross-curricular activities

Skills

LITERARY CONCEPTS
- Structure

GENRE STUDY
- Essay

GRAMMAR
- Noun clauses

SPEAKING, LISTENING, AND VIEWING
- Interviews
- Group discussion
- Oral presentation

CUSTOMIZING FOR
Students Acquiring English

- Use **ACCESS FOR STUDENTS ACQUIRING ENGLISH,** *Reading Support.*
- "Black Men and Public Space" contains deft phrasing, figurative language, sophisticated vocabulary, and sentence structure and references to urban life that may be troubling to some students. Encourage students to read for overall comprehension of what Staples experienced, how it made him feel, and what he eventually chose as a solution to his problem.
- In addition to these boxes, you may want to use the suggestions under Strategic Reading for Less-Proficient Readers.

PRINT AND MEDIA RESOURCES

UNIT TWO RESOURCE BOOK
Strategic Reading: Literature, p. 57
Vocabulary SkillBuilder, p. 58

GRAMMAR MINI-LESSONS
Transparencies, p. 50

ACCESS FOR STUDENTS ACQUIRING ENGLISH
Selection Summaries
Reading Support

FORMAL ASSESSMENT
Selection Test, p. 57
 Test Generator

 AUDIO LIBRARY
See Reference Card

THE LANGUAGE OF LITERATURE TEACHER'S EDITION   **297**

Black Men and Public Space

Brent Staples

Homage to Sterling Brown (1972), Charles White. Collection of Dr. Edmund Gordon, courtesy of the Heritage Gallery, Los Angeles.

My first victim was a woman—white, well dressed, probably in her early twenties. I came upon her late one evening on a deserted street in Hyde Park, a relatively <u>affluent</u> neighborhood in an otherwise mean, impoverished section of Chicago. As I swung onto the avenue behind her, there seemed to be a discreet, uninflammatory[1] distance between us. Not so. She cast back a worried glance. To her, the youngish black man—a broad six feet two inches with a beard and billowing hair, both hands shoved into the pockets of a bulky military jacket—seemed menacingly close. After a few more quick glimpses, she picked up her pace and was soon running in earnest. Within seconds she disappeared into a cross street.

That was more than a decade ago. I was twenty-two years old, a graduate student newly arrived at the University of Chicago. It was in the echo of that terrified woman's footfalls that I first began to know the <u>unwieldy</u> inheritance I'd

---

1. **uninflammatory** (ŭn´ĭn-flăm´ə-tôr´ē): not likely to rouse excitement, anger, or violence.

WORDS TO KNOW
affluent (ăf´lōō-ənt) *adj.* prosperous; rich
unwieldy (ŭn-wēl´dē) *adj.* hard to handle; awkward

298

WORDS TO KNOW

affluent (ăf´lōō-ənt) *adj.* prosperous, rich (p. 298)
avid (ăv´ĭd) *adj.* marked by keen interest and enthusiasm (p. 299)
congenial (kən-jēn´yəl) *adj.* agreeable, sociable; sympathetic (p. 300)
cursory (kûr´sə-rē) *adj.* performed with haste and little attention to detail (p. 300)
elicit (ĭ-lĭs´ĭt) *v.* to bring out, to call forth (p. 299)
errant (ĕr´ənt) *adj.* straying from the proper course or standards (p. 299)
retrospect (rĕt´rə-spĕkt´) *n.* a review or examination of things in the past (p. 300)
solace (sŏl´ĭs) *n.* comfort; consolation (p. 299)
taut (tôt) *adj.* tense, strained (p. 299)
unwieldy (ŭn-wēl´dē) *adj.* hard to handle, awkward (p. 298)

come into—the ability to alter public space in ugly ways. It was clear that she thought herself the quarry[2] of a mugger, a rapist, or worse. Suffering a bout of insomnia, however, I was stalking sleep, not defenseless wayfarers. As a softy who is scarcely able to take a knife to a raw chicken—let alone hold one to a person's throat—I was surprised, embarrassed, and dismayed all at once. Her flight made me feel like an accomplice in tyranny. It also made it clear that I was indistinguishable from the muggers who occasionally seeped into the area from the surrounding ghetto. That first encounter, and those that followed, signified that a vast, unnerving gulf lay between nighttime pedestrians—particularly women—and me. And I soon gathered that being perceived as dangerous is a hazard in itself. I only needed to turn a corner into a dicey[3] situation, or crowd some frightened, armed person in a foyer somewhere, or make an errant move after being pulled over by a policeman. Where fear and weapons meet—and they often do in urban America—there is always the possibility of death.

In that first year, my first away from my hometown, I was to become thoroughly familiar with the language of fear. At dark, shadowy intersections, I could cross in front of a car stopped at a traffic light and elicit the *thunk, thunk, thunk, thunk* of the driver—black, white, male, or female—hammering down the door locks. On less traveled streets after dark, I grew accustomed to but never comfortable with people crossing to the other side of the street rather than pass me. Then there were the standard unpleasantries with policemen, doormen, bouncers, cabdrivers, and others whose business it is to screen out troublesome individuals *before* there is any nastiness.

I moved to New York nearly two years ago, and I have remained an avid night walker. In central Manhattan, the near-constant crowd cover minimizes tense one-on-one street encounters. Elsewhere—in SoHo,[4] for example, where sidewalks are narrow and tightly spaced buildings shut out the sky—things can get very taut indeed.

After dark, on the warrenlike[5] streets of Brooklyn where I live, I often see women who fear the worst from me. They seem to have set their faces on neutral, and with their purse straps strung across their chests bandolier-style, they forge ahead as though bracing themselves against being tackled. I understand, of course, that the danger they perceive is not a hallucination. Women are particularly vulnerable to street violence, and young black males are drastically overrepresented among the perpetrators of that violence. Yet these truths are no solace against the kind of alienation that comes of being ever the suspect, a fearsome entity[6] with whom pedestrians avoid making eye contact.

It is not altogether clear to me how I reached the ripe old age of twenty-two without being conscious of the lethality[7] nighttime pedestrians attributed to me. Perhaps it was because in Chester, Pennsylvania, the small, angry industrial town where I came of age in the 1960s, I was scarcely noticeable against a backdrop of

---

2. **quarry:** prey; object of pursuit.
3. **dicey:** risky; hazardous.
4. **SoHo** (sō′hō′): a neighborhood in Manhattan.
5. **warrenlike** (wôr′ən-līk): like a rabbit warren, the area in which a colony of rabbits lives in burrows; like a maze, a place where one may easily become lost.
6. **entity** (ĕn′tĭ-tē): thing or being.
7. **lethality** (lē-thăl′ĭ-tē): the ability to cause extreme harm or death.

WORDS TO KNOW
errant (ĕr′ənt) *adj.* straying from the proper course or standards
elicit (ĭ-lĭs′ĭt) *v.* to bring out; to call forth
avid (ăv′ĭd) *adj.* marked by keen interest and enthusiasm
taut (tôt) *adj.* tense; strained
solace (sŏl′ĭs) *n.* comfort; consolation

299

Mini-Lesson Grammar

NOUN CLAUSES Tell students that a noun clause is a subordinate clause used in a sentence as a noun. Consequently, noun clauses can function as subjects, direct objects, indirect objects, predicate nominatives, and objects of prepositions. Noun clauses are introduced by pronouns or by subordinating conjunctions. Have students study the chalkboard as shown here, then point out the sentence  on this page as an example. Ask students to scan this page for other examples of noun clauses.

"I understand, of course, *that the danger they perceive is not a hallucination.*" (noun clause used as a direct object)

Application Have students write three sentences with subordinate clauses, one of which functions as the subject, one as a direct object, and one as the object of a preposition.

Reteaching/Reinforcement
• *Grammar Mini-Lessons* transparencies, p. 50

The Writer's Craft
Noun Clauses, pp. 615–616

NOUN CLAUSES
Pronouns: who, whom, which, what, that, whoever, whomever, whatever
Subordinating Conjunctions: how, that, when, where, whether, why

---

CUSTOMIZING FOR Students Acquiring English

1 Go over what the author means when he says he "alter[s] public space in ugly ways." Point out that the public space he is referring to is more mental than physical; he alters it by arousing fear in people.

Literary Concept: IRONY

B Help students see the irony in Staple's situation: the fact that people are afraid he will injure them makes it more likely that he himself will be injured.

Literary Concept: DESCRIPTION

C Invite students to visualize the scene Staples describes here. Then ask why they think he included the repetitive and onomatopoeic phrase "thunk, thunk, thunk, thunk." (Possible responses: to appeal to readers' sense of hearing; to show how startling and insulting the sound is)

CUSTOMIZING FOR Students Acquiring English

2 Explain that the women the author sees can be compared to a car in neutral gear, which goes neither one way nor the other. Staples is emphasizing that the women are neither friendly nor openly rude, but that they are tensed to meet a possible attack.

Cultural Note

D African Americans also make up the majority of crime victims in this country. In 1991, for example, there were 10,628 African-American male homicide victims compared to 9,581 white male homicide victims.

Literary Concept: STRUCTURE

E Ask students why they think Staples presents several examples of his own and other African-American men's encounters with frightened people. *(Possible responses: to stress that his experience is not unique; to support the essay's thesis that black men are often stereotyped as criminals.)*

Critical Thinking: MAKING JUDGMENTS

F Ask students if they agree with Staples's approach of smothering his rage and avoiding others before they can avoid him. *(Answers will vary.)*

CUSTOMIZING FOR
Multiple Learning Styles

G **Musical Learners** You may wish to play Vivaldi's "Four Seasons" or a Beethoven piece. Ask students to discuss how whistling this type of tune might allay people's fears.

CUSTOMIZING FOR
Gifted and Talented Students

In America, a person is presumed innocent until proven guilty. Ask students to discuss this precept in relation to the essay.

COMPREHENSION CHECK

1. How does Staples know people fear him? *(They lock their doors; women are defensive; police are suspicious of him.)*
2. Why does Staples now whistle classical music when he walks after dark? *(to give the impression that he is harmless)*

---

gang warfare, street knifings, and murders. I grew up one of the good boys, had perhaps a half-dozen fistfights. In retrospect, my shyness of combat has clear sources.

As a boy, I saw countless tough guys locked away; I have since buried several, too. They were babies, really—a teenage cousin, a brother of twenty-two, a childhood friend in his mid-twenties—all gone down in episodes of bravado[8] played out in the streets. I came to doubt the virtues of intimidation early on. I chose, perhaps unconsciously, to remain a shadow—timid, but a survivor.

E The fearsomeness mistakenly attributed to me in public places often has a perilous flavor. The most frightening of these confusions occurred in the late 1970s and early 1980s, when I worked as a journalist in Chicago. One day, rushing into the office of a magazine I was writing for with a deadline story in hand, I was mistaken for a burglar. The office manager called security and, with an ad hoc posse,[9] pursued me through the labyrinthine[10] halls, nearly to my editor's door. I had no way of proving who I was. I could only move briskly toward the company of someone who knew me.

Another time I was on assignment for a local paper and killing time before an interview. I entered a jewelry store on the city's affluent Near North Side. The proprietor excused herself and returned with an enormous red Doberman pinscher straining at the end of a leash. She stood, the dog extended toward me, silent to my questions, her eyes bulging nearly out of her head. I took a cursory look around, nodded, and bade her good night.

Relatively speaking, however, I never fared as badly as another black male journalist. He went to nearby Waukegan, Illinois, a couple of summers ago to work on a story about a murderer who was born there. Mistaking the reporter for the killer, police officers hauled him from his car at gunpoint and but for his press credentials would probably have tried to book him. Such episodes are not uncommon. Black men trade tales like this all the time.

F Over the years, I learned to smother the rage I felt at so often being taken for a criminal. Not to do so would surely have led to madness. I now take precautions to make myself less threatening. I move about with care, particularly late in the evening. I give a wide berth[11] to nervous people on subway platforms during the wee hours, particularly when I have exchanged business clothes for jeans. If I happen to be entering a building behind some people who appear skittish,[12] I may walk by, letting them clear the lobby before I return, so as not to seem to be following them. I have been calm and extremely congenial on those rare occasions when I've been pulled over by the police.

G And on late-evening constitutionals[13] I employ what has proved to be an excellent tension-reducing measure: I whistle melodies from Beethoven and Vivaldi and the more popular classical composers. Even steely New Yorkers hunching toward nighttime destinations seem to relax, and occasionally they even join the tune. Virtually everybody seems to sense that a mugger wouldn't be warbling bright, sunny selections from Vivaldi's *Four Seasons*. It is my equivalent to the cowbell that hikers wear when they know they are in bear country. ❖

---

8. **bravado** (brə-vä′dō): pretended courage or defiant confidence when there is really little or none.
9. **ad hoc posse:** a group of people that has been brought together to form a search party.
10. **labyrinthine** (lăb′ə-rĭn′thĭn): like a labyrinth, or maze.
11. **wide berth:** ample space or distance to avoid an unwanted consequence.
12. **skittish:** nervous; jumpy.
13. **constitutionals:** walks taken for one's health.

WORDS TO KNOW
retrospect (rĕt′rə-spĕkt′) *n.* a review or examination of things in the past
cursory (kûr′sə-rē) *adj.* performed with haste and little attention to detail
congenial (kən-jēn′yəl) *adj.* agreeable; sociable; sympathetic

300

Mini-Lesson   Genre Study

NONFICTION Remind students that **essays** are short nonfiction pieces that usually deal with a single subject. The purpose of an essay can be to entertain readers, to persuade readers of something, to inform readers about a topic, or to give the author's opinion on a subject. Often, essays have more than one purpose.

Application Invite students to analyze Staples's purpose in writing "Black Men and Public Space." Suggest that they look back through the essay for sentences and phrases that provide clues to his purpose, such as "I first began to know the unwieldy inheritance . . ." and "Yet these truths are no solace." Also have them note that Staples does not exhort the reader to action. Students should recognize that his primary purposes are to inform readers about the predicament of black men in public spaces and to give his opinion about this predicament.

RESPONDING OPTIONS

FROM PERSONAL RESPONSE TO CRITICAL ANALYSIS

REFLECT
1. What is your response to this essay? Record your response in your notebook.

RETHINK

Close Textual Reading

2. How would you describe Brent Staples? **Consider**
   - his description of himself in the first two paragraphs
   - what he says about his childhood
   - the fact that he takes precautions to make himself "less threatening"
3. What is your opinion of the way people respond to Staples? Be sure to draw on examples from the selection in explaining your point of view.
4. Do you approve of the ways Staples chooses to deal with the fears of others? Explain your opinion.
5. Why do you think Staples concludes his essay with the image of a hiker wearing a bell in bear country?

RELATE
6. Think back to your discussion in the Personal Connection and to what you wrote for the Writing Connection on page 297. Did anything in Staples's essay cause you to reexamine your own feelings and behavior?

LITERARY CONCEPTS

Structure is the way in which a work of literature is put together. In prose, structure is the arrangement of units or parts of a selection. Staples begins his essay "Black Men and Public Space" by describing a woman's perception of him that contrasts with his true identity. Next, he describes the predicament he faces as an African American and elaborates on his experience by providing specific examples. He concludes by explaining how he has adapted his behavior over time. With a partner, discuss how the structure of the essay affected your thoughts and feelings about the author. How did your ideas about him change from the beginning to the end of the selection?

Multimodal Learning
ANOTHER PATHWAY

Write a review of "Black Men and Public Space" for a column in a student newspaper. Explain your opinion about the essay and about the problems Staples describes. Be sure to include a summary of the essay in your review.

QUICKWRITES

1. Write a **descriptive paragraph** of Staples from the point of view of the female "victim" presented in the first paragraph of the essay. Then write another paragraph that describes Staples as he sees himself.
2. Write a **dramatic scene** based on one of the incidents in Staples's essay. Include dialogue as well as stage directions describing action.
3. In an **editorial** for your school or local newspaper, explain how people's prejudices or fears have threatened or damaged the dignity of African-American men or some other group.
4. Draft a **personal narrative** describing a time when another person did not perceive the truth about you.

 **PORTFOLIO** Save your writing. You may want to use it later as a springboard to a piece for your portfolio.

BLACK MEN AND PUBLIC SPACE **301**

From Personal Response to Critical Analysis

1. Accept all reasonable responses.
2. Possible responses: physically large; sensitive to other people's feelings; timid; intelligent; adaptable
3. Possible responses: it's racist and insulting, particularly the incident with the woman and the Doberman; it's understandable, considering that women alone on the street at night are vulnerable, and, as Staples himself says, a large proportion of crimes are committed by black men.
4. Possible responses: yes, because he shows sensitivity to others' feelings, and more aggressive reactions might just lead to violence; no, because his actions implicitly condone a racist fear.
5. Possible responses: to emphasize the fact that he feels he is the victim; to emphasize the fact that he is harmless
6. Accept all reasonable, well-supported responses.

Another Pathway
If your school has no newspaper, students can post their reviews on a hallway bulletin board or make copies to distribute to other classes.

Rubric

3 Full Accomplishment Students summarize the essay accurately and support their critique with facts and details.

2 Substantial Accomplishment Students summarize and critique the essay, but they fail to support their opinions with details.

1 Little or Partial Accomplishment Students do not accurately summarize the essay or support their critique.

Literary Concepts
Accept all reasonable, well-supported responses. Most students will sympathize with the frustration an innocent man feels at being constantly suspected and misjudged, noting that their outrage grows as the essay progresses.

QuickWrites
1. Make sure that students note that two different first-person points of view are required.
2. Remind students that to be most effective, their scenes should include some kind of conflict.
3. Point out that an editorial writer states an opinion and then supports it with facts and details.
4. Remind students that a personal narrative tells a story and describes the writer's feelings.

The Writer's Craft
Character Sketch, pp. 78–82
Editorial, pp. 228–232
Dramatic Scene, p. 112
Autobiographical Narrative, pp. 26–41

Words to Know

1. c
2. b
3. c
4. a
5. c
6. b
7. a
8. a
9. b
10. c

Reteaching/Reinforcement
- Unit Two Resource Book, p. 58.

Literary Links

Possible responses: Some students may say they would have applauded his nonviolent solution; others may suggest they would have encouraged him to work peacefully toward changing people's perceptions of black men.

Art Connections

Possible responses: because of the target on the central figure, this painting underscores Staples' idea that black men are victims of, or "targets" of, society's prejudice and misconceptions; the inclusion of many background faces makes the painting resemble a police line-up, reinforcing the stereotype of African-American men as criminals.

Across the Curriculum

Psychology Cooperative Learning Encourage students to conduct group interviews with the police officer. One student could write down the group's interview questions, another could actually conduct the interview, and a third could report on the results of the group's interview to the rest of the class.

LITERARY LINKS
What do you think Martin Luther King, Jr., Coretta Scott King, or another person featured in "Montgomery Boycott" might have said to Staples about his predicament and about the way he altered his behavior to make himself seem less threatening?

ART CONNECTION
Why do you think the painting on page 298, titled *Homage to Sterling Brown*, was chosen to accompany the essay "Black Men and Public Space"?

Detail of *Homage to Sterling Brown* (1972), Charles White. Collection of Dr. Edmund Gordon, courtesy of Heritage Gallery, Los Angeles.

WORDS TO KNOW

EXERCISE A Write the letter of the word that is most nearly the opposite of the word in bold print.

1. **cursory:** (a) polite, (b) unclear, (c) thorough
2. **unwieldy:** (a) clumsy, (b) manageable, (c) huge
3. **congenial:** (a) ill, (b) unspoken, (c) unfriendly
4. **taut:** (a) relaxed, (b) stern, (c) ignorant
5. **retrospect:** (a) review, (b) test, (c) forecast
6. **affluent:** (a) dry, (b) poor, (c) bilingual
7. **avid:** (a) uninterested, (b) wet, (c) eager
8. **solace:** (a) distress, (b) friendship, (c) dimness
9. **elicit:** (a) allow, (b) stifle, (c) accuse
10. **errant:** (a) roaming, (b) false, (c) truthful

EXERCISE B Working with a partner, write the ten Words to Know on small pieces of paper, fold the pieces, and mix them up. Then take turns choosing a word and drawing a picture to illustrate the word for your partner. To make the game more challenging, set a time limit for drawing and guessing the words.

Multimodal Learning
ACROSS THE CURRICULUM

Psychology Interview a police officer to find out how to avoid becoming a victim of a street crime or how to avoid being perceived as a threat. Share your findings with the class in an oral report.

BRENT STAPLES

1951–

The incidents Brent Staples recounts in this essay were incorporated into his 1994 memoir, *Parallel Time: Growing Up in Black and White,* a work that shows how he escaped his difficult home life and impoverished neighborhood in the racially mixed industrial city of Chester, Pennsylvania. Staples came from a family of nine children, and gang violence, drugs, and street crime were prevalent in his community. In fact, Staples's own brother Blake became a drug dealer and was shot to death at the age of 22 by a former customer. By the time his younger brother was killed, however, Staples had already graduated from college and earned his doctorate in psychology from the University of Chicago. He then became a journalist, writing for the *Chicago Sun Times* and other publications before joining the staff of the *New York Times* in 1985. He is now on that paper's editorial board, and he writes on politics and culture.

Alternative Activities

1. Invite students to make collages showing how they think different ethnic groups in the United States perceive each other. They can use their own drawings as well as words and pictures cut out from newspapers and magazines.
2. Suggest that student groups create skits about an encounter of the type Staples describes in his essay, but with three alternative endings. After each skit, the class can discuss which of the alternatives they thought was the best response and why.

PREVIEWING

POETRY

Miss Rosie
Lucille Clifton United States

Kitchenette Building
Gwendolyn Brooks United States

PERSONAL CONNECTION *Activating Prior Knowledge*

Think about a person or a place in your everyday life that means something to you. How would you describe your subject? What essential images would you use if you were to write a poem about that person or place? Brainstorm a list of words or phrases to describe your subject. Remember that sometimes you can define what something is by showing what it is not.

Building Background

BIOGRAPHICAL CONNECTION

The poems you are about to read were written by two widely read and critically acclaimed African-American poets. Lucille Clifton, author of "Miss Rosie," has been inspired to write by the urban community in which she lives. She also acknowledges that she writes from her experience as a woman, or more particularly, as a black woman. Like Lucille Clifton, Gwendolyn Brooks writes from personal experience and from what she sees and hears in her community. She says, "In my writing I am proud to feature people and their concerns, their troubles as well as their joys." Her poem "Kitchenette Building" is about everyday life in a type of apartment house found in low-income urban areas, in which the small apartments have compact kitchens and the bathrooms are shared by the tenants on a floor.

Active Reading/Setting a Purpose

READING CONNECTION

Making Inferences in Poetry An inference is a logical guess or conclusion based on known facts or evidence. When reading a poem, you can make inferences from ideas that are stated directly as well as from ideas that are presented in figurative language. In the two poems that follow, the literal and figurative details allow you to make inferences about the everyday people and places they describe. In your notebook, make a chart like the one below for each of the two poems and fill it out as you read.

Detail from Poem	Inference
"old man's shoes with the little toe cut out"	She's too poor to buy shoes for herself.

Public housing project in Chicago. AP/Wide World Photos.

MISS ROSIE / KITCHENETTE BUILDING **303**

OVERVIEW

Objectives

- To understand and appreciate lyric poetry that explores how poverty can imprison people
- To identify and examine the speaker in poetry
- To express understanding of the poems through a choice of writing forms, including a poem and a report card
- To extend understanding of the poems through a variety of multimodal and cross-curricular activities

Skills

READING SKILLS/ STRATEGIES
- Making inferences

THE WRITER'S STYLE
- Sound devices

LITERARY CONCEPTS
- Speaker

SPEAKING, LISTENING, AND VIEWING
- Choral reading
- Group discussion
- Oral presentation

Thematic Link: *Prisoners of Circumstance* Poverty and old age imprison the subjects of these two lyric poems.

CUSTOMIZING FOR
Students Acquiring English

- Use **ACCESS FOR STUDENTS ACQUIRING ENGLISH,** *Reading Support.*
- These poems do not have the kind of set rhythm and rhyme schemes students often associate with poetry. In addition, the compressed language may cause students some problems. Have them jot down puzzling lines and then help them to rephrase these into prose.
- In addition to these boxes, you may want to use the suggestions under Strategic Reading for Less-Proficient Readers.

PRINT AND MEDIA RESOURCES

UNIT TWO RESOURCE BOOK
Strategic Reading: Literature, p. 61

ACCESS FOR STUDENTS ACQUIRING ENGLISH
Reading Support

FORMAL ASSESSMENT
Selection Test, p. 59
 Test Generator

 AUDIO LIBRARY
See Reference Card

 LASERLINKS
Author Background

THE LANGUAGE OF LITERATURE TEACHER'S EDITION **303**

Literary Concept:
FIGURATIVE LANGUAGE

A Invite students to identify and discuss the similes and metaphors in this poem. Ask them to explain the meaning of *wrapped up like garbage*, *next week's grocery*, and *wet brown bag of a woman*. Ask what mood they feel these figures of speech evoke. *(dismal; depressing)*

Literary Concept: IMAGERY

B Ask students to note all the sensory images Clifton uses in this poem and to discuss the impact these images have on their reading of the poem.

Literary Concept: SPEAKER

C Ask students how they think the speaker's attitude changes from line 15 to line 16. *(Possible response: from one of sorrow or scorn to one of pride and self assurance)*

CUSTOMIZING FOR
Students Acquiring English

1 Tell students that *waiting for your mind* means "waiting for one's sanity to return; trying to orient oneself."

From Personal Response to Critical Analysis

1. Accept all reasonable responses.
2. Accept all reasonable, well-supported responses.
3. Possible responses: the speaker is intrigued by Miss Rosie; the speaker is angry that Miss Rosie has to live this way; the speaker is sorrowful that Miss Rosie's beauty has faded; the speaker admires Miss Rosie's endurance.
4. Possible responses: She used to be admired and have fun, but now she is decrepit and impoverished; she used to be popular, but now no one cares about her.

Miss Rosie
Lucille Clifton

A When I watch you
     wrapped up like garbage
B sitting, surrounded by the smell
     of too old potato peels
5   or
     when I watch you
     in your old man's shoes
     with the little toe cut out
  sitting, waiting for your mind
10   like next week's grocery
     I say
     when I watch you
     you wet brown bag of a woman
     who used to be the best looking gal in Georgia
15   used to be called the Georgia Rose
C I stand up
     through your destruction
     I stand up

FROM PERSONAL RESPONSE TO CRITICAL ANALYSIS

REFLECT 1. What person or persons does Miss Rosie remind you of? Discuss your response with a partner.

RETHINK 2. Describe your mental picture of Miss Rosie.

3. How do you think the speaker feels about Miss Rosie?
   Consider
   • why the speaker keeps repeating "when I watch you"
   • the meaning of "I stand up / through your destruction" (lines 16–17)

Close Textual Reading

4. What speculations can you make about the way Miss Rosie used to live and about the way she lives now? Use information from the chart you created for the Reading Connection on page 303.

304   UNIT TWO   PART 2: PRISONERS OF CIRCUMSTANCE

Mini-Lesson: Speaking, Listening, and Viewing

CHORAL READING Remind students that effective choral readings are synchronized recitations designed to emphasize a poem's meaning and highlight certain passages. Useful methods include reading in rounds, reading alternative stanzas, and using a musical instrument as accompaniment.

Application Have students form groups of four or five and plan a choral reading of one of these poems. Groups can present their readings in class.

Kitchenette Building

Gwendolyn Brooks

Shaded Lives (1988), Phoebe Beasley. Collage, 40″ × 30″, collection of Alex Gallery, Washington, D.C.

We are things of dry hours and the involuntary plan,
Grayed in, and gray. "Dream" makes a giddy sound, not strong
Like "rent," "feeding a wife," "satisfying a man."

But could a dream send up through onion fumes
5 Its white and violet, fight with fried potatoes
And yesterday's garbage ripening in the hall,
Flutter, or sing an aria[1] down these rooms

Even if we were willing to let it in,
Had time to warm it, keep it very clean,
10 Anticipate a message, let it begin?

We wonder. But not well! not for a minute!
Since Number Five is out of the bathroom now,
We think of lukewarm water, hope to get in it.

---

1. **aria** (är′ē-ə): a song or melody for a solo voice in an opera.

Literary Concept: IMAGERY

D Ask students to identify and discuss the sensory details Brooks uses to create images in this poem. *(Possible responses: "grayed in and gray," "giddy sound," "onion fumes," "white and violet," "fried potatoes," "garbage ripening," "flutter," "sing an aria," "lukewarm water")* Then have students divide these images into those associated with dreams and those with the tenement. How might students characterize each group of images? *(images associated with dreams are light and airy; those with the tenement are heavy, pungent, and dark)*

Literary Concept: THEME

E Ask students what they think the speaker's message is about the role of dreams in the setting she describes? *(Possible responses: Dreams have a hard time surviving in the struggle for everyday necessities; dreams are important but difficult to nurture in a tenement.)*

Art Note

Shaded Lives by Phoebe Beasley
This collage, made of found objects, cutout tissue paper forms, Japanese block print paper, and paint, deals with the secret and fleeting glimpses that people often get of one another's lives. The canvas frame is used to create four separate "windows," each of which partially reveals the interiors and inhabitants inside. This collage can also be seen as a metaphor for people's inner selves. As Beasley states, "Each of our lives are shaded and compartmentalized, physically and mentally."

Reading the Art *What does this collage say to you about separateness? about living in close quarters? about poverty?*

Mini-Lesson — The Writer's Style

SOUND DEVICES Point out that each of these poems effectively uses sound devices. "Miss Rosie" relies on alliteration in phrases like "sitting, surrounded by the smell," "potato peels," and "brown bag" to emphasize images. The repetition of phrases such as "when I watch you" and "I stand up" emphasizes the speaker's attitude toward Miss Rosie. "Kitchenette Building" uses the sound device of rhyme (plan/man, fumes/rooms, in/begin, minute/in it), perhaps to emphasize the ongoing pattern of poverty in these people's lives.

Application Invite students to create poems about their own homes or an elderly person they know. Encourage them to use one or more sound devices in their poems. Besides the ones mentioned here, they could use assonance, consonance, and rhythm.

Reteaching/Reinforcement

The Writer's Craft
Sound Devices, p. 427

From Personal Response to Critical Analysis

1. Accept all reasonable responses.
2. Possible responses: drab; noisy; smelly; hopeless; impoverished; hard; no choices; focused on everyday survival
3. Possible responses: the dream is about improving lives, as lines like "its white and violet, fight with . . ." show; the dream is about fulfilling hopes or finding beauty, as phrases like "giddy sound" and "sing an aria" show.
4. Possible responses: no, the people have no time for dreams; the ugliness and routine of life there would kill dreams; yes, but only with constant attention and care.
5. Accept all reasonable responses. Possible responses: the characters are all prisoners of poverty; Miss Rosie is alone while the characters in "Kitchenette Building" are crowded together. Miss Rosie was known as a beauty, and the tenants of "Kitchenette Building" are seeking beauty.
6. Accept all reasonable, well-supported responses.

Another Pathway

Cooperative Learning Suggest that one student lead the group in a discussion to figure out each poem's meaning and tone; another student can record the group's ideas. Other group members can actually perform the reading or give feedback to readers as they practice.

Rubric

3 Full Accomplishment The reading is presented well and insightfully incorporates the poems' meanings and tones.

2 Substantial Accomplishment The general meaning and tone of each poem is conveyed, but the reading shows lack of rehearsal.

1 Little or Partial Accomplishment The reading is disorganized and doesn't express the meanings or tones of the poems.

RESPONDING OPTIONS

FROM PERSONAL RESPONSE TO CRITICAL ANALYSIS

REFLECT 1. What images from everyday life came to mind as you were reading "Kitchenette Building"? Describe or draw them in your notebook.

RETHINK 2. What words and phrases would you use to describe the kind of life the tenants of the kitchenette building lead?
   Consider
   - what the phrases "dry hours," "involuntary plan," and "grayed in, and gray" might mean (lines 1–2)
   - what lines 4–7 say about the tenants' environment
   - the concerns named in lines 3 and 12–13
   - information from the chart you created for the Reading Connection on page 303

Close Textual Reading

3. How would you describe the kind of dream this poem is talking about? Use details from the poem to support your response.
4. Does the speaker seem to think a dream can survive in this building?

RELATE 5. Do you think that the characters in "Miss Rosie" and "Kitchenette Building" are prisoners of the same circumstances? What is similar and what is different about their situations?

Thematic Link

Literary Link 6. Which poem's imagery do you think has stronger sensory appeal? Why?

Multimodal Learning
ANOTHER PATHWAY
Cooperative Learning
With a small group of classmates, prepare a dramatic reading of the poems. To do this, you will first need to discuss the meaning of each poem and determine the tone. Present your reading to the entire class.

LITERARY CONCEPTS

The **speaker** in a poem is the voice that talks to the reader, similar to the narrator in fiction. Through inference the reader can learn many things about the speaker in a poem, insights that in turn enhance the poem's meaning. Who is the speaker in "Miss Rosie"? What do you think is that speaker's relationship to Rosie? Who is the speaker in "Kitchenette Building"? Why do you think the speaker uses the pronoun "we"?

CONCEPT REVIEW: Theme Do the messages about life communicated in these two poems apply to both the rich and the poor? Explain your answer.

QUICKWRITES

1. Adapt each poem into a new **poem** with a different speaker. For example, you might make Miss Rosie the speaker of one poem.
2. Prepare a **report card** for Clifton and Brooks in which you evaluate each poem on the basis of theme, imagery, word choice, and overall effectiveness.

📁 **PORTFOLIO** Save your writing. You may want to use it later as a springboard to a piece for your portfolio.

306 UNIT TWO PART 2: PRISONERS OF CIRCUMSTANCE

Literary Concepts

The speaker in "Miss Rosie" may be a relative, neighbor, or friend. The speaker in "Kitchenette Building" seems to be one of the tenants; she uses the pronoun we because she speaks for all of the building's inhabitants, and perhaps for everyone who is in a similar situation.

Theme Some students may feel the messages do apply to both rich and poor, especially the message of "Miss Rosie," because loneliness and senility can strike anyone. Also, focusing on day-to-day existence could lead someone from any economic level to lose his or her dreams. Others may think that the messages are specifically about the indignities of poverty and therefore cannot be applied to the rich.

QuickWrites

1. Remind students that if Miss Rosie is the speaker, the poem should reflect her wandering train of thought.
2. Suggest that students set up these report cards like real ones, with each category listed as a "subject." Remind students that most report cards give not only a grade for each subject, but also comment about the student's (poet's) strengths, weaknesses, and areas where "improvement is needed."

Poetry, pp. 88–101
Standards of Evaluation, p. 97

Multimodal Learning

ALTERNATIVE ACTIVITIES

1. Working with a small group of classmates, select additional poems by Gwendolyn Brooks and Lucille Clifton for **oral reading**. After presenting the poems, try to identify the speaker of each one, and compare the content and style of the new poems with that of "Miss Rosie" and "Kitchenette Building."

2. Paint or sketch two **portraits** of Miss Rosie, one showing her as she is today and another showing her when she was called the Georgia Rose.

CRITIC'S CORNER

According to critic Audrey T. McCluskey, "Lucille Clifton writes with conviction; she always takes a moral and hopeful stance." Based on your reading of "Miss Rosie," do you think this statement is true? Would you say the observation is true of Gwendolyn Brooks? Explain your opinions.

THE WRITER'S STYLE

Lucille Clifton once said, "I am interested in trying to render big ideas in a simple way." To what extent does "Miss Rosie" illustrate Clifton's approach to writing?

LUCILLE CLIFTON

1936–

Lucille Clifton writes frequently about the struggles and triumphs of African-American families living in urban communities, emphasizing "endurance and strength through adversity." Of her youth in Depew, New York, Clifton says, "I grew up a well-loved child in a loving family, and so I have always known that being poor, which we were, had nothing to do with lovingness or familyness or character." She tries to bring this understanding to her writing, particularly to her works for young people. A mother of six, Clifton has published more than 20 books for children, including a popular series about a little boy named Everett Anderson. Among her collections of poetry for adults are *Good Times*, which includes "Miss Rosie," and *Book of Light*. She also coauthored the Emmy Award–winning television program *Free to Be . . . You and Me*. Clifton has received many awards and honors for her writing, including a Pulitzer Prize nomination and National Endowment for the Arts awards. She served as the poet laureate of Maryland from 1979 to 1982.

OTHER WORKS *Good News About the Earth: New Poems; Generations: A Memoir* Extended Reading

GWENDOLYN BROOKS

1917–

A lifelong resident of Chicago, Illinois, Gwendolyn Brooks frequently writes about the lives of the urban poor. As a child she was an avid reader, and she began writing poetry at a very early age. Brooks was encouraged by such well-known poets as James Weldon Johnson and Langston Hughes after sending them samples of her work, and she became a published poet at the age of 13.

In 1950, Brooks became the first African-American author to win a Pulitzer Prize. She was named the poet laureate of Illinois in 1968, and at the age of 68, she became the first African-American woman appointed Poetry Consultant to the Library of Congress. Brooks is a great champion of young writers, visiting schools nationwide and sponsoring literary awards programs in her home state. Through her poetry, Brooks reveals what she calls the "neglected miracles of everyday experience," and she encourages her students to do the same. She offers students this reminder: "Your poem does not need to tell your reader everything. A little mystery is fascinating."

OTHER WORKS *Annie Allen, Maud Martha, Selected Poems, The World of Gwendolyn Brooks, Blacks*

Extended Reading

Literary Links

Ask students to compare the ways "Miss Rosie" and "Those Winter Sundays" use repetition effectively. (They both use it to emphasize how the subject of the poem affects the speaker: repetition shows how Miss Rosie's condition both angers and empowers the speaker; in "Those Winter Sundays," repetition stresses the speaker's sadness and regret about his father.)

Critic's Corner

Possible responses: Yes, because Clifton implies that Miss Rosie has made her determined; no, the portrait of Miss Rosie makes life seem dismal. Regarding Gwendolyn Brooks, some students may think her "Kitchenette Building" exhorts readers to keep dreams alive, while others may feel that it says dreams die in poverty.

The Writer's Style

Possible response: The poem is a very simple portrait of one old woman, but it deals with big ideas like poverty and growing old.

Across the Curriculum

Science The phrase *waiting for your mind* in "Miss Rosie" suggests that Miss Rosie suffers from forgetfulness, which may be caused by any of several conditions, including Alzheimer's disease, a crippling condition that destroys one's mental abilities. Ask students to research Alzheimer's disease, seeking answers to questions such as: What causes Alzheimer's? Has a cure been suggested? How many people does Alzheimer's affect? How do caretakers deal with Alzheimer's patients? Students can present their findings orally or in writing.

Alternative Activities

1. Remind students that they should think about the meaning and tone of each poem as they prepare their readings. Groups may wish to hand out copies of the poems so that classmates can read along silently as they listen. Suggest that the audience participate in the discussion of speakers, content, and style.

2. Students may wish to make character webs for Miss Rosie before they begin their portraits. For the present portrait they can use details from the poem, but for the past portrait they will have to imagine how she might have looked when she was a young woman.

AUTHOR BACKGROUND

Lucille Clifton In these excerpts from an interview with Bill Moyers, Lucille Clifton shares her thoughts about poetry and about life. The interview was filmed at the Geraldine R. Dodge Poetry Festival in Waterloo, New Jersey.

Side A, Frame 15545

OVERVIEW

Objectives

- To understand and appreciate an autobiographical excerpt that explores the nightmare of the Holocaust
- To understand and appreciate style
- To express understanding of the selection through a choice of writing forms, including an excerpt, an eyewitness account, and a list of questions
- To extend understanding of the selection through a variety of multimodal and cross-curricular activities

Skills

THE WRITER'S STYLE
- Considering your audience

GRAMMAR
- Auxiliary verbs

LITERARY CONCEPTS
- Style
- Setting

SPEAKING, LISTENING, AND VIEWING
- Dramatic reading
- Film
- Group discussion
- Oral presentation

ALTERNATIVE
Previewing

In lieu of writing words and phrases that describe the thoughts and feelings of someone living in a death camp, students can choose partners and discuss their ideas.

Discussion Prompts *Describe to a partner your ideas about life in a concentration camp. Then listen as your partner shares his or her ideas. Use the following questions as prompts:*

- *What would you eat; where would you sleep; what would you do?*
- *How might it feel to live with the threat of death constantly hovering over you?*
- *How might it feel to witness the terrible deaths of friends and relatives?*

As you read this excerpt from Night, see if your ideas match Elie Wiesel's description.

HISTORICAL CONNECTION
The Holocaust Photographs of concentration camp prisoners, including one of Elie Wiesel at Auschwitz, show the brutal existence that the author describes in *Night*.

Side A, Frame 49409

PREVIEWING

NONFICTION

from Night
Elie Wiesel (ĕl′ē vē-sĕl′) Romania / United States

PERSONAL CONNECTION *Activating Prior Knowledge*
With a small group of classmates, share what you know about the Holocaust, the slaughter of millions of Jews in Europe during World War II. Where did you learn what you know? How did you react when you learned it?

Building Background
HISTORICAL CONNECTION

In the 1920s and 1930s, Germany was in the throes of a major economic depression; millions were unemployed. When Adolph Hitler became chancellor in 1933, he promised people jobs while providing them with a scapegoat for the nation's problems: the Jews. Hitler's Nazi party began its campaign against the Jews by revoking their citizenship, boycotting their businesses, and banning them from certain professions.

Germany's invasion of Poland in 1939 marked the beginning of World War II. Hitler's goal was to expand his empire across Europe and to eliminate the Jews at the same time. In Germany and from each nation Germany occupied, Jews—as well as gypsies, homosexuals, and intellectuals and artists who opposed Hitler—were transported to the concentration camps. Everyone entering the camps was tattooed with a number on the left forearm, replacing people's names with numbers. Most of the 6 million Jews who were killed during World War II died in concentration camps. They were put to death in gas chambers, were shot by firing squads, or succumbed to starvation, torture, and disease. This selection is from the memoir of a survivor who was only 15 when he was imprisoned.

Setting a Purpose
WRITING CONNECTION

In your notebook, list words and phrases that you think might describe the thoughts and feelings of someone living in a death camp during the Holocaust. As you read, compare your list with Elie Wiesel's thoughts and feelings.

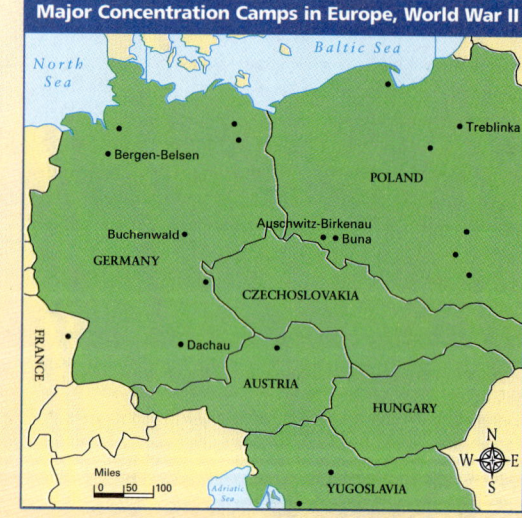

- HISTORICAL CONNECTION

 UNIT TWO PART 2: PRISONERS OF CIRCUMSTANCE

PRINT AND MEDIA RESOURCES

UNIT TWO RESOURCE BOOK
Strategic Reading: Literature, p. 65
Vocabulary SkillBuilder, p. 66

WRITING MINI-LESSONS
Transparencies, p. 34

ACCESS FOR STUDENTS ACQUIRING ENGLISH
Selection Summaries
Reading Support

FORMAL ASSESSMENT
Selection Test, p. 61
Test Generator

AUDIO LIBRARY
See Reference Card

See Reference Card

Historical Connection

INTERNET RESOURCES
McDougal Littell Literature Center at http://www.hmco.com/mcdougal/lit

308 THE LANGUAGE OF LITERATURE TEACHER'S EDITION

Survivors of a Nazi concentration camp, 1945. The Bettmann Archive.

FROM
NIGHT

Elie Wiesel

The SS[1] gave us a fine New Year's gift. We had just come back from work. As soon as we had passed through the door of the camp, we sensed something different in the air. Roll call did not take so long as usual. The evening soup was given out with great speed and swallowed down at once in anguish.

---

1. SS: an elite military unit of the Nazi party that served as Hitler's personal guard and as a special security force.

WORDS TO KNOW

din (dĭn) *n.* a jumble of loud noises (p. 313)
emaciated (ĭ-mā′shē-ā-tĭt) *adj.* extremely thin, especially as a result of starvation **emaciate** *v.* (p. 311)
interminable (ĭn-tûr′mə-nə-bəl) *adj.* endless or seemingly endless (p. 311)

notorious (nō-tôr′ē-əs) *adj.* having a widely known, usually very bad reputation; infamous (p. 311)
stature (stăch′ər) *n.* a person's height (p. 310)

I was no longer in the same block as my father. I had been transferred to another unit, the building one, where, twelve hours a day, I had to drag heavy blocks of stone about. The head of my new block was a German Jew, small of stature, with piercing eyes. He told us that evening that no one would be allowed to go out after the evening soup. And soon a terrible word was circulating—selection.

We knew what that meant. An SS man would examine us. Whenever he found a weak one, a *musulman* as we called them, he would write his number down: good for the crematory.

After soup, we gathered together between the beds. The veterans said:

"You're lucky to have been brought here so late. This camp is paradise today, compared with what it was like two years ago. Buna[2] was a real hell then. There was no water, no blankets, less soup and bread. At night we slept almost naked, and it was below thirty degrees. The corpses were collected in hundreds every day. The work was hard. Today, this is a little paradise. The Kapos[3] had orders to kill a certain number of prisoners every day. And every week—selection. A merciless selection. . . . Yes, you're lucky."

"Stop it! Be quiet!" I begged. "You can tell your stories tomorrow or on some other day."

They burst out laughing. They were not veterans for nothing.

"Are you scared? So were we scared. And there was plenty to be scared of in those days."

The old men stayed in their corner, dumb, motionless, haunted. Some were praying.

An hour's delay. In an hour, we should know the verdict—death or a reprieve.

And my father? Suddenly I remembered him. How would he pass the selection? He had aged so much. . . .

The head of our block had never been outside concentration camps since 1933. He had already been through all the slaughterhouses, all the factories of death. At about nine o'clock, he took up his position in our midst:

"Achtung!"[4]

There was instant silence.

"Listen carefully to what I am going to say." (For the first time, I heard his voice quiver.) "In a few moments the selection will begin. You must get completely undressed. Then one by one you go before the SS doctors. I hope you will all succeed in getting through. But you must help your own chances. Before you go into the next room, move about in some way so that you give yourselves a little color. Don't walk slowly, run! Run as if the devil were after you! Don't look at the SS. Run, straight in front of you!"

He broke off for a moment, then added:

"And, the essential thing, don't be afraid!"

Here was a piece of advice we should have liked very much to be able to follow.

I got undressed, leaving my clothes on the bed. There was no danger of anyone stealing them this evening.

Tibi and Yossi, who had changed their unit at the same time as I had, came up to me and said:

"Let's keep together. We shall be stronger."

Yossi was murmuring something between his teeth. He must have been praying. I had never realized that Yossi was a believer. I had even always thought the reverse. Tibi was silent, very pale. All the prisoners in the block stood naked

---

2. **Buna** (bōō′nə): a forced-labor camp in Poland, near the Auschwitz concentration camp.
3. **Kapos** (kä′pōz): the prisoners who served as foremen, or heads, of each building or cell block.
4. **Achtung!** (äkH-tŏŏng′) *German:* Attention!

WORDS TO KNOW
stature (stăch′ər) *n.* a person's height

310

Mini-Lesson Grammar

AUXILIARY VERBS Remind students that an auxiliary verb, also known as a helping verb, joins with the main verb to make up a verb phrase. Write the common auxiliary verbs listed here on the chalkboard. Then direct students' attention to the sentence highlighted on this page and ask them to identify the auxiliary verbs (*should have*). Point out that Wiesel uses many auxiliary verbs because he is telling about events that took place in the past. Many verb forms that show past action, such as the present perfect, the past perfect, and the past subjunctive, are formed with auxiliary verbs.

Application Divide the class into groups of four or five and have them write sentences about *Night*, using the auxiliary verbs listed on the board.

Reteaching/Reinforcement

Auxilliary Verbs, p. 536

Common auxiliary Verbs
be (all forms), have (all forms), do (all forms), can, could, will, would, shall, should, may, might, must

between the beds. This must be how one stands at the last judgment.

"They're coming!"

There were three SS officers standing around the notorious Dr. Mengele,⁵ who had received us at Birkenau.⁶ The head of the block, with an attempt at a smile, asked us:

"Ready?"

Yes, we were ready. So were the SS doctors. Dr. Mengele was holding a list in his hand: our numbers. He made a sign to the head of the block: "We can begin!" As if this were a game!

The first to go by were the "officials" of the block: Stubenaelteste,⁷ Kapos, foremen, all in perfect physical condition of course! Then came the ordinary prisoners' turn. Dr. Mengele took stock of them from head to foot. Every now and then, he wrote a number down. One single thought filled my mind: not to let my number be taken; not to show my left arm.

There were only Tibi and Yossi in front of me. They passed. I had time to notice that Mengele had not written their numbers down. Someone pushed me. It was my turn. I ran without looking back. My head was spinning: you're too thin, you're too weak, you're too thin, you're good for the furnace. . . . The race seemed interminable. I thought I had been running for years. . . . You're too thin, you're too weak. . . . At last I had arrived exhausted. When I regained my breath, I questioned Yossi and Tibi:

"Was I written down?"

"No," said Yossi. He added, smiling: "In any case, he couldn't have written you down, you were running too fast. . . ."

I began to laugh. I was glad. I would have liked to kiss him. At that moment, what did the others matter! I hadn't been written down.

Those whose numbers had been noted stood apart, abandoned by the whole world. Some were weeping in silence.

> ONE SINGLE THOUGHT FILLED MY MIND: NOT TO LET MY NUMBER BE TAKEN; NOT TO SHOW MY LEFT ARM.

The SS officers went away. The head of the block appeared, his face reflecting the general weariness.

"Everything went off all right. Don't worry. Nothing is going to happen to anyone. To anyone."

Again he tried to smile. A poor, emaciated, dried-up Jew questioned him avidly in a trembling voice:

"But . . . but, Blockaelteste,⁸ they did write me down!"

The head of the block let his anger break out. What! Did someone refuse to believe him!

"What's the matter now? Am I telling lies then? I tell you once and for all, nothing's going to happen to you! To anyone! You're wallowing

---

5. **Dr. Mengele** (měng'ə-lə): Josef Mengele, a German doctor who personally selected nearly half a million prisoners to die in gas chambers at Auschwitz. He also became infamous for his medical experiments on inmates.
6. **Birkenau** (bîr'kə-nou): a large section of the Auschwitz concentration camp.
7. **Stubenaelteste** (shtōō'bən-ĕl'tə-stə): a rank of Kapos; literally "elders of the rooms."
8. **Blockaelteste** (blŏk'ĕl'tə-stə): a rank of Kapos; literally "elders of the building."

WORDS TO KNOW
notorious (nō-tôr'ē-əs) *adj.* having a widely known, usually very bad reputation; infamous
interminable (ĭn-tûr'mə-nə-bəl) *adj.* endless or seemingly endless
emaciated (ĭ-mā'shē-ā-tĭd) *adj.* extremely thin, especially as a result of starvation
emaciate *v.*

311

 Mini-Lesson   The Writer's Style

CONSIDERING YOUR AUDIENCE Ask students to determine whether Wiesel wrote his autobiography only for other Holocaust survivors or for a more general audience. To guide discussion, ask them to consider explanatory phrases that he uses, such as "the first to go by were the 'officials' of the block: Stubenaelteste, Kapos, foremen . . ." Point out that if he had been writing for an audience of Holocaust survivors, he wouldn't have needed to explain who the block "officials" were. Usually, the more general a writer's audience is going to be, the more the writer explains things and the less he or she uses jargon or dialect.

Application Invite students to write two paragraphs describing an experience they have had at school: one for their classmates and another for people who don't go to their school. Ask students to point out the similarities and differences between the paragraphs.

Reteaching/Reinforcement
- Writing Handbook, anthology p. 1019
- *Writing Mini-Lessons*, transparencies p. 34

 The Writer's Craft

Considering Your Audience pp. 319–320

Linking to Geography

E The Auschwitz–Birkenau concentration camp was in Poland, near the city of Kraków. The Nazis built the camp after Germany invaded and annexed Poland in 1939. Invite students to locate the camp's site on a map.

Linking to History

F In fact, to the SS, selections were perilously close to being a game. As the Italian writer Primo Levi points out in his concentration camp memoir, *Survival in Auschwitz*, one of the most terrible aspects of the selections was the triviality of the reasons for holding them. According to Levi, selections were often held simply because new arrivals were coming and the Nazis needed to free up beds. Therefore, being fit and able was not always a guarantee of survival.

Literary Concept: STYLE

G Ask students why they think the writer uses repetitive phrases and multiple sets of ellipses in this passage. (*Possible responses: to capture the narrator's anxious state of mind; to emphasize the narrator's fears and his weak physical condition, which keep him from thinking clearly.*)

Critical Thinking: ANALYZING

H Ask students why they think the Blockaelteste attempts to reassure the condemned prisoners. (*Possible responses: he is compassionately trying to allay their fears; he is in charge of keeping orders, and doesn't want the prisoners to become hysterical and "disorderly."*)

THE LANGUAGE OF LITERATURE **TEACHER'S EDITION** **311**

CUSTOMIZING FOR

Students Acquiring English

I Ask a volunteer to clarify this sentence. *(Wiesel's father had found a piece of rubber at the warehouse, and he traded it to another prisoner in exchange for some bread. The other prisoner could use the rubber to make a new sole, or bottom, for a worn shoe.)*

Literary Concept: SETTING

I Ask students how this passage helps them better understand the setting of the camp. *(The description of the bells emphasizes the camp's regimentation and the Nazis' total control over the prisoners' lives.)*

Linking to History

J Dr. Mengele is considered one of the most vicious criminals of the Nazi death camps: a man trained as a healer who instead oversaw the torture and murder of hundreds of thousands of Jews, Gypsies, and Slavs. Many inmates were killed or maimed in medical "experiments" under Mengele's direction.

Critical Thinking: ANALYZING

K Ask students why the Blockaelteste shut himself in his room. *(Possible responses: He didn't want the condemned men to bother him; he couldn't face the fact that these men were going to die and that he was partially responsible.)*

Literary Concept: SETTING

L Ask students how comparing the camp to hell helps readers visualize it. *(Possible responses: we all have an idea of hell, and now we can apply it to the camp; since hell is full of torments, this comparison emphasizes the torment suffered by the camp prisoners.)*

---

in your own despair, you fool!"

The bell rang, a signal that the selection had been completed throughout the camp.

With all my might I began to run to Block 36. I met my father on the way. He came up to me:

"Well? So you passed?"

"Yes. And you?"

"Me too."

How we breathed again, now! My father had brought me a present—half a ration of bread obtained in exchange for a piece of rubber, found at the warehouse, which would do to sole a shoe.

The bell. Already we must separate, go to bed. Everything was regulated by the bell. It gave me orders, and I automatically obeyed them. I hated it. Whenever I dreamed of a better world, I could only imagine a universe with no bells.

Several days had elapsed. We no longer thought about the selection. We went to work as usual, loading heavy stones into railway wagons. Rations had become more meager: this was the only change.

We had risen before dawn, as on every day. We had received the black coffee, the ration of bread. We were about to set out for the yard as usual. The head of the block arrived, running.

"Silence for a moment. I have a list of numbers here. I'm going to read them to you. Those whose numbers I call won't be going to work this morning; they'll stay behind in the camp."

And, in a soft voice, he read out about ten numbers. We had understood. These were numbers chosen at the selection. Dr. Mengele had not forgotten.

The head of the block went toward his room. Ten prisoners surrounded him, hanging onto his clothes:

"Save us! You promised . . . ! We want to go to the yard. We're strong enough to work. We're good workers. We can . . . we will . . . ."

He tried to calm them to reassure them about their fate, to explain to them that the fact that they were staying behind in the camp did not mean much, had no tragic significance.

> "THOSE WHOSE NUMBERS I CALL WON'T BE GOING TO WORK THIS MORNING; THEY'LL STAY BEHIND IN THE CAMP."

"After all, I stay here myself every day," he added.

It was a somewhat feeble argument. He realized it, and without another word went and shut himself up in his room.

The bell had just rung.

"Form up!"

It scarcely mattered now that the work was hard. The essential thing was to be as far away as possible from the block, from the crucible of death, from the center of hell.

I saw my father running toward me. I became frightened all of a sudden.

"What's the matter?"

Out of breath, he could hardly open his mouth.

"Me, too . . . me, too . . . ! They told me to stay behind in the camp."

They had written down his number without his being aware of it.

"What will happen?" I asked in anguish.

But it was he who tried to reassure me.

"It isn't certain yet. There's still a chance of escape. They're going to do another selection today . . . a decisive selection."

I was silent.

312 UNIT TWO PART 2: PRISONERS OF CIRCUMSTANCE

Mini-Lesson  Literary Concepts

REVIEWING SETTING Remind students that the setting of a piece of literature is the time and place in which it occurs. This can be the present, past, or future, at any time of the day or night, and in any real or imaginary place. In some pieces of literature the setting plays an important role and is clearly defined. In others, it is left more to the reader's imagination.

Application Have students consider the importance of the setting to this excerpt from *Night*. What words and phrases does Wiesel use to help a reader visualize the setting? How is the reader's reaction to the event affected by Wiesel's description of the setting? Suggest that students get together in groups and discuss their responses to these questions.

He felt that his time was short. He spoke quickly. He would have liked to say so many things. His speech grew confused; his voice choked. He knew that I would have to go in a few moments. He would have to stay behind alone, so very alone.

"Look, take this knife," he said to me. "I don't need it any longer. It might be useful to you. And take this spoon as well. Don't sell them. Quickly! Go on. Take what I'm giving you!"

The inheritance.

"Don't talk like that, Father." (I felt that I would break into sobs.) "I don't want you to say that. Keep the spoon and knife. You need them as much as I do. We shall see each other again this evening, after work."

He looked at me with his tired eyes, veiled with despair. He went on:

"I'm asking this of you. . . . Take them. Do as I ask, my son. We have no time. . . . Do as your father asks."

Our Kapo yelled that we should start.

The unit set out toward the camp gate. Left, right! I bit my lips. My father had stayed by the block, leaning against the wall. Then he began to run, to catch up with us. Perhaps he had forgotten something he wanted to say to me. . . . But we were marching too quickly . . . Left, right!

We were already at the gate. They counted us, to the din of military music. We were outside.

The whole day, I wandered about as if sleepwalking. Now and then Tibi and Yossi would throw me a brotherly word. The Kapo, too, tried to reassure me. He had given me easier work today. I felt sick at heart. How well they were treating me! Like an orphan! I thought: even now, my father is still helping me.

I did not know myself what I wanted—for the day to pass quickly or not. I was afraid of finding myself alone that night. How good it would be to die here!

At last we began the return journey. How I longed for orders to run!

The military march. The gate. The camp.

I ran to Block 36.

Were there still miracles on this earth? He was alive. He had escaped the second selection. He had been able to prove that he was still useful. . . . I gave him back his knife and spoon. ❖

WORDS TO KNOW
din (dĭn) *n.* a jumble of loud noises

313

Mini-Lesson — Study Skills

SUMMARIZING Explain that summarizing is a useful skill because it requires students to identify important details in a work. Suggest that one way students can decide if a detail belongs in a summary is by asking themselves the question: Will the summary make sense if I leave this out?

Application Invite students to write brief summaries of this excerpt from *Night.* Then have them swap summaries with a partner. Pairs should discuss ways of improving the summaries, such as adding important details that were left out or deleting unimportant details to make the summary more concise.

Literary Concept: STYLE

M Ask students why they think Wiesel chose to start every sentence in this paragraph with "he" or "his." *(Possible responses: to focus on the father's words; to stress urgency; to reflect the sound of his father's speech)*

CUSTOMIZING FOR
Students Acquiring English

2 Explain that an *inheritance* is property or money received at the bequest of someone who has died. In Europe, a traditional inheritance from one's father would include the family home, savings, and all personal property. In this case, the only thing the father can leave to his son is a knife and a spoon.

STRATEGIC READING FOR
Less-Proficient Readers

N Have students describe what happened to the narrator and his father during and after the selections. *(The narrator passes the selection and survives, but his father's number is written down. Several days later his father is told to remain in camp with the rest of the selected men. However, he is not killed because he proves that he is still useful.)*
Summarizing

CUSTOMIZING FOR
Gifted and Talented Students

Point out that many prisoners prayed for courage or solace during the selection. Invite students to discuss why people might embrace religion at times of great crisis or hardship.

COMPREHENSION CHECK
1. Why are the narrator and his father in the concentration camp? *(because they are Jews and the Nazis want to exterminate the Jews)*
2. What is the prisoners' greatest fear? *(that they will be selected as unfit and sent to the gas chambers to be killed)*
3. What was the miracle Elie found when he returned to camp from work? *(His father was still alive.)*

INSIGHT

from Nobel Prize Acceptance Speech

Elie Wiesel

It is with a profound sense of humility that I accept the honor you have chosen to bestow upon me. I know: your choice transcends me. This both frightens and pleases me.

It frightens me because I wonder: do I have the right to represent the multitudes who have perished? Do I have the right to accept this great honor on their behalf? I do not. That would be presumptuous. No one may speak for the dead, no one may interpret their mutilated dreams and visions.

It pleases me because I may say that this honor belongs to all the survivors and their children, and through us, to the Jewish people with whose destiny I have always identified.

I remember: it happened yesterday or eternities ago. A young Jewish boy discovered the kingdom of night. I remember his bewilderment, I remember his anguish. It all happened so fast. The ghetto. The deportation. The sealed cattle car. The fiery altar upon which the history of our people and the future of mankind were meant to be sacrificed.

I remember: he asked his father: "Can this be true? This is the 20th century, not the Middle Ages. Who would allow such crimes to be committed? How could the world remain silent?"

And now the boy is turning to me: "Tell me," he asks. "What have you done with my future? What have you done with your life?"

And I tell him that I have tried. That I have tried to keep memory alive, that I have tried to fight those who would forget. Because if we forget, we are guilty, we are accomplices.

And then I explained to him how naive we were, that the world did know and remain silent. And that is why I swore never to be silent whenever and wherever human beings endure suffering and humiliation. We must always take sides. Neutrality helps the oppressor, never the victim. Silence encourages the tormentor, never the tormented.

Multicultural Perspectives

GENOCIDE The Holocaust is not the only example of attempted genocide or ethnic cleansing to have occurred. Others include the Turkish slaughter of more than 1,000,000 Armenians around the turn of the 20th century; Pol Pot and the Khmer Rouge's brutal murder of about 3,000,000 Cambodians in the 1970s; and, more recently, the killing of over 400,000 Tutsi people in Rwanda by the rival Hutu people, and the "ethnic cleansing" of Bosnian Muslims by Bosnian Serbs in the former Yugoslavia. Closer to home, millions of Native Americans died due to war, starvation, disease, and brutal slavery that took place during the colonization of North and South America by the British and the Spanish.

RESPONDING OPTIONS

FROM PERSONAL RESPONSE TO CRITICAL ANALYSIS

REFLECT
1. Make a sketch, painting, or drawing that depicts your reaction to this selection about the Holocaust.

RETHINK
2. What do you consider the worst circumstance in this portion of Wiesel's concentration camp experiences? Explain.
3. What are your impressions of the people portrayed in this excerpt?

RELATE
4. How would you describe Wiesel's tone?
   Consider
   - his saying that the SS "gave us a fine New Year's gift"
   - his calling the knife and spoon his "inheritance"
5. Why do you think Wiesel called his book *Night*?
   Consider
   - the circumstances he recounts
   - what the word *night* might symbolize
   - Wiesel's remarks on accepting the Nobel Peace Prize, provided in the Insight
6. Do you agree with Wiesel's statement from his Nobel Prize acceptance speech that "neutrality helps the oppressor, never the victim"? Support your opinion.

LITERARY CONCEPTS

Style is the way in which a literary work is written. Style refers not to what is said but to how it is said. Elements that contribute to a writer's personal style include word choice; sentence length, structure, and variety; tone; imagery; and use of dialogue. In this selection, for example, Wiesel tends to use simple vocabulary and short sentences along with questions and exclamations. How do you think these elements of style affect Wiesel's tone? What overall impact does this style have on readers? Review the selection again and identify other elements of Wiesel's style.

ANOTHER PATHWAY
Cooperative Learning
What can you glean about life—and death—in a concentration camp on the basis of this short excerpt from *Night*? Get together with a small group of classmates and make a list of generalizations you can draw about people's experiences in the camps. Also list the words and phrases from the selection that have led you to your conclusions.

QUICKWRITES

1. Rewrite the **excerpt** from Wiesel's father's point of view. Try to show what it might have felt like to fear for your life—and that of your son—in these circumstances.
2. Imagine that you are one of the soldiers who helped to liberate a concentration camp at the end of World War II and that the first thing you saw when you arrived was the group of prisoners pictured on page 309. Using the photo and Wiesel's description of his experiences as your inspiration, write an **eyewitness account** of your experience.
3. Make a **list of questions** you would ask Wiesel if you had the chance to talk to him.

📁 **PORTFOLIO** Save your writing. You may want to use it later as a springboard to a piece for your portfolio.

NIGHT **315**

From Personal Response to Critical Analysis

1. Accept all reasonable responses.
2. Accept all reasonable, well-supported responses.
3. Possible responses: some are inhuman, like Dr. Mengele; some are forced to do despicable things to save themselves, like the Blockaelteste; some are tragic, like the prisoners; some are loving, supportive friends.
4. Possible responses: Some students may say his tone is ironic, because "gift" and "inheritance" denote something positive, while the actual experience is dreadful. Others may say his tone is sad or bitter.
5. Possible responses: it refers to the "kingdom of night" that Wiesel discusses in his Noble Prize acceptance speech; it might symbolize death, or evil, or suggest the "darkest hour" of Jews.
6. Accept all reasonable, well-supported responses.

Another Pathway

Cooperative Learning Suggest that one group member lead the discussion and another record the group's generalizations. Other students might search the selection for specific words and phrases to support their generalizations. Remind the group to keep their conclusions based on information in the selection.

Rubric
3 Full Accomplishment The generalizations are accurate and are supported by words and phrases from the selection.
2 Substantial Accomplishment The generalizations are accurate but are unsupported by selection details.
1 Little or Partial Accomplishment The generalizations are inaccurate and are not supported by textual details.

Literary Concepts

Some students might suggest that Wiesel's style conveys the constant state of anxiety, despair, and helplessness in which he lived. This, combined with sarcastic phrases that give him cynical and ironic tone, helps readers better understand his experience and how it affected him. Students might also note his use of stark, bleak images, and his use of dialogue to show the personalities of all the characters.

QuickWrites

1. Students should refer to the details that Wiesel supplies about his father.
2. Suggest that students study the photograph on page 309 and pick out specific details to include in their accounts.
3. Students might compile their questions into a class list and send it to Wiesel's publisher.

The Writer's Craft

Point of View, pp. 447–451
Observing Situations and Settings, pp. 58–71
Interview, pp. 72–77

Words to Know

1. interminable
2. notorious
3. emaciated
4. stature
5. din

Reteaching/Reinforcement
- *Unit Two Resource Book*, p. 66

Literary Links

Refer students to Tim O'Brien's comment in "On the Rainy River," that "there were occasions . . . when a nation was justified in using military force to achieve its ends, to stop a Hitler or some comparable evil . . ." Based on what students know about Elie Wiesel, do they think he would agree or disagree with O'Brien's statement? *(Possible responses: He would agree, because he says in his Noble Prize acceptance speech that people should act in the face of evil and not remain neutral; he would disagree because that's exactly what Germany did: It used military force to achieve its "ends.")*

Across the Curriculum

Media Students might read the book *Schindler's List* by Thomas Keneally on which the movie is based.

Music Invite students to find out more about the Auschwitz orchestra that played during role call and as the prisoners marched to and from work and even to the gas chamber. What kind of music did the musicians play? What was its probable purpose? Students can report their findings in oral or written form. Students might also view a videotape of *Playing for Time*, a movie recounting the story of those prisoners who played in the orchestra.

ALTERNATIVE ACTIVITIES

1. Perform a **dramatic reading** of Wiesel's Nobel Prize acceptance speech. You may read the portion on page 314 or obtain a copy of the complete speech from the *New York Times*, December 11, 1986.
2. Read all of *Night* to find out more about Wiesel's experiences during the Holocaust, as well as what his life was like before being deported and imprisoned. Present a summary in an **oral report**.

ACROSS THE CURRICULUM

Media Obtain and view a video recording of *Schindler's List,* the 1993 film about a man who enabled more than a thousand Jews to escape the Holocaust. Discuss the impact of the film in an oral review.

WORDS TO KNOW

Review the Words to Know at the bottom of the selection pages. Then, on your paper, indicate which of these words could best replace the italicized word or phrase in each sentence below.

1. To those in concentration camps, the war seemed *as if it would never end*.
2. Auschwitz was *famous in a negative way* for torture and mass murder.
3. Those not killed immediately were fed little and soon grew *incredibly skinny*.
4. Backbreaking labor bent once tall prisoners to half their *size*.
5. Daily, the *clashing background sound* of German patriotic music tore at the prisoners' ears.

ELIE WIESEL

1928–

Elie Wiesel was born in the town of Sighet (sē´gĕt), Transylvania, an area of Romania that the Germans made part of Hungary when they overran both nations in 1940, during World War II. Cut off by the war from most communication, the 15,000 Jews of Sighet had no idea where they were going when, in the spring of 1944, the Nazis ordered their deportation and shipped them on a cattle train to Auschwitz in Poland. Wiesel's mother and one of his three sisters were murdered there. In 1945, Wiesel and his father were sent to Buchenwald concentration camp in Germany, but sadly, Wiesel's father died of starvation and dysentery less than three months before the camp was liberated by the Allies.

After the war, Wiesel settled in France. He studied at the Sorbonne and worked as a writer and journalist, but he made a vow to write nothing about his concentration camp experience for ten years. "I didn't want to use the wrong words," he later explained. "I was afraid that words might betray it." Wiesel's 800-page autobiographical account was first written in Yiddish, the language of his childhood, and published in 1956. He condensed the work to just over 100 pages and published it in French as *La Nuit* in 1958. Two years later, the book was published in English as *Night*. Wiesel has written numerous histories, novels, and stories about the Holocaust and its survivors, and he has received scores of literary awards. A U.S. citizen since 1963, Wiesel has worked tirelessly to call attention to human rights violations in countries around the world, including South Africa, Cambodia, Bangladesh, and Bosnia. He was awarded the Nobel Peace Prize in 1986.

OTHER WORKS *Dawn, The Accident, A Beggar in Jerusalem, Legends of Our Time, A Jew Today, The Oath, One Generation After*

Alternative Activities

1. Point out that successful dramatic readings depend upon close attention to such details as tone of voice, facial expressions, gestures, speaking pace, and pauses for emphasis.
2. Remind students that an oral report about a book should include a plot summary, a statement of theme, and the reader's own response to the book.

PREVIEWING

OVERVIEW

Objectives
- To understand and appreciate a lyric poem that explores the social restrictions faced by Bulgarian women and the women's need to give voice to their suffering
- To identify and examine stanzas
- To express understanding of the poem through a choice of writing forms, including a speech, a poem, and a letter
- To extend understanding of the selection through a variety of multimodal and cross-curricular activities

Skills
LITERARY CONCEPTS
- Stanzas

SPEAKING, LISTENING, AND VIEWING
- Collaborative translation

POETRY

The Women Who Are Poets in My Land
Blaga Dimitrova (blä′gä dĭ-mē′trə-və) Bulgaria

PERSONAL CONNECTION — Activating Prior Knowledge

Do you think that there are equal opportunities in our society for both men and women? Create a chart like the one shown, indicating whether you think there is equal opportunity in each category. Then, in a group discussion, debate these issues.

	Yes	No
Education		
Careers		
Social Customs		

Building Background
HISTORICAL/CULTURAL CONNECTION

During its long history, Blaga Dimitrova's native country of Bulgaria has experienced many forms of oppression and strife. For centuries, it was ruled by Turkey's Ottoman Empire, and much of its native culture was suppressed. It became a fully independent monarchy in 1908 but was torn by competing political factions until World War II, after which it became a Communist state. In the late 1980s, when communism began to crumble throughout Eastern Europe, Bulgaria moved toward democracy. Despite continued unrest, the nation elected its first non-Communist government in 1991.

During its four decades of communism, Bulgaria moved away from its centuries-old agricultural economy. However, other traditions proved more deep-seated. Though the Communists paid lip service to the idea of equality of the sexes, the traditional dominance of males continued in Bulgarian society. Dimitrova recognized this discrepancy; thus her writing often focuses on the lives and concerns of women.

Setting a Purpose
WRITING CONNECTION

Imagine yourself living in a society in which your choices of career, marriage, and lifestyle were not your own. In your notebook, describe how you would feel about this situation. As you read the following poem, decide whether the world portrayed by the speaker is one in which freedom and equality are valued.

Thematic Link: *Prisoners of Circumstance* Bulgarian women, imprisoned by social restrictions and the loss of control over their lives, need to express their own voices after "centuries of silence."

CUSTOMIZING FOR
Students Acquiring English

- Use **ACCESS FOR STUDENTS ACQUIRING ENGLISH**, *Reading Support*.
- You may wish to review with these students the importance of attending to punctuation as they read poems. Generally, the reader should continue on from line to line, unless a comma or a period indicates a pause or stop. Demonstrate how this strategy contributes to understanding by reading the first stanza aloud to students. Then invite volunteers to read the same stanza aloud.
- In addition to these boxes, you may want to use the suggestions under Strategic Reading for Less-Proficient Readers.

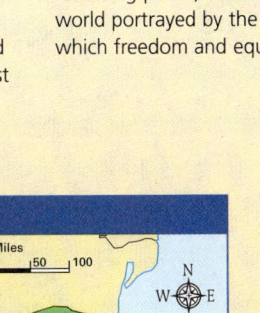

THE WOMEN WHO ARE POETS IN MY LAND **317**

PRINT AND MEDIA RESOURCES

UNIT TWO RESOURCE BOOK
Strategic Reading: Literature, p. 69

ACCESS FOR STUDENTS ACQUIRING ENGLISH
Selection Summaries
Reading Support

FORMAL ASSESSMENT
Selection Test, p. 63
 Test Generator

AUDIO LIBRARY
See Reference Card

THE LANGUAGE OF LITERATURE TEACHER'S EDITION **317**

CUSTOMIZING FOR
Multiple Learning Styles

A **Musical Learners** Have students note the musical images in this first stanza. Ask students what type of music might reflect events from ordinary life, such as "humming at the cradle," "the reaper's harmonies," and "strumming at the loom." (*Possible responses: folk music, work songs, spirituals, country music*) Invite students to recite lyrics from such songs or to hum the melodies. Then tell students to note the contrasts between musical images in the first stanza and the images of silence in the rest of the poem.

Literary Concept: HYPERBOLE

B Discuss how hyperbole is a figure of speech in which an exaggeration is made for emphasis. As an example, discuss "grown mute" (line 11), "dumb as a doornail" (line 15), and "without / a word" (lines 22–23). Does the speaker mean literally that the women will never say a word during their entire lives? (*No*) What does this hyperbole contribute to the meaning of the poem? (*Possible response: It stresses that women have no influence over their own lives, the women must play a subservient role in their households*)

Literary Concept: STANZA

C Ask students to analyze Dimitrova's use of transitions to get from one stanza to the next and to consider how each stanza is linked to the preceding one. (*Possible response: the second stanza provides a contrast to the first, marked by "instead"; the third stanza is a continuation of the second, marked by "And"; the fourth stanza explains the first three, continuing a sentence begun in the third stanza, "That's why."*)

Art Note

Never Ending Work by Lelde Vinters-Ore Lelde Vinters-Ore, born in Latvia, emigrated to Chicago in 1950, where she continues to live and work. Her paintings are expressionistic, conveying her emotional response to her subjects, and characterized by strong colors, which are applied with a palette knife.

Reading the Art Why do you think the artist has blurred the border between the woman and the background in this painting? What does this suggest about the woman's life and her identity?

The Women Who Are Poets in My Land

Blaga Dimitrova

When I think of them,
numberless, armorless,
it's not the distant
humming at the cradle that I hear,
5   nor the reaper's[1] harmonies,
unbearable, or any strumming
at the loom—the rug they weave
of many strings—or widows winding
graves into their song.

10 Instead I think of cruel
silences: the girl grown mute
in wedlock, so as not
to talk back; and the bride
sworn in her home to be
15 dumb as a doornail all her life,
nor bother her mother-in-law;
the lonely schoolteachers
in every little town,
pale-lipped, home-bound.

20 And all the beauties taken abroad
and wed for life unto a foreign tongue,
all those who died without
a word—O future in my blood—to lose
in silence what is most your own,
25 before your lover and your world,
before your hearth[2] and self, unsung,
misunderstood—That's why

there are so many poets
among women in my land.
30 The mute whose speech
is suddenly restored
will rend[3] the air
with a moan or a shout—
centuries of silence
35 crying to come out.

*Translated by Niko Boris and
Heather McHugh*

Never Ending Work (1990), Lelde Vinters-Ore. Private collection.

1. **reaper:** a person who cuts and gathers grain or another crop.
2. **hearth** (härth): the paved floor of a fireplace, which usually extends into a room; figuratively, one's home or family life.
3. **rend:** split apart in rage; pierce or disturb with sound.

318 UNIT TWO PART 2: PRISONERS OF CIRCUMSTANCE

Mini-Lesson: Speaking,  Listening, and Viewing

COLLABORATIVE TRANSLATIONS Remind students that this poem has been translated from the Bulgarian. Point out that there are special considerations translators have to make when translating poetry. Besides translating the meanings of words and phrases, they must also pay attention to poetic devices such as rhyme, rhythm, and alliteration. This often makes the job of translating poetry difficult, and sometimes poetic devices are sacrificed in translation.

Application Have students form groups that include a member—the group leader—who speaks a language other than English. The group leader should find a short poem in the language with which he or she is familiar and then translate it literally for the group. Group members can then work together to transform the poem into an English-language poem, proposing various versions of each phrase or line. After completing the translations, the group can discuss the problems they faced as translators.

RESPONDING OPTIONS

FROM PERSONAL RESPONSE TO CRITICAL ANALYSIS

REFLECT
1. Which lines of the poem did you find most memorable, powerful, or surprising? Share your response with your classmates.

RETHINK

Close Textual Reading

2. How would you describe the world portrayed by the speaker of this poem?
   Consider
   - what has caused the "cruel silences" described in stanzas 2 and 3
   - why so many poets inhabit this world
   - how a woman in this world might fill out the chart for the Personal Connection on page 317

3. What do you predict will happen when "speech is suddenly restored" (lines 30–35)? Give reasons for your prediction.

4. Review the description you wrote for the Writing Connection on page 317. Now that you have read the poem, would you change anything about your description?

5. Assuming that the subject matter in this poem remained the same, how do you think this poem would be different if Dimitrova were a man?

RELATE
6. Compare and contrast your own ideas about the institution of marriage with the speaker's ideas as reflected in this poem.

LITERARY CONCEPTS

Many poems are organized into **stanzas,** or groups of two or more lines, that can work the same way paragraphs do in prose. This poem, for example, is organized into four stanzas, each of which presents a different, complete idea. Notice that the third stanza is linked to the fourth with the transitional phrase, "That's why." Write down in your own words the main idea of each stanza.

CONCEPT REVIEW: Imagery List five images in the poem. Why do you think so many of the images appeal to the sense of sound?

ANOTHER PATHWAY

Cooperative Learning

Working with a few classmates, take turns reading the poem aloud. Remember that the punctuation can guide your reading. Commas, dashes, and colons indicate a brief pause; semicolons and periods signal a complete stop. After each period, stop and discuss what you think the speaker is saying.

QUICKWRITES

1. Use the description you wrote for the Writing Connection as a starting point for a **speech** you deliver to classmates on the importance of a person's determining his or her own direction in life.

2. Write your own **poem** called "The Women Who Are Poets in My Land," but instead of Bulgaria, use your native country as the setting. Try to express what you know about the ways women's lives are affected by your country's social norms and conventions.

3. Imagine that you are one of the "beauties taken abroad and wed for life unto a foreign tongue." Write a **letter** to your sister in Bulgaria. Explain how your life changed.

 **PORTFOLIO** Save your writing. You may want to use it later as a springboard to a piece for your portfolio.

THE WOMEN WHO ARE POETS IN MY LAND 319

Literary Concepts

Possible responses: The first stanza deals with images of traditional women's work in Bulgaria. The second stanza describes women in unhappy marriages or confined by traditional roles; the third one describes women who have married foreigners and live misunderstood and lonely abroad. The fourth stanza deals with how this unhappiness might make women "poets."

Imagery Students may list images such as "humming at the cradle," "reaper's harmonies," "strumming at the loom," "whose speech is suddenly restored," and "rend the air with a moan or a shout." Students may suggest that many of the images appeal to the sense of sound because Dimitrova feels that sexist attitudes and traditions have silenced women.

QuickWrites

1. Suggest that students choose partners and rehearse their speeches.
2. Encourage students to use concrete images based on what they know about women's lives in their native country.
3. Remind students to include details about their everyday lives in the letters.

The Writer's Craft

Persuasive Speech, pp. 222–227
Poetry, pp. 88–101

From Personal Response to Critical Analysis

1. Accept all reasonable responses.
2. Possible responses: Some students may note the cruel oppression that women face in this world; some may discuss all that is lost by keeping women silent and subservient; others may focus on the anger and sorrow simmering beneath the surface of the women's lives.
3. Possible responses: The women will feel free to express their anger; they will write about their experiences; they will give voice to all that has been lost in their lives.
4. Some students may feel that their Writing Connection responses fully predicted the feelings in the poem. Others may feel that the poem changed or expanded their insights.
5. Possible responses: A man sympathetic to the plight of women might express similar views; a male speaker might express puzzlement or frustration about the women's discontent; some men might be incapable of understanding why women would not be content with such narrowly defined roles.
6. Accept all reasonable, well-supported responses.

Another Pathway

Cooperative Learning Encourage students to give constructive advice to one another about their oral readings. Make sure students realize that each reading is itself an interpretation of the poem. You might even wish to conduct a competition among the groups to see which group provides the most compelling reading.

Rubric

3 Full Accomplishment Students pause appropriately for punctuation, convey a consistent tone, and express understanding of the poem's ideas.

2 Substantial Accomplishment Students make occasional inappropriate pauses and exhibit trouble with communicating some of the ideas in the poem.

1 Little or Partial Accomplishment Students don't adjust for punctuation and have trouble expressing the poem's ideas.

THE LANGUAGE OF LITERATURE TEACHER'S EDITION **319**

Literary Links

Possible response: In "The Censors" government policies and laws silence people, while in the poem the silencing is accomplished through customs, traditions, and social roles.

Critic's Corner

Possible response: The entire poem is about the need for women to express their own needs and wants, to restore their "speech" and "rend the air with a moan or a shout." In speech lies power and freedom.

Across the Curriculum

Music Students should keep the following questions in mind while listening: What instruments are being used? What is the mood of the song? Help students see that even if they can't understand the words to the songs, they can interpret the mood by focusing on such things as the tone and the pace of the music.

Multimodal Learning

ALTERNATIVE ACTIVITIES

1. Create a **bulletin-board display** of original drawings and/or art and photo reproductions to illustrate the women described in this poem.
2. Working with a partner, **dramatize** "The Women Who Are Poets in My Land." Use pantomime and facial expressions to depict the images in each stanza. Present your drama to the class.

LITERARY LINKS

Compare the ways in which voices are silenced in Blaga Dimitrova's poem "The Women Who Are Poets in My Land" with the ways they are silenced in Luisa Valenzuela's story "The Censors."

CRITIC'S CORNER

The poet and scholar Alexander Shurbanov once wrote that "words are especially dear to Blaga Dimitrova. . . . [She said,] 'If they should put a ban on my words, how could I quench this thirst of mine?'" What kind of "thirst" do you think Dimitrova is talking about? What evidence can you find in the poem to show how important language is to her?

ACROSS THE CURRICULUM

Music Obtain recordings of Bulgarian folk music, and play the recordings in class. Share information that accompanying printed materials provide about the songs' lyrics or histories.

Folk dancers in Bulgaria. Balkan Holidays-USA.

BLAGA DIMITROVA

Blaga Dimitrova (1922–) is one of the most popular and respected writers in Eastern Europe today. Remarkably, she was able to write and publish despite Bulgaria's long-time repressive Communist regime and its totalitarian control over the arts. She was an outspoken opponent of communism and in 1989 joined the "Club for the Promotion of Glasnost and Perestroika." She stayed at the forefront of the struggle for human rights, women's rights, and democracy and was elected to the Bulgarian parliament in 1991. She became vice president of Bulgaria in January 1992, but she resigned her post 18 months later because she opposed the president's policies and feared her nation was headed toward dictatorship.

Born in northwestern Bulgaria, Dimitrova attended Sofia University in Bulgaria's capital and earned her Ph.D. at Moscow University's A. M. Gorky Institute of World Literature. Later, she worked as an editor for a Sofia publishing house. She has written more than 20 works of poetry, fiction, drama, criticism, and translation; much of her own work has been translated into eight languages. Among her poetry volumes are *Forbidden Sea*, which includes poems about her harrowing experiences as a cancer victim, and *Night Diary*, a collection of poems written between 1989 and 1992, the years of Bulgaria's transition from communism to democracy.

OTHER WORKS *Because the Sea Is Black, Journey to Oneself*, poems in *Poets of Bulgaria* and in *The Devil's Dozen: Thirteen Contemporary Bulgarian Women Poets, The Last Rock Eagle* Extended Reading

---

Alternative Activities

1. You may wish to suggest that students copy the poem onto a separate sheet of paper and use it as the centerpiece of the display. You could also create a resource shelf of old magazines from which students could cut pictures. Encourage students to donate old magazines for the shelf.
2. Students could start by breaking each stanza down into separate images and deciding on a way to dramatize each one. Then they could put the dramatized images together to create their interpretation of the whole poem.

PREVIEWING

FICTION

House Taken Over
Julio Cortázar (hōō'lyô kôr-tä'sär) **Argentina**

PERSONAL CONNECTION Activating Prior Knowledge

Sometimes the images in our dreams fade as soon as we open our eyes; sometimes the images stay with us. Can you remember a dream you had last night? last week? years ago? Try to recall one of your dreams, and think about what real-life details or situations it contained. Did it also contain fantastic events that could never actually occur? In your notebook, jot down what you remember about the dream, and indicate whether the events belong to the world of reality or to the world of fantasy. You might organize them in a diagram like this one.

Event 1
Reality: I'm heading home from school.
Fantasy: Airplanes are lined up in middle of street.

→ **Event 2**
Reality: I fall crossing the street.
Fantasy: I try crawling to the curb, but it keeps moving away from me.

→ **Event 3**
Reality: A traffic light turns green.
Fantasy: Airplanes rush at me.

Building Background
BIOGRAPHICAL CONNECTION

Dreams and fantasy play a large role in the writings of Argentine author Julio Cortázar—a role evident in the story you are about to read. Cortázar's taste for fantasy developed in childhood, when he was fond of horror and mystery stories. It was further nurtured by his early association with the great Argentine writer Jorge Luis Borges (hôr'hĕ lōō-ēs' bôr'hĕs), whose experimental prose often blurred the borders between fact and fiction.

Cortázar was deeply dissatisfied with life under the dictators who ruled Argentina for decades, and his discomfort with his country's political situation helped inspire some of his darker fantasies. "House Taken Over" first appeared in 1946 in a literary journal that Borges edited. The story takes place in Argentina's capital, Buenos Aires, not far from where Cortázar grew up. It is based on one of the author's recurring nightmares.

Setting a Purpose
READING CONNECTION

Recognizing Fantasy As you read the story, consider its dreamlike qualities. What true-to-life details does it contain? How does it mingle real-life experiences with events that could never happen?

Street scene from the 1940s, Buenos Aires, Argentina. Culver Pictures.

OVERVIEW
Objectives
- To understand and appreciate a short story that explores the tenuous border between dreams and reality
- To understand and appreciate magical realism
- To express understanding of the story through a choice of writing forms, including an essay and a story
- To extend understanding of the story through a variety of multimodal and cross-curricular activities

Skills

LITERARY CONCEPTS
- Magical realism
- Description

READING SKILLS/ STRATEGIES
- Recognizing fantasy

GENRE STUDY
- Fantasy

THE WRITER'S STYLE
- Paragraphs with different purposes

GRAMMAR
- Semicolons

SPEAKING, LISTENING, AND VIEWING
- Group discussions
- Oral presentations

HOUSE TAKEN OVER **321**

PRINT AND MEDIA RESOURCES

UNIT TWO RESOURCE BOOK
Strategic Reading: Literature, p. 73
Vocabulary SkillBuilder, p. 74

GRAMMAR MINI-LESSONS
Transparencies, p. 49
Copymasters, p. 41

WRITING MINI-LESSONS
Transparencies, p. 37

ACCESS FOR STUDENTS ACQUIRING ENGLISH
Selection Summaries
Reading Support

FORMAL ASSESSMENT
Selection Test, p. 65
 Test Generator

 AUDIO LIBRARY
See Reference Card

 **LASERLINKS**
Art Gallery

THE LANGUAGE OF LITERATURE TEACHER'S EDITION **321**

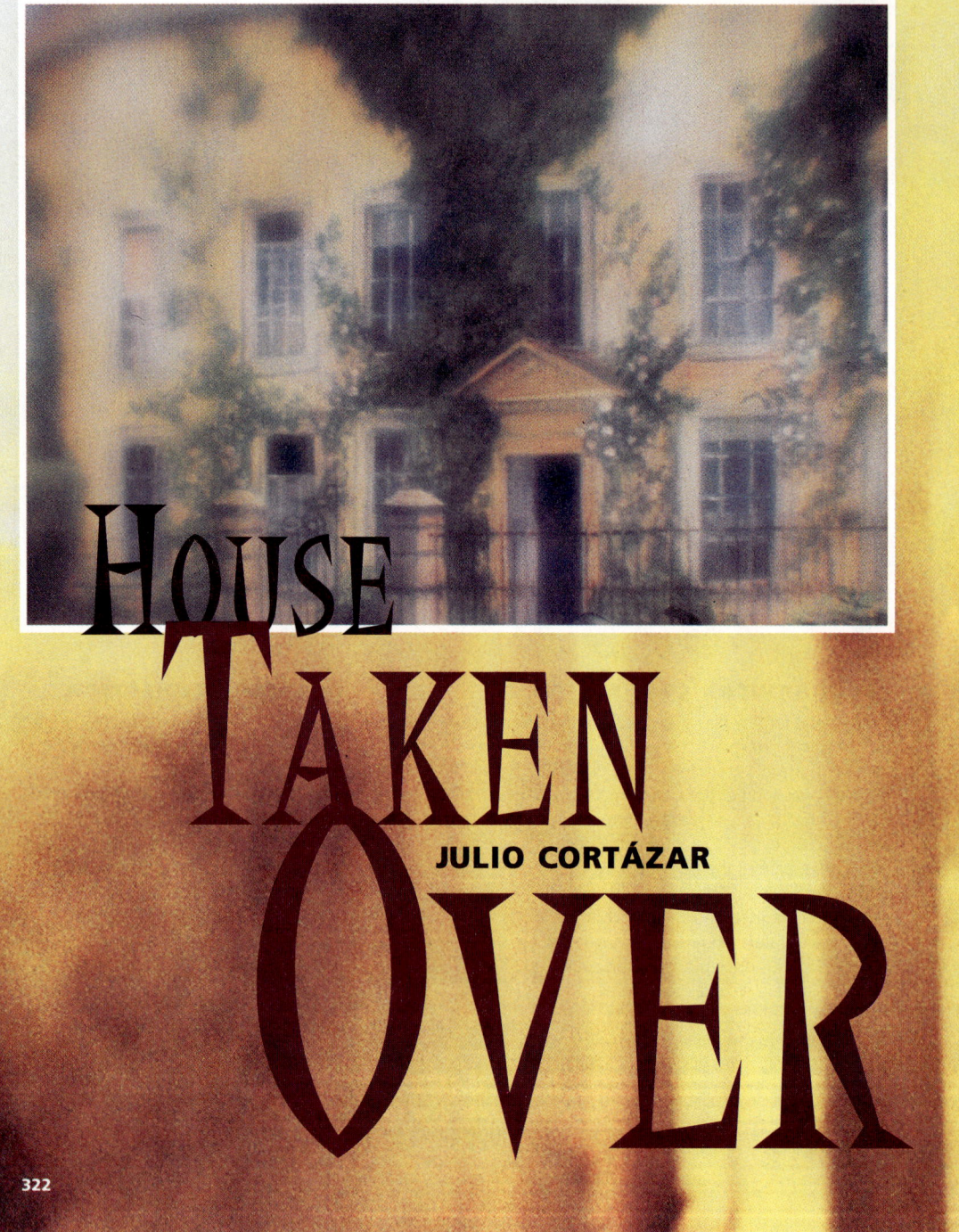

HOUSE TAKEN OVER

JULIO CORTÁZAR

SUMMARY

A brother and sister live complacently alone together in a big old house that holds memories of great-grandparents, a grandfather, their parents, and their childhood. The sister, Irene, sits in her room and knits each day, while her brother stays by her side and watches. Then, one day, the brother hears a sound at the back of the house. He hurls the door shut, locks it, and bolts it. He and his sister resolve to live only in the front part of the house because the back part has been "taken over." Both brother and sister adjust to the smaller space and the loss of some favorite items. For a time, life goes on as before. One night, however, both brother and sister hear noises in the kitchen; the rest of the house has been taken over. The siblings flee the house without time to take anything along. The brother locks the door and throws the keys down the sewer to protect other people from entering the taken-over house.

Thematic Link: *Prisoners of Circumstance*
In this story, two siblings become prisoners of an amorphous and unexplained "they" who take over their home.

CUSTOMIZING FOR
Students Acquiring English

- Use **ACCESS FOR STUDENTS ACQUIRING ENGLISH**, *Reading Support*.
- The calm, matter-of-fact narration might make it difficult for students to recognize the fantastic elements of the story. Pause after each section and invite students to summarize what has happened so far.

STRATEGIC READING FOR
Less-Proficient Readers

Invite students to talk about ghost or horror movies they have seen that feature houses that are the site of strange, unexplainable events. Discuss how reality and fantasy are blended in such dramas.

Set a Purpose Have students read to find out what changes occur in the house featured in this story.

Use **UNIT TWO RESOURCE BOOK**, p. 73, for guidance in reading the selection.

WORDS TO KNOW

brusquely (brŭsk′lē) *adv.* abruptly and curtly (p. 327)

commune (kə-myōōn′) *v.* to be in a state of heightened sensitivity, as with one's surroundings (p. 323)

dexterity (dĕk-stĕr′ĭ-tē) *n.* skill and grace in physical movement, especially in the use of the hands (p. 323)

obscure (ŏb-skyōōr′) *adj.* not well-known (p. 323)

replete (rĭ-plēt′) *adj.* abundantly supplied; filled (p. 323)

We liked the house because, apart from its being old and spacious (in a day when old houses go down for a profitable auction of their construction materials), it kept the memories of great-grandparents, our paternal grandfather, our parents and the whole of childhood.

Irene and I got used to staying in the house by ourselves, which was crazy; eight people could have lived in that place and not have gotten in each other's way. We rose at seven in the morning and got the cleaning done, and about eleven I left Irene to finish off whatever rooms and went to the kitchen. We lunched at noon precisely; then there was nothing left to do but a few dirty plates. It was pleasant to take lunch and commune with the great, hollow, silent house, and it was enough for us just to keep it clean. We ended up thinking, at times, that that was what had kept us from marrying. Irene turned down two suitors for no particular reason, and María Esther went and died on me before we could manage to get engaged. We were easing into our forties with the unvoiced concept that the quiet, simple marriage of sister and brother was the indispensable end to a line established in this house by our grandparents. We would die here someday, obscure and distant cousins would inherit the place, have it torn down, sell the bricks and get rich on the building plot; or more justly and better yet, we would topple it ourselves before it was too late.

Irene never bothered anyone. Once the morning housework was finished, she spent the rest of the day on the sofa in her bedroom, knitting. I couldn't tell you why she knitted so much; I think women knit when they discover that it's a fat excuse to do nothing at all. But Irene was not like that, she always knitted necessities, sweaters for winter, socks for me, handy morning robes and bedjackets for herself. Sometimes she would do a jacket, then unravel it the next moment because there was something that didn't please her; it was pleasant to see a pile of tangled wool in her knitting basket fighting a losing battle for a few hours to retain its shape. Saturdays I went downtown to buy wool; Irene had faith in my good taste, was pleased with the colors and never a skein¹ had to be returned. I took advantage of these trips to make the rounds of the bookstores, uselessly asking if they had anything new in French literature. Nothing worthwhile had arrived in Argentina since 1939.²

But it's the house I want to talk about, the house and Irene; I'm not very important. I wonder what Irene would have done without her knitting. One can reread a book, but once a pullover is finished you can't do it over again; it's some kind of disgrace. One day I found that the drawer at the bottom of the chiffonier,³ replete with mothballs, was filled with shawls: white, green, lilac. Stacked amid a great smell of camphor—it was like a shop; I didn't have the nerve to ask her what she planned to do with them. We didn't have to earn our living, there was plenty coming in from the farms each month, even piling up. But Irene was only interested in the knitting and showed a wonderful dexterity, and for me the hours slipped away watching her, her hands like silver sea urchins, needles flashing, and one or two knitting baskets on the floor, the balls of yarn jumping about. It was lovely.

---

1. **skein** (skān): a length of yarn or thread wound into a loose coil.
2. **1939**: the year in which World War II began. The war prevented most exports from France to South America.
3. **chiffonier** (shĭf′ə-nîr′): a narrow, high chest of drawers, often with a mirror attached.

WORDS TO KNOW

commune (kə-myōōn′) *v.* to be in a state of heightened sensitivity, as with one's surroundings
obscure (ŏb-skyoor′) *adj.* not well-known
replete (rĭ-plēt′) *adj.* abundantly supplied; filled
dexterity (dĕk-stĕr′ĭ-tē) *n.* skill and grace in physical movement, especially in the use of the hands

CUSTOMIZING FOR
Multiple Learning Styles

D **Spatial or Graphic Learners** Invite students to draw a simple floor plan of the house based on the description that begins here. Encourage students to share their floor plans as a means of furthering understanding of the setting and action of the story.

Literary Concept: DESCRIPTION

E Ask students to share their mental pictures of the house, as described in this paragraph. Encourage students to identify words and phrases from the selection that helped to stimulate those pictures. *(Responses will vary; accept all reasonable responses)*

Linking to Geography

F The port city of Buenos Aires, the capital of Argentina, is considered by many to be South America's most elegant city. Located on the Rio de la Plata estuary, its metropolitan area is the second largest in the Southern Hemisphere and one of the world's largest. The inhabitants of Buenos Aires are known as *Portenos* (pôr-tĕ′nôs), which means "people of the port." The majority of them are descended from European (mainly Italian) immigrants. Today Buenos Aires has its share of ethnic communities, among them French, German, English, Polish, Russian, Portuguese, Syrian, and Turkish.

Linking to History

G In Argentina, as in all areas colonized by Europeans, "old world" traditions—such as tea time—were adapted to indigenous materials available such as *yerba maté* (yĕr′bä mä-tĕ′), an indigenous Paraguayan tea plant. In Argentina, yerba maté is traditionally brewed in conical silver cups. Long silver stirrers are used to mix the maté with hot water and sugar.

CUSTOMIZING FOR
Students Acquiring English

I Point out that *ran* here means "pushed or shoved."

D How not to remember the layout of that house. The dining room, a living room with tapestries, the library and three large bedrooms in the section most recessed, the one that faced toward Rodríguez Peña.[4] Only a corridor with its massive oak door separated that part from the front wing, where there was a bath, the kitchen, our bedrooms and the hall. One entered the house through a vestibule with enameled tiles, **E** and a wrought-iron grated door opened onto the living room. You had to come in through the vestibule and open the gate to go into the living room; the doors to our bedrooms were on either side of this, and opposite it was the corridor leading to the back section; going down the passage, one swung open the oak door beyond which was the other part of the house; or just before the door, one could turn to the left and go down a narrower passageway which led to the kitchen and the bath. When the door was open, you became aware of the size of the house; when it was closed, you had the impression of an apartment, like the ones they build today, with barely enough room to move around in. Irene and I always lived in this part of the house and hardly ever went beyond the oak door except to do the cleaning. Incredible how much dust collected on the furniture. It may be Buenos **F** Aires is a clean city, but she owes it to her population and nothing else. There's too much dust in the air, the slightest breeze and it's back on the marble console tops and in the diamond patterns of the tooled-leather desk set. It's a lot of work to get it off with a feather duster; the motes[5] rise and hang in the air, and settle again a minute later on the pianos and the furniture.

I'll always have a clear memory of it because it happened so simply and without fuss. Irene was knitting in her bedroom, it was eight at night, and I suddenly decided to put the water **G** up for maté.[6] I went down the corridor as far as the oak door, which was ajar, then turned into the hall toward the kitchen, when I heard something in the library or the dining room. The sound came through muted and indistinct, a chair being knocked over onto the carpet or the muffled buzzing of a conversation. At the same time or a second later, I heard it at the end of the passage which led from those two rooms toward the door. I hurled myself against the door before it was too late and shut it, leaned on it with the weight of my body; luckily, the key was on our side; moreover, I ran the great bolt into place, just to be safe. **H**

I went down to the kitchen, heated the kettle, and when I got back with the tray of maté, I told Irene:

"I had to shut the door to the passage. They've taken over the back part."

She let her knitting fall and looked at me with her tired, serious eyes.

"You're sure?"

I nodded.

"In that case," she said, picking up her needles again, "we'll have to live on this side."

I sipped at the maté very carefully, but she took her time starting her work again. I remember it was a gray vest she was knitting. I liked that vest. **J**

The first few days were painful, since we'd both left so many things in the part that had been taken over. My collection of French literature, for example, was still in the library. Irene had left several folios of stationery and a pair of slippers that she used a lot in the winter. I missed my briar pipe, and Irene, I think, regretted the loss of an ancient bottle of Hesperidin.[7] It happened repeatedly (but only in the first few days) that we would close some drawer or

---

4. **Rodríguez Peña** (rô-drē′gĕz pĕ′nyä): a wealthy, mostly residential street in central Buenos Aires.
5. **motes:** small particles; specks.
6. **maté** (mä-tĕ′): a tealike beverage popular in South America.
7. **Hesperidin** (hĕ-spĕr′ĭ-dĭn): a natural citrus flavoring.

324 UNIT TWO PART 2: PRISONERS OF CIRCUMSTANCE

Mini-Lesson — Literary Concepts

REVIEWING DESCRIPTION Remind students that a description is writing that helps readers picture a setting, a character, or an event. Descriptions often contain figurative language, including imagery and sensory detail.

Application Have students point out examples of description in "House Taken Over." Ask them to find at least one example of figurative language and four examples of sensory details. They can arrange the descriptive words and phrases in a chart like the one shown.

Figurative Language	
Simile	her hands like silver sea urchins
Metaphor	this voice from a parrot or a statue
Sensory Details	
sight	oak door
hearing	metallic click rustle
smell	camphor
touch	dust on furniture
taste	sipped the maté cold supper

---

324 THE LANGUAGE OF LITERATURE TEACHER'S EDITION

El novio [The groom] (1974), Jacobo Borges. Oil on canvas, 120.5 cm × 120.5 cm, collection of Clara Diament Sujo, New York.

Critical Thinking: SPECULATING

H Ask students what they think the narrator hears. *(Possible responses: ghosts; intruders; noises created by his own imagination)*

Art Note

The Groom by Jacobo Borges
Borges, a Venezuelan, is known for the dreamlike quality of his paintings, which raise questions about the nature of reality. Many of his paintings overlay a real-life situation with images that seem ghostly and fragmented.

Reading the Art *What realistic figure appears in the painting? What might the other components of the painting symbolize? How does the painting relate to the story?*

STRATEGIC READING FOR
Less-Proficient Readers

I Make sure that students understand what has upset the routine of Irene and her brother.

- What do the brother and sister fear? *("they," the mysterious, unseen intruders)* **Noting Relevant Details**
- What about this situation seems unrealistic? *(that unseen intruders could provoke the house's residents to seal off half the building; the intruders themselves seem fantastic)* **Classifying**

Set a Purpose Have students read on to find out what happens now that part of the house is closed.

Mini-Lesson Genre Study

FICTION Remind students that **fantasy** is a type of highly imaginative fiction that generally recounts events that could not happen in real life. In some fantasies, however, certain elements remain realistic. In "House Taken Over," for example, the characters and setting are realistic, but the plot seems fantastic.

Application Invite students to think about and discuss other fantasies that they have read or seen in movies or on television. Which elements of these stories are fantastic? Which elements are realistic?

Art Note

That Which I Should Have Done, I Did Not Do by Ivan Albright
Albright was born in Illinois in 1897. This painting, his most famous work, took ten years to complete. A meticulous painter, Albright could work for days on minute parts of his canvases, creating the vibrant layers of color that make his subjects come alive.

Reading the Art What do you think the title of this painting means? How does it relate to the painting?

CUSTOMIZING FOR
Students Acquiring English

2 Ask students to assume an "arms-folded" position. What does this posture suggest about the lives of the narrator and his sister? *(They were bored and had little to fill their time; they were passive.)*

Critical Thinking: ANALYZING

J Ask students what "living without thinking" involves. *(Possible responses: just going about daily life without analyzing anything, as if one were operating by rote; not thinking about painful or difficult things, such as losing part of one's house and prized possessions.)*

Literary Concept: DESCRIPTION

K Ask students what the narrator might mean when he describes Irene talking in her sleep as having a "voice from a statue or a parrot." *(Possible responses: The voice sounds disembodied, as if it is not coming from her; the voice sounds emotionless and mechanical, as if, like a parrot or a statue, she is uncomprehendingly repeating something she heard.)*

That Which I Should Have Done I Did Not Do (1931–1941), Ivan Le Lorraine Albright. Oil on canvas, 246.5 cm × 91.5 cm, The Art Institute of Chicago, Mary and Leigh B. Block Charitable Fund (1955.645). Photo Copyright © 1994, The Art Institute of Chicago, all rights reserved.

326   UNIT TWO   PART 2: PRISONERS OF CIRCUMSTANCE

---

cabinet and look at one another sadly.

"It's not here."

One thing more among the many lost on the other side of the house.

But there were advantages, too. The cleaning was so much simplified that, even when we got up late, nine-thirty for instance, by eleven we were sitting around with our arms folded. Irene got into the habit of coming to the kitchen with me to help get lunch. We thought about it and decided on this: while I prepared the lunch, Irene would cook up dishes that could be eaten cold in the evening. We were happy with the arrangement because it was always such a bother to have to leave our bedrooms in the evening and start to cook. Now we made do with the table in Irene's room and platters of cold supper.

Since it left her more time for knitting, Irene was content. I was a little lost without my books, but so as not to inflict myself on my sister, I set about reordering papa's stamp collection; that killed some time. We amused ourselves sufficiently, each with his or her own thing, almost always getting together in Irene's bedroom, which was more comfortable. Every once in a while, Irene might say:

"Look at this pattern I just figured out, doesn't it look like clover?"

After a bit it was I, pushing a small square of paper in front of her so that she could see the excellence of some stamp or another from Eupen-et-Malmédy.[8] We were fine, and little by little we stopped thinking. You can live without thinking.

(Whenever Irene talked in her sleep, I woke up immediately and stayed awake. I never could get used to this voice from a statue or a parrot, a voice that came out of the dreams, not from a throat. Irene said that in my sleep I flailed about

---

8. **Eupen-et-Malmédy** (ə-pĕ′nā-mäl-mā′dē): a region in Belgium.

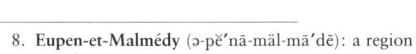

PARAGRAPHS WITH DIFFERENT PURPOSES Point out that writers construct paragraphs to serve different purposes. For example, in this story, some paragraphs primarily describe setting, such as the first paragraph on page 324. Other paragraphs describe actions that move the plot along, such as the paragraph on page 327 that begins "Except for the consequences." Discuss how both kinds of paragraphs help to involve the reader in the mood and action of the story.

Application Invite students to write a brief narrative in which the first paragraph describes a setting and the second paragraph relates a series of actions. After students have shared their narratives, discuss how descriptions of setting and actions support one another to build an interesting and cohesive story.

Reteaching/Reinforcement
- *Writing Handbook*, anthology pp. 1026–1029
- *Writing Mini-Lessons* transparencies, p. 37

Developmental Paragraphs, pp. 360–362

326   THE LANGUAGE OF LITERATURE **TEACHER'S EDITION**

enormously and shook the blankets off. We had the living room between us, but at night you could hear everything in the house. We heard each other breathing, coughing, could even feel each other reaching for the light switch, when, as happened frequently, neither of us could fall asleep.

Aside from our nocturnal rumblings, everything was quiet in the house. During the day there were the household sounds, the metallic click of knitting needles, the rustle of stamp-album pages turning. The oak door was massive; I think I said that. In the kitchen or the bath, which adjoined the part that was taken over, we managed to talk loudly, or Irene sang lullabies. In a kitchen there's always too much noise, the plates and glasses, for there to be interruptions from other sounds. We seldom allowed ourselves silence there, but when we went back to our rooms or to the living room, then the house grew quiet, half-lit, we ended by stepping around more slowly so as not to disturb one another. I think it was because of this that I woke up irremediably[9] and at once when Irene began to talk in her sleep.)

Except for the consequences, it's nearly a matter of repeating the same scene over again. I was thirsty that night, and before we went to sleep, I told Irene that I was going to the kitchen for a glass of water. From the door of the bedroom (she was knitting) I heard the noise in the kitchen; if not the kitchen, then the bath, the passage off at that angle dulled the sound. Irene noticed how brusquely I had paused, and came up beside me without a word. We stood listening to the noises, growing more and more sure that they were on our side of the oak door, if not the kitchen then the bath, or in the hall itself at the turn, almost next to us.

We didn't wait to look at one another. I took Irene's arm and forced her to run with me to the wrought-iron door, not waiting to look back. You could hear the noises, still muffled but louder, just behind us. I slammed the grating and we stopped in the vestibule. Now there was nothing to be heard.

"They've taken over our section," Irene said. The knitting had reeled off from her hands and the yarn ran back toward the door and disappeared under it. When she saw that the balls of yarn were on the other side, she dropped the knitting without looking at it.

"Did you have time to bring anything?" I asked hopelessly.

"No, nothing."

We had what we had on. I remembered fifteen thousand pesos in the wardrobe in my bedroom. Too late now.

I still had my wristwatch on and saw that it was 11 P.M. I took Irene around the waist (I think she was crying), and that was how we went into the street. Before we left, I felt terrible; I locked the front door up tight and tossed the key down the sewer. It wouldn't do to have some poor devil decide to go in and rob the house, at that hour and with the house taken over. ❖

Translated by Paul Blackburn

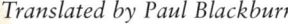
9. **irremediably** (ĭr´ĭ-mē´dē-ə-blē): in a way that cannot be remedied, corrected, or repaired.

WORDS TO KNOW
brusquely (brŭsk´lē) *adv.* abruptly and curtly

327

Assessment Option

SELF ASSESSMENT To help students assess their understanding of the story, have them write a review of "House Taken Over" for an upcoming collection of short stories in the magical realism mode. Remind students that reviews first briefly summarize the plot and important story details without revealing the ending, then focus on the story's theme or meaning, and finally give the reviewer's opinion about the story.

To help students assess their own work, have them respond to the following questions:
1. Have I accurately summarized the story and included all the important details?
2. Have I analyzed the story's meaning?
3. Have I given my opinion of the story?

Critical Thinking: SPECULATING

L Ask students to suggest why the brother and sister go to such trouble to ignore the noises from the part of the house that is taken over. (*Possible responses: The sounds depress them because they are a reminder of what has been lost; the sounds scare them, and ignoring them is a way of escaping; the brother and sister are so passive that they simply cannot take meaningful action.*)

STRATEGIC READING FOR
Less-Proficient Readers

M Ask students to describe what happens as the house is completely taken over. (*The brother and sister get used to living in only part of the house, but when the rest is taken over, they are forced to flee.*) Summarizing

CUSTOMIZING FOR
Gifted and Talented Students

Ask students to discuss the themes of this story. (*Possible responses: The story reflects the madness that can be caused by reclusiveness and passivity; the story is a kind of allegory about the loss of individual freedom in political dictatorships, with the house representing freedom and "they" the strong intrusive arm of the state; the story depicts the social changes sweeping through Latin America, with the idle, wealthy landowners being threatened by the masses.*)

COMPREHENSION CHECK
1. Who are the main characters in this story? (*a brother and sister*)
2. Where do they live? (*in a large, old house in Buenos Aires that has been in their family for a long time*)
3. Why do they close off part of the house? (*Something or someone has taken it over.*)
4. Why do they flee at the end? (*They cannot cope with the mysterious invaders, who have moved beyond the oak door barrier.*)

From Personal Response to Critical Analysis

1. Accept all reasonable responses.
2. Possible responses: upper-class, wealthy; educated and well-off; members of an aristocratic family
3. Possible responses: In a sense, the brother and sister seem just as fantastic as the voices; they are incredibly passive and quickly resign themselves to the presence of the intruders; their lack of emotion is unnerving, as if they themselves are not fully human; their response is understandable because they clearly feel that they cannot control their own fate.
4. Possible responses: ghosts; suppressed fears; political oppressors; the unconscious realm of the author
5. Possible responses: They are prisoners of a haunted house; of their age and lifestyle; of a dictatorship; of their own passivity.
6. Possible responses: They will find a place where they can continue their quiet life; they will confront the presences that haunt them; they will be unable to cope with life and die.
7. Accept all reasonable responses.

Another Pathway

Students may see the old house and the lifestyle of the brother and sister as realistic, but see other details, such as the sister's prodigious knitting and the house being taken over by ghosts, as fantastic.

Rubric

3 Full Accomplishment Charts reflect students' ability to identify realistic and fantastic details. The charts incorporate a substantial number of details.

2 Substantial Accomplishment Students list major details, but have trouble classifying them as realistic or fantastic; the charts could profit from additional details.

1 Little or Partial Accomplishment Students do not identify major details, and cannot distinguish between the fantastic and the realistic.

RESPONDING OPTIONS

FROM PERSONAL RESPONSE TO CRITICAL ANALYSIS

REFLECT
1. What is your reaction to this story? Record your thoughts in your notebook and share them with classmates.

RETHINK
2. How would you describe the background and social class of the narrator and his sister?
3. What is your opinion of the way the brother and sister react to the discovery that "they" have taken over the back part of the house?
4. The story is intentionally ambiguous, or open to different interpretations. What might the mysterious invaders represent?

Thematic Link
5. In what sense might the narrator and his sister be considered prisoners of circumstance? Explain your view.
6. Judging from the details in the story, predict what will happen to the brother and sister after the story's end.

RELATE
7. How do you think the dreams we have at night are related to our daytime experiences? Explain your views in a class discussion.

ANOTHER PATHWAY

In a chart like the one below, differentiate between the situations and details from the story that can be considered realistic and those that can be considered fantastic. If any details about the lives of the two characters can be considered absurd or inconsistent with what is customary—even before the house is "taken over"—list them in the "Fantastic" category.

Realistic	Fantastic

LITERARY CONCEPTS

Julio Cortázar is considered a master of **magical realism**, a style of writing that often includes exaggeration, unusual humor, magical and bizarre events, dreams that come true, and superstitions that prove warranted. Magical realism differs from pure fantasy in that it combines fantastic elements with realistic elements such as recognizable characters, believable dialogue, a true-to-life setting, a matter-of-fact tone, and a plot that sometimes contains historic events. How does "House Taken Over" fit this definition of magical realism? Cite details from the story to support your answer.

CONCEPT REVIEW: Setting Why do you think Cortázar describes the house in such detail? What role does the house play in the lives of the two main characters?

QUICKWRITES

1. Draft an **essay** in which you explain your interpretation of "House Taken Over." Be sure to defend your point of view with details from the story.
2. Write a **story,** in the style of magical realism, based on the dream you described in the Personal Connection on page 321.

📁 **PORTFOLIO** Save your writing. You may want to use it later as a springboard to a piece for your portfolio.

328 UNIT TWO PART 2: PRISONERS OF CIRCUMSTANCE

Literary Concepts

Students may cite as realistic the description of the house, the narrator's matter-of-fact tone, the historically accurate references (such as the one about French literature), and the believable dialogue. Students may cite the following fantastic elements: the bizarre event of the house being taken over, and the brother and sister vacating the house to leave it to "them."

Setting Some students may feel that Cortázar describes the house in such detail in order to establish a realistic setting; others may note that the realistic descriptions of the house provide an interesting contrast to the fantastic elements of the story.

QuickWrites

1. Remind students that an essay begins with a statement of viewpoint or opinion, continues with supporting ideas or facts, and concludes with an interesting restatement of the opinion.
2. Students might consider adopting the matter-of-fact tone of "House Taken Over" for their own stories. Volunteers can read their stories aloud to the class.

 **The Writer's Craft**

Interpretive Essay, pp. 238–253
Story, pp. 102–107

Multimodal Learning

ALTERNATIVE ACTIVITIES

1. Create a **painting** of the "house taken over" or its mysterious invaders. Blend realistic details with fantastic ones.
2. Put together a **recording** of several pieces of music that evoke the same mood of suspense and mystery as this story does.

ART CONNECTION

Examine the painting on page 325 titled *The Groom*. In what way might the term *magical realism* be applied to it?

Detail of *El Novio* [The groom] (1974), Jacobo Borges. Oil on canvas, 120.5 cm x 120.5 cm, collection of Clara Diament Sujo, New York.

WORDS TO KNOW

On a separate sheet of paper, answer each question below.

1. If you answer a question **brusquely,** are you more likely to seem rude or to seem long-winded?
2. If a waiter displays **dexterity,** does he or she serve smoothly or clumsily?
3. Will a person who **communes** with nature be more likely to leave a camping site virtually unchanged or to leave litter behind?
4. If your shelf is **replete** with trophies, have you won or have you lost many tournaments?
5. Is an **obscure** actress famous, or is she known to few people?

CRITIC'S CORNER

In commenting on this story, student Kevin Schatzman said, "The thing I liked best about it was the suspense. It kept me wondering what was going to happen next and made me want to read more." How does this compare with your own experience reading the story?

JULIO CORTÁZAR

1914–1984

Although Julio Cortázar was born in Brussels, Belgium, he was raised by his Argentine parents in a suburb of Buenos Aires from the time he was four years old. Even as a child, Cortázar was an avid reader and writer. He attended the Teachers College of Buenos Aires and then taught literature at both the high school and the university level before working as a translator and publishing his own writing.

Cortázar opposed Argentine dictator Juan Perón (hwän pĕ-ron'), who rose to power in the 1940s. In 1951, dissatisfied with the Perón regime, Cortázar immigrated to Paris, France, and continued to write. A lifelong jazz fan and trumpet player, he won much attention with his 1959 novella *The Pursuer*, whose hero is modeled after American jazz musician Charlie "Bird" Parker. Cortázar's fame increased with the publication of *Rayuela*, an experimental novel that was translated into English and published as *Hopscotch* in 1966. In that same year, one of his stories was used as the basis for the critically acclaimed film *Blow-Up*. By the end of the 1960s, Cortázar—despite his self-imposed exile in Europe—was internationally acknowledged as one of Latin America's most influential authors. Cortázar was also a "man of conscience," remaining politically active throughout his life.

OTHER WORKS *The Winners, End of the Game and Other Stories, We Love Glenda So Much and Other Tales*

Extended Reading

LASERLINKS
• ART GALLERY

HOUSE TAKEN OVER **329**

Words To Know

1. rude
2. smoothly
3. virtually unchanged
4. won
5. known to few people

Reteaching/Reinforcement
• *Unit Two Resource Book,* p. 74

Critic's Corner

Ask students to tell whether they had the same reaction to the story as Kevin did and to explain why or why not.

Art Connection

Possible response: Fantastic images are combined with realistic ones.

Literary Links

Ask students to compare and contrast "House Taken Over" with "The Censors," another story by an Argentine writer. What elements do the two stories share? *(Both tell about people trapped in bizarre circumstances; both can be interpreted politically, and both end with strange and unexpected resolutions to a problem.)*

Across the Curriculum

Drama Cooperative Learning Suggest that students work in groups to dramatize "House Taken Over." Tasks for group members include writing the adaptation, directing the play, designing the set, handling the props, managing the special effects, and playing the characters.

ART GALLERY
Magical Realism Julio Cortazar uses a writing style known as magical realism, which combines elements of realism with exaggeration, unusual humor, dreams, and bizarre events. Other artists, including Latin American painter Frida Kahlo, have used a similar style in their work. These paintings will enhance students' understanding of magical realism

Side A, Frame 49417

Alternative Activities

1. Encourage students to vary the textures and materials they use in their paintings. Besides using paint, students can glue objects and pieces of material to their canvases. They can also apply the paint with different tools to achieve varied effects.
2. Suggest that students start by identifying the kinds of music that they have heard in suspense and mystery films. They may find it helpful to study the soundtracks of movies that made an impression on them. Students with a strong musical background might record their own improvisational pieces to accompany the story.

OBJECTIVES

- To promote independent active reading
- To practice and apply skills learned in previous lessons
- To provide an opportunity to assess students' performance through an alternative assessment instrument.

Reading Pathways

- Divide students into groups and have group members alternate reading sections of the selection aloud. Ask students to pay special attention to the description of life in Manzanar as they listen to other group members read. After the group finishes reading, suggest that members discuss literary strategies the authors use to create their images of Manzanar.

- Ask students to read the selection twice. After the first reading the class can make a list of questions about the piece. During the second reading, students can try to answer the questions.

- Invite students to use sketch pads as visual notebooks as they read the selection. Students can sketch impressions the piece creates in their minds. When the reading is completed, students might discuss within a small group the ways in which sketching a scene enables them to understand it better.

- Evaluate how well students can read, interpret, discuss, and write about the selection on their own by using the Integrated Assessment for Unit Two, located in the Alternative Assessment booklet. Set aside two class periods, or about two hours, to administer the assessment after students have completed the final writing assignment for the unit.

from FAREWELL TO MANZANAR

Jeanne Wakatsuki Houston and James D. Houston

United States

Surrounded by her family's belongings, a young Japanese girl awaits transfer to a relocation center. The Bettmann Archive.

PRINT AND MEDIA RESOURCES

UNIT TWO RESOURCE BOOK
Strategic Reading: Literature, p. 77

FORMAL ASSESSMENT
Selection Test, p. 67
Part Test, pp. 69–70
Test Generator

ALTERNATIVE ASSESSMENT
Unit Two Integrated Assessment
pp. 7–12

ACCESS FOR STUDENTS ACQUIRING ENGLISH
Selection Summaries

AUDIO LIBRARY
See Reference Card

When Japan's attack on Pearl Harbor drew the United States into World War II in December, 1941, people on the West Coast began to fear further attacks from those of Japanese descent living in their communities. The fears were racist and completely irrational (most of the Japanese had become U.S. citizens or legal residents and had been living and working on the coast for decades), yet suspicion fueled public policy. In February, 1942, President Franklin D. Roosevelt signed an order that cleared the way for the removal of Japanese people from their homes. Virtually the entire Japanese American population of the West Coast, about 110,000 people, was bused to ten inland "relocation" centers in the western states and Arkansas, where they were interned, or confined, for the duration of the war. With sometimes only twenty-four hours notice, they were forced to abandon their homes, farms, and businesses and to leave behind most of their possessions in what has been called "the most blatant mass violation of civil liberties in American history."

Jeanne Wakatsuki was seven years old and living in Ocean Park, California, when the United States entered the war. On the night after the Pearl Harbor attack, her father showed his loyalty to his adoptive land by burning the Japanese flag he had brought with him from Japan thirty-five years before. Nevertheless, he was arrested and sent to a detention camp in North Dakota. The rest of the family moved to a Japanese-American community in Terminal Island, California, but the area was soon declared off-limits to Japanese Americans because of its proximity to the Long Beach Naval Station. The Wakatsukis were forced to relocate to a minority ghetto in Los Angeles, where they are living when the following selection begins. The selection is an excerpt from the memoir that Jeanne Wakatsuki Houston wrote with her husband three decades after the war.

The American Friends Service[1] helped us find a small house in Boyle Heights, another minority ghetto, in downtown Los Angeles, now inhabited briefly by a few hundred Terminal Island refugees. Executive Order 9066 had been signed by President Roosevelt, giving the War Department authority to define military areas in the western states and to exclude from them anyone who might threaten the war effort. There was a lot of talk about internment, or moving inland, or something like that in store for all Japanese Americans. I remember my brothers sitting around the table talking very intently about what we were going to do, how we would keep the family together. They had seen how quickly Papa was removed, and they knew now that he would not be back for quite a while. Just before leaving Terminal Island, Mama had received her first letter, from Bismarck, North Dakota. He had been imprisoned at Fort Lincoln, in an all-male camp for enemy aliens.

1. **American Friends Service:** a Quaker charity often aiding political and religious refugees and other displaced persons.

FAREWELL TO MANZANAR   **331**

SUMMARY

Days of quiet, desperate waiting, during which Japanese Americans are the targets of undisguised hostility, follow the signing of Executive Order 9066. President Roosevelt had signed this order after Japan attacked the United States during World War II. The narrator is part of a Japanese-American family, and her father is unjustly imprisoned. After being relocated for about a month in Boyle Heights, the narrator's family and many others are evacuated to the cold, barren, and dust-blown Manzanar. The narrator, who was a young girl at the time, looks back at the daily and continual indignities that camp life brought: unpalatable food, hastily erected and drafty barracks, lack of privacy, inadequate numbers of blankets, and clownish clothing. As she recreates life during those early days at Manzanar, she punctuates her grim tale with the moments of humor and resourcefulness that made life more tolerable and humane. She also recounts in some detail the discomfort and embarrassment—especially for the oldest and most modest women—of rows of toilets with no walls between them. This was a humiliation that, like all the others, they learned to endure.

Thematic Link: *Prisoners of Circumstance*
West Coast Japanese Americans were not only literal prisoners in internment camps, but also prisoners of the circumstances surrounding World War II: prejudice, fear, and the state of war between Japan and the United States.

OPTION 1

Individual Activity
WRITING A LETTER
Invite each student to imagine that he or she is the narrator and is writing a letter to her father, describing life in Manzanar and giving news of the family.

Teacher's Role Help students assume and maintain the narrator's voice by suggesting that as they write they keep in mind important details, such as the narrator's age and the feelings she describes in the selection.

Rubric

3 Full Accomplishment The letters are written in the narrator's voice and contain details from the selection.

2 Substantial Accomplishment Letters contain details from the selection, but are not written in the correct voice.

1 Little or Partial Accomplishment Letters display little understanding of selection details and have inappropriate narrative voices.

Papa had been the patriarch.[2] He had always decided everything in the family. With him gone, my brothers, like councilors in the absence of a chief, worried about what should be done. The ironic thing is, there wasn't much left to decide. These were mainly days of quiet, desperate waiting for what seemed at the time to be inevitable. There is a phrase the Japanese use in such situations, when something difficult must be endured.

You would hear the older heads, the Issei,[3] telling others very quietly, *"Shikata ga nai"* (It cannot be helped). *"Shikata ga nai"* (It must be done).

Mama and Woody went to work packing celery for a Japanese produce dealer. Kiyo and my sister May and I enrolled in the local school, and what sticks in my memory from those few weeks is the teacher—not her looks, her remoteness. In Ocean Park my teacher had been a kind, grandmotherly woman who used to sail with us in Papa's boat from time to time and who wept the day we had to leave. In Boyle Heights the teacher felt cold and distant. I was confused by all the moving and was having trouble with the classwork, but she would never help me out. She would have nothing to do with me.

This was the first time I had felt outright hostility from a Caucasian. Looking back, it is easy enough to explain. Public attitudes toward the Japanese in California were shifting rapidly. In the first few months of the Pacific war, America was on the run. Tolerance had turned to distrust and irrational fear. The hundred-year-old tradition of anti-Orientalism on the west coast soon resurfaced, more vicious than ever. Its result became clear about a month later, when we were told to make our third and final move.

The name Manzanar meant nothing to us when we left Boyle Heights. We didn't know where it was or what it was. We went because the government ordered us to. And, in the case of my older brothers and sisters, we went with a certain amount of relief. They had all heard stories of Japanese homes being attacked, of beatings in the streets of California towns. They were as frightened of the Caucasians as Caucasians were of us. Moving, under what appeared to be government protection, to an area less directly threatened by the war seemed not such a bad idea at all. For some it actually sounded like a fine adventure.

★ **Tolerance had turned to distrust and irrational fear.** ★

Our pickup point was a Buddhist church in Los Angeles. It was very early, and misty, when we got there with our luggage. Mama had bought heavy coats for all of us. She grew up in eastern Washington and knew that anywhere inland in early April would be cold. I was proud of my new coat, and I remember sitting on a duffel bag trying to be friendly with the Greyhound driver. I smiled at him. He didn't smile back. He was befriending no one. Someone tied a numbered tag to my collar and to the duffel bag (each family was given a number, and that became our official designation until the camps were closed), someone else passed out box lunches for the trip, and we climbed aboard.

I had never been outside Los Angeles County, never traveled more than ten miles from the coast, had never even ridden on a bus. I was full of excitement, the way any kid would be, and wanted to look out the window. But for the first few hours the shades were drawn. Around me other people played cards, read magazines,

---

2. **patriarch** (pā′trē-ärk′): the man who heads his family or clan.
3. **Issei** (ēs′sā′): people born in Japan who immigrate to the United States.

332 UNIT TWO PART 2: PRISONERS OF CIRCUMSTANCE

Multicultural Perspectives

ASIANS IN AMERICA Many historians view the internment of Japanese Americans as the low point in a long history of discriminatory U.S. policies toward Asians and Americans of Asian descent. These policies began in 1882 with the Chinese Exclusion Act, which prohibited the immigration of Chinese laborers for ten years. The act was renewed in 1892, and in 1902 Chinese immigration was suspended indefinitely. (This law was not repealed until 1943.) The United States also continued to pass laws discriminating against Asians already living here. During a certain period, the court testimony of Chinese Americans was declared void. Separate schools for Asian Americans were legal until 1936, and an alien land law that sought to keep Asians from owning land was not ruled unconstitutional until 1956.

dozed, waiting. I settled back, waiting too, and finally fell asleep. The bus felt very secure to me. Almost half its passengers were immediate relatives. Mama and my older brothers had succeeded in keeping most of us together, on the same bus, headed for the same camp. I didn't realize until much later what a job that was. The strategy had been, first, to have everyone living in the same district when the evacuation began, and then to get all of us included under the same family number, even though names had been changed by marriage. Many families weren't as lucky as ours and suffered months of anguish while trying to arrange transfers from one camp to another.

We rode all day. By the time we reached our destination, the shades were up. It was late afternoon. The first thing I saw was a yellow swirl across a blurred, reddish setting sun. The bus was being pelted by what sounded like splattering rain. It wasn't rain. This was my first look at something I would soon know very well, a billowing flurry of dust and sand churned up by the wind through Owens Valley.[4]

We drove past a barbed-wire fence, through a gate, and into an open space where trunks and sacks and packages had been dumped from the baggage trucks that drove out ahead of us. I could see a few tents set up, the first rows of black barracks, and beyond them, blurred by sand, rows of barracks that seemed to spread for miles across this plain. People were sitting on cartons or milling around, with their backs to the wind, waiting to see which friends or relatives might be on this bus. As we approached, they turned or stood up, and some moved toward us expectantly. But inside the bus no one stirred. No one waved or spoke. They just stared out the windows, ominously silent. I didn't understand this. Hadn't we finally arrived, our whole family intact? I opened a window, leaned out, and yelled happily. "Hey! This whole bus is full of Wakatsukis!"

Outside, the greeters smiled. Inside there was an explosion of laughter, hysterical, tension-breaking laughter that left my brothers choking and whacking each other across the shoulders.

We had pulled up just in time for dinner. The mess halls weren't completed yet. An outdoor chow line snaked around a half-finished building that broke a good part of the wind. They issued us army mess kits, the round metal kind that fold over, and plopped in scoops of canned Vienna sausage, canned string beans, steamed rice that had been cooked too long, and on top of the rice a serving of canned apricots. The Caucasian servers were thinking that the fruit poured over rice would make a good dessert. Among the Japanese, of course, rice is never eaten with sweet foods, only with salty or savory foods. Few of us could eat such a mixture. But at this point no one dared protest. It would have been impolite. I was horrified when I saw the apricot syrup seeping through my little mound of rice. I opened my mouth to complain. My mother jabbed me in the back to keep quiet. We moved on through the line and joined the others squatting in the lee[5] of half-raised walls, dabbing courteously at what was, for almost everyone there, an inedible concoction.

After dinner we were taken to Block 16, a cluster of fifteen barracks that had just been finished a day or so earlier—although finished was hardly the word for it. The shacks were built of one thickness of pine planking covered with tarpaper. They sat on concrete footings, with about two feet of open space between the floorboards and the ground. Gaps showed between the planks, and as the weeks passed

---

4. **Owens Valley:** referring to the valley of the Owens River in south central California west of Death Valley, where Manzanar was built. The once lush and green valley had become dry and deserted in the 1930s after water was diverted to an aquaduct supplying Los Angeles.
5. **lee:** the side sheltered from the wind.

Linking to Geography

Like Manzanar, most of the internment camps were located in desolate, arid regions. The two exceptions were Camp Rohwer and Camp Jerome in Arkansas. These were built in swampy lowlands infested with poisonous snakes and other vermin.

Cultural Note

Japanese Americans had specific terms for each generation of Japanese living in the United States. Those who were born in Japan but immigrated to the United States, like the narrator's father, were known as *Issei*. The second generation, those born in the United States of Japanese immigrant parents, were known as *Nisei*. The narrator's mother was *Nisei*. The third generation of Japanese Americans, born to *Nisei* parents, were known as *Sansei*. Both the *Nisei* and the *Sansei*, because they were born in the United States, were American citizens by birth.

The 550-acre Manzanar internment camp was located 200 miles northeast of Los Angeles at the foot of the Sierra Nevada. When the war ended in 1945, the camp's staff buildings and barracks were quickly disassembled and auctioned off. AP/Wide World Photos.

and the green wood dried out, the gaps widened. Knotholes gaped in the uncovered floor.

Each barracks was divided into six units, sixteen by twenty feet, about the size of a living room, with one bare bulb hanging from the ceiling and an oil stove for heat. We were assigned two of these for the twelve people in our family group; and our official family "number" was enlarged by three digits—16 plus the number of this barracks. We were issued steel army cots, two brown army blankets each, and some mattress covers, which my brothers stuffed with straw.

The first task was to divide up what space we had for sleeping. Bill and Woody contributed a blanket each and partitioned off the first room: one side for Bill and Tomi, one side for Woody and Chizu and their baby girl. Woody also got the stove, for heating formulas.

The people who had it hardest during the first few months were young couples like these, many of whom had married just before the evacuation began, in order not to be separated and sent to different camps. Our two rooms were crowded, but at least it was all in the family. My oldest

night—the parents wanted their boys asleep by 9:00 p.m.—and they continued arguing over matters like that for six months, until my sister and her husband left to harvest sugar beets in Idaho. It was grueling work up there, and wages were pitiful, but when the call came through camp for workers to alleviate the wartime labor shortage, it sounded better than their life at Manzanar. They knew they'd have, if nothing else, a room, perhaps a cabin of their own.

That first night in Block 16, the rest of us squeezed into the second room—Granny; Lillian, age fourteen; Ray, thirteen; May, eleven; Kiyo, ten; Mama; and me. I didn't mind this at all at the time. Being youngest meant I got to sleep with Mama. And before we went to bed I had a great time jumping up and down on the mattress. The boys had stuffed so much straw into hers, we had to flatten it some so we wouldn't slide off. I slept with her every night after that until Papa came back.

We woke early, shivering and coated with dust that had blown up through the knotholes and in through the slits around the doorway. During the night Mama had unpacked all our clothes and heaped them on our beds for warmth. Now our cubicle looked as if a great laundry bag had exploded and then been sprayed with fine dust. A skin of sand covered the floor. I looked over Mama's shoulder at Kiyo, on top of his fat mattress, buried under jeans and overcoats and sweaters. His eyebrows were gray, and he was starting to giggle. He was looking at me, at my gray eyebrows and coated hair, and pretty soon we were both giggling. I looked at Mama's face to see if she thought Kiyo was funny. She lay very still next to me on our mattress, her eyes scanning everything—bare rafters, walls, dusty kids—scanning slowly, and I think the mask of her face would have cracked had not Woody's voice just then come at us through the wall. He was rapping on the

sister and her husband were shoved into one of those sixteen-by-twenty-foot compartments with six people they had never seen before—two other couples, one recently married like themselves, the other with two teenage boys. Partitioning off a room like that wasn't easy. It was bitter cold when we arrived, and the wind did not abate. All they had to use for room dividers were those army blankets, two of which were barely enough to keep one person warm. They argued over whose blanket should be sacrificed and later argued about noise at

Linking to History

Ironically, Japanese immigration was encouraged in the United States as a result of American sentiment against Chinese immigrants. As a result, many Japanese emigrated from Japan to California and became prosperous farmers. By 1920, they controlled more than ten percent of California's farmland. This, in turn, led to a growing resentment of Japanese Americans, which was compounded by Japan's alliance with Germany in World War II.

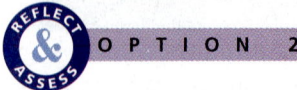

OPTION 2

Cooperative Learning
CREATE A DISPLAY

Have students work in groups of four to six to create displays about the internment of Japanese Americans. The groups might begin with collaborative meetings to plan their displays, which should consist of not only written materials but also visuals such as charts, maps, and photographs. One student in each group should act as a recorder during the meeting, and another act as an encourager of participation. Group researchers can look for more information on the subject.

Teacher's Role Suggest that for more information students can write or call the Manzanar National Historic Site, which since 1992 has commemorated the internment of Japanese Americans. Have students contact the site at the following address: c/o Death Valley, P. O. Box 579, Death Valley, CA 92328 (tel: 619-786-2331). Encourage students to use creative visuals in their displays.

Rubric

3 Full Accomplishment Displays creatively show a variety of information about the subject, taken from both the selection and from outside sources.

2 Substantial Accomplishment Students use only information from the story to create their displays.

1 Little or Partial Accomplishment Displays are lackluster and contain little or inaccurate information.

---

planks as if testing to see if they were hollow.

"Hey!" he yelled. "You guys fall into the same flour barrel as us?"

"No," Kiyo yelled back. "Ours is full of Japs." All of us laughed at this.

"Well, tell 'em it's time to get up," Woody said. "If we're gonna live in this place, we better get to work."

He gave us ten minutes to dress, then he came in carrying a broom, a hammer, and a sack full of tin can lids he had scrounged somewhere. Woody would be our leader for a while now, short, stocky, grinning behind his mustache. He had just turned twenty-four. In later years he would tour the country with Mr. Moto, the Japanese tag-team wrestler, as his sinister assistant Suki— karate chops through the ropes from outside the ring, a chunky leg reaching from under his kimono to trip up Mr. Moto's foe. In the ring Woody's smile looked sly and crafty; he hammed it up. Offstage it was whimsical, as if some joke were bursting to be told.

"Hey, brother Ray, Kiyo," he said. "You see these tin can lids?"

"Yeah, yeah," the boys said drowsily, as if going back to sleep. They were both young versions of Woody.

"You see all them knotholes in the floor and in the walls?"

They looked around. You could see about a dozen.

Woody said, "You get those covered up before breakfast time. Any more sand comes in here through one of them knotholes, you have to eat it off the floor with ketchup."

"What about sand that comes in through the cracks?" Kiyo said.

Woody stood up very straight, which in itself was funny, since he was only about five-foot-six.

"Don't worry about the cracks," he said. "Different kind of sand comes in through the cracks."

He put his hands on his hips and gave Kiyo a sternly comic look, squinting at him through one eye the way Papa would when he was asserting his authority. Woody mimicked Papa's voice: "And I can tell the difference. So be careful."

The boys laughed and went to work nailing down lids. May started sweeping out the sand. I was helping Mama fold the clothes we'd used for cover, when Woody came over and put his arms around her shoulder. He was short; she was even shorter, under five feet.

He said softly, "You okay, Mama?"

She didn't look at him, she just kept folding clothes and said, "Can we get the cracks covered too, Woody?"

Outside the sky was clear, but icy gusts of wind were buffeting our barracks every few minutes, sending fresh dust puffs up through the floorboards. May's broom could barely keep up with it, and our oil heater could scarcely hold its own against the drafts.

"We'll get this whole place as tight as a barrel, Mama. I already met a guy who told me where they pile all the scrap lumber."

"Scrap?"

"That's all they got. I mean, they're still building the camp, you know. Sixteen blocks left to go. After that, they say maybe we'll get some stuff to fix the insides a little bit."

Her eyes blazed then, her voice quietly furious. "Woody, we can't live like this. Animals live like this."

> ★ The simple truth is the camp was no more ready for us when we got there than we were ready for it. ★

It was hard to get Woody down. He'd keep smiling when everybody else was ready to explode. Grief flickered in his eyes. He blinked it away and hugged her tighter. "We'll make it better, Mama. You watch."

We could hear voices in other cubicles now. Beyond the wall Woody's baby girl started to cry.

"I have to go over to the kitchen," he said, "see if those guys got a pot for heating bottles. That oil stove takes too long—something wrong with the fuel line. I'll find out what they're giving us for breakfast."

"Probably hotcakes with soy sauce," Kiyo said, on his hands and knees between the bunks.

"No." Woody grinned, heading out the door. "Rice. With Log Cabin syrup and melted butter."

I don't remember what we ate that first morning. I know we stood for half an hour in cutting wind waiting to get our food. Then we took it back to the cubicle and ate huddled around the stove. Inside, it was warmer than when we left, because Woody was already making good his promise to Mama, tacking up some ends of lath[6] he'd found, stuffing rolled paper around the door frame.

Trouble was, he had almost nothing to work with. Beyond this temporary weather stripping, there was little else he could do. Months went by, in fact, before our "home" changed much at all from what it was the day we moved in— bare floors, blanket partitions, one bulb in each compartment dangling from a roof beam, and open ceilings overhead so that mischievous boys like Ray and Kiyo could climb up into the rafters and peek into anyone's life.

The simple truth is the camp was no more ready for us when we got there than we were ready for it. We had only the dimmest ideas of what to expect. Most of the families, like us, had moved out from southern California with as much luggage as each person could carry. Some old men left Los Angeles wearing Hawaiian shirts and Panama hats and stepped off the bus at an altitude of 4000 feet, with nothing available but sagebrush and tarpaper to stop the April winds pouring down off the back side of the Sierras.[7]

The War Department was in charge of all the camps at this point. They began to issue military surplus from the First World War—olive-drab knit caps, earmuffs, peacoats, canvas leggings. Later on, sewing machines were shipped in, and one barracks was turned into a clothing factory. An old seamstress took a peacoat of mine, tore the lining out, opened and flattened the sleeves, added a collar, put arm holes in and handed me back a beautiful cape. By fall, dozens of seamstresses were working full-time transforming thousands of these old army clothes into capes, slacks, and stylish coats. But until that factory got going and packages from friends outside began to fill out our wardrobes, warmth was more important than style. I couldn't help laughing at Mama walking around in army earmuffs and a pair of wide-cuffed, khaki-colored wool trousers several sizes too big for her. Japanese are generally smaller than Caucasians, and almost all these clothes were oversize. They flopped, they dangled, they hung.

It seems comical, looking back; we were a band of Charlie Chaplins[8] marooned in the California desert. But at the time, it was pure chaos. That's the only way to describe it. The evacuation had been so hurriedly planned, the camps so hastily thrown together, nothing was completed when we got there, and almost nothing worked.

I was sick continually, with stomach cramps and diarrhea. At first it was from the shots they

---

6. **lath** (lăth): a thin strip of wood.
7. **Sierras** (sē-ĕr′əz): referring to the Sierra Nevada mountain range in eastern California.
8. **Charlie Chaplins:** referring to actor and director Charlie Chaplin, who portrayed a tramp in baggy clothing in several comedy films of the 1920s and 1930s.

> **Linking to History**
>
> Manzanar was the first of the internment camps to be set up. It was opened in March, 1942, and closed in November, 1945. During this two-and-a-half-year period, more than 11,000 Japanese-Americans were interned there.

Multicultural Perspectives

XENOPHOBIA The United States is not the only country to have problems with anti-immigration sentiment and prejudice. Today, as millions of immigrants and refugees worldwide flee starvation, unemployment, conflict, and war, many countries must cope with local resentment of new immigrant arrivals. In England and Germany, for example, there is an increasing incidence of bias crimes as immigrant populations swell.

OPTION 3

Class Discussion
SHARING IDEAS

Teacher's Role After students have read the selection, engage them in a whole-class discussion using the following questions.

1. *Describe daily life at Manzanar. How would you feel about living there?* (Possible responses: life at Manzanar was hard; the food was bad, there wasn't adequate clothing or blankets, and the lack of privacy made things difficult. Most students will probably feel that living there would have made them unhappy, because life was difficult and because they would have left behind their homes, their possessions, and their friends.)

2. *Why do you think the author was unable to talk about Manzanar for 25 years?* (Possible responses: the experience was so horrible that she didn't want to talk about it and bring back memories; it was not until 25 years later that Americans were willing to recognize that the internment was wrong; it was only as an adult that she could come to terms with what had happened to her.)

3. *Why do you think the Houstons titled their book* Farewell to Manzanar? (Possible responses: With this book Jeanne Wakatsuki Houston finally dealt with her memories of Manzanar and so could leave the experience behind; the title is ironic because she and other internees can never say good-bye to this episode in their lives.)

4. *How do you feel about the internment of Japanese Americans during World War II?* (Accept all reasonable responses. Possible responses: it was a blatant violation of civil rights that was motivated by racism; although it was wrong, the climate of World War II makes it more understandable.)

---

gave us for typhoid, in very heavy doses and in assembly-line fashion: swab, jab, swab, *Move along now*, swab, jab, swab, *Keep it moving*. That knocked all of us younger kids down at once, with fevers and vomiting. Later, it was the food that made us sick, young and old alike. The kitchens were too small and badly ventilated. Food would spoil from being left out too long. That summer, when the heat got fierce, it would spoil faster. The refrigeration kept breaking down. The cooks, in many cases, had never cooked before. Each block had to provide its own volunteers. Some were lucky and had a professional or two in their midst. But the first chef in our block had been a gardener all his life and suddenly found himself preparing three meals a day for 250 people.

"The Manzanar runs" became a condition of life, and you only hoped that when you rushed to the latrine, one would be in working order.

That first morning, on our way to the chow line, Mama and I tried to use the women's latrine in our block. The smell of it spoiled what little appetite we had. Outside, men were working in an open trench, up to their knees in muck—a common sight in the months to come. Inside, the floor was covered with excrement, and all twelve bowls were erupting like a row of tiny volcanoes.

Mama stopped a kimono-wrapped woman stepping past us with her sleeve pushed up against her nose and asked, "What do you do?"

"Try Block Twelve," the woman said, grimacing. "They have just finished repairing the pipes."

It was about two city blocks away. We followed her over there and found a line of women waiting in the wind outside the latrine. We had no choice but to join the line and wait with them.

Inside it was like all the other latrines. Each block was built to the same design just as each of the ten camps, from California to Arkansas, was built to a common master plan. It was an open room, over a concrete slab. The sink was a long metal trough against one wall, with a row of spigots for hot and cold water. Down the center of the room twelve toilet bowls were arranged in six pairs, back to back, with no partitions. My mother was a very modest person, and this was going to be agony for her, sitting down in public, among strangers.

One old woman had already solved the problem for herself by dragging in a large cardboard carton. She set it up around one of the bowls, like a three-sided screen. OXYDOL was printed in large black letters down the front. I remember this well, because that was the soap we were issued for laundry; later on, the smell of it would permeate these rooms. The upended carton was about four feet high. The old woman behind it wasn't much taller. When she stood, only her head showed over the top.

She was about Granny's age. With great effort she was trying to fold the sides of the screen together. Mama happened to be at the head of the line now. As she approached the vacant bowl, she and the old woman bowed to each other from the waist. Mama then moved to help her with the carton, and the old woman said very graciously, in Japanese, "Would you like to use it?"

Happily, gratefully, Mama bowed again and said, *"Arigato"* (Thank you). *"Arigato gozaimas"* (Thank you very much). "I will return it to your barracks."

"Oh, no. It is not necessary. I will be glad to wait."

The old woman unfolded one side of the cardboard, while Mama opened the other; then she bowed again and scurried out the door.

Those big cartons were a common sight in the spring of 1942. Eventually sturdier partitions appeared, one or two at a time. The first were built of scrap lumber. Word would get around that Block such and such had partitions now, and Mama and my older sisters would walk halfway across the camp to use them. Even after every latrine in camp was screened, this quest for privacy continued. Many would wait in line at night. Ironically, because of this, midnight was often the most crowded time of all.

Like so many of the women there, Mama never did get used to the latrines. It was a humiliation she just learned to endure: *shikata ga nai*, this cannot be helped. She would quickly subordinate her own desires to those of the family or the community, because she knew cooperation was the only way to survive. At the same time, she placed a high premium on personal privacy, respected it in others and insisted upon it for herself. Almost everyone at Manzanar had inherited this pair of traits from the generations before them who had learned to live in a small, crowded country like Japan. Because of the first, they were able to take a desolate stretch of wasteland and gradually make it livable. But the entire situation there, especially in the beginning—the packed sleeping quarters, the communal mess halls, the open toilets—all this was an open insult to that other, private self, a slap in the face you were powerless to challenge. ❖

JEANNE WAKATSUKI HOUSTON AND JAMES D. HOUSTON

1934–

1933–

The daughter of a Japanese father and a Japanese-American mother, Jeanne Wakatsuki Houston and her mother, brothers, and sisters were among the first to be interned at Manzanar and among the last to be released. In the foreword to her book *Farewell to Manzanar,* Houston says that it took her 25 years to be able to talk about what happened to her and her family in the internment camp. Writing the book, she says, was "a way of coming to terms with the impact these years have had on my entire life." The book, coauthored with her writer husband, James D. Houston, won instant attention and critical praise when it was published in 1973; three years later, the Houstons collaborated on an award-winning screenplay based on the book.

The Houstons have spent most of their lives on the West Coast and have written mainly about their home state of California. They met as students at San Jose State University in California and married in 1957. James Houston served in the U.S. Air Force from 1957 to 1960 and went on to become an award-winning writer of novels and short stories as well as nonfiction.

OTHER WORKS by Jeanne Wakatsuki Houston: *Don't Cry, It's Only Thunder* (with Paul G. Hensler); *Beyond Manzanar and Other Views of Asian-American Womanhood*

OTHER WORKS by James D. Houston: *Between Battles; Gig; Californians: Searching for the Golden State* Extended Reading

OVERVIEW

To gain a deeper understanding of the selections they have read in this unit, students will explore the characteristics of a persuasive essay and then create a well-developed example in this lesson.

Objectives

- To plan a persuasive essay by considering elements such as research, bias, use of sources and supporting evidence, format, and method of organization
- To draft a persuasive essay and solicit response
- To revise, edit, and publish a persuasive essay
- To reflect on the process of writing a persuasive essay

Skills

WRITING AND LANGUAGE
- Creating emphasis

GRAMMAR AND USAGE
- Using pronouns

MEDIA LITERACY
- Evaluating news articles
- Reading a pie chart
- Analyzing controversial issues
- Using on-line services

SPEAKING, LISTENING, AND VIEWING
- Conducting interviews
- Conferencing
- Conducting a poll
- Debating

CRITICAL THINKING
- Evaluating sources

RESEARCH SKILLS
- Using periodical indexes
- Conducting interviews
- Using the computer

Teaching Strategy: MODELING

A To help students see how a news article can serve as a springboard for a persuasive essay, ask them to identify the major issue in the news article on this page. *(Possible response: whether an 11-year-old can choose the family he wants to live with)* Call on volunteers to share their reactions to the issue. *(Reactions will vary.)*

Critical Thinking: ANALYZING

B Have students probe the news article about Gregory K. for bias or gaps in coverage. Call on volunteers to share their analyses of the article. *(Possible responses: Adjectives such as "neglectful," "sad," and "abusive" betray some bias; the biological father's point of view is only briefly mentioned.)*

WRITING FROM EXPERIENCE

WRITING TO PERSUADE

In Unit Two, "Reflecting on Society," many challenged unjust systems and brought about change. To right society's wrongs, it is necessary to take a stand, present convincing arguments, and ask for support. In this lesson you will learn techniques that will help you gain the support of others.

GUIDED ASSIGNMENT

Write a Persuasive Essay Did you ever find a situation that made you say, "Someone ought to do something!"? Have you ever thought that the someone could be you? Fight for your cause! Write an essay persuading readers to correct a situation or to support your position on an issue.

❶ Explore Issues

Find an issue you feel strongly about. Your issue may involve a local, a national, or an international problem.

Looking Close to Home Look into local or state issues that affect your family or that affect you personally. Think about school policies you disagree with or support.

Exploring the Media Scan magazine and newspaper articles, letters to the editor, and political cartoons. Television news stories, documentaries, and movies may also present controversial issues. For example, the news articles and statistics on these pages concern children's rights. Note your initial reactions to each item. What issues are involved in each situation?

A

❷ Look for Bias

As you come across interesting topics, ask yourself:

- Are all sides of the story reported here?
- What is the writer's position? What is left out?
- What would I need to know before I could take a stand on this issue?

B

In a small group, discuss issues that interest you and your classmates. Note the feelings and opinions of group members on these issues.

340 UNIT TWO: REFLECTING ON SOCIETY

Newspaper Article

Fed up with custody shuffle, boy seeks 'divorce' from parents

Gregory K. wants a divorce. From his parents.

This isn't the movies, where a poor little rich girl . . . pouts precociously as her Hollywood-gorgeous parents bicker about their marriage.

It's the sad life of a real 11-year-old . . . boy, who–according to court records–has been passed from an abusive, alcoholic dad to a neglectful mom, to a foster home, back to Mom, to another foster home, to a boys ranch and finally to another foster family.

Enough already, Gregory pleads in [his lawsuit]. All he has ever wanted is "a place to be," Gregory once tearfully told a social worker, the lawsuit says.

The boy's attorney . . . says the bespectacled 5th grader, who likes to read and is now making A's and B's, wants to stay with his latest foster family–a couple with eight children of their own. They want to adopt Gregory as their ninth.

The biological parents say no.

Patty Shillington,
from *Chicago Tribune*, April 22, 1992

I think this boy was old enough to decide where he wants to live.

PRINT AND MEDIA RESOURCES

UNIT TWO RESOURCE BOOK
Prewriting, p. 81
Elaboration, p. 82
Peer Response Guide, pp. 83–84
Revising and Proofreading
Student Model, pp. 86–87
Rubric, p. 88

GRAMMAR MINI-LESSONS
Transparencies, pp. 7, 12
Copymasters, pp. 9, 37

WRITING MINI-LESSONS
Transparencies, pp. 50, 57–59, 72

FORMAL ASSESSMENT
Guidelines for Writing Assessment

 LASERLINKS
Writing Springboard

Persuasion, pp. 205–232

340 THE LANGUAGE OF LITERATURE TEACHER'S EDITION

Newspaper Article

Don't laws protect adopted children from being "reclaimed" by their biological parents?

"Baby Michael" to be taken from the only parents he has ever known

"Baby Michael" will be sleeping in an unfamiliar bed tonight. For the four years of his life, since he was three days old, he has been tucked into bed each night by the adoptive parents who have raised him.

After weeks of hostile negotiations between lawyers for the biological father and the adoptive parents of the boy and hours of sessions with both sets of parents and psychiatric experts, the time has arrived for Michael to be turned over to the biological father he has never met.

"This is the most moving of experience I have ever had," said the attorney for the biological father, Melvin Nelson. "We are so happy and excited!"

"This is a tragedy for the boy and for my clients," said the attorney for the adoptive parents. "We thought this could never be allowed to happen."

Negotiations over the transfer of Michael began November 22, the day the Wisconsin Supreme Court, for the second time in six months, ordered Michael to Nelson's custody.

Nelson's efforts to obtain custody of Michael began more than three years ago. He was unaware of the boy's birth and adoption because he was out of the country at the time. Michael's mother, Margaret Clinton, gave the child up for adoption and told the father the child had died. Nelson—now married and the father of a second child—sued for custody of Michael as soon as he learned the truth about him.

This really upsets me! What if I was taken from my adoptive parents?

The State of America's Children
Living Arrangements of Children, 1970–1990

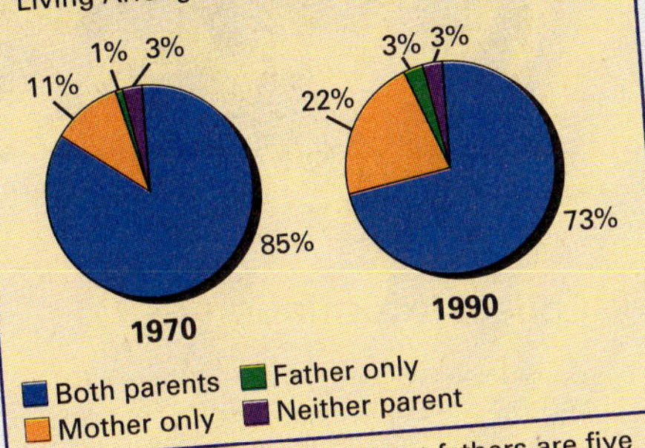

1970: Both parents 85%, Mother only 11%, Father only 1%, Neither parent 3%
1990: Both parents 73%, Mother only 22%, Father only 3%, Neither parent 3%

- Children who grow up without fathers are five times more likely to drop out of high school
- 3 million children were reported abused and neglected in 1993—a number triple that of 1980
- 1 in 4 homeless people in 1994 was a child under the age of 18
- 9.4 million children were without health insurance in 1993
- Suicide is the third-leading cause of death for young people ages 15–27
- 5,379 children and teens were killed by gunfire in 1992

Sources: Statistical Abstract of the United States, 1992, 1994

Graph & Data
C Circle graphs do not show actual numbers. What do they show?

3 Record Your Reactions

D Spend five to ten minutes writing down your ideas about an issue that has aroused your emotions. What do you already know about this issue? What is your initial position on it? Why do you feel this way? Write freely to see where your thoughts lead you. You may decide to explore another topic if your QuickWrite does not lead you in a satisfying direction.

- LASERLINKS
  • WRITING SPRINGBOARD
- WRITING COACH

Media Literacy: READING A CIRCLE GRAPH

C Have students look at the circle graphs. Remind them that these graphs show percentages of a whole amount rather than actual numbers. Point out that the complete circle represents 100% of the population. The graph legend identifies four categories, represented on each circle by wedges in different shadings of color. Invite students to give the ratio of children in 1990 who lived with their mother only to children who lived in the same kind of family in 1970. *(Answer: The percentages are 22% and 11%, making the ratio 2:1.)*

Teaching Strategy: USING THE COMPUTER

D Students may find that their ideas and reactions flow more freely when they compose on a computer because they can refine or add to a thought as quickly as they can input.

Critical Thinking: DRAWING CONCLUSIONS

E Have students examine the self-stick notes at the top and bottom of the news article on this page. Invite them to use the notes to draw a conclusion about the writer's reactions to this issue so far. *(Possible response: Both notes suggest that the writer feels sympathetic to the adoptive parents, not to the biological parents.)*

Critical Thinking: COMPARING/CONTRASTING

F Have students meet in small groups to compare and contrast the newspaper articles on pages 340 and 341. How would students rate the complexity of the issues? Is the coverage in one article more evenhanded than in the other? *(Possible response: The case of "Baby Michael" presents more complex issues than does the case of Gregory K., and the article on page 341 is more evenhanded.)*

WRITING SPRINGBOARD
David vs. Goliath Andrew Holliman was only 16-years-old when he fought developers who planned to turn a beautiful wetlands into a condominium development. Through persistence and hard work, Holliman succeeded in stopping the development and saving the wetlands.

Side B, Frame 9867

Writing Prompt Think about a situation in your community that you feel is wrong and should be changed. Write a persuasive essay that convinces readers that the situation is a problem and it should be corrected.

**Teaching Strategy:
STUMBLING BLOCK**

G If students seem overwhelmed by the different categories of ideas shown on the tree diagram, tell them that their most important goal at this point should be to develop a strong position statement and supporting reasons. Suggest, for example, that writing a simplified outline for a speech they might give to their classmates about a school policy will also help them focus on their first goal.

H Share the following practical hints about conducting telephone interviews:

- before the interview, prepare a list of questions or a script in modified outline form
- introduce yourself and immediately state your reason for calling
- take notes as your interviewee answers your questions; if you have your interviewee's permission to use a tape recorder, do so
- if appropriate, ask your interviewee's permission to quote him or her directly
- thank the interviewee

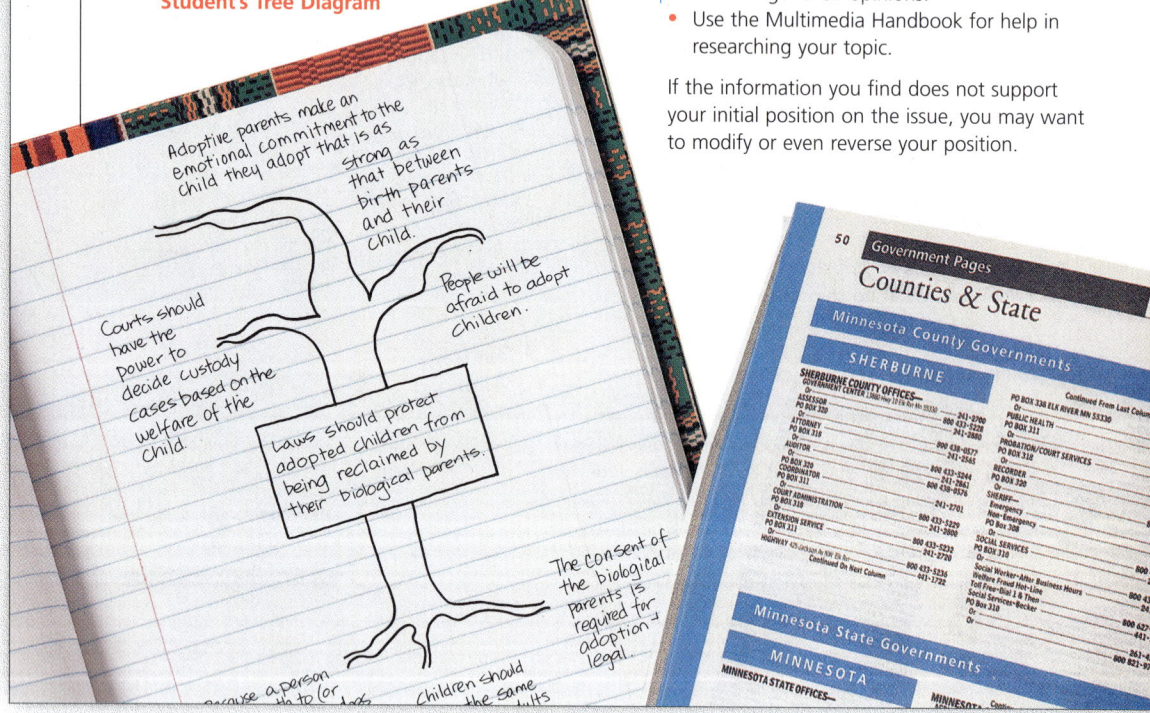

PREWRITING

Investigating the Issue

Filling In the Gaps It is not enough to care about an issue and want to do something about it. You must make sure that your feelings are based on good information and that you've examined the issue from other viewpoints. You must identify questions you have about the issue and begin to answer them.

1 Analyze Your Position

Examine why you feel strongly about your issue. A tree diagram like the one below may help you to do this. A student's stance on the issue is written on the trunk. Arguments that support his position are written as branches, and basic beliefs underlying his position are written as roots.

Decision Point After thinking about why you feel as you do on an issue, you may decide to change your position or to choose another issue.

Student's Tree Diagram

2 Collect Information

Consider a variety of sources to fill gaps in your knowledge and to find evidence that supports your position.

- Check magazine, newspaper, and on-line indexes for articles on your topic.
- Interview people directly involved in or affected by your issue.
- Scan the phone book for organizations or agencies concerned with your issue.
- Poll your classmates or computer on-line users to get their opinions.
- Use the Multimedia Handbook for help in researching your topic.

If the information you find does not support your initial position on the issue, you may want to modify or even reverse your position.

 SkillBuilder **RESEARCH SKILLS**

DESIGNING OPINION POLLS Remind students that designing an opinion poll requires thoughtful work. Offer the following guidelines:
- Plan to survey a statistically significant number of respondents. On an issue like children's rights, 15–20 responses may be an adequate sample.
- Design questions that are direct and easy to answer. Make sure that filling out the survey does not impose on respondents' time or patience.
- Ask respondents to return the survey within a specified period of time.

Applying What You've Learned Encourage students to work in small groups to develop opinion poll questions on the topics they have selected for a persuasive essay.

Additional Suggestions Suggest that students include at least a few open-ended questions in their opinion survey.

Reteaching/Reinforcement

 **The Writer's Craft**

Opinion poll, p. 209

3 Define Your Audience and Purpose

In a persuasive essay, it is not enough to support your position with valid evidence. To change your readers' minds, you must know who they are. Listing some characteristics of your audience may help you know how you can speak directly to them. Ask yourself the following questions:

- How much does my audience know about the issue?
- What does my audience need to know in order to believe or do what I ask?
- What are some other ways I could publish the arguments in my essay in order to reach my audience? (See Share Your Work, page 347.)

4 Look Through Others' Eyes

Be aware that there are more viewpoints than yours on your issue. Readers who disagree with your position or who haven't made up their minds will be more likely to consider your arguments if they see that you have considered other points of view. To prepare to defend your position, try any of these activities.

- In a group, brainstorm arguments against your position.
- Do a tree diagram listing arguments and underlying beliefs from another viewpoint.
- With a partner, debate the issue. Ask your partner to argue your position. You should play "devil's advocate" and argue opposing positions in order to understand them better.

SkillBuilder
CRITICAL THINKING

Evaluating Sources

As you collect material for your essay, include information that supports your position as well as opinions of experts with whom you agree. To evaluate information and opinions, ask yourself questions like the following:

- Do my sources seem to be unbiased and reliable?
- Does information in my sources come from experts in the field?
- Is information in different sources consistent? If not, why?
- Are my sources up-to-date?
- Are the opinions in my sources those of experts?
- Are opinions supported by good arguments or by evidence?
- Will the ideas and information help to accomplish my purpose?

APPLYING WHAT YOU'VE LEARNED
Evaluate the facts and opinions in one of your sources.

THINK & PLAN

Reflecting on Your Ideas

1. What additional kinds of information would support your argument? Where might you locate this information? Have you contacted anyone representing the opposing side?
2. Do your sources address other points of view? If so, can you use any of their thinking in your own argument?

WRITING FROM EXPERIENCE 343

Critical Thinking: MAKING INFERENCES

 To emphasize the importance of students' making inferences about their audience and its preconceptions, compare this essay to advertising—persuasive writing created for certain target groups and markets. Ask students to state how an essay about children's rights would differ if its audience were (a) a convention of family court judges, (b) a neighborhood gathering of young people, or (c) a panel of social workers from adoption agencies in the region.

Teaching Strategy: STUMBLING BLOCK

J Some students may be reluctant to devote much time to this step on the grounds that they need to focus on developing reasons to support their view. Remind them, however, that people disagree about controversial issues precisely because those issues are complex and debatable. To argue effectively for one point of view, an advocate must understand other people's stances.

SkillBuilder CRITICAL THINKING

EVALUATING SOURCES In addition to answering the questions listed in the text, students will find the following guidelines helpful for evaluating sources:

1. Analyze the relationship of the source to the subject.
   - Is the author of a source thoroughly familiar with the topic?
   - Is the author so closely identified with one side or the other that his or her opinion on an issue is not likely to sway your audience?
2. Analyze the reasoning behind opinions stated in the source.

- Are there any hasty generalizations?
- Is there circular reasoning?
- Does the writer assume that there are only two possible sides to the issue?

Applying What You've Learned Have students examine newspaper editorials and Op-Ed columns. Invite them to focus particularly on how the writers quoted or alluded to the opinions of experts.

Reteaching/Reinforcement
- Writing Handbook, anthology p. 1045
- *Writing Mini-Lessons* transparencies, p. 58

THE LANGUAGE OF LITERATURE TEACHER'S EDITION 343

Research Skill: USING THE COMPUTER

K If students compose their drafts on a computer, suggest that they keep a separate file for discarded arguments. They may want to come back to those arguments later on in the writing process. Also remind students to save frequently in order to avoid losing an entire evening's work to a single computer error.

Critical Thinking: ANALYZING

L Have students get together in small groups to analyze the writer's questions and comments for the draft on this page. Make sure they understand that these marginal notes cover several areas, including the introduction, the writer's purpose, and opposing points of view. Suggest that students list revision ideas for their own writing.

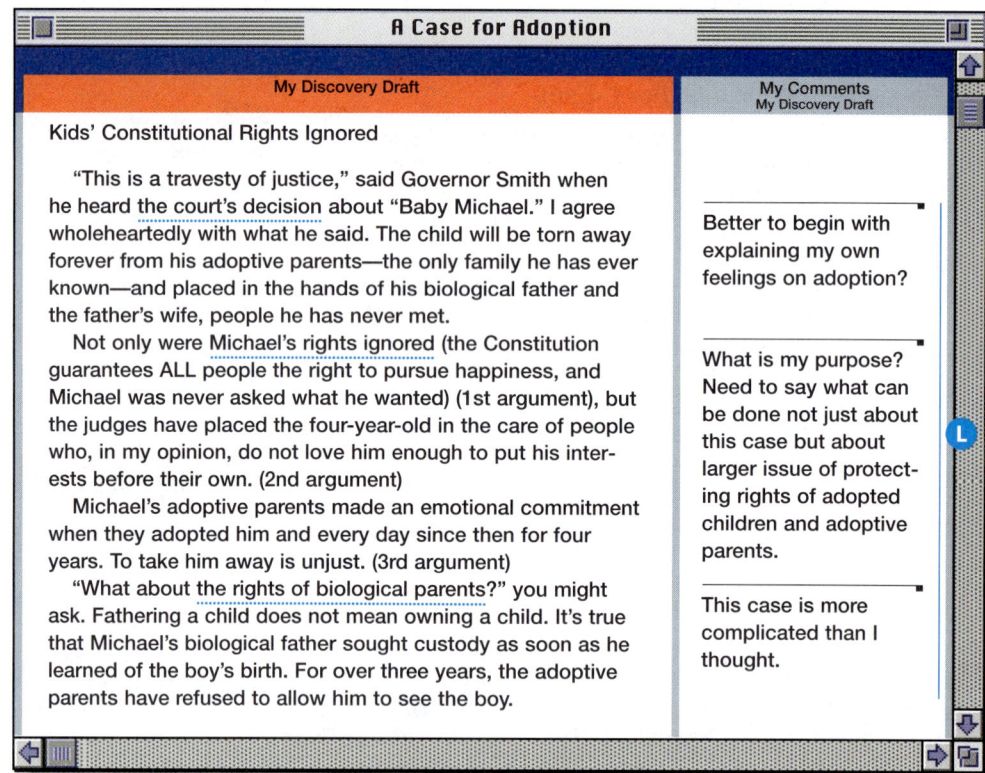

WRITING SPRINGBOARD
Motorcycle Helmet Laws Should motorcyclists be required by law to wear helmets? This film presents two opposing views on this issue.

Side B, Frames 14838

Writing Prompt Take a position on a controversial law or proposed law. In a persuasive essay, state your arguments for or against the law.

② Review with Your Purpose in Mind

As you read your discovery draft, focus on your ideas. Is your position clear on this issue? Decide whether the arguments and information in your draft support your position and whether they will be clear to your audience and will accomplish your purpose. Think about how you could order your arguments in a way that will convince your readers.

③ Rework and Share

As you write your second draft, the suggestions below may help you.

Hook Them from the Start Ask a question, tell an anecdote, list statistics, or provide a quotation. Make it clear why your audience should care about the issue.

Decide What Comes Next Before giving your arguments, you could give background information or explain the problem. Look over the organizing patterns in the Writing Handbook on page 1042, and choose one that fits your subject.

Order Your Evidence Win the trust of your audience by beginning with statements everyone can agree with. Then progress to more controversial or more emotional arguments.

Call to Action If you want your audience to take specific action, say so clearly and forcefully. Then give them the information they need to take the recommended action.

End on a Powerful Note Restate your original position. It will now carry with it the strength of your evidence and arguments.

 PEER RESPONSE

Before you begin to revise your writing, ask a peer to review your draft and to give you feedback. Questions like the following will help you target your strengths and weaknesses.

- What do you think I'm trying to accomplish?
- What are my strongest arguments?
- Where do you think I need to add more support?

SkillBuilder

 WRITER'S CRAFT

Creating Emphasis
Your sentence structure and your choice of words can help you emphasize certain ideas.

- Short, simple sentences and clauses help to make important ideas easy to understand.
- Parallel construction emphasizes relationships between ideas.
- Inverted sentence order can emphasize important words.
- Repetition and alliteration call attention to important points.
- Questions invite your audience to get involved.

APPLYING WHAT YOU'VE LEARNED
With a partner, discuss ways to revise your sentences or change certain words in order to emphasize important ideas in your essay.

📖 WRITING HANDBOOK

For more information on persuasive writing, see page 1042 of the Writing Handbook.

RETHINK & EVALUATE

Preparing to Revise

1. Which ideas need more emphasis? How can you revise sentences to emphasize these ideas?
2. What information, if any, have you left out?
3. How can you reorganize your ideas to make your point more powerfully?

WRITING FROM EXPERIENCE **345**

Teaching Strategy: USING THE SKILLBUILDER

Ⓜ You may wish to teach the SkillBuilder on Creating Emphasis at this time. An understanding of how to make muddled sentences more clear will aid students as they review their drafts.

CUSTOMIZING FOR
Less-Proficient Writers

Ⓝ Point out that questions, anecdotes, statistics, or quotations are effective in an introduction when they fulfill at least two criteria:

- They must be unusual or striking enough to attract readers' interest.
- They must provide a direct, apparent lead-in to the topic of the essay.

Teaching Strategy: PEER REVIEW

Ⓞ Have peer reviewers read the entire essay before they offer feedback. During a second reading, they should jot down brief comments and suggestions. Remind students to include specific ideas for revision, such as, "Why not lead off with a quotation?"

SkillBuilder WRITER'S CRAFT

CREATING EMPHASIS Point out that devices like underlining or adding exclamation points are often overused to create emphasis. Consequently, they fail to make an impression. Far more effective are vivid word choices, variations in sentence structure, repetitions, and sound effects.

Applying What You've Learned Encourage students to examine the final draft on page 346 for specific examples of the techniques listed in the text. For instance, the writer uses short, simple sentences in the third paragraph to emphasize the position statement, and poses a question at the beginning of the fifth paragraph to signal awareness of a conflicting point of view.

Additional Suggestions Ask students to examine a famous persuasive speech such as "I Have a Dream" by Dr. Martin Luther King, Jr., to see the writer's effective use of repetition, parallelism, sound devices, and variations in sentence structure.

THE LANGUAGE OF LITERATURE TEACHER'S EDITION **345**

Writing Skill: REVISING

P Suggest that students try the following techniques to improve their drafts:
1. add new material
2. cut repetitive or unnecessary material
3. substitute appropriate or relevant words, sentences, and paragraphs for deleted material if necessary
4. rearrange parts of the text to achieve coherence and unity
5. prepare appropriate visuals

Teaching Strategy: MODELING

Q Discuss how this model meets the standards for evaluation on page 347. For example, in the first paragraph of the essay the writer's personal situation captures readers' attention and appeals to their emotions.

R In the quotation in the final paragraph, the student cites an authoritative source on the existence of laws protecting adopted children's rights. The source is someone who is a professional in the field of law and an expert on the subject of the paper. The fact that the source agrees with the student adds weight to the student's position.

REVISING AND PUBLISHING

Fine-Tuning Your Essay

Polishing Before Publishing Before presenting your essay, prepare any visuals you'll use when you present your ideas to your audience. Read your draft aloud and listen for places where language could be more precise or powerful. The tips on this page will help you correct and improve your draft.

Student's Final Draft

A Case for Adoption

When I first heard the news that "Baby Michael" would be taken from his adoptive family—the only family he had ever known—and placed in the custody of his biological parents—people he had never met—I was overcome with a familiar feeling of fear. You see, I'm adopted. And for many of my younger years I lived with the haunting dread that something like this could happen to me.

As I watched my nightmare being played out on the six o'clock news, I wondered how one of the highest courts of this land could impose such a horrible sentence upon an innocent boy.

The laws that allowed this must be changed. Courts must protect the rights of adopted children. We must make sure that other children do not suffer Michael's fate.

The institution of adoption itself is endangered. Since 1970, adoptions have decreased by nearly fifty percent, and as more and more cases like Michael's are publicized, the number of children in foster homes grows: 276,000 in 1986; 470,000 now.

What about the rights of biological parents? Just because a person gives birth to or fathers a child does not mean that the person owns that child. The legal system has made some advances from the days of ancient Rome, when a father had the legal right to kill his unwanted children. There are now laws that protect children. "Where we haven't made sufficient progress," says Diane Geraghy, a professor of law at Loyola University and an expert on children's rights, "is in the aggressive implementation of these laws."

❶ Revise and Edit

Put your draft aside for a day, and then return to it with a fresh, critical eye. Revise your essay to eliminate anything that could detract from your arguments.

- Be sure that you explain the issue and your position in an introduction.
- Check that you have provided support for your arguments and addressed opposing views.
- Use peer comments to identify arguments that are not logical or that need additional support.

Why does the student tell about his own situation?

How does the quotation from an expert help support the student's position and add credibility?

S Words are not your only tools of persuasion. How might these visual aids clarify ideas, convey additional information, or intensify interest?

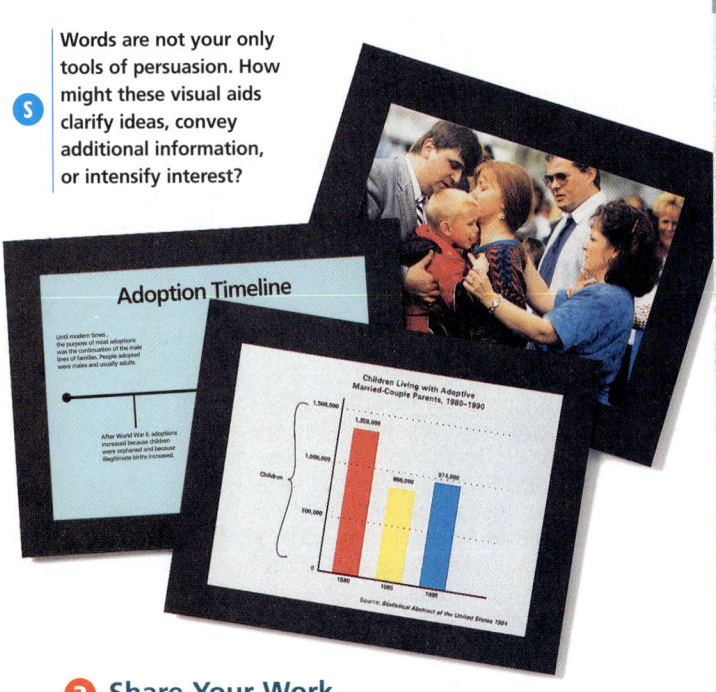

② Share Your Work

When you feel strongly about an issue, you want to get your message to as many people as possible. You could publish your essay as an illustrated pamphlet. Charts, photographs, and other illustrations could help to persuade your audience. Also consider these options:

- A letter to the editor of a local newspaper will reach a wide audience.
- Your essay could be an editorial in a school newspaper.
- You could argue your case in a persuasive speech.

Standards for Evaluation

An effective persuasive essay
- sets forth the issue and the writer's position in the introduction
- uses logical arguments that are supported by evidence
- anticipates and answers possible challenges
- uses language effectively and precisely

T

SkillBuilder

Using Pronouns

Use the first- and second-person pronouns *we, us, our, you,* and *your* to make your audience feel more involved and responsive to your arguments. Revise these sentences by adding pronouns.

1. Citizens should not tolerate another tax hike.
2. The school board has made plans to use the money without reporting its plans.

 GRAMMAR HANDBOOK

For more information on using pronouns, see page 1069 of the Grammar Handbook.

Editing Checklist Use the following editing tips as you revise.

- Have I checked the spelling of names and accuracy of dates?
- Do the visual aids I'm using accurately represent the information in my essay?

REFLECT & ASSESS

Evaluating the Experience

1. Has this assignment changed your thinking about your issue?
2. How could you have argued your point differently?

 PORTFOLIO How well did you argue your position? Put this evaluation in your portfolio along with your published essay.

U

WRITING FROM EXPERIENCE **347**

Teaching Strategy: MODELING

S Call on student volunteers to suggest the likely impact of the visual aids. For example, students may suggest that a photograph might intensify emotions or interest in the issue and that an adoption timeline might lend graphic support to the writer's argument.

Teaching Strategy: MANAGING THE PAPER LOAD

T Whenever possible, phrase your written comments as questions that will encourage students to reflect on and assess their work. For example, instead of writing "unsupported," try "Why not use a reason or quotation to support this claim?"

Standards for Evaluation

Ideas and Content
- Clearly states the issue and writer's opinion in the introduction.
- Supports opinions and ideas with observations, facts, and expert opinions.
- Takes into account and answers opposing views.
- Uses sound logic and effective language.
- Concludes with a strong argument, summary, or call to action.

Structure and Form
- Uses well-organized paragraphs and a clear organization.
- Includes transitional words and phrases to show relationships among ideas.

Grammar, Usage, and Mechanics
- Contains no more than two or three minor errors in grammar and usage.
- Contains no more than two or three minor errors in spelling, capitalization, and punctuation.

PORTFOLIO

U Encourage students to base their evaluations on the Standards for Evaluation as well as information they received from peer readers.

 SkillBuilder  GRAMMAR FROM WRITING

USING PRONOUNS Possible responses might include the following:
1. We citizens should not tolerate another hike in our taxes.
2. The members of the school board have made plans to use your money without reporting their plans to you.

Applying What You've Learned Students can work in pairs to edit each other's essays for the appropriate use of first- and second-person pronouns.

Reteaching/Reinforcement
- *Writing Mini-Lessons,* transparencies, p. 55

The Writer's Craft
Point of View, pp. 447–450

THE LANGUAGE OF LITERATURE TEACHER'S EDITION **347**

UNIT REVIEW

This feature has been designed to help students assess what they have learned in Unit Two. It also provides opportunities for them to evaluate the theme and to test their understanding of specific literary concepts. As students complete at least one of the optional activities for each section, you may want to conduct your own informal assessment of their performance, including their speaking and listening skills and their ability to engage in cooperative work.

Objectives

- To allow students to reflect on and assess their understanding of theme
- To allow students to reflect on and assess their understanding of literary concepts such as irony and point of view
- To provide students with the opportunity to assess and build their portfolios

REFLECTING ON THEME

OPTION 1

Suggest that students use the following procedure as they create a mirror for each selection. First, have them write on the mirror whatever words and phrases they can come up with without reviewing the selection. Then have them skim each selection, looking for the images that made strong impressions on them, and use those ideas to generate additional entries. Finally, have them check the mirror that most closely reflects their own view of society.

OPTION 2

If students have trouble identifying issues that they care about, ask them to think about what selections affected them the most; they can explore their responses to those selections by freewriting, which may help them identify social issues that matter to them.

OPTION 3

Have the class name examples of people who seem in control of their fate, and discuss what those people have in common. Then invite students to complete the activity in pairs or small groups.

 **Self-Assessment** Some students may conceive of their place in society only in terms of age, sex, socioeconomic status, and educational level. Encourage them to consider other factors such as personal relationships, ambitions and goals, and special interests or abilities.

REFLECT & ASSESS

UNIT TWO: REFLECTING ON SOCIETY

What insights have you gained into the relationship between society and individuals as a result of your readings in this unit? Explore this question by completing one or more of the options in each of the following sections.

REFLECTING ON THEME

OPTION 1 Drawing a Mirror of Society Consider the different views of society presented in this unit. Choose three selections that made you think about the power of society and its impact on individuals' lives. For each selection, draw a mirror containing words, phrases, and images that suggest your view of the society portrayed in the selection. Then put a check by the mirror that most closely reflects your own views about society.

OPTION 2 Social-Issues Freewriting Review the selections you have read, jotting down the problems they address. Circle two or three issues that seem particularly relevant to your life. Then do some freewriting about one or more of those issues. Consider why each issue matters to you and whether your opinions about it have changed as a result of your reading.

OPTION 3 Charting One's Destiny Can individuals control their own destinies in society? Working with a partner, decide which of this unit's selections suggest an affirmative answer to that question and which suggest a negative answer. Then create a two-column chart. In the first column, list examples—drawn both from the selections and from your experience—of individuals who seem to control their own destinies. In the second, list examples of individuals who seem to be controlled by society. On the basis of your perception of your own life, put yourself in one of the two categories.

Self-Assessment: Now that you have had a chance to reflect upon society and its relationship to individuals, create two cluster diagrams. The first should be centered on the topic "My Views of Society"; the second, on the topic "My Place in Society." Put an X next to any entry that represents an insight prompted by a selection in this unit.

REVIEWING LITERARY CONCEPTS

OPTION 1 Identifying Irony After reviewing the definition of *irony* on page 246, identify at least four selections in this unit that contain examples of irony. Then fill out a chart similar to the one shown. For each selection, list one or more examples of irony, putting each example in the appropriate column. When finished, pair up with a classmate and compare charts.

Selection	Examples of		
	Situational Irony	Verbal Irony	Dramatic Irony
"The Thrill of the Grass"	Responsible adults break into a stadium and destroy private property—all for the love of a game.		

348 UNIT TWO: REFLECTING ON SOCIETY

OPTION 2 **Discussing Point of View** The use of point of view in writing fiction may be compared to the use of a camera in making a movie. A close-up shot brings viewers very close to the subject, offering an intimate view. A wide-angle shot, on the other hand, presents a large scene. Which stories in this unit offer the most intimate view of their subjects? Are those stories told from a first-person or a third-person point of view? Discuss how point of view can affect a reader's sense of closeness to a character.

Self-Assessment: On a sheet of paper, copy the following list of literary terms introduced in this unit. Put a check next to the terms that you believe you could easily define in your own words. Underline the terms that you feel are not easy to define. Then get together with a small group of classmates to discuss the meanings of the terms that seem difficult to define.

stage directions
simile
tone
author's purpose
third-person point of view
irony
theme

first-person point of view
satire
structure
speaker
style
stanza
magical realism

PORTFOLIO BUILDING

- **QuickWrites** In many of the QuickWrites features in this unit, you were asked to write in order to persuade others to adopt or understand a certain view on a social issue. Choose the two of your responses that you think would be most successful at persuading people. Write a cover note supporting your choices, and add the note and the two pieces of writing to your portfolio.

- **Writing About Literature** Earlier, you analyzed a setting presented in one of the selections in this unit. Review your analysis and write a journal entry about it. How easy or difficult was it for you to write the analysis? How successful do you think your analysis is? Why? What did you learn about setting as you wrote your analysis? You may wish to include a copy of your journal entry in your portfolio.

- **Writing from Experience** Review your persuasive essay. As you researched and wrote the essay, what did you discover about your topic? Did your attitude toward your topic change as you worked? If so, how and why do you think it changed? What advice would you give to someone who wants to write persuasively? Jot down your answers to these questions and attach them to your essay.

- **Personal Choice** Look back through all the activities and writing you have completed for this unit, including any work you have done on your own. Which of the activities or writing assignments was the most challenging to work on? Write a note explaining your choice, and add it to your portfolio.

Self-Assessment: Think about the pieces you have just added to your portfolio. How do they compare with the items you added previously? Are your choices beginning to reveal any preferences you may have for certain types of writing or activities?

SETTING GOALS

As you worked through the reading and writing activities in this unit, you probably encountered some people or issues you would like to learn more about. Look back through the unit, making a list of subjects you would like to follow up on in your personal reading.

REFLECT & ASSESS **349**

REVIEWING LITERARY CONCEPTS

OPTION 1

Be sure that students understand that irony can be found in real life too. Invite them to describe ironic events that have occurred in their lives. If you feel comfortable doing so, you might start them off by describing an ironic situation from your own experience. Help them to see that an incident in real life can reveal situational, verbal, or dramatic irony.

OPTION 2

Suggest that students describe how point of view affects the reader by contrasting two characters in stories told from different points of view. For the first-person narrative, students should list the facts they learned and the feelings they became aware of as they read. For the third-person limited point of view, they should list the things they don't know about one of the main characters after reading the story.

Self-Assessment Suggest that groups of students write the most difficult terms on a sheet of chart paper. Appoint recorders to take notes as the groups brainstorm ideas to use in defining each term. After the groups come up with definitions, ask them to look for specific examples in the unit selections to illustrate each concept.

PORTFOLIO BUILDING

Review the main elements of the portfolio system that the class is using. Encourage students to include first drafts as well as final revisions so that they can reflect on and assess their progress in analyzing setting, explaining issues, and writing persuasive essays.

Self-Assessment Invite students to answer the following questions: *Which kinds of writing do I enjoy most? least? Which kinds of writing activities are easy for me? Which ones are hard? Why? What do my personal comments about the writing process tell me about my development as a writer?*

THE LANGUAGE OF LITERATURE **TEACHER'S EDITION 349**

UNIT THREE

UNIT THEMES

Unit Three

In the Name of Love In Unit Three, students will read selections which explore the meaning of love. This unit contains two parts: Part 1, "The Ties that Bind," and Part 2, "Mysteries of the Heart." Selections in both Parts 1 and 2 contribute to the unit theme by recounting the effects of emotional ties, both painful and exhilarating, on a variety of characters.

Part 1

The Ties that Bind Selections in Part 1 emphasize the endurance of love over time, separation, and other difficulties. For example, in "Lalla," a young woman realizes that wealth, luxury, and excitement cannot bring her the contentment she found with her first love.

Part 2

Mysteries of the Heart Selections in Part 2 emphasize the destructive power of possessive and romantic love. For example, in "The Californian's Tale," a man, unable to face his wife's death, has pretended for 19 years that she is only away on a visit and will soon return.

The Lovers (Somali Friends) (1950), Lois Mailou Jones. Casein on canvas, The Evans-Tibbs Collection, Washington, D.C.

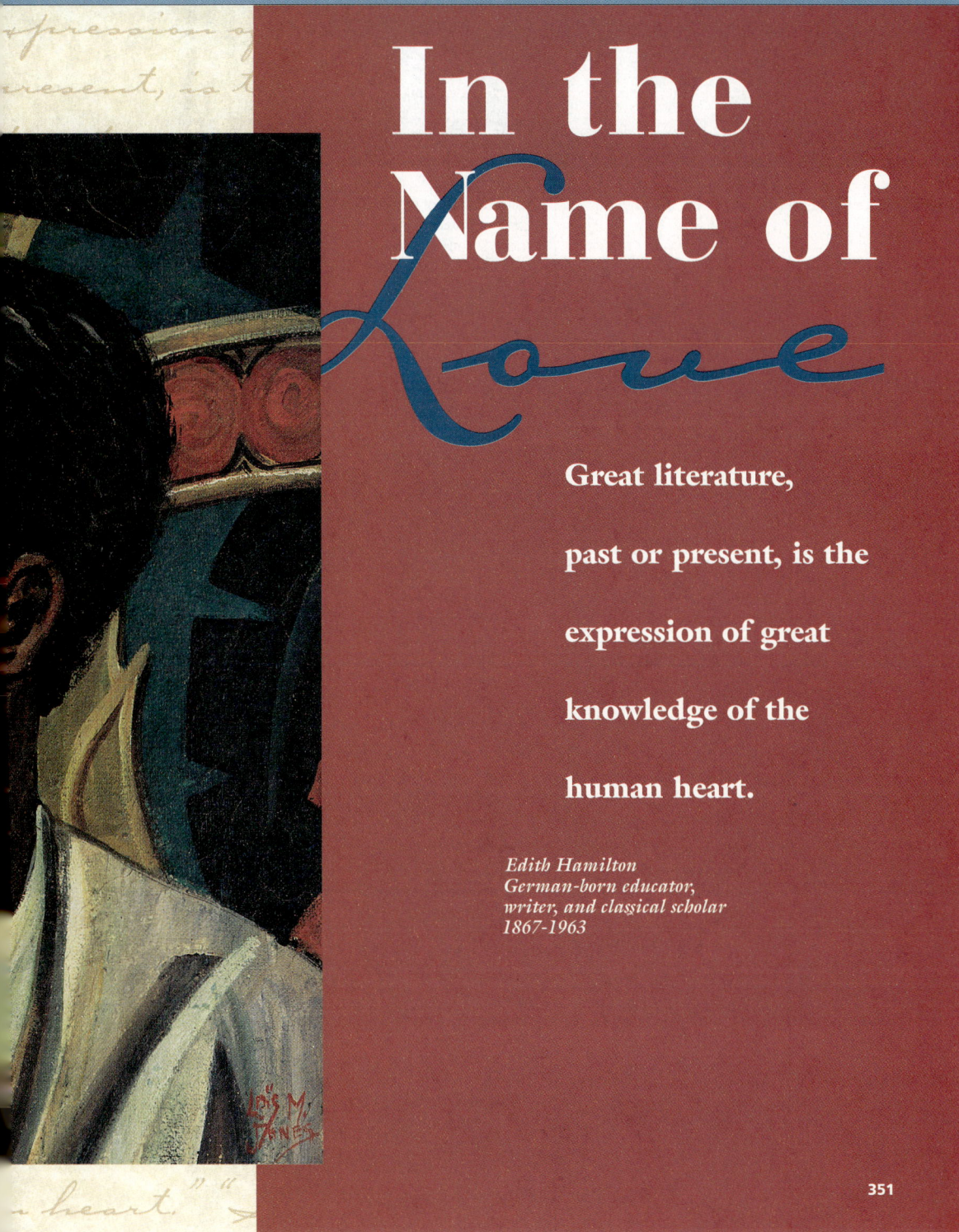

In the Name of *Love*

Great literature, past or present, is the expression of great knowledge of the human heart.

Edith Hamilton
German-born educator,
writer, and classical scholar
1867-1963

Discussion Questions

To help students explore the connections between the art, the quotation, and the unit theme, have them consider the following questions:

1. Do you think that love is an important theme to explore? Why? *(Accept all reasonable responses.)*

2. Have students paraphrase Edith Hamilton's statement. *(Possible responses: All first-class written works express the emotions of the writer; the purpose of writing is to express one's feelings; the most important themes to write about involve human emotions.)*

3. How do you think the two subjects of this painting feel about each other? Why do you think so? *(Accept all reasonable, well-supported responses. Possible responses: They know one another well, because they are looking into one another's eyes and standing close together; they trust one another, because their expressions are open and not defensive or frightened.)*

4. What kinds of stories and experiences might you expect to read about in this unit? *(Possible response: various relationships involving love—romantic love, love between parents and children, or love between friends)*

5. Discuss an experience which helped you understand the phrase "knowledge of the human heart." *(Responses will vary.)*

Art Note

The Lovers (Somali Friends) by Lois Mailou Jones

Jones was born in Boston in 1905. In 1930, she became a professor of design and painting at Howard University—a position she held until retirement in 1977. Jones is noted as among the first African-American women artists who explored African themes in their paintings.

Reading the Art *Why do you think the artist called the people in this painting both "lovers" and "friends"?*

UNIT THREE
Part 1 Skills Trace

ML DENOTES MINI-LESSON IN TEACHER'S EDITION

Selections	Reading Skills and Strategies	Literary Concepts	Writing Opportunities	Speaking, Listening, and Viewing
FICTION **Lalla** Rosamunde Pilcher	Understanding point of view, PE p. 354	Exposition, PE p. 368 Reviewing plot, ML TE p. 357 Fiction, ML TE p. 362	Write a proposal, PE p. 368 Create two lists of pros and cons, PE p. 368 Write a script, PE p. 368 Conclusions for narratives, ML TE p. 367	Act out an imaginary conversation, PE p. 368 Discussion, PE p. 368 Brainstorm with a partner, TE p. 369
POETRY **Love Without Love** Luis Lloréns Torres **The Taxi** Amy Lowell		Metaphor, PE p. 373 Reviewing simile, PE p. 373 Reviewing sensory details, ML TE p. 372	Create an image of romantic love, PE p. 370 Write a poem, PE p. 373 Develop a list of images, PE p. 373 Write a journal entry, PE p. 373 Imaging, ML TE p. 371	Stage a TV talk-show/Interview couples, PE p. 373
POETRY **Sonnet 18** William Shakespeare **Sonnet 30** Edna St. Vincent Millay	Understanding sonnet structure, PE p. 376 Rhyme scheme/quatrain, couplet, PE p. 378	Rhythm/Meter, PE p. 379	Create a Venn diagram, PE p. 379 Create a personality profile, PE p. 379 Write a sonnet or poem, PE p. 379 Comparison and contrast, ML TE p. 378	Present a weather report, PE p. 380 Perform a sonnet as a popular song, PE p. 380
NONFICTION **A Case of Cruelty** James Herriot		Narrative, PE p. 394 Nonfiction, ML TE p. 385 Reviewing style, ML TE p. 389 Reviewing characterization, ML TE p. 390	Describe a memorable experience, PE p. 381 Create a chart, PE p. 381 Create a pamphlet, PE p. 394 Write a nonfiction narrative, PE p. 394 Write diary entries, PE p. 394 Write an editorial, PE p. 394 Vivid, specific words, ML TE p. 383	View episode of *All Creatures Great and Small*, PE p. 395 Oral review, PE p. 395 Tape an interview, PE p. 395 Motivating individuals, ML TE p. 388 Role-play, ML TE p. 388
FICTION **Love Must Not Be Forgotten** Zhang Jie	Understanding flashbacks, PE p. 396 Using your reading log, PE p. 396	Theme, PE p. 409 Reviewing narrative, ML TE p. 403	Prepare a eulogy, PE p. 409 Write a newspaper advice column, PE p. 409 Write a monologue, PE p. 409 Write a character evaluation, PE p. 409 Choosing quotations, ML TE p. 407 Prepare an outline, TE p. 409	Present a eulogy, PE p. 409 Dramatic reading, ML TE p. 406
FICTION ON YOUR OWN **Brigid** Mary Lavin				Paired reading, TE p. 411 Dramatic presentation, TE p. 411

Writing	Reading Skills and Strategies	Literary Concepts	Writing Opportunities	Speaking, Listening, and Viewing
WRITING ABOUT LITERATURE **Creative Response**	Analyzing figurative language, PE pp. 420–421 Responding to literature, PE pp. 422–425	Analyzing figurative language, PE pp. 420–421 Poetry, PE pp. 422–425	Practice personification, PE p. 421 Spice it up, PE p. 421 Make the comparison, PE p. 421 Avoiding clichés, PE p. 421 Poem, PE pp. 422–425 Using sound devices, PE p. 423	Viewing an image, PE p. 427 Interpreting an image, PE p. 427 Discussion, PE p. 427 Making observations, PE p. 427

Grammar, Usage, Mechanics, and Spelling	Multimodal Learning	Research and Study Skills	Vocabulary
Gerunds, ML TE p. 359	Act out an imaginary conversation, PE p. 368 Discussion, PE p. 368 Create a poster, PE p. 369 Create valentines, PE p. 369 Making decisions, ML TE p. 361	Using references/periodicals, ML TE p. 364	benign ludicrous bereft resignation decipher trepidation enmity unnervingly impeccably vacillating
	Draw a picture of romantic love, PE p. 370 Stage a TV talk show/Interview couples, PE p. 373 Tape-recording of love songs, PE p. 374 Create a sketch, PE p. 374 Photographic essay, PE p. 374	Explore many genres of music, TE p. 374	
	Create a Venn diagram, PE p. 379 Present a weather report, PE p. 380 Perform a sonnet as a popular song, PE p. 380		
Prefixes, ML TE p. 386	Create a chart, PE p. 381 Create a two-part drawing, PE p. 395 View episode of *All Creatures Great and Small*, PE p. 395 Oral review, PE p. 395 Tape an interview, PE p. 395 Motivating individuals, ML TE p. 388 Role-play, ML TE p. 388		adamant indignation beneficent mystic callousness placidly convalescence rank coquettishly transcend
Using progressive verb forms, ML TE p. 398	Present a eulogy, PE p. 409 Dramatic reading, ML TE p. 406	Research the cultural revolution in China, PE p. 410 Reading a time line, ML TE p. 404 Research Red Guards, TE p. 410 Research Mao Zedong, TE p. 410	ardent heretic atonement naiveté aversion parry censure renounce coyness wistful
	Dramatic presentation, TE p. 411 Sketching vivid images, TE p. 411 Before-and-after chart, TE p. 417	Researching Irish life, TE p. 418	

Grammar, Usage, Mechanics, and Spelling	Multimodal Learning	Research and Study Skills	Media Literacy
Using punctuation in poetry, PE p. 425 Participial phrases, PE p. 425	Viewing an image, PE p. 427 Interpreting an image, PE p. 427 Discussion, PE p. 427 Making observations, PE p. 427	Analyzing literature, PE pp. 420–421 Analyzing an image, PE p. 427	Interpreting visual metaphors, PE pp. 426–427

UNIT THREE
Part 2 Skills Trace

ML DENOTES MINI-LESSON IN TEACHER'S EDITION

Selections	Reading Skills and Strategies	Literary Concepts	Writing Opportunities	Speaking, Listening, and Viewing
FICTION **The Californian's Tale** Mark Twain	Interpreting details about setting, PE p. 430	Foreshadowing, PE p. 439 Reviewing surprise ending, **ML** TE p. 437	Write a literary analysis, PE p. 439 Write the wife's letter, PE p. 439 Write a comic scene, PE p. 439 Write a script, PE p. 440 Position of adjectives, **ML** TE p. 432	Role-play, PE p. 439 Pantomime, PE p. 440 Reading aloud, **ML** TE p. 435 Improvisation, TE p. 440
POETRY **Simile** N. Scott Momaday **Tonight I Can Write... /Puedo Escribir Los Versos...** Pablo Neruda	Understanding comparisons, PE p. 441	Repetition, PE p. 446 Reviewing figurative language, PE p. 446 Reviewing figurative language, **ML** TE p. 443	Draft a paragraph, PE p. 446 Write a monologue, PE p. 446 Write a poem, PE p. 446	Choral reading, **ML** TE p. 444
POETRY **To...** Aleksandr Pushkin	Understanding chronological order, PE p. 448	Rhyme, PE p. 450 Reviewing rhythm and meter, PE p. 450 Poetry, **ML** TE p. 449	Write a song lyric, PE p. 450 Write an extended definition, PE p. 450 Write a poem, PE p. 450	Compare/Contrast translations, PE p. 451
FICTION **Metonymy, or The Husband's Revenge** Rachel de Queiroz		Frame story, PE p. 458 Reviewing tone, **ML** TE p. 455	Describe a time you were wronged, PE p. 452 Sketch out plan for TV talk show, PE p. 458 Write the investigative notes, PE p. 458 Write a letter, PE p. 458 Write an opening statement, PE p. 458	Stage a TV talk show, PE p. 458 Deliver a newscast, PE p. 459 Appropriate use of modifiers, **ML** TE p. 456
FICTION **The First Seven Years** Bernard Malamud	Interpreting motivation, PE p. 460 Using your reading log, PE p. 460	Allusion, PE p. 471 Reviewing foreshadowing, PE p. 471 Reviewing point of view, **ML** TE p. 465	Rewrite section from first-person point of view, PE p. 470 Write a wedding announcement, PE p. 470 Write two public service announcements, PE p. 470 Write a biographical sketch, PE p. 470	Discussion, PE p. 470 Role-play a conversation, PE p. 471 Give the wedding toast, PE p. 471 Style, **ML** TE p. 463 View art, **ML** TE p. 468
DRAMA **The Bear** Anton Chekhov		Farce, PE p. 486 Stereotypes, PE p. 486 Drama, **ML** TE p. 476 Reviewing stage directions, **ML** TE p. 478	Write a humorous description, PE p. 473 Create dialogue and action, PE p. 486 Write an analysis, PE p. 486 Write a review, PE p. 486	Stage a sequel, PE p. 486 Prepare class presentation, PE p. 487 Dramatic reading, **ML** TE p. 482
FOLK TALE ON YOUR OWN **The Lady Who Was a Beggar** Anonymous			Writing and performing a play, TE p. 488	Grouped reading, TE p. 488 Retelling the story, TE p. 488

Writing	Reading Skills and Strategies	Literary Concepts	Writing Opportunities	Speaking, Listening, and Viewing
WRITING FROM EXPERIENCE **Writing to Explain**			Writing a compare-and-contrast essay, PE pp. 500–507 Drafting, PE pp. 504–505 Using parallel structure, PE p. 505 Revising and publishing, PE pp. 506–507	Interpreting illustrations, PE p. 500 Listening to music, PE p. 502 Watching videotapes, PE p. 502 Interviewing, PE p. 502

Grammar, Usage, Mechanics, and Spelling	Multimodal Learning	Research and Study Skills	Vocabulary
	Role-play, PE p. 439 Create a painting, PE p. 440 Pantomime, PE p. 440 Improvisation, TE p. 440	Using a reading log, ML TE p. 434	balmy imploring boding predecessor desolation sedate furtive sever grizzled supplicating
	Choose a contemporary song, PE p. 447		
	Create visual representations, PE p. 450 Create an exhibition of 19th-century paintings, PE p. 451 Choreograph a dance, PE p. 451	Find additional translations of poem, PE p. 451 Research 19th-century Europe in art history books, TE p. 451	
Adverb phrases, ML TE p. 454	Stage a TV talk show, PE p. 458 Draw a cartoon, PE p. 459 Deliver a newscast, PE p. 459 Draw pictures of key scenes, PE p. 459	Research diseases: beriberi, asthma, jaundice, TE p. 459	deplorable rebuke embellish refined eminently scrutinize ingratiating tepid illicit vile
Appositives, ML TE p. 462	Role-play a conversation, PE p. 471 Give the wedding toast, PE p. 471 Make a sketch for "The First Seven Years," ML TE p. 468	Job application forms, ML TE p. 467 Consult encyclopedias and biographical dictionaries, ML TE p. 470	apt pittance deft profuse direst repugnant discern seethe pallid vehemently
Who vs. whom, ML TE p. 480	Stage a sequel, PE p. 486 Class presentation, PE p. 487 Display photographs from stage productions, PE p. 487	Research Chekov's contributions to theater, PE p. 487 Literary reference sources, ML TE p. 484	emancipation futile languish liberty sniveling
	Sketching characters and scenes, TE p. 488 Flow chart, TE p. 488 Charting folk tale elements, TE p. 497		

Grammar, Usage, Mechanics, and Spelling	Multimodal Learning	Research and Study Skills	Media Literacy
Using parallel structure, PE p. 505 Avoiding double comparisons, PE p. 507	Interpreting illustrations, PE p. 500 Listening to music, PE p. 502 Watching videotapes, PE p. 502 Creating multimedia presentations, PE p. 507 Creating photo essays, PE p. 507 Writing a newspaper article, PE p. 507	Using card catalogs, PE p. 502 Using on-line services, PE p. 502 Using library resources, PE p. 503 Organizing information, PE p. 503	Interpreting illustrations, PE p. 500 Interpreting magazine articles, PE p. 501

UNIT THREE
Recommended Resources   ENRICHMENT   RESEARCH

Recommended Novels and Plays

LITERATURE CONNECTIONS WITH SOURCEBOOK FOR TEACHERS

Thematic Link The line between illusion and reality becomes blurred in this comedy featuring the escapades of mischievous fairies and spellbound young lovers in an enchanted forest.

About the Author William Shakespeare (1564–1616), the gifted playwright and poet, probed the mysteries of human nature, creating memorable characters whose experiences transcend time and place.

Other Works by William Shakespeare *Hamlet, Prince of Denmark; Julius Caesar; Macbeth; Antony and Cleopatra*

LITERATURE CONNECTIONS WITH SOURCEBOOK FOR TEACHERS

Thematic Link A spirited, independent governess wins the love of her employer.

About the Author Generally considered a pioneer of women writers, Charlotte Brontë (1816–1854) passionately addressed the inequalities and contradictions inherent in the society she lived in.

Other Works by Charlotte Brontë *Villette, The Professor, Shirley*

LITERATURE CONNECTIONS WITH SOURCEBOOK FOR TEACHERS

Thematic Link *The Tragedy of Romeo and Juliet* is a classic drama of love, hate, revenge, and realization set in Renaissance Italy.

About the Author William Shakespeare (1564–1616) was an actor, poet, and playwright whose work was popular among the working class and the educated upper classes. He is considered by many to be the greatest playwright of all time.

Other Works by William Shakespeare *Othello, the Moor of Venice; King Lear; As You Like It; The Taming of the Shrew*

Thematic Link In the funniest and sharpest of Austen's novels, strangers who take an instant dislike to one another overcome their first impressions and fall in love.

About the Author Jane Austen (1775–1817) began her literary career at the age of 15. She produced six major novels and is best known for the deftness of her comic touch and her sharp wit.

Other Works by Jane Austen *Sense and Sensibility, Emma, Northanger Abbey, Persuasion*

Thematic Link An early love is rekindled under unlikely circumstances after more than 50 years.

About the Author Marquez (born 1928) is one of the literary giants of South America. His work is rich in particulars and epic in its scope. He earned the Nobel Prize for Literature in 1982.

Other Works by Gabriel García Marquez *One Hundred Years of Solitude, The General and His Labyrinth*

Professional Development   TEACHING THE NOVEL

Chekhov, Anton. *Lady with Lapdog and Other Stories.* NY: Penguin, 1975.

Person, Ethel. *Dreams of Love and Fateful Encounters.* NY: Penguin, 1988.

Singer, Irving. *The Pursuit of Love.* Baltimore, MD: John Hopkins University Press, 1994.

Twain, Mark. "How to Tell a Story," *Selected Shorter Writings of Mark Twain.* Boston, MA: Houghton Mifflin Company, 1962.

CROSS-CURRICULAR TEACHING   PROFESSIONAL DEVELOPMENT

✓ Recommended Readings in Cross-Curricular Areas

SOCIAL STUDIES

The Age of Shakespeare by Francoise Larogue (1993) Beautiful presentation of the social situation and the daily life that gives context to Shakespeare's brilliance. Links to Shakespeare's "Sonnet 18."

Celebrating Life: Jewish Rites of Passage by Malka Drucker (1984) The cultural and religious beliefs and practices of Jewish people are explored. Links to Bernard Malamud's "The First Seven Years."

Anton Chekhov's Life and Thought: Selected Letters and Commentary (1975) The colorful character of a literary giant shines through these pages of intimate reflections. Links to Anton Chekhov's "The Bear."

Professional Development — CROSS-CURRICULAR INSTRUCTION

Day, Francis Ann. *Multicultural Voices in Contemporary Literature: A Resource for Teachers.* Portsmouth, NH: Heinmann, 1994.

Fagan, Edward R. "Interdisciplinary English: Science, Technology, and Society," *English Journal.* 76 (September 1987) 81–83.

Giroux, Henry A. *Teachers as Intellectuals.* NY: Bergin and Garvey, 1988.

✓ Recommended Media Resources

THE LANGUAGE OF LITERATURE

ELECTRONIC LIBRARY
CD-ROM
Additional literature selections for Unit Three can be found on the Electronic Library CD-ROM.

LASERLINKS
Videodisc, Gr.10
See Laserlinks Teacher's Source Book, pages 28–29, for overview of Unit Three.

AUDIO LIBRARY
Tapes
Gr. 10, Tapes 9–12: Sides A & B

Novel in Spanish
Romeo y Julieta

WRITING COACH
Writing Coach Software: Writing About Literature—Poem, Compare-and-Contrast Essay

OUTSIDE RESOURCES

Films/Videos/Film Strips/Audiocassettes
Shakespeare: The Man and His Times, video, Educational Audio Visual, 1989, (38 minutes).
Pablo Neruda, video, Library Video Company, 1995, (30 minutes).
N. Scott Momaday Reads, audiocassette, American Audio Prose Library, (40 minutes).
All Things Bright and Beautiful, audiocassette, Listen for Pleasure, (150 minutes).

Internet Resources
McDougal Littel Literature Center at http://www.hmco.com/mcdougal/lit

Professional Development — TEACHING WITH TECHNOLOGY

Cowan, Hilary. "Software for Teaching Earth Science, Math, Shakespeare, and More," *Electronic Learning.* 15:1 (September 1995) 52.

Schuster, James. "Learning to Improve Learning," *Educational Technology.* 35:3 (May/June 1995) 23.

Education Technology. Business Publishers, Inc., 951 Pershing Drive, Silver Springs, MD 20910.

UNIT THREE

Professional Enrichment

from Poetry Browsing: You Can't Explicate 'Em All
David S. Burk

Read any engaging poems lately? . . . You may even have read some on your own, apart from graduate work or course planning. But most other adults or adolescents would find the question itself surprising or even humorous. Why is this? Is poetry not for everyone? Or has education steered readers away from it?

I can't accept the first possibility. I've never known a preschooler who didn't enjoy children's poetry, nor a high school or middle school student who couldn't do the poetry reading and writing in my classes. I have worked with students who disliked poetry, or weren't comfortable with it, or who were convinced it wasn't important; but those are learned responses. No, I'm convinced poetry is, to use Lionel Trilling's phrase, "indigenous to the very constitution of the mind." . . . Myra Cohn Livingston agrees. Near the end of *The Child as Poet: Myth or Reality?*, she writes:

> Children have the potential for growth, for creativity, and for the writing of poetry—and . . . given this, with guidance by caring parents, educators, teachers, and poet-teachers, they can be led to learn the value of craft and the work that it requires to make a poem.

If all children are potential poets, all are potential poetry lovers. There is nothing fundamentally wrong with poetry itself, but we need to rethink the guidance we give poetry readers. We could give more guidance, certainly. But devoting more time to poetry is only part of the answer. My breakthrough came when I changed my focus in teaching poetry from explication to exposure, moving to a workshop approach where students experience as much as possible of the wide terrain of poetry.

EXPLICATION IN ITS PLACE

M. H. Abrams defines explication, or "close reading," as "the detailed and subtle analysis of the complex interrelations and ambiguities (multiple meanings) of the component elements within a work." If you were in college during the "reign" of New Criticism, that may sound like fun to you. It does to me. A part of me still thinks close reading is the only approach to poetry that counts.

One way New Criticism continues to influence instruction, I've noticed, is in how much time is devoted to each poem in class. Whatever our critical stance, we tend to feel guilty turning the page when there's more to be said about a poem. Many types of response may be encouraged, but we feel duty bound that the response be at length. Reading and literature textbooks support this tendency, surrounding each poem with its encapsulating lesson, demanding equal time, and lots of it, for each poem.

Certainly, there is nothing wrong with taking long looks at individual poems. Students need to see just how much a skilled, enthusiastic reader or group can discover and savor in a single text. But the mechanical, chew-each-bite-20-times-before-you-swallow-it rhythm of much poetry instruction isn't consistent with the way poetry is read outside of school. Those who read poetry outside of school do many things with poems besides fully explicating them:

- We sample and reject poems.
- We let meaning accumulate through rereadings spread over months or years.
- We start explications and don't finish.
- We fall in love with poems we don't understand.
- We respond in ways that are personal or even quirky, ways that can't be supported by the text.
- We find poems that resonate so forcefully with our experiences or yearnings that for us they need no explication.

Outside of school, readers choose whether or not to explore the riches of a given poem, whether to explore them all at once or in stages, when to stop exploring . . . and what counts for riches in the first place. To get good at making these decisions, and to build momentum to continue, students need to start making them more often in school.

I used to prepare for the year's first poetry lesson by making overheads of a few carefully selected poems I could perform my interpretive magic on. I looked for poems I thought would engage my students, but it seemed even my best, field-tested poems left too large a minority either mystified or bored. My solution was to look for better poems but, of course, I never found one that engaged everybody.

Now I begin poetry by wheeling out my collection of literature textbook examination copies, wiping out the school library poetry shelves, and then raiding the public library. I bag up most of the poetry books from my own shelves, then the books from my son's room. Finally I add collections of poems my students and I have written in past years. I still get my overheads ready—we'll still need poems we can all look at together. But I remind myself to spend less class time with each one, less time insisting on my own interpretations and evaluations. What I'm after is browsing.

At first glance, the word *browsing* may not seem forceful enough. A browsing shopper might be inattentive, just passing time, just looking. However, browsers (in stores as well as among poems) see and learn volumes in a short time. And when, as eventually happens, browsers become buyers, they can be more sure of their selections, having explored their options. I use browsing here in its richest library and antique shop sense.

BENEFITS OF BROWSING

Of the many good things that happen when students browse through poetry, two stand out:

Students create their own definition of poetry based on sufficient evidence. The more poems readers see, the richer definition of the genre they can build for themselves. Those who have only seen Dr. Seuss, Shel Silverstein, and the poems in the basal readers have a narrow and skewed lens through which to view new poems. Students occasionally prove this point by blurting out, "That's not poetry!" in response to texts that clearly are poems. Such narrow definitions of poetry harden quickly and are difficult to dislodge. And many students who grudgingly give them up seize upon the opposite misconception: "Anything's poetry!" [Through browsing, students learn] to distinguish poetry from nonpoetry, and eventually good poems from bad. . . .

The second thing that happens when students browse through poetry is that **students have a chance to be engaged by poems.** Of course, we don't expose students to poetry just so they can learn to define the term. We want students to enter poetry for life, convinced that it will enrich their spirits and intellects. How does one become convinced? Well, from the looks of things it's seldom through explicating poems someone else has chosen. That's a chancy, blind date approach. By inviting students to look at many poems in a short time we increase their chances of encountering poems that engage them, set their minds rambling, perhaps even sweep them off their feet.

Every child is a potential poetry lover, but the practical fact remains that for most readers poetry is an acquired taste. Good experiences with poetry accumulate . . . we reach a threshold—a certain number of good experiences, different for each reader—and love blossoms. Those for whom love hasn't blossomed simply may not have seen enough poems.

HOW MANY POEMS ARE ENOUGH?

This past year in my classes, I began our first browsing session by handing out various poetry books at random. I asked students to start with the first poem in the book, read the first four lines, then decide if they understood them and found them interesting. If not, the students were free to move to the next poem. If the beginning of the poem was understandable and interesting, they were to finish reading it. When they found a whole poem they understood and found interesting, I asked them to answer some questions about it. I also asked students to keep track of how many poems they browsed through before finding a "keeper."

It was a limited study—involving 53 students—and very loosely structured, each student deciding for him- or herself how to define the terms "understand" and "find interesting." Here are some of the findings.

- Four students hit it off with the very first poem they read.
- Twenty students (over a third) found a poem to discuss within the first five poems.
- The average student read 22 poems before stopping to respond.
- Five students needed to see more than 70 poems before responding.
- One student didn't stop and respond until poem number 167.

One must generalize cautiously from such an informal study. But what if these numbers hold true? What if the average student in each reading class needs to see 22 poems before one motivates him or her enough to study it further? A little explicate-'em-all voice inside of me is saying, "What a waste of perfectly good poetry. Go back. Look at them again. Let me show you why you shouldn't reject so many." But the truth is, I too reject quite a few poems for each one I savor. Even in the poetry book that engages me most— that continues truly to sweep me off my feet—Frost's *A Boy's Will*, 10 of the 30 poems leave me with nothing to say.

If these numbers hold true, many students in classrooms where poetry is a low priority or where explication is the main approach stand little chance of being engaged by even one poem.

ENGAGEMENT

Once each of my students located a poem he or she both enjoyed and understood, I asked for four types of response about it. Samples include:

- In your own words, tell what the poem means.
- Tell why you enjoyed the poem. What about the poem got your attention?
- Copy out your favorite line from the poem, and tell why it is your favorite.
- Tell what you noticed about the way the poet wrote the poem—the special way he or she used words, lines, stanzas, sounds, ideas, comparisons.

When students browse, it is important that they stop and reflect on some poems. Otherwise poetry reading might become a race to see who can "read" the most poems, just another form of channel surfing. Students should browse purposefully, expecting to be engaged.

I can report that my students browsed purposefully. All 53 found poems to respond to, and with just a couple exceptions all wrote satisfying responses, many quite focused and insightful. . . . This suggests that engagement works the same way for my students as it does for me: I begin to be engaged by subject matter that resonates in some way with my own experience. The engagement deepens as I read further and find myself saying, "Why yes, that's it exactly! I couldn't have said it better." For me and for my students, that kind of engagement leads naturally into curiosity and insight about poetic technique and subtleties of meaning. . . .

CONCLUSION

Good teachers do more than structure opportunities and time for students. Through their attitudes and actions, they turn students on to poetry. They model delight and curiosity. With a deep knowledge both of poems and of their students, they match up the two, increasing the opportunities for engagement. They respect student responses and help students elaborate them. Through modeling and direct instruction, they give students tools with which to capitalize on their inborn potential to love and make use of poetry.

Copyrighted material reprinted with permission.

UNIT THREE
Starting Points for Unit Projects

The following suggestions will help you initiate individual and group projects during the course of this unit.

Staging a Poetry Slam

LITERATURE PROJECT Have students review all the poems in the unit and have each choose a favorite. Each student can then write his or her own poem, using the selection as an inspiration. Students can imitate the poet's style, or they can write a poem dealing with the same subject. Then have students stage a poetry slam, in which they read the poems from the unit, as well as their own poems.

Collecting Fine Art About Love

GROUP ART PROJECT Ask groups of students to assemble a booklet of paintings that depict romantic love. Students can use photocopies from library resources or the inexpensive postcard reproductions sold in many museums. Ask students to identify the artist, date, and title of each painting and to include a commentary about what they think each piece suggests about love.

Producing a Booklet of Advice

PSYCHOLOGY PROJECT Ask small groups of students to solicit questions about romantic relationships from other class members or other students in the school. The group can then select a number of questions and confer about an appropriate and sensitive response to each. Students can present their advice in an oral presentation or in a booklet.

Making a Valentine

ART PROJECT Have students make a valentine for any person to whom they are especially close. Students can draw or design text and images, or they can make collages with images gleaned from photographs or magazines, photocopies from books, or original sketches. Find a place in class to display the finished valentines. Reassure students that they need not include their name or the recipient's name!

Presenting a Skit About Love

GROUP DRAMA PROJECT Invite groups of students to write and produce a skit about teenage characters facing the problems of love: a misunderstanding between a boyfriend and girlfriend, for example, or a conflict between a character's romantic relationship and other friendships and commitments. Suggest that the group initiate a class discussion on the resolution of the conflict.

Taping a Medley of Love Songs

GROUP MUSIC PROJECT Ask groups of students to tape a medley of excerpts from love songs. Their selections should have a connecting theme: young love, love gone wrong, love fulfilled, love in the time of war, playful love, etc. As resources, students can use school and public libraries, family collections, and local music schools and radio stations. Suggest that students include their own commentaries on the tape.

Family and Community Involvement

Family

The selections in Unit Three present a variety of characters who learn important things about themselves through love or the lack of it. The following activities will help students, family, and community members to think about the meaning of love in their own lives.

OPTION 1 SHARE FAVORITE STORIES ABOUT LOVE

- **Connection** All the selections in Unit Three consider the effects of love on characters' lives.
- **Activity** *Copymaster 1* Students and family members can share a favorite story, either from real life or from a family library, that shows someone acting out of love. Each family member can tell why the story he or she chose is particularly affecting.

OPTION 2 DISCOVER LOVE IN THE NEWS

- **Connection** "The First Seven Years" describes one man's sacrifices in the name of love.
- **Activity** *Copymaster 2* Students and family members can look in the daily newspaper and magazines to find news stories and articles that feature love in some context, including people caring for ill family members, rescuing children from fires or drowning, or rescuing and providing homes for stray animals.

OPTION 3 WRITE A LOVE SONG

- **Connection** "Love Must Not Be Forgotten" describes a love that went unexpressed.
- **Activity** *Copymaster 3* Have students and family members try to express love via a love song—a ballad, a rock-and-roll number, a rap, an aria, or any form that interests them.

Community

OPTION 1

- **Connection** All of the selections in Unit Three consider the effects of love on characters' lives
- **Activity** Have students visit a local cemetery and write down or photograph some of the inscriptions on the headstones, collecting words and images that describe the enduring nature of love.

OPTION 2

- **Connection** "The Californian's Tale" considers the painful consequences of love on a man's life.
- **Activity** Invite a local novelist to come and talk to the class about his or her work. Ask the novelist to discuss how he or she approaches the topic of love.

OPTION 3

- **Connection** "Tonight I Can Write . . ." deals with a man's struggle to express how the loss of his lover has affected him.
- **Activity** Invite someone from a local dance group to talk to your class about some of the great love stories conveyed by their art, such as the ballets *Romeo and Juliet*, *Giselle*, and *Swan Lake*.

UNIT THREE
Part 1 Lesson Planner

TIME ALLOTMENTS SHOWN ARE APPROXIMATE. DEPENDING ON YOUR GOALS AND THE NEEDS OF YOUR STUDENTS, YOU MAY WISH TO ALLOW MORE OR LESS TIME FOR CERTAIN PORTIONS OF THE LESSON.

Table of Contents	Discussion	Previewing the Selection	Reading the Selection
PART OPENER **The Ties That Bind** page 352	**20 MINUTES** • Reflect on the part theme		
SELECTION **Lalla** page 355 EASY		**20 MINUTES** • PERSONAL CONNECTION • GEOGRAPHICAL CONNECTION • READING CONNECTION: Understanding point of view	**90 MINUTES** • Introduce vocabulary • Read pp. 355–367 (13 pp.)
SELECTIONS **Love Without Love/ The Taxi** page 371 AVERAGE		**20 MINUTES** • PERSONAL CONNECTION • LITERARY CONNECTION • WRITING CONNECTION	**15 MINUTES** • Read pp. 371–372 (2 pp.)
SELECTIONS **Sonnet 18/Sonnet 30** page 377 CHALLENGING		**20 MINUTES** • PERSONAL CONNECTION • LITERARY CONNECTION • READING CONNECTION: Understanding sonnet structure	**20 MINUTES** • Read pp. 377–378 (2 pp.)
SELECTION **A Case of Cruelty** page 382 EASY		**20 MINUTES** • PERSONAL CONNECTION • BIOGRAPHICAL CONNECTION • WRITING CONNECTION	**60 MINUTES** • Introduce vocabulary • Read pp. 382–391 (10 pp.)
SELECTION **Love Must Not Be Forgotten** page 397 AVERAGE		**20 MINUTES** • PERSONAL CONNECTION • CULTURAL CONNECTION • READING CONNECTION: Understanding flashbacks/Using your reading log	**60 MINUTES** • Introduce vocabulary • Read pp. 397–408 (12 pp.)
FICTION ON YOUR OWN **Brigid** page 411 AVERAGE			**50 MINUTES** • Read pp. 411–419 (9 pp.)
Writing **WRITING ABOUT LITERATURE** **Creative Response**	**Writer's Style** **20 MINUTES**	**Prewriting** **25 MINUTES**	**Drafting and Revising** **55 MINUTES**

Time estimates assume in-class work. You may wish to assign some of these stages as homework.

Responding to the Selection

FROM PERSONAL RESPONSE TO CRITICAL ANALYSIS	OR	ANOTHER PATHWAY	LITERARY CONCEPTS	QUICKWRITES
50 MINUTES				
• Discussion questions	OR	• Imaginary conversation	• Exposition	• Proposal • Two lists of pros and cons • Script
50 MINUTES				
• Discussion questions	OR	• Television talk show	• Metaphor • Simile	• Poem • List of images • Journal entry
50 MINUTES				
• Discussion questions	OR	• Venn diagram	• Rhythm/Meter	• Personality profile • Sonnet/Poem
40 MINUTES				
• Discussion questions	OR	• Pamphlet	• Narrative	• Nonfiction narrative • Diary entries • Editorial
50 MINUTES				
• Discussion questions	OR	• Eulogy	• Theme	• Advice column • Monologue • Character evaluation

Extension Activities

• ALTERNATIVE ACTIVITIES • LITERARY LINKS • CRITIC'S CORNER • THE WRITER'S STYLE • ACROSS THE CURRICULUM • ART CONNECTION • WORDS TO KNOW • BIOGRAPHY

ALTERNATIVE ACTIVITIES	LITERARY LINKS	CRITIC'S CORNER	THE WRITER'S STYLE	ACROSS THE CURRICULUM	ART CONNECTION	WORDS TO KNOW	BIOGRAPHY
30 MINUTES							
✔	✔				✔	✔	
15 MINUTES							
✔							✔
30 MINUTES							
✔		✔					✔
40 MINUTES							
✔	✔		✔	HEALTH		✔	✔
30 MINUTES							
✔				HISTORY	✔	✔	✔

Publishing and Reflecting	Grammar in Context	Reading the World
25 MINUTES	**15 MINUTES**	**35 MINUTES**

PART 1

REFLECTING ON THEME

Ask students how they react to the metaphor that compares love to ties that bind people. Is love a prison, or does it set a person free? Does it have aspects of both? Are ties that bind necessarily a restriction of freedom? Have students discuss these questions with a partner.

What Do You Think?

Before students begin their graphs, remind them that there are many kinds of love relationships, as reflected in the subjects of the selections in this part of the unit. The love relationship they graph need not necessarily be romantic love. Suggest that they choose the relationship which brings out the strongest feelings in them. Students will return to this activity on pages 410 and 508.

UNIT THREE **PART 1**

THE TIES THAT BIND

REFLECTING ON THEME

The writers who created the original Star Trek series for television imagined an entire race of people—the Vulcans—defined by their logic and absence of emotion. For the Vulcans, love's passions posed a threat to reason. In this part of Unit Three, you will read selections that would certainly puzzle the Vulcans. Here, you will encounter a variety of ties created by love.

What Do You Think? Think about a love relationship in your own life. In your notebook, list various feelings that you experience in that relationship. Then create a bar graph that shows the relative frequencies of these feelings. For example, the longest bar might be used to represent contentment, while the shortest bar might be used to represent anger. As you read, compare your experience of love with those described in the selections.

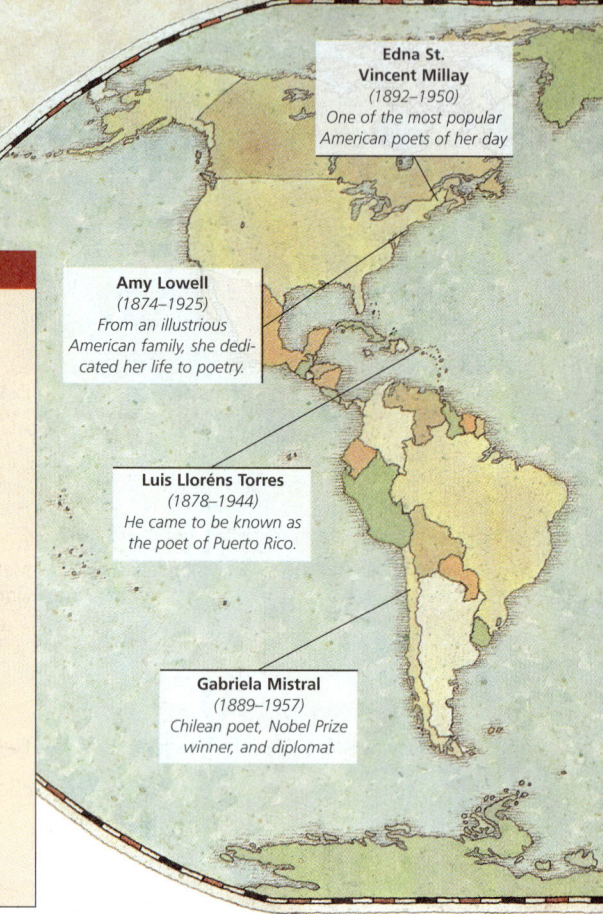

Edna St. Vincent Millay (1892–1950) One of the most popular American poets of her day

Amy Lowell (1874–1925) From an illustrious American family, she dedicated her life to poetry.

Luis Lloréns Torres (1878–1944) He came to be known as the poet of Puerto Rico.

Gabriela Mistral (1889–1957) Chilean poet, Nobel Prize winner, and diplomat

Rosamunde Pilcher	**Lalla** *Which boy will she choose?*	354
Luis Lloréns Torres	**Love Without Love** *What he asks of his love*	370
Amy Lowell	**The Taxi** *Raw emotions with an urban edge*	370
William Shakespeare	**Sonnet 18** *"Shall I compare thee to a summer's day?"*	375
Edna St. Vincent Millay	**Sonnet 30** *All that love is not*	375

352

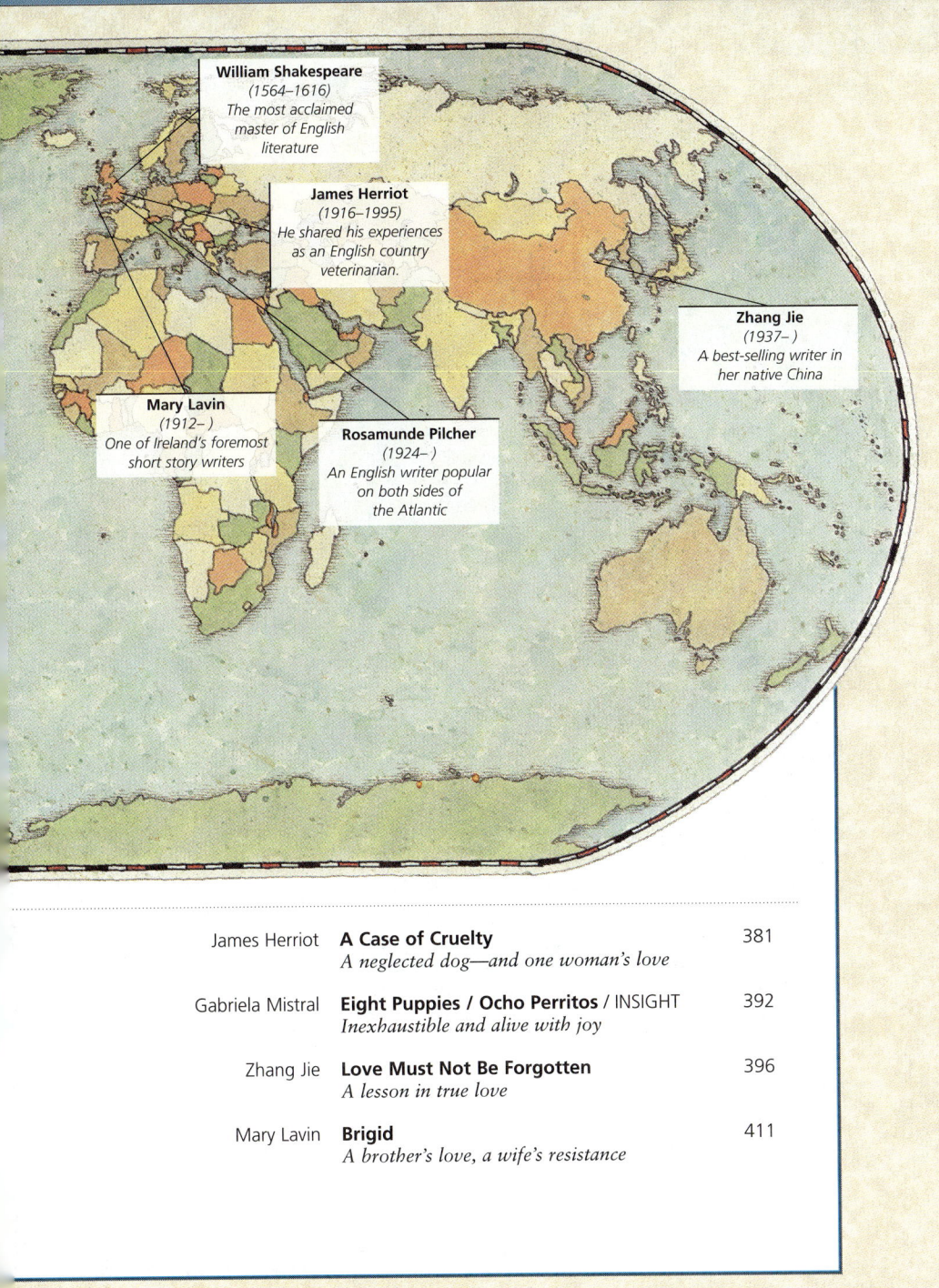

James Herriot	**A Case of Cruelty** *A neglected dog—and one woman's love*	381
Gabriela Mistral	**Eight Puppies / Ocho Perritos** / INSIGHT *Inexhaustible and alive with joy*	392
Zhang Jie	**Love Must Not Be Forgotten** *A lesson in true love*	396
Mary Lavin	**Brigid** *A brother's love, a wife's resistance*	411

Map Note

This map shows the native countries of the authors featured in this part of the unit. In order to help students think about the variety of ties of love, you may want to ask them one or more of the following questions:

- What do you know about modern China that might influence the way Zhang Jie writes about love?
- Can you name other works by William Shakespeare? What influence has he had on English literature?
- Are you familiar with James Herriot? What might a veterinarian's experiences teach readers about love?

OVERVIEW

Objectives

- To understand and appreciate a love story that explores how a young woman learns to value intangibles
- To identify and understand exposition
- To express understanding of the selection through a choice of writing forms, including a proposal, a list of pros and cons, and a script
- To extend understanding of the story through a variety of multimodal and cross-curricular activities

Skills

LITERARY CONCEPTS
- Exposition
- Plot

READING SKILLS/ STRATEGIES
- Understanding point of view

THE WRITER'S STYLE
- Conclusions for narratives

GENRE STUDY
- Fiction: love story

GRAMMAR
- Gerunds

SPEAKING, LISTENING, AND VIEWING
- Group discussion
- Role playing

GEOGRAPHICAL CONNECTION
London and Cornwall The main character in this story must decide whether she wants to live the cosmopolitan life of London or the rural life of Cornwall. Photographs of London and Cornwall will help students visualize Lalla's two worlds.

Side A, Frame 49426

PREVIEWING

FICTION

Lalla
Rosamunde Pilcher Great Britain

Activating Prior Knowledge
PERSONAL CONNECTION

When you set a goal for your life or make another important decision, you probably base that decision on your values, the ideals or beliefs that are most important to you. Think about the values that you would consider when setting a goal or making a major decision. In your notebook, list five values that are important to you, then rank them from one to five, with one being the most important.

Building Background
GEOGRAPHICAL CONNECTION

In the selection you are about to read, Lalla, the main character, makes several life decisions based on her values. One choice she faces is whether to live in the cosmopolitan capital city of London or in a rural village in the county of Cornwall, on the remote southwest coast of England.

Cornwall is popular with tourists and artists for its rugged beauty. The county occupies a long, narrow peninsula that juts into the Atlantic Ocean. The area is mainly rural, with small farming villages scattered through the inland countryside and picturesque fishing towns along the coast. By contrast, London has been one of the world's largest and busiest cities for centuries. The city boasts many famous museums, art galleries, parks, and cathedrals. It also offers a wide variety of job opportunities, fine shops, and exciting night life. In choosing between the excitement of London and the attractions of Cornwall, Lalla discovers what she values most.

Active Reading/Setting a Purpose
READING CONNECTION

Understanding Point of View Point of view refers to the type of narrator used in a story. The short story "Lalla" uses a first-person point of view, in which the narrator is a character in the story who tells everything in his or her own words. This narrator, a young girl named Jane, describes characters and relates events as she sees and understands them. As you read the selection, look for clues to Jane's values in the comments she makes.

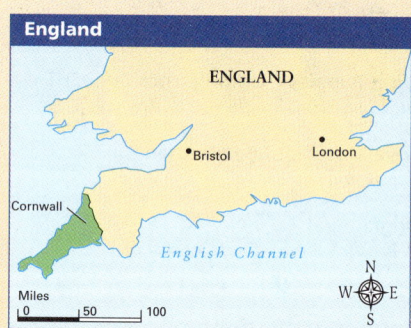

- GEOGRAPHICAL CONNECTION
- VISUAL VOCABULARY

354 UNIT THREE PART 1: THE TIES THAT BIND

PRINT AND MEDIA RESOURCES

UNIT THREE RESOURCE BOOK
Strategic Reading: Literature, p. 4
Vocabulary SkillBuilder, p. 5

ACCESS FOR STUDENTS ACQUIRING ENGLISH
Selection Summaries
Reading Support

TEACHER'S GUIDE TO ASSESSMENT AND PORTFOLIO USE

FORMAL ASSESSMENT
Selection Test, pp. 71–72
 Test Generator

 **AUDIO LIBRARY**
See Reference Card

 **LASERLINKS**
Geographical Connection
Visual Vocabulary

354 THE LANGUAGE OF LITERATURE TEACHER'S EDITION

Lalla

Rosamunde Pilcher

There was a Before and After. Before was before our father died, when we lived in London, in a tall narrow house with a little garden at the back. When we went on family skiing holidays every winter and attended suitable—and probably very expensive—day schools.

Portrait of Amber (1991), Charles Warren Mundy. Oil on canvas, 8" × 10", private collection.

SUMMARY

Jane tells the story of her beautiful sister, Lalla, who is horrified to leave London and move to rural Cornwall after their father dies. She avoids making new friends in Cornwall until she meets Godfrey Howard. Though Godfrey is a veterinary student in Bristol, he and Lalla write and spend holidays together. At a dance given by an acquaintance, Lalla meets, and is attracted to, wealthy Allan Sutton. She moves to London and eventually becomes engaged to Allan. The next Easter, however, Lalla breaks up with Allan and leaves behind her glamorous city life. She returns home to Godfrey and to the companionship and warmth that no wealth could bring.

Thematic Link: *The Ties That Bind* Lalla discovers how strong her ties are to an old love.

CUSTOMIZING FOR
Students Acquiring English

- Use **ACCESS FOR STUDENTS ACQUIRING ENGLISH.**
- This story is filled with British idioms, many of which are defined in the footnotes. You may wish to go over these unfamiliar words and expressions.

STRATEGIC READING FOR
Less-Proficient Readers

Set a Purpose Ask students to read about "Before" at the start of the story and then predict what "After" will be like. Then have them read on to find out how the narrator's life changes after her father's death.

Use **UNIT THREE RESOURCE BOOK**, p. 4, for guidance in reading the selection.

 VISUAL VOCABULARY
- **estuary** (ĕs′chōō-ĕr′ē)
- **portico** (pôr′tĭ-kō′)

Side A, Frame 49433

WORDS TO KNOW

benign (bĭ-nīn′) *adj.* mild; gentle (p. 367)
bereft (bĭ-rĕft′) *adj.* suffering the death of a loved one; deprived of someone or something important (p. 356)
decipher (dĭ-sī′fər) *v.* to read or interpret something unclear; to figure out (p. 361)
enmity (ĕn′mĭ-tē) *n.* the hatred between enemies; antagonism; hostility (p. 361)
impeccably (ĭm-pĕk′ə-blē) *adv.* flawlessly; perfectly (p. 362)
ludicrous (lōō′dĭ-krəs) *adj.* laughably absurd; ridiculous (p. 356)

resignation (rĕz′ĭg-nā′shən) *n.* the act of giving up; submission (p. 357)
trepidation (trĕp′ĭ-dā′shən) *n.* a state of alarm or dread; apprehension; anxiety (p. 357)
unnervingly (ŭn-nûrv′ĭng-lē) *adv.* in a way that causes someone to become nervous or upset; disturbingly (p. 364)
vacillating (văs′ə-lāt′ĭng) *adj.* swinging indecisively from one course of action or opinion to another **vacillate** *v.* (p. 361)

CUSTOMIZING FOR
Gifted and Talented Students

As students read the story, ask them how the social pressures of status and wealth affect Lalla and her family.

Possible responses:

- *Page 358*—As the tenants, Lalla's family feels they have less status than the Roystons.
- *Page 360*—Lalla sees Carwheal as a step down from her old life in London.
- *Page 363*—Lalla's jilting of Godfrey may have been due to his lack of money.
- *Page 364*—Material things seem more important than intangibles to Lalla.
- *Page 364*—Despite Allan's character flaws, his wealth attracted Lalla.

CUSTOMIZING FOR
Students Acquiring English

① Explain to students that *immortal* means "living forever."

② Ask students to figure out the meaning of *limbo* using context clues. (state of uncertainty)

Critical Thinking:
HYPOTHESIZING

Ⓐ Have students suggest why the family has decided to move from London so soon after the father's death. (*Possible responses:* They can no longer afford to live life in London; Mother wants to return to her old home now that she is alone.)

Literary Concept: EXPOSITION

Ⓑ Have students discuss the background information provided so far. (Readers learn the family had lived well in London.) Ask how the exposition heightens their interest in the story. (Readers want to know whether the family will adjust to life in Cornwall.)

---

① Our father was a big man, outgoing and immensely active. We thought he was immortal, but then most children think that about their father. The worst thing was that Mother thought he was immortal too, and when he died, keeling over on the pavement between the insurance offices where he worked, and the company car into which he was just about to climb, there followed a period of ghastly ② limbo. Bereft, uncertain, lost, none of us knew what to do next. But after the funeral and a little talk with the family lawyer, Ⓐ Mother quietly pulled herself together and told us.

At first we were horrified. "Leave London? Leave school?" Lalla could not believe it. "But I'm starting 'O' levels[1] next year."

"There are other schools," Mother told her.

"And what about Jane's music lessons?"

"We'll find another teacher."

"I don't mind about leaving school," said Barney. "I don't much like my school anyway."

Mother gave him a smile, but Lalla persisted in her inquisition.[2] "But where are we going to *live?*"

Ⓑ "We're going to Cornwall."

And so it was After. Mother sold the lease of the London house and a removals firm[3] came and packed up all the furniture and we traveled, each silently thoughtful, by car to Cornwall. It was spring, and because Mother had not realized how long the journey would take, it was dark by the time we found the village and, finally, the house. It stood just inside a pair of large gates, backed by tall trees. When we got out of the car, stiff and tired, we could smell the sea and feel the cold wind.

"There's a light in the window," observed Lalla.

"That'll be Mrs. Bristow," said Mother, and I knew she was making a big effort to keep her voice cheerful. She went up the little path and knocked at the door, and then, perhaps realizing it was ludicrous to be knocking at her own door, opened it. We saw someone coming down the narrow hallway towards us—a fat and bustling lady with grey hair and a hectically flowered pinafore.[4]

"Well, my dear life," she said, "what a journey you must have had. I'm all ready for you. There's a kettle on the hob[5] and a pie in the oven."

The house was tiny compared to the one we had left in London, but we all had rooms to ourselves, as well as an attic for the dolls' house, the books, bricks,[6] model cars and paintboxes we had refused to abandon, and a ramshackle shed alongside the garage where we could keep our bicycles. The garden was even smaller than the London garden, but this didn't matter because now we were living in the country and there were no boundaries to our new territory.

> We were living in the country and there were no boundaries to our new territory.

---

1. **'O' levels:** in Britain, a series of secondary-school examinations given before students can advance to higher studies.
2. **inquisition** (ĭn′kwĭ-zĭsh′ən): a lengthy series of questions.
3. **removals firm:** chiefly British term for a moving company.
4. **pinafore** (pĭn′ə-fôr): an apron.
5. **hob:** a warming shelf, especially on the back or side of a fireplace.
6. **bricks:** chiefly British term for building blocks.

| WORDS TO KNOW | **bereft** (bĭ-rĕft′) *adj.* suffering the death of a loved one; deprived of someone or something important |
| | **ludicrous** (lōō′dĭ-krəs) *adj.* laughably absurd; ridiculous |

We explored, finding a wooded lane which led down to a huge inland estuary[7] where it was possible to fish for flounder from the old sea wall.[8] In the other direction, a sandy right-of-way[9] led past the church and over the golf links[10] and the dunes to another beach—a wide and empty shore where the ebb tide[11] took the ocean out half a mile or more.

The Roystons, father, mother and two sons, lived in the big house and were our landlords. We hadn't seen them yet, though Mother had walked, in some trepidation, up the drive to make the acquaintance of Mrs. Royston, and to thank her for letting us have the house. But Mrs. Royston hadn't been in, and poor Mother had had to walk all the way down the drive again with nothing accomplished.

"How old are the Royston boys?" Barney asked Mrs. Bristow.

"I suppose David's thirteen and Paul's about eleven." She looked at us. "I don't know how old you lot are."

"I'm seven," said Barney, "and Jane's twelve and Lalla's fourteen."

"Well," said Mrs. Bristow. "That's nice. Fit in nicely, you would."

"They're far too young for me," said Lalla. "Anyway, I've seen them. I was hanging out the washing for Mother, and they came down the drive and out of the gate on their bicycles. They didn't even look my way."

"Come now," said Mrs. Bristow, "they're probably shy as you are."

"We don't particularly want to know them," said Lalla.

"But . . ." I started and then stopped. I wasn't like Lalla. I wanted to make friends. It would be nice to know the Royston boys. They had a tennis court; I had caught a glimpse of it through the trees. I wouldn't mind being asked to play tennis.

But for Lalla, of course, it was different. Fourteen was a funny age, neither one thing nor the other. And as for the way that Lalla looked! Sometimes I thought that if I didn't love her, and she wasn't my sister, I should hate her for her long, cloudy brown hair, the tilt of her nose, the amazing blue of her eyes, the curve of her pale mouth. During the last six months she seemed to have grown six inches.

I was short and square and my hair was too curly and horribly tangly. The awful bit was, I couldn't remember Lalla ever looking the way I looked, which made it fairly unlikely that I should end up looking like her.

A few days later Mother came back from shopping in the village to say that she had met Mrs. Royston in the grocer's and we had all been asked for tea.

Lalla said, "I don't want to go."

"Why not?" asked Mother.

"They're just little boys. Let Jane and Barney go."

"It's just for tea," pleaded Mother.

She looked so anxious that Lalla gave in. She shrugged and sighed, her face closed in resignation.

We went, and it was a failure. The boys didn't want to meet us any more than Lalla wanted to

---

7. **estuary** (ĕs′chōō-ĕr′ē): the wide part of a river where its currents meet the tides of an ocean or sea.
8. **sea wall:** a wall or embankment built to shelter the coast from storms or erosion.
9. **right-of-way:** a path or road on which the public is allowed to cross private property.
10. **golf links:** a golf course.
11. **ebb tide:** the outgoing tide.

WORDS TO KNOW

trepidation (trĕp′ĭ-dā′shən) *n.* a state of alarm or dread; apprehension; anxiety
resignation (rĕz′ĭg-nā′shən) *n.* the act of giving up; submission

357

Critical Thinking: ANALYZING

G Invite students to suggest an explanation for the tension that arises between the families. *(Possible responses: The Roystons may be shy or snobbish; the landlord/tenant relationship may make the children uncomfortable.)*

Cultural Note

H Pilcher alludes to a social value important to British society and to cultures all over the world: that invitations to social events be reciprocated quickly.

STRATEGIC READING FOR
Less-Proficient Readers

I Make sure students have grasped the main events of the story.

- What has the family done since the father died in London? *(moved to a house near the sea in Cornwall)* **Summarizing**

- Who is narrating this story? *(Jane, Lalla's younger sister)* **Drawing Conclusions**

- How are the children adjusting to their new home? *(Jane and Barney seem to like Cornwall, but Lalla is less positive; they haven't made friends with the Royston boys.)* **Summarizing**

Set a Purpose Have students read on to find out how the family's relationship with the Roystons changes.

Critical Thinking: SYNTHESIZING

J Point out the sentence fragment *Until one Sunday* and ask students what they think it signals. *(Possible responses: Some students may suggest that something is about to change. Others may predict that the two families will become friends.)*

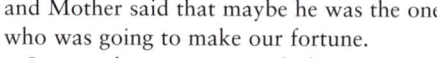

meet them. Lalla was at her coolest, her most remote. I knocked over my teacup, and Barney, who usually chatted to everybody, was silenced by the superiority of his hosts. When tea was over, Lalla stayed with the grown-ups, but Barney and I were sent off with the boys.

"Show Jane and Barney your tree house," Mrs. Royston told them as we trailed out of the door.

They took us out into the garden and showed us the tree house. It was a marvelous piece of construction, strong and roomy. Barney's face was filled with longing. "Who built it?" he asked.

"Our cousin Godfrey. He's eighteen. He can build anything. It's our club, and you're not members."

They whispered together and went off, leaving us standing beneath the forbidden tree house.

When the summer holidays came, Mother appeared to have forgotten about our social debt to the Royston boys, and we were careful not to remind her. So their names were never raised, and we never saw them except at a distance, cycling off to the village or down to the beach. Sometimes on Sunday afternoons they had guests and played tennis on their court. I longed to be included, but Lalla, deep in a book, behaved as though the Roystons didn't exist. Barney had taken up gardening, and, with his usual single-mindedness, was concentrating on digging himself a vegetable patch. He said he was going to sell lettuces,

and Mother said that maybe he was the one who was going to make our fortune.

It was a hot summer, made for swimming. Lalla had grown out of her old swimsuit, so Mother made her a cotton bikini out of scraps. It was pale blue, just right for her tan and her long, pale hair. She looked beautiful in it, and I longed to look just like her. We went to the beach most days and often saw the Royston boys there. But the beach was so vast that there was no necessity for social contact, and we all avoided each other.

Until one Sunday. The tide came in during the afternoon that day, and Mother packed us a picnic so we could set off after lunch. When we got to the beach, Lalla said she was going to swim right away, but Barney and I decided we would wait. We took our spades and went down to where the outgoing tide had left shallow pools in the sand. There we started the construction of a large and complicated harbor. Absorbed in our task, we lost track of time, and never noticed the stranger approaching. Suddenly a long shadow fell across the sparkling water.

I looked up, shading my eyes against the sun. He said "Hello" and squatted down to our level.

"Who are you?" I asked.

"I'm Godfrey Howard, the Roystons' cousin. I'm staying with them."

Illustration by Robbin Gourley

Barney suddenly found his tongue. "Did you build the tree house?"

"That's right."

"How *did* you do it?"

Godfrey began to tell him. I listened and wondered how any person apparently so nice could have anything to do with those hateful Royston boys. It wasn't that he was particularly good-looking. His hair was mousey, his nose too big and he wore spectacles. He wasn't even very tall. But there was something warm and friendly about his deep voice and his smile.

"Did you go up and look at it?"

Barney went back to his digging. Godfrey looked at me. I said, "They wouldn't let us. They said it was a club. They didn't like us."

"They think you don't like them. They think you come from London and that you're very grand."

This was astonishing. "Grand? *Us?*" I said indignantly. "We never even pretended to be grand." And then I remembered Lalla's coolness, her pale, unsmiling lips. "I mean—Lalla's older—it's different for her." His silence at this was encouraging. "I wanted to make friends," I admitted.

He was sympathetic. "It's difficult sometimes. People are shy." All at once he stopped, and looked over my shoulder. I turned to see what had caught his attention and saw Lalla coming towards us across the sand. Her hair lay like wet silk over her shoulders, and she had knotted her red towel around her hips like a sarong.¹² As she approached, Godfrey stood up. I said, introducing them the way Mother introduced people, "This is Lalla."

"Hello, Lalla," said Godfrey.

"He's the Roystons' cousin," I went on quickly. "He's staying with them."

"Hello," said Lalla.

Godfrey said, "David and Paul are wanting to play cricket. It's not much good playing cricket with just three people and I wondered if you'd come and join us?"

"Lalla won't want to play cricket," I told myself. "She'll snub him and then we'll never be asked again."

But she didn't snub him. She said, uncertainly, "I don't think I'm much good at cricket."

"But you could always try?"

"Yes." She began to smile, "I suppose I could always try."

And so we all finally got together. We played a strange form of beach cricket invented by Godfrey, which involved much lashing out at the ball and hysterical running. When we were too hot to play any longer, we swam. The Roystons had a couple of wooden surfboards, and they let us have turns, riding in on our stomachs on the long, warm breakers of the flood tide.¹³ By five o'clock we were ready for tea, and we collected our various baskets and haversacks¹⁴ and sat around in a circle on the sand. Other people's picnics are always much nicer than one's own, so we ate the Royston sandwiches and chocolate biscuits, and they ate Mother's scones with loganberry jam in the middle.

We had a last swim before the tide turned, and then gathered up our belongings and walked slowly home together. Barney and the two Roystons led the way, planning the next day's activities, and I walked with Godfrey and Lalla. But gradually, in the natural manner of events, they fell behind me. Plodding up and over the springy turf of the golf course, I listened to their voices.

---

12. **sarong:** a skirtlike garment formed by wrapping cloth around the waist.
13. **flood tide:** the incoming tide.
14. **haversacks** (hăv′ər-săks′): supply bags carried over one shoulder, popular with hikers.

Art Note

***First Sail* by C. W. Mundy** "I attempt to use as few brush strokes as possible, making each one really count," explains the artist. In this painting, Mundy has used a few simple, broad brush strokes on the woman's dress and on the water to emphasize the sunny pleasantness of the scene.

Reading the Art Describe the mood captured in *First Sail.* How does it reflect the mood in the story now that the main characters have made new friends?

Critical Thinking:
MAKING JUDGMENTS

N Ask students whether they agree or disagree with Jane's comment that Lalla and Godfrey sound like "grown-ups talking." Have students explain their answers. *(Possible responses: Agree—They are taking turns asking each other polite questions, just as grown-ups would; disagree— they sound like two teenagers interested in each other, asking personal questions to learn more about one another.)*

Literary Concept:
CHARACTERIZATION

O Have students suggest what the observation "After today, things would be different" reveals about Jane. *(Possible response: She is quite mature for her age; she is intuitive.)*

Critical Thinking: SPECULATING

P Have students speculate on how things might be different for Lalla and Jane. *(Possible responses: Lalla may be more accepting of living in Cornwall; they will have a more active social life; with Godfrey and the Roystons as friends, they will meet new people and go places.)*

First Sail (1993), Charles Warren Mundy. Oil on canvas, 30″ × 40″, private collection.

"Do you like living here?"

"It's different from London."

"That's where you lived before?"

"Yes, but my father died, and we couldn't afford to live there any more."

"I'm sorry, I didn't know. Of course, I envy your living here. I'd rather be at Carwheal than anywhere else in the world."

"Where do you live?"

"In Bristol."

"Are you at school there?"

"I've finished with school. I'm starting college in September. I'm going to be a vet."

"A vet?" Lalla considered this. "I've never met a vet before."

He laughed. "You haven't actually met one yet."

I smiled to myself in satisfaction. They sounded like two grown-ups talking. Perhaps a grown-up friend of her own was all that Lalla had needed. I had a feeling that we had crossed another watershed.[15] After today, things would be different.

---
15. **watershed:** a critical point that marks a division or a change of course; a turning point.

360 THE LANGUAGE OF LITERATURE **TEACHER'S EDITION**

The Roystons were now our friends. Our relieved mothers—for Mrs. Royston, faced with our unrelenting <u>enmity</u>, had been just as concerned and conscience-stricken as Mother—took advantage of the truce, and after that Sunday we were never out of each other's houses. Through the good offices[16] of the Roystons, our social life widened, and Mother found herself driving us all over the county to attend various beach picnics, barbecues, sailing parties and teenage dances. By the end of the summer we had been accepted. We had dug ourselves in. Carwheal was home. And Lalla grew up.

She and Godfrey wrote to each other. I knew this because I would see his letters to her lying on the table in the hall. She would take them upstairs to read them in secret in her room, and we were all too great respecters of privacy ever to mention them. When he came to Carwheal, which he did every holiday, to stay with the Roystons, he was always around first thing in the morning on the first day. He said it was to see us all, but we knew it was Lalla he had come to see.

He now owned a battered second-hand car. A lesser man might have scooped Lalla up and taken her off on her own, but Godfrey was far too kind, and he would drive for miles, to distant coves and hilltops, with the whole lot of us packed into his long-suffering car, and the boot[17] filled with food and towels and snorkels and other assorted clobber.[18]

But he was only human, and often they would drift off on their own and walk away from us. We would watch their progress and let them go, knowing that in an hour or two they would be back—Lalla with a bunch of wild flowers or some shells in her hand, Godfrey sunburned and tousled—both of them smiling and content in a way that we found reassuring and yet did not wholly understand.

Lalla had always been such a certain person, so positive, so unveering from a chosen course, that we were all taken by surprise by her <u>vacillating</u> indecision as to what she was going to do with her life. She was nearly eighteen, with her final exams over and her future spread before her like a new country observed from the peak of some painfully climbed hill.

Mother wanted her to go to university.

"Isn't it rather a waste of time if I don't know what I'm going to do at the end of it? How can I decide now what I'm going to do with the rest of my life? It's inhuman. Impossible."

"But darling, what do you want to do?"

"I don't know. Travel, I suppose. Of course, I could be really original and take a typing course."

"It might at least give you time to think things over."

This conversation took place at breakfast. It might have continued forever, reaching no satisfactory conclusion, but the post arrived as we sat there over our empty coffee cups. There was the usual dull bundle of envelopes, but, as well, a large square envelope for Lalla. She opened it idly, read the card inside and made a face. "Goodness, how grand, a proper invitation to a proper dance."

"How nice," said Mother, trying to <u>decipher</u> the butcher's bill. "Who from?"

"Mrs. Menheniot," said Lalla.

We were all instantly agog, grabbing at the invitation in order to gloat over it. We had once been to lunch with Mrs. Menheniot, who lived with Mr. Menheniot and a tribe of junior Menheniots in a beautiful house on the Fal.[19] For

---

16. **offices:** kind acts performed to help someone else.
17. **boot:** British term for the trunk of a car.
18. **clobber:** British slang for clothing or equipment.
19. **Fal:** a river in western Cornwall.

WORDS TO KNOW

enmity (ĕn′mĭ-tē) *n.* the hatred between enemies; antagonism; hostility
vacillating (văs′ə-lāt′ĭng) *adj.* swinging indecisively from one course of action or opinion to another **vacillate** *v.*
decipher (dĭ-sī′fər) *v.* to read or interpret something unclear; to figure out

361

STRATEGIC READING FOR
Less-Proficient Readers

Q Make sure students understand how relationships in the story have changed.

- How has Jane and Lalla's relationship with the Roystons changed? *(With the help of the Roystons' cousin Godfrey, the young people have all become friends.)* **Summarizing**
- How does the new friendship help Lalla's family adjust to life in Cornwall? *(The Roystons include their tenants in their active social life, and the newcomers are accepted by their new neighbors.)* **Summarizing**

Set a Purpose Ask students to read on to find out what important choices Lalla makes about her life.

Literary Concept: THEME

R Ask students how they would describe the relationship between Lalla and Godfrey. *(They are in love.)* Have students suggest how Pilcher depicts this love as wholesome and positive. *(Possible responses: Their relationship is open and part of the ongoing family activities; the lovers are portrayed as being closely connected to the natural seaside setting—Lalla holds shells and wildflowers, Godfrey is sunburned.)*

Literary Concept: SIMILE

S To help students understand the simile in this sentence, ask to what the "new country" is being compared. *(to Lalla's future)* To what does the "peak of some painfully climbed hill" refer? *(to Lalla's long years of schooling and the completion of her final exams)* Ask students to explain why they do or do not find this an effective comparison. *(Accept all reasonable responses.)*

Mini-Lesson Workplace Literacy

SCANS Goal: Acquires and Evaluates Information

MAKING DECISIONS In this story, Lalla has to make several difficult choices regarding her future. Tell students that making decisions is one of the most important things people do. When faced with decisions, people often follow their feelings. Sometimes, however, it's helpful to follow this decision-making procedure:

1. Consider your options.
2. Outline the pros and cons for each option.
3. Brainstorm to include as many different pros and cons as possible.
4. Evaluate the entries on your chart and see which way the chart is weighted.
5. Consider the chart as you make your final decision.

Application Ask students to imagine they are Lalla, and fill in a chart like the one shown.

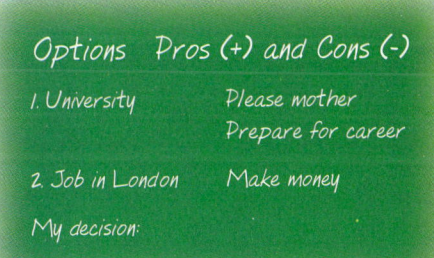

THE LANGUAGE OF LITERATURE TEACHER'S EDITION **361**

Literary Concept:
CHARACTERIZATION

T Ask students what this sentence tells the reader about Godfrey. *(Possible responses: He is determined to finish school; he has ambition.)*

Critical Thinking: SPECULATING

U Ask students which famous fairy tale character needed a new dress for a ball. *(Cinderella)* Have students recall what happened to her and then speculate on what Lalla might experience. *(Possible response: She will meet her "prince.")*

Literary Note

V Diana was the Roman goddess of the moon, of hunting, and of young living things. She symbolized chastity and modesty, and is often portrayed with bow and arrows.

Literary Concept: CONTRAST

W Have students contrast this first description of Allan Sutton with the first description of Godfrey on page 359. *(Allan is very good-looking and tall while Godfrey is not; Allan has "rather wooden features" while Godfrey is warm, friendly, and smiling.)*

Literary Concept: PLOT

X Point out that at this stage in the plot, the action rises fast as Allan whisks Lalla away for the evening. Have students speculate on what climax this rising action might lead to. *(Possible response: Lalla will have to decide between Allan and Godfrey.)*

---

some unspecified reason they were very rich, and their house was vast and white with a pillared portico[20] and green lawns which sloped down to the tidal inlets of the river.

"Are you going to go?" I asked.

Lalla shrugged. "I don't know."

"It's in August. Perhaps Godfrey will be here and you can go with him."

"He's not coming down this summer. He has to earn money to pay his way through college."

he would not make up her mind whether or not she would go to Mrs. Menheniot's party and probably never would have come to any decision if it had not been for the fact that, before very long, I had been invited too. I was really too young, as Mrs. Menheniot's booming voice pointed out over the telephone when she rang Mother, but they were short of girls and it would be a blessing if I could be there to swell the numbers. When Lalla knew that I had been asked as well, she said of course we would go. She had passed her driving test, and we would borrow Mother's car.

We were then faced with the problem of what we should wear, as Mother could not begin to afford to buy us the sort of evening dresses we wanted. In the end she sent away to Liberty's[21] for yards of material, and she made them for us, beautifully, on her sewing machine. Lalla's was pale blue lawn and in it she looked like a goddess—Diana the Huntress perhaps. Mine was a sort of tawny-gold, and I looked quite presentable in it, but of course not a patch on[22] Lalla.

When the night of the dance came, we put on our dresses and set off together in Mother's Mini,[23] giggling slightly with nerves. But when we reached the Menheniots' house, we stopped giggling because the whole affair was so grand as to be awesome. There were floodlights and car parks[24] and hundreds of sophisticated-looking people all making their way towards the front door.

Indoors, we stood at the foot of the crowded staircase, and I was filled with panic. We knew nobody. There was not a single familiar face. Lalla whisked a couple of glasses of champagne from a passing tray and gave me one. I took a sip, and at that very moment a voice rang out above the hubbub. "Lalla!" A girl was coming down the stairs, a dark girl in a strapless satin dress that had very obviously not been made on her mother's sewing machine.

Lalla looked up. "Rosemary!"

She was Rosemary Sutton from London. She and Lalla had been at school together in the old days. They fell into each other's arms and embraced as though this was all either of them had been waiting for. "What are you doing? I never thought I'd see you here. How marvelous. Come and meet Allan. You remember my brother Allan, don't you? Oh, this is exciting."

Allan was so good-looking as to be almost unreal. Fair as his sister was dark, <u>impeccably</u> turned out. Lalla was tall, but he was taller. He looked down at her, and his rather wooden features were filled with both surprise and obvious pleasure. He said, "But of course I remember." He smiled and laid down his glass. "How could I forget? Come and dance."

I scarcely saw her again all evening. He took her away from me, and I was bereft, as though I had lost my sister forever. At one point I was

---

20. **pillared portico** (pĭl′ərd pôr′tĭ-kō′): a porch with a roof supported by columns.
21. **Liberty's:** a London store especially famous for the fabric it sells.
22. **not a patch on:** not nearly as good as.
23. **Mini** (mĭn′ē): a small, fairly inexpensive, popular British car.
24. **car parks:** British term for parking lots.

WORDS TO KNOW
impeccably (ĭm-pĕk′ə-blē) *adv.* flawlessly; perfectly

362

Mini-Lesson   Genre Study

FICTION Use a web like the one shown to list the main characteristics of a **love story**.

Application Ask students to copy the web into their notebooks. Then have them write a brief essay describing these characteristics in the story "Lalla."

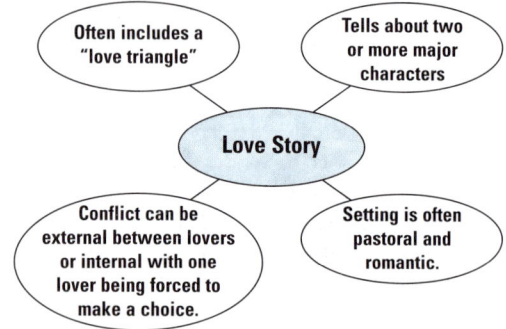

362 THE LANGUAGE OF LITERATURE TEACHER'S EDITION

rescued by Mrs. Menheniot herself, who dragooned[25] some young man into taking me to supper, but after supper even he melted away. I found an empty sofa in a deserted sitting-out room,[26] and collapsed into it. It was half-past-twelve, and I longed for my bed. I wondered what people would think if I put up my feet and had a little snooze.

Somebody came into the room and then withdrew again. I looked up and saw his retreating back view. I said, "Godfrey." He turned back. I got up off the sofa, back on to my aching feet.

"What are you doing here? Lalla said you were working."

"I am, but I wanted to come. I drove down from Bristol. That's why I'm so late." I knew why he had wanted to come. To see Lalla. "I didn't expect to see you."

"They were short of girls, so I got included."

We gazed glumly at each other, and my heart felt very heavy. Godfrey's dinner jacket looked as though he had borrowed it from some larger person, and his bow tie was crooked. I said, "I think Lalla's dancing."

"Why don't you come and dance with me, and we'll see."

I thought this a rotten idea but didn't like to say so. Together we made our way towards the ballroom. The ceiling lights had been turned off, and the disco lights now flashed red and green and blue across the smoky darkness. Music thumped and rocked an assault on our ears, and the floor seemed to be filled with an unidentifiable confusion of people, of flying hair and arms and legs. Godfrey and I joined in at the edge, but I could tell that his heart wasn't in it.

> I couldn't say any more. I couldn't tell Godfrey to go and claim her for himself.

I wished that he had never come. I prayed that he would not find Lalla.

But of course, he saw her, because it was impossible not to. It was impossible to miss Allan Sutton as well. They were both so tall, so beautiful. Godfrey's face seemed to close up.

"Who's she with?" he asked.

"Allan Sutton. He and his sister have come down from London. Lalla used to know them."

I couldn't say any more. I couldn't tell Godfrey to go and claim her for himself. I wasn't even certain by then what sort of a reception she would have given him. And anyway, as we watched them, Allan stopped dancing and put his arm around Lalla, drawing her towards him, whispering something into her ear. She slipped her hand into his, and they moved away towards the open French window.[27] The next moment they were lost to view, swallowed into the darkness of the garden beyond.

At four o'clock in the morning Lalla and I drove home in silence. We were not giggling now. I wondered sadly if we would ever giggle together again. I ached with exhaustion, and I was out of sympathy with her. Godfrey had never even spoken to her. Soon after our dance he had said

---

25. **dragooned** (drə-gōōnd′): compelled by threats or force. The term is used humorously here.
26. **sitting-out room:** a room used by those not dancing.
27. **French window:** a type of window that extends to the floor.

LALLA 363

Multicultural Perspectives

GIRL INTO WOMAN Point out that in polite English society, wealthy, upper-class young women of about 18 years of age often had a debutante party or coming-out ball after they finished school. In cities such as London, these balls made up a "social season." During this period, young women hoped to meet eligible bachelors from their own social circle whom they might marry. These balls were often lavish affairs with dance bands, huge tents, and champagne. These formal dances are still popular in America. Other cultures also hold dances as rites of passage for young women, although usually at an earlier age. For instance, among the Sioux or Cheyenne the mother of a girl reaching puberty has the village crier invite everyone to a huge feast. A Tlingit father would give huge party called a *potlatch*. In Japan, every January 15, ceremonies are held in each town for youngsters coming of age.

Literary Concept: DESCRIPTION

Y Have students discuss what these descriptive details reveal about Godfrey. (*Possible responses: Godfrey is not wealthy; he's not used to attending formal parties; he is out of place among the rich and beautiful.*)

Linking to Social Studies

Z You might point out that the mention of "disco lights" is one of the few details which place the story in the late 1970s or early 1980s.

Critical Thinking: ANALYZING

AA Ask students why the unexpected arrival of Godfrey upsets Jane. (*Possible responses: Jane is fond of Godfrey and is worried that he will be hurt if he learns Lalla is with Allan; she is afraid Godfrey will be embarrassed and feel out of place; she is afraid Godfrey will no longer want to date Lalla when he sees her with Allan.*)

Critical Thinking: SPECULATING

BB Ask students what they think would have happened if Godfrey had gone and "claimed" Lalla for himself. (*Possible responses: He would have embarrassed or angered Lalla; Lalla would have resented him; he would have made an uncomfortable situation worse; Lalla may have chosen to go with him.*)

Critical Thinking:
MAKING JUDGMENTS

CC Ask students what this passage tells them about Lalla's values. *(Possible responses: She prefers the big city; she is interested in wealth and appearance.)*

Literary Concept:
CHARACTERIZATION

DD Ask students what Lalla's reaction to learning of Godfrey's presence at the dance suggests about her. *(Possible response: She seems callous; she is so infatuated with Allan that she no longer cares for Godfrey.)*

Literary Concept: PLOT

EE Have students note how the author speeds up the pace and condenses story events here. Tremendous changes occur in Lalla's life in the space of three sentences.

STRATEGIC READING FOR
Less-Proficient Readers

FF Ask students what changes have come to pass in Lalla's life *(She has moved to London, gotten a glamorous job, and fallen in love with Allan.)* **Noting Relevant Details**

- Ask students whether they think Godfrey and Lalla have maintained any contact with one another. *(Possible response: No; Godfrey would not fit in with Lalla's new life.)* **Drawing Conclusions**

Set a Purpose Have students complete the story to find out whether Lalla marries Allan.

Critical Thinking:
MAKING JUDGMENTS

GG Ask students whether or not they think Lalla should marry Allan. *(Accept all reasonable responses.)*

Critical Thinking:
MAKING INFERENCES

HH Ask students what Lalla's mother means when she says that Lalla may have "grown out of laughter." *(Possible response: She has absorbed too much of Allan's manner; maybe she's not truly happy; she's too sophisticated for laughter.)*

---

goodbye and disappeared, presumably to make the long, lonely journey back to Bristol.

She, on the other hand, had an aura of happiness about her that was almost tangible. I glanced at her and saw her peaceful, smiling profile. It was hard to think of anything to say.

It was Lalla who finally broke the silence. "I know what I'm going to do. I mean, I know what I'm going to do with my life. I'm going back to London. Rosemary says I can live with her. I'll take a secretarial course or something, then get a job."

"Mother will be disappointed."

"She'll understand. It's what I've always wanted. We're buried down here. And there's another thing; I'm tired of being poor. I'm tired of homemade dresses and never having a new car. We've always talked about making our fortunes, and as I'm the eldest, I might as well make a start. If I don't do it now, I never will."

I said, "Godfrey was there this evening."

"Godfrey?"

"He drove down from Bristol."

She did not say anything, and I was angry. I wanted to hurt her and make her feel as bad as I felt. "He came because he wanted to see you. But you didn't even notice him."

"You can scarcely blame me," said Lalla, "for that."

And so she went back to London, lived with Rosemary, and took a secretarial course, just as she said she would. Later, she got a job on the editorial staff of a fashionable magazine, but it was not long before one of the photographers spied her potential, seduced her from her typewriter, and started taking pictures of her. Soon her lovely face smiled at us from the cover of the magazine.

"How does it feel to have a famous daughter?" people asked Mother, but she never quite accepted Lalla's success, just as she never quite accepted Allan Sutton. Allan's devotion to Lalla had proved unswerving and he was her constant companion.

"Let's hope he doesn't marry her," said Barney, but of course eventually, inevitably, they decided to do just that. "We're engaged!" Lalla rang up from London to tell us. Her voice sounded, <u>unnervingly</u>, as though she was calling from the next room.

"Darling!" said Mother, faintly.

"Oh, do be pleased. Please be pleased. I'm so happy and I couldn't bear it if you weren't happy, too."

So of course Mother said that she was pleased, but the truth was that none of us really liked Allan very much. He was—well—spoilt. He was conceited. He was too rich. I said as much to Mother, but Mother was loyal to Lalla. She said, "*Things* mean a lot to Lalla. I think they always have. I mean, possessions and security. And perhaps someone who truly loves her."

I said, "Godfrey truly loved her."

"But that was when they were young. And perhaps Godfrey couldn't give her love."

"He could make her laugh. Allan never makes her laugh."

"Perhaps," said Mother sadly, "she's grown out of laughter."

And then it was Easter. We hadn't heard from Lalla for a bit and didn't expect her to come to Carwheal for the spring holiday. But she rang up, out of the blue, and said that she hadn't been well and was taking a couple of weeks off. Mother was delighted, of course, but concerned about her health.

By now we were all more or less grown-up. David was studying to be a

| WORDS TO KNOW | **unnervingly** (ŭn-nûrv′ĭng-lē) *adv.* in a way that causes someone to become nervous or upset; disturbingly |

364

Mini-Lesson — Study Skills

USING REFERENCES—PERIODICALS
Point out that many of Pilcher's short stories first appeared in the periodical *Good Housekeeping*. Have knowledgeable students describe the services available in your local or school library that they would use to locate issues of this magazine with a Pilcher story. Such services should include a computerized periodical search service and the *Reader's Guide to Periodical Literature*.

Application Have students locate and list short stories by Pilcher published in popular magazines. Listings should appear in proper bibliographic style. You might also wish to have students include a list of the sources they used to compile this information. Encourage interested students to read one or more of Pilcher's stories on their own.

doctor, and Paul had a job on the local newspaper. I had achieved a place at the Guildhall School of Music, and Barney was no longer a little boy but a gangling teenager with an insatiable appetite. Still, however, we gathered for the holidays, and that Easter Godfrey abandoned his sick dogs and ailing cows to the ministrations[28] of his partner and joined us.

It was lovely weather, almost as warm as summer. The sort of weather that makes one feel young again—a child. There was scented thyme on the golf links, and the cliff walks were starred with primroses and wild violets. In the Roystons' garden the daffodils blew in the long grass beneath the tree house, and Mrs. Royston put up the tennis net and swept the cobwebs out of the summer house.

It was during one of these sessions that Godfrey and I talked about Lalla. We were in the summer house together, sitting out while the others played a set.

"Tell me about Lalla."

"She's engaged."

"I know. I saw it in the paper." I could think of nothing to say. "Do you like him—Allan Sutton, I mean?"

I said "Yes," but I was never much good at lying.

Godfrey turned his head and looked at me. He was wearing old jeans and a white shirt, and I thought that he had grown older in a subtle way. He was more sure of himself and somehow more attractive.

He said, "That night of the Menheniots' dance, I was going to ask her to marry me."

"Oh, Godfrey."

"I hadn't even finished my training, but I thought perhaps we'd manage. And when I saw her, I knew that I had lost her. I'd left it too late."

On the day that Lalla was due to arrive, I took Mother's old car into the neighboring town to do some shopping. When the time came to return home, the engine refused to start. After struggling for a bit, I walked to the nearest garage and persuaded a kindly, oily man to come and help me. But he told me it was hopeless.

We walked back to the garage, and I telephoned home. But it wasn't Mother who answered the call, it was Godfrey.

I explained what had happened. "Lalla's train is due at the junction in about half an hour and we said someone would meet her."

There was a momentary hesitation, then Godfrey said, "I'll go. I'll take my car."

When I finally reached home, exhausted from carrying the laden grocery bags from the bus stop, Godfrey's car was nowhere to be seen.

A short time later the telephone rang. But it wasn't Lalla, explaining where they were, it was a call from London and it was Allan Sutton.

"I have to speak to Lalla."

His voice sounded frantic. I said cautiously, "Is anything wrong?"

"She's broken off our engagement. I got back from the office and found a letter from her and my ring. She said she was coming home. She doesn't want to get married."

---

28. **ministrations** (mĭn´ĭ-strā´shəns): services performed to aid someone or something.

Illustration by Robbin Gourley

LALLA **365**

Art Note

The Cove by Fairfield Porter Fairfield Porter (1907–1975), an American painter who lived most of his life on Great Spruce Head Island, Maine, painted many landscapes and seascapes. He was also a prominent writer on art. In this painting, Porter uses soft pastels to depict a quiet landscape of green and gold.

Reading the Art *Imagine the figure in the art is Godfrey. How does the painting seem to express his feelings about losing Lalla?*

Literary Concept: CHARACTERIZATION

MM Allan says that Lalla's decision came "as a bolt out of the blue" and he thought she was "just tired." What do these comments suggest about Allan? *(Possible responses: He isn't very perceptive; he isn't sensitive to Lalla's feelings.)*

Critical Thinking: INFERRING

NN Ask students whether they think Jane is likely to talk to Lalla and try to make her "see sense" *(Possible responses: No, because Jane is delighted by this turn of events; Jane thinks Lalla has finally seen sense.)*

The Cove (1964), Fairfield Porter. Oil on canvas, 37″ × 53½″, The Metropolitan Museum of Art, New York, bequest of Arthur M. Bullowa, 1993 (1993.406.7). Copyright © 1995 The Metropolitan Museum of Art.

I found it in my heart to be very sorry for him. "But Allan, you must have had *some* idea."

"None. Absolutely none. It's just a bolt from the blue. I know she's been a bit off-color lately, but I thought she was just tired."

"She must have her reasons, Allan," I told him, as gently as I could.

"Talk to her, Jane. Try to make her see sense."

He rang off at last. I put the receiver back on the hook and stood for a moment, gathering my wits about me and assessing this new and startling turn of events. I found myself caught up in a tangle of conflicting emotions. Enormous sympathy for Allan; a reluctant admiration for

366 UNIT THREE PART 1: THE TIES THAT BIND

Assessment Option

INFORMAL ASSESSMENT You can informally assess your students' understanding of the story by asking pairs of students to compose the journal entry that Lalla writes when she breaks her engagement. The entry should reveal Lalla's feelings and shed some light on her motives.

Rubric

3 Full Accomplishment Students demonstrate insight into Lalla's character and accurately portray the reasons behind her decision.

2 Substantial Accomplishment Students grasp some of Lalla's feelings or motivations, but do not communicate them clearly.

1 Little or Partial Accomplishment Students show little understanding of Lalla's motivations.

Lalla, who had had the courage to take this shattering decision; but, as well, a sort of rising excitement.

Godfrey. Godfrey and Lalla. Where were they? I knew then that I could not face Mother and Barney before I had found out what was going on. Quietly, I opened the door and went out of the house, through the gates, down the lane. As soon as I turned the corner at the end of the lane, I saw Godfrey's car parked on the patch of grass outside the church.

It was a marvelously warm, <u>benign</u> sort of evening. I took the path that led past the church and towards the beach. Before I had gone very far, I saw them, walking up over the golf links towards me. The wind blew Lalla's hair over her face. She was wearing her London high-heeled boots so was taller than Godfrey. They should have appeared ill-assorted, but there was something about them that was totally right. They were a couple, holding hands, walking up from the beach as they had walked innumerable times, together.

I stopped, suddenly reluctant to disturb their intimacy. But Lalla had seen me. She waved and then let go of Godfrey's hand and began to run towards me, her arms flailing like windmills.

"Jane!" I had never seen her so exuberant.

"Oh, Jane." I ran to meet her. We hugged each other, and for some stupid reason my eyes were full of tears.

"Oh, darling Jane . . ."

"I had to come and find you."

"Did you wonder where we were? We went for a walk. I had to talk to Godfrey. He was the one person I could talk to."

"Lalla, Allan's been on the phone."

"I had to do it. It was all a ghastly mistake."

"But you found out in time. That's all that matters."

"I thought I was going after what I wanted. I thought I had what I wanted, and then I found out that I didn't want it at all. Oh, I've missed you all so much. There wasn't anybody I could talk to."

Over her shoulder I saw Godfrey coming, tranquilly, to join us. I let go of Lalla and went to give him a kiss. I didn't know what they had been discussing as they paced the lonely beach, and I knew that I never would. But still, I had the feeling that the outcome could be nothing but good for all of us.

I said, "We must go back. Mother and Barney don't know about anything. They'll be thinking that I've dissolved into thin air, as well as the pair of you."

"In that case," said Godfrey, and he took Lalla's hand in his own once more, "perhaps we'd better go and tell them."

And so we walked home, the three of us. In the warm evening, in the sunshine, in the fresh wind. ❖

WORDS TO KNOW
benign (bĭ-nīn′) *adj.* mild; gentle

367

Literary Concept: CHARACTERIZATION

OO Ask students what they think Lalla has found out about herself. *(Possible responses: She has realized that she values her family and home; material things and social prestige won't make her happy; she values being with people she can talk to.)*

CUSTOMIZING FOR
Gifted and Talented Students

PP Have students note Lalla's comment, "I thought I had what I wanted, and then I found out that I didn't want it at all." Discuss why this is such a common human experience.

STRATEGIC READING FOR
Less-Proficient Readers

QQ Have students explain what important decision Lalla makes at the end of the story. *(She decides to break off her engagement to Allan; she seems to realize that she really loves Godfrey.)*
Summarizing

COMPREHENSION CHECK

1. Why does Lalla's family move to Cornwall? *(as a result of the father's death)*
2. As teenagers, how do Lalla and Godfrey feel about each other? *(They are in love.)*
3. Who is Allan Sutton? *(The rich, handsome brother of Lalla's old classmate.)*
4. Why does Lalla move to London? *(She wants a job and career; she wants to be with Allan.)*
5. Why does Lalla break her engagement with Allan? *(She realizes she doesn't love him and doesn't want the kind of life he represents.)*

Mini-Lesson — The Writer's Style

CONCLUSIONS FOR NARRATIVES Discuss with students why they think Pilcher ended the tale in a "quiet" and understated way. Also ask students to suggest why she did not close the story with Lalla's engagement to Godfrey. *(Possible responses: She wanted readers to draw their own conclusions; the story is not about Lalla's relationship with Godfrey, but about Lalla's achievement of self-knowledge.)*

Application Invite students to write a new conclusion for the story that could begin after the sentence, "Over her shoulder I saw Godfrey coming, tranquilly, to join us." Ask them to write a few sentences that spell out exactly what Lalla has decided to do. Ask students whether they find their new endings more satisfying than the original.

Reteaching/Reinforcement
- Writer's Handbook, anthology pp. 1032–1033

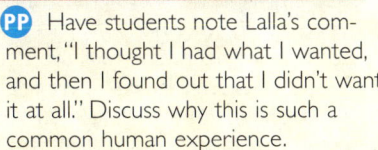

Conclusions for Narratives, pp. 388–389

THE LANGUAGE OF LITERATURE TEACHER'S EDITION **367**

From Personal Response to Critical Analysis

1. Accept all reasonable responses.
2. Accept all reasonable responses. Some students may say it was wise not to marry Allan since she did not love him.
3. Possible response: As a teen, she values the excitement of city life. She resents leaving London and returns at the first opportunity. After a while, though, the allure of sophisticated city life appeals to her less, and she comes to value her family ties and close friends in Cornwall more.
4. Accept all reasonable, well-supported responses. Some students may say they don't like the way Lalla treats Jane even though Jane idolizes her. Others may say that since Jane clearly adores Godfrey and wants Lalla to marry him, we tend to feel similarly.
5. Accept all reasonable responses.

Another Pathway

Cooperative Learning Before they act out the conversation, have group members discuss what they know about the characters and why the characters acted the way they did. Encourage students to suggest imaginative new details that account for their actions in the story and for why the characters have all gotten together.

Rubric

3 Full Accomplishment Conversation demonstrates thorough understanding of the characters; presentation is well-rehearsed and convincing.

2 Substantial Accomplishment Conversation demonstrates adequate understanding of characters; presentation is fairly smooth.

1 Little or Partial Accomplishment Conversation has little relation to events and characterization as established in the story; presentation is awkward.

RESPONDING OPTIONS

FROM PERSONAL RESPONSE TO CRITICAL ANALYSIS

REFLECT
1. What was your reaction to the story? Describe your reaction in your notebook.

RETHINK
2. Do you think Lalla made a wise choice in the end? Why or why not?
3. In what ways, if any, do you think Lalla's values change as she gets older? Use examples from the story to support your opinion.

Close Textual Reading

Consider
- her reaction to moving to Cornwall
- her relationships with Godfrey and Allan
- her comments to Jane after the Menheniots' dance
- her final decision

4. How does Jane's view of her older sister affect what you think of Lalla?

RELATE
5. What values do you think are most important for people to consider when they choose a mate?

LITERARY CONCEPTS

Many stories open with **exposition,** background information that usually introduces the characters, describes the setting, and summarizes significant events that took place before the story's action begins. In "Lalla," the exposition tells us about Lalla and her family and explains why they are moving to Cornwall. How does this exposition help explain Lalla's later interest in Allan and in living in London?

Multimodal Learning

ANOTHER PATHWAY

Cooperative Learning
With three or four other classmates, act out an imaginary conversation that takes place ten years after the story. Choose among the roles of Lalla, Godfrey, Jane, Mother, and Allan, and reminisce about "the old days." In the role of your character, talk about what happened and why you made the decisions you did.

QUICKWRITES

1. Imagine that this story is being turned into a television movie. Write a **proposal** for a new title that will attract viewers. Be sure to explain your reasoning.
2. Create the **two lists of pros and cons** Lalla might have made before she decided to return to Cornwall. On one list, show the benefits and problems of staying with Allan. On the other, analyze the advantages and disadvantages of returning to Godfrey.
3. Write a **script** for a telephone conversation between Lalla and Allan in which she explains why she is leaving him and moving back to Cornwall.

PORTFOLIO Save your writing. You may want to use it later as a springboard to a piece for your portfolio.

Literary Concepts

Point out that in the exposition, Lalla objected to leaving London for Cornwall. Lalla seemed unwilling to adjust to Cornwall at first, and her "grand" London manners put off the Roystons. Lalla's interest in Allan, the rich brother of her old London schoolmate, might be seen as an attempt to recapture the London lifestyle she had enjoyed when her father was alive.

QuickWrites

1. Suggest that the new title emphasize that the movie is a love story partially set in London's world of fashion.
2. Remind students that the list should reflect Lalla's growing dissatisfaction with her glamorous life in London and with the social world Allan represents.
3. Suggest that students first decide whether Lalla will be frank or gentle with Allan.

 **The Writer's Craft**

Guidelines for Problem Solving, p. 473
Using Dialogue in Plays and Skits, pp. 453–454

Multimodal Learning

ALTERNATIVE ACTIVITIES

1. Create a **poster**. One side should include images that represent Allan's values; the other side should represent Godfrey's values.
2. Create **valentines** that Godfrey and Allan might have sent Lalla. In each, try to reflect the background and personality of the sender.

CRITIC'S CORNER

A magazine editor once noted, "When Rosamunde Pilcher writes about people, in crisis or at peace, falling in or out of love, discovering new life or accepting death, readers see themselves . . . or their children . . . or their parents." Did you agree? Explain.

WORDS TO KNOW

EXERCISE A Review the Words to Know at the bottom of the selection pages and write the word that is closest in meaning to the italicized word or phrase in each sentence.

1. Allan spoke with *grudging acceptance* of Lalla's engagement to Godfrey.
2. Jane knew she would feel *very lonely* after Lalla got married.
3. Mother was exasperated with Lalla for *changing her mind* so often about the wedding plans.
4. For Lalla's sake, Godfrey and Allan put aside their *intense dislike* for each other.
5. On the wedding day the weather turned sunny and *mild*.
6. Before the ceremony, Uncle Peter spoke *distressingly* to Godfrey about the responsibilities of married life.
7. Remembering Uncle Peter's advice, Godfrey felt some *anxiety* about getting married.
8. Aunt Fran arrived wearing a *very silly* green feathered hat.
9. Allan missed the wedding because he could not *figure out* the map Barney sent him.
10. The ceremony went exactly as planned, and the organist played the wedding music *without a single mistake*.

EXERCISE B With a partner, take turns using facial expressions and/or body gestures to act out the meaning of three Words to Know each and guessing what word is being shown.

ROSAMUNDE PILCHER

1924–

Although she now lives in Scotland, Rosamunde Pilcher grew up in Cornwall, the setting of her story "Lalla." She joined the Women's Royal Naval Service during World War II and became a writer soon after the war ended. From 1949 to 1987 she published more than 20 romantic novels. Though her work was largely ignored by British critics, some of it was well received in America. Praise from the *New York Times* for her novel *Sleeping Tiger* (1967) brought Rosamunde Pilcher to the attention of *Good Housekeeping* magazine, which has since published many of her stories. Nevertheless, it was not until *The Shell Seekers* appeared in 1988 that she found herself treated as a serious novelist.

Pilcher accepts being called a writer of "light fiction," but she dislikes the label "romantic fiction" and the contempt that often goes with it. After winning respect with *The Shell Seekers,* she commented, "All my life I've had people coming up and saying, 'Sat under the hair dryer and read one of your little stories, dear. So clever of you. Wish I had the time to do it myself.' . . . And now I'm hoping that nobody will ever, ever say that again."

OTHER WORKS *The Blue Bedroom and Other Stories, September, Flowers in the Rain and Other Stories*

Extended Reading

LALLA **369**

Words to Know

1. resignation
2. bereft
3. vacillating
4. enmity
5. benign
6. unnervingly
7. trepidation
8. ludicrous
9. decipher
10. impeccably

Reteaching/Reinforcement
- *Unit Three Resource Book,* p. 5

Critic's Corner

Students might point out that readers identify with Pilcher's characters because they are ordinary people living ordinary lives.

ROSAMUNDE PILCHER

The author considers her childhood in an artists' colony in Cornwall, surrounded by potters, painters, and sculptors, as "a lovely life." Pilcher decided to become a writer at age seven, sold her first story as a young woman, and continued to write while raising four children. Despite the international success of her novel *The Shell Seekers,* Pilcher still works on a small portable typewriter in her family's guest bedroom.

Alternative Activities

1. Suggest that students brainstorm with a partner to generate ideas for images appropriate to each character. Encourage students to review the story for ideas.
2. Encourage students to consider the personality traits of each character before they begin their work. The students' valentines might reflect the fact that Allan is less warm than Godfrey and so probably less apt to express personal feelings. You may have students work in pairs, with one partner writing the text and the other drawing the images.

OVERVIEW

Objectives

- To understand and appreciate lyric poetry that explores the bonds between lovers
- To identify and understand metaphor
- To express understanding of the poems through a choice of writing forms, including a poem, a list of images, and a journal entry
- To extend understanding of the poems through a variety of multimodal and cross-curricular activities

Skills

LITERARY CONCEPTS
- Metaphor
- Sensory details

THE WRITER'S STYLE
- Imaging

SPEAKING, LISTENING, AND VIEWING
- Music
- Role playing
- Art
- Group discussion

Thematic Link: *The Ties That Bind*
In these two poems, spiritual and physical ties bind the speakers to their lovers.

CUSTOMIZING FOR
Students Acquiring English

- Use **ACCESS FOR STUDENTS ACQUIRING ENGLISH.**
- Students may not have difficulty with the two poems, for they use concrete images to convey meaning. You may wish to take this opportunity to have them discuss courtship practices and images of love in their own cultures.
- You may also want to use the suggestions under Strategic Reading for Less-Proficient Readers.

STRATEGIC READING FOR
Less-Proficient Readers

Set a Purpose Have students read to find how the speaker in each poem feels about being separated from the one he or she loves.

- Use **UNIT THREE RESOURCE BOOK,** p. 9, for guidance in reading the selection.

PREVIEWING

POETRY

Love Without Love
Luis Lloréns Torres (loo-ēs′ yô-rĕns′ tô′rĕs) Puerto Rico

The Taxi
Amy Lowell United States

Activating Prior Knowledge
PERSONAL CONNECTION

In a small group, identify images that suggest romantic love in our culture. For example, you might think of a movie scene with two lovers on a moonlit walk or a television commercial that portrays a man and a woman nestled before a fireplace. Then discuss what these images reveal about our views of romantic love. Use a chart like the one shown to keep track of your images and what they reveal. Share your findings with your classmates.

Romantic Love in Our Culture	
Image	**What It Reveals**
a man and a woman on a moonlit walk	• peacefulness of love • love removed from the harsh realities of ordinary life

Building Background
LITERARY CONNECTION

The following two poems use vivid, unexpected images to convey the poets' ideas about romantic love. The first poem is by Luis Lloréns Torres, a famous Puerto Rican poet who began publishing his verse in 1899 and was noted for his love poems and his patriotic verse. The second poem is by Amy Lowell, an American poet who won fame just a few years after Lloréns Torres. This poem reflects Lowell's interest in **imagism,** a literary movement that stressed the importance of using clear, precise images in poetry.

Setting a Purpose
WRITING CONNECTION

In your notebook, create your own image of romantic love, one that conveys your own thoughts and feelings. You may either draw a picture of that image or describe it in words. Then explain how your image communicates what love means to you. As you read the following poems, look for the images the poets use to describe their feelings about love.

370 UNIT THREE PART 1: THE TIES THAT BIND

PRINT AND MEDIA RESOURCES

UNIT THREE RESOURCE BOOK
Strategic Reading: Literature, p. 9

WRITING MINI–LESSONS
Transparencies, p. 46

ACCESS FOR STUDENTS ACQUIRING ENGLISH
Reading Support

FORMAL ASSESSMENT
Selection Test, p. 73
 Test Generator

AUDIO LIBRARY
See Reference Card

---

370 THE LANGUAGE OF LITERATURE **TEACHER'S EDITION**

Love Without Love

Luis Lloréns Torres

I love you, because in my thousand and one nights of dreams,
I never once dreamed of you.
I looked down paths that traveled from afar,
but it was never you I expected.
5   Suddenly I've felt you flying through my soul
in quick, lofty flight,
and how beautiful you seem way up there, far
from my always idiot heart!
Love me that way, flying over everything.
10   And, like the bird on its branch, land in my arms
only to rest,
then fly off again.
Be not like the romantic ones who,
   in love, set me on fire.
When you climb up my mansion,
15   enter so lightly, that as you enter
the dog of my heart will not bark.

Translated by Julio Marzán

FROM PERSONAL RESPONSE TO CRITICAL ANALYSIS

REFLECT 1. Think about the image from this poem that stands out the most to you. In your notebook, jot down what this image makes you think of.

RETHINK 2. What does the speaker's choice of images say to you about his attitude toward his relationship with his loved one?
   Consider
   - the image of the bird flying through his soul in lines 5–6
   - the speaker's reference to his "idiot heart" in line 8
   - the contrast between his beloved and "the romantic ones" in line 13
   - the speaker's request in lines 15–16

   Close Textual Reading

   3. What does the title of the poem mean to you?

RELATE 4. Compare and contrast your ideas about love with those of the speaker.

Literary Concept: METAPHOR

A Have students discuss why they think the speaker describes his heart as an idiot. *(Possible response: Some students might say he feels his love is not worthy of her. Others might say his heart acts foolishly.)*

Literary Concept: METAPHOR

B Have students discuss what the "dog" of the speaker's heart might be and why the speaker doesn't want it to bark. *(Possible response: it stands for romantic passion, which the speaker feels might jeopardize the cool, tranquil relationship he describes.)*

From Personal Response to Critical Analysis

1. Accept all reasonable responses.
2. Accept all well-supported responses. Possible responses: He wants their relationship to be on a higher, more spiritual level than the earthy, passionate relationships he's had before; he wants some distance and freedom between them; he wants their relationship to be steady, quiet, not upsetting.
3. Possible responses: a spiritual love without typical, romantic passions; a love that comes and goes quietly and freely.
4. Accept all reasonable, well-supported responses.

 Mini-Lesson The Writer's Style

IMAGING Tell students that imaging is an effective prewriting technique that writers often use. A writer begins by clearing his or her mind of distracting thoughts, then concentrating on a subject and noting the images that come to mind. In addition to people or objects, the images might include colors, sounds, tactile sensations, or smells. Suggest that "Love Without Love" could be a result of the imaging technique, because the poet has refined various bird images to present a compelling picture of love.

Application Encourage students to use the imaging technique to begin work on love poems of their own. Once they have chosen a subject, ask them to clear their minds, focus on that subject, and jot down any and all images that come to mind.

Reteaching/Reinforcement
- *Writer's Handbook*, anthology pp. 1030–1032
- *Writing Mini-Lessons* transparencies, p. 46

 The Writer's Craft
Imaging, p. 323

Art Note

Times Square, New York City by Robert Gniewek For Detroit-born photorealist Robert Gniewek (1951–), the first step in creating art is taking photographs. Once he has an intriguing photo, he uses paint to "push reality over the edge." *Times Square* is an extraordinary nightscape of light-splashed images and reflections.

Reading the Art How does the light in this painting "prick" a viewer's eyes?

Literary Concept: SIMILE

C Ask students what a slackened drum would feel and sound like. *(Possible responses: It would have no tension; it would feel dead; it would sound dull.)*

Literary Concept: SENSORY DETAILS

D Ask students to describe the feelings evoked in them by the images of "jutted stars," "the ridges of the wind," city streets that "wedge" the speaker, and lights that "prick" the eye appeal. *(Possible responses: pain; loneliness; fear)*

STRATEGIC READING FOR Less-Proficient Readers

E Invite students to restate in their own words how the speaker of "The Taxi" feels about leaving her beloved. Then have them compare and contrast that view with the way the speaker in "Love Without Love" feels. *(Possible responses: Leaving her beloved causes the speaker in "The Taxi" to suffer; the speaker in "Love Without Love" accepts, even welcomes, the unpredictable behavior of his beloved.)* **Comparing/Contrasting**

THE TAXI

AMY LOWELL

When I go away from you
The world beats dead
C Like a slackened drum.
I call out for you against the jutted stars
D 5 And shout into the ridges of the wind.
Streets coming fast,
One after the other,
Wedge you away from me,
And the lamps of the city prick my eyes
10 So that I can no longer see your face.
Why should I leave you,
E To wound myself upon the sharp edges of the night?

Times Square, New York City No. 2 (1990), Robert Gniewek. Oil on linen, 38" × 60", courtesy of Louis K. Meisel Gallery, New York. Photo by Steve Lopez.

372   UNIT THREE   PART 1: THE TIES THAT BIND

Mini-Lesson Literary Concepts

REVIEWING SENSORY DETAILS Remind students that sensory details are words and phrases that appeal to the five senses. Have students identify which of the five senses Lowell appeals to in the first three lines of the poem. *(sound)* Have students read lines 4–8 and identify the sense or senses to which the images appeal. *(touch and sight)*

Application Invite the students to imagine that they must leave someone they love. What sensory details might they use to evoke what they are feeling? Challenge students to list details for each of the five senses: sight, sound, smell, touch, and taste.

RESPONDING OPTIONS

FROM PERSONAL RESPONSE TO CRITICAL ANALYSIS

REFLECT
1. What questions would you like to ask the speaker in "The Taxi"? Jot down those questions in your notebook.

RETHINK
2. Based on the images used in this poem, how would you describe the speaker's feelings about love?

Close Textual Reading

Consider
- the sound a slackened drum would make, as described in lines 2–3
- her sense of the streets wedging her loved one away from her (line 8)
- the last two lines, where she compares leaving her loved one to being wounded

3. Do you think "The Taxi" is a good title for this poem? Explain your reasoning.

RELATE
Literary Link
4. Compare and contrast the speakers' attitudes toward love in "Love Without Love" and "The Taxi."

Thematic Link
5. Which speaker's view of love appeals more to you? Explain your choice.

LITERARY CONCEPTS

A **metaphor** is a form of figurative language that makes a comparison between two things that have something in common. Some metaphors make the comparison directly, while others imply it. Explain the metaphor in lines 5–9 of "Love Without Love." How does the image of love expressed in this metaphor compare to some of the images you identified and discussed for the Personal Connection on page 370?

CONCEPT REVIEW: Simile Identify a **simile** in each poem. What ideas are being communicated in each simile?

metaphor	simile
is	like or as

Multimodal Learning
ANOTHER PATHWAY

With the class as a whole, stage a television talk show in which one student, the host, interviews four classmates posing as the two couples represented in "Love Without Love" and "The Taxi." The rest of the class will act as the studio audience. Have the host and members of the audience ask the couples about their views of love and the relationship they have or want.

QUICKWRITES

1. Using the image you created for the Writing Connection on page 370, write a **poem** that expresses your feelings about the nature of love.

2. The images in "The Taxi" convey feelings about love by describing the pain of being separated from the loved one. Develop a **list of images** that the speaker might use to convey how she feels when she is with her loved one.

3. Write a **journal entry** in which the speaker of "Love Without Love" records a perfect day with his loved one.

 **PORTFOLIO** Save your writing. You may want to use it later as a springboard to a piece for your portfolio.

LOVE WITHOUT LOVE / THE TAXI **373**

From Personal Response to Critical Analysis

1. Accept all reasonable responses.
2. Possible response: Love is a vital part of the speaker's life; the speaker's romance offers shelter from harsh urban life; the speaker has a strong need to be with the beloved.
3. Possible responses: Yes, since it helps readers see the speaker in a cab, reluctantly moving away from his or her lover; no, because the taxi is not central to the poem.
4. Possible responses: The speaker of "Love Without Love" wants a distant, restrained, more spiritual relationship. The speaker of "The Taxi" wants a strong commitment and a more intense, physical relationship.
5. Accept all reasonable, well-supported responses.

Another Pathway

Cooperative Learning Student "couples" should work together ahead of time to define their relationship. The student host and audience also should prepare questions before the activity.

Rubric

3 Full Accomplishment The host poses meaningful questions, the couples clearly articulate their positions based on the poems, and audience participation is appropriate.

2 Substantial Accomplishment The host asks pertinent questions, the couples are able to respond in most cases, and the audience participates to some degree.

1 Little or Partial Accomplishment The host is unprepared or asks irrelevant questions, the couples responses are not based on the text, and the audience is unresponsive.

Literary Concepts

The poet uses "lofty flight," and "flying through my soul" to develop a metaphor comparing the loved one to a bird in flight. Have students share their notes and ideas from the Personal Connection on page 370.

Simile In "Love Without Love," the simile in lines 10–12 compares his love to "the bird on the branch," emphasizing her freedom to come and go. In "The Taxi," lines 1–3 compare the speaker's world when away from her lover to a "slackened drum." This suggests that the lover adds fullness and rhythm to life, and that life without the lover lacks vitality.

QuickWrites

1. Suggest that students use the imaging technique as a prewriting device.
2. Have students create images that appeal to the same senses as the images in the poem.
3. Suggest that the entry focus on a few key incidents.

The Writer's Craft

Poetry, pp. 88–101
Types of Figurative Language, pp. 425–426
Sensory Details, p. 366

LUIS LLORÉNS TORRES

In addition to love poems, Luis Lloréns Torres wrote poems and plays based on his patriotic and political ideals. Many of his most famous works celebrate the lives and heritage of the peasants, or *jíbaros*, of his homeland.

AMY LOWELL

Amy Lowell's two best-known poems are "Lilacs" and "Patterns." In addition to her poetry, Lowell is remembered for a ground-breaking, two-volume biography of the English poet John Keats. The year after her death, Lowell was awarded the 1926 Pulitzer Prize for poetry for her collection *What's O'Clock*.

Multimodal Learning

ALTERNATIVE ACTIVITIES

1. Make a **tape-recording** of songs that reflect the views about love expressed in either one of the poems.
2. Create a **sketch** showing a figurative expression from one of the poems in a literal way. For example, you might show a night scene that literally has sharp edges.
3. Put together a **photographic essay** that contrasts the ideas of love expressed in these two poems.

LUIS LLORÉNS TORRES

One of Puerto Rico's most respected modern poets, Luis Lloréns Torres (1878–1944) said the goal of the poet "consists of the presentation in a sensitive manner of scenes and landscapes of the ideal world . . . existing in every poet's imagination." Lloréns Torres took up writing poetry when he was studying law in Spain. He was still in Spain when he published his first book of verse, *At the Foot of the Alhambra*, in 1899. On returning to Puerto Rico, he served in the Puerto Rican legislature and joined with other political leaders who supported independence from the United States. Lloréns Torres also founded and edited the *Antilles Journal*, a literary journal that was highly respected in Puerto Rico and the rest of Latin America. In the journal, he published his own poetry along with works by other leading Latin American writers. Lloréns Torres's association with the *Antilles Journal*, as well as subsequent work, won him a place as a major poet of Latin America.

OTHER WORKS Poems in *The Puerto Rican Poets* and in *Inventing a Word* Extended Reading

AMY LOWELL

1874–1925

A member of an illustrious American family, Amy Lowell was the sister of a noted astronomer, the granddaughter of the founder of Lowell, Massachusetts, and a descendant of the famous American poet James Russell Lowell (1819–1891). She spent much of her early adulthood involved in civic activities. Then, deciding to become a poet herself, Lowell spent ten years studying the craft before she published her first collection of poems, *A Dome of Many-Colored Glass*, in 1912. Soon afterward, while visiting England, she met the American poet Ezra Pound (1885–1972) and adopted his theories of imagism. Pound wanted poetry to rely on clear, concrete images and the patterns of ordinary speech. Such images in "The Taxi" as the world beating dead "like a slackened drum" and the lights of the city pricking the speaker's eyes reflect this imagist approach.

OTHER WORKS *Sword Blades and Poppy Seeds, Selected Poems, The Complete Poetical Works of Amy Lowell* Extended Reading

374 UNIT THREE PART 1: THE TIES THAT BIND

Alternative Activities

1. Suggest that students explore many genres of music in their search for appropriate songs.
2. Encourage students to read the figurative expressions in the poems quite literally before they choose one to illustrate.
3. Have students work in small groups, with each group designating members to summarize ideas, to research appropriate photographs, and to integrate photos and text.

PREVIEWING

POETRY

Sonnet 18
William Shakespeare Great Britain

Sonnet 30
Edna St. Vincent Millay United States

Activating Prior Knowledge
PERSONAL CONNECTION

With a partner, come up with different ideas for completing these statements about love shown to the right. You may use lyrics from popular music or any other phrases that come to mind. Share your best responses with your classmates. Then discuss what the completed statements reveal about people's attitudes toward love.

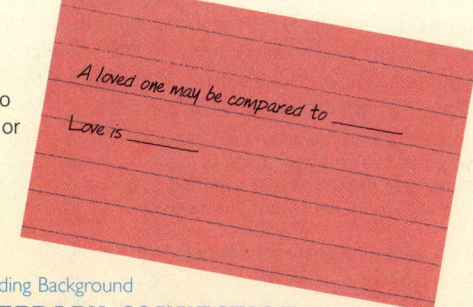

A loved one may be compared to _____

Love is _____

Building Background
LITERARY CONNECTION

Poets have often explored the topic of love in **sonnets,** 14-line poems that have been a popular form of expression for many centuries. The sonnet originated in Italy; in fact, the word *sonnet* comes from the Italian for "little song." The form was first popularized by the Italian poet Petrarch (1304–1374), who wrote a famous **sonnet sequence,** or series, expressing his love for a woman named Laura. From Italy, the form spread to France, Spain, and England, where many poets, including William Shakespeare, experimented with the form. Shakespeare's 154 sonnets are widely regarded as the finest in English. Like Petrarch's, Shakespeare's sonnets often focus on romantic love; they also address the love between friends. Since Shakespeare's day, many English-language poets have tried their hand at writing sonnets. Among them is the 20th-century American poet Edna St. Vincent Millay.

OVERVIEW

Objectives

- To understand and appreciate sonnets that express feelings and thoughts about love and its importance
- To understand and identify meter
- To identify and understand archaic words and expressions
- To express understanding of the selection through a choice of writing forms, including a personality profile, a sonnet, or another poem
- To extend understanding of the sonnets through a variety of multimodal and cross-curricular activities

Skills

LITERARY CONCEPTS
- Meter

THE WRITER'S STYLE
- Comparison and contrast

SPEAKING, LISTENING, AND VIEWING
- Group discussion
- Oral presentation

PRINT AND MEDIA RESOURCES

UNIT THREE RESOURCE BOOK
Strategic Reading: Literature, p. 13

WRITING MINI–LESSONS
Transparencies, pp. 18–19

ACCESS FOR STUDENTS ACQUIRING ENGLISH
Reading Support

FORMAL ASSESSMENT
Selection Test, p. 75
 Test Generator

 AUDIO LIBRARY
See Reference Card

 LASERLINKS
Author Background

INTERNET RESOURCES
McDougal Littell Literature Center at http://www.hmco.com/mcdougal/lit

Thematic Link: *The Ties That Bind*
In these two sonnets, the speakers explore the depth and meaning of their feelings for their lovers.

CUSTOMIZING FOR
Students Acquiring English

- Use ACCESS FOR STUDENTS ACQUIRING ENGLISH.
- The formal language of these sonnets may challenge some students. Before students begin reading, you may find it helpful to discuss traditions of love poetry and love music from their native cultures. As students read, encourage them to paraphrase each unit of thought.
- In addition to these boxes, you may want to use the suggestions under Strategic Reading for Less-Proficient Readers.

CUSTOMIZING FOR
Gifted and Talented Students

Point out to students that these sonnets have numbers rather than titles. These numbers reflect the sonnets' place in their respective sequences. (In St. Vincent Millay's case, the poet herself placed the poems in a specific order, but whether Shakespeare's sonnets have been numbered in an order which he intended is a matter of some speculation.) Suggest that students provide titles for these hitherto untitled poems, and ask them to explain their reasons for the titles they gave.

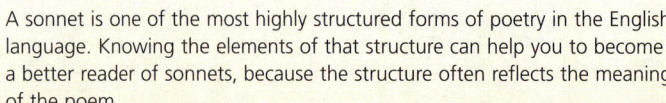

READING CONNECTION Active Reading

Understanding Sonnet Structure

A sonnet is one of the most highly structured forms of poetry in the English language. Knowing the elements of that structure can help you to become a better reader of sonnets, because the structure often reflects the meaning of the poem.

Rhyme Scheme Poets use rhyme not only to please the ear but also to mark units of thought. In a sonnet, the **rhyme scheme,** which is the rhyme pattern of the poem, can help you to follow the progression of thought. To identify a sonnet's rhyme scheme, you assign a letter of the alphabet to each line according to the rhymed sound at the end of the line. The example below, from another Shakespeare sonnet, illustrates an *abab* rhyme scheme. Note that *fled* rhymes with *dead* and that *bell* rhymes with *dwell*.

No longer mourn for me when I am *dead*	a
Than you shall hear the ruly sullen *bell*	b
Give warning to the world that I am *fled*	a
From this vile world, with vilest worms to *dwell*.	b

The English, or Shakespearean, Sonnet A sonnet by Shakespeare is characterized by the fixed rhyme pattern *abab cdcd efef gg*. The rhymes reflect the logical organization of the poem, dividing it into three quatrains and one couplet. A **quatrain** is a group of four rhymed lines; a **couplet** is a rhymed pair of lines. This structure is so common in English poetry, and in Shakespeare's poems in particular, that it is recognized as a separate type of sonnet.

In a typical English sonnet, the first quatrain introduces a situation, identifies a problem, or raises a question. In subsequent quatrains the issue is further explored. Toward the end of the poem, a turning point usually occurs, after which the situation is clarified, the problem is resolved, or the question is answered. This turning point often takes place at the beginning of the third quatrain or at the couplet, though it may take place elsewhere.

Modern poets, such as Millay, have continued to experiment with the sonnet form, stretching the Shakespearean mold in fresh and original ways.

Strategies for Reading Sonnets

As you read the Shakespeare and Millay sonnets, apply these strategies to find out how the speakers feel about love.

1. Identify the rhyme scheme and the major units of thought.
2. In your own words, describe the situation, problem, or question that is introduced at the beginning of the poem.
3. Identify the turning point, if there is one.
4. Find out how the situation is clarified, the problem resolved, or the question answered.
5. Summarize the message of the poem in your own words.

376 UNIT THREE PART 1: THE TIES THAT BIND

Critic's Corner

"He was not for an age, but for all time!"

Ben Jonson

Tell students that Ben Johnson was a contemporary of Shakespeare's and a rival poet and dramatist, regarded as one of the finest writers of the English Renaissance. Ask students to explain Jonson's meaning and to tell whether they agree with the sentiment it expresses.

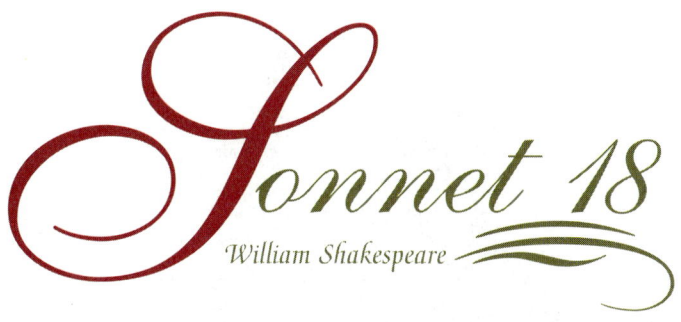
Sonnet 18
William Shakespeare

Shall I compare thee to a summer's day?
Thou art more lovely and more temperate:
Rough winds do shake the darling buds of May,
And summer's lease hath all too short a date:
5 Sometime too hot the eye of heaven shines,
And often is his gold complexion dimmed;
And every fair from fair sometime declines,
By chance or nature's changing course untrimmed;
But thy eternal summer shall not fade,
10 Nor lose possession of that fair thou owest;
Nor shall Death brag thou wander'st in his shade,
When in eternal lines to time thou growest:
  So long as men can breathe, or eyes can see,
  So long lives this, and this gives life to thee.

2 temperate (tĕm′pər-ĭt): moderate; mild.

8 untrimmed: stripped of beauty.

10 thou owest (ō′əst): you own; you possess.

FROM PERSONAL RESPONSE TO CRITICAL ANALYSIS

REFLECT

1. Working with a partner, strike a pose that expresses your response to "Sonnet 18," then invite your partner to interpret that pose. In your notebook, explain your response and what you learned about your partner's response to the poem.

RETHINK
Close Textual Reading

2. How did your knowledge of sonnet structure help you to understand the poem?
   Consider
   • the question raised in the first line
   • the rhyme scheme
   • the main point of each quatrain and the couplet

3. What words would you use to describe how the speaker feels about the person being addressed? Support your opinion with details from the poem.

CUSTOMIZING FOR
Students Acquiring English

1. Explain to students that *thee* and *thou* are informal second-person pronouns which have fallen out of common use in the English language.

2. Explain that *lease* here means "the amount of time that summer lasts."

STRATEGIC READING FOR
Less-Proficient Readers

Set a Purpose Point out that even experts in literature typically do not fully understand a poem in one reading. Encourage students to grasp whatever meaning they can at first reading. Challenge them to learn what they can about the speakers' feelings for their loved ones.

Use **UNIT THREE RESOURCE BOOK**, p. 13, for guidance in reading the selection.

Literary Concept: RHYME

A Make sure students can identify the rhyme scheme. Then point out that the poet rhymes *temperate* with *date*. Such rhymes are called *slant rhymes*, or *eye rhymes*, because they appeal more to the eye than to the ear. This type of rhyme is common in English-language sonnets because English contains far fewer rhyming words than Italian.

Literary Concept: METER

B Ask students to identify the meter of the sonnet. *(iambic pentameter)* Ask what advantages this meter gives the poet. *(Possible responses: long lines; close approximation of natural human speech; a predictable rhythm to the language, creating a musical quality.)*

Literary Concept: SONNET

C Point out to students that the speaker claims that his beloved's beauty is eternal, and that death will not affect it. Ask students how the speaker feels this has been accomplished. *(The poem has immortalized her beauty; as long as there is someone to read about her, her image will remain as it is described.)*

From Personal Response to Critical Analysis

1. Accept all thoughtful, sincere responses.
2. Possible responses: A knowledge of sonnet structure tells us that the poet will use the first two quatrains to explore the question posed in the first line. The third quatrain and the couplet answer the question, saying that the loved one is better than a summer day because the sonnet has immortalized the beloved's beauty.
3. Possible response: Some students may describe the speaker as head-over-heels in love, as evidenced by his extravagant praise of his beloved's beauty. Other students may feel that the speaker is enamored not only by his beloved but also of his own ability as a poet to immortalize that love.

Art Note

***Lovers III* by Eng Tay** Eng Tay (1947–) was born and raised in Malaysia, though he has lived in New York City for the last two decades. An internationally recognized printmaker and artist, Tay's works are characterized by a quiet play of color harmonies.

Reading the Art Make sure that students realize that that there are two central figures, though at first glance there may seem to be only one. *How does the painter show the difference between the two figures? Why does the boundary between the two figures seem blurred? What does this suggest about the relationship between the lovers?*

Literary Concept: METER

D Have a volunteer read the first four lines of "Sonnet 18." Then, working collaboratively, have the entire class scan each line. Ask students to identify possible exceptions to the iambic pattern. *(Possible responses: The first foot in Line 1 may be considered an exception, with an accent on "Love"; the third foot in Line 1 might be considered a spondee with both syllables being accented.)*

Critical Thinking: ANALYZING

E Ask students where they think the turning point of this sonnet occurs. *(Possible response: It occurs in line 7 when the speaker stops listing what love is not and begins to point out how essential love can be in one's life.)*

Literary Concept: REPETITION

F Ask students to point out the repetition in the last six lines of the phrases "may be" and "might be." Ask students what they feel this indicates about the speaker. *(Possible responses: The speaker is deliberately understating her conviction about the primacy of love—she would not "sell" or "trade" love for anything.)*

STRATEGIC READING FOR
Less-Proficient Readers

G Why does the speaker in "Sonnet 18" feel that the beloved is superior to a summer day? *(The beloved is more beautiful, and that beauty has been made immortal by its description in a sonnet.)* **Summarizing**

- In "Sonnet 30" what value does the speaker place on the beloved's affection? *(It may be more precious than life itself.)* **Drawing Conclusions**

Lovers III (1990), Eng Tay. Edition 175, intaglio. Published by Tapir Editions, New York.

Sonnet 30
Edna St. Vincent Millay

D Love is not all: it is not meat nor drink
Nor slumber nor a roof against the rain;
Nor yet a floating spar to men that sink
And rise and sink and rise and sink again;
5 Love can not fill the thickened lung with breath,
Nor clean the blood, nor set the fractured bone;
E Yet many a man is making friends with death
Even as I speak, for lack of love alone.
It well may be that in a difficult hour,
10 Pinned down by pain and moaning for release,
F Or nagged by want past resolution's power,
I might be driven to sell your love for peace,
Or trade the memory of this night for food.
It well may be. I do not think I would.
G

3 spar: a pole used to support a ship's sails.

11 want: need.

378   UNIT THREE   PART 1: THE TIES THAT BIND

Mini-Lesson   The Writer's Style

COMPARISON AND CONTRAST Explain that Edna St. Vincent Millay uses comparison and contrast in "Sonnet 30" to organize her ideas about love. In the first six lines she uses negative comparisons, focusing on what love is not, rather than what it is. In the last eight lines she compares love with such necessities as food and peace, and concludes that love is more important to her than they are.

Application Invite students to brainstorm ideas about an important concept such as success, happiness, or friendship. Then, working with the class as a whole, ask students to define that concept. Like Millay, they should begin with negative comparisons, telling what the concept is not. Then have them provide some positive comparisons, telling what it is or what it is like.

Reteaching/Reinforcement
- *Writer's Handbook*, anthology p. 1037
- *Writing Mini-Lessons* transparencies pp. 18–19

 **The Writer's Craft**

Comparison and Contrast, pp. 118–132

378 THE LANGUAGE OF LITERATURE **TEACHER'S EDITION**

RESPONDING OPTIONS

FROM PERSONAL RESPONSE TO CRITICAL ANALYSIS

REFLECT
1. Which lines of Millay's "Sonnet 30" did you find most memorable? Describe your response to those lines in your notebook.

RETHINK
2. Consider all the details that the speaker uses to explain why "Love is not all." In your opinion, what do these details have in common?
3. What seems to be the speaker's overall opinion of love?

RELATE
Literary Link
4. Do you think Shakespeare's "Sonnet 18" and Millay's "Sonnet 30" follow the same structure? Explain, using your knowledge of sonnet structure and details from the poems.
5. Do you think these poems convey attitudes about love that are still common today? Draw upon the discussion for the Personal Connection on page 375 to support your opinion.

Multimodal Learning
ANOTHER PATHWAY

Work with a partner to create a Venn diagram like the one below. In it, show what the two poems have in common and what sets each poem apart. Your diagram should include information about the meaning and structure of each poem.

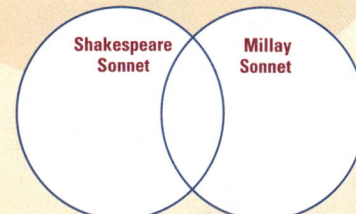

LITERARY CONCEPTS

Sonnets usually follow a regular **rhythm** called **meter**. The meter of a poem is like the beat of a song. Each unit of meter is known as a foot. In English, the most commonly used type of metrical foot is an iamb, an unstressed syllable followed by a stressed syllable (˘ ´).

Two words are used to identify the meter of a line of poetry. The first word describes the predominant type of metrical foot in the line. The second word describes the number of feet in the line: trimeter (three feet), tetrameter (four feet), pentameter (five feet), and so on. Thus, the meter of a poem might be iambic trimeter or iambic pentameter. The following example from Millay's sonnet illustrates iambic pentameter, the most common pattern.

Nŏr yét ă floátĭng spár tŏ mén thăt sínk
Ănd rísĕ ănd sínk ănd rísĕ ănd sínk ăgáin;

Work in a small group to identify the metrical pattern of Shakespeare's sonnet.

QUICKWRITES

1. Create a **personality profile** of one of the speakers in the two poems. Use details from the poem to support your opinion of the speaker's personality.

2. Write a **sonnet** or another **poem** in which, like Millay, you express your own view of love by defining what it is not.

 **PORTFOLIO** Save your writing. You may want to use it later as a springboard to a piece for your portfolio.

SONNET 18 / SONNET 30   **379**

From Personal Response to Critical Analysis

1. Accept all reasonable, well-supported responses.
2. Possible responses: All the details name necessities of life such as food, drink, sleep, shelter; they all describe things a person needs to stay alive; all of the details relate to practical necessities, which, unlike love, do not involve human emotion.
3. Possible response: Love is as necessary as food or drink, perhaps more so; love is more important to the well-being of people than any physical necessity.
4. Possible responses: Yes, because they both follow the same rhyme scheme; no, because Shakespeare develops his idea in three quatrains and a final couplet, while Millay develops an idea in lines 1-6, refutes it in lines 7-8, and resolves the question in a final sestet
5. Accept all reasonable, well-supported responses.

Another Pathway

Cooperative Learning Students might begin by having each partner prepare a list of attributes: one listing similarities and the other listing differences. They can then combine their lists while making their Venn diagram.

Rubric

3 Full Accomplishment Students' Venn diagrams correctly express an exhaustive catalog of similarities and differences.

2 Substantial Accomplishment Students' Venn diagrams express an adequate catalog of similarities and differences.

1 Little or Partial Accomplishment Students' Venn diagrams are incorrectly structured; information expressed is incorrect or severely lacking in detail.

Literary Concepts

Suggest that students read aloud a few lines from the sonnet and then mark the syllables that they tend to stress with a (´) and the syllables they do not stress with a (˘). Students should note that there are five iambs in each line and the metrical pattern is therefore iambic pentameter. Make sure that students realize that there are exceptions to the pattern, which adds to the rich texture of the sonnet.

QuickWrites

1. Before beginning, students should discuss the speakers of both poems. Ask them to think about the type of person who might have the ideas and feelings expressed about love in each poem.
2. If students decide to write a sonnet, suggest that they review the information about sonnet structure on page 376.

The Writer's Craft

Figurative Language, pp. 425–426
Sound Devices, p. 427

WILLIAM SHAKESPEARE

Shakespeare's sonnets circulated in manuscript for about ten years before they were collected and published in 1609, probably without the poet's consent. It is possible that they were not addressed to any particular person—a convention in sonnet writing in Elizabethan times. Two years after their publication, Shakespeare gave up acting and the theater and retired to his home in Stratford. He wrote very little in his last years.

EDNA ST. VINCENT MILLAY

Millay was born in Rockland, Maine, and raised in near-poverty by a widowed mother. Her poem "Renascence," which catapulted her to fame at age 19, describes a personal spiritual experience. Her early themes include youthful rebellion, love and death, the self and the universe. Her later work, which was less well-received, tends to deal with modern history and social issues.

AUTHOR BACKGROUND
William Shakespeare Although Shakespeare grew up in the town of Stratford-upon-Avon, he spent most of his life in London. Pictures of Stratford, Elizabethan London, and the Globe Theatre will enhance students' understanding of the life and times of this great poet and playwright.

Side A, Frame 49436

Multimodal Learning

ALTERNATIVE ACTIVITIES

1. Present a **weather report** that is not about the weather at all but about the qualities of a person whom you know well. In your report, try to imitate some of the techniques used by Shakespeare to make comparisons.
2. Turn either sonnet into a **popular song** and perform it before the class.

THE WRITER'S STYLE

Shakespeare wrote almost 500 years ago. Study his sonnet for words or expressions that are no longer commonly used. Then create a list of those terms and try to come up with a modern substitute for each one. Compare your results with those of your classmates.

WILLIAM SHAKESPEARE

1564–1616

The son of a merchant, William Shakespeare grew up in the market town of Stratford-upon-Avon, England, where he attended the local grammar school. In 1582 he married Anne Hathaway, who was to give birth to three children. Shakespeare probably moved to London in the 1580s and began a career as an actor with the Lord Chamberlain's Men, London's leading theater company. In the 1590s he began writing plays for the group. Great acclaim followed, under both Queen Elizabeth I and her successor, King James I, who became the theater company's patron. From then on known as the King's Players, the group performed mainly at London's Globe Theatre, where Shakespeare was a part owner. When he died, Shakespeare was able to leave his heirs a large inheritance. Of course, Shakespeare's greatest legacy was his writing—over 150 sonnets and over 35 dramas that are generally regarded as the world's finest. These include tragedies such as *Hamlet* and *King Lear* and comedies such as *The Taming of the Shrew* and *A Midsummer Night's Dream*.
OTHER WORKS *Romeo and Juliet, Macbeth, As You Like It, Twelfth Night*

Extended Reading

EDNA ST. VINCENT MILLAY

1892–1950

Edna St. Vincent Millay was still a student when she burst on the literary scene in 1912 with her poem "Renascence." After graduating from Vassar College, she settled in Greenwich Village, a New York City neighborhood then enjoying its heyday as a center for poets and artists. Millay quickly became one of Greenwich Village's social lions, admired as much for her offbeat, romantic lifestyle as for her skill with the pen. Though Millay lived the life of a nonconformist, her well-crafted verse usually conformed to poetic traditions of the past. She was one of the few poets of her day who did not abandon rhyme and meter, and her sonnets are still considered masterpieces. In 1923, Millay became the first woman to win the Pulitzer Prize in poetry. Her work reflected many of the social changes that swept through the United States during that era and won her international acclaim. "Love is not all," which appears as Sonnet 30 in her *Collected Sonnets* (1941), was first published in her sonnet sequence *Fatal Interview* (1931).
OTHER WORKS *A Few Figs from Thistles, The Harp-Weaver and Other Poems, Conversation at Midnight*

Extended Reading

• AUTHOR BACKGROUND

380 UNIT THREE PART 1: THE TIES THAT BIND

The Writer's Style

Some terms from the sonnet and their modern-day substitutes are listed below.

thee	you
thou	you
hath	have
darling	beautiful
eye of heaven	sun
nature's changing course	time and the seasons
wander'st	wander

Varieties of Language, pp. 428–429

Alternative Activities

1. Students might focus on a change in the weather—a thaw in midwinter, the sunshine after a thunderstorm—to suggest the range of qualities in their subjects.
2. Students may adapt or shorten the sonnets, if necessary. Allow them to create their own melodies or to choose existing melodies from any musical styles.

380 THE LANGUAGE OF LITERATURE TEACHER'S EDITION

PREVIEWING

NONFICTION

A Case of Cruelty
James Herriot Great Britain

Activating Prior Knowledge
PERSONAL CONNECTION

Think about animals you have owned or about the people you know who feel strong ties to animals. Why do you think people have such strong feelings about pets or other animals? Discuss your ideas with your classmates, drawing on your own experiences.

Building Background
BIOGRAPHICAL CONNECTION

James Herriot, the author of the selection you are about to read, felt very strong ties to animals of all kinds. For years Herriot worked as a veterinarian, treating both pets and farm animals in a rural part of the northern English county of Yorkshire. Recognizing that his experiences with animals and their owners might make for good reading, he eventually began to put them down on paper. Herriot won fame with a series of charming books about the veterinary practice he shared with his partner in a Yorkshire village called Darrowby. "A Case of Cruelty," from that series, recounts an experience involving the "small animal" side of the two men's practice.

Countryside in Yorkshire, England.
Copyright © Colin Raw/Tony Stone Images.

Setting a Purpose
WRITING CONNECTION

In your notebook describe a memorable experience that you have had with a pet or with another animal. Create a chart like the one shown, substituting answers for the questions in the boxes. As you read, compare your own memorable experience with Herriot's recollection.

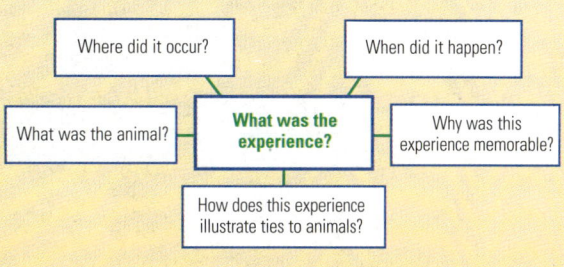

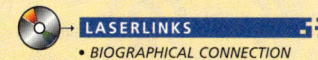
• BIOGRAPHICAL CONNECTION

381

OVERVIEW

Objectives

- To understand and appreciate a nonfiction narrative that recounts the strong ties that an old woman has with her pets
- To identify and understand the elements of a narrative
- To appreciate and write detailed description
- To express understanding of a selection through a choice of writing forms including a nonfiction narrative, diary entries, and an editorial
- To extend understanding of the selection through a variety of multimodal and cross-curricular activities.

Skills

LITERARY CONCEPTS	GRAMMAR
• Narrative	• Prefixes
• Style	**SPEAKING, LISTENING,**
• Characterization	**AND VIEWING**
THE WRITER'S STYLE	• Film
• Vivid, specific words	• Interviews
GENRE STUDY	• Art
• Nonfiction: memoir	• Oral presentation

 **BIOGRAPHICAL CONNECTION**
James Herriot This famous veterinarian lived and worked in the English county of Yorkshire. Photographs of the Yorkshire countryside and the author at work provide a sense of Herriot's world.

Side A, Frame 49448

PRINT AND MEDIA RESOURCES

UNIT THREE RESOURCE BOOK
Strategic Reading: Literature, p. 17
Vocabulary SkillBuilder, p. 18

WRITING MINI–LESSONS
Transparencies, pp. 46, 54

ACCESS FOR STUDENTS ACQUIRING ENGLISH
Selection Summaries
Reading Support

FORMAL ASSESSMENT
Selection Test, pp. 77–78
 Test Generator

 AUDIO LIBRARY
See Reference Card

 **LASERLINKS**
Biographical Connection
Social Studies Connection

THE LANGUAGE OF LITERATURE TEACHER'S EDITION **381**

A Case of Cruelty

SUMMARY

The veterinarian James Herriot recalls Mrs. Donovan, an old woman who used to walk miles throughout Darrowby with her small terrier. When Mrs. Donovan's dog died, the old woman declared she would never have another dog. However, when Herriot found an emaciated, sore-covered golden retriever living in a filthy shed, Mrs. Donovan took the dog and transformed it into a happy, healthy pet. Whenever the old woman saw Herriot, she always exclaimed, "Haven't I made a difference to this dog!"

Thematic Link: *The Ties That Bind* A lonely woman heals a badly-mistreated dog, forging strong ties of love and devotion.

CUSTOMIZING FOR
Students Acquiring English

- Use **ACCESS FOR STUDENTS ACQUIRING ENGLISH.**
- You may want to preteach some of the more difficult Briticisms that appear in the footnotes.
- In addition to these boxes, you may want to use the suggestions under Strategic Reading for Less-Proficient Readers.

Art Note

***Golden Retriever #1* by Fairfield Porter**
Fairfield Porter (1907–1975), a classic American figurative painter, uses pale pastels in his carefully composed works.

Reading the Art *What feelings about the retriever does this painting evoke?*

Golden Retriever (1972), Fairfield Porter. Oil on wood panel, 14⅛" × 15⅛", The Parrish Art Museum, Southampton, New York, gift of the Estate of Fairfield Porter (1980.10.124). Photo by Jim Strong, Inc.

WORDS TO KNOW

adamant (ăd′ə-mənt) *adj.* remaining firm despite the pleas or reasoning of others; stubbornly unyielding (p. 384)

beneficent (bə-nĕf′ĭ-sənt) *adj.* producing a benefit; kind; charitable (p. 391)

callousness (kăl′əs-nĭs) *n.* emotional hardness; lack of feeling (p. 383)

convalescence (kŏn′və-lĕs′əns) *n.* the gradual return to health and strength after an illness or an injury (p. 384)

coquettishly (kō-kĕt′ĭsh-lē) *adv.* in a flirtatious manner (p. 391)

indignation (ĭn′dĭg-nā′shən) *n.* anger aroused by something unjust, mean, or unworthy (p. 383)

mystic (mĭs′tĭk) *adj.* showing supernatural powers; spiritual; inspiring mystery or wonder (p. 385)

placidly (plăs′ĭd-lē) *adv.* in an undisturbed manner; quietly; calmly (p. 391)

rank (răngk) *adj.* growing abundantly or excessively (p. 386)

transcend (trăn-sĕnd′) *v.* to move above and beyond; to be greater than (p. 384)

James Herriot

The silvery haired old gentleman with the pleasant face didn't look the type to be easily upset, but his eyes glared at me angrily, and his lips quivered with indignation.

"Mr. Herriot," he said. "I have come to make a complaint. I strongly object to your callousness in subjecting my dog to unnecessary suffering."

"Suffering? What suffering?" I was mystified.

"I think you know, Mr. Herriot. I brought my dog in a few days ago. He was very lame, and I am referring to your treatment on that occasion."

I nodded. "Yes, I remember it well . . . but where does the suffering come in?"

"Well, the poor animal is going around with his leg dangling, and I have it on good authority that the bone is fractured and should have been put in plaster immediately." The old gentleman stuck his chin out fiercely.

WORDS TO KNOW
indignation (ĭn′dĭg-nā′shən) *n.* anger aroused by something unjust, mean, or unworthy
callousness (kăl′əs-nĭs) *n.* emotional hardness; lack of feeling

---

Mini-Lesson The Writer's Style

VIVID, SPECIFIC WORDS Use the opening scene on page 383 to illustrate how Herriot uses vivid, specific words to create a clear description of a character. Point out that the specific verbs *glared* and *quivered* and the exact nouns *indignation* and *callousness* help us see this man's wrought-up emotional state.

Application Have students write a brief description of Mrs. Donovan examining the old gentleman's dog. Ask them to use specific nouns, verbs, and modifiers that show she is kind and loving toward dogs, but less than charitable to Herriot.

Reteaching/Reinforcement
- Writer's Handbook, anthology pp. 1029–1032
- Writing Mini-Lessons transparencies, pp. 46, 54

Achieving Clarity, pp. 402–406

Literary Concept: DESCRIPTION

B Ask students to list specific details in this paragraph that help them see Mrs. Donovan. *(Possible responses: a dumpy little figure; walnut face; black-button eyes)*

Critical Thinking: INFERRING

C Ask students what the people who "took an uncharitable view of her acute curiosity" might say about Mrs. Donovan. *(Possible response: She's a nosy old busybody.)*

Critical Thinking: DRAWING CONCLUSIONS

D Ask students what they think Herriot's true opinion is of Mrs. Donovan's "armory" of homemade medicines. *(Possible responses: He doesn't think highly of them; he feels Mrs. Donovan overestimates the value of her remedies.)*

"All right, you can stop worrying," I said. "Your dog has a radial paralysis[1] caused by a blow on the ribs, and if you are patient and follow my treatment he'll gradually improve. In fact I think he'll recover completely."

"But he trails his leg when he walks."

"I know—that's typical, and to the layman it does give the appearance of a broken leg. But he shows no sign of pain, does he?"

"No, he seems quite happy, but this lady seemed to be absolutely sure of her facts. She was adamant."

"Lady?"

"Yes," said the old gentleman. "She is very clever with animals, and she came around to see if she could help in my dog's convalescence. She brought some excellent condition powders[2] with her."

"Ah!" A blinding shaft pierced the fog in my mind. All was suddenly clear. "It was Mrs. Donovan, wasn't it?"

"Well . . . er, yes. That was her name."

Old Mrs. Donovan was a woman who really got around. No matter what was going on in Darrowby—weddings, funerals, house-sales—you'd find the dumpy little figure and walnut face among the spectators, the darting, black-button eyes taking everything in. And always, on the end of its lead, her terrier dog.

When I say "old," I'm only guessing, because she appeared ageless; she seemed to have been around a long time, but she could have been anything between fifty-five and seventy-five. She certainly had the vitality of a young woman because she must have walked vast distances in her dedicated quest to keep abreast of events. Many people took an uncharitable view of her acute curiosity, but whatever the motivation, her activities took her into almost every channel of life in the town. One of these channels was our veterinary practice.

She could talk at length on the ailments of small animals.

Because Mrs. Donovan, among her other widely ranging interests, was an animal doctor. In fact I think it would be safe to say that this facet of her life <u>transcended</u> all the others.

She could talk at length on the ailments of small animals, and she had a whole armory of medicines and remedies at her command, her two specialities being her miracle-working condition powders and a dog shampoo of unprecedented value for improving the coat. She had an uncanny ability to sniff out a sick animal, and it was not uncommon when I was on my rounds to find Mrs. Donovan's dark, gypsy face poised intently over what I had thought was my patient, while she administered calf's foot jelly[3] or one of her own patent nostrums.[4]

I suffered more than Siegfried because I took a more active part in the small animal side of our practice. I was anxious to develop this aspect and to improve my image in this field, and Mrs. Donovan didn't help at all. "Young Mr. Herriot," she would confide to my clients, "is all right with cattle and such like, but he don't know nothing about dogs and cats."

---

1. **radial paralysis:** loss of movement in the lower part of the leg.
2. **condition powders:** medicines for keeping an animal in good condition.
3. **calf's foot jelly:** meat gelatin made by boiling calves' feet; an old-fashioned, nutritious remedy.
4. **patent nostrums** (păt'nt nŏs'trəmz): nonprescription medicines whose effectiveness has not been proven scientifically; quack remedies.

WORDS TO KNOW

adamant (ăd'ə-mənt) *adj.* remaining firm despite the pleas or reasoning of others; stubbornly unyielding
convalescence (kŏn'və-lĕs'əns) *n.* the gradual return to health and strength after an illness or an injury
transcend (trăn-sĕnd') *v.* to move above and beyond; to be greater than

384

Multicultural Perspectives

PETS As in Darrowby, England, dogs are popular pets around the world. In many cultures, however, pets less commonly seen in the United States are also cherished. In China, where the population is dense and space is limited, children keep small pets like silkworms and goldfish. Similarly, children in Japan make pets out of singing insects, especially crickets and beetles. Children keep crickets, a symbol of good luck in Japanese culture, in bamboo cages and feed them cucumber slices. Cricket concerts are often held in neighborhood parks. Many Thai farmers keep water buffalo. The animal works in the rice paddies and is devoted to its master. Children often ride the buffalo the way Americans might ride a horse.

And of course they believed her and had implicit faith in her. She had the irresistible <u>mystic</u> appeal of the amateur, and on top of that there was her habit, particularly endearing in Darrowby, of never charging for her advice, her medicines, her long periods of diligent nursing.

Older folk in the town told how her husband, an Irish farm worker, had died many years ago and how he must have had a "bit put away" because Mrs. Donovan had apparently been able to indulge all her interests over the years without financial strain. Since she inhabited the streets of Darrowby all day and every day, I often encountered her, and she always smiled up at me sweetly and told me how she had been sitting up all night with Mrs. So-and-so's dog that I'd been treating. She felt sure she'd be able to pull it through.

There was no smile on her face, however, on the day when she rushed into the surgery[5] while Siegfried and I were having tea.

"Mr. Herriot!" she gasped. "Can you come? My little dog's been run over!"

I jumped up and ran out to the car with her. She sat in the passenger seat with her head bowed, her hands clasped tightly on her knees.

"He slipped his collar and ran in front of a car," she murmured. "He's lying in front of the school half way up Cliffend Road. Please hurry."

I was there within three minutes, but as I bent over the dusty little body stretched on the pavement, I knew there was nothing I could do. The fast-glazing eyes, the faint, gasping respirations, the ghastly pallor of the mucous membranes[6] all told the same story.

"I'll take him back to the surgery and get some saline[7] into him, Mrs. Donovan," I said. "But I'm afraid he's had a massive internal hemorrhage.[8] Did you see what happened exactly?"

She gulped. "Yes, the wheel went right over him."

Ruptured liver, for sure. I passed my hands under the little animal and began to lift him gently, but as I did so, the breathing stopped, and the eyes stared fixedly ahead.

Mrs. Donovan sank to her knees, and for a few moments she gently stroked the rough hair of the head and chest. "He's dead, isn't he?" she whispered at last.

"I'm afraid he is," I said.

She got slowly to her feet and stood bewilderedly among the little group of bystanders on the pavement. Her lips moved, but she seemed unable to say any more.

I took her arm, led her over to the car and opened the door. "Get in and sit down," I said. "I'll run you home. Leave everything to me."

I wrapped the dog in my calving overall[9] and laid him in the boot[10] before driving away. It wasn't until we drew up outside Mrs. Donovan's house that she began to weep silently. I sat there without speaking till she finished. Then she wiped her eyes and turned to me.

"Do you think he suffered at all?"

"I'm certain he didn't. It was all so quick—he wouldn't know a thing about it."

She tried to smile. "Poor little Rex, I don't know what I'm going to do without him. We've traveled a few miles together, you know."

"Yes, you have. He had a wonderful life, Mrs. Donovan. And let me give you a bit of

---

5. **surgery:** in Britain, a general term for a physician's or veterinarian's office.
6. **mucous membranes:** thin layers of tissue lining the nose, mouth, and other body passages.
7. **saline** (sā′lēn′): a salt solution used to stem the effects of blood loss.
8. **internal hemorrhage** (hĕm′ər-ĭj): excessive bleeding inside the body.
9. **calving overall:** a special heavy overall worn by the veterinarian assisting in the birth of a calf.
10. **boot:** British term for the trunk of a car.

WORDS TO KNOW

mystic (mĭs′tĭk) *adj.* showing supernatural powers; spiritual; inspiring mystery or wonder

385

Mini-Lesson  Genre Study

NONFICTION Tell students that "A Case of Cruelty," is a type of nonfiction called a **memoir** because it is based on an actual event in which the author participated, but the story focuses primarily on a person other than Herriot himself. Use the word web shown here to explain the typical features of a memoir.

Application Have students copy the web into their notebooks. Ask them to list specific examples of the characteristics of a memoir that they find in "A Case of Cruelty."

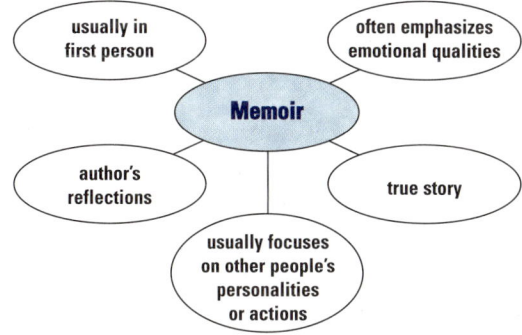

CUSTOMIZING FOR
Students Acquiring English

2 Point out to students that, in this instance, *lost* means "unable to function, helpless."

Critical Thinking:
MAKING JUDGMENTS

I Ask students whether they agree or disagree with James Herriot's advice to replace a lost pet quickly. Have students explain their responses. *(Answers will vary.)*

Literary Concept:
CHARACTERIZATION

J Ask students if they believe Mrs. Donovan will keep her vow never to have another dog, based on what they know about her. *(Possible responses: No; she loves dogs too much not to have one. Yes; she will be loyal to Rex.)*

Linking to Geography

K Because England's moist, mild climate is ideal for growing things, the country is sometimes called "a nation of gardeners." Many English homeowners devote more yard space to flower beds than to lawn.

Literary Concept: STYLE

L Point out to students that the author uses one long sentence to list the jumble of debris in the shed, then introduces the dog in a simple sentence fragment. Ask students how this use of sentence structure affects their reading of the paragraph. *(Possible response: it contrasts the mess in the shed with the dog's solitude)*

CUSTOMIZING FOR
Students Acquiring English

3 Tell students that *emaciation* means "a state of being abnormally thin."

Linking to Science

M Dogs, like humans, have 12 sets of ribs.

---

2 advice—you must get another dog. You'd be lost without one."

She shook her head. "No, I couldn't. That little dog meant too much to me. I couldn't let another take his place."

I "Well I know that's how you feel just now, but I wish you'd think about it. I don't want to seem callous—I tell everybody this when they lose an animal, and I know it's good advice."

"Mr. Herriot, I'll never have another one." She shook her head again, very decisively. "Rex was my faithful friend for many years, and I just want

J to remember him. He's the last dog I'll ever have."

I often saw Mrs. Donovan around the town after this, and I was glad to see she was still as active as ever, though she looked strangely incomplete without the little dog on its lead. But it must have been over a month before I had the chance to speak to her.

It was on the afternoon that Inspector Halliday of the R.S.P.C.A.[11] rang me.

"Mr. Herriot," he said. "I'd like you to come and see an animal with me. A cruelty case."

"Right, what is it?"

"A dog, and it's pretty grim. A dreadful case of neglect." He gave me the name of a row of old brick cottages down by the river and said he'd meet me there.

Halliday was waiting for me, smart and business-like in his dark uniform, as I pulled up in the back lane behind the houses. He was a big, blond man with cheerful blue eyes, but he didn't smile as he came over to the car.

"He's in here," he said and led the way towards one of the doors in the long, crumbling wall. A few curious people were hanging around, and with a feeling of inevitability I recognized a gnome-like brown face. Trust Mrs. Donovan, I thought, to be among those present at a time like this.

We went through the door into the long garden. I had found that even the lowliest dwellings in Darrowby had long strips of land at the back as though the builders had taken it for granted that the country people who were going to live in them would want to occupy themselves with the pursuits of the soil; with vegetable and fruit growing, even stock keeping[12] in a small way. You usually found a pig there, a few hens, often pretty beds of flowers.

But this garden was a wilderness. A chilling air of desolation hung over the few gnarled apple and plum trees standing among a tangle of <u>rank</u> grass as though the place had been forsaken by all living creatures.

Halliday went over to a ramshackle wooden shed with peeling paint and a rusted corrugated iron roof. He produced a key, unlocked the padlock and dragged the door partly open. There was no window, and it wasn't easy to identify the jumble inside; broken gardening tools, an ancient mangle, rows of flower pots and partly used paint tins.[13] And right at the back, a dog sitting quietly.

I didn't notice him immediately because of the gloom and because the smell in the shed started me coughing, but as I drew closer, I saw that he was a big animal, sitting very upright, his collar secured by a chain to a ring in the wall. I had seen some thin dogs, but this advanced emaciation reminded me of my textbooks on anatomy; nowhere else did the bones of pelvis, face and rib cage stand out with such horrifying clarity. A deep, smoothed out hollow in the earth floor showed where he had lain, moved about, in fact lived, for a very long time.

---

11. **R.S.P.C.A.:** the Royal Society for the Prevention of Cruelty to Animals.
12. **stock keeping:** keeping farm animals.
13. **tins:** British term for cans.

WORDS TO KNOW

rank (răngk) *adj.* growing abundantly or excessively

386

Mini-Lesson ✏ Grammar

PREFIXES Remind students that a prefix is a word part that is added to the beginning of a word or another word part. Explain that the prefixes *in-* and *im-* mean "not" when added to a word. Point out the word *incomplete* on this page and ask students for other examples, such as *immodest, incompetent,* or *immature.* Explain that *in-* and *im-* can also mean "in" or "into," usually when they are added to a word part. Point out the  words *inhabited* ("lived in") and *inspector* ("someone who looks into things") on pages 385 and 386.

Application Invite students to tell whether the prefix in each of the following words *in-* or *im-* means "not" or "in; into."

1. inject *(in; into)*
2. inaccurate *(not)*
3. involved *(in; into)*
4. improper *(not)*
5. investigate *(in; into)*
6. immerse *(in; into)*
7. indescribable *(not)*
8. imbalance *(not)*
9. infection *(in; into)*
10. immobile *(not)*

Reteaching/Reinforcement

📖 **The Writer's Craft**
Analyzing Word Parts, pp. 460–462

Old Farmhouse (1872), Edward Henry Fahey, RI. Watercolor and bodycolor, heightened with gum arabic, 13¼″ × 9¾″, Anthony Reed Gallery, London.

Art Note

***Old Farm House* by Edward Henry Fahey** Romantic watercolorist Edward Henry Fahey (1844–1907) recorded everyday scenes in the English countryside in the late nineteenth century. This painting has been described as "an essay in the textures of crumbling plaster."

Reading the Art *What details of this painting remind you of the row house and shed where the neglected dog was chained?*

The sight of the animal had a stupefying effect on me; I only half took in the rest of the scene—the filthy shreds of sacking scattered nearby, the bowl of scummy water.

"Look at his back end," Halliday muttered.

I carefully raised the dog from his sitting position and realized that the stench in the place was not entirely due to the piles of excrement. The hindquarters were a welter of pressure sores which had turned gangrenous,[14] and strips of sloughing tissue[15] hung down from them. There were similar sores along the sternum[16] and ribs. The coat, which seemed to be a dull yellow, was matted and caked with dirt.

The inspector spoke again. "I don't think he's ever been out of here. He's only a young dog—about a year old—but I understand he's been in this shed since he was an eight-week-old pup.

---

14. **gangrenous** (găng′grə-nəs): infected with gangrene, which is the death or decay of body tissue due to loss of blood supply.
15. **sloughing** (slŭf′ĭng) **tissue**: dead body tissue separating from the surrounding living tissue.
16. **sternum**: the breastbone, from which the ribs branch off.

A CASE OF CRUELTY

Literary Concept:
CHARACTERIZATION

N Ask students why they think Herriot characterizes the dog in such a sympathetic way. *(Possible responses: Some students may say it's Herriot's natural inclination to care about animals. Others may say he wants to build sympathy for the dog, he wants us to know the dog as a story character, or he wants to prepare the reader for the next event in the story.)*

Critical Thinking: SPECULATING

O Ask students what they think will soon happen, based on Herriot's comment about "letting out" the lovely retriever and on what they know about Herriot and Mrs. Donovan so far. *(Possible responses: Herriot will not destroy the dog; he may keep it himself; he may ask Mrs. Donovan to nurse the dog to health.)*

Critical Thinking: ANALYZING

P Ask students why they think Herriot makes these comments about a "good shampoo" and "a long course of condition powders" while pretending not to notice Mrs. Donovan. *(Possible response: He knows the old lady is just the person to nurse the dog to health, but he remembers what she said about never wanting another dog. These comments are a sly way to induce her to take the dog.)*

Literary Note

Q The name *Rex* is the Latin word for "king" while *Roy* comes from the French word *roi*, also meaning "king." The English word *royal* is also derived from the same French word.

Somebody out in the lane heard a whimper, or he'd never have been found."

I felt a tightening of the throat and a sudden nausea which wasn't due to the smell. It was the thought of this patient animal sitting starved and forgotten in the darkness and filth for a year. I looked again at the dog and saw in his eyes only a calm trust. Some dogs would have barked their heads off and soon been discovered, some would have become terrified and vicious, but this was one of the totally undemanding kind, the kind which had complete faith in people and accepted all their actions without complaint. Just an occasional whimper perhaps as he sat interminably in the empty blackness which had been his world and at times wondered what it was all about.

"Well, Inspector, I hope you're going to throw the book at whoever's responsible," I said.

Halliday grunted. "Oh, there won't be much done. It's a case of diminished responsibility. The owner's definitely simple. Lives with an aged mother who hardly knows what's going on either. I've seen the fellow, and it seems he threw in a bit of food when he felt like it, and that's about all he did. They'll fine him and stop him keeping an animal in the future but nothing more than that."

"I see." I reached out and stroked the dog's head, and he immediately responded by resting a paw on my wrist. There was a pathetic dignity about the way he held himself erect, the calm eyes regarding me, friendly and unafraid. "Well, you'll let me know if you want me in court."

"Of course, and thank you for coming along." Halliday hesitated for a moment. "And now I expect you'll want to put this poor thing out of his misery right away."

I continued to run my hand over the head and ears while I thought for a moment. "Yes . . . yes, I suppose so. We'd never find a home for him in this state. It's the kindest thing to do. Anyway, push the door wide open will you so that I can get a proper look at him."

In the improved light I examined him more thoroughly. Perfect teeth, well-proportioned limbs with a fringe of yellow hair. I put my stethoscope on his chest, and as I listened to the slow, strong thudding of the heart, the dog again put his paw on my hand.

I turned to Halliday, "You know, Inspector, inside this bag of bones there's a lovely healthy golden retriever. I wish there was some way of letting him out."

As I spoke, I noticed there was more than one figure in the door opening. A pair of black pebble eyes were peering intently at the big dog from behind the inspector's broad back. The other spectators had remained in the lane, but Mrs. Donovan's curiosity had been too much for her. I continued conversationally as though I hadn't seen her.

"You know, what this dog needs first of all is a good shampoo to clean up his matted coat."

"Huh?" said Halliday.

"Yes. And then he wants a long course of some really strong condition powders."

"What's that?" The inspector looked startled.

"There's no doubt about it," I said. "It's the only hope for him, but where are you going to find such things? Really powerful enough, I mean." I sighed and straightened up. "Ah well, I suppose there's nothing else for it. I'd better put him to sleep right away. I'll get the things from my car."

When I got back to the shed, Mrs. Donovan was already inside examining the dog despite the feeble remonstrances[17] of the big man.

"Look!" she said excitedly, pointing to a name roughly scratched on the collar. "His name's Roy.' She smiled up at me. "It's a bit like Rex, isn't it, that name?"

"You know, Mrs. Donovan, now you mention it, it is. It's very like Rex, the way it comes off your tongue." I nodded seriously.

---

17. **remonstrances** (rĭ-mŏn'strəns-ĭz): protests; complaints; objections.

388 UNIT THREE PART 1: IN THE NAME OF LOVE

Mini-Lesson Workplace Literacy

SCANS Goal: Exercises Leadership

MOTIVATING INDIVIDUALS Ask students what part they think Herriot played in Mrs. Donovan's decision to adopt Roy. Point out that his carefully-phrased statements about what the dog needed may have suggested the idea to her. Help students see that Herriot cleverly realized what was required and that Mrs. Donovan needed to feel the idea of adopting Roy was her own.

Application Tell students that motivating and encouraging others to take a certain action are important leadership skills that are often necessary in the workplace. Have students work in pairs to role-play one of the following situations, in which one character tries to motivate the other character to take a certain action or change his or her behavior.

- A nursery school teacher must convince a belligerent child to join the story circle.
- The director of a volunteer organization needs someone to make phone calls or to distribute pamphlets door-to-door.
- A store manager needs to get a sales clerk to be more polite and friendly to customers.

She stood silent for a few moments, obviously in the grip of a deep emotion, then she burst out.

"Can I have 'im? I can make him better, I know I can. Please, please let me have 'im!"

"Well I don't know," I said. "It's really up to the inspector. You'll have to get his permission."

Halliday looked at her in bewilderment, then he said: "Excuse me, Madam," and drew me to one side. We walked a few yards through the long grass and stopped under a tree.

"Mr. Herriot," he whispered, "I don't know what's going on here, but I can't just pass over an animal in this condition to anybody who has a casual whim. The poor beggar's had one bad break already—I think it's enough. This woman doesn't look a suitable person . . ."

I held up a hand. "Believe me, Inspector, you've nothing to worry about. She's a funny old stick, but she's been sent from heaven today. If anybody in Darrowby can give this dog a new life it's her."

Halliday still looked very doubtful. "But I still don't get it. What was all that stuff about him needing shampoos and condition powders?"

"Oh never mind about that. I'll tell you some other time. What he needs is lots of good grub, care and affection, and that's just what he'll get. You can take my word for it."

"All right, you seem very sure." Halliday looked at me for a second or two then turned and walked over to the eager little figure by the shed.

I had never before been deliberately on the lookout for Mrs. Donovan: she had just cropped up wherever I happened to be, but now I scanned the streets of Darrowby anxiously day by day without sighting her. I didn't like it when Gobber Newhouse got drunk and drove his bicycle determinedly through a barrier into a ten-foot hole where they were laying the new sewer and Mrs. Donovan was not in evidence among the happy crowd who watched the council workmen[18] and two policemen trying to get him out; and when she was nowhere to be seen when they had to fetch the fire engine to the fish and chip shop the night the fat burst into flames, I became seriously worried.

Maybe I should have called round to see how she was getting on with that dog. Certainly I had trimmed off the necrotic tissue[19] and dressed the sores before she took him away, but perhaps he needed something more than that. And yet at the time I had felt a strong conviction that the main thing was to get him out of there and clean him and feed him, and nature would do the rest. And I had a lot of faith in Mrs. Donovan—far more than she had in me—when it came to animal doctoring; it was hard to believe I'd been completely wrong.

It must have been nearly three weeks, and I was on the point of calling at her home, when I noticed her stumping briskly along the far side of the market place, peering closely into every shop window exactly as before. The only difference was that she had a big yellow dog on the end of the lead.

I turned the wheel and sent my car bumping over the cobbles till I was abreast of her. When she saw me getting out, she stopped and smiled impishly, but she didn't speak as I bent over Roy and examined him. He was still a skinny dog, but he looked bright and happy, his wounds

---

18. **council workmen:** construction workers for the local government, here putting in the new sewer.
19. **necrotic tissue:** tissue in which the cells have died through injury or disease.

> I had a lot of faith in Mrs. Donovan—far more than she had in me.

A CASE OF CRUELTY   389

Art Note

Portrait of Fridel Battenberg by Max Beckmann In this portrait, German painter Max Beckmann (1884–1950) sought to express both the trust and warmth of a close friend.

Reading the Art Does this figure remind you of Mrs. Donovan?

Critical Thinking: INFERRING

V Ask students why they think Mrs. Donovan repeats the comment "Haven't I made a difference to this dog!" Ask what they think Roy means to her. *(Possible response: The dog's remarkable recovery validates Mrs. Donovan's claims as a healer; she wants Herriot to acknowledge her abilities; Roy gives her life purpose and meaning.)*

Linking to Health

W In general, malnutrition or a poor diet limits the growth of hair and affects the hair's texture. It also affects the production of melanin and other pigments that color the hair.

Literary Concept: STYLE

X Ask students to note the vivid action verbs that make this description of Roy lively. *(Possible responses: His new collar* glittered; *his tail* fanned *the air; he* plunked *his paws on Herriot's chest.)*

Critical Thinking: SPECULATING

Y Ask students if they think Herriot really wants to know what's in the condition powders. *(No; he's only teasing Mrs. Donovan.)* Ask whether they think Mrs. Donovan really believes in the powders. *(Yes, she does.)*

Portrait of Fridel Battenberg (1920), Max Beckmann. Oil on canvas, 97 cm × 48.5 cm, Kunstmuseum Hannover (Germany) mit Sammlung Sprengel. Copyright © 1996 Artists Rights Society (ARS), New York/VG Bild-Kunst, Bonn, Germany.

were healthy and granulating[20] and there was not a speck of dirt in his coat or on his skin. I knew then what Mrs. Donovan had been doing all this time; she had been washing and combing and teasing at that filthy tangle till she had finally conquered it.

As I straightened up, she seized my wrist in a grip of surprising strength and looked up into my eyes.

"Now, Mr. Herriot," she said. "Haven't I made a difference to this dog!"

"You've done wonders, Mrs. Donovan," I said. "And you've been at him with that marvelous shampoo of yours, haven't you?"

She giggled and walked away, and from that day I saw the two of them frequently but at a distance, and something like two months went by before I had a chance to talk to her again. She was passing by the surgery as I was coming down the steps, and again she grabbed my wrist.

"Mr. Herriot," she said, just as she had done before. "Haven't I made a difference to this dog!"

I looked down at Roy with something akin to awe. He had grown and filled out, and his coat, no longer yellow but a rich gold, lay in luxuriant shining swathes over the well-fleshed ribs and back. A new, brightly studded collar glittered on his neck, and his tail, beautifully fringed, fanned the air gently. He was now a golden retriever in full magnificence. As I stared at him, he reared up, plunked his forepaws on my chest and looked into my face, and in his eyes I read plainly the same calm affection and trust I had seen in that black, noisome[21] shed.

"Mrs. Donovan," I said softly, "he's the most beautiful dog in Yorkshire." Then, because I knew she was waiting for it. "It's those wonderful condition powders. Whatever do you put in them?"

---

20. **granulating:** healing by forming fleshy new growth and tiny new blood vessels.
21. **noisome** (noi′səm): foul; disgusting.

390 UNIT THREE PART 1: IN THE NAME OF LOVE

Mini-Lesson  Literary Concepts

REVIEWING CHARACTERIZATION
Remind students that characterization refers to the techniques a writer uses to create and develop a character. The reader learns about character through the character's words, actions and feelings; through descriptions of the character; and through what others in the work say about the character and how they react to him or her.

Application Ask students what qualities of character the highlighted passage on this page shows about Mrs. Donovan. *(Possible responses: kindness; patience; affection for animals; pride in her abilities to care for animals)* Remind students that the writer has shown other qualities of Mrs. Donovan elsewhere in the story. Have students locate other passages in which Mrs. Donovan is characterized and explain the qualities shown. *(p. 384–385—a nosy busybody; p. 388–curiosity, compassion)*

"Ah, wouldn't you like to know!" She bridled[22] and smiled up at me coquettishly and indeed she was nearer being kissed at that moment than for many years.

I suppose you could say that that was the start of Roy's second life. And as the years passed, I often pondered on the beneficent providence which had decreed that an animal which had spent his first twelve months abandoned and unwanted, staring uncomprehendingly into that unchanging, stinking darkness, should be whisked in a moment into an existence of light and movement and love. Because I don't think any dog had it quite so good as Roy from then on.

His diet changed dramatically from odd bread crusts to best stewing steak and biscuit, meaty bones and a bowl of warm milk every evening. And he never missed a thing. Garden fêtes,[23] school sports, evictions, gymkhanas[24]—he'd be there. I was pleased to note that as time went on, Mrs. Donovan seemed to be clocking up an even greater daily mileage. Her expenditure on shoe leather must have been phenomenal, but of course it was absolute pie[25] for Roy—a busy round in the morning, home for a meal then straight out again; it was all go.

Mrs. Donovan didn't confine her activities to the town center; there was a big stretch of common land down by the river where there were seats, and people used to take their dogs for a gallop, and she liked to get down there fairly regularly to check on the latest developments on the domestic scene. I often saw Roy loping majestically over the grass among a pack of assorted canines, and when he wasn't doing that, he was submitting to being stroked or patted or generally fussed over. He was handsome, and he just liked people; it made him irresistible.

It was common knowledge that his mistress had bought a whole selection of brushes and combs of various sizes with which she labored over his coat. Some people said she had a little brush for his teeth, too, and it might have been true, but he certainly wouldn't need his nails clipped—his life on the roads would keep them down.

Mrs. Donovan, too, had her reward; she had a faithful companion by her side every hour of the day and night. But there was more to it than that; she had always had the compulsion to help and heal animals, and the salvation of Roy was the high point of her life—a blazing triumph which never dimmed.

I know the memory of it was always fresh because many years later I was sitting on the sidelines at a cricket match, and I saw the two of them; the old lady glancing keenly around her, Roy gazing placidly out at the field of play, apparently enjoying every ball. At the end of the match I watched them move away with the dispersing crowd; Roy would be about twelve then, and heaven only knows how old Mrs. Donovan must have been, but the big golden animal was trotting along effortlessly, and his mistress, a little more bent perhaps and her head rather nearer the ground, was going very well.

When she saw me, she came over, and I felt the familiar tight grip on my wrist.

"Mr. Herriot," she said, and in the dark probing eyes the pride was still as warm, the triumph still as bursting new as if it had all happened yesterday.

"Mr. Herriot, haven't I made a difference to this dog!" ❖

---

22. **bridled:** lifted the head and drew in the chin, like a horse restrained by its bridle.
23. **fêtes** (fāts): outdoor parties; festivals.
24. **gymkhanas** (jĭm-kä′nəz): sporting events in which gymnastics, horse-jumping, or other contests are held.
25. **pie:** slang for something highly desirable; a treat.

WORDS TO KNOW
coquettishly (kō-kĕt′ĭsh-lē) *adv.* in a flirtatious manner
beneficent (bə-nĕf′ĭ-sənt) *adj.* producing a benefit; kind; charitable
placidly (plăs′ĭd-lē) *adv.* in an undisturbed manner; quietly; calmly

---

Critic's Corner

"What the world needs now, and does every so often, is a warm, G-rated, down-home, and unadrenalized prize of a book that sneaks onto the bestseller lists for no apparent reason other than a certain floppy-eared puppy appeal."

William R. Doerner
Time

Ask students to describe the appeal of "A Case of Cruelty." Suggest that they come up with a list of unusual and colorful adjectives to describe the story's appeal to them.

INSIGHT

1. Do you ever feel that animals, and especially dogs, seem to enjoy life more fully than humans do? Explain. *(Accept all reasonable responses.)*
2. If you could be any animal for a single day, what would you choose? Explain your reasons. *(Accept all reasonable responses.)*
3. Why do you think Gabriela Mistral sees an animal as God's "secret, divine servant"? *(Possible responses: They live life fully; they help people see the miracle of creation.)*

GABRIELA MISTRAL

Gabriela Mistral (1889–1957) was a Chilean poet and educator who was awarded the Nobel Prize for literature in 1945. She was the first female poet and the first Latin American to receive this honor. Upon hearing that she had been chosen, she commented, "Perhaps it was because I was the candidate of women and children." Mistral's poetry, inspired by her personal tragedies, is rich in themes of sorrow and frustrated motherhood. The suicide of her fiancé left her devastated and discouraged her from ever marrying. It also led to three of her poetry collections: *Desolation, Tenderness,* and *Destruction.* Her later life was also plagued by suicide: two close friends killed themselves in 1942, and her nephew, whom she had helped to raise, drank arsenic a year later. Mistral taught widely in Chile and in the United States.

INSIGHT

Eight Puppies
GABRIELA MISTRAL

Between the thirteenth and the
   fifteenth day
the puppies opened their eyes.
Suddenly they saw the world,
anxious with terror and joy.
5 They saw the belly of their mother,
saw the door of their house,
saw a deluge of light,
saw flowering azaleas.

They saw more, they saw all,
10 the red, the black, the ash.
Scrambling up, pawing and clawing
more lively than squirrels,
they saw the eyes of their mother,
heard my rasping cry and my laugh.

15 And I wished I were born with them.
Could it not be so another time?
To leap from a clump of banana
   plants
one morning of wonders—
a dog, a coyote, a deer;
20 to gaze with wide pupils,
to run, to stop, to run, to fall,
to whimper and whine and jump with
   joy,
riddled with sun and with barking,
a hallowed child of God, his secret,
   divine servant.

Translated by Doris Dana

Ocho Perritos
GABRIELA MISTRAL

Los perrillos abrieron sus ojos
del treceavo al quinceavo día.
De golpe vieron el mundo,
con ansia, susto y alegría.
5 Vieron el vientre de la madre,
la puerta suya que es la mía,
el diluvio de la luz,
las azaleas floridas.

Vieron más: se vieron todos,
10 el rojo, el negro, el ceniza,
gateando y aupándose,
más vivos que las ardillas;
vieron los ojos de la madre
y mi grito rasgado, y mi risa.

15 Y yo querría nacer con ellos.
¿Por qué otra vez no sería?
Saltar de unos bananales
una mañana de maravilla,
en can, en coyota, en venada;
20 mirar con grandes pupilas,
correr, parar, correr, tumbarme
y gemir y saltar de alegría,
acribillada de sol y ladridos
hija de Dios, sierva oscura y divina.

Still Life with Three Puppies (1888), Paul Gauguin. Oil on wood, 36⅛" × 24⅝", The Museum of Modern Art, New York, Mrs. Simon Guggenheim Fund. Photo Copyright © 1995 The Museum of Modern Art, New York.

Art Note

Still Life with Three Puppies by Paul Gauguin "Don't paint too much from nature," French painter Paul Gauguin (1848–1903) advised his disciples. "Art is an abstraction! Study nature, brood on it and think more of the creation which will result...." This painting shows Gauguin's deliberate distortion of nature by enclosing broad, flat areas of color with heavy contours.

Reading the Art *Does Gauguin's deliberate distortion of these puppies help you see or understand them in a new way?*

From Personal Response to Critical Analysis

1. Accept all reasonable responses.
2. Possible response: Mrs. Donovan is clearly a busybody. She has distinct opinions about treating sick animals, but she is far less knowledgeable about veterinary medicine than Herriot. She is a caring person, especially when it comes to pets.
3. Accept all reasonable, well-supported responses.
4. Possible response: Herriot's and Donovan's mutual desire to help the neglected Roy changes their initial rivalry into a relationship based on respect and admiration.
5. Accept all reasonable responses.
6. Possible responses: The eight puppies in the poem joyously explore their natural surroundings; Roy was chained and starved in a dark and filthy shed.

Another Pathway

Cooperative Learning Encourage the group members to collaborate on their pamphlets. One student can research dog care books to find background information, which a pair of student writers can use along with the selection to compose the do's and don'ts. A fourth student can edit the pamphlet, and a fifth student can illustrate it.

Rubric

3 Full Accomplishment Pamphlets offer a great deal of useful, well-organized information, accompanied by appropriate illustrations and graphics.

2 Substantial Accomplishment Pamphlets offer basic information, adequately organized, and supported by some illustrations or graphics.

1 Little or Partial Accomplishment Pamphlets' information is incorrect or inadequate; organization is poor; illustrations and graphics are lacking.

SOCIAL STUDIES CONNECTION

Animal Rights Protests Some people believe that practices such as hunting whales and using animals in laboratory tests are cruel and should be stopped. These photographs of animal-rights demonstrations can be used to prompt a discussion about the treatment of animals.

Side A, Frame 49456

RESPONDING OPTIONS

FROM PERSONAL RESPONSE TO CRITICAL ANALYSIS

REFLECT
1. What one event in this selection stands out the most for you? Describe it in your notebook, then share what you have written with a partner.

RETHINK
2. How would you describe Mrs. Donovan?
   Consider
   - her reaction to Herriot's treatment of local pets
   - her presence at every community event
   - her reaction to the death of her terrier
   - her attitude and behavior toward Roy

Close Textual Reading

3. What is your opinion of Mr. Herriot, the narrator of the selection?

Thematic Link

4. In your judgment, how is the relationship between Mr. Herriot and Mrs. Donovan affected by the ties each character feels to animals?

RELATE
5. What rights, if any, do you think animals have? Give some examples to illustrate your views.

Literary Link

6. Compare and contrast the life of the dogs in the poem "Eight Puppies" with the experiences Roy probably had as a puppy.

LITERARY CONCEPTS

Although "A Case of Cruelty" is nonfiction, it is nevertheless a **narrative,** or writing that tells a story, and as such it has many of the same elements as fiction. Review Understanding Fiction on pages 16–17, which lists the major elements of fiction. Then show how the plot of "A Case of Cruelty" develops by completing the plot diagram begun below. Finish labeling the four stages of a typical plot at the appropriate places on the diagram, and then describe the events from the story that fit each stage.

394 UNIT THREE PART 1: THE TIES THAT BIND

Multimodal Learning
ANOTHER PATHWAY

Cooperative Learning
Working with a small group of classmates, create a pamphlet titled "How to Care for a Dog." In the pamphlet list the do's and don'ts of dog care based on the treatment of dogs in the selection. Include examples from the selection to illustrate each point. You might use graphics on your computer to make your pamphlet more interesting.

QUICKWRITES

1. Expand the description you wrote for the Writing Connection on page 381 into a **nonfiction narrative** featuring a pet or another animal. Be sure to include all necessary plot elements and make your narrative as entertaining as possible.

2. Write the **diary entries** that Mrs. Donovan might have written about Herriot's treatment of the old gentleman's dog, the death of her terrier, her decision to accept Roy, and her progress in bringing Roy back to health.

3. For the local Darrowby paper, write an **editorial** on the discovery of Roy in the garden shed.

📁 **PORTFOLIO** Save your writing. You may want to use it later as a springboard to a piece for your portfolio.

Literary Concepts

Bring out that the exposition of "A Case of Cruelty" ends at the top of page 385, just before Mrs. Donovan's dog Rex is hit by a car. The rising action includes Rex's death as well as finding Roy in the shed. The climax comes on pages 389 and 390, when Herriot finally spots Mrs. Donovan and the revitalized Roy. The falling action occurs in the final scenes, in which Herriot meets Mrs. Donovan from time to time over the years and reflects on the ramifications of her saving Roy's life.

QuickWrites

1. Encourage students to use details that help readers better see the characters, setting, and events.
2. Suggest that the diary entries include specific details from the story and show Mrs. Donovan's mellowing attitude toward Mr. Herriot.
3. Remind students that editorials usually have a persuasive purpose. Ask them to suggest a remedy that would limit or eliminate cruelty to animals.

 **The Writer's Craft**

Narrative conclusions, pp. 388–389
Autobiographical Incident, pp. 26–40
Editorial, pp. 228–232

Multimodal Learning

ALTERNATIVE ACTIVITIES

1. Think about Roy's living conditions in the garden shed and in his "second life" with Mrs. Donovan. Create a two-part **drawing** that reflects both parts of Roy's life and your feelings about them.
2. On videocassette, view an episode of *All Creatures Great and Small*, the aired PBS television series based on Herriot's books. In an **oral review**, compare the episode to "A Case of Cruelty."

LITERARY LINKS

Based on this selection, what advice do you think Herriot might give Godfrey, the character in "Lalla" (page 354) who plans to become a veterinarian?

Multimodal Learning

ACROSS THE CURRICULUM

Health Tape an **interview** with a veterinarian to find out more about the treatment and mistreatment of animals in your area.

THE WRITER'S STYLE

James Herriot's writing abounds with lively, detailed descriptions of his characters and settings. Reread the description on page 386 of Herriot's first encounter with Roy in the garden shed. In your notebook, list the specific details that make this part of the story come alive for you. Compare your list with those of your classmates.

WORDS TO KNOW

On a separate sheet of paper, indicate whether the words in each numbered pair below are synonyms or antonyms.

1. beneficent / heartless
2. callousness / compassion
3. placidly / tranquilly
4. coquettishly / teasingly
5. rank / overgrown
6. indignation / pleasure
7. transcend / surpass
8. adamant / flexible
9. convalescence / recuperation
10. mystic / supernatural

JAMES HERRIOT

1916–1995

James Herriot, whose real name was James Alfred Wight, was only 13 when he read a magazine article about a veterinarian's life and decided to become a vet himself. After training in Scotland, he returned to his native England and in 1938 began working in Yorkshire. "The life of a country vet was dirty, uncomfortable, sometimes dangerous," he once told an interviewer. "It was terribly hard work and I loved it." For over 25 years he kept coming home from work and telling his wife about interesting on-the-job experiences, always promising to write a book about them. One day she finally challenged him, observing that vets of 50 do not write first books. "Well, that did it," Herriot later explained. "I stormed out and bought some paper and taught myself to type."

The result was *If Only They Could Talk*, published in England in 1970 and followed two years later by *It Shouldn't Happen to a Vet*. For his first American edition Herriot joined the two books together under the title *All Creatures Great and Small* (1972), and the new version became a bestseller. Three similar books followed.

OTHER WORKS *All Things Wise and Wonderful, The Lord God Made Them All, Every Living Thing*

Extended Reading

LASERLINKS
• SOCIAL STUDIES CONNECTION

A CASE OF CRUELTY **395**

Words to Know

1. antonyms
2. antonyms
3. synonyms
4. synonyms
5. synonyms
6. antonyms
7. synonyms
8. antonyms
9. synonyms
10. synonyms

Reteaching/Reinforcement
• *Unit Three Resource Book*, p. 18

Literary Links

Students might note that Herriot would advise Godfrey Howard to settle in rural Cornwall and to take people's love and feelings for their pets very seriously.

Across the Curriculum

Encourage students to telephone a local veterinarian for an appointment to interview him or her. Have students prepare a list of questions that they wish to ask.

You might refer students to The Writer's Craft, pp. 72–76, for information on preparing for and conducting interviews.

JAMES HERRIOT

Herriot adopted a pen name because he feared that publishing under his real name might seem an unprofessional attempt to solicit new veterinary business. Four years of hard practice at writing passed before Herriot could create narratives that satisfied both himself and his publisher.

The Writer's Style

Suggest that students categorize the details according to whether they describe the pathetic dog or the dismal shed. Details about the dog include "a welter of pressure sores which had turned gangrenous," "strips of sloughing tissue," and "the coat . . . matted and caked with dirt." Details about the shed include "a deep, smoothed out hollow in the earth floor," "filthy shreds of sacking," and "the bowl of scummy water."

Alternative Activities

1. Before they begin their two part drawings, have students read the descriptions of Roy in the shed on page 386 and Roy walking with Mrs. Donovan on page 391.
2. Suggest that students begin with a brief summary of the episode, giving the title and their general opinion of it. Then ask them to list first any similarities, then the major differences, between the two stories.

OVERVIEW
Objectives

- To understand and appreciate a short story that explores a woman's lifelong ties to a secret love
- To enrich reading by using active reading strategies
- To identify and understand the theme of a story
- To express understanding of a selection through a choice of writing forms, including an advice column, a monologue, and a character evaluation
- To extend understanding of the selection through a variety of multimodal and cross-curricular activities

Skills

LITERARY CONCEPTS
- Theme
- Narrative
- Flashback

READING SKILLS/STRATEGIES
- Understanding chronological order
- Clarifying

THE WRITER'S STYLE
- Choosing quotations

GRAMMAR
- Using progressive verb forms

SPEAKING, LISTENING, AND VIEWING
- Dramatic reading
- Group discussion

CULTURAL CONNECTION
China's Cultural Revolution What events led to Mao Zedong's Cultural Revolution of the 1960s? This film provides historical background about this disastrous "revolution" and will help students understand the characters in "Love Must Not Be Forgotten."

Side A, Frame 19309

CUSTOMIZING FOR
Students Acquiring English

- Use **ACCESS FOR STUDENTS ACQUIRING ENGLISH**.
- This selection should not be too challenging for most students. Be sensitive to the fact that some students may have parents or grandparents in arranged marriages or marriages of convenience.
- In addition to these boxes, you may also want to use the suggestions under Strategic Reading for Less-Proficient Readers.

PREVIEWING

FICTION

Love Must Not Be Forgotten
Zhang Jie (jäng' jē-ĕ') China

Activating Prior Knowledge
PERSONAL CONNECTION
Think about the married couples you know. Based on your observations, what components are necessary to a good marriage? Share your ideas in a class discussion.

Building Background
CULTURAL CONNECTION
In the 1960s and 1970s, when this selection takes place, many institutions of Chinese life, including marriage, were subjected to intense questioning. Since 1949, Mao Zedong (sometimes spelled Mao Tse-tung) and his Communist forces had been in control of China. By the mid 1960s Mao felt that new blood was needed to keep the ideals of Communism alive, so he implemented the Cultural Revolution in 1966. For the next three years, groups of young students and other radicals removed and replaced older Communist Party leaders. Many leaders were executed; others were sent to prison or to the countryside to be "re-educated" in communist thought.

Despite sweeping political changes, many Chinese customs were slow to change. For example, centuries-old traditions dictated that marriages be arranged by the couple's families when the prospective spouses were still young children. Although new laws enacted by the Communists allowed individuals to choose their own marriage partners, marrying for love was still frowned upon because communist teachings encouraged individuals to suppress personal desires for the greater social good.

Active Reading/Setting a Purpose
READING CONNECTION
Understanding Flashbacks In this selection, which opens in 1979, a young woman examines the role that love should play in her own marriage. Throughout the story her thoughts are interwoven with flashbacks to her mother's advice and diary entries from her mother's past. You may find it easier to keep track of the events in the story if you refer to the time line below as you read.

Using Your Reading Log Use your reading log to record your responses to the questions inserted throughout the selection. Also, jot down other thoughts and feelings that come to mind as you read.

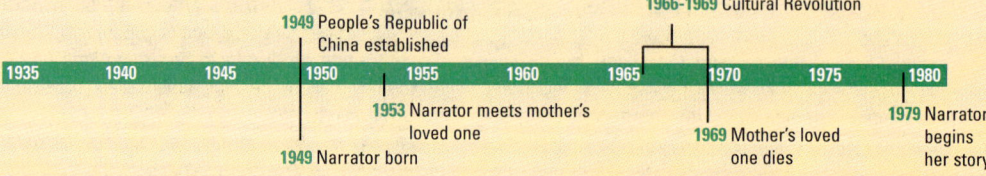

- CULTURAL CONNECTION

396 UNIT THREE PART 1: THE TIES THAT BIND

PRINT AND MEDIA RESOURCES

UNIT THREE RESOURCE BOOK
Strategic Reading: Literature, p. 21
Vocabulary SkillBuilder, p. 22

GRAMMAR MINI-LESSONS
Transparencies, pp. 29–30
Copymasters, pp. 29–30, 45–46

WRITING MINI-LESSONS
Transparencies, p. 68

ACCESS FOR STUDENTS ACQUIRING ENGLISH
Selection Summaries
Reading Support

FORMAL ASSESSMENT
Selection Test, pp. 79–80
 Test Generator

AUDIO LIBRARY
See Reference Card

LASERLINKS
Cultural Connection

INTERNET RESOURCES
McDougal Littell Literature Center at http://www.hmco.com/mcdougal/lit

Love Must Not Be Forgotten

Zhang Jie

Red Peonies (1929), Ch'i Pai-Shih. Arthur M. Sackler Museum, Harvard University.

I am thirty, the same age as our People's Republic. For a republic thirty is still young. But a girl of thirty is virtually on the shelf.

Actually, I have a bona fide[1] suitor. Have you seen the Greek sculptor Myron's *Discobolus*? Qiao Lin[2] is the image of that discus thrower. Even the padded clothes he wears in winter fail to hide his fine physique. Bronzed, with clear-cut features, a broad forehead and large eyes, his appearance alone attracts most girls to him.

But I can't make up my mind to marry him. I'm not clear what attracts me to him, or him to me.

---

1. **bona fide** (bō′nə fīd): authentic; genuine.
2. **Qiao Lin** (chou′lĭn′).

WORDS TO KNOW

ardent (är′dnt) *adj.* displaying great warmth of feeling; passionate (p. 401)

atonement (ə-tōn′mənt) *n.* the act of making up for a serious error, sin, or wrong (p. 400)

aversion (ə-vûr′zhən) *n.* a strong, definite dislike (p. 398)

censure (sĕn′shər) *v.* to criticize severely; to blame (p. 407)

coyness (coi′nĭs) *n.* the pretense of being more modest and innocent than one really is (p. 399)

heretic (hĕr′ĭ-tĭk) *n.* a person who holds controversial opinions that do not conform to the prevailing opinions of a society, religion, or group (p. 407)

naiveté' (nä′ēv-tā′) *n.* lack of sophistication; childlike innocence (p. 399)

parry (păr′ē) *v.* to turn aside or avoid (a question) with a clever reply (p. 399)

renounce (rĭ-nouns′) *v.* to give up, especially as a matter of principle (p. 402)

wistful (wĭst′fəl) *adj.* full of wishful longing; sad (p. 399)

CUSTOMIZING FOR
Gifted and Talented Students

Suggest that students note specific passages that show how living in a Communist society has shaped attitudes toward love and marriage.

Possible responses:

- Page 398—"In a society where commercial production still exists, marriage . . . is a form of barter." / Narrator thinks bad marriages occur because society is not completely communist yet, and families arrange marriages for their own benefit.

- Page 401—"Out of . . . class feeling, he had unhesitatingly married the girl." / Communist ideals led the man to marry someone he didn't love.

- Page 407—"I am a materialist, yet I wish there were a Heaven" / Communist beliefs make a lover's death very difficult to accept.

CUSTOMIZING FOR
Students Acquiring English

2 Explain to students that *playing hard to get* means "turning a suitor down repeatedly so he or she tries harder to win you."

Cultural Note

A As a Communist, the narrator looks forward to a time when society evolves beyond the buying and selling of goods and services. The Communist ideal is for people to share all that they have equally.

Critical Thinking:
SYNTHESIZING

B Ask students why they think Qiao Lin's response floods the narrator's heart with loneliness. *(Possible responses: Some students may say she realizes that he is an unsuitable mate for her. Others might suggest that living with him would be as lonely as living alone.)*

I know people are gossiping behind my back, "Who does she think she is, to be so choosy?"

To them, I'm a nobody playing hard to get. They take offense at such preposterous behavior.

Of course, I shouldn't be captious.³ In a society where commercial production still exists, marriage like most other transactions is still a form of barter.

I have known Qiao Lin for nearly two years, yet still cannot fathom whether he keeps so quiet from aversion to talking or from having nothing to say. When, by way of a small intelligence test, I demand his opinion of this or that, he says "good" or "bad" like a child in kindergarten.

Once I asked, "Qiao Lin, why do you love me?" He thought the question over seriously for what seemed an age. I could see from his normally smooth but now wrinkled forehead that the little grey cells in his handsome head were hard at work cogitating.⁴ I felt ashamed to have put him on the spot.

Finally he raised his clear childlike eyes to tell me, "Because you're good!"

Loneliness flooded my heart. "Thank you, Qiao Lin!" I couldn't help wondering, if we were to marry, whether we could discharge our duties to each other as husband and wife. Maybe, because law and morality would have bound us together. But how tragic simply to comply with law and morality! Was there no stronger bond to link us?

When such thoughts cross my mind, I have the strange sensation that instead of being a girl contemplating marriage I am an elderly social scientist.

Perhaps I worry too much. We can live like most married couples, bringing up children together, strictly true to each other according to the law. . . . Although living in the seventies of the twentieth century, people still consider marriage the way they did millennia ago, as a means of continuing the race, a form of barter or a business transaction in which love and marriage can be separated. As this is the common practice, why shouldn't we follow suit?

But I still can't make up my mind. As a child, I remember, I often cried all night for no rhyme or reason, unable to sleep and disturbing the whole household. My old nurse, a shrewd though uneducated woman, said an ill wind had blown through my ear. I think this judgment showed prescience,⁵ because I still have that old weakness. I upset myself over things which really present no problem, upsetting other people at the same time. One's nature is hard to change.

I think of my mother too. If she were alive, what would she say about my attitude to Qiao Lin and my uncertainty about marrying him?

My thoughts constantly turn to her, not because she was such a strict mother that her ghost is still watching over me since her death. No, she was not just my mother but my closest

> *How tragic simply to comply with law and morality! Was there no stronger bond to link us?*

---

3. **captious** (kăp′shəs): quick to find fault; quibbling.
4. **cogitating** (kŏj′ĭ-tā′tĭng): thinking carefully; pondering.
5. **prescience** (prē′shē-əns): knowledge of things before they happen; foresight.

WORDS TO KNOW
aversion (ə-vûr′zhən) *n.* a strong, definite dislike

398

Mini-Lesson Grammar

USING PROGRESSIVE VERB FORMS
Remind students that progressive forms of verbs show ongoing action. A progressive is made by combining the present participle of the verb with a form of the verb *be*. Point out the progressive form *are gossiping*  on this page. Explain that this progressive is in the present tense. Progressives can also show ongoing action in the past (people *were gossiping*), past perfect (people *had been gossiping*), and future (people *will be gossiping*).

Application Have students change the verb in each sentence to its progressive form.

1. My thoughts constantly turn to her. *(are turning)*
2. Perhaps I worry to much. *(am worrying)*
3. They stood face to face. *(were standing)*
4. Haven't you managed fine without a husband? *(been managing)*

Reteaching/Reinforcement
- *Grammar Mini-Lessons* copymasters, pp. 29–30

The Writer's Craft
Progressive verb forms, pp. 665–666

friend. I loved her so much that the thought of her leaving me makes my heart ache.

She never lectured me, just told me quietly in her deep, unwomanly voice about her successes and failures, so that I could learn from her experience. She had evidently not had many successes—her life was full of failures.

During her last days she followed me with her fine, expressive eyes, as if wondering how I would manage on my own and as if she had some important advice for me but hesitated to give it. She must have been worried by my naiveté and sloppy ways. She suddenly blurted out, "Shanshan,[6] if you aren't sure what you want, don't rush into marriage—better live on your own!"

Other people might think this strange advice from a mother to her daughter, but to me it embodied her bitter experience. I don't think she underestimated me or my knowledge of life. She loved me and didn't want me to be unhappy.

"I don't want to marry, mum!" I said, not out of bashfulness or a show of coyness. I can't think why a girl should pretend to be coy. She had long since taught me about things not generally mentioned to girls.

"If you meet the right man, then marry him. Only if he's right for you!"

"I'm afraid no such man exists!"

"That's not true. But it's hard. The world is so vast, I'm afraid you may never meet him." Whether I married or not was not what concerned her, but the quality of the marriage.

"Haven't you managed fine without a husband?"

"Who says so?"

"I think you've done fine."

"I had no choice. . . ." She broke off, lost in thought, her face wistful. Her wistful lined face reminded me of a withered flower I had pressed in a book.

"Why did you have no choice?"

"You ask too many questions," she parried, not ashamed to confide in me but afraid that I might reach the wrong conclusion. Besides, everyone treasures a secret to carry to the grave. Feeling a bit put out, I demanded bluntly, "Didn't you love my dad?"

"No, I never loved him."

"Did he love you?"

"No, he didn't."

"Then why get married?"

She paused, searching for the right words to explain this mystery, then answered bitterly, "When you're young, you don't always know what you're looking for, what you need, and people may talk you into getting married. As you grow older and more experienced, you find out your true needs. By then, though, you've done many foolish things for which you could kick yourself. You'd give anything to be able to make a fresh start and live more wisely. Those content with their lot will always be happy, they say, but I shall never enjoy that happiness." She added, self-mockingly, "A wretched idealist, that's all I am."

Did I take after her? Did we both have genes which attracted ill winds?

"Why don't you marry again?"

"I'm afraid I'm still not sure what I really want." She was obviously unwilling to tell me the truth.

I cannot remember my father. He and Mother split up when I was very small. I just recall her telling me sheepishly that he was a fine handsome fellow. I could see she was ashamed of having judged by appearances and made a futile choice. She told me, "When I can't sleep at night, I force myself to sober up by recalling all those

---

6. **Shanshan** (shän'shän').

WORDS TO KNOW	**naiveté** (nä'ēv-tā') *n.* lack of sophistication; childlike innocence
	coyness (coi'nĭs) *n.* the pretense of being more modest and innocent than one really is
	wistful (wĭst'fəl) *adj.* full of wishful longing; sad
	parry (păr'ē) *v.* to turn aside or avoid (a question) with a clever reply

399

STRATEGIC READING FOR
Less-Proficient Readers

H Ask students how the narrator's mother feels about marriage. *(It is not something to be rushed into; you must find the absolutely right person to marry.)*
Making Inferences

- What experience had the mother had with marriage? *(She had married a handsome man whom she did not really love; the marriage did not last.)*
Summarizing

Set a Purpose Ask students to read on to find out more about why the mother didn't remarry.

Active Reading: CLARIFY

I Students should see that the narrator thinks they would have been happier had her mother remarried; she also thinks that her mother would have made a fine wife.

Critical Thinking: INFERRING

J Invite students to suggest why the mother might feel so strongly about her volumes of Chekhov. *(Possible responses: They may be stories that have a special meaning to her; they may have sentimental value; perhaps she admires Chekhov's writing.)*

Literary Concept: THEME

K Point out that the title of the story reflects the title of the mother's diary. Ask students whether they agree that love must not be forgotten. *(Accept all reasonable responses.)*

---

stupid blunders I made. Of course it's so distasteful that I often hide my face in the sheet for shame, as if there were eyes watching me in the dark. But distasteful as it is, I take some pleasure in this form of **atonement**."

H I was really sorry that she hadn't remarried. She was such a fascinating character, if she'd married a man she loved, what a happy household ours would surely have been. Though not beautiful, she had the simple charm of an ink landscape. She was a fine writer too. Another author who knew her well used to say teasingly, "Just reading your works is enough to make anyone love you!"

CLARIFY

I Why does the narrator think that her mother should have remarried?
Using a Reading Log

She would retort, "If he knew that the object of his affection was a white-haired old crone, that would frighten him away."

At her age, she must have known what she really wanted, so this was obviously an evasion. I say this because she had quirks which puzzled me.

For instance, whenever she left Beijing on a trip, she always took with her one of the twenty-seven volumes of Chekhov's[7] stories published between 1950 and 1955. She also warned me, "Don't touch these books. If you want to read Chekhov, read that set I bought you." There was no need to caution me. Having a set of my own why should I touch hers? Besides, she'd told me this over and over again. Still she was on her guard. She seemed bewitched by those books.

So we had two sets of Chekhov's stories at home. Not just because we loved Chekhov, but to parry other people like me who loved Chekhov. Whenever anyone asked to borrow a volume, she would lend one of mine. Once, in her absence, a close friend took a volume from her set. When she found out, she was frantic and at once took a volume of mine to exchange for it.

Ever since I can remember, those books were on her bookcase. Although I admire Chekhov as a great writer, I was puzzled by the way she never tired of reading him. Why, for over twenty years, had she had to read him every single day? **J**

Sometimes, when tired of writing, she poured herself a cup of strong tea and sat down in front of the bookcase, staring raptly at that set of books. If I went into her room then, it flustered her, and she either spilt her tea or blushed like a girl discovered with her lover.

I wondered: Has she fallen in love with Chekhov? She might have if he'd still been alive.

When her mind was wandering just before her death, her last words to me were: "That set. . . ." She hadn't the strength to give it its complete title. But I knew what she meant. "And my diary . . . 'Love Must Not Be Forgotten'. . . . Cremate them with me." **K**

I carried out her last instruction regarding the works of Chekhov, but couldn't bring myself to destroy her diary. I thought, if it could be published, it would surely prove the most moving thing she had written. But naturally publication was out of the question.

At first I imagined the entries were raw material she had jotted down. They read neither like stories, essays, a diary or letters. But after reading the whole I formed a hazy impression, helped out by my imperfect memory. Thinking it over, I finally realized that this was no lifeless manuscript I was holding, but an anguished, loving heart. For over twenty years one man had occupied her heart, but he was not for her. She used these diaries as a substitute for him, a means of pouring out her feelings to him, day after day, year after year.

---

7. **Chekhov's** (chĕk´ôfs): Anton Chekhov (1860–1904; also spelled Chekov), a Russian author, whose short stories were first published in Chinese in the 1950s.

WORDS TO KNOW
atonement (ə-tōn´mənt) *n.* the act of making up for a serious error, sin, or wrong

400

No wonder she had never considered any eligible proposals, had turned a deaf ear to idle talk whether well-meant or malicious. Her heart was already full, to the exclusion of anybody else. "No lake can compare with the ocean, no cloud with those on Mount Wu."[8] Remembering those lines I often reflected sadly that few people in real life could love like this. No one would love me like this.

I learned that towards the end of the thirties, when this man was doing underground work for the Party[9] in Shanghai, an old worker had given his life to cover him, leaving behind a helpless wife and daughter. Out of a sense of duty, of gratitude to the dead and deep class feeling, he had unhesitatingly married the girl. When he saw the endless troubles caused by "love" of couples who had married for "love," he may have thought, "Thank Heaven, though I didn't marry for love, we get on well, able to help each other." For years, as man and wife they lived through hard times.

He must have been my mother's colleague. Had I ever met him? He couldn't have visited our home. Who was he?

In the spring of 1962, Mother took me to a concert. We went on foot, the theatre being quite near.

A black limousine pulled up silently by the pavement. Out stepped an elderly man with white hair in a black serge tunicsuit. What a striking shock of white hair! Strict, scrupulous, distinguished, transparently honest—that was my impression of him. The cold glint of his flashing eyes reminded me of lightning or swordplay. Only <u>ardent</u> love for a woman really deserving his love could fill cold eyes like those with tenderness.

He walked up to Mother and said, "How are you, Comrade Zhong Yu?[10] It's been a long time."

"How are you!" Mother's hand holding mine suddenly turned icy cold and trembled a little.

They stood face to face without looking at

Forbidden Fruit, Simon Ng. Reprinted with the permission of Simon & Schuster Books for Young Readers, an imprint of Simon & Schuster Children's Publishing Division. From *Tales from Gold Mountain: Stories of the Chinese in the New World*, a Groundwood Book/Douglas & McIntyre. Text Copyright © 1989 by Paul Yee, illustrations Copyright © 1989 by Simon Ng.

each other, each appearing upset, even stern. Mother fixed her eyes on the trees by the roadside, not yet in leaf. He looked at me. "Such a big girl already. Good, fine—you take after your mother."

Instead of shaking hands with Mother he shook hands with me. His hand was as icy as

---

8. **Mount Wu:** a high mountain in southern China.
9. **the Party:** the Communist Party.
10. **Zhong Yu** (jŏng′yōō′).

WORDS TO KNOW
ardent (är′dnt) *adj.* displaying great warmth of feeling; passionate

---

Multicultural Perspectives

DUTY AND OBLIGATION Ancient traditions remain at the heart of modern Chinese life. These traditions are based on the Buddhist virtues of austerity and enlightenment and the Confucian ideals of unselfishness, courage, and honor. Confucianism has rigid rules about behavior toward the living and toward one's departed ancestors. According to one tradition, it is a man's duty to marry the widow or the daughter of a man who has saved his life, and this duty must come before everything else. To Confucius, a person's inner virtues can only be fully realized through such "ritual propriety." These demands compel the story's lovers to deny themselves a life together.

Literary Concept:
CHARACTERIZATION

P Ask students what the narrator's rather rude behavior here reveals about her. *(Possible responses: She is frank and feisty; she isn't always willing to show devotion to her mother.)*

Critical Thinking: INFERRING

Q Ask students to try to find another meaning behind the man's criticism of the mother's story. *(Possible responses: He was stating the situation of their love disguised in his reaction to the story; he may have been trying to tell the mother he loved her.)*

Literary Concept: SYMBOL

R Ask students what the puff of smoke, and the narrator's lasting memory of it, might symbolize. *(Possible response: It might symbolize the brief and insubstantial physical contact between the lovers, in contrast with their intense and enduring emotional connection.)*

Literary Concept: FLASHBACK

S Point out that the diary entry, in the form of a conversation, is a sort of flashback. Have students tell what this dialogue reveals about the man. *(Possible response: He was a considerate, sensitive man; he was in love with the mother.)*

---

hers and trembling a little. As if transmitting an electric current, I felt a sudden shock. Snatching my hand away I cried, "There's nothing good about that!"

"Why not?" he asked with the surprised expression grown-ups always have when children speak out frankly.

I glanced at Mother's face. I did take after her, to my disappointment. "Because she's not beautiful!"

He laughed, then said teasingly, "Too bad that there should be a child who doesn't find her own mother beautiful. Do you remember in '53, when your mum was transferred to Beijing, she came to our ministry to report for duty? She left you outside on the verandah,[11] but like a monkey you climbed all the stairs, peeped through the cracks in doors, and caught your finger in the door of my office. You sobbed so bitterly that I carried you off to find her."

"I don't remember that." I was annoyed at his harking back to a time when I was still in open-seat pants.[12]

"Ah, we old people have better memories." He turned abruptly and remarked to Mother, "I've read that last story of yours. Frankly speaking, there's something not quite right about it. You shouldn't have condemned the heroine. . . . There's nothing wrong with falling in love, as long as you don't spoil someone else's life. . . . In fact, the hero might have loved her too. Only for the sake of a third person's happiness, they had to <u>renounce</u> their love. . . ."

A policeman came over to where the car was parked and ordered the driver to move on. When the driver made some excuse, the old man looked around. After a hasty "Goodbye" he strode to the car and told the policeman, "Sorry. It's not his fault, it's mine. . . ."

I found it amusing watching this old cadre[13] listening respectfully to the policeman's strictures.[14] When I turned to Mother with a mischievous smile, she looked as upset as a first-form[15] primary schoolchild standing forlornly in front of the stern headmistress. Anyone would have thought she was the one being lectured by the policeman.

The car drove off, leaving a puff of smoke. Very soon even this smoke vanished with the wind, as if nothing at all had happened. But the incident stuck in my mind.

Analyzing it now, he must have been the man whose strength of character won Mother's heart. That strength came from his firm political convictions, his narrow escapes from death in the revolution, his active brain, his drive at work, his well-cultivated mind. Besides, strange to say, he and Mother both liked the oboe. Yes, she must have worshipped him. She once told me that unless she worshipped a man, she couldn't love him even for one day.

But I could not tell whether he loved her or not. If not, why was there this entry in her diary?

> "This is far too fine a present. But how did you know that Chekhov's my favorite writer?"
> "You said so."
> "I don't remember that."

---

11. **verandah** (və-răn'də): a partly enclosed porch.
12. **open-seat pants:** pants with a slit down the back, worn by young children.
13. **cadre** (kăd'rē): a member of a tightly knit revolutionary party or military group.
14. **strictures** (strĭk'chərz): rules or remarks setting limits or making restrictions.
15. **first-form:** first-grade.

WORDS TO KNOW
renounce (rĭ-nouns') *v.* to give up, especially as a matter of principle

"I remember. I heard you mention it when you were chatting with someone."

So he was the one who had given her the *Selected Stories of Chekhov*. For her that was tantamount[16] to a love letter.

Maybe this man, who didn't believe in love, realized by the time his hair was white that in his heart was something which could be called love. By the time he no longer had the right to love, he made the tragic discovery of this love for which he would have given his life. Or did it go deeper than that?

This is all I remember about him.

How wretched Mother must have been, deprived of the man to whom she was devoted! To catch a glimpse of his car or the back of his head through its rear window, she carefully figured out which roads he would take to work and back. Whenever he made a speech, she sat at the back of the hall watching his face rendered hazy by cigarette smoke and poor lighting. Her eyes would brim with tears, but she swallowed them back. If a fit of coughing made him break off, she wondered anxiously why no one persuaded him to give up smoking. She was afraid he would get bronchitis again. Why was he so near yet so far?

He, to catch a glimpse of her, looked out of the car window every day, straining his eyes to watch the streams of cyclists, afraid that she might have an accident. On the rare evenings on which he had no meetings, he would walk by a roundabout way to our neighborhood, to pass our compound gate. However busy, he would always make time to look in papers and journals for her work.

His duty had always been clear to him, even

> *We agreed to forget each other. But I deceived you, I have never forgotten.*

in the most difficult times. But now confronted by this love he became a weakling, quite helpless. At his age it was laughable. Why should life play this trick on him? Yet when they happened to meet at work, each tried to avoid the other, hurrying off with a nod. Even so, this would make Mother blind and deaf to everything around her. If she met a colleague named Wang, she would call him Guo[17] and mutter something unintelligible.

It was a cruel ordeal for her. She wrote:

> *We agreed to forget each other. But I deceived you, I have never forgotten. I don't think you've forgotten either. We're just deceiving each other, hiding our misery. I haven't deceived you deliberately, though; I did my best to carry out our agreement. I often stay far away from Beijing, hoping time and distance will help me to forget you. But on my return, as the train pulls into the station, my head reels. I stand on the platform looking around intently, as if someone were waiting for me. Of course there is no one. I realize then that I have forgotten nothing. Everything is unchanged. My love is like a tree the roots of which strike deeper year after year—I have no way to uproot it.*
>
> *At the end of every day, I feel as if I've forgotten something important. I may wake with a start from my dreams wonder-*

---

16. **tantamount** (tăn′tə-mount′): equal in effect or value.
17. **Guo** (gwō): The Chinese characters for this family name are similar to those for the name *Wang*.

Active Reading: CLARIFY

Y Invite students to identify the narrator's mother's dream. *(She wanted to be married to the man she loved.)* Then have them describe the obstacles that stood in her way. *(Possible responses: The man is married to someone else; the man and the mother subscribe to ideals that place duty and honor ahead of individual emotional needs.)*

Literary Concept: ALLUSION

Z Remind students that an allusion can be a reference to a well-known work of literature. Invite volunteers to suggest how this story's lovers are like the two lovers in Shakespeare's *Romeo and Juliet*. *(Possible responses: Both sets of lovers are prisoners of circumstance; both spend little time together.)*

Literary Concept: CHARACTERIZATION

AA Have students note what this scene reveals about the old man. *(Possible response: He was brave; he'd rather die than turn his back on his ideals.)*

Literary Concept: IRONY

BB Ask students what might be considered ironic about the mother's wearing the black armband. *(Possible response: Only after her beloved is dead does the mother openly display her love.)*

Linking to History

CC During the Cultural Revolution writers like the narrator's mother were often persecuted for being "too personal." Tell students that Zhang Jie herself left China in 1989 after the Communists cracked down on "Western thinking" among students and intellectuals.

---

ing what has happened. But nothing has happened. Nothing. Then it comes home to me that you are missing! So everything seems lacking, incomplete, and there is nothing to fill up the blank. We are nearing the ends of our lives, why should we be carried away by emotion like children? Why should life submit people to such ordeals, then unfold before you your lifelong dream? Because I started off blindly, I took the wrong turning, and now there are insuperable[18] obstacles between me and my dream.

Yes, Mother never let me go to the station to meet her when she came back from a trip, preferring to stand alone on the platform and imagine that he had met her. Poor mother with her greying hair was as infatuated as a girl.

CLARIFY
Why was the mother unable to fulfill her dream?
Using a Reading Log

Not much space in the diary was devoted to their romance. Most entries dealt with trivia: Why one of her articles had not come off; her fear that she had no real talent; the excellent play she missed by mistaking the time on the ticket; the drenching she got by going out for a stroll without her umbrella. In spirit they were together day and night, like a devoted married couple. In fact, they spent no more than twenty-four hours together in all. Yet in that time they experienced deeper happiness than some people in a whole lifetime. Shakespeare makes Juliet say, "I cannot sum up half my sum of wealth." And probably that is how Mother felt.

He must have been killed in the "cultural revolution." Perhaps because of the conditions then, that section of the diary is ambiguous and obscure. Mother had been so fiercely attacked for her writing, it amazed me that she went on keeping a diary. From some veiled allusions I gathered that she had queried the theories advanced by that "theoretician" then at the height of favor, and had told someone, "This is sheer Rightist[19] talk." It was clear from the tear-stained pages of Mother's diary that he had been harshly denounced; but the steadfast old man never knuckled under to the authorities. His last words were, "When I go to meet Marx,[20] I shall go on fighting my case!"

That must have been in the winter of 1969, because that was when Mother's hair turned white overnight, though she was not yet fifty. And she put on a black arm band. Her position then was extremely difficult. She was criticized for wearing this old-style mourning, and ordered to say for whom she was in mourning.

"For whom are you wearing that, mum?" I asked anxiously.

"For my lover." Not to frighten me she explained, "Someone you never knew."

"Shall I put one on too?" She patted my cheeks, as she had when I was a child. It was years since she had shown me such affection. I often felt that as she aged, especially during these last years of persecution, all tenderness had left her, or was concealed in her heart, so that she seemed like a man.

She smiled sadly and said, "No, you needn't wear one."

Her eyes were as dry as if she had no more tears to shed. I longed to comfort her or do something to please her. But she said, "Off you go."

I felt an inexplicable dread, as if dear Mother had already half left me. I blurted out, "Mum!"

Quick to sense my desolation, she said gently, "Don't be afraid. Off you go. Leave me alone for a little."

I was right. She wrote:

---

18. **insuperable** (ĭn-sōō′pər-ə-bəl): impossible to overcome; insurmountable.
19. **Rightist:** belonging to a conservative or reactionary politics.
20. **Marx:** Karl Marx (1818–1883) a German economic philosopher revered by communists.

404 UNIT THREE PART 1: THE TIES THAT BIND

Mini-Lesson — Study Skills

READING A TIME LINE Point out that much of the narrative on this page refers to the year 1969. Then ask students to turn back to the time line on page 396. To read the time line, students should begin at the left, with the earliest event, and then read on to the right. Point out that this time line also distinguishes between types of events by showing them above or below the line.

Application Ask students the following questions to make sure they understand the time line.
1. What type of events are shown above the line? *(events in Chinese history)* Below the line? *(family events)*
2. How old was the narrator when she first met the man her mother loved? *(four)*
3. What events coincide in time? *(the beginning of the Republic of China and the birth of the narrator; the last part of the Cultural Revolution and the old man's death)*

404 THE LANGUAGE OF LITERATURE TEACHER'S EDITION

A painting in the class-education exhibition, Niutung People's Commune No. 4 (about 1970), Niutung People's Commune Spare-Time Art Group.

Art Note

A Painting in the Class-Education Exhibition by Niutung People's Commune Spare-Time Art Group
Painted by peasants during the Great Proletarian Cultural Revolution, this revolutionary art was meant "for uniting and educating the people and for attacking and destroying the enemy." These lines accompany the painting:

Dancing are the Chinling Mountains
Laughing are the Weishui River.
The revolutionary committee's been set up,
Revisionism's on the run; our
Rivers and mountains will be red forever.

Reading the Art This painting was done by a commune, or group of people, not a single artist. Can you point out details of the work that seem to have been done by different artists, or does this appear to be the work of one artist? What does your response tell you about the people who created the painting?

Literary Concept: TONE

DD Have the students discuss the tone of the mother's diary entry. What attitudes does she express toward the events she writes about? *(Possible responses: Students may say her tone is bitter, angry, or defiant when describing the Cultural Revolution. Some students may point out that the account of the couple's meeting is bittersweet.)*

Literary Concept: FIGURATIVE LANGUAGE

EE Ask students what the narrator means when she says her mother has a "locked heart." *(Possible responses: Although her heart was full of love for the man, this love was secret and carefully protected.)*

Literary Concept: NARRATIVE

FF The narrator gives her impressions here of events already described by her mother in the preceding diary entry. Ask students to describe how this retelling from separate viewpoints affects the story, and what effects the exclusion of one version or the other would have. *(Possible response: Because the mother tells the reader how sorrowful the road makes her feel—and the daughter implies that her sorrow never showed—the reader gains an additional image of, and appreciation for, the mother's stoicism.)*

DD You have gone. Half my soul seems to have taken flight with you.

I had no means of knowing what had become of you, much less of seeing you for the last time. I had no right to ask either, not being your wife or friend. . . . So we are torn apart. If only I could have borne that inhuman treatment for you, so that you could have lived on! You should have lived to see your name cleared and take up your work again, for the sake of those who loved you. I knew you could not be a counter-revolutionary. You were one of the finest men killed. That's why I love you— I am not afraid now to avow it.

Snow is whirling down. Heavens, even God is such a hypocrite, he is using this whiteness to cover up your blood and the scandal of your murder.

I have never set store by my life. But now I keep wondering whether anything I say or do would make you contract your shaggy eyebrows in a frown. I must live a worthwhile life like you and do some honest work for our country. Things can't go on like this—those criminals will get what's coming to them.

I used to walk alone along that small asphalt road, the only place where we once walked together, hearing my footsteps in the silent night. . . . I always paced to and fro and lingered there, but never as wretchedly as now. Then, though you were not beside me, I knew you were still in this world and felt that you were keeping me company. Now I can hardly believe that you have gone.

> *I must live a worthwhile life like you and do some honest work for our country.*

At the end of the road I would retrace my steps, then walk along it again. Rounding the fence I always looked back, as if you were still standing there waving goodbye. We smiled faintly, like casual acquaintances, to conceal our undying love. That ordinary evening in early spring, a chilly wind was blowing as we walked silently away from each other. You were wheezing a little because of your chronic bronchitis. That upset me. I wanted to beg you to slow down, but somehow I couldn't. We both walked very fast, as if some important business were waiting for us. How we prized that single stroll we had together, but we were afraid we might lose control of ourselves and burst out with "I love you"—those three words which had tormented us for years. Probably no one else could believe that we never once even clasped hands!

No, Mother, I believe it. I am the only one able to see into your locked heart. **EE**

Ah, that little asphalt road, so haunted by bitter memories. We shouldn't overlook the most insignificant spots on earth. For who knows how much secret grief and joy they may hide. **FF**

No wonder that when tired of writing, she would pace slowly along that little road behind our window. Sometimes at dawn after a sleepless night, sometimes on a moonless, windy evening. Even in winter during howling gales which hurled sand and pebbles against the windowpane. . . . I thought this was one of her

406 UNIT THREE PART 1: THE TIES THAT BIND

Mini-Lesson: Speaking, Listening, and Viewing

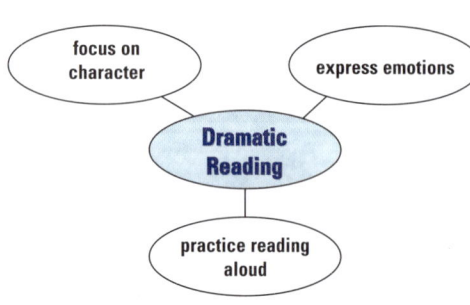

DRAMATIC READING Point out that a dramatic reading of a passage can give the readers and the listeners a deeper understanding and appreciation of a work. Use the word web shown to help you discuss some tips for giving an effective dramatic reading.
- Focus on the character whose words you are reading and try to speak as he or she would speak.
- Think about the emotions the character is experiencing and try to express them.
- Become thoroughly familiar with the passage by practicing reading it aloud.

Application Ask a group of students to reread the long excerpt from the mother's diary on this page and discuss the best ways to express the mother's emotions through a dramatic reading. Then have them coordinate a reading, each student reading one paragraph aloud. Suggest that they perform their reading for the entire class.

406 THE LANGUAGE OF LITERATURE TEACHER'S EDITION

eccentricities, not knowing that she had gone to meet him in spirit.

She liked to stand by the window too, staring at the small asphalt road. Once I thought from her expression that one of our closest friends must be coming to call. I hurried to the window. It was a late autumn evening. The cold wind was stripping dead leaves from the trees and blowing them down the small empty road.

She went on pouring out her heart to him in her diary as she had when he was alive. Right up to the day when the pen slipped from her fingers. Her last message was:

> I am a materialist,[21] yet I wish there were a Heaven. For then, I know, I would find you there waiting for me. I am going there to join you, to be together for eternity. We need never be parted again or keep at a distance for fear of spoiling someone else's life. Wait for me, dearest, I am coming—

I do not know how Mother, on her death bed, could still love so ardently with all her heart. To me it seemed not love but a form of madness, a passion stronger than death. If undying love really exists, she reached its extreme. She obviously died happy, because she had known true love. She had no regrets.

Now these old people's ashes have mingled with the elements. But I know that, no matter what form they may take, they still love each other. Though not bound together by earthly laws or morality, though they never once clasped hands, each possessed the other completely. Nothing could part them. Centuries to come, if one white cloud trails another, two grasses grow side by side, one wave splashes another, a breeze follows another . . . believe me, that will be them.

Each time I read that diary "Love Must Not Be Forgotten" I cannot hold back my tears. I often weep bitterly, as if I myself experienced their ill-fated love. If not a tragedy it was too laughable. No matter how beautiful or moving I find it, I have no wish to follow suit!

Thomas Hardy[22] wrote that "the call seldom produces the comer, the man to love rarely coincides with the hour for loving." I cannot censure them from conventional moral standards. What I deplore is that they did not wait for a "missing counterpart" to call them.

If everyone could wait, instead of rushing into marriage, how many tragedies could be averted!

When we reach communism,[23] will there still be cases of marriage without love? Maybe, because since the world is so vast, two kindred spirits may be unable to answer each other's call. But how tragic! However, by that time, there may be ways to escape such tragedies.

Why should I split hairs?

Perhaps after all we are responsible for these tragedies. Who knows? Maybe we should take the responsibility for the old ideas handed down from the past. Because if someone never marries, that is a challenge to these ideas. You will be called neurotic, accused of having guilty secrets or having made political mistakes. You may be regarded as an eccentric who looks down on ordinary people, not respecting age-old customs—a heretic. In short they will trump up endless vulgar and futile charges to ruin your

---

21. **materialist** (mə-tîr'ē-ə-lĭst): here, a person who believes that the physical world is the only reality.
22. **Thomas Hardy** (1840–1928): a British author.
23. **When we reach communism:** When we reach the ideal state by following communist principles.

WORDS TO KNOW
censure (sĕn'shər) *v.* to criticize severely; to blame
heretic (hĕr'ĭ-tĭk) *n.* a person who holds controversial opinions that do not conform to the prevailing opinions of a society, religion, or group

---

Cultural Note

GG The word *materialist* here reflects the Communist belief that everything can be explained through science, not through spiritual or supernatural beliefs. This view of the world is encouraged in Communist countries, and religion is discouraged.

Active Reading: EVALUATE

HH Some students might find the mother's devotion to her beloved emotionally moving and profound; others might consider such devotion tragically misplaced.

Cultural Note

II This vision of life after death reflects the Buddhist belief that a person's station in life is determined by behavior in past lives. The lovers are together as a reward.

Literary Note

JJ In Thomas Hardy's novels, the characters usually fight a losing battle against an impersonal fate. In *Jude the Obscure*, Hardy describes a character waiting for her soulmate this way: "But nobody did come because nobody does." In that novel, Hardy describes another couple's marriage this way: "The fundamental error of their matrimonial union; that of having based a permanent contract on a temporary feeling."

Literary Concept: THEME

KK Have students compare this statement of the theme with that on page 399: "If you meet the right man, then marry him. Only if he's right for you." Have students discuss how the statements are similar. (*Possible response: Both stress the seriousness of marriage and the importance of being certain that a mate is right for you.*)

CUSTOMIZING FOR Students Acquiring English

4 Tell students that the phrase *split hairs* means "to make trivial distinctions."

Mini-Lesson   The Writer's Style

CHOOSING QUOTATIONS Tell students that quoting someone else's words is an effective way to incorporate that person's ideas in their own writing. Caution students to choose quotations carefully, however; quoted material should be to the point and preferably from recognized authorities. Remind students to cite quotations exactly and to attribute the quotation to the person who said it.

Application Point out the highlighted quotations from Shakespeare and Thomas Hardy on pages 404 and 407. Ask students what these quotations add to the story. Then ask students to think of a well-known line from a popular song or poem that could also be used in this story.

Reteaching/Reinforcement
- *Writer's Handbook*, anthology p. 1030
- *Writing Mini-Lessons* transparencies, p. 68
- *Grammar Mini-Lessons* copymasters, pp. 45–46

Quotations, p. 367

Art Note

New Look of a Village by Niutung People's Commune Spare-Time Art Group

Reading the Art *What does this painting suggest to you about the ideal village under a Communist government?*

Critical Thinking:
MAKING INFERENCES

LL To whom does the narrator long to shout, "Mind your own business!" *(to anyone who would pressure her into marriage or criticize or disdain her for not being married)*

Literary Concept: THEME

MM Ask students how this final sentence takes the story theme a step further than simply warning against hasty marriages. *(Living singly, the author suggests, may improve a person's quality of life.)*

STRATEGIC READING FOR
Less-Proficient Readers

NN Have students explain what happened to the two lovers. *(The old man was killed by radicals during the Cultural Revolution; the mother aged and died some time later.)* Summarizing

- Ask students how the narrator learned the details of her mother's unusual love affair. *(by reading the mother's diary)* Summarizing

---

CUSTOMIZING FOR
Gifted and Talented Students

Have students discuss why the mother wanted her diary cremated with her. Ask students if they think the daughter did the right thing in not following this request. *(Accept all reasonable responses.)*

COMPREHENSION CHECK
1. What decision does the narrator face? *(whether or not to marry)*
2. What does her mother advise her to do? *(marry only the right man)*
3. How does the narrator learn about her mother's love? *(from a diary)*
4. What prevented the mother and her lover from marrying? *(a sense of duty)*

New Look of a Village (about 1970), Niutung People's Commune Spare-Time Art Group.

reputation. Then you have to knuckle under to those ideas and marry willy-nilly. But once you put the chains of a loveless marriage around your neck, you will suffer for it for the rest of your life.

I long to shout: "Mind your own business! Let us wait patiently for our counterparts. Even waiting in vain is better than willy-nilly marriage. To live single is not such a fearful disaster. I believe it may be a sign of a step forward in culture, education and the quality of life." ❖

Translated by Gladys Yang

408 UNIT THREE PART 1: THE TIES THAT BIND

Critic's Corner

"I found the fact that the narrator's mother could love so deeply and keep it a secret her entire life astonishing."

Amy Dobelstein
Student Advisory Board

Ask students if they agree or disagree with Amy's statement. Why is it usually difficult to keep love a secret?

RESPONDING OPTIONS

FROM PERSONAL RESPONSE TO CRITICAL ANALYSIS

REFLECT
1. Write down your impressions of the narrator and her mother in your notebook. Share your thoughts with your classmates.

RETHINK
2. How do you think the narrator is affected by her mother's advice and experiences?
   Consider
   Close Textual Reading
   - the narrator's feelings about her relationship with Qiao Lin
   - the narrator's views on love and marriage
   - how the narrator says she is viewed by society

3. Do you think that the mother and the man she loved made the right choices about their relationship? Explain your opinion.

Thematic Link
4. Do you agree or disagree with the mother that it is better to live on one's own than to rush into marriage? Use examples from the story to support your opinion.

5. Predict the narrator's future. Will she marry, and if so, will she be happy?

RELATE
6. Do you think our society puts pressure on people to get married? Discuss your views with your classmates.

Multimodal Learning
ANOTHER PATHWAY
Cooperative Learning

In a small group, prepare a eulogy that the narrator might have spoken at her mother's funeral. Be sure to include details from the story about the mother's life, comments from her friends, and the narrator's personal thoughts about her mother. Read your eulogy aloud to classmates.

QUICKWRITES

1. Recall the ideas on marriage that you discussed for the Personal Connection on page 396 and the advice that the mother gives her daughter in the story. Then write a newspaper **advice column** in which you give the best advice you can on the subject of marriage. State your opinions and support them with strong reasons.

2. Write a **monologue** in which the mother describes her feelings about and concerns for her daughter.

3. Write a **character evaluation** of any prominent figure in the selection. First provide an objective description of the character and then state your opinion of that character. Be sure to base your statements on details in the selection.

 PORTFOLIO Save your writing. You may want to use it later as a springboard to a piece for your portfolio.

LOVE MUST NOT BE FORGOTTEN **409**

LITERARY CONCEPTS

The **theme** of a work of literature is the central idea or message of the work. Theme should not be confused with subject, or what the work is about. Rather, theme is a perception about life or human nature that the writer shares with the reader. In most fiction, the reader uses details from the story to figure out a theme. In this story, however, the writer states the theme directly. Find quotations from the selection that could serve as the theme. Then, in a class discussion, decide which quotations best communicate the theme of the story.

From Personal Response to Critical Analysis

1. Accept all reasonable responses.
2. Possible responses: Some students might say the narrator is uncertain about her mother's advice at first. Others may suggest that she is willing to take her mother's advice and wait.
3. Accept all reasonable responses. Possible responses: The couple should have risked society's censure in order to be together; the couple dutifully did the right thing.
4. Accept all reasonable, well-supported responses. Possible response: It is better to live on your own than to rush into marriage. The narrator seems better off single than marrying Qiao Lin, whom she does not respect; the narrator's mother regretted her marriage.
5. Accept all reasonable, well-supported responses. Possible responses: Some students will predict that the narrator will take her mother's advice and wait until she finds the right man, or she will remain single. Others might predict that she will have to settle for someone less than ideal if she does get married.
6. Accept all reasonable, well-supported responses.

Another Pathway

Cooperative Learning Have students prepare an outline, listing the aspects about the mother they wish to eulogize. Suggest that one or two students find illustrative details in the story, and another student record the outline and references. The group can then write the text of the eulogy from the outline. Groups may wish to designate one member to read the eulogy aloud.

Rubric

3 Full Accomplishment Students develop an insightful, appropriate eulogy that is consistent with the characters and includes story details.

2 Substantial Accomplishment The eulogy is consistent with the characters and includes some story details, but lacks any profound insight into the mother's life.

1 Little or Partial Accomplishment Students have difficulty conveying the character and using relevant details from the story.

Literary Concepts

Some examples of direct statements of the theme for students to discuss include:

Page 407—"If everyone could wait instead of rushing into marriage, how many tragedies could be averted!"

Page 399—"Shanshan, if you aren't sure what you want, don't rush into marriage—better live on your own."

Page 399—"When you're young, you don't always know what you're looking for, what you need, and people may talk you into getting married."

QuickWrites

1. Suggest that students use a question-and-answer format, first formulating questions that explore common concerns about marriage.
2. In their monologues, students might choose to invent details about the mother's unsuccessful marriage or her feelings for the man she loves.
3. Ask students to evaluate the character's goals, achievements, and personal and political beliefs.

The Writer's Craft

Advice Essay, pp. 190–194
Monologue, pp. 108–112
Character Sketch, pp. 78–82

Literary Links

Possible response: In "Lalla," the title character almost rushes into an ill-advised early marriage, like the narrator's mother. Also like the narrator's mother, the speaker in "The Taxi" suffers pain and loneliness at being separated from her lover.

Across the Curriculum

Suggest that in addition to searching under *Cultural Revolution*, students might search under the heading *Red Guards*. Students may also search under *Mao Zedong* (also spelled *Mao Tse-Tung*), the leader of the Chinese people during the Cultural Revolution.

Art Connection

Possible responses: Some students may point out that the masses of people at the meeting suggest that everyone in the society must obey and attend. Others might suggest that there seems to be very little room for individual expression or action.

Words to Know

1. c
2. b
3. c
4. b
5. a
6. b
7. c
8. a
9. b
10. a

Reteaching/Reinforcement
• Unit Three Resource Book, p. 22

ZHANG JIE

Zhang Jie was born in Beijing, and like the story's narrator, was raised by her mother alone. Many of her stories focus on relationships between individuals and the problems of modernization. She has also written two successful screenplays for China's movie industry, *The Search* and *We Are Still Young*.

LITERARY LINKS

What similarities, if any, do you see between the attitudes toward love expressed in this selection and those conveyed in other selections in this unit? Explain your reasoning.

Multimodal Learning

ACROSS THE CURRICULUM

History Find out more about the Cultural Revolution in China. Use current books, encyclopedia entries, and articles about China and determine what happened and what impact the Cultural Revolution has had on life in China. Present your findings in an oral report.

ART CONNECTION

The painting on page 405 shows workers at a political meeting in China. What does this painting tell you about the power of the Communist government over the lives of the characters in this selection?

Detail of a painting in the class-education exhibition, Niutung People's Commune No. 4.

WORDS TO KNOW

Determine the relationship between each pair of capitalized words below. On your paper, write the letter of the choice that shows the most similar relationship.

1. RENOUNCE : ACCEPT :: (a) agree : approve (b) despise : disapprove (c) abandon : join
2. WISTFUL : SAD :: (a) warm : hot (b) bashful : shy (c) cheerful : gloomy
3. ATONEMENT : SIN :: (a) question : answer (b) fact : opinion (c) apology : insult
4. NAIVETÉ : WORLDLINESS :: (a) beauty : youth (b) simplicity : complexity (c) love : marriage
5. PARRY : QUESTION :: (a) dodge : bullet (b) donate : gift (c) suffer : injury
6. COYNESS : MODESTY :: (a) intelligence : foolishness (b) bravado : courage (c) cowardice : fear
7. CENSURE : OPPONENT :: (a) advise : counselor (b) ridicule : mockery (c) praise : hero
8. ARDENT : FOND :: (a) hilarious : funny (b) cool : icy (c) wicked : evil
9. HERETIC : SOCIETY :: (a) criminal : prison (b) outlaw : community (c) voter : democracy
10. AVERSION : DISLIKE :: (a) passion : fondness (b) innocence : guilt (c) elm : tree

ZHANG JIE

1937–

Zhang Jie has been one of China's most highly acclaimed and, at times, controversial authors. Brought up in poverty and forced by the government to pursue college studies in economics instead of in literature as she had dreamed, Zhang Jie developed a strong sensitivity to injustices within the Communist system. After college Zhang Jie was directed to become a statistician, and during the Cultural Revolution, she, like many other college graduates, was sent to southern China to work in a factory. Finally, in 1976, Zhang Jie was able to move to Beijing and begin a writing career. Her first story, published in 1978, won her the first of many writing awards. By the early 1980s, Zhang Jie was a best-selling writer in her homeland.

Zhang Jie's stories highlight injustices and other problems in China's Communist system. Strongly committed to socialism, she has described her role as a writer as being to encourage readers to work to improve society. With "Love Must Not Be Forgotten" she became the first Chinese author in years to write about romantic love, marriage and the role of women.

OTHER WORKS *As Long as Nothing Happens, Nothing Will*; *Heavy Wings* (also translated as *Leaden Wings*)

Extended Reading

410   UNIT THREE   PART 1: THE TIES THAT BIND

REFLECTING ON THEME
What Do You Think?

Have students look back at the bar graph they created at the beginning of this part of Unit Three and ask if there is anything they would like to add to or change on their graphs after reading this selection.

ON YOUR OWN

Brigid

Mary Lavin

"Brigid" is set in Ireland, a rainy, largely agricultural land that is also one of western Europe's poorer nations. Irish farms are small by American standards, and most farm families must struggle to support themselves. Farmers were even poorer five or six decades ago, when "Brigid" takes place. Farms like that of the family in the story often lacked electricity and indoor plumbing and many of the other conveniences we associate with modern life. Despite the poverty—or perhaps because of it—Irish farming families remained close-knit, with children expected to care for aging parents and for other relatives unable to care for themselves. As author Joe McCarthy noted in the 1960s, "The bonds of an Irish family are deep between brothers and sisters and their uncles, aunts and grandparents. . . . It is a disgrace for a family to let old relatives live alone and a scandalous shame to put a granduncle or an aged aunt among strangers in a nursing home or public institution." Such values play a prominent role in the story you are about to read.

BRIGID **411**

OBJECTIVES

- To promote independent active reading
- To practice and apply skills learned in previous selections

Reading Pathways

- Suggest that students choose partners and do a paired reading of the story, alternating each four or five paragraphs.
- Encourage individuals to work together to create a dramatic presentation of selected scenes.
- Suggest that students use a sketch pad to record some of the vivid imagery in the story as they read.

PRINT AND MEDIA RESOURCES

UNIT THREE RESOURCE BOOK
Strategic Reading: Literature, p. 25

FORMAL ASSESSMENT
Selection Test, pp. 81–82
Part Test, pp. 83–84
Test Generator

ACCESS FOR STUDENTS ACQUIRING ENGLISH
Selection Summaries
Reading Support

AUDIO LIBRARY
See Reference Card

THE LANGUAGE OF LITERATURE TEACHER'S EDITION **411**

> ## SUMMARY
>
> Owen and his wife are quarreling about the weather, the food, and the children when the topic of his mentally challenged sister Brigid comes up. Owen's wife complains that Brigid's presence makes it difficult for their daughters to attract husbands, but Owen insists that he will not let his sister be put away—that she will remain in her nearby home, where they can care for her. Then he goes to check on Brigid. After suppertime comes and goes, the wife sets out to find Owen. She walks to Brigid's house, where she discovers him lying dead on the hearth by the fire. Brigid does not understand that her brother has suffered a stroke and died. In the moments that follow, the wife recognizes that she has failed her husband. She resolves, in spite of her neighbors' opinions, to bring Brigid home with her.
>
> **Thematic Link: *The Ties That Bind*** After Owen's death, the ties of affection and responsibility that bound Owen to his sister are transferred to Owen's wife.

The rain came sifting through the air and settled like a bloom on the fields. But under the trees it fell in single heavy drops, noisily, like cabbage water running through the holes of a colander.[1]

The house was in the middle of the trees.

"Listen to that rain!" said the woman to her husband. "Will it never stop?"

"What harm is a sup[2] of rain?" he said.

"That's you all over again," she said. "What harm is anything, as long as it doesn't affect yourself?"

"How do you mean, when it doesn't affect me? Look at my feet. They're sopping. And look at my hat. It's soused."[3] He took the hat off and shook the rain from it onto the spitting bars of the grate.

"Quit that," said the woman. "Can't you see you're raising ashes?"

"What harm is ashes?"

"I'll show you what harm," she said, taking down a plate of cabbage and potato from the shelf over the fire. "There's your dinner destroyed with them." The yellow cabbage was lightly sprayed with ash.

"Ashes is healthy, I often heard said. Put it here!" He sat down at the table, taking up his knife and fork, and indicating where the plate was to be put by tapping the table with the handle of the knife. "Is there no bit of meat?" he asked, prodding the potato critically.

"There's plenty in the town, I suppose."

"In the town? And why didn't somebody go to the town, might I ask?"

"Who was there to go? You know as well as I do there's no one here to be traipsing in and out every time there's something wanted from the town."

"I suppose one of our fine daughters would think it the end of the world if she was asked to go for a bit of a message? Let me tell you they'd get husbands for themselves quicker if they were seen doing a bit of work once in a while."

"Who said anything about getting husbands for them?" said the woman. "They're time enough getting married."

"Is that so? Mind you now, anyone would think that you were anxious to get them off your hands with the way every penny that comes into the house goes out again on bits of silks and ribbons for them."

"I'm not going to let them be without their bit of fun just because you have other uses for your money than spending it on your own children!"

"What other uses have I? Do I smoke? Do I drink? Do I play cards?"

"You know what I mean."

"I suppose I do." The man was silent. He left down his fork. "I suppose you're hinting at poor Brigid again?" he said. "But I told you forty times, if she was put into a home[4] she'd be just as much of an expense to us as she is in the little house above there." He pointed out of the window with his fork.

"I see there's no use in talking about it," said the woman. "All I can say is God help the girls, with you, their own father, putting a drag on them so that no man will have anything to do with them after hearing about Brigid."

"What do you mean by that? This is something new. I thought it was only the bit of bread and tea she got that you grudged the poor thing. This is something new. What is this?"

"You oughtn't to need to be told, a man like you that saw the world, a man that traveled like you did, a man that was in England and London."

---

1. **colander** (kŭl´ən-dər): a bowl-shaped, perforated kitchen utensil for draining off liquid and rinsing food.
2. **sup:** a small quantity of liquid.
3. **soused** (soust): soaking wet; drenched.
4. **home:** here, a residential institution where people are cared for.

Rebecca (about 1947), Raphael Soyer. Oil on canvas, 26″ × 20″, courtesy of Forum Gallery, New York.

BRIGID **413**

Art Note

***Rebecca* by Raphael Soyer** Russian-born artist Raphael Soyer (1899–1987) has a subdued, realistic style that expresses an intimate sympathy for people. For much of his career, Soyer portrayed the ordinary people of New York City going about their daily tasks.

Reading the Art *What is your impression of the woman in this portrait? What details create this impression?*

Multicultural Perspectives

EDUCATING THE MENTALLY CHALLENGED At one time in Europe and the United States, it was common for the mentally challenged to be kept at home, largely hidden from the outside world. In the 1830s, however, a French doctor by the name of Edouard Séguin developed a method of teaching the severely retarded. Séguin established a school in 1839 to apply his methods. Later he emigrated to the United States where he established similar schools. Séguin's publications about his methods influenced Maria Montessori. Between 1899 and 1901, she served as director of a state school in Rome where her own educational methods were applied successfully. (Montessori later applied her methods to students of all abilities.) Today experts believe that, whenever possible, mentally challenged people should receive all necessary education to live and work in the community.

THE LANGUAGE OF LITERATURE TEACHER'S EDITION **413**

"I don't know what you're talking about." He took up his hat and felt it to see if the side he had placed near the fire was dry. He turned the other side toward the fire. "What are you trying to say?" he said. "Speak plain!"

"Is any man going to marry a girl when he hears her aunt is a poor half-witted creature, soft in the head, and living in a poke of a hut, doing nothing all day but sitting looking into the fire?"

> *"You don't want to listen to anything unpleasant. You don't want to listen to anything that's right."*

"What has that got to do with anybody but the poor creature herself? Isn't it her own trouble?"

"Men don't like marrying into a family that has the like of her in it."

"Is that so? I didn't notice that you were put off marrying me, and you knew all about poor Brigid. You used to bring her bunches of primroses. And one day I remember you pulling the flowers off your hat and giving them to her when she started crying over nothing. You used to say she was a harmless poor thing. You used to say you'd look after her."

"And didn't I? Nobody can say I didn't look after her. Didn't I do my best to have her taken into a home, where she'd get proper care? You can't deny that."

"I'm not denying it. You never gave me peace or ease since the day we were married. But I wouldn't give in. I wouldn't give in then, and I won't give in now, either. I won't let it be said that I had hand or part in letting my own sister be put away."

"But it's for her own good." This time the woman's voice was softer, and she went over and turned the wet hat again on the fender.[5] "It's nearly dry," she said, and she went back to the table and took up the plate from which he had eaten and began to wash it in a basin of water at the other end of the table. "It's for her own good. I'm surprised you can't see that; you, a sensible man, with two grown-up daughters. You'll be sorry one of these days when she's found dead in the chair—the Lord between us and all harm—or falls in the fire and gets scorched to death—God preserve us from the like! I was reading, only the other day, in a paper that came round something from the shop, that there was a case like that up in the Midlands."

"I don't want to hear about it," said the man, shuffling his feet. "The hat is dry, I think," he said, and he put it on his head and stood up.

"That's the way you always go on. You don't want to listen to anything unpleasant. You don't want to listen to anything that's right. You don't want to listen because you know what I'm saying is true and you know you have no answer to it."

"You make me tired," said the man; "it's always the one story in this house. Why don't you get something else to talk about for a change?"

The woman ran to the door and blocked his way.

"Is that your last word?" she said. "You won't give in?"

"I won't give in. Poor Brigid. Didn't my mother make me promise I'd never have hand or part in putting the poor creature away? 'Leave her alone,' my mother used to say, 'she's doing no harm to anyone.'"

---

5. **fender:** a metal screen in front of a fireplace to keep hot coals and ashes from falling out.

"She's doing harm to our daughters," said the woman, "and you know that. Don't you?" She caught his coat and stared at him. "You know the way Matty Monaghan[6] gave up Rosie after dancing with her all night at a dance in the Town Hall last year. Why did he do that, do you suppose? It's little you know about it at all! You don't see Mamie crying her eyes out some nights after coming in from a walk with the girls and hearing bits of talk from this one and that one, and putting two and two together, and finding out for herself the talk that goes on among the men about girls and the kind of homes they come from!"

"There'd be a lot more talk if the poor creature was put away. Let me tell you that, if you don't know it for yourself! It's one thing to have a poor creature, doing no one any harm, living quiet, all by herself, up at the end of a boreen[7] where seldom or never anyone gets a chance of seeing her. It's another thing altogether to have her taken away in a car and everyone running to the window to see the car pass and talking about her and telling stories from one to another till in no time at all they'd be letting on she was twice as bad as she is, and the stories about her would be getting so wild that none of us could go down the streets without being stared at as if we were all queer!"

"You won't give in?" his wife asked once more.

"I won't give in."

"Poor Mamie. Poor Rosie." The woman sighed. She put the plate up on the dresser.

Owen shuffled his feet. "If you didn't let it be seen so plain that you wanted to get them off, they might have a better chance. I don't know what they want getting married for, in any case. They'd be better off to be interested in this place, and raise a few hens, and make a bit of money for themselves so they could be independent and take no notice of people and their gossip!"

"It's little you know about anything, that's all I have to say," said the woman.

Owen moved to the door.

"Where are you going now?"

"There's no use in my telling you and drawing down another stream of abuse on myself when I mention the poor creature's name."

The woman sighed and then stood up and walked over to the fire.

"If that's where you're going you might as well take over these clean sheets." She took down a pair of sheets from where they were airing on the shelf over the fire. "You can't say but I look after her, no matter what," she said.

"If you remembered her the way I do," said the man, "when she was only a little bit of a child, and I was growing up and going to school, you'd know what it feels like to hear talk of putting her in a home. She used to have lovely hair. It was like the flossy heads of the dandelions when they are gone past their best. No one knew she was going to be a bit soft[8] until she was toddling around and beginning to talk, and even then it was thought she was only slow, that she'd grow out of it."

"I know how you feel," said the woman. "I could cry sometimes myself when I think about her. But she'd be so happy in a home! We could visit her any time we wanted. We could hire a car and drive over to see her, all of us, on a fine Sunday now and again. It would be some place to go. And it would cost no more than it costs to keep her here."

She didn't know whether he had heard the end of the sentence because he had gone out through the yard and was cutting across the field, with his ash plant[9] in his hand.

---

6. **Monaghan** (mŏn′ə-hăn).
7. **boreen** (bôr-ēn′): a narrow country lane.
8. **a bit soft**: simple-minded; mentally slow.
9. **ash plant**: a walking stick made from a young ash tree.

Linking to History

Children and Marriage Worrying about children who had grown old enough to marry was common in Ireland at the time of this story, some 40 years ago. Then, and to a lesser extent today, most young people in Ireland remained single and lived with their parents until they were well over the age of 30. Because both farmland and jobs were scarce, young people simply could not afford to marry and raise children.

Art Note

Fire and Water by Winifred Nicholson
Winifred Nicholson (1893–1981) was a distinguished English artist and thinker in the 1920s and 1930s. According to one art critic, Nicholson's "life of paintings led to a deeper explorations of the colours at the edge of the rainbow."

Reading the Art *How do the colors in this painting by Nicholson express the fire's intensity?*

Fire and Water (1927), Winifred Nicholson. Copyright © artist's family.

"He was cutting across the field with the ash plant in his hand when we were starting off on our walk," said Rosie, when she and Mamie came in to their supper and her mother asked her if she had seen their father out in the yard.

"He was going up to your Aunt Brigid then," said their mother. "Did you not see him after that?"

"That was three hours ago," said Mamie, looking worried. "He wouldn't be over there all this time. Would he? He must be doing something for Aunt Brigid—chopping wood or mending something. He wouldn't be just sitting over there all this time."

"Ah, you wouldn't know what he'd be doing," the mother said, and the girls looked at each other. They knew then there had been words between their father and mother while they were out.

"Maybe one of you ought to run over and see what's keeping him?" said their mother.

"Oh, leave him alone," said Mamie. "If he wants to stay over there, let him! He'll have to be home soon anyway to put in the calves. It's nearly dark."

But soon it was very dark, and the calves were still out. The girls had gone out again to a dance, and it was beginning to rain when Owen's wife put on her coat and went across the field herself and up the boreen to Brigid's.

How can she sit there in the dark? she thought, when she didn't see a light in the window. But as she got nearer she saw there was a faint glow from the fire on the hearth. She felt sure Owen wasn't there. He wouldn't be there without lighting a lamp, or a bit of a candle! There was no need to go in. She was going to turn back, but it seemed an unnatural thing not to call to the door and see if the poor creature was all right.

Brigid was the same as ever, sitting by the fire with a silly smile and not looking up till she was called three or four times.

"Brigid, did you see Owen?" his wife asked without much hope of a reply.

Brigid looked up. "Owen is a queer man," she said. That was all the answer she gave.

"So he was here! What time did he leave?"

Brigid grumbled something.

"What are you saying, Brigid?"

"He wouldn't go home," Brigid said. "I told him it was time to go home for his tea, but he wouldn't answer me. 'Go home,' I said, 'go home, Owen.'"

"When did he go? What time was it? Did you notice?"

Brigid could be difficult sometimes. Was she going to be difficult now?

"He wouldn't go home," Brigid said again.

Suddenly Owen's wife saw his ash plant lying on the table.

"Is he still here?" she said, sharply, and she glanced back at the door. "I didn't see him in the yard! I didn't hear him!"

"He wouldn't speak to me," Brigid said again stubbornly.

The other woman couldn't see her in the dark. The fire was flickering too irregularly to see by its light.

"But where is he? Is there anything the matter with him?" She ran to the door and called out into the dark. But there was no answer. She stood there trying to think. She heard Brigid talking to herself, but she didn't trouble to listen. She might as well go home, she thought. Wherever he was, he wasn't here. "If he comes back, Brigid, tell him I was here looking for him," she said. "I'll go home through the other field."

Brigid said something then that made her turn sharply and look at her.

"What did you say?"

"Tell him yourself," said Brigid, and then she seemed to be talking to herself again. And she was leaning down in the dark before the fire.

"Why don't you talk?" she said. "Why don't you talk?"

Before Owen's Death
- resentful towards Brigid
- angry at husband for caring for Brigid
- fearful about how Brigid might affect her daughters' future

After Owen's Death
- remorseful for her inability to love Owen
- determined to care for Brigid
- unconcerned about what people think about Brigid

Cooperative Learning
RESEARCHING IRISH LIFE

Students can form into groups to research and prepare oral reports on topics related to Irish life in the first half of this century. These topics should pertain to issues important to the story, such as family life, marriage, the care of the mentally challenged, and village life. Suggest that students assign roles within their groups once they have agreed upon topics: one student might obtain research materials, one might compile information, another might ensure that the information is coherently organized, and so on. All group members should take part in presenting the information to the class.

Teacher's Role Offer suggestions for research resources (school library, local library, encyclopedias, and so forth). Provide time after the reading of "Brigid" for students to deliver their oral reports.

Rubric

3 **Full Accomplishment** The oral report develops the topic in a well-organized way and is clear and easy to understand.

2 **Substantial Accomplishment** The oral report develops the topic fairly well and is delivered with only a little difficulty or hesitation.

1 **Little or Partial Accomplishment** The oral report is poorly organized and hard to understand.

Owen's wife began to pull out the old settle bed[10] that was in front of the fire, not knowing why she did it, but she could feel the blood pounding in her ears and behind her eyes.

"He fell down there and he wouldn't get up!" Brigid said. "I told him to get up. I told him that his head was getting scorched. But he wouldn't listen to me. He wouldn't get up. He wouldn't do anything."

Owen's wife closed her eyes. All of a sudden she was afraid to look. But when she looked, Owen's eyes stared up at her, wide open, from where he lay on his back on the hearth.

"Owen!" she screamed, and she tried to pull him up.

His shoulders were stiff and heavy. She caught his hands. They were cold. Was he dead? She felt his face. But his face was hot, so hot she couldn't put her hand on it. If he was dead he'd be cold. She wanted to scream and run out of the house, but first she tried to drag him as far as she could from the ashy hearth. Then suddenly feeling the living eyes of Brigid watching her, and seeing the dead eyes staring up from the blistered red face, she sprang up, knocking over a chair, and ran out of the house, and ran screaming down the boreen.

Her screams brought people running out to their doors, the light streaming out each side of them. She couldn't speak, but she pointed up the hill and ran on. She wanted to get to the pump.

It was dark at the pump, but she could hear people running the way she had pointed. Then when they had reached the cottage, there was no more running, but great talking and shouting. She sat down at the side of the pump, but there was a smell off her hands and desperately she bent forward and began to wash them under the pump, but when she saw there was hair stuck to her fingers she wanted to scream again, but there was a great pain gathering in her heart, not yet the pain of loss, but the pain of having failed; failed in some terrible way.

> *"I told him to get up. I told him that his head was getting scorched. But he wouldn't listen to me."*

I failed him always, she thought, from the very start. I never loved him like he loved me; not even then, long ago, the time I took the flowers off my hat. It wasn't for Brigid, like he thought. I was only making myself out to be what he imagined I was. I didn't know enough about loving to change myself for him. I didn't even know enough about it to keep him loving me. He had to give it all to Brigid in the end.

He gave it all to Brigid; to a poor daft thing that didn't know enough to pull him back from the fire or call someone when he fell down in a stroke. If it was anyone else was with him, he might have had a chance.

Oh, how had it happened? How could love be wasted and go to loss like that?

It was like the way the tossy balls of cowslips[11] they used to make as children were forgotten and left behind in the fields, till they were trodden into the muck by the cattle and the sheep.

---

10. **settle bed:** a long bench used both as a seat and as a bed.
11. **tossy balls of cowslips:** strung-together flowers and stems of cowslips. A cowslip is a wildflower that grows in Britain and Ireland.

Critic's Corner

"Miss Lavin possesses the strength of gentleness. A serene radiance illuminates all her writing: the radiance of one who observes, accepts, and meditates on the human condition . . . She invites us to contemplate with her the infinite sadness and beauty of the world, the divine inconsequence of life. . . ."

Jean Stubbs, a novelist and reviewer, commenting on Mary Lavin's short stories.

Read the quote aloud. Then ask students to cite details from "Brigid" that support or refute this description of Lavin's writing.

Suddenly she thought of the heavy feet of the neighbors tramping the boards of the cottage up in the fields behind her, and rising up, she ran back up the boreen.

"Here's the poor woman now," someone said, as she thrust past the crowd around the door.

They began to make a way for her to where, on the settle bed, they had laid her husband. But instead she parted a way through the people and went toward the door of the room off the kitchen.

"It's Brigid I'm thinking about," she said. "Where is she?"

"Something will have to be done about her now all right," someone said.

"It will," she said, decisively, and her voice was as true as a bell.

She had reached the door of the room.

"That's why I came back," she said, looking around her defiantly. "She'll need proper minding[12] now. To think she hadn't the strength to run for help or pull him back a bit from the fire." She opened a door.

Sitting on the side of the bed, all alone, she saw Brigid.

"Get your hat and coat, Brigid," she said. "You're coming home with me." ❖

---
12. **minding:** tending; watching; caring for.

MARY LAVIN

Although she was born in Massachusetts, Mary Lavin (1912–) has spent most of her life in Ireland and writes about Ireland in virtually all of her fiction. The daughter of an Irish couple who spent a few years in America, Lavin immigrated to Ireland when she was nine and attended a convent school in the Irish capital of Dublin. Four years later, her father became the manager of the Bective estate in Ireland's County Meath, an area that Lavin came to know and love. In fact, Lavin's first collection of short stories, published in 1942, was called *Tales from Bective Bridge;* later, she and her family purchased Abbey Farm in Bective and made it their residence.

With her stories being published on both sides of the Atlantic Ocean, Lavin became one of Ireland's foremost short story writers. "Mary Lavin is a great artist," said the eminent British critic V. S. Pritchett; "we are excited by her sympathy, her acute knowledge of the human heart, her truthfulness and, above all, by the controlled revelation of untidy powerful emotion." "Brigid," which first appeared in a 1944 edition of *Dublin Magazine,* was later chosen for the Dell anthology *Great Irish Short Stories* (1964).

OTHER WORKS *Collected Stories, The Shrine and Other Stories, Mary Lavin: Selected Stories, A Family Likeness*

OPTION 3

Class Discussion

SHARING IDEAS

Teacher's Role After students have read the selections, engage them in a whole-class discussion using the following questions:

1. What does Owen's relationship with his sister Brigid tell you about him? *(Possible responses: He is loving and generous; he takes his family responsibilities seriously; he is stubborn and unbending in his devotion to his sister.)*

2. Do you think Owen's wife has other reasons, besides the ones stated, for wanting Brigid to be put in a home? *(Possible responses: Yes, Owen's wife seems to be jealous of all the attention that her husband gives Brigid; also, she may be envious of the warmth of his relationship with Brigid, considering her own lack of emotional warmth; she is probably embarrassed of having her family associated with Brigid. No, Owen's wife is an attentive mother who places the well-being of her daughters ahead of Brigid's needs.)*

3. Why does Owen's wife change her attitude towards Brigid after the death of her husband? *(Possible response: She realized that she had failed her husband by not loving him; she resolved to make up for her failure to love Owen by loving Brigid.)*

4. At the end of the story, the woman realizes, "I didn't even know enough about loving to change myself for him [Owen]." What sorts of changes should people make in themselves for those they love? *(Accept all reasonable responses.)*

5. Do you think people should take care of family members who are too old or disabled to take care of themselves? Or is it better to have them placed in special homes? *(Possible responses: Some students may suggest that it is one's responsibility to care for one's own family members; others might say that such difficult work is better left to professionals.)*

MARY LAVIN

Mary Lavin graduated from University College, Dublin, and the National University of Ireland with first-class honors. In addition to publishing over a dozen collections of short stories and two novels, Ms. Lavin has worked as a farmer and has taught French. She is the mother of three daughters.

OVERVIEW

In the Guided Assignment for this section, students will compose a poem by exploring their thoughts and feelings and creating images. They will also use poetry-writing techniques to generate personal responses and to refine and condense poetic expression through revision. The Writer's Style will help them understand the use of punctuation in poetry. In Reading the World, students will consider the use of metaphor in the mass media.

Objectives

- To identify the uses of different forms of figurative language
- To enliven description by employing fresh and original figures of speech
- To weave images, thoughts, and feelings into a draft of a poem
- To examine some common uses of metaphor in magazines and newspapers

Skills

LITERATURE
- Identifying figurative language

GRAMMAR AND USAGE
- Using punctuation in poetry

MEDIA LITERACY
- Identifying metaphors in the media

SPEAKING, LISTENING, AND VIEWING
- Reading poetry aloud
- Group discussion

CRITICAL THINKING
- Making observations

Teaching Strategy: MODELING

In the models that follow, figurative language suggests an image that enables the reader to see a familiar thing in a fresh way. Figurative language is one of the essential devices of poetry.

A Lowell Possible responses: streets (which seem to be moving); lamps (which assault the eyes of the speaker)

B Su Tung Po Possible responses: Snow is compared to white willow cotton; in a reversal of the simile, willow cotton is compared to snow.

WRITING ABOUT LITERATURE

Capturing a Moment

Does the language in this unit's poetry captivate you or create a picture in your mind? Poetic language uses sound devices, figurative language, and sensory details to surprise or enlighten you. Even such everyday writing as TV jingles, rock lyrics, and phrases in your journal can sparkle with the language of poetry. On the next few pages you will

- explore the figures of speech that poets use
- write a poem of your own
- make observations about the use of metaphor in media

The Writer's Style: Figurative Language Figurative language, which is often used in poetry, conveys a message beyond the literal meaning of words. Some types of figurative language are simile, metaphor, and personification.

Read the Literature

Notice how these poets use figurative language to help you see familiar things in unusual ways. How do personification, simile, and metaphor form pictures in your mind?

Literature Models

Personification
Personification gives human characteristics to inanimate objects. What objects does this poet personify?

> Streets coming fast,
> One after the other,
> Wedge you away from me,
> And the lamps of the city prick my eyes
> So that I can no longer see your face.
>
> Amy Lowell, from "The Taxi"

A

Simile
A simile uses the word *like* or *as* to make a comparison. What two unlike things is this poet comparing?

> The snow was flying, like white willow cotton.
> This year, Spring has come again,
> And the willow cotton is like snow.
>
> Su Tung Po, from "To a Traveler," translated by Kenneth Rexroth

B

PRINT AND MEDIA RESOURCES

UNIT THREE RESOURCE BOOK
Writer's Style, p. 29
Prewriting Guide, p. 30
Elaboration, p. 31
Peer Response Guide, pp. 32–33
Revising and Proofreading, p. 34
Student Model, p. 35
Rubric, p. 36

FORMAL ASSESSMENT
Guidelines for Writing Assessment

GRAMMAR MINI-LESSONS
Transparencies, pp. 39–47
Copymasters, pp. 38–44

WRITING MINI-LESSONS
Transparencies, pp. 46, 47, 53, 58

 WRITING COACH

 The Writer's Craft
Poetry, pp. 87–101
Literal and Figurative Language, pp. 425–426

Connect to Music

Whenever you listen to a song, you are also listening to a poem. A song lyric is really a short verse that expresses the writer's emotion. The following song lyric makes an unusual direct comparison. Notice how figurative language is used.

Song Lyric

> We have come for LIGHT
> WHOLLY, we have come for light
> it's TRUE
> I am the SUN
> I am the new year
> I am the rain
>
> the Breeders,
> from "New Year,"
> *Last Splash*

Metaphors
A metaphor makes a comparison by speaking of one thing as though it were something else. What direct comparisons does this lyricist make?

Try Your Hand: Using Figurative Language

1. **Practice Personification** Write a sentence or phrase that gives human characteristics to each of the following: a river, time, a computer.

2. **Spice It Up** Make the following scene richer by using figurative language.

    We stood motionless and afraid. An eerie silence began to fill the town. Before we could decide what to do, we heard a deafening sound. Then, the tornado hit without fair warning and we were caught in its mighty winds.

3. **Make the Comparison** In a sentence, create a metaphor and a simile of your own. You might want to describe a feeling, an object, or a person you know.

SkillBuilder

WRITER'S CRAFT

Avoiding Clichés

Clichés are phrases or figures of speech that are so overused that they are no longer effective. Because they lack creative thought, they give you nothing new to think about.

For example, instead of saying that his love is *"as pretty as a picture,"* Shakespeare writes

> *Shall I compare thee to a summer's day?*
> *Thou art more lovely and more temperate: . . .*
>
> from Sonnet 18

Following are some examples of clichés. Can you think of more?

- as big as a house
- squeaky clean
- happy as a clam
- working my fingers to the bone
- a sight for sore eyes

APPLYING WHAT YOU'VE LEARNED
Rewrite the phrases above to provide fresh, interesting alternatives.

WRITING ABOUT LITERATURE **421**

Teaching Strategy: MODELING

C **The Breeders** Possible responses: In lines 4-6, the speaker compares himself or herself to the sun, the new year, and the rain. The speaker suggests that the sun, the new year, and the rain bring light or the promise of something new.

Try Your Hand

1. Responses will vary. Suggest that students reverse the metaphor by comparing three people to a river, time, and a computer. Then challenge them to turn the metaphors around by describing what a river, time, and a computer would be like if they resembled the three people.

2. Answers will vary. Students' paragraphs should show proper use of figurative language.

3. To help students choose a rich metaphor or simile, suggest that they make a list of qualities that can be ascribed to the feeling, object, or person they choose to describe. Then ask them to use this list to decide which quality promises to produce the most vivid figure of speech.

SkillBuilder WRITER'S CRAFT

AVOIDING CLICHÉS Write the following examples of clichés on the chalkboard: "He's as old as the hills"; "They're as different as night and day"; "I cried like a baby"; and "Last but not least." Invite students to offer a critique of each cliché that describes its limitations and explains why a fresh way of saying something can lead to an insightful description.

Applying What You've Learned Possible answers include:
- as big as the sky
- clean as a white bed sheet
- happy as a new rose
- working like an Iowa tractor
- daybreak in Alaska

Additional Suggestions Ask students to think about a delicious meal that they ate and to use that recollection to rewrite the trite statement below:

I had a meal. It was out of this world. It was awesome. It was unbelievable. It was to die for.

Reteaching/Reinforcement
- *Writing Handbook,* anthology pp. 1030–1032
- *Writing Mini-Lessons* transparencies, p. 46, 47

The Writer's Craft
Clichés, p. 430

Critical Thinking: IDENTIFYING

D Have students look through the poems in this unit and note phrases that capture a moment, make surprising observations, or tell stories. List their responses on the chalkboard.

Speaking and Listening: GROUP DISCUSSION

E Have students use the list as a springboard for a discussion of things they have seen, heard about, or thought about that might make a compelling subject for an evocative poem. Encourage them to describe and talk about poems that they like.

WRITING ABOUT LITERATURE

Creative Response

D Poems like those in Unit Three capture a moment of experience, make a surprising observation, or tell a story. Poetry may take any form and may be written about anything, yet poetry is unique. The sounds and rhythms of words, the look of a poem, the mental images that poems evoke—all make poetry the closest thing in words to music and to visual art.

GUIDED ASSIGNMENT

Write a Poem To better understand a piece of writing, you can do the same kind of writing yourself. On these pages you'll explore your own response to the poems in Unit Three. Then you'll discover a poem that could be written only by you.

Student's Poetry Sketchbook

1 Prewrite and Explore

Poets seldom plan what they will write before they compose. Usually, they begin with a phrase, a feeling, or an image, in language that brings forth a certain direction.

SEARCHING FOR IDEAS

The following methods might help you to discover the poem inside of you:

- Listen to conversation.
- Observe events and situations.
- Read the poetry of others.
- Recall a mood or feeling.
- Think about images.
- Reread literature that evokes a memory.

E

RECORDING YOUR THOUGHTS

Your search for subjects or images can take on many forms. You might like to keep a notebook of ideas, create webs, draw pictures, or talk over your ideas with a friend. Many times the best way to begin a poem is just to start writing. The example at the left is one student's approach to recording thoughts at the beach that might be used in future poems.

422 UNIT THREE: IN THE NAME OF LOVE

 **Assessment Option**

SELF-ASSESSMENT Offer these self-assessment questions for Recording Your Thoughts:
- Do your ideas for poems reflect subjects that really matter to you?
- Did you freewrite your ideas without worrying about how good they might be or how much sense they might make?
- Would you understand your notes if you went back to them six months from now?

422 THE LANGUAGE OF LITERATURE TEACHER'S EDITION

② Freewrite

Now it's time to freewrite. Record words, phrases, and feelings that come to you. Play with language, write as much as you can, and don't censor yourself. All you need to do is write!

The yellow notes show how one student analyzed his freewriting.

Student's Freewriting

I look at the horizon and see layers of pale blue, gray blue, bright blue. It is a hot sunny day. Waves ruin sand creations. What does this scene remind me of? My childhood memories of the beach at the lake. What feelings does this memory give me? calm, secure, free

Now I think about the present. As I stand at the edge of the ocean, I am surprised the water is warm. I feel the fresh mist from the sea and lick my lips to taste the salt and summer.

Children squeal and sand crabs scurry across the sand. umbrellas dot the beach.

I look back to the horizon and feel peace.

— *Do I want to write about my childhood memories or my present impressions?*

— *What kinds of images might I add?*

③ Draft and Share

How will you change your freewriting into a poem? Remember that poetry is written in lines, not sentences. First, mark the sections, phrases, even words that you think you want to keep. Next, condense your poem by including only your most important ideas and details. Consider how your poem can make a strong impression. When you are finished, think about these questions and share your poem with a friend.

- Does my poem make sense?
- Do I use interesting figurative language?
- Is every word necessary? How might I condense my ideas?

PEER RESPONSE

- What is your first reaction when you read my poem?
- Does the figurative language appeal to you? Why?
- What images could be stronger?

SkillBuilder
WRITER'S CRAFT

Using Sound Devices

Poets use various techniques such as sound devices to add dimension to poetry. Two sound devices, consonance and assonance, can help add interest to your poems.

Consonance Notice the repetition of consonant sounds within words.

To leap from a clump of banana plants
one morning of wonders—

— Gabriela Mistral
from "Eight Puppies"

Assonance Watch for the repetition of vowel sounds within words.

Tonight I can write the saddest lines.
I loved her, and sometimes she loved me too.

— Pablo Neruda
from "Tonight I Can Write . . ."
translated by W. S. Merwin

APPLYING WHAT YOU'VE LEARNED

Try your hand at using these sound devices. Write one line of poetry using consonance and one line using assonance.

WRITING ABOUT LITERATURE   423

Writing Skill: FREEWRITING

F Freewriting will give students an opportunity to mine their thoughts. Remind them not to pay attention to spelling, punctuation, and grammar. Encourage students to keep writing without pausing to think. If they get stuck, they can discharge their frustration by repeating phrases they have already written until they unearth other thoughts. Suggest a specific period of time, such as ten minutes, for the whole class to freewrite.

Teaching Strategy: USING WRITING SPRINGBOARDS

G Help students see that poetry is a special kind of writing that requires much less explication and background information than narrative forms such as fiction or journalism. Discuss the concept of line breaks, and mention that in most poetry, a line won't exceed the number of words that a reader can say in one breath.

SkillBuilder   WRITER'S CRAFT

USING SOUND DEVICES Remind students that poets are especially concerned with the sounds of words. One common way poets stress sounds is by rhyming the final sounds on consecutive or alternate lines. Tell students that consonance and assonance are sound devices that poets use to create sound patterns that reinforce or emphasize the mood or meaning of the work.

Applying What You've Learned Sample responses:

Consonance: What w<u>r</u>ecked <u>r</u>ock and <u>r</u>oll <u>r</u>ecords?

Assonance: Their r<u>ou</u>nd old h<u>ou</u>nd-dog s<u>ou</u>nds have been gr<u>ou</u>nd and p<u>ou</u>nded.

Additional Suggestions Challenge students to identify consonance and assonance in a poem that you have selected.

Reteaching/Reinforcement

The Writer's Craft

Sound devices, pp. 94, 427

Critical Thinking: ANALYZING

H Tell students that poets almost always rework their first drafts by adding, deleting, and changing language. Like other writers, poets strive to make their writing as concise, precise, fresh, and evocative as possible.

Offer these suggestions for revision:
- Read the poem to yourself or to a partner and locate places where the poem drags or has words that can be cut.
- Ask yourself if you have said everything you want to say about the subject of the poem.
- Identify unsatisfactory word choices or a line that has been constructed awkwardly, and provide new wording.
- A poem does not have to be long to be effective; if a word or phrase doesn't help you make your point, be willing to cut it out.

Teaching Tip: MODELING

I Discuss how this sample meets the Standards for Evaluation on this page. Some interesting language choices include the phrases: "Waves kiss the shore," and "Damp heat presses." Figurative language is used to create a contemplative mood. The author conveys a feeling of sensory pleasure.

Standards for Evaluation

Ideas and Content
- Usually focuses on one memorable or interesting experience, event, or person.
- Uses precise and fresh language.
- Uses sensory and figurative language to support the meaning and the effect.
- May use poetic sound devices.

Structure and Form
- May use lines of varying lengths.
- May use stanza breaks to show changes in mood, images, or emphases.
- Uses a variety of sentence structures.

Grammar, Usage, and Mechanics
- Contains no more than two or three minor errors in grammar and usage.
- Contains no more than two or three minor errors in spelling, capitalization, and punctuation.

WRITING ABOUT LITERATURE

4 Revise and Edit

H Even poems need revision. Reread your poem aloud and listen to decide if each word you chose adds to the poem's effect. Check the callouts below and consider the Standards for Evaluation as you prepare your final draft.

Student's Final Draft

What language choices seem interesting?

How is figurative language used?

What feeling does the student convey?

June Day at the Seashore

Perched between the sand and sea, I gaze upon the horizon.
Soft layers of blue put me in a trance.
I am lost inside the cloudless day.

Waves kiss the shore and topple sand castles.
Expecting cold, I am surprised at the warmth.
After the misty sea sprays me,
I lick my lips to taste the salt and summer.

Damp heat presses, children squeal in delight, sand crabs scurry.
Scents of sunscreen and stickiness float between breezes.
Graceful umbrellas dot the straight beige beach.

The seashore is all of these things,
but it's always the horizon that calls me back—
showing me a dream, a promise, an answer.

Standards for Evaluation

The poem
- accurately captures an experience, observation, or emotion
- uses precise and fresh language
- uses sounds and figurative language to support the meaning and effect

424 UNIT THREE: IN THE NAME OF LOVE

Assessment Option

SELF-ASSESSMENT To help students evaluate their own writing, offer the following questions:
- Does my poem have an identifiable subject?
- Have I used concise language that contains no unnecessary description or explanation?
- Have I read the poem aloud to hear how it sounds?
- Have I chosen words that convey precise meanings?
- Does my poem express thoughts and feelings that intrigue me?

Grammar in Context

Participial Phrases A **participle** is a verb form that is used as a modifier. A participial phrase contains a participle and any words that modify it. Participial phrases are often used in poetry because they are useful in compressing ideas. However, a writer must use them carefully. If a participial phrase is not placed near the word it modifies, the result can be very confusing.

> I gaze upon the horizon, perched between the sand and sea.

In the example above, the participial phrase should be moved to the beginning of the line because it modifies the word *I*, not *horizon*.

> I am surprised at the warmth, expecting cold.

The example above shows that the participial phrase, *expecting cold*, should be placed near *I*, the word it modifies.

Try Your Hand: Using Participial Phrases

On a separate piece of paper, identify which of the following sentences contain misplaced participial phrases. Rewrite the sentences correctly.

1. The crabs were hidden from view buried in the sand.
2. Sparkling in the sun, the shells were beautiful treasures.
3. Walking across the beach, the sun set as I headed home.

SkillBuilder

GRAMMAR FROM WRITING

Using Punctuation in Poetry

The rules of punctuation are usually relaxed in the writing of poetry. It is important, though, to follow some punctuation rules. Even though you've written a poem to express yourself, you need to make your poem reader-friendly. Punctuation is your reader's "roadmap."

Look at this excerpt from "I Love Words" by Louis Ginsberg:

> Some love jewels
>   And gems that daze:
> Topaz, onyx,
>   Chrysoprase.
>
> Others love Beauty
>   That haunts swans
> In permanent
>   Repose of bronze.

Ginsberg uses a colon to alert the reader to an upcoming list. He uses commas to separate items and a period at the end of a thought. He also capitalizes the first letter of each new line.

APPLYING WHAT YOU'VE LEARNED

Go back to your final poem and decide whether there are places you can improve punctuation use. Modify your poem's punctuation.

GRAMMAR HANDBOOK

For more information on punctuation, see page 1089 of the Grammar Handbook.

WRITING ABOUT LITERATURE 425

Teaching Strategy: STUMBLING BLOCK

Explain that a participle is a verb form that can be used to describe a noun. Tell students that participial phrases are sometimes used to add information to a sentence.

Examples:
- *Exhausted by the events of the day*, Phoebe collapsed on the couch.
- *Confused by my feelings*, I did not extend the invitation.

Try Your Hand

The sentences that need to be rewritten can be modified as follows:
1. Buried in the sand, the crabs were hidden from view.
2. correct
3. The sun set as I headed home, walking across the beach.

PORTFOLIO

Invite students to compare their finished poems to poems that they have previously written. Then ask students to write a brief description of what they have learned about writing poetry as a result of this assignment. They may wish to include their description and their finished poem in their portfolio.

SkillBuilder — GRAMMAR FROM WRITING

USING PUNCTUATION IN POETRY

Inform students that one of the most important functions of punctuation in poetry is to designate specific kinds of stops. Offer students a list of punctuation techniques similar to the following:

Period, Question Mark, Exclamation Point—ends a sentence; can be used at the end of a line or within a line

Comma—creates a pause; can be used at the end of a line or within a line

Colon—alerts readers to information that follows

Applying What You've Learned Invite pairs of students to read their poems out loud to each other. Have the partner note whether the pauses match those indicated by the punctuation. If not, encourage the poet to eliminate or add punctuation as needed.

Additional Suggestions Provide students with the unpunctuated text of a poem. Encourage them to use their own judgment about where to insert punctuation. Then ask them to compare their marks to the poet's original format. Did the meaning of the poem change due to differences in punctuation?

Reteaching/Reinforcement
- *Grammar Handbook,* anthology pp. 1089–1097
- *Grammar Mini-Lessons* copymasters pp. 39–47, transparencies pp. 38–44

The Writer's Craft
End Marks and Commas, pp. 782–803
Semicolons, Colons, and Other Punctuation, pp. 804–811

READING THE WORLD

On pages 420–425, students considered some of the techniques of writing poetry. Remind them that writers use poetic language to describe aspects of everyday life in newspapers, magazines, and other kinds of mass communication. In this lesson, students will explore the use of metaphor in such sources as advertisements, cartoons, and newspaper and magazine features.

Critical Thinking: ANALYZING

K Students' answers will vary. Students are likely to notice the images before they notice the words on each page.

Critical Thinking: SPECULATING

L Hayun Cho is described as "a rising star." Acme Widgets Company is described as a sinking ship. Invite students to explain the meaning of these expressions and to speculate about what each image suggests about the subject.

Speaking and Listening: GROUP DISCUSSION

M Encourage students to come up with metaphors for the magazine article and the cartoon that will create impressions that are similar to those conveyed in the original versions. Have them discuss and evaluate the effectiveness of their metaphors and suggest ways in which their metaphors could be conveyed visually.

READING THE WORLD

SEEING METAPHOR

Literature is not the only place you will find metaphors. In articles, advertisements, and cartoons, for example, metaphors can be effective shortcuts for communicating ideas. By using familiar images, writers can instantly convey an idea or opinion to their readers.

View Look at the magazine and newspaper pages shown here. Which words and pictures catch your attention first?

Interpret What ideas are being expressed on each page? What metaphors are used to help present each idea?

Discuss In a group, discuss how effective the metaphors were in helping you get a quick sense of the ideas. How would the message have been different if the writer or artist had used a more straightforward approach? Refer to the SkillBuilder at the right to help you think about what you observe.

SkillBuilder

CRITICAL THINKING

Making Observations
What is going on around you? Making observations is more than just looking. It's paying close attention to your environment by using your senses to gather information. Becoming aware of what makes each person, place, thing, or situation special is the key to making successful observations.

To effectively observe, zero in on ideas or images that help you make connections in your world. Take notes on what you perceive. Look beyond the surface. That's what metaphors teach you. In effect, that's what all of your experiences teach you. Making observations helps you to interpret those experiences.

When making observations, remember the following:

- Use all five of your senses.
- Ask *who, what, why, where, when,* and *how.*
- Recall past experiences.
- Create lists.

APPLYING WHAT YOU'VE LEARNED
Over the next few days, practice making observations. Consider the ideas above and remember to expect the unexpected!

READING THE WORLD 427

SkillBuilder — CRITICAL THINKING

MAKING OBSERVATIONS Journalists and advertisers often use common phrases such as "interactive," "lifestyle," and "the 90s" as if they had a set meaning rather than the range of meanings ascribed to them by individual readers. Have students create a list of such "buzzwords" used in the popular media. Then invite them to choose and render their own interpretations of several of these trumpeted phrases, and remind them to be aware of such potentially empty terms when they are used.

Applying What You've Learned Encourage students to carry a notebook for recording their observations of television, newspapers, magazines, and ads. After two days invite them to discuss and categorize what they have observed and what they have learned from reviewing their notes.

UNIT THREE
Part 2 Lesson Planner

TIME ALLOTMENTS SHOWN ARE APPROXIMATE. DEPENDING ON YOUR GOALS AND THE NEEDS OF YOUR STUDENTS, YOU MAY WISH TO ALLOW MORE OR LESS TIME FOR CERTAIN PORTIONS OF THE LESSON.

Table of Contents	Discussion	Previewing the Selection	Reading the Selection
PART OPENER **Mysteries of the Heart** page 428	**20 MINUTES** • Reflect on the part theme		
SELECTION **The Californian's Tale** page 431 CHALLENGING		**20 MINUTES** • PERSONAL CONNECTION • HISTORICAL CONNECTION • READING CONNECTION: Interpreting details about setting	**40 MINUTES** • Introduce vocabulary • Read pp. 431–437 (7 pp.)
SELECTIONS **Simile/Tonight I Can Write . . .** Page 442 AVERAGE		**20 MINUTES** • PERSONAL CONNECTION • LITERARY CONNECTION • READING CONNECTION: Understanding comparisons	**20 MINUTES** • Read pp. 442–444 (3 pp.)
SELECTION **To . . .** page 449 CHALLENGING		**20 MINUTES** • PERSONAL CONNECTION • LITERARY CONNECTION • READING CONNECTION: Understanding chronological order	**10 MINUTES** • Read p. 449 (1 p.)
SELECTION **Metonymy, or The Husband's Revenge** page 453 CHALLENGING		**20 MINUTES** • PERSONAL CONNECTION • LITERARY CONNECTION • WRITING CONNECTION	**30 MINUTES** • Introduce vocabulary • Read pp. 453–457 (5 pp.)
SELECTION **The First Seven Years** page 461 AVERAGE		**20 MINUTES** • PERSONAL CONNECTION • HISTORICAL/CULTURAL CONNECTION • READING CONNECTION: Interpreting motivation/Using your reading log	**50 MINUTES** • Introduce vocabulary • Read pp. 461–469 (9 pp.)
SELECTION **The Bear** page 474 AVERAGE		**20 MINUTES** • PERSONAL CONNECTION • CULTURAL CONNECTION • WRITING CONNECTION	**60 MINUTES** • Introduce vocabulary • Read pp. 474–485 (12 pp.)
FOLK TALE ON YOUR OWN **The Lady Who Was a Beggar** page 488 AVERAGE			**60 MINUTES** • Read pp. 488–499 (12 pp.)
Writing WRITING FROM EXPERIENCE **Informative Exposition**	**Exploring Topics** **25 MINUTES**	**Prewriting** **35 MINUTES**	**Drafting and Revising** **70 MINUTES**

Time estimates assume in-class work. You may wish to assign some of these stages as homework.

427a   UNIT THREE   IN THE NAME OF LOVE

Responding to the Selection

Extension Activities

FROM PERSONAL RESPONSE TO CRITICAL ANALYSIS	OR	ANOTHER PATHWAY	LITERARY CONCEPTS	QUICKWRITES	ALTERNATIVE ACTIVITIES	LITERARY LINKS	CRITIC'S CORNER	THE WRITER'S STYLE	ACROSS THE CURRICULUM	ART CONNECTION	WORDS TO KNOW	BIOGRAPHY
50 MINUTES					**40 MINUTES**							
• Discussion questions	OR	• Character conversation	• Foreshadowing	• Literary analysis • Letter • Comic scene			✓		DRAMA		✓	✓
50 MINUTES					**20 MINUTES**							
• Discussion questions	OR	• Speaker situation	• Repetition	• Monologue • Poem		✓			MUSIC			✓
50 MINUTES					**30 MINUTES**							
• Discussion questions	OR	• Visualizing emotional states	• Rhyme/rhyme schemes • Rhythm and meter	• Song lyric • Definition • Poem	✓				WORLD LAN-GUAGES	✓		✓
50 MINUTES					**30 MINUTES**							
• Discussion questions	OR	• Television talk show	• Frame story	• Investigative notes • Letter • Opening statement	✓	✓	✓				✓	✓
50 MINUTES					**50 MINUTES**							
• Discussion questions	OR	• Character's point of view	• Allusion • Foreshadowing	• Wedding announcement • Public-service announcement • Biographical sketch	✓	✓	✓			✓	✓	✓
50 MINUTES					**40 MINUTES**							
• Discussion questions	OR	• Drama sequel	• Farce/stereotypes	• Analysis • Review • Dramatic Scene		✓	✓		DRAMA		✓	✓

Publishing and Reflecting

20 MINUTES

PART 2

REFLECTING ON THEME

Have students reflect on different ways love affects people's lives. Ask volunteers to offer examples, from literature or from their own experience, of ways people react to the mysterious powers of love.

What Do You Think?

You may want to invite students to coin a few terms to describe love. Encourage students to be as creative as they like when inventing these new phrases and words. Students will return to this activity on pages 472 and 508.

UNIT THREE PART 2

MYSTERIES OF THE HEART

REFLECTING ON THEME

Consider the Roman god of love, Cupid. Young, beautiful, mischievous—even cruel—he shoots his arrows of love, and the results are almost always unpredictable. His characteristics reflect love's mysterious powers. As you will see in this part of Unit Three, love can have a profound impact, for better or worse, on people's lives.

What Do You Think? With a group of classmates, create a brief glossary of expressions that convey the strange, wonderful, and even frightful effects of love. You may want to include phrases such as *love-crazed* and *head over heels in love*, as well as expressions that you have heard at home or through the media. Define each expression, give an example of its use, and provide a visual illustration if one would be appropriate. After reading these selections, you may have ideas for additions to the glossary.

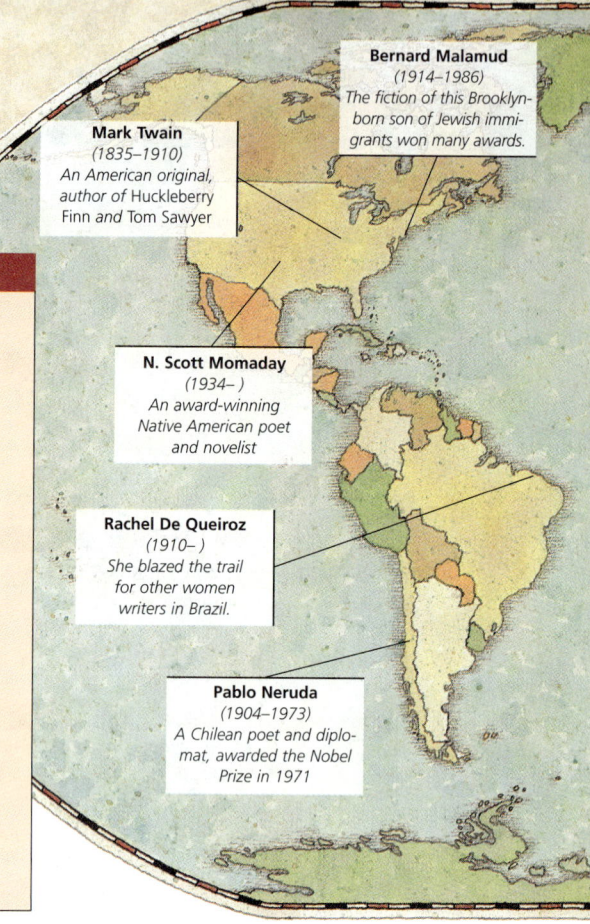

Bernard Malamud (1914–1986)
The fiction of this Brooklyn-born son of Jewish immigrants won many awards.

Mark Twain (1835–1910)
An American original, author of Huckleberry Finn and Tom Sawyer

N. Scott Momaday (1934–)
An award-winning Native American poet and novelist

Rachel De Queiroz (1910–)
She blazed the trail for other women writers in Brazil.

Pablo Neruda (1904–1973)
A Chilean poet and diplomat, awarded the Nobel Prize in 1971

Mark Twain	**The Californian's Tale** *When will she return to her devoted husband?*	430
Su Dong Po	**To a Traveler** / INSIGHT *Absence and remembrance*	438
N. Scott Momaday	**Simile** *How did love go wrong?*	441
Pablo Neruda	**Tonight I Can Write . . . /** **Puedo Escribir Los Versos . . .** *The "saddest lines" about love*	441
Aleksandr Pushkin	**To . . .** *He can't forget her.*	448

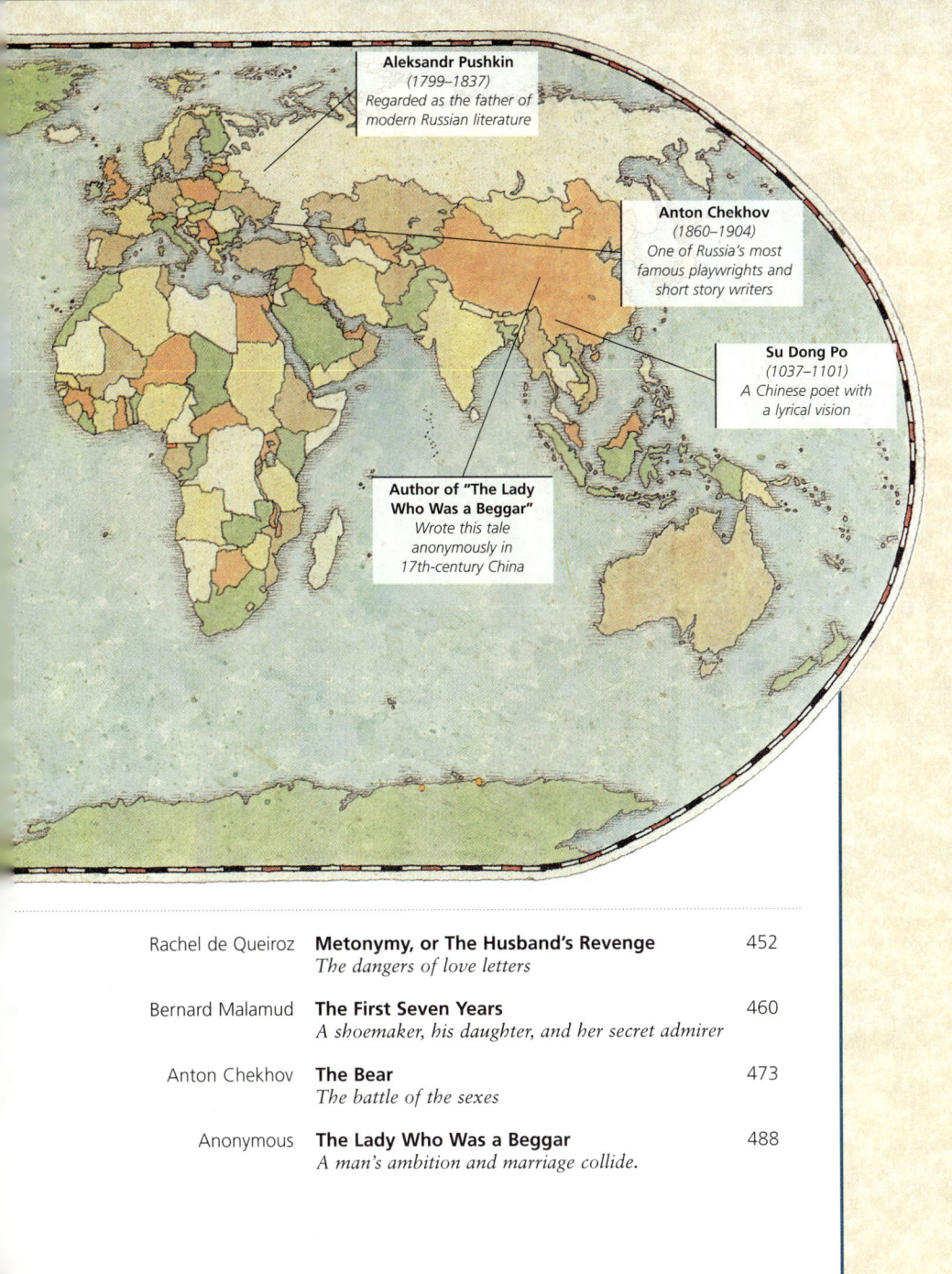

Map Note

This map emphasizes the fact that the effects of love know no geographic or political divisions. To stress this point, ask students the following questions:

- Why do you think love, as a topic for writers, crosses boundaries of nationality and ethnicity?
- What differences might you expect between Su Dong Po's interpretation of love and Mark Twain's?

Rachel de Queiroz	**Metonymy, or The Husband's Revenge** *The dangers of love letters*	452
Bernard Malamud	**The First Seven Years** *A shoemaker, his daughter, and her secret admirer*	460
Anton Chekhov	**The Bear** *The battle of the sexes*	473
Anonymous	**The Lady Who Was a Beggar** *A man's ambition and marriage collide.*	488

OVERVIEW

Objectives

- To understand and appreciate a short story about a man ensnared by the memory of love
- To identify and understand foreshadowing
- To appreciate and write dialogue
- To express understanding of a selection through a choice of writing forms, including a literary analysis, a letter, and a comic scene
- To extend understanding of the selection through a variety of multimodal and cross-curricular activities

Skills

LITERARY CONCEPTS
- Foreshadowing
- Surprise ending

READING SKILLS/ STRATEGIES
- Interpreting details about setting

THE WRITER'S STYLE
- Position of adjectives

SPEAKING, LISTENING, AND VIEWING
- Oral reading
- Art
- Pantomime
- Group discussion

HISTORICAL CONNECTION

The Gold Rush Mining towns seemed to spring up overnight in 1849 as people rushed to California to prospect for gold. Photographs of mining camps and gold prospectors offer a look at this famous period in California history.

Side A, Frame 49462

PREVIEWING

FICTION

The Californian's Tale
Mark Twain United States

Activating Prior Knowledge
PERSONAL CONNECTION

What do you think makes a house a home? Is a home created by its comfortable furnishings or the personal touches in its decoration? Is it created by the feelings of the people who live there or by the way guests are welcomed? For five minutes, do some focused freewriting in your notebook about what it takes to make a house a home.

Building Background
HISTORICAL CONNECTION

The comforts of home have a special significance for the characters in "The Californian's Tale," who live in a lonely environment in the aftermath of the California Gold Rush. Gold was first discovered in 1848 at Sutter's Mill east of Sacramento. During 1849 alone, more than 80,000 so-called "forty-niners" rushed to the California territory to prospect, or hunt, for gold in the region's many rivers and creeks. Dozens of mining towns sprang up along these waterways, and by 1850 California had grown so much that it was admitted as a state in the Union. Most settlers who came to California to strike it rich were men. In fact, women were so seldom seen that miners were known to walk miles to catch sight of one.

Once the precious ore became harder to find, many Gold Rush "boom" towns turned into ghost towns. A number of the miners returned to their families in the East. Some moved on to other regions in the West that promised gold or silver. Other veteran prospectors, however, did remain to continue their search for gold or to try their hand at farming.

Active Reading/Setting a Purpose
READING CONNECTION

Interpreting Details About Setting As you read the story, pay attention to the little domestic touches that make Henry's house seem so pleasant to the narrator. What do the details about the house reveal about Henry's wife? What do they reveal about Henry?

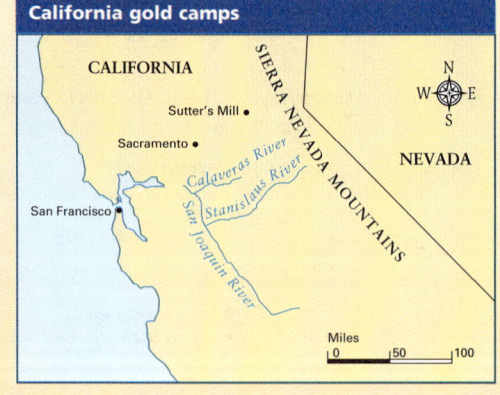

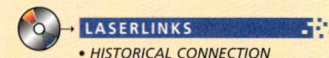
• HISTORICAL CONNECTION

430 UNIT THREE PART 2: MYSTERIES OF THE HEART

PRINT AND MEDIA RESOURCES

UNIT THREE RESOURCE BOOK
Strategic Reading: Literature, p. 39
Vocabulary SkillBuilder, p. 40

GRAMMAR MINI-LESSONS
Transparencies, pp. 22–26
Copymasters, pp. 24–27

ACCESS FOR STUDENTS ACQUIRING ENGLISH
Selection Summaries
Reading Support

FORMAL ASSESSMENT
Selection Test, pp. 85–86
 Test Generator

 **AUDIO LIBRARY**
See Reference Card

 **LASERLINKS**
Historical Connection
Author Background

INTERNET RESOURCES
McDougal Littell Literature Center at http://www.hmco.com/mcdougal/lit

---

430 THE LANGUAGE OF LITERATURE TEACHER'S EDITION

The Californian's Tale

Mark Twain

Old-Time Cabin, Maynard Dixon. Courtesy of Museum of Art, Brigham Young University. Copyright © Museum of Art, Brigham Young University, all rights reserved.

Thirty-five years ago I was out prospecting on the Stanislaus,[1] tramping all day long with pick and pan and horn, and washing a hatful of dirt here and there, always expecting to make a rich strike, and never doing it.

---

1. **Stanislaus:** a river in California where gold was mined.

WORDS TO KNOW

balmy (bä′mē) *adj.* soothingly fragrant; mild and pleasant (p. 432)
boding (bō′dĭng) *n.* a warning or omen about the future, especially of evil **bode** *v.* (p. 436)
desolation (dĕs′ə-lā′shən) *n.* the state of being empty, deserted, or forlorn; barrenness; loneliness (p. 433)
furtive (fûr′tĭv) *adj.* shifty; having a hidden motive or purpose (p. 434)
grizzled (grĭz′əld) *adj.* streaked with or partly gray (p. 432)

imploring (ĭm-plôr′ĭng) *adj.* begging; making an urgent appeal **implore** *v.* (p. 436)
predecessor (prĕd′ĭ-sĕs′ər) *n.* someone who came before and has been succeeded or replaced by another (p. 432)
sedate (sĭ-dāt′) *adj.* serenely deliberate, composed, and dignified (p. 435)
sever (sĕv′ər) *v.* to cut or break off (p. 432)
supplicating (sŭp′lĭ-kāt′ĭng) *adj.* humbly or sincerely asking, begging, or praying **supplicate** *v.* (p. 435)

SUMMARY

After prospecting all day near a lonesome old mining town, the narrator meets an ex-miner named Henry, who invites him into his rose-clad cottage. The narrator accepts the man's hospitality and walks inside a delightful home full of lovely feminine touches. Henry praises his young wife and her decorating talents. He shows the narrator a picture of his bride and begs him to stay three days until his wife's return. During the next few days, three friends drop by to ask about Henry's wife. After listening to Henry read a letter from her, they plan a party for the evening of her arrival. The night of the party, they celebrate with their friend until the hour she is to arrive, and then they drug Henry and put him to bed. They explain to the puzzled visitor that Henry's wife disappeared 19 years before. The miner lost his mind, and his friends have visited him, listened to him read the letter, and held this party each year to help him through the anniversary of her death.

Thematic Link: *Mysteries of the Heart*
Sympathetic friends keep alive a man's illusion about his beloved wife.

Art Note

Old Time Cabin by **Maynard Dixon**
Dixon portrayed not the melodramatic "Wild West" but rather the reality of day-to-day life. This painting is one of many he created during a sojourn in Utah in 1933.

Reading the Art *Who might have lived in this cabin?*

CUSTOMIZING FOR
Students Acquiring English

- Use **ACCESS FOR STUDENTS ACQUIRING ENGLISH,** Reading Support.
- The use of detailed description and imagery in this selection may prove challenging to some students. You may want to read certain sections aloud to help clarify meanings.

STRATEGIC READING FOR
Less-Proficient Readers

Set a Purpose Have students read on to find out about the cottage's owner.

Use **UNIT THREE RESOURCE BOOK,** p. 39, for guidance in reading the selection.

CUSTOMIZING FOR
Gifted and Talented Students
Tell students that while Mark Twain considered himself a foe of sentimentality, he succumbed to it in some of his works. Ask students whether "The Californian's Tale" is sentimental or realistic. Encourage them to support their opinions with details from the selection. *(Possible responses: Some students may say the story is sentimental in its exaggerated picture of a lover's grief and its manipulation of readers' emotions. Others might say it is realistic in showing a man possessed by illusion.)*

Literary Concept: DESCRIPTION
A Ask students why Twain includes descriptions of long-gone inhabitants in this exposition. *(Possible responses: to stress the present loneliness and desolation; to add to the sense of passing time.)*

CUSTOMIZING FOR
Multiple Learning Styles
B **Bodily-Kinesthetic Learners** Ask a volunteer to pantomime the changes in the traveler's attitude when he spots the owner of the cottage.

Literary Concept: FORESHADOWING
C Ask students what the description of the cottage suggests about the occupants. *(A woman also lives there.)*

Literary Concept: DESCRIPTION
D Ask students to discuss Twain's use of contrast in his description. *(He emphasizes the comforts of the cottage by contrasting it with the barren cabins.)*

> At last, in the early part of the afternoon, when I caught sight of a human creature, I felt a most grateful uplift.

A It was a lovely region, woodsy, balmy, delicious, and had once been populous, long years before, but now the people had vanished and the charming paradise was a solitude. They went away when the surface diggings gave out. In one place, where a busy little city with banks and newspapers and fire companies and a mayor and aldermen had been, was nothing but a wide expanse of emerald turf, with not even the faintest sign that human life had ever been present there. This was down toward Tuttletown.[2] In the country neighborhood thereabouts, along the dusty roads, one found at intervals the prettiest little cottage homes, snug and cozy, and so cobwebbed with vines snowed thick with roses that the doors and windows were wholly hidden from sight—sign that these were deserted homes, forsaken years ago by defeated and disappointed families who could neither sell them nor give them away. Now and then, half an hour apart, one came across solitary log cabins of the earliest mining days, built by the first gold miners, the predecessors of the cottage builders. In some few cases these cabins were still occupied; and when this was so, you could depend upon it that the occupant was the very pioneer who had built the cabin; and you could depend on another thing, too—that he was there because he had once had his opportunity to go home to the States rich, and had not done it; had rather lost his wealth, and had then in his humiliation resolved to sever all communication with his home relatives and friends, and be to them thenceforth as one dead. Round about California in that day were scattered a host of these living dead men—pride-smitten poor fellows, grizzled and old at forty, whose secret thoughts were made all of regrets and longings—regrets for their wasted lives, and longings to be out of the struggle and done with it all.

It was a lonesome land! Not a sound in all those peaceful expanses of grass and woods but the drowsy hum of insects; no glimpse of man or beast; nothing to keep up your spirits and make you glad to be alive. And so, at last, in the early part of the afternoon, when I caught sight of a human creature, I felt a most grateful uplift. This person was a man about forty-five years old, and he was standing at the gate of one of those cozy little rose-clad cottages of the sort already referred to. However, this one hadn't a deserted look; it had the look of being lived in and petted and cared for and looked after; and so had its front yard, which was a garden of flowers, abundant, gay, and flourishing. I was invited in, of course, and required to make myself at home—it was the custom of the country. **B**

It was delightful to be in such a place, after long weeks of daily and nightly familiarity with miners' cabins—with all which this implies of dirt floor, never-made beds, tin plates and cups, **C**

D

---

[2] **Tuttletown:** a mining town near the Stanislaus River.

WORDS TO KNOW
balmy (bä′mē) *adj.* soothingly fragrant; mild and pleasant
predecessor (prĕd′ĭ-sĕs′ər) *n.* someone who came before and has been succeeded or replaced by another
sever (sĕv′ər) *v.* to cut or break off
grizzled (grĭz′əld) *adj.* streaked with or partly gray

Mini-Lesson The Writer's Style

POSITION OF ADJECTIVES Remind students that an adjective is a word that describes a noun or a pronoun. Direct students' attention to the passages highlighted on this page. Point out that adjectives usually appear before the nouns or pronouns that they modify. ("It was a *lonesome* land!") Then show students that sometimes, for variety, for emphasis, or to add details, a writer might put adjectives both before and after the noun. ("It was a *lovely* region, *woodsy, balmy, delicious. . . .*")

Application Ask students to discuss what effect Twain creates by using adjectives in this way. Then invite them to write a paragraph describing the setting of "The Californian's Tale," using adjectives before and after nouns or the pronouns they modify.

Reteaching/Reinforcement
- *Grammar Handbook*, anthology pp. 1076–1080
- *Grammar Mini-Lessons* copymasters, pp. 24–27, transparencies pp. 22–26

 The Writer's Craft
Adjectives, pp. 541–543

bacon and beans and black coffee, and nothing of ornament but war pictures from the Eastern illustrated papers tacked to the log walls. That was all hard, cheerless, materialistic desolation, but here was a nest which had aspects to rest the tired eye and refresh that something in one's nature which, after long fasting, recognizes, when confronted by the belongings of art, howsoever cheap and modest they may be, that it has unconsciously been famishing and now has found nourishment. I could not have believed that a rag carpet could feast me so, and so content me; or that there could be such solace to the soul in wallpaper and framed lithographs,³ and bright-colored tidies⁴ and lamp mats, and Windsor chairs,⁵ and varnished whatnots,⁶ with seashells and books and china vases on them, and the score of little unclassifiable tricks and touches that a woman's hand distributes about a home, which one sees without knowing he sees them, yet would miss in a moment if they were taken away. The delight that was in my heart showed in my face, and the man saw it and was pleased; saw it so plainly that he answered it as if it had been spoken.

"All her work," he said, caressingly; "she did it all herself—every bit," and he took the room in with a glance which was full of affectionate worship. One of those soft Japanese fabrics with which women drape with careful negligence the upper part of a picture frame was out of adjustment. He noticed it, and rearranged it with cautious pains, stepping back several times to gauge the effect before he got it to suit him. Then he gave it a light finishing pat or two with his hand, and said: "She always does that. You can't tell just what it lacks, but it does lack something until you've done that—you can see it yourself after it's done, but that is all you know; you can't find out the law of it. It's like the finishing pats a mother gives the child's hair after she's got it combed and brushed, I reckon. I've seen her fix all these things so much that I can do them all just her way, though I don't know the law of any of them. But she knows the law. She knows the why and the how both; but I don't know the why; I only know the how."

He took me into a bedroom so that I might wash my hands; such a bedroom as I had not seen for years: white counterpane,⁷ white pillows, carpeted floor, papered walls, pictures, dressing table, with mirror and pincushion and dainty toilet things; and in the corner a washstand, with real chinaware bowl and pitcher, and with soap in a china dish, and on a rack more than a dozen towels—towels too clean and white for one out of practice to use without some vague sense of profanation.⁸ So my face spoke again, and he answered with gratified words:

"All her work; she did it all herself—every bit. Nothing here that hasn't felt the touch of her hand. Now you would think—But I mustn't talk so much."

---

3. **lithographs:** prints made by a process in which portions of a flat surface are treated either to retain or to repel ink.
4. **tidies:** decorative coverings for the arms or headrest of a chair or sofa.
5. **Windsor chairs:** wooden chairs with high-spoked backs, outward-slanting legs, and saddle seats.
6. **whatnots:** a set of light, open shelves for displaying ornaments.
7. **counterpane:** bedspread.
8. **profanation:** the showing of contempt for something regarded as sacred.

WORDS TO KNOW
desolation (dĕs′ə-lā′shən) *n.* the state of being empty, deserted, or forlorn; barrenness; loneliness

433

Critic's Corner

"... the lie, as a virtue, a principle, is eternal; the lie, as a recreation, a solace, a refuge in time of need, the fourth Grace, the tenth Muse, man's best and surest friend, is immortal...."

Mark Twain
"On the Decay of the Art of Lying"

Ask students to consider Twain's meaning in the light of this tale.

Art Note

***Into the Past* by Hananiah Harari** This oil painting by Harari (1912–) recaptures the atmosphere of earlier times through a collage of items including an old, stamped envelope; a postcard of an old building; and antique photographs of a child and a woman in 19th-century dress.

Reading the Art *How does the artist portray the passage of time? What mood or feeling does the picture create?*

CUSTOMIZING FOR
Students Acquiring English

(2) Tell students that *apt* means "likely."

Critical Thinking: SPECULATING

(H) Ask students to pause here and guess what the "something" might be that the man wishes the narrator to discover. Then have them read on to find out what the "something" is *(a picture)*. Discuss whether this answer is what students expected. Some students may sense that a further mystery is foreshadowed.

Into the Past (1941), Hananiah Harari. Oil on canvas, 15″ × 12⅞″, Richard York Gallery, New York.

By this time I was wiping my hands and glancing from detail to detail of the room's belongings, as one is apt to do when he is in a new place, where everything he sees is a comfort to his eye and his spirit; and I became conscious, in one of those unaccountable ways, you know, that there was something there somewhere that the man wanted me to discover for myself. I knew it perfectly, and I knew he was trying to help me by furtive indications with his eye, so I tried hard to get on the right track, being eager to gratify him. I failed several times, as I could see out of the corner of my eye without being told; but at last I knew I must be looking straight at the thing—knew it from the pleasure issuing in invisible waves from him. He broke into a happy laugh, and rubbed his hands together, and cried out:

"That's it! You've found it. I knew you would. It's her picture."

WORDS TO KNOW

furtive (fûr′tĭv) *adj.* shifty; having a hidden motive or purpose

434 THE LANGUAGE OF LITERATURE TEACHER'S EDITION

I went to the little black-walnut bracket[9] on the farther wall, and did find there what I had not yet noticed—a daguerreotype case.[10] It contained the sweetest girlish face, and the most beautiful, as it seemed to me, that I had ever seen. The man drank the admiration from my face, and was fully satisfied.

"Nineteen her last birthday," he said, as he put the picture back; "and that was the day we were married. When you see her—ah, just wait till you see her!"

"Where is she? When will she be in?"

"Oh, she's away now. She's gone to see her people. They live forty or fifty miles from here. She's been gone two weeks today."

"When do you expect her back?"

"This is Wednesday. She'll be back Saturday, in the evening—about nine o'clock, likely."

I felt a sharp sense of disappointment.

"I'm sorry, because I'll be gone then," I said, regretfully.

"Gone? No—why should you go? Don't go. She'll be so disappointed."

She would be disappointed—that beautiful creature! If she had said the words herself they could hardly have blessed me more. I was feeling a deep, strong longing to see her—a longing so supplicating, so insistent, that it made me afraid. I said to myself: "I will go straight away from this place, for my peace of mind's sake."

"You see, she likes to have people come and stop with us—people who know things, and can talk—people like you. She delights in it; for she knows—oh, she knows nearly everything herself, and can talk, oh, like a bird—and the books she reads, why, you would be astonished. Don't go; it's only a little while, you know, and she'll be so disappointed."

I heard the words, but hardly noticed them, I was so deep in my thinkings and strugglings. He left me, but I didn't know. Presently he was back, with the picture case in his hand, and he held it open before me and said:

"There, now, tell her to her face you could have stayed to see her, and you wouldn't."

That second glimpse broke down my good resolution. I would stay and take the risk. That night we smoked the tranquil pipe, and talked till late about various things, but mainly about her; and certainly I had had no such pleasant and restful time for many a day. The Thursday followed and slipped comfortably away. Toward twilight a big miner from three miles away came—one of the grizzled, stranded pioneers—and gave us warm salutation, clothed in grave and sober speech. Then he said:

"I only just dropped over to ask about the little madam, and when is she coming home. Any news from her?"

"Oh yes, a letter. Would you like to hear it, Tom?"

"Well, I should think I would, if you don't mind, Henry!"

Henry got the letter out of his wallet, and said he would skip some of the private phrases, if we were willing; then he went on and read the bulk of it—a loving, sedate, and altogether charming and gracious piece of handiwork, with a postscript full of affectionate regards and messages to Tom, and Joe, and Charley, and other close friends and neighbors.

As the reader finished, he glanced at Tom, and cried out:

"Oho, you're at it again! Take your hands away, and let me see your eyes. You always do

---

9. **bracket:** a small shelf.
10. **daguerreotype** (də-gâr′ə-tīp′) **case:** a frame-like case holding an early type of photograph.

| WORDS TO KNOW | **supplicating** (sŭp′lĭ-kāt′ĭng) *adj.* humbly or sincerely asking, begging, or praying
supplicate *v.*
sedate (sĭ-dāt′) *adj.* serenely deliberate, composed, and dignified |

435

Literary Concept:
FORESHADOWING

L Ask students what the miners' crying may indicate. *(Possible responses: They are easily moved because they are getting old, as Tom says; they feel nostalgic; they are moved by the letter from Henry's wife.)* Ask students what they think all this emotion is foreshadowing. *(Possible responses: a sad ending; an accident)*

CUSTOMIZING FOR
Students Acquiring English

3 Explain to students that *broke the old fellow all up* means "made him cry."

Critical Thinking:
MAKING JUDGMENTS

M Encourage students to discuss the emotions displayed in the narrator's flare-up at Henry. Suggest that they consider how they feel about Henry's behavior and whether the narrator was justified in getting angry. *(Accept all reasonable responses.)*

Literary Concept:
FORESHADOWING

N Ask students how they respond to Charley's hearty reassurances that nothing has happened to Henry's wife. *(Many students will guess that this means something disastrous has happened to her.)*

> *"I'm getting old, you know, and any little disappointment makes me want to cry. I thought she'd be here herself, and now you've got only a letter."*

that when I read a letter from her. I will write and tell her."

"Oh no, you mustn't, Henry. I'm getting old, you know, and any little disappointment makes me want to cry. I thought she'd be here herself, and now you've got only a letter."

"Well, now, what put that in your head? I thought everybody knew she wasn't coming till Saturday."

"Saturday! Why, come to think, I did know it. I wonder what's the matter with me lately? Certainly I knew it. Ain't we all getting ready for her? Well, I must be going now. But I'll be on hand when she comes, old man!"

Late Friday afternoon another gray veteran tramped over from his cabin a mile or so away, and said the boys wanted to have a little gaiety and a good time Saturday night, if Henry thought she wouldn't be too tired after her journey to be kept up.

"Tired? She tired! Oh, hear the man! Joe, *you* know she'd sit up six weeks to please any one of you!"

When Joe heard that there was a letter, he asked to have it read, and the loving messages in it for him broke the old fellow all up; but he said he was such an old wreck that *that* would happen to him if she only just mentioned his name. "Lord, we miss her so!" he said.

Saturday afternoon I found I was taking out my watch pretty often. Henry noticed it, and said, with a startled look:

"You don't think she ought to be here so soon, do you?"

I felt caught, and a little embarrassed; but I laughed, and said it was a habit of mine when I was in a state of expectancy. But he didn't seem quite satisfied; and from that time on he began to show uneasiness. Four times he walked me up the road to a point whence we could see a long distance; and there he would stand, shading his eyes with his hand, and looking. Several times he said:

"I'm getting worried, I'm getting right down worried. I know she's not due till about nine o'clock, and yet something seems to be trying to warn me that something's happened. You don't think anything has happened, do you?"

I began to get pretty thoroughly ashamed of him for his childishness; and at last, when he repeated that <u>imploring</u> question still another time, I lost my patience for the moment, and spoke pretty brutally to him. It seemed to shrivel him up and cow[11] him; and he looked so wounded and so humble after that, that I detested myself for having done the cruel and unnecessary thing. And so I was glad when Charley, another veteran, arrived toward the edge of the evening, and nestled up to Henry to hear the letter read, and talked over the preparations for the welcome. Charley fetched out one hearty speech after another, and did his best to drive away his friend's <u>bodings</u> and apprehensions.

"Anything *happened* to her? Henry, that's pure nonsense. There isn't anything going to happen to her; just make your mind easy as to that. What did the letter say? Said she was well,

---
11. **cow:** to intimidate; to frighten with threats or a show of force.

WORDS TO KNOW
imploring (ĭm-plôr´ĭng) *adj.* begging; making an urgent appeal **implore** *v.*
boding (bō´dĭng) *n.* a warning or omen about the future, especially of evil **bode** *v.*

436

Assessment Option

INFORMAL ASSESSMENT Have students write a journal entry in the first-person voice of the narrator or of one of Henry's friends, recounting the events of the story and giving the journal writer's views about Henry, Henry's wife, and the strange annual ritual. If students wish, they may read their journal entries aloud or exchange them with partners to read and compare.

Rubric

3 Full Accomplishment The journal entries accurately recount the events of the story, and show insight into such themes as the endurance of love and the role of illusion.

2 Substantial Accomplishment Journal entries sketch in the events.

1 Little or Partial Accomplishment Journal entries contain inaccuracies about significant events of the story and fail to recognize its themes.

436 THE LANGUAGE OF LITERATURE TEACHER'S EDITION

didn't it? And said she'd *be* here by nine o'clock, didn't it? Did you ever know her to fail of her word? Why, you know you never did. Well, then, don't you fret; she'll be here, and that's absolutely certain, and as sure as you are born. Come, now, let's get to decorating—not much time left."

Pretty soon Tom and Joe arrived, and then all hands set about adorning the house with flowers. Toward nine the three miners said that as they had brought their instruments they might as well tune up, for the boys and girls would soon be arriving now, and hungry for a good, old-fashioned breakdown.[12] A fiddle, a banjo, and a clarinet—these were the instruments. The trio took their places side by side, and began to play some rattling dance music, and beat time with their big boots.

It was getting very close to nine. Henry was standing in the door with his eyes directed up the road, his body swaying to the torture of his mental distress. He had been made to drink his wife's health and safety several times, and now Tom shouted:

"All hands stand by! One more drink, and she's here!"

Joe brought the glasses on a waiter,[13] and served the party. I reached for one of the two remaining glasses, but Joe growled, under his breath:

"Drop that! Take the other."

Which I did. Henry was served last. He had hardly swallowed his drink when the clock began to strike. He listened till it finished, his face growing pale and paler; then he said:

"Boys, I'm sick with fear. Help me—I want to lie down!"

They helped him to the sofa. He began to nestle and drowse, but presently spoke like one talking in his sleep, and said: "Did I hear horses' feet? Have they come?"

One of the veterans answered, close to his ear: "It was Jimmy Parrish come to say the party got delayed, but they're right up the road a piece, and coming along. Her horse is lame, but she'll be here in half an hour."

"Oh, I'm *so* thankful nothing has happened!"

He was asleep almost before the words were out of his mouth. In a moment those handy men had his clothes off, and had tucked him into his bed in the chamber where I had washed my hands. They closed the door and came back. Then they seemed preparing to leave; but I said: "Please don't go, gentlemen. She won't know me; I am a stranger."

They glanced at each other. Then Joe said:

"She? Poor thing, she's been dead nineteen years!"

"Dead?"

"That or worse. She went to see her folks half a year after she was married, and on her way back, on a Saturday evening, the Indians captured her within five miles of this place, and she's never been heard of since."

"And he lost his mind in consequence?"

"Never has been sane an hour since. But he only gets bad when that time of the year comes round. Then we begin to drop in here, three days before she's due, to encourage him up, and ask if he's heard from her, and Saturday we all come and fix up the house with flowers, and get everything ready for a dance. We've done it every year for nineteen years. The first Saturday there was twenty-seven of us, without counting the girls; there's only three of us now, and the girls are all gone. We drug him to sleep, or he would go wild; then he's all right for another year—thinks she's with him till the last three or four days come round; then he begins to look for her, and gets out his poor old letter, and we come and ask him to read it to us. Lord, she was a darling!" ❖

---

12. **breakdown:** a noisy, energetic American country dance.
13. **waiter:** a tray.

THE CALIFORNIAN'S TALE **437**

Mini-Lesson Literary Concepts

SURPRISE ENDING Remind students that a surprise ending is an unexpected twist in plot at the conclusion of a story. In some works a surprise ending is foreshadowed, or subtly hinted at, throughout the course of the work. Some of the most effective surprise endings are those for which the author has prepared the reader. The writer E.M. Forster once said, "The shock of the unexpected, followed by the feeling 'oh, that's all right' is a sign that all is well with the plot."

Application Invite students to discuss the pros and cons of surprise endings. Suggest that they base their discussion on examples from and their reactions to this selection.

INSIGHT

1. Who do you think the speaker of the poem is? *(Possible responses: a lover, husband, or wife, whose partner has left and not returned)*
2. How does the speaker console him/herself during the absence of the beloved? *(Possible responses: toasts the beloved with wine; imagines that they are united in thought; imagines the moon's light connecting them)*
3. How is the speaker's attitude different from Henry's in "The Californian's Tale"? *(Possible response: the speaker in the poem has a good grasp of reality; Henry in the story is deluded. The poem's speaker seems resigned; Henry is impatient and worried.)*

SU DONG PO

Like many other Chinese poets, Su Dong Po (the pen name of Su Shih) was a public official as well as a poet. Born in 1036 into a distinguished literary family, he performed brilliantly in the official examinations that were required for office. Though he was a popular administrator, his career took many twists and turns because of political intrigue. He was exiled to remote provinces and even imprisoned for three months because of his views. His poetry is distinguished by realistic details of ordinary life, optimism, and philosophical musing. In addition to being one of the greatest Chinese poets, he was also an excellent essayist, painter, and calligrapher.

INSIGHT

To a Traveler
Su Dong Po

Last year when I accompanied you
As far as the Yang Chou Gate,
The snow was flying, like white willow cotton.
This year, Spring has come again,
5 And the willow cotton is like snow.
But you have not come back.
Alone before the open window,
I raise my wine cup to the shining moon.
The wind, moist with evening dew,
10 Blows the gauze curtains.

Maybe Chang-O the moon goddess,
Will pity this single swallow
And join us together with the cord of light
That reaches beneath the painted eaves of your home.

Translated by Kenneth Rexroth

Multicultural Perspectives

TRAVEL LITERATURE Travel literature, a popular genre in the modern United States, was a highly developed literary form centuries ago in both Asia and Europe. *The Travels of Marco Polo* (1254–1324?) chronicle the adventures of a young Venetian merchant in the court of the Chinese emperor Kublai Khan. The extent to which they were fictionalized is still a matter for scholarly debate, but the book remains very readable. A beautiful travel book by a great Asian poet is *The Narrow Road to the Deep North*, by the Japanese haiku master Basho (1644–1694). Interspersing seemingly offhand travel jottings with haiku, Basho achieves rare insight into the beauty of life's transience.

RESPONDING OPTIONS

FROM PERSONAL RESPONSE TO CRITICAL ANALYSIS

REFLECT
1. Were you surprised by the outcome of this story? Explain why or why not in your notebook, and then share your writing with a classmate.

RETHINK
2. How would you describe Henry?
   Consider
   Close Textual Reading
   - how Henry has taken care of his home
   - Henry's expectation of his wife's return
   - the anxiety that Henry experiences on Saturday night

3. Why do you think the narrator becomes so fascinated by Henry's wife?
   Consider
   Close Textual Reading
   - the narrator's description of the cottage and the wife's photograph
   - what Henry says about her
   - the type of life the narrator has led

4. Do you think the miners exercise good judgment in staging a welcome home party for Henry's wife year after year? Why or why not?

RELATE
Thematic Link
5. What does the speaker in Su Dong Po's poem "To a Traveler" have in common with Henry?

Multimodal Learning
ANOTHER PATHWAY
Cooperative Learning
What happens after the story ends? Get together with three other classmates and continue the conversation among the narrator, Tom, Charley, and Joe, with each student acting out a role. Talk over what happened that night, tell stories about past gatherings and share impressions of the wife.

QUICKWRITES

1. Write a **literary analysis** in which you explain what the setting—the house and its surroundings—reveals about the lives of Henry and his wife.

2. Write the wife's **letter** that Henry has treasured for so many years. Be sure to incorporate the details about the letter's content that the story provides.

3. Imagine that Henry's wife actually returns, 19 years after leaving. Write a **comic scene** in which Henry and his wife are reunited but find it difficult to adjust to the changes in each other. Be sure to include the wife's explanation for her absence.

 PORTFOLIO Save your writing. You may want to use it later as a springboard to a piece for your portfolio.

LITERARY CONCEPTS

Foreshadowing is a writer's use of hints or clues to indicate events that will occur later in a narrative. This technique often creates suspense and prepares the reader for what is to come. In "The Californian's Tale," for example, the crying of Henry's friends upon hearing the wife's letter foreshadows the ending of the story, where we learn that the wife has been long gone. With a partner, find three more examples of foreshadowing in "The Californian's Tale." Which of them—if any—did you recognize as foreshadowing when you first read the story? What effect did they have on you? Share your responses with the rest of the class.

THE CALIFORNIAN'S TALE **439**

From Personal Response to Critical Analysis

1. Accept all reasonable responses.
2. Accept all well-supported responses. Possible responses include loving, devoted, lovesick, deluded, crazy, pitiful.
3. Possible responses: Some students may say the narrator's fascination results from his roving, prospecting life, which has isolated him from women and comfort for a long time. Others might say Henry's description of his wife and the photograph of her make her very appealing to the narrator.
4. Possible responses: Yes—they are acting from kindness and concern, helping Henry bear grief which he would not otherwise survive; no—they are keeping an illusion alive rather than helping Henry face reality.
5. Both the speaker of the poem and Henry miss a beloved partner; both wait longingly for the beloved's return.

Another Pathway

Cooperative Learning Student actors should review the story beforehand. One member of the group might summarize the events and record the group's ideas for extending the story, while another member checks the accuracy of the character portrayals. During rehearsals, one student might give support to the actors.

Rubric

3 Full Accomplishment The conversation is faithful to the characters and the events of Twain's story and extends the story imaginatively.

2 Substantial Accomplishment The conversation is faithful to the facts of the story but may portray characters inaccurately.

1 Little or Partial Accomplishment Students do not convincingly play the characters or discuss the events.

Literary Concepts

Students will find many examples of foreshadowing in this story. Some will have enjoyed guessing the outcome, while others may find that it was too obvious. Discuss the technique of foreshadowing by asking:
- When and how did you guess the ending of the story?
- Did you think the foreshadowing was too heavy-handed, too subtle, or just right?

QuickWrites

1. Remind students that their analyses should have strong thesis statements and that they should support their theses with specific details from the story.
2. Challenge students to study the dialogue and diction in Twain's story and try to replicate it in their letters.
3. Students may write their scenes either in narrative form or in play form.

The Writer's Craft

Writing About Literature, pp. 237–253
Components of Voice, pp. 420–422
Story, pp. 102–107

Words To Know

1. d
2. b
3. c
4. b
5. d
6. a
7. a
8. c
9. b
10. c

Reteaching/Reinforcement
• *Unit Three Resource Book*, p. 4

Across the Curriculum

Drama *Cooperative Learning*
Improvisation will allows students to create dialogue that expands upon the dialogue in the story. After assigning roles, students might first improvise dialogue, tape-recording it as they do so. A production editor can listen to the tape and suggest changes. Then each actor can write his or her own dialogue for the script. One group member can write stage directions, and another can plan sets, costumes, and props.

MARK TWAIN

Twain wrote "The Californian's Tale" in the summer of 1892, after a trip through Switzerland and Italy. The subject of a husband's grief over the death of his beloved wife may have been connected to Twain's concern over the health of his wife Livy, although at the time he wrote the story, she had received a promising report from her physicians. The background for the story's setting dates back to Twain's experiences at Angel's Camp in gold-mining country in 1864–1865, when he had met grizzled, failed miners like those he later described.

AUTHOR BACKGROUND
Mark Twain Mark Twain began his writing career, developed his unique voice, and gained his first measure of fame in the American West. This film shows some of the people, places, and events that influenced Twain early in his career.

Side A, Frame 22676

Multimodal Learning
ALTERNATIVE ACTIVITIES

1. Create a **painting** of either the landscape described at the beginning of the story or the interior of Henry's house. Try to capture the mood of either setting.

2. In a small group, act out the story in **pantomime**, using movement and facial expressions to convey the action and emotions of the characters.

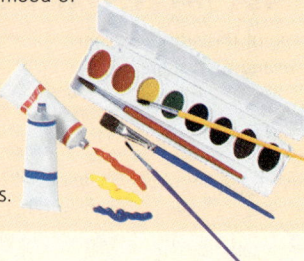

Multimodal Learning
THE WRITER'S STYLE

Mark Twain developed a distinctly American style. He wrote for the ear, capturing the voices of his characters like no other author of his time. In a small group, take turns reading aloud the dialogue from the story. What do you notice about Twain's use of dialogue?

ACROSS THE CURRICULUM

Drama Working in a small group, write a script for a dramatic presentation of "The Californian's Tale." In your stage directions, include information about sets, costumes, and props.

MARK TWAIN

Mark Twain—whose real name was Samuel Clemens—grew up in the Mississippi River port of Hannibal, Missouri. Before becoming a writer, Twain worked first as a printer and then as a steamboat pilot on the Mississippi, but when the river was closed to commercial traffic during the Civil War, he headed west to prospect for gold. He supported himself by writing for local newspapers, adopting his pen name from a riverman's term for water two fathoms deep, or just deep enough for safe navigation.

Although Twain never struck it rich in the western mines, he did successfully mine his western experiences to win fame and fortune as a writer. In 1865, one of his California tall tales, "The Celebrated Jumping Frog of Calaveras County," was published in a New York newspaper. The story became an immediate hit, launching a writing career that earned international acclaim. Twain's two most famous books, *The Adventures of Tom Sawyer* and *The Adventures of Huckleberry Finn,* drew their inspiration from his own wild and spirited boyhood along the Mississippi River. He is also remembered for his satires, his humorous tall tales, his travel sketches, and his public lectures.

1835–1910

OTHER WORKS *Innocents Abroad, A Connecticut Yankee in King Arthur's Court, Mark Twain's Speeches*

Extended Reading
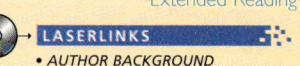
• AUTHOR BACKGROUND

440 UNIT THREE PART 2: MYSTERIES OF THE HEART

WORDS TO KNOW

Write the letter of the word that is not similar in meaning to the other words in each numbered set.

1. (a) calm (b) sedate (c) controlled (d) disturbed
2. (a) forefather (b) follower (c) ancestor (d) predecessor
3. (a) sever (b) cut (c) join (d) amputate
4. (a) mild (b) irritating (c) balmy (d) refreshing
5. (a) supplicating (b) seeking (c) appealing (d) denying
6. (a) cheerfulness (b) emptiness (c) bleakness (d) desolation
7. (a) memory (b) prediction (c) boding (d) foretelling
8. (a) old (b) grizzled (c) young (d) aged
9. (a) deceitful (b) open (c) mysterious (d) furtive
10. (a) imploring (b) pleading (c) commanding (d) begging

The Writer's Style

Twain's style of dialogue may seem elaborate to students today because styles of speech have changed drastically in the hundred years since he wrote. In its time, however, Twain's dialogue was considered refreshingly informal, as in his use of interrupted sentences, such as, ". . . for she knows-oh, she knows nearly everything herself, and can talk, oh, like a bird—" (page 435). Students may also note that Twain uses dialogue to develop characters and move the plot along. You might suggest that students rewrite Twain's dialogue in present-day style.

The Writer's Craft
Using Dialogue in Fiction, pp. 452–453

Alternative Activities

1. Encourage students to reread the passages that describe their chosen settings, and to make rough annotated sketches. Remind students that color, line, and shading are powerful conveyors of mood.

2. Students may wish to use a sheet of paper as a prop to symbolize the wife's letter to Henry. Pantomiming the musicians at the party might also be an effective, enjoyable part of the show. An ambitious mime might wish to perform all the characters, while a partner narrates the action.

440 THE LANGUAGE OF LITERATURE

PREVIEWING

POETRY

Simile
N. Scott Momaday (mä′mə-dā) United States

Tonight I Can Write . . . / Peudo Escribir Los Versos . . .
Pablo Neruda (nĕ-rōō′də) Chile

Activating Prior Knowledge
PERSONAL CONNECTION

The natural world can sometimes seem to hold up a mirror to your emotions. For example, if you are in a bad mood on a rainy day, you may think that the weather reflects how you feel. In a small group, discuss how elements in nature may seem to reflect various human emotions. Together, brainstorm a list of images from nature that suggest feelings such as sadness, love, or regret. Share your ideas with the rest of the class.

Building Background
LITERARY CONNECTION

Poets often illuminate human emotions and experiences by drawing comparisons to the natural world. In the first part of this unit, you saw how Shakespeare compared a loved one to a summer's day, while Luis Lloréns Torres described his loved one in terms of a bird. Frequently, poets employ figures of speech, such as similes and metaphors, to make their comparisons. Another common figure of speech is **personification,** which attributes human qualities to an object, animal, or idea. In the following two poems, various figures of speech are used to express the emotions felt by the speakers.

Active Reading/Setting a Purpose
READING CONNECTION

Understanding Comparisons As you read, pay careful attention to descriptions of the natural world and what they suggest about the speaker's emotions and experience. Complete a chart like the one below for each poem. In the first column, list each image from nature that you find. In the second column, describe the human emotions or experiences that are suggested by that image.

Image from nature	Suggested human emotions or experiences

SIMILE / TONIGHT I CAN WRITE . . . **441**

OVERVIEW

Objectives
- To understand and appreciate two poems about love and loss
- To examine repetition in poetry
- To review figurative language in poetry
- To express understanding of the selection through a choice of writing forms, including a monologue and a poem
- To extend understanding of the poem through a variety of multimodal and cross-curricular activities

Skills

LITERARY CONCEPTS
- Repetition
- Figurative language

SPEAKING, LISTENING, AND VIEWING
- Choral reading
- Music
- Group discussion

ALTERNATIVE
Previewing

Students can choose partners and use the following prompts to preview the poems orally.

Personal Connection

Discussion Prompts *People often feel that nature reflects their emotions. With a partner, discuss the connection between nature and human emotions. Ask the following questions:*

- *What aspects of nature have the greatest effect on your life?*
- *What feelings do those aspects of nature stir in you?*

As you read "Simile" and "Tonight I Can Write . . .," notice how the writers make use of images from nature to express their feelings.

CUSTOMIZING FOR
Students Acquiring English

- Use **ACCESS FOR STUDENTS ACQUIRING ENGLISH**, Reading Support.
- You may want to guide students line by line through the poems, paraphrasing the meaning as you go.
- In addition to these boxes, you may want to use the suggestions under Strategic Reading for Less-Proficient Readers.

PRINT AND MEDIA RESOURCES

UNIT THREE RESOURCE BOOK
Strategic Reading: Literature, p. 43

ACCESS FOR STUDENTS ACQUIRING ENGLISH
Reading Support

FORMAL ASSESSMENT
Selection Test, p. 87
 Test Generator

AUDIO LIBRARY
See Reference Card

 Simile

N. Scott Momaday

What did we say to each other
that now we are as the deer
who walk in single file
with heads high
with ears forward
with eyes watchful
with hooves always placed on
    firm ground
in whose limbs there is latent flight

8 **latent** (lāt′nt): present but not active; potential.

FROM PERSONAL RESPONSE TO CRITICAL ANALYSIS

REFLECT 1. Draw a quick sketch of the first image that came to mind when you finished reading "Simile." Share your drawing with a partner.

RETHINK 2. Review the chart that you created for the Reading Connection on page 441. In your opinion, what human emotions and experiences are being compared to "the deer who walk in single file"?

Close Textual Reading

Consider
- the relationship between the speaker and the person being addressed
- the physical description of the deer
- what is suggested by the first line of the poem

3. How do you think the speaker feels about the future of the relationship that he is describing? Explain your opinion.

RELATE 4. Is it possible for two people to remain close without sometimes quarreling? Share your opinions with classmates.

Corn Maiden (1982), David Dawangyumptewa.
Photo Copyright © 1987 by Jerry Jacka.

442   UNIT THREE PART 2: MYSTERIES OF THE HEART

Art Note

Corn Maiden by David Dawangyumptewa In this watercolor painting, Hopi artist David Dawangyumptewa portrays the Corn Maiden legend of his people. In the top center, the sun shines in the starry sky. Below the sun are stylized clouds, the rainbringers. The two Corn Maidens signify ripeness and plenty.

Reading the Art Study the composition of the painting. Why do you think the sun and the maidens are placed where they are?

CUSTOMIZING FOR
Gifted and Talented Students

To link "Simile" with the bilingual presentation of "Tonight I Can Write . . . ," invite students working singly or in pairs to translate "Simile" into a foreign language they are studying. You may also wish to encourage students who do not know Spanish to decipher as much as they can of Neruda's original verse by comparing it to W. S. Merwin's translation.

Mini-Lesson Literary Concepts

REVIEWING FIGURATIVE LANGUAGE
Remind students that figurative language communicates ideas beyond the literal meaning of words. It can make descriptions and unfamiliar or difficult ideas easier to understand. The most common types of figurative language, called figures of speech, are simile, metaphor, personification, and hyperbole.

Application Invite pairs or small groups of students to brainstorm about natural phenomena or natural objects, other than animals, to which a human couple might be compared. Ask each group to choose the comparison it likes best and to develop the comparison, using a list like the one shown.

> COUPLE = THUNDER & LIGHTNING
> • both are found together
> • they are different aspects of the same thing but they have separate identities
> • they travel together
> • their effects are electrical

STRATEGIC READING FOR
Less-Proficient Readers

Set a Purpose Have a volunteer read the title and the first line aloud. Invite students to predict what this poem will be about.

Use **UNIT THREE RESOURCE BOOK**, p. 43, for guidance in reading the selection.

CUSTOMIZING FOR
Students Acquiring English

I Have students who are fluent in Spanish read the original version aloud for the class. Then ask them to compare the original with the English translation, and encourage them to explain any aspects of the translation with which they disagree. Invite them to suggest other ways in which these lines could be translated.

Literary Concept:
FIGURATIVE LANGUAGE

C Ask students what type of figure of speech is used in the phrase "the blue winds shiver" *(personification)* What purpose does this use of personification serve? *(Possible response: It reflects the speaker's emotions.)*

Literary Concept: **REPETITION**

D Ask students to identify the ways in which this line repeats line 6. *(Both lines follow the same grammatical structure, and most of the words are identical. However, line 6 suggests that the woman was not constant in her love, while this line suggests the opposite.)*

Critical Thinking: **ANALYZING**

E Ask students to analyze the speaker's feelings here. *(Possible responses: The speaker seems internally divided. On one hand, he tries to minimize the ending of the relationship, stating "What does it matter." On the other hand, he seems sad, lonely, and regretful; his "soul is not satisfied that it has lost her.")*

Critical Thinking: **SPECULATING**

F Ask students to speculate about why the speaker uses the third-person pronoun "it" to refer to his soul. *(Possible response: Perhaps the speaker feels separated from the deepest part of himself, what he calls "my soul." His use of the pronoun may be a further indication of his divided feelings about the woman.)*

TONIGHT
I Can Write...
PABLO NERUDA

I Tonight I can write the saddest lines.

C Write, for example, 'The night is shattered
and the blue stars shiver in the distance.'
The night wind revolves in the sky and sings.

5 Tonight I can write the saddest lines.
I loved her, and sometimes she loved me too.
Through nights like this one I held her in my arms.
I kissed her again and again under the endless sky.

D She loved me, sometimes I loved her too.
10 How could one not have loved her great still eyes.

Tonight I can write the saddest lines.
To think that I do not have her. To feel that I have lost her.
To hear the immense night, still more immense without her.
And the verse falls to the soul like dew to the pasture.

15 What does it matter that my love could not keep her.
The night is shattered and she is not with me.

E This is all. In the distance someone is singing. In the distance.
My soul is not satisfied that it has lost her.

My sight searches for her as though to go to her.
20 My heart looks for her, and she is not with me.

The same night whitening the same trees.
We, of that time, are no longer the same.

I no longer love her, that's certain, but how I loved her.
My voice tried to find the wind to touch her hearing.

25 Another's. She will be another's. Like my kisses before.
Her voice. Her bright body. Her infinite eyes.

I no longer love her, that's certain, but maybe I love her.
Love is so short, forgetting is so long.

F Because through nights like this one I held her in my arms
30 my soul is not satisfied that it has lost her.

Though this be the last pain that she makes me suffer
and these the last verses that I write for her.

Translated by W. S. Merwin

444

Mini-Lesson: Speaking, Listening, and Viewing

CHORAL READING In choral reading, a small group reads a work of literature aloud. Some passages may be read in unison by the whole group. Other passages may be read by solo voices or by two or three voices together. Visual and sound effects can be added, if the performers desire.

Application Invite small groups to give choral readings of "Simile" and "Tonight I Can Write..." If possible, readings of "Tonight I Can Write..." should be given in both Spanish and English, either by the same group or by different groups. You might suggest that groups alternate lines or passages from the two languages in creative ways. Point out that although the speakers of these poems are individuals, both poems are about relationships between two people; therefore, duets and call-and-response patterns may be used to enhance the readings.

444 THE LANGUAGE OF LITERATURE TEACHER'S EDITION

PUEDO *Escribir Los Versos . . .*

PABLO NERUDA

Puedo escribir los versos más tristes esta noche.

Escribir, por ejemplo: 'La noche está estrellada,
y tiritan, azules, los astros, a lo lejos.'

El viento de la noche gira en el cielo y canta.

Puedo escribir los versos más tristes esta noche.
Yo la quise, y a veces ella también me quiso.

En las noches como ésta la tuve entre mis brazos.
La besé tantas veces bajo el cielo infinito.

Ella me quiso, a veces yo también la quería.
Cómo no haber amado sus grandes ojos fijos.

Puedo escribir los versos más tristes esta noche.
Pensar que no la tengo. Sentir que la he perdido.

Oir la noche inmensa, más inmensa sin ella.
Y el verso cae al alma como al pasto el rocío.

Qué importa que mi amor no pudiera guardarla.
La noche está estrellada y ella no está conmigo.

Eso es todo. A lo lejos alguien canta. A lo lejos.
Mi alma no se contenta con haberla perdido.

Como para acercarla mi mirada la busca.
Mi corazón la busca, y ella no está conmigo.

La misma noche que hace blanquear los mismos arboles.
Nosotros, los de entonces, ya no somos los mismos.

Ya no la quiero, es cierto, pero cuánto la quise.
Mi voz buscaba el viento para tocar su oído.

De otro. Será de otro. Como antes de mis besos.
Su voz, su cuerpo claro. Sus ojos infinitos.

Ya no la quiero, es cierto, pero tal vez la quiero.
Es tan corto el amor, y es tan largo el olvido.

Porque en noches como ésta la tuve entre mis brazos,
mi alma no se contenta con haberla perdido.

Aunque éste sea el último dolor que ella me causa,
y éstos sean los últimos versos que yo le escribo.

G

STRATEGIC READING FOR

Less-Proficient Readers

G Invite students to go back to the predictions they made about the poem.

- What is this poem about? *(lost love)* **Finding the Main Idea**
- How did this match students' predictions? *(Answers will vary.)* **Predicting**

CUSTOMIZING FOR

Gifted and Talented Students

Invite students to locate poems from different cultures and different periods of history in which a speaker bewails a lost love or an unhappy romance. Small groups of students might give readers' theater presentations of poems that they especially like.

COMPREHENSION CHECK

1. To what does "Simile" compare two people? *(a pair of deer walking in single file)*
2. Why is the soul of the speaker of "Tonight I Can Write . . ." unsatisfied? *(He has lost his love.)*
3. What aspects of nature are most prominent in "Tonight I Can Write . . ."? *(the sky; stars; wind; night)*

Assessment Option

SELF-ASSESSMENT Ask students to respond to the following questions as a way of assessing their own work:

- Which poem moved you more and why?
- Which poem do you think used figurative language more imaginatively? Explain.
- If a friend asked you, "What are these poems about?" what would you say?
- Why do you think these two poems were placed together?

From Personal Response to Critical Analysis

1. Accept all reasonable, well-supported responses.
2. Possible responses: he himself may be shivering and feel shattered; the night feels immense because he is lonely; the night reminds him of nights he held her in his arms. Some students may say that the woman left the speaker feeling uncertain of his own feelings.
3. Accept all well-supported opinions. Possible responses: Some students might say the speaker is ambivalent about his feelings for the woman; in line 27 he says both that he certainly does not love her but that he still may. Others may suggest that he really does love her but is trying to deny his love.
4. Some students will accept the poet's claim that he is finished with thinking about or writing about the woman; others will see either self-deception or conscious irony in the statement.
5. Possible responses: Both poems explore the mysteries of love relationships. In both poems, the speaker seems uncertain about why his relationship has changed; both speakers struggle to make sense of their complex feelings about love.

Another Pathway
Students may wish to write either from their own perspective as critical readers or from the first-person points of view of the speakers of the poems.

Rubric
3 Full Accomplishment Students show insight into the emotional situation of the speakers in the two poems and back up insights with appropriate quotations or details from the poems.
2 Substantial Accomplishment Students explain the situations of the speakers but do not present supporting quotations or details from the poems.
1 Little or Partial Accomplishment Explanations of the speakers' situations are not accurate; textual support is missing.

RESPONDING OPTIONS

FROM PERSONAL RESPONSE TO CRITICAL ANALYSIS

REFLECT 1. Which lines of "Tonight I Can Write . . ." are the most memorable for you? Why? Jot down your thoughts in your notebook.

RETHINK 2. Review the chart that you created for the Reading Connection on page 441. What do the images from nature reveal about the speaker's emotions and experience?
Consider
- why the speaker says "The night is shattered and the blue stars shiver"
- what you learn about the speaker's relationship with the woman
- why the night feels "still more immense without her"
- what this night reminds him of

Close Textual Reading

3. Do you think the speaker still loves the woman? Support your opinion.
4. Reread the last two lines of the poem. What is your opinion of the speaker's conclusion?

RELATE 5. How do you think "Simile" and "Tonight I Can Write" relate to the theme of this part of the unit, "Mysteries of the Heart"? Explain.

Thematic Link

Multimodal Learning
ANOTHER PATHWAY
For each poem, draft a paragraph that explains the speaker's situation. Include details or quotations from each poem. Then share your writing with a classmate and discuss your respective explanations.

LITERARY CONCEPTS

Repetition is a literary technique in which sounds, words, phrases, or lines are repeated for emphasis or unity. In "Tonight I Can Write . . ." Neruda repeats the first line three times to emphasize the speaker's sorrow and to help unify the poem. With a partner, make a list of repeated words, phrases, or lines.

Then discuss how each instance of repetition affects your understanding of the speaker's feelings. Why do you think Neruda sometimes repeats part of a line and then adds new information.

CONCEPT REVIEW: Figurative Language Review both poems and identify each metaphor, simile, or personification. Then create one metaphor, one simile, and one personification of your own to compare your feelings to objects in nature.

QUICKWRITES

1. In a **monologue,** give the other side of the story for one of the two poems. In other words, assume the identity of the loved one in the poem and express your feelings and ideas about the relationship described by the speaker.
2. Express your own ideas about love and loss in a **poem.** Try to include images from nature as well as repetition and figurative language to help emphasize and unify your ideas. The images you generated in the Personal Connection on page 441 may help you get started.

📁 **PORTFOLIO** Save your writing. You may want to use it later as a springboard to a piece for your portfolio.

446 UNIT THREE PART 2: MYSTERIES OF THE HEART

Literary Concepts
Repetition is found throughout the poem, ranging from entire lines (1, 5, 11) to single words ("immense," "her"). Some students may feel that such repetition conveys the strength of the speaker's feelings towards the woman; others may regard the repetition as a sign of the speaker's emotional turmoil and ambivalence about the ending of the relationship.

Figurative Language The major figures of speech are the deer simile in "Simile," the personifications of night, the stars, the sight, the voice, and the heart in "Tonight I Can Write . . . ," the simile comparing verse to dew, and the metaphor of night as something that shatters.

QuickWrites
1. Students' monologues may be in prose or in free verse. Suggest that they use clues from the poem to imagine what the loved one is like before they begin to write from the loved one's point of view.
2. Suggest that students structure their poems as a sustained simile as Momaday did.

 **The Writer's Craft**
Monologue, pp. 108–112
Poetry, pp. 88–101

LITERARY LINKS

Which of the two poems do you think has the most in common with Amy Lowell's "Taxi"? Cite details from the two poems to support your evaluation.

ACROSS THE CURRICULUM

Music Find a contemporary song that reveals some of the same emotions conveyed by "Simile" or "Tonight I Can Write . . . ." Share the song with your classmates and discuss how it relates to the poem.

Literary Links

Some students may say that "Tonight I Can Write . . ." has more in common with "The Taxi" because both poems utilize imagery of night, stars, and wind to describe love; in both poems the speaker is anguished, intense, and physically distant from the other person. Other students may find "Simile" to have more in common with "The Taxi" because both of these poems describe a still existent relationship.

N. SCOTT MOMADAY

1934–

N. Scott Momaday's poetry and prose reflect his deeply felt love for his Kiowa Indian ancestry—its culture, history, and native traditions. His father, a member of the Kiowa tribe, was one of the finest Native American artists of his day; his mother, who was part Cherokee, was a writer and a teacher. When asked about how his heritage has affected his work, Momaday told an interviewer, "When I was growing up on the reservations of the Southwest, I saw people who were deeply involved in their traditional life, in the memories of their blood. They had, as far as I could see, a certain strength and beauty that I find missing in the modern world at large. I like to celebrate that involvement in my writing."

Momaday has received a number of honors and awards for his writing, including the Pulitzer Prize for fiction in 1969 for his novel *House Made of Dawn*. In fact, he was the first Native American to earn that prestigious award. Momaday has since published several books of poetry and fiction, as well as essays and articles on the importance of preserving the environment. Momaday says, "I sometimes think [writing] is a very lonely sort of work. But when you get into it, it can be exhilarating, tremendously fulfilling and stimulating."
OTHER WORKS *The Way to Rainy Mountain, Angle of Geese and Other Poems, The Names: A Memoir*

Extended Reading

N. SCOTT MOMADAY

Momaday was born in Lawton, Oklahoma. He is a professor of English at Arizona State University and previously taught at Stanford University and other universities.

PABLO NERUDA

1904–1973

Pablo Neruda, the pen name of Ricardo Eliecer Neftalí Reyes y Basoalto, was drawn to poetry at an early age, even though his working-class family scoffed at his literary ambitions. He began publishing poems at the age of 15. When just 20, he won celebrity throughout his native Chile with *Twenty Love Poems and a Song of Despair* in which "Tonight I Can Write . . ." first appeared.

After he served in his nation's diplomatic corps—an honor then commonly granted to talented Latin American writers—he shifted the focus of his poetry to political and social criticism. In the early 1970s, Neruda supported Chile's socialist leader Salvador Allende and served as his nation's ambassador to France. When the poet received the 1971 Nobel Prize for Literature, the event was celebrated as a national holiday in his homeland. Neruda produced more than 40 volumes of poetry, translations, and verse drama during his literary career.
OTHER WORKS *Residence on Earth, Elemental Odes, The Heights of Macchu Picchu, Pablo Neruda: Selected Poems, Extravagaria*

Extended Reading

PABLO NERUDA

Neruda's poetic output was enormous—his collected poems contain almost 2,000 pages—and represents an ever-changing stream of sometimes contradictory feelings. Much of his work is comparable to that of Walt Whitman, who greatly influenced him. Neruda's youthful poems were imitative of French symbolist poetry. His next creative period was surrealistic. Later, becoming a poet of social and political issues, he renounced his earlier work for being too preoccupied with the self, though even his political poems reflect his personality and experience.

Across the Curriculum

Cooperative Learning Suggest that students work in small groups and brainstorm to generate a list of songs. One member can record all suggestions, another can encourage the participation of all group members, and a third can clarify or summarize aspects of the songs that relate to the poems. A fourth group member can present the results to the class.

OVERVIEW

Objectives

- To understand and appreciate a lyric poem about the effects of love at first sight
- To identify and appreciate rhyme, rhythm, and meter
- To express understanding of the selection through a choice of writing forms, including a song lyric, an extended definition, and a poem
- To extend understanding of the poem through a variety of multimodal and cross-curricular activities

Skills

LITERARY CONCEPTS
- Rhyme
- Rhythm and meter

GENRE STUDY
- Poetry: lyric poem

SPEAKING, LISTENING, AND VIEWING
- Group discussion

ALTERNATIVE
Previewing

Students can choose partners and use the following prompts to preview "To . . ." orally.

Personal Connection

Discussion Prompts *Recall a time when you met a person who made a strong first impression on you, either positive or negative. Share your memories with a partner, using the following questions to start you off:*

- *What did you first notice about the person?*
- *How did your opinion of the person change over time?*

As you read "To . . . ," notice who the speaker met and how time affected his first impression.

STRATEGIC READING FOR
Less-Proficient Readers

Set a Purpose Invite students to identify the positive and negative effects of the love that is experienced by the speaker in this poem.

Use **UNIT THREE RESOURCE BOOK**, p. 47, for guidance in reading the selection.

PREVIEWING

POETRY

To . . .

Aleksandr Pushkin (pōōsh′kĭn) Russia

Activating Prior Knowledge
PERSONAL CONNECTION

Recall a time when you met a person who made a very positive first impression. What was it about the person that you found remarkable? What feelings did he or she inspire? In your notebook, explore your experience in a tree diagram like the one on the right. Note which details about the person most impressed you, as well as your thoughts and feelings after your first meeting.

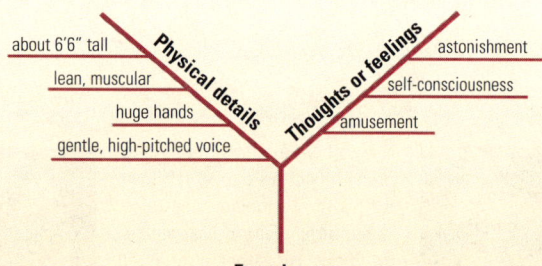

Building Background
BIOGRAPHICAL CONNECTION

In 1819, the 20-year-old Russian poet Aleksandr Pushkin met an attractive young woman named Anna Kern, the niece of a friend. Anna made a very strong first impression on Pushkin, who frequently fell in love with beautiful women. Unfortunately, the poet was exiled shortly thereafter to a remote part of southern Russia by a government that did not care for some of his political poems, and he was not to see Anna Kern for six years. It seems that Anna's first impression had become a lasting one, however, because soon after meeting her again in June 1825, Pushkin was inspired to write the following poem to her. Though his romantic interest faded as he got to know her better, the two remained friends.

Portrait of the Princess Saltikova, 1802–1863 (1837), Karl Pavlovitch Briullov. Oil on canvas, 200 cm × 142 cm, Russian State Museum, St. Petersburg, Russia, Giraudon/Art Resource, New York.

Active Reading/Setting a Purpose
READING CONNECTION

Understanding Chronological Order
As you read the poem, pay attention to the order of the events and the feelings associated with them. Which details refer to the speaker's first meeting with the woman addressed? Which refer to a second meeting? Which refer to the period in between? Look for words and phrases that indicate time sequence, and think about how the speaker communicates that his first impressions have become lasting ones.

448 UNIT THREE PART 2: MYSTERIES OF THE HEART

PRINT AND MEDIA RESOURCES

UNIT THREE RESOURCE BOOK
Strategic Reading: Literature, p. 47

FORMAL ASSESSMENT
Selection Test, p. 89
 Test Generator

ACCESS FOR STUDENTS ACQUIRING ENGLISH
Reading Support

AUDIO LIBRARY
See Reference Card

LASERLINKS
Author Background

To...

Aleksandr Pushkin

Couple Above St. Paul (1970–1971), Marc Chagall. Collection Chagall, St. Paul de Vence, France, Scala/Art Resource, New York. Copyright © 1996 Artists Rights Society (ARS), New York/ADAGP, Paris.

I recollect that wondrous meeting,
That instant I encountered you,
When like an apparition fleeting,
Like beauty's spirit, past you flew.
5 Long since, when hopeless grief distressed me,
When noise and turmoil vexed, it seemed
Your voice still tenderly caressed me,
Your dear face sought me as I dreamed.

Years passed; their stormy gusts confounded
10 And swept away old dreams apace.
I had forgotten how you sounded,
Forgot the heaven of your face.

In exiled gloom and isolation
My quiet days meandered on,
15 The thrill of awe and inspiration,
And life, and tears, and love, were gone.

My soul awoke from inanition,
And I encountered you anew,
And like a fleeting apparition,
20 Like beauty's spirit, past you flew.

My pulses bound in exultation,
And in my heart once more unfold
The sense of awe and inspiration,
The life, the tears, the love of old.

Translated by Walter Arndt

---

3 apparition (ăp′ə-rĭsh′ən): a ghost or ghostly figure; a sudden or unusual sight.

6 vexed (vĕkst): annoyed; bothered.

9 confounded (kən-foun′dĭd): confused; mixed up; made hard to distinguish.

10 apace (ə-pās′): at a rapid pace; swiftly.

14 meandered (mē-ăn′dərd): followed a winding course; moved aimlessly and idly, without a fixed direction or purpose.

17 inanition (ĭn′ə-nĭsh′ən): exhaustion caused by lack of nourishment or vitality; emptiness.

From Personal Response to Critical Analysis

1. Accept all reasonable responses.
2. Possible responses: she was beautiful; the brevity of their meeting made her more attractive; the speaker's sorrow during the years of separation made her appeal grow in memory.
3. Some students might feel that the speaker is a romantic person who remains faithful over the years; they may note the intensity of his feelings and his idealization of the woman; others might find his attraction to someone he hardly knows superficial, suggesting that the speaker is too easily swayed by emotion.
4. Accept all reasonable responses.
5. Accept all reasonable responses.

Another Pathway

Cooperative Learning Suggest to students that "visual representations" can include captioned photos and drawings, montages of words and phrases clipped from periodicals, and videotapes accompanied by readings of the poem. The group as a whole can brainstorm possible representations. Two members might be responsible for finding or creating images, and another member might choose the words or phrases from the poem to accompany each image. A fourth member might present the results to the class.

Rubric

3 Full Accomplishment The visual representations convey the three time periods and the speaker's three emotional states with textual support.

2 Substantial Accomplishment The three states are pictured in a recognizable way, but textual support is lacking.

1 Little or Partial Accomplishment The three representations do not convey the three emotional states and lack textual references.

RESPONDING OPTIONS

FROM PERSONAL RESPONSE TO CRITICAL ANALYSIS

REFLECT
1. What impression do you have of the speaker and his experience? Describe your response in your notebook.

RETHINK
2. Why do you think the woman made such a lasting impression on the speaker?
   Consider
   Close Textual Reading
   - what he remembers about their first encounter
   - how he has been affected by his memories of her
   - the way he describes his life during their years apart

3. In your judgment, what does the poem reveal about the personality and values of the speaker? Cite details from the poem to support your opinion.

Thematic Link
4. Compare your own views about romantic love with the speaker's. How much do you have in common?

RELATE
5. Do you believe that too much attention is paid to romantic love in our culture today? Why or why not?

Multimodal Learning
ANOTHER PATHWAY

Cooperative Learning

In a small group, create visual representations of the speaker's various emotional states. For example, you might create three different images to convey his feelings about first meeting the woman, their separation, and their second meeting. Use words or phrases from the poem to accompany each image.

LITERARY CONCEPTS

Rhyme is the occurrence of a similar or identical sound at the ends of words, as in *tether* and *together*. Rhyme that occurs at the ends of lines of poetry is called **end rhyme**. End rhymes that are not exact but approximate are called **off rhymes,** for example *other* and *bother*. A **rhyme scheme** is the pattern of end rhyme in a poem. With a partner, review the explanation of how to determine rhyme scheme on page 376; then identify the poem's rhyme scheme, noting where off rhyme is used. Share your findings with the class.

CONCEPT REVIEW: Rhythm and Meter Review the explanation of rhythm and meter on page 379. Then copy one of the poem's stanzas and mark it for stressed and unstressed syllables. In a small group, check each other's work and decide what kind of metrical pattern is represented.

QUICKWRITES

1. Write a **song lyric** that describes the relationship between the speaker and the woman to whom the poem is addressed. In your lyric, describe their first meeting and the different stages of their relationship.

2. Write an extended **definition** of love that conveys what love means to the speaker. Before writing, check the definitions of love in two or three dictionaries.

3. Write a **poem** about the encounter that you described in the Personal Connection on page 448.

 **PORTFOLIO** Save your writing. You may want to use it later as a springboard to a piece for your portfolio.

450 UNIT THREE PART 2: MYSTERIES OF THE HEART

Literary Concepts

The rhyme scheme for the poem is as follows: *abab, cdcd, efef, ghgh, ijij, klkl, imim*. Make sure that students notice the repetition of the *-ation* sound in the 4th and 6th stanzas, a slight difference from the *-ition* sound in the 5th stanza. The rhyme *on-gone* is an off-rhyme

Rhythm and Meter The metrical pattern is iambic tetrameter with an extra unaccented syllable at the end of the first and third lines in each stanza. This use of an extra syllable is called a feminine ending.

QuickWrites

1. Students may find it helpful to study examples of song lyrics before writing their own.
2. Suggest that students consult a large dictionary to explore the various definitions of love. They may find it interesting to look up some famous quotations about love in *Bartlett's Familiar Quotations*.
3. Suggest that students use similes and metaphors, as Pushkin did, to engage the imagination of their readers.

The Writer's Craft

Poetry, pp. 88–101
Definition, pp. 134–137

Multimodal Learning

ALTERNATIVE ACTIVITIES

1. With a partner, create an **exhibition** of 19th-century paintings that feature women who might have appealed to Pushkin. To do this, bring in reproductions of paintings from art books or printouts from on-line computer-based encyclopedias. For each painting, provide a caption from Pushkin's poem.

2. Choreograph a **dance** based on "To . . . ." Through movement, try to capture the mood of the poem, as well as the speaker's changing emotions from the beginning to the end. Then perform your dance for your classmates.

ART CONNECTION

Why do you think the painting on page 449, *Couple Above St. Paul,* was chosen to accompany Pushkin's poem?

Detail of *Couple Above St. Paul* (1970–1971), Marc Chagall. Collection Chagal, St. Paul de Vence, France, Scala/Art Resource, New York. Copyright © 1996 Artists Rights Society (ARS), New York/ADAGP, Paris.

ACROSS THE CURRICULUM

World Languages With a partner, find one or more additional translations of this poem, which is often called "To Anna Kern." Then compare and contrast the translations. What do the differences suggest about the process of translation?

ALEKSANDR PUSHKIN

1799–1837

Aleksandr Pushkin is widely regarded as the father of modern Russian literature. He began writing at a time when Russia's upper class regarded their own language as an "uncultured" tongue and preferred to speak and write in French. Pushkin went on to prove the versatility and beauty of the Russian language in his many poems and prose writings. Though he was descended from the upper class, he took pride in his maternal great grandfather, Ibrahim Hannibal, an Ethiopian who had been brought to Russia as a slave and who rose to comrade-in-arms of the Russian czar Peter the Great (1672–1725). Perhaps because of his ancestry, Pushkin was sympathetic to the plight of Russia's peasants. His sympathies, expressed in several early political poems, made him hugely popular with the Russian people but also led to his exile to southern Russia in 1820. While he was not imprisoned, he was forced to live far from the cultural centers of St. Petersburg and Moscow. Nonetheless, he was immensely productive during this period, writing or beginning some of his greatest works, including his verse novel *Eugene Onegin* and his historic drama *Boris Godunov.*

After Nicholas I became Russia's czar, he allowed Pushkin to return to Moscow in the fall of 1826, in part so that his ministers could keep an eye on the poet. A few years later, Pushkin married one of the many beautiful women with whom he had fallen in love over the years, but the marriage brought him little happiness. After discovering that she was carrying on a flirtation with another man, Pushkin fought a duel to defend her honor. Although he had survived duels in the past, this time he was not so lucky. Two days after fighting, Pushkin died of his wounds.

OTHER WORKS "Mozart and Salieri," *The Captain's Daughter, The Bronze Horseman: Selected Poems of Aleksandr Pushkin* Extended Reading

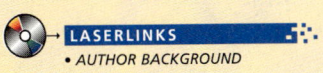
• AUTHOR BACKGROUND

TO . . . 451

Across the Curriculum

World Languages Suggest to your students that they ask a school or community librarian for help in finding catalogue entries or bibliographical citations for other translations. Student opinions of the translation process will vary: some students will be impressed by the amount of creativity involved and the difficulty of being both poetic and faithful to the original. Other students may be impatient with the differences in translation, wishing for a "correct" version.

Art Connection

Students may cite the romantic mood of the painting as the reason for its inclusion; others find the dreamlike images of the painting appropriate to the poem.

ALEKSANDR PUSHKIN

Pushkin was tutored at home and later educated at the Lyceum, where he studied Latin and French literature. He began publishing poetry during his student days, and at the age of 20 he was acknowledged as the leading Russian poet. His greatest works were written during the next few years. His verse novel *Eugene Onegin* inspired an opera by Tchaikovsky.

AUTHOR BACKGROUND
Aleksandr Pushkin Pictures of the author, a palace ball, and a 19th-century duel are among the images giving students a sense of Pushkin's life and times.

Side A, Frame 49469

Alternative Activities

1. Suggest that students begin their research by looking in general art-history books that include art in 19th-century Europe. They might go on from there to books about individual artists. Although Pushkin was Russian, French paintings are likely to play a major role in this activity.

2. The dance might be a solo, expressing the speaker's feelings directly, or a *pas de deux* in which the woman addressed by the speaker plays a part.

OVERVIEW

Objectives

- To understand and appreciate a short story that explores the effects of jealousy
- To identify and understand the frame story form.
- To express understanding of a selection through a choice of writing forms, including investigative notes, a letter, and an opening statement
- To extend understanding of the selection through a variety of multimodal and cross-curricular activities

Skills

LITERARY CONCEPTS
- Frame story
- Tone

THE WRITER'S STYLE
- Appropriate use of modifiers

GRAMMAR
- Adverb phrases

SPEAKING, LISTENING, AND VIEWING
- Newscast
- Role-playing
- Group discussion

ALTERNATIVE

Previewing

Students can chose partners and use the following prompts to preview "Metonymy" orally.

Writing Connection

Discussion Prompts With a partner, share reflections about a time when you felt someone wronged you. Use these questions to help start your conversation:

- What happened, and what caused the incident?
- How did you respond?
- How do you feel now about the incident and your response?

As you read "Metonymy," notice who wrongs whom, and what the response is.

PREVIEWING

FICTION

Metonymy, or The Husband's Revenge

Rachel de Queiroz (rä-chĕl′ dĕ kĕ-ē-rôs′) Brazil

Activating Prior Knowledge
PERSONAL CONNECTION

Get together with another student and role-play a situation in which one of you has wronged the other. If you wish, you may base your role playing on one of the situations on the right. Afterward, discuss the reactions expressed. Were feelings conveyed in an open manner, or did feelings remain hidden? Did revenge enter into the scene? Compare your reactions to those of other pairs of students.

- being deceived in love
- having a friend break a promise
- having something stolen
- being cheated

Building Background
LITERARY CONNECTION

Rachel de Queiroz, a prominent Brazilian writer, is considered a master of the *crônica* (krô′nē-kä), a form of short fiction that combines elements of the essay and the short story. This form, which has become especially popular in Brazil, is characterized by a simple and direct style and an interest in contemporary issues and events. "Metonymy," which was published in a collection of her *crônicas,* is representative of the form. It has an informal, conversational tone, which makes it seem as if the narrator is carrying on a conversation with an interested listener. The narrator begins by discussing a figure of speech and from there launches into a compelling tale that explores the ways in which people react when they feel they have been wronged.

WRITING CONNECTION Setting a Purpose

In your notebook, describe a time when you felt that someone had wronged you. What caused the incident and how did you respond to it? How do you feel now about your response? As you read, compare your own response to wrongdoing to that of the husband in the story.

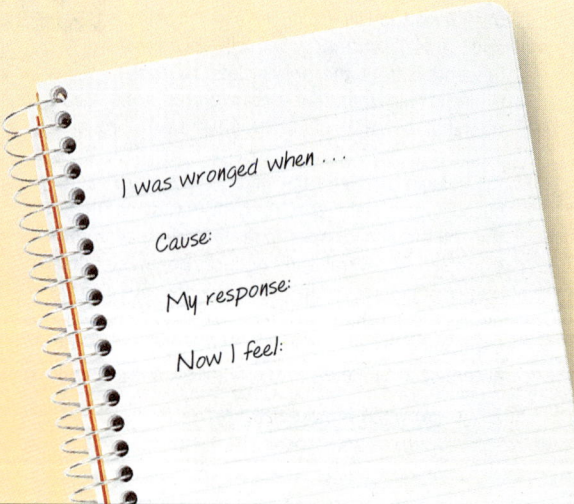

I was wronged when...

Cause:

My response:

Now I feel:

452 UNIT THREE PART 2: MYSTERIES OF THE HEART

PRINT AND MEDIA RESOURCES

UNIT THREE RESOURCE BOOK
Strategic Reading: Literature, p. 51
Vocabulary SkillBuilder, p. 52

GRAMMAR MINI-LESSONS
Transparencies, pp. 22–26
Copymasters, pp. 24–27

WRITING MINI-LESSONS
Transparencies, pp. 53–54

ACCESS FOR STUDENTS ACQUIRING ENGLISH
Selection Summaries
Reading Support

FORMAL ASSESSMENT
Selection Test, pp. 91–92
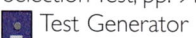 Test Generator

 **AUDIO LIBRARY**
See Reference Card

---

452 THE LANGUAGE OF LITERATURE TEACHER'S EDITION

METONYMY, or The Husband's Revenge

Rachel de Queiroz

Metonymy. I learned the word in 1930 and shall never forget it. I had just published my first novel. A literary critic had scolded me because my hero went out into the night "chest unclosed."

"What deplorable nonsense!" wrote this eminently sensible gentleman. "Why does she not say what she means? Obviously, it was his shirt that was unclosed, not his chest."

I accepted his rebuke with humility, indeed with shame. But my illustrious Latin professor, Dr. Matos Peixoto,[1] came to my rescue. He said that what I had written was perfectly correct; that I had used a respectable figure of speech known as metonymy; and that this figure consisted in the use of one word for another word associated with it—for example, a word representing a cause instead of the effect, or representing the container when the content is intended. The classic instance, he told me, is "the sparkling cup"; in reality, not the cup but the wine in it is sparkling.

The professor and I wrote a letter, which was published in the newspaper where the review had appeared. It put my unjust critic in his place. I hope he learned a lesson. I know I did. Ever since, I have been using metonymy—my only bond with classical rhetoric.

Moreover, I have devoted some thought to it, and I have concluded that metonymy may be more than a figure of speech. There is, I believe, such a thing as practical or applied metonymy. Let me give a crude example, drawn from my own experience. A certain lady of my acquaintance suddenly moved out of the boardinghouse where she had been living for years and became a mortal enemy of the woman who owned it.

---

1. Matos Peixoto (mä′tŏŏs pĕ-ē-hô′tô).

WORDS TO KNOW
deplorable (dĭ-plôr′ə-bəl) *adj.* worthy of strong criticism or disapproval; terrible
eminently (ĕm′ə-nənt-lē) *adv.* highly; notably
rebuke (rĭ-byōōk′) *n.* sharp criticism

453

WORDS TO KNOW

deplorable (dĭ-plôr′ə-bəl) *adj.* worthy of strong criticism or disapproval; terrible (p. 453)
embellish (ĕm-bĕl′ĭsh) *v.* to make more beautiful; to decorate (p. 454)
eminently (ĕm′ə-nənt-lē) *adv.* highly; notably (p. 453)
ingratiating (ĭn-grā′shē-ā′tĭng) *adj.* pleasing; agreeable (p. 455)
illicit (ĭ-lĭs′ĭt) *adj.* unlawful; not allowed by custom or law (p. 456)
rebuke (rĭ-byōōk′) *n.* sharp criticism (p. 453)
refined (rĭ-fīnd′) *adj.* free from coarseness or vulgarity; polite (p. 457)
scrutinize (skrōōt′n-īz′) *v.* to examine or observe with great care (p. 456)
tepid (tĕp′ĭd) *adj.* lacking emotional warmth or enthusiasm; halfhearted (p. 454)
vile (vīl) *adj.* disgusting; objectionable; wicked (p. 457)

I asked her why. We both knew that the woman was a kindly soul; she had given my friend injections when she needed them, had often loaned her a hot-water bag, and had always waited on her when she had her little heart attacks. My friend replied:

"It's the telephone in the hall. I hate her for it. Half the time when I answered it, the call was a hoax or joke of some sort."

"But the owner of the boardinghouse didn't perpetrate these hoaxes. She wasn't responsible for them."

"No. But whose telephone was it?"

I know another case of applied metonymy, a more disastrous one for it involved a crime. It happened in a city of the interior,[2] which I shall not name for fear that someone may recognize the parties and revive the scandal. I shall narrate the crime but conceal the criminal.

Well, in this city of the interior there lived a man. He was not old but he was spent, which is worse than being old. In his youth he had suffered from beriberi.[3] His legs were weak, his chest was tired and asthmatic, his skin was yellowish, and his eyes were rheumy.[4] He was, however, a man of property: he owned the house in which he lived and the one next to it, in which he had set up a grocery store. Therefore, although so unattractive personally, he was able to find himself a wife. In all justice to him, he did not tempt fate by marrying a beauty. Instead, he married a poor, emaciated girl, who worked in a men's clothing factory. By her face one would have thought she had consumption.[5] So our friend felt safe. He did not foresee the effects of good nutrition and a healthful life on a woman's appearance. The girl no longer spent eight hours a day at a sewing table. She was the mistress of her house. She ate well: fresh meat, cucumber salad, pork fat with beans and manioc mush,[6] all kinds of sweets, and oranges, which her husband bought by the gross for his customers. The effects were like magic. Her body filled out, especially in the best places. She even seemed to grow taller. And her face—what a change! I may have forgot to mention that her features, in themselves, were good to begin with. Moreover, money enabled her to <u>embellish</u> her natural advantages with art: she began to wear makeup, to wave her hair, and to dress well.

Lovely, attractive, she now found her sickly, prematurely old husband a burden and a bore. Each evening, as soon as the store was closed, he dined, mostly on milk (he could not stomach meat), took his newspaper, and rested on his chaise longue[7] until time to go to bed. He did not care for the movies or for soccer or for radio. He did not even show much interest in love. Just a sort of <u>tepid</u>, tasteless cohabitation.

And then Fate intervened: it produced a sergeant.

Granted, it was unjust for a young wife, after being reconditioned at her husband's expense, to employ her charms to the prejudice of the aforesaid husband. Unjust; but, then, this world

---

2. **city of the interior:** an inland Brazilian city, as opposed to one of Brazil's more populous coastal cities.
3. **beriberi** (bĕr′ē-bĕr′ē): a disease caused by a deficiency of thiamine in the diet.
4. **rheumy** (rōō′mē): filmy with a watery or thin mucous discharge.
5. **consumption** (kən-sŭmp′shən): tuberculosis, a lung disease that causes weight loss and chest pain.
6. **manioc mush:** mashed cassava, a tropical plant with starchy, edible roots.
7. **chaise longue** (shāz-lông′): a reclining chair with a seat long enough to support a person's outstretched legs.

WORDS TO KNOW
embellish (ĕm-bĕl′ĭsh) *v.* to make more beautiful; to decorate
tepid (tĕp′ĭd) *adj.* lacking emotional warmth or enthusiasm; halfhearted

454

ADVERB PHRASES An adverb phrase is a phrase that is used as an adverb to modify a verb, an adjective, or another adverb. Like adverbs, adverb phrases tell *where, when, why, how,* or *to what extent.*

Application Write the following excerpts on the chalkboard.
- "<u>Every day at the fateful hour of lunch</u>, she replaced her husband <u>at the counter</u>." (p. 456)
- "<u>On the sidewalk in front of the shopkeeper's house</u> they saw his wife <u>on her knees</u>..." (p. 457)

Ask students to tell what question each phrase answers. (*very day*—when; *at the fateful hour of lunch*—when; *at the counter*—where; *on the sidewalk*—where; *in front of the shopkeeper's house*—where; *on her knees*—how or where)

Reteaching/Reinforcement
- *Grammar Handbook,* anthology pp. 1076–1080
- *Grammar Mini-Lessons* copymasters pp. 24–27, transparencies pp. 22–26

The Writer's Craft
Adverb Phrases, p. 587

Le coeur [The heart] (1947), Henri Matisse. Plate 7 from *Jazz*, published by Tériade. The Metropolitan Museum of Art, New York, gift of Lila Acheson Wallace, 1983 (1983.1009). Copyright © 1985 The Metropolitan Museum of Art, all rights reserved.

Art Note

***Le Coeur (The Heart)* by Henri Matisse** Matisse (1869–1954), a French painter, studied law, but turned seriously to painting in 1892. He is known for his vibrant use of color and his expressive, flowing line. This 1947 *pochoir*, or stenciled print, is a typical example of his love for sharply contrasting shapes and colors.

Reading the Art *What is your response to this picture? Compare and contrast that response with your response to the story.*

Literary Concept: TONE

F Invite students to describe the author's attitude toward the sergeant. Have them support their comments with specific words and phrases from the passage. *(Possible response: Some students may say her tone is sarcastic and that she thinks very little of the sergeant. Others may say she sees him as a strong, pleasing contrast to the husband. Either view could be supported by the phrases "a manly, commanding voice . . ." and "gloriously martial.")*

---

thrives on injustice, doesn't it? The sergeant—I shall not say whether he was in the Army, the Air Force, the Marines, or the Fusileers, for I still mean to conceal the identities of the parties—the sergeant was muscular, young, ingratiating, with a manly, commanding voice and a healthy spring in his walk. He looked gloriously martial in his high-buttoned uniform.

One day, when the lady was in charge of the counter (while her husband lunched), the sergeant came in. Exactly what happened and what did not happen, is hard to say. It seems that the sergeant asked for a pack of cigarettes. Then he wanted a little vermouth.[8] Finally, he asked permission to listen to the sports broadcast on the radio next to the counter. Maybe it was just an excuse to remain there awhile. In any case, the girl said it would be all right. It is hard to refuse a favor to a sergeant, especially a sergeant like this one. It appears that the sergeant asked nothing more that day. At most, he and the girl exchanged expressive glances and a few agreeable words, murmured so softly that the customers, always alert for something to gossip about, could not hear them.

Three times more the husband lunched while his wife chatted with the sergeant in the store. The flirtation progressed. Then the husband fell ill with a grippe,[9] and the two others went far beyond flirtation. How and when they met, no one was able to discover. The important thing is that they were lovers and that they loved with a

---

8. **vermouth** (vər-mōōth′): a type of wine.
9. **grippe** (grĭp): the flu.

WORDS TO KNOW
ingratiating (ĭn-grā′shē-ā′tĭng) *adj.* pleasing; agreeable

Mini-Lesson Literary Concepts

REVIEWING TONE Remind students that tone is a writer's attitude toward his or her subject. A writer communicates tone through word choice, sentence structure, choice of details, and direct statements of his or her position. Point out that tone can also apply to a speaker's attitude about a subject. When people speak, their voice, gestures, and facial expressions help convey their attitude.

Application Direct students' attention to the highlighted passage on this page. Have students work in pairs to identify the tone of this passage. *(Possible responses: gossipy, confiding, light and conversational, mocking)* Then one student from each pair should read the passage aloud to the other, trying to convey the writer's tone. Ask students if reading the passage aloud affected their original perception of the tone.

Literary Note

G The story of Tristan and Isolde has been called one of literature's greatest love stories. In this Arthurian epic, Tristan goes to Ireland to fetch the bride-to-be of his uncle, King Mark. On the way home to Cornwall, the two young people drink a magic potion and fall irrevocably in love. The other pair of lovers, Paolo and Francesca, are adulterers who appear in Dante's *Divine Comedy*, an Italian epic poem written in 1321.

Critical Thinking: ANALYZING

H Ask students why it has taken so long for the husband to become suspicious. *(Possible responses: He is too self-absorbed to have noticed the healthy change in his wife's appearance; he only notices disruptive events, like tears.)*

Literary Concept: CHARACTERIZATION

I Ask students what the husband's behavior during the five months hints about his feelings. *(Possible responses: He may get a strange kind of pleasure from contemplating his wife's infidelity; he is unable to act; he may feel guilty over invading his wife's privacy.)*

Courtesy of the National Postal Museum, Smithsonian Institution, Washington, D.C.

G forbidden love, like Tristan and Isolde or Paolo and Francesca.[10]

Then Fate, which does not like <u>illicit</u> love and generally punishes those who engage in it, transferred the sergeant to another part of the country.

It is said that only those who love can really know the pain of separation. The girl cried so much that her eyes grew red and swollen. She lost her appetite. Beneath her rouge could be seen the consumptive complexion of earlier times. **H** And these symptoms aroused her husband's suspicion, although, curiously, he had never suspected anything when the love affair was flourishing and everything was wine and roses.

He began to observe her carefully. He <u>scrutinized</u> her in her periods of silence. He listened to her sighs and to the things she murmured in her sleep. He snooped around and found a postcard and a book, both with a man's name in the same handwriting. He found the insignia of the sergeant's regiment and concluded that the object of his wife's murmurs, sighs, and silences was not only a man but a soldier. Finally he made the supreme discovery: that they had indeed betrayed him. For he discovered the love letters, bearing airmail stamps, a distant postmark, and the sergeant's name. They left no reasonable doubt.

For five months the poor fellow twisted the poisoned dagger of jealousy in his thin, sickly chest. Like a boy who discovers a bird's nest and, hiding nearby, watches the eggs increasing in number every day, so the husband, using a duplicate key to the wood chest where his wife put her valuables, watched the increase in the number of letters concealed there. He had given her the chest during their honeymoon, saying, "Keep your secrets here." And the ungrateful girl had obeyed him. **I**

Every day at the fateful hour of lunch, she replaced her husband at the counter. But he was not interested in eating. He ran to her room, pulled out a drawer of her bureau, removed the chest from under a lot of panties, slips, and such, took the little key out of his pocket, opened the chest, and anxiously read the new letter. If there was no new letter, he reread the one dated August 21st; it was so full of realism that it sounded like dialogue from a French movie. Then he put everything away and hurried to the kitchen, when he swallowed a few spoonfuls of broth and gnawed at a piece of bread. It was almost impossible to swallow with the passion of those two thieves sticking in his throat.

When the poor man's heart had become utterly saturated with jealousy and hatred, he

---

10. **Tristan and Isolde or Paolo and Francesca:** two legendary pairs of lovers.

| WORDS TO KNOW | **illicit** (ĭ-lĭs′ĭt) *adj.* unlawful; not allowed by custom or law
scrutinize (skrōōt′n-īz′) *v.* to examine or observe with great care |

456

 Mini-Lesson   The Writer's Style

APPROPRIATE USE OF MODIFIERS

Explain to students that modifiers—adjectives and adverbs—can enhance a description by adding details that help the reader visualize characters, events, places, or things, and by affecting tone. Caution them that modifiers should not be used just for their own sake, however. Point out that extraneous modifiers can slow a piece of writing down.

Application In the highlighted passages, students will notice many well-chosen modifiers, such as "the *supreme* discovery," and "the *fateful* hour of lunch," which contribute to a comic tone. However, students will also notice instances where nouns and verbs are unmodified so as to create a feeling of urgency, as in, "He *ran* to her room, *pulled* out a drawer of her bureau, *removed* the chest . . ." Invite students to share other passages in the story that show the appropriate use of modifiers.

Reteaching/Reinforcement

• *Writing Handbook*, anthology pp. 1030–1032
• *Writing Mini-Lessons* transparencies, pp. 53–54

 **The Writer's Craft**

Avoiding Overuse of Modifiers, p. 411

---

456 THE LANGUAGE OF LITERATURE TEACHER'S EDITION

took a revolver and a box of bullets from the counter drawer; they had been left, years before, by a customer as security for a debt, which had never been paid. He loaded the revolver.

One bright morning at exactly ten o'clock, when the store was full of customers, he excused himself and went through the doorway that connected the store with his home. In a few seconds the customers heard the noise of a row,[11] a woman's scream, and three shots. On the sidewalk in front of the shopkeeper's house they saw his wife on her knees, still screaming, and him, with the revolver in his trembling hand, trying to raise her. The front door of the house was open. Through it, they saw a man's legs, wearing khaki trousers and boots. He was lying face down, with his head and torso in the parlor, not visible from the street.

The husband was the first to speak. Raising his eyes from his wife, he looked at the terror-stricken people and spotted among them his favorite customer. He took a few steps, stood in the doorway, and said:

"You may call the police."

At the police station he explained that he was a deceived husband. The police chief remarked:

"Isn't this a little unusual? Ordinarily you kill your wives. They're weaker than their lovers."

The man was deeply offended.

"No," he protested, "I would be utterly incapable of killing my wife. She is all that I have in the world. She is refined, pretty, and hard-working. She helps me in the store, she understands bookkeeping, she writes the letters to the wholesalers. She is the only person who knows how to prepare my food; I have a special diet. Why should I want to kill my wife?"

"I see," said the chief of police. "So you killed her lover."

The man shook his head.

"Wrong again. The sergeant—her lover—was transferred to a place far away from here. I discovered the affair only after he had gone. By reading his letters. They tell the whole story. I know one of them by heart, the worst of them...."

The police chief did not understand. He said nothing and waited for the husband to continue, which he presently did:

"Those letters! If they were alive, I would kill them, one by one. They were shameful to read—almost like a book. I thought of taking an airplane trip. I thought of killing some other sergeant here so that they would all learn a lesson not to fool around with another man's wife. But I was afraid of the rest of the regiment; you know how these military men stick together. Still, I had to do something. Otherwise I would have gone crazy. I couldn't get those letters out of my head. Even on days when none arrived I felt terrible, worse than my wife. I had to put an end to it, didn't I? So today, at last, I did it. I waited till the regular time and, when I saw the wretch appear on the other side of the street, I went into the house, hid behind a door, and lay there for him."

"The lover?" asked the police chief stupidly.

"No, of course not. I told you I didn't kill her lover. It was those letters. The sergeant sent them—but he delivered them. Almost every day, there he was at the door, smiling, with the vile envelope in his hand. I pointed the revolver and fired three times. He didn't say a word; he just fell. No, Chief, it wasn't her lover. It was the mailman."

Translated by William L. Grossman

---

11. **row:** a noisy quarrel; a brawl.

WORDS TO KNOW
refined (rĭ-fīnd′) *adj.* free from coarseness or vulgarity; polite
vile (vīl) *adj.* disgusting; objectionable; wicked

From Personal Response to Critical Analysis

1. Accept all reasonable responses.
2. Accept all reasonable responses.
3. Possible responses: Some students might predict that the husband would have killed the sergeant. Others may say that the wife and the sergeant would have run away together, or that the affair would have eventually ended.
4. Possible responses: ironic; humorous; comical; mocking
5. Accept all reasonable, well-supported responses.
6. Accept all reasonable, well-supported responses.

Another Pathway

Cooperative Learning The roles for the performance divide naturally into husband, wife, sergeant, and talk show host. During the planning stage, the group can decide whether they will treat the situation seriously or mockingly. One student can serve as director of the talk show, reviewing questions with the host and presentations with each guest.

Rubric
- **3 Full Accomplishment** The performance is lively and offers insights into the characters and their motives.
- **2 Substantial Accomplishment** The performance is lively but actors may not reflect the characters accurately.
- **1 Little or Partial Accomplishment** The performance is lackluster and the characters are not true to the story.

RESPONDING
OPTIONS

FROM PERSONAL RESPONSE TO CRITICAL ANALYSIS

REFLECT
1. How do you feel about the husband's action at the end of the story? Briefly express your feelings in your notebook.

RETHINK
2. Which character do you sympathize with most, and why?
3. What do you think would have happened if the sergeant had not been transferred?
4. How would you describe the story's tone, which conveys the attitude a writer takes toward a subject?

Close Textual Reading
Consider
- the narrator's introductory anecdote about the word metonymy
- the narrator's commentary interspersed throughout the story
- the outcome of the story

5. Do you think the story has a message, or theme? Explain your view.

RELATE
6. The idea of "killing the messenger" goes back to ancient times, when people sometimes killed a messenger because they disliked the message or its sender. Can you think of instances in real life in which a "messenger" is blamed for the "message"? Share your ideas with classmates.

LITERARY CONCEPTS

"Metonymy, or The Husband's Revenge" is an example of a **frame story,** a story within a narrative setting—or frame. The first four paragraphs describing the narrator's use of metonymy in her writing provide the frame for the two stories-within-a-story: the tale about the woman in the boardinghouse and the tale of the husband's revenge. Why do you think the author included the frame instead of just telling about the husband's revenge?

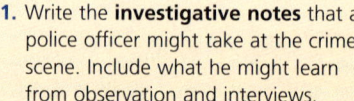
Multimodal Learning
ANOTHER PATHWAY
Cooperative Learning
What would happen if the characters in "Metonymy, or The Husband's Revenge" were invited to appear on a television talk show to share their scandalous story with a public audience? With a group of classmates, sketch out a plan for the show. Then stage it for the rest of the class.

QUICKWRITES

1. Write the **investigative notes** that a police officer might take at the crime scene. Include what he might learn from observation and interviews.
2. Write a **letter** from the wife to the sergeant, telling him what has happened and what she has decided to do next.
3. Imagine that the husband decides to defend himself at his trial. Write his **opening statement** before the jury.

📁 **PORTFOLIO** Save your writing. You may want to use it later as a springboard to a piece for your portfolio.

458   UNIT THREE   PART 2: MYSTERIES OF THE HEART

Literary Concepts

You might want to use the following questions as prompts for discussion:
- *How does the presence of the narrator in the frame affect the tone of the story? (It allows the narrator to make personal comments and observations, adding to the story's humor.)*
- *How did the anecdote about the landlady's boarder help "set you up" for the main tale? (Both the boarder and the husband make the same mistake.)*

QuickWrites

1. Suggest that students use a graphic organizer such as a double-column journal with quotes from interviews on one side and observations on the other.
2. Suggest that students review the story for insights into the wife's character.
3. Encourage students to use pompous legal and rhetorical phrases.

The Writer's Craft
Interview, pp. 72–76
Voice and Style, pp. 420–423

Multimodal Learning

ALTERNATIVE ACTIVITIES

1. Draw a **cartoon** to illustrate a scene from the story. Use a quotation from the story to serve as a caption. Then display your artwork on a classroom or school bulletin board.
2. Imagine that you are a radio or television journalist and prepare and deliver a **newscast** about the mailman's murder. If your report is for television, you may want to draw pictures of key scenes and present visuals as part of your story.

CRITIC'S CORNER

Fred P. Ellison, one of Queiroz's translators, has praised her work for its "acute perception of human motives." How well do you think his observation applies to "Metonymy, or The Husband's Revenge"? Explain your view.

LITERARY LINKS

Compare and contrast the husband in this story to Henry in "The Californian's Tale" by Mark Twain.

WORDS TO KNOW

EXERCISE A Identify the word that is closest in meaning to the word in bold print.

1. **refined:** (a) scarce, (b) polished, (c) expensive
2. **embellish:** (a) adorn, (b) create, (c) ring
3. **scrutinize:** (a) struggle, (b) twist, (c) inspect
4. **tepid:** (a) enthusiastic, (b) hot, (c) indifferent
5. **deplorable:** (a) bad, (b) favorable, (c) capable
6. **eminently:** (a) prominently, (b) quickly, (c) weakly
7. **rebuke:** (a) response, (b) praise, (c) scolding
8. **vile:** (a) hidden, (b) wretched, (c) pleasant
9. **ingratiating:** (a) charming, (b) harsh, (c) unappreciative
10. **illicit:** (a) sick, (b) incapable, (c) illegal

EXERCISE B Play a game of charades with the Words to Know, pantomiming their meanings for classmates. Try to present each word in its entirety instead of syllable-by-syllable.

RACHEL DE QUEIROZ

1910–

Rachel de Queiroz once wrote, "The . . . merit I may possess is in my free and easy countrywoman's way of saying things, of telling stories about what I know and what I like." For more than 60 years, Queiroz has done just that, writing novels, plays, stories, and essays on political and social issues that deeply interest her. The status and role of women in Brazilian society have always been among Queiroz's primary concerns, and much of her writing features strong female protagonists.

As a child, Queiroz lived on her family's ranch in northeastern Brazil. Her first novel, *The Year '15*, was inspired by family stories of the great drought that hit northeastern Brazil in 1915. Hailed as part of a new wave of Brazilian writers who focused on real-life social and economic problems, Queiroz wrote three more realistic novels.

Queiroz devoted herself to journalism in the early 1940s, writing political articles and *crônicas*, which gained her a wide following in Brazil. In recognition of her life's work, she was elected to the Brazilian Academy of Letters, the first woman to receive that honor.

OTHER WORKS *The Three Marias; Dôra, Doralina*

Extended Reading

METONYMY, OR THE HUSBAND'S REVENGE 459

Alternative Activities

1. Urge students to try to incorporate each level of the frame story into their cartoons.
2. Encourage students to use a mock-serious tone similar to that used in the story. Their aim would be to give the facts of the case while implicitly making fun of sensationalist journalism.

WORDS TO KNOW

Exercise A
1. b
2. a
3. c
4. c
5. a
6. a
7. c
8. b
9. a
10. c

Exercise B
Responses will vary.

Reteaching/Reinforcement
- *Unit Three Resource Book*, p. 52

Literary Links

Possible responses: Both husbands are deeply, even unhealthily, attached to their wives and remain so after they have lost them (though the loss in Henry's case is permanent). Both take bizarre, illogical actions. Henry, however, is a tragic and sympathetic character; the husband in "Metonymy" is comical and less sympathetic.

Across the Curriculum

Health The husband suffers from a variety of symptoms: yellow skin, rheumy eyes, asthmatic chest, fatigue, weak legs. Have students research the diseases mentioned in the story—beriberi, asthma, and jaundice—investigating the causes, effects, treatment and prevention of each disease. Have students recommend a health regimen the husband should follow.

RACHEL DE QUEIROZ

Queiroz explores themes of social conflict, poverty, and the oppression of women in her writing. She frequently sets her stories in her native state of Cear, and her writing has helped raise awareness of issues and problems facing that region.

OVERVIEW

Objectives

- To understand and appreciate a short story about love among Jewish immigrants shortly after World War II
- To enrich reading by using active reading strategies
- To identify and understand allusion
- To express understanding of a selection through a choice of writing forms, including a wedding announcement, public service announcements, and a biographical sketch
- To extend understanding of the selection through a variety of multimodal and cross-curricular activities

Skills

LITERARY CONCEPTS
- Allusion
- Point of view
- Style

READING SKILLS/STRATEGIES
- Interpreting motivation
- Question

THE WRITER'S STYLE
- Style

GRAMMAR
- Appositives

SPEAKING, LISTENING, AND VIEWING
- Art
- Role play
- Group discussion

CULTURAL CONNECTION
Immigrant's World, New York City

Many of Bernard Malamud's fictional characters are Jewish immigrants or children of such immigrants (as was Malamud himself). These photographs of Jewish immigrants in New York City in the mid-1900s will help students visualize Malamud's world.

Side A, Frame 49477

PREVIEWING

FICTION

The First Seven Years
Bernard Malamud (măl′ə-məd) United States

Activating Prior Knowledge
PERSONAL CONNECTION

Think about the qualities or characteristics that you would consider especially important in a husband or wife. Would a sense of humor be important, or physical appearance, or shared interests and goals? Would your parents or guardians find the same qualities important in the spouse of your choice? In your notebook, make a Venn diagram like the one shown.

Building Background
HISTORICAL/CULTURAL CONNECTION

In "The First Seven Years," Feld the shoemaker expresses his ideas about the qualities that his daughter Miriam should seek in a husband. Feld is one of the millions of eastern European Jews who immigrated to America from 1880 to 1930 to escape religious persecution and seek economic opportunity. Though often not educated themselves, these Jewish immigrants placed great value on education and saw it as the means by which their children would achieve the American dream. Many of them settled in New York City, where "The First Seven Years" is set. This story takes place in the years just after World War II, when a new and far smaller group of European Jews arrived in America. These refugees—including Sobel in the story—were survivors of the Holocaust.

Ship bringing immigrants to the United States. Photo courtesy of Brown Brothers.

Active Reading/Setting a Purpose
READING CONNECTION

Interpreting Motivation As you read this story, pay attention to the hopes and dreams that Feld the shoemaker has for his daughter. What type of man does he want his daughter to marry? What qualities does he believe her husband should possess? What motivates him to have such qualities in mind?

Using Your Reading Log Use your reading log to record your responses to the questions inserted throughout the selection. Also jot down other thoughts and feelings as you read.

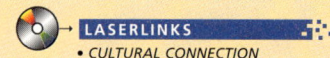
- CULTURAL CONNECTION

460 UNIT THREE PART 2: MYSTERIES OF THE HEART

PRINT AND MEDIA RESOURCES

UNIT THREE RESOURCE BOOK
Strategic Reading: Literature, p. 51
Vocabulary SkillBuilder, p. 52

GRAMMAR MINI-LESSONS
Transparencies, p. 20
Copymasters, p. 22

WRITING MINI-LESSONS
Transparencies, pp. 44–56

ACCESS FOR STUDENTS ACQUIRING ENGLISH
Selection Summaries
Reading Support

FORMAL ASSESSMENT
Selection Test, pp. 93–94
Test Generator

AUDIO LIBRARY
See Reference Card

LASERLINKS
Cultural Connection

INTERNET RESOURCES
McDougal Littell Literature Center at http://www.hmco.com/mcdougal/lit

460 THE LANGUAGE OF LITERATURE TEACHER'S EDITION

Les souliers [A pair of boots] (1887), Vincent van Gogh. Oil on canvas, 13″ × 16⅛″, The Baltimore Museum of Art, The Cone Collection, formed by Dr. Claribel Cone and Miss Etta Cone of Baltimore, Maryland (BMA 1950.302).

THE FIRST SEVEN YEARS

BERNARD

Feld, the shoemaker, was annoyed that his helper, Sobel, was so insensitive to his reverie that he wouldn't for a minute cease his fanatic pounding at the other bench.

SUMMARY

Feld, a shoemaker, wishes that his daughter Miriam would go to college, but she is content to read the books she gets from Feld's poor assistant, Sobel. One day, Feld asks Max, a college student he admires, if Max will introduce himself to Miriam, hoping that the encounter will awaken her desire to go to college, or if not, that at least she might marry Max and have a life with a scholarly man. Overhearing, Sobel reacts furiously to Feld's plan by leaving the shop and intending not to return. The shop begins to suffer, and so does Feld's health, especially when he discovers that his new assistant has been stealing from him. In the meantime, Miriam dates Max twice and pronounces him a boring materialist. Finally, Feld goes to Sobel and begs him to come back. At that meeting, he faces what he sensed all along: his assistant loves his daughter. Although upset that if she marries Sobel, (she will be the wife of a shoemaker), he gives Sobel permission to ask for her hand in two years. When Feld opens his shop the next day, he finds the faithful Sobel working steadily.

Thematic Link: *Mysteries of the Heart*
This story offers a glimpse of unspoken love that patiently endures years of waiting.

Art Note

***Les Souliers (A Pair of Boots)* by Vincent van Gogh** The Dutch post-Impressionist Van Gogh (1853–1890) could infuse the most humble, ordinary objects—such as a pair of unlaced boots—with the light of compassionate insight.

Reading the Art *What feelings does this simple still life evoke?*

CUSTOMIZING FOR
Students Acquiring English

- Use **ACCESS FOR STUDENTS ACQUIRING ENGLISH**, Reading Support.

- Explain to students that much of the narration reflects speech patterns of the Yiddish language commonly spoken by Jewish immigrants at the time the story takes place. Although Yiddish itself is not spoken in the story, Feld's sentence structure often employs the inverted syntax common in that language.

WORDS TO KNOW

apt (ăpt) *adj.* quick to learn or understand (p. 465)
deft (dĕft) *adj.* skillful (p. 467)
direst (dīr′ĕst) *adj.* most terrible; worst (p. 462)
discern (dĭ-sûrn′) *v.* to perceive with the eyes or intellect; to recognize (p. 462)
pallid (păl′ĭd) *adj.* abnormally pale (p. 468)
pittance (pĭt′ns) *n.* a small amount of money (p. 465)

profuse (prə-fyōōs′) *adj.* plentiful; given freely and abundantly (p. 465)
repugnant (rĭ-pŭg′nənt) *adj.* offensive; repulsive (p. 466)
seethe (sēth) *v.* to be violently agitated or excited; to churn as if boiling (p. 468)
vehemently (vē′ə-mənt-lē) *adv.* forcefully; with intensity of emotion (p. 468)

STRATEGIC READING FOR
Less-Proficient Readers

Set a Purpose Explain that the first paragraph of the story introduces all four of the story's characters. Ask students to read on to find out how Feld influences the lives of the other characters.

Use **UNIT THREE RESOURCE BOOK**, p. 51, for guidance in reading the selection.

CUSTOMIZING FOR
Multiple Learning Styles

Ⓐ Interpersonal Learners Ask students to describe Feld's personality based on details they read in this paragraph. *(Possible responses: Feld is philosophical; resigned; sad; disappointed, yet hopeful; hard-working; practical.)*

Ⓐ He gave him a look, but Sobel's bald head was bent over the last[1] as he worked, and he didn't notice. The shoemaker shrugged and continued to peer through the partly frosted window at the near-sighted haze of falling February snow. Neither the shifting white blur outside, nor the sudden deep remembrance of the snowy Polish village where he had wasted his youth could turn his thoughts from Max the college boy, (a constant visitor in the mind since early that morning when Feld saw him trudging through the snowdrifts on his way to school) whom he so much respected because of the sacrifices he had made throughout the years—in winter or <u>direst</u> heat—to further his education. An old wish returned to haunt the shoemaker: that he had had a son instead of a daughter, but this blew away in the snow for Feld, if anything, was a practical man. Yet he could not help but contrast the diligence of the boy, who was a peddler's son, with Miriam's unconcern for an education. True, she was always with a book in her hand, yet when the opportunity arose for a college education, she had said no she would rather find a job. He had begged her to go, pointing out how many fathers could not afford to send their children to college, but she said she wanted to be independent. As for education, what was it, she asked, but books, which Sobel, who diligently read the classics, would as usual advise her on. Her answer greatly grieved her father.

A figure emerged from the snow, and the door opened. At the counter the man withdrew from a wet paper bag a pair of battered shoes for repair. Who he was the shoemaker for a moment had no idea, then his heart trembled as he realized, before he had thoroughly <u>discerned</u> the face, that Max himself was standing there, embarrassedly explaining what he wanted done to his old shoes. Though Feld listened eagerly, he couldn't hear a word, for the opportunity that had burst upon him was deafening.

He couldn't exactly recall when the thought had occurred to him, because it was clear he had more than once considered suggesting to the boy that he go out with Miriam. But he had not dared speak, for if Max said no, how would he face him again? Or suppose Miriam, who harped so often on independence, blew up in anger and shouted at him for his meddling? Still, the chance was too good to let by: all it meant was an introduction. They might long ago have become friends had they happened to meet somewhere, therefore was it not his duty—an obligation—to bring them together, nothing more, a harmless connivance[2] to replace an accidental encounter in the subway, let's say, or a mutual friend's introduction in the street? Just let him once see and talk to her, and he would for sure be interested. As for Miriam, what possible harm for a working girl in an office, who met only loud-mouthed salesmen and illiterate shipping clerks, to make the acquaintance of a fine scholarly boy? Maybe he would awaken in her a desire to go to college; if not—the shoemaker's mind at last came to grips with the truth—let her marry an educated man and live a better life.

When Max finished describing what he wanted done to his shoes, Feld marked them, both with enormous holes in the soles which he pretended not to notice, with large white-chalk *x*'s, and the rubber heels, thinned to the nails, he marked with *o*'s, though it troubled him he might have mixed up the letters. Max inquired the price, and the shoemaker cleared his throat and asked the boy, above Sobel's insistent hammering, would he please step through the side door there into the hall. Though surprised, Max did

---

1. **last:** a block or form shaped like a human foot and used in making or repairing shoes.
2. **connivance** (kə-nī′vəns): a scheme; a plot.

WORDS TO KNOW
direst (dīr′ĕst) *adj.* most terrible; worst
discern (dĭ-sûrn′) *v.* to perceive with the eyes or intellect; to recognize

---

Mini-Lesson Grammar

APPOSITIVES Remind students that an appositive is a noun or pronoun that usually follows another noun or pronoun and identifies or explains it.

- Feld, <u>the shoemaker</u>, hopes his daughter will marry well.
- his helper, <u>Sobel</u>
- Max <u>the college boy</u>
- my daughter <u>Miriam</u>

Point out that in writing, commas may be used for clarity to set off an appositive from the rest of the sentence, as in the first example given.

Application Have students work in pairs or small groups to compose several appositives identifying the characters in this story. Encourage students to use the appositives in sentences.

Reteaching/Reinforcement
- *Grammar Mini-Lessons* copymasters p. 22, transparencies, p. 20

 **The Writer's Craft**

Appositives and Appositive Phrases, pp. 589–590

as the shoemaker requested, and Feld went in after him. For a minute they were both silent, because Sobel had stopped banging, and it seemed they understood neither was to say anything until the noise began again. When it did, loudly, the shoemaker quickly told Max why he had asked to talk to him.

"Ever since you went to high school," he said, in the dimly-lit hallway, "I watched you in the morning go to the subway to school, and I said always to myself, this is a fine boy that he wants so much an education."

"Thanks," Max said, nervously alert. He was tall and grotesquely thin, with sharply cut features, particularly a beak-like nose. He was wearing a loose, long slushy overcoat that hung down to his ankles, looking like a rug draped over his bony shoulders, and a soggy, old brown hat, as battered as the shoes he had brought in.

"I am a business man," the shoemaker abruptly said to conceal his embarrassment, "so I will explain you right away why I talk to you. I have a girl, my daughter Miriam—she is nineteen—a very nice girl and also so pretty that everybody looks on her when she passes by in the street. She is smart, always with a book, and I thought to myself that a boy like you, an educated boy—I thought maybe you will be interested sometime to meet a girl like this." He laughed a bit when he had finished and was tempted to say more but had the good sense not to.

Max stared down like a hawk. For an uncomfortable second he was silent, then he asked, "Did you say nineteen?"

"Yes."

"Would it be all right to inquire if you have a picture of her?"

"Just a minute." The shoemaker went into the store and hastily returned with a snapshot that Max held up to the light.

"She's all right," he said.

Feld waited.

"And is she sensible—not the flighty kind?"

"She is very sensible."

After another short pause, Max said it was okay with him if he met her.

"Here is my telephone," said the shoemaker,

> "She is smart, always with a book, and I thought to myself that a boy like you, an educated boy—I thought maybe you will be interested sometime to meet a girl like this."

hurriedly handing him a slip of paper. "Call her up. She comes home from work six o'clock."

Max folded the paper and tucked it away into his worn leather wallet.

"About the shoes," he said. "How much did you say they will cost me?"

"Don't worry about the price."

"I just like to have an idea."

"A dollar—dollar fifty. A dollar fifty," the shoemaker said.

At once he felt bad, for he usually charged two twenty-five for this kind of job. Either he should have asked the regular price or done the work for nothing.

Later, as he entered the store, he was startled by a violent clanging and looked up to see Sobel pounding with all his might upon the naked last. It broke, the iron striking the floor

THE FIRST SEVEN YEARS 463

Mini-Lesson   The Writer's Style

STYLE Remind students that style is the distinctive way in which a work of literature is written. Style refers not so much to what is said but how it is said. Word choice, sentence length, tone, imagery, and use of dialogue all contribute to a writer's style.

Application Copy the chart shown here on to the chalkboard. Invite the class to point out aspects of Malamud's style that impress them and fill in the chart with their ideas.

Reteaching/Reinforcement
- *Writing Mini-Lessons* transparencies, pp. 44–56

Voice and Style, pp. 420–423

Bernard Malamud STYLE

Word Choice	• sometimes bookish or poetic (*grieved, unconcern, diligently*)
	• sometimes plain (*she was always with a book in her hand*)
Sentence Length	•
Tone	•
Imagery	•
Dialogue	•

Art Note

Girl with a Book by Matej Sternen
Using thick brush strokes, the painter portrays a young woman with head down, intent on the pages of a book. Sternen was a noted member of the Slovene Impressionist movement, which was active in Slovenia, formerly part of Yugoslavia, during the first part of the 1900s.

Reading the Art *How does the woman in this painting resemble, or differ from, your image of Miriam in the story?*

Linking to History

F The nations of Eastern Europe had large Jewish populations before World War II. Malamud's forebears came from Russia; Feld, in the story, is a Polish refugee. According to historian Lucy S. Dawidowicz in *The War Against the Jews 1933–1945*, 90% of the Jews in Poland (three million people) were annihilated by the Nazis. In Russia, which was partially occupied by the Nazis, the losses were 107,000 out of 975,000 (11%).

Girl with a Book (1927), Matej Sternen. National Gallery, Ljubljana, Slovenia.

464 UNIT THREE PART 2: MYSTERIES OF THE HEART

Critic's Corner

"In Malamud's fictional world, there is always a prison."

Leslie and Joyce Field
Bernard Malamud: A Collection of Critical Essays

"Necessity is the primary prison, though the bars are not visible to all."

Bernard Malamud in an interview with Leslie and Joyce Field

Ask students what "prison" might be represented in "The First Seven Years."

and jumping with a thump against the wall, but before the enraged shoemaker could cry out, the assistant had torn his hat and coat from the hook and rushed out into the snow.

QUESTION
What do you think has made Sobel so angry?
Using a Reading Log

So Feld, who had looked forward to anticipating how it would go with his daughter and Max, instead had a great worry on his mind. Without his temperamental helper he was a lost man, especially since it was years now that he had carried the store alone. The shoemaker had for an age suffered from a heart condition that threatened collapse if he dared exert himself. Five years ago, after an attack, it had appeared as though he would have either to sacrifice his business upon the auction block and live on a pittance thereafter, or put himself at the mercy of some unscrupulous employee who would in the end probably ruin him. But just at the moment of his darkest despair, this Polish refugee, Sobel, appeared one night from the street and begged for work. He was a stocky man, poorly dressed, with a bald head that had once been blond, a severely plain face and soft blue eyes prone to tears over the sad books he read, a young man but old—no one would have guessed thirty. Though he confessed he knew nothing of shoemaking, he said he was apt and would work for a very little if Feld taught him the trade. Thinking that with, after all, a landsman,³ he would have less to fear than from a complete stranger, Feld took him on and within six weeks the refugee rebuilt as good a shoe as he, and not long thereafter expertly ran the business for the thoroughly relieved shoemaker. Feld could trust him with anything and did, frequently going home after an hour or two at the store, leaving all the money in the till,⁴ knowing Sobel would guard every cent of it. The amazing thing was that he demanded so little. His wants were few; in money he wasn't interested—in nothing but books, it seemed—which he one by one lent to Miriam, together with his profuse, queer written comments, manufactured during his lonely rooming house evenings, thick pads of commentary which the shoemaker peered at and twitched his shoulders over as his daughter, from her fourteenth year, read page by sanctified page, as if the word of God were inscribed on them. To protect Sobel, Feld himself had to see that he received more than he asked for. Yet his conscience bothered him for not insisting that the assistant accept a better wage than he was getting, though Feld had honestly told him he could earn a handsome salary if he worked elsewhere, or maybe opened a place of his own. But the assistant answered, somewhat ungraciously, that he was not interested in going elsewhere, and though Feld frequently asked himself what keeps him here? why does he stay? he finally answered it that the man, no doubt because of his terrible experiences as a refugee, was afraid of the world.

After the incident with the broken last, angered by Sobel's behavior, the shoemaker decided to let him stew for a week in the rooming house, although his own strength was taxed dangerously and the business suffered. However, after several sharp nagging warnings from both his wife and daughter, he went finally in search of Sobel, as he had once before, quite recently, when over some fancied slight—Feld had merely asked him not to give Miriam so many books to read because her eyes were strained and red—the assistant had left the

---

3. **landsman:** a fellow Jew who comes from the same district or town, especially in eastern Europe.
4. **till:** a drawer or compartment for holding money.

WORDS TO KNOW
pittance (pĭt′ns) *n.* a small amount of money
apt (ăpt) *adj.* quick to learn or understand
profuse (prə-fyo͞os′) *adj.* plentiful; given freely and abundantly

465

Active Reading: QUESTION

G Discuss students' insights or ideas about Sobel's feelings. You might wish to use the following model to show students a possible line of inquiry.
Think-Aloud Model *I think Sobel's anger has been building during Max's visit. I recall all that banging he does as he works, and then the silence while Feld and Max talk, as if Sobel is eavesdropping. Sobel might resent Feld's catering to Max. Perhaps Sobel is jealous of Max.)*

Literary Concept: FLASHBACK

H Point out the beginning of a flashback with the words "Five years ago...." Ask students what purposes this flashback serves. *(Possible responses: to provide details about Feld's and Sobel's backgrounds; to explain their working relationship; to indicate how Sobel and Miriam became attached to one another)*

Mini-Lesson Literary Concepts

REVIEWING POINT OF VIEW Remind students that most fictional narratives are written in the first-person or the third-person point of view. In a story told from the first-person point of view, the narrator refers to himself or herself as *I* and is usually a character in the story relating his or her own experiences, attitudes, and opinions. In a story told from the third-person point of view, such as "The First Seven Years," the narrator does not participate in the story, but rather relates events as an observer.

Application Ask pairs of students to imagine an event in Miriam's life and write a paragraph about the event from a third-person point of view. Encourage students to use insights into Miriam's character that they've learned from reading the story. Invite students to read their paragraphs aloud.

THE LANGUAGE OF LITERATURE TEACHER'S EDITION **465**

place in a huff, an incident which, as usual, came to nothing, for he had returned after the shoemaker had talked to him, and taken his seat at the bench. But this time, after Feld had plodded through the snow to Sobel's house—he had thought of sending Miriam but the idea became repugnant to him—the burly landlady at the door informed him in a nasal voice that Sobel was not at home, and though Feld knew this was a nasty lie, for where had the refugee to go? still for some reason he was not completely sure of—it may have been the cold and his fatigue—he decided not to insist on seeing him. Instead he went home and hired a new helper.

Having settled the matter, though not entirely to his satisfaction, for he had much more to do than before, and so, for example, could no longer lie late in bed mornings because he had to get up to open the store for the new assistant, a speechless, dark man with an irritating rasp[5] as he worked, whom he would not trust with the key as he had Sobel. Furthermore, this one, though able to do a fair repair job, knew nothing of grades of leather or prices, so Feld had to make his own purchases; and every night at closing time it was necessary to count the money in the till and lock up. However, he was not dissatisfied, for he lived much in his thoughts of Max and Miriam. The college boy had called her, and they had arranged a meeting for this coming Friday night. The shoemaker would personally have preferred Saturday, which he felt would make it a date of the first magnitude, but he learned Friday was Miriam's choice, so he said nothing. The day of the week did not matter. What mattered was the aftermath. Would they like each other and want to be friends? He sighed at all the time that would have to go by before he knew for sure. Often he was tempted to talk to Miriam about the boy, to ask whether she thought she would like his type—he had told her only that he considered Max a nice boy and had suggested he call her—but the one time he tried she snapped at him—justly—how should she know?

At last Friday came. Feld was not feeling particularly well, so he stayed in bed, and Mrs. Feld thought it better to remain in the bedroom with him when Max called. Miriam received the boy, and her parents could hear their voices, his throaty one, as they talked. Just before leaving, Miriam brought Max to the bedroom door, and he stood there a minute, a tall, slightly hunched figure wearing a thick, droopy suit, and apparently at ease as he greeted the shoemaker and his wife, which was surely a good sign. And Miriam, although she had worked all day, looked fresh and pretty. She was a large-framed girl with a well-shaped body, and she had a fine open face and soft hair. They made, Feld thought, a first-class couple.

Miriam returned after 11:30. Her mother was already asleep, but the shoemaker got out of bed and after locating his bathrobe went into the kitchen, where Miriam, to his surprise, sat at the table, reading.

"So where did you go?" Feld asked pleasantly.

"For a walk," she said, not looking up.

"I advised him," Feld said, clearing his throat, "he shouldn't spend so much money."

"I didn't care."

The shoemaker boiled up some water for tea and sat down at the table with a cupful and thick slice of lemon.

"So how," he sighed after a sip, "did you enjoy?"

"It was all right."

He was silent. She must have sensed his disappointment, for she added, "You can't

---

5. **rasp:** a harsh, grating sound.

WORDS TO KNOW

repugnant (rĭ-pŭg′nənt) *adj.* offensive; repulsive

really tell much the first time."

"You will see him again?"

Turning a page, she said that Max had asked for another date.

"For when?"

"Saturday."

"So what did you say?"

"What did I say?" she asked, delaying for a moment—"I said yes."

Afterwards she inquired about Sobel, and Feld, without exactly knowing why, said the assistant had got another job. Miriam said nothing more and began to read. The shoemaker's conscience did not trouble him; he was satisfied with the Saturday date.

During the week, by placing here and there a deft question, he managed to get from Miriam some information about Max. It surprised him to learn that the boy was not studying to be either a doctor or lawyer but was taking a business course leading to a degree in accountancy. Feld was a little disappointed because he thought of accountants as bookkeepers and would have preferred "a higher profession." However, it was not long before he had investigated the subject and discovered that certified public accountants were highly respected people, so he was thoroughly content as Saturday approached. But because Saturday was a busy day, he was much in the store and therefore did not see Max when he came to call for Miriam. From his wife he learned there had been nothing especially revealing about their meeting. Max had rung the bell, and Miriam had got her coat and left with him—nothing more. Feld did not probe, for his wife was not particularly observant. Instead, he waited up for Miriam with a newspaper on his lap, which he scarcely looked at so lost was he in thinking of the future. He awoke to find her in the room with him, tiredly removing her hat.

Greeting her, he was suddenly inexplicably afraid to ask anything about the evening. But since she volunteered nothing, he was at last forced to inquire how she had enjoyed herself. Miriam began something noncommittal but apparently changed her mind, for she said after a minute, "I was bored."

When Feld had sufficiently recovered from

Greeting her, he was suddenly inexplicably afraid to ask anything about the evening.

his anguished disappointment to ask why, she answered without hesitation, "Because he's nothing more than a materialist."

"What means this word?"

"He has no soul. He's only interested in things."

He considered her statement for a long time but then asked, "Will you see him again?"

"He didn't ask."

"Suppose he will ask you?"

"I won't see him."

He did not argue; however, as the days went by he hoped increasingly she would change her mind. He wished the boy would telephone, because he was sure there was more to him than Miriam, with her inexperienced eye, could discern. But Max didn't call. As a matter of fact he took a different route to school, no longer passing the shoemaker's store, and Feld was deeply hurt.

Then one afternoon Max came in and asked for his shoes. The shoemaker took them down from the shelf where he had placed them, apart

EVALUATE

Why didn't Miriam and Max get along?
Using a Reading Log

WORDS TO KNOW

deft (dĕft) *adj.* skillful

467

**Literary Concept:
CHARACTERIZATION**

O Invite students to discuss what this exchange adds to the reader's understanding of Max and Feld. (Possible responses: Max is happy he is getting a bargain even though the special price hinged on Max's relationship with Miriam, which has gone awry; Feld is a man of his word, even when disappointed.)

Literary Concept: STYLE

P Point out Malamud's use of the word "toiled" to describe how Feld walks up the stairs to Sobel's room. Invite students to discuss what that word adds to the story. (Possible responses: It emphasizes Feld's failing strength; it stresses Feld's reluctance to ask for Sobel's help.)

Critical Thinking: ANALYZING

Q Ask students what they think Sobel really wants from Feld. (Possible responses: Some students may say Sobel wants Miriam; others might say respect or trust.)

Literary Concept: MOTIVATION

R As the tension between Feld and Sobel builds during their urgent conversation, Sobel's motivation—his reason for behaving as he does—bursts into the open. Invite students to summarize it. (He is in love with Miriam.)

---

from the other pairs. He had done the work himself, and the soles and heels were well built and firm. The shoes had been highly polished and somehow looked better than new. Max's Adam's apple went up once when he saw them, and his eyes had little lights in them.

"How much?" he asked, without directly looking at the shoemaker.

"Like I told you before," Feld answered sadly. "One dollar fifty cents."

Max handed him two crumpled bills and received in return a newly-minted silver half dollar.

He left. Miriam had not been mentioned. That night the shoemaker discovered that his new assistant had been all the while stealing from him, and he suffered a heart attack.

Though the attack was very mild, he lay in bed for three weeks. Miriam spoke of going for Sobel, but sick as he was Feld rose in wrath against the idea. Yet in his heart he knew there was no other way, and the first weary day back in the shop thoroughly convinced him, so that night after supper he dragged himself to Sobel's rooming house.

He toiled up the stairs, though he knew it was bad for him, and at the top knocked at the door. Sobel opened it, and the shoemaker entered. The room was a small, poor one, with a single window facing the street. It contained a narrow cot, a low table and several stacks of books piled haphazardly around on the floor along the wall, which made him think how queer Sobel was, to be uneducated and read so much. He had once asked him, Sobel, why you read so much? and the assistant could not answer him. Did you ever study in a college someplace? he had asked, but Sobel shook his head. He read, he said, to know. But to know what, the shoemaker demanded, and to know, why? Sobel never explained, which proved he read much because he was queer.

Feld sat down to recover his breath. The assistant was resting on his bed with his heavy back to the wall. His shirt and trousers were clean, and his stubby fingers, away from the shoemaker's bench, were strangely pallid. His face was thin and pale, as if he had been shut in this room since the day he had bolted from the store.

"So when you will come back to work?" Feld asked him.

To his surprise, Sobel burst out, "Never."

Jumping up, he strode over to the window that looked out upon the miserable street. "Why should I come back?" he cried.

"I will raise your wages."

"Who cares for your wages!"

The shoemaker, knowing he didn't care, was at a loss what else to say.

"What do you want from me, Sobel?"

"Nothing."

"I always treated you like you was my son."

Sobel vehemently denied it. "So why you look for strange boys in the street they should go out with Miriam? Why you don't think of me?"

The shoemaker's hands and feet turned freezing cold. His voice became so hoarse he couldn't speak. At last he cleared his throat and croaked, "So what has my daughter got to do with a shoemaker thirty-five years old who works for me?"

"Why do you think I worked so long for you?" Sobel cried out. "For the stingy wages I sacrificed five years of my life so you could have to eat and drink and where to sleep?"

"Then for what?" shouted the shoemaker.

"For Miriam," he blurted—"for her."

The shoemaker, after a time, managed to say, "I pay wages in cash, Sobel," and lapsed into silence. Though he was seething with excitement, his mind was coldly clear, and he had to

WORDS	**pallid** (păl′ĭd) *adj.* abnormally pale
TO	**vehemently** (vē′ə-mənt-lē) *adv.* forcefully; with intensity of emotion
KNOW	**seethe** (sēth) *v.* to be violently agitated or excited; to churn as if boiling

468

Mini-Lesson: Speaking, Listening, and Viewing

ART Point out to students that illustrations can bring out or heighten the mood of a story through the artist's use of color, composition, line, shadow and light, and choice of medium.

Application Focus student attention on the van Gogh painting on page 461 and the Sternen on page 464. Invite volunteers to describe the mood or feeling that they perceive in the two pictures, and to discuss how each artist achieves that feeling. Then invite students to sketch an illustration for "The First Seven Years," which captures a mood of the story. Invite students to show their illustrations and ask classmates to interpret it.

admit to himself he had sensed all along that Sobel felt this way. He had never so much as thought it consciously, but he had felt it and was afraid.

"Miriam knows?" he muttered hoarsely.

"She knows."

"You told her?"

"No."

"Then how does she know?"

"How does she know?" Sobel said, "because she knows. She knows who I am and what is in my heart."

Feld had a sudden insight. In some devious way, with his books and commentary, Sobel had given Miriam to understand that he loved her. The shoemaker felt a terrible anger at him for his deceit.

"Sobel, you are crazy," he said bitterly. "She will never marry a man so old and ugly like you."

Sobel turned black with rage. He cursed the shoemaker, but then, though he trembled to hold it in, his eyes filled with tears, and he broke into deep sobs. With his back to Feld, he stood at the window, fists clenched, and his shoulders shook with his choked sobbing.

Watching him, the shoemaker's anger diminished. His teeth were on edge with pity for the man, and his eyes grew moist. How strange and sad that a refugee, a grown man, bald and old with his miseries, who had by the skin of his teeth escaped Hitler's incinerators, should fall in love, when he had got to America, with a girl less than half his age. Day after day, for five years he had sat at his bench, cutting and hammering away, waiting for the girl to become a woman, unable to ease his heart with speech, knowing no protest but desperation.

"Ugly I didn't mean," he said half aloud.

Then he realized that what he had called ugly was not Sobel but Miriam's life if she married him. He felt for his daughter a strange and gripping sorrow, as if she were already Sobel's bride—the wife, after all, of a shoemaker—and had in her life no more than her mother had had. And all his dreams for her—why he had slaved and destroyed his heart with anxiety and labor—all these dreams of a better life were dead.

The room was quiet. Sobel was standing by the window reading, and it was curious that when he read he looked young.

"She is only nineteen," Feld said brokenly. "This is too young yet to get married. Don't ask her for two years more, till she is twenty-one, then you can talk to her."

Sobel didn't answer. Feld rose and left. He went slowly down the stairs, but once outside, though it was an icy night and the crisp falling snow whitened the street, he walked with a stronger stride.

But the next morning, when the shoemaker arrived, heavy-hearted, to open the store, he saw he needn't have come, for his assistant was already seated at the last, pounding leather for his love. ❖

From Personal Response to Critical Analysis

1. Accept all reasonable responses.
2. Accept all reasonable responses. Some students might admire Feld for his hard work and devotion to family. Others might dislike him for his harshness toward Sobel and his meddling in Miriam's life.
3. Some students might say that Sobel's poverty, age, personality, and background make him a bad marriage prospect; others may say that love and intellectual affinity are more important than those factors.
4. Accept either choice as long as the explanation refers to the student's Venn diagram and is supported with details from the selection. "Neither" may also be an acceptable choice.
5. Accept all reasonable, well-supported responses.

Another Pathway

Students may work individually or with a partner. Suggest that before they write, students review the story and jot down words or phrases that give insight into the character they have chosen.

Rubric

3 Full Accomplishment Rewritten passage displays mastery of first-person point of view, correctly recounts events of the story, and shows insight into the character.

2 Substantial Accomplishment Passage shows basic understanding of first-person point of view but may fail to relate story events or the personality of the character accurately.

1 Little or Partial Accomplishment Passage is not consistently written in the first-person point of view and does not accurately relate the story or a sense of the character.

RESPONDING OPTIONS

FROM PERSONAL RESPONSE TO CRITICAL ANALYSIS

REFLECT
1. What do you think of Sobel at the end of the story? Write down your impressions in your notebook, then share your ideas with a classmate.

RETHINK
2. What is your opinion of Feld? Explain your views.

Close Textual Reading

   Consider
   - his relationship with his daughter
   - his treatment of Sobel
   - what you learn about his life and values

3. If Miriam were your daughter, would you want her to marry Sobel?

Close Textual Reading

   Consider
   - what Sobel and Miriam have in common
   - whether you believe they will be happy together
   - whether Sobel possesses the qualities that you value in a mate

RELATE
4. Review the Venn diagram you created for the Personal Connection on page 460. Which character do you think would be more likely to earn the respect of your parents or guardians, Max or Sobel? Explain your choice.

5. In today's society, do you think parents should exert an influence in their child's choice of mate?

Multimodal Learning
ANOTHER PATHWAY

Think about how the story would have been different if told from a first-person point of view. For example, if Sobel had narrated the story, how might he have described Feld's actions? Choose one section of the story and rewrite it from the point of view of one of the characters. Discuss the effects of altering the point of view.

QUICKWRITES

1. Write the **wedding announcement** that might appear in the neighborhood newspaper if Miriam agrees to marry Sobel in two years. Be sure to include information on each character's background.

2. Write two **public service announcements** about the value of education that might appear in a magazine. One should present the views of Max and Feld; the other should present the views of Miriam and Sobel.

3. Choose one of the characters and imagine what his or her life will be like over the next 20 years. Write a **biographical sketch** in which you convey possible events in the character's life.

PORTFOLIO Save your writing. You may want to use it later as a springboard to a piece for your portfolio.

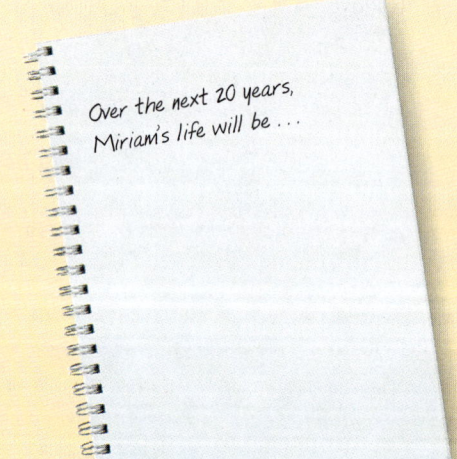

Over the next 20 years, Miriam's life will be...

470

QuickWrites

1. Invite the class to bring wedding announcements from the newspaper to class for models. Encourage students to compose an article-length announcement rather than a simple note.
2. Before beginning the activity, invite students to discuss the educational views of the characters. Tell students that good public service announcements generally have the same qualities as good advertisements: they are brief, catchy, and often include mottoes or slogans.
3. Encourage students to begin by consulting encyclopedias and biographical dictionaries to see how biographical sketches are organized.

The Writer's Craft

Focusing a Topic, pp. 338–341
Editorials, pp. 230–232

LITERARY CONCEPTS

An **allusion** is a reference to a historical or literary person, place, thing, or event with which the reader is assumed to be familiar. Malamud's title "The First Seven Years" makes an allusion to events recounted in the Old Testament of the Bible. According to chapter 29, verses 15–30, of the Book of Genesis, Jacob worked for Laban for seven years in return for Laban's beautiful daughter Rachel's hand in marriage. When the seven years were up, however, Laban tricked Jacob into marrying Leah, Rachel's elder sister, because it was not the custom for a younger sister to marry first. Jacob then agreed to work for Laban for seven more years to earn the right to Rachel's hand. How does the title of Malamud's story—and the biblical story to which it alludes—apply to Sobel's situation? Why do you think Malamud makes this allusion?

CONCEPT REVIEW: Foreshadowing Did you realize before the end of the story that Sobel was in love with Miriam? Find clues in the story that foreshadow Sobel's confession to Feld.

LITERARY LINKS

What do you think this story has in common with the Unit One story "Two Kinds" by Amy Tan?

ART CONNECTION

Take another look at the painting on page 464. Do you think it captures the essence of Miriam in "The First Seven Years"? Explain why or why not.

Detail of *Girl with a Book* (1927), Matej Sternen. National Gallery, Ljubljana, Slovenia.

CRITIC'S CORNER

Critic Edward A. Abramson wrote that Malamud deprives his characters of emotional well-being, physical comfort, and the ability to achieve their life's goals. "He pushes them down to bedrock in order to test them, to make them come to grips with what he feels to be the centrally important facets of life—selflessness and love." Do you think Abramson's generalization holds true for "The First Seven Years"? Why or why not?

Multimodal Learning

ALTERNATIVE ACTIVITIES

1. With a partner, **role-play** the conversation Miriam might have had with Sobel when she sees that he has returned to work at her father's shop. As an alternative, role-play the conversation Miriam and her father might have had in which they discuss her desire to find a job.

2. Imagine that Miriam and Sobel are marrying and that you are a friend at the wedding. Give the **wedding toast** to the bride and groom.

Alternative Activities

1. Encourage pairs to review the lines of dialogue their characters speak in the story as models for their own role playing. Students may wish to list their characters' traits and motivations. Allow students to try out their role-playing more than once if time permits.

2. **Cooperative Learning** At many weddings, several guests give toasts in turn. A group of four students can first discuss different reactions guests might have to the marriage of Miriam and Sobel, while one group member acts as a recorder of ideas. A facilitator-editor can help "toasters" phrase their toasts to reflect the different ideas. A director can rehearse "toasters."

Literary Links

Possible responses: Both stories deal with parents who have immigrated to the United States but cling to traditional ideas about parent-child and intergenerational conflict.

Critic's Corner

Possible responses: Agree, because Malamud pushes Feld down to "bedrock" by forcing him, through a heart attack, business losses, and interpersonal conflict, to give up his idea that he can control other people; disagree, because Feld is never really pushed down to bedrock—because he has his business and his family.

Literary Concepts

Like Jacob, Sobel must work patiently for years to gain his prospective father-in-law's approval to ask for the hand of his daughter. Moreover, like Jacob, Sobel must wait an additional amount of time to actually win his true love. Malamud may make this allusion because the story of Jacob comes from the Old Testament, a holy scripture for the characters in his story. Malamud probably expects his readers to be familiar with Jacob's example of patient fidelity. "The First Seven Years" refers to the seven years that Sobel must wait before actually proposing to Miriam.

Foreshadowing Many students will have guessed Sobel's feelings because of his angry reaction to the date between Miriam and Max. The fact that both Sobel and Miriam are bookish is a subtler foreshadowing grounded in characterization.

Words to Know

1. seethe
2. vehemently
3. deft
4. pallid
5. repugnant
6. apt
7. profuse
8. pittance
9. discern
10. direst

Reteaching/Reinforcement
- *Unit Three Resource Book*, p. 52

BERNARD MALAMUD

Malamud taught at Erasmus Hall High School in New York City as an evening instructor of English, beginning in 1940. From 1948 to 1949 he taught English at Harlem High School. Two of his novels have been made into feature films: *The Fixer* (1969, directed by John Frankenheimer, starring Alan Bates) and *The Natural* (1984, directed by Barry Levinson, starring Robert Redford, Robert Duvall, Glenn Close, and Kim Basinger.) Malamud said of his writing habits, "The idea is to get the pencil moving quickly . . . I go over and over a page. . . ." He says that he kept revising a novel or story until he "can no longer stand working on it."

WORDS TO KNOW

EXERCISE A Review the Words to Know at the bottom of the selection pages. Then, on your paper, indicate which word could best replace the italicized word or phrase in each sentence below.

1. When Tillie learned that her father had arranged a blind date for her, she began to *boil with anger*.
2. She *strongly* refused to meet the young man.
3. Finally, her father's *crafty* maneuvers convinced her to give the fellow a chance.
4. At their first encounter, she noticed his *very pale* complexion.
5. Though hardly handsome, he was not *disgusting*.
6. They went bowling on their first date; although he had never bowled before, Tillie found him to be *quick to learn*.
7. He was impressed with Tillie's strength and agility, and his compliments were *many*.
8. When Tillie asked about his job, he informed her that he earned more than a *tiny sum*.
9. From the twinkle in his eye, Tillie could *figure out* that he was teasing her.
10. By the time their date was over, Tillie was in the *gravest* danger of falling in love.

EXERCISE B Draw pictures that communicate the meaning of five of the Words to Know. Then exchange your drawings with a classmate and identify which words have been depicted.

BERNARD MALAMUD

1914–1986

Born and raised in Brooklyn, New York, Bernard Malamud was the son of poor Russian-Jewish immigrants who, according to the author, "taught me their values. . . . Theirs was a person-centered world, one that regarded the qualities of people. When I think of my father, I'm filled with a sense of sweet humanity." As a child, Malamud was often taken to theaters on New York's Second Avenue, where his mother's relatives performed plays in Yiddish, the language of European Jews. He also pored over his *Book of Knowledge*, a 20-volume encyclopedia that his father, though he could ill afford it, bought to encourage his son's pursuit of learning. Malamud was only a teenager when he began writing stories in the back room of the family grocery store, where he worked part time after his mother died. In the 1940s he published stories in noted magazines such as *Harper's Bazaar* and *Partisan Review*. "The First Seven Years" is one of several stories collected in *The Magic Barrel*, which won Malamud a National Book Award in 1959. Malamud was awarded a Pulitzer Prize, as well as a second National Book Award, for his novel *The Fixer*, published in 1966.

For most of his professional life, Malamud combined his writing activities with teaching. He held positions in the English departments at Oregon State University, Harvard University, and Bennington College in Vermont. Although his first novel, *The Natural*, is a fantasy about baseball and many of his stories draw on his wife's Italian-American heritage, Malamud is best known for writing about the experiences of European and American Jews. "I write about Jews," he explained, "because they set my imagination going . . . because I think I will understand them better as people."

OTHER WORKS *The Assistant, Idiots First, Rembrandt's Hat, The Stories of Bernard Malamud*

Extended Reading

REFLECTING ON THEME
What Do You Think?

Have students refer back to the glossary of expressions they made before beginning this part of Unit Three. Ask if there is anything they would like to add to or change about the glossary as a result of reading this selection.

PREVIEWING

DRAMA

The Bear
Anton Chekhov (chĕk′ôf) Russia

Activating Prior Knowledge
PERSONAL CONNECTION

What does the phrase "battle of the sexes" mean to you? In a class discussion, share your definition of the term and your opinions about it. Also describe examples of the battle of the sexes from books, movies, plays, or television shows.

Building Background
CULTURAL CONNECTION

In the following one-act comedy, the battle of the sexes takes place on a country estate in 19th-century Russia. The two combatants are both members of what was then Russia's privileged land-owning class. One is a woman who would describe herself as a genteel widow with delicate sensibilities, while the other is an outspoken gentleman farmer whose hot temper makes him seem like a bear, or a crude, insensitive person. Like others of his class, he is educated enough to know French—considered a language of refinement by upper-class Russians of the day—but he pokes fun at those who insist on speaking it. Far more at home with the "manly" pursuits of his class, such as riding, dueling, and managing his farm, he seems out of place in the widow's elegant drawing room, the formal room for receiving guests that is the setting of the play's "battle."

Scene from a 1995 stage performance of *The Bear*. Writers Theatre Chicago. Photo by Alexander Guezentsvey.

Setting a Purpose
WRITING CONNECTION

In your notebook, provide a humorous description of one particular battle of the sexes. You may describe an actual event from your own experience or one that is imaginary. Use actual terms of battle to describe the conflict. Feel free to make use of exaggeration in describing the participants and the event. As you read *The Bear*, compare your battle to the one that takes place in the widow's drawing room.

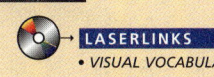
• VISUAL VOCABULARY

OVERVIEW
Objectives

- To understand and appreciate a one-act play that explores the war between the sexes
- To identify and understand farce and stereotype
- To appreciate diction
- To express understanding of a selection through a choice of writing forms, including an analysis, a review, and a dramatic scene
- To extend understanding of the selection through a variety of multimodal and cross-curricular activities

Skills

LITERARY CONCEPTS
- Farce
- Stereotype
- Stage directions

GRAMMAR
- *Who* vs. *whom*

SPEAKING, LISTENING, AND VIEWING
- Dramatic reading
- Group discussion
- Oral presentations

ALTERNATIVE
Previewing

Students can choose partners and use the following prompts to preview *The Bear* orally.

Writing Connection

Discussion Prompts *With a partner, talk about an experience that involved a "battle of the sexes." The experience can be factual or imaginary. You might use the following questions to help you get started.*

- *What caused the battle?*
- *Who were the combatants and what "weapons" did they use?*
- *Who won the battle, and how and why?*

As you read The Bear, *look for elements of the battle of the sexes.*

PRINT AND MEDIA RESOURCES

UNIT THREE RESOURCE BOOK
Strategic Reading: Literature, p. 59
Vocabulary SkillBuilder, p. 60

GRAMMAR MINI–LESSONS
Transparencies, p. 19
Copymasters, p. 21

ACCESS FOR STUDENTS ACQUIRING ENGLISH
Selection Summaries
Reading Support

FORMAL ASSESSMENT
Selection Test, pp. 95–96
 Test Generator

 **AUDIO LIBRARY**
See Reference Card

LASERLINKS
Drama Connection
Visual Vocabulary

SUMMARY

In this humorous one-act play, the servant Luke reproves his mistress—Mrs. Popov, a young widow—for continuing to mourn over her husband. She vows to remain inside the four walls of her house and orders extra oats for her husband's horse, Toby. Then Gregory Smirnov, a landed gentleman, unexpectedly comes to collect on a debt of her late husband's. The two aristocrats argue over the debt, and the conflict degenerates until Smirnov challenges Mrs. Popov to a duel. She accepts. As Mrs. Popov leaves to get the pistols and Luke runs out to find help, Smirnov marvels at the woman's spirit. When she returns to fight the duel, he declares his love. At first she resists, but when the frantic servant returns with help, he finds the combatants kissing. Lowering her eyes, Mrs. Popov asks Luke to make sure Toby gets no oats that day.

Thematic Link: *Mysteries of the Heart*
Unexpectedly, a fierce quarrel ends in a first kiss.

CUSTOMIZING FOR
Students Acquiring English

- Use **ACCESS FOR STUDENTS ACQUIRING ENGLISH,** Reading Support.
- Students may have difficulty with the colloquial expressions in this play. Encourage them to use context clues to find general meanings for these expressions.

STRATEGIC READING FOR
Less-Proficient Readers

Set a Purpose Have students read to find out who comes to visit, and why.

Use **UNIT THREE RESOURCE BOOK,** p. 59, for guidance in reading the selection.

Literary Concept:
CHARACTERIZATION

Ⓐ Invite students to discuss how the opening dialogue establishes the contrast between the characters' personalities.

The Bear
A Farce in One Act
by Anton Chekhov

Cast of Characters

Mrs. Helen Popov, a young widow with dimpled cheeks, a landowner
Gregory Smirnov, a landowner in early middle age
Luke, Mrs. Popov's old manservant

The action takes place in the drawing room of Mrs. Popov's country house.

Scene 1

(Mrs. Popov, *in deep mourning, with her eye fixed on a snapshot, and* Luke)

Ⓐ **Luke.** This won't do, madam; you're just making your life a misery. Cook's out with the maid picking fruit, every living creature's happy, and even our cat knows how to enjoy herself—she's parading round the yard trying to pick up a bird or two. But here you are cooped up inside all day like you was in a convent cell[1]—you never have a good time. Yes, it's true. Nigh on twelve months it is since you last set foot outdoors.

Mrs. Popov. And I'm never going out again; why should I? My life's finished. He lies in his grave; I've buried myself inside these four walls—we're both dead.

Luke. There you go again! I don't like to hear such talk, I don't. Your husband died and that was that—God's will be done, and may he rest in peace. You've shed a few tears and that'll

---

1. **convent cell:** a small room occupied by an individual nun in a convent, a community of nuns living under strict religious vows.

474 UNIT THREE PART 2: MYSTERIES OF THE HEART

WORDS TO KNOW

emancipation (ĭ-măn′sə-pā′shən) *n.* a setting free from restraint or controls (p. 480)
futile (fyōōt′l) *adj.* serving no useful purpose (p. 481)
languish (lăng′gwĭsh) *v.* to suffer with longing (p. 480)
liberty (lĭb′ər-tē) *n.* an action that is too bold or forward (p. 480)
sniveling (snĭv′əl-ĭng) *adj.* whining (p. 478)

VISUAL VOCABULARY
- convent cell (kŏn′vənt sĕl′)
- sackcloth (săk′klôth′)

Side A, Frame 49487

Portrait of the Pianist, Conductor, and Composer A. G. Rubinstein (1881), Ilya Efimovich Repin. Oil on canvas, 80 cm × 62.3 cm, The State Tretyakov Gallery, Moscow, acquired by P. M. Tretyakov from the artist.

Art Note

Portrait of the Pianist, Conductor, and Composer A. G. Rubinstein by Ilya Efimovich Repin Repin (1844–1930) was a member of the Wanderers group, which in the 1870s supported traveling art exhibits to win new patrons outside of St. Petersburg and Moscow. Rubinstein (1829–1894) was the founder of the Petersburg Conservatory. This painting was commissioned for a portrait gallery of distinguished figures in Russian culture.

Reading the Art *How would you describe the subject's personality based on this painting?*

CUSTOMIZING FOR
Gifted and Talented Students

Encourage students to find hints of serious themes in this play, such as unfulfillment, misunderstanding, and the quirkiness of human emotion. Invite them to write or talk about their interpretations.

Director's Note

Ask students to imagine, as they read, how they would stage Scene 1 of *The Bear*. Suggest that they jot down a few director's notes.

Critic's  Corner

"No more honest mind has ever observed the spectacle of mankind. He [Chekhov] was a great artist.... But he was more than an artist; he was a man who, without being dogmatic, revealed, taught and practiced a way of living and thinking which was heroic without ever being pretentious, and well suited to keep hope alive even in moments of despair.... Modesty was his only weakness."

André Maurois
The Art of Writing

Ask students to think about the play and decide how it does or doesn't reflect an "honest mind;" "the spectacle of mankind;" and a way of keeping "hope alive."

Literary Concept: FARCE

B Ask students to read lines or phrases in this passage that they find particularly exaggerated. *(Possible responses: "When Nicholas died, my life lost all meaning…." "You may think I'm alive, but I'm not really.")* Ask what impression they have of Mrs. Popov. *(Possible responses: She's a silly woman; her grief is too burlesque to be sincere.)*

Critical Thinking: ANALYZING

C Ask students why they think Mrs. Popov orders extra oats for Toby. *(Possible responses: to demonstrate her love for her late husband; to be kind to Toby because she thinks the horse misses her husband)*

Actor's Note

D Invite students to talk about how they would play Mrs. Popov's soliloquy. Ask volunteers to try reading the speech aloud in character.

---

do; it's time to call it a day—you can't spend your whole life a-moaning and a-groaning. The same thing happened to me once, when my old woman died, but what did I do? I grieved a bit, shed a tear or two for a month or so, and that's all she's getting. Catch me wearing sackcloth and ashes[2] for the rest of my days; it'd be more than the old girl was worth! *(sighs)* You've neglected all the neighbors—won't go and see them or have them in the house. We never get out and about, lurking here like dirty great spiders, saving your presence. The mice have been at my livery[3] too. And it's not for any lack of nice people either—the county's full of 'em, see. There's the regiment stationed at Ryblovo, and them officers are a fair treat; a proper sight for sore eyes they are. They have a dance in camp of a Friday, and the brass band plays most days. This ain't right, missus. You're young, and pretty as a picture with that peaches-and-cream look, so make the most of it. Them looks won't last forever, you know. If you wait another ten years to come out of your shell and lead them officers a dance, you'll find it's too late.

Mrs. Popov *(decisively)*. Never talk to me like that again, please. When Nicholas died, my life lost all meaning, as you know. You may think I'm alive, but I'm not really. I swore to wear this mourning and shun society till my dying day, do you hear? Let his departed spirit see how I love him! Yes, I realize you know what went on—that he was often mean to me, cruel and, er, unfaithful even; but I'll be true to the grave and show him how much I can love. And he'll find me in the next world just as I was before he died.

Luke. Don't talk like that—walk round the garden instead. Or else have Toby or Giant harnessed and go and see the neighbors.

Mrs. Popov. Oh dear! *(weeps)*

Luke. Missus! Madam! What's the matter? For heaven's sake!

Mrs. Popov. He was so fond of Toby—always drove him when he went over to the Korchagins' place and the Vlasovs'. He drove so well too! And he looked so graceful when he pulled hard on the reins, remember? Oh Toby, Toby! See he gets an extra bag of oats today.

Luke. Very good, madam.

(A loud ring.)

Mrs. Popov *(shudders)*. Who is it? Tell them I'm not at home.

Luke. Very well, madam. *(goes out)*

Scene 2

(Mrs. Popov, alone)

Mrs. Popov *(looking at the snapshot)*. Now you shall see how I can love and forgive, Nicholas. My love will only fade when I fade away myself, when this poor heart stops beating. *(laughs, through tears)* Well, aren't you ashamed of yourself? I'm your good, faithful little wifie; I've locked myself up, and I'll be faithful to the grave, while you—aren't you ashamed, you naughty boy? You deceived me, and you used to make scenes and leave me alone for weeks on end.

Scene 3

(Mrs. Popov and Luke)

Luke *(comes in, agitatedly)*. Someone's asking for you, madam. Wants to see you—

Mrs. Popov. Then I hope you told them I haven't received visitors since the day my husband died.

---

2. **sackcloth and ashes:** rough, scratchy clothing and ashes worn as symbols of mourning.
3. **livery:** a servant's uniform.

476 UNIT THREE PART 2: MYSTERIES OF THE HEART

Luke. I did, but he wouldn't listen—his business is very urgent, he says.

Mrs. Popov. *I am not at home!*

Luke. So I told him, but he just swears and barges straight in, drat him. He's waiting in the dining room.

Mrs. Popov (*irritatedly*). All right, ask him in here then. Aren't people rude?

(*Luke goes out.*)

Mrs. Popov. Oh, aren't they all a bore? What do they want with me; why must they disturb my peace? (*sighs*) Yes, I see I really shall have to get me to a nunnery.[4] (*reflects*) I'll take the veil;[5] that's it.

Scene 4

(Mrs. Popov, Luke *and* Smirnov)

Smirnov (*coming in, to* Luke). You're a fool, my talkative friend. An ass. (*seeing* Mrs. Popov, *with dignity*) May I introduce myself, madam? Gregory Smirnov, landed gentleman[6] and lieutenant of artillery retired. I'm obliged to trouble you on most urgent business.

Mrs. Popov (*not holding out her hand*). What do you require?

Smirnov. I had the honor to know your late husband. He died owing me twelve hundred roubles[7]—I have his two IOUs. Now I've some interest due to the land bank tomorrow, madam, so may I trouble you to let me have the money today?

Mrs. Popov. Twelve hundred roubles—How did my husband come to owe you that?

Smirnov. He used to buy his oats from me.

Mrs. Popov (*sighing, to* Luke). Oh yes—Luke, don't forget to see Toby has his extra bag of oats. (Luke *goes out. To* Smirnov.) Of course I'll pay if Nicholas owed you something, but I've nothing on me today, sorry. My manager will be back from town the day after tomorrow, and I'll get him to pay you whatever it is then, but for the time being I can't oblige. Besides, it's precisely seven months today since my husband died, and I am in no fit state to discuss money.

Smirnov. Well, I'll be in a fit state to go bust with a capital B if I can't pay that interest tomorrow. They'll have the bailiffs[8] in on me.

Mrs. Popov. You'll get your money the day after tomorrow.

Smirnov. I don't want it the day after tomorrow; I want it now.

Mrs. Popov. I can't pay you now, sorry.

Smirnov. And I can't wait till the day after tomorrow.

Mrs. Popov. Can I help it if I've no money today?

Smirnov. So you can't pay then?

Mrs. Popov. Exactly.

Smirnov. I see. And that's your last word, is it?

Mrs. Popov. It is.

Smirnov. Your last word? You really mean it?

Mrs. Popov. I do.

Smirnov (*sarcastic*). Then I'm greatly obliged to you; I'll put it in my diary! (*shrugs*) And people expect me to be cool and collected! I met the local excise man[9] on my way here just now. "My dear Smirnov," says he, "why are you always losing your temper?" But how can I help it, I ask you? I'm in desperate need of money! Yesterday morning I left home at

---

4. **get me to a nunnery:** go and live in a convent. This is probably a reference to a line from Shakespeare's *Hamlet* in which Hamlet angrily tells his girlfriend, "Get thee to a nunnery."
5. **veil:** the outer covering of a nun's headdress and, by extension, the life of a nun.
6. **landed gentleman:** a land owner. In Russia before the Russian Revolution, only a few people owned land.
7. **roubles:** units of Russian money; often spelled *rubles*.
8. **bailiffs:** assistants or deputies to the police chief.
9. **excise man:** tax man.

THE BEAR **477**

Critic's Corner

"When I've written myself out I'm going to write vaudevilles [farces] and live on them. I think I could write about a hundred of them every year. Vaudeville subjects gush out of me like oil from the wells of Baku."

Anton Chekhov

Ask students to consider why Chekhov liked writing farces so much.

Literary Concept: IRONY

J Ask a volunteer to interpret Smirnov's statement that he has been too nice: in what sense does Chekhov mean the opposite of what the character says? *(Smirnov has actually been aggressive rather than nice.)*

CUSTOMIZING FOR
Students Acquiring English

I Help students understand that when Smirnov says "It doesn't pay to wear kid gloves with this lot," he means that it doesn't help to ask for his money nicely with these debtors. He therefore plans to get tough with them.

Critical Thinking:
MAKING JUDGMENTS

K Students may feel indignant at Smirnov's anti-female outbursts here and later in the play. Encourage them to discuss how these passages contribute to the characterization. *(Possible response: The diatribe against women points up Smirnov's bad temper and bad manners.)*

---

crack of dawn. I call on everyone who owes me money, but not a soul forks out. I'm dog tired. I spend the night in some God-awful place. Then I fetch up here, fifty miles from home, hoping to see the color of my money, only to be fobbed off[10] with this "no fit state" stuff! How *can* I keep my temper?

Mrs. Popov. I thought I'd made myself clear. You can have your money when my manager gets back from town.

Smirnov. It's not your manager I'm after; it's you. What the blazes, pardon my language, do I want with your manager?

Mrs. Popov. I'm sorry, my dear man, but I'm not accustomed to these peculiar expressions and to this tone. I have closed my ears. (*hurries out*)

Scene 5

(Smirnov, *alone*)

Smirnov. Well, what price that! "In no fit state!" Her husband died seven months ago, if you please! Now have I got my interest to pay or not? I want a straight answer—yes or no? All right, your husband's dead, you're in no fit state and so on and so forth, and your blasted manager's hopped it. But what am I supposed to do? Fly away from my creditors by balloon, I take it! Or go and bash the old brain-box against a brick wall? I call on Gruzdev—not at home. Yaroshevich is in hiding. I have a real old slanging match[11] with Kuritsyn and almost chuck him out of the window. Mazutov has the bellyache, and this creature's "in no fit state." Not one of the swine will pay. This is what comes of being too nice to them and behaving like some sniveling no-hoper or old woman. It doesn't pay to wear kid gloves with this lot! All right, just you wait—I'll give you something to remember me by! You don't make a monkey out of me, blast you! I'm staying here—going to stick around till she coughs up. Pah! I feel well and truly riled today. I'm shaking like a leaf, I'm so furious—choking I am. Phew, my God, I really think I'm going to pass out! (*shouts*) Hey, you there!

Scene 6

(Smirnov *and* Luke)

Luke (*comes in*). What is it?

Smirnov. Bring me some kvass[12] or water, will you?

(Luke *goes out*)

Smirnov. What a mentality, though! You need money so bad you could shoot yourself, but she won't pay, being "in no fit state to discuss money," if you please! There's female logic for you and no mistake! That's why I don't like talking to women. Never have. Talk to a woman—why, I'd rather sit on top of a powder magazine![13] Pah! It makes my flesh creep, I'm so fed up with her, her and that great trailing dress! Poetic creatures they call 'em! Why, the very sight of one gives me cramp in both legs, I get so aggravated.

Scene 7

(Smirnov *and* Luke)

Luke (*comes in and serves some water*). Madam's unwell and won't see anyone.

---

10. **fobbed off:** put off with a trick or an excuse.
11. **slanging match:** the exchange of angry, abusive language.
12. **kvass** (kväs): Russian beer.
13. **powder magazine:** a room in which gun powder and other explosives are stored in a fort or on a ship.

WORDS TO KNOW
sniveling (snĭv′ə-lĭng) *adj.* whining

478

Mini-Lesson   Literary Concepts

REVIEWING STAGE DIRECTIONS Remind students that stage directions are the instructions for the director, the performers, and the stage crew of a play. Usually set in italics, stage directions are located at the beginning of and throughout a script. Stage directions usually tell the time and place of the action and explain how actors should move and speak. They may also describe scenery, props, lighting, costumes, music, or sound effects.

Application Invite students to write fuller stage directions for Scene 5, Smirnov's monologue. Suggest that students visualize themselves or a professional actor playing the scene and write directions based on these visualizations. At the beginning, their stage directions should identify the character and describe the set, as if the speech were the first scene of the play. Within the speech, directions should specify gestures and tones of voice for Smirnov and may have him use props. Invite students to read their stage directions aloud; or, students might perform the monologue according to their stage directions.

478 THE LANGUAGE OF LITERATURE TEACHER'S EDITION

A Room in the Brasovo Estate (1916), Stanislav Iulianovich Zhukovskii. Oil on canvas, 80 cm × 107 cm, The State Tretyakov Gallery, Moscow, accessioned from the People's Commissariate of Foreign Affairs, 1941.

Smirnov. You clear out!

(Luke *goes out*)

Smirnov. "Unwell and won't see anyone." All right then, don't! I'm staying put, chum, and I don't budge one inch till you unbelt.[14] Be ill for a week, and I'll stay a week; make it a year, and a year I'll stay. I'll have my rights, lady! As for your black dress and dimples, you don't catch me that way—we know all about those dimples! (*shouts through the window*) Unhitch, Simon; we're here for some time—I'm staying put. Tell the stable people to give my horses oats. And you've got that animal tangled in the reins again, you great oaf! (*imitates him*) "I don't care." I'll give you don't care! (*moves away from the window*) How ghastly—it's unbearably hot, no one will pay up, I had a bad night, and now here's this female with her long black dress and her states. I've got a headache. How about a glass of vodka? That might be an idea. (*shouts*) Hey, you there!

Luke (*comes in*). What is it?

Smirnov. Bring me a glass of vodka.

(Luke *goes out*)

Smirnov. Phew! (*sits down and looks himself over*) A fine specimen I am, I must say—dust all over me, my boots dirty, unwashed, hair unbrushed, straw on my waistcoat. I bet the little woman took me for a burglar. (*yawns*) It's not exactly polite to turn up in a drawing room in this rig! Well, anyway, I'm not a guest here; I'm collecting money. And there's no such thing as correct wear for the well-dressed creditor.

---

14. **unbelt:** take off a belt designed to hold money; in this case, to pay what is due.

Literary Concept:
CHARACTERIZATION

M Discuss what this brief exchange reveals about Luke's character. *(Possible responses: He is easily cowed by rough manners; he is anxious to maintain order and civility in the house.)*

Literary Concept:
STAGE DIRECTIONS

N Point out the stage directions for Mrs. Popov's entrance and ask students how these directions hint at the way the actress is to deliver her lines. *(Possible responses: "Downcast eyes" suggests modesty and quietness. Some students might suggest that her modesty is fake, and should be exaggerated.)*

Cultural Note

O During much of the Czarist period, the Russian aristocracy spoke only French. Russian was considered to be the language of the serfs until the Russian-language poetry of Aleksandr Pushkin became popular in the 1820s (see pages 448–451) and that language began to gain acceptance among the upper class. Later in the 19th century, Chekhov and the novelist Leo Tolstoy (1828–1910) customarily used French for the characters they intended to present as snobs. Smirnov, mimicking the French of the aristocracy, is appealing to the anti-snob feelings of the audience.

STRATEGIC READING FOR
Less-Proficient Readers

P Have students suggest what is further enraging Smirnov. *(Possible responses: Mrs. Popov's insistence on fine manners; her way of making him appear to be an oaf; her strategies for avoiding payment of the debt)* **Clarifying**

Set a Purpose Ask students to read on to find out what crisis the two characters reach.

Luke (*comes in and gives him the vodka*). This is a liberty, sir.

Smirnov (*angrily*). What!

Luke. I, er, it's all right, I just—

Smirnov. Who do you think you're talking to? You hold your tongue!

Luke (*aside*). Now we'll never get rid of him, botheration take it! It's an ill wind brought him along.

(*Luke goes out*)

Smirnov. Oh, I'm so furious! I could pulverize the whole world, I'm in such a rage. I feel quite ill. (*shouts*) Hey, you there!

(*Mrs. Popov and Smirnov*)

Mrs. Popov (*comes in, with downcast eyes*). Sir, in my solitude I have grown unaccustomed to the sound of human speech, and I can't stand shouting. I must urgently request you not to disturb my peace.

Smirnov. Pay up and I'll go.

Mrs. Popov. As I've already stated quite plainly, I've no ready cash. Wait till the day after tomorrow.

Smirnov. I've also had the honor of stating quite plainly that I need the money today, not the day after tomorrow. If you won't pay up now, I'll have to put my head in a gas oven tomorrow.

Mrs. Popov. Can I help it if I've no cash in hand? This is all rather odd.

Smirnov. So you won't pay up now, eh?

Mrs. Popov. I can't.

Smirnov. In that case I'm not budging; I'll stick around here till I do get my money. (*sits down*) You'll pay the day after tomorrow, you say?

Very well, then I'll sit here like this till the day after tomorrow. I'll just stay put exactly as I am. (*jumps up*) I ask you—have I got that interest to pay tomorrow or haven't I? Think I'm trying to be funny, do you?

Mrs. Popov. Kindly don't raise your voice at me, sir—we're not in the stables.

Smirnov. I'm not discussing stables; I'm asking whether my interest falls due tomorrow. Yes or no?

Mrs. Popov. You don't know how to treat a lady.

Smirnov. Oh yes I do.

Mrs. Popov. Oh no you don't. You're a rude, ill-bred person. Nice men don't talk to ladies like that.

Smirnov. Now, this *is* a surprise! How do you want me to talk then? In French, I suppose? (*in an angry, simpering voice*) Madame, je voo pree. You won't pay me—how perfectly delightful. Oh, *pardong*, I'm sure—sorry you were troubled! Now isn't the weather divine today? And that black dress looks too, too charming! (*bows and scrapes*)

Mrs. Popov. That's silly. And not very clever.

Smirnov (*mimics her*). "Silly, not very clever." I don't know how to treat a lady, don't I? Madam, I've seen more women in my time than you have house sparrows. I've fought three duels over women. There have been twenty-one women in my life. Twelve times it was me broke it off; the other nine got in first. Oh yes! Time was I made an ass of myself, slobbered, mooned around, bowed and scraped and practically crawled on my belly. I loved; I suffered; I sighed at the moon; I languished; I melted; I grew cold. I loved passionately, madly, in every conceivable fashion, damn me, burbling nineteen to the dozen about women's emancipation and wasting half

---

| WORDS
TO
KNOW | liberty (lĭb′ər-tē) *n.* an action that is too bold or forward
languish (lăng′gwĭsh) *v.* to suffer with longing
emancipation (ĭ-măn′sə-pā′shən) *n.* a setting free from restraint or controls |

480

Mini-Lesson Grammar

WHO VS. WHOM Remind students that *who* is used as the subject of a verb or as a predicate pronoun. *Whom* is used as a direct object or as the object of a preposition. Write the following sentences on the board and ask volunteers to explain how *who* and *whom* are used.
1. Who is Smirnov? (*Who* is the subject.)
2. Whom did Smirnov challenge to a duel? (*Whom* is the direct object.)
3. With whom did she speak? (*Whom* is the object of the preposition *with*.)

Application Explain that colloquial speech often is not grammatically correct. Have students identify incorrect usages of *who* and *whom* in the play, correct them, and discuss which version is more effective.

Reteaching/Reinforcement
• *Grammar Handbook*, anthology pp. 1073–1074
• *Grammar Mini-Lessons* copymasters p. 21, transparencies p. 19

Who and *Whom*, p. 720

my substance[15] on the tender passion. But now—no thank you very much! I can't be fooled anymore; I've had enough. Black eyes, passionate looks, crimson lips, dimpled cheeks, moonlight, "Whispers, passion's bated breathing"[16]—I don't give a tinker's cuss[17] for the lot now, lady. Present company excepted, all women, large or small, are simpering, mincing, gossipy creatures. They're great haters. They're eyebrow deep in lies. They're futile; they're trivial; they're cruel; they're outrageously illogical. And as for having anything upstairs (*taps his forehead*)—I'm sorry to be so blunt, but the very birds in the trees can run rings round your average bluestocking.[18] Take any one of these poetical creations. Oh, she's all froth and fluff, she is; she's half divine; she sends you into a million raptures. But you take a peep inside her mind, and what do you see? A common or garden crocodile! (*clutches the back of a chair, which cracks and breaks*) And yet this crocodile somehow thinks its great lifework, privilege and monopoly is the tender passion—that's what really gets me! But damn and blast it, and crucify me upside down on that wall if I'm wrong—does a woman know how to love any living creature apart from lap dogs? Her love gets no further than sniveling and slobbering. The man suffers and makes sacrifices, while she just twitches the train of her dress and tries to get him squirming under her thumb; that's what her love adds up to! You must know what women are like, seeing you've the rotten luck to be one. Tell me frankly, did you ever see a sincere, faithful, true woman? You know you didn't. Only the old and ugly ones are true and faithful. You'll never find a constant woman, not in a month of Sundays you won't, not once in a blue moon!

Mrs. Popov. Well, I like that! Then who is true and faithful in love to your way of thinking? Not men by any chance?

Smirnov. Yes, madam. Men.

Mrs. Popov. *Men!* (*gives a bitter laugh*) Men true and faithful in love! That's rich, I must say. (*vehemently*) What right have you to talk like that? Men true and faithful! If it comes to that, the best man I've ever known was my late husband, I may say. I loved him passionately, with all my heart as only an intelligent young woman can. I gave him my youth, my happiness, my life, my possessions. I lived only for him. I worshiped him as an idol. And—what do you think? This best of men was shamelessly deceiving me all along the line! After his death I found a drawer in his desk full of love letters, and when he was alive—oh, what a frightful memory!—he used to leave me on my own for weeks on end, he carried on with other girls before my very eyes, he was unfaithful to me, he spent my money like water, and he joked about my feelings for him. But I loved him all the same, and I've been faithful to him. What's more, I'm still faithful and true now that he's dead. I've buried myself alive inside these four walls, and I shall go round in these widow's weeds[19] till my dying day.

Smirnov (*with a contemptuous laugh*). Widow's weeds! Who do you take me for? As if I didn't know why you wear this fancy dress and bury yourself indoors! Why, it sticks out a mile! Mysterious and romantic, isn't it? Some army

---

15. **substance:** wealth or fortune.
16. **bated breathing:** breathing held in, due to excitement or fear. Smirnov is quoting the first lines of a well-known lyric by A. A. Fet.
17. **a tinker's cuss:** the smallest degree or amount; same as a tinker's damn.
18. **bluestocking:** a woman having intellectual or literary interests.
19. **widow's weeds:** the black mourning clothes of a widow.

WORDS TO KNOW

futile (fyōōt′l) *adj.* serving no useful purpose

481

Art Note

Portrait of M. K. Oliv by Valentin Aleksandrovich Serov This portrait of a young Russian married woman is notable for its interplay of deep shadows and light, in the manner of Rembrandt. Serov (1865–1911) remarked about the subject of his 1895 oil painting, "She resembles a young mouse peeking out of a dark corner with two sharp eyes."

Reading the Art *Do you agree with Serov's description of Oliv? Why?*

CUSTOMIZING FOR
Students Acquiring English

(2) Translate *Let me call a spade a spade* as "Let me be honest." Invite students to share other idioms, in any language, which mean the same thing.

Portrait of M. K. Oliv (1895), Valentin Aleksandrovich Serov. Oil on canvas, 88 cm × 68.5 cm, The State Russian Museum, St. Petersburg, accessioned from I. A. Mamontov, 1904.

cadet or hack poet[20] may pass by your garden, look up at your windows and think: "There dwells Tamara,[21] the mysterious princess, the one who buried herself alive from love of her husband." Who do you think you're fooling?

Mrs. Popov (*flaring up*). What! You dare to take that line with me!

Smirnov. Buries herself alive—but doesn't forget to powder her nose!

Mrs. Popov. You dare adopt that tone!

Smirnov. Don't you raise your voice to me, madam; I'm not one of your servants. Let me call a spade a spade. Not being a woman, I'm used to saying what I think. So stop shouting, pray.

Mrs. Popov. It's you who are shouting, not me. Leave me alone, would you mind?

Smirnov. Pay up, and I'll go.

Mrs. Popov. You'll get nothing out of me.

Smirnov. Oh yes I shall.

Mrs. Popov. Just to be awkward, you won't get one single copeck.[22] And you can leave me alone.

---

20. **hack poet:** a poet who writes shallow or ordinary verse, usually just to make a living.
21. **Tamara:** a reference to the heroine of the poem "Tamara" by Russian Romantic poet Mikhail Lermontov.
22. **copeck:** a Russian coin of little value, similar to a penny.

482 UNIT THREE PART 2: MYSTERIES OF THE HEART

Mini-Lesson: Speaking, Listening, and Viewing

DRAMATIC READING Tell students that in dramatic reading, actors take roles and read their characters' dialogue aloud while looking at the script. Unlike a full-fledged performance, a dramatic reading does not use scenery, costumes, props, lighting, sound effects, or the movements of the actors. Its emphasis is on the actors' oral interpretation of the characters. Tones of voice and pace are of primary importance.

Application Ask one male and one female volunteer to prepare and perform a dramatic reading of any of the crucial scenes between Smirnov and Mrs. Popov, from Scene 8 on. Encourage the rest of the class, the audience, to listen to the actors as they bring the characters to life. Invite class discussion afterward, focusing on the question, "What did listening to a performance show you about the play that reading it on the page didn't?"

2 THE LANGUAGE OF LITERATURE TEACHER'S EDITION

Smirnov. Not having the pleasure of being your husband or fiancé, I'll trouble you not to make a scene. (*sits down*) I don't like it.

Mrs. Popov. (*choking with rage*). Do I see you sitting down?

Smirnov. You most certainly do.

Mrs. Popov. Would you mind leaving?

Smirnov. Give me my money. (*aside*) Oh, I'm in such a rage! Furious I am!

Mrs. Popov. I've no desire to bandy words with cads,[23] sir. Kindly clear off! (*pause*) Well, are you going or aren't you?

Smirnov. No.

Mrs. Popov. No?

Smirnov. No!

Mrs. Popov. Very well then! (*rings*)

(*The above and* Luke)

Mrs. Popov. Show this gentleman out, Luke.

Luke (*goes up to* Smirnov). Be so good as to leave, sir, when you're told, sir. No point in—

Smirnov (*jumping up*). You hold your tongue! Who do you think you're talking to? I'll carve you up in little pieces.

Luke (*clutching at his heart*). Heavens and saints above us! (*falls into an armchair*) Oh, I feel something terrible—fair took my breath away, it did.

Mrs. Popov. But where's Dasha? Dasha! (*shouts*) Dasha! Pelegeya! Dasha! (*rings*)

Luke. Oh, they've all gone fruit picking. There's no one in the house. I feel faint. Fetch water.

Mrs. Popov. Be so good as to clear out!

Smirnov. Couldn't you be a bit more polite?

Mrs. Popov (*clenching her fists and stamping*). You uncouth oaf! You have the manners of a bear! Think you own the place? Monster!

Smirnov. What! You say that again!

Mrs. Popov. I called you an ill-mannered oaf, a monster!

Smirnov (*advancing on her*). Look here, what right have you to insult me?

Mrs. Popov. All right, I'm insulting you. So what? Think I'm afraid of you?

Smirnov. Just because you look all romantic, you can get away with anything—is that your idea? This is dueling talk!

Luke. Heavens and saints above us! Water!

Smirnov. Pistols at dawn!

Mrs. Popov. Just because you have big fists and the lungs of an ox, you needn't think I'm scared, see? Think you own the place, don't you!

Smirnov. We'll shoot it out! No one calls me names and gets away with it, weaker sex or no weaker sex.

Mrs. Popov (*trying to shout him down*). You coarse lout!

Smirnov. Why should it only be us men who answer for our insults? It's high time we dropped that silly idea. If women want equality, let them damn well have equality! I challenge you, madam!

Mrs. Popov. Want to shoot it out, eh? Very well.

Smirnov. This very instant!

Mrs. Popov. Most certainly! My husband left some pistols; I'll fetch them instantly. (*moves hurriedly off and comes back*) I'll enjoy putting a bullet through that thick skull, damn your infernal cheek![24] (*goes out*)

Smirnov. I'll pot[25] her like a sitting bird. I'm not one of your sentimental young puppies. She'll get no chivalry from me!

---

23. **bandy . . . cads:** exchange words with a scoundrel.
24. **infernal cheek:** hellish sass or boldness.
25. **pot:** shoot.

Literary Concept: STEREOTYPE

X Invite students to read Luke's lines as they think he should say them. Discuss how Luke is a stereotype of an elderly servant, whom Chekhov's audience would recognize.

Literary Concept: FARCE

Y Point out that Smirnov's tone changes with comic exaggeration, so that within a few lines he has changed from hostility to admiration for Mrs. Popov. Invite volunteers to read aloud the last few speeches in Scene 9.

Director's Notes

Z Ask students what physical movements and gestures might accompany the lines in which Smirnov shows Mrs. Popov how to shoot a gun. *(Possible response: Smirnov might use the opportunity to get close to Mrs. Popov and touch her hand; she might remain serious, pointing the gun at him.)*

Cultural Note

AA Firing in the air was a frequent, chivalrous gesture on the part of duelists. The object of a duel was not necessarily to kill or wound, but to answer a challenge or an affront.

Literary Concept: STAGE DIRECTIONS

BB Ask students to read these stage directions to determine how good actors can make "actions speak louder than words." What might Smirnov's demeanor indicate here? *(Possible responses: his understanding that he doesn't want to harm Mrs. Popov; his realization that he loves her; his realization that their quarrel is ridiculous)*

Luke. Kind sir! (*kneels*) Grant me a favor; pity an old man and leave this place. First you frighten us out of our wits; now you want to fight a duel.

Smirnov (*not listening*). A duel! There's true women's emancipation for you! That evens up the sexes with a vengeance! I'll knock her off as a matter of principle. But what a woman! (*mimics her*) "Damn your infernal cheek! I'll put a bullet through that thick skull." Not bad, eh? Flushed all over, flashing eyes, accepts my challenge! You know, I've never seen such a woman in my life.

Luke. Go away, sir, and I'll say prayers for you till the day I die.

Smirnov. There's a regular woman for you, something I do appreciate! A proper woman—not some namby-pamby, wishy-washy female, but a really red-hot bit of stuff, a regular pistol-packing little spitfire. A pity to kill her, really.

Luke (*weeps*). Kind sir—do leave. Please!

Smirnov. I definitely like her. Definitely! Never mind her dimples; I like her. I wouldn't mind letting her off what she owes me, actually. And I don't feel angry anymore. Wonderful woman!

Scene 10

(*The above and* Mrs. Popov)

Mrs. Popov (*comes in with the pistols*). Here are the pistols. But before we start would you mind showing me how to fire them? I've never had a pistol in my hands before.

Luke. Lord help us! Mercy on us! I'll go and find the gardener and coachman. What have we done to deserve this? (*goes out*)

Smirnov (*examining the pistols*). Now, there are several types of pistol. There are Mortimer's special dueling pistols with percussion caps.[26] Now, yours here are Smith and Wessons, triple action with extractor,[27] center-fired. They're fine weapons, worth a cool ninety roubles the pair. Now, you hold a revolver like this. (*aside*) What eyes, what eyes! She's hot stuff all right!

Mrs. Popov. Like this?

Smirnov. Yes, that's right. Then you raise the hammer and take aim like this. Hold your head back a bit; stretch your arm out properly. Right. And then with this finger you press this little gadget; and that's it. But the great thing is—don't get excited, and do take your time about aiming. Try and see your hand doesn't shake.

Mrs. Popov. All right. We can't very well shoot indoors; let's go in the garden.

Smirnov. Very well. But I warn you, I'm firing in the air.

Mrs. Popov. Oh, this is the limit! Why?

Smirnov. Because, because—That's my business.

Mrs. Popov. Got cold feet, eh? I see. Now don't shilly-shally, sir. Kindly follow me. I shan't rest till I've put a bullet through your brains, damn you. Got the wind up, have you?

Smirnov. Yes.

Mrs. Popov. That's a lie. Why won't you fight?

Smirnov. Because, er, because you, er, I like you.

Mrs. Popov (*with a vicious laugh*). He likes me! He dares to say he likes me! (*points to the door*) I won't detain you.

Smirnov (*puts down the revolver without speaking, picks up his peaked cap and moves off; near the door he stops, and for about half a minute the two look at each other without speaking; then he speaks, going up to her hesitantly*). Listen. Are you still angry? I'm absolutely furious myself, but you must see—how can I put it? The fact is that, er, it's this

---

26. **percussion caps:** small powder caps used to set off some older guns.
27. **extractor:** the part of a gun that pulls the shell case out of the chamber so that it may be ejected after firing.

484 UNIT THREE PART 2: MYSTERIES OF THE HEART

Mini-Lesson — Study Skills

LITERARY REFERENCE SOURCES Discuss with students the various specialized sources of information about authors and their works. Biographical dictionaries contain factual information and sometimes critical commentary and quotations. Literary reference works include *Twentieth Century Authors*, *Contemporary Authors*, and Benet's *The Reader's Encyclopedia*. More extensive entries can be found in *American Writers: A Collection of Literary Biographies* and *Writers at Work*. *Book Review Digest* provides reviews arranged alphabetically by author. *The Cyclopedia of Literary Characters* identifies the main characters in 1,300 works from world literature. The *Oxford Companion* series offers articles on topics in the history and theory of literature. Biographies of authors are found in the nonfiction stacks, in the 900 section in the Dewey Decimal system; literary criticism is in the 800's.

Application Ask pairs of students to plan a library search for a report on the performance history of Chekhov's *The Bear* or on a broader related topic such as Chekhov's life and work, or Russian literature of the 19th century.

way, actually—(*shouts*) Anyway, can I help it if I like you? (*clutches the back of a chair, which cracks and breaks*) Damn fragile stuff, furniture! I like you! Do you understand? I, er, I'm almost in love.

Mrs. Popov. Keep away from me; I loathe you.

Smirnov. God, what a woman! Never saw the like of it in all my born days. I'm sunk! Without trace! Trapped like a mouse!

Mrs. Popov. Get back or I shoot.

Smirnov. Shoot away. I'd die happily with those marvelous eyes looking at me; that's what you can't see—die by that dear little velvet hand. Oh, I'm crazy! Think it over and make your mind up now, because once I leave this place we shan't see each other again. So make your mind up. I'm a gentleman and a man of honor, I've ten thousand a year, I can put a bullet through a coin in midair and I keep a good stable. Be my wife.

Mrs. Popov (*indignantly brandishes the revolver*). A duel! We'll shoot it out!

Smirnov. I'm out of my mind! Nothing makes any sense. (*shouts*) Hey, you there—water!

Mrs. Popov (*shouts*). We'll shoot it out!

Smirnov. I've lost my head, fallen for her like some damfool boy! (*Clutches her hand. She shrieks with pain.*) I love you! (*kneels*) I love you as I never loved any of my twenty-one other women—twelve times it was me broke it off; the other nine got in first. But I never loved anyone as much as you. I've gone all sloppy, soft and sentimental. Kneeling like an imbecile, offering my hand! Disgraceful! Scandalous! I haven't been in love for five years, I swore not to, and here I am crashing head over heels, hook, line and sinker! I offer you my hand. Take it or leave it. (*gets up and hurries to the door*)

Mrs. Popov. Just a moment.

Smirnov (*stops*). What is it?

Mrs. Popov. Oh, never mind, just go away. But wait. No, go, go away. I hate you. Or no—don't go away. Oh, if you knew how furious I am! (*throws the revolver on the table*) My fingers are numb from holding this beastly thing. (*tears a handkerchief in her anger*) Why are you hanging about? Clear out!

Smirnov. Good-bye.

Mrs. Popov. Yes, yes, go away! (*shouts*) Where are you going? Stop. Oh, go away then. I'm so furious! Don't you come near me, I tell you.

Smirnov. (*going up to her*). I'm so fed up with myself! Falling in love like a schoolboy! Kneeling down! It's enough to give you the willies! (*rudely*) I love you! Oh, it's just what the doctor ordered, this is! There's my interest due in tomorrow, hay making's upon us—and *you* have to come along! (*takes her by the waist*) I'll never forgive myself.

Mrs. Popov. Go away! You take your hands off me! I, er, hate you! We'll sh-shoot it out!

(*A prolonged kiss*)

Scene 11

(*The above,* Luke *with an axe, the gardener with a rake, the coachman with a pitchfork and some workmen with sundry sticks and staves*)

Luke (*seeing the couple kissing*). Mercy on us! (*pause*)

Mrs. Popov (*lowering her eyes*). Luke, tell them in the stables—Toby gets no oats today.

Curtain

Translated by Ronald Hingley

From Personal Response to Critical Analysis

1. Accept all reasonable responses.
2. Accept all reasonable, well-supported responses.
3. Possible responses: Some students will agree, saying that his behavior is rude and uncouth. Others might say he's simply reacting to Mrs. Popov and his frustration, but he's not so bad
4. Possible responses: hypocritical; snobbish; fearless; temperamental
5. Accept all reasonable, well-supported responses.
6. Possible responses: Luke is like a narrator who points out the other characters' faults. Toby, though offstage, represents Mrs. Popov's changing opinion of her fate and her widowhood.
7. Accept all reasonable, well-supported responses.

Another Pathway

Cooperative Learning Group members should work together to decide what direction their sequel will take. One student should record the group's ideas, and two or three others could write actual dialogue. Groups should also decide what props, scenery, and costumes they want to use, and appoint individuals to take responsibility for these aspects.

Rubric

3 Full Accomplishment The sequel is cohesive and entertaining and reflects valid insights into the characters.

2 Substantial Accomplishment The sequel reflects an adequate understanding of the characters, but may lack cohesiveness or humor as drama.

1 Little or Partial Accomplishment The sequel shows that students do not understand the central conflict or characters in "The Bear."

RESPONDING OPTIONS

FROM PERSONAL RESPONSE TO CRITICAL ANALYSIS

REFLECT
1. In your notebook, rate this comedy on a 1 to 10 scale, with 10 representing "very funny" and 1 representing "not funny at all." Share your response.

RETHINK
2. What is your opinion of Smirnov's attitude toward women? Cite examples from the play to support your opinion.
3. Do you think that Smirnov is really a bear, as the title implies? Explain your answer.
4. How would you describe Mrs. Popov?
   Consider
   - how she responded to her husband's death
   - what her marriage was really like
   - why she agrees to the duel
   - her change of heart at the end of the play

   Close Textual Reading

5. Of the sayings "Birds of a feather flock together" and "Opposites attract," which do you think is more appropriate to the romance in *The Bear*? Explain your answer.
6. In a well-made play, even minor characters contribute to its success. In your opinion, what do Luke and the horse, Toby, contribute to this play?

RELATE
7. Do you think men or women most often win the battle of the sexes? Explain your reasoning.

LITERARY CONCEPTS

A **farce** is a play that prompts laughter through ridiculous situations, exaggerated behavior and language, and physical comedy. Characters are often **stereotypes;** that is, they conform to a fixed pattern or are defined by a single trait. In *The Bear*, for example, Luke might be seen as a stereotype of a loyal but critical servant who tells his superior more than she wants to hear. Cite examples of ridiculous situations, exaggerated behavior and language, and physical comedy in *The Bear*. Would you say that the main characters are stereotypes? Why or why not?

486 UNIT THREE PART 2: MYSTERIES OF THE HEART

Multimodal Learning
ANOTHER PATHWAY

Cooperative Learning
With a group of classmates, stage a sequel to *The Bear*, set at the wedding reception after the two main characters marry. Create dialogue and action in keeping with the characters' earlier portrayal. Guests at the reception can share stories about the couple's odd courtship.

QUICKWRITES

1. Why do you think the two main characters in *The Bear* fall in love? Write an **analysis** that explains their behavior, citing details from the play to support your ideas.
2. Imagine that you are a theater critic. Write a **review** of *The Bear* that focuses on your opinion of the play itself, though you may also include imaginary details about the quality of the production.
3. Write your own **dramatic scene** from a farce about the battle of the sexes. The description you created for the Writing Connection on page 473 might serve as the basis of your plot.

📁 **PORTFOLIO** Save your writing. You may want to use it later as a springboard to a piece for your portfolio.

Literary Concepts

Opinions may differ on whether the main characters are fundamentally stereotypical, but there is no doubt that they contain stereotypical elements, such as Mrs. Popov's false show of grief and Smirnov's loutishness. Remind students that a Russian audience in Chekhov's time may have perceived stereotypical elements more readily than would an audience of American students today. Other farcical elements are discussed in annotations B, E, H, Y, and DD.

QuickWrites

1. Suggest that students take notes to prewrite and that they include a tentative thesis statement in their notes.
2. Encourage students to cite specific details from the play in their reviews.
3. Remind students to use stage directions as well as dialogue, and to use physical comedy, exaggerated language, and ridiculous situations.

 **The Writer's Craft**

Paragraphs That Analyze, p. 361
Using Dialogue in Plays, pp. 453–454

486 THE LANGUAGE OF LITERATURE TEACHER'S EDITION

THE WRITER'S STYLE

Chekhov's diction, or word choice, plays a strong role in reinforcing characterization in *The Bear*. Find examples of slang and formal language in the play. What do these examples reveal about the characters who speak in such a manner?

CRITIC'S CORNER

A student reviewer, Cynthia Villicana, found Chekhov's play to be interesting because it is "romantic and funny at the same time." How does her judgment of the play compare with your own?

ACROSS THE CURRICULUM

Drama Find out more about Chekhov's contributions to the theater. Prepare a class presentation of this information and, if possible, share with the class various photographs from stage productions of his plays.

Logo Moscow Arts Theatre

WORDS TO KNOW

Review the Words to Know at the bottom of the selection pages. Then write the word that best completes each sentence.

1. That ill-mannered man overstepped his bounds and took the _____ of asking a woman out on a date just one week after her husband's funeral!
2. Giving him a book on etiquette would be _____, since rude people don't see any point to politeness.
3. "Why," he might whine, "should I _____ with desire instead of just asking for what I want?"
4. Overwhelmed by his rudeness, the woman cried, "You inconsiderate, _____ idiot!"
5. One who wants _____ from the restrictions imposed by good manners will find that there is a price to pay for such freedom.

ANTON CHEKHOV

1860–1904

One of his country's greatest authors, Anton Chekhov was born to a poor family in Taganrog in the south of Russia. After finishing high school, Chekhov enrolled in medical school in Moscow, but since his family needed his financial support, he began writing comical sketches and selling them to popular newspapers and journals. Although Chekhov obtained his degree in 1884, he practiced medicine only sporadically throughout his writing career.

By 1887 Chekhov had published three story collections and was beginning to experiment with drama, producing *The Bear* and several more one-act farces, as well as full-length plays. The first performance of one of these plays, *The Seagull*, received such poor reviews that Chekhov nearly stopped writing drama; however, a successful restaging at the Moscow Art Theater turned the criticism around. In the next few years Chekhov wrote three more plays for which he is best remembered: *Uncle Vanya, The Three Sisters,* and *The Cherry Orchard*. Chekhov died of tuberculosis in 1904, just three years after marrying actress Olga Knipper, whom he met when the Moscow Art Theater staged his plays.

OTHER WORKS *Stories of Russian Life, The Brute and Other Farces, Chekhov: The Major Plays, Forty Stories*

Extended Reading

• DRAMA CONNECTION

THE BEAR **487**

Words to Know

1. liberty
2. futile
3. languish
4. sniveling
5. emancipation

Reteaching/Reinforcement
• *Unit Three Resource Book*, p. 60

Across the Curriculum

Drama Encourage students to use the research methods suggested in the Mini-Lesson: Study Skills on page 484, and to consult general reference sources such as encyclopedias. Critical commentary contained in editions of Chekhov's plays might also prove useful.

ANTON CHEKHOV

Chekhov's father—a strict, intensely religious man—was a gifted singer and artist; his mother was a gifted storyteller and taught Chekhov to read and write. As a boy, Chekhov spent many hours behind the counter of his father's shop; this, and his later experience as a physician, strengthened his power of observing human beings. Discussing his early, comic stories, Chekhov once wrote, "I wrote as naturally as a bird sings. I just sat down and the writing came.... To write an essay, a story, a short sketch, caused me no trouble at all. Like a calf or foal let loose in a green and sunlit field, I jumped and sweated, flicking my tail and waggling my head in the funniest way. I laughed and made those round me laugh."

DRAMA CONNECTION
Scenes from The Bear Although Chekhov wrote *The Bear* approximately 100 years ago, this one-act comedy continues to entertain audiences today. Photographs of scenes from a contemporary production of *The Bear* may lead to a discussion about the casting, costuming, and staging of the play.

Side A, Frame 49490

The Writer's Style

Students might use the many of Smirnov's lines as examples of slang diction. Examples of formal diction might be found more readily in Mrs. Popov's lines, such as, "Kindly don't raise your voice at me, sir." Invite students to select passages from the play that they feel are slangy and ones that they feel are formal, and to rewrite each in the opposite style.

THE LANGUAGE OF LITERATURE **TEACHER'S EDITION** **487**

OBJECTIVES

- To promote independent active reading
- To practice and apply skills learned in previous selections
- To provide an opportunity to assess students' performance through an alternative assessment instrument

Reading Pathways

- Invite students to form small groups, with members taking turns reading the story aloud.

- Have students read the story individually. Then have them form small groups to retell the story, each member telling a part of it. Students may look at the text to refresh their memories, but should use their own words rather than reading verbatim.

- Invite students to sketch the characters and scenes as they read independently, using the illustrations in the text for ideas.

- Suggest that students keep track of the plot twists and turns by tracking them on a flow chart of the events of the story. They might begin their chart with a statement of why Chin Lao-ta's former occupation limits his chances to find a suitable husband for his daughter. Encourage students to be creative with their charts. For example, they might develop two branches to show the different roads Jade Slave and Mo Chi take after he leaves her in the river.

- Evaluate how well students can read, interpret, discuss, and write about the selection on their own by using the Intergrated Assessment for Unit Three, located in the Alternative Assessment booklet. Administer the assessment after students have completed the final writing assignment for the unit.

ON YOUR OWN REFLECT & ASSESS

The Lady Who Was a Beggar

Anonymous

488 UNIT THREE PART 2: MYSTERIES OF THE HEART

PRINT AND MEDIA RESOURCES

UNIT THREE RESOURCE BOOK
Strategic Reading: Literature, p. 63

FORMAL ASSESSMENT
Selection Test, pp. 97–98
Part Test, pp. 99–100
Test Generator

ALTERNATIVE ASSESSMENT
Unit Three Integrated Assessment, pp. 13–18

ACCESS FOR STUDENTS ACQUIRING ENGLISH
Selection Summaries

AUDIO LIBRARY
See Reference Card

INTERNET RESOURCES
McDougal Littell Literature Center at http://www.hmco.com/mcdougal/lit

The Bride Wore Red (about 1988–1989), Yang Hsien Min. Copyright © 1989, The Greenwich Workshop, Inc., Shelton, Connecticut. Reproduced with the permission of the Greenwich Workshop, Inc.

SUMMARY

Chin Lao-ta, the wealthy former leader of a band of beggars, is eager to rise in society. To accomplish his goal, he seeks a husband from the educated upper class for his daughter, Jade Slave. A poor young scholar, Mo Chi, agrees to marry her. Jade Slave does all she can financially and emotionally to advance her husband's learning and position, but he becomes ashamed of her background. Eventually, Mo Chi tries to drown his loyal wife, but she is rescued by Hsü Te-hou, her husband's superior officer, who hears her weeping on the riverbank. He and his wife adopt her and devise a scheme that will make Mo Chi rectify his wrong. Without revealing Jade Slave's identity, Hsü Te-hou offers her as a bride to Mo Chi, who sees the marriage as fulfillment of his ambition. After the wedding, the unsuspecting bridegroom is beaten by several women and brought before the furious Jade Slave, who feels a duty toward her husband but shames him for exploiting her. Mo Chi begs forgiveness, and the two finally reach an accord. Touched by the kindness of his wife's new family, the repentant husband even takes care of his first father-in-law, Chin Lao-ta.

Thematic Link: *Mysteries of the Heart* A young man learns a lesson about valuing social status more than love.

Although the following folk tale was not published until the early 1620s, it was probably first composed in the 12th century. At that time, China was ruled by the Song dynasty (960–1279) and its magnificent capital was in the eastern city of Lin-an, later called Hangzhou. During the Song dynasty, literature, music, and art flourished, and oral storytelling in the everyday language of the people became an art form. Audiences gathered in a variety of settings—including street corners and market places—to hear their favorite artists.

Each teller had a specialty, such as crime stories, stories from Buddhist scripture, or love stories. The tales themselves were always meant to entertain, but they also communicated the values of the society, teaching proper, moral behavior through the deeds of the characters and the punishments they suffered.

Cautionary tales and romances were two types of love stories that were particularly popular in Lin-an during the 12th and 13th centuries, and "The Lady Who Was a Beggar," is considered a typical romance tale. Such lines in the story as, "Let us digress no longer," or "Don't you agree that . . ." are evidence that the tale was once shared aloud. Look for other such evidence as you read.

Art Note

The Bride Wore Red by Yang Hsien Min This twentieth-century print celebrates the traditional Chinese wedding ritual, in which the bride and groom were carried in sedan chairs to the groom's home. The chairs are draped in red silk and decorated with phoenix and dragons. Musicians precede the married couple, and porters follow the couple. In China the color red has long been associated with joy, good luck, and prosperity.

Reading the Art *What aspects of this wedding scene remind you of weddings you have known, and what aspects look unfamiliar?*

DESIGN NOTE

The Chinese character used as a background for the title of the folk tale means *marriage*.

Reading the Art *What does the presence of this particular character, coupled with the art at the top of the page, suggest to you about the story being told?*

It is told that in the Shao-hsing[1] reign period of the Sung dynasty (1131–1163), although Lin-an had been made the capital city and was a wealthy and populous district, still the great number of beggars had not diminished. Among them was one who acted as their head. He was called the "tramp-major," and looked after all the beggars. Whenever they managed to beg something, the tramp-major would demand a fee for the day. Then when it was raining or snow lay on the ground, and there was nowhere to go to beg, the tramp-major would boil up a drop of thin gruel and feed the whole beggar band. Their tattered robes and jackets were also in his care. The result was that the whole crowd of the beggars were careful to obey him, with bated breath like a lot of slaves, and none of them dared offend him.

The tramp-major was thus provided with a regular income, and as a rule he would lend out sums of money among the beggars and extort a tidy interest. In this way, . . . he could build up a going concern out of it. He depended on this for his livelihood, and never for a moment thought of changing his profession. There was only one drawback: a tramp-major did not have a very good name. Though he acquired land by his efforts, and his family had prospered for generations, still he was a boss of the beggars and not to be compared with ordinary respectable people. No one would salute him with respect if he showed himself out-of-doors, and so the only thing for him to do was to shut his doors and play the great man in his own home.

And yet, distinguishing the worthy from the base, we count among the latter only . . . actors, yamen-runners[2] and soldiers: we certainly do not include beggars. For what is wrong with beggars is not that they are covered in sores, but simply that they have no money. There have been men like the minister Wu Tzu-hsü,[3] of Ch'un-ch'iu times,[4] who as a fugitive from oppression played his pipes and begged his food in the marketplace of Wu; or Cheng Yüan-ho[5] of T'ang times[6] who sang the beggar's song of "Lien-hua lo,"[7] but later rose to wealth and eminence and covered his bed with brocade. These were great men, though beggars: clearly, we may hold beggars in contempt, but we should

---

1. **Shao-hsing** (shou′shĭng′).
2. **yamen-runners** (yä′mən-rŭn′ərz): people who run errands for a Chinese government official or department.
3. **Wu Tzu-hsü** (wōō′ tsōō′shü′).
4. **Ch'un ch'iu** (chŏŏn′chē-ōō′) **times**: 722–479 B.C.
5. **Cheng Yüan-ho** (jəng yü-än′hō′).
6. **T'ang** (täng) **times**: the T'ang (now usually spelled Tang) dynasty, which ruled from A.D. 618–907.
7. **Lien-hua lo** (lē-ĕn′hwä′ lō′).

not compare them with the . . . actors, the runners, and [the] soldiery.

Let us digress no longer, but tell now how in the city of Hangchow there was once a tramp-major by the name of Chin Lao-ta. In the course of seven generations his ancestors had developed the profession into a perfect family business, so that Chin Lao-ta ate well and dressed well, lived in a fine house and cultivated good land. His barns were well-stocked with grain and his purse with money, he made loans and kept servants; if not quite the wealthiest, he was certainly one of the rich. Being a man of social aspirations, he decided to relinquish this post of tramp-major into the hands of a relative, "Scabby" Chin, while he himself took his ease with what he had and mingled no more with the beggar band. But unfortunately, the neighbors were used to speaking of the "tramp-major's family," and the name persisted in spite of his efforts.

Chin Lao-ta was over fifty. He had lost his wife and had no son, but only a daughter whose name was Jade Slave. Jade Slave was beautiful, as we are told by a verse about her:

> *Pure to compare with jade,*
> *Gracious to shame the flowers,*
> *Given the adornments of the court*
> *Here would be another Chang Li-hua.*[8]

Chin Lao-ta prized his daughter as a jewel, and taught her from an early age to read and write. By the age of fifteen she was adept in prose and verse, composing as fast as her hand could write. She was equally proficient in the womanly crafts, and in performing on the harp or flute: everything she did proclaimed her skill. Her beauty and talent inspired Chin Lao-ta to seek a husband for her among the scholar class. But the fact was that among families of name and rank it would be difficult to find anyone anxious to marry the girl—no one wanted a tramp-major's daughter. On the other hand, Lao-ta had no desire to cultivate a liaison[9] with humble and unaspiring tradespeople. Thus, while her father hovered between high and low, the girl reached the age of seventeen without betrothal.

And then one day an old man of the neighborhood came along with news of a student by the name of Mo Chi who lived below the T'ai-ping Bridge. This was an able youth of nineteen, full of learning, who remained unmarried only because he was an orphan and had no money. But he had graduated recently, and was hoping to marry some girl in whose family he could find a home.

"This youth would be just right for your daughter," said the neighbor. "Why not take him as your son-in-law?"

"Then do me the favor of acting as go-between," said Chin Lao-ta; and off went the old man on his errand, straight to the T'ai-ping Bridge.

> *Unfortunately, the neighbors were used to speaking of the "tramp-major's family."*

---

8. **Chang Li-hua** (jäng′ lē′hwä′): beautiful girlfriend of the Chen dynasty's last emperor, who ruled from A.D. 583–589.
9. **liaison** (lē′ā-zŏn′): a close relationship, connection, or link.

Multicultural Perspectives

SOCIAL STATUS Traditionally, social status in China has been based more upon profession than upon wealth. During the Song dynasty, government officials, who were also scholars and had to pass rigorous civil service examinations, held the highest social rank. Not everyone was privileged to receive an education, but the opportunity was available to the most talented men whether rich or poor. Other societies have used different yardsticks for measuring one's status. Among "potlatch" societies such as the Kwakiutl of the Northwest Coast, the amount of goods a person gave away in huge feasts was a mark of prestige. Some Native American peoples of the Great Plains counted "coups"—points awarded to warriors for brave actions according to their degree of fearlessness, such as striking an armed enemy with the bare hand. Among Orthodox Jews, Talmudic learning is a highly prized achievement. In many European countries in past centuries, one's title, family history, and inherited income determined one's status. In the United States today, fame and wealth produce high status.

Cultural Note

Although other types of marriages did exist during the Song dynasty, traditional Chinese families followed an established ritual in the marriage ceremony. Before modern times, Chinese tradition called for a young woman to live with her husband in the home of his parents. The ceremony itself was always held in the groom's home; the bride's family did not attend. On the day of the wedding, the bride was carried from her home to the groom's home in a red bridal chair. Carrying the bride in this fashion was said to protect her from evil spirits. The wedding ceremony was followed by an elaborate feast, after which the couple retired to a room in the same house. The day after the wedding, the bride began to learn the domestic responsibilities she would have in her new family, with whom she would live the rest of her life. The training was conducted under the supervision of her mother-in-law. Families who could afford such arrangements often had several generations living together in one house—parents, sons, grandsons, and their wives and children. Traditionally, marriage was a lifetime commitment for a Chinese wife. This commitment was never to be broken, and remarrying was considered improper even for a widow.

There he sought out the graduate Mo Chi, to whom he said, "There is one thing I am obliged to tell you: the ancestors of Chin Lao-ta followed the profession of tramp-major. But this was long ago: and think, what a fine girl she is, this daughter of his—and what's more, what a prosperous and flourishing family! If it is not against the young gentleman's wishes, I will take it upon myself to arrange the whole thing at once."

Before giving his reply, Mo Chi turned the matter over in his mind: "I am not very well-off for food and clothes just now, and I am certainly not in a position to take a wife in the usual way. Why not make the best of it and marry into this family? It would be killing two birds with one stone; and I needn't take any notice of ridicule." Turning to the old man, he said, "Uncle,[10] what you propose seems an admirable plan. But I am too poor to buy the usual presents. What do you suggest?"

"Provided only that you accept this match," replied the old man, "you will not even be called on to supply so much as the paper for the exchange of horoscopes.[11] You may leave everything to me."

With this he returned to report to Chin Lao-ta. They selected an auspicious[12] day, and the Chin family even provided clothes for Mo Chi to wear at the wedding.

When Mo Chi had entered the family and the ceremony was over, he found that Jade Slave's beauty and talents exceeded his wildest hopes. And this perfect wife was his without the outlay of a single copper! He had food and clothes in abundance, and indeed everything he could wish. Even the ridicule he had feared from his friends was withheld, for all were willing to make allowances for Mo Chi's penniless condition.

When their marriage had lasted a month, Chin Lao-ta prepared a generous banquet at which his son-in-law could feast his graduate friends and thus enhance the dignity of the house. The drinking went on for a week: but what was not foreseen was the offense which all this gave to the kinsman "Scabby" Chin. Nor was Scabby without justification.

"You're a tramp-major just as much as I am," said he in his heart, "the only thing is that you've been one for a few generations longer and have got some money in your pocket. But if it comes to ancestors, aren't yours the very same as mine? When my niece Jade Slave gets married, I expect to be invited to drink a toast—here's a load of guests drinking for a week on end to celebrate the first month, but not so much as a one-inch by three-inch invitation card do I receive. What is this son-in-law of yours—he's a graduate, I know, but is he a President of a Board or a Prime Minister as well? Aren't I the girl's own uncle, and entitled to a stool at your party? Very well," he concluded, "if they're so ready to ignore my existence, I'll go and stir them up a bit and see how that pleases them."

Thereupon he called together fifty or sixty of his beggars, and took the lot of them along to Chin Lao-ta's house. What a sight—

Hats bursting into flower, shirts tied up in knots,
A rag of old matting or a strip of worn rug, a bamboo stick and a rough chipped bowl.
Shouting "Father!," shouting "Mother!," shouting "Benefactor!," what a commotion before the gate!
Writhing snakes, yapping dogs, chattering apes and monkeys, what sly cunning they all display!

---

10. **Uncle:** in China, a respectful way of addressing any elderly man.
11. **exchange of horoscopes:** Before marriage, astrological forecasts based on the Chinese calendar were traditionally exchanged to make sure the partners were compatible.
12. **auspicious:** favorable; lucky.

> *Beating clappers, singing "Yang Hua,"*[13] *the clamor deafens the ear;*
> *Clattering tiles, faces white with chalk,*[14] *the sight offends the eye.*
> *A troop of rowdies banded together, not Chung K'uei*[15] *himself could contain them.*

When Chin Lao-ta heard the noise they made, he opened the gate to look out, whereupon the whole crowd of beggars, with Scabby at their head, surged inside and threw the house into commotion. Scabby himself hurried to a seat, snatched the choicest of the meats and wines and began to stuff himself, calling meanwhile for the happy couple to come and make their obeisances[16] before their uncle.

So terrified were the assembled graduates that they gave up at once and fled the scene, Mo Chi joining in their retreat. Chin Lao-ta was at his wits' end, and pleaded repeatedly, "My son-in-law is the host today; this is no affair of mine. Come another day when I will buy some wine specially for you and we will have a chat together."

He distributed money among the beggar band, and brought out two jars of fine wine and some live chickens and geese, inviting the beggars to have a banquet of their own over at Scabby's house; but it was late at night before they ceased their rioting and took their leave, and Jade Slave wept in her room from shame and rage.

That night Mo Chi stayed at the house of a friend, returning only when morning came. At the sight of his son-in-law, Chin Lao-ta felt keenly the disgrace of what had happened, and his face filled with shame. Naturally enough, Mo Chi on his part was strongly displeased; but no one was anxious to say a word. Truly,

> *When a mute tastes the bitterness of cork-tree wood*
> *He must swallow his disgust with his medicine.*

Let us rather tell how Jade Slave, conscious of her family's disrepute and anxious that her husband should make his own name for himself, exhorted[17] him to labor at his books. She grudged neither the cost of the works, classical and recent, which she bought for his use, nor the expense of engaging tutors for learned discussion with him. She provided funds also for the entertaining that would widen her husband's circle of acquaintances. As a result, Mo Chi's learning and reputation made daily advances.

He gained his master's degree at the age of twenty-two, and ultimately his doctorate, and at last the day came when he left the great reception for successful candidates and, black hat, doctor's robes and all, rode back to his father-in-law's house. But as he entered his own ward of the city, a crowd of urchins pressed about him,

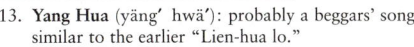

---

13. **Yang Hua** (yäng′ hwä′): probably a beggars' song similar to the earlier "Lien-hua lo."
14. **white with chalk:** Beggars sometimes whitened their faces to simulate poverty and hunger.
15. **Chung K'uei** (jŏŏng′ kwä′): a legendary Chinese demon slayer whose image is often posted on festival days to ward off evil spirits.
16. **obeisances** (ō-bā′sən-səz): bows, curtsies, or other body movements that show submission or respect.
17. **exhorted** (ĭg-zôr′tĭd): urged very strongly.

Art Note

The Han dynasty lasted from 202 B.C. to A.D. 220. During that period the arts flourished in China and the empire prospered. This painted clay figurine of a female servant was found in a tomb of the Han period. Although the woman's pose is stylized, her facial expression is very lifelike.

Reading the Art *What in the woman's pose might indicate that she is a servant?*

Literary Note

A common feature of folk tales is a brief summary of the story's plot to that point, inserted within a tale. This technique was introduced when the stories were being told orally, since it was often necessary to update listeners who arrived after the story started. Another storytelling technique aimed at the audience is the use of comments or questions on the part of the storyteller, perhaps to keep the audience's attention, as in the sentence, "But don't you agree that 'there is such a thing as coincidence'?" on page 495. Both techniques are combined in the passage beginning, "But what an absurd figure, this Mo Chi!" on page 494.

---

pointing and calling—"Look at the tramp-major's son-in-law! He's an official now!"

From his elevated position Mo Chi heard them, but it was beneath his dignity to do anything about it. He simply had to put up with it; but his correct observance of etiquette on greeting his father-in-law concealed a burning indignation. "I always knew that I should attain these honors," he said to himself, "yet I feared that no noble or distinguished family would take me in as a son-in-law, and so I married the daughter of a tramp-major. Without question, it is a lifelong stain. My sons and daughters will still have a tramp-major for their grandfather, and I shall be passed from one man to the next as a laughing stock! But the thing is done now. What is more, my wife is wise and virtuous; it would be impossible for me to divorce her on any of the seven counts.[18] 'Marry in haste, repent at leisure'—it's a true saying after all!"

His mind seethed with such thoughts, and he was miserable all day long. Jade Slave often questioned him, but received no reply and remained in ignorance of the cause of his displeasure. But what an absurd figure, this Mo Chi! Conscious only of his present eminence, he has forgotten the days of his poverty. His wife's assistance in money and effort are one with the snows of yesteryear,[19] so crooked are the workings of his mind.

Before long, Mo Chi presented himself for appointment and received the post of Census Officer at Wu-wei-chün. His father-in-law provided wine to feast his departure, and this time awe of the new official deterred the beggar band from breaking up the party.

It so happened that the whole journey from Hangchow to Wu-wei-chün was by water, and Mo Chi took his wife with him, boarded a junk[20] and proceeded to his post. After several days their voyage brought them to the eddies and whirlpools below the Colored Stone Cliff,[21] and they tied up to the northern bank. That night the moon shone bright as day. Mo Chi, unable to sleep, rose and dressed and sat in the prow enjoying the moonlight. There was no one about; and as he sat there brooding on his relationship with a tramp-major, an evil notion came into his head. The only way for him to be rid of lifelong disgrace was for his wife to die and a new one to take her place. A plan formed in his mind. He entered the cabin and inveigled[22] Jade Slave into getting up to see the moon in its glory.

Jade Slave was already asleep, but Mo Chi repeatedly urged her to get up, and she did not like to contravene[23] his wishes. She put on her

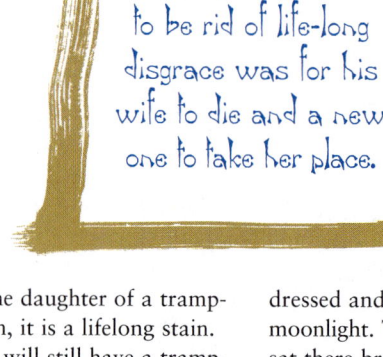

The only way for him to be rid of life-long disgrace was for his wife to die and a new one to take her place.

---

18. **any of the seven counts:** In Chinese tradition, a wife could be divorced for failing to bear a son, adultery, disobedience to her in-laws, nagging, stealing, jealousy, or contracting an evil disease.
19. **are one with the snows of yesteryear:** that is, have melted away; are completely forgotten.
20. **junk:** a Chinese flat-bottomed ship.
21. **Colored Stone Cliff:** a spur of the mountain Niu-chu that projects from the south bank of the Yangtze (yăng′sē′) River.
22. **inveigled** (ĭn-vā′gəld): convinced by clever or deceitful means; lured.
23. **contravene** (kŏn′trə-vēn′): to act in opposition to.

gown and crossed over to the doorway, where she raised her head to look at the moon. Standing thus, she was taken unawares by Mo Chi, who dragged her out on to the prow and pushed her into the river.

Softly he then woke the boatmen and ordered them to get under way at once—extra speed would be handsomely rewarded. The boatmen, puzzled but ignorant, seized pole and flourished oar. Mo Chi waited until the junk had covered three good miles before he moored again and told them that his wife had fallen in the river while gazing at the moon, and that no effort would have availed to save her. With this, he rewarded the boatmen with three ounces of silver to buy wine. The boatmen caught his meaning, but none dared open his mouth. The silly maidservants who had accompanied Jade Slave on board accepted that their mistress had really fallen in the river. They wept for a little while and then left off, and we will say no more of them. There is a verse in evidence of all this:

The name of tramp-major pleases him ill;
Hardened by pride he casts off his mate.
The ties of Heaven are not easily broken;
All he gains is an evil name.

But don't you agree that "there is such a thing as coincidence"? It so happened that the newly-appointed Transport Commissioner for Western Huai, Hsü Te-hou,[24] was also on his way to his post; and his junk moored across from the Colored Stone Cliff just when Mo Chi's boat had disappeared from view. It was the very spot where Mo Chi had pushed his wife into the water. Hsü Te-hou and his lady had opened their window to enjoy the moonlight, and had not yet retired but were taking their ease over a cup of wine. Suddenly they became aware of someone sobbing on the riverbank. It was a woman, from the sound, and her distress could not be ignored.

At once Hsü ordered his boatmen to investigate. It proved indeed to be a woman, alone, sitting on the bank. Hsü made them summon her aboard, and questioned her about herself. The woman was none other than Jade Slave, Madam Chin, the wife of the Census Officer at Wu-wei-chün. What had happened was that when she found herself in the water, her wits all but left her, and she gave herself up for dead. But suddenly she felt something in the river which held up her feet, while the waves washed her close to the bank. Jade Slave struggled ashore; but when she opened her eyes, there was only the empty expanse of the river, and no sign of the Census Officer's junk. It was then that she realized what had happened: "My husband, grown rich, has forgotten his days of hardship. It was his deliberate plan to drown his true wife to pave the way for a more advantageous marriage. And now, though I have my life, where am I to turn for support?"

Bitter reflections of this kind brought forth piteous weeping, and confronted by Hsü's questioning she could hold nothing back, but told the whole story from beginning to end. When she had finished she wept without ceasing. Hsü and his wife in their turn were moved to tears, and Hsü Te-hou tried to comfort her: "You must not grieve so; but if you will agree to become my adopted daughter, we will see what provision can be made."

Hsü had his wife produce a complete change of clothing for the girl and settle her down to rest in the stern cabin.[25] He told his servants to treat her with the respect due to his daughter, and prohibited the boatmen from disclosing anything of the affair. Before long he reached his place of office in Western Huai. Now it so happened that among the places under his juris-

---

24. **Huai** (hwī); **Hsü Te-hou** (shü′də-hou′).
25. **stern cabin:** the cabin at the rear end of a boat.

THE LADY WHO WAS A BEGGAR

OPTION 1

Cooperative Activity
WRITING AND PERFORMING A PLAY

Encourage a group of interested students to write the script for a short drama based on "The Lady Who Was a Beggar" and to perform their play before the class. One student might act as producer and coordinate the group members' roles, such as writing the script; acting; directing; and designing costumes, scenery, props, lighting, and sound effects. To a great extent the producer will be a support giver and an encourager of participation. An associate producer can take on tasks that keep the group working smoothly and on schedule—such as noise monitor, clarifier, and accuracy coach. A director should guide the actors in learning and refining their roles.

Teacher's Role After encouraging participation, allow students maximum freedom in creating their own performance, including freedom to reshape the tale imaginatively. As one of the audience, initiate and moderate discussion after the play.

Rubric

3 Full Accomplishment The play shows insight into the folk tale and is imaginatively rendered.

2 Substantial Accomplishment The play reflects an understanding of the basic content of the folk tale but lacks dramatic excitement.

1 Little or Partial Accomplishment The play shows neither understanding of the folk tale nor an imaginative interpretation of it.

---

diction was Wu-wei-chün. He was therefore the superior officer of Mo Chi, who duly appeared with his fellows to greet the new Commissioner. Observing the Census Officer, Hsü sighed that so promising a youth should be capable of so callous an action.

Hsü Te-hou allowed several months to pass, and then he addressed the following words to his staff: "I have a daughter of marriageable age, and possessing both talent and beauty. I am seeking a man fit to be her husband, whom I could take into my family. Does any of you know of such a man?"

All his staff had heard of Mo Chi's bereavement early in life, and all hastened to commend his outstanding ability and to profess his suitability as a son-in-law for the Commissioner. Hsü agreed: "I myself have had this man in mind for some time. But one who has graduated at such a youthful age must cherish high ambitions: I am not at all sure that he would be prepared to enter my family."

"He is of humble origin," the others replied. "It would be the happiest of fates for him to secure your interest, to 'cling as the creeper to the tree of jade'—there can be no doubt of his willingness."

"Since you consider it practicable," said Hsü, "I should like you to approach the Census Officer. But to discover how he reacts, say that this plan is of your own making: it might hinder matters if you disclose my interest."

They accepted the commission and made their approach to Mo Chi, requesting that they should act as go-betweens. Now to rise in society was precisely Mo Chi's intention; moreover, a matrimonial alliance with one's superior officer was not a thing to be had for the asking. Delighted, he replied, "I must rely entirely on you to accomplish this; nor shall I be slow in the material expression of my gratitude."

"You may leave it to us," they said; and thereupon they reported back to Hsü.

But Hsü demurred: "The Census Officer may be willing to marry her," said he, "but the fact is that my wife and I have doted on our daughter and have brought her up to expect the tenderest consideration. It is for this reason that we wish her to remain in her own home after marriage. But I suspect that the Census Officer, in the impatience of youth, might prove insufficiently tolerant; and if the slightest discord should arise, it would be most painful to my wife and myself. He must be prepared to be patient in all things, before I can accept him into my family."

They bore these words to Mo Chi, who accepted every condition.

The Census Officer's present circumstances were very different from those of his student days. He signified acceptance of the betrothal by sending fine silks and gold ornaments on the most ample scale. An auspicious date was selected, and Mo Chi itched in his very bones as he awaited the day when he should become the son-in-law of the Transport Commissioner.

But let us rather tell how Hsü Te-hou gave his wife instructions to prepare Jade Slave for her marriage. "Your stepfather," Mrs. Hsü said to her, "moved by pity for you in widowhood, wishes to invite a young man who has gained his doctorate to become your husband and enter our family. You must not refuse him."

But Jade Slave replied, "Though of humble family, I am aware of the rules of conduct. When Mo Chi became my husband I vowed to remain faithful to him all my life. However cruel and lawless he may have been, however shamefully he may have rejected the companion of his poverty, I shall fulfill my obligations. On no account will I forsake the true virtue of womanhood by remarrying."

With these words her tears fell like rain. Mrs. Hsü, convinced of her sincerity, decided to tell her the truth, and said, "The young graduate of

496 UNIT THREE PART 2: MYSTERIES OF THE HEART

whom my husband spoke is none other than Mo Chi himself. Appalled by his mean action, and anxious to see you reunited with him, my husband passed you off as his own daughter, and told the members of his staff that he was seeking a son-in-law who would enter our family. He made them approach Mo Chi, who was delighted by the proposal. He is to come to us this night; but when he enters your room, this is what you must do to get your own back. . . ."

As she disclosed her plan, Jade Slave dried her tears. She remade her face and changed her costume, and made preparations for the coming ceremony.

With evening, there duly appeared the Census Officer Mo Chi, all complete with mandarin's hat and girdle:[26] he was dressed in red brocade and had gold ornaments in his cap, under him was a fine steed with decorated saddle, and before him marched two bands of drummers and musicians. His colleagues were there in force to see him married, and the whole procession was cheered the length of the route. Indeed,

> *To the roll and clang of music the white steed advances,*
> *But what a curious person, this fine upstanding groom:*
> *Delighted with his change of families, beggar for man of rank,*
> *For memories of the Colored Stone Cliff his glad heart has no room.*

That night the official residence of the Transport Commissioner was festooned with flowers and carpeted, and to the playing of pipe and drum all awaited the arrival of the bridegroom. As the Census Officer rode up to the gate and dismounted, Hsü Te-hou came out to receive him, and then the accompanying junior officers took their leave. Mo Chi walked straight through to the private apartments, where the bride was brought out to him, veiled in red and supported

by a maidservant on either side. From beyond the threshold the master of ceremonies took them through the ritual. The happy pair made obeisances to heaven and earth and to the parents of the bride; and when the ceremonial observances were over, they were escorted into the nuptial chamber for the wedding feast. By this time Mo Chi was in a state of indescribable bliss, his soul somewhere above the clouds. Head erect, triumphant, he entered the nuptial chamber.

But no sooner had he passed the doorway than from positions of concealment on either

---

26. **mandarin's hat and girdle:** a distinctive hat and belt indicating that the wearer is a high government official.

THE LADY WHO WAS A BEGGAR **497**

OPTION 2

Individual Activity
CHARTING FOLK TALE ELEMENTS
Provide students with the following list of traditional folk-tale elements. Ask students to identify which of these elements appear in "The Lady Who Was a Beggar." Have them make a chart to show where these elements appear in the selection.

- flat characters exemplifying a single trait such as loyalty or greed
- events in the plot caused by miracles, magic, or extraordinary coincidence
- passages in which the storyteller addresses the reader or listener
- teaching or moralizing
- foreshadowing
- opposites appearing together, such as rich and poor, joy and grief, or triumph and humiliation
- justice, retribution, or revenge

Teacher's Role As coach for the activity, you might want to hint that all the listed elements can be found in the selection. Make yourself available to answer questions and guide chart construction. Set aside a couple of minutes to confer with each student about his or her chart.

Rubric
3 Full Accomplishment Students accurately place examples of all the listed elements on their charts.
2 Substantial Accomplishment Students accurately list and support most of the elements in their charts.
1 Little or Partial Accomplishment Students omit several elements and/or fail to support them with examples.

Art Note

***Beggars and Street Characters* by Zhou Chen** This figure, along with the figure pictured on page 490, was painted in 1516 by the Chinese artist Zhou Chen (about 1450–1535) who lived during the Ming dynasty, which lasted from 1368 to 1644. Although the figures seem comical, they represent the uprooted people who crowded the streets of Chinese towns during the turbulent years of the Ming period. During the Song period, also, cultural advances had been offset by an increase in the number of people living in poverty. Bands of beggars were a common sight on Song streets.

Reading the Art *What do you think the man with the snakes is doing?*

THE LANGUAGE OF LITERATURE TEACHER'S EDITION **497**

Cultural Note

Kowtowing specifically showed respect for a superior. A woman might kowtow before her husband, and children before their parents, but traditionally husbands would not kowtow before their wives, who were considered inferior to men. Therefore, Mo Chi's kowtowing to Jade Slave is an extraordinary gesture, which would have made a strong impression on the storyteller's audience.

---

side there suddenly emerged seven or eight young maids and old nannies, each one armed with a light or heavy bamboo. Mercilessly they began to beat him. Off came his silk hat; blows fell like rain on his shoulders; he yelled perpetually, but try as he might he could not get out of the way.

Under the beating the Census Officer collapsed, to lie in a terrified heap on the floor, calling on his parents-in-law to save him. Then he heard, from within the room itself, a gentle command issued in the softest of voices: "Beat him no more, our hardhearted young gentleman, but bring him before me."

At last the beating stopped, and the maids and nannies, tugging at his ears and dragging at his arms like the six senses tormenting Amida Buddha in the parable,[27] hauled him, his feet barely touching the ground, before the presence of the bride. "What is the nature of my offense?" the Census Officer was mumbling; but when he opened his eyes, there above him, correct and upright in the brilliance of the candlelight, was seated the bride—who was none other than his former wife, Jade Slave, Madam Chin.

Now Mo Chi's mind reeled, and he bawled, "It's a ghost! It's a ghost!" All began to laugh, until Hsü Te-hou came in from outside and addressed him: "Do not be alarmed, my boy: this is no ghost, but my adopted daughter, who came to me below the Colored Stone Cliff."

Mo Chi's heart ceased its pounding. He fell to his knees and folded his hands in supplication. "I, Mo Chi, confess my crime," he said. "I only beg your forgiveness."

"This is no affair of mine," replied Hsü, "unless my daughter has something to say. . . ."

Jade Slave spat in Mo Chi's face and cursed him: "Cruel wretch! Did you never think of the words of Sung Hung?[28] 'Do not exclude from your mind the friends of your poverty, nor from your house the wife of your youth.' It was empty-handed that you first came into my family, and thanks to our money that you were able to study and enter society, to make your name and enjoy your present good fortune. For my part, I looked forward to the day when I should share in your glory. But you—forgetful of the favors you had received, oblivious of our early love, you repaid good with evil and threw me into the river to drown. Heaven took pity on me and sent me a savior, whose adopted daughter I became. But if I had ended my days on the riverbed, and you had taken a new wife—how could your heart have been so callous? And now, how can I so demean myself as to rejoin you?"

Her speech ended in tears and loud wails, and "Cruel, cruel!" she continued to cry. Mo Chi's whole face expressed his shame. He could find no words, but pleaded for forgiveness by kowtowing[29] before her. Hsü Te-hou, satisfied with her demonstration of anger, raised Mo Chi to his feet and admonished Jade Slave in the following words: "Calm your anger, my child. Your husband has now repented his crime, and we may be sure that he will never again treat you ill. Although in fact your marriage took place some years ago, so far as my family is concerned you are newly wed; in all things, therefore, show consideration to me, and let an end be made here and now to recriminations."[30] Turning to Mo Chi, he said, "My son, your crime is upon your own head; lay no blame on others. Tonight I

---

27. **six senses tormenting Amida Buddha in the parable:** sight, hearing, smell, taste, touch, and thought, tormenting a godlike being that is worshipped in Buddhism.
28. **Sung Hung** (soŏng′ hoŏng′): Chinese minister who in A.D. 26 refused to leave his lowborn wife after being elevated to the nobility, even though the emperor told him to marry a princess.
29. **kowtowing** (kou-tou′ĭng): kneeling and touching the forehead to the ground as a sign of respect.

498 UNIT THREE PART 2: MYSTERIES OF THE HEART

Critic's Corner

"Emotions such as love, hate, joy, sorrow, happiness, and sadness are found again and again [in folk tales], and often the same tale deals with such phenomena in contrasting pairs, that is success versus failure, wealth versus poverty, luck versus misfortune, kindness versus meanness, compassion versus indifference, or, simply put, good versus evil."

Wolfgang Mieder
Tradition and Innovation in Folk Literature

Ask students to discuss this tale and other folk tales they know that deal with contrasting pairs of emotions or conditions.

ask you only to show tolerance. I will send your mother-in-law to make peace between you."

He left the room, and shortly his wife came in to them. Much mediation was required from her before the two were finally brought into accord.

On the following day Hsü Te-hou gave a banquet for his new son-in-law, during which he returned all the betrothal gifts, the fine silks and gold ornaments, saying to Mo Chi, "One bride may not receive two sets of presents. You took such things as these to the Chin family on the previous occasion; I cannot accept them all over again now." Mo Chi lowered his head and said nothing, and Hsü went on: "I believe it was your dislike of the lowly status of your father-in-law which put an end to your love and almost to your marriage. What do you think now of my own position? I am only afraid that the rank I hold may still be too low for your aspirations."

Mo Chi's face flushed crimson, and he was obliged to retire a few steps and acknowledge his errors. There is a verse to bear witness:

Full of fond hopes of bettering himself by marriage,
Amazed to discover his bride to be his wife;
A beating, a cursing, an overwhelming shame:
Was it really worth it for a change of in-laws?

From this time on, Mo Chi and Jade Slave lived together twice as amicably as before. Hsü Te-hou and his wife treated Jade Slave as their own daughter and Mo Chi as their proper son-in-law, and Jade Slave behaved towards them exactly as though they were her own parents. Even the heart of Mo Chi was touched, so that he received Chin Lao-ta, the tramp-major, into his official residence and cared for him to the end of his days. And when in the fullness of time Hsü Te-hou and his wife died, Jade Slave, Madam Chin, wore the heaviest mourning of coarse linen for each of them in recompense for their kindness to her; and generations of descendants of Mo and Hsü regarded each other as cousins and never failed in friendship. A verse concludes:

Sung Hung remained faithful and was praised for his virtue;
Huang Yün[31] divorced his wife and was reviled for lack of feeling.
Observe the case of Mo Chi, remarrying his wife:
A marriage is predestined:[32] no objection can prevail. ❖

---

30. **recriminations** (rĭ-krĭm′ə-nā′shənz): countercharges; accusations made in return.
31. **Huang Yün** (hwăng′ yün′): a famous figure of third-century China who left his wife in the hopes of marrying a noblewoman.
32. **predestined** (prē-dĕs′tĭnd): determined in advance by fate or divine will.

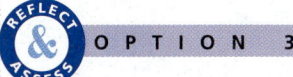

Class Discussion
SHARING IDEAS

Teacher's Role After students have read the selection, engage them in a whole-class discussion using the following questions. In the course of discussion, be aware of cultural issues in relation to students' backgrounds. Chinese-American students may reasonably be asked about traditional Chinese history and culture, but it cannot be assumed that they will know much about it.

1. What lessons do you think can be gathered from this tale? *(Possible responses: Selfish ambition will be punished; loyalty, unselfishness, forgiveness, and repentance will be rewarded; marriages should not be destroyed.)*
2. What impressions do you have of the society being described in this tale? *(Possible responses: Some students may say the culture's attitudes toward crime, women, and marriage are now outdated in many cultures. Others might point out that the culture placed importance on family, loyalty, and forgiveness.)*
3. Does social position still play an important role in contemporary life? Give your opinion. *(Many students will say it is still important, citing their own experiences in school and adults' efforts to gain professional and personal prestige. Encourage students to consider attributes that might outweigh social position, such as talent and character.)*

EDITOR'S NOTE With the permission of the copyright holder, potentially offensive material has been deleted from the selection.

SONG DYNASTY STORYTELLERS

In 1126, the Chinese court was driven south across the Yangtse River from its previous capital at Kaifeng by the Chin Tartars. The Song rulers established a new capital at Lin-an, which soon became a major center of civilization to which artists and intellectuals from the north flocked. Storytelling by traveling professionals took place in marketplaces, in amusement parks, and occasionally at imperial galas. It appealed to audiences from all classes and professions. Eventually, the oral folk tales were written down, and many were published in collections put together by two scholars, Feng Meng-lung and Ling Meng-chu. "The Lady Who Was a Beggar" is one of the stories in Feng Meng-lung's collection. These tales are valued today not only for their literary merit but also for their description of life among the common people during the Song dynasty. "The Lady Who Was a Beggar," although a typical romance tale, is notable for its attack on snobbism and for the realism with which Jade Slave, the spurned wife, berates Mo Chi before accepting his apology.

OVERVIEW

To gain a deeper appreciation of the selections they have read in this unit, students will explore the characteristics of a compare-and-contrast essay and then create a well-developed example in this lesson.

Objectives

- To plan a compare-and-contrast essay by considering elements such as library research, interviews, organizational techniques, and publication formats
- To draft a compare-and-contrast essay and solicit a response
- To revise, edit, and publish a compare-and-contrast essay
- To reflect on the process of writing a compare-and-contrast essay

Skills

WRITING AND LANGUAGE
- Using parallel structure
- Organizing information

GRAMMAR AND USAGE
- Avoiding double comparisons

MEDIA LITERACY
- Reading newspaper and magazine articles
- Interpreting pictorial references

- Using on-line services

SPEAKING, LISTENING, AND VIEWING
- Conducting interviews
- Conferencing

RESEARCH SKILLS
- Using library resources
- Conducting interviews

Critical Thinking: ANALYZING

A Have students analyze the essential elements of compare-and-contrast writing. Guide the class to realize that a writer needs to identify at least two categories of a subject area. Compare-and-contrast essays can focus on similarities, on differences, or on both.

Teaching Strategy: MODELING

B Point out to students that illustrations can show or imply details of a culture's foods, modes of dress and transport, values, climatological pressures, or religion, among others—anything that can be depicted visually.

WRITING FROM EXPERIENCE

WRITING TO EXPLAIN

As Unit Three, "In the Name of Love," shows, the ties that bind couples and families together vary from culture to culture and change over time within cultures. As you learn about different families and different ways of life, you will often find yourself comparing cultures so that you will better understand other people and the ways they behave.

YOUR ASSIGNMENT
Write a Compare-and-Contrast Essay In this lesson you will learn how to compare and contrast aspects of two or more cultures or historical periods that interest you.

❶ Read the Articles

Read the articles on these pages. What aspect or era of a country's culture does each discuss? What interests or surprises you about each article? What do you learn from the illustrations?

❷ Think About Topics

A Using these articles as starting points, list some aspects of culture that might be interesting to explore across different countries or time periods. Consider such topics as marriages, extended families, schools, or death and mourning.

- You may want to learn more about a custom or practice you have read about.
- You may want to explore a culture that is part of your family's history.

Think about how you might compare unfamiliar practices or customs with those that are familiar. Then discuss your ideas for comparison essays in a group.

Pictorial Reference
B How can illustrations provide insights into a culture?

500 UNIT THREE: IN THE NAME OF LOVE

My sister wants a traditional Hindu ceremony. Does she realize how different that will be?

Hindu Rites of Passage

Hindus consider marriage the most important rite of passage. In India, parents arrange most marriages, which are viewed as family alliances. They look for similar family traditions, languages, and backgrounds. On the wedding day the bride's parents greet the groom and present gifts. Before the ceremony, guests sing songs and throw rice. During the ceremony the couple, wearing special clothes, exchange garlands and face each other over a sacred fire. They pour *ghee* (melted butter) into the fire as they pray for healthy children, a long life, and wealth and as priests chant mantras.

Excerpt from Social Studies Text

Folk and Festival Costumes of the World
Wedding Costume
TURKEY

PRINT AND MEDIA RESOURCES

UNIT THREE RESOURCE BOOK
Prewriting Activity, p. 67
Elaboration, p. 68
Peer Response Guide, pp. 69–70
Revising and Proofreading, p. 71
Student Model, pp. 72–73
Rubric, p. 74

GRAMMAR MINI-LESSONS
Transparencies, pp. 23–24
Copymasters, pp. 26–27

WRITING MINI-LESSONS
Transparencies, pp. 18–19, 26–27, 60–63

FORMAL ASSESSMENT
Guidelines for Writing Assessment

 WRITING COACH

 LASERLINKS
Writing Springboard

 The Writer's Craft
Informative Exposition: Classification, pp. 118–133

Magazine Article

1940s–1950s
Dating DO's & DON'Ts

DO be fascinated by the same subjects he is. Say things like, "I see you have your football letter. It looks wonderful."

DON'T keep him waiting. Be ready when he arrives and introduce him with obvious pleasure to your parents

1980s–1990s
Dating DO's & DON'Ts

DO stop looking to guys as your only source of excitement and self-esteem. Then you will graduate from flings to more lasting love.

DON'T go out with a guy who verbally or physically abuses you.

Rebecca Barry
from *Seventeen*

Custom of the Country

When I was in India last spring I went to visit my cousin, a quiet and thoughtful woman with a teenage daughter, who lives in the frenetic, modern, Westernized, commerce-conscious city of Bombay. We had a peaceful cup of tea, countless little delicacies both sweet and salty, which she had gone to some pains to prepare, and a long, chatty, family-gossip kind of conversation in which we exchanged our news. The particular item that occupied her mind at the time was that her daughter was of an age to get married and that she had to do something about it.

"But the girl is so *young*," I said, talking like a foreigner.

"Old enough to be betrothed," she replied with a puzzled severity. "She's nearly eighteen."

Meekly, I nodded acceptance of her point of view, and asked whether there was someone the girl was particularly keen on. Was she in love? Who was the young man? (It always takes me a little time to get readjusted to India, and I had forgotten that arranged marriages are a very ordinary matter.)

My cousin looked as though she thought I had lost my reason. "Love?" she said in amazement. "A young man?" With quiet dignity she remarked, "Naturally there are several who seek her hand. This is a good family. Of course there would be several. They have all sent their horoscopes in the proper way."

"Yes, yes," I said quickly, "yes, *of course*." Thinking back rapidly to my grandmother and her ways I asked, as casually as I could, "Do any of the horoscopes match?"

"Match!" she repeated scornfully. "We are a modern family. Certainly we aren't as old-fashioned as *that!*"

Santha Rama Rau
from *Travel Holiday*, June 1991

Amazing! Are marriages still arranged by parents in India?

3 Choose Your Topic

Examine your list. Which customs do you think would be most similar or most different across cultures or across time? Which topic interests you the most? Freewrite about the topic you've chosen, predicting what you might find as you begin your research.

Magazine Article

WRITING FROM EXPERIENCE **501**

WRITING SPRINGBOARD

Culture Gap, Generation Gap The high-school students interviewed in this film come from families that have immigrated to the United States. The students comment on how their parents' views of teenage behavior differ from those of most American parents.

Side B, Frame 17929

Writing Prompt Write a compare-and-contrast essay about the expectations and rules that parents from different cultures have for their children.

Critical Thinking:
DRAWING CONCLUSIONS

C Make sure that students recognize that this article provides information for comparing and contrasting dating customs in two time periods. Ask students to draw a conclusion about the focus of an essay that features this information. Would the essay be likely to emphasize similarities or differences between the dating customs of the two eras? *(differences)*

CUSTOMIZING FOR
Students Acquiring English

D Some students may have difficulty with some words and phrases in the magazine article. Explain the following:

frenetic: "frantic, frenzied"

betrothed: "engaged to be married"

keen on: "fond of"

horoscope: "chart showing the position of the planets and stars at the time of a person's birth, often consulted in the planning stages for a Hindu wedding"

Teaching Strategy:
STUMBLING BLOCK

E Remind students that they should not be concerned with grammar, spelling, etc. during the freewriting process. Should they change their opinions in mid-thought, they should feel free to abandon a sentence unfinished and begin a new one.

THE LANGUAGE OF LITERATURE TEACHER'S EDITION **501**

Teaching Strategy:
STUMBLING BLOCK

F Suggest that students who are having difficulty finding or focusing on a topic work in a group to create three comparison-and-contrast charts: one using two representative objects from different cultures, another two people, and another two ideas. Then guide students to evaluate the contents of each chart as the basis for an essay.

Research Skill:
USING SOURCES

G Emphasize that students can use a wide range of sources for many essay topics, especially topics that compare and contrast the customs of two cultures. Source materials could include the following: books, magazines, newspapers, maps, posters, almanacs, atlases, museum brochures, pamphlets from cultural centers, interviews, audiocassettes, videotapes, and CD-ROMs.

PREWRITING

Exploring Information

Making Decisions Your discussion and freewriting so far have probably helped you zero in on a culture or time period you want to know more about. These pages will help you to narrow your topic and to collect and organize information about it.

❶ Focus Your Exploration

You will find it easier to explore your topic if you narrow it down. For example, don't try to compare ceremonies in India with ceremonies in the United States. Instead, perhaps you could compare a traditional Hindu wedding ceremony with a typical wedding in the United States.

Find a reason to write. Could a comparison help you make a decision? solve a problem? understand an unfamiliar subject?

Student's Research Materials

❷ Collect Information

As you look for information on your topic, remember that you will want to explain the ideas behind customs or rituals, not just the customs themselves.

- Visit museums or cultural centers for information about cultures you intend to compare.
- Listen to music from these cultures, watch movies or videotapes; talk to classmates or other people who are familiar with these cultures.
- Use the SkillBuilder on the next page and the Multimedia Handbook to help you access library sources and information from on-line services.

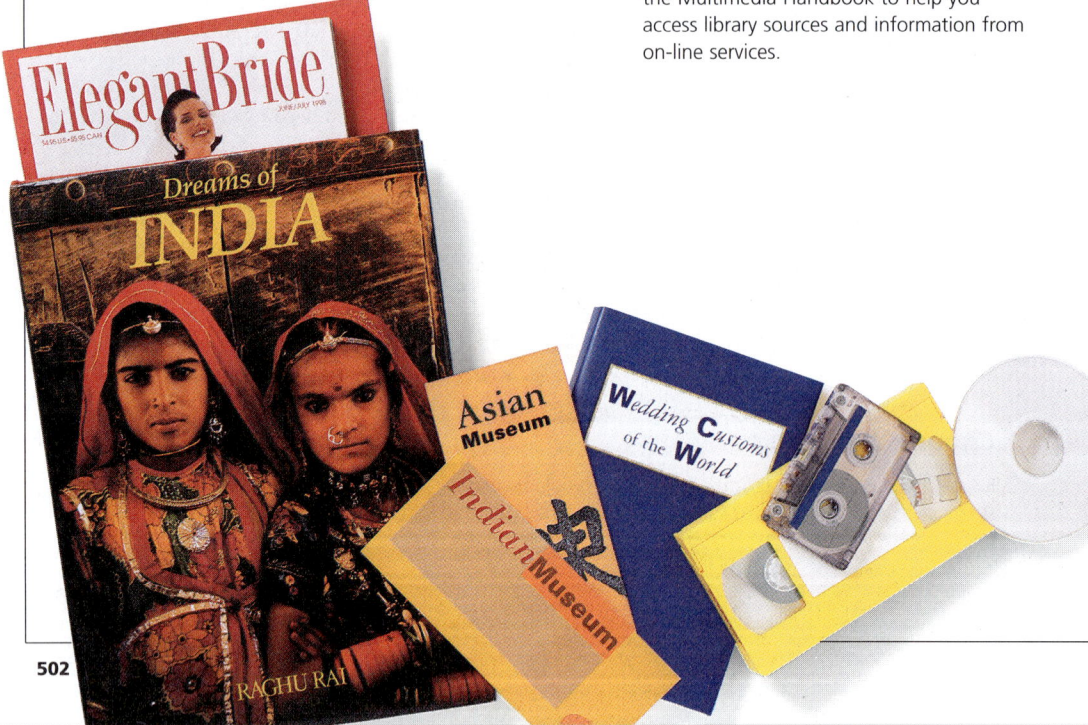

502

 SkillBuilder **RESEARCH SKILLS**

Reteaching/Reinforcement
- Writing Handbook, anthology pp. 1044–1047
- Writing Mini-Lessons transparencies, pp. 60–63

 **The Writer's Craft**
Card Catalog, pp. 486–488

USING CARD CATALOGS Review information that will help students use library card catalogs productively in their research. The traditional library card catalog is a cabinet of small drawers containing cards arranged in alphabetical order by title, author, or subject. Each card carries a classification number, or call number, in the upper left-hand corner. In many libraries, the on-line catalog—a computer workstation with screen and keyboard—has replaced the card catalog. The electronic entries provide the same information as that provided by a card catalog.

Applying What You've Learned Suggest that students start their library research by using a key word or words to search cards or electronic entries by subject area.

Additional Suggestions Point out that catalog cards or electronic entries give helpful information about a source, such as the number of pages and the presence of illustrations, as well as valuable cross-references to related headings or topics.

❸ Organize Information

Use a graphic organizer to keep track of information you find.

- A Venn diagram can help you think about similarities and differences. The example below shows how one student organized his thoughts about different wedding customs.
- After organizing information, you may decide that the topics you chose to compare have too few features in common to make an interesting essay.

Student's Venn Diagram

❹ Define Your Audience

Now that you have reviewed information on your topic, you probably have some ideas about who your audience is and how you could share your comparison with them.

- You may have a special audience for your comparison—for example, the families participating in a wedding.
- You may want to write your comparison as a newspaper or magazine article or as a photo essay for a general audience.
- You may want to add music and pictures to your information and make a multimedia presentation.

SkillBuilder

 RESEARCH SKILLS

Using Library Resources

Begin your search for information on your topic by looking up key words related to the topic in the subject index of your library's card or computer catalog. Use the call numbers for books indexed under these key words to locate books. One of the books may have a bibliography that will direct you to other books or articles on the subject. Find magazine articles by looking in the *Readers' Guide to Periodical Literature*.

When taking notes from sources, summarize information or paraphrase the author's sentences. If you want to quote a passage directly, be careful to copy the author's sentences exactly. Make careful notes of the source's title, author, publishing information, and page numbers so that you can credit it in your essay.

APPLYING WHAT YOU'VE LEARNED
Find at least one book or article on your topic. In a group, discuss how you located this resource and what new information it provided.

THINK & PLAN

Getting Ready to Write

1. How will you make your comparison clear?
2. What generalizations are you beginning to see?
3. How will you use your graphic organizer as you draft?

WRITING FROM EXPERIENCE 503

Critical Thinking: ANALYZING

Encourage students to analyze the Venn diagram by breaking it down into its essential parts. Guide them to recognize that the headings on the left and the right represent the principal subjects or categories being compared and contrasted: customary Western weddings and Hindu weddings. The standards for evaluation, however, must be extracted from the body of the diagram: (1) planning, (2) ceremony, and (3) aftermath. These features have both similarities (listed in the space where the circles overlap) and differences (listed to the left and to the right).

Teaching Strategy: MODELING

Point out that focusing on the audience is especially important to writers. It helps them gauge how much background information to provide to make the comparison and contrast meaningful and effective for the audience.

SkillBuilder RESEARCH SKILLS

USING LIBRARY RESOURCES Point out that students may use subject indexes not only to locate relevant books and articles but also to extract further information from sources. For example, book indexes are often the most efficient means for determining how helpful a source is likely to be. Book indexes frequently offer cross-references to related topics or passages.

Applying What You've Learned Invite students to work with partners to locate books and articles. Then have two or three pairs join together to share results, ideas, and research tips.

Additional Suggestions Recommend that when students take notes, they use a modified outline form, listing main ideas on the left-hand side of a page or card and using dashes and indentations to indicate details.

Reteaching/Reinforcement
- Writing Handbook, anthology pp. 1044–1047
- *Writing Mini-Lessons* transparencies, pp. 60–63

 **The Writer's Craft**
The Library, pp. 486–496

CUSTOMIZING FOR
Less-Proficient Writers

J Emphasize that the important goal for writers now is to record their ideas. Reassure students that they will have plenty of time later to correct any errors in spelling, grammar, or mechanics.

Teaching Strategy: MANAGING THE PAPER LOAD

K Suggest that each student affix a self-stick note to his or her draft, bearing his or her most important question or concern. You can concentrate on that issue as you read and allow more minor issues to be addressed in a peer-review setting.

DRAFTING

Getting Your Ideas Down

Putting Ideas into Words Review any graphic organizers you made during prewriting. They can help you to think about the information you gathered as well as help you to organize your draft.

❶ Try a Rough Draft

As you write your rough draft, remember to explain the history or meaning behind the customs you describe as well as the customs themselves.

The Writing Coach can help you as you draft.

Student's Rough Draft

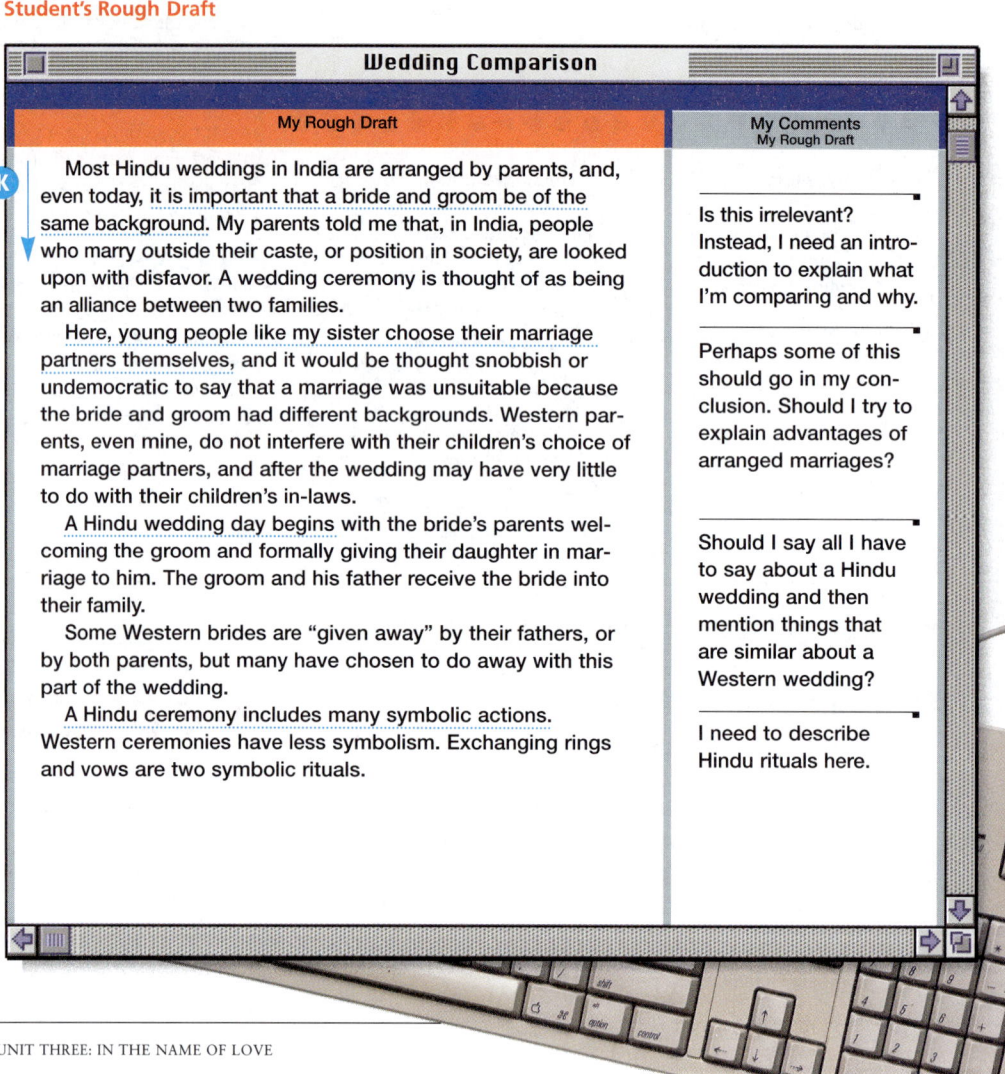

Wedding Comparison

My Rough Draft

Most Hindu weddings in India are arranged by parents, and, even today, it is important that a bride and groom be of the same background. My parents told me that, in India, people who marry outside their caste, or position in society, are looked upon with disfavor. A wedding ceremony is thought of as being an alliance between two families.

Here, young people like my sister choose their marriage partners themselves, and it would be thought snobbish or undemocratic to say that a marriage was unsuitable because the bride and groom had different backgrounds. Western parents, even mine, do not interfere with their children's choice of marriage partners, and after the wedding may have very little to do with their children's in-laws.

A Hindu wedding day begins with the bride's parents welcoming the groom and formally giving their daughter in marriage to him. The groom and his father receive the bride into their family.

Some Western brides are "given away" by their fathers, or by both parents, but many have chosen to do away with this part of the wedding.

A Hindu ceremony includes many symbolic actions. Western ceremonies have less symbolism. Exchanging rings and vows are two symbolic rituals.

My Comments
My Rough Draft

Is this irrelevant? Instead, I need an introduction to explain what I'm comparing and why.

Perhaps some of this should go in my conclusion. Should I try to explain advantages of arranged marriages?

Should I say all I have to say about a Hindu wedding and then mention things that are similar about a Western wedding?

I need to describe Hindu rituals here.

504 UNIT THREE: IN THE NAME OF LOVE

WRITING SPRINGBOARD
Comparing Artistic Styles Different painters may use very different artistic styles in portraying a similar subject. This collection of images includes paintings of landscapes and paintings of people. Notice how, within these two categories, a similar subject is rendered in different styles.

Side B, Frame 50346

Writing Prompt Choose one pair of paintings and study the similarities and differences between them. Write a compare/contrast essay dealing with the two paintings.

504 THE LANGUAGE OF LITERATURE TEACHER'S EDITION

2 Organize Your Ideas

Think about how you can best order the information and ideas. The patterns in the Writing Handbook will show you different ways. Either of the patterns below could be used to organize the student writer's draft.

COMPARE-AND-CONTRAST PATTERNS

Subject-by-Subject	Feature-by-Feature
1. Western Wedding	1. Planning
• *Planning*	• Western Wedding
• *Ceremony*	• Hindu Wedding
• *Reception*	2. Ceremony
2. Hindu Wedding	• Western Wedding
• *Planning*	• Hindu Wedding
• *Ceremony*	3. Reception
• *Reception*	• Western Wedding
	• Hindu Wedding

3 Rework and Share

With your rough draft in front of you and your organizational structure in mind, write your second draft.

- Consider writing an introduction to establish what you will compare or to explain your purpose.
- Consider adding a conclusion to pull together what you learned.
- The SkillBuilder on the right will help you use parallel sentence structures to emphasize similarities and differences.

PEER RESPONSE

A peer reviewer can help identify strengths and weaknesses of your draft. Ask him or her questions like the following:

- Which specific points of comparison were most interesting to you? Which were least interesting?
- Where have I strayed from my topic?
- What additional information might support my conclusion?

SkillBuilder

WRITER'S CRAFT

Using Parallel Structure
One way to make comparisons clear to your readers is to use parallel structures for the ideas you are comparing. Using similar grammatical structures or sentence patterns calls attention to similarities or differences. Compare these two sets of sentences:

The wedding cake serves as part of a modern ritual. Another use for it is that people eat it for dessert.

The wedding cake is part of modern ritual. It is also a dessert.

In the second set, the sentences are grammatically parallel.

APPLYING WHAT YOU'VE LEARNED
Rewrite the following sentences, using similar sentence patterns.

The groom's family plays a major role in planning a Hindu wedding. A minor role is played by the groom's family in planning a Western wedding.

RETHINK & EVALUATE

Preparing to Revise

1. How can you improve the organization of your draft?
2. How can you use parallel structures to make similarities and differences more clear?
3. How can you pull your generalizations together in a conclusion?

WRITING FROM EXPERIENCE **505**

Writing Skill: ORGANIZATION

L As students examine each pattern, guide them to see that both organizational patterns shown in the text use chronological order (planning, ceremony, reception). Also, point out that whichever pattern students select, they should be consistent in following a specific kind of order such as chronological order.

Teaching Strategy: PEER REVIEW

M Have reviewers read the essay before they make any comments. During the second reading, they should jot down brief comments and suggestions. Remind students to include specific ideas for revision, such as "Wouldn't a word like *likewise* or *similarly* make the sequence of thought clearer in this paragraph?"

  **WRITER'S CRAFT**

USING PARALLEL STRUCTURE Remind students that the use of parallel sentence structure is a stylistic matter. Parallel structure is desirable when it is appropriate to the content: for example, to call attention to similarities or contrasts. Overuse of parallelism, however, may result in awkwardly choppy, monotonous sentences.

Applying What You've Learned Sample response: For a Hindu wedding, the groom's family plays a major role in the planning. For a Western wedding, the groom's family plays a minor role.

Additional Suggestions Remind students that parallelism also extends to parts within sentences. Ask them to correct the error in parallelism in this example: *Roberto enjoyed playing baseball and to improvise on the guitar.* (*Roberto enjoyed playing baseball and improvising on the guitar.*)

Reteaching/Reinforcement

📘 **The Writer's Craft**

Parallelism, p. 797

THE LANGUAGE OF LITERATURE TEACHER'S EDITION **505**

Writing Skill: REVISING

 As students revise and edit their essays, they will work to improve their drafts by:
1. adding needed words, sentences, and paragraphs
2. cutting unnecessary material by focusing on repetitive or unrelated details
3. substituting words, sentences, and paragraphs for deleted material if necessary
4. rearranging parts of the text to create coherence and unity

Teaching Strategy: MODELING

 Discuss how this model meets the Standards for Evaluation on page 507. For example, the introduction identifies the customs being compared (Hindu weddings and Western weddings) and indicates that the essay will focus on both differences and similarities.

 Be sure that students recognize that the writer used the feature-by-feature organizational pattern. The writer first discussed planning with reference to Hindu and then Western arrangements (second and third paragraphs of the final draft). The writer then turned to the wedding ceremony, first giving details about Hindu rites and then commenting on Western wedding symbolism (fourth and fifth paragraphs). If necessary, review the outline of the feature-by-feature pattern on page 505.

REVISING AND PUBLISHING

Finishing Your Essay

Making Final Changes Once you have worked at improving your draft, read it again to make sure that comparisons will be clear to your readers and that paragraphs are well developed. If you've decided to publish your essay in a special format, you may want to make additional changes to the text or to choose music or visual aids to accompany the information in your essay.

A Comparison of Hindu and Western Weddings

When my sister became engaged, she decided she wanted to include customs and rituals from her Hindu heritage as well as Western customs. She asked us all to help her do some research. To our surprise, we found that although Hindu weddings are very different from Western weddings, the meaning behind some Western customs is similar to the meaning behind some Hindu rituals.

Even today, most marriages in India are arranged by parents and are thought of as alliances between families. The ceremony is held in the bride's home and begins after the groom is welcomed by the bride's parents and is formally given their daughter. The groom's parents give the bride gifts and welcome her into their family.

Here, men and women usually choose their marriage partners without parental advice or interference. Some Western brides are "given away" by their fathers, or by both parents, but many couples have chosen to do away with this particular wedding tradition.

The Hindu ceremony includes many symbolic actions. At the beginning the couple stands as the guests chant blessings and throw rice at the couple. The bride and groom exchange garlands. Then a sacred fire is lit, and the couple pour clarified butter on it as they pray for healthy children, long life, and wealth. The couple takes seven paces around the fire to symbolize the following: a long married life, power, prosperity, happiness, children, enjoyment of seasonal pleasures, and a lifelong friendship.

Western ceremonies also include symbolism. Exchanging rings and vows are two symbolic rituals. Lighting a unity candle is another.

① Revise and Edit

Read your draft again slowly and carefully. Mark parts you want to revise.

- Use peer comments and the Standards for Evaluation as you reorganize your essay.
- Make sure your introduction and conclusion help to accomplish your purpose.
- Use the Editing Checklist and the SkillBuilder on the next page to make sure that comparisons are made correctly.

Student's Final Draft
What information does the introduction provide.

Which of the two types of organization did the writer use?

❷ Share Your Work

You may decide to adapt the information in your essay for a multimedia presentation including music, text, and pictures. (For help, see the Multimedia Handbook on page 1055.) The revisions you make will depend on the audience with whom you want to share your ideas.

PUBLISHING IDEAS

- A newspaper story could include photographs and charts.
- A photo essay could make your points dramatically.
- Your class could publish a collection of essays and share them with social studies classes at a junior high school.

Standards for Evaluation

A compare-and contrast-essay

- identifies clearly the things being compared
- includes specific, relevant details
- follows a clear plan of organization
- concludes with generalizations that are supported by information in the essay

---

SkillBuilder

GRAMMAR FROM WRITING

Avoiding Double Comparisons

When making comparisons, be careful to avoid double comparisons. A double comparison is one that uses both an adjective ending in *-er* or *-est* and *more* or *most*. Look at these examples:

Incorrect: *A bride's bouquet is more fancier than a bridesmaid's.*

Correct: *A bride's bouquet is fancier than a bridesmaid's.*

GRAMMAR HANDBOOK

For more information on writing correct comparisons, see page 1077 of the Grammar Handbook.

Editing Checklist Use these tips as you revise.

- Is spelling correct?
- Is punctuation used correctly?
- Are comparisons written correctly?

REFLECT & ASSESS

Evaluating the Experience

1. What did you learn by writing a compare-and-contrast essay?
2. How can you use compare-and-contrast organizational patterns in other writing situations?

 PORTFOLIO What would you do differently if you were writing your compare-and-contrast essay? Add your thoughts to your portfolio.

WRITING FROM EXPERIENCE 507

Teaching Strategy: COLLABORATIVE OPPORTUNITY

Q Invite students who have written about similar topics to work in small groups to develop photo essays as a means of sharing their work. Remind them that a photo essay uses pictures and brief captions to tell a story or present an insight about human life or behavior.

Teaching Strategy: MANAGING THE PAPER LOAD

R Whenever possible, phrase your written comments as questions that will encourage students to reflect on and assess their work. For example, instead of writing "broad generalization," try "Do the facts you've presented support this claim adequately?"

Standards for Evaluation

Ideas and Content
- Contains an introduction that clearly identifies the subjects being compared.
- Indicates a reason or purpose for the comparison.
- Elaborates on similarities and differences, using specific and relevant details.
- Concludes with generalizations that are supported by information in the essay.

Structure and Form
- Organizes ideas logically, using either a feature-by-feature or subject-by-subject organization.
- Uses transitions to signal similarities and differences.
- Devotes one paragraph to each main idea.

Grammar, Usage, and Mechanics
- Contains no more than two or three minor errors in grammar, usage, spelling, capitalization, and punctuation.

SkillBuilder  GRAMMAR FROM WRITING

AVOIDING DOUBLE COMPARISONS

Remind students that double comparisons can also occur when irregular adjectives or adverbs are used, as shown by this example: *We played more worse in yesterday's game than in any other game this season.*

Applying What You've Learned Have students practice by correcting the following sentences:
1. This was the most happiest day of her life.
2. The house was more busier than ever.
3. We wanted a more bigger place to hold the reception, but we couldn't get one.

Reteaching/Reinforcement
- *Grammar Handbook*, anthology, p. 1077
- *Grammar Mini-Lessons* copymasters, pp. 25–27, transparencies pp. 23–25

The Writer's Craft

Avoiding Double Comparisons, pp. 746–747

PORTFOLIO

Ask students to jot down what they like best about their compare-and-contrast essays. Then invite them to make a brief list of the weaknesses or trouble spots in their essays. Students may wish to include their informal evaluations along with their essays in their portfolio.

THE LANGUAGE OF LITERATURE TEACHER'S EDITION 507

UNIT REVIEW

This feature has been designed to help students assess what they have learned in Unit Three. It also provides opportunities for them to evaluate the theme and to test their understanding of specific literary concepts. As students complete at least one of the optional activities for each section, you may want to conduct your own informal assessment of their performance, including their speaking and listening skills and their ability to engage in cooperative work.

Objectives

- To allow students to reflect on and assess their understanding of theme
- To allow students to reflect on and assess their understanding of literary concepts such as metaphor, mood, and sonnet form
- To provide students with the opportunity to assess and build their portfolios

REFLECTING ON THEME

OPTION 1

Remind students that love exists in many kinds of relationships. As they consider this activity, suggest that they think of the love between siblings, the love between best friends, and the love a person shares with a cherished pet.

OPTION 2

Ask students to describe various images that come to mind when they think of love's extremes. Encourage students to go beyond the commonplace and to come up with fresh ways of suggesting love's emotions.

Self-Assessment Invite students to spend some time rereading key passages in the selections before they compile their lists. Suggest that students add brief notes to any entries that consist of only a word or a name, explaining how the entries reflect their views about the nature of love.

REFLECT & ASSESS

UNIT THREE: IN THE NAME OF LOVE

Have the selections in this unit changed your opinions about love or deepened your understanding of its effects? What new things have you learned as a reader and writer? Explore these questions by completing one or more of the options in each of the following sections.

REFLECTING ON THEME

OPTION 1 **Comparing Love's Emotions** Review the activity on page 352, which asked you to create a bar graph identifying the different feelings that you have experienced in a love relationship. Then review the selections in the unit to identify which one comes closest to your own experience of love; also identify the selection that seemed furthest removed from your experience. Write a note explaining why you have chosen those two selections instead of other selections in the unit. Consider how the selections that you have chosen affect your own understanding of love.

OPTION 2 **Portraying Love's Agony and Ecstasy** As you saw in this unit, love can lead people to great happiness or to the depths of misery. Consider which selections in the unit depict the agony of love, which portray its ecstasy, and which, if any, capture both extremes. Then create a collage with images and words that suggest your own views about the extremes of love. Your images may be based on ones described in the selections, as well as from your own experience. Share your collage with a small group of classmates. Explain how your collage represents your views, and discuss whether your opinions of love were changed by your readings.

Self-Assessment: *Put together your reflections about love by creating two lists, one titled* What Love Is *and one titled* What Love Is Not. *Each list may comprise words or phrases, names of characters from the selections, or brief descriptions of people and events from your own life. In other words, you may include virtually anything in your lists as long as it represents your own views about the nature of love. Underline those items on your lists that are inspired by your readings in this unit.*

REVIEWING LITERARY CONCEPTS

OPTION 1 **Understanding Metaphor and Mood** After reviewing the definition of *metaphor* on page 373, search through the selections in this unit to find at least five metaphors that you find interesting or memorable. Create a chart like the one shown. For each metaphor, identify the two things being compared and tell what mood is evoked by the metaphor. Compare your chart with those created by other students.

Selection	Metaphor	Things Compared	Mood Evoked
"Tonight I Can Write . . ."	"The night is shattered and she is not with me."	The night is being compared with something that can be broken, such as a piece of fine china or a fragile glass.	sadness; an overwhelming sense of loss

508 UNIT THREE: IN THE NAME OF LOVE

OPTION 2 **Appreciating the Sonnet** Review the information on page 376 about the sonnet. Then work with a partner to create a poster, pamphlet, or multimedia display about the sonnet. Include information about its history, offer your own definitions of sonnet and related terms, and present a variety of sonnets drawn from different centuries and countries. You may wish to include decorative art and, if possible, present recordings of sonnet readings.

Self-Assessment: On a sheet of paper, copy down the following list of terms from this unit, all of which are related to poetry. Create a test to measure students' understanding of these terms. One section of your test might require that students match terms with their definitions. Another section might include poems or excerpts of poems, along with questions focused on how the terms can be applied to the poetry. Take a test created by one of your classmates, and note any terms that give you trouble. Work with the classmate to clarify the meaning of these terms.

metaphor	couplet
sonnet	rhythm
sonnet sequence	meter
rhyme scheme	repetition
English sonnet	rhyme
quatrain	

PORTFOLIO BUILDING

- **QuickWrites** Many of the QuickWrites assignments in this unit ask for creative responses to the selections. These responses include the writing of poems, scripts, and monologues. Review the creative assignments that you completed, and pick out one or two pieces that you feel contain the best use of descriptive language. Write a note that explains your opinion of those pieces. If you feel that the pieces are worthy of your portfolio, add the note and the pieces to your portfolio.

- **Writing About Literature** By now you've written your own poem as a response to a poem in this unit. Write a note about your poem to include in your portfolio. How well does your poem stand on its own? What would you change, if anything? What about this experience can you bring to your reading of other poems?

- **Writing from Experience** Earlier in this unit you wrote a comparison-contrast essay. As you review your essay, what questions do you have about it, if any? Would you do anything differently if you were to rewrite it? Note one or two other potential subjects for a comparison-contrast essay.

- **Personal Choice** Reflect upon the various writing assignments and other activities that you have worked on during the course of this unit, including work that you may have done on your own. You may also want to review any evaluations or peer responses that you received about your work. Which activity or piece of writing proved the most difficult? Write a note explaining the difficulty and what you learned as a result.

Self-Assessment: Consider all the pieces that you now have in your portfolio. Have you changed your opinion about the quality of any of the pieces? Is there some item that you feel no longer represents your ability or interests? You may wish to weed out some pieces or to replace them.

SETTING GOALS

You probably have a good idea of your likes and dislikes in literature and writing, as well as your strengths and weaknesses. Set a new challenge for yourself to turn a weakness into a strength or to come to a new appreciation of certain genres of literature. For example, if you have struggled with poetry in the past, set a goal to improve in that area.

REVIEWING LITERARY CONCEPTS

OPTION 1

The poems in this unit contain a variety of vivid metaphors. For example, in "Love Without Love" the speaker says, "Suddenly I felt you flying through my soul in quick, lofty flight..." Here love is compared to the majesty of a bird in flight, evoking the sense of wonder and elation that often accompanies the experience of falling in love.

OPTION 2

Offer guidance and support to all students who choose this option, helping them locate a variety of background materials and sources of sonnets. Suggest that they hold off on deciding what form the presentation will take until after they have gathered their information.

Self-Assessment Remind students who choose to create a matching exercise that they can use the Literary Concepts features that appear in the unit as a source of definitions. They can also use the Handbook of Literary Terms at the back of the textbook.

PORTFOLIO BUILDING

Review the main elements of the portfolio system. Encourage students to rewrite the poem or the comparison-contrast essay to include more descriptive language and to reflect on what they have learned since they wrote it. Ask them to retain all drafts as well as final revisions so that they can reflect on and assess their development and progress.

Self-Assessment As students review their portfolios and eliminate various items, be sure that they understand that the materials they are removing are not wasted efforts. Remind them that learning involves trial and error. Emphasize that writing each draft has contributed to their understanding of the selections while helping them develop and refine their writing skills.

SETTING GOALS

Help students come up with specific statements of their goals along with some concrete steps that they can take to meet those goals. If they choose to work on developing their writing skills, ask them to list two or three elements that they will focus on such as using sensory imagery to describe scenes and evoke moods or using vivid verbs. If they choose to increase their appreciation of a certain genre, ask other students to suggest works in that genre that they have found interesting.

UNIT FOUR

Unit Four

Moments of Truth In Unit Four students will read selections which explore moments when people achieve an important understanding about life. This unit contains two parts: Part 1, "Unexpected Realizations," and Part 2, "What Matters Most." Selections in both Parts 1 and 2 contribute to the unit theme by describing a variety of characters as they come to important insights about their lives.

Part 1

Unexpected Realizations Selections in Part 1 emphasize characters' realizations about the world around them. For example, in "The Meeting," a man realizes that a duel he once witnessed may have been controlled by forces beyond the duelists themselves.

Part 2

What Matters Most Selections in Part 2 highlight a variety of characters' realizations about what is most important to them in life. For example, in "A White Heron," a lonely child refuses an attractive offer in order to protect a magnificent bird.

UNIT FOUR

MOMENTS OF TRUTH

Truth resides in every human heart, and one has to search for it there.

Mohandas K. Gandhi
Indian nationalist and spiritual leader
1869–1948

The Flooded Field (1992), Claire B. Cotts. Courtesy of the artist.

Discussion Questions

To help students explore the connections between the art, the quotation, and the unit theme, have them consider the following questions:

1. Why do you think "Moments of Truth" might be an important theme to explore? *(Possible response: Some students might say that reading about other people's realizations can help us understand our own "moments of truth." Other students might suggest that characters' insights can point to general truths about the world.)*

2. Do you agree with Ghandi's statement? Why? *(Accept all reasonable responses.)*

3. Do you feel that this painting is a good illustration of the theme "Moments of Truth"? Why? *(Responses will vary.)*

4. What kinds of stories and experiences might you expect to read about in this unit? *(Possible response: These selections may deal with characters who are confronted with something which gives them a greater understanding of themselves, of their personal relationships, or of the world around them.)*

5. Discuss a moment of truth which you have experienced. *(Responses will vary.)*

Art Note

The Flooded Field by Claire B. Cotts
This painting by American artist Cotts (1964–) portrays a sense of waiting and renewal as the waters recede after a flood. For this work, Cotts began with a dark canvas, pulling images out as she found them in the painting.

Reading the Art *How do the subject of this painting and the artist's method of moving from darkness into light in this work affect your understanding of the Unit theme, Moments of Truth?*

UNIT FOUR
Part 1 Skills Trace

ML DENOTES MINI-LESSON IN TEACHER'S EDITION

Selections	Reading Skills and Strategies	Literary Concepts	Writing Opportunities	Speaking, Listening, and Viewing
FICTION **The Meeting** Jorge Luis Borges	Identifying causes, PE p. 514	Narrator, PE p. 521 Reviewing magical realism, PE p. 521 Reviewing conflict, ML TE p. 517 Fiction, ML TE p. 518	Write a ballad, PE p. 521 Write a police report, PE p. 521 Create a brochure, PE p. 521 Tone, ML TE p. 519	Produce a TV newscast, PE p. 521 Begin tall tale in circle, PE p. 522 Monologue, ML TE p. 520 Listen to music, TE p. 522
FICTION **The Witness for the Prosecution** Agatha Christie	Finding clues, PE p. 523	Suspense, PE p. 542 Reviewing point of view, PE p. 542 Reviewing characterization, ML TE p. 535 Mystery, ML TE p. 537	Prepare a time line, PE p. 542 Write a script, PE p. 542 Write a newspaper article, PE p. 542 Make a cast list of characters, PE p. 542 Write a review, PE p. 543 Write a report, PE p. 543 Surprise endings, ML TE p. 539	Role-play prosecution's examination or defense's cross-examination, PE p. 543 View instructional videos, PE p. 543 Class discussion, TE p. 542
FICTION **Games at Twilight** Anita Desai		Diction, PE p. 554 Reviewing description, ML TE p. 551	Write about importance of childhood games, PE p. 545 Write a first-person narrative, PE p. 553 Write an episode, PE p. 553 Write an article about competition, PE p. 553 Sensory details, ML TE p. 549	Role-playing, PE p. 553 Oral monologue, PE p. 554 Oral presentation, PE p. 554 Class discussion, TE p. 554
POETRY **The Street/La Calle** Octavio Paz **I Am Not I/Yo No Soy Yo** Juan Ramón Jiménez	Understanding modern poetry, PE p. 557	Alliteration, PE p. 560 Reviewing repetition, PE p. 560 Write a poem as a diary entry, PE p. 560	Write a poem about who you are, PE p. 560 Create a horoscope, PE p. 560 Comparison and contrast order, ML TE p. 559	Prepare a dramatic scene, PE p. 561 Listening to an audiotape, ML TE p. 558 Perform or tape-record musical adaptations of poems, TE p. 561
NONFICTION **from The Unexpected Universe** Loren Eiseley		Reflective essay, PE p. 565 Reviewing setting, PE p. 565	Write about a personal experience, PE p. 562 Write a dramatic soliloquy, PE p. 565 Write a reflective essay, PE p. 565 Write a character analysis, PE p. 565 Write an eyewitness account, PE p. 565 Personification, ML TE p. 564	Present a soliloquy, PE p. 565 Create a radio drama, TE p. 566
FICTION **Two Friends** Guy de Maupassant	Understanding contrast, PE p. 567	Protagonist and antagonist, PE p. 578 Reviewing irony, PE p. 578 Realism, PE p. 579 Reviewing imagery, ML TE p. 569	Create a storyboard of events, PE p. 578 Write a letter, PE p. 578 Write an alternative ending, PE p. 578 Word choice, ML TE p. 570	Read aloud passages, PE p. 579 Group brainstorming, ML TE p. 574 Interviews, ML TE p. 576 Oral presentation, TE p. 579
FICTION ON YOUR OWN **When Greek Meets Greek** Samuel Selvon			Writing predictions, TE p. 580 Writing from a different perspective, TE p. 581	Paired reading, TE p. 580 Dramatizing, TE p. 582

Writing	Reading Skills and Strategies	Literary Concepts	Writing Opportunities	Speaking, Listening, and Viewing
WRITING ABOUT LITERATURE **Interpretation**	Analyzing tone, PE pp. 584–585 Responding to literature, PE pp. 586–589	Analyzing tone, PE pp. 584–585 Poetry, PE pp. 586–589	What tone?, PE p. 585 A new tone, PE p. 585 Your own tone, PE p. 585 Interpretation of a poem, PE pp. 586–589 Writing a thesis statement, PE p. 587	Viewing a scene, PE p. 591 Interpreting a scene, PE p. 591 Discussion, PE p. 591 Discussing observations, PE p. 591

Grammar, Usage, Mechanics, and Spelling	Multimodal Learning	Research and Study Skills	Vocabulary	
Simple past tense, ML TE p. 516	Produce TV newscast, PE p. 521 Begin tall tale in circle, PE p. 522 Create an illustration, PE p. 522 Illustrations or diagrams of knives, TE p. 521	Find examples of Argentine popular and folk music, TE p. 522	archetype exacerbated incipient versed wary	
Quotation marks, ML TE p. 531	Prepare a time line, PE p. 542 Role-play prosecution's examination or defense's cross-examination, PE p. 543 Draw courtroom sketches, PE p. 543 Create instructional video, PE p. 543	Research current scientific techniques for gathering evidence, PE p. 543 Developing a strategy, ML TE p. 527	amicable animosity assiduously averse cajole churlish cultivate dastardly	impotently infatuated infernal insolence quell unfathomable vindicate
Participial phrases, ML TE p. 548	Role-playing, PE p. 553 Draw a map, PE p. 554 Oral monologue, PE p. 554 Create a pie chart, PE p. 554 Oral presentation, PE p. 554 Create bar graphs, PE p. 554 Class discussion, TE p. 554	Research history of a childhood game, PE p. 554 Research average monthly temperatures and rainfall in India, PE p. 554 Sentence completion, ML TE p. 550	arid defunct fray ignominy melancholy	slaking stifle stridently superciliously temerity
	Prepare a dramatic scene, PE p. 561 Create a mask, PE p. 561 Use charts, graphs, and other visual aids, TE p. 561 Set two modern poems to music, TE p. 561	Research psychological concept of an identity crisis, TE p. 561		
	Present a soliloquy, PE p. 565 Draw a pencil sketch of a major scene, TE p. 566 Create a radio drama, TE p. 566	Research the last Ice Age, the animals that lived then, and their place in the food chain, PE p. 566	appraise augment chide recede utterance	
Adjective clauses, ML TE p. 572	Create a storyboard, PE p. 578 Create a paper patchwork quilt, PE p. 579 Create a multimedia presentation, PE p. 579 Design a greeting card, PE p. 579 Brainstorming, ML TE p. 574 Oral presentation, TE p. 579 Dramatizing, TE p. 582	Research famous sieges, TE p. 579	atrocity fanatical pensive rejuvenated respite	

Grammar, Usage, Mechanics, and Spelling	Multimodal Learning	Research and Study Skills	Media Literacy
Styling titles of literary texts, PE p. 589 Quoting from poetry, PE p. 589	Viewing a scene, PE p. 591 Interpreting a scene, PE p. 591 Discussion, PE p. 591 Discussing observations, PE p. 591	Analyzing literature, PE pp. 584–589 Making observations, PE pp. 590–591	Interpreting a scene, PE pp. 590–591

UNIT FOUR
Part 2 Skills Trace

ML DENOTES MINI-LESSON IN TEACHER'S EDITION

Selections	Reading Skills and Strategies	Literary Concepts	Writing Opportunities	Speaking, Listening, and Viewing
FICTION **A White Heron** Sarah Orne Jewett	Making inferences, PE p. 594 Using your reading log, PE p. 594	Third-person point of view, PE p. 606 Omniscient point of view, PE p. 606 Reviewing symbolism, **ML** TE p. 602	Create a bar graph, PE p. 605 Rewrite "A White Heron" as children's book, PE p. 605 Write a haiku, PE p. 605 Travel brochure, PE p. 605 Draft an epilogue, PE p. 605 Using dialogue in fiction, **ML** TE p. 599	Give a speech, PE p. 606 Group discussion, TE p. 605
FICTION **Like the Sun** R.K. Narayan		Humor of situation, PE p. 613 Humor of character, PE p. 613 Humor of language, PE p. 613 Reviewing conflict, **ML** TE p. 612	Describe an incident, PE p. 608 Rewrite Sekhar's conversations, PE p. 613 Write two notes, PE p. 613 Literary analysis, PE p. 613 Questions, PE p. 614	Group discussion, PE p. 613 Enact story scenes, TE p. 613 Report survey results, TE p. 614
POETRY **Once Upon a Time** Gabriel Okara **Making the Jam Without You** Maxine Kumin		Free verse, PE p. 620 Reviewing speaker, **ML** TE p. 616 Simile, **ML** TE p. 618	Description, PE p. 615 Biographical sketches, PE p. 620 Write a letter, PE p. 620 Write a definition, PE p. 620 Brainstorm, PE p. 620 Figurative language, **ML** TE p. 617	Group discussion, PE p. 620 Role-play conversations, PE p. 621
FICTION **The Cabuliwallah** Rabindranath Tagore	Comparing characters, PE p. 622	Characterization, PE p. 630 Reviewing point of view, PE p. 630 Reviewing imagery, **ML** TE p. 628	Letter to editor, PE p. 629 Retell as fairy tale, PE p. 629 Write a diary entry, PE p. 629 Euphemism, **ML** TE p. 625	Panel discussion, PE p. 629 Oral reading, PE p. 629 Class discussion, PE p. 630 Multimedia presentation, PE p. 630 Oral report, PE p. 630 Dance, **ML** TE p. 627
POETRY **For the New Year, 1981** Denise Levertov **Pride** Dahlia Ravikovitch	Understanding images, PE p. 632	Personification, PE p. 636 Reviewing rhythm, PE p. 636 Reviewing rhythm, **ML** TE p. 635	Brainstorm titles, PE p. 636 Thesaurus entries, PE p. 636 Poem, PE p. 636 Repetition, **ML** TE p. 633 Sound devices, **ML** TE p. 634	Evaluation, PE p. 636 Listen to music, PE p. 637 Translate poem, PE p. 637
FICTION **As the Night the Day** Abioseh Nicol		Internal conflict, PE p. 650 Reviewing allusion, PE p. 650 Reviewing figurative language, **ML** TE p. 644	Describe a conflict, PE p. 638 Chart, PE p. 649 Job evaluation, PE p. 649 Story ending, PE p. 649 Dialogue, PE p. 649 Explanation, PE p. 649 Chart, PE p. 650 List, PE p. 650 Chronological order, **ML** TE p. 643	Improvisation, PE p. 650 Interview, PE p. 650 Discussion, PE p. 650 Speeches, **ML** TE p. 648
NONFICTION ON YOUR OWN *from* **A Precocious Autobiography** Yevgeny Yevtushenko			Questions, TE p. 652 List, TE p. 654	Paired reading, TE p. 652

Writing	Reading Skills and Strategies	Literary Concepts	Writing Opportunities	Speaking, Listening, and Viewing
WRITING FROM EXPERIENCE **Informative Exposition**			Writing a cause-and-effect essay, PE pp. 685–665 Drafting, PE pp. 662–663 Creating coherence in paragraphs, PE p. 663 Revising and publishing, PE pp. 664–665	Observing nature, PE p. 658 Graphs, PE p. 659 Interviewing, PE p. 661

Grammar, Usage, Mechanics, and Spelling	Multimodal Learning	Research and Study Skills	Vocabulary	
Concrete and abstract nouns, ML TE p. 598	Give a speech, PE p. 606 Create a painting, PE p. 606 Group discussion, TE p. 605 Make a mural, TE p. 606 Make a guide book, TE p. 607	Research old-growth forests, TE p. 606 Research the spotted owl, TE p. 606 Research local birds, TE p. 606	discreetly elusive ponderous squalor traverse	
Subjects in imperative sentences, ML TE p. 610	Group discussion, PE p. 613 Take a survey, PE p. 614 Math word problem, PE p. 614		essence incessantly shirk stupefied tempering	
	Group discussion, PE p. 620 Role-play conversations, PE p. 621 Make a collage, PE p. 621 Draw or paint pictures, TE p. 621			
Appositives, ML TE p. 624	Panel discussion, PE p. 629 Make a sketch, PE p. 630 Oral reading, PE p. 629 Class discussion, PE p. 630 Multimedia presentations, PE p. 630 Oral report, PE p. 630 Dance, ML TE p. 627	Research economics of Afghanistan and India, PE p. 630 Investigate poetry for which Raban Dranath Tagore is famous, PE p. 630 Research traditional Hindu marriage customs, PE p. 630 Dictionary skills, ML TE p. 626	composure euphemism fettered impending intervene	judicious pervade prattle precarious quaint
	Evaluation, PE p. 636 Choose a piece of music, PE p. 637 Create a narrative cartoon, PE p. 637 Translate poem, PE p. 637			
Interjections, ML TE p. 647	Chart, PE p. 649 Improvisation, PE p. 650 Chart, PE p. 650 Interview, PE p. 650 Contact university, medical, or company laboratories, TE p. 650	Notetaking, ML TE p. 641 Research fundamental safety rules of laboratory behavior, TE p. 650	coalesce enigmatically imperiously inconsolable indignation	malevolence protracted recrimination self-righteous wanly
	Sketching characters, TE p. 652 Make a career choice chart, TE p. 655			

Grammar, Usage, Mechanics, and Spelling	Multimodal Learning	Research and Study Skills	Media Literacy
Creating coherence in paragraphs, PE p. 663 Avoiding sentence fragments, PE p. 665	Observing nature, PE p. 658 Graphs, PE p. 659 Interviewing, PE p. 661 Using graphics to explain, PE p. 663 Using graphic organizers, PE p. 660	Looking for sources, PE p. 661 Using graphic organizers, PE p. 660 Using Indexes, ML TE p. 660 Searching using key words, ML TE p. 660	Reading graphs, PE p. 659

UNIT FOUR
Recommended Resources   ENRICHMENT   RESEARCH

✓ Recommended Novels and Play

LITERATURE CONNECTIONS WITH SOURCEBOOK FOR TEACHERS

Thematic Link In this novel about a Mexican village, several characters are forced to balance their own desires and family demands as they try to determine what really matters.

About the Author Raised in Mexico, El Salvador, and the American Midwest, Sarah Benítez is a versatile writer of essays and fiction who also teaches creative writing.

LITERATURE CONNECTIONS WITH SOURCEBOOK FOR TEACHERS

Thematic Link An African-American family pursuing the American dream of their own home encounters racism and must decide what is really important.

About the Author Lorraine Hansberry (1930–1965) was the youngest child of a real estate broker. *A Raisin in the Sun* dramatizes her family's attempt to move to an all-white suburb.

Other Works by Lorraine Hansberry *The Sign in Sidney Brustein's Window, The Drinking Gourd, Les Blancs, To Be Young, Gifted, and Black*

Thematic Link A restless young man vacillates between the active and the contemplative life, eventually finding a truth that does not waver.

About the Author Hermann Hesse (1877–1962) received the Nobel Prize for literature in 1946. His work is scrupulous in its exploration of the subconscious and was influenced by his experiences with psychoanalysis.

Other Works by Hermann Hesse *Demian, Steppenwolf, Magister Ludi*

LITERATURE CONNECTIONS WITH SOURCEBOOK FOR TEACHERS

Thematic Link While traveling down the Mississippi with a runaway slave, an adolescent boy learns to decide for himself what matters most.

About the Author Mark Twain (1835–1910) drew upon his vast knowledge of the Mississippi River to write this classic picaresque novel.

Other Works by Mark Twain *Innocents Abroad, Roughing It, The Adventures of Tom Sawyer, The Prince and the Pauper, Life on the Mississippi, A Connecticut Yankee in King Arthur's Court*

Novel available in Spanish: *Las aventuras de Huckleberry Finn*

LITERATURE CONNECTIONS WITH SOURCEBOOK FOR TEACHERS

Thematic Link The weary inhabitants of a bleak farm struggle to ignore their household's truth.

About the Author Edith Wharton (1862–1937) based many of her novels on the upper-class New York City society in which she grew up and by which she felt imprisoned until she began to write. *Summer* and *Ethan Frome* are unusual among her novels for their settings, one a small quiet town and the other an isolated farm.

Other Works by Edith Wharton *The House of Mirth, The Custom of the Country, Summer, The Age of Innocence*

Professional Development   TEACHING THE NOVEL

Farr, Judith. *The Passion of Emily Dickinson.* Cambridge, MA: Harvard University Press, 1980.

Kumin, Maxine. "Enough Jam for a Lifetime," *Women, Animals, and Vegetables.* NY: Norton, 1994.

Molloy, Sylvia. *Signs of Borges.* Durham, NC: Duke University Press, 1994.

Spence, Donald P. *Narrative Truth and Historical Truth.* NY: Norton, 1982.

Walker, Scott, ed. *Multicultural Literacy.* St. Paul, MN: The Greywolf Press, 1988.

CROSS-CURRICULAR TEACHING   PROFESSIONAL DEVELOPMENT

Recommended Readings in Cross-Curricular Areas

SOCIAL STUDIES

Argentina's Lost Patrol by Maria José Moyano (1995) An impressively detailed vision of a political situation that gives context to contemporary Argentina. Links to Borges's "The Meeting."

Jamaica: A Guide to Its People, Politics, and Culture by Marcel Bayer (1993) Highly readable and concise introduction to one of our most vibrant cultures. Links to Selvon's "When Greek Meets Greek."

The Illusionless Man by Allen Wheelis (1966) Philosophical approach that claims life is impossible without daily illusions to propel us forward. Links to Narayan's "Like the Sun."

Soccer: Images of World Cup USA by Patrick Barclay (1995) Plausible presentation of this popular sport and its grand journey across America. Links to Yevtushenko's "A Precocious Autobiography."

Professional Development — CROSS-CURRICULAR INSTRUCTION

Anderson, J.D. "Students' Reflections on Community Service Learning," *Equity and Excellence in Education.* 28:3 (December 1995) 42.

Christiensen, C. Roland, et al. *Education for Judgement: The Artistry of Discussion Leadership.* Cambridge, MA: Harvard Business School Press, 1991.

Coles, Robert. *The Call of Stories.* Boston, MA: Houghton Mifflin Company, 1989.

Reissman, Rose C. "News Links to Literature: Bridging the Gap Between Literature and the News," *English Journal.* 83 (January 1994) 57–59.

Recommended Media Resources

THE LANGUAGE OF LITERATURE

ELECTRONIC LIBRARY
CD-ROM
Additional literature selections for Unit Four can be found on the Electronic Library CD-ROM.

LASERLINKS
Videodisc, Gr. 10
See *LaserLinks Teacher's SourceBook,* pages 40–41, for overview of Unit Four.

AUDIO LIBRARY
Tapes
Unit Four: Moments of Truth Gr. 10, Tapes 13–15: Sides A & B

WRITING COACH
Writing Coach Software: Writing About Literature—Interpretive Response, Cause and Effect Analysis

OUTSIDE RESOURCES

Films/Videos/Film Strips/Audiocassettes
The White Heron, video, Learning Corp. of America, 1978 (26 minutes).
Yevgeny Yevtushenko: A Poet's Journey, video, Films for the Humanities & Sciences, 1970 (29 minutes).
The Witness for the Prosecution, video, MGA/UA Home Video/CBS/Fox Video, 1957 (116 minutes).

Internet Resources
McDougal Littell Literature Center at http://www.hmco.com/mcdougal/lit

Professional Development — TEACHING WITH TECHNOLOGY

Kinnaman, Daniel E., and Dyrli, Odvard Egil. "Part 2: Developing a Technology-Powered Curriculum (What Every Teacher Needs to Know about Technology)," *Technology-Learning* 15:46 (February 1995) 6.

Means, Barbara, et al. *Using Technology to Support Education Reform.* Newton, MA: Education Development Center, Inc.

Educational Technology. Educational Technology Publications, Inc., 720 Palisade Avenue, Englewood Cliffs, NJ 07632.

UNIT FOUR
Professional Enrichment

On Translation Octavio Paz

In this article, a Nobel Prize-winning poet discusses issues related to translation—issues that the reader of a translated work should keep in mind.

Each text is unique, yet at the same time it is the translation of another text. No text is entirely original, because language itself is essentially a translation. In the first place, it translates from the non-verbal world. Then, too, each sign, each sentence, is the translation of another sign, another sentence. The reasoning may even be reversed without losing any of its force and we may assert that all texts are original because every translation is different. To a certain extent every translation is an original invention and thus constitutes a unique text.

The original text never reappears in the other language: this would be impossible. Nevertheless, it is always present because, although the translation does not explicitly state as much, it refers to the original text constantly, or else converts it into a verbal object that differs from it, yet reproduces it by metonymy or metaphor. Both of these, as distinct from explanatory or free translations, are strict forms that are not incompatible with exactness. Metonymy is an indirect description; metaphor is a verbal equation.

Poetry has always been considered the form of writing that lends itself least to translation. This prejudice is surprising when we stop to think that many of the best poems in every Western language are translations, and that many of these translations have been made by outstanding poets.

The reason why many poets are unable to translate poetry is not purely psychological in nature—though the cult of self does enter into it — but functional. Poetic translation is an operation similar to poetic creation, except that it is executed in reverse.

Meaning tends to be univocal in prose, whereas one of the characteristics of poetry, as has often been noted, and possibly its chief quality, is that it retains the several meanings of a word. In reality, this is a property of language in general. Poetry accentuates it, but it is also to be found in everyday speech and even in prose.

The poet, caught up in the whirl of language — which is a constant verbal coming and going — selects a few words, or is selected by them. He fashions his poem by combining them and it then becomes a verbal object made up of irreplaceable and irremovable signs. The translator's starting point is not language in motion, which is the poet's raw material, but the fixed language of the poem. It is a frozen language, and yet it is quite alive. His operation is the opposite of the poet's. He is not called upon to forge an unchangeable text with changing signs, but to take the text apart, set the signs in motion again and return them to the language. Up to this point the translator's work is similar to that of a reader or a critic, since every reading is a translation and every criticism is, or begins by being, an interpretation.

Reading, however, is a translation within the same language and criticism is a free version, or more exactly a transposition, of the poem. For the critic a poem is the jumping-off place towards another text, his own, whereas the translator, using another language and different signs, must compose a poem similar to the original.

Thus at the second stage the translator's activity is comparable to that of the poet, but with this important difference: when the poet writes, he does not know what his poem is going to be like; when the translator translates, he knows that the poem must reproduce the poem he has before him.

Translation and creation are twin operations. As the cases of Baudelaire and Pound show, it is often impossible to distinguish translation from creation. Moreover, there is a constant give and take between them, a continual and mutual creative influence. The great ages of poetry in the West have been preceded or accompanied by the interweaving of various poetic traditions. These cross-currents have sometimes taken the form of imitation and at other times that of translation.

Critics say "influences," but this term is equivocal. All styles have been translinguistic.

Styles are collective and pass from one language to another; written works, rooted in their verbal soil, are unique. They are unique but not isolated, for each of them is born and lives in relation to other works in different languages.

In every period European poets—and now those of the two Americas as well—write the same poem in their several languages, and each of these versions is likewise an original and different poem.

The synchronization may not be perfect, but if we withdraw a certain distance, we find that we are listening to a concert in which the musicians, playing different instruments and without following any orchestra leader or score, are composing a collective work in which improvisation is inseparable from translation, and invention is closely bound up with imitation. Occasionally one of the musicians launches into an inspired solo. The others soon take their cue from him and then go on to introduce variations, while the original motif becomes lost in the new creation.

Copyrighted material reprinted with permission.

UNIT FOUR
Starting Points for Unit Projects

The following suggestions will help you initiate individual and group projects during the course of this unit.

Creating a Time Line

ART/WRITING PROJECT Ask students to create a visual or verbal time line of their development over time. Students may choose to include photographs of themselves at various ages or images that represent the changes in their concerns and interests. For a verbal approach, students can write a series of poems exploring their own evolution.

Finding Truth in Art

GROUP ART HISTORY PROJECT Ask groups of students to visit museums or skim books of art history to find paintings that depict a subject or subjects undergoing a moment of truth. Suggest that students organize a panel discussion about what they think the moment means in each painting, based on the picture itself, the title, and any textual commentary.

Creating a Poster Series

GROUP ART PROJECT Ask small groups of students to compile a list of five values each member agrees is important, such as honesty, loyalty, or respect for the environment. Then the group should plan and execute a series of posters illustrating each of these values. Suggest that students support each visual image with an apt quotation selected from a book of quotations.

Dramatizing the Moment of Decision

GROUP DRAMA PROJECT Ask groups of students to prepare several skits in which the characters are faced with a conflict of values. Direct students to present their skits only to the point of decision and then to engage the class in discussion:
- What values are in conflict?
- What should each character do? Why?
- What will be the consequence of each decision?

Recording the World's Surprises

GROUP RESEARCH PROJECT Ask groups of students to collect newspaper articles that reflect unexpected turns: new developments in a police investigation, a verdict that surprises the community, a question to an advice columnist about how to deal with something the writer just found out, a comic strip in which a character is surprised. Encourage students to speculate about what good or ill can come of each situation and to compile their commentaries in a booklet.

Analyzing Advertising

GROUP MARKETING RESEARCH PROJECT Ask groups of students to collect magazine or newspaper ads that seem to be selling a value as well as a product: for example, a makeup ad that sells youth. Have students analyze each ad to judge its probable truthfulness and to identify its overt and implied messages. Suggest that students present their findings in a booklet, in a series of labeled posters, or in an oral presentation.

Family and Community Involvement

 Family

The selections in Unit Four explore those moments at which characters realize important truths. The following activities will help students, family, and community members to learn about some of the ways people encounter, and struggle to live with, their moments of truth.

OPTION 1 SHARE FAMILY MEMORIES
- **Connection** Some selections in Unit Four contain moments when the truth is revealed.
- **Activity** *Copymaster 1* Students and family members can discuss their own moments of truth. For example, people may recall the moment when they knew what they wanted to do with their lives or the moment they realized they wanted to marry a specific person.

OPTION 2 PERFORM A HUMOROUS SKETCH
- **Connection** "Like the Sun" explores the ways people deal with the knowledge gained from their moments of truth.
- **Activity** *Copymaster 2* Students and family members can work together to create a humorous sketch that shows what might happen if everyone told the truth constantly, no matter what the situation. They can use the selection "Like the Sun" for ideas.

OPTION 3 WRITE A DIARY ENTRY
- **Connection** "A White Heron" is about a girl who finds that what matters most to her is the preservation of the natural world.
- **Activity** *Copymaster 3* Students and family members may write in their journals or diary about an important truth they have learned about themselves. How is that truth connected with what matters most to each person?

 Community

OPTION 1
- **Connection** All of the selections in Unit Four contain moments when the truth is revealed.
- **Activity** Invite a prosecuting attorney or a police detective to discuss the variety of ways in which truth is sought in the legal system—the collecting of evidence, the kinds of questions asked a suspect, the tracking down of witnesses. The speaker might also discuss the gulf between the verdicts of guilty or not guilty and the question of absolute truth.

OPTION 2
- **Connection** "A Precocious Autobiography" tells about a moment of truth that enables a person to make a career choice.
- **Activity** Have students seek out and interview professionals respected in their local community to find out about their own "moments of truth." What made each decide upon his or her chosen profession?

OPTION 3
- **Connection** Some of the characters in "As the Night the Day" learn the truth about themselves but try to keep this truth from others.
- **Activity** Ask a psychologist or social worker to address the class about how he or she works with people who are having family problems. How does the person help people to express their true feelings to one another?

UNIT FOUR
Part 1 Lesson Planner

TIME ALLOTMENTS SHOWN ARE APPROXIMATE. DEPENDING ON YOUR GOALS AND THE NEEDS OF YOUR STUDENTS, YOU MAY WISH TO ALLOW MORE OR LESS TIME FOR CERTAIN PORTIONS OF THE LESSON.

Table of Contents	Discussion	Previewing the Selection	Reading the Selection
PART OPENER **Unexpected Realizations** page 512	**20 MINUTES** • Reflect on the part theme		
SELECTION **The Meeting** page 515 AVERAGE		**20 MINUTES** • PERSONAL CONNECTION • CULTURAL CONNECTION • READING CONNECTION: Identifying clauses	**40 MINUTES** • Introduce vocabulary • Read pp. 515–520 (6 pp.)
SELECTION **The Witness for the Prosecution** page 524 CHALLENGING		**20 MINUTES** • PERSONAL CONNECTION • CULTURAL CONNECTION • READING CONNECTION: Finding clues	**90 MINUTES** • Introduce vocabulary • Read pp. 524–541 (18 pp.)
SELECTION **Games at Twilight** page 546 EASY		**20 MINUTES** • PERSONAL CONNECTION • CULTURAL CONNECTION • WRITING CONNECTION	**40 MINUTES** • Introduce vocabulary • Read pp. 546–552 (7 pp.)
SELECTIONS **The Street/La Calle** **I Am Not I/Yo No Soy Yo** page 558 CHALLENGING		**20 MINUTES** • PERSONAL CONNECTION • LITERARY CONNECTION • READING CONNECTION: Understanding modern poetry	**15 MINUTES** • Read pp. 558–559 (2 pp.)
SELECTION *from* **The Unexpected Universe** page 563 AVERAGE		**20 MINUTES** • PERSONAL CONNECTION • SCIENTIFIC CONNECTION • WRITING CONNECTION	**15 MINUTES** • Introduce vocabulary • Read pp. 563–564 (2 pp.)
SELECTION **Two Friends** page 568 AVERAGE		**20 MINUTES** • PERSONAL CONNECTION • HISTORICAL CONNECTION • READING CONNECTION: Understanding contrast	**60 MINUTES** • Introduce vocabulary • Read pp. 568–576 (9 pp.)
FICTION ON YOUR OWN **When Greek Meets Greek** page 580 AVERAGE			**30 MINUTES** • Read pp. 580–583 (4 pp.)
Writing	**Writer's Style**	**Prewriting**	**Drafting and Revising**
WRITING ABOUT LITERATURE **Interpretation**	**20 MINUTES**	**25 MINUTES**	**65 MINUTES**

Time estimates assume in-class work. You may wish to assign some of these stages as homework.

Responding to the Selection

FROM PERSONAL RESPONSE TO CRITICAL ANALYSIS	OR	ANOTHER PATHWAY	LITERARY CONCEPTS	QUICKWRITES
		50 MINUTES		
• Discussion questions	OR	• Television newscast	• Narrator • Magical realism	• Ballad • Police report • Brochure
		50 MINUTES		
• Discussion questions	OR	• Time line	• Suspense • Point of view	• Script • Newspaper article • Cast list
		50 MINUTES		
• Discussion questions	OR	• Role-playing	• Diction	• Personal narrative • Episode • Article
		40 MINUTES		
• Discussion questions	OR	• Diary entry	• Alliteration • Repetition	• Poem • Horoscope
		40 MINUTES		
• Discussion questions	OR	• Dramatic soliloquy	• Reflective essay • Setting	• Reflective essay • Character analysis • Eyewitness account
		50 MINUTES		
• Discussion questions	OR	• Storyboard	• Protagonist/ Antagonist • Irony	• Letter • Alternative ending

Extension Activities

• ALTERNATIVE ACTIVITIES • LITERARY LINKS • CRITIC'S CORNER • THE WRITER'S STYLE • ACROSS THE CURRICULUM • ART CONNECTION • WORDS TO KNOW • BIOGRAPHY

Alternative Activities	Literary Links	Critic's Corner	The Writer's Style	Across the Curriculum	Art Connection	Words to Know	Biography
30 MINUTES							
✔	✔					✔	✔
60 MINUTES							
✔		✔	✔	SCIENCE	✔	✔	✔
40 MINUTES							
✔	✔	✔		SCIENCE ANTHRO- POLOGY		✔	✔
15 MINUTES							
✔							✔
15 MINUTES							
			✔	SCIENCE		✔	✔
30 MINUTES							
✔		✔				✔	✔

Publishing and Reflecting	Grammar in Context	Reading the World
25 MINUTES	**15 MINUTES**	**30 MINUTES**

LESSON PLANNER TEACHER'S EDITION 511I

PART 1

REFLECTING ON THEME

Ask students to define irony (the contrast between what is expected and what really happens). Remind them that much of literary irony is built upon "unexpected realizations." Have students name examples of irony from their own experience.

What Do You Think?

In addition to the writing exercise, have students draw a diagram of the moments preceding, during, and after their important insight. Some of these diagrams may resemble plot diagrams of a story or a novel, with an introduction leading to rising action, climax, and falling action. If so, point this out and explain that many literary plots involve unexpected insights and changes. Students will return to this activity on page 555.

UNIT FOUR **PART 1**

UNEXPECTED REALIZATIONS

REFLECTING ON THEME

Oliver Wendell Holmes, a poet and U.S. Supreme Court justice, once said, "A moment's insight is sometimes worth a life's experience." All of us have probably had moments when a flash of insight illuminated the truth about a situation, another person, or ourselves. Such insights often catch us by surprise, overturning our expectations and assumptions. In this part of Unit Four, you will read about characters who come to unexpected realizations about the truth. The results, as you will see, range from the humorous to the tragic.

What Do You Think? In your notebook, describe a time when a moment of insight altered your perception of a situation, another person, or yourself. How did the insight affect you, and what were its consequences?

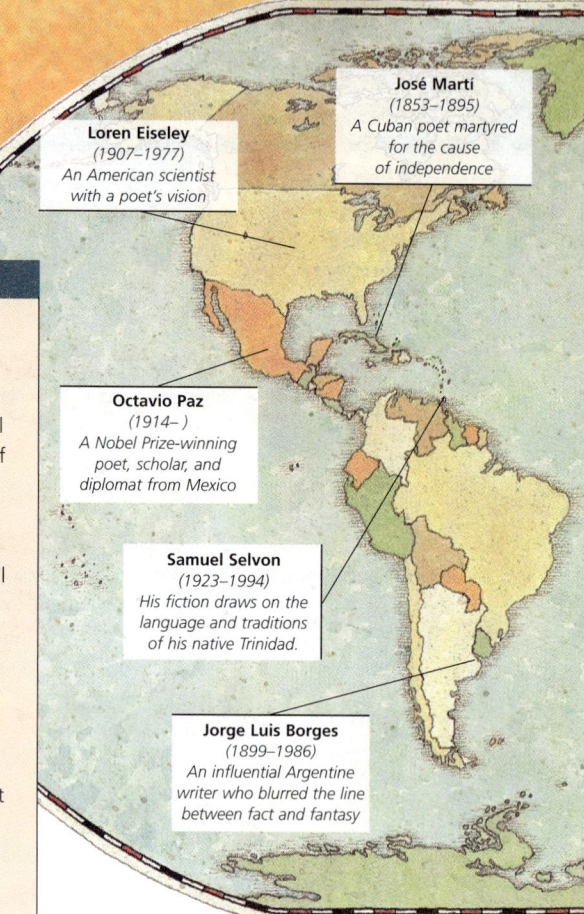

Loren Eiseley (1907–1977)
An American scientist with a poet's vision

José Martí (1853–1895)
A Cuban poet martyred for the cause of independence

Octavio Paz (1914–)
A Nobel Prize-winning poet, scholar, and diplomat from Mexico

Samuel Selvon (1923–1994)
His fiction draws on the language and traditions of his native Trinidad.

Jorge Luis Borges (1899–1986)
An influential Argentine writer who blurred the line between fact and fantasy

Jorge Luis Borges	**The Meeting** *Two men, two knives*	514
Agatha Christie	**The Witness for the Prosecution** *Did he really murder the woman?*	523
Anita Desai	**Games at Twilight** *A young boy dreams of victory.*	545
Octavio Paz	**The Street / La Calle** *Who—or what—is following him?*	556
Juan Ramón Jiménez	**I Am Not I / Yo No Soy Yo** *Seeing two selves*	556

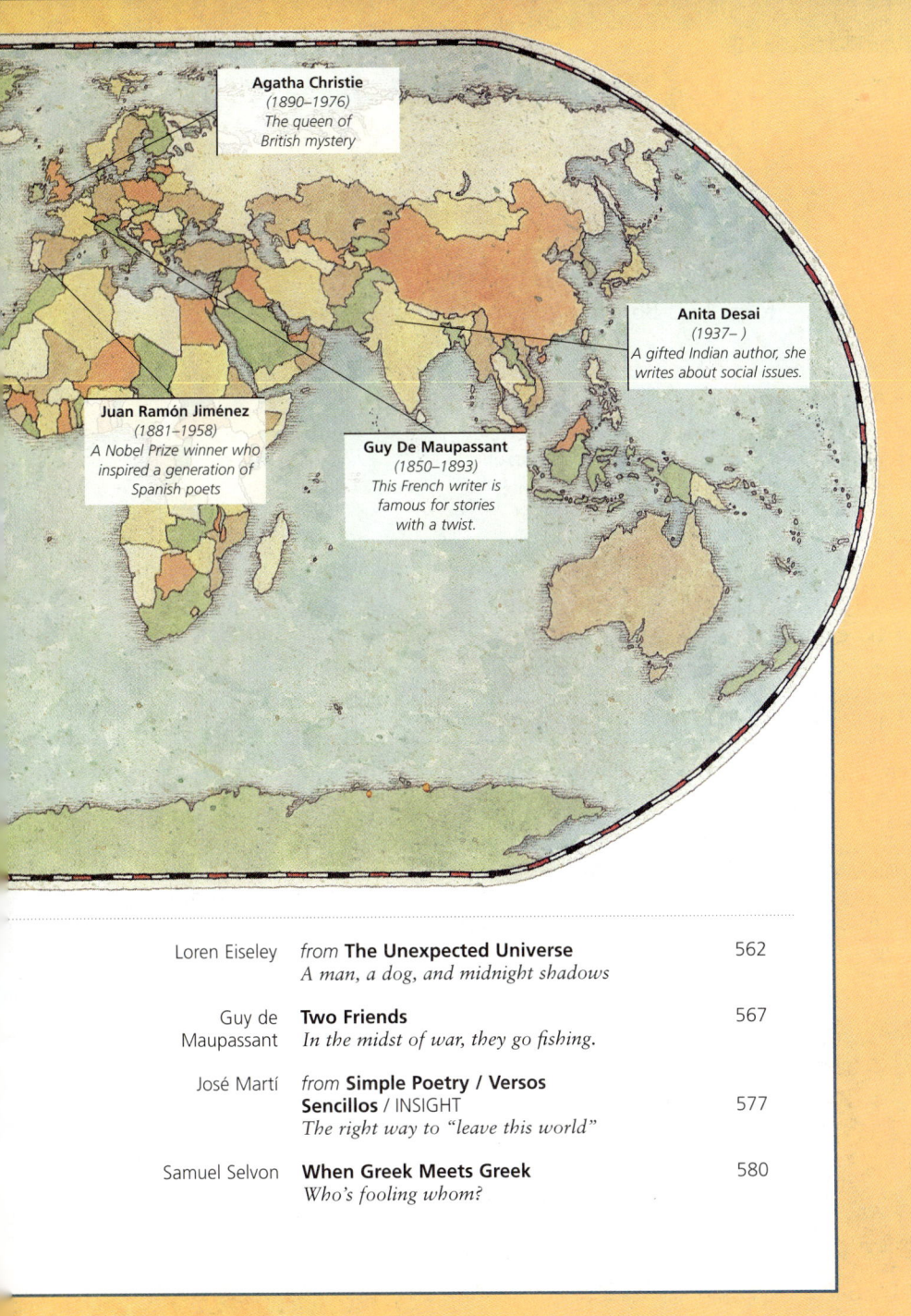

Loren Eiseley	from **The Unexpected Universe** *A man, a dog, and midnight shadows*	562
Guy de Maupassant	**Two Friends** *In the midst of war, they go fishing.*	567
José Martí	from **Simple Poetry / Versos Sencillos** / INSIGHT *The right way to "leave this world"*	577
Samuel Selvon	**When Greek Meets Greek** *Who's fooling whom?*	580

Map Note

This map shows the varied backgrounds of the authors featured in this part of the unit. To help students anticipate the ironic twists in the upcoming selections, you may want to ask them the following questions:

- What do you know about Agatha Christie? Why might her writing be included in this part of the unit?
- What kinds of unexpected realizations might you expect from a scientist like Loren Eiseley to write about?

OVERVIEW

Objectives

- To understand and appreciate a short story that explores the effect of a mysterious duel on a young eyewitness
- To enrich reading by using active reading strategies
- To identify and understand the concept of a narrator
- To express understanding of the story through a choice of writing forms, including a ballad, a police report, and a brochure
- To extend understanding of the story through a variety of multimodal and cross-curricular activities

Skills

LITERARY CONCEPTS
- Narrator
- Conflict

READING SKILLS/STRATEGIES
- Identifying causes
- Predicting
- Clarifying

GENRE STUDY
- Fiction: magical realism

GRAMMAR
- Simple past tense

SPEAKING, LISTENING, AND VIEWING
- Monologue
- Group discussion
- Oral presentation

CULTURAL CONNECTION

Gauchos Like the cowboys in the Old West in the United States, the gauchos of Argentina have been romanticized as colorful heroes of a bygone era. Use these photographs to help students build prior knowledge about the world of the Argentine gaucho.

Side A, Frame 49494

CUSTOMIZING FOR
Students Acquiring English

- Use **ACCESS FOR STUDENTS ACQUIRING ENGLISH**, *Reading Support*.

- Ask students if there has ever been a tradition of dueling or other fights of honor in the history of their home cultures. If so, ask them to describe the events that might lead up to such combat and the weapons that would be used.

- In addition to these boxes, you may want to use the suggestions under Strategic Reading for Less-Proficient Readers.

PREVIEWING

FICTION

The Meeting
Jorge Luis Borges (hôr'hĕ loo-ēs' bôr'hĕs) Argentina

Activating Prior Knowledge
PERSONAL CONNECTION

Recall a time when you witnessed a fight that began with words and moved on to physical violence, or at least to the threat of violence. What caused the fight? What pushed the participants over the edge? Describe the incident and its causes in your notebook, and explain how you felt about witnessing such a conflict.

Building Background
CULTURAL CONNECTION

In "The Meeting," the narrator recalls a violent conflict that he witnessed in his youth. This tale, like many stories by Jorge Luis Borges, draws upon the history and culture of the author's native Argentina.

Though the story takes place in the early 20th century, it makes reference to the gauchos of Argentina's frontier past. The gauchos, like the cowboys in the Old West in the United States, were wandering cattlemen known for their skillful horsemanship, distinctive clothes, and fighting abilities. Eventually, gauchos were romanticized and became folk heroes. Three gauchos mentioned in this story, Juan Moreira, Martín Fierro, and Segundo Sombra, are still celebrated today.

The duels fought by gauchos were often the result of insults to honor; typically, the knife was the weapon of choice. Among Argentina's upper classes, duels of honor were fought with the sword, a weapon regarded as more appropriate to polite society. In both cases, spectators did not interfere, and the killing of an opponent in a duel was considered a less serious offense than murder.

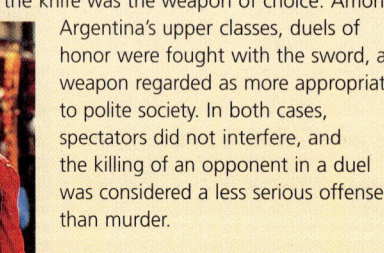

Gaucho in Argentina. Copyright © Carlos Goldin / DDB Stock Photo.

514

Active Reading/Setting a Purpose
READING CONNECTION

Identifying Causes In "The Meeting," an argument spins out of control and leads to a duel. As you read, identify the various explanations that are offered as causes of the conflict. Fill in a chart, like the one below, to keep track of the possible causes. Feel free to add to your chart more boxes than those shown here.

Causes of the Duel

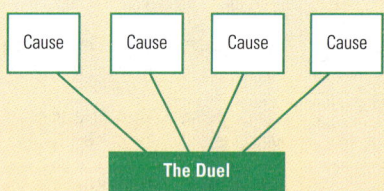

• CULTURAL CONNECTION

PRINT AND MEDIA RESOURCES

UNIT FOUR RESOURCE BOOK
Strategic Reading: Literature, p. 4
Vocabulary SkillBuilder, p. 5

GRAMMAR MINI–LESSONS
Transparencies, pp. 29–31
Copymasters, p. 28

WRITING MINI–LESSONS
Transparencies, p. 53

ACCESS FOR STUDENTS ACQUIRING ENGLISH
Selection Summaries
Reading Support

TEACHER'S GUIDE TO ASSESSMENT AND PORTFOLIO USE

FORMAL ASSESSMENT
Selection Test, p. 101
 Test Generator

AUDIO LIBRARY
See Reference Card

 **LASERLINKS**
Cultural Connection
Literary Concept

2 Draft Your Story

As you write your draft, think carefully about the effects that one change can have on other elements of the story. If you're stuck, write the ending first and work backwards.

In the student draft below, the plot of "The Sound of Thunder" has been changed. Note the student's own questions.

Student's Draft

> Travis and Eckels looked down at the shoes. "What's that?" asked Travis, noticing the butterfly.
> Eckels backed away and mumbled, "Uh, I . . ."
> "That's it! I won't have you ruin our business. You're staying here," said Travis.
> The time machine made a tremendous noise and left abruptly. Eckels' head began to spin. He had never been so afraid and uncertain in his life. As he was thinking about his choices, an eerie feeling came over him. Looking up, he saw a pterodactyl. As it swooped down at him, he feared for his life. "What am I going to do?" he thought. Just then, an idea hit him. He stood perfectly still while the giant bird flew by him. Then, with all the courage he could find, he walked the narrow metal path towards a clearing in the trees ahead.

Does my plot progression make sense?

Do I show how other elements change when the plot changes?

3 Share Your Work

When you've finished your draft, ask yourself

- How does my writing show a changed story element?
- Do story events still flow logically?
- How well does my writing imitate the writer's style?

 PEER RESPONSE

Then ask a classmate to read your rewritten portion of the story and respond to the following questions.

- What story element have I changed?
- How does the change affect the story?

SkillBuilder

 **CRITICAL THINKING**

Using Graphic Organizers

As you develop ideas for your draft, you might create a graphic organizer showing how you'll change a scene in your chosen story.

- If you are changing a character or the setting, for example, you could make a web showing aspects of the character's personality or of the setting.

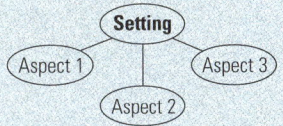

- If you are changing the point of view or the narrator of a story, you could make a Venn diagram showing differences and similarities between the original story and the story as it will be told from a different point of view or a different narrator.

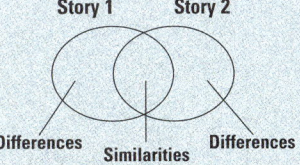

- If you are changing the plot of a story you could develop a cause-effect chain like the one on page 736 showing how one event leads to the next.

APPLYING WHAT YOU'VE LEARNED
Develop a web, Venn diagram, or cause-effect chain to show how you will change a story element.

WRITING ABOUT LITERATURE   737

Writing Skill: USING THE COMPUTER

H Writing a discovery draft gives students the opportunity to let their ideas flow. Reassure writers that there will be plenty of time later to revise and edit their drafts for errors in spelling, grammar, and mechanics. Using a computer to compose a discovery draft may help students get their ideas down rapidly because they can easily adjust, reverse, or expand a thought as they input.

Teaching Strategy: MANAGING THE PAPER LOAD

I As you read the drafts, concentrate on the single element that each student finds most troublesome, such as a logical plot progression or suitable dialogue. Reassure students that they can work out less serious story problems in a peer review setting.

Teaching Strategy: COLLABORATIVE OPPORTUNITY

J Have peer reviewers read the story twice before they make any comments. During the second reading, they should jot down brief reactions and suggestions. Remind students to include specific ideas for revision, such as "Would a teenager speak like this in real life?"

SkillBuilder  CRITICAL THINKING

USING GRAPHIC ORGANIZERS

K Point out that graphic organizers work well for certain story elements but are not particularly useful for others, such as dialogue. Remind students to carefully plan out all important aspects of the story.

Applying What You've Learned Point out that students may need to develop several different kinds of graphic organizers to show the connections between story elements that are interdependent.

Reteaching/Reinforcement
- *Writing Mini-Lessons* transparencies, pp. 2–33

The Writer's Craft
Graphic Devices, pp. 330–337

THE LANGUAGE OF LITERATURE TEACHER'S EDITION   737

Critical Thinking: ANALYZING

L Point out to students that revising their drafts involves molding the text to fit their purposes. To evaluate and revise their scenes, students should

- check to see that they have changed a story element and integrated the new element smoothly
- make sure that they have presented the altered element consistently through the scene

Teaching Tip: MODELING

M Discuss how the writer's final draft meets the Standards for Evaluation on this page. Point out that when the writer changed the plot of "A Sound of Thunder," the mood of the narrative also changed from somber and fatalistic to exciting and suspenseful.

WRITING ABOUT LITERATURE

4 Revise and Edit

As you write a final draft, check to see that your writing is unified. Refer to the Grammar in Context on the opposite page and the Standards for Evaluation below. Consider sharing your final version with other students and discussing changes you made in various stories.

Student's Final Draft

> Eckels had spent two long days under the cover of a tree in the jungle. During that time, a change had come over him. He felt brave. Although he was tired and hungry, he had become used to the eerie jungle sounds. He was sometimes afraid of the creatures in the jungle, but now he was very good at remaining still when an animal was near. Suddenly, he heard the noise he had been waiting for. Whhrrrrr! Chink, chink, chink! Thud!
>
> He heard the familiar voice, "Here we are! Everyone, remember what I told you about stepping off the path. One member of the last group stepped off the path and found himself in a grave situation!" With that last sentence, Travis howled an evil laugh. Members of the group sighed nervously.
>
> "What happened to him?" one man asked.
>
> Travis laughed again, only louder. "Well, my friend, I don't think you'd care to know!"
>
> As he hid behind the leaves, Eckels could hear the group coming toward him. A creature from the distance approached. Eckels could feel the ground shake.
>
> Then, there was the clicking sound of a rifle. With his newfound bravery, Eckels came face to face with his target.
>
> Bang! A sound of thunder.

What other story elements changed when the plot changed? How did they change?

Standards for Evaluation

A creative response that changes a story element
- skillfully retells a story part while changing an element
- retains the element change throughout the story part
- changes other story elements in order to make sense with the new element

738 UNIT FIVE: NOTHING STAYS THE SAME

Assessment ✓ Option

SELF-ASSESSMENT To help students assess their own writing, have them answer the following questions:
- *Have I retold a scene in the story after changing a single element?*
- *Have I maintained the shift in one story element consistently throughout the scene?*
- *Have I considered the implications of my change for other elements of the story?*

Grammar in Context

Past Perfect Tense To clearly present events, you need to use the correct verb tense. Sometimes when writing a narrative, you will need to use the past perfect tense to show an action that came before another past action. To form the past perfect tense, use the helping verb *had* with the past participle. Look at the following student draft of a story with actions that took place in the past.

> Eckels ^had^ spent two long days under the cover of a tree in the jungle. During that time, a change ~~came~~ ^had come^ over him. He felt brave. Although he was tired and hungry, he ~~became~~ ^had become^ used to the eerie jungle sounds. He was sometimes afraid of the creatures in the jungle, but now he was very good at remaining still when an animal was near.

This story part takes place in the past, but some of the action took place even earlier. Therefore, the helping verb *had* plus the past participle was inserted to create the past perfect verb tense. Notice how the past perfect verb tense makes sense in the story. Consult the lessons on verb tenses and forms in the Grammar Handbook on page 1081 for more help.

Try Your Hand: Using Past Perfect Tense

Create past perfect verb tenses in the following paragraph.

> The change in Eckels occurred suddenly. His confidence grew. He no longer shuddered at the sound of a prehistoric animal approaching him. As for shelter and food, he built a rough little hut out of bunches of leaves. Luckily, he brought a survival kit with a basic food supply. He waited patiently until Travis and the time machine finally returned.

SkillBuilder

 GRAMMAR FROM WRITING

Past Participles of Irregular Verbs

When you use the past perfect tense, you will be using past participles too. Most past participles of regular verbs are formed by adding *-d* or *-ed* to the present verb form. Some examples follow.

*Travis had **guided** safaris for ten years.* (guide)

*Eckels had **pointed** the rifle at his target.* (point)

Past participles of irregular verbs are not formed by adding *-d* or *-ed*. Since they are formed irregularly, you may need to consult a dictionary or grammar handbook. Check the following samples.

*Eckels **built** a hut with materials he had **found**.* (build, find)

*He felt lucky that he had **brought** a survival kit.* (bring)

APPLYING WHAT YOU'VE LEARNED
Create three sentences that contain the past participles of irregular verbs. Refer to a dictionary if you need help.

 GRAMMAR HANDBOOK

For more information on past participles of irregular verbs, see page 1082 of the Grammar Handbook.

WRITING ABOUT LITERATURE **739**

CUSTOMIZING FOR

Students Acquiring English

N Before you begin this page, be sure that students understand the definitions of past perfect tense, past participle, and irregular verb. The past perfect tense is formed by placing the auxiliary verb *had* before the past participle. The past participle is the fourth and last principal part of a verb. An irregular verb is a verb that does not form its past participle by adding *-d* or *-ed* to the present form.

Try Your Hand

Answers will vary slightly. Possible response: The change in Eckels had occurred suddenly. His confidence had grown. He no longer shuddered at the sound of a prehistoric animal approaching him. As for shelter and food, he had built a rough little hut out of bunches of leaves. Luckily, he had brought a survival kit with a basic food supply. He waited patiently until Travis and the time machine finally returned.

Standards for Evaluation

Have students review their stories for the following:

Ideas and Content
- Retells a scene from a story by changing a story element: point of view, plot, setting, or character.
- Keeps new element the same throughout scene.
- Changes other story elements and adds or removes information to make sense with new element.
- Begins with introduction that catches reader's attention and makes clear what element has changed.

Structure and Form
- Displays a clear order of events.
- Demonstrates proper and effective paragraphing.
- Includes sentences with a variety of structures.

Grammar, Usage, and Mechanics
- Contains no more than two or three minor errors in grammar and usage.
- Contains no more than two or three minor errors in spelling, capitalization, and punctuation.

PORTFOLIO

Invite students to discuss the effectiveness of their story revisions. Then ask students to write a brief reflection on what they learned as a result of this assignment. Students may wish to include their reflections along with their rewrites in their portfolios.

SkillBuilder  GRAMMAR FROM WRITING

PAST PARTICIPLES OF IRREGULAR VERBS First, use a regular verb to model the principal forms of a verb: *look, looking, looked, (have) looked*. Then model an irregular verb—*break, breaking, broke, (have) broken*—and discuss irregular verbs' unpredictability.

Applying What You've Learned Pair less-proficient writers and students acquiring English with more proficient partners for this activity.

Additional Suggestions Have students give the principal form of all the irregular verbs that appear in the excerpt from the student's draft on this page. *(spend, come, feel, be, become)*

Reteaching/Reinforcement
- *Grammar Handbook*, anthology pp. 1082–1084
- *Grammar Mini-Lessons*, copymasters pp. 30–32, transparencies pp. 32–33

 The Writer's Craft

Irregular Verbs, pp. 650–651

THE LANGUAGE OF LITERATURE TEACHER'S EDITION **739**

READING THE WORLD

On pages 736–739, students rewrote a scene from a story by changing one story element. Then they examined how changing that element changed to whole story. Students should be aware that a change in any element of packaging is designed to have similarly sweeping effects upon consumers' buying decisions. In this lesson, students will examine changes in meaning suggested by changes in packaging.

Critical Thinking: OBSERVING

O Students' lists of differences will vary. They may mention, for example, that the juice shown at the left is canned and that the juice at the right is packaged in a jar. The labels are different as well. The can displays the words "All Natural" in larger type, and the fruit pictured on the label, which sports a modern graphic design, is more prominent.

Critical Thinking: MAKING INFERENCES

P Students' answers will vary. In general, they may suggest that the juice in the jar seems more healthful. The label for the canned juice, however, may seem more attractive to some students.

Speaking and Listening: GROUP DISCUSSION

Q Group members may say that many factors combine to make a package appealing: materials (aluminum can versus glass jar, for example), color, shape, label design and size of type, and so on.

READING THE WORLD

NEW AND IMPROVED?

You've seen how changing an element changes a story. How might changing an element on a product's package change the way you think about that product? Imagine you're in a grocery store looking for fruit juice. How might the differences between the packages affect your buying decision?

View Look at the two products below. In your notebook, list differences between the two. What do you notice first? **O**

Interpret Review your list of differences. Which product do you like better? Which seems healthier? Which would you buy? **P**

Discuss What did you base your choice on? In a small group, talk about the power of a package. What makes a package appealing? Refer to the SkillBuilder on comparing and contrasting for more ideas. **Q**

SkillBuilder

 CRITICAL THINKING

Comparing and Contrasting Products

Can you really judge a book by its cover? Do colors, shapes, and specific words persuade you to buy a product? Believe it or not, many consumers choose one product instead of another because of the packaging rather than the content. A product's packaging might cause you to believe that one product is better than another—or that you'll be "better" for having purchased it.

When you evaluate by comparing and contrasting, you are recognizing similarities and differences. Each time you taste a different food, consider buying a new product, or listen to a new musical group, you judge similarities and differences. The key to making smart judgments is to look beyond the surface, or package, to discover the facts.

APPLYING WHAT YOU'VE LEARNED
Try the following with a partner.

- Flip through a newspaper or magazine and find an advertisement that compares and contrasts two products. In two columns, list similarities and differences of the two products. Which product would you purchase?
- Discuss a time when you made a choice based on a product's packaging. What was the outcome? What were your reasons for your decision?

READING THE WORLD **741**

SkillBuilder CRITICAL THINKING

COMPARING AND CONTRASTING Point out that words' connotations are especially important in packaging. For example, the phrase "all natural" on the containers of juice makes the juice seem as if it were filled with apples straight from the tree and with cranberries right out of the bog. The label ignores the harvesting, processing, and packaging stages of getting this product to market because packagers wish to appeal to health-conscious consumers.

Applying What You've Learned Students could also use Venn diagrams to chart the similarities and differences between products. This approach may help students distinguish attributes common to all labels—those functions that a label must perform—from elements designed to set a particular product apart as uniquely worthy.

Reteaching/Reinforcement
- *Writing Mini-Lessons* transparencies, pp. 18–19

 **The Writer's Craft**

Comparison-and-Contrast Charts; pp. 334–335

UNIT FIVE
Part 2 Lesson Planner

TIME ALLOTMENTS SHOWN ARE APPROXIMATE. DEPENDING ON YOUR GOALS AND THE NEEDS OF YOUR STUDENTS, YOU MAY WISH TO ALLOW MORE OR LESS TIME FOR CERTAIN PORTIONS OF THE LESSON.

Table of Contents	Discussion	Previewing the Selection	Reading the Selection
PART OPENER **Cultural Crossroads** page 742	**20 MINUTES** • Reflect on the part theme		
SELECTION **No Witchcraft for Sale** page 745 AVERAGE		**20 MINUTES** • PERSONAL CONNECTION • HISTORICAL CONNECTION • READING CONNECTION: Interpreting characterizations to discover an author's viewpoint/Using reading log	**40 MINUTES** • Introduce vocabulary • Read pp. 745–751 (7 pp.)
SELECTION **Thoughts of Hanoi** page 755 AVERAGE		**20 MINUTES** • PERSONAL CONNECTION • CULTURAL CONNECTION • WRITING CONNECTION	**30 MINUTES** • Read pp. 755–758 (4 pp.)
SELECTION **The Son from America** page 762 AVERAGE		**20 MINUTES** • PERSONAL CONNECTION • HISTORICAL/CULTURAL CONNECTION • READING CONNECTION: Making predictions	**50 MINUTES** • Read pp. 762–768 (7 pp.)
SELECTION **By Any Other Name** page 773 AVERAGE		**20 MINUTES** • PERSONAL CONNECTION • CULTURAL CONNECTION • WRITING CONNECTION	**30 MINUTES** • Reading pp. 773–777 (5 pp.)
SELECTION **Marriage Is a Private Affair** page 781 CHALLENGING		**20 MINUTES** • PERSONAL CONNECTION • CULTURAL CONNECTION • WRITING CONNECTION	**40 MINUTES** • Introduce vocabulary • Read pp. 781–785 (5 pp.)
SELECTION **Lost Sister** page 790 AVERAGE		**20 MINUTES** • PERSONAL CONNECTION • CULTURAL CONNECTION • READING CONNECTION: Defining cultural roles	**20 MINUTES** • Read pp. 790–791 (2 pp.)
POETRY ON YOUR OWN **Bora Ring** page 794 CHALLENGING			**20 MINUTES** • Read pp. 794–795 (2 pp.)

Writing	Exploring Topics	Prewriting	Drafting and Revising
WRITING FROM EXPERIENCE **Narrative and Literary Writing**	**25 MINUTES**	**30 MINUTES**	**65 MINUTES**

Time estimates assume in-class work. You may wish to assign some of these stages as homework.

Responding to the Selection

FROM PERSONAL RESPONSE TO CRITICAL ANALYSIS	OR	ANOTHER PATHWAY	LITERARY CONCEPTS	QUICKWRITES		Extension Activities						
						ALTERNATIVE ACTIVITIES	LITERARY LINKS	CRITIC'S CORNER	THE WRITER'S STYLE	ACROSS THE CURRICULUM	ART CONNECTION	WORDS TO KNOW	BIOGRAPHY

50 MINUTES / 30 MINUTES

From Personal Response	OR	Another Pathway	Literary Concepts	Quickwrites	Alt. Act.	Lit. Links	Critic's Corner	Writer's Style	Across Curriculum	Art Conn.	Words to Know	Biography
• Discussion questions	OR	• Newspaper editorial	• Climax	• Afterword • Dialogue	✓				HEALTH	✓	✓	
• Discussion questions	OR	• Letter	• Dramatic monologue	• Dramatic monologue • Extended definitions • Essay	✓	✓	✓		HISTORY			✓
	OR	• Discussion questions	• Comparison and contrast chart	• Situational irony • Voice	✓		✓	✓	WORLD RELIGION WORLD LANGUAGES			✓
• Newsletter article • Review • Character sketches	OR	• Discussion questions	• Annotated time line	• Title			✓		HISTORY			✓
• Opinion column • Note	OR	• Discussion questions	• Chart	• Cultural setting • Point of view	✓	✓	✓		ANTHROPOLOGY HISTORY	✓	✓	✓
• Letter • Diary entries • List	OR	• Discussion questions	• Paragraph	• Cultural/literary symbols	✓	✓			WORLD CULTURES			✓

Time allotments by row: 50 MINUTES (Responding) / 30, 40, 40, 30, 60, 30 MINUTES (Extension Activities)

Publishing and Reflecting

25 MINUTES

LESSON PLANNER TEACHER'S EDITION 741b

PART 2

REFLECTING ON THEME

After students read the opening paragraph, explore with the class what the word "culture" means to them. You may wish to create a word web on the board to record students' ideas. Here is a sample:

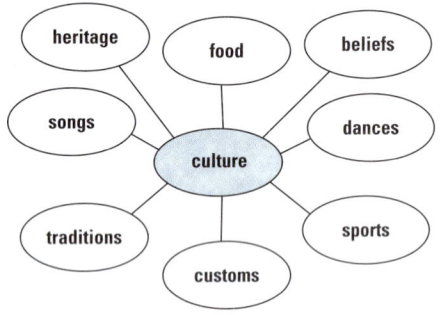

What Do You Think?

Suggest that students consult newsmagazines such as *Time, Newsweek,* and *US News and World Report* as well as newspapers. If students decide to use a televised newscast, encourage them to videotape the show so they can watch it again to verify details. Students will return to this activity on pages 771 and 788.

UNIT FIVE **PART 2**

CULTURAL CROSSROADS

REFLECTING ON THEME

The phrase *cultural crossroads* has two distinct meanings. On the one hand, it can refer to an intersection of two or more cultures—an intersection that may produce mutual enrichment, conflict, or misunderstanding. On the other hand, it can refer to a critical turning point within a single culture. For example, a traditional society may reach a crossroads when it seeks to adopt modern ways of living. As you read this part of Unit Five, consider which meaning best applies to each selection.

What Do You Think? Working with a partner, find two or three news stories dealing with cultural crossroads. For example, a newspaper might have a report about a conflict between two cultural groups, or a newscast might feature a story about a culture in the process of change. Discuss your findings with your classmates.

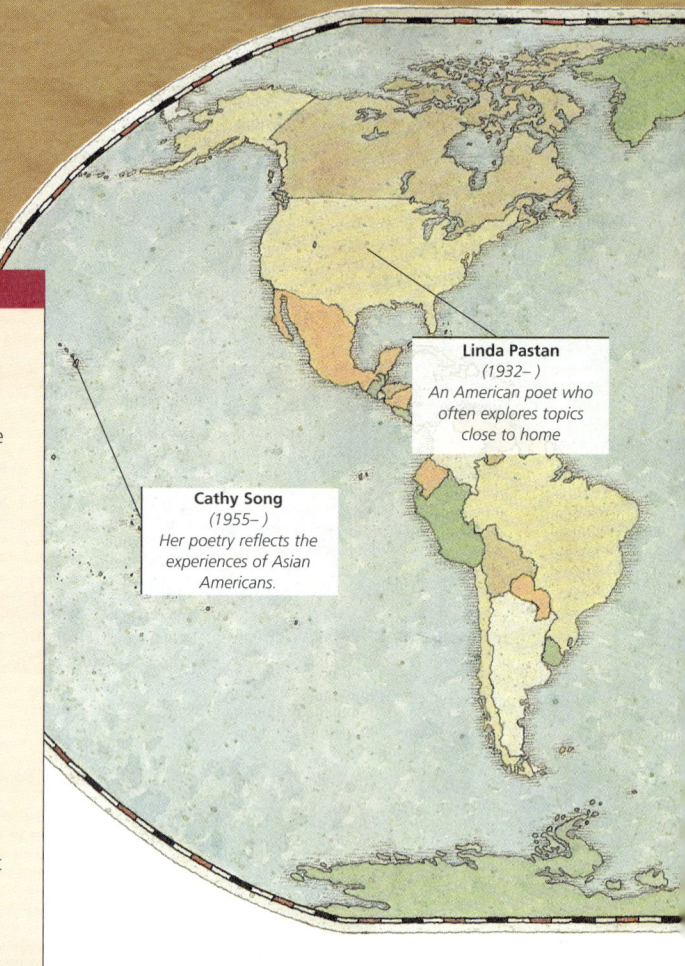

Linda Pastan (1932–)
An American poet who often explores topics close to home

Cathy Song (1955–)
Her poetry reflects the experiences of Asian Americans.

Doris Lessing	**No Witchcraft for Sale** *An African servant resists his British masters.*	744
Nguyen Thi Vinh	**Thoughts of Hanoi** *The friends of his youth are now civil-war enemies.*	754
Isaac Bashevis Singer	**The Son from America** *When he returns home, two worlds meet.*	761
Linda Pastan	**Grudnow** / INSIGHT *Visions of the old country*	768

742 THE LANGUAGE OF LITERATURE TEACHER'S EDITION

Map Note

The purpose of the map is to show the diversity of cultural experiences represented by the authors in this section. You may want to ask students one or more of the following questions:

- What different cultures are represented on this map?
- Which countries represented here do you think have faced important cultural crossroads? Why?

Santha Rama Rau	**By Any Other Name** *When school becomes a test of cultural pride*	772
Chinua Achebe	**Marriage Is a Private Affair** *He defied tradition by choosing his own wife.*	780
Cathy Song	**Lost Sister** *Links to one's cultural past*	789
Judith Wright	**Bora Ring** *Faint traces of a lost culture*	794

OVERVIEW

Objectives

- To understand and appreciate a short story that explores a profound misunderstanding between two cultures
- To enrich reading by using active reading strategies
- To identify and understand climax
- To express understanding of a selection through a choice of writing forms, including an afterword and a dialogue
- To extend understanding of the selection through a variety of multimodal and cross-curricular activities

Skills

LITERARY CONCEPTS
- Climax
- Conflict

READING SKILLS/ STRATEGIES
- Interpreting characterizations to discover an author's viewpoint
- Evaluating
- Predicting

THE WRITER'S STYLE
- Chronological order

GRAMMAR
- Modifiers that follow verbs

SPEAKING, LISTENING, AND VIEWING
- Group discussion
- Oral tale

GEOGRAPHICAL CONNECTION
Zimbabwe This story takes place in southern Africa before 1965 in the British colony of Southern Rhodesia. Today this land is the independent nation of Zimbabwe. A map and photographs of Zimbabwe will help students visualize the setting of this story.

Side A, Frame 49630

CUSTOMIZING FOR
Students Acquiring English

- Use **ACCESS FOR STUDENTS ACQUIRING ENGLISH,** *Reading Support.*
- Ask students what they think the word *witchcraft* means. Explain that in the context of this story, it does not have to do with supernatural ceremonies, but rather with the secret knowledge of the medicinal uses of herbs.
- Point out that the story contains colloquial language and subtle patterns of behavior that reflect the racially segregated, colonial British society of Southern Rhodesia in the time the story is set.

PREVIEWING

FICTION

No Witchcraft for Sale

Doris Lessing Southern Rhodesia / England

Activating Prior Knowledge
PERSONAL CONNECTION

Think of an incident in which people from different cultures or races have misjudged or misunderstood one another. Perhaps you have personally experienced such a misunderstanding, or perhaps you have read about one. Describe the incident in your notebook, offering your explanation of what happened. Then share your description with your classmates. In a class discussion, try to identify some of the causes and effects of cultural or racial misunderstanding. You might use a diagram like the one shown to help you organize your ideas.

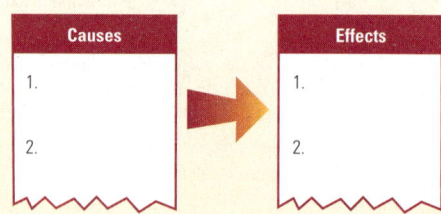

Building Background
HISTORICAL CONNECTION

Africa has long been a setting for misunderstanding and confrontation between cultures and races. In the 1800s and early 1900s, most African countries became colonies of European powers. Although many of the African countries had been strong kingdoms with well-developed economies and cultures, they came to be dominated politically, economically, and culturally by their European rulers.

In the 1890s, the region that would become Southern Rhodesia fell under British control. A land of great beauty and mineral wealth, Southern Rhodesia had a large population of British settlers that for decades dominated the country, both as a British colony and, after 1965, as an independent nation. Following a sometimes violent struggle, the black majority gained control of the country—in 1980 renaming it Zimbabwe, after the ancient African capital city of the region. "No Witchcraft for Sale" takes place in Southern Rhodesia during the time of white rule.

Active Reading / Setting a Purpose
READING CONNECTION

Interpreting Characterizations to Discover an Author's Viewpoint
Writers of fiction seldom state their viewpoints directly. The ways in which an author presents characters, however, may provide clues to his or her opinions. For example, a character treated sympathetically may embody values that the author approves of. As you read Doris Lessing's story, decide which characters are portrayed sympathetically. What do these portrayals suggest about Lessing's views on the misunderstandings described?

Using Your Reading Log Use your reading log to record your responses to the questions inserted in the selection. Also jot down other thoughts and feelings that come to you as you read.

- GEOGRAPHICAL CONNECTION

744   UNIT FIVE   PART 2: CULTURAL CROSSROADS

PRINT AND MEDIA RESOURCES

UNIT FIVE RESOURCE BOOK
Strategic Reading: Literature, p. 41
Vocabulary SkillBuilder, p. 42

GRAMMAR MINI–LESSONS
Transparencies, p. 22
Copymasters, p. 24

WRITING MINI–LESSONS
Transparencies, pp. 8–9

ACCESS FOR STUDENTS ACQUIRING ENGLISH
Selection Summaries
Reading Support

FORMAL ASSESSMENT
Selection Test, p. 147
 Test Generator

 LASERLINKS
Geographical Connection
Health Connection

INTERNET RESOURCES
McDougal Littell Literature Center at http://www.hmco.com/mcdougal/lit

---

744   THE LANGUAGE OF LITERATURE   **TEACHER'S EDITION**

Conjur Woman (1975), Romare Bearden. Collage on board, 46″ × 36″, private collection, courtesy of Sheldon Ross Gallery, Birmingham, Michigan, and the Estate of Romare Bearden.

No Witchcraft for Sale

Doris Lessing

SUMMARY

The Farquars live in Southern Rhodesia, where their African cook Gideon is close to their only child, Teddy. Gideon watches sadly as the boy becomes like a white man who expects black people to obey his commands. One day, a tree snake spits into Teddy's eyes. Gideon runs into the bush and comes back with a root that he uses to save the boy's eyesight. Because they believe others could benefit from this medicine, the Farquars ask Gideon for samples of the root. Gideon feels betrayed and refuses to cooperate, leading the whites on a long hike—a wild goose chase—to "discover" a bunch of common blue flowers. After a time, the family and Gideon reconcile, yet clearly a rift remains between the African cook and his employers.

Thematic Link: *Cultural Crossroads* A man must choose between loyalty to his African heritage and his employer.

Art Note

***Conjur Woman* by Romare Bearden** Romare Bearden (1914–1988) grew up in New York City during the Harlem Renaissance, and many celebrities of that movement regularly visited his house, including Duke Ellington, Fats Waller, and Langston Hughes. Bearden specialized in collages, which are notable for the striking colors and dramatic juxtapositions of images.

Reading the Art *What images from nature do you see in the collage?*

STRATEGIC READING FOR
Less-Proficient Readers

Set a Purpose Ask volunteers to read aloud the first two paragraphs and suggest words that describe the relationship between Gideon and Teddy. Then have them read to find out how what Gideon does to make the Farquars indebted to him.

Use **UNIT FIVE RESOURCE BOOK**, p.41, for guidance in reading the selection.

WORDS TO KNOW

anecdote (ăn′ĭk-dōt) *n.* a short account of an interesting or humorous incident (p. 749)

annul (ə-nŭl′) *v.* to do away with or make invalid; cancel (p. 750)

distasteful (dĭs-tāst′fəl) *adj.* unpleasant; disagreeable (p. 749)

efficacy (ĕf′ĭ-kə-sē) *n.* the power to produce a desired effect; effectiveness (p. 747)

indifferently (ĭn-dĭf′ər-ənt-lē) *adv.* in a way showing no particular interest or concern (p. 750)

CUSTOMIZING FOR
Gifted and Talented Students

Invite students to note elements of the story that draw upon the Judeo-Christian tradition.

Literary Concept:
CHARACTERIZATION

A Ask students what these details—making "curious little toys" from plants and wetted earth—suggest about Gideon. *(Possible responses: He has a close connection with nature and the earth; he is good with his hands.)*

Critical Thinking: COMPARING/CONTRASTING

B Ask students to compare and contrast the attitudes of Gideon and Mrs. Farquar about class and race. Why does each see the situation as God's will? *(Possible response: They are both saddened by the separation of the races and are both caught in a system that they did not create. Gideon is powerless in the system so his blaming it on God's will may be more justified than Mrs. Farquar, who might be able to bring about some change in the racist order.)*

The Farquars had been childless for years when little Teddy was born; and they were touched by the pleasure of their servants, who brought presents of fowls and eggs and flowers to the homestead when they came to rejoice over the baby, exclaiming with delight over his downy golden head and his blue eyes. They congratulated Mrs. Farquar as if she had achieved a very great thing, and she felt that she had—her smile for the lingering, admiring natives was warm and grateful.

Later, when Teddy had his first haircut, Gideon the cook picked up the soft gold tufts from the ground and held them reverently in his hand. Then he smiled at the little boy and said: "Little Yellow Head." That became the native name for the child. Gideon and Teddy were great friends from the first. When Gideon had finished his work, he would lift Teddy on his shoulders to the shade of a big tree, and play with him there, forming curious little toys from twigs and leaves and grass, or shaping animals from wetted soil. When Teddy learned to walk, it was often Gideon who crouched before him, clucking encouragement, finally catching him when he fell, tossing him up in the air till they both became breathless with laughter. Mrs. Farquar was fond of the old cook because of his love for her child.

There was no second baby; and one day Gideon said: "Ah, missus, missus, the Lord above sent this one; Little Yellow Head is the most good thing we have in our house." Because of that "we" Mrs. Farquar felt a warm impulse towards her cook; and at the end of the month she raised his wages. He had been with her now for several years; he was one of the few natives who had his wife and children in the compound and never wanted to go home to his kraal,[1] which was some hundreds of miles away. Sometimes a small piccanin[2] who had been born the same time as Teddy, could be seen peering from the edge of the bush, staring in awe at the little white boy with his miraculous fair hair and Northern blue eyes. The two little children would gaze at each other with a wide, interested gaze, and once Teddy put out his hand curiously to touch the black child's cheeks and hair.

Gideon, who was watching, shook his head wonderingly, and said: "Ah, missus, these are both children, and one will grow up to be a baas,[3] and one will be a servant"; and Mrs. Farquar smiled and said sadly, "Yes, Gideon, I was thinking the same." She sighed. "It is God's

> **"Gideon, look at me!" And Gideon would laugh and say: "Very clever, Little Yellow Head."**

will," said Gideon, who was mission boy.[4] The Farquars were very religious people; and this shared feeling about God bound servant and masters even closer together.

Teddy was about six years old when he was given a scooter, and discovered the intoxications of speed. All day he would fly around the homestead, in and out of flowerbeds, scattering squawking chickens and irritated dogs, finishing with a wide dizzying arc into the kitchen door. There he would cry: "Gideon, look at me!" And Gideon would laugh and say: "Very clever, Little Yellow Head." Gideon's youngest son, who was now a herdsboy, came especially up

---

1. **kraal** (kröl): a native village in southern Africa.
2. **piccanin** (pĭk′ə-nĭn′): a native child (usually considered offensive).
3. **baas:** boss.
4. **mission boy:** a boy educated at a school run by Christian missionaries.

746 UNIT FIVE PART 2: CULTURAL CROSSROADS

from the compound to see the scooter. He was afraid to come near it, but Teddy showed off in front of him. "Piccanin," shouted Teddy, "get out of my way!" And he raced in circles around the black child until he was frightened and fled back to the bush.

"Why did you frighten him?" asked Gideon, gravely reproachful.

Teddy said defiantly: "He's only a black boy," and laughed.

Then, when Gideon turned away from him without speaking, his face fell. Very soon he slipped into the house and found an orange and brought it to Gideon, saying: "This is for you." He could not bring himself to say he was sorry; but he could not bear to lose Gideon's affection either. Gideon took the orange unwillingly and sighed. "Soon you will be going away to school, Little Yellow Head," he said wonderingly, "and then you will be grown up." He shook his head gently and said, "And that is how our lives go." He seemed to be putting a distance between himself and Teddy, not because of resentment, but in the way a person accepts something inevitable. The baby had lain in his arms and smiled up into his face: the tiny boy had swung from his shoulders and played with him by the hour. Now Gideon would not let his flesh touch the flesh of the white child. He was kind, but there was a grave formality in his voice that made Teddy pout and sulk away. Also, it made him into a man: with Gideon he was polite, and carried himself formally, and if he came into the kitchen to ask for something, it was in the way a white man uses towards a servant, expecting to be obeyed.

But on the day that Teddy came staggering into the kitchen with his fists to his eyes, shrieking with pain, Gideon dropped the pot full of hot soup that he was holding, rushed to the child, and forced aside his fingers. "A snake!" he exclaimed. Teddy had been on his scooter and had come to a rest with his foot on the side of a big tub of plants. A tree snake, hanging by its tail from the roof, had spat full into his eyes. Mrs. Farquar came running when she heard the commotion. "He'll go blind," she sobbed, holding Teddy close against her. "Gideon, he'll go blind!" Already the eyes, with perhaps half an hour's sight left in them, were swollen up to the size of fists: Teddy's small white face was distorted by great purple oozing protuberances.[5] Gideon said: "Wait a minute, missus, I'll get some medicine." He ran off into the bush.

Mrs. Farquar lifted the child into the house and bathed his eyes with permanganate.[6] She had scarcely heard Gideon's words; but when she saw that her remedies had no effect at all, and remembered how she had seen natives with no sight in their eyes because of the spitting of a snake, she began to look for the return of her cook, remembering what she heard of the efficacy of native herbs. She stood by the window, holding the terrified, sobbing little boy in her arms, and peered helplessly into the bush. It was not more than a few minutes before she saw Gideon come bounding back, and in his hand he held a plant.

"Do not be afraid, missus," said Gideon, "this will cure Little Yellow Head's eyes." He stripped the leaves from the plant, leaving a small white fleshy root. Without even washing it, he put the root in his mouth, chewed it

---

EVALUATE

D How does Teddy view Gideon?

---

5. **protuberances** (prō-tōō′bər-ən-səz): bulges or swellings.
6. **permanganate** (pər-măng′gə-nāt′): a solution of the chemical potassium permanganate, formerly used as an antidote to snake poison.

WORDS TO KNOW
efficacy (ĕf′ĭ-kə-sē) *n.* the power to produce a desired effect; effectiveness

747

Literary Concept: CONFLICT

C Ask students what conflict Teddy's comment about Gideon's son reveals. *(Possible response: Teddy, even at a young age, feels superior to all black people and believes that he can treat them any way he wants; Gideon clearly disapproves of such an attitude, but he is powerless to voice his opposition.)*

Active Reading: EVALUATE

D Invite students to suggest what the details here show about Teddy's relationship to the cook.
Think-Aloud Model *I think Teddy's inability to say he's sorry shows how he has internalized the racist views of the colonial British. On one hand, Teddy views Gideon as his inferior. On the other hand, his deep need for Gideon's affection shows that the cook is like a parent or nurturing relative to him.*

Literary Concept: CONFLICT

E Ask students how Gideon's changed attitude about touching Teddy is symptomatic of race relations in Southern Rhodesia. *(Possible response: Now that Teddy is growing up, his relationship with the cook becomes more formal, suggesting a master-servant relationship based upon the racial injustice of the society at large.)*

Literary Concept: SETTING

F Ask students how the emergency caused by the snake reveals the differences between Gideon's attitude toward the "bush" and the Farquars'. *(Possible response: Gideon obviously feels comfortable finding his way in the "bush," and he is knowledgeable of its uses. For the Farquars, the "bush" is more mysterious, perhaps even hostile, because they lack Gideon's knowledge and understanding.)*

Mini-Lesson Literary Concepts

REVIEWING CONFLICT Remind students that conflict is the struggle between opposing forces. External conflict occurs between a character and any force outside himself or herself, such as another character, society, or some force of nature. Internal conflict occurs when a character has an inner struggle within himself or herself, for example, when trying to make a decision.

Application Have students work in pairs to fill out a chart like the one shown. Each pair should try to list as many internal and external conflicts in "No Witchcraft for Sale" as possible. When students have finished their charts, they should discuss them with the entire class. You may wish to create a "master chart" on the board to synthesize the discussion.

External Conflicts	Internal Conflicts

THE LANGUAGE OF LITERATURE **TEACHER'S EDITION** 747

CUSTOMIZING FOR
Students Acquiring English

F Write the words *swelling, inflamed,* and *tender* on the board. Ask students to describe injuries or illnesses they have had that resulted in these symptoms. Then ask them to define each term.

Literary Concept:
CHARACTERIZATION

G Ask students what the "presents" and "big increase in wages" suggest about how the Farquars' treated Gideon before he saved their son's life. *(Possible response: They probably did not pay any attention to Gideon's family; it is also likely that they paid Gideon very low wages.)*

STRATEGIC READING FOR
Less-Proficient Readers

H Have students explain why the Farquars are in Gideon's debt. *(Gideon's knowledge of healing herbs saved their son's sight.)* **Summarizing**

Set a Purpose Have students read on to find out how the drug used to heal Teddy causes a conflict between the Farquars and Gideon and how the conflict is resolved.

Cultural Note

I Aboriginal groups of people all over the world are deeply connected to the land and possess knowledge of its powers. Often, the more "civilized" a culture becomes, the farther it goes away from these natural connections. Ask students to discuss examples of cultures that maintain these connections to the "ancient wisdom of leaf and soil and season," even in the modern world.

The Ukimwi Road (1994), John Harris.

vigorously, and then held the spittle there while he took the child forcibly from Mrs. Farquar. He gripped Teddy down between his knees, and pressed the balls of his thumbs into the swollen eyes, so that the child screamed and Mrs. Farquar cried out in protest: "Gideon, Gideon!" But Gideon took no notice. He knelt over the writhing child, pushing back the puffy lids till chinks of eyeball showed, and then he spat hard, again and again, into first one eye, and then the other. He finally lifted Teddy gently into his mother's arms, and said: "His eyes will get better." But Mrs. Farquar was weeping with terror, and she could hardly thank him: it was impossible to believe that Teddy could keep his sight. In a couple of hours the swellings were gone: the eyes were inflamed and tender but Teddy could see. Mr. and Mrs. Farquar went to Gideon in the kitchen and thanked him over and over again. They felt helpless because of their gratitude: it seemed they could do nothing to express it. They gave Gideon presents for his wife and children, and a big increase in wages, but these things could not pay for Teddy's now completely cured eyes. Mrs. Farquar said: "Gideon, God chose you as an instrument for His goodness," and Gideon said: "Yes, missus, God is very good."

Now, when such a thing happens on a farm, it cannot be long before everyone hears of it. Mr. and Mrs. Farquar told their neighbors and the story was discussed from one end of the district to the other. The bush is full of secrets. No one can live in Africa, or at least on the veld,[7] without learning very soon that there is an ancient wisdom of leaf and soil and season— and, too, perhaps most important of all, of the darker tracts of the human mind—which is the black man's heritage. Up and down the district

---
7. **veld** (vĕlt): an open, grass-covered plain of southern Africa.

748 UNIT FIVE PART 2: CULTURAL CROSSROADS

Mini-Lesson • The Writer's Style

CHRONOLOGICAL ORDER Point out that "No Witchcraft for Sale" is written in chronological order, with events progressing in the order in which they occur in time. Elicit that chronological order is the most common way to organize details in fiction and nonfiction. Suggest that students identify the main events of the story as a series of simple statements in a numbered list.

Application Invite students to reorder the statements on their list to retell the story in a way that does not follow strict chronological order. For example, they might begin with the arrival of the scientist, flash back to Teddy's blinding and healing, and then move forward to Gideon's refusal to cooperate. Students should discuss their reorderings of events and speculate about how such changes would affect the reader.

Reteaching/Reinforcement
- *Writing Handbook,* anthology pp. 1027–1028
- *Writing Mini-Lessons* transparencies, pp. 8–9

 **The Writer's Craft**

Chronological Order, pp. 343–344

748 THE LANGUAGE OF LITERATURE TEACHER'S EDITION

people were telling anecdotes, reminding each other of things that had happened to them.

"But I saw it myself, I tell you. It was a puff-adder bite. The kaffir's[8] arm was swollen to the elbow, like a great shiny black bladder. He was

> **The scientist explained how humanity might benefit if this new drug could be offered for sale.**

groggy after a half a minute. He was dying. Then suddenly a kaffir walked out of the bush with his hands full of green stuff. He smeared something on the place, and next day my boy was back at work, and all you could see was two small punctures in the skin."

This was the kind of tale they told. And, as always, with a certain amount of exasperation, because while all of them knew that in the bush of Africa are waiting valuable drugs locked in bark, in simple-looking leaves, in roots, it was impossible to ever get the truth about them from the natives themselves.

The story eventually reached town; and perhaps it was at a sundowner party, or some such function, that a doctor, who happened to be there, challenged it. "Nonsense," he said. "These things get exaggerated in the telling. We are always checking up on this kind of story, and we draw a blank every time."

Anyway, one morning there arrived a strange car at the homestead, and out stepped one of the workers from the laboratory in town, with cases full of test-tubes and chemicals.

Mr. and Mrs. Farquar were flustered and pleased and flattered. They asked the scientist to lunch, and they told the story all over again, for the hundredth time. Little Teddy was there too, his blue eyes sparkling with health, to prove the truth of it. The scientist explained how humanity might benefit if this new drug could be offered for sale; and the Farquars were even more pleased: they were kind, simple people, who liked to think of something good coming about because of them. But when the scientist began talking of the money that might result, their manner showed discomfort. Their feelings over the miracle (that was how they thought of it) were so strong and deep and religious, that it was distasteful to them to think of money. The scientist, seeing their faces, went back to his first point, which was the advancement of humanity. He was perhaps a trifle perfunctory: it was not the first time he had come salting the tail of[9] a fabulous bush-secret.

Eventually, when the meal was over, the Farquars called Gideon into their living-room and explained to him that this baas, here, was a big Doctor from the Big City, and he had come all that way to see Gideon. At this Gideon seemed afraid; he did not understand; and Mrs. Farquar explained quickly that it was because of the wonderful thing he had done with Teddy's eyes that the Big Baas had come.

Gideon looked from Mrs. Farquar to Mr. Farquar, and then at the little boy, who was showing great importance because of the occasion. At last he said grudgingly: "The Big

---

8. **kaffir's** (kăf′ərz): belonging to a black African (usually considered offensive).
9. **salting the tail of:** trying to capture (from the childhood belief that birds can be caught by putting salt on their tail).

WORDS TO KNOW
anecdote (ăn′ĭk-dōt′) *n.* a short account of an interesting or humorous incident
distasteful (dĭs-tāst′fəl) *adj.* unpleasant; disagreeable

749

Mini-Lesson — Grammar

MODIFIERS THAT FOLLOW VERBS Explain that both adverbs and adjectives can follow verbs. Point out the highlighted verb and modifier *said grudgingly* and elicit that *grudgingly* is an adverb that modifies the verb *said*. Next point out the highlighted *seemed afraid* and elicit that *afraid* is a predicate adjective; it follows a linking verb—*seemed*—and modifies the sentence subject—*Gideon*.

Application Have students tell whether the underlined word is an adverb or adjective.

1. Teddy said defiantly, "He's only a black boy." (adverb)

2. He could not say he was sorry. (adjective)

3. ...with Gideon he was polite, and carried himself formally. (adjective; adverb)

Reteaching/Reinforcement
- *Grammar Handbook*, anthology p. 1076
- *Grammar Mini-Lessons* copymasters p. 24, transparencies p. 22

 **The Writer's Craft**

Modifiers That Follow Verbs, pp. 738–739

THE LANGUAGE OF LITERATURE TEACHER'S EDITION **749**

Literary Concept: CONFLICT

M Ask students why Gideon is so uncomfortable at the suggestion he give the scientist the root. (*Possible response: Gideon wants to be loyal to the Farquars, but he owes more loyalty to his traditions as medicine man.*)

Critical Thinking: ANALYZING

N Ask students to analyze the two sides of the conflict here. (*The whites want Gideon's secret herbal lore; the Farquars are disappointed and annoyed by his lack of cooperation; Gideon feels that sharing his secret would be an act of betrayal.*) Have students predict what climax this conflict might reach. (*Possible responses: Gideon will make it perfectly clear that his secret is not for sale; Gideon will be forced to reveal his secrets.*)

CUSTOMIZING FOR

Students Acquiring English

2 Explain that Gideon's chewing the root and spitting the liquid into Teddy's eyes looked strange and impolite—the meaning of *uncouth*.

Critical Thinking: ANALYZING

O Ask students whether they think Gideon is trying to be convincing; what message is he sending by contradicting himself? (*Possible response: He is not trying to sound convincing. By contradicting himself, he is trying to tell them that the secret of the root is "off limits."*)

Literary Concept:
FIGURATIVE LANGUAGE

P Ask how the simile here builds tension. (*Possible response: Likening the whites to a yelping dog pack emphasizes the danger Gideon feels.*)

Baas want to know what medicine I used?" He spoke incredulously, as if he could not believe his old friends could so betray him. Mr. Farquar began explaining how a useful medicine could be made out of the root, and how it could be put on sale, and how thousands of people, black and white, up and down the continent of Africa, could be saved by the medicine when that spitting snake filled their eyes with poison. Gideon listened, his eyes bent on the ground, the skin of his forehead puckering in discomfort. When Mr. Farquar had finished he did not

> **But they went on persuading and arguing, with all the force of their exasperation.**

reply. The scientist, who all this time had been leaning back in a big chair, sipping his coffee and smiling with skeptical good-humor, chipped in and explained all over again, in different words, about the making of drugs and the progress of science. Also, he offered Gideon a present.

There was silence after this further explanation, and then Gideon remarked indifferently that he could not remember the root. His face was sullen and hostile, even when he looked at the Farquars, whom he usually treated like old friends. They were beginning to feel annoyed; and this feeling annulled the guilt that had been sprung into life by Gideon's accusing manner. They were beginning to feel that he was unreasonable. But it was at that moment that they all realized he would never give in. The magical drug would remain where it was, unknown and useless except for the tiny scattering of Africans who had the knowledge, natives who might be digging a ditch for the municipality in a ragged shirt and a pair of patched shorts, but who were still born to healing, hereditary healers, being the nephews or sons of the old witch doctors whose ugly masks and bits of bone and all the uncouth properties of magic were the outward signs of real power and wisdom.

The Farquars might tread on that plant fifty times a day as they passed from house to garden, from cow kraal[10] to mealie[11] field, but they would never know it.

But they went on persuading and arguing, with all the force of their exasperation; and Gideon continued to say that he could not remember, or that there was no such root, or that it was the wrong season of the year, or that it wasn't the root itself, but the spit from his mouth that had cured Teddy's eyes. He said all these things one after another, and seemed not to care they were contradictory. He was rude and stubborn. The Farquars could hardly recognize their gentle, lovable old servant in this ignorant, perversely obstinate[12] African, standing there in front of them with lowered eyes, his hands twitching his cook's apron, repeating over and over whichever one of the stupid refusals that first entered his head.

And suddenly he appeared to give in. He lifted his head, gave a long, blank angry look at the circle of whites, who seemed to him like a circle of yelping dogs pressing around him, and said: "I will show you the root."

They walked single file away from the homestead down a kaffir path. It was a blazing December afternoon, with the sky full of hot

---

10. **cow kraal:** a livestock enclosure or corral.
11. **mealie:** corn.
12. **perversely obstinate:** stubbornly and wrongly insistent on having one's own way.

WORDS TO KNOW
indifferently (ĭn-dĭf′ər-ənt-lē) *adv.* in a way showing no particular interest or concern
annul (ə-nŭl′) *v.* to do away with or make invalid; cancel

750

Critic's Corner

Doris Lessing's African Stories "confirm in precise and painful detail, like stitches in a wound, the abuse of the native population of Southern Rhodesia by the white settlers...."

J. M. Edelstein

Invite students to discuss whether Gideon suffered abuse at the hands of the Farquars. In what sense, if any, might Gideon be considered "wounded" by his relationship with the Farquars?

rain-clouds. Everything was hot: the sun was like a bronze tray whirling overhead, there was a heat shimmer over the fields, the soil was scorching underfoot, the dusty wind blew gritty and thick and warm in their faces. It was a terrible day, fit only for reclining on a verandah[13] with iced drinks, which is where they would normally have been at that hour.

From time to time, remembering that on the day of the snake it had taken ten minutes to find the root, someone asked: "Is it much further, Gideon?" And Gideon would answer over his shoulder, with angry politeness: "I'm looking for the root, baas." And indeed, he would frequently bend sideways and trail his hand among the grasses with a gesture that was insulting in its perfunctoriness. He walked them through the bush along unknown paths for two hours, in that melting destroying heat, so that the sweat trickled coldly down them and their heads ached. They were all quite silent: the Farquars because they were angry, the scientist because he was being proved right again; there was no such plant. His was a tactful silence.

PREDICT
Do you think Gideon will find the root?

At last, six miles from the house, Gideon suddenly decided they had had enough; or perhaps his anger evaporated at that moment. He picked up, without an attempt at looking anything but casual, a handful of blue flowers from the grass, flowers that had been growing plentifully all down the paths they had come.

He handed them to the scientist without looking at him, and marched off by himself on the way home, leaving them to follow him if they chose.

When they got back to the house, the scientist went to the kitchen to thank Gideon: he was very very polite, even though there was an amused look in his eyes. Gideon was not there. Throwing the flowers casually into the back of his car, the eminent visitor departed on his way back to his laboratory.

Gideon was back in his kitchen in time to prepare dinner, but he was sulking. He spoke to Mr. Farquar like an unwilling servant. It was days before they liked each other again.

The Farquars made inquiries about the root from their laborers. Sometimes they were answered with distrustful stares. Sometimes the natives said: "We do not know. We have never heard of the root." One, the cattle boy, who had been with them a long time, and had grown to trust them a little, said: "Ask your boy in the kitchen. Now, there's a doctor for you. He's the son of a famous medicine man who used to be in these parts, and there's nothing he cannot cure." Then he added politely: "Of course, he's not as good as the white man's doctor, we know that, but he's good for us."

After some time, when the soreness had gone from between the Farquars and Gideon, they began to joke: "When are you going to show us the snake-root, Gideon?" And he would laugh and shake his head, saying, a little uncomfortably: "But I did show you, missus, have you forgotten?"

Much later, Teddy, as a schoolboy, would come into the kitchen and say: "You old rascal, Gideon! Do you remember that time you tricked us all by making us walk miles all over the veld for nothing? It was so far my father had to carry me!"

And Gideon would double up with polite laughter. After much laughing, he would suddenly straighten himself up, wipe his old eyes, and look sadly at Teddy, who was grinning mischievously at him across the kitchen: "Ah, Little Yellow Head, how you have grown! Soon you will be grown up with a farm of your own . . ."

---

13. **verandah** (və-răn′də): a long porch.

NO WITCHCRAFT FOR SALE 751

Multicultural Perspectives

Robert Mugabe, the first leader of Zimbabwe, took great pains to prevent "white flight" from his country when it gained independence. Mugabe felt that the former colonizers of Southern Rhodesia had a right to continue living in the country if they so desired. He also wanted his country to benefit from their technical knowledge and skills. As a result of Mugabe's policy, only a small minority of the Europeans left Zimbabwe once its independence was recognized.

Literary Concept: SETTING

Q Ask students how the description of the setting contributes to an understanding of how the whites view Africa. (Possible responses: The weather and landscape seem hostile and unwelcoming; the whites seem more concerned with their own comfort than learning to adapt to a different land and climate.)

Active Reading: PREDICT

R Students will probably predict that Gideon won't find the root. The two-hour trek is just a tactic to wear out the whites.

Literary Concept: CLIMAX

S Ask students whether this climax—Gideon handing the scientist the blue flowers—surprises them. (Answers will vary. Students may feel that it was clear from the beginning that Gideon wasn't going to cooperate; others may be surprised by Gideon's refusal to give in to the whites.)

STRATEGIC READING FOR
Less-Proficient Readers

T Have students explain how the conflict was resolved. (The Farquars pressured Gideon to reveal his secret, but he refused, more loyal to his traditional role as medicine man than to his white employers. In time, both parties made a joke of the disagreement.) Summarizing

---

COMPREHENSION CHECK

1. What happens to Teddy's eyes? (A snake spits venom in them.)
2. How is Teddy saved from blindness? (Gideon presses liquid from a root into his eyes.)
3. What does Gideon give the scientist? (blue flowers, not the curing root)

From Personal Response to Critical Analysis

1. Accept all reasonable responses.
2. Possible responses: Gideon was right to refuse cooperation; he probably considered his knowledge of the healing roots a sacred trust; Gideon was wrong not to share his knowledge; because of his secret, lives will probably be lost in the future.
3. Possible responses: Yes, the Farquars seem kindhearted because they reward Gideon for saving Teddy's sight, do not wish to profit personally from the drug, and even laugh about Gideon's refusal to share his knowledge. No, the Farquars profit from an unjust society, and they treat Africans as their inferiors, which makes their "goodwill" only superficial and self-serving.
4. Possible responses: The racial misunderstanding is caused by the whites' lack of awareness of African traditions and the condescending attitudes that result from this ignorance.
5. Possible responses: A society based on racial injustice is harmful to all its members. Gideon and other black people in the story are treated as children by the whites, which violates the Africans' personal dignity and cultural traditions; the ignorance and false sense of superiority possessed by the whites is tragically passed on to the next generation.
6. Accept all reasonable, well-supported responses.

Another Pathway

Cooperative Learning Have students work in groups, deciding beforehand who will write the editorial and the letters and the different opinions each will present.

Rubric

3 Full Accomplishment The letters and editorial present varying and thoughtful viewpoints.

2 Substantial Accomplishment The letters and editorial lack variety but show that students are familiar with main issues of the story.

1 Little or Partial Accomplishment The letters and editorial suggest an incomplete grasp of the story.

RESPONDING OPTIONS

FROM PERSONAL RESPONSE TO CRITICAL ANALYSIS

REFLECT
1. Which part of this story evoked the strongest response in you? In your notebook, describe your reaction to that part of the story.

RETHINK
2. How do you feel about Gideon's refusal to share his knowledge of the medicinal plant?
Consider

Close Textual Reading
- the relationship between the whites and the blacks
- the title of the story
- the plant's effectiveness against snake poison
- what you think motivates Gideon's actions

3. The Farquars believe themselves to be people of goodwill. Do you agree? Support your opinion.
4. In your judgment, what are the causes and effects of cultural and racial misunderstanding in the story? You may find it helpful to review the chart that you made for the Personal Connection on page 744.
5. What do you think is the author's view of the characters and society that she depicts?

RELATE
Thematic Link
6. In this story, Gideon stands up for his own dignity and the dignity of his culture. Think of other instances you know of in which an individual has taken a stand to protect his or her culture. How successful do you think such actions can be in influencing people's attitudes?

ANOTHER PATHWAY

Cooperative Learning

Work to develop a newspaper editorial page focusing on the events in this story. Include an editorial presenting the paper's position on whether Gideon was right to keep his secret. Express other points of view about Gideon's decision in letters to the editor from doctors, snakebite victims, and traditional healers.

QUICKWRITES

1. Assume the identity of Doris Lessing and write an **afterword** to the story, explaining the story's theme. Also explain which characters reflect values that you support.
2. Write a **dialogue** between Gideon and his son, in which Gideon explains why he did not give the scientist the healing root.

📁 **PORTFOLIO** Save your writing. You may want to use it later as a springboard to a piece for your portfolio.

LITERARY CONCEPTS

In the plot of a story, the **climax** is the moment when the reader's interest and emotional intensity reach their highest point. This moment is also called the turning point, since it usually determines how the conflict of the story will be resolved. What would you identify as the climax of "No Witchcraft for Sale"? With a partner, create a plot diagram, marking each event as a point on a line that rises to a peak at the climax, then falls off as the conflict is resolved.

752 UNIT FIVE   PART 2: CULTURAL CROSSROADS

Literary Concepts

On their diagrams, students might note the stages of the plot. The exposition of the plot includes the opening scenes in which we meet Gideon, Teddy, and Farquars; Teddy's run-in with the snake and Gideon's healing effort are part of the rising action; the climax comes when, confronted by the Farquars and the scientist, Gideon refuses to divulge the secret that would betray his medicine man traditions; the falling action includes the final scenes in which the Farquars and the cook attempt to reestablish their relationship.

QuickWrites

1. In their afterwords, students should suggest how Lessing's view of Gideon differs from the Farquars' view. Encourage students to consistently write from Lessing's viewpoint and to identify what she would regard as the theme of the story.
2. Ask students to keep in mind that Gideon was a highly regarded medicine man among his people.

 **The Writer's Craft**

Writing Dialogue, pp. 452–455

Multimodal Learning

ALTERNATIVE ACTIVITIES

1. Prepare an **oral tale** that Gideon might tell his neighbors about his "helping" the scientist, and tell it to your classmates.
2. Create a **bar graph** in which you rate each character's power in society, with the longest bar representing the most powerful character. Then explain your ratings to the class.

ACROSS THE CURRICULUM

Health With a partner, research the medicinal properties of plants native to your part of the country. Present your findings by displaying a sample or picture of each plant along with an explanation of its medicinal use.

WORDS TO KNOW

Answer the following questions.

1. Is a **distasteful** activity one that is popular, one that is difficult, or one that is unappealing?
2. Are you most likely to react **indifferently** to a remark that angers you, that bores you, or that surprises you?
3. Is an **anecdote** a story that is amusing, that is boring, or that is instructional?
4. Would a medicine known for its **efficacy** have a reputation for working well, for being expensive, or for having side effects?
5. In an effort to **annul** the effects of an insulting remark you made, would you repeat it, add to it, or say you were kidding?

DORIS LESSING

1919–

Born to British parents in Persia (now Iran), Doris Lessing grew up in Southern Rhodesia, where her family went to farm when she was about five. Her childhood was fairly solitary, and she spent most of her time reading or walking outdoors. "The storms, the winds, the silences of the bush; the sunlit or rain-whipped mountains; fields of maize miles long; sunflowers that turned their heads after the sun; cotton plants with their butterfly-like pink and white flowers—these, and the neighbors, were my education," she reports.

Lessing left school at 14 and worked as a nursemaid and telephone operator in Salisbury, Southern Rhodesia, until she married at the age of 19. In 1949, after two failed marriages, she moved to England, which remains her place of residence. Not long afterward, Lessing published her first novel, *The Grass Is Singing* (1950), and the story collection *This Was the Old Chief's Country* (1951). These stories were based on her intimate knowledge of Southern Rhodesia, especially the problems between blacks and whites. Because of her outspoken criticism of racism and her radical political sympathies, Lessing was banned from her homeland and South Africa. Nonetheless, her works have been praised for their honest portrayal of colonial Africa and its mysterious, often harsh, natural beauty.

Another major theme in Lessing's writing is the role of women in modern society. *The Golden Notebook* (1962), an experimental novel about a woman coming to terms with her personal relationships and her role in the world, is regarded as her masterpiece.

OTHER WORKS *Going Home; African Stories; The Doris Lessing Reader; Under My Skin: Volume One of My Autobiography, to 1949*

Extended Reading

LASERLINKS
• HEALTH CONNECTION

NO WITCHCRAFT FOR SALE 753

Words to Know

1. unappealing
2. a remark that bores you
3. amusing
4. working well
5. say you were kidding

Reteaching/Reinforcement
• *Unit Five Resource Book,* p. 42

Across the Curriculum

Health Students might note that aspirin, developed from willow tree bark, was used by Native Americans.

HEALTH CONNECTION

Medicinal Plants Lessing's story suggests that certain plants have medicinal properties. These photographs show several of the most famous medicinal plants, including the purple foxglove, the yew tree, and the cinchona tree.

Side A, Frame 49641

DORIS LESSING

"Africa," Doris Lessing once commented, "gives you the knowledge that man is a small creature among other creatures, in a large landscape." By contrast, she noted that "England," where Lessing moved at age 30, "seems the ideal country to live in because it is quiet and unstimulating and leaves you in peace."

Alternative Activities

1. Students might choose to represent the events as a trickster tale in which Gideon fools the scientist and protects his culture's traditions.
2. Some students may wish to represent this information in a double-bar graph, with one bar showing a character's power in traditional African society and a second bar showing the same character's power in white colonial society.

OVERVIEW

Objectives

- To understand and appreciate a poem that explores the effects of civil war
- To identify and understand a dramatic monologue
- To express understanding of a selection through a choice of writing forms, including a dramatic monologue, extended definitions, and an essay
- To extend understanding of the selection through illustrations and recordings

Skills

LITERARY CONCEPTS
- Dramatic monologue
- Mood

THE WRITER'S STYLE
- Concrete language

SPEAKING, LISTENING, AND VIEWING
- Group discussion
- Oral presentation
- Dramatic monologue

CUSTOMIZING FOR
Students Acquiring English

- Use **ACCESS FOR STUDENTS ACQUIRING ENGLISH,** *Reading Support.*
- Invite students to examine the alphabet letters, punctuation symbols, and accent marks of the original Vietnamese version of the poem. Have students compare these linguistic symbols to symbols in English or in their native languages. If someone in the class knows Vietnamese, invite him or her to read the original aloud.
- In addition to these boxes, you may want to use the suggestions under Strategic Reading for Less-Proficient Readers.

PREVIEWING

POETRY

Thoughts of Hanoi

Nguyen Thi Vinh (nwĭn′ tē′ vĭng′) Vietnam

Activating Prior Knowledge
PERSONAL CONNECTION

Imagine finding yourself in the midst of a civil war and having to move halfway across the country to support the side that you favored. How do you think you would feel about your former home? How would you feel about your friends who were fighting for the opposite side? Discuss your ideas with classmates.

Building Background
CULTURAL CONNECTION

Like all civil wars, the war between Communist North Vietnam and anti-Communist South Vietnam pitted friend against friend, relative against relative. The situation was particularly difficult in a small country whose people had traditionally viewed themselves as one large extended family—an attitude reflected in the Vietnamese language, in which there is no word corresponding to *you*. The Vietnamese address even strangers as "Brother," "Sister," "Uncle," "Aunt," "Grandfather," and "Grandmother."

The poet Nguyen Thi Vinh was born near Hanoi, the capital of North Vietnam. Because of her anti-Communist convictions, however, she moved during the civil war to South Vietnam, where she published this poem.

Setting a Purpose
WRITING CONNECTION

In your notebook, make a simple chart like the one shown. In the first column, list images that suggest war; in the second column, list images that suggest peace. Then, as you read Nguyen Thi Vinh's poem, compare your images of war and peace with those in the poem.

War	Peace
• an exploding gun	• a peaceful lake on a summer afternoon

754 UNIT FIVE PART 2: CULTURAL CROSSROADS

PRINT AND MEDIA RESOURCES

UNIT FIVE RESOURCE BOOK
Strategic Reading: Literature, p. 45

WRITING MINI-LESSONS
Transparencies, p. 46

ACCESS FOR STUDENTS ACQUIRING ENGLISH
Reading Support

FORMAL ASSESSMENT
Selection Test, p. 149
 Test Generator

 **AUDIO LIBRARY**
See Reference Card

INTERNET RESOURCES
McDougal Littell Literature Center at http://www.hmco.com/mcdougal/lit

754 THE LANGUAGE OF LITERATURE TEACHER'S EDITION

Thoughts of Hanoi

Nguyen Thi Vinh

The night is deep and chill
as in early autumn. Pitchblack,
it thickens after each lightning flash.
I dream of Hanoi:
Co-ngu Road[1]
ten years of separation
the way back sliced by a frontier of hatred.
I want to bury the past
to burn the future
still I yearn
still I fear
those endless nights
waiting for dawn.

Brother,
how is Hang Dao[2] now?
How is Ngoc Son[3] temple?
Do the trains still run
each day from Hanoi
to the neighboring towns?
To Bac-ninh, Cam-giang, Yen-bai,[4]
the small villages, islands
of brown thatch in a lush green sea?

---

1. **Co-ngu** (kông′ōō′).
2. **Hang Dao** (häng′ dou′).
3. **Ngoc Son** (ngôk′ sôn′).
4. **Bac-ninh** (bäk′nĭn′), **Cam-giang** (käm′gē-äng′), **Yen-bai** (yĕn′bī′).

Đêm sâu thẳm, thâm u
từng cơn chớp lóe
càng tăng thêm cảnh mịt mù
hơi mưa lành lạnh
dường như trời đã sang Thu

Tôi mơ về Hà nội
tôi nhớ đường Cổ Ngư
mười năm cách biệt
ngăn lối về bằng biên giới hận thù

Anh ơi phố Hàng Đào giờ ra sao
đền Ngọc Sơn thế nào
ga Hàng Cỏ có còn
những toa tàu hỏa
hằng ngày bao chuyến đi về
qua khắp các vùng lân cận?

Bắc Ninh Cẩm Giàng, Yên Báy . . .
tôi nhớ những xóm làng nho nhỏ
chừng vài trăm mái tranh
chung quanh toàn đồng xanh

 Multicultural Perspectives

BUDDHIST INFLUENCE Although discouraged by the Communists, Buddhism has been a dominant religion and a major cultural force in Vietnam for centuries, and certain Buddhist influences are evident in the poem. For example, the Buddhist ideal of nonattachment to worldly things and emotions helps explain lines 10–11. By saying, "still I yearn / still I fear," the speaker is sadly admitting his attachment to these negative emotions. Similarly, in lines 8 and 9, the desire "to bury the past / to burn the future" speaks to the Buddhist concept that time is an illusion created by the mind.

Cultural Note

D Explain that "raven-bill scarves" are cloth scarves folded into a stiff triangular shape that resembles the bill of a raven. Such headgear is traditional for rural women in Vietnam.

Literary Concept: STYLE

E Ask students why the poet might have chosen to use so many participles in these stanzas. *(Possible response: To help express the constant motion and round of activities of village life)*

Literary Concept: IMAGERY

F Have students point out words and phrases that appeal to different senses. *(Possible responses: "Stainless blue sky"—sight; "jubilant voices"—sound; "chewing betel leaves"—taste.)*

> The girls
>   bright eyes
> 25   ruddy cheeks
>   four-piece dresses
>   raven-bill scarves
>   sowing harvesting
>   spinning weaving
> 30 all year round,
> the boys
>   ploughing
>   transplanting
>   in the fields
> 35 in their shops
>   running across
>   the meadow at evening
>   to fly kites
>   and sing alternating songs.[5]
>
> 40 Stainless blue sky,
>   jubilant voices of children
> stumbling through the alphabet,
>   village graybeards strolling to the temple,
> grandmothers basking in twilight sun,
> 45   chewing betel leaves[6]
> while the children run—

---

5. **alternating songs:** songs sung in rounds.
6. **betel** (bĕt′l) **leaves:** the leaves of the betel palm, which are wrapped around the seed of the plant and chewed like chewing gum.

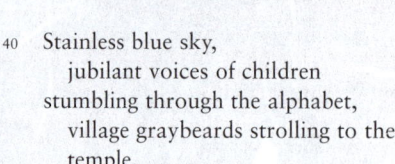

> 20 Các nàng con gái
>   mắt sáng má hồng
>   mặc áo tứ thân
>   chít khăn mỏ qua
>
>   Các chàng trai da rám, ngực đầy
> 25 đi cấy đi cày
>   làm thợ sơn thợ khảm
>   Nền trời cao trong xanh
>   tiếng trẻ reo vui nói ngọng
>   ê . . . a tập đánh vần
>
>   Các ông già tóc bạc râu dài
> 30 thong thả thăm đình thăm miếu
>   Các bà già ngồi sưởi nắng hoàng hôn
>   nhai trầu bỏm bẻm
>   mắt nhìn con trẻ thương yêu

756 UNIT FIVE PART 2: CULTURAL CROSSROADS

Mini-Lesson The Writer's Style

CONCRETE LANGUAGE Remind students that concrete words describe things that can be seen, heard, smelled, and touched, while abstract words refer to conditions, qualities, emotions, and ideas that cannot be sensed directly. Have students identify concrete phrases in the first stanza of page 756 that describe the girls. *("bright eyes," "ruddy cheeks," "four-piece dresses," "raven-bill scarves")* Discuss the benefits of using concrete language in a description.

Application Encourage students to write a description of what they would miss most about their own community if they were forced to leave it. Suggest that they use only concrete words in their descriptions.

Reteaching/ Reinforcement
- Writing Handbook, anthology pp. 1030–1032
- *Writing Mini-Lessons* transparencies, p. 46

Concrete and Abstract Language, pp. 424–425

756 THE LANGUAGE OF LITERATURE TEACHER'S EDITION

Brother,
how is all that now?
Or is it obsolete?
50 Are you like me,
reliving the past,
imagining the future?
Do you count me as a friend
or am I the enemy in your eyes?
55 Brother, I am afraid
that one day I'll be with the March-North Army[7]
meeting you on your way to the South.
I might be the one to shoot you then
or you me
60 but please
not with hatred.

7. **March-North Army:** the South Vietnamese army marching north to invade Communist North Vietnam.

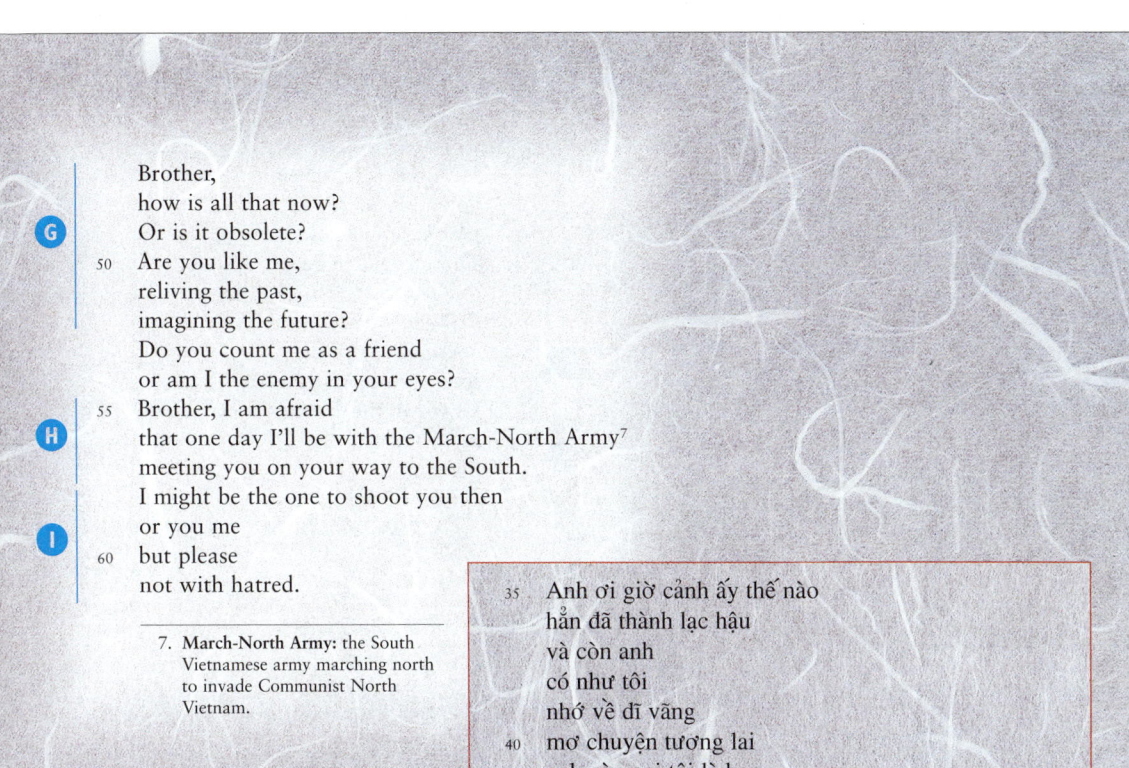

35 Anh ơi giờ cảnh ấy thế nào
hẳn đã thành lạc hậu
và còn anh
có như tôi
nhớ về dĩ vãng
40 mơ chuyện tương lai
anh còn coi tôi là bạn
hay đã chuyển thành thù

Nhớ không anh, ngày trước
hai chúng mình cùng trường, chung lớp
45 bảo nhau rằng tình bạn thâm sâu
Giờ đây Bến Hải chia đôi đất nước
gà nhà bôi mặt đá nhau
bởi các tay cá độ

Tôi sợ có ngày tôi theo đoàn quân Bắc tiến
50 anh vào xâm chiếm miền Nam
gặp nhau trên chiến trận
anh bắn tôi, tôi bắn anh
trong ánh mắt nhìn nhau thù hận!
Có thể nào như thế không anh?

Critical Thinking: SPECULATING

K In what way was the Vietnamese War about people's "material needs"? *(Possible response: Communist and free-market forces struggled over their competing visions of the best way to meet people's material needs.)* What might the speaker mean by "more than material needs"? *(Possible responses: people require peace, friendship, family ties, love for one's homeland)*

Literary Concept: DRAMATIC MONOLOGUE

L Ask how this paradoxical ending—calling the brother both friend and foe—adds to the drama of the monologue. *(It points out the speaker is torn between his patriotic duty and his love for his "brother.")*

CUSTOMIZING FOR
Gifted and Talented Students

Have students discuss how a partisan Vietnamese Communist fighting for the North might have answered the final question of the poem.

COMPREHENSION CHECK

1. To whom does the speaker address his poem? *(a "brother," a friend from childhood)*
2. What separates the speaker and this person? *(political differences that have divided Vietnam into North and South)*
3. How does the speaker feel about the village life of his youth. *(His memories are happy ones, filled with images of peace and contentment; he misses that life now.)*
4. What does the speaker seem to fear most? *(that he and his "brother" will confront each other in battle)*

For don't you remember how it was,
you and I in school together,
plotting our lives together?
65 Those roots go deep!

Brother, we are men,
conscious of more
than material needs.
How can this happen to us
70 my friend
my foe?

Translated by Nguyen Ngoc Bich

55 Ngày xưa Hà Nội hiền lành
tình người như bánh cốm xanh
   ngọt ngào
Mùa Thu hồng chín nao nao
lá sen gói thủy chung vào dậy
   hương . . .

758 UNIT FIVE PART 2: CULTURAL CROSSROADS

DESIGN NOTE

The illustrations throughout the selection present various scenes of Vietnamese life. These illustrations came from a Vietnamese greeting card.

RESPONDING OPTIONS

FROM PERSONAL RESPONSE TO CRITICAL ANALYSIS

REFLECT
1. Draw a picture to convey the feelings that this poem evoked in you. Share your drawing with a classmate and discuss your response to the poem.

RETHINK
2. How do you think the speaker feels about being a soldier in the civil war?
   Consider
   Close Textual Reading
   - his description, in the first stanza, of his current situation
   - the feelings he expresses in his memories of Hanoi
   - his fear of encountering his "brother" in battle (lines 55–61)

3. How would you describe the relationship between the speaker and the person he is addressing?
   Consider
   Close Textual Reading
   - why the speaker uses the word brother
   - the effects that the civil war has had on both men
   - the meaning of the last stanza

4. Why do you think the poet chose to create a male speaker for this poem? Explain your opinion.

5. What does the poem suggest to you about the poet's view of the civil war?

RELATE
6. Do you think that countries ever fully recover from the wounds of civil wars? Cite examples from history or current events to support your opinion.

LITERARY CONCEPTS

"Thoughts of Hanoi" is a **dramatic monologue**, the speech of a character in a dramatic situation. In a dramatic monologue, the speaker usually addresses a silent or absent listener, as if engaged in a private conversation. Practice reading this poem aloud as if you were the Vietnamese soldier who is the speaker. Then perform your dramatic reading for the rest of the class.

ANOTHER PATHWAY

With a partner, rewrite this poem as a letter from the speaker to a friend in the north. Try to express the speaker's feelings about the war and about the contrast between his current situation and his memories of his past. Add details as needed to make your letter sound authentic. Then read the letter to your class.

QUICKWRITES

1. Write your own **dramatic monologue** about civil war. Use ideas prompted by your reading of the poem or by your work for the Personal Connection and the Writing Connection on page 754.

2. Write **extended definitions** of the words *war* and *peace* that reflect the speaker's views of the subjects. If your views are different from the speaker's, also write your own definitions of the two terms.

3. Draft an **essay** in which you compare the feelings expressed in this poem with those expressed in Tim O'Brien's "On the Rainy River" (page 266) or in the excerpt from Le Ly Hayslip's *When Heaven and Earth Changed Places* (page 140).

📁 **PORTFOLIO** *Save your writing. You may want to use it later as a springboard to a piece for your portfolio.*

THOUGHTS OF HANOI **759**

From Personal Response to Critical Analysis

1. Accept all reasonable responses.
2. Possible responses: The speaker is dismayed to be caught in a war that destroys his country and his people; though the speaker does not approve of war, he still seems to support the South Vietnamese cause.
3. Possible responses: The speaker feels tenderness and closeness for the person he addresses; the speaker seems convinced that the enmity caused by war cannot change the friendship.
4. Accept all reasonable, well-supported responses.
5. Possible responses: The poet seems convinced that the common roots of the Vietnamese people, symbolized by the land and village life, go much deeper than the causes of the war; she is afraid of all that might be lost because of the war, including such intangibles as friendship and love.
6. Accept all reasonable, well-supported responses.

Another Pathway

Suggest that the ideas and details in each paragraph of the letter correspond to the content of each stanza in the poem. Remind students that a personal letter should be informal in tone.

Rubric

3 Full Accomplishment Students' letter insightfully expresses the speaker's feelings and makes use of convincing details.

2 Substantial Accomplishment Students' letter adequately reproduces the speaker's feelings, but more details are needed.

1 Little or Partial Accomplishment Students' letter does not adequately capture the speaker's feelings or present details.

Literary Concepts

Remind students that reading poetry aloud offers them an opportunity to express their feelings about a poem and their understanding of it. Encourage them to use their voice, facial expressions, and gestures to interpret the poem.

QuickWrites

1. Like Nguyen Thi Vinh, students might choose to address their monologues to a person on the other side of the conflict.
2. Encourage students to draw upon their Writing Connection notes as they develop their extended definitions.
3. Have all students who choose this option discuss the two selections. Then have students work individually on their essays.

The Writer's Craft

Monologue, pp. 108–112
Definition, pp. 134–137
Comparison and Contrast, pp. 118–132

THE LANGUAGE OF LITERATURE TEACHER'S EDITION **759**

Literary Links

Like the speaker of this poem who feels separated from his brother countryman, the main character in Hwang Sunwŏn's "Cranes" has also seen the struggle against Communism divide his country—Korea—and separate him from his boyhood friend.

Critic's Corner

Possible responses: In the first stanza, the speaker sincerely admits his fears and longing. His simple, glowing account of life in pre-war Vietnam also suggest his sincerity. The questions in the final stanzas, such as "Do you count me as a friend," also express an honest openness.

Across the Curriculum

History Suggest that students start with the encyclopedia. They might also interview any people they know who had direct experience of the war, either in the armed forces or as a civilian.

NGUYEN THI VINH

As a young woman, Nguyen Thi Vinh was active in the struggle against the French colonizers of Vietnam; however, she and her husband, a well-known revolutionary, were not Communists and so left Hanoi when Ho Chi Minh came to power there. Many of Nguyen Thi Vinh's short stories are set during the early years of the Indochinese War and present characters struggling to survive and maintain their traditional way of life amid civil war.

ALTERNATIVE ACTIVITIES

1. Create two **illustrations** for this poem, one representing the speaker's current situation and one showing his recollection of a past event. Your illustrations should convey the contrasting moods of the two experiences.

2. Find **recordings** of songs about the American Civil War and share them with the class. In a discussion, compare the feelings expressed in the American songs with the feelings conveyed in this poem.

ACROSS THE CURRICULUM

History Research the aftermath of the war in Vietnam. What steps were taken to rebuild the country? How were members of the defeated army treated? What has life in Vietnam been like since the war? Share your findings in an oral report.

LITERARY LINKS

What does the speaker of this poem have in common with the main character in Hwang Sunwŏn's story "Cranes" (page 33)?

CRITIC'S CORNER

Nguyen Ngoc Bich, who translated this poem into English, has said that Nguyen Thi Vinh's "sincerity shines right through her work." Cite details from the poem that support this statement.

NGUYEN THI VINH

Born into a middle-class family in northern Vietnam, Nguyen Thi Vinh (1924–) spent most of her childhood in the city of Hanoi. Her first husband was a well-known activist in the Vietnamese nationalist movement seeking to free the country from French control, but neither he nor Nguyen Thi Vinh supported the Communists. After World War II, when the Communists began taking over the North, the couple fled to Hong Kong.

In 1952, Nguyen Thi Vinh settled in Saigon (now Ho Chi Minh City), then the capital of South Vietnam. She began contributing stories to magazines and in 1953 published her first story collection, *Two Sisters*. From 1954 until the fall of South Vietnam two decades later, she published several works of fiction as well as a collection of poetry. She also helped found the literary magazine *Tan Phong* ("New Wind"), which specialized in works by women, and later edited another magazine, *Dong Phuong* ("The East").

Like other South Vietnamese, Nguyen Thi Vinh suffered great hardship after South Vietnam surrendered to the North Vietnamese in 1975. Nine years later, she escaped in a small boat with family members and others. They were rescued in the South China Sea by a Norwegian fishing vessel, and she now lives in Norway, where she has resumed her writing career. Her most recent story collection, *Norway and I* (1994), appeared in both Vietnamese and Norwegian editions.

Alternative Activities

1. To prompt ideas, encourage students to find news photos of Vietnam taken during the years of American involvement there that express the suffering and destruction that occurred. Also have them contrast these photos with rural scenes of traditional Vietnamese village life.

2. If possible, have students write out the lyrics to the songs and reproduce them for the entire class. Then students can refer to the lyrics in their discussion of the feelings conveyed.

PREVIEWING

FICTION

The Son from America
Isaac Bashevis Singer Poland / United States

Activating Prior Knowledge
PERSONAL CONNECTION
What kinds of changes do you think people who immigrate to the United States go through as they adapt to a new way of life? How might their departure from their native lands affect the family and friends they leave behind? In a small-group discussion, explore the answers to these questions, sharing personal experiences of immigration if possible.

Building Background
HISTORICAL/CULTURAL CONNECTION
Millions of eastern European Jews immigrated to the United States near the beginning of the 20th century, often fleeing religious persecution or seeking a better way of life. Life in America at the time bore little resemblance to the life these immigrants had left behind. In the "old country"—particularly in rural villages—change occurred slowly, if at all, and people lived simply, as their ancestors before them had lived. In the United States, however, change was occurring at a rapid pace as economic and urban development transformed the nation and its people.

To meet the challenge of living in a new country, immigrants learned English, found jobs, and often became assimilated, or absorbed, into mainstream American culture. In order to fit in, some abandoned the cultural and religious traditions that had formerly shaped their lives. However, as they adapted to their newfound freedom and relative prosperity, most tried to maintain the feeling of community they had left behind. Typically, they settled among other Jews from the same towns or regions in eastern Europe. They also formed social groups, or societies, that raised money to help support those still living in their native villages.

Active Reading / Setting a Purpose
READING CONNECTION
Making Predictions In this story, a man who emigrated to the United States returns to the Polish village of his youth to visit his aging parents. In your notebook, make a prediction about what will happen during his visit. As you read, compare your prediction with the events of the story.

An Eastern European village during the 1930s. Sovfoto.

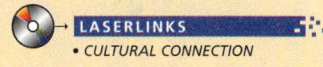
• CULTURAL CONNECTION
761

OVERVIEW

Objectives
- To understand and appreciate a short story that explores a man's return to his native Jewish village in Poland
- To identify and understand situational irony
- To express understanding of the story through a choice of writing forms, including a newsletter article, a review, and character sketches
- To extend understanding of the selection through a variety of multimodal and cross-curricular activities

Skills

LITERARY CONCEPTS
- Situational irony
- Voice

READING SKILLS/STRATEGIES
- Making predictions

THE WRITER'S STYLE
- Ending with a resolution

GRAMMAR
- Appositives

SPEAKING, LISTENING, AND VIEWING
- Group discussion
- Oral presentation

 CULTURAL CONNECTION
Village Life in Poland Singer's short story is set in a small rural hamlet in Poland. These photographs show scenes from Polish villages that are similar to Lentshin, the village in the story. The images will help students picture the setting of "The Son from America."

Side A, Frame 49646

CUSTOMIZING FOR
Students Acquiring English
- Use **ACCESS FOR STUDENTS ACQUIRING ENGLISH,** *Reading Support.*
- Discuss with students some ways in which their view of the world is different from their parents'. Explain that this story shows the contrasting views of a man who immigrated to the United States and his parents who stayed behind in Poland.
- In addition to these boxes, you may want to use the suggestions under Strategic Reading for Less-Proficient Readers.

PRINT AND MEDIA RESOURCES

UNIT FIVE RESOURCE BOOK
Strategic Reading: Literature, p. 49

GRAMMAR MINI-LESSONS
Copymasters, p. 42

ACCESS FOR STUDENTS ACQUIRING ENGLISH
Selection Summaries
Reading Support

FORMAL ASSESSMENT
Selection Test, p. 151
 Test Generator

 AUDIO LIBRARY
See Reference Card

 **LASERLINKS**
 Cultural Connection
Storyteller

THE LANGUAGE OF LITERATURE TEACHER'S EDITION **761**

The Son from America

Isaac Bashevis Singer

The village of Lentshin was tiny—a sandy marketplace where the peasants of the area met once a week. It was surrounded by little huts with thatched roofs or shingles green with moss. The chimneys looked like pots. Between the huts there were fields, where the owners planted vegetables or pastured their goats.

In the smallest of these huts lived old Berl, a man in his eighties, and his wife, who was called Berlcha (wife of Berl). Old Berl was one of the Jews who had been driven from their villages in Russia and had settled in Poland. In Lentshin, they mocked the mistakes he made while praying aloud. He spoke with a sharp "r." He was short, broad-shouldered, and had a small white beard, and summer and winter he wore a sheepskin hat, a padded cotton jacket, and stout boots. He walked slowly, shuffling his feet. He had a half acre of field, a cow, a goat, and chickens.

The couple had a son, Samuel, who had gone to America forty years ago. It was said in Lentshin that he became a millionaire there. Every month, the Lentshin letter carrier brought old Berl a money order and a letter that no one could read because many of the words were English. How much money Samuel sent his parents remained a secret. Three times a year, Berl and his wife went on foot to Zakroczym[1] and cashed the money orders there. But they never seemed to use the money. What for? The garden, the

---
1. **Zakroczym** (zä-krô′chəm).

The Grey House (1917), Marc Chagall. Thyssen-Bornemisza Museum, Madrid, Spain, Nimatallah/Art Resource, New York. Copyright © 1996 Artists Rights Society (ARS), New York/ADAGP, Paris.

Art Note

The Grey House by Marc Chagall Marc Chagall (1889–1985), a Russian painter, was influenced by a number of movements in modern art, including surrealism. But many of his subjects were drawn from the Jewish village life and folklore of his boyhood. This 1917 painting of Chagall's native town Vitebsk contrasts the towers of the gracious town center with a simple and ramshackle hut.

Reading the Art *Would you consider this painting to be realistic or abstract? Use details from the painting to support your opinion.*

CUSTOMIZING FOR
Gifted and Talented Students

As students read the story, have them think about how the faith rituals of Judaism define life for Berl and Berlcha.

Possible responses:

- Page 764— "Only for the Sabbath would Berlcha buy three tallow candles..." / The Sabbath and holy days are the only special times in their lives.

- Page 764— "But since the [Talmud] teacher said so, it must be true..." / The couple have utter confidence in their rabbi and faith.

- Page 767— "On what? Thank God we have everything" / Although they seem poverty-stricken to us, the couple is totally content and grateful to God.

THE LANGUAGE OF LITERATURE **TEACHER'S EDITION** **763**

Literary Concept: SITUATIONAL IRONY

C Ask students why it's ironic that Berl doesn't use the money Samuel sends. *(Possible responses: Normally, poor people want and use any money they get from well-off relatives or charity; we can imagine countless ways for Berl to use the money.)*

Literary Concept: CHARACTERIZATION

D Ask students what these details about their hut tell us about Berl and Berlcha. *(Possible responses: They are very simple people; they live close to the earth; they have few possessions and no pretensions.)*

Critical Thinking: MAKING JUDGMENTS

E Ask students whether Berl and Berlcha seem happy with the way they live. *(Possible response: They seem very content, living in harmony with nature and their age-old traditions.)*

Critical Thinking: ANALYZING

F Have students suggest why so many young have men left Lentshin. *(Possible response: They wanted opportunity and excitement; they were not satisfied with traditional life; they needed work.)*

C cow, and the goat provided most of their needs. Besides, Berlcha sold chickens and eggs, and from these there was enough to buy flour for bread.

No one cared to know where Berl kept the money that his son sent him. There were no thieves in Lentshin. The hut consisted of one room, which contained all their belongings: the table, the shelf for meat, the shelf for milk foods, the two beds, and the clay oven. Sometimes the chickens roosted in the woodshed and sometimes, when it was cold, in a coop near the oven. The goat, too, found shelter inside when the weather was bad. The more prosperous villagers had kerosene lamps, but Berl and his wife did not believe in newfangled gadgets. What was wrong with a wick in a dish of oil? Only for the Sabbath[2] would Berlcha buy three tallow candles at the store. In summer, the couple got up at sunrise and retired with the chickens. In the long winter evenings, Berlcha spun flax at her spinning wheel, and Berl sat beside her in the silence of those who enjoy their rest.

Once in a while when Berl came home from the synagogue after evening prayers, he brought news to his wife. In Warsaw there were strikers who demanded that the czar abdicate. A heretic by the name of Dr. Herzl[3] had come up with the idea that Jews should settle again in Palestine. Berlcha listened and shook her bonneted head. Her face was yellowish and wrinkled like a cabbage leaf. There were bluish sacks under her eyes. She was half deaf. Berl had to repeat each word he said to her. She would say, "The things that happen in the big cities!"

Here in Lentshin nothing happened except usual events: a cow gave birth to a calf, a young couple had a circumcision party,[4] or a girl was born and there was no party. Occasionally, someone died. Lentshin had no cemetery, and the corpse had to be taken to Zakroczym. Actually, Lentshin had become a village with few young people. The young men left for Zakroczym, for Nowy Dwor, for Warsaw, and sometimes for the United States. Like Samuel's, their letters were illegible, the Yiddish[5] mixed with the languages of the countries where they were now living. They sent photographs in which the men wore top hats and the women fancy dresses like squiresses.[6]

Berl and Berlcha also received such photographs. But their eyes were failing, and neither he nor she had glasses. They could barely make out the pictures. Samuel had sons and daughters with Gentile[7] names—and grandchildren who had married and had their own offspring. Their names were so strange that Berl and Berlcha could never remember them. But what difference do names make? America was far, far away on the other side of the ocean, at the edge of the world. A Talmud[8] teacher who came to Lentshin had said that Americans walked with their heads down and their feet up. Berl and Berlcha could not grasp this. How was it possible? But since the teacher said so, it must be true. Berlcha pondered for some time, and then she said, "One can get accustomed to everything."

---

2. **the Sabbath:** a weekly day of rest and worship for Jews, beginning at sundown Friday and ending at sundown Saturday.
3. **Dr. Herzl** (hĕrt′səl): Theodor Herzl, an Austrian writer and journalist who, in response to anti-Jewish feeling in Europe in the late 1800s, called for the establishment of a Jewish state.
4. **circumcision party:** a party following the Jewish ceremony called *brith milah* (brĭt′ mē-lä′), in which a baby boy is circumcised and given a Hebrew name on the eighth day after birth.
5. **Yiddish:** a language—containing elements of German, Hebrew, and several other languages—spoken by Jews in central and eastern Europe and by their descendants in other countries.
6. **squiresses:** wives of country gentlemen (squires).
7. **Gentile** (jĕn′tīl′): not Jewish (usually applied to people and things Christian).
8. **Talmud** (täl′mŏŏd): the writings that are the basis of Jewish civil and religious law.

764   UNIT FIVE   PART 2: CULTURAL CROSSROADS

Mini-Lesson  Literary Concepts

REVIEWING VOICE Remind students that just as people's speaking voices differ, so do their writing voices. A writer's voice is the identity that he or she reveals through his or her writing style. Point out that some writers, such as Ernest Hemingway, Virginia Woolf, and William Faulkner, have such distinctive voices that their writing can be easily recognized.

Application Have students think about Isaac Bashevis Singer's voice in "The Son from America." What identity does he reveal? Point out that his voice is that of a person who is very much at home in the 19th-century world of Eastern European Jewry. For example, have them find sympathetic portrayals of synagogue worshippers on pages 766 and 767. Also have them cite examples that show Singer's sympathies for village life, its traditions, and faith.

And so it remained. From too much thinking—God forbid—one may lose one's wits.

One Friday morning, when Berlcha was kneading the dough for the Sabbath loaves, the door opened and a nobleman entered. He was so tall that he had to bend down to get through the door. He wore a beaver hat and a cloak bordered with fur. He was followed by Chazkel, the coachman from Zakroczym, who carried two leather valises with brass locks. In astonishment Berlcha raised her eyes.

The nobleman looked around and said to the coachman in Yiddish, "Here it is." He took out a silver ruble and paid him. The coachman tried to hand him change, but he said, "You can go now."

When the coachman closed the door, the nobleman said, "Mother, it's me, your son Samuel—Sam."

Berlcha heard the words and her legs grew numb. Her hands, to which pieces of dough were sticking, lost their power. The nobleman hugged her, kissed her forehead, both her cheeks. Berlcha began to cackle like a hen, "My son!" At that moment Berl came in from the woodshed, his arms piled with logs. The goat followed him. When he saw a nobleman kissing his wife, Berl dropped the wood and exclaimed, "What is this?"

The nobleman let go of Berlcha and embraced Berl. "Father!"

For a long time Berl was unable to utter a sound. He wanted to recite holy words that he had read in the Yiddish Bible, but he could remember nothing. Then he asked, "Are you Samuel?"

"Yes, Father, I am Samuel."

"Well, peace be with you." Berl grasped his son's hand. He was still not sure that he was not being fooled. Samuel wasn't as tall and heavy as this man, but then Berl reminded himself that Samuel was only fifteen years old when he had left home. He must have grown in that faraway country. Berl asked, "Why didn't you let us know that you were coming?"

"Didn't you receive my cable?" Samuel asked.

Berl did not know what a cable was.

Berlcha had scraped the dough from her hands and enfolded her son. He kissed her again and asked, "Mother, didn't you receive a cable?"

"What? If I lived to see this, I am happy to die," Berlcha said, amazed by her own words. Berl, too, was amazed. These were just the words he would have said earlier if he had been able to remember. After a while Berl came to himself and said, "Pescha, you will have to make a double Sabbath pudding in addition to the stew."

It was years since Berl had called Berlcha by her given name. When he wanted to address her, he would say, "Listen," or "Say." It is the young or those from the big cities who call a wife by her name. Only now did Berlcha begin to cry. Yellow tears ran from her eyes, and everything became dim. Then she called out, "It's Friday—I have to prepare for the Sabbath." Yes, she had to knead the dough and braid the loaves. With such a guest, she had to make a larger Sabbath stew. The winter day is short, and she must hurry.

THE SON FROM AMERICA 765

Mini-Lesson Grammar

APPOSITIVES Remind students that an appositive is a noun or pronoun that usually follows another noun or pronoun and identifies or explains it. As an example, point out the highlighted word "Samuel" on page 762. Explain that an appositive phrase consists of an appositive and its modifiers and draw their attention to the highlighted example on page 765—"the coachman from Zakroczym."

Application Have students combine each set of sentences using an appositive or appositive phrase.
1. Samuel visited his parents' village. It was Lentshin.
2. Berlcha made a special Sabbath meal. It was tasty gefilte fish and chicken soup.
3. Samuel belonged to an organization in New York that wanted to help the people. The organization was called the Lentshin Society.

Reteaching/Reinforcement
- Grammar Mini-Lessons copymasters, p. 42

 **The Writer's Craft**
Appositives and Appositive Phrases, pp. 589–590

Art Note

Le juif en vert [Jew in green] by Marc Chagall For Chagall, rabbis were quasi-mythical figures, and he often used them as subjects for his paintings. The rabbis themselves, however, were sometimes offended by Chagall's attempts to paint them because religious strictures forbid such representation. Chagall painted this rabbi from the village of Slousk as he slept.

Reading the Art What feelings do you think are conveyed by this painting. Use details from the painting to support your opinion.

Literary Concept: CHARACTERIZATION

K Ask students what this detail tells us about Samuel. (Possible response: Despite his wealth and status, he is still kind and open.)

Literary Concept: VOICE

L Ask students what Berl's comment reveals about Singer's attitudes toward the world. (Possible response: Although seemingly obvious, this statement paradoxically suggests a profound acceptance of and resignation to things as they are; traditions seem to be the crucial, defining factor in human behavior.)

Le juif en vert [Jew in green] (1914), Marc Chagall. Oil on cardboard 38 ¼" × 30 ¼", private collection, Geneva, Switzerland. Copyright © 1996 Artists Rights Society (ARS), New York/ADAGP, Paris.

Kaddish[9] for me." She wept raspingly. Her strength left her, and she slumped onto the bed.

Berl said, "Women will always be women." And he went to the shed to get more wood. The goat sat down near the oven; she gazed with surprise at this strange man—his height and his bizarre clothes.

The neighbors had heard the good news that Berl's son had arrived from America, and they came to greet him. The women began to help Berlcha prepare for the Sabbath. Some laughed; some cried. The room was full of people, as at a wedding. They asked Berl's son, "What is new in America?"

And Berl's son answered, "America is all right."

"Do Jews make a living?"

"One eats white bread there on weekdays."

"Do they remain Jews?"

"I am not a Gentile."

After Berlcha blessed the candles, father and son went to the little synagogue across the street. A new snow had fallen. The son took large steps, but Berl warned him, "Slow down."

In the synagogue the Jews recited "Let Us Exult" and "Come, My Groom." All the time, the snow outside kept falling. After prayers, when Berl and Samuel left the Holy Place, the village was unrecognizable. Everything was covered in snow. One could see only the contours

Her son understood what was worrying her, because he said, "Mother, I will help you."

Berlcha wanted to laugh, but a choked sob came out. "What are you saying? God forbid."

The nobleman took off his cloak and jacket and remained in his vest, on which hung a solid-gold watch chain. He rolled up his sleeves and came to the trough. "Mother, I was a baker for many years in New York," he said, and he began to knead the dough.

"What! You are my darling son who will say

---

9. **Kaddish** (kä′dĭsh): a Jewish prayer recited by mourners after the death of a close relative.

of the roofs and the candles in the windows. Samuel said, "Nothing has changed here."

Berlcha had prepared gefilte fish,[10] chicken soup with rice, meat, carrot stew. Berl recited the benediction over a glass of ritual wine. The family ate and drank, and when it grew quiet for a while, one could hear the chirping of the house cricket. The son talked a lot, but Berl and Berlcha understood little. His Yiddish was different and contained foreign words.

After the final blessing Samuel asked, "Father, what did you do with all the money I sent you?"

Berl raised his white brows. "It's here."

"Didn't you put it in a bank?"

"There is no bank in Lentshin."

"Where do you keep it?"

Berl hesitated. "One is not allowed to touch money on the Sabbath, but I will show you." He crouched beside the bed and began to shove something heavy. A boot appeared. Its top was stuffed with straw. Berl removed the straw, and the son saw that the boot was full of gold coins. He lifted it.

"Father, this is a treasure!" he called out.

"Well."

"Why didn't you spend it?"

"On what? Thank God, we have everything."

"Why didn't you travel somewhere?"

"Where to? This is our home."

The son asked one question after the other, but Berl's answer was always the same: they wanted for nothing. The garden, the cow, the goat, the chickens provided them with all they needed. The son said, "If thieves knew about this, your lives wouldn't be safe."

"There are no thieves here."

"What will happen to the money?"

"You take it."

Slowly, Berl and Berlcha grew accustomed to their son and his American Yiddish. Berlcha could hear him better now. She even recognized his voice. He was saying, "Perhaps we should build a larger synagogue."

"The synagogue is big enough," Berl replied.

"Perhaps a home for old people."

"No one sleeps in the street."

The next day after the Sabbath meal was eaten, a Gentile from Zakroczym brought a paper—it was the cable. Berl and Berlcha lay down for a nap. They soon began to snore. The goat, too, dozed off. The son put on his cloak and his hat and went for a walk. He strode with his long legs across the marketplace. He stretched out a hand and touched a roof. He wanted to smoke a cigar, but he remembered it was forbidden on the Sabbath. He had a desire to talk to someone, but it seemed that the whole of Lentshin was asleep. He entered the synagogue. An old man was sitting there, reciting psalms. Samuel asked, "Are you praying?"

"What else is there to do when one gets old?"

"Do you make a living?"

The old man did not understand the meaning of these words. He smiled, showing his empty gums, and then he said, "If God gives health, one keeps on living."

Samuel returned home. Dusk had fallen. Berl went to the synagogue for the evening prayers, and the son remained with his mother. The room was filled with shadows.

Berlcha began to recite in a solemn singsong, "God of Abraham, Isaac, and Jacob, defend the

---

10. **gefilte** (gə-fĭl′tə) **fish:** a traditional Jewish food made from finely chopped fish.

THE SON FROM AMERICA 767

Mini-Lesson  The Writer's Style

ENDING WITH A RESOLUTION Remind students that a writer often ends a story by showing how the main conflict is resolved and answering any remaining questions the reader may have. This technique is called resolution. Ask students to discuss what is resolved by the ending of this story. *(Samuel realizes that his plans for gift-giving are inappropriate for his parents and their village; he realizes that their religion gives them more than can be purchased by his money; Samuel learns to appreciate the traditional world that he left and to realize the shortcomings of the modern pursuit of wealth and possessions.)*

Application Invite the students to write a scene or two to continue the story and expand the resolution. Will Samuel return to New York and his familiar way of life? Or will his insights in Lentshin change him in a lasting way?

Reteaching/Reinforcement
- Writing Handbook, anthology pp. 1034–1035

📁 **The Writer's Craft**
Conclusions for Narratives, pp. 388–389

Literary Concept: SETTING

M Ask students what Samuel's statement—"Nothing has changed here"—suggests to them about Lentshin. *(Possible response: Lentshin seems to exist in a dimension outside time, unaffected by outside events.)*

Literary Concept: SITUATIONAL IRONY

N Have students explain why Berl's offering the money back to Samuel is humorous. *(Possible response: That someone so poor as Berl would have no use for money and even offer it back to rich Samuel is totally unexpected.)*

Critical Thinking: ANALYZING

O Ask students why Berl and Berlcha believe that the village has no use for Samuel's money. *(Possible responses: Their religious faith and traditional ways have fostered a deep contentment; in this village, everyone in need is taken care of by the community.)*

Literary Concept: VOICE

P Ask students what the old man's inability to understand the phrase "Do you make a living?" and his simple comment about God might reveal about the author's attitudes. *(Possible response: Singer's world view is religious, not economic; he is intrigued by people whose entire lives are defined by their traditions of faith.)*

DESIGN NOTE

These coins are Russian rubles from 1886–1890; two of the coins show Nicholas II (1868–1918), the last czar of Russia.

poor people of Israel and Thy name. The Holy Sabbath is departing; the welcome week is coming to us. Let it be one of health, wealth, and good deeds."

"Mother, you don't need to pray for wealth," Samuel said. "You are wealthy already."

Berlcha did not hear—or pretended not to. Her face had turned into a cluster of shadows.

In the twilight Samuel put his hand into his jacket pocket and touched his passport, his checkbook, his letters of credit. He had come here with big plans. He had a valise filled with presents for his parents. He wanted to bestow gifts on the village. He brought not only his own money but funds from the Lentshin Society in New York, which had organized a ball for the benefit of the village. But this village in the hinterland needed nothing. From the synagogue one could hear hoarse chanting. The cricket, silent all day, started again its chirping. Berlcha began to sway and utter holy rhymes inherited from mothers and grandmothers:

*Thy holy sheep
In mercy keep,
In Torah and good deeds;
Provide for all their needs,
Shoes, clothes, and bread
And the Messiah's tread.* ❖

Translated by the author and Dorothea Straus

INSIGHT

GRUDNOW
LINDA PASTAN

When he spoke of where he
   came from,
my grandfather could have been
clearing his throat
of that name, that town
5 sometimes Poland, sometimes Russia,
the borders penciled in
with a hand as shaky as his.
He left, I heard him say,
because there was nothing there.

10 I understood what he meant
when I saw the photograph
of his people standing
against a landscape emptied
of crops and trees, scraped raw
15 by winter. Everything
was in sepia, as if the brown earth
had stained the faces,
stained even the air.

I would have died there, I think
20 in childhood maybe
of some fever,
my face pressed for warmth
against a cow with flanks
like those of the great-aunts
25 in the picture. Or later
I would have died of history
like the others, who dug
their stubborn heels into that earth,
heels as hard as the heels
30 of the bread my grandfather tore
from the loaf at supper. He always
sipped his tea through a cube of sugar
clenched in his teeth, the way
he sipped his life here, noisily,
35 through all he remembered
that might have been sweet in
   Grudnow.

INSIGHT

1. Why do you think the grandfather left Grudnow? *(Possible responses: He says "there was nothing there"; he may have been searching for a better life in America.)*
2. What do you think the speaker means in line 24 when she says "she would have died of history"? *(Possible response: Like millions of other Polish and Russian Jews, she might have been a victim of the pogroms or of the Holocaust.)*

LINDA PASTAN

Linda Pastan (1932–) was born in New York City and graduated from Radcliffe College. During the 1950s and 1960s, Pastan postponed her desire to write to focus on raising a family, and the tension between the roles of wife and mother and poet remains a theme in her work. Pastan has published over ten collections of poetry and is a lecturer at the Breadloaf Writer's Conference in Vermont.

RESPONDING OPTIONS

FROM PERSONAL RESPONSE TO CRITICAL ANALYSIS

REFLECT
1. How close was the prediction you made for the Reading Connection on page 761 to what actually happened in the story? Share your thoughts with a classmate.

RETHINK
2. What are your impressions of Berl and Berlcha?

Close Textual Reading

   Consider
   - the description of their home and their community
   - their understanding of what's going on in the world
   - their reasons for not spending the money their son has sent
   - the role of tradition and religion in their life

3. What are your impressions of their son, Samuel?

Close Textual Reading

   Consider
   - why he returns to Lentshin
   - how he has adapted to life in his new country
   - how he reacts to his parents' life

Thematic Link

4. What do you think are the advantages and the disadvantages of life in Lentshin, and how do these compare with the advantages and the disadvantages of life in America? Cite details from the story in explaining your response.

5. How would you explain what Samuel has realized by the end of the story?

RELATE
6. Would you say that the grandfather in the Insight poem "Grudnow" has more in common with Samuel or with Samuel's parents? Why?

7. Do aspects of life in Lentshin exist anywhere in the United States today? Cite details from the story as you share your opinion with classmates.

ANOTHER PATHWAY
Cooperative Learning
Get together with classmates and compare Samuel's values and attitudes with those of his parents. First, create a list of categories, such as "attitude toward money" and "attitude toward life," to use in making your comparisons. Then organize your ideas in a comparison-and-contrast chart.

QUICKWRITES

1. Imagine that you are Samuel. Write a **newsletter article** for the Lentshin Society, describing your trip to Lentshin, Poland. Be sure to explain why you have returned to New York with the money that the society has raised for the village.

2. Write a **review** of this story, providing a brief summary of the story and discussing your opinion of Singer's merits as a writer.

3. Write **character sketches** of Berl and Berlcha. Use quotations from the story to help you describe the characters' appearance and show how they live and relate to each other.

📁 **PORTFOLIO** *Save your writing. You may want to use it later as a springboard to a piece for your portfolio.*

THE SON FROM AMERICA 769

From Personal Response to Critical Analysis

1. Accept all reasonable responses.
2. Possible response: While Berl and Berlcha are simple peasants with little education or knowledge of the world, they have a religious world view that provides them with deep contentment.
3. Possible response: Samuel is a well-meaning and kind son who genuinely wants to help his parents and their village; although he does not have their traditional religious views, he respects their faith and way of life.
4. Accept all reasonable, well-supported responses.
5. Accept all reasonable, well-supported responses.
6. Possible response: The grandfather is more like Samuel; both left their native villages in Poland to go to America in search of opportunity and wealth; both were somewhat dissatisfied.
7. Accept all reasonable, well-supported responses.

Another Pathway
Cooperative Learning Assign one student in each group to create a list of categories for comparison. A second student can then go back through the story finding evidence about the characters' attitudes for each category. A third student can then create the chart.

Rubric
3 Full Accomplishment Charts contain a number of categories that are thoughtfully filled in, accurately reflecting the major issues in the story.

2 Substantial Accomplishment Charts contain a number of categories and most are filled in appropriately.

1 Little or Partial Accomplishment Charts contain few categories and are filled in with irrelevant details.

QuickWrites

1. Make sure that students consider the type of audience that Samuel would be addressing.
2. Before students write their reviews, you may wish to point out that as a teenager, Singer absorbed Jewish history and culture in his grandfather's village, a place that had remained virtually unchanged since the Middle Ages.
3. As part of their sketches, students might note the subtle changes that occurred in the old couple after the arrival of Samuel.

 **The Writer's Craft**

Character Sketch, pp. 78–82

The Writer's Style

Singer includes elements of history, such as the mention of the Russian pogroms and the news items about the Warsaw strikers and Dr. Hertzl's Zionism. Elements of folklore and fable include such aspects as the mysterious appearance of a wealthy donor, the sharp contrast between the simple peasants and the distinguished visitor, the simple language, and the mythical innocence and contentment that mark life in the village.

Critic's Corner

Possible response: The story deals with two universal, and perhaps contradictory, conditions: the desire to better one's condition in life and the desire to experience lasting contentment.

Across the Curriculum

World Religions You might ask Jewish students to share information with their classmates. Remind students that there are various traditions within Judaism and that customs vary a great deal.

World Languages Yiddish developed in the 900s from several languages, including German and Hebrew. It uses the Hebrew alphabet and is the mother language of European Jews. Later, as Jews migrated to Eastern Europe, Yiddish absorbed elements from Slavic languages. Some Yiddish words commonly used in America include *bagel, chutzpah, nebbish, shtick, schlock, pastrami,* and *mensch.*

STORYTELLER
Susan Stone Tells "Yossele, the Holy Miser" In this film performance, the storyteller Susan Stone tells a centuries-old Polish-Jewish folk-tale, which is reminiscent of Singer's story in its irony and compassion.

Side B, Frame 40095

LITERARY CONCEPTS

As you may recall, **situational irony** is a contrast between what a character or reader expects and what actually happens in a literary work. If the detective in a mystery story turns out to be the criminal, for example, most readers would consider the situation ironic. With a partner, review and discuss "The Son from America," listing examples of situational irony that the story contains. What point might Isaac Bashevis Singer have been making by means of these ironies?

CONCEPT REVIEW: Voice How would you describe Singer's writing voice? What does his voice suggest about his personality and attitudes?

Multimodal Learning

ALTERNATIVE ACTIVITIES

1. Draw or paint a **portrait** of Samuel as seen through his parents' eyes.
2. Work with two classmates to create a **scrapbook** of Samuel's trip to Lentshin. Use old photos, art reproductions, bits of writing or clippings, and drawings of your own to depict the most important aspects of his visit. Include captions explaining how the images reflect Samuel's encounters and realizations.
3. Conduct an interview with someone you know who has immigrated to America. The discussion you had for the Personal Connection on page 761 can give you ideas for questions to ask the person about his or her experiences. Prepare a summary statement comparing that person's experiences with Samuel's.

770 UNIT FIVE PART 2: CULTURAL CROSSROADS

Literary Concepts

Possible responses: Examples of irony include Samuel's skill as a baker, Berl's lack of interest in money, and the contentment that pervades the ostensibly poor village; Singer may have intended to point out that a small village can care for its own without everyone having to pay money for help.

Voice Possible response: In the story, Singer's voice is that of a warm and humane traditionalist, giving a gentle and humorous warning to modern readers that contentment does not depend on material well-being.

THE WRITER'S STYLE

Singer's short fiction is noted for its blend of modern attitudes with elements of folklore, fable, and history. Which of these elements do you detect in "The Son from America"? Explain your ideas, citing details from the story.

CRITIC'S CORNER

In awarding Singer its prize for literature, the Nobel Prize committee praised his "impassioned narrative art which, with roots in a Polish-Jewish cultural tradition, brings universal human conditions to life." Would you say that "The Son from America" deals with universal human conditions? Why or why not?

Multimodal Learning

ACROSS THE CURRICULUM

World Religions Do some research into the Jewish celebration of the Sabbath. Look for information on the symbolism of candles, bread, and wine and on the traditional laws governing behavior on the Sabbath, some of which are mentioned in the story. Present your findings to your classmates in an oral report.

World Languages Find out more about Yiddish, the language in which Singer wrote his works. Make a list of Yiddish words and expressions that have entered into the English language.

Alternative Activities

1. Have students review the selection for clues to Samuel's appearance and personality.
2. Students might want to work together on this activity. Have them review the story for highlights of the visit.
3. Students might also explore the experiences of immigrants who have returned to their native lands for visits.

770 THE LANGUAGE OF LITERATURE TEACHER'S EDITION

ISAAC BASHEVIS SINGER

1904–1991

One of the world's foremost Yiddish-language authors, Isaac Bashevis Singer was born in a tiny village in rural Poland and spent most of his youth in Warsaw, the country's capital. His father and both of his grandfathers were rabbis, so he received a traditional religious education. Singer was very close with his older brother, I. J. Singer, a writer who rejected some traditional beliefs and supported the modernization of Judaism. "I was fascinated both with my brother's rationalism and with my parents' mysticism," he once remarked, and both interests are evident in his writings. He also said that he preferred "to write about the world which I knew, which I know best." As a result, much of his fiction is set in the Polish-Jewish communities of his boyhood, which no longer exist.

In the 1920s, while working in Warsaw as a proofreader for a Yiddish literary journal edited by his brother, Singer began writing and publishing his own stories and book reviews. In 1932 he became coeditor of *Globus,* a literary magazine in which he published portions of what would become his first novel, *Satan in Goray.* The complete novel appeared in 1935, the same year that Singer left for America to join his brother, who had emigrated the year before. He settled in New York City and began writing articles, book reviews, and short stories for the *Daily Forward,* a Yiddish newspaper.

Over the course of his career, Singer won a great number of honors and awards for his writing, including the 1978 Nobel Prize in literature. He won a National Book Award for children's literature for *A Day of Pleasure,* an account of his boyhood in Warsaw, as well as a National Book Award for fiction for the story collection *A Crown of Feathers,* in which "The Son from America" appeared. He always wrote in Yiddish, his native tongue, even though he learned English and even collaborated on English translations of his works. Singer once said in an interview, "When I was a boy, they called me a liar . . . for telling stories. Now they call me a writer. It's more advanced, but it's the same thing." He also believed that "every experience becomes important when it's told, not before."

OTHER WORKS *The Family Moskat; Gimpel the Fool and Other Stories; In My Father's Court; Yentl, the Yeshiva Boy; Shosha; The Collected Stories of Isaac Bashevis Singer*   Extended Reading

ISAAC BASHEVIS SINGER

When Singer was elected to the National Institute of Arts and Letters in 1964, he became the only American member to write in a language other than English. In his Nobel Prize acceptance speech, Singer expressed his gratitude for the award as a "recognition of the Yiddish language—a language of exile, without a land, without frontiers, not supported by any government, a language which possesses no words for weapons, ammunition, military exercises, war tactics."

THE SON FROM AMERICA   771

REFLECTING ON THEME
What Do You Think?

Have students review the cultural-crossroads activity that they completed at the beginning of this part of the unit (see pp. 742–743). Discuss what cultural crossroads are depicted in Singer's story and how these crossroads compare to the examples that students found earlier.

OVERVIEW

Objectives

- To understand and appreciate an autobiographical essay that explores a clash of cultures
- To identify and understand the title of a literary work
- To express understanding of a selection through a choice of writing forms, including an opinion column and a note
- To extend understanding of the selection through a variety of multimodal and cross-curricular activities

Skills

LITERARY CONCEPTS
- Title
- Minor characters

THE WRITER'S STYLE
- Topic sentence

GENRE STUDY
- Nonfiction: autobiographical essay

GRAMMAR
- The dash

SPEAKING, LISTENING, AND VIEWING
- Group discussion

CUSTOMIZING FOR
Students Acquiring English

- Use **ACCESS FOR STUDENTS ACQUIRING ENGLISH**, *Reading Support*.
- Ask students if the name they are called in school is the same as the one their family and friends use outside of school. If they use a different name, have them explain its origin.
- In addition to using these boxes, you may want to use the suggestions under Strategic Reading for Less-Proficient Readers.

PREVIEWING

NONFICTION

By Any Other Name

Santha Rama Rau (săn'thä rä'mä rou') India

Activating Prior Knowledge
PERSONAL CONNECTION

With your classmates, discuss what it might be like to live in a country ruled by a foreign government. How do you think your everyday life might be affected? What conflicts might arise? Use a cluster map like the one shown to help you generate ideas.

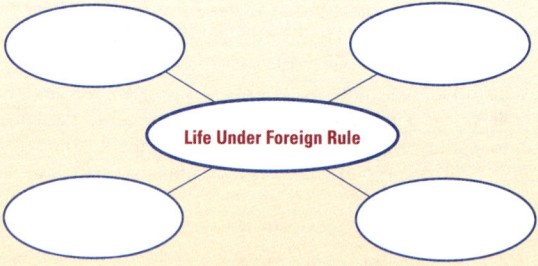

Building Background
CULTURAL CONNECTION

India was a British colony from the late 1700s until 1947, when it gained its independence. During these years, the British came to dominate nearly all aspects of Indian life—the economy, the military, education, and government—and Indians often had to adapt to British ways and attitudes in order to succeed. They faced the difficulty of choosing between their own native customs and those of their foreign colonial "masters." Santha Rama Rau, the author of this selection, grew up in a well-to-do Indian household during the time of British rule.

Setting a Purpose
WRITING CONNECTION

Imagine that you are an Indian child during British colonial rule. In your notebook, write about how attending a British school and being taught by British teachers might make you feel. Then, as you read the selection, compare your ideas with the feelings of the main characters.

772 UNIT FIVE PART 2: CULTURAL CROSSROADS

PRINT AND MEDIA RESOURCES

UNIT FIVE RESOURCE BOOK
Strategic Reading: Literature, p. 53

WRITING MINI-LESSONS
Transparencies, p. 38

ACCESS FOR STUDENTS ACQUIRING ENGLISH
Selection Summaries
Reading Support

FORMAL ASSESSMENT
Selection Test, p. 153
 Test Generator

AUDIO LIBRARY
See Reference Card

INTERNET RESOURCES
McDougal LIttell Literature Center at http://www.hmco.com/mcdougal/lit

772 THE LANGUAGE OF LITERATURE TEACHER'S EDITION

By Any Other Name

Santha Rama Rau

At the Anglo-Indian[1] day school in Zorinabad[2] to which my sister and I were sent when she was eight and I was five and a half, they changed our names. On the first day of school, a hot, windless morning of a north Indian September, we stood in the headmistress's study, and she said, "Now you're the *new* girls. What are your names?"

My sister answered for us. "I am Premila, and she"—nodding in my direction—"is Santha."

The headmistress had been in India, I suppose, fifteen years or so, but she still smiled her helpless inability to cope with Indian names. Her rimless half-glasses glittered, and the precarious bun on the top of her head trembled as she shook her head. "Oh, my dears, those are much too hard for me. Suppose we give you pretty English names. Wouldn't that be more jolly? Let's see, now—Pamela for you, I think." She shrugged in a baffled way at my sister. "That's as close as I can get. And for *you*," she said to me, "how about Cynthia? Isn't that nice?"

My sister was always less easily intimidated than I was, and while she kept a stubborn silence, I said, "Thank you," in a very tiny voice.

We had been sent to that school because my father, among his responsibilities as an officer of the civil service, had a tour of duty to perform in the villages around that steamy little provincial town, where he had his headquarters at that time. He used to make his shorter inspection tours on horseback, and a week before, in the stale heat of a typically postmonsoon[3] day, we had waved good-by to him and a little procession—an assistant, a secretary, two bearers, and the man to look after the bedding rolls and luggage. They rode away through our large garden, still bright green from the rains, and we turned back into the twilight of the house and the sound of fans whispering in every room.

Up to then, my mother had refused to send Premila to school in the British-run establishments of that time, because, she used to say,

---
1. **Anglo-Indian:** belonging to the British colonists in India.
2. **Zorinabad** (zə-rĭn′ə-bäd′).
3. **postmonsoon:** following the Indian rainy season.

BY ANY OTHER NAME **773**

CUSTOMIZING FOR
Gifted and Talented Students

Have students think about other details, in addition to the girls' names, that Rau uses to dramatize the wide-ranging conflict between Indian and English traditions.

Possible responses:

- Page 774—"These [verandas], in the tradition of British schools, were painted dark brown . . ."/ The English replace the bright Indian colors with a somber, heat-retaining color.

- Page 774—". . . ask my mother if I couldn't wear a dress"/ Santha feels self-conscious about her traditional clothing.

- Page 775—". . . the little Indian girl . . . looked at my food longingly"/ The Indians feel they must eat English-style sandwiches.

Literary Concept: MINOR CHARACTERS

B Ask students how the headmistress serves to illustrate the "insular" Britisher. *(Possible response: She has to have things just as they were in England, even though it means insulting and confusing her new students.)*

CUSTOMIZING FOR
Students Acquiring English

I Help students find synonyms for *detached* and *disbelieving*. Point out that the prefixes *de-* and *dis-* mean "not." *Detached* means "not attached," *Disbelieving* means "not believing."

Literary Concept: TITLE

C Recall the title of the essay and explain that Santha's name change is the central event. Ask what it means when Santha says she doesn't know her name. *(Possible response: Caught between two cultures, Santha doesn't really know who she is and what name defines her.)*

B "you can bury a dog's tail for seven years and it still comes out curly, and you can take a Britisher away from his home for a lifetime and he still remains insular." The examinations and degrees from entirely Indian schools were not, in those days, considered valid. In my case, the question had never come up, and probably never would have come up if Mother's extraordinary good health had not broken down. For the first time in my life, she was not able to continue the lessons she had been giving us every morning. So our Hindi[4] books were put away, the stories of the Lord Krishna[5] as a little boy were left in midair, and we were sent to the Anglo-Indian school.

I That first day at school is still, when I think of it, a remarkable one. At that age, if one's name is changed, one develops a curious form of dual personality. I remember having a certain detached and disbelieving concern in the actions of "Cynthia," but certainly no responsibility. Accordingly, I followed the thin, erect back of the headmistress down the veranda to my classroom feeling, at most, a passing interest in what was going to happen to me in this strange, new atmosphere of School.

The building was Indian in design, with wide verandas opening onto a central courtyard, but Indian verandas are usually whitewashed, with stone floors. These, in the tradition of British schools, were painted dark brown and had matting on the floors. It gave a feeling of extra intensity to the heat.

I suppose there were about a dozen Indian children in the school—which contained perhaps forty children in all—and four of them were in my class. They were all sitting at the back of the room, and I went to join them. I sat next to a small, solemn girl who didn't smile at me. She had long, glossy-black braids and wore a cotton dress, but she still kept on her Indian jewelry—a gold chain around her neck, thin gold bracelets, and tiny ruby studs in her ears. Like most Indian children, she had a rim of black kohl[6] around her eyes. The cotton dress should have looked strange, but all I could think of was that I should ask my mother if I couldn't wear a dress to school, too, instead of my Indian clothes.

I can't remember too much about the proceedings in class that day, except for the beginning. The teacher pointed to me and asked me to stand up. "Now, dear, tell the class your name."

I said nothing.

"Come along," she said, frowning slightly. "What's your name, dear?" **C**

"I don't know," I said, finally.

The English children in the front of the class—there were about eight or ten of them—giggled and twisted around in their chairs to look at me. I sat down quickly and opened my eyes very wide, hoping in that way to dry them off. The little girl with the braids put out her hand and very lightly touched my arm. She still didn't smile.

Most of that morning I was rather bored. I looked briefly at the children's drawings pinned to the wall and then concentrated on a lizard clinging to the ledge of the high, barred window behind the teacher's head. Occasionally it would shoot out its long yellow tongue for a fly, and then it would rest, with its eyes closed and

---

4. **Hindi** (hĭn′dē): the principal language of northern India.
5. **Lord Krishna:** one of the chief gods of Hinduism, the major religion of India.
6. **kohl** (kōl): a powder used in some Eastern countries to darken the eyelids and eyelashes.

774

Mini-Lesson The Writer's Style

TOPIC SENTENCES Point out that Santha Rama Rau occasionally uses topic sentences to state the main ideas of her paragraphs. As an example, point out the highlighted opening sentence in the last paragraph of page 774. Draw attention to the details and examples in the paragraph that support the main idea that Santha was bored. Then identify the highlighted topic sentences in the paragraphs on pages 776 and 777, and have students explain how the sentences in each paragraph develop these main ideas.

Application Have students imagine a scene in which Premila, Santha, and their mother return to the school to explain why the girls have left. Ask students to write a paragraph describing this scene, beginning with a topic sentence.

Reteaching/Reinforcement
- Writing Handbook, anthology p. 1026
- Writing Mini-Lessons transparencies, p. 38

Topic Sentences, pp. 355–356

774 THE LANGUAGE OF LITERATURE TEACHER'S EDITION

its belly palpitating, as though it were swallowing several times quickly. The lessons were mostly concerned with reading and writing and simple numbers—things that my mother had already taught me—and I paid very little attention. The teacher wrote on the easel blackboard words like "bat" and "cat," which seemed babyish to me; only "apple" was new and incomprehensible.

When it was time for the lunch recess, I followed the girl with braids out onto the veranda. There the children from the other classes were assembled. I saw Premila at once and ran over to her, as she had charge of our lunchbox. The children were all opening packages and sitting down to eat sandwiches. Premila and I were the only ones who had Indian food—thin wheat chapatties,[7] some vegetable curry,[8] and a bottle of buttermilk. Premila thrust half of it into my hand and whispered fiercely that I should go and sit with my class, because that was what the others seemed to be doing.

The enormous black eyes of the little Indian girl from my class looked at my food longingly, so I offered her some. But she only shook her head and plowed her way solemnly through her sandwiches.

I was very sleepy after lunch, because at home we always took a siesta. It was usually a pleasant time of day, with the bedroom darkened against the harsh afternoon sun, the drifting off into sleep with the sound of Mother's voice reading a story in one's mind, and, finally, the shrill, fussy voice of the ayah[9] waking one for tea.

Two Indian girls in their native clothing. Copyright © Bill Cardoni/Bruce Coleman Inc.

At school, we rested for a short time on low, folding cots on the veranda, and then we were expected to play games. During the hot part of the afternoon we played indoors, and after the shadows had begun to lengthen and the slight breeze of the evening had come up, we moved outside to the wide courtyard.

I had never really grasped the system of competitive games. At home, whenever we

---

7. **chapatties** (chə-päd′ēz): flat, thin pieces of bread.
8. **curry**: a stew seasoned with curry powder (a combination of spices).
9. **ayah** (ä′yə): a native nurse or lady's maid in India.

BY ANY OTHER NAME **775**

STRATEGIC READING FOR
Less-Proficient Readers

D Make sure students understand why Santha wasn't able to tell the class her name and why things in general seem so strange to her.

- What name can't Santha remember? *(Cynthia)* Why? *(The headmistress just gave it to her.)* **Summarizing**
- Why do things seem so strange to Santha? *(It's her first day at school; she isn't used to English ways.)* **Drawing Conclusions**

Set a Purpose Have students read on to find out whether Santha continues to go to the school.

Critical Thinking: ANALYZING

E Why do you think none of the other Indian students eat Indian food? *(Possible responses: It was probably discouraged by the school authorities; their English classmates might have made fun of them.)*

Literary Concept:
MINOR CHARACTERS

F Have students speculate on why the author introduces this little girl as a minor character in the essay. *(Possible response: She serves as a mirror for Santha, suggesting the sadness that comes from giving up one's traditional ways.)*

DESIGN NOTE

The cloth behind the photograph of the two young girls represents the centuries-old Indian tradition of hand-crafted clothing.

Reading the Art What does this cloth and the photograph of the two girls suggest about the differences between Indian and British styles of clothing?

CUSTOMIZING FOR
Students Acquiring English

② Ask volunteers to imitate the shrill fussy voice of the children's maid as she wakes them.

Mini-Lesson Grammar

THE DASH Remind students that dashes show an abrupt change of thought or a pause in a sentence. Point out that Santha Rama Rau uses dashes, not commas, in the first highlighted sentence on this page to set off the explanatory statement "things that my mother had already taught me." In the second highlighted sentence, the dash is used to set off a list of particular Indian foods.

Application Ask students to add the necessary dashes in these sentences.

1. I suppose there were about a dozen Indian children in the school(—)which contained perhaps forty children in all(—)and four of them were in my class.
2. The English children in the front of the class(—)there were about eight or ten of them(—)giggled and twisted around in their chairs to look at me.

Reteaching/Reinforcement
- Grammar Handbook, anthology p. 1092

The Dash, pp. 810–811

Literary Concept:
POINT OF VIEW

G Have students discuss Rau's possible reasons for choosing to write her essay from the first-person point of view of a five-year-old child. *(Possible response: The innocence of young Santha emphasizes the injustice done to the Indian people.)*

CUSTOMIZING FOR
Students Acquiring English

3 Read this sentence aloud and ask students to figure out what Santha did wrong. Invite volunteers to explain the problem to the class. *(Santha didn't realize that the children only played to win and would make no allowances.)*

Literary Concept: THEME

H Ask students why Rau includes these details about Premila using a British slang term and asking to take sandwiches to school. *(Possible response: These details illustrate the cultural crossroads at which the girls find themselves; Premila finds herself imitating British ways in order to fit in.)*

Literary Concept:
MINOR CHARACTERS

I Have students discuss how this scene presents an important contrast to Santha's school experience. *(Possible response: With the cook's son, a familar Indian, Santha enjoys the beauty and wonder of India's natural world and folklore; this scene is free of the British influences that make school so uncomfortable.)*

---

played tag or guessing games, I was always allowed to "win"—"because," Mother used to tell Premila, "she is the youngest, and we have to allow for that." I had often heard her say it, and it seemed quite reasonable to me, but the result was that I had no clear idea of what "winning" meant.

When we played twos-and-threes that afternoon at school, in accordance with my training, I let one of the small English boys catch me but was naturally rather puzzled when the other children did not return the courtesy. I ran about for what seemed like hours without ever catching anyone, until it was time for school to close. Much later I learned that my attitude was called "not being a good sport," and I stopped allowing myself to be caught, but it was not for years that I really learned the spirit of the thing.

When I saw our car come up to the school gate, I broke away from my classmates and rushed toward it yelling, "Ayah! Ayah!" It seemed like an eternity since I had seen her that morning—a wizened,[10] affectionate figure in her white cotton sari, giving me dozens of urgent and useless instructions on how to be a good girl at school. Premila followed more sedately, and she told me on the way home never to do that again in front of the other children.

When we got home, we went straight to Mother's high, white room to have tea with her, and I immediately climbed onto the bed and bounced gently up and down on the springs. Mother asked how we had liked our first day in school. I was so pleased to be home and to have left that peculiar Cynthia behind that I had nothing whatever to say about school, except to ask what "apple" meant. But Premila told Mother about the classes, and added that in her class they had weekly tests to see if they had learned their lessons well.

I asked, "What's a test?"

Premila said, "You're too small to have them.

You won't have them in your class for donkey's years." She had learned the expression that day and was using it for the first time. We all laughed enormously at her wit. She also told Mother, in an aside, that we should take sandwiches to school the next day. Not, she said, that *she* minded. But they would be simpler for me to handle.

That whole lovely evening I didn't think about school at all. I sprinted barefoot across the lawns with my favorite playmate, the cook's son, to the stream at the end of the garden. We quarreled in our usual way, waded in the tepid water under the lime trees, and waited for the night to bring out the smell of the jasmine. I listened with fascination to his stories of ghosts and demons, until I was too frightened to cross the garden alone in the semidarkness. The ayah found me, shouted at the cook's son, scolded me, hurried me in to supper—it was an entirely usual, wonderful evening.

It was a week later, the day of Premila's first test, that our lives changed rather abruptly. I was sitting at the back of my class, in my usual inattentive way, only half listening to the teacher. I had started a rather guarded friendship with the girl with the braids, whose name turned out to be Nalini (Nancy, in school). The three other Indian children were already fast friends. Even at that age it was apparent to all of us that friendship with the English or Anglo-Indian children was out of the question. Occasionally, during the class, my new friend and I would draw pictures and show them to each other secretly.

The door opened sharply, and Premila marched in. At first, the teacher smiled at her in a kindly and encouraging way and said, "Now, you're little Cynthia's sister?"

---
10. **wizened** (wĭz′ənd): withered; shriveled.

Mini-Lesson ⟡ Literary Concepts

REVIEWING MINOR CHARACTERS Remind students that generally a narrative focuses on a number of main characters, who often grow or change as the story progresses. In addition to these major characters, there are often minor characters who are usually static, or unchanging. Explain that these minor characters help move events along or serve as foils, or contrasts, for the main characters.

Application Have students think about how the minor characters in this narrative help keep events moving. For example, ask them how the headmistress in the opening scene and later Premila's teacher establish and develop the Anglo-Indian conflict. Then have them discuss the ayah, the cook's boy, and the girl Nalini (Nancy), and tell how these minor characters help readers see Santha's traditional Indian side more fully.

Premila didn't even look at her. She stood with her feet planted firmly apart and her shoulders rigid and addressed herself directly to me. "Get up," she said. "We're going home."

I didn't know what had happened, but I was aware that it was a crisis of some sort. I rose obediently and started to walk toward my sister.

"Bring your pencils and your notebook," she said.

I went back for them, and together we left the room. The teacher started to say something just as Premila closed the door, but we didn't wait to hear what it was.

In complete silence we left the school grounds and started to walk home. Then I asked Premila what the matter was. All she would say was "We're going home for good."

It was a very tiring walk for a child of five and a half, and I dragged along behind Premila with my pencils growing sticky in my hand. I can still remember looking at the dusty hedges, and the tangles of thorns in the ditches by the side of the road, smelling the faint fragrance from the eucalyptus trees and wondering whether we would ever reach home. Occasionally a horse-drawn tonga[11] passed us, and the women, in their pink or green silks, stared at Premila and me trudging along on the side of the road. A few coolies[12] and a line of women carrying baskets of vegetables on their heads smiled at us. But it was nearing the hottest time of day, and the road was almost deserted. I walked more and more slowly and shouted to Premila, from time to time, "Wait for me!" with increasing peevishness.[13] She spoke to me only once, and that was to tell me to carry my notebook on my head, because of the sun.

When we got to our house, the ayah was just taking a tray of lunch into Mother's room. She immediately started a long, worried questioning about what are you children doing back here at this hour of the day.

Mother looked very startled and very concerned and asked Premila what had happened.

Premila said, "We had our test today, and she made me and the other Indians sit at the back of the room, with a desk between each one."

Mother said, "Why was that, darling?"

"She said it was because Indians cheat," Premila added. "So I don't think we should go back to that school."

Mother looked very distant and was silent a long time. At last she said, "Of course not, darling." She sounded displeased.

We all shared the curry she was having for lunch, and afterward I was sent off to the beautifully familiar bedroom for my siesta. I could hear Mother and Premila talking through the open door.

Mother said, "Do you suppose she understood all that?"

Premila said, "I shouldn't think so. She's a baby."

Mother said, "Well, I hope it won't bother her."

Of course, they were both wrong. I understood it perfectly, and I remember it all very clearly. But I put it happily away, because it had all happened to a girl called Cynthia, and I never was really particularly interested in her. ❖

---

11. **tonga:** a small two-wheeled carriage.
12. **coolies:** unskilled laborers in India or China.
13. **peevishness:** irritability.

BY ANY OTHER NAME **777**

Multicultural Perspectives

NAMING Every culture has its own naming traditions. The Chinese were the first to use more than one name. Emperor Fuxi in 2852 B.C. decreed that everyone must have a family name. Today, the Chinese usually have three names. Traditionally, the family name comes first. A "generation" name comes second, which comes from a family poem. The last name is similar to an American given name. In European cultures, family names come from a variety of sources, such as ancestors, occupations, place names, and geographic features. Among Native Americans, names are always symbolic, but every group has its own naming traditions. Often, the names come from animal totems. In many cultures, a child has one name at birth and receives different names at later times in life.

From Personal Response to Critical Analysis

1. Accept all reasonable responses.
2. Possible responses: Yes, she was absolutely right to refuse to stand for an unjust accusation; yes, an Indian child would have had no hearing if she had appealed to the school authorities; no, she should have tried resolving the issue, even though she may not have succeeded.
3. Possible responses: She wanted the children to be proud of themselves and proud of their heritage; she wanted them to reach their full potential.
4. Possible responses: The Indian children were torn from their own traditions and were made to see their heritage as inferior to British culture; the children themselves were made to feel inferior to their British counterparts.
5. Possible responses: Rau tells a lively story; she has the ability to see the world through the eyes of a five-year-old and to use small details to express important conflicts.
6. Accept all reasonable, well-supported responses.

Another Pathway

Cooperative Learning In each group, one student can review the story to determine the exact amount of time that passes. A second can construct a time line based on this information. A third student can label the events above the line while a fourth records below the lines the characters' feelings.

Rubric
3 Full Accomplishment Time lines show what happened during the girls' one week at school and their reactions to these events.

2 Substantial Accomplishment Time lines adequately reflect chronology, but more events might be noted or more attention might be given to the girls' feelings.

1 Little or Partial Accomplishment Time lines suggest that students are unaware of the chronology of events or do not understand the girls' feelings.

RESPONDING OPTIONS

FROM PERSONAL RESPONSE TO CRITICAL ANALYSIS

REFLECT
1. In your notebook, jot down your immediate reaction to the selection. Share your reaction with a partner.

RETHINK
2. Do you think Premila did the right thing by walking out in the middle of school? Explain your position.

3. What do you think were the mother's goals for her daughters' education?
   Consider
   - why she taught them at home and told them stories about Lord Krishna
   Close Textual Reading
   - what she said about the British
   - why she sent Santha and Premila to a British school when she was no longer able to teach them herself
   - the family's position in society

4. How do you think the Indian children were affected by the Britishers' treatment of them?
   Consider
   - Santha's two personalities as "Santha" and "Cynthia"
   Close Textual Reading
   - how Premila responded to school
   - why other children adapted to British ways
   - how the teachers viewed the Indians
   - what you wrote for the Writing Connection on page 772

5. How would you evaluate Rama Rau as a storyteller? Support your opinion with examples from the selection.

RELATE
6. Premila was able to walk out of school rather than remain and face continued humiliation. On the basis of what you know about Premila and other people, what personal characteristics do you think an individual needs in order to reject unjust treatment?

ANOTHER PATHWAY
Cooperative Learning
With a small group of classmates, create an annotated time line that shows the key events in this selection. Above the time line, label each event. Below the line, write a brief description of how Santha and Premila felt about the event.

QUICKWRITES

1. Write an **opinion column** for the Zorinabad newspaper, in which you report and comment on the incident presented in this selection. You may show support either for Santha and Premila's family or for the British school.

2. Imagine you are the girls' mother and write a **note** to the headmistress of the British school, explaining why your daughters will not be returning to the school.

   📁 **PORTFOLIO** *Save your writing. You may want to use it later as a springboard to a piece for your portfolio.*

778 UNIT FIVE PART 2: CULTURAL CROSSROADS

QuickWrites

1. You may wish to bring in examples of such columns from local newspapers. Point out that students can be firm in their opinions without being insulting.
2. Suggest to students that the letter be formal in tone and polite and civil in diction, appropriate to the mother's character.

Formal English, pp. 428–429

LITERARY CONCEPTS

The **title** of a literary work often reflects the meaning of the work. Sometimes the title contains an allusion that can help readers better understand and appreciate the work. Santha Rama Rau's title is an allusion to these lines from Act Two, Scene 2, of William Shakespeare's *Romeo and Juliet*:

> What's in a name? That which we call a rose
> By any other name would smell as sweet.

Explain in your own words what the quotation means and how it applies to Rama Rau's autobiographical essay.

ACROSS THE CURRICULUM

History Many immigrants found their names changed when they entered the United States because officials who could not spell or pronounce the names simply wrote down familiar approximations of what they heard. For example, "Jurek" (yoor'ĕk) might become "George," and "Iorizzo" (yō-rēt'tsō) might become "Rice." Research other name changes and create a chart showing various original names along with their "Americanized" variations. Share your chart with the class.

CRITIC'S CORNER

A reviewer for the *Providence Journal* once observed that Rama Rau "can see the color and catch the flavor of a scene. She can give the complete atmosphere of quite different ways of life. Best of all, she has a sharp and amused eye for people." Explain whether you agree with this statement, supporting your opinion with details from the selection.

SANTHA RAMA RAU

1923–

Born in the city of Madras, Santha Rama Rau came from a wealthy and distinguished family. Her father was a diplomat in the Anglo-Indian government, and her mother was a leading social reformer. Although her father's job required the family to move frequently, she and her sister sometimes lived with their grandmother, surrounded by stability and tradition. Rama Rau once wrote, "The two strong strains of my childhood—the shifting life of district touring and the unshakable little universe of the family—were both vividly a part of my experience."

When Rama Rau was six, her family moved to London, and she attended school in England for the next ten years. She later enrolled at Wellesley College in Massachusetts, where she began composing *Home to India*, an account of a 1939 trip to her homeland. The book won instant acclaim as a "refreshing, readable contrast" to the "serious and weighty works" about Indian nationalism that were then flooding the market.

After graduating from Wellesley, Rama Rau lived in Bombay, India, and worked as editor of a magazine called *Trend*. In 1947, after India gained independence from Britain, she accompanied her father to Tokyo when he became India's first ambassador to Japan. Her experiences in eastern Asia are recounted in her travel book *East of Home* (1950). In subsequent years Rama Rau has produced several more travel books and articles, as well as novels, personal essays, and even an Indian cookbook. "By Any Other Name" first appeared in *The New Yorker*.

OTHER WORKS *Remember the House, View to the Southeast, The Adventuress, A Princess Remembers: The Memoirs of the Maharani of Jaipur*

Extended Reading

Literary Links

Have students contrast the attitudes of the teachers in "By Any Other Name" with those of Mrs. Hurd, described by Nicholas Gage in "The Teacher Who Saved My Life." Bring out that Mrs. Hurd attempted to break down the emotional barriers that stood between students of different backgrounds, while the teachers at the Anglo-Indian school seemed to reinforce them.

Across the Curriculum

History Suggest that students interview immigrants and their children for details about name changes. Books about immigration will also contain anecdotal information.

As an alternative history activity, ask a group of students to research India's independence movement and the major historical figures who played a role in it.

Critic's Corner

Students who agree with this statement might cite the description of the English headmistress as a good example of the author's "sharp and amused eye for people." The description of the road along which Premila and Santha walk seems to capture much of the color and flavor of British India.

SANTHA RAMA RAU

Santha Rama Rau began her writing career when a famous Indian poet, Madame Sarojini Naidu, encouraged her to write about her travels and experiences. Ms. Rau won great praise for her stage adaptation of E. M. Forster's *A Passage to India*, a 1924 novel that describes the clash between British and traditional Indian cultures in India.

Literary Concepts

Help students to realize that Shakespeare is saying that the name of a person or thing does not affect or change its essential traits. Even if a rose were called something else, it would still be a fragrant flower with soft petals, a lovely color, thorns, and so on. Some students may believe that Rau is being ironic by alluding to Shakespeare because Santha's name is very important to her and reflects her cultural identity. Others might think that the two girls are still the same people, regardless of the British names given them.

OVERVIEW

Objectives

- To understand and appreciate a short story that explores contrasting attitudes toward marriage
- To identify and understand setting
- To express understanding of a selection through a choice of writing forms, including a letter, diary entries, and a list
- To extend understanding of the selection through a variety of multimodal and cross-curricular activities

Skills

LITERARY CONCEPTS
- Setting
- Irony

THE WRITER'S STYLE
- Plot device: letters

GRAMMAR
- Punctuating direct quotations

SPEAKING, LISTENING, AND VIEWING
- Group discussion
- Role-playing
- Improvisational scene

ALTERNATIVE

Previewing

Students can choose partners and use the following prompts to preview the story orally.

Writing Connection

Discussion Prompts Tell your partner about situations you have read or heard about in which family members did not speak to each other because of their choice of marriage partners.

- What caused the breakdown in communications?
- Did the situation get worse or better over time? Why?

As you read the story, notice why communication breaks down between two main characters.

PREVIEWING

FICTION

Marriage Is a Private Affair

Chinua Achebe (chĭn'wä ä-chä'bā) Nigeria

Activating Prior Knowledge
PERSONAL CONNECTION

Marriage customs vary greatly throughout the world. In some cultures, people's marriages are traditionally arranged by their parents; in others, parents play little part. Discuss what you know about arranged marriages. Then create a comparison-contrast chart, like the one shown, to compare arranged marriages with marriages based on the choice of the partners.

	Parents Choose Mates	Partners Choose Each Other
Reason for marriage		
Benefits of this method of choice		
Drawbacks		

Building Background
CULTURAL CONNECTION

This story takes place in the West African country of Nigeria, a land of great cultural diversity. Centuries-old traditions continue to govern life in Nigerian villages, where parents often play a decisive role in choosing mates for their children. In the cities, however, modern practices have displaced many of the village traditions, including the role of parent as matchmaker. The tension between the old and new ways of living sometimes creates conflict within families, especially between generations.

The story focuses on a conflict between a father and son about the choice of the son's marriage partner. Both men are Ibo (ē'bō), members of one of the largest ethnic groups in Nigeria. The son, like many of his contemporaries, has moved away from the village of his birth and lives in a city—in this case, Lagos (lā'gŏs), the economic and commercial center of the nation, with a population of 1.4 million. In the villages of Nigeria, the Ibo live apart from other peoples, maintaining their traditional way of life. Life in Lagos, however, is characterized by a mingling of ethnic groups, cultures, and religions.

Setting a Purpose
WRITING CONNECTION

With another student, brainstorm some common objections that parents raise to their children's choice of marriage partners. Record the objections in your notebook, putting an *R* by the ones that you think are reasonable and a *U* by those that seem unreasonable. Then, as you read the story, think about what is reasonable and unreasonable in the father's reaction to his son's choice of a spouse.

780 UNIT FIVE PART 2: CULTURAL CROSSROADS

PRINT AND MEDIA RESOURCES

UNIT FIVE RESOURCE BOOK
Strategic Reading: Literature, p. 57
Vocabulary SkillBuilder, p. 58

GRAMMAR MINI-LESSONS
Transparencies, p. 44
Copymasters, pp. 45–46

WRITING MINI-LESSONS
Transparencies, p. 55

ACCESS FOR STUDENTS ACQUIRING ENGLISH
Selection Summaries
Reading Support

FORMAL ASSESSMENT
Selection Test, p. 155
Test Generator

AUDIO LIBRARY
See Reference Card

LASERLINKS
Cultural Connection
Author Background

INTERNET RESOURCES
McDougal Littell Literature Center at http://www.hmco.com/mcdougal/lit

780 THE LANGUAGE OF LITERATURE TEACHER'S EDITION

Marriage Is a Private Affair
Chinua Achebe

"Have you written to your dad yet?" asked Nene[1] one afternoon as she sat with Nnaemeka[2] in her room at 16 Kasanga Street, Lagos.

"No. I've been thinking about it. I think it's better to tell him when I get home on leave!"

"But why? Your leave is such a long way off yet—six whole weeks. He should be let into our happiness now."

Nnaemeka was silent for a while and then began very slowly as if he groped for his words: "I wish I were sure it would be happiness to him."

"Of course it must," replied Nene, a little surprised. "Why shouldn't it?"

"You have lived in Lagos all your life, and you know very little about people in remote parts of the country."

"That's what you always say. But I don't believe anybody will be so unlike other people that they will be unhappy when their sons are engaged to marry."

"Yes. They are most unhappy if the engagement is not arranged by them. In our case it's worse—you are not even an Ibo."

This was said so seriously and so bluntly that Nene could not find speech immediately. In the cosmopolitan atmosphere of the city it had always seemed to her something of a joke that a person's tribe could determine whom he married.

At last she said, "You don't really mean that he will object to your marrying me simply on that account? I had always thought you Ibos were kindly disposed to other people."

"So we are. But when it comes to marriage, well, it's not quite so simple. And this," he added, "is not peculiar to the Ibos. If your father were alive and lived in the heart of Ibibio-land, he would be exactly like my father."

"I don't know. But anyway, as your father is

---

1. **Nene** (nā'nā).
2. **Nnaemeka** (ən-nä'ā-mä'kä).

WORDS TO KNOW
cosmopolitan (kŏz'mə-pŏl'ĭ-tn) *adj.* worldly; sophisticated

WORDS TO KNOW

commiserate (kə-mĭz'ə-rāt') *v.* to express sorrow or pity for another's trouble (p. 784)
cosmopolitan (kŏz'mə-pŏl'ĭ-tn) *adj.* worldly; sophisticated (p. 781)
deference (dĕf'ər-əns) *n.* courteous regard or respect (p. 785)
dissuasion (dĭ-swā'zhən) *n.* the persuading of someone not to perform an action (p. 783)
forsaken (fŏr-sā'kən) *adj.* abandoned **forsake** *v.* (p. 785)

homily (hŏm'ə-lē) *n.* a tedious, moralizing lecture; sermon (p. 783)
perfunctorily (pər-fŭngk'tə-rĭ-lē) *adv.* in a careless, uninterested way (p. 785)
persevere (pûr'sə-vēr) *v.* to persist in the face of difficulties (p. 785)
remorse (rĭ-môrs') *n.* a deep sense of guilt over a wrong one has done (p. 785)
theological (thē'ə-lŏjĭ-kəl) *adj.* having to do with the study of God and religion (p. 784)

CUSTOMIZING FOR
Gifted and Talented Students

Ask students to note how Okeke uses Christianity to reinforce his desire to follow African traditions.

Possible responses:

- Page 782—"She has a proper Christian upbringing"/Okeke believes that the religious upbringing of Nweke's daughter makes her a suitable wife for his son.

- Page 782—"... I should like to point out to you, Emeka, that no Christian woman should teach. St. Paul in his letter to Corinthians says that women should keep silence."/Okeke uses the Bible to find fault with his son's choice of wife.

CUSTOMIZING FOR
Students Acquiring English

I Explain that *negotiation* means "the act or process of settling an agreement or contract." Point out the negotiations here concern financial arrangements for a marriage. In many traditional cultures, money or property is exchanged as a condition for marriage.

Critical Thinking:
MAKING JUDGMENTS

B Have students discuss Okeke's feeling that love is not necessary for marriage. Do they agree or disagree? Why? *(Accept all reasonable responses.)*

Literary Concept:
CHARACTERIZATION

C Have students discuss what this "pet subject" about women reveals about Okeke. *(Possible responses: He is very traditional and literal-minded; he is rather didactic, or preachy.)*

---

so fond of you, I'm sure he will forgive you soon enough. Come on then, be a good boy and send him a nice lovely letter . . ."

"It would not be wise to break the news to him by writing. A letter will bring it upon him with a shock. I'm quite sure about that."

"All right, honey, suit yourself. You know your father."

As Nnaemeka walked home that evening, he turned over in his mind different ways of overcoming his father's opposition, especially now that he had gone and found a girl for him. He had thought of showing his letter to Nene but decided on second thoughts not to, at least for the moment. He read it again when he got home and couldn't help smiling to himself. He remembered Ugoye[3] quite well, an Amazon[4] of a girl who used to beat up all the boys, himself included, on the way to the stream, a complete dunce at school.

> *I have found a girl who will suit you admirably—Ugoye Nweke, the eldest daughter of our neighbor, Jacob Nweke. She has a proper Christian upbringing. When she stopped schooling some years ago, her father (a man of sound judgment) sent her to live in the house of a pastor where she has received all the training a wife could need. Her Sunday school teacher has told me that she reads her Bible very fluently. I hope we shall begin negotiations when you come home in December.*

On the second evening of his return from Lagos Nnaemeka sat with his father under a cassia tree. This was the old man's retreat where he went to read his Bible when the parching December sun had set and a fresh, reviving wind blew on the leaves.

"Father," began Nnaemeka suddenly, "I have come to ask for forgiveness."

"Forgiveness? For what, my son?" he asked in amazement.

"It's about this marriage question."

"Which marriage question?"

"I can't—we must—I mean it is impossible for me to marry Nweke's daughter."

"Impossible? Why?" asked his father.

"I don't love her."

"Nobody said you did. Why should you?" he asked.

"Marriage today is different . . ."

"Look here, my son," interrupted his father, "nothing is different. What one looks for in a wife are a good character and a Christian background."

Nnaemeka saw there was no hope along the present line of argument.

"Moreover," he said, "I am engaged to marry another girl who has all of Ugoye's good qualities, and who . . ."

His father did not believe his ears. "What did you say?" he asked slowly and disconcertingly.

"She is a good Christian," his son went on, "and a teacher in a girls' school in Lagos."

"Teacher, did you say? If you consider that a qualification for a good wife, I should like to point out to you, Emeka, that no Christian woman should teach. St. Paul in his letter to the Corinthians says that women should keep silence." He rose slowly from his seat and paced forwards and backwards. This was his pet subject, and he condemned vehemently those church leaders who encouraged women to teach in their schools. After he had spent his emotion on a long

---

3. **Ugoye** (ōō-gō′yā).
4. **Amazon:** an exceptionally tall, strong woman.

782 UNIT FIVE PART 2: CULTURAL CROSSROADS

Mini-Lesson Grammar

PUNCTUATING DIRECT QUOTATIONS

Point out the highlighted dialogue on page 782. Remind students that the exact words of a speaker are enclosed in quotation marks with the first word capitalized. Commas are placed inside the quotation marks; when the end of the quotation is also the end of a sentence, the period is inside the quotation. Question marks and exclamation points are inside the quotation marks if they are part of the quotation.

Application Invite students to punctuate this dialogue from the story

1. Of course it must replied Nene, a little surprised. Why shouldn't it?
2. Father began Nnaemeka suddenly I have come to ask forgiveness.
3. Forgiveness? For what, my son? he asked in amazement.

Reteaching/Reinforcement
- *Grammar Handbook*, anthology pp. 1096–1097
- *Grammar Mini-Lessons* copymasters pp. 45–46, transparencies p. 44

Quotation Marks, pp. 825–830

Wooing (1984), Varnette Honeywood. Collage. Copyright © 1984 Varnette P. Honeywood.

homily, he at last came back to his son's engagement, in a seemingly milder tone.

"Whose daughter is she, anyway?"

"She is Nene Atang."

"What!" All the mildness was gone again. "Did you say Neneataga; what does that mean?"

"Nene Atang from Calabar.⁵ She is the only girl I can marry." This was a very rash reply, and Nnaemeka expected the storm to burst. But it did not. His father merely walked away into his room. This was most unexpected and perplexed Nnaemeka. His father's silence was infinitely more menacing than a flood of threatening speech. That night the old man did not eat.

When he sent for Nnaemeka a day later, he applied all possible ways of dissuasion. But the young man's heart was hardened, and his father eventually gave him up as lost.

"I owe it to you, my son, as a duty to show you what is right and what is wrong. Whoever put this idea into your head might as well have cut your throat. It is Satan's work." He waved his son away.

"You will change your mind, Father, when you know Nene."

"I shall never see her" was the reply. From that night the father scarcely spoke to his son. He did not, however, cease hoping that he would realize how serious was the danger he was heading for. Day and night he put him in his prayers.

Nnaemeka, for his own part, was very deeply affected by his father's grief. But he kept hoping that it would pass away. If it had occurred to him that never in the history of his people had a man married a woman who spoke a different tongue, he might have been less optimistic. "It has never been heard," was the verdict of an old man speaking a few weeks later. In that

---

5. **Calabar:** a seaport in southeastern Nigeria.

WORDS TO KNOW
homily (hŏm'ə-lē) *n.* a tedious, moralizing lecture; sermon
dissuasion (dĭ-swā'zhən) *n.* the persuading of someone not to perform an action

Literary Concept: SETTING

G Have students suggest what the neighbors' comments tell them about the village. *(Possible responses: Villagers get little input from the outside world; there is little variation from the traditional ways of doing things; they view things in religious terms.)*

Critical Thinking: SUMMARIZING

H Invite students to explain the gist of what the elders are gossiping about. *(A neighbor woman has killed a local medicine man by secretly trying out a love potion on him that was meant for her husband.)*

Literary Concept: SETTING

I Ask students what the anecdote about Mrs. Ochuba tells us about the cultural environment of the village. *(Possible response: The old traditions are alive, coexisting uneasily with Christianity; villagers are divided about the role of traditional native doctors.)*

Literary Concept: IRONY

J Ask students why Okeke's response to the photograph is ironic. *(Possible response: Normally, parents treasure photos of their children's weddings; Okeke thinks it's "unfeeling" for his son to send him one.)*

---

short sentence he spoke for all of his people. This man had come with others to commiserate with Okeke[6] when news went round about his son's behavior. By that time the son had gone back to Lagos.

"It has never been heard," said the old man again with a sad shake of his head.

"What did Our Lord say?" asked another gentleman. "Sons shall rise against their fathers; it is there in the Holy Book."

"It is the beginning of the end," said another.

The discussion thus tending to become theological, Madubogwu, a highly practical man, brought it down once more to the ordinary level.

"Have you thought of consulting a native doctor about your son?" he asked Nnaemeka's father.

"He isn't sick" was the reply.

"What is he then? The boy's mind is diseased, and only a good herbalist[7] can bring him back to his right senses. The medicine he requires is *Amalile*, the same that women apply with success to recapture their husbands' straying affection."

"Madubogwu is right," said another gentleman. "This thing calls for medicine."

"I shall not call in a native doctor." Nnaemeka's father was known to be obstinately ahead of his more superstitious neighbors in these matters. "I will not be another Mrs. Ochuba. If my son wants to kill himself, let him do it with his own hands. It is not for me to help him."

"But it was her fault," said Madubogwu. "She ought to have gone to an honest herbalist. She was a clever woman, nevertheless."

"She was a wicked murderess," said Jonathan, who rarely argued with his neighbors because, he often said, they were incapable of reasoning.

"The medicine was prepared for her husband, it was his name they called in its preparation, and I am sure it would have been perfectly beneficial to him. It was wicked to put it into the herbalist's food and say you were only trying it out."

Six months later, Nnaemeka was showing his young wife a short letter from his father:

It amazes me that you could be so unfeeling as to send me your wedding picture. I would have sent it back. But on further thought I decided just to cut off your wife and send it back to you because I have nothing to do with her. How I wish that I had nothing to do with you either.

When Nene read through this letter and looked at the mutilated picture, her eyes filled with tears, and she began to sob.

"Don't cry, my darling," said her husband. "He is essentially good-natured and will one day look more kindly on our marriage." But years passed, and that one day did not come.

For eight years, Okeke would have nothing to do with his son, Nnaemeka. Only three times (when Nnaemeka asked to come home and spend his leave) did he write to him.

"I can't have you in my house," he replied on one occasion. "It can be of no interest to me where or how you spend your leave—or your life, for that matter."

The prejudice against Nnaemeka's marriage was not confined to his little village. In Lagos, especially among his people who worked there,

---

6. Okeke (ō-kā′kā).
7. herbalist (ûr′bə-lĭst): a person who is expert in the use of medicinal herbs.

WORDS TO KNOW
commiserate (kə-mĭz′ə-rāt′) *v.* to express sorrow or pity for another's trouble
theological (thē′ə-lŏj′ĭ-kəl) *adj.* having to do with the study of God and religion

784

Mini-Lesson — The Writer's Style

PLOT DEVICE: LETTERS Point out the letter from Okeke on page 784 and the letter from Nene on page 785 and elicit that these are in the first person. Have students suggest why the author breaks the third-person narration to include these letters. Bring out that the letters are an efficient way to advance the plot and to show how people feel about an issue that divides them.

Application Suggest that students rewrite the ending of the story so that it is told entirely in the third person—with no letter. Then ask them which version they prefer.

Reteaching/Reinforcement
- *Writing Mini-Lessons* transparencies, p. 55

The Writer's Craft
Point of View, pp. 447–448
Narrative Conclusions, pp. 388–389

---

784 THE LANGUAGE OF LITERATURE **TEACHER'S EDITION**

it showed itself in a different way. Their women, when they met at their village meeting, were not hostile to Nene. Rather, they paid her such excessive deference as to make her feel she was not one of them. But as time went on, Nene gradually broke through some of this prejudice and even began to make friends among them. Slowly and grudgingly they began to admit that she kept her home much better than most of them.

The story eventually got to the little village in the heart of the Ibo country that Nnaemeka and his young wife were a most happy couple. But his father was one of the few people in the village who knew nothing about this. He always displayed so much temper whenever his son's name was mentioned that everyone avoided it in his presence. By a tremendous effort of will he had succeeded in pushing his son to the back of his mind. The strain had nearly killed him, but he had persevered and won.

Then one day he received a letter from Nene, and in spite of himself he began to glance through it perfunctorily until all of a sudden the expression on his face changed and he began to read more carefully.

> . . . Our two sons, from the day they learnt that they have a grandfather, have insisted on being taken to him. I find it impossible to tell them that you will not see them. I implore you to allow Nnaemeka to bring them home for a short time during his leave next month. I shall remain here in Lagos . . .

The old man at once felt the resolution he had built up over so many years falling in. He was telling himself that he must not give in. He tried to steel his heart against all emotional appeals. It was a reenactment of that other struggle. He leaned against a window and looked out. The sky was overcast with heavy black clouds, and a high wind began to blow, filling the air with dust and dry leaves. It was one of those rare occasions when even Nature takes a hand in a human fight. Very soon it began to rain, the first rain in the year. It came down in large sharp drops and was accompanied by the lightning and thunder which mark a change of season. Okeke was trying hard not to think of his two grandsons. But he knew he was now fighting a losing battle. He tried to hum a favorite hymn, but the pattering of large raindrops on the roof broke up the tune. His mind immediately returned to the children. How could he shut his door against them? By a curious mental process he imagined them standing, sad and forsaken, under the harsh angry weather—shut out from his house.

That night he hardly slept, from remorse—and a vague fear that he might die without making it up to them. ❖

WORDS TO KNOW
deference (dĕf′ər-əns) *n.* courteous regard or respect
persevere (pûr′sə-vîr′) *v.* to persist in the face of difficulties
perfunctorily (pər-fŭngk′tə-rĭ-lē) *adv.* in a careless, uninterested way
forsaken (fôr-sā′kən) *adj.* abandoned **forsake** *v.*
remorse (rĭ-môrs′) *n.* a deep sense of guilt over a wrong one has done

785

Literary Concept: IRONY

K Have students discuss the irony in this situation. *(Possible response: that the father is the one who doesn't know how his own family is doing)*

Literary Concept: SETTING

L Ask students how Achebe uses a description of the outside world to help us see Okeke's internal conflict. *(Possible responses: The violent thunderstorm suggests the father's emotional turmoil; the rain after a long dry spell symbolizes Okeke coming to his emotional senses.)*

STRATEGIC READING FOR
Less-Proficient Readers

M How does Okeke feel about his son's family now? *(reconciled to the marriage; hopeful of seeing his grandsons)*
Summarizing

CUSTOMIZING FOR
Gifted and Talented Students

Ask students to discuss whether young people today are too quick to scorn "old-fashioned" cultural traditions. Have them discuss specific traditions and the practical concerns these traditions might be based on.

COMPREHENSION CHECK
1. What does Nnaemeka's father try to do for him in the village while Nnaemeka works in Lagos? *(He tries to arrange a marriage.)*
2. Give two reasons why Okeke objects to Nene? *(She is not of his tribe; she is a teacher; he has not arranged the marriage himself.)*
3. In the end, what causes Okeke to change his attitude? *(the thought of his grandsons)*

Mini-Lesson Literary Concepts

REVIEWING IRONY Remind students that irony is the contrast between what is expected and what really happens. Situational irony occurs when a reader or character expects one thing to happen but something entirely different occurs. For example, Nnaemeka expects his father to look favorably on Nene since she is a good Christian and a teacher; instead, the father condemns her for these very things. Similarly, when Nene and Nnaemeka send Okeke their wedding photograph, they probably expect him to keep it and perhaps change his mind about them. Instead, he cuts Nene out of the picture and sends it back.

Application Invite students to cite other examples of situational irony from the story.

THE LANGUAGE OF LITERATURE TEACHER'S EDITION **785**

From Personal Response to Critical Analysis

1. Accept all reasonable, well-supported responses.
2. Possible responses: The marriage offends Okeke's sense of tradition; he feels that his own authority and beliefs are mocked by the marriage; his attitude changes because he is finally able to enter into another point of view.
3. Possible responses: Nnaemeka handles the situation well; he calmly and lovingly tries to explain his choice; he accepts his father's rejection without anger; he makes attempts to re-establish contact.
4. Accept all reasonable, well-supported responses.
5. Possible response: The title suggests that individuals should make their own choices about whom to marry.
6. Accept all reasonable, well-supported responses.

Another Pathway

Invite students to discuss together reasons for each man's choice. Also have them discuss drawbacks and benefits that might come from each match.

Rubric
- **3 Full Accomplishment** Chart lists a number of reasons for both men's choices, with benefits and drawbacks.
- **2 Substantial Accomplishment** Chart is accurate but not as detailed as possible.
- **1 Little or Partial Accomplishment** Chart is inaccurate or lacks detail.

RESPONDING OPTIONS

FROM PERSONAL RESPONSE TO CRITICAL ANALYSIS

REFLECT 1. Which character did you have the strongest feelings about? Explain your reaction in your notebook.

RETHINK 2. How would you explain Okeke's persistent opposition to his son's marriage, and his change of attitude at the end of the story?
Consider
- the traditions that influence Okeke
- how he feels about his son's actions
- how he is affected by Nene's letter

Close Textual Reading

3. How well do you think Nnaemeka handles his father's opposition to his marriage?
4. What is your opinion of Nene's personality and judgment?
5. How do you think the story's title relates to its theme?

RELATE 6. What do you think is gained and lost when a society undergoes a transformation from traditional ways of life to modern ways? Draw upon your knowledge of history and current events, as well as your interpretation of this story.

Thematic Link

ANOTHER PATHWAY

Fill out a chart similar to the one you created for the Personal Connection on page 780. In one column, give reasons why Okeke wants Nnaemeka to marry Ugoye, and list the benefits and the drawbacks of his choice. In the other column, list the reasons why Nnaemeka has chosen Nene, along with the benefits and the drawbacks of his choice.

LITERARY CONCEPTS

As you have learned, the **setting** of a literary work is the time and place in which the action of the work takes place. A setting does not consist only of a physical location, however—it also includes the cultural environment in which the events unfold. The Ibo traditions of village life and the modern ways of city life can be considered parts of this story's cultural setting. With a partner, create two lists of details that convey the story's **cultural setting.** In one list, note what the story tells you about village life and attitudes; in the other, what it tells you about city life and attitudes. Share your lists with the rest of the class, and discuss how the story's setting contributes to your understanding of its characters and theme.

CONCEPT REVIEW: Point of View From what point of view is this selection narrated? How does the use of that point of view affect your reaction to the story?

QUICKWRITES

1. Write a **letter** that Okeke might send in response to Nene's letter. Your letter should reflect the father's personality and communicate how he now feels about his son and his son's family.
2. Write a series of **diary entries** in which Nene describes the problems she encounters as a result of her marriage, as well as her feelings about the problems.
3. Create a **list** of Okeke's objections to modern life. For each objection, include a supporting quotation from the story. Then write a response to each objection, defending modern life as Nnaemeka and Nene might.

📁 **PORTFOLIO** Save your writing. You may want to use it later as a springboard to a piece for your portfolio.

786 UNIT FIVE PART 2: CULTURAL CROSSROADS

Literary Concepts

Possible responses:

Traditional Village Life
- Tribal membership is central.
- Fathers arrange marriages for their children.
- People rely on traditional native medicine.
- Christianity is a strong influence.
- Women have fewer opportunities to work.

City Life
- People choose their own mates.
- Women have more opportunities.
- People of different tribes mingle and mix.

QuickWrites

1. Suggest that Okeke might include an apology in his letter as well as an account of what he plans to do to make amends.
2. Students should spread out their diary entries over the eight or more years that pass in the course of the story.
3. Encourage students to make use of their lists from the Literary Concepts activity.

 **The Writer's Craft**

Pro-and-Con Charts, p. 331

Multimodal Learning

ALTERNATIVE ACTIVITIES

1. With two of your classmates, perform an **improvisational scene** depicting the first meeting of Nene, Nnaemeka, and Okeke.

2. Do research to find two contrasting **photographs** of life in Nigeria today—one showing a way of life that Okeke would find appealing, the other showing a way of life that would appeal to his son. Display reproductions of the photographs to your class, explaining why you chose them.

3. With a group of classmates, role-play a **conversation** that might take place in the village where Okeke lives. Share news about the letter from Nene, being sure to convey the various attitudes of the villagers.

4. Create a **Venn diagram** to compare Okeke and Nnaemeka. In the nonoverlapping parts of the circles, list characteristics that are unique to the father and to the son. Where the circles overlap, list characteristics they have in common. Consider their personalities, beliefs, attitudes, and actions.

ART CONNECTION

Take another look at *Wooing,* the painting shown on page 783. What does the image suggest to you about the relationship between Nnaemeka and Nene?

Detail of *Wooing* (1984), Varnette Honeywood. Collage. Copyright © 1984 Varnette P. Honeywood.

CRITIC'S CORNER

About Achebe's writing, the critic G. D. Killam has said, "Through it all the spirit of man and the belief in the possibility of triumph endures." Do you think this comment is relevant to "Marriage Is a Private Affair"? Explain your opinion.

LITERARY LINKS

Compare the attitudes toward love and marriage expressed in this story with those expressed in "The First Seven Years" (page 460). What do the two stories have in common?

ACROSS THE CURRICULUM

Anthropology Find out more about Ibo traditions and village life. You may find information by looking up *Ibo* or *Igbo* (a variation of the name) in reference works or in a library card catalog. Then create a poster that displays information about life in an Ibo village.

History When did romantic love become a basis of marriage? What countries are associated with the origins of romantic love as we know it? Research an aspect of love or marriage that interests you, and draft a report on your findings.

MARRIAGE IS A PRIVATE AFFAIR **787**

Art Connection

Students might say that the painting expresses the strong physical and emotional closeness between Nene and Nnaemeka.

Critic's Corner

Students might point out that for eight years Nnaemeka and Nene maintain their spirits while hoping to reestablish ties with Okeke, and at story's end, they finally succeed.

Literary Links

In "The First Seven Years," Feld comes to see that Sobel, not Max, is the right spouse for his daughter. Similarly, Okeke must accept Nene although he would have much preferred a daughter-in-law from his own tribe and of his own choosing.

Across the Curriculum

Anthropology Nigerian students at local universities might be a good source of information for this activity. Tell students that the Ibo, during the period of British rule in the 1900s, accepted Western education and ways of life more quickly than other Nigerian peoples such as the Hausa and Yoruba. As a result, the Ibo held most important positions in government and business during colonial rule.

History To arouse interest in this project, you might point out that the word *romance* is derived from the Latin word *Romanus,* meaning a citizen of ancient Rome.

Alternative Activities

1. Remind students that improvisational means without practice. Point out that any awkwardness or discomfort they bring to the scene might be expressive of what the characters would have felt in the situation.

2. In researching their pictures, encourage students to use a CD-ROM data base at the library to find current events articles about Nigeria.

3. Before their role-play, students should discuss the various responses that one might expect from the villagers.

4. Students might note that Okeke and Nnaemeka both seem sure of themselves, confident in their ability to make decisions, and firm in their resolution to carry out decisions. Nnaemeka, a city-dweller, has more liberal and modern ideas, while Okeke is more traditional.

Words to Know

Exercise A
1. b
2. c
3. c
4. a
5. a

Exercise B
1. homily
2. forsaken
3. commiserate
4. theological
5. deference

Exercise C
Responses will vary.

Reteaching/Reinforcement
• *Unit Five Resource Book*, p. 58

CHINUA ACHEBE

Achebe has this to say about his own Christian upbringing in a Nigerian village: "When I was growing up I remember we tended to look down on the others. We were called in our language "the people of the church," and we called the others . . . "the people of nothing."

AUTHOR BACKGROUND
Chinua Achebe In this candid film interview, Bill Moyers speaks with the great African writer. Achebe talks about the Ibo philosophy of life and the place of the storyteller in society.

Side A, Frame 32340

CULTURAL CONNECTION
Marriage in Nigeria This is a film interview with Bassey Até, a Nigerian political scientist from Calabar, the same town where the wife in the story was born. Até speaks about marriage customs in his country.

Side A, Frame 39946

WORDS TO KNOW

EXERCISE A For each group of words below, write the letter of the word that is an antonym of the boldfaced word.

1. **persevere:** (a) praise, (b) quit, (c) accept
2. **dissuasion:** (a) improvement, (b) silence, (c) encouragement
3. **remorse:** (a) attraction, (b) improvement, (c) satisfaction
4. **cosmopolitan:** (a) provincial, (b) widespread, (c) elegant
5. **perfunctorily:** (a) thoroughly, (b) naturally, (c) wisely

EXERCISE B Review the Words to Know at the bottom of the selection pages. Then read each title below and write the vocabulary word, not used in Exercise A, that you might expect to find in a magazine article with that title.

1. "When Know-It-Alls Start Talking: A Guide for Self-Defense"
2. "The Tragedy of America's Cast-Off Pets"
3. "How to Help When a Loved One Hurts"
4. "Prayer in the Schools: The Debate Goes On"
5. "The Wisdom of Age: Honoring Our Elderly"

EXERCISE C With a partner, pantomime a situation that suggests the meaning of one of the vocabulary words. For example, one of you might act in a fawning manner toward the other to suggest the word *deference*. Invite your classmates to try to guess the word.

CHINUA ACHEBE

1930–

Chinua Achebe is one of contemporary Africa's most famous authors. A member of the Ibo people of eastern Nigeria, Achebe was born in the village of Ogidi, where his father taught at a Christian mission school. As a child, Achebe learned both the Ibo and the English language. "I have always been fond of stories and intrigued by language—first my mother tongue, Ibo, and later English," he reports. He first considered a writing career while a student at Nigeria's University of Ibadan. "I read some appalling European novels about Africa," he explains, ". . . and realized that our story could not be told for us by anyone else."

After college, Achebe taught briefly and then took a job with the Nigerian Broadcasting Corporation, eventually becoming the company's director of external broadcasting. In 1958 he published his first novel, *Things Fall Apart*, now a modern African classic. Like much of his subsequent fiction, this book, set in an Ibo village in the late 1800s, explores the effects of European colonialism in Africa and the clash between traditional and modern ways.

During the Nigerian civil war of 1967–1970, Achebe supported the independence effort of Biafra, a predominantly Ibo region in eastern Nigeria. He served on diplomatic missions representing Biafra and traveled in the United States with his fellow writer Gabriel Okara, lecturing and raising funds. After the fall of Biafra, Achebe took a university position in Nigeria; he has devoted his life to teaching and writing ever since.

Though fluent in Ibo, Achebe usually writes in English. He is generally regarded as the most accomplished of the many African novelists who write in English, and his works have sold well on three continents. In addition to novels and short stories, Achebe has produced a number of children's books, as well as collections of essays and poetry. "Marriage Is a Private Affair" is from *Girls at War and Other Stories*, published in 1973.

OTHER WORKS *Arrow of God; A Man of the People; Beware, Soul-Brother, and Other Poems; Anthills of the Savannah*

Extended Reading

LASERLINKS
• AUTHOR BACKGROUND
• CULTURAL CONNECTION

REFLECTING ON THEME
What Do You Think?

Have students compare the cultural crossroads that are described in this story with those that they examined for the activity on pages 742-743. You may also have them compare Achebe's story with Isaas Bashevis Singer's "The Son from America" in terms of the attitudes toward traditional and modern ways that are conveyed in the two stories.

PREVIEWING

POETRY

Lost Sister
Cathy Song United States

Activating Prior Knowledge

PERSONAL CONNECTION

Think about various situations that might prompt a woman to immigrate to the United States. What part might the social conditions in her native country play in her decision to leave? How do you think the experience of an immigrant woman in the United States might differ from that of an immigrant man? In a class discussion, share what you know about the lives of female immigrants in this country. Draw upon personal experience, or share what you have read or have seen in films or television shows.

Immigrants in Chinatown, San Francisco.
Copyright © Underwood Photo Archives.

Building Background

CULTURAL CONNECTION

In "Lost Sister," the poet Cathy Song contrasts the traditional life of women in China with the life of a Chinese woman who has emigrated to the United States. For many centuries, Chinese marriages were arranged when the partners were children. Before marriage, a girl was subservient to the adults in her family; afterward, when she moved into her husband's family's home, she was subservient to her husband, his male relations, and his older female relations. Only after having children of her own did she gain some measure of authority.

In some parts of China, it was considered essential for a girl to have small feet if she was to be married, so female children were subjected to the practice of foot binding—the tight wrapping of the feet to stunt their growth—between the ages of five and seven. Because this process bent the feet, breaking the bones of the insteps, the girls would hobble for the rest of their lives.

Active Reading / Setting a Purpose

READING CONNECTION

Defining Cultural Roles As you read this poem, notice the details that are used to characterize the traditional life of women in China and those that are used to characterize the life of a Chinese woman who has emigrated to the United States. In a chart like the one shown, jot down words or phrases, contained in or suggested by the poem, that describe the two ways of life.

A Woman in China	A Chinese Woman in U.S.
1.	1.
2.	2.
3.	3.

LOST SISTER **789**

OVERVIEW

Objectives

- To understand and appreciate a poem that explores the contrast between women's life in China and the experience of a Chinese immigrant woman in the United States
- To identify and understand symbols
- To express understanding of the poem through a choice of writing forms, including letters and an alternative title
- To extend understanding of the selection through a variety of multimodal and cross-curricular activities

Skills

LITERARY CONCEPTS
- Symbol
- Imagery

THE WRITER'S STYLE
- Simile

SPEAKING, LISTENING, AND VIEWING
- Group discussion
- Oral presentation

ALTERNATIVE
Previewing

Students can choose partners and use the following prompts to preview the poem orally.

Personal Connection

Discussion Prompts *Tell your partner about any links you have to the countries from which your parents or ancestors have come. Use these questions to direct you:*

- *What things tend to symbolize your links to another country?*
- *Did you ever wish to visit the country from which your family emigrated? Why?*

As you read the poem, think about the lost sister's relationship to China.

CUSTOMIZING FOR
Students Acquiring English

- Use **ACCESS FOR STUDENTS ACQUIRING ENGLISH**, *Reading Support*.
- Help students use punctuation marks such as dashes and periods to divide each stanza into meaningful groups of words. For example, in the first stanza the first four lines form a single thought; the next five lines go together, elaborating the role of jade in Chinese culture.
- In addition to these boxes, you may want to use the suggestions under Strategic Reading for Less-Proficient Readers.

PRINT AND MEDIA RESOURCES

UNIT FIVE RESOURCE BOOK
Strategic Reading: Literature, p. 61

WRITING MINI-LESSONS
Transparencies, p. 47

ACCESS FOR STUDENTS ACQUIRING ENGLISH
Reading Support

FORMAL ASSESSMENT
Selection Test, p. 157
 Test Generator

 AUDIO LIBRARY
See Reference Card

INTERNET RESOURCES
McDougal Littell Literature Center at http://www.hmco.com/mcdougal/lit

THE LANGUAGE OF LITERATURE TEACHER'S EDITION **789**

Thematic Link: *Cultural Crossroads*
This poem explores the feelings of a Chinese woman who has rebelled against the culture of her homeland but feels lost in the West.

Cultural Note

A Hard, tough, and usually green in color, jade has been China's most popular precious material for centuries.

Literary Concept: SIMILE

B Point out the simile in line 9 and ask how this image helps the reader appreciate jade. *(Possible response: By likening jade to a slice of melon, Song suggests that jade is a living substance, providing pleasure and sustenance.)*

Literary Concept: SYMBOL

C Ask students to speculate on what the binding of girls' feet might symbolize about the role of women in China. *(Possible response: It symbolizes their loss of freedom.)*

Critical Thinking: ANALYZING

D Have students explain the phrase "traveled far in surviving." *(Possible response: the women learned how to survive, despite their restrictions, even in times of famine and scarcity.)*

Lost Sister

CATHY SONG

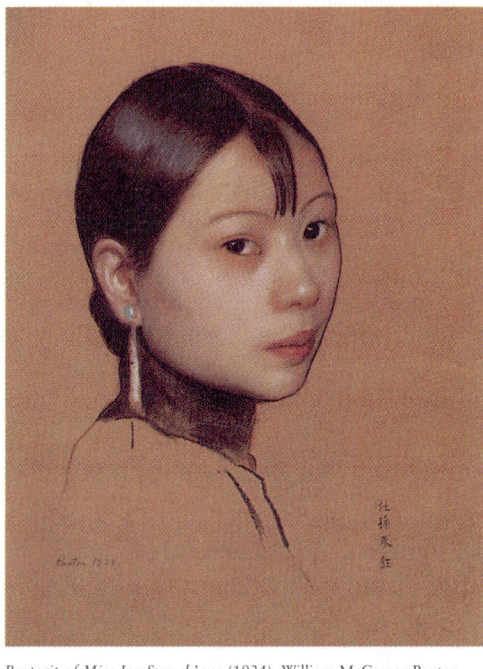

Portrait of Miss Jen Sun-ch'ang (1934), William McGregor Paxton. Courtesy Robert Douglas Hunter.

1

In China,
even the peasants
named their first daughters
Jade—
5   the stone that in the far fields
could moisten the dry season,
could make men move mountains
for the healing green of the inner hills
glistening like slices of winter melon.

10 And the daughters were grateful:
they never left home.
To move freely was a luxury
stolen from them at birth.
Instead, they gathered patience,
15 learning to walk in shoes
the size of teacups,
without breaking—
the arc of their movements
as dormant as the rooted willow,
20 as redundant as the farmyard hens.
But they traveled far
in surviving,
learning to stretch the family rice,
to quiet the demons,
25 the noisy stomachs.

19 **dormant** (dôr′mənt): inactive.
20 **redundant** (rĭ-dŭn′dənt): needlessly repetitive.

790   UNIT FIVE   PART 2: CULTURAL CROSSROADS

Mini-Lesson   The Writer's Style

SIMILES Review the definition of *simile*, a figure of speech using the words *like* or *as* that reveals similarities in very different things. Invite students to note the two similes in lines 19–20. Ask how Chinese daughters were similar to rooted willow trees. *(They are both dormant, or seemingly asleep, waiting for a time to bloom.)* Ask how the daughters are like farmyard hens. *(They are redundant, that is, there are more daughters than necessary; no great importance is placed on them.)* Ask students to share their thoughts about why these similes paint vivid images.

Application Invite students to write similes that describe the role of women in the United States. Encourage students to make comparisons to things in nature as Song does.

Reteaching/Reinforcement
• *Writing Handbook*, anthology pp. 1031–1032
• *Writing Mini-Lessons* transparencies, p. 47

 **The Writer's Craft**
Figurative Language, pp. 425–426

790   THE LANGUAGE OF LITERATURE   TEACHER'S EDITION

2

There is a sister
across the ocean,
who relinquished her name,
diluting jade green
30 with the blue of the Pacific.
Rising with a tide of locusts,
she swarmed with others
to inundate another shore.
In America,
35 there are many roads
and women can stride along with men.

But in another wilderness,
the possibilities,
the loneliness,
40 can strangulate like jungle vines.
The meager provisions and sentiments
of once belonging—
fermented roots, Mah-Jongg tiles and firecrackers—
set but a flimsy household
45 in a forest of nightless cities.
A giant snake rattles above,
spewing black clouds into your kitchen.
Dough-faced landlords
slip in and out of your keyholes,
50 making claims you don't understand,
tapping into your communication systems
of laundry lines and restaurant chains.

You find you need China:
your one fragile identification,
55 a jade link
handcuffed to your wrist.
You remember your mother
who walked for centuries,
footless—
60 and like her,
you have left no footprints,
but only because
there is an ocean in between,
the unremitting space of your rebellion.

28 relinquished (rĭ-lĭng′kwĭsht): gave up; abandoned.

29 diluting (dī-lōō′tĭng): lessening the strength or purity of.

33 inundate (ĭn′ŭn-dāt′): overwhelm as if by a flood; overflow.

43 Mah-Jongg (mä′zhŏng′): a game of Chinese origin, played with tiles resembling dominoes.

64 unremitting (ŭn′rĭ-mĭt′ĭng): continuing without interruption; unceasing.

LOST SISTER 791

Literary Concept: IMAGERY

E Have students discuss what this image of locusts suggests about Chinese immigration. *(Possible response: Countless people left China during that time, so many that they seemed to lose their individual identity; the image suggests an uncontrollable and destructive force.)*

Literary Concept: SYMBOL

F Have students suggest what the fermented roots, Mah-Jongg tiles, and firecrackers symbolize. *(Possible response: These odd bits, all that are left of the woman's Chinese heritage, symbolize the devastating loss that the woman experiences.)*

Literary Concept: IMAGERY

G Have students discuss what this imagery suggests about the life of the immigrant. *(Possible responses: The images all suggest persecution and entrapment; the immigrant seems to face real obstacles, such as the landlord, and imaginary ones, such as the "giant snake.")*

CUSTOMIZING FOR
Students Acquiring English

I Point out that *fragile* means "weak or easily broken" while *identification* refers to the speaker's sense of her own identity and her ties to China.

COMPREHENSION CHECK

1. Why did the sister go to America? *(to rebel against the repression of women in China and gain new freedom)*
2. What difficulties does the sister face in America? *(loneliness and the difficulty of adjusting to a strange culture)*

Mini-Lesson Literary Concepts

REVIEWING IMAGERY Remind students that imagery refers to words and phrases that appeal to the reader's senses, sometimes in a startling way. Most imagery appeals to the sense of sight, but imagery can appeal to other senses as well.

Application Have students discuss particular images in "Lost Sister" that they find startling. For example, they might discuss the image of Chinese women walking in teacup-sized shoes in line 15, the image likening immigrants to locusts in line 31, or the image of the giant snake in line 46.

THE LANGUAGE OF LITERATURE **Teacher's Edition** 791

From Personal Response to Critical Analysis

1. Accept all reasonable responses.
2. Possible responses: The speaker feels that traditional Chinese families systematically repressed their daughters by binding their feet and limiting their movement. Naming a first daughter Jade turned her into a lucky charm without individual identity.
3. Possible responses: The immigrant woman faces problems that are nearly opposite those faced in China: life in her new land is lonely, her choices are overwhelming, and there are few traditions to guide her.
4. Accept all reasonable, well-supported responses.
5. Accept all reasonable, well-supported responses.

Another Pathway

Once students have written their paragraphs, you might have a whole-class discussion so students can share their ideas.

Rubric

3 Full Accomplishment Students' paragraphs insightfully explore the pros and cons of both situations.

2 Substantial Accomplishment Students' paragraphs adequately discuss the pros and cons of both situations.

1 Little or Partial Accomplishment Students list the pros and cons of both situations but fail to explore them.

RESPONDING
OPTIONS

FROM PERSONAL RESPONSE TO CRITICAL ANALYSIS

REFLECT 1. What kind of mood did this poem leave you with? Explain your response to a classmate.

RETHINK 2. How do you think the speaker feels about the traditional life of Chinese women, as described in the first part of the poem?
Consider
- the significance of the name Jade (lines 1–9)
- the speaker's description of the lives of daughters (lines 10–25)

Close Textual Reading

3. What conclusions can you reach about the life of the immigrant Chinese woman, as described in the second part of the poem?
Consider
- the "many roads" she can take (lines 35–36)
- the use of the word strangulate (line 40)
- the comparison between the "footless" mother and the immigrant daughter with "no footprints" (lines 57–61)

Close Textual Reading

4. How might the poem be different if the immigrant described were male instead of female?

RELATE 5. Do you think other immigrant women, from different times and places, might have feelings similar to those expressed in this poem? Explain your opinion.

ANOTHER PATHWAY

Imagine you are a Chinese woman of about 100 years ago who must decide whether to emigrate to the United States. Write a paragraph on the pros and cons of staying in China and another paragraph on the pros and cons of living as an immigrant in the United States. Use the chart you created for the Reading Connection on page 789 to support your ideas.

QUICKWRITES

1. Imagine that you are the woman portrayed in the second part of the poem. Write two **letters** to a sister in China, telling her about your experience—one conveying your thoughts shortly after leaving home, the other describing your feelings after living in America for a while. Be sure to express your feelings about immigration.

2. Compose an **alternative title** for the poem, providing an explanation of the title's meaning and the reasons you think it appropriate.

📁 **PORTFOLIO** Save your writing. You may want to use it later as a springboard to a piece for your portfolio.

792 UNIT FIVE PART 2: CULTURAL CROSSROADS

QuickWrites

1. Make sure students realize that the first letter should deal mainly with her resentments about the role of women in China as well as her hopes for life in America. The second letter should focus on the serious difficulties the writer is having adjusting to her new homeland and can elaborate on some of the nightmarish imagery from lines 37–52.

2. Suggest that the new title might include mention of the woman's role as a daughter or an immigrant. Or it might focus on the idea of an ocean of time and space dividing her two homelands.

 **The Writer's Craft**

Paragraphs That Narrate and Describe, p. 361

LITERARY CONCEPTS

A **symbol** is a person, a place, or an object that represents something beyond itself. **Cultural symbols** are things with symbolic meaning for people in a particular culture. The stone jade, for example, is a cultural symbol in China, where carved jade objects and jewelry are equated with such abstract values as toughness, durability, and moral and physical beauty. **Literary symbols** are things that are given symbolic meaning within the context of literary works. How does an understanding of the cultural symbolism of jade influence your interpretation of its use as a literary symbol in "Lost Sister"? Discuss each of the three mentions of the stone in the poem.

Multimodal Learning
ACROSS THE CURRICULUM

World Cultures Do some research on one of the poem's references to aspects of Chinese or Chinese-American life, and share your findings with your classmates in an oral report. For example, you might report on foot binding, rice, Mah-Jongg (also spelled *mahjong*), firecrackers, or the businesses in which Chinese immigrants to the United States have traditionally found jobs.

LITERARY LINKS

Compare the immigrant experience depicted in "Lost Sister" with that depicted in "The Son from America" by Isaac Bashevis Singer (page 761).

CRITIC'S CORNER

The poet Richard Hugo has written, "Taste and touch are strong elements in [Cathy Song's] poems, although it is our sight that is most often engaged." Does this comment apply to "Lost Sister"? Support your answer with details from the poem.

Teapot belonging to Chinese woman who emigrated to the United States, 1880s. Photo by Karen Yamauchi for Chermayeff & Geismar Inc./MetaForm Inc.

CATHY SONG

1955–

In 1982 Cathy Song's first poetry collection, *Picture Bride*, was published as the winner of the Yale Series of Younger Poets competition, a contest open to any American writer under the age of 40 who has not previously published a volume of poetry. Many of the poems in the book, like "Lost Sister," chronicle the Chinese-American experience. Noting that *Picture Bride* is divided into sections named for different flowers, the contest judge, Richard Hugo, compared Song's poems to "flowers—colorful, sensual and quiet—offered almost shyly as bouquets to those moments in life that seemed minor but in retrospect count the most."

Song was born and raised in Hawaii and attended the University of Hawaii and Wellesley College; she earned her master's degree at Boston University. In addition to publishing poems in a number of anthologies and literary journals, she has coedited the anthology *Sister Stew: Fiction and Poetry by Women*. She now lives and teaches in Honolulu, Hawaii.

OTHER WORKS *Frameless Windows, Squares of Light*; poems in *The Open Boat: Poems from Asian America*

Extended Reading

Literary Links

Possible responses: In general it seems that Samuel in "The Son from America" has a much better immigrant experience than the immigrant in "Lost Sister." Samuel prospered in his new home, maintained ties to his old culture, and upon returning to Poland, appreciated his village in a new and deeper way. The lost sister experiences alienation and fear in America and remains cut off from the China against which she rebelled.

Critic's Corner

If they agree, students might point to such visual images as the blue Pacific diluting the green jade, the giant snake spewing black clouds into the kitchen, the dough-faced landlords slipping in keyholes, and so on.

Across the Curriculum

World Cultures *Cooperative Learning* Have students work in small groups to do the research. Students may divide research responsibilities according to topics, such as foot binding, Mah-Jongg, employment opportunities in the United States, and so on.

CATHY SONG

Cathy Song believes that poets, like artists, capture the moment, knowing that it is always dissolving. Indeed, the work of two well-known artists, the modern American painter Georgia O'Keeffe and the 19th-century Japanese printmaker Kitagawa Utamaro, have inspired many of Cathy Song's poems. Song has also looked to people for inspiration, using imagination to enter into their life experiences.

Literary Concepts

When it is first mentioned in line 4, jade functions as a cultural symbol, calling forth associations of beauty, power, and health, suggesting the strength of Chinese heritage. In line 29, jade functions as a literary symbol; the dilution of the green jade by the blue Pacific symbolizes the lost sister's rejection and the weakening of her Chinese heritage by going overseas. In line 55, the jade is reduced to an ornamental cufflink, a reminder of the past, but hardly the healing stone of Chinese heritage.

OBJECTIVES

- To promote independent active reading
- To practice and apply skills learned in previous selections
- To provide an opportunity to assess students' performance through an alternative assessment instrument

Reading Pathways

- Suggest that students choose partners and do a paired reading of the poem, alternating stanza by stanza.
- Encourage individuals to present a dramatic oral reading.
- Suggest that students use a sketch pad to record some of the vivid imagery in the poem.
- Evaluate how well students can read, interpret, discuss, and write about the selection on their own by using the Integrated Assessment for Unit Five, located in the Alternative Assessment booklet. Administer the assessment at the end of the unit after students have completed the final writing assignment.

Thematic Link: *Cultural Crossroads*
A modern-day Australian muses on the aboriginal culture that has all but disappeared from Australia.

ON YOUR OWN

BORA RING

JUDITH WRIGHT AUSTRALIA

Rock engravings done by aborigines in eastern Australia. Superstock.

Before the English began to colonize Australia at the end of the 18th century, the Australian Aborigines (ăb′ə-rĭj′ə-nēz)—the native peoples of the continent—probably numbered around 300,000. Seminomadic and dependent on the natural environment for survival, they felt a deep spiritual connection to the land and marked life's passages—such as birth, maturity, marriage, and death—with sacred rituals and ceremonies. The bora ritual, performed in a "bora ring," celebrated a boy's entry into manhood.

English colonization greatly reduced the number of Australian Aborigines and destroyed much of their way of life. Bloodshed, disease, forced resettlement, agricultural expansion, and urbanization all contributed to the destruction of their traditional culture.

794

PRINT AND MEDIA RESOURCES

UNIT FIVE RESOURCE BOOK
Strategic Reading: Literature, p. 65

ACCESS FOR STUDENTS ACQUIRING ENGLISH
Reading Support

FORMAL ASSESSMENT
Selection Test, p. 159
Part Test, pp. 161–162
Test Generator

ALTERNATIVE ASSESSMENT
Unit Five Integrated Assessment, pp. 25–30

AUDIO LIBRARY
See Reference Card

INTERNET RESOURCES
McDougal Littell Literature Center at http://www.hmco.com/mcdougal/lit

The song is gone; the dance
is secret with the dancers in the earth,
the ritual useless, and the tribal story
lost in an alien tale.

5 Only the grass stands up
to mark the dancing-ring: the apple-gums
posture and mime a past corroboree,
murmur a broken chant.

The hunter is gone: the spear
10 is splintered underground; the painted bodies
a dream the world breathed sleeping and forgot.
The nomad feet are still.

Only the rider's heart
halts at a sightless shadow, an unsaid word
15 that fastens in the blood the ancient curse,
the fear as old as Cain.

6 **apple-gums:** eucalyptus trees, native to Australia.

7 **corroboree** (kə-rŏb′ə-rē): a nighttime festival in which the Australian Aborigines celebrate important events with songs and symbolic dances.

16 **Cain** (kān): the eldest son of Adam and Eve, who was condemned to be a fugitive after he murdered his brother Abel out of jealousy.

JUDITH WRIGHT

1915–

The acclaimed poet Judith Wright is a descendant of English settlers who arrived on the continent of Australia in 1828. She grew up in a small farming town in the New England district of the Australian state of New South Wales. Educated at home until she was 13, she spent much of her childhood out of doors, on horseback. "The country was deep in my bones," she recalls, "and I loved to look at it."

Wright attended the University of Sydney and then traveled in Europe for a year before returning to Australia and embarking on her literary career. "Bora Ring" appeared in Wright's first volume of poetry, *The Moving Image*, which was published in 1946. The poems in this collection and in *Woman to Man*, which followed in 1949, concern the plight of Australian Aborigines, the role of women, and the need to protect Australia's natural landscape. These themes have continued to concern the poet throughout her writing career, during which she has produced more than a dozen volumes of verse, as well as short stories, essays, children's books, and plays.

An active environmentalist, Wright helped found a wildlife preservation society in Queensland, Australia, and has fought to preserve Australia's Great Barrier Reef, to establish national parks, and to protect the land from deforestation. "Four generations of my forebears spent a lot of their time battling against Australian trees," she once observed; ". . . I spend a good deal of my time in the reverse process, battling *for* trees."

OTHER WORKS *The Generations of Men; Because I Was Invited; The Double Tree: Selected Poems, 1942–1976*

Extended Reading

BORA RING **795**

JUDITH WRIGHT

In addition to her poetry and children's books, Wright wrote two books largely based on the diary of her grandfather: *The Generations of Men* and *The Cry for the Dead*. These books deal with the story of the land, as well as that of her family. Albert Wright's diary told a good deal about the unwise use of the land and about the brutal extermination of the Aborigines.

OPTION 1

Individual Activity
RESEARCHING AUSTRALIA'S ABORIGINES

Assign students to choose and research an aspect of Australian Aborigine culture. Possible topics include the following:

- family and tribal relationships, including local descent groups and bands
- bark and stone paintings
- "Dreaming" religious beliefs
- the purpose of body painting

Ask students to present their findings orally to the group.

Teacher's Role If possible, work with students at the school library or media resource center to help them find and evaluate sources of information.

Rubric

3 Full Accomplishment Report is detailed, entertaining, and informative about the chosen topic.

2 Substantial Accomplishment Report is accurate and informative; delivery is adequate.

1 Little or Partial Accomplishment Report is superficial; delivery is disorganized.

OPTION 2

Class Discussion
SHARING IDEAS

Teacher's Role After students have read the poem, engage them in a whole-class discussion, using the following prompts:

1. Who is the speaker in the poem? What is the speaker doing? *(a modern-day Australian on horseback riding though the countryside)*

2. How would you describe the speaker's tone, or attitude, toward the aboriginal culture? *(Possible response: The tone is one of mourning for a lost culture and perhaps guilt for the role English-settler ancestors played in this loss.)*

3. What does stanza two suggest about the relationship of nature and aboriginal culture? *(Possible response: The forms of nature somehow suggest the lost rituals of the Australian Aborigines; it's as if nature and their culture were one.)*

4. Think about the concluding stanza of the poem. How does the story of Cain and Abel apply to the poem? *(Possible response: like Cain, the white settlers can be held responsible for the murder of their brothers, or the Australian Aborigine culture.)*

THE LANGUAGE OF LITERATURE TEACHER'S EDITION **795**

OVERVIEW

To gain a deeper appreciation of the selections they have read in this unit, students will explore the characteristics of a dramatic scene and then create a well-developed example in this lesson.

Objectives

- To plan a dramatic scene by considering elements such as conflict, characters, setting, stage directions, dialogue, audience, and script format
- To draft a dramatic scene and solicit a response
- To revise, edit, and publish a dramatic scene
- To reflect on the process of writing a dramatic scene

Skills

WRITING AND LANGUAGE
- Writing stage directions
- Writing dialogue

GRAMMAR AND USAGE
- Formatting a script

MEDIA LITERACY
- Understanding headlines, news stories, and news photographs
- Producing and performing a play

SPEAKING, LISTENING, AND VIEWING
- Listening
- Conferencing

RESEARCH SKILLS
- Using the computer

CUSTOMIZING FOR
Students Acquiring English

A If some students are put off by the negative connotations of the word *conflict*, guide them to recognize the literary meaning of this word. Real-life examples might include deciding whether to work or to attend college after high school.

CUSTOMIZING FOR
Less-Proficient Writers

B Thinking of ideas is one of the biggest sticking points for young writers when they face creative writing assignments. One productive strategy is to supply a title to students who lack confidence in their imaginations. Tell students that the stories, poems, and essays listed in the Table of Contents might suggest good ideas for plays even if (or especially if) students have not yet read the selections.

WRITING FROM EXPERIENCE

WRITING A PLAY

Selections in Unit Five, "Nothing Stays the Same," show the effects of change and the conflicts that arise among people affected by change. What conflicts are there among people in your school? your town? the world? How many of these conflicts are related to change?

GUIDED ASSIGNMENT
Write a Scene for a Play Because all of the action in a play takes place before an audience, drama is a very effective medium for showing change and conflict. In this lesson, you will write a scene that dramatizes a challenging situation.

❶ Identify Changes

A Most good stories and plays have their beginnings in some sort of real-world conflict. For example, the stories in Unit Five involved conflicts between different groups of people or between people and changing situations. Look at the headlines and articles on these pages. What change or conflict is at the center of each one? How might a writer build a story around one of these conflicts?

❷ Consider the Possibilities

You, too, may discover the seeds of a story in situations and images that you see around you. Try one or more of these activities to find an idea that you can turn into a play.

- Think about stories in the news that you've read or heard about. Would any of the conflicts behind these stories make good plays? What details would you need to add or change?
- Discuss changes that may happen in the future, such as a woman becoming president or global warming. What conflicts might result? Could the conflicts be dramatized?
- **B** Discuss stories in this book that would make good plays. Look through the Table of Contents for ideas.

News Photograph
People often organize to protest situations they believe are unfair. What kinds of conflicts do public protests involve?

796   UNIT FIVE: NOTHING STAYS THE SAME

PRINT AND MEDIA RESOURCES

UNIT FIVE RESOURCE BOOK
Prewriting, p. 69
Elaboration, p. 70
Peer Response Guide, pp. 71–72
Revising and Proofreading, p. 73
Student Model, pp. 74–75
Rubric, p. 76

FORMAL ASSESSMENT
Guidelines for Writing Assessment

GRAMMAR MINI-LESSONS
Transparencies, p. 44
Copymasters, pp. 1, 47

WRITING MINI-LESSONS
Transparencies, pp. 44, 54, 56

WRITING COACH

LASERLINKS
Writing Springboard

Article Headlines

A play set in the future could have conflicts over the environment.

Newspaper headlines often emphasize conflict. What stories might follow each of these headlines?

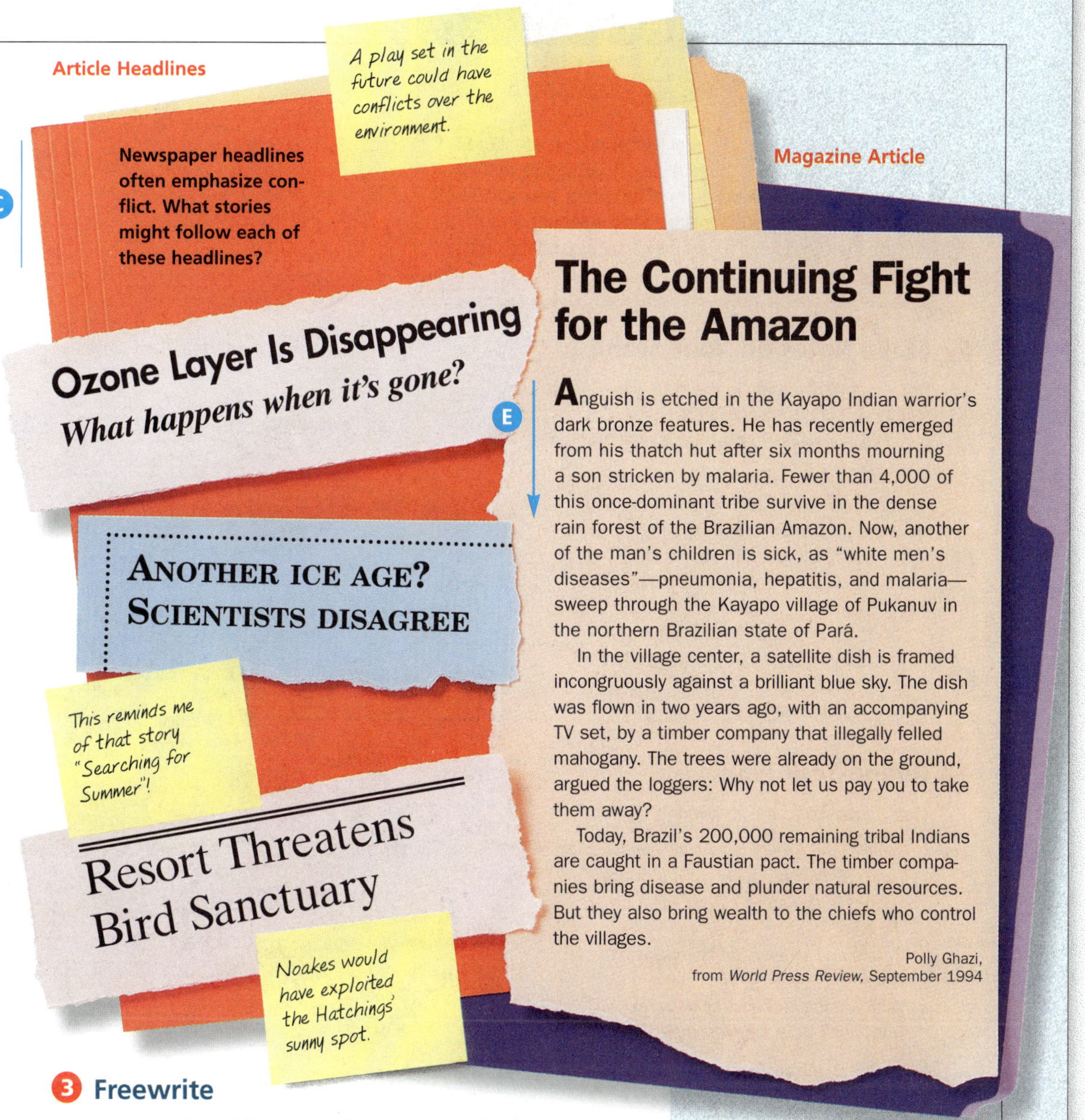

Magazine Article

Ozone Layer Is Disappearing
What happens when it's gone?

The Continuing Fight for the Amazon

Anguish is etched in the Kayapo Indian warrior's dark bronze features. He has recently emerged from his thatch hut after six months mourning a son stricken by malaria. Fewer than 4,000 of this once-dominant tribe survive in the dense rain forest of the Brazilian Amazon. Now, another of the man's children is sick, as "white men's diseases"—pneumonia, hepatitis, and malaria—sweep through the Kayapo village of Pukanuv in the northern Brazilian state of Pará.

In the village center, a satellite dish is framed incongruously against a brilliant blue sky. The dish was flown in two years ago, with an accompanying TV set, by a timber company that illegally felled mahogany. The trees were already on the ground, argued the loggers: Why not let us pay you to take them away?

Today, Brazil's 200,000 remaining tribal Indians are caught in a Faustian pact. The timber companies bring disease and plunder natural resources. But they also bring wealth to the chiefs who control the villages.

Polly Ghazi,
from *World Press Review*, September 1994

ANOTHER ICE AGE?
SCIENTISTS DISAGREE

This reminds me of that story "Searching for Summer"!

Resort Threatens Bird Sanctuary

Noakes would have exploited the Hatchings' sunny spot.

3 Freewrite

Try some of your ideas. For each situation, think of things that could happen that would create conflict. Ask "What if . . . ?" and then freewrite about the situation for a few minutes.

Decision Point Decide which story or real-life situation you are going to dramatize.

→ LASERLINK
→ WRITING COACH

WRITING FROM EXPERIENCE 797

Teaching Strategy: MODELING

C Discuss with students how they might generate ideas for a play from real-life conflicts. Have students examine these headlines and volunteer ideas about the stories that could be inspired by them. Possible responses include science fiction or fantasy stories showing what might happen if these headlines came true.

Teaching Strategy: STUMBLING BLOCK

D Reassure students that they do not need to look for conflicts in the areas of politics, economics, or the environment. Headlines in such fields as sports and the arts should also offer many possibilities. "Human interest" feature stories in newspapers and magazines are often built around conflicts in the lives or careers of interesting people.

CUSTOMIZING FOR
Students Acquiring English

E Some of the vocabulary in the article may cause problems for readers. Explain the following:
satellite dish: "large, dish-shaped antenna for receiving television signals"
felled mahogany: "cut down mahogany trees"
Faustian pact: "contract like that made by the legendary philosopher Faust, who sold his soul to the devil in exchange for power and knowledge"

WRITING SPRINGBOARD
Interview with a Screenwriter In this film interview, Gordon Lewis, a Hollywood screenwriter, offers keen insights into the process of writing a script. Students may draw on his insights as they write their own scripts for a scene of a play.

Writing Prompt Keeping in mind Gordon Lewis's comments about the organization of a script, write your own screenplay for one scene of an animated film for children.

Side B, Frame 26907

Writer's Craft: USING DIALOGUE

F Point out that students will have to use dialogue to convey essential background information for their dramatic scenes. Encourage them to make a list of background facts and then plan how they can incorporate those facts smoothly in the characters' dialogue.

Speaking and Listening: COLLABORATIVE OPPORTUNITY

G Have students work in pairs or small groups to help one another develop their characters. Students can take turns reading aloud their notes about each character. Then collaborators can ask questions about the character's physical appearance, background, motivation, and role in the plot. As students try to answer these questions, they will identify what they know about the character and what they still have to determine in order to create a credible character.

Teaching Strategy: MODELING

H Remind students that even if they do not draw sketches of their characters, as the student writer did in the planning notes shown in the text, they should try to visualize each character on stage. Students may want to make a checklist or chart listing items such as the following: eye color, height and weight, clothing, characteristic facial expression, hair color and style, special physical characteristics, and distinctive ways of speaking, gesturing, and moving.

PREWRITING

Setting the Stage

Conflict Through Action You've decided on a real or fictional story that you want to dramatize. Now it's time to think about the people and events that will be part of your scene. These pages can help you to make decisions about how to dramatize the conflict and about the characters, setting, and action of your scene.

❶ Make Notes on Your Scene

Note important events in the story you want to tell. As you choose a specific scene to dramatize, look for an event that has a clear starting point and end point.

F
- Make some notes on what will happen, where and when it will happen, and who will make it happen in your scene.
- Decide which events will be included in your scene.

G
- Jot down a few sentences or phrases that describe the key characters. Include personality traits as well as physical characteristics and clothing.

❷ Refine Your Plan

Questions such as the following may help you improve your plan.

- How will I set up the most important conflict in the scene? How will it be resolved?
- Where and when does the play take place?
- Who are the characters? How do they look? How are they dressed?

H Notice how one student noted what she wanted to show in a scene based on the story "Searching for Summer."

Student's Planning Notes

798 UNIT FIVE: NOTHING STAYS THE SAME

Mini-Lesson: Speaking, Listening, and Viewing

DIALOGUE As students prepare to write dialogue of their own, they should be encouraged to pay close attention to how people speak. Point out to students that people do not always speak in complete—or even entirely grammatical—sentences. While dialogue should be written clearly enough to be easily understood, it need not be so pristinely grammatical as to obliterate a character's personal speech patterns.

Application Encourage students to discretely listen to people speaking to one another in public places. They may even wish to transcribe verbatim the dialogue of people around them for future reference.

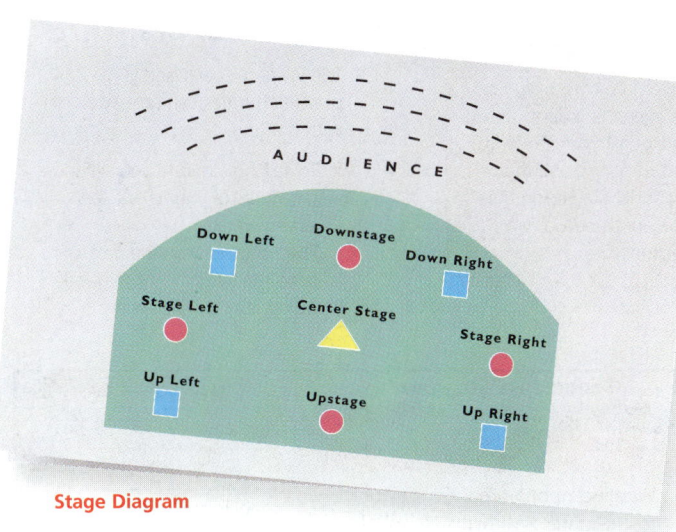

Stage Diagram

3 Visualize Your Staging

Now that you've made some basic decisions about your scene, imagine how it will look and sound as it is performed.

- Picture what the audience will see when the scene opens and where the actors will be on the stage. Then imagine each event as your story unfolds.
- The stage diagram above and the SkillBuilder on the right may help you imagine the placement of scenery and props and the movement of characters on stage.
- When you have finished playing out the scene in your mind, jot down ideas that you want to include in your script.

4 Consider Your Audience

Who will this play be for—people your own age, a general audience, or children? Once you have identified your audience, think about how you can plan setting, dialogue, action, and costumes that will appeal to this audience. For example, a play for children would probably include more action and less dialogue than a play for adults.

SkillBuilder

 WRITER'S CRAFT

Writing Stage Directions

Scripts for plays include stage directions—descriptions of how characters look, speak, and move and of scenery, props, and lighting. Characters are described where each appears on stage.

Include speaking directions for actors with dialogue. Most directions are a word or phrase, such as *(sadly)* or *(looking at him)*. Other directions describe complicated actions. *(He smiles with satisfaction as he looks in mirror.)* Review plays in this book for more examples.

The setting is described at the beginning of each scene. A setting should fit the mood of a scene. For example, a set for a realistic play could include real furniture. Some plays are performed with only lighting or music to evoke a mood.

APPLYING WHAT YOU'VE LEARNED
Describe a setting that would be appropriate for your scene.

THINK & PLAN

Reflecting on Your Ideas

1. What details can you include in your opening to describe the setting and characters?
2. How can you make the conflict in your story clear through dialogue and stage directions?
3. If you are adapting a story, what changes will you make?

WRITING FROM EXPERIENCE   799

Teaching Strategy: STUMBLING BLOCK

I Encourage kinesthetic learners who find it hard to visualize setting and movement to form small groups and block out their scenes by rehearsing movements, gestures, and lines in a designated performance space. This technique often reveals what will "play" on stage and helps actors develop effective gestures and movements.

Writer's Craft: THINKING ABOUT AUDIENCE

J Discuss how a scene might be affected if the audience were composed of young children. Guide students to recognize that most young children interpret actions and dialogue literally, whereas most teenagers and adults respond to hints, innuendoes, symbolism, and abstract ideas.

SkillBuilder WRITER'S CRAFT

WRITING STAGE DIRECTIONS Explain that because plays are written to be performed, students should not treat stage directions as a secondary element or an afterthought. On the contrary, they should remember that stage directions are a crucial element in play writing, second in importance only to the dialogue that is actually delivered by actors on stage. Because stage directions have such a critical impact on the visual dimension of drama, they require careful planning and precise wording.

Applying What You've Learned You may wish to have students work with partners or in small groups for this activity. Students can read their stage directions to a partner, who briefly sketches what is described. The writer can then verify whether or not his or her description is adequate.

Additional Suggestions Remind students that in addition to guiding actions, movements, and gestures on stage, stage directions can call for offstage music or special effects.

THE LANGUAGE OF LITERATURE TEACHER'S EDITION   799

Teaching Strategy: MANAGING THE PAPER LOAD

K Rather than reading the written scripts, you may wish to have groups of students present dramatic readings of their drafts for your comments.

DRAFTING

Developing Your Script

Conflict Shown Through Dialogue In a play, dialogue and stage directions must communicate everything about the story. Keep this in mind as you draft a script for your scene. If you feel more comfortable with one part of your scene than with another, begin with that part. Put your characters in the scene and have them start talking to one another. You can clarify their situation and add stage directions later.

1 Begin Your Draft

The Writing Coach and your prewriting notes can help you with drafting.

- Try talking aloud to yourself in the voices of your characters as you write.
- The SkillBuilder on the next page can help you write good dialogue.

Student's Rough Draft

Scene for "Summer"

My Rough Draft

Mr. Noakes. Old nuisances! Wasting public time. Every week that business goes on, taking the old man to Midwick Hospital Outpatients and back again. I know what I'd do with 'em. Put away somewhere, that sort ought to be!

Garage owner. Mr. Noakes, Mr. Noakes! Here's two young people wanting you. They need a room for the night.

Mr. Noakes. Honeymooners, eh? Want a bed for the night, eh? Heh, heh, heh, heh.

Lily. Well, we WERE looking for some sunshine. Now we'll have to stay until the bike's fixed, I guess.

Mr. Noakes. Sunshine! Oh my gawd! That's a good one! Hear that? They're looking for a bit of sunshine. Heh, heh, heh, heh, heh, heh! Why if I could find a bit of sunshine near here, permanent bit, that is, do you know what I'd do? Beach, trailer site, country club, holiday camp—you wouldn't know the place. Land around here is dirt cheap; I'd buy up the lot. Nothing but woods. I'd advertise—I'd have people flocking to this little dump from all over the country. But what a hope, what a hope, eh? Well, come on then. Almost bedtime! Ready for bed? Heh, heh, heh, heh, bed's ready for you! Follow me.

Lily. I—I'd like to go for a bit of a walk first, Tom. Look, I picked up that old lady's bag on the pavement. I didn't notice it till we'd done talking to Mr. Noakes, and by then she was out of sight. Should we take it back to her?

Tom. Good Idea! Do you know where she lives, Mr. Noakes?

Mr. Noakes. Who, old Ma Hatching? Sure, she lives in the wood. But you don't want to take her bag back. Let her worry.

My Comments *My Rough Draft*

I need to tell what Mr. Noakes looks like and what important characters are wearing. Also, how can I get characters off the bus?

Here, in the original story, they go to the inn, but I can't change the scenery in the middle of the scene. Instead, have them talking on the road. Is there a way to get them off for their walk before they go to the inn?

800 UNIT FIVE: NOTHING STAYS THE SAME

WRITING SPRINGBOARD

Stories in Pictures Photographs of dramatic scenes and people in conflict will help students generate ideas for a scene of a play. Challenge students to write the conversation that they imagine is occurring in one of the photographs.

Writing Prompt Choose one of the photographs and imagine the conversation that is occurring between the people in the picture. Write a script, shaping the conversation into a scene with a beginning, middle, and end.

Side B, Frames 50369

2 Review Your Draft

Read your draft aloud to yourself to catch unnatural sounding dialogue. Mark places where dialogue must be added to supply necessary background information. Also, ask yourself these questions:

- Does the part of the story shown in my scene make sense?
- Is the conflict in the story developed in an interesting way?
- Could I move more quickly into the conflict?
- Do my characters have distinct personalities? Can I change the dialogue or add stage directions to make them more real? Would it help to have them wear certain costumes?
- Is my setting clear? What details can I add to make it more vivid? Do I want to describe the setting in dialogue, or should I add stage directions for scenery and lighting?

Ask a few of your friends to read your script aloud or to act out your script and follow your stage directions.

3 Rework and Share

Before you write a second draft, think about changes that you want to make based on your attempt to act out your scene.

- If the action in your scene was too slow or too fast, add or take out dialogue or action.
- Make sure that your opening stage directions identify the setting and describe the stage as the scene opens, including the positions of the actors.
- Wherever it is needed, add stage directions to describe how the characters talk and move.
- The stage diagram and SkillBuilder on page 799 can help you write good stage directions.

PEER RESPONSE

Ask a few peer readers to once again act out your script and follow your stage directions. These questions may help readers to identify the strengths and weaknesses of your scene:

- Were you interested in the scene from the beginning? If not, how could I change the opening to make it more involving?

- What details would tell more about setting and characters?
- Do my characters seem real? Is their dialogue natural?
- Are any parts of the scene unclear to you? What parts?

SkillBuilder

 WRITER'S CRAFT

Writing Dialogue

Use dialogue to show characters' personalities, describe settings, and advance plot. For example, if characters are in danger, have them discuss what they see and hear, how they feel, and how to escape. Keep dialogue natural by using short sentences, fragments, contractions, and slang. With some dialogue, you may want to add stage directions.

If you are adapting a story you have read, use some of the original dialogue. You will also have to invent dialogue to give necessary information about background, characters, and plot.

APPLYING WHAT YOU'VE LEARNED
Write dialogue to dramatize passages from a story of your choice.

 GRAMMAR HANDBOOK

For information on punctuating dialogue in narrative, see page 1096 of the Grammar Handbook.

RETHINK & EVALUATE

Preparing to Revise

1. How could your stage directions better direct actors or communicate mood?
2. What changes could you make to dialogue to clarify events or make characters more real?
3. How could you improve the opening or end of the scene?

WRITING FROM EXPERIENCE **801**

Teaching Strategy:
COLLABORATIVE OPPORTUNITY

 Have reviewers read the scene before they make any comments. During a second reading, they should jot down brief comments and suggestions. Remind students to include specific ideas for revision, such as "The action seems too slow here. How about cutting these two speeches?"

SkillBuilder — WRITER'S CRAFT

WRITING DIALOGUE Remind students that many people in real life have characteristic ways of speaking: They use favorite words or idioms, for example, or they utter certain exclamations or slang expressions. It is precisely these idiosyncratic, character-revealing aspects of dialogue for which good playwrights develop an ear.

Applying What You've Learned Suggest that students work with partners for this activity. The partners could first attempt to improvise the scene using the source material for guidance.

Additional Suggestions Tell students that deliberately leaving a line of dialogue unfinished may sometimes be an effective device for suggesting a character's internal conflict, doubts, or hesitancy.

Reteaching/Reinforcement
- *Writing Mini-lessons*, transparencies, p. 56

Using Dialogue in Plays, pp. 453–454

THE LANGUAGE OF LITERATURE **TEACHER'S EDITION** **801**

Writing Skill: REVISING

M Many students think that good writers always get it right the first time and therefore never have to revise their work. Explain that *all* writers revise and that extensive revision is the mark of a thoughtful writer. As students revise and edit their scenes, they should try the following techniques:
1. adding needed words, sentences, or stage directions
2. cutting unnecessary material by identifying repetitive or unrelated speeches that do not advance the plot or the character development
3. substituting vivid words and sentences for material that sounds dull
4. rearranging parts of the text to improve logic, coherence, and audience appeal

Teaching Strategy: MODELING

N Discuss how this model meets the standards for evaluation on page 803. Point out that the opening stage directions contain several sentence fragments that establish the setting of the scene.

REVISING AND PUBLISHING

Staging Your Scene

On with the Show! You've worked to make your dialogue and stage directions tell a story. Now share your scene by preparing a final draft. This draft should incorporate your own and your peers' ideas for improvements and should use correct scriptwriting conventions. If you decide to produce your scene, choose your actors, design your scenery, and start rehearsals. You're the producer, director, and the star of your show.

Student's Final Script

The future. Molesworth village. A road in front of a garage, gray sky above. Lily, in a yellow wedding dress, and Tom, in a suit, stand with their scooter beside Garage owner, who waves at people getting off a bus, which is offstage left.

Garage owner. There's Mr. Noakes now. He'll have room for you.

William, blind and with a white stick, and Mrs. Hatching, old and frail in a black dress and hat, enter. William is helped along by George. Mr. Noakes, who is fat, red-faced, and dirty-looking, follows them.

Mrs. Hatching. Careful now, George, mind ee be careful with my son William. (*She drops her purse. They move off right.*)

Mr. Noakes (*furiously*). Old nuisances! Wasting public time. Every week that business goes on, taking the old man to Midwick Hospital Outpatients and back again. I know what I'd do with 'em. Put away somewhere, that sort ought to be!

Garage owner (*calling*). Mr. Noakes, Mr. Noakes! Here's two young people wanting you. They need a room for the night.

Mr. Noakes (*leering with false sentimentality at Lily*). Honeymooners, eh? Want a bed for the night, eh? (*Laughs suggestively and pinches Lily's arm*).

Lily (*sadly*). Well, we WERE looking for some sunshine. Now we'll have to stay until the bike's fixed, I guess.

802

---

1 Revise and Edit

Use peer comments on dialogue and stage directions and the Standards for Evaluation on the next page as you revise. The SkillBuilder on the next page will help you to make your scene ready for its opening.

N The writer describes the setting of the scene and the characters' positions on stage in an introductory paragraph.

The writer changes some story events to allow all the action to take place in the same setting.

Student's Idea for Stage Set

2 Share Your Scene

 You may want to expand your scene into a complete play before having it performed. For a play based on "Searching for Summer," the writer designed a set for a forest scene. The trees pull back to give the illusion of sun breaking through clouds.

You may also adapt your play as a radio script or film script.

- Radio plays have sound effects and often have narrators.
- Scripts for television and films describe what is shown on the screen while the characters are speaking and specify the point of view from which a shot is seen.
- Record your play on audiotape or videotape and share it.

Standards for Evaluation

 An effective dramatic scene
- deals with a conflict that is clearly conveyed by the plot
- uses characters and setting to create a world of its own
- includes complete stage directions as necessary
- uses dialogue that advances the plot
- uses appropriate format for dramatic writing

SkillBuilder

GRAMMAR FROM WRITING

Formatting Your Script
Look over the plays in this book before preparing the final draft of your script. Notice the beginning of the play and the dialogue.

- Describe the setting and opening situation in a paragraph.
- If you list characters, arrange them by order of appearance.
- Begin a new line when the speaker changes. Give the name of the speaker, followed by a period.
- Give directions for an actor within parentheses between the name and the dialogue.
- Use italic type for stage directions and boldface type for characters' names, if possible.

Editing Checklist Use the following editing tips as you revise.

- Did you correctly use scriptwriting conventions?
- Are capitalization, punctuation, and spelling correct?

REFLECT & ASSESS

Evaluating the Experience

1. How well did your scene communicate to your audience?
2. How would you change your scene if you adapted it for film?

   PORTFOLIO How well did you communicate the idea of the story you dramatized? Put this evaluation in your portfolio.

WRITING FROM EXPERIENCE 803

Teaching Strategy: COLLABORATIVE OPPORTUNITY

In many cases, the most practical alternative for students will be pooling their resources to expand and produce one writer's dramatic scene. You may wish to organize a play competition judged by a panel of students who select the winning script for production.

Teaching Strategy: MANAGING THE PAPER LOAD

Whenever possible, phrase your written comments as questions that will encourage students to reflect on and assess their work. For example, instead of writing "needs more detail," try "Could you use a stage direction here to call for lighting that sets the mood?"

Standards for Evaluation

Have students review their scripts for the following:

Ideas and content
- Uses realistic dialogue that enhances and advances the plot.
- Presents central problem or conflict through plot.
- Includes stage directions that establish setting, describe action, and give clues to character.
- Reveals mood and character through dialogue and action.

Structure and Form
- Is formatted clearly and accurately according to guidelines.
- Organizes scene effectively so audience can follow story line.

Grammar, Usage, and Mechanics
- Contains no more than two or three minor errors in grammar, usage, spelling, capitalization, and punctuation.

PORTFOLIO

With the class as a whole, discuss which scenes seemed to be the most effective. Students should consider the class discussion when evaluating their own works.

SkillBuilder — GRAMMAR FROM WRITING

FORMATTING YOUR SCRIPT Point out that formatting conventions for a play script are different from those for a screenplay. In a screenplay, the directions must cover camera angles and movements in addition to the actors' movements, gestures, and motivations.

Applying what you've learned Suggest that students work with partners to review each other's scenes for proper formatting. Such needed corrections are often easier for someone other than the author to spot.

UNIT REVIEW

This feature has been designed to help students assess what they have learned in Unit Five. It also provides opportunities for them to evaluate the theme and to test their understanding of specific literary concepts. As students complete at least one of the optional activities for each section, you may want to conduct your own informal assessment of their performance, including their speaking and listening skills and their ability to engage in cooperative work.

Objectives

- To allow students to reflect on and assess their understanding of theme
- To allow students to reflect on and assess their understanding of literary concepts, such as the personal essay and symbols
- To provide students with the opportunity to assess and build their portfolios

REFLECTING ON THEME

OPTION 1

To help students get started listing things that have changed in their own lives, conduct a class brainstorming session. Volunteers will probably mention such changes as the birth of a brother or sister, the death of a grandparent or a pet, changing schools, moving to another city, making friends, and growing three inches in a year. Encourage them to record in both columns any changes that had both welcome and unwelcome aspects.

OPTION 2

After students have prepared their lists, suggest that they find key passages from the readings that illustrate each character's or author's point of view about change. They can refer to those sections and perhaps read them aloud when they compare their lists and discuss their thinking with classmates.

OPTION 3

Give students a starting point for establishing the causes of change that will be shown in their pie charts. For example, you might draw attention to "Searching for Summer," which shows how changes in the earth's environment affect people's lives. You might also note how the political upheaval in "Thoughts of Hanoi," changed people's relationships with others. Invite volunteers to add to the list, citing examples from other selections in this unit and from their own lives.

REFLECT & ASSESS

UNIT FIVE: NOTHING STAYS THE SAME

The selections in this unit show many dimensions of change, from changes that mark an individual's life to ones that affect an entire culture. How has your own understanding of change been affected by the selections? Explore this question by completing one or more of the options in each section.

REFLECTING ON THEME

OPTION 1 Charting Responses to Change Are you a person who welcomes change, or do you tend to approach change with fear or regret? Make a two-column chart, with one column labeled "Welcome Changes" and the other labeled "Unwelcome Changes." Fill in the chart by listing, in the appropriate columns, some changes that are presented in this unit's selections, as well as ones that you have faced in your own life. Underline the entries that you have the strongest feelings about. Then write an evaluation of your own attitude toward change, describing how your attitude has been affected by your reading.

OPTION 2 Evaluating a Quotation Consider the quotation from the ancient philosopher Heraclitus at the beginning of this unit: "There is nothing permanent except change." Which of the characters and authors in this unit might agree with that statement? Which might disagree? Make two lists of characters and authors—one list showing those who would agree, the other showing those who would disagree. Include yourself in one of the lists.

OPTION 3 Graphing the Causes of Change Work with a partner to create a pie chart showing what you believe to be the major causes of change affecting individuals and societies. To identify these causes, consider the changes presented in this unit's selections and reflect on your own experiences with change. Remember that the largest section of your chart should represent the most important or most common cause of change. Compare your pie chart with those of your classmates, and discuss their similarities and differences.

Self-Assessment: Which of the selections in this unit might have the greatest influence on you in the future—those dealing with the price of progress (Part 1) or those examining cultural issues (Part 2)? Create a list of the selection titles, arranging them in their order of impact.

REVIEWING LITERARY CONCEPTS

OPTION 1 Analyzing Personal Essays Review the information about personal essays on page 703. Then identify at least four personal essays in this textbook or other sources, and create a chart, like the one shown, to analyze them. After you complete

Essay	Author's Purpose	Theme	Tone	Style
"Once More to the Lake" by E. B. White	To offer his reflections on revisiting a lake where he had vacationed as a child	Memory can bring the past to life, but only partially.	Thoughtful, nostalgic, tranquil	Complex; characterized by long, elaborate sentences; full of sensory details

804 UNIT FIVE: NOTHING STAYS THE SAME

Self-Assessment Invite students to explain the reasoning behind their ordering of the selections. If students have difficulty relating the selections to their own lives, ask them to consider which characters they had the strongest feelings about. Invite them to list the changes those characters had to face and to circle the changes that they themselves may have to face in the future.

your chart, identify the essay that had the greatest impact on you. Write a note explaining your choice.

OPTION 2 Identifying Symbols Review the definition of *symbol* in the Handbook of Literary Terms on page 1000. Then identify at least five symbols in this unit's selections and write a brief explanation of each. After sharing your work with a small group of classmates, work with the group to choose a symbol that conveys the idea expressed by the unit title, "Nothing Stays the Same." The symbol can be one of those you identified in the selections, or it can invented.

 Self-Assessment: Imagine that a rich, eccentric patron of your school is offering a $5,000 prize to students who show mastery of the following terms. There is a catch, however—you have only 15 minutes to review the terms. To help you use your time efficiently, divide the terms into three categories: those you don't need to review, those you need to review only briefly, and those for which you require extensive review. Then spend 15 minutes reviewing the necessary terms (and hope that you find that rich patron!).

imagery	tone	situational irony
science fiction	first-person point of view	title
mood		setting
personal essay	naive narrator	cultural setting
voice	climax	cultural symbols
sentence structure	dramatic monologue	literary symbols
diction		

PORTFOLIO BUILDING

- **QuickWrites** Imagine that you are applying for a job and your prospective employer has asked to see a writing sample. Review your QuickWrites for this unit, paying particular attention to any that reflects the world of work, such as an advertisement, a newsletter article, or a press release. Choose the one that you feel would most impress an employer. Write a note explaining your choice. Then add the piece and the note to your portfolio.

- **Writing About Literature** Earlier in this unit, you changed a story element in one of the selections. Review your rewritten portion of the story, noting your impressions of your work now. How does it sound to you? What do you remember most about this experience of writing it? How might you apply what you learned to your future reading or writing?

- **Writing from Experience** By now you have written a scene for a play. How well does it work as a dramatic moment? Write a brief yet thoughtful review of your scene. What are its strengths and weaknesses? What did you learn from writing it that you can apply to other writing assignments? You may want to include your review in your portfolio.

- **Personal Choice** Look back through your records and evaluations of all the activities and writing that you completed in this unit, including any work that you did on your own. Which activity or piece of writing would you most like to expand into a larger project? Write a note explaining your choice, and add it, along with your record of the original work, to your portfolio.

 Self-Assessment: Compare the recent additions to your portfolio with pieces that you included earlier in the year. In what ways has your writing improved? How have your interests changed since the beginning of the year? How satisfied are you with your progress? Write an evaluation of your development as a writer up to this point in the year.

SETTING GOALS

Make a list of things that you would like to change about yourself as a reader and writer. Then circle the changes that seem realistically achievable by the end of the year. Use the circled items as goals for your work in the next unit.

REFLECT & ASSESS **805**

REVIEWING LITERARY CONCEPTS

OPTION 1

The following sample response for "By Any Other Name" shows how students might complete the chart.

Purpose: *To show how two children resisted imposed cultural changes*

Tone: *Critical, innocent, bemused*

Theme: *Each person's cultural identity should be preserved and treated with respect.*

Style: *Simple, clear sentences that impart vivid descriptions of people and places*

OPTION 2

Lead a full-class discussion to help students to realize that when ideas are communicated through explanation and argument, the listener needs to reflect on and assess the merits of the ideas. In contrast, when an effective symbol is used to communicate an idea, the message may go straight to the heart.

Self-Assessment After students have assessed their own knowledge of the terms, you may wish to conduct an informal oral exam. Call on students at random and ask them to define the terms and to illustrate their meaning by citing examples from the selections. You may wish to form study groups for those students who need additional work on the terms.

PORTFOLIO BUILDING

Encourage students to include first drafts as well as final revisions so that they can reflect on and assess their development and progress. Set up a conference with each student so that you can review the contents of his or her portfolio. Provide positive feedback and point out specific examples of progress that each student has made.

 Self-Assessment Guide students to evaluate their growth as writers by helping them discover which aspects of their writing would be the most useful to examine now. Some students might benefit from looking at mechanics, such as the use of capital letters, appropriate punctuation, and complete sentences.

SETTING GOALS

Help students come up with specific statements of what they would like to change about their reading and writing habits as well as some concrete steps that they can take to meet those goals. If they choose to work on writing, help them tailor their goals to their expectations. If they choose to improve their reading skills, encourage them to set concrete goals.

THE LANGUAGE OF LITERATURE Teacher's Edition **805**

UNIT SIX

UNIT SIX

Unit Six

The Making of Heroes In Unit Six, students will encounter many kinds of heroes, from ancient and contemporary times. This unit has two parts: Part 1, "A Strength from Within," and Part 2, "The Heroic Tradition." Selections in both parts contribute to the unit theme by examining the qualities and circumstances that make people heroes.

Part 1

A Strength from Within Selections in Part 1 emphasize the qualities within everyday human beings which make them stand out as heroes. For example, in "The Man in the Water," an ordinary man gives up his chance of surviving a plane crash to help other victims to safety.

Part 2

The Heroic Tradition Part 2 includes various classic works which feature larger-than-life heroes. For example, in "Sir Launcelot du Lake" from *Le Morte d'Arthur*, a knight wins a victory over his enemies by using his superior strength and intelligence.

THE MAKING OF HEROES

THE HERO IN ONE AGE WILL BE A HERO IN ANOTHER.

CHARLOTTE LENNOX
BRITISH NOVELIST AND POET
1720–1804

Still Life #31 (1993), Tom Wesselmann. Mixed-media construction with television, 48″ × 60″ × 10 ¾″, Frederick R. Weisman Art Foundation, Los Angeles. Copyright © 1996 Tom Wesselmann / Licensed by VAGA, New York.

Art Note

Still Life #31 by Tom Wesselmann
This painting by American artist Wesselmann includes symbols of everyday life in the United States.
Reading the Art Why do you think the artist chose these particular items for his still life?

Discussion Questions

To help students explore the connections between the art, the quotation, and the unit theme, have them consider the following questions:

1. Why do you think heroism has been such a popular theme of literature through the ages? *(Possible responses: Some students might say many people would like to think of themselves as being capable of heroic acts if necessary. Others might say stories about heroism are exciting and full of adventure.)*

2. Have students paraphrase Lennox's statement about heroes. *(Possible response: Some may say a true hero will transcend the passage of time and retain his or her heroic status; others might say that the qualities that make people heroes are enduring and will always be important, admired qualities in a person.)*

3. What details can you find in this painting that make it an appropriate illustration for "The Making of Heroes?" Why? *(Possible responses: The presence of George Washington's portrait in a modern kitchen shows that a hero of the 1770s is still a hero in the 20th century; television is a major factor in determining who our heroes are today.)*

4. What kinds of stories and experiences might you expect to read about in this unit? *(Possible response: adventure stories; stories with brave characters in dangerous situations; stories about people who, in one way or another, stand out among their fellow men and women as heroes)*

5. Discuss a particular experience of your own which helped you understand the meaning of heroism. *(Responses will vary.)*

THE LANGUAGE OF LITERATURE **TEACHER'S EDITION**

UNIT SIX
Part 1 Skills Trace

ML DENOTES MINI-LESSON IN TEACHER'S EDITION

Selections	Reading Skills and Strategies	Literary Concepts	Writing Opportunities	Speaking, Listening, and Viewing
FICTION **A Chip of Glass Ruby** Nadine Gordimer	Visualizing setting, PE p. 810 Using your reading log, PE p. 810	Dialogue, PE p. 821 Reviewing simile, ML TE p. 815	Prepare dramatic monologues, PE p. 820 Draft an essay, PE p. 820 Write diary entries, PE p. 820 Write a literary analysis, PE p. 820 Rewrite an episode as a dramatic scene, PE p. 820 Write a scene with an implied main idea, ML TE p. 818 Write a dialogue, TE p. 819	Present dramatic monologues, PE p. 820 Conduct an interview, PE p. 821 Oral report, PE p. 821 Lead a meeting, ML TE p. 816
NONFICTION **The Man in the Water** Roger Rosenblatt		Tone, PE p. 827	Generalizations about human nature responding to disaster, PE p. 823 Create a two-column chart to convey views, PE p. 827 Write statements, PE p. 827 Write a tribute, PE p. 827 Write a newspaper article, PE p. 827 Write a personal essay, PE p. 827 Write compare-contrast paragraphs, TE p. 826	Stage a TV report, PE p. 828 Videotape a TV report, PE p. 828
FICTION **And of Clay Are We Created** Isabel Allende	From fact to fiction, PE p. 830	Internal/External conflict, PE p. 842 Reviewing narrator, PE p. 842 Reviewing foreshadowing, ML TE p. 837	Draft a monologue, PE p. 841 Write a love letter, PE p. 841 Create a two-column chart, PE p. 841 Write a short story with chronological order, ML TE p. 832 Write diary entries, TE p. 839	Small group discussion, PE p. 841 Deliver a eulogy, PE p. 842 Listen to a musical composition, PE p. 842 Act out impromptu phone dialogue, ML TE p. 840
FICTION **The Leap** Louise Erdrich	Recognizing flashbacks, PE p. 844	Flashback, PE p. 853 Reviewing imagery, ML TE p. 848	Create an annotated time line of events, PE p. 852 Write a tabloid article, PE p. 852 Write an analysis, PE p. 852 Draft a comparison-contrast essay, PE p. 852 Write a story, ML TE p. 851	Class discussion, PE p. 852 Stage a TV or radio talk show, PE p. 853 Prepare an oral report on the circus, PE p. 853
NONFICTION **from Back from Tuichi** Yossi Ghinsberg		True-life adventure, PE p. 867 Reviewing suspense, PE p. 867 Reviewing setting, ML TE p. 866	Write ideas for an adventure story, PE p. 855 Create a chart, PE p. 867 Write book jacket copy, PE p. 867 Write a book report, PE p. 867 True-life adventure, PE p. 867 Describe an adventure, ML TE p. 865	Class discussion, PE p. 867 Present an oral reading, PE p. 868 View Back From Tuichi, ML TE p. 859
DRAMA **The Ring of General Macías** Josephina Niggli	Visualizing drama, PE p. 869	Foil, PE p. 885 Reviewing verbal irony, PE p. 885 Reviewing stage directions, ML TE p. 874 Reviewing character, ML TE p. 878	Write director's notes, PE p. 884 Write a letter, PE p. 884 Write a psychological profile, PE p. 884 Write a speech, PE p. 884 Write dialogues, ML TE p. 877	View Viva Zapata, (1952), PE p. 885
NONFICTION ON YOUR OWN **Gift from a Son Who Died** Doris Herold Lund				Group reading, TE p. 886
Writing **WRITING ABOUT LITERATURE** **Criticism**	Reading Skills and Strategies Analyzing elaboration, PE pp. 894–895 Responding to literature, PE pp. 896–899	Literary Concepts Analyzing elaboration, PE pp. 894–895 Story elements, PE pp. 896–897	Writing Opportunities Elaborate on an idea, PE p. 895 A QuickWrite check, PE p. 805 Work together, PE p. 805 Critical essay, PE pp. 896–899	Speaking, Listening, and Viewing Viewing a scene, PE p. 900 Interpreting a scene, PE p. 900 Discussion, PE p. 900

Grammar, Usage, Mechanics, and Spelling	Multimodal Learning	Research and Study Skills	Vocabulary
Direct objects, ML TE p. 812	Present dramatic monologues, PE p. 820 Create an illustration, PE p. 821 Conduct an interview, PE p. 821 Create a political cartoon, PE p. 821 Oral report, PE p. 821 Lead a meeting, ML TE p. 816	Research anti-apartheid protests led by African National Congress, PE p. 821 Research earlier protests led by Mohandas Gandhi, PE p. 821	disarm morose patronize presumption sallow
Infinitives, ML TE p. 825	Stage and videotape a TV report, PE p. 828 Draw a picture, PE p. 828 Compose a song or create an instrumental piece, PE p. 828 Create a bulletin board display, PE p. 828	Research the role weather plays in plane crashes, PE p. 828	abiding anonymity chaotic flail implacable
Compound-complex sentences, ML TE p. 834	Small group discussion, PE p. 841 Deliver a eulogy, PE p. 842 Listen to a musical composition, PE p. 842 Create a budget, ML TE p. 835 Act out impromptu phone dialogue, ML TE p. 840 Prepare a TV science report, TE p. 842	Research repression and its causes and treatment, PE p. 842 Research volcanoes in the ring of fire, TE p. 842	embody stupor equanimity tenacity fortitude tribulation irreparably visceral pandemonium vulnerable
Adverb phrases, ML TE p. 849	Class discussion, PE p. 852 Stage a TV or radio talk show, PE p. 853 Make a collage, PE p. 853 Prepare an oral report on the circus, PE p. 853 Build a model or diorama or find photos and fine-art reproductions, PE p. 852	Research history of circuses, PE p. 853 Research flying trapeze act, PE p. 853 Using indexes, ML TE p. 846	constricting destined extricating flair perpetually
Exclamation points, ML TE p. 860	Class discussion, PE p. 867 Create a chart, PE p. 867 Create a map, PE p. 868 Present an oral reading, PE p. 868 View *Back from Tuichi*, ML TE p. 859	K-W-L charts, ML TE p. 857 Research the rain forest ecosystem, TE p. 869	
Sentence fragments, ML TF p. 872	Design costumes or set, PE p. 885 Create a poster, PE p. 885 View *Viva Zapata*, PE p. 885		farce ostentatiously regally sanctuary stealthily
	Sketching a character, TE p. 886 Create a comic strip, TE p. 891 Create a character web, TE p. 892		

Grammar, Usage, Mechanics, and Spelling	Multimodal Learning	Research and Study Skills	Media Literacy
Using adjective clauses, PE p. 895 Positioning adverbs correctly, PE p. 899 Using adverbs, PE p. 899	Viewing a scene, PE p. 900 Interpreting a scene, PE p. 900 Discussion, PE p. 900	Analyzing literature, PE pp. 894–899 Analyzing controversies, PE p. 900	Evaluating controversies, PE pp. 900–901

UNIT SIX
Part 2 Skills Trace

ML DENOTES MINI-LESSON IN TEACHER'S EDITION

Selections	Reading Skills and Strategies	Literary Concepts	Writing Opportunities	Speaking, Listening, and Viewing
ROMANCE *from* **Le Morte d' Arthur: The Crowning of Arthur Sir Lancelot du Lake** Sir Thomas Malory, retold by Keith Baines		Romance, PE p. 920 Reviewing plot, ML TE p. 914	Write about what makes a hero, PE p. 904 Prepare a guidebook to Arthurian World, PE p. 920 Write a plot synopsis, PE p. 920 Write a magazine article, PE p. 920 Write an editorial, PE p. 920 Diction, ML TE p. 916	Oral movie review, PE p. 921 Create a television commercial, PE p. 921 Dramatic reading, ML TE p. 911
ROMANCE *from* **The Acts of King Arthur and His Noble Knights** John Steinbeck	Making inferences, PE p. 923 Using your reading log, PE p. 923	Style, PE p. 934 Reviewing romance, ML TE p. 927 Reviewing plot, ML TE p. 929 Elaboration, ML TE p. 930	Prepare a storyboard, PE p. 933 Write a brief feature article, PE p. 933 Write an interview, PE p. 933 Write an advice column, PE p. 933 Write a soap opera scene, PE p. 933 Develop a menu, PE p. 934	Create a dramatization, PE p. 934 Give a demonstration of ways of walking, PE p. 934 Share a menu, PE p. 934
DRAMA **Antigone** Sophocles	Understanding classical drama, PE p. 937 The theater, PE p. 937 Actors and chorus, PE p. 937 Tragedy and the tragic hero, PE p. 937 Tragedy, ML TE p. 941	Irony and dramatic irony, PE p. 980 Reviewing characterization, ML TE p. 953 Dialogue in drama, ML TE p. 957	Create a flow chart: Cause and effect, PE p. 979 Write a letter, PE p. 979 Write a diary entry, PE p. 979 Write a lecture, PE p. 979 Create a chart to compare father and daughter, PE p. 980	View flow chart, PE p. 979 Perform a readers theater production of a scene, PE p. 980 View a film/drama, ML TE p. 949 Press conference, ML TE p. 965
POETRY **Old Song** Traditional, West Africa			Double-entry journal, TE p. 982	Paired and choral reading, TE p. 982

Writing	Reading Skills and Strategies	Literary Concepts	Writing Opportunities	Speaking, Listening, and Viewing
WRITING FROM EXPERIENCE **Report**			Writing a biographical research paper, PE pp. 984–991 Drafting, PE pp. 988–989 Revising and publishing, PE pp. 990–991	Interpreting a cartoon, PE p. 985 Brainstorming a group list, PE p. 984 Analyzing a photograph, PE p. 984

Grammar, Usage, Mechanics, and Spelling	Multimodal Learning	Research and Study Skills	Vocabulary	
Commas in a series, ML TE p. 908	Prepare a tourist's guidebook to Arthurian World, PE p. 920 Oral movie review, PE p. 921 Create a drawing or painting, PE p. 921 Create a TV commercial, PE p. 921 Create a program for a tournament, PE p. 921 Dramatic reading, ML TE p. 911	Research medieval tournaments, PE p. 921 Inferring word meanings, ML TE p. 907 Taking essay tests, ML TE p. 909	adversary champion fidelity prowess recompense	
Subordinating conjunctions, ML TE p. 925	Design a storyboard, PE p. 933 Create a dramatization, PE p. 934 Give a demonstration of ways of walking, PE p. 934 Develop a menu, PE p. 934 Create a model or diagram of Arthur's castle, PE p. 934 Create a poster, PE p. 934	Research food at a medieval feast, PE p. 934 Research the design and construction of medieval castles, PE p. 934 Note-taking, ML TE p. 928 Research Winchester today, TE p. 934	carriage decorous disparagement exalt fallible	haggard intemperate penitence reprisal vagrant
Parallel structure, ML TE p. 945	View a flow chart, PE p. 979 Perform a readers theater production of a scene, PE p. 980 Create a mask, PE p. 980 Comparison chart, PE p. 980 Create a model, PE p. 980 Create a Venn diagram, PE p. 980 View a film/drama, ML TE p. 949 Press conference, ML TE p. 965	Research the typical role of noblewomen during 15th-century B.C., PE p. 980 Research allusions to myths, PE p. 980 Taking objective tests: Sentence completion, ML TE p. 961 Taking tests: Planning your time, ML TE p. 970	auspicious compulsive defile dirge edict	lamentation lithe perverse sated transgress

Grammar, Usage, Mechanics, and Spelling	Multimodal Learning	Research and Study Skills	Media Literacy
Using ellipses and brackets, PE p. 991	Analyzing a photograph, PE p. 984 Interpreting a cartoon, PE p. 985	Finding reference sources, PE p. 987 Primary and secondary sources, PE p. 986 Evaluating sources, PE p. 989	Primary and secondary sources, PE p. 986 Evaluating sources, PE p. 989 Analyzing a photograph, PE p. 984 Interpreting a cartoon, PE p. 985

UNIT SIX
Recommended Resources

ENRICHMENT   RESEARCH

✓ Recommended Novels and Play

LITERATURE CONNECTIONS WITH SOURCEBOOK FOR TEACHERS

Thematic Link Beryl Markham, the world-famous pilot, reveals her heroic and adventurous spirit in this poetic memoir of her life in Africa—a land of spectacular beauty and diversity.

About the Author Beryl Markham (1902–1985), best-known for her solo flight westward across the Atlantic Ocean in 1936, grew up in Kenya, where she learned to hunt wild animals, to train and breed horses, and to fly a plane.

Other Work by Beryl Markham *The Splendid Outcast*

Thematic Link Gardner retells the epic of Beowulf from the viewpoint of the monster.

About the Author John Gardner (1933–1982) was a popular writer with an uncommon vision of ordinary circumstances and daily life.

Other Works by John Gardner *Mickelson's Ghosts, October Light, Stillness and Shadows*

LITERATURE CONNECTIONS WITH SOURCEBOOK FOR TEACHERS

Thematic Link As witchcraft accusations fly in Puritan New England, John Proctor must choose between his own personal safety and the truth.

About the Author Arthur Miller (born 1915), accused of being a Communist in the 1950s, has examined the morality of American life in his plays.

Other Works by Arthur Miller *All My Sons, Death of a Salesman, A View from the Bridge, After the Fall*

Thematic Link Two heroines must each weigh the consequences of the choices they have made and ask themselves what is heroic.

About the Author With her mastery of linguistic nuances, Toni Morrison (born 1931) earned a permanent place in world literature, as well as a Nobel Prize.

Other Works by Toni Morrison *Song of Solomon, The Bluest Eye, Beloved, Jazz*

Professional Development — TEACHING THE NOVEL

Gallop, Jane. *Pedagogy.* Bloomington, IN: Indiana University Press, 1995.

Raglan, Lord. "The Hero: A Study in Tradition, Myth, and Drama," *In Quest of the Hero.* Princeton, NJ: Princeton University Press, 1990.

Rank, Otto. "The Myth of the Birth of the Hero," *In Quest of the Hero.* Princeton, NJ: Princeton University Press, 1990.

Rich, Adrienne. *What Is Found There.* NY: Norton, 1993.

CROSS-CURRICULAR TEACHING   PROFESSIONAL DEVELOPMENT

✓ Recommended Readings in Cross-Curricular Areas

SOCIAL STUDIES

The Mythic Image by Joseph Campbell (1974) Expansive and dazzling scan of myth and heroism and their function over five millenia of the world's civilizations. Links to all selections in the unit.

The Hero, Manhood and Power by John Lasch (1995) Beautifully illustrates and explores the double-sided role of the cult of the hero: one that leads to grandeur or devastation. Links to all selections in the unit.

White Water Rafting by Cecil Kuhne (1995) An informative introduction into the dangers and pleasures of rafting that details the skills it requires. Links to Yossi Ghinsberg's *Back from Tuichi.*

Working It Through by Elisabeth Kubler-Ross (1982) Intimate portraits of compelling individuals and the situations the author guided them through to find acceptance and peace. Links to many selections in the unit.

Professional Development — CROSS-CURRICULAR INSTRUCTION

Knopp, Sharon L. "Columbus in the Curriculum: Shoring Up a Hero," *Equity and Excellence in Education* (December 1995) Vol. 28: 3: 57.

Kozol, Jonathan. *On Being a Teacher.* NY: Oneworld Publications, 1993.

Nitze, William A. *Arthurian Romance and Modern Poetry and Music.* Arthurian Legend and Literature Series, Number 1. New York: Haskell Booksellers, 1970.

✓ Recommended Media Resources

THE LANGUAGE OF LITERATURE

ELECTRONIC LIBRARY
CD-ROM
Additional literature selections for Unit Six can be found on the Electronic Library CD-ROM.

LASERLINKS
Videodisc, Gr. 10
See *LaserLinks Teacher's SourceBook,* pages 64–65, for overview of Unit Six.

AUDIO LIBRARY
Tapes
Unit Six: The Making of Heroes Gr. 10. Tapes 19–22: Sides A & B

WRITING COACH
Writing Coach Software: Writing About Literature—Critical Response, Research Paper

OUTSIDE RESOURCES

Films/Videos/Film Strips/Audiocassettes
A Chip of Glass Ruby, video, Films for the Humanities & Sciences, 1988 (20 minutes).
Antigone, video, Films for the Humanities & Sciences, 1987 (120 minutes).
Isabel Allende, video, Films for the Humanities & Sciences, 1994 (56 minutes).
Louise Erdrich Reads, audiocassette, American Audio Prose Library (81 minutes).

Internet Resources
McDougal Littell Literature Center at http://www.hmco.com/mcdougal/lit

Professional Development — TEACHING WITH TECHNOLOGY

Bracey, Gerald. "New Pathways: Technology's Empowering Influence on Teaching," *Electronic Learning* 12:7 (April 1993) 8–9.

Cuban, Larry. "Software on Indians, Astronomy, the Nile, Yukon Trial, and Sesame Street," *Electronic Learning* 15:2 (October 1995) 52.

Teaching and Computers. Scholastic, Inc., 730 Broadway, New York, NY 10003-9538.

UNIT SIX
Professional Enrichment

The Timeless World of a Play
Tennessee Williams

This article by the renowned American playwright Tennessee Williams provides insights that enrich and extend the dramatic offerings included in this unit.

Carson McCullers concludes one of her lyric poems with the line: "Time, the endless idiot, runs screaming 'round the world." It is this continual rush of time, so violent that it appears to be screaming, that deprives our actual lives of so much dignity and meaning, and it is, perhaps more than anything else, the *arrest of time* which has taken place in a completed work of art that gives to certain plays their feeling of depth and significance. In the London notices of *Death of a Salesman* a certain notoriously skeptical critic made the remark that Willy Loman was the sort of man that almost any member of the audience would have kicked out of an office had he applied for a job or detained one for conversation about his troubles. The remark itself possibly holds some truth. But the implication that Willy Loman is consequently a character with whom we have no reason to concern ourselves in drama, reveals a strikingly false conception of what plays are. Contemplation is something that exists outside of time, and so is the tragic sense. Even in the actual world of commerce, there exists in some persons a sensibility to the unfortunate situations of others, a capacity for concern and compassion, surviving from a more tender period of life outside the present whirling wire-cage of business activity. Facing Willy Loman across an office desk, meeting his nervous glance and hearing his querulous voice, we would be very likely to glance at our wrist watch and our schedule of other appointments. We would not kick him out of the office, no, but we would certainly *ease* him out with more expedition than Willy had feebly hoped for. But suppose there had been no wrist watch or office clock and suppose there had *not* been the schedule of pressing appointments, and suppose that we were not actually facing Willy across a desk—and facing a person is *not* the best way to *see* him!—suppose, in other words, that the meeting with Willy Loman had somehow occurred in a world *outside* of time. Then I think we would receive him with concern and kindness and even with respect. If the world of a play did not offer us this occasion to view its characters under that special condition of a *world without time,* then, indeed, the characters and occurrences of drama would become equally pointless, equally trivial, as corresponding meetings and happenings in life.

The classic tragedies of Greece had tremendous nobility. The actors wore great masks, movements were formal, dance-like, and the speeches had an epic quality which doubtless was as removed from the normal conversation of their contemporary society as they seem today. Yet they did not seem false to the Greek audiences: the magnitude of the events and the passions aroused by them did not seem ridiculously out of proportion to common experience. And I wonder if this was not because the Greek audiences knew, instinctively or by training, that the created world of a play is removed from that element which makes people *little* and their emotions fairly inconsequential.

Great sculpture often follows the lines of the human body: yet the repose of great sculpture suddenly transmutes those human lines to something that has an absoluteness, a purity, a beauty, which would not be possible in a living mobile form.

A play may be violent, full of motion: yet it has that special kind of repose which allows contemplation and produces the climate in which tragic importance is a possible thing, provided that certain modern conditions are met.

In actual existence the moments of love are succeeded by the moments of satiety and sleep. The sincere remark is followed by a cynical distrust. Truth is fragmentary, at best: we love and betray each other in not quite the same breath but in two breaths that occur in fairly close sequence. But the fact that passion occurred in *passing,* that it then declined into a more familiar sense of indifference, should not be regarded as proof of its inconsequence. And this is the very truth that drama wished to bring us. . . .

Whether or not we admit it to ourselves, we are all haunted by a truly awful sense of impermanence. I have always had a particularly keen sense of this at New York cocktail parties, and perhaps that is why I drink the martinis almost as fast as I can snatch them from the tray. This sense is the febrile thing that hangs in the air. Horror of insincerity, of *not meaning,* overhangs these affairs like the cloud of cigarette smoke and the hectic chatter. This horror is the only thing, almost, that is left unsaid at such functions. All social functions involving a group of people not intimately known to each other are always under this shadow. They are almost always (in an unconscious way) like that last dinner of the condemned: where steak or turkey, whatever the doomed man wants, is served in his cell as a mock-

> Whether or not we admit it to ourselves, we are all haunted by a truly awful sense of impermanence.

ingly cruel reminder of what the great-big-little-transitory world had to offer.

In a play, time is arrested in the sense of being confined. By a sort of legerdemain, *events* are made to remain events, rather than being reduced so quickly to mere *occurrences.* The audience can sit back in a comforting dusk to watch a world which is flooded with light and in which emotion and action have a dimension and dignity that they would likewise have in real existence, if only the shattering intrusion of time could be locked out.

About their lives, people ought to remember that when they are finished, everything in them will be contained in a marvelous state of repose which is the same as that which they unconsciously admired in drama. The rush is temporary. The great and only possible dignity of man lies in his power deliberately to choose certain moral values by which to live as steadfastly as if he, too, like a character in a play, were immured against the corrupting rush of time. Snatching the eternal out of the desperately fleeting is the great magic trick of human existence. As far as we know, as far as there exists any kind of empiric evidence, there is no way to beat the game of *being* against *nonbeing,* in which nonbeing is the predestined victor on realistic levels.

Yet plays in the tragic tradition offer us a view of certain moral values in violent juxtaposition. Because we do not participate, except as spectators, we can view them clearly, within the limits of our emotional equipment. These people on the stage do not return our looks. We do not have to answer their questions no make any sign of being in company with them, nor do we have to compete with their virtues nor resist their offenses. All at once, for this reason, we are able to see them! Our hearts are wrung by recognition and pity, so that the dusky shell of the auditorium where we are gathered anonymously together is flooded with an almost liquid warmth of unchecked human sympathies, relieved of selfconsciousness, allowed to function. . . .

Men pity and love each other more deeply than they permit themselves to know. The moment after the phone has been hung up, the hand reaches for a scratch pad and scrawls a notation: "Funeral Tuesday at five, Church of the Holy Redeemer, don't forget flowers." And the same hand is only a little shakier than usual as it reaches, some minutes later, for a highball glass that will pour a stupefaction over the kindled nerves. Fear and evasion are the two little beasts that chase each other's tails in the revolving wire-cage of our nervous world. They distract us from feeling too much about things. Time rushes toward us with its hospital tray of infinitely varied narcotics, even while it is preparing us for its inevitably fatal operation. . . .

So successfully have we disguised from ourselves the intensity of our own feelings, the sensibility of our own hearts, that plays in the tragic tradition have begun to seem untrue. For a couple of hours we may surrender ourselves to a world of fiercely illuminated values in conflict, but when the stage is covered and the auditorium lighted, almost immediately there is a recoil of disbelief. "Well, well!" we say as we shuffle back up the aisle, while the play dwindles behind us with the sudden perspective of an early Chirico painting. By the time we have arrived at Sardi's, if not as soon as we pass beneath the marquee, we have convinced ourselves once more that life has as little resemblance to the curiously stirring and meaningful occurrences on the stage as a jingle has to an elegy of Rilke.

This modern condition of his theater audience is something that an author must know in advance. The diminishing influence of life's destroyer, time, must be somehow worked into the context of his play. Perhaps it is a certain foolery, a certain distortion toward the grotesque, which will solve the problem for him. Perhaps it is only restraint, putting a mute on the strings that would like to break all bounds. But almost surely, unless he contrives in some way to relate the dimensions of his tragedy to the dimensions of a world in which time is *included*—he will be left among his magnificent debris on a dark stage, muttering to himself: "Those fools . . ."

And if they could hear him above the clatter of tongues, glasses, chinaware, and silver, they would give him this answer: "But you have shown us a world not ravaged by time. We admire your innocence. But we have seen our photographs, past and present. Yesterday evening we passed our first wife on the street. We smiled as we spoke but we didn't really see her! It's too bad, but we know what is true and not true, and at 3 A.M. your disgrace will be in print!"

Copyrighted material reprinted with permission.

> So successfully have we disguised from ourselves the intensity of our own feelings, the sensibility of our own hearts, that plays in the tragic tradition have begun to seem untrue.

UNIT SIX

Starting Points for Unit Projects

The following suggestions will help you initiate individual and group projects during the course of this unit.

Staging a Myth

GROUP DRAMA PROJECT Ask groups of students to choose a mythological hero and present a dramatization of his or her story. Suggest that students distill the story into one or two scenes, write the script, and assign roles. Encourage students to come up with costumes, props, and at least rudimentary backdrops.

Creating a Superhero

GROUP ART/DRAMA PROJECT Invite groups of students to create a comic or serious teenage superhero whose undercover identity is that of a student in your school. Suggest that students "discover" the source and nature of the hero's power and set several adventures in the school or community. Have students introduce their character via a comic book or a dramatization.

Listening to Heroic Music

GROUP MUSIC PROJECT Ask groups of students to tape-record a medley of music that stirs feelings of loyalty, pride, or awe in listeners. Their selections should have a unifying theme, such as national anthems of different countries, military music, or operatic or Broadway show music sung by heroic characters (such as "C'est moi" from Lerner and Loewe's *Camelot* or "Nessun dorma" from Puccini's *Turandot*). Students can identify and comment on the pieces either on the tape or in a class presentation, pausing the tape between songs.

Creating a Poster Campaign

GROUP ART PROJECT Have groups of students create a series of posters, each developing the theme "If you can _____, you could save a life." Encourage students to think beyond the obvious examples of CPR and swimming to skills like reading, speaking a foreign language, keeping your head, etc. Suggest that students display their posters in school or community building hallways.

Filming Small Acts of Heroism

GROUP FILM PROJECT Ask groups of students to plan, stage, and videotape a sequence of small acts of heroism right in the school: the student who sits down for lunch with the lonely newcomer, the one who picks up the litter tossed by another, the one who steps in to stop a fight.

Creating a Diorama

GROUP ART PROJECT Ask groups of students to research the social structure of the Middle Ages and to construct a diorama with a castle, manor houses, and peasant dwellings, as well as fields and forests. Encourage students to include miniature figures dressed in the costumes of the era. As a variation, students can produce a mural or an illustrated booklet.

Family and Community Involvement

Family

Most people think of heroism in terms of war, sports, or other active and visible areas of endeavor. However, a hero is also anyone who does what is called for in an important situation. The selections in Unit Six present a variety of heroes. The following activities will help students, families, and community members recognize the presence of heroes and heroism in their own lives.

OPTION 1 WRITE A DEFINITION OF HEROES

- **Connection** All of the selections in Unit Six explore different kinds of heroism.
- **Activity** *Copymaster 1* Have students and family members watch a regular news program for a week and document instances of heroism. Working together, students and family members can write a definition of a hero, based on real-life examples that students can share with the class.

OPTION 2 CREATE A *FAMILY HERO BOOK*

- **Connection** "The Leap" describes a mother who is her daughter's hero for many reasons.
- **Activity** *Copymaster 2* Have students and family members make a *Family Hero Book* to document acts of heroism performed within the family. For example, a father might document the time his children made his work deliveries while he was laid up with a broken leg.

OPTION 3 SHARE STORIES OF COURAGE

- **Connection** "The Man in the Water" describes a heroic rescue.
- **Activity** *Copymaster 3* Students and family members can read aloud from books, magazines, and newspapers about dangerous undertakings that involve rescue.

Community

OPTION 1

- **Connection** All of the selections in Unit Six explore different kinds of heroism.
- **Activity** Plan a field trip to a site that documents heroism of one kind or another, for example, a war memorial or an AIDS exhibit.

OPTION 2

- **Connection** "And of Clay Are We Created" describes a man's attempts to help a girl in mortal danger.
- **Activity** Have students interview a doctor or other person involved in an organ donor program, or a local resident who has either donated or received an organ, to discuss the value of such a program.

OPTION 3

- **Connection** "Sir Launcelot du Lake" describes a heroic rescue.
- **Activity** Contact a local police officer, fire fighter, Coast Guard officer, or other person whose job entails rescuing citizens from danger. Invite the person to speak to the class about why he or she is willing to take such great risks to help other people.

UNIT SIX
Part 1 Lesson Planner

TIME ALLOTMENTS SHOWN ARE APPROXIMATE. DEPENDING ON YOUR GOALS AND THE NEEDS OF YOUR STUDENTS, YOU MAY WISH TO ALLOW MORE OR LESS TIME FOR CERTAIN PORTIONS OF THE LESSON.

Table of Contents	Discussion	Previewing the Selection	Reading the Selection
PART OPENER **A Strength From Within** page 808	**20 MINUTES** • Reflect on the part theme		
SELECTION **A Chip of Glass Ruby** page 811 AVERAGE		**20 MINUTES** • PERSONAL CONNECTION • HISTORICAL CONNECTION • READING CONNECTION: Visualizing setting/Using your reading log	**60 MINUTES** • Introduce vocabulary • Read pp. 811–819 (9 pp.)
SELECTION **The Man in the Water** page 824 AVERAGE		**20 MINUTES** • PERSONAL CONNECTION • HISTORICAL CONNECTION • WRITING CONNECTION	**30 MINUTES** • Introduce vocabulary • Read pp. 824–826 (3 pp.)
SELECTION **And of Clay Are We Created** page 831 AVERAGE		**20 MINUTES** • PERSONAL CONNECTION • SCIENTIFIC CONNECTION • READING CONNECTION: From fact to fiction	**60 MINUTES** • Read pp. 831–839 (9 pp.)
SELECTION **The Leap** page 845 CHALLENGING		**20 MINUTES** • PERSONAL CONNECTION • CULTURAL CONNECTION • READING CONNECTION: Recognizing flashbacks	**50 MINUTES** • Introduce vocabulary • Read pp. 845–851 (7 pp.)
SELECTION *from* **Back from Tuichi** page 856 CHALLENGING		**20 MINUTES** • PERSONAL CONNECTION • BIOGRAPHICAL CONNECTION • WRITING CONNECTION	**40 MINUTES** • Read pp. 856–866 (11 pp.)
SELECTION **The Ring of General Macías** page 870 AVERAGE		**20 MINUTES** • PERSONAL CONNECTION • HISTORICAL CONNECTION • READING CONNECTION: Visualizing drama	**90 MINUTES** • Introduce vocabulary • Read pp. 870–883 (14 pp.)
NONFICTION ON YOUR OWN **Gift from a Son Who Died** page 886 CHALLENGING			**40 MINUTES** • Read pp. 886–893 (8 pp.)
Writing WRITING ABOUT LITERATURE **Criticism**	**Writer's Style** **15 MINUTES**	**Prewriting** **20 MINUTES**	**Drafting and Revising** **40 MINUTES**

Time estimates assume in-class work. You may wish to assign some of these stages as homework.

Responding to the Selection

FROM PERSONAL RESPONSE TO CRITICAL ANALYSIS	OR	ANOTHER PATHWAY	LITERARY CONCEPTS	QUICKWRITES
	**50 MINUTES**				
• Discussion questions	OR	• Dramatic monologues	• Dialogue	• Essay • Diary entries • Literary analysis • Dramatic scene
	**50 MINUTES**				
• Discussion questions	OR	• Chart	• Tone	• Tribute • Newspaper article • Personal essay
	**50 MINUTES**				
• Discussion questions	OR	• Character evaluation	• Internal/external conflicts • Narrator	• Monologue • Love letter • Chart
	**50 MINUTES**				
• Discussion questions	OR	• Annotated time line	• Flashback • Foreshadowing	• Tabloid article • Analysis • Comparison/contrast chart
	**50 MINUTES**				
• Discussion questions	OR	• Ability chart	• True-life adventure • Suspense	• Book jacket copy • Book report • True-life adventure
	**50 MINUTES**				
• Discussion questions	OR	• Play	• Foil • Verbal irony	• Letter • Psychological profile • Speech

Extension Activities

ALTERNATIVE ACTIVITIES	LITERARY LINKS	CRITIC'S CORNER	THE WRITER'S STYLE	ACROSS THE CURRICULUM	ART CONNECTION	WORDS TO KNOW	BIOGRAPHY
	**60 MINUTES**							
✔	✔	✔	✔	HISTORY	✔	✔	✔
	**50 MINUTES**							
✔				SCIENCE TECHNOLOGY	✔	✔	✔
	**60 MINUTES**							
✔	✔			PSYCHOLOGY	✔	✔	✔
	**60 MINUTES**							
✔	✔	✔		HISTORY SPORTS	✔	✔	✔
	**20 MINUTES**							
✔	✔						✔
	**40 MINUTES**							
✔	✔			FILM		✔	✔

Publishing and Reflecting
15 MINUTES

Grammar in Context
15 MINUTES

Reading the World
25 MINUTES

PART 1

REFLECTING ON THEME

Explore with the class various sources of inner strength. Some possibilities might include family, friends, religion, values, pride, and physical prowess. List the class's responses on the board and ask students to rank them from most to least important as sources of personal strength. You might want to discuss with students why certain sources seem more important than others.

What Do You Think?

Remind students that heroic acts can be private as well as public, small as well as large. If students are having difficulty generating names, suggest they write the letters of the alphabet and brainstorm the name of a hero for each one. Students will return to this activity on page 992.

UNIT SIX **PART 1**

A STRENGTH FROM WITHIN

REFLECTING ON THEME

Are you a strong person? In times of trial, can you find the strength to do what needs to be done—to overcome obstacles, to withstand opposition, even to face danger? Often, people never know what they are capable of doing until circumstances push them to the limit. In this part of Unit Six, you will encounter a number of ordinary people who must confront extraordinary challenges. As you will see, such challenges can produce unexpected heroes.

What Do You Think? In your notebook, list the names of three people whom you regard as heroes. These may be figures from history, people in the news, or personal acquaintances. Write a brief explanation of what makes each of the people heroic. Then compare your list with those of your classmates and discuss what you regard as essential ingredients of heroism.

Roger Rosenblatt (1940–) An award-winning American journalist known for his literary flair

Louise Erdrich (1954–) An American writer influenced by her Native American heritage

Josephina Niggli (1910–1983) Vividly portrayed the history and village life of her native Mexico

Doris Herold Lund (1919–) An American writer, illustrator, and cartoonist

Rosario Castellanos (1925–1974) A respected poet and diplomat who championed Mexico's native cultures

Isabel Allende (1942–) A Chilean journalist turned fiction writer, living in exile in the United States

Nadine Gordimer	**A Chip of Glass Ruby** *Fighting for rights in South Africa*	810
Roger Rosenblatt	**The Man in the Water** *Why did he sacrifice himself?*	823
Isabel Allende	**And of Clay Are We Created** *Amid disaster, heroism*	829
Rosario Castellanos	**Nocturne** / INSIGHT *A question for the night*	840
Louise Erdrich	**The Leap** *How far would you go to save your child?*	844

Map Note

This map reflects the diverse backgrounds of the authors in this section. You may want to ask students one or more of the following questions:

- Which of these countries would you like to visit the most? Explain your answer.
- Which areas represented here might provide the greatest opportunity for heroism? Why?

Yossi Ghinsberg	from **Back from Tuichi** *Battling a treacherous river and a hostile jungle*	855
Josephina Niggli	**The Ring of General Macías** *Revolution, love, and honor*	869
Doris Herold Lund	**Gift from a Son Who Died** *His spirit never quit.*	886

THE LANGUAGE OF LITERATURE TEACHER'S EDITION **809**

OVERVIEW

Objectives

- To understand and appreciate a short story that explores a woman's commitments
- To enrich reading by using active reading strategies
- To identify and understand dialogue
- To appreciate a writer's style
- To express understanding of the story through a choice of writing forms, including an essay, diary entries, a literary analysis, and a dramatic scene
- To extend understanding of the story through a variety of multimodal and cross-curricular activities

Skills

LITERARY CONCEPTS
- Dialogue
- Simile

READING SKILLS/STRATEGIES
- Visualizing setting
- Clarifying
- Questioning
- Evaluating

THE WRITER'S STYLE
- Implied main ideas

GRAMMAR
- Direct objects

SPEAKING, LISTENING, AND VIEWING
- Dramatic monologue
- Interview

HISTORICAL CONNECTION

A Struggle for Freedom For over four decades the nonwhites of South Africa fought against apartheid, the government's rigid system of racial segregation. These photographs of civil rights demonstrations in South Africa during the period of apartheid will help students understand the historical context of Gordimer's short story.

Side A, Frame 49653

PREVIEWING

FICTION

A Chip of Glass Ruby
Nadine Gordimer South Africa

Activating Prior Knowledge
PERSONAL CONNECTION

Think of a household where one parent is heavily involved in political or charitable activities outside the home. With a small group of classmates, discuss how the family might be affected by such activities. Make a chart, like the one shown, listing the positive and negative effects that such involvement might have on the family.

Possible Effects on Family	
Positive	Negative

Building Background
HISTORICAL CONNECTION

In this story, an Indian woman living in South Africa juggles the responsibilities of family life with her work as a political activist. The story takes place during the time of apartheid (ə-pärt′hīt′), a system of racial segregation. Under apartheid, every citizen was classified as either white, colored (mixed race), Asian (of East Indian ancestry), or Bantu (native black). Complex laws set limits on the lives of those who were not white. For example, the Group Areas Act, mentioned in this story, forced nonwhites to live in certain areas. Pass laws required that black South Africans carry passes identifying where they lived and what areas they could visit. While Asians did not have to carry passes, their movements also were restricted.

For decades, many South Africans struggled against apartheid, despite the threat of being jailed. Among the most influential antiapartheid groups was the African National Congress (ANC), called simply "Congress" in the story. As a result of protests led by the ANC and others, the pass laws were among the first apartheid laws to be fought successfully; they were abolished in 1986. Apartheid was completely dismantled in the early 1990s.

Active Reading/Setting a Purpose
READING CONNECTION

Visualizing Setting As you read this story, create mental pictures of the domestic life that the writer describes. Notice details about the house, the clothing, the food, and the routines of daily life. Consider what these details reveal about the family members, the society in which they live, and how their lives are affected by the political activities of Mrs. Bamjee.

Using Your Reading Log Use your reading log to record your responses to the questions throughout the selection. Also jot down any questions, thoughts, and feelings you have as you read.

- HISTORICAL CONNECTION

810 UNIT SIX PART 1: A STRENGTH FROM WITHIN

PRINT AND MEDIA RESOURCES

UNIT SIX RESOURCE BOOK
Strategic Reading: Literature, p. 4
Vocabulary SkillBuilder, p. 5

GRAMMAR MINI-LESSONS
Transparencies, p. 19
Copymasters, p. 17

WRITING MINI-LESSONS
Transparencies, p. 54

ACCESS FOR STUDENTS ACQUIRING ENGLISH
Selection Summaries
Reading Support

TEACHER'S GUIDE TO ASSESSMENT AND PORTFOLIO USE

FORMAL ASSESSMENT
Selection Test, p. 163
Test Generator

 AUDIO LIBRARY
See Reference Card

 LASERLINKS
Historical Connection
Author Background

 INTERNET RESOURCES
McDougal Littell Literature Center at http://www.hmco.com/mcdougal/lit

A Chip of Glass Ruby

Nadine Gordimer

When the duplicating machine was brought into the house, Bamjee said, "Isn't it enough that you've got the Indians' troubles on your back?" Mrs. Bamjee said, with a smile that showed the gap of a missing tooth but was confident all the same, "What's the difference, Yusuf? We've all got the same troubles."

"Don't tell me that. We don't have to carry passes; let the natives protest against passes on their own; there are millions of them. Let them go ahead with it."

WORDS TO KNOW

disarm (dĭs-ärm′) *v.* to overcome or reduce the intensity of suspicion or hostility; to win the confidence of (p. 814)

morose (mə-rōs′) *adj.* gloomy; sullen (p. 814)

patronize (pā′trə-nīz) *v.* to behave in a manner that shows feelings of superiority (p. 814)

presumption (prĭ-zŭmp′shən) *n.* behavior or language that is boldly arrogant or offensive (p. 813)

sallow (săl′ō) *adj.* of a sickly, yellowish color or complexion (p. 814)

SUMMARY

Zanip Bamjee, an Indian woman living in South Africa, runs off political leaflets on a duplicating machine in her kitchen and holds secret anti-apartheid meetings with prominent Indian leaders. Her husband, Yusuf, does not share in or understand his wife's political activities. At three o'clock one morning, the police come to arrest Zanip, leaving their nine children in Yusuf's care. Gradually, the children help Yusuf to understand her deep commitment. When Zanip sends his stepdaughter over to celebrate his birthday, which he has forgotten, Yusuf realizes that it is her very humanity and concern for others that made him love her in the first place.

Thematic Link: *A Strength from Within*
After his wife is arrested, a husband finally understands the strength from within that enables her to fight against injustice.

CUSTOMIZING FOR
Students Acquiring English

- Use **ACCESS FOR STUDENTS ACQUIRING ENGLISH,** *Reading Support.*
- Make sure students refer to the Historical Connection on the Previewing page for essential background information.
- In addition to these boxes, you may want to use the suggestions under Strategic Reading for Less-Proficient Readers.

STRATEGIC READING FOR
Less-Proficient Readers

Set a Purpose To help students establish context for this story, you may wish to have them read the first few pages and then respond to any questions they may have. Then have students read to find out how one woman fights for causes she believes are right.

Use **UNIT SIX RESOURCE BOOK,** p. 4, for guidance in reading the selection.

CUSTOMIZING FOR
Gifted and Talented Students

As students read the selection, ask them to pay close attention to Bamjee's relationship with his children. How does his behavior with them follow the same pattern as his relationship with his wife? *(Possible response: Bamjee assumes a passive role with his children. For example, Jimmy and Girlie take charge of finding out where their mother has been imprisoned. Yet Bamjee also seems to feel affection for his children though he does not express his feelings openly.)*

Literary Concept: SIMILE

A Point out the simile used here and ask students what aspect of the children Gordimer might be trying to emphasize with this comparison. *(Possible responses: The children pick up on everything around them; Mrs. Bamjee's children have taken her activism to heart, "closing on" it, so to speak.)*

Linking to Geography

B Tell students that most of South Africa's Indian population lives in urban areas in the provinces of Transvaal and Natal.

Active Reading: CLARIFY

C You may wish to use this model to give students an example of how to report their thinking process.

Think-Aloud Model: *Bamjee seems removed from his wife's activities. He complains when she brings home the duplicator and does not show any interest in what she is doing.*

The nine Bamjee and Pahad children were present at this exchange as they were always; in the small house that held them all there was no room for privacy for the discussion of matters they were too young to hear, and so they had never been too young to hear anything. Only their sister and half-sister, Girlie, was missing; she was the eldest, and married. The children looked expectantly, unalarmed and interested, at Bamjee, who had neither left the room nor settled down again to the task of rolling his own cigarettes, which had been interrupted by the arrival of the duplicator. He had looked at the thing that had come hidden in a washbasket and conveyed in a black man's taxi, and the **A** children turned on it too, their black eyes surrounded by thick lashes like those still, open flowers with hairy tentacles that close on whatever touches them.

"A fine thing to have on the table where we eat," was all he said at last. They smelled the machine among them; a smell of cold black grease. He went out, heavily on tiptoe, in his troubled way.

"It's going to go nicely on the sideboard!" Mrs. Bamjee was busy making a place by removing the two pink glass vases filled with plastic carnations and the hand-painted velvet runner with the picture of the Taj Mahal.[1]

After supper she began to run off leaflets on the machine. The family lived in that room—the three other rooms in the house were full of beds—and they were all there. The older children shared a bottle of ink while they did their homework, and the two little ones pushed a couple of empty milk bottles in and out the chair legs. The three-year-old fell asleep and was carted away by one of the girls. They all drifted off to bed eventually; Bamjee himself went before the older children—he was a fruit-and-vegetable hawker[2] and was up at half past four every morning to get to the market by five. "Not long now," said Mrs. Bamjee. The older children looked up and smiled at him. He turned his back on her. She still wore the traditional clothing of a Moslem woman, and her body, which was scraggy and unimportant as a dress on a peg when it was not host to a child, was wrapped in the trailing rags of a cheap sari,[3] and her thin black plait[4] was greased. When she was a girl, in the Transvaal[5] town where they lived still, her mother fixed a chip of glass ruby in her nostril; but she had abandoned that adornment as too old-style, even for her, long ago. **B**

She was up until long after midnight, turning out leaflets. She did it as if she might have been pounding chilies.

Bamjee did not have to ask what the leaflets were. He had read the papers. All the past week Africans had been destroying their passes and then presenting themselves for arrest. Their leaders were jailed on charges of incitement,[6] campaign offices were raided—someone must be helping the few minor leaders who were left to keep the campaign going without offices or equipment. What was it the leaflets would say—"Don't go to work tomorrow," "Day of Protest," "Burn Your Pass for Freedom"? He didn't want to see.

CLARIFY

Why doesn't Bamjee want to see the leaflets?
Using a Reading Log

He was used to coming home and finding his wife sitting at the table deep in discussion with strangers or people whose names **C**

---

1. **Taj Mahal** (täzh′ mə-häl′): a beautiful white marble building in India, built in the seventeenth century by Shah Jahan as a tomb for his wife and himself.
2. **hawker:** a peddler who sells goods by calling out.
3. **sari** (sä′rē): a garment worn by East Indian women and girls, consisting of a long cloth wrapped around the body, with one end draped over the shoulder.
4. **plait** (plāt): a braid of hair.
5. **Transvaal** (trăns-väl′): a province in northeast South Africa.
6. **incitement** (ĭn-sīt′mənt): a rousing, stirring up, or calling to action.

812 UNIT SIX PART 1: A STRENGTH FROM WITHIN

Mini-Lesson Grammar

DIRECT OBJECTS Direct objects are words or groups of words that receive the action of action verbs. Direct objects answer the questions *What?* or *Whom?* about a verb. Point out the highlighted sentence on this page and ask *What was fixed in her nostril?* (a glass ruby) and *What was abandoned?* (that adornment) Invite students to find other examples of direct objects on this page.

Application Write the words below on the chalkboard and have students create sentences in which the words are used as direct objects.

| sari | duplicating machine | Dr. Khan |
| tome | bread | neighbors |

Reteaching/Reinforcement
- *Grammar Handbook,* anthology p. 1074
- *Grammar Mini-Lessons* copymasters p. 17, transparencies p. 19,

Direct Objects, p. 577

News from the Gulf (about 1991), Robert A. Wade. Watercolor, 19″ × 29″, private collection. Copyright © Robert A. Wade. From *Painting Your Vision in Watercolor*, North Light Books.

were familiar by repute.[7] Some were prominent Indians, like the lawyer, Dr. Abdul Mohammed Khan, or the big businessman, Mr. Moonsamy Patel, and he was flattered, in a suspicious way, to meet them in his house. As he came home from work next day, he met Dr. Khan coming out of the house, and Dr. Khan—a highly educated man—said to him, "A wonderful woman." But Bamjee had never caught his wife out in any presumption; she behaved properly, as any Moslem woman should, and once her business with such gentlemen was over would never, for instance, have sat down to eat with them. He found her now back in the kitchen, setting about the preparation of dinner and carrying on a conversation on several different wavelengths with the children. "It's really a shame if you're tired of lentils, Jimmy, because that's what you're getting—Amina, hurry up, get a pot of water going—don't worry, I'll mend that in a minute; just bring the yellow cotton, and there's a needle in the cigarette box on the sideboard."

"Was that Dr. Khan leaving?" said Bamjee.

"Yes, there's going to be a stay-at-home on Monday. Desai's ill, and he's got to get the word around by himself. Bob Jali was up all last night

---

7. **repute** (rĭ-pyo͞ot′): reputation; fame.

WORDS TO KNOW
presumption (prĭ-zŭmp′shən) *n.* behavior or language that is boldly arrogant or offensive

Linking to History

D This conversation helps to establish the historical frame for the story. The South African government passed the Group Areas Act in 1950, dividing all cities and towns into segregated residential and business areas. This segregation entailed government-forced removal of thousands of Asians and Coloreds from areas that had been newly classified as White.

Literary Concept: DIALOGUE

E Ask students what inferences they can make about the Bamjees' standard of living from the dialogue in this passage. *(Possible responses: Bamjee owns one suit and can afford to send it to the cleaners; family members routinely borrow clothes from one another because there is little money to spend on clothing; the family is poor, but it is not totally impoverished.)*

CUSTOMIZING FOR
Students Acquiring English

3 Help students paraphrase this long sentence. If necessary, discuss the meaning of specific terms such as *commonplaces, does service as, unthinking doze,* and *jerks and starts* before students attempt their restatements. You may want to have mixed-ability pairs work on this task together and share their statements with the class.

Active Reading: CLARIFY

F Discuss students' thoughts about Bamjee's attitude toward Mrs. Bamjee and invite them to share any other thoughts or questions they have at this point in the story.

---

printing leaflets, but he's gone to have a tooth out." She had always treated Bamjee as if it were only a mannerism that made him appear uninterested in politics, the way some woman will persist in interpreting her husband's bad temper as an endearing gruffness hiding boundless goodwill, and she talked to him of these things just as she passed on to him neighbors' or family gossip.

"What for do you want to get mixed up with these killings and stonings and I don't know what? Congress should keep out of it. Isn't it enough with the Group Areas?"

She laughed. "Now, Yusuf, you know you don't believe that. Look how you said the same thing when the Group Areas started in Natal. You said we should begin to worry when we get moved out of our own houses here in the Transvaal. And then your own mother lost her house in Noorddorp,[8] and there you are; you saw that nobody's safe. Oh, Girlie was here this afternoon; she says Ismail's brother's engaged—that's nice, isn't it? His mother will be pleased; she was worried."

"Why was she worried?" asked Jimmy, who was fifteen, and old enough to <u>patronize</u> his mother.

"Well, she wanted to see him settled. There's a party on Sunday week at Ismail's place—you'd better give me your suit to give to the cleaners tomorrow, Yusuf."

One of the girls presented herself at once. "I'll have nothing to wear, Ma."

Mrs. Bamjee scratched her <u>sallow</u> face. "Perhaps Girlie will lend you her pink, eh? Run over to Girlie's place now and say I say will she lend it to you."

The sound of commonplaces often does service as security, and Bamjee, going to sit in the armchair with the shiny armrests that was wedged between the table and the sideboard, lapsed into an unthinking doze, that, like all times of dreamlike ordinariness during those weeks, was filled with uneasy jerks and starts back into reality. The next morning, as soon as he got to market, he heard that Dr. Khan had been arrested. But that night Mrs. Bamjee sat up making a new dress for her daughter; the sight <u>disarmed</u> Bamjee, reassured him again, against his will, so that the resentment he had been making ready all day faded into a <u>morose</u> and accusing silence. Heaven knew, of course, who came and went in the house during the day. Twice in that week of riots, raids, and arrests, he found black women in the house when he came home; plain ordinary native women in doeks,[9] drinking tea. This was not a thing other Indian women would have in their homes, he thought bitterly; but then his wife was not like other

> This was not a thing other Indian women would have in their homes, he thought bitterly...

CLARIFY

What seems to be Bamjee's attitude toward his wife?

Using a Reading Log

---

8. **Natal** (nə-tăl') . . . **Noorddorp** (nōrt'dôrp): provinces in South Africa.
9. **doeks** (dūks): cloth head coverings.

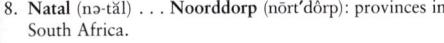

WORDS TO KNOW
patronize (pā'trə-nīz) *v.* to behave in a manner that shows feelings of superiority
sallow (săl'ō) *adj.* of a sickly, yellowish color or complexion
disarm (dĭs-ärm') *v.* to overcome or reduce the intensity of suspicion or hostility; to win the confidence of
morose (mə-rōs') *adj.* gloomy; sullen

people, in a way he could not put his finger on, except to say what it was not: not scandalous, not punishable, not rebellious. It was, like the attraction that had led him to marry her, Pahad's widow with five children, something he could not see clearly.

When the Special Branch[10] knocked steadily on the door in the small hours of Thursday morning, he did not wake up, for his return to consciousness was always set in his mind to half past four, and that was more than an hour away. Mrs. Bamjee got up herself, struggled into Jimmy's raincoat which was hanging over a chair, and went to the front door. The clock on the wall—a wedding present when she married Pahad—showed three o'clock when she snapped on the light, and she knew at once who it was on the other side of the door. Although she was not surprised, her hands shook like a very old person's as she undid the locks and the complicated catch on the wire burglar-proofing. And then she opened the door and they were there—two colored policemen in plain clothes. "Zanip Bamjee?"

"Yes."

As they talked, Bamjee woke up in the sudden terror of having overslept. Then he became conscious of men's voices. He heaved himself out of bed in the dark and went to the window, which, like the front door, was covered with a heavy mesh of thick wire against intruders from the dingy lane it looked upon. Bewildered, he appeared in the room, where the policemen were searching through a soapbox of papers beside the duplicating machine. "Yusuf, it's for me," Mrs. Bamjee said.

At once, the snap of a trap, realization came. He stood there in an old shirt before the two policemen, and the woman was going off to prison because of the natives. "There you are!" he shouted, standing away from her. "That's what you've got for it. Didn't I tell you? Didn't I? That's the end of it now. That's the finish. That's what it's come to." She listened with her head at the slightest tilt to one side, as if to ward off a blow, or in compassion.

Jimmy, Pahad's son, appeared at the door with a suitcase; two or three of the girls were behind him. "Here, Ma, you take my green jersey." "I've found your clean blouse." Bamjee had to keep moving out of their way as they helped their mother to make ready. It was like the preparation for one of the family festivals his wife made such a fuss over; wherever he put himself, they bumped into him. Even the two policemen mumbled, "Excuse me," and pushed past into the rest of the house to continue their search. They took with them a tome[11] that Nehru[12] had written in prison; it had been bought from a persevering traveling salesman and kept, for years, on the mantelpiece. "Oh, don't take that, please," Mrs. Bamjee said suddenly, clinging to the arm of the man who had picked it up.

The man held it away from her.

"What does it matter, Ma?"

It was true that no one in the house had ever read it; but she said, "It's for my children."

"Ma, leave it." Jimmy, who was squat and plump, looked like a merchant advising a client against a roll of silk she had set her heart on. She went into the bedroom and got dressed. When she came out in her old yellow sari with a brown coat over it, the faces of the children were behind her like faces on the platform at a railway station. They kissed her goodbye. The policemen did not hurry her, but she seemed to be in a hurry just the same.

"What am I going to do?" Bamjee accused them all.

The policemen looked away patiently.

"It'll be all right. Girlie will help. The big

---

10. **Special Branch:** the South African secret police.
11. **tome:** a book, especially a large or scholarly one.
12. **Nehru** (nā′rōō): Jawaharlal (jə-wä′hər-läl′) Nehru, nationalist leader in India's movement for self-governance and the first prime minister of independent India.

Active Reading: EVALUATE

J Encourage students to think about what kind of person Bamjee is. What aspects of his personality would enable him to ignore such an important part of his wife's life? *(Possible responses: Bamjee is too self-centered to pay attention to his wife's activities; he probably thinks that his wife should spend all her time taking care of him and the family; he may resent his wife's involvment.)*

CUSTOMIZING FOR
Multiple Learning Styles

K **Intrapersonal Learners** Suggest that students try putting themselves in the place of Mrs. Bamjee's children. In their notebooks they should describe how it would feel to have their mother taken away and not know where she is or be able to see her.

---

children can manage. And Yusuf—" The children crowded in around her; two of the younger ones had awakened and appeared, asking shrill questions.

"Come on," said the policemen.

"I want to speak to my husband." She broke away and came back to him, and the movement of her sari hid them from the rest of the room for a moment. His face hardened in suspicious anticipation against the request to give some message to the next fool who would take up her pamphleteering until he, too, was arrested. "On Sunday," she said. "Take them on Sunday." He did not know what she was talking about. "The engagement party," she whispered, low and urgent. "They shouldn't miss it. Ismail will be offended."

They listened to the car drive away. Jimmy bolted and barred the front door and then at once opened it again; he put on the raincoat that his mother had taken off. "Going to tell Girlie," he said. The children went back to bed. Their father did not say a word to any of them; their talk, the crying of the younger ones and the argumentative voices of the older, went on in the bedrooms. He found himself alone; he felt the night all around him. And then he happened to meet the clock face and saw with a terrible sense of unfamiliarity that this was not the secret night but an hour he should have recognized: the time he always got up. He pulled on his trousers and his dirty white hawker's coat and wound his grey muffler up to the stubble on his chin and went to work.

The duplicating machine was gone from the sideboard. The policemen had taken it with them, along with the pamphlets and the conference reports and the stack of old newspapers that had collected on top of the wardrobe in the bedroom—not the thick dailies of the white men but the thin, impermanent-looking papers that spoke up, sometimes interrupted by suppression or lack of money, for the rest. It was all gone. When he had married her and moved in with her and her five children, into what had been the Pahad and became the Bamjee house, he had not recognized the humble, harmless, and apparently useless routine tasks—the minutes of meetings being written up on the dining-room table at night, the government blue books that were read while the latest baby was suckled, the employment of the fingers of the older children in the fashioning of crinkle-paper Congress rosettes—as activity intended to move mountains. For years and years he had not noticed it, and now it was gone.

EVALUATE

Why do you think Bamjee hadn't paid attention to his wife's political activities?
Using a Reading Log

The house was quiet. The children kept to their lairs, crowded on the beds with the doors shut. He sat and looked at the sideboard, where the plastic carnations and the mat with the picture of the Taj Mahal were in place. For the first few weeks he never spoke of her. There was the feeling, in the house, that he had wept and raged at her, that boulders of reproach had thundered down upon her absence, and yet he had said not one word. He had not been to inquire where she was; Jimmy and Girlie had gone to Mohammed Ebrahim, the lawyer, and when he found out that their mother had been taken—when she was arrested, at least—to a prison in the next town, they had stood about outside the big prison door for hours while they waited to be told where she had been moved from there. At last they had discovered that she was fifty miles away, in Pretoria.[13] Jimmy asked Bamjee for five shillings to help Girlie pay the train fare to Pretoria, once she had been interviewed by the police and had been given a permit to visit her mother; he put three two-shilling pieces on the

---

13. **Pretoria** (prĭ-tôr′ē-ə): the administrative capital of South Africa.

816 UNIT SIX PART 1: A STRENGTH FROM WITHIN

Mini-Lesson — The Writer's Style

SCANS GOAL: Participates as a Member of a Team

LEADING A MEETING Point out that part of Mrs. Bamjee's political activity consisted of meetings with other activists. Explain that leading a meeting is an important management skill. Competent leaders pass out copies of the meeting agenda so that all participants will know in advance about the matters to be discussed. They also appoint someone to take minutes—a written record of the proceedings. Leaders take steps to ensure that all viewpoints are presented during the meeting.

Application Divide students into groups of five or six and have them play the role of Mrs. Bamjee's activist friends. Each group should discuss what can be done to assist Mrs. Bamjee and her family. Appoint a leader in each group who can set an agenda for the meeting; the leader should designate someone to take minutes of the meeting. Each group should share its recommendations with the class.

Light in the Souk, (about 1991), Robert A. Wade. Watercolor, 19″ × 29″, private collection. Copyright © Robert A. Wade. From *Painting Your Vision in Watercolor*, North Light Books.

table for Jimmy to pick up, and the boy, looking at him keenly, did not know whether the extra shilling meant anything, or whether it was merely that Bamjee had no change.

It was only when relations and neighbors came to the house that Bamjee would suddenly begin to talk. He had never been so expansive in his life as he was in the company of these visitors, many of them come on a polite call rather in the nature of a visit of condolence. "Ah, yes, yes, you can see how I am—you see what has been done to me. Nine children, and I am on the cart all day. I get home at seven or eight. What are you to do? What can people like us do?"

"Poor Mrs. Bamjee. Such a kind lady."

"Well, you see for yourself. They walk in here in the middle of the night and leave a houseful of children. I'm out on the cart all day; I've got a living to earn." Standing about in his shirt-sleeves, he became quite animated; he would call for the girls to bring fruit drinks for the visitors. When they were gone, it was as if he, who was orthodox[14] if not devout and never drank liquor, had been drunk and abruptly sobered up; he looked dazed and could not have gone over in his mind what he had been saying. And as he cooled, the lump of resentment and wrongedness stopped his throat again.

---

14. **orthodox:** conforming to established religious rules or principles.

A CHIP OF GLASS RUBY **817**

Art Note

Light in the Souk by Robert A. Wade
This watercolor, also produced with the "visioneering" method, portrays the market in Marrakesh, Morocco.

Reading the Art What impact do the vaguely defined figures have on the painting as a whole?

Literary Concept: DIALOGUE

L Ask students what the responses of the "relations and neighbors" reveal about Mrs. Bamjee. *(Possible responses: Mrs. Bamjee has obviously touched many lives; people seem to be drawn to her kindness.)*

Cultural Note

M Explain that in the Islamic religion, the consumption of alcohol is prohibited. The phrase "orthodox if not devout" suggests that Bamjee followed Islamic teachings but did not pray or go to the mosque regularly.

STRATEGIC READING FOR
Less-Proficient Readers

N Make sure that students are following the events of the story by asking the following questions.

- How would you describe life in the Bamjee household since Mrs. Bamjee has been arrested. *(It has been very quiet, with both Bamjee and the children keeping to themselves; a number of visitors have come to pay condolences.)* Summarizing

- How has his wife's arrest affected Bamjee? *(He seems to be lonely and lost without her presence and resents her for causing this trouble; he complains about his fate to visitors.)* Evaluating

Set a Purpose Have students read to find out how the Bamjees' situation is resolved.

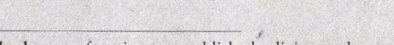

Critic's Corner

"Gordimer examines, with passionate precision, the intricacies both of individual lives and of the wide-ranging political and historical forces that contain them."

Margo Jefferson

Ask students to discuss how this quote applies to "A Chip of Glass Ruby."

THE LANGUAGE OF LITERATURE **TEACHER'S EDITION** 817

CUSTOMIZING FOR
Students Acquiring English

4 Ask students what they think the expression *championing brothers and sisters* means. Have them look up the word *champion* in the dictionary and ask them to pay attention to the definition of the verb form of the word. Lead them to understand that the children were defending and supporting their brother who had been verbally attacked by his teacher.

Critical Thinking: ANALYZING

O Point out that both Bamjee and one of the children are unable to eat because of Mrs. Bamjee's hunger strike, although they seem to lose their appetites for different reasons. Ask students to analyze Bamjee's reaction. Is he using anger as a shield for his sorrow? *(Accept all reasonable responses.)*

Active Reading: CLARIFY

P Discuss with students the reasons why Bamjee feels as he does about his life. If students are having trouble understanding Bamjee's feelings, suggest they look back through the story for descriptions of Bamjee's life since his wife has been arrested.

---

4 Bamjee found one of the little boys the center of a self-important group of championing brothers and sisters in the room one evening. "They've been cruel to Ahmed."

"What has he done?" said the father.

"Nothing! Nothing!" The little girl stood twisting her handkerchief excitedly.

An older one, thin as her mother, took over, silencing the others with a gesture of her skinny hand. "They did it at school today. They made an example of him."

"What is an example?" said Bamjee impatiently.

"The teacher made him come up and stand in front of the whole class, and he told them, 'You see this boy? His mother's in jail because she likes the natives so much. She wants the Indians to be the same as natives.'"

"It's terrible," he said. His hands fell to his sides. "Did she ever think of this?"

He had a sudden vision of her at the duplicating machine...

"That's why Ma's *there*," said Jimmy, putting aside his comic and emptying out his schoolbooks upon the table. "That's all the kids need to know. Ma's there because things like this happen. Petersen's a colored teacher, and it's his black blood that's brought him trouble all his life, I suppose. He hates anyone who says everybody's the same because that takes away from him his bit of whiteness that's all he's got. What d'you expect? It's nothing to make too much fuss about."

"Of course, you are fifteen and you know everything," Bamjee mumbled at him.

"I don't say that. But I know Ma, anyway." The boy laughed.

There was a hunger strike among the political prisoners, and Bamjee could not bring himself to ask Girlie if her mother was starving herself too. He would not ask; and yet he saw in the young woman's face the gradual weakening of her mother. When the strike had gone on for nearly a week, one of the elder children burst into tears at the table and could not eat. Bamjee pushed his own plate away in rage. **O**

Sometimes he spoke out loud to himself while he was driving the vegetable lorry.[15] "What for?" Again and again: "What for?" She was not a modern woman who cut her hair and wore short skirts. He had married a good plain Moslem woman who bore children and stamped her own chilies. He had a sudden vision of her at the duplicating machine, that night just before she was taken away, and he felt himself maddened, baffled, and hopeless. He had become the ghost of a victim, hanging about the scene of a crime whose motive he could not understand and had not had time to learn. **P**

CLARIFY
How does Bamjee feel about his life?

Using a Reading Log

15. **lorry:** a truck.

818 UNIT SIX PART 1: A STRENGTH FROM WITHIN

Mini-Lesson The Writer's Style

IMPLIED MAIN IDEAS Most fiction writers don't reveal their main ideas directly. Instead they imply them through story details. This is certainly true of "A Chip of Glass Ruby." One of Gordimer's main ideas is Bamjee's disconnection from his wife's political activity. However, instead of stating this idea directly to her readers, Gordimer implies it through Bamjee's actions, thoughts, and words. For instance, after Mrs. Bamjee is arrested, the absence of her political activity is shown to both disconcert and puzzle Bamjee. "For years and years he had not noticed it, and now it was gone."

Application Invite students to write a scene from a short story in which a main idea is implied instead of stated. Suggest that they exchange their scenes with a partner to find out if they have implied their ideas effectively.

Reteaching/Reinforcement
- Writing Handbook, anthology pp. 1034–1035
- *Writing Mini-Lessons* transparencies, p. 54

Story, pp. 102–107

The hunger strike at the prison went into the second week. Alone in the rattling cab of his lorry, he said things that he heard as if spoken by someone else, and his heart burned in fierce agreement with them. "For a crowd of natives who'll smash our shops and kill us in our houses when their time comes." "She will starve herself to death there." "She will die there." "Devils who will burn and kill us." He fell into bed each night like a stone and dragged himself up in the mornings as a beast of burden is beaten to its feet.

One of these mornings, Girlie appeared very early, while he was wolfing bread and strong tea—alternate sensations of dry solidity and stinging heat—at the kitchen table. Her real name was Fatima, of course, but she had adopted the silly modern name along with the clothes of the young factory girls among whom she worked. She was expecting her first baby in a week or two, and her small face, her cut and curled hair, and the sooty arches drawn over her eyebrows did not seem to belong to her thrust-out body under a clean smock. She wore mauve lipstick and was smiling her cocky little white girl's smile, foolish and bold, not like an Indian girl's at all.

"What's the matter?" he said.

She smiled again. "Don't you know? I told Bobby he must get me up in time this morning. I wanted to be sure I wouldn't miss you today."

"I don't know what you're talking about."

She came over and put her arm up around his unwilling neck and kissed the grey bristles at the side of his mouth. "Many happy returns! Don't you know it's your birthday?"

"No," he said. "I didn't know, didn't think—" He broke the pause by swiftly picking up the bread and giving his attention desperately to eating and drinking. His mouth was busy, but his eyes looked at her, intensely black. She said nothing but stood there with him. She would not speak, and at last he said, swallowing a piece of bread that tore at his throat as it went down, "I don't remember these things."

The girl nodded, the Woolworth baubles in her ears swinging. "That's the first thing she told me when I saw her yesterday—don't forget it's Bajie's birthday tomorrow."

He shrugged over it. "It means a lot to children. But that's how she is. Whether it's one of the old cousins or the neighbor's grandmother, she always knows when the birthday is. What importance is my birthday, while she's sitting there in a prison? I don't understand how she can do the things she does when her mind is always full of woman's nonsense at the same time—that's what I don't understand with her."

"Oh, but don't you see?" the girl said. "It's because she doesn't want anybody to be left out. It's because she always remembers; remembers everything—people without somewhere to live, hungry kids, boys who can't get educated—remembers all the time. That's how Ma is."

"Nobody else is like that." It was half a complaint.

"No, nobody else," said his stepdaughter.

She sat herself down at the table, resting her belly. He put his head in his hands. "I'm getting old"—but he was overcome by something much more curious, by an answer. He knew why he had desired her, the ugly widow with five children; he knew what way it was in which she was not like the others; it was there, like the fact of the belly that lay between him and her daughter. ❖

A CHIP OF GLASS RUBY 819

From Personal Response to Critical Analysis

1. Accept all reasonable responses.
2. Accept all reasonable, well-supported responses.
3. Possible responses: They seem ill-suited for one another; although they appear to be opposites, they seem to love each other; Mrs. Bamjee's personality appears to both torment and enthrall Bamjee.
4. Possible responses: On the positive side, their children will grow with a strong sense of justice and a belief in political activism; on the negative side, her political activism has taken her away from her children, who need her.
5. Possible responses: It is a very stratified society in which every color and ethnic group has its place; it is like a police state, in which dissent or protest is not tolerated.
6. Accept all reasonable, well-supported responses.

Another Pathway

Cooperative Learning An accuracy coach can help group members rehearse their monologues, a criticizer of ideas can help review and revise monologue ideas, and an options generator can think of creative ways of extending the monologues.

Rubric

3 Full Accomplishment Monologues are consistent with the story's portrayal of each character.

2 Substantial Accomplishment Monologues are slightly inconsistent with story information.

1 Little or Partial Accomplishment Students have trouble working together or demonstrate a poor understanding of the story or the form of a monologue.

Literary Links

Accept all reasonable, well-supported responses.

RESPONDING OPTIONS

FROM PERSONAL RESPONSE TO CRITICAL ANALYSIS

REFLECT
1. With which character did you sympathize more, Bamjee or Mrs. Bamjee? Share your response with a partner.

RETHINK
2. Do you think that Mrs. Bamjee is a heroic character? Explain your views, citing details from the story to support your opinion.

3. How would you describe the relationship between the husband and wife?
   Consider
   - what Bamjee realizes at the story's conclusion about "why he had desired her"
   - how he feels about his wife's political involvement
   - how each of them handles the responsibilities of marriage and parenthood
   - the differences in their values and personalities

   Close Textual Reading

4. In your judgment, what are the positive and negative effects of Mrs. Bamjee's political activities on her family?
   Consider
   - how Mrs. Bamjee's children and husband respond to her imprisonment
   - how her actions might influence the future lives of family members
   - the chart that you created for the Personal Connection on page 810

   Close Textual Reading

5. How would you describe life under apartheid, based on your understanding of this story?

RELATE
6. In what ways might this story be relevant to people living in your country?

LITERARY LINKS

Review Coretta Scott King's "Montgomery Boycott" on page 221. If Mrs. King and Mrs. Bamjee were to meet, what might they say to each other?

820 UNIT SIX PART 1: A STRENGTH FROM WITHIN

Multimodal Reading
ANOTHER PATHWAY
Cooperative Learning

With a small group of classmates, prepare and present four dramatic monologues in which each of the following characters expresses his or her view of Mrs. Bamjee: Girlie, Jimmy, Yusuf, and a neighbor. You may wish to include quotations from the story in your monologues.

QUICKWRITES

1. A character in one of Gordimer's novels says, "The real definition of loneliness . . . is to live without social responsibility." Draft an **essay** explaining how Yusuf and Zanip Bamjee would respond to such a statement and how they would define their own responsibilities.

2. Write the **diary entries** that Yusuf and Girlie might have written soon after Mrs. Bamjee's arrest.

3. Write a **literary analysis** in which you offer your own explanation of the significance of this story's title.

4. Rewrite an episode from the story as a **dramatic scene** with stage directions and dialogue.

   PORTFOLIO Save your writing. You may want to use it later as a springboard to a piece for your portfolio.

QuickWrites

1. Remind students to include introductions and conclusions in their essays.
2. Suggest that students go back through the story and focus on the two characters' different attitudes towards Mrs. Bamjee.
3. Point out that a literary analysis does not necessarily have to have a story summary.
4. Students should use the correct format for setting up their dramatic scene. Remind them to describe the setting in their stage directions.

The Writer's Craft

Interpretive Essay, pp. 238–253
Using Dialogue, pp. 453–454

LITERARY CONCEPTS

Writers often use **dialogue** as a method of developing characters. Working with a partner, choose three characters from this story whom you would like to study. Then review the story to find examples of dialogue that reveal those characters' traits. Create three diagrams like the one shown to record your findings.

Jimmy	
Dialogue	Trait(s) Revealed
"Ma's there because things like this happen."	—respect for mother —concern about social justice

THE WRITER'S STYLE

Cooperative Learning With a small group of classmates, take turns reading aloud the description of Mrs. Bamjee's late-night arrest. After completing your oral reading, discuss Gordimer's style. Consider her choice of words, her **tone**, her handling of **dialogue**, her use of **descriptive language**, and any other aspects of **style** that you notice.

CRITIC'S CORNER

The critic Brigitte Weeks wrote that "Gordimer insists that her readers face South African life as she does: with affection and horror." How do you think this statement applies to "A Chip of Glass Ruby"?

ART CONNECTION

Choose one of the two paintings that accompany the selection (page 813 or 817) and explain how it reflects the mood of "A Chip of Glass Ruby."

Detail of *Light in the Souk*, (about 1991), Robert A. Wade. Watercolor, 19″ × 29″, private collection. Copyright © Robert A. Wade. From *Painting Your Vision in Watercolor*, North Light Books.

Detail of *News from the Gulf* (about 1991), Robert A. Wade. Watercolor, 19″ × 29″, private collection. Copyright © Robert A. Wade. From *Painting Your Vision in Watercolor*, North Light Books.

Multimodal Reading

ALTERNATIVE ACTIVITIES

1. Create an **illustration** that shows an interior scene of the Bamjee household, based on details in the story. You may work in any medium that you like. Try to portray the household as you visualized it while reading.

2. Conduct an **interview** of someone who is involved in political or charitable activities in your community. Determine why he or she is involved in this work and what—if anything—he or she has sacrificed to provide time for such a commitment.

3. Create a **political cartoon** that offers a reflection on apartheid.

ACROSS THE CURRICULUM

History Find out more about antiapartheid protests led by the African National Congress or about earlier protests in South Africa led by India's Mohandas Gandhi. Share your findings in an oral report.

Literary Concepts

Encourage students to make their lists as comprehensive as possible. Tell the pairs that they do not always have to agree on what traits are revealed by the dialogue; where disagreement occurs, each student can list his or her interpretation of the trait revealed.

Across the Curriculum

History Students may also wish to find out about international policies, such as boycotts and divestment, that put world pressure on South Africa to dismantle the apartheid system. Students researching Gandhi and the ANC might want to think about common traits shared by Gandhi and Nelson Mandela.

Critic's Corner

Possible responses: Gordimer has an obvious affection for Mrs. Bamjee, who is portrayed as a strong and loving character; however, Mrs. Bamjee's fate evokes horror. She is arrested in the middle of the night and torn from her family.

Art Connection

Students should support their explanations with both story and painting details.

The Writer's Style

Cooperative Learning Groups should appoint a turn-taking monitor to ensure that everyone gets a chance to read. A recorder can write down the group's ideas about Gordimer's style, and a summarizer can finalize statements that include everyone's opinions and comments.

Alternative Activities

1. Students should share and compare their illustrations with their classmates. How do students' visualizations of the Bamjee household differ from one another? Encourage students to post their illustrations on the bulletin board.

2. Remind students that good interviewers research their subjects so that they can ask informed questions. Suggest that students make up a list of questions ahead of time, but caution them to be flexible; unplanned digressions in interviews can reveal fascinating information.

Words to Know

1. look down on
2. has spent a lot of time indoors
3. depressed
4. rude
5. friendly

Reteaching/Reinforcement
- *Unit Six Resource Book,* p. 5.

NADINE GORDIMER

To Gordimer, writing is essentially an internal and solitary craft from start to finish. She shows no one her work before submitting it for publication. In fact, after she won the Nobel Prize, she was amused by the photographs that appeared in newspapers showing her surrounded by family. "It's very nice, but nobody in that group ever sees a word that I write before it's printed; I never discuss it. Writing makes one a bit schizophrenic, or maybe it's just a behavior pattern that leads one to writing."

 AUTHOR BACKGROUND
Nadine Gordimer Much of Gordimer's work has focused on the destructive influence of apartheid in South Africa. In this Bill Moyers interview with Gordimer, the South African Nobel Prize winner talks about the problems facing her country.

Side A, Frame 43925

 **WORDS TO KNOW**

Answer the following questions.

1. Would people be most likely to **patronize** someone they fear, look up to, or look down on?
2. Would a person with a **sallow** appearance be more likely to look as if he or she has spent a lot of time indoors, out in the sun, or at the gym lifting weights?
3. Does a **morose** person typically act conceited, depressed, or frightened?
4. Is a **presumption** an act that is usually seen as being humorous, bashful, or rude?
5. If you were trying to **disarm** someone, would you be most likely to behave in a friendly, bossy, or insulting manner?

NADINE GORDIMER

1923–

Nadine Gordimer was born and raised in Springs, South Africa, a small mining town near Johannesburg, the country's largest city. She attended an all-white school and spent much of her free time reading at the local library. Gordimer realized early on that she had little in common with her peers, however, and she began questioning the racial attitudes of white South Africa. She discovered, in her words, that she "was not merely part of a suburban white life aping Europe" but "lived with and among a variety of colors and kinds of people. This discovery was a joyous personal one, not a political one, at first; but, of course, as time has gone by it has hardened into a sense of political opposition to abusive white power."

Gordimer knew she would be a writer when, at the age of 15, she had her first short story published; her first story collection, *Face to Face,* appeared 10 years later. She was recognized almost immediately as a serious and talented artist, and she gained an American audience by publishing her stories in such magazines as the *New Yorker* and *Harper's.* She has also won praise for her novels—including *A World of Strangers, A Guest of Honour, Burger's Daughter,* and *July's People*—and has written numerous essays, television plays, and documentaries.

Much of Gordimer's writing has focused on the theme of the destructive influence of apartheid on relationships among South Africans of all colors; as a result, several of her books were banned in her homeland for many years. Although she has said that she's not by nature a political person, she joined the African National Congress (ANC) and also helped found the Congress of South African Writers. "The real influence of politics on my writing is the influence of politics on people," she said. "Their lives, and I believe their very personalities, are changed by the extreme political circumstances one lives under in South Africa." On learning that she had won the 1991 Nobel Prize for literature, she called the event the second greatest thrill of recent years; the first, she said, was the release of ANC leader Nelson Mandela after 27 years as a political prisoner.

OTHER WORKS *Selected Stories, Six Feet of the Country, My Son's Story, Jump and Other Stories*

Extended Reading

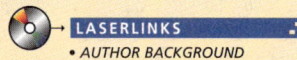
• AUTHOR BACKGROUND

822 UNIT SIX PART 1: A STRENGTH FROM WITHIN

REFLECTING ON THEME
What Do You Think?

Ask students to review what they wrote about the heroes they chose for the activity on page 806. Which of these heroes, if any, would most likely appreciate Mrs. Bamjee? Ask students to consider whether their own ideas about heroism have been affected by reading this selection.

PREVIEWING

NONFICTION

The Man in the Water
Roger Rosenblatt United States

Activating Prior Knowledge
PERSONAL CONNECTION
In a disaster—such as an earthquake, a flood, a tornado, or a plane crash—people react in many different ways. With your classmates, discuss how such disasters can bring out the best—or worst—in people. Draw upon your own knowledge for examples.

Building Background
HISTORICAL CONNECTION
One of the most publicized disasters in recent aviation history occurred on January 13, 1982, when a passenger jet crashed in Washington, D.C., during the evening rush hour. The jet was taking off in freezing rain and failed to gain enough altitude. Crashing onto the 14th Street Bridge, which crosses the Potomac River, the plane broke in two and fell into the icy river. Seventy-eight people died in the disaster—some of them in the plane, some in their cars on the bridge, and some in the frigid waters of the Potomac.

Following the crash of Flight 90, news reports on television and in newspapers provided extensive details of the tragedy. This essay offers more than a news report. It presents the author's viewpoints on the meaning of the events that took place immediately following the crash. In particular, the author looks at how one passenger behaved in those confusing, terrifying moments and considers what his behavior says about all of us.

Setting a Purpose
WRITING CONNECTION
Think about the discussion you had for the Personal Connection, and jot down in your notebook a list of the generalizations you can make about human nature based on the way people respond to a disaster. As you read this essay, see how your views of human nature compare with the author's.

● **LASERLINKS**
• HISTORICAL CONNECTION

OVERVIEW
Objectives
- To understand and appreciate an essay that explores one man's inner strength and heroism
- To identify and understand an author's tone
- To express understanding of the selection through a choice of writing forms, including a tribute, a newspaper article, and a personal essay
- To extend understanding of the selection through a variety of multimodal and cross-curricular activities

Skills
LITERARY CONCEPTS
• Tone

GRAMMAR
• Infinitives

SPEAKING, LISTENING, AND VIEWING
• Group discussion
• Oral report

HISTORICAL CONNECTION
The Crash of Air Florida Flight 90
The 1982 crash in Washington, D.C., of a passenger jet was one of the most publicized airline disasters. These photographs of the rescue efforts at the crash site will help to build students' prior knowledge about this event.

Side A, Frame 49660

CUSTOMIZING FOR
Students Acquiring English
- Use **ACCESS FOR STUDENTS ACQUIRING ENGLISH**, *Reading Support*.
- Some of the sentences in this article are long and complex. Suggest that students break up the long sentences into smaller chunks.
- In addition to these boxes, you may also want to use the suggestions under Strategic Reading for Less-Proficient Readers.

PRINT AND MEDIA RESOURCES

UNIT SIX RESOURCE BOOK
Strategic Reading: Literature, p. 9
Vocabulary SkillBuilder, p. 10

WRITING MINI-LESSONS
Transparencies, pp. 18-19

ACCESS FOR STUDENTS ACQUIRING ENGLISH
Selection Summaries
Reading Support

FORMAL ASSESSMENT
Selection Test, p. 165
 Test Generator

 **AUDIO LIBRARY**
See Reference Card

● **LASERLINKS**
Historical Connection

The Man in the Water

Roger Rosenblatt

A paramedic pulls a woman from the Potomac River following the crash of Air Florida Flight 90. AP / Wide World Photos.

A woman holds on to a safety ring as she is pulled from the Potomac River. AP / Wide World Photos.

As disasters go, this one was terrible, but not unique, certainly not among the worst on the roster of U.S. air crashes. There was the unusual element of the bridge, of course, and the fact that the plane clipped it at a moment of high traffic, one routine thus intersecting another and disrupting both. Then, too, there was the location of the event. Washington, the city of form and regulations, turned chaotic, deregulated, by a blast of real winter and a single slap of metal on metal. The jets from Washington National Airport that normally swoop around the presidential monuments like famished gulls are, for the moment, emblemized by the one that fell; so there is that detail. And there was the aesthetic[1] clash as well—blue-and-green Air Florida, the name a flying garden, sunk down among gray chunks in a black river. All that was worth noticing, to be sure. Still, there was nothing very special in any of it, except death, which, while always special, does not necessarily bring millions to tears or to attention. Why, then, the shock here?

Perhaps because the nation saw in this disaster something more than a mechanical failure. Perhaps because people saw in it no

---
1. **aesthetic** (ĕs-thĕt′ĭk): relating to that which is beautiful or pleasing to the senses.

WORDS TO KNOW
chaotic (kā-ŏt′ĭk) *adj.* extremely confused or disordered

WORDS TO KNOW

abiding (ə-bī′dĭng) *adj.* lasting or enduring **abide** *v.* (p. 826)
anonymity (ăn′ə-nĭm′ĭ-tē) *n.* the state of being unknown or unidentified (p. 825)
chaotic (kā-ŏt′ĭk) *adj.* extremely confused or disordered (p. 824)
flail (flāl) *v.* to wave or swing vigorously; thrash (p. 825)
implacable (ĭm-plăk′ə-bəl) *adj.* impossible to appease or satisfy; relentless (p. 826)

failure at all, but rather something successful about their makeup. Here, after all, were two forms of nature in collision: the elements and human character. Last Wednesday, the elements, indifferent as ever, brought down Flight 90. And on that same afternoon, human nature—groping and <u>flailing</u> in mysteries of its own—rose to the occasion.

Of the four acknowledged heroes of the event, three are able to account for their behavior. Donald Usher and Eugene Windsor, a park police helicopter team, risked their lives every time they dipped the skids into the water to pick up survivors. On television, side by side in bright blue jumpsuits, they described their courage as all in the line of duty. Lenny Skutnik, a twenty-eight-year-old employee of the Congressional Budget Office, said: "It's something I never thought I would do"—referring to his jumping into the water to drag an injured woman to shore. Skutnik added that "somebody had to go in the water," delivering every hero's line that is no less admirable for its repetitions. In fact, nobody had to go into the water. That somebody actually did so is part of the reason this particular tragedy sticks in the mind.

But the person most responsible for the emotional impact of the disaster is the one known at first simply as "the man in the water." (Balding, probably in his fifties, an extravagant mustache.) He was seen clinging with five other survivors to the tail section of the airplane. This man was described by Usher and Windsor as appearing alert and in control. Every time they lowered a lifeline and flotation ring to him, he passed it on to another of the passengers. "In a mass casualty, you'll find people like him," said Windsor. "But I've never seen one with that commitment." When the helicopter came back for him, the man had gone under. His selflessness was one reason the story held national attention; his <u>anonymity</u> another. The fact that he went unidentified invested him with a universal character. For a while he was Everyman, and thus proof (as if one needed it) that no man is ordinary.

Still, he could never have imagined such a capacity in himself. Only minutes before his character was tested, he was sitting in the ordinary plane among the ordinary passengers, dutifully listening to the stewardess telling him to fasten his seat belt and saying something about the "no smoking sign." So our man relaxed with the others, some of whom would owe their lives to him. Perhaps he started to read, or to doze, or to regret some harsh remark made in the office that morning. Then suddenly he knew that the trip would not be ordinary. Like every other person on that flight, he was desperate to live, which makes his final act so stunning.

For at some moment in the water he must have realized that he would not live if he continued to hand over the rope and ring to others. He *had* to know it, no matter how gradual the effect of the cold. In his judgment he had no choice. When the helicopter took off with what was to be the last survivor, he watched everything in the world move away from him, and he deliberately let it happen.

Yet there was something else about the man that kept our thoughts on him, and which

| WORDS TO KNOW | **flail** (flāl) *v.* to wave or swing vigorously; thrash |
| | **anonymity** (ăn′ə-nĭm′ĭ-tē) *n.* the state of being unknown or unidentified |

825

Mini-Lesson — Grammar

INFINITIVES Remind students that an infinitive is a verb form that usually begins with *to* and functions as a noun, adjective, or an adverb.

Adverb: "Perhaps he started *to read,...*"

Adjective: Was it his time *to die*?

Noun: To live must have been the man's greatest wish.

Be sure that students can distinguish an infinitive from a prepositional phrase.

Infinitive: "He was desperate *to live.*"

Prepositional Phrase: He passed the flotation ring *to others.*

Application Tell students to create three sentences containing infinitives, all of which describe the actions of the man in the water. Challenge them to create infinitives that function as a noun, an adjective, and an adverb.

Infinitives and Infinitive Phrases, pp. 592–593

Critical Thinking:
MAKING INFERENCES

A Ask students why they think the author includes this physical description of the man in the water. *(Possible responses: to emphasize his ordinary, rather than heroic, appearance; to make him come alive for readers since no one knows his name.)*

STRATEGIC READING FOR
Less-Proficient Readers

B Make sure students comprehend both the crash and the rescue effort.

- What conditions surrounded the crash of Flight 90? *(It was freezing rain and the jet crashed into a bridge.)* Noting Relevant Details

- What did the first three heroes do? *(They pulled people out of the water.)* Summarizing

- What was unusual about "the man in the water"? *(He kept handing the life ring to others and never tried to save himself.)* Making Inferences

Set a Purpose Have students read to find out Rosenblatt's analysis of the man's actions.

Literary Concept: TONE

C Ask students to analyze how Rosenblatt feels about the man in the water at this point. How can they tell this? *(Possible responses: He is amazed because the man's actions were deliberate; he is astonished that someone would choose to save others rather than first save himself.)*

CUSTOMIZING FOR
Multiple Learning Styles

D Logical-Mathematical Learners Invite students to debate the logic of what the man in the water did. Doesn't it go against our biological instinct for self-preservation to save others instead of ourselves?

CUSTOMIZING FOR
Students Acquiring English

2 Make two lists on the board to help students understand the contrast between the forces of nature (the wind, cold weather, and icy water) and humans (in the form of the man in the water). Review the meanings of the words *distinctions, principles,* and *faith* and show how these elements are part of the makeup of humans, but not of nature.

Critical Thinking:
MAKING JUDGMENTS

E The author states that this incident reminds us that people are not powerless in this world, although the opposite seems to be true. Ask students if they agree or disagree. *(Accept all reasonable responses.)*

STRATEGIC READING FOR
Less-Proficient Readers

F Make sure students understand that according to Rosenblatt, the man in the water represents the timeless battle between humans and nature.

- What is the "timeless battle" that occurred during the tragedy? *(the battle of man against nature)* **Clarifying**
- What were the "natural powers" that the man in the water had? *(the power to hand life over to a stranger)* **Drawing Conclusions**

COMPREHENSION CHECK
1. What disaster happened on January 13, 1982? *(A passenger plane crashed into a bridge in Washington, D.C.)*
2. What did "the man in the water" do? *(He saved the lives of five people.)*
3. What finally happened to him? *(He drowned)*
4. Whom does the author think the man represents? *(everyone)*

keeps our thoughts on him still. He was *there*, in the essential, classic circumstance. Man in nature. The man in the water. For its part, nature cared nothing about the five passengers. Our man, on the other hand, cared totally. So the timeless battle commenced in the Potomac. For as long as that man could last, they went at each other, nature and man: the one making no distinctions of good and evil, acting on no principles, offering no lifelines; the other acting wholly on distinctions, principles, and, one supposes, on faith.

Since it was he who lost the fight, we ought to come again to the conclusion that people are powerless in the world. In reality, we believe the reverse, and it takes the act of the man in the water to remind us of our true feelings in this matter. It is not to say that everyone would have acted as he did, or as Usher, Windsor, and Skutnik. Yet whatever moved these men to challenge death on behalf of their fellows is not peculiar to them. Everyone feels the possibility in himself. That is the <u>abiding</u> wonder of the story. That is why we would not let go of it. If the man in the water gave a lifeline to the people gasping for survival, he was likewise giving a lifeline to those who observed him.

The odd thing is that we do not even really believe that the man in the water lost his fight. "Everything in Nature contains all the powers of Nature," said Emerson. Exactly. So the man in the water had his own natural powers. He could not make ice storms, or freeze the water until it froze the blood. But he could hand life over to a stranger, and that is a power of nature too. The man in the water pitted himself against an <u>implacable</u>, impersonal enemy; he fought it with charity; and he held it to a standoff. He was the best we can do. ❖

January 25, 1982

Two more survivors are pulled from the icy water. UPI/Bettmann.

A section of the plane's fuselage is hoisted from the river several days after the crash. UPI/Bettmann.

WORDS TO KNOW	**abiding** (ə-bī′dĭng) *adj.* lasting or enduring **abide** *v.* **implacable** (ĭm-plăk′ə-bəl) *adj.* impossible to appease or satisfy; relentless

826

Mini-Lesson The Writer's Style

COMPARISON AND CONTRAST
Comparison and contrast is a frequently used technique in writing. Roger Rosenblatt creates a memorable contrast in this essay, when he juxtaposes man with nature. On page 825, for example, he states that "nature cared nothing about the five passengers. Our man, on the other hand, cared totally." This contrast serves to highlight both the eternal struggle of humans against nature and the extraordinariness of someone who stood out in this struggle.

Application Invite students to write paragraphs in which they compare and contrast two things or people. Remind them that this device should lead to some sort of conclusion or insight.

Reteaching/Reinforcement
- Writer's Handbook, anthology p. 1028
- *Writing Mini-Lessons* transparencies, pp. 18–19

The Writer's Craft

Comparision and Contrast, pp. 118–132

RESPONDING OPTIONS

FROM PERSONAL RESPONSE TO CRITICAL ANALYSIS

REFLECT
1. What do you think about the behavior of the man in the water? Record your response in your notebook.

RETHINK
2. Why do you think Rosenblatt chose to focus on the anonymous man in the water rather than on one of the other three acknowledged heroes of the tragedy?
3. Rosenblatt concludes that "we do not even really believe that the man in the water lost his fight" with nature. Do you agree or disagree?
   Consider
   - Rosenblatt's view of nature *(Close Textual Reading)*
   - the lessons that Rosenblatt draws from the man's sacrifice
   - the power that enabled the man to "hand life over to a stranger"
4. What does the essay's final statement—"He was the best we can do"—mean to you? Explain your response.

RELATE
5. Do you think that everyone is capable of acting as heroically as the man in the water? You may wish to review the generalizations you made for the Writing Connection on page 823. *(Thematic Link)*

ANOTHER PATHWAY
Cooperative Learning
In a small group, create a two-column chart. Label one column Nature and the other column Human Nature. In each column, list words and phrases from the essay that convey Rosenblatt's views about that subject. Then write statements summarizing his view of nature and his view of human nature.

QUICKWRITES
1. Write a **tribute** to the man in the water that would be appropriate for a memorial plaque to be placed on the 14th Street Bridge.
2. Using information from this essay and from the Historical Connection on page 823, write a **newspaper article** about the man in the water.
3. Write a **personal essay** about a disaster, an emergency, or some other event that you witnessed or learned about and that made you reflect about human nature. You may find it helpful to review the generalizations that you made for the Writing Connection on page 823.

📁 **PORTFOLIO** Save your writing. You may want to use it later as a springboard to a piece for your portfolio.

LITERARY CONCEPTS
Tone is the attitude a writer takes toward a subject. In nonfiction a writer's tone is influenced by his or her purpose for writing, as well as the writing format. For example, the tone of an informative newspaper article is typically detached and objective. In contrast, the tone of an editorial may be angry or pleading, urging readers to action, while a personal narrative may have a nostalgic tone, appropriate to the recollection of one's past. Read aloud several paragraphs of "The Man in the Water." What word or words would you use to describe Roger Rosenblatt's tone? How might the tone be related to Rosenblatt's purpose for writing the essay?

From Personal Response to Critical Analysis
1. All responses are valid.
2. Possible responses: The man in the water was unknown and therefore could have been anyone; his actions were more heroic than those of the other three men.
3. Possible responses: No, he did lose the fight because he lost his life in freezing water; yes, he managed to save five people from drowning, so he won the fight.
4. Possible responses: This man's heroic self-sacrifice exemplified the best that human beings can do in the face of tragedy; He set an ideal that people should aspire to.
5. Possible responses: Yes, everyone has a spark of goodness that can come out in a crisis; no, most people are too self-centered and too worried about self-preservation.

Another Pathway
Cooperative Learning Be sure that students recognize that Rosenblatt feels nature is impersonal and implacable while human nature at its best is self-sacrificing.

Rubric
- **3 Full Accomplishment** The chart is thorough, and the statements are concise and based upon essay details.
- **2 Substantial Accomplishment** Some details are missing from the chart, or the statements are not completely accurate.
- **1 Little or Partial Accomplishment** The chart contains irrelevant details, or the statements are not based upon essay details.

Literary Concepts
Students might find Rosenblatt's tone admiring, respectful, serious, or contemplative. Since his main purpose for writing the essay is to express his opinion about the man in the water, his somewhat formal tone signals readers to take what he says quite seriously.

QuickWrites
1. Remind students that tributes on plaques are generally short and formal. Students may wish to include appropriate quotes in their tribute.
2. Students' articles should answer the questions *Who? What? Why? When? Where?* and *How?* and should be as objective as possible.
3. Remind students that a personal essay should include both the description of an event and the writer's reflections about the meaning or significance of that event.

 **The Writer's Craft**
Autobiographical Incident, pp. 26–40

Words to Know

1. flail
2. abiding
3. chaotic
4. anonymity
5. implacable

Reteaching/Reinforcement
- *Unit Six Resource Book*, p. 10.

Art Connection

Linguistic learners may not feel that the photographs added to the selection, while more visually oriented students, such as spatial and graphic learners, may feel that the photographs had a larger impact than the essay. Students should give reasons for their opinions.

Literary Links

Ask students to compare this brief essay to Brent Staples's brief essay "Black Men and Public Space." Which essay do they find more effective? Do the two essays share similarities of tone or structure? Which do students like better? Why? *(Students should give reasons for their opinions.)*

Across the Curriculum

Science/Technology Weather-related plane crashes include the 1985 crash in Dallas that was caused by wind shear and microburst and the 1993 crash in New York that was caused by ice on the wings. Students could form research groups, with each group taking one weather problem, such as wind shear, ice, or fog.

Multimodal Learning

ALTERNATIVE ACTIVITIES

1. Stage a **television report** from the scene of the airplane crash. A reporter can interview people on the scene, such as Lenny Skutnik, a rescued person, and a witness to the disaster. If possible, videotape the report and show the tape to other classes.
2. Draw a **picture** of the man in the water, using Rosenblatt's description of him as your inspiration.
3. Compose a **song** that reflects your own response to the events described by Rosenblatt. You might, for example, write a ballad about the man in the water or create an instrumental piece to express your feelings about him.

ART CONNECTION

Look over the photographs of the rescue efforts made at the scene of the Air Florida crash. What kind of impact did they make on you? Would Rosenblatt's article have affected you the same way if the photographs had not been presented along with the selection? Explain why or why not.

ACROSS THE CURRICULUM

Science/Technology Do research to learn about the role that weather can play in plane crashes. For example, you might investigate wind shear or the effects of ice on a plane's wings. Present your findings in a bulletin-board display.

WORDS TO KNOW

Review the Words to Know at the bottom of the selection pages. Then write the word that applies to each description below.

1. Tree limbs may do this during a windstorm.
2. A crush will not be this, but true love is supposed to be.
3. Riots, wild scenes, rowdy classrooms, and some children's bedrooms are this.
4. Beloved movie stars often wish for this when they go out in public.
5. Nothing is good enough for this kind of person, and apologies to him or her may be met with stony silence.

ROGER ROSENBLATT

1940–

A journalist and essayist who has won many awards for his writing, Roger Rosenblatt is a New York City native with a Ph.D. from Harvard University. After teaching literature at Harvard, he served for two years as the director of education for the National Endowment for the Humanities. In 1975 he turned to journalism, working first as the literary editor of the Washington-based magazine *The New Republic* and then as an editorial writer for the *Washington Post.* He has also been a senior writer for *Time* and *U.S. News and World Report* and has regularly contributed oral essays to the TV news show *The MacNeil/Lehrer Newshour.*

Known for his sensitivity and literary flair, Rosenblatt has won praise for several nonfiction books on controversial topics, including *Witness: The World Since Hiroshima,* which examines the impact of the atomic bomb on different aspects of modern life. Perhaps the best known of Rosenblatt's books is *Children of War* (1983), an investigation into the lives of children in war-torn Ireland, Israel, Lebanon, Cambodia, and Vietnam.

OTHER WORKS *Black Fiction, The Man in the Water: Essays and Stories*

Extended Reading

Alternative Activities

1. Remind students that live television reports should give background information about what is going on. For instance, the reporter should give details about the flight, such as its airline, its flight number, its departure point, its destination, and its time of takeoff before interviewing people.
2. Students can share their pictures with one another. How are the pictures alike? How are they different? Have students explain which part of Rosenblatt's description inspired them the most.
3. Some students may wish to do this activity in groups. Suggest that both groups and individuals perform their songs for the class. Instruct listeners to concentrate on the mood of the piece as it is being performed.

PREVIEWING

FICTION

And of Clay Are We Created
Isabel Allende (ä-yĕn'dĕ) Chile / United States

Activating Prior Knowledge
PERSONAL CONNECTION

Think about the novels or stories you have read that are based upon actual events, such as wars, natural disasters, or other thought-provoking occurrences. Why do you think certain fiction writers choose to use factual events in their writing, often altering details to suit their stories? Do you enjoy reading such fictionalized accounts? Or would you rather read a nonfiction account of those events? As a class, discuss your experience in reading fiction that is based upon fact. Then discuss your views about the relationship between fact and imagination in storytelling.

Building Background
SCIENTIFIC CONNECTION

In this story, which is based on an actual disaster, a reporter becomes involved in rescue efforts following a deadly volcanic eruption. When a volcano erupts, it releases lava, hot gases, rock fragments, and ash. Such eruptions can be disastrous not only because of what is released during the explosion but also because of the mud slides and avalanches that may follow. Volcanoes have caused some of the worst disasters in human history, even burying entire cities. Scientists often monitor the activities of volcanoes in an effort to predict eruptions and save lives. Some volcanoes, such as the one in this story, emit early warning signals of an eruption. Small earthquakes and clouds of gas signal that the pressure within the volcano is building.

Preliminary eruption of Nevado del Ruiz volcano, September 1985, three months before the major eruption. U.S. Geological Survey.

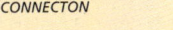
LASERLINKS
• HISTORICAL CONNECTION

OVERVIEW

Objectives

- To understand and appreciate a story that explores how a tragic event elicits both strength and sorrow
- To identify and understand internal and external conflicts
- To express understanding of the story through a choice of writing forms, including a monologue, a love letter, and a chart
- To extend understanding of the story through a variety of multimodal and cross-curricular activities

Skills

LITERARY CONCEPTS
- Conflict
- Foreshadowing

READING SKILL/STRATEGIES
- Analyzing the relationship between fact and fiction

GRAMMAR
- Compound-complex sentences

SPEAKING, LISTENING, AND VIEWING
- Group discussion
- Eulogy

HISTORICAL CONNECTION
The Eruption of Nevado del Ruiz

Allende's story is based on a tragic incident in the aftermath of one of the most disastrous volcanic eruptions in modern times. These photographs show the Nevado del Ruiz volcano and scenes at Armero, Colombia, where rescue workers struggled to help townspeople trapped in an avalanche of ash and mud.

Side A, Frame 49667

PRINT AND MEDIA RESOURCES

UNIT SIX RESOURCE BOOK
Strategic Reading: Literature, p. 13
Vocabulary SkillBuilder, p. 14

GRAMMAR MINI-LESSONS
Transparencies, pp. 39–40
Copymasters, pp. 41

WRITING MINI-LESSONS
Transparencies, pp. 8–9

ACCESS FOR STUDENTS ACQUIRING ENGLISH
Selection Summaries
Reading Support

FORMAL ASSESSMENT
Selection Test, p. 167
 Test Generator

 AUDIO LIBRARY
See Reference Card

 LASERLINKS
Historical Connection

INTERNET RESOURCES
McDougal Littell Literature Center at http://www.hmco.com/mcdougal/lit

SUMMARY

An unnamed narrator tells about the aftermath of a volcanic eruption in South America, when a girl named Azucena is discovered, almost completely buried in mud. Rolf Carle is the first reporter to reach the girl. He wades into the mud and learns her name. Then he struggles valiantly to free Azucena, but she is trapped by both the rubble and her dead siblings, who cling to her legs. As Rolf reassures the girl, the narrator, watching on television, feels her love for Rolf grow. He radios for a water pump, but none is available, so he stays with Azucena and waits for help. During his second night with the girl in the cold mud, Rolf faces the pain of his own life for the first time. He relives unspeakable memories from his childhood. The next day, he assures Azucena, who claims that no boy has ever loved her, that she is loved—that he loves her more than he's ever loved anyone. That night, he holds her gaze until she dies, then closes her eyes and lets her sink.

Thematic Link: *A Strength from Within*
Both Rolf and Azucena find a strength from within, she to face death and he to comfort her and face his repressed past.

CUSTOMIZING FOR
Students Acquiring English

- Use **ACCESS FOR STUDENTS ACQUIRING ENGLISH,** *Reading Support.*
- Help set the scene for the story by reviewing the description of the actual eruption of the Nevado del Ruiz volcano on page 830. Make sure that students understand key words used to describe the eruption and its aftermath, such as *crater, icecap, ash, avalanche, rubble,* and so forth.
- In addition to these boxes, you may want to use the suggestions under Strategic Reading for Less-Proficient Readers.

Active Reading/Setting a Purpose
READING CONNECTION

From Fact to Fiction

Writers often draw upon real-life events to create their fictional stories. Isabel Allende, a former reporter herself, found inspiration for this story in news reports and photographs of a volcanic disaster. On November 13, 1985, the Nevado del Ruiz (nĕ-vä'dô dĕl rōō-ēs') volcano in Colombia, South America, erupted after more than a century of inactivity. The intense heat from the erupting crater inside the volcano melted the mountain's icecap and sent a thick torrent of water, ash, mud, and rocks into the valley below. The liquid avalanche buried the town of Armero and damaged several others, killing more than 20,000 people.

The plight of one of the volcano's victims became known to people around the world. Omeira Sanchez, a teenage girl, was submerged up to her neck in mud, trapped by rubble and by the bodies of her relatives. The girl featured in this story is based upon Omeira Sanchez, pictured on this page.

As you read Allende's story, you may find it helpful to consider the following questions:

- Which parts of the story seem factually accurate, and which do you think were invented by Allende?
- Why do you think Allende chose to use a narrator who is not present at the scene of the disaster?
- Why would Allende decide to write about this occurrence in fiction rather than nonfiction?
- What does the story suggest to you about the relationship between fact and fiction?

Aftermath of disaster caused by Nevado del Ruiz eruption. Allan Tannenbaum/Sygma.

Rescue efforts to save Omeira Sanchez, the Colombian teenage girl who inspired this story. Carraro/Rex USA Ltd.

830 UNIT SIX PART 1: A STRENGTH FROM WITHIN

WORDS TO KNOW

embody (ĕm-bŏd'ē) *v.* to give concrete shape to; to personify or represent (p. 835)
equanimity (ē'kwə-nĭm'ĭ-tē) *n.* the quality of being calm and even-tempered; composure (p. 832)
fortitude (fôr'tĭ-tōōd') *n.* strength of mind to endure misfortune or pain with courage (p. 832)
irreparably (ĭ-rĕp'ər-ə-blē) *adv.* in a way that is impossible to repair or correct (p. 834)
pandemonium (păn'də-mō'nē-əm) *n.* a wild uproar or noise (p. 834)
stupor (stōō'pər) *n.* a state of mental numbness, as from shock (p. 837)
tenacity (tə-năs'ĭ-tē) *n.* the state or quality of holding persistently to something; firm determination (p. 832)
tribulation (trĭb'yə-lā'shən) *n.* great distress or suffering (p. 838)
visceral (vĭs'ər-əl) *adj.* instinctive or emotional rather than intellectual (p. 837)
vulnerable (vŭl'nər-ə-bəl) *adj.* unprotected and easily hurt; sensitive (p. 839)

830 THE LANGUAGE OF LITERATURE TEACHER'S EDITION

And of Clay Are We Created

Isabel Allende

They discovered the girl's head protruding from the mud pit, eyes wide open, calling soundlessly. She had a First Communion name,[1] Azucena.[2] Lily. In that vast cemetery where the odor of death was already attracting vultures from far away, and where the weeping of orphans and wails of the injured filled the air, the little girl obstinately clinging to life became the symbol of the tragedy. The television cameras transmitted so often the unbearable image of the head budding like a black squash from the clay that there was no one who did not recognize her and know her name. And every time we saw her on the screen, right behind her was Rolf Carlé,[3] who had gone there on

---

1. **First Communion name:** a name traditionally given to a Roman Catholic child at the time of the child's first participation in the rite of Holy Communion.
2. **Azucena** (ä′zōō-kĕ′nä).
3. **Rolf Carlé** (rälf kär-lĕ′).

Literary Concept:
FORESHADOWING

B Ask students what the narrator suggests will happen to Rolf Carle. *(Possible responses: He will meet someone he hasn't seen for over thirty years; something about the disaster will remind Rolf of something that he has forgotten.)*

Linking to History

C Perhaps the most famous volcanic eruption in the Western world occurred in what is now Italy in A.D. 79, when Mount Vesuvius erupted, burying the cities of Pompeii, Herculaneum, and Stabiae. The mud and ash from the eruption formed a sort of hermetic seal, effectively preserving many of the towns' sites and giving modern archeologists much insight into Mediterranean life during that time period. A more recent major volcanic eruption occurred in 1883, when a volcano on the island of Krakatau, Indonesia, erupted. The resulting tidal wave killed over 36,000 people. William Pène du Bois wrote a fanciful novel, *The Twenty-One Balloons,* based on this incident.

CUSTOMIZING FOR
Students Acquiring English

Help students divide this sentence into manageable parts and paraphrase the complex phrases it contains. You might focus on the meaning of a *prolonged roar announced the end of the world* and *beneath unfathomable meters of telluric vomit.*

Literary Concept:
FORESHADOWING

D Ask students what the narrator implies about this particular trip of Rolf's. *(Possible responses: It will last a lot longer than she suspects; something will happen to him while he is gone.)*

B assignment, never suspecting that he would find a fragment of his past, lost thirty years before.

First a subterranean[4] sob rocked the cotton fields, curling them like waves of foam. Geologists had set up their seismographs[5] weeks before and knew that the mountain had awakened again. For some time they had predicted that the heat of the eruption could detach the eternal ice from the slopes of the volcano, but no one heeded their warnings; they sounded like the tales of frightened old women. The towns in the valley went about their daily life, deaf to the moaning of the earth, until that fateful Wednesday night in November when a prolonged roar announced the end of the world, and walls of snow broke loose, rolling in an avalanche of clay, stones, and water that descended on the villages and buried them beneath unfathomable meters of telluric[6] vomit. As soon as the survivors emerged from the paralysis of that first awful terror, they could see that houses, plazas, churches, white cotton plantations, dark coffee forests, cattle pastures—all had disappeared. Much later, after soldiers and volunteers had arrived to rescue the living and try to assess the magnitude of the cataclysm,[7] it was calculated that beneath the mud lay more than twenty thousand human beings and an indefinite number of animals putrefying in a viscous soup.[8] Forests and rivers had also been swept away, and there was nothing to be seen but an immense desert of mire.

When the station called before dawn, Rolf Carlé and I were together. I crawled out of bed, dazed with sleep, and went to prepare coffee while he hurriedly dressed. He stuffed his gear in the green canvas backpack he always carried, and we said goodbye, as we had so many times before. I had no presentiments.[9] I sat in the kitchen, sipping my coffee and planning the long hours without him, sure that he would be back the next day.

He was one of the first to reach the scene, because while other reporters were fighting their way to the edges of that morass in jeeps, bicycles, or on foot, each getting there however he could, Rolf Carlé had the advantage of the television helicopter, which flew him over the avalanche. We watched on our screens the footage captured by his assistant's camera, in which he was up to his knees in muck, a microphone in his hand, in the midst of a bedlam of lost children, wounded survivors, corpses, and devastation. The story came to us in his calm voice. For years he had been a familiar figure in newscasts, reporting live at the scene of battles and catastrophes with awesome <u>tenacity</u>. Nothing could stop him, and I was always amazed at his <u>equanimity</u> in the face of danger and suffering; it seemed as if nothing could shake his <u>fortitude</u> or deter his curiosity. Fear seemed never to touch him, although he had confessed to me that he was not a courageous man, far from it. I believe that the lens of a camera had a strange effect on him; it was as if it transported him to a different time from which he could watch events without actually participating in them. When I knew him better, I came to realize

---

4. **subterranean** (sŭb′tə-rā′nē-ən): underground.
5. **seismographs** (sīz′mə-grăfs): instruments that record the intensity and duration of earthquakes and other tremors.
6. **telluric** (tĕ-loor′ĭk): relating to the earth.
7. **cataclysm** (kăt′ə-klĭz′əm): a violent and sudden change in the earth's crust; upheaval that destroys.
8. **putrefying** (pyoo′trə-fī′ĭng) . . . **soup:** rotting in a thick soup.
9. **presentiments** (prĭ-zĕn′tə-mənts): feelings that something is about to happen; forebodings.

WORDS TO KNOW

tenacity (tə-năs′ĭ-tē) *n.* the state or quality of holding persistently to something; firm determination
equanimity (ē′kwə-nĭm′ĭ-tē) *n.* the quality of being calm and even-tempered; composure
fortitude (fôr′tĭ-tood′) *n.* strength of mind to endure misfortune or pain with courage

832

CHRONOLOGICAL ORDER One way that writers give structure to their stories is by organizing them chronologically. This means that story events are told in the order in which they occurred. In this story, the chronological structure has added importance, because Azucena will not live very long unless a pump arrives. Therefore, the author's references to each successive day become loaded with meaning. Allende alludes to the story's chronological structure by using such time-order words and phrases as *first, for some time, then,* and *later.*

Application Invite students to write short stories that have a chronological structure. They should use time-order words and phrases to let the reader know the chronology of events.

Reteaching/Reinforcement
- *Writing Handbook,* anthology p. 1027
- *Writing Mini-Lessons* transparencies, pp. 8–9

The Writer's Craft

Chronological Order, pp. 343–344

The Volcanos (1950), Dr. Atl (Gerardo Murillo). Oil on masonite, 137 cm × 260 cm, Instituto Cultural Cabañas, Patrimonio de Jalisco, Guadalajara, Mexico.

that this fictive[10] distance seemed to protect him from his own emotions.

Rolf Carlé was in on the story of Azucena from the beginning. He filmed the volunteers who discovered her, and the first persons who tried to reach her; his camera zoomed in on the girl, her dark face, her large desolate eyes, the plastered-down tangle of her hair. The mud was like quicksand around her, and anyone attempting to reach her was in danger of sinking. They threw a rope to her that she made no effort to grasp until they shouted to her to catch it; then she pulled a hand from the mire and tried to move but immediately sank a little deeper. Rolf threw down his knapsack and the rest of his equipment and waded into the quagmire, commenting for his assistant's microphone that it was cold and that one could begin to smell the stench of corpses.

"What's your name?" he asked the girl, and she told him her flower name. "Don't move, Azucena," Rolf Carlé directed, and kept talking to her, without a thought for what he was saying, just to distract her, while slowly he worked his way forward in mud up to his waist. The air around him seemed as murky as the mud.

It was impossible to reach her from the approach he was attempting, so he retreated and circled around where there seemed to be firmer footing. When finally he was close enough, he took the rope and tied it beneath her arms, so they could pull her out. He smiled at her with that smile that crinkles his eyes and makes him look like a little boy; he told her that everything was fine, that he was here with

---

10. **fictive** (fĭk′tĭv): imaginary or fictional.

Critic's Corner

"Part of the [book's] power comes from the fact that real events form the background for the fictional story."

Marjorie Agosin
reviewing Allende's first novel

CUSTOMIZING FOR
Students Acquiring English

3 Ask students what "ancestral resignation" might mean. (*an inherited quality that allows one to accept one's fate*)

Literary Concept: CONFLICT

F Ask students to make predictions about who they think will win this battle, Rolf or nature. (*Students should give reasons for their opinions. Some may think that Rolf is so determined he will eventually free Azucena, while others may feel that his efforts will be in vain.*)

Literary Concept: FORESHADOWING

G Ask students what the words "premature optimism" suggest. (*Possible responses: It will not be as easy to free Azucena as Rolf thinks; something else bad will happen before Rolf is able to free her.*)

STRATEGIC READING FOR
Less-Proficient Readers

H Make sure students understand what has happened so far.

- What has happened to Azucena? (*She has been trapped in a mudslide caused by an erupting volcano.*) **Making Inferences**

- Describe Rolf Carlé as a reporter? (*Possible responses: always calm in the midst of danger or disaster; determined; tough; curious; fearless*) **Clarifying**

- Why is Rolf unable to pull Azucena from the mud? (*She is trapped by the collapsed walls of her house and by the bodies of her brothers and sisters.*) **Noting Relevant Details**

Set a Purpose Have students read to find out what happens to Rolf, Azucena, and the narrator.

---

her now, that soon they would have her out. He signaled the others to pull, but as soon as the cord tensed, the girl screamed. They tried again, and her shoulders and arms appeared, but they could move her no farther; she was trapped. Someone suggested that her legs might be caught in the collapsed walls of her house, but she said it was not just rubble, that she was also held by the bodies of her brothers and sisters clinging to her legs.

"Don't worry, we'll get you out of here," Rolf promised. Despite the quality of the transmission, I could hear his voice break, and I loved him more than ever. Azucena looked at him but said nothing.

During those first hours Rolf Carlé exhausted all the resources of his ingenuity to rescue her. He struggled with poles and ropes, but every tug was an intolerable torture for the imprisoned girl. It occurred to him to use one of the poles as a lever but got no result and had to abandon the idea. He talked a couple of soldiers into working with him for a while, but they had to leave because so many other victims were calling for help. The girl could not move, she barely could breathe, but she did not seem desperate, as if an ancestral resignation allowed her to accept her fate. The reporter, on the other hand, was determined to snatch her from death. Someone brought him a tire, which he placed beneath her arms like a life buoy, and then laid a plank near the hole to hold his weight and allow him to stay closer to her. As it was impossible to remove the rubble blindly, he tried once or twice to dive toward her feet but emerged frustrated, covered with mud, and spitting gravel. He concluded that he would have to have a pump to drain the water, and radioed a request for one but received in return a message that there was no available transport and it could not be sent until the next morning.

"We can't wait that long!" Rolf Carlé shouted, but in the <u>pandemonium</u> no one stopped to commiserate. Many more hours would go by before he accepted that time had stagnated[11] and reality had been <u>irreparably</u> distorted.

A military doctor came to examine the girl and observed that her heart was functioning well and that if she did not get too cold she could survive the night.

"Hang on, Azucena, we'll have the pump tomorrow," Rolf Carlé tried to console her.

"Don't leave me alone," she begged.

"No, of course I won't leave you."

Someone brought him coffee, and he helped the girl drink it, sip by sip. The warm liquid revived her, and she began telling him about her small life, about her family and her school, about how things were in that little bit of world before the volcano erupted. She was thirteen, and she had never been outside her village. Rolf Carlé, buoyed by a premature optimism, was convinced that everything would end well: the pump would arrive, they would drain the water, move the rubble, and Azucena would be transported by helicopter to a hospital where she would recover rapidly and where he could visit her and bring her gifts. He thought, She's already too old for dolls, and I don't know what would please her; maybe a dress. I don't know much about women, he concluded, amused, reflecting that although he had known many women in his lifetime, none had taught him these details. To pass the hours he began to tell Azucena about his travels and adventures as a news hound, and when he exhausted his memory, he called upon imagination, inventing things he thought might entertain her. From time to time she dozed, but he kept talking in the darkness, to assure her that he was still there and to overcome the menace of uncertainty.

That was a long night.

---
11. **stagnated:** stopped moving.

WORDS TO KNOW
pandemonium (păn´də-mō´nē-əm) *n.* a wild uproar or noise
irreparably (ĭ-rĕp´ər-ə-blē) *adv.* in a way that is impossible to repair or correct

834

Mini-Lesson ✏ Grammar

COMPOUND-COMPLEX SENTENCES

Remind students that a compound-complex sentence has two or more independent clauses and one or more subordinate clauses. Point out the <u>highlighted</u> example in the text. Make sure students notice that there are two independent clauses ("He concluded . . . and radioed a request for one but received in return a message . . ." and "it could not be sent until the next morning") and two subordinate clauses ("that he would have to have a pump . . ." and "that there was no available transport").

Application Have students work in groups of four. Set a time limit and challenge each group to find as many compound-complex sentences from the selections in this textbook as possible. The entire class can check the accuracy of each group's work.

Reteaching/Reinforcement
- *Grammar Handbook*, anthology p. 1089
- *Grammar Mini-Lessons* copymasters p. 41, transparencies pp. 39–40

 **The Writer's Craft**

Compound-Complex Sentences, p. 623

Many miles away, I watched Rolf Carlé and the girl on a television screen. I could not bear the wait at home, so I went to National Television, where I often spent entire nights with Rolf editing programs. There, I was near his world, and I could at least get a feeling of what he lived through during those three decisive days. I called all the important people in the city, senators, commanders of the armed forces, the North American ambassador, and the president of National Petroleum, begging them for a pump to remove the silt, but obtained only vague promises. I began to ask for urgent help on radio and television, to see if there wasn't *someone* who could help us. Between calls I would run to the newsroom to monitor the satellite transmissions that periodically brought new details of the catastrophe. While reporters selected scenes with most impact for the news report, I searched for footage that featured Azucena's mud pit. The screen reduced the disaster to a single plane and accentuated the tremendous distance that separated me from Rolf Carlé; nonetheless, I was there with him. The child's every suffering hurt me as it did him; I felt his frustration, his impotence.[12] Faced with the impossibility of communicating with him, the fantastic idea came to me that if I tried, I could reach him by force of mind and in that way give him encouragement. I concentrated until I was dizzy—a frenzied and futile activity. At times I would be overcome with compassion and burst out crying; at other times, I was so drained I felt as if I were staring through a telescope at the light of a star dead for a million years.

I watched that hell on the first morning broadcast, cadavers[13] of people and animals awash in the current of new rivers formed overnight from the melted snow. Above the mud rose the tops of trees and the bell towers of a church where several people had taken refuge and were patiently awaiting rescue teams. Hundreds of soldiers and volunteers from the civil defense were clawing through rubble searching for survivors, while long rows of ragged specters[14] awaited their turn for a cup of hot broth. Radio networks announced that their phones were jammed with calls from families offering shelter to orphaned children. Drinking water was in scarce supply, along with gasoline and food. Doctors, resigned to amputating arms and legs without anesthesia, pled that at least they be sent serum and painkillers and antibiotics; most of the roads, however, were impassable, and worse were the bureaucratic obstacles that stood in the way. To top it all, the clay contaminated by decomposing bodies threatened the living with an outbreak of epidemics.

Azucena was shivering inside the tire that held her above the surface. Immobility and tension had greatly weakened her, but she was conscious and could still be heard when a microphone was held out to her. Her tone was humble, as if apologizing for all the fuss. Rolf Carlé had a growth of beard, and dark circles beneath his eyes; he looked near exhaustion. Even from that enormous distance I could sense the quality of his weariness, so different from the fatigue of other adventures. He had completely forgotten the camera; he could not look at the girl through a lens any longer. The pictures we were receiving were not his assistant's but those of other reporters who had appropriated Azucena, bestowing on her the pathetic responsibility of <u>embodying</u> the horror of what had happened in that place. With the

---

12. **impotence:** powerlessness.
13. **cadavers** (kə-dăv′ərz): dead bodies.
14. **specters:** ghosts or ghostlike visions.

WORDS TO KNOW

embody (ĕm-bŏd′ē) *v.* to give a concrete shape to; personify or represent

835

Illustration by David Loew / ARTCO.

first light Rolf tried again to dislodge the obstacles that held the girl in her tomb, but he had only his hands to work with; he did not dare use a tool for fear of injuring her. He fed Azucena a cup of the cornmeal mush and bananas the army was distributing, but she immediately vomited it up. A doctor stated that she had a fever but added that there was little he could do: antibiotics were being reserved for cases of gangrene.[15] A priest also passed by and blessed her, hanging a medal of the Virgin around her neck. By evening a gentle, persistent drizzle began to fall.

"The sky is weeping," Azucena murmured, and she, too, began to cry.

"Don't be afraid," Rolf begged. "You have to keep your strength up and be calm. Everything will be fine. I'm with you, and I'll get you out somehow."

Reporters returned to photograph Azucena and ask her the same questions, which she no longer tried to answer. In the meanwhile, more television and movie teams arrived with spools of cable, tapes, film, videos, precision lenses, recorders, sound consoles, lights, reflecting screens, auxiliary motors, cartons of supplies, electricians, sound technicians, and cameramen: Azucena's face was beamed to millions of screens around the world. And all the while Rolf Carlé kept pleading for a pump. The improved technical facilities bore results, and National Television began receiving sharper pictures and clearer sound, the distance seemed suddenly compressed, and I had the horrible sensation that Azucena and Rolf were by my side, separated from me by impenetrable glass. I was able to follow events hour by hour; I knew everything my love did to wrest the girl from her prison and help her endure her suffering; I overheard fragments of what they said to one another and could guess the rest; I was present when she taught Rolf to pray and when he distracted her with the stories I had told him in a thousand and one nights beneath the white mosquito netting of our bed.

When darkness came on the second day, Rolf tried to sing Azucena to sleep with old Austrian folk songs he had learned from his mother, but she was far beyond sleep. They spent most of the night talking, each in a stupor of exhaustion and hunger and shaking with cold. That night, imperceptibly, the unyielding floodgates that had contained Rolf Carlé's past for so many years began to open, and the torrent of all that had lain hidden in the deepest and most secret layers of memory poured out, leveling before it the obstacles that had blocked his consciousness for so long. He could not tell it all to Azucena; she perhaps did not know there was a world beyond the sea or time previous to her own; she was not capable of imagining Europe in the years of the war. So he could not tell her of defeat, nor of the afternoon the Russians had led them to the concentration camp to bury prisoners dead from starvation. Why should he describe to her how the naked bodies piled like a mountain of firewood resembled fragile china? How could he tell this dying child about ovens and gallows? Nor did he mention the night that he had seen his mother naked, shod in stiletto-heeled red boots, sobbing with humiliation. There was much he did not tell, but in those hours he relived for the first time all the things his mind had tried to erase. Azucena had surrendered her fear to him and so, without wishing it, had obliged Rolf to confront his own. There, beside that hellhole of mud, it was impossible for Rolf to flee from himself any longer, and the visceral terror he had lived as a boy suddenly invaded him. He reverted to the years when he was the age of Azucena and younger, and, like her, found himself trapped in a pit without escape, buried in life, his head barely

---

15. **gangrene:** death and decay of body tissue, usually resulting from injury or disease.

WORDS TO KNOW
stupor (stōō'pər) *n.* a state of mental numbness, as from shock
visceral (vĭs'ər-əl) *adj.* instinctive or emotional rather than intellectual

837

Literary Concept: CONFLICT

O Invite students to discuss why Rolf is finally able to weep for his sister's death and what internal conflict of his this passage reveals. *(Possible responses: Rolf had made himself numb in response to the tragedies brought on by the war; because of his experience with Azucena, he can now release his true feelings; he did not allow himself to fully feel the loss of his sister because he felt that he had abandoned her.)*

STRATEGIC READING FOR
Less-Proficient Readers

P Make sure students understand how this situation has affected all three of the characters.

- How does the narrator feel as she watches the television broadcasts? *(Possible responses: very close to Rolf and Azucena; frustrated at not being able to help; sad; exhausted)* **Clarifying**

- How does Rolf seem to change as a reporter? *(Possible responses: He can no longer view the story at a distance; he has become emotionally involved with his subject.)* **Evaluating**

- Why does Rolf begin telling stories? *(to keep Azucena from thinking about her suffering)* **Clarifying**

- What makes Rolf cry and "hurt all over"? *(guilt and sorrow for his sister's death that he has kept hidden for years)* **Making Inferences**

Set a Purpose Have students read to find out what happens to Azucena and Rolf.

---

above ground; he saw before his eyes the boots and legs of his father, who had removed his belt and was whipping it in the air with the never-forgotten hiss of a viper coiled to strike. Sorrow flooded through him, intact and precise, as if it had lain always in his mind, waiting. He was once again in the armoire[16] where his father locked him to punish him for imagined misbehavior, there where for eternal hours he had crouched with his eyes closed, not to see the darkness, with his hands over his ears to shut out the beating of his heart, trembling, huddled like a cornered animal. Wandering in the mist of his memories he found his sister, Katharina, a sweet, retarded child who spent her life hiding, with the hope that her father would forget the disgrace of her having been born. With Katharina, Rolf crawled beneath the dining room table, and with her hid there under the long white tablecloth, two children forever embraced, alert to footsteps and voices. Katharina's scent melded with his own sweat, with aromas of cooking, garlic, soup, freshly baked bread, and the unexpected odor of putrescent[17] clay. His sister's hand in his, her frightened breathing, her silk hair against his cheek, the candid gaze of her eyes. Katharina . . . Katharina materialized before him, floating on the air like a flag, clothed in the white tablecloth, now a winding sheet, and at last he could weep for her death and for the guilt of having abandoned her. He understood then that all his exploits as a reporter, the feats that had won him such recognition and fame, were merely an attempt to keep his most ancient fears at bay, a stratagem for taking refuge behind a lens to test whether reality was more tolerable from that perspective. He took excessive risks as an exercise of courage, training by day to conquer the monsters that tormented him by night. But he had to come face to face with the moment of truth; he could not continue to escape his past. He *was* Azucena; he was buried in the clayey mud; his terror was not the distant emotion of an almost forgotten childhood, it was a claw sunk in his throat. In the flush of his tears he saw his mother, dressed in black and clutching her imitation-crocodile pocketbook to her bosom, just as he had last seen her on the dock when she had come to put him on the boat to South America. She had not come to dry his tears, but to tell him to pick up a shovel: the war was over and now they must bury the dead.

"Don't cry. I don't hurt anymore. I'm fine," Azucena said when dawn came.

"I'm not crying for you," Rolf Carlé smiled. "I'm crying for myself. I hurt all over."

The third day in the valley of the cataclysm began with a pale light filtering through storm clouds. The president of the republic visited the area in his tailored safari jacket to confirm that this was the worst catastrophe of the century; the country was in mourning; sister nations had offered aid; he had ordered a state of siege; the armed forces would be merciless; anyone caught stealing or committing other offenses would be shot on sight. He added that it was impossible to remove all the corpses or count the thousands who had disappeared; the entire valley would be declared holy ground, and bishops would come to celebrate a solemn mass for the souls of the victims. He went to the army field tents to offer relief in the form of vague promises to crowds of the rescued, then to the improvised hospital to offer a word of encouragement to doctors and nurses worn down from so many hours of <u>tribulations</u>. Then he asked to be taken to see Azucena, the little

---

16. **armoire** (ärm-wär′): a large, ornate wardrobe or cabinet.
17. **putrescent** (pyo̅o̅-trĕs′ənt): rotting and foul smelling.

WORDS TO KNOW
tribulation (trĭb′yə-lā′shən) *n.* great distress or suffering

girl the whole world had seen. He waved to her with a limp statesman's hand, and microphones recorded his emotional voice and paternal tone as he told her that her courage had served as an example to the nation. Rolf Carlé interrupted to ask for a pump, and the president assured him that he personally would attend to the matter. I caught a glimpse of Rolf for a few seconds kneeling beside the mud pit. On the evening news broadcast, he was still in the same position; and I, glued to the screen like a fortuneteller to her crystal ball, could tell that something fundamental had changed in him. I knew somehow that during the night his defenses had crumbled and he had given in to grief; finally he was <u>vulnerable</u>. The girl had touched a part of him that he himself had no access to, a part he had never shared with me. Rolf had wanted to console her, but it was Azucena who had given him consolation.

I recognized the precise moment at which Rolf gave up the fight and surrendered to the torture of watching the girl die. I was with them, three days and two nights, spying on them from the other side of life. I was there when she told him that in all her thirteen years no boy had ever loved her and that it was a pity to leave this world without knowing love. Rolf assured her that he loved her more than he could ever love anyone, more than he loved his mother, more than his sister, more than all the women who had slept in his arms, more than he loved me, his life companion, who would have given anything to be trapped in that well in her place, who would have exchanged her life for Azucena's, and I watched as he leaned down to kiss her poor forehead, consumed by a sweet, sad emotion he could not name. I felt how in that instant both were saved from despair, how they were freed from the clay, how they rose above the vultures and helicopters, how together they flew above the vast swamp of corruption and laments. How, finally, they were able to accept death. Rolf Carlé prayed in silence that she would die quickly, because such pain cannot be borne.

By then I had obtained a pump and was in touch with a general who had agreed to ship it the next morning on a military cargo plane. But on the night of that third day, beneath the unblinking focus of quartz lamps and the lens of a hundred cameras, Azucena gave up, her eyes locked with those of the friend who had sustained her to the end. Rolf Carlé removed the life buoy, closed her eyelids, held her to his chest for a few moments, and then let her go. She sank slowly, a flower in the mud.

ou are back with me, but you are not the same man. I often accompany you to the station, and we watch the videos of Azucena again; you study them intently, looking for something you could have done to save her, something you did not think of in time. Or maybe you study them to see yourself as if in a mirror, naked. Your cameras lie forgotten in a closet; you do not write or sing; you sit long hours before the window, staring at the mountains. Beside you, I wait for you to complete the voyage into yourself, for the old wounds to heal. I know that when you return from your nightmares, we shall again walk hand in hand, as before. ❖

Translated by Margaret Sayers Peden

WORDS TO KNOW
vulnerable (vŭl′nər-ə-bəl) *adj.* unprotected and easily hurt; sensitive

INSIGHT

1. What do you think is the message of this poem? *(Possible responses: Life is fleeting; we do not fully understand our reason for living; the line between dream and reality is a blurred one.)*
2. What do you think is the mood of this poem? *(Possible responses: sad, resigned, wistful)*
3. Do you think the speaker has a positive or negative attitude towards life? Support your opinion with details from the poem. *(Accept all reasonable and well-supported responses.)*

ROSARIO CASTELLANOS

One of Mexico's most respected writers, Rosario Castellanos grew up in the Chiapas region of southern Mexico. From her Indian nursemaid, Castellanos developed a lifelong interest in Mexico's native cultures and a love of oral poems and stories. As an adult, she joined the group of prominent writers known as the Generation of the '50s. In 1952, however, Castellanos' childhood affections drew her southward. As she described it: "I put my hair up in a tight bun, threw away my make-up, and went to Chiapas to work with the Indians." For several years she served as cultural promoter for the Chiapas Institute of Arts and Sciences and also directed a regional theater. At the same time, she wrote sympathetically about the plight of Mexico's native population. She was serving as Mexico's ambassador to Israel when she died in a tragic accident caused by faulty wiring in her hotel room.

INSIGHT

Nocturne   Nocturno

Rosario Castellanos

Time is too long for life;
for knowledge not enough.
 	
What have we come for, night, heart
   of night?
 	
All we can do is dream, or die,
5 dream that we do not die
and, at times, for a moment, wake.
 	
Translated by Magda Bogin
	Para vivir es demasiado el tiempo;
	para saber no es nada.
	
	¿A qué vinimos, noche, corazón de la
	   noche?
	
	No es posible sino soñar, morir,
	5 soñar que no morimos
	y, a veces, un instante, despertar.

Nocturnal Landscape (1947), Diego Rivera. Oil on canvas, 111 cm × 91 cm, courtesy of Museo de Arte Moderno (INBA), Mexico City. Photo Copyright © 1995, Dirk Bakker/The Detroit Institute of Arts.

Mini-Lesson: Speaking, Listening, and Viewing

TELEPHONE CONVERSATION The narrator made a number of frantic phone calls to seek help for Azucena. People often miss vital information on the telephone because they fail to listen attentively. Ask students to share examples from their own experience in which mistakes were made due to inattentive telephone listening.

Application Invite a pair of students to role-play one of the telephone conversations that the narrator might have had. One student should play the role of the narrator and the other should take the part of an official. Encourage the pair to invent details as needed to make their conversation as plausible as possible. After the conversation is completed, quiz the participants and the rest of the class on exactly what was said. If possible, tape-record the conversations and play back the recording to verify the answers.

FROM PERSONAL RESPONSE TO CRITICAL ANALYSIS

REFLECT
1. How did you react to the outcome of the story? In your notebook, jot down a few words and phrases that best describe your emotions.

RETHINK
2. How would you describe the relationship that develops between Rolf and Azucena?
   Consider
   - why Rolf becomes a participant in the effort to save her
   - what they learn from each other
   - the painful childhood memories he is able to recall
   - why he tells Azucena that he loves her more than he could ever love anyone

   Close Textual Reading

3. How do you think Rolf's experience with Azucena will affect him in the future?
   Consider
   - his career as a reporter
   - his relationship with the narrator
   - his understanding of his past

   Close Textual Reading

4. According to the narrator, the name Azucena means "lily." Why do you think the author might have given her this name?

5. Now that you have read this story, how would you respond to the questions in the Reading Connection on page 830?

RELATE
6. What connection do you see between the Insight poem on page 840 and Allende's story?

7. Although Azucena had the attention of her entire nation, she died partly because no one transported a pump to the disaster site. Could a similar situation happen in your own country? Why or why not?

Multimodal Learning
ANOTHER PATHWAY
Cooperative Learning
Do you think this story has a hero or heroes? In a small group, evaluate the actions and attitudes of the characters and narrator in terms of heroism. Then decide which characters, if any, can be considered heroic. Share the results of your discussion with other groups.

QUICKWRITES

1. Draft the **monologue** Rolf might give in a retrospective television broadcast one year after the tragic destruction of the town.

2. Write the **love letter** that the narrator might write to Rolf in the months following the disaster.

3. Read articles in newsmagazines to learn what really happened when the Nevado del Ruiz volcano erupted. Then, in a two-column **chart,** list those details that the author derived from news accounts and those details that the author probably invented for her story.

📁 **PORTFOLIO** Save your writing. You may want to use it later as a springboard to a piece for your portfolio.

AND OF CLAY ARE WE CREATED **841**

From Personal Response to Critical Analysis

1. All responses are valid.
2. Possible responses: Despite profound differences in their life experience, Rolf and Azucena become very close, even dependent on each other, as Rolf tries to rescue Azucena and refuses to abandon her; Rolf thinks of Azucena as the sister he has lost.
3. Possible responses: He will participate more in life and not hide behind his camera so much; he will be the same because once life goes back to normal, he will repress his memories again.
4. Possible responses: It implies that she is beautiful and delicate, like a flower; it implies that she is pure and good, since lilies, especially white ones, are Christian symbols of purity, and this contrasts with the mud and destruction around her.
5. Accept all reasonable, well-supported responses.
6. Accept all reasonable, well-supported responses.
7. Accept all reasonable, well-supported responses.

Another Pathway
Cooperative Learning Assign one student to be the recorder for each group.

Rubric
3 Full Accomplishment Groups clearly define their views of heroism and thoughtfully evaluate the characters in the selection.
2 Substantial Accomplishment Groups adequately define their views of heroism and apply them aptly to the characters, though not always satisfactorily.
1 Little or Partial Accomplishment Groups fail to formulate their ideas of heroism and make few applications to the characters.

QuickWrites

1. Students' monologues should review the details of the disaster and then give Rolf's reactions to it; they should conclude by telling about how Rolf has been affected by his experience.

2. Suggest that students go back through the story and look for details that give clues to the narrator's state of mind and the extent of her love for Rolf. They should also try to capture her narrative voice in the letter.

3. Remind students to give their charts headings. They can look for information in issues of *Time, Newsweek, U.S. News and World Report,* and other newsmagazines for the week of November 25th, 1985.

📁 **The Writer's Craft**
Monologue, pp. 108–112

Critic's Corner

Students should give reasons for their opinions. You may wish to suggest they begin thinking about their response by first defining what it means to "get under one's skin."

Literary Links

Some students may appreciate the elaborateness of Allende's descriptive style, while others may prefer Staple's more matter-of-fact approach, Rosenblatt's philosophical outlook, or Gage's directness. Remind students to explain their opinions.

Art Connection

Students should support their responses with details from the picture.

Across the Curriculum

Psychology Students might want to report on some specific examples of repression if they find such examples in their reading. They may also wish to explore the controversy surrounding the "recovered memory" syndrome that is going on in the United States today.

Science Both Isabel Allende's homeland, Chile, and Colombia are part of the Pacific Ring of Fire, a region that contains most of the world's active volcanoes. Ask students to use an encyclopedia or earth-science text to discover why there is so much volcanic activity in this part of the world. Then have them prepare a script, complete with diagrams or maps, for a television science report on the causes of these eruptions.

LITERARY CONCEPTS

The events of a story almost always involve one or more **conflicts**, or struggles between opposing forces. A conflict may be **external**, pitting a character against an outside force—such as another character, a physical obstacle, or an aspect of nature or society—or it may be **internal**, occurring within a character. What kinds of conflicts do Rolf, Azucena, and the narrator each experience in this story? Cite passages in the story that support your conclusions.

CONCEPT REVIEW: Narrator How do the narrator's relationship with Rolf and her feelings for him affect your understanding of the story? Explain, using story details to support your response.

Multimodal Learning

ALTERNATIVE ACTIVITIES

1. Assume the identity of Rolf or the narrator and deliver a **eulogy** for Azucena.
2. If this story were made into a movie, what music might be used in the soundtrack? Write your own **musical composition** or find an existing piece of music that would help create the mood of one of the scenes in the story. Play it for your classmates and ask them what part of the story it was intended to accompany.

ACROSS THE CURRICULUM

Psychology Look up the word *repression* in a psychology textbook to better understand how some people, like Rolf in the story, deal with very painful memories. Also find out what the experts believe about the causes of repression and how it can be treated. Share your findings.

842 UNIT SIX PART 1: A STRENGTH FROM WITHIN

CRITIC'S CORNER

After reading "And of Clay Are We Created," student reviewer Quoleshna Elbert wrote, "The story got under my skin; that's what makes a good story." Do you feel the same way about this story? What makes a good story for you?

LITERARY LINKS

Compare Allende's descriptive passages with those of another reporter or news commentator, such as Nicholas Gage, Brent Staples, or Roger Rosenblatt. Whose style of description do you prefer? Explain your opinion.

ART CONNECTION

What is your interpretation of the illustration on page 836? Why do you think it was chosen to accompany this story?

Detail of illustration by David Loew/ARTCO.

Literary Concepts

Possible responses:
- Rolf's conflicts include his fight with nature and his struggle to deal with painful memories.
- Azucena's conflicts include her struggle with nature and her attempt to fight off feelings of despair.
- The narrator's conflicts include her struggle to get a pump for Rolf and her struggle with her feelings of frustration.

Narrator Students may say that since the story is told through the narrator's eyes, we only get her view of Rolf; others may note that she assigns only good motives to his actions. Because the narrator is removed from the events herself, the reader is kept at a distance, as if we are watching the story unfold from afar.

Alternative Activities

1. Remind students that eulogies often offer inspiring and uplifting tributes.
2. Students should decide what style of music would best convey the story's mood.

WORDS TO KNOW

EXERCISE A Identify each pair of words as synonyms or antonyms.

1. visceral—logical
2. fortitude—endurance
3. tenacity—doubt
4. equanimity—hysteria
5. stupor—daze
6. pandemonium—disturbance
7. vulnerable—immune
8. tribulation—blessing
9. embody—symbolize
10. irreparably—correctably

EXERCISE B In a small group, tell a "round robin" story using the Words to Know. One person should begin a story and continue to speak until he or she has used one of the words in a sentence. Then the next person picks up the story where the first person left off, continuing until another of the words is used. Continue this process until all ten words are used and the story is brought to a conclusion.

ISABEL ALLENDE

1942–

Born in Lima, Peru, Isabel Allende moved with her mother to Santiago, Chile, when she was three years old and grew up in the home of her maternal grandparents. Her mother nurtured her creativity from the time she was very young, encouraging her to record her thoughts in a notebook and to draw anything she wanted on a bedroom wall. After graduating from high school, Allende worked for many years as a journalist and television interviewer. "My love for words induced me to work as a journalist since I was seventeen, but my vicious imagination was a great handicap," she said. "I could never be objective, I exaggerated and twisted reality, I would put myself in the middle of every feature."

Isabel Allende's uncle and godfather, Salvador Allende, became president of Chile in 1970 but was murdered when the military seized power in 1973. As a result, Isabel Allende and her family—along with many Chilean artists and intellectuals—went into exile, moving first to Venezuela and later to the United States. In her words, she felt "like a Christmas tree, cut off from all roots" after fleeing from her homeland, and for several years she was unable to write or to find work as a journalist.

After receiving word in 1981 that her nearly 100-year-old grandfather was dying, however, she began writing a long letter to him. Her grandfather believed that people died only when you forgot them, and Allende says she wanted to prove to him that she had forgotten nothing, "that his spirit was going to live with us forever." Allende's letter became her first novel, *The House of the Spirits,* which was published in Spanish in 1982 and in English translation three years later. Written in the style of magical realism, the novel is based on her own family history and the political upheaval in modern Chile. The work became an international bestseller, hailed by critics as a powerful and original piece of historical fiction.

Although she is fluent in English, Allende writes her novels and short stories in Spanish, then has her work translated. Recent works include *The Infinite Plan,* her first novel set in the United States, and *Paula,* an autobiographical work.

OTHER WORKS *Of Love and Shadows, Eva Luna, The Stories of Eva Luna*

Extended Reading

AND OF CLAY ARE WE CREATED 843

Words to Know

Exercise A
1. A
2. S
3. A
4. A
5. S
6. S
7. A
8. A
9. S
10. A

Exercise B
Remind students not to use the words in nonsensical or incorrect ways.

Reteaching/Reinforcement
- *Unit Six Resource Book,* p. 14

ISABEL ALLENDE
Allende's autobiographical book *Paula* chronicles her experiences and emotions during her daughter's illness and death from the hereditary disease porphyria.

REFLECTING ON THEME
What Do You Think?

Ask students to review what they wrote about their heroes for the activitiy on page 806. Discuss how Rolf and Azucena compare to their heroes, and whether the students' views of heroism have changed as a result of reading this selection.

OVERVIEW

Objectives

- To understand and appreciate a short story that explores courage
- To identify and understand flashback
- To express understanding of the story through a choice of writing forms, including a tabloid article, an analysis, and a comparison-contrast essay
- To extend understanding of the story through a variety of multimodal and cross-curricular activities

Skills

LITERARY CONCEPTS
- Flashback
- Imagery

READING SKILLS/STRATEGIES
- Recognizing flashbacks

GRAMMAR
- Adverb phrases

SPEAKING, LISTENING, AND VIEWING
- Group discussion
- Oral report

CUSTOMIZING FOR
Students Acquiring English

- Use **ACCESS FOR STUDENTS ACQUIRING ENGLISH**, *Reading Support*.
- This story is full of vivid descriptive passages, each of them containing numerous dramatic details relating to an incident that took only seconds to occur. You may wish to have students work together in pairs to paraphrase key passages.
- As you guide students through the selection, you may want to use the suggestions in these boxes as well as the suggestions under Strategic Reading for Less-Proficient Readers.

PREVIEWING

FICTION

The Leap
Louise Erdrich United States

Activating Prior Knowledge
PERSONAL CONNECTION

Are you the sort of person who would risk injury—perhaps even death—for the sake of an activity that you loved? Would you be willing to put yourself in physical danger for the sake of someone else? In your notebook, describe your attitude toward taking physical risks and the circumstances that might lead you to do so.

Building Background
CULTURAL CONNECTION

This story focuses on the life of a woman who took great physical risks as a blindfolded trapeze performer. Although trapeze acts often appear to be foolhardy stunts, the risks are well calculated by the trained performer, who may spend several years perfecting a single maneuver. Working on the trapeze requires not only tremendous strength, precise timing, and delicate balance but also considerable mental effort. Alfred Codona, one of the world's greatest trapeze artists, repeatedly emphasized the importance of "brain coordination" in aerial routines, warning other performers that any lack of mental clarity could result in death.

Active Reading/Setting a Purpose
READING CONNECTION

Recognizing Flashbacks The narrator of "The Leap" is a woman who owes her life to the risks her mother took. She tells her story using flashbacks—interruptions in the chronological order of events. She begins in the present, when she is an adult, but then recounts several events that happened in the past, some even before she was born. Be aware of these shifts in time as you read.

Poster reproduced with the permission of Ringling Bros. and Barnum & Bailey Combined Shows, Inc.

844 UNIT SIX PART 1: A STRENGTH FROM WITHIN

PRINT AND MEDIA RESOURCES

UNIT SIX RESOURCE BOOK
Strategic Reading: Literature, p. 17
Vocabulary SkillBuilder, p. 18

GRAMMAR MINI-LESSONS
Transparencies, p. 46

ACCESS FOR STUDENTS ACQUIRING ENGLISH
Selection Summaries
Reading Support

FORMAL ASSESSMENT
Selection Test, p. 169
 Test Generator

 **AUDIO LIBRARY**
See Reference Card

LASERLINKS
Art Gallery

---

844 THE LANGUAGE OF LITERATURE TEACHER'S EDITION

The Leap

Louise Erdrich

My mother is the surviving half of a blindfold trapeze act, not a fact I think about much even now that she is sightless, the result of encroaching and stubborn cataracts.[1] She walks slowly through her house here in New Hampshire, lightly touching her way along walls and running her hands over knickknacks, books, the drift of a grown child's belongings and castoffs. She has never upset an object or as much as brushed a magazine onto the floor. She has never lost her balance or bumped into a closet door left carelessly open.

Illustration by Sarah Figlio.

---

1. **encroaching . . . cataracts:** Cataracts are clouded areas on the lens of the eye. When they encroach, or advance beyond previous limits, they can cause total blindness.

WORDS TO KNOW

constricting (kən-strĭk′tĭng) *adj.* limiting; without much opportunity or freedom (p. 850)
destined (dĕs′tĭnd) *adj.* determined beforehand; fated **destine** *v.* (p. 848)
extricating (ĕk′strĭ-kā′tĭng) *n.* releasing from entanglement **extricate** *v.* (p. 849)
flair (flâr) *n.* distinctive elegance or style (p. 846)
perpetually (pər-pĕch′o͞o-əl-ē) *adv.* always, continually (p. 850)

CUSTOMIZING FOR
Multiple Learning Styles

A **Bodily-Kinesthetic Learners** Invite students to try identifying objects by running their hands over them or making their way around the classroom by "lightly touching" the walls. This may give them a better sense of appreciation for how difficult it might be to move so gracefully after becoming blind.

Literary Concept: FLASHBACK

B Ask students to identify one indication that the story has switched to another time period. *(the use of the past tense)* Then have students discuss why an author might choose to tell a story through flashbacks. *(Possible responses: to examine the impact of a past act upon the present; to emphasize the fact that the events described are over and done with)*

Literary Concept: IMAGERY

C Draw attention to the vivid imagery in this passage. Ask students to describe what they visualize. *(Possible responses: a pair of trapeze artists in colorful costumes swooping through the air as gracefully as birds; trapeze artists kissing in midair like lovebirds)*

CUSTOMIZING FOR
Students Acquiring English

I Ask students to name the three actions in this passage that describe the flight of birds. *(beat their way up, hovering, swooped).* Then have them explain and pantomime the differences among the three motions.

A It has occurred to me that the catlike precision of her movements in old age might be the result of her early training, but she shows so little of the drama or <u>flair</u> one might expect from a performer that I tend to forget the Flying Avalons. She has kept no sequined costume, no photographs, no fliers or posters from that part of her youth. I would, in fact, tend to think that all memory of double somersaults and heart-stopping catches had left her arms and legs were it not for the fact that sometimes, as I sit sewing in the room of the rebuilt house in which I slept as a child, I hear the crackle, catch a whiff of smoke from the stove downstairs, and suddenly the room goes dark, the stitches burn beneath my fingers, and I am sewing with a needle of hot silver, a thread of fire.

I owe her my existence three times. The first was when she saved herself. In the town square a replica tent pole, cracked and splintered, now stands cast in concrete. It commemorates the disaster that put our town smack on the front page of the Boston and New York tabloids.² It is from those old newspapers, now historical records, that I get my information. Not from my mother, Anna of the Flying Avalons, nor from any of her in-laws, nor certainly from the other half of her particular act, Harold Avalon, her first husband. In one news account it says, "The day was mildly overcast, but nothing in the air or temperature gave any hint of the sudden force with which the deadly gale would strike."

I have lived in the West, where you can see the weather coming for miles, and it is true that out here we are at something of a disadvantage. When extremes of temperature collide, a hot and cold front, winds generate instantaneously behind a hill and crash upon you without warning. That, I think, was the likely situation on that day in June. People probably commented on the pleasant air, grateful that no hot sun beat upon the striped tent that stretched over the entire center green. **B**

They bought their tickets and surrendered them in anticipation. They sat. They ate caramelized popcorn and roasted peanuts. There was time, before the storm, for three acts. The White Arabians of Ali-Khazar rose on their hind legs and waltzed. The Mysterious Bernie folded himself into a painted cracker tin, and the Lady of the Mists made herself appear and disappear in surprising places. As the clouds gathered outside, unnoticed, the ringmaster cracked his whip, shouted his introduction, and pointed to the ceiling of the tent, where the Flying Avalons were perched.

It is from those old newspapers, now historical records, that I get my information.

They loved to drop gracefully from nowhere, like two sparkling birds, and blow kisses as they threw off their plumed helmets and high-collared capes. They laughed and flirted openly as they beat their way up again on the trapeze bars. In the final vignette³ of their act, they actually would kiss in midair, pausing, almost hovering as they swooped past one another. On the ground, between bows, Harry Avalon would skip quickly to the front rows and point out the smear of my mother's lipstick, just off the edge of his mouth. They made a romantic pair all right, especially in the blindfold sequence. **I** **C**

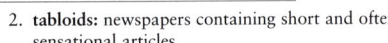

2. **tabloids:** newspapers containing short and often sensational articles.
3. **vignette** (vĭn-yĕt′): a short sketch or scene.

WORDS TO KNOW
flair (flâr) *n.* distinctive elegance or style

846

Mini-Lesson · Study Skills

INDEXES Explain to students that indexes are useful tools for locating the particular information they need to find. Most reference works and other nonfiction books contain indexes at the back which list all the citations of a particular subject in the text.

Application Divide students into two teams and play a quiz game based on the indexes of this textbook. Ask questions that require students to give pages numbers from the text. Award points for the first team to find the correct page number, using the index.

846 THE LANGUAGE OF LITERATURE **TEACHER'S EDITION**

Copyright © Michelle Barnes / The Image Bank.

Art Note

Untitled by Michelle Barnes This illustration by Michelle Barnes shows the skills and thrills of trapeze artistry. Through a subtle use of color, the artist suggests the spotlights and dizzying height of the act. The elongated bodies of the flyers stretching for contact emphasize the energy and tension concentrated into a single instant.

Reading the Art As you look at the picture, what do you think are the most important skills or qualities Anna Avalon needed to perform her act?

Linking To History

The first circus tent was put up in 1825 in Wilmington, Delaware, by Joshua Purdy Brown. Early tents were small, providing seating for only a few hundred spectators. At the height of traveling circuses' popularity, however, these huge canvas structures would shelter from 10,000 to 20,000 people. The big top of the Ringling Brothers and Barnum and Bailey Circus covered more than two acres. It was supported by huge main poles that were 65 feet long. In addition to the main, or king poles, the tent was supported by side poles and, between the king and side poles, quarter poles.

Critic's  Corner

"I liked the imagery of this selection because I could imagine what the author was describing and I can picture what the author is saying in my head."

Ronnie Pigao
Student Critic

Ask students to share their opinions on the imagery of "The Leap."

Art Note

Sketches from Calder's Circus by Alexander Calder Noted sculptor Alexander Calder (1898–1976) first gained worldwide fame and success over fifty years ago with his miniature circus. The figure here and the one on page 845 are sketches from Calder's work on the circus.

Reading the Art *Based on these sketches, what type of material do you think Calder used to make his circus sculpture?*

Literary Concept: CHARACTERIZATION

D Call attention to the statement "my mother lives comfortably in extreme elements." Ask students to discuss what the narrator might mean by this. *(Possible response: The narrator's mother has no trouble adjusting to unusual or dangerous situations, such as blindness or swinging from a trapeze.)*

Linking To History

E The flying-trapeze act was invented in 1859 by the French acrobat J. Leotard when, at the Cirque Napoleon in Paris, he let go of one metal swing and flew through the air to grab another. Trapeze acts, which often involve several members of the same family, have grown more and more daring as aerialists have added somersaults and twists. The first triple somersault from a flying trapeze was accomplished in 1897 by Lena Jordan of the Flying Jordans. In the 1930s and 1940s the Concellos, a husband-and-wife team, dominated circus flying with their double and triple somersaults and passing leaps. In 1982 Miguel Vazquez did a quadruple somersault into the hands of his brother Juan.

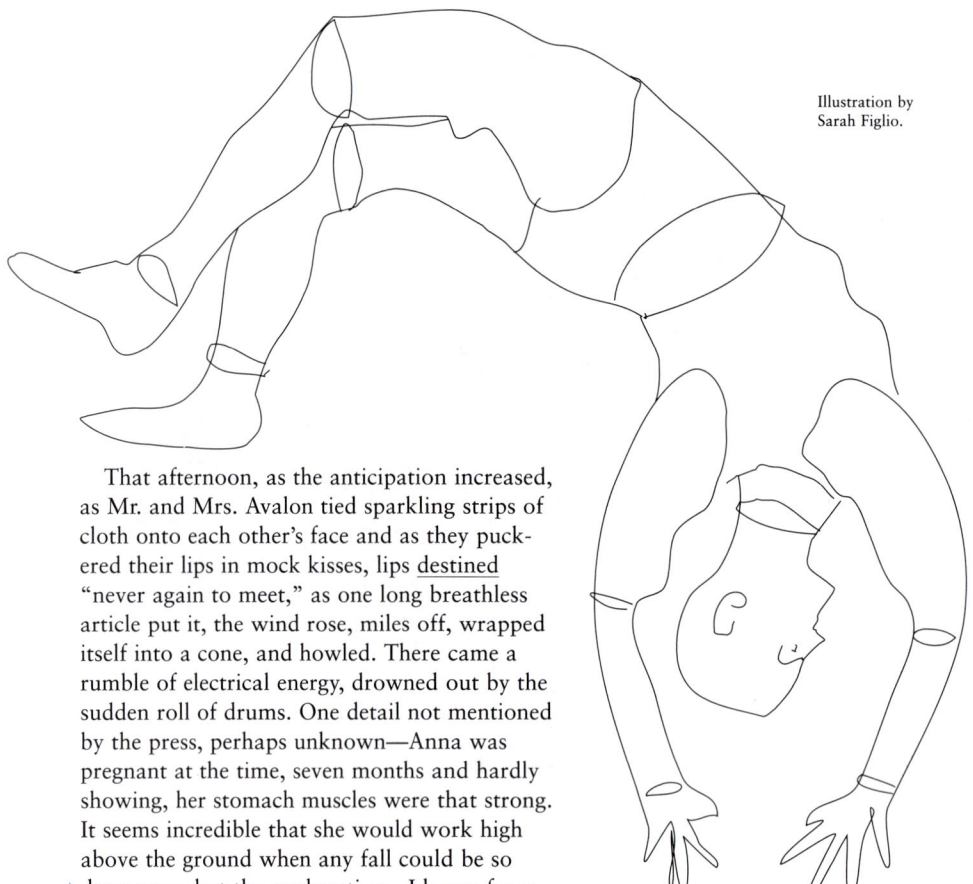

Illustration by Sarah Figlio.

That afternoon, as the anticipation increased, as Mr. and Mrs. Avalon tied sparkling strips of cloth onto each other's face and as they puckered their lips in mock kisses, lips destined "never again to meet," as one long breathless article put it, the wind rose, miles off, wrapped itself into a cone, and howled. There came a rumble of electrical energy, drowned out by the sudden roll of drums. One detail not mentioned by the press, perhaps unknown—Anna was pregnant at the time, seven months and hardly showing, her stomach muscles were that strong. It seems incredible that she would work high above the ground when any fall could be so dangerous, but the explanation—I know from watching her go blind—is that my mother lives comfortably in extreme elements. She is one with the constant dark now, just as the air was her home, familiar to her, safe, before the storm that afternoon.

From opposite ends of the tent they waved, blind and smiling, to the crowd below. The ringmaster removed his hat and called for silence, so that the two above could concentrate. They rubbed their hands in chalky powder, then Harry launched himself and swung, once, twice, in huge calibrated[4] beats across space. He hung from his knees and on the third swing stretched wide his arms, held his hands out to receive his pregnant wife as she dove from her shining bar.

It was while the two were in midair, their hands about to meet, that lightning struck the main pole and sizzled down the guy wires, filling the air with a blue radiance that Harry Avalon must certainly have seen through the

---

4. **calibrated:** measured.

WORDS TO KNOW

destined (dĕs′tĭnd) *adj.* determined beforehand; fated **destine** *v.*

848

Mini-Lesson Literary Concepts

REVIEWING IMAGERY Remind students that imagery refers to a writer's use of descriptive details that appeal to the senses. Visual details are the most common form of imagery, but authors also use details that appeal to the senses of touch, taste, hearing, and smell. Images such as "filling the air with a blue radiance" help to create a picture in the reader's mind. Such sensory details help a reader to imagine the settings, characters, and events in a story.

Application Students pairs can create a list of the vivid images found in the story. Have them identify the sense to which each image appeals. Ask them to discuss which kinds of images they usually find most powerful: ones that appeal to taste, touch, sight, hearing, or smell. Encourage students to explain the reasons for their answers.

848 THE LANGUAGE OF LITERATURE TEACHER'S EDITION

cloth of his blindfold as the tent buckled and the edifice[5] toppled him forward, the swing continuing and not returning in its sweep, and Harry going down, down into the crowd with his last thought, perhaps, just a prickle of surprise at his empty hands.

My mother once said that I'd be amazed at how many things a person can do within the act of falling. Perhaps, at the time, she was teaching me to dive off a board at the town pool, for I associate the idea with midair somersaults. But I also think she meant that even in that awful doomed second one could think, for she certainly did. When her hands did not meet her husband's, my mother tore her blindfold away. As he swept past her on the wrong side, she could have grasped his ankle, the toe end of his tights, and gone down clutching him. Instead, she changed direction. Her body twisted toward a heavy wire, and she managed to hang on to the braided metal, still hot from the lightning strike. Her palms were burned so terribly that once healed they bore no lines, only the blank scar tissue of a quieter future. She was lowered, gently, to the sawdust ring just underneath the dome of the canvas roof, which did not entirely settle but was held up on one end and jabbed through, torn, and still on fire in places from the giant spark, though rain and men's jackets soon put that out.

Three people died, but except for her hands my mother was not seriously harmed until an overeager rescuer broke her arm in extricating her and also, in the process, collapsed a portion of the tent bearing a huge buckle that knocked her unconscious. She was taken to the town hospital, and there she must have hemorrhaged,[6] for they kept her, confined to her bed, a month and a half before her baby was born without life.

Harry Avalon had wanted to be buried in the circus cemetery next to the original Avalon, his uncle, so she sent him back with his brothers. The child, however, is buried around the corner, beyond this house and just down the highway. Sometimes I used to walk there just to sit. She was a girl, but I rarely thought of her as a sister or even as a separate person really. I suppose you could call it the egocentrism[7] of a child, of all young children, but I considered her a less finished version of myself.

When the snow falls, throwing shadows among the stones, I can easily pick hers out from the road, for it is bigger than the others and in the shape of a lamb at rest, its legs curled beneath. The carved lamb looms larger as the years pass, though it is probably only my eyes, the vision shifting, as what is close to me blurs and distances sharpen. In odd moments, I think it is the edge drawing near, the edge of everything, the unseen horizon we do not really speak of in the eastern woods. And it also seems to me, although this is probably an idle fantasy, that the statue is growing more sharply etched, as if, instead of weathering itself into a porous mass, it is hardening on the hillside with each snowfall, perfecting itself.

It was during her confinement in the hospital that my mother met my father. He was called in to look at the set of her arm, which was complicated. He stayed, sitting at her bedside, for he was something of an armchair traveler and had spent his war quietly, at an air force training grounds, where he became a specialist in arms and legs broken during parachute training exercises. Anna Avalon had been to many of the places he

---

5. **edifice** (ĕd′ə-fĭs): structure; building.
6. **hemorrhaged** (hĕm′ər-ĭjd): bled heavily from a blood vessel.
7. **egocentrism**: self-centeredness; the belief that everything revolves around oneself.

WORDS TO KNOW
extricating (ĕk′strĭ-kā′tĭng) *n.* releasing from an entanglement **extricate** *v.*

849

Mini-Lesson Grammar

ADVERB PHRASES Remind students that a prepositional phrase that functions as an adverb is known as an adverb phrase. Like an adverb, an adverb phrase modifies a verb, an adjective, or another adverb. Write this sentence from "The Leap" on the chalkboard and ask students to identify both the adverb phrase and the word it modifies.

From opposite ends of the tent they waved, blind and smiling, to the crowd below.

Application Ask students to use each of the following adverb phrases in a sentence.
1. inside the circus tent
2. from the roof of the house
3. beside her hospital bed

Reteaching/Reinforcement
• *Grammar Mini-Lessons* transparencies, p. 46

Adverb Phrases, p. 587

Literary Concept: IMAGERY

F Ask students why blank palms might point to "a quieter future." (*Possible response: It would be impossible to be a trapeze artist with palms that couldn't grip well.*)

STRATEGIC READING FOR Less-Proficient Readers

G Make sure that students understand what has happened up to this point in the story.
• What job did the narrator's mother have as a young woman? (*She was a trapeze artist.*) Noting Relevant Details
• On "that day in June," what causes Harry Avalon to fall? (*Lightning strikes the main pole of the tent.*) Noting Relevant Details
• Summarize what happens to the narrator's mother after she grabs the heavy wire? (*She burns her palms, and then her arm is accidentally broken and she is knocked out.*) Summarizing

Set a Purpose Have students read to find out what happens to the mother after the accident.

Literary Concept: SYMBOL

H Ask students what the lamb tombstone might represent to the narrator. Note that the narrator says she considered the dead child "a less finished version of myself." She may identify with the child and with the lamb, which "looms larger as the years pass." Her vision seems to shift as death, "the edge of everything," draws nearer. The statue seems to be "growing more sharply etched." Perhaps that is how she sees her own life.

longed to visit—Venice, Rome, Mexico, all through France and Spain. She had no family of her own and was taken in by the Avalons, trained to perform from a very young age. They toured Europe before the war, then based themselves in New York. She was illiterate.

It was in the hospital that she finally learned to read and write, as a way of overcoming the boredom and depression of those weeks, and it was my father who insisted on teaching her. In return for stories of her adventures, he graded her first exercises. He bought her her first book, and over her bold letters, which the pale guides of the penmanship pads could not contain, they fell in love.

I wonder if my father calculated the exchange he offered: one form of flight for another. For after that, and for as long as I can remember, my mother has never been without a book. Until now, that is, and it remains the greatest difficulty of her blindness. Since my father's recent death, there is no one to read to her, which is why I returned, in fact, from my failed life where the land is flat. I came home to read to my mother, to read out loud, to read long into the dark if I must, to read all night.

Once my father and mother married, they moved onto the old farm he had inherited but didn't care much for. Though he'd been thinking of moving to a larger city, he settled down and broadened his practice in this valley. It still seems odd to me, when they could have gone anywhere else, that they chose to stay in the town where the disaster had occurred, and which my father in the first place had found so constricting. It was my mother who insisted upon it, after her child did not survive. And then, too, she loved the sagging farmhouse with its scrap of what was left of a vast acreage of woods and hidden hay fields that stretched to the game park.

I owe my existence, the second time then, to the two of them and the hospital that brought them together. That is the debt we take for granted since none of us asks for life. It is only once we have it that we hang on so dearly.

I was seven the year the house caught fire, probably from standing ash. It can rekindle, and my father, forgetful around the house and perpetually exhausted from night hours on call, often emptied what he thought were ashes from cold stoves into wooden or cardboard containers. The fire could have started from a flaming box, or perhaps a buildup of creosote[8] inside the chimney was the culprit. It started right around the stove, and the heart of the house was gutted. The baby sitter, fallen asleep in my father's den on the first floor, woke to find the stairway to my upstairs room cut off by flames. She used the phone, then ran outside to stand beneath my window.

When my parents arrived, the town volunteers had drawn water from the fire pond and were spraying the outside of the house, preparing to go inside after me, not knowing at the time that there was only one staircase and that it was lost. On the other side of the house, the superannuated[9] extension ladder broke in half. Perhaps the clatter of it falling against the walls woke me, for I'd been asleep up to that point.

As soon as I awakened, in the small room that I now use for sewing, I smelled the smoke. I followed things by the letter then, was good at memorizing instructions, and so I did exactly what was taught in the second-grade home fire drill. I got up; I touched the back of my door before opening it. Finding it hot, I left it closed and stuffed my rolled-up rug beneath the crack. I did not hide under my bed or crawl into my closet. I put on my flannel robe, and then I sat down to wait.

---

8. **creosote** (krē′ə-sōt′): an oily tar deposit from burned wood, which collects in a chimney.
9. **superannuated** (soo̅′pər-ăn′yoo̅-ā′tĭd): too old or worn for further work or service.

WORDS TO KNOW	**constricting** (kən-strĭk′tĭng) *adj.* limiting; without much opportunity or freedom 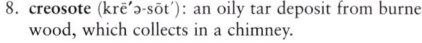 **constrict** *v.* **perpetually** (pər-pĕch′oo̅-əl-ē) *adv.* always; continually

Outside, my mother stood below my dark window and saw clearly that there was no rescue. Flames had pierced one side wall, and the glare of the fire lighted the massive limbs and trunk of the vigorous old elm that had probably been planted the year the house was built, a hundred years ago at least. No leaf touched the wall, and just one thin branch scraped the roof. From below, it looked as though even a squirrel would have had trouble jumping from the tree onto the house, for the breadth of that small branch was no bigger than my mother's wrist.

Standing there, beside Father, who was preparing to rush back around to the front of the house, my mother asked him to unzip her dress. When he wouldn't be bothered, she made him understand. He couldn't make his hands work, so she finally tore it off and stood there in her pearls and stockings. She directed one of the men to lean the broken half of the extension ladder up against the trunk of the tree. In surprise, he complied. She ascended. She vanished. Then she could be seen among the leafless branches of late November as she made her way up and, along her stomach, inched the length of a bough that curved above the branch that brushed the roof.

Once there, swaying, she stood and balanced. There were plenty of people in the crowd and many who still remember, or think they do, my mother's leap through the ice-dark air toward that thinnest extension, and how she broke the branch falling so that it cracked in her hands, cracked louder than the flames as she vaulted with it toward the edge of the roof, and how it hurtled down end over end without her, and their eyes went up, again, to see where she had flown.

I didn't see her leap through air, only heard the sudden thump and looked out my window. She was hanging by the backs of her heels from the new gutter we had put in that year, and she was smiling. I was not surprised to see her, she was so matter-of-fact. She tapped on the window. I remember how she did it, too. It was the friendliest tap, a bit tentative, as if she was afraid she had arrived too early at a friend's house. Then she gestured at the latch, and when I opened the window, she told me to raise it wider and prop it up with the stick so it wouldn't crush her fingers. She swung down, caught the ledge, and crawled through the opening. Once she was in my room, I realized she had on only underclothing, a bra of the heavy stitched cotton women used to wear and step-in, lace-trimmed drawers. I remember feeling light-headed, of course, terribly relieved, and then embarrassed for her to be seen by the crowd undressed.

I was still embarrassed as we flew out the window, toward earth, me in her lap, her toes pointed as we skimmed toward the painted target of the fire fighter's net.

I know that she's right. I knew it even then. As you fall, there is time to think. Curled as I was, against her stomach, I was not startled by the cries of the crowd or the looming faces. The wind roared and beat its hot breath at our back; the flames whistled. I slowly wondered what would happen if we missed the circle or bounced out of it. Then I wrapped my hands around my mother's hands. I felt the brush of her lips and heard the beat of her heart in my ears, loud as thunder, long as the roll of drums. ❖

> From below, it looked as though even a squirrel would have had trouble jumping from the tree onto the house . . .

THE LEAP **851**

 Mini-Lesson The Writer's Style

ENDING WITH A RESOLUTION Point out that many short stories end by resolving conflicts or dilemmas faced by their characters, and "the Leap" is no exception. In the story's last, lyrical paragraph, Erdrich manages to tie together the flashbacks about the circus accident and the house fire, the story title, and the mother's assertion that there is time to think while falling. Such a resolution can satisfy readers by providing them with a sense of closure.

Application Have students write their own stories in which conflicts or problems are resolved at the end. Suggest that they try to do what Erdrich does so successfully: use the story's resolution to tie together several seemingly disparate threads.

Reteaching/Reinforcement
• Writing Handbook, anthology pp. 1034–1035

 The Writer's Craft
Conclusions for Narratives, pp. 388–389

Literary Concept: IMAGERY

L Ask students how the imagery here echoes the circus disaster. *(Possible responses: The daughter is curled against her mother's stomach, like the unborn child during the circus fall; each event involves wind and flames; the mother's heartbeat is compared to thunder, again recalling the circus storm, and to the roll of drums, which preceded the circus fall.)*

STRATEGIC READING FOR
Less-Proficient Readers

M Make sure students understand the sequence of events that have occurred after the tragic circus accident.

• How do the narrator's parents meet? *(Her father, a doctor, is called to look at her mother's arm. She tells him stories about the circus, he teaches her to read and write, and they fall in love.)*
Summarizing

• Where does the fire start? What probably causes it? *(The fire starts near the stove, probably caused by the rekindling of standing ash or by creosote buildup inside the chimney.)*
Noting Relevant Details

COMPREHENSION CHECK
1. How does Anna save herself when lightening strikes the tent? *(She catches hold of a wire.)*
2. What is the shape of Anna's dead child's tombstone? *(a lamb)*
3. What does the narrator's father teach Anna to do? *(to read and write)*
4. How do the narrator and her mother get out of the house during the fire? *(They jump into a net.)*
5. What does the narrator, as an adult, regularly do for her mother? *(She reads to her.)*

From Personal Response to Critical Analysis

1. Accept all reasonable responses.
2. Possible responses: her courage; her love for her child; her ability to think and act calmly and quickly in emergencies; her ability to adapt to changes in her life; her survival instincts; her will to live; her daring; her integrity
3. Possible responses: loving and caring; based on a deep bond of love and respect; an extreme and perhaps unhealthy attachment because she has given up her own life to come home and take care of her mother, who has clearly demonstrated that she is capable of taking care of herself.
4. Possible responses: admiring, the narrator clearly admires her mother; wistful, the narrator wishes that her life had been as eventful as her mother's.
5. Accept all reasonable, well-supported responses.

Another Pathway

Remind students that the flashbacks disrupt the chronology; they will have to read carefully to determine the chronological order of story events.

Rubric

3 Full Accomplishment Time line details are in correct chronological order, and all invented details are plausible.

2 Substantial Accomplishment Some details are in the wrong place on the time line, but invented details show an understanding of story characters.

1 Little or Partial Accomplishment Time line details are in story order, not chronological order, or made-up details are implausible.

RESPONDING OPTIONS

FROM PERSONAL RESPONSE TO CRITICAL ANALYSIS

REFLECT 1. In your notebook, describe what you would say if you could meet the narrator's mother.

RETHINK 2. What, in your opinion, are the mother's most admirable qualities?
Consider
- how she saved herself after the lightning struck
- what she did in the years following the aerial accident
- the risk she took to save her daughter's life
- how she manages with her present blindness

Close Textual Reading

3. How would you describe the narrator's relationship with her mother?
Consider
- the narrator's statement "I owe her my existence three times"
- why the narrator has returned to live with her mother
- the feelings that the narrator expresses about her mother

Close Textual Reading

4. In your opinion, what tone is conveyed by the story? Cite evidence from the story to support your opinion.

RELATE 5. Why do you think some people find ways of coping with a tragedy that forever alters their lives, while others seem unable to recover from tragedy?

ANOTHER PATHWAY

Create an annotated time line of the events in "The Leap." Add as many details from the story as you can, including information about the mother's early life. You may also invent plausible details about the characters' lives. Compare your completed time line with those of other classmates.

QUICKWRITES

1. Write the **tabloid article** that might have appeared after the lightning struck the circus tent. Use information presented in "The Leap," but feel free to invent details.

2. Think about the different kinds of leaps people can make, such as a physical leap, a leap of faith, and so on. Then write an **analysis** of the title of this selection, explaining the multiple leaps that take place in the story.

3. Draft a **comparison-contrast essay** in which you analyze your own attitude toward taking physical risks and draw comparisons between yourself and the narrator's mother.

📁 **PORTFOLIO** *Save your writing. You may want to use it later as a springboard to a piece for your portfolio.*

852 UNIT SIX PART 1: A STRENGTH FROM WITHIN

QuickWrites

1. Remind students that tabloid articles are usually sensational. Students may wish to review the references to the press coverage on page 848.
2. Students should think about how they want to organize their analysis. They could devote a paragraph to each kind of leap, or they might wish to group similar aspects of the leaps together in a paragraph.
3. Before beginning their essays, students can organize their thoughts by creating a Venn diagram.

The Writer's Craft

Comparison and Contrast, pp. 118–132

LITERARY CONCEPTS

As you know, a **flashback** is a description of a conversation, an episode, or an event that happened before the beginning of a story. Often a flashback interrupts the chronological flow of a story to give the reader information helpful in understanding a character's present situation. Identify the main flashbacks in "The Leap." How are they related to one another?

CONCEPT REVIEW: Foreshadowing Which passages foreshadow the disaster in the circus tent and the fire in the house?

Multimodal Learning
ALTERNATIVE ACTIVITIES

1. **Cooperative Learning** With a group of classmates, stage a **television** or **radio talk show** in which Harry Avalon, the narrator, and the narrator's mother and father are interviewed. Have each character tell his or her remarkable story and answer questions from the audience.
2. Make a **collage** of the most powerful images in "The Leap." Use clippings from magazines and your own artwork as you piece together a visual portrait of the story.

ART CONNECTION

In what way does the illustration on page 847 capture the mood of the story? Support your response.

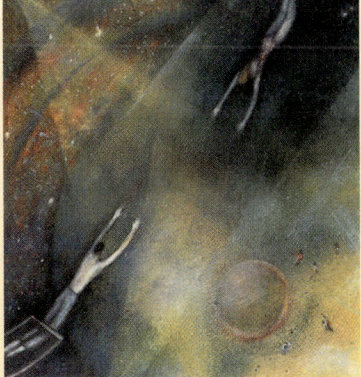

LITERARY LINKS

Compare and contrast the heroism of the mother in "The Leap" with that of the anonymous hero in "The Man in the Water." Which of the two do you have the strongest feelings about?

CRITIC'S CORNER

"Louise Erdrich's stories celebrate the ordinary parts of life," said the critic Jeanne Kinney. "Like many women authors, she seems to appreciate the balance between the commonplace and the sensational." What elements of "The Leap" do you find sensational? Do you agree that the story ultimately celebrates the more ordinary parts of life?

ACROSS THE CURRICULUM

History Investigate the history of circuses and present your findings in an oral report for your classmates. Consider focusing your report on the small traveling circuses of the 19th century, or tell the story of the Ringling Brothers and Barnum & Bailey Circus. You may wish to build a model or diorama, or bring in photos and fine-art reproductions.

Sports Find out more about the flying trapeze act: how it has changed since it was invented in 1859; the kinds of stunts it includes; and the famous families who have popularized the act. Share your findings with interested classmates.

THE LEAP 853

Across the Curriculum

History Students may find it interesting to investigate newspaper accounts of circus performances that occurred earlier in the 20th century.

Sports Students might consider turning their research into a bulletin board display or an oral report.

Literary Links

Some students may have stronger feelings about the mother because they know a lot more about her, while others may be more touched by the anonymity of "the man in the water." Students may suggest that "the man in the water" was more of a hero because he saved people he didn't know, while the mother saves her own daughter.

Critic's Corner

Students might find the blind trapeze act and the mother's leaping onto the roof during the fire sensational. Some students will agree that the story celebrates the more ordinary parts of life, claiming that it is ultimately about such ordinary things as love, marriage, and old age. Others will feel that the story celebrates and highlights the mother's sensational acts.

Art Connection

Students might feel that the illustration captures the mood of excitement and uncertainty that characterizes the situations in the story.

Literary Concepts

The main two flashbacks in the story are the description of the circus accident and the description of the fire. They are related by the fact that in both instances the narrator's mother managed to think quickly, calmly, and ingeniously during an emergency, thereby saving her own life and her daughter's life.

Foreshadowing The passage at the beginning of the story and the one that begins "I owe her my existence three times" (p. 846) foreshadow the circus accident. The passage that begins "as I sit sewing in the room of the rebuilt house" (p. 846) foreshadows the fire.

Alternative Activities

1. Advise groups to review the story to gather details about the characters. Some groups may want to write a script for their show.
2. Reminds students that they can include words as well as images in their collages, but the words should be presented artistically and be visually interesting. Students may wish to display their collages on a classroom or school bulletin board.

THE LANGUAGE OF LITERATURE TEACHER'S EDITION 853

Words to Know

1. d
2. a
3. b
4. e
5. c

Reteaching/Reinforcement
- Unit Six Resource Book, p. 18.

LOUISE ERDRICH

When discussing how she became interested in writing, Erdrich gives credit to her Native American heritage and the Native American storytelling tradition. "People just sit and the stories start coming, one after another. I suppose that when you grow up constantly hearing the stories rise, break, and fall, it gets into you somehow." Like the mother in "The Leap," Erdrich has held some interesting jobs, including a prison poetry teacher and a construction flag signaler.

ART GALLERY
Art of the Circus The heroine of Erdrich's "The Leap" was once a trapeze performer, one of the star attractions of a circus. Posters and paintings of circus acts provide students with visual context for understanding the protagonist's world.

Side A, Frame 49676

WORDS TO KNOW

For each phrase in the first column, write the letter of the synonymous phrase from the second column.

1. perpetually lonely   a. hair with flair
2. a dashing "do"   b. disentangle the wrangler
3. extricate the cowboy   c. presumed to be doomed
4. moistly constricting   d. endlessly friendless
5. thought to be destined   e. damply cramping

LOUISE ERDRICH

1954–

Chippewa on her mother's side and German on her father's, Louise Erdrich was born in Little Falls, Minnesota, and grew up in the small town of Wahpeton, North Dakota, near the Minnesota border. Both of her parents taught at the Bureau of Indian Affairs boarding school in Wapheton, and her grandfather was a tribal leader of the nearby Turtle Mountain Reservation. Her childhood love of writing was encouraged by both her father, who gave her a nickel for every story she wrote, and her mother, who stapled the tales into construction paper covers. "So at an early age," Erdrich humorously notes, "I felt myself to be a published author earning substantial royalties."

Erdrich enrolled in Dartmouth in 1972, the first year in which the New Hampshire college admitted women. There she took courses in the new Native American studies department—chaired by anthropologist Michael Dorris—and began coming to terms with the importance of her Native American heritage. After working at several jobs and obtaining a master's degree, she returned to Dartmouth as a writer-in-residence and began a close professional friendship with Dorris, who was also part Native American. Their mutual interests blossomed into love, and they married in 1981.

Erdrich's first novel, *Love Medicine*, grew out of a short story that she and Dorris worked on together. Winner of the 1984 National Book Critics Circle Award, *Love Medicine* traces the lives of several Native American families in a series of interconnected stories. Many of the characters in *Love Medicine* appear in three of Erdrich's subsequent novels. "My characters choose me," she once said, "and once they do it's like standing in a field and hearing echoes. All I can do is trace their passage."

Erdrich and Dorris continue to work in unusually close collaboration, reading and revising each other's drafts; they have even jointly published one novel, *The Crown of Columbus*. Their large family includes several adopted children, one of whom became the subject of Dorris's award-winning nonfiction book *The Broken Cord*. Erdrich has published two highly regarded volumes of poetry and a number of prize-winning short stories. Her first major work of nonfiction, *The Blue Jay's Dance: A Birth Year*, was published in 1995.

OTHER WORKS *Jacklight, Baptism of Desire, The Beet Queen, Tracks, The Bingo Palace*

Extended Reading

- ART GALLERY

854 UNIT SIX PART 1: A STRENGTH FROM WITHIN

REFLECTING ON THEME
What Do You Think?

Ask students to reflect upon the activity on page 806. How does the narrator's mother compare to the heroes that students wrote about and discussed? Do students think that physical courage and quick thinking in the face of danger are important ingredients in heroism?

PREVIEWING

NONFICTION

from Back from Tuichi (tōō'ē-chē)
Yossi Ghinsberg (yō'sē gǐnz'bûrg) Israel

Activating Prior Knowledge
PERSONAL CONNECTION
As a class, discuss the ingredients needed for an exciting adventure story. You may consider either real-life adventures or fictional ones portrayed in books, in movies, or on television. Identify the types of characters, settings, plot lines, and other elements that make for an interesting story. Use a diagram like the one shown to organize your ideas.

Building Background
BIOGRAPHICAL CONNECTION
Yossi Ghinsberg experienced the adventure of a lifetime while backpacking through South America in the early 1980s. He recounts his perilous journey in his book *Back from Tuichi: The Harrowing Life-and-Death Story of Survival in the Amazon Rainforest*. While in Bolivia, Yossi met three men, Kevin, Marcus, and Karl, who would journey with him by river raft deep into the jungle. They were searching for a remote Indian village and gold, but all they found was adventure. After several weeks of rough traveling, Marcus and Karl—who had lived and worked in the rain forest and knew best how to survive there—decided to head back to civilization on foot. As this selection begins, Yossi and Kevin are getting ready to continue on their own down the Tuichi River in Bolivia.

Setting a Purpose
WRITING CONNECTION
What exciting adventures have you had? Have you ever had an experience that might have been more exciting had something gone awry? In your notebook, jot down ideas for an adventure story—real or fictional. Then see how your ideas compare to Yossi Ghinsberg's experiences as you read the following excerpt from *Back from Tuichi*.

LASERLINKS
• GEOGRAPHICAL CONNECTION

BACK FROM TUICHI **855**

OVERVIEW

Objectives
- To understand and appreciate a narrative that explores a struggle for survival
- To understand and appreciate a true-life adventure
- To express understanding of the selection through a choice of writing forms, including book jacket copy, a book report, and a true-life adventure
- To extend understanding of the selection through a variety of multimodal and cross-curricular activities

Skills

LITERARY CONCEPTS
- True-life adventure
- Setting

GRAMMAR
- Exclamation points

SPEAKING, LISTENING, AND VIEWING
- Film
- Group discussion
- Oral reading

GEOGRAPHICAL CONNECTION
The Amazon Rain Forest
Ghinsberg's journey takes him through the Amazon rainforest, a dense, remote jungle abundant in plant and animal life. These color photographs of wildlife and other natural wonders of the rainforest will help students visualize the setting of *Back from Tuichi*.

Side A, Frame 49688

PRINT AND MEDIA RESOURCES

UNIT SIX RESOURCE BOOK
Strategic Reading: Literature, p. 21

GRAMMAR MINI-LESSONS
Transparencies, p.48

WRITING MINI-LESSONS
Transparencies, p. 42

ACCESS FOR STUDENTS ACQUIRING ENGLISH
Selection Summaries
Reading Support

FORMAL ASSESSMENT
Selection Test, p. 171
 Test Generator

 AUDIO LIBRARY
See Reference Card

LASERLINKS
Geographical Connection

 INTERNET RESOURCES
McDougal Littell Literature Center at http://www.hmco.com/mcdougal/lit

THE LANGUAGE OF LITERATURE TEACHER'S EDITION **855**

SUMMARY

Rafting down a South American river, Yossi Ghinsberg and his friend Kevin are battered by white-water rapids, enormous rocks, and whirlpools. When the current gets too strong, Kevin ties up the raft and goes ashore. The raft breaks free of its mooring with Yossi and the supplies still aboard. Yossi goes down a waterfall but comes out uninjured. After trying to keep sight of the life pack but losing it, he staggers ashore, improvises a shelter, and settles in for a nerve-rattling night in the wilds. He spends the next day finding and retrieving the life pack. He manages to pick some fruit for dinner, after encountering a deadly snake and fire ants. Then he beds down for the night and makes plans to travel on his own. During the night, he has visions of Kevin calling to him.

Thematic Link: *A Strength from Within*
In this selection, a young man has to find the strength within himself to survive alone in the wilderness.

CUSTOMIZING FOR
Students Acquiring English

- Use **ACCESS FOR STUDENTS ACQUIRING ENGLISH,** *Reading Support.*

- This selection contains a great deal of colloquial dialogue, beginning with the very first words of the story, "Get a move on, Yossi." Students can use context clues to guess what each colloquial expression means and keep a list of any expressions they can't figure out.

- In addition to these boxes, you may also want to use the suggestions under Strategic Reading for Less-Proficient Readers.

STRATEGIC READING FOR
Less-Proficient Readers

Set a Purpose Have students read to find out what happens to Yossi and Kevin.

Use **UNIT SIX RESOURCE BOOK,** p. 21, for guidance in reading the selection.

from BACK FROM TUICHI
YOSSI GHINSBERG

Kevin broke the silence. "Get a move on, Yossi. We still have a lot to do."

We crossed back to the other side of the Ipurama[1] and set to work. Kevin uncoupled the four logs we had added to the raft in Asriamas.[2] Then, using *panchos*[3] the way Karl had taught us, we tied the logs to one another to make a smaller raft.

"This," Kevin explained, "will serve as our life raft. We'll fasten all of our equipment down to it."

We bound the small raft tightly to the center of the larger one using the ropes and leather strips that Marcus had left us.

"The main raft will take all the knocks from the rocks, and if anything happens to it, all we'll have to do is to chop the straps with the machete, and the life raft will be set free. We just jump onto it and use it to get ashore."

It sounded reasonable to me.

Kevin emptied the backpacks and rearranged our possessions. In the larger of the two packs he put the bulk of our equipment: the pot and utensils, the sheets of nylon that served as tenting, his extra clothes and sandals, the large stalk of bananas, and the smoked monkey meat. He lined the smaller pack, which he called the life pack, with a waterproof rubber bag. Then he filled the bag with the first-aid kit, the map of Bolivia, the two green mosquito nets, Dede's[4] red poncho, the flashlight, the lighter and matches, and his camera along with an extra lens and film. He placed our documents and what money we had into a watertight metal box. I reluctantly took my wallet with my uncle's tiny book[5] from my pocket. Kevin was watching me. He carefully, wordlessly placed the wallet into the metal box. Finally we fitted the rice and beans into additional waterproof bags. Kevin cinched the mouth of the rubber

---

1. **Ipurama** (ē-pōō-rä′mä): a broad river that empties into the Tuichi River.
2. **Asriamas** (äs-rē-ä′mäs): a small, remote jungle settlement.
3. ***panchos*** (pän′chōs) *Spanish:* ropes made from tree fibers.
4. **Dede's** (dĕ′dĕz): belonging to a friend Yossi made in La Paz, Bolivia, before heading into the jungle.
5. **my uncle's tiny book:** a special book given to Yossi by his Uncle Nissim just before Nissim died; it was believed to have the power to save and protect the person who carried it.

bag tightly shut and closed the pack over it. To the top of the pack he tied two large, sealed tin cans to keep the pack afloat if it should fall from the raft. He placed the entire pack into a nylon bag, which he filled with balsa[6] chips to make it buoyant. The packs were tied firmly to the life raft, and we were ready to go.

① We combed the camp area one last time, but we hadn't forgotten anything. Kevin was very thorough. He kicked through the blanket of leaves that had served as our ground cover and poked through the charred remains of the fire. Nothing was overlooked.

Excited, my stomach fluttering, I boarded the raft. Kevin stood in the water, gave the raft a good shove, and then jumped up beside me.

"Everything's going to be just fine," he assured me. "Just remember what you said yourself: your grandmother could do it. And one other thing: keep alert and pay attention to my instructions."

"You're the captain," I answered.

I wanted to believe that Kevin knew what he was talking about, but at that moment I was pretty nervous. The current seized the raft, and Kevin instructed me to change the pole for an oar.

"All we have to do is to keep the front of the raft pointed straight ahead," he said. "We'll let the current carry us along. We should make the bank Karl was talking about sometime today."

We were rapidly coming upon the first difficult pass. I could see jagged rocks jutting out of white-water rapids.

"To the right, Yossi! Pull hard!"

We ran into a rock, and the raft climbed

On a handmade raft of balsa logs, Yossi Ghinsberg navigated dangerous rapids like the ones shown here and on the following pages. Kenneth Garrett / National Geographic Image Collection.

I could see jagged rocks jutting out of white-water rapids.

partway up, the logs shuddering under our feet. Then we were back in the current and about to ram another rock. I made no attempt at rowing but held on to ② the leather straps for dear life. Kevin was doing the same in the bow. The raft, tossed from rock to rock, descended churning falls, most of the time tilted to one side.

"Hold on tight, Yossi! Don't let go!"

My eyes were squeezed shut.

Just as suddenly we found ourselves drifting once again on a placid[7] river. Looking behind me, I could see the white waters that we had just come through.

"Hey, we made it!" I shouted joyously.

Kevin smiled back at me and gave me a thumbs up. Now we both realized how dangerous this journey was. We had discovered how little we could control the raft. While we were being carried along by the powerful current, we hadn't even been able to keep the front of the raft pointed straight ahead. No, my grandmother wouldn't have come along on this trip. Now that there was no one else along with us sniveling, I Ⓐ no longer felt the need to act the tough guy.

We spent the next two hours drifting easily,

---

6. **balsa** (bôl′sə): a tropical tree having wood that is buoyant and very lightweight, and that is used as a substitute for cork in insulation, floats, and crafts.

7. **placid** (plăs′ĭd): pleasantly calm, quiet, or peaceful.

CUSTOMIZING FOR
Gifted and Talented Students

As students read the selection, ask them to analyze Yossi's and Kevin's relationship. *(Possible response: Yossi seems to both look up to and depend on Kevin, which makes it all that much harder when Yossi is left on his own.)*

CUSTOMIZING FOR
Students Acquiring English

① Ask students to explain the connection between the expressions "We combed the camp" and "Kevin was very thorough." Help them understand that it means they searched the camp as carefully as if they were combing it with the same kind of comb they use on their hair.

CUSTOMIZING FOR
Students Acquiring English

② Ask students to guess what the phrase *held on for dear life* means. Then invite them to cite equivalent expressions in their first languages and give a word-for-word translation of the native language idiom.

Literary Concept:
TRUE-LIFE ADVENTURE

Ⓐ Ask students whether they think that Yossi's admission about the danger of the trip makes the story more exciting or suspenseful. *(Possible responses: yes, because it gets the reader excited about what's going to happen to Yossi and Kevin next; no, because it takes away the unexpected; now the reader knows the trip will be dangerous.)*

Mini-Lesson — Study Skills

KWL Explain to students that *KWL* is a helpful technique for reading nonfiction. This technique is a three-step process. Before reading a selection, a student writes down *What I Know* about the subject of the nonfiction piece. Then the student creates a list of questions on *What I Want to Know* about the subject. After reading the selection, the students jots down *What I Learned*.

Application Have students use the *KWL* technique to read about the rain forests of South America or another topic related to *Back from Tuichi*. Have students bring in materials to read in class, and check their application of the technique.

Literary Concept: SETTING

B Point out that the setting is an integral part of this story. In this passage, the setting impresses Kevin and Yossi so much that Kevin wants to take a picture. Invite students to use the description to form a "photograph" in their own minds. Then invite students to share their "photographs" with the class.

CUSTOMIZING FOR
Students Acquiring English

3 Invite students to read aloud the descriptions of Yossi's actions and pantomime each one. Focus on the terms *craning my neck, trying to catch a glimpse of him,* and *froze.*

James P. Blair / National Geographic Image Collection.

convinced that we would reach our destination. The scenery was breathtaking. Evergreen-covered mountains towered over reddish cliffs along the shore. Occasionally we passed a narrow waterfall, cascading from the heights to the river. From time to time a family of monkeys accompanied us downstream, jumping from tree to tree. Kevin considered taking the camera out but decided it would be too risky and gave up on the idea.

Around noon we ran into trouble. A large rock jutted out from the shore, and the water pounding against it formed a treacherous whirlpool. The current carried us into its center. We tried for two hours to get out of it without success. Finally seeing no other way, Kevin swam to shore, climbed onto the rock, and tried to use the rope that was tied to the front of the raft to pull it out of the whirlpool. Twice he slipped, fell into the water, and was swept away by the current but quickly recovered. On his third try the rope broke off in his hands, and he fell once again into the water, but this time he didn't return so quickly. I was left whirling with the raft, fear churning in my stomach. What if Kevin had drowned? What would become of me? I sat on the raft, craning my neck, trying desperately to catch a glimpse of him. When I saw his straw hat carried downstream, I froze.

Kevin returned about fifteen minutes later, bleeding from a deep wound on his knee.

"The undertow here is incredible," he said. "I thought I was drowning. My air was gone, but just in time the current threw me to the surface, and I made it to shore."

"What about your leg?"

"Oh, I didn't even notice. I guess I must have hit it against a rock. I lost my straw hat."

858   UNIT SIX   PART 1: A STRENGTH FROM WITHIN

Instead of attempting to navigate out of the whirlpool, we moored the raft to the riverbank. It was a great relief to have solid ground under my feet.

The next time we tried something else. We pulled the raft upriver, jumped aboard, and, rowing with all our strength, tried to get past the whirlpool and back into the middle of the river. We succeeded on the third try. After our cries of joy had died down, Kevin remarked thoughtfully, "Maybe we should have just stayed back there. It wouldn't have been such a bad place to camp."

"But we've still got a while before dark," I said. "Anyway, it's better that we should get all the way to the mouth of the *cajón*[8] and camp on the bank that Karl showed us on the map. It would be nice to know that we start walking tomorrow."

"Maybe you're right," Kevin agreed.

The reddish cliffs encroached upon the riverbank. It was as if suddenly the river had no banks at all.

"This must be it," Kevin declared. "Get ready. We should sight the island any minute now. When we do, you start rowing to the left as hard as you can. If we run into any serious trouble, jump overboard and swim for shore. This is starting to look like it must be the canyon."

We were both on edge, alert. The current grew stronger. Where was the island?

There was a large rock near the right-hand bank. We were swiftly being drawn toward it. To its left the riverbed dropped sharply, though it was impossible to see just how far. Nevertheless the water cascaded over the edge with a mighty roar. Maybe we could pass to the right of the rock, between it and the riverbank.

"To the right, to the right! Harder, faster!"

I was rowing desperately with all my strength. I closed my eyes, and we rammed into the rock with tremendous force.

"Are you all right, Yossi?"

Like me, Kevin was in the river, hanging on to the ropes of the raft. The water rushed past us on both sides, but the raft wasn't moving. It was protruding from the river at a sixty-degree angle, stuck on a sandbar, riding up against the rock. The pressure of the water slammed us up against the rock and held us fast.

We climbed back onto the raft. Kevin instructed me to tie the oar down so that it wouldn't be swept into the river. I looked over at the waterfall to our left. The river cascaded downward ten or twelve feet. God, why hadn't I turned back with Karl and Marcus?

My legs quivered. If we could maneuver to the right, we would make it through. We tried to get the raft off the rock but were helpless against the current. We tried everything we could think of—pushing, pulling, rowing, prying the raft off with the poles—but the raft didn't budge.

Kevin quickly sized up the situation.

"I don't see much chance of the current getting us out of here. It's only six or seven yards to the right bank, while the waterfall is here on our left, and after that it's probably twenty yards to the left bank. The river is narrow, and the current is terrifically strong. You see what it means? The canyon must start here. We must be really close to the island. If we can just make it ashore, we can go on from here by foot and easily bypass the canyon overland to Curiplaya."[9]

Kevin paused for a moment and looked around before he made up his mind.

"We don't have any choice. I'm going in. I'll try to reach the right bank. When I do, you throw me the machete. I'll climb up into the jungle and cut a vine. I'll throw the vine to you, and you'll pass the packs over to me on it. Then you tie yourself to the vine, and I'll pull you ashore."

---

8. *cajón* (kä-hôn′) *Spanish*: a narrow canyon.
9. **Curiplaya** (kōō-rē-plä′yä): a gold-mining camp, deserted most of the year.

BACK FROM TUICHI **859**

Mini-Lesson: Speaking, Listening, and Viewing

FILM Ask students how camera work, lighting, and special effects can contribute to their enjoyment of a film. Discuss examples from films that they have seen. The following questions may help students pay closer attention to these elements of film.

Camera work: What angles am I viewing scenes from? When the camera zooms in for a close-up, why is it focusing on a particular person or thing?

Lighting: Is the lighting natural-looking all the time, or do some scenes have interesting color overcasts to them, meant to suggest a mood?

Special Effects: Are there any special effects being used? How do they add to the movie?

Application View the movie version of *Back from Tuichi* with students. Before viewing, discuss why this story might be particularly suited for a visual medium. After viewing, have a discussion comparing and contrasting the film with the excerpt they have read.

Literary Concept: SIMILE

F Ask students to point out the simile Yossi uses here. Why is a fallen leaf a particularly apt comparison for Yossi in his present predicament? *(Possible responses: Like a fallen leaf, he did not choose to be where he is; like a fallen leaf, he cannot make any movements himself; where he goes and what he does is completely dictated by the force of the water.)*

Literary Concept: SETTING

G Point out that the river, the focal point of the story's setting, is almost like a character in the story because of the way in which it affects Yossi and Kevin. Invite students who have been white-water rafting or who have seen it on TV or in the movies to describe it and its dangers for classmates.

"Don't go in, Kevin. It's much too dangerous. Wait awhile," I called to him, but Kevin didn't hesitate. He took off his shoes and socks.

"I'll make it, Yossi," he shouted, and jumped into the river.

The current's tremendous force pulled him along. He disappeared for a moment but then bobbed up again. He was washed up against a rock about twenty-five yards downstream, grabbed onto it, and from there made it to the riverbank. I sighed with relief but then caught my breath. I felt the raft moving under me, slowly breaking free of the rock.

"Kevin! Kevin! The raft is moving, Kevin!"

It was slowly slipping away. Kevin ran swiftly toward me.

"Throw me my shoes, fast!"

I obeyed him automatically and threw his shoes as hard in his direction as I could. They landed on the rocky bank. The raft was almost free. It was headed toward the waterfall. I was trembling all over, looking at Kevin in terror, pleading. He was already hurriedly putting his shoes on.

"The machete! Throw me the machete!" he shouted.

The large blade whistled through the air and thudded to the ground. The raft had begun moving.

"You're leaving me, Kevin!" I shouted.

"Hang on as tight as you can, Yossi! Don't let go of the leather straps, no matter what! Don't let go! You're heading for the waterfall. You're going to go over it! Hang on tight!"

"Kevin, you're leaving me!"

"I'll catch up with you. Just hang on! Hang on!"

The raft came off the rock and edged vertically toward the waterfall. I could feel the surge of the river beneath me and held on to the leather straps for dear life. I was thrown into the air, raging water swallowing my screams; amidst the water I felt as helpless as a fallen leaf. The moment of terror lingered, then abruptly ended with a crash. The raft was pulled under the surface of the river, taking me with it. Darkness enveloped me. My lungs were bursting. I had no air.

Don't, don't let go of the raft! I told myself as the undertow dragged the raft along rapidly below the surface. The pressure on my lungs grew unbearable.

God, help me please.

I thought this was the end. Then I found myself above water, the raft floating again. I jerked my head around and saw Kevin, a hundred yards or more behind me, running in my direction. Relief washed over me.

"I'll wait for you wherever I manage to make shore!" I shouted, and waved at him.

Kevin couldn't hear me, but he waved back and kept running.

Suddenly I understood where I was: I had entered the canyon and was being swept swiftly toward the treacherous Mal Paso San Pedro.[10] The raft bounced from wall to wall. It crashed into the rocks, tilted on its sides, was tossed over falls, and swept through foaming rapids. I held on desperately, closing my eyes and praying *God, God.* Then the raft dove under again, taking me with it. I rammed into a rock so violently that I was twice thrown into the air, landing in the water, vulnerable to the torments of the river, sucked down to its depths. If I hit another rock, I would be smashed to pieces. I was running out of air. When I resurfaced, I saw the bound logs of the raft nearby. I managed to grab hold of them and climb aboard again.

The horrible dance of death went endlessly on. The current was incredibly swift. The raft was swept along like lightning. There was another small bend in the river, and then, still far away, I saw it: a mountain of rock in the middle of the river, almost blocking its entire

---

10. **Mal Paso San Pedro** (mäl pä′sô sän pĕ′drô) *Spanish:* Bad Pass of St. Peter.

860 UNIT SIX PART 1: A STRENGTH FROM WITHIN

EXCLAMATION POINTS Remind students that exclamation points are used at the end of exclamatory sentences or after strong interjections. Exclamation points can add a sense of excitement to writing, which is why writers of adventure stories often use them. The overuse of exclamation points in a story, however, dulls their impact and becomes intrusive.

Application Have students write a short narrative about an adventure, which includes exclamatory sentences and interjections; however, the students should leave out all end punctuation. Then have them exchange narratives with a partner. Partners should decide which of the sentences they are reading deserve exclamation points.

Reteaching/Reinforcement
- *Grammar Mini-Lessons* transparencies, p. 48

The Writer's Craft

The Exclamation Point, p. 783

Frank & Helen Schreider / National Geographic Image Collection.

I knew that I had to get to the life raft. I mustn't lose the life packs. I couldn't survive without it.

breadth. The water pounded against it with a terrible roar. White foam sprayed in all directions, the white-capped maelstrom[11] swirling at the foot of the terrifying crag,[12] and I knew that I would never make it past.

I lay down on the raft facing the stern, not wanting to watch as death approached. I squeezed my eyes tightly shut and clutched at the straps for all I was worth. There was a crash. I felt nothing. I was simply flying through the air, then landing back in the water, my eyes still squeezed shut. I was sucked under the black waters for what seemed an eternity. I could feel the pressure in my ears, my nose, the sockets of my eyes. My chest was bursting. Then once more an invisible hand plucked me out of the current and, just in time, drew me to the surface. I lifted my head, gasped for air—a lot of air—before I would be pulled back under. Far behind me I could see the mountain of rock receding. I couldn't believe it. I had passed it. But how? I didn't feel any pain. No, I was uninjured. It was a miracle.

The raft was in front of me not far away. The logs had become loosened from one another. I managed to climb up onto what was left of it. The leather straps were torn, and I had nothing to cling to. I knew that I had to get to the life raft. I mustn't lose the life pack. I couldn't survive without it.

I jumped into the water, and two strokes brought me to the life raft. Again I crashed into the stone walls of the canyon, only now I no longer had a wide, solid raft to protect me. The life raft was small and narrow. Every blow lifted it half out of the water. Once again I rammed into a rock, injuring my knee, but much worse than that, the precious life pack came loose and fell into the water. I grabbed hold of it just as it was about to float away, but it was heavy, and I was afraid that it would drown me. I tied the waist belt to one of the logs and hoped that it would hold. But I was wrong. One more knock,

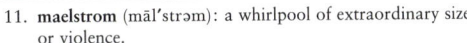

11. **maelstrom** (māl′strəm): a whirlpool of extraordinary size or violence.
12. **crag:** a steeply projecting mass of rock forming part of a rugged cliff.

BACK FROM TUICHI

CUSTOMIZING FOR

Students Acquiring English

④ Write the expression *wonder of wonders* on the board and ask students to find other English expressions to substitute in this sentence. *(amazingly, by some miracle, although I couldn't believe it)* Invite students to share similar idioms in other languages with the class.

Critical Thinking: ANALYZING

Ⓙ Ask students to analyze Yossi's state of mind at this point. Does he really believe what he is saying, or is he just trying to reassure himself? *(Possible responses: He is just trying to reassure himself because he is very scared; it's a little bit of both; he's trying to reassure himself but he does think that Kevin will find him and that they will walk to Curiplaya.)*

How would you find shelter from continual rainfall; protection from poisonous snakes, biting insects, and other wild animals; and nourishing food if left alone in the heart of the jungle? Copyright © Luiz C. Marico / Peter Arnold, Inc.

one more dive over a fall, and the precious pack was bobbing behind me, out of my reach. I couldn't take my eyes off it.

I mustn't lose sight of it, I told myself. *I mustn't lose it, no matter what.*

I was fairly certain that I was already through the pass but still in a canyon. Steep stone walls rose on both sides, but the river was getting wider, the current milder, and I could have swum to the bank, but I couldn't abandon the pack. As long as I could still see it bobbing behind me followed by the large raft, I didn't swim ashore.

The river turned a bend, and I waited in vain for the pack to make the bend behind me. It must have gotten caught on something. Nor did the raft appear. So, as the life raft neared the right bank, I took the chance to leap ashore, having no other choice but to abandon the big pack and raft.

I landed in the water close to the bank and, ④ wonder of wonders, felt sand beneath my feet. I could actually stand up. I staggered out of the river, unbelieving. I had landed on a rocky strip of shore. Solid ground. I was alive!

It was a few moments before my breathing became regular. Then my thoughts returned to my present situation. The life pack was lost, nowhere to be seen, but maybe it would turn up. Couldn't the current knock it free?

And what about Kevin? Surely he would find me. I had seen him running in my direction. He would certainly make it this far today—or tomorrow at the latest. Yes, everything would be all right. I was sure. He would find me, and together we would walk to Curiplaya. How far could we be from each other? I didn't know. How long had I spent on the river? I didn't know. Maybe twenty minutes. The thought of the river made me shudder.

A steady rain had been falling and now grew stronger. There was no more point in waiting. It would be better to climb up into the jungle to find shelter for the night. I clawed my way up the stone wall. When I reached a height of about fifteen feet, I looked down and was overcome with joy. I could see the big raft. It was trapped between some rocks near the shore, bobbing and banging softly, maybe three hundred yards upstream. Now that I could see it, I could hear the sound that it made as it hit against the rocks. What luck! I thought that the pack was probably stuck there too.

I hurried down to the bank, but the bend in the river blocked my view, and except for the spot where I was standing, the river had no bank at all. I wouldn't be able to get any closer to the raft by foot. I waded into the river, very close to the bank, and tried to walk upriver, fighting the current. I progressed a few feet but then slipped and fell as if the bottom had been pulled out from under me. I was terror-stricken and scrambled back to shore.

Now what would I do? I was seething with anger and frustration. I desperately needed the pack. Maybe I could reach it by land, but scaling the stone walls could take hours. I choked back tears.

No, don't cry. Be strong. Don't give up. You're

862 UNIT SIX PART 1: A STRENGTH FROM WITHIN

a man of action. Get on with it, do whatever must be done.

I knew I couldn't make it to the raft that day. It was already growing dark and still raining. I had to find some kind of shelter. I started climbing again, chanting to myself in a whisper, "Man of action, man of action." I could see the raft bobbing among the rocks.

Please stay there until tomorrow. Please stay put.

Improvising a shelter was no easy task. I uprooted small bushes, broke off branches, tore off leaves, and dragged it all back to a little alcove in the stony hillside. I scattered leaves about on the floor and piled branches in the opening until they formed some kind of barrier.

I was famished. I hadn't eaten since morning. A way down the hillside I saw a palmetto tree. I could eat the palm heart, as Karl had taught us. The tree was small, but its roots went deep into the rocky ground. I dug around them with my hands until I finally succeeded in uprooting it. The heart was at the very top. I took a large rock and smashed it against the trunk until I uncovered the soft, white heart. It was a small amount of nourishment, but I gathered every bit.

Suddenly I heard shouting.

It must be Kevin, I said to myself, and roared, "Kevin! Kevin! Kevin!" but there was no reply.

It must have been my imagination. No, I could hear something. A family of monkeys. I trembled with fear. Karl had told us that there were always jaguars in the vicinity of bands of monkeys.

God, let Kevin get here.

I was wearing a blue T-shirt that Marcus had given me, a brown flannel shirt, rough underwear, jeans, socks, walking shoes, and a large bandanna tied around my neck. I crawled into my camouflaged little niche. The stones cut into my back, but they weren't as bad as the cold. I was soaking wet and had no fire or anything with which to cover myself. I took the bandanna from around my neck and tied it over my face, and the warmth of my own breath gave me at least the illusion of comfort. Frightening thoughts filled my mind: wild animals, snakes. What if I didn't find the pack? What if Kevin didn't get here? I would either be devoured by wild beasts or die of starvation. I felt desperate, desolate, and I leapt out of the niche.

"Kevin! Kevin! Kevin!"

"Oha, oha," the cursed monkeys chattered.

I fled back to my alcove. I was choked with tears.

Don't cry. Don't break now. Be a man of action, I coaxed myself.

It was already dark. I replaced the bandanna over my face. I couldn't sleep, couldn't get the frightening thoughts out of my mind. . . .

I told myself that when morning came, I would find Kevin, and together we would make it out of this. When I found myself feeling hopeless, I whispered my mantra,[13] "Man of action, man of action." I don't know where I had gotten the phrase. Perhaps I had picked it up from one of Carlos Castaneda's books.[14] I repeated it over and over: a man of action does whatever he must, isn't afraid, and doesn't worry. But when I heard the rustle of branches outside, my motto wasn't all that encouraging. I held my breath and waited for the rustling to recede into the jungle.

I felt better in the morning. I pushed the branches aside and crawled outside. I roared Kevin's name a few times but then went back to being a man of action and sized up my situation. For starters I was absolutely certain that I was past the canyon. I remembered Karl's description well: the waterfalls, the rapids, the gigantic rock blocking the river. Yes, I was sure

---

13. **mantra:** a verbal formula repeated in prayer or during meditation.
14. **Carlos Castaneda's** (käs-tä-nĕ′däz) **books:** books written by Carlos Castaneda, a Latin American mystic and novelist born in 1931.

Linking to Geography

N It is not surprising that there should be a four days' walk between settlements in this part of Bolivia. Bolivia, the most sparsely populated country in South America, has a particularly sparsely populated rain-forest region. Although jungle and river terrain covers about half of Bolivia, only about one-third of its population lives there. Most Bolivians live on the high, barren Andean plateau known as the *altiplano*.

Critical Thinking:
MAKING JUDGMENTS

O Ask students if they agree with Yossi's reasoning. Would they have spent a day trying to find the life pack or would they have set out immediately for Curiplaya? *(Possible responses: yes, because without food Yossi won't have the strength to walk; no, the sooner he gets to a settlement of some sort, the better off he is; if he doesn't find the life pack, he will have wasted an entire day.)*

Literary Note

P Kevin did eventually find Yossi, but not for another 19 days. Kevin was swept into the river, and the current rushed him downstream past Yossi. Eventually someone along the riverbank spotted Kevin and rescued him. Kevin then organized a search party organized by a guide named Tico Tudela. Today, Tico has transformed his knowledge of the Bolivian jungle into a thriving adventure tourism business. Each year, he takes hundreds of tourists up the Tuichi river, teaching them survival skills like the ones Yossi used to stay alive during his ordeal.

---

that that had been the *mal paso*, and Curiplaya was supposed to be not far from the pass, on the right bank, the bank I was standing on. There was a chance that I could make it there. There were cabins and equipment in Curiplaya. Karl had said that there was also a banana grove. And from Curiplaya it was four days' walk to San José de Uchupiamonas.[15] There should even be a path cut through the jungle. I allowed myself to feel optimistic. I could do it. Not more than one day's walk to Curiplaya and from there on a path to San José. There might even be someone left in Curiplaya.

I hunted around for something for breakfast but found nothing. I decided to try to retrieve the pack once again. It would be worth investing an entire day looking for it as long as there was even the slightest chance of finding it. There was food in the pack, along with matches, a map, and a flashlight. If I could only find it, I'd be set.

It was no easy task. I started walking upriver. The route took me over jagged cliffs and smooth rock faces. I walked for two hours, climbing higher to progress and then back down to see if I could reach the shore. The stony walls were steep and smooth. I lost my footing a few times but luckily was caught by trees and bushes. Finally, from a cliff that towered fifty feet over the river, I spotted the raft in the water, still beating against the rocks. I was positive that the pack must be nearby.

At that point the bank of the river was a thin strip of land. I had no choice but to take the risk and started slowly climbing down, clawing at the sharp rocks. I took tiny steps, groping with my foot for a hold that would support my weight, my body covered with cold sweat. I said a silent prayer, *Don't slip. Don't fall.* If I broke an arm or leg, I didn't stand a chance. The last time I had gone rock climbing, I had fallen but had been saved by a miracle: Uncle Nissim's little book had been in my pocket. Now it was in the backpack. I should never have left it there.

It was still raining, hadn't let up at all since yesterday. The stones were damp and slick, but I kept climbing. My pants caught on a jagged edge and ripped. My knee was scratched, my fingers bloody. The strain on my legs was tremendous, terribly painful. I could tell that the rash was spreading over my wet feet again. When I was about ten feet above the ground, I turned and slid down the rock face on my rear end. My back was scraped, but I landed safely on the riverbank. I started searching, skipping over rocks until I reached the raft.

It was hard to believe, but the raft was still in one piece. All seven logs were still bound together. . . .

Before I began my search for the pack, I secured the raft well, just in case I met up with Kevin and the two of us might make use of it. I looked around among the rocks and crevices, and there, about ten yards away, in the cleft of a small rock, sat the precious pack, soaking wet but still afloat.

Thank you, God.

Words could not describe my happiness. I laid down on the rock and fished the pack out of the river and hurriedly opened it. I was saved! The contents were only slightly damp. The rubber bag had protected them well. There was everything: rice and beans, the flashlight and matches, the lighter, map, mosquito netting, red poncho, medicines, and, most important, my wallet with Uncle Nissim's little book. Now I wouldn't die. I felt safe. . . .

Somebody up there likes me, I thought. *Just let Kevin find me.*

Up until now I had thought him the better off of the two of us—at least he had the machete—but now I was a wealthy man, and he, poor guy, had only the clothes on his back. Poor Kevin had nothing; he must need me. I had food and could start a fire. He just had

---

15. **San José de Uchupiamonas** (sän hô-sě' dě ōō'chōō-pē-ä-mô'näs): Yossi and Kevin's final destination.

Three weeks after becoming separated from Kevin, Yossi Ghinsberg was rescued. His poncho had been dinner for millions of termites that had invaded his final campsite. Courtesy of Yossi Ghinsberg.

to find me. Without me he didn't have a chance.

It was still pouring rain, and I shivered with cold. I hurriedly closed the pack and set it down in a niche of the cliff. I kept only the poncho to protect me from the rain. Then it occurred to me that I should hang it up in some conspicuous place. It was bright red and might catch Kevin's eye. I saw a crag jutting prominently over the river. I climbed up to it and spread the poncho out over it, weighting it down with heavy stones so that it wouldn't blow away in the wind. Again I called out to Kevin, but I knew the shouts were pointless. The roar of the water was deafening, and there was no chance of anyone's hearing me.

On my way back to the pack I noticed a few yellow fruits lying on the shore and stopped to pick them up. Most of them were rotten, but I found one hard, fresh fruit and took a bite. It was delicious. I looked up and spotted the source: a tree laden with wild yellow plums at the edge of the stone wall.

Someone really is looking out for me, I thought.

I looked for a way up to the tree and found a slight hollow in the rock face where the rainwater ran off the mountain and down to the river. It was wet and slippery, but the incline was not so steep there. I had almost reached the tree—just a few more steps—when I saw a snake. It was green and coiled and just a few inches from my foot. I recognized it immediately as the deadly lora. Karl had told me they could blind their victims by spraying venom even from a distance.

I froze in my place. The snake, too, was motionless. Only its tongue flicked in and out of

BACK FROM TUICHI **865**

Mini-Lesson The Writer's Style

SHOWING ACTION THROUGH DETAIL
Adventure stories, like many others, rely on a sequence of details to show action. Direct students' attention to the passage on this page that begins "On my way back to the pack." Point out that in this passage Ghinsberg describes a series of details that culminate in his encounter with the snake. First he notices the fruit and tries one, then he spots the tree, then he figures out how to climb up towards it, and then he spots the snake. Instead of just writing, "I went to pick fruit and encountered a snake," he shows what happens through a series of details.

Application Invite students to write brief descriptions of an adventure, using details to show the action. Encourage them to read their writing aloud to the class.

Reteaching/Reinforcement
- *Writing Handbook,* anthology pp. 1029–1032
- *Writing Mini-Lessons* transparencies, p. 42

Adequate Detail, pp. 405–406

Literary Concept: SUSPENSE

Q Ask students to discuss how Ghinsberg builds suspense in this scene. *(Possible responses: The reader thinks that things will finally get easier for Yossi because he has nearly reached the fruit tree, then the reader is surprised by the snake.)*

CUSTOMIZING FOR
Gifted and Talented Students

Have students create a list of items for a life pack they would take into the Bolivian jungle, based upon what they have read about Yossi's experiences. *(Students' lists might include the things in Yossi's pack as well as snakebite venom, warm or waterproof clothing, insect repellent, anti-fungal and anti-bacterial creams, and a compass.)*

Literary Concept: SETTING

R Have students discuss whether or not this story would be as effective if it were set somewhere else, such as the American Rockies. Ask them to cite details from the story to support their opinions. *(Accept all reasonable responses.)*

STRATEGIC READING FOR
Less-Proficient Readers

S Have students describe what happens to Yossi while he is waiting for Kevin to catch up with him. *(He sets up shelter for the night and retrieves the life pack the next day. He tries to pick some yellow fruit and encounters a deadly snake, which he kills. On the second night he sets up camp again and waits for Kevin.)* **Summarizing**

EDITOR'S NOTE With the permission of the author or copyright holder, potentially offensive material has been deleted from the selection.

COMPREHENSION CHECK

1. What are Yossi and Kevin preparing to do at the beginning of the story? *(raft down the Tuichi river)*
2. How do the two become separated? *(Kevin swims ashore to see if they can travel overland. While he is gone, the raft breaks free of its mooring with Yossi on it.)*
3. What happens to Yossi when he is alone on the raft? *(He plunges down a waterfall and is thrown off the raft. He nearly drowns.)*
4. What piece of good luck befalls Yossi after he is washed ashore? *(He finds the raft with the life pack.)*
5. What happens when Yossi tries to pick fruit from a tree? *(He encounters a lora, a deadly tree snake.)*

---

its mouth. It held the upper half of its body erect. I was afraid to move a muscle, but my fear and desperation soon turned to hatred. I took a step backward, picked up a huge rock, and flung it at the snake. Its body convulsed and then thickened, as if tied in knots. I picked up a flat, narrow rock, bent over, and started hitting the snake in a rage, over and over, until I'd sliced its head from its body. I was trembling, knowing that if the snake had bitten me, I would have died.

I picked up its green body and peeled its skin like a banana, revealing its pinkish flesh. I cleaned the internal organs out with one flick of my finger and was left holding the flesh. What should I do with it? Eat it or use it for bait? I threw it down to the riverbank. I would decide what to do with it after I got down.

R I went over to the fruit tree, looking cautiously before every step. The lora was a tree climber, and I was afraid its mate might be nearby. I climbed up into the tree, eating ripe fruit as I went. The tree was heavily laden, but I had competition: tiny yellow ants swarmed on the trunk. I was all too familiar with them: fire ants. They stung me all over, but I didn't give in to them. I hurriedly picked as much fruit as I could, tossing it down to the riverbank. Then I climbed down and shook the cursed ants off. I felt as if I was on fire but was glad I hadn't let them drive me away. Now I would eat my fill.

Down on the riverbank I took one of the large tin cans that had been tied to the pack. It had two cups and a spoon inside. I drank from the river and then gathered up the fruit, filling the can with those I didn't eat.

I no longer had any desire to make a meal of the snake. I couldn't have started a fire anyway, because everything was still damp, and I certainly wasn't about to eat it raw. I found the fishing line in the pack, but the river was too rocky and the water too turbulent to fish.

I sat on the pack awhile, leaning against the cliff, the rain still beating down on me. Kevin couldn't have continued walking along the riverbank, I reasoned, so he must be walking up on the ledge above the stone walls. There wasn't much chance of his seeing the poncho from there. I couldn't see any point in waiting by the river any longer. I might as well climb up to the ledge myself. I retrieved the poncho, folded it into the pack, put the pack on my back, and started scaling the wall back toward the plum tree.

Marching the length of the ledge, I searched for a cranny that would shelter me for the night and found an ideal place: a shallow niche cut into the stone wall about six feet above ground level. I climbed up to it. I would have liked to have started a fire now that I had matches and a lighter, but all the branches were wet, so I abandoned the idea.

In the second tin I discovered a large lump of salt, some spices, garlic cloves, and three lemons. I had a well-balanced supper: one lemon, three cloves of garlic, a pinch of salt, and a handful of the plumlike fruit.

This night was kinder to me than the last one had been. I covered myself with the two mosquito nets, which, although damp, were comforting. I spread the poncho over them and covered my face with its hood. I breathed into the hood, and waves of warmth spread over my body.

What if Kevin doesn't make it here? I asked myself.

Tomorrow I will check the map, try to figure out approximately where I am and how far it is to San José. I'll spend tomorrow here waiting for Kevin, and if he doesn't show up, then I'll set out myself on the following day.

During the night I started hallucinating. Kevin was calling in desperation, *Help! Help! Yossi, save me. Wait for me. Don't leave, Yossi! Yossi! Help!*

I was sweating under my wet clothes. ❖

S *Translated by Yael Politis and Stanley Young*

866 UNIT SIX PART 1: A STRENGTH FROM WITHIN

Mini-Lesson — Literary Concepts

REVIEWING SETTING Remind students that the setting of a true-life adventure is the time and place in which the adventure occurs. Usually, the setting plays an important part in true-life adventures because the protagonist is battling against a force of nature. The settings of true-life adventures, unlike those of fiction, are limited to real places and always take place in the past.

Application Have students work in small groups to make a chart, like the one shown, to identify the different ways that the setting affects this selection.

You might get students started by telling them one effect of the story's setting is Yossi's complete isolation after he is separated from Kevin.

Setting Element	How It Affects the Story

RESPONDING OPTIONS

FROM PERSONAL RESPONSE TO CRITICAL ANALYSIS

REFLECT
1. What feelings did you experience while reading the selection? Describe your reaction in your notebook, and share your writing with a classmate.

RETHINK
2. How would you rate this selection as an adventure story? Consider the ingredients for a good adventure story that you identified in the Personal Connection on page 855.
3. What do you think was the most difficult challenge that Yossi Ghinsberg faced? Explain your opinion.
4. What sort of person does Yossi Ghinsberg reveal himself to be?

   Consider
   - how he responds to danger and adversity
   - his thoughts in italics
   - why he repeats "man of action"
   - his relationship with Kevin

   Close Textual Reading

RELATE
5. How does Yossi Ghinsberg compare to your personal definition of a hero? Use evidence from the story to support your point of view.
6. Why do you think some people have such a strong need for adventure, while others have little desire for such experiences?

LITERARY CONCEPTS

A **true-life adventure** is a nonfiction account of heroic deeds or exciting adventures, usually organized chronologically. Often, a true-life adventure is narrated from the first-person point of view, presenting the experience as it happened to the writer. A true-life adventure may also be written from a third-person point of view, as reported to the writer. Choose an exciting passage from this selection and rewrite it from a third-person point of view. Discuss the differences between the two versions.

CONCEPT REVIEW: Suspense How does Yossi Ghinsberg create suspense in Back from Tuichi? At what point or points did the tension reach a peak?

Multimodal Learning
ANOTHER PATHWAY
Cooperative Learning

Working with a group of your classmates, review the story to see which of Kevin's and Yossi's actions require physical prowess and which require clever thinking. Create a chart like the one shown to report your findings. Then discuss which of these abilities is more important in a test of survival.

Physical Ability	Mental Ability

QUICKWRITES

1. Write the **book jacket copy** for *Back from Tuichi* on the basis of what you know about the book from the Biographical Connection on page 855 and from the selection.
2. Read the rest of *Back from Tuichi* and share your opinion of Yossi's adventures in a **book report**. If possible, use a computer to compose and edit your draft.
3. Draft your own **true-life adventure**. The notes you made for the Writing Connection on page 855 can help you to get started.

📁 **PORTFOLIO** Save your writing. You may want to use it later as a springboard to a piece for your portfolio.

From Personal Response to Critical Analysis

1. All responses are valid.
2. Possible responses: It's a good adventure story because it has an exciting plot, interesting characters, an exotic setting, and suspense; it's not a very good adventure story because the reader knows from the beginning that Yossi will be fine.
3. Possible responses: surviving the waterfall; finding food; facing the jungle alone; maintaining mental focus in the face of disaster; battling the snake
4. Possible responses: warm and caring; slightly dependent on Kevin and unsure of himself; optimistic; scared and uncertain
5. Possible responses: He is a hero because he adapts to face unexpected challenges; he isn't a hero because the only person he is saving is himself, and he often breaks down and shows fear.
6. Accept all reasonable, well-supported responses.

Another Pathway
Cooperative Learning A direction-giver can explain the assignment and monitor its completion; recorders can create the chart; and an extender can lead students into the discussion about the importance of each in a test of survival.

Rubric
3 **Full Accomplishment** Charts are thorough and contain most story details; discussions are even-handed and in-depth.
2 **Substantial Accomplishment** Charts leave out some story details; discussions are dominated by only a few students.
1 **Little or Partial Accomplishment** Charts are incomplete and lacking in many story details; students have trouble starting discussions and keeping to the subject.

Literary Concepts
Some students may feel that the passages written in the third-person lack the immediacy and excitement of the original, while others may feel that there is greater suspense in the third-person passages because readers don't know if Yossi will make it out alive.

Suspense He creates suspense by setting up situations about which the reader is unsure of the outcome. Students might feel that the tension reached a peak when the raft breaks free and Yossi goes through the Mal Paso San Pedro or when he encounters the lora.

QuickWrites
1. Remind students that book jacket copy is meant to entice readers and should emphasize the most exciting or interesting points of a story.
2. Students should keep the summaries in their book reports brief. Remind them that the book reports should include their personal responses to the story.
3. Encourage students to make use of sensory details to make the adventure come alive for the reader.

The Writer's Craft
Interpretive Essay, pp. 238–253

Critic's Corner

Some students may agree with the reviewer and cite Yossi's loyalty to Kevin and the description of his ordeal to support their opinion. Others may feel that this excerpt doesn't necessarily bear out the reviewer's comments because students don't know the whole story and therefore cannot judge the accuracy of the reviewers' comment.

Across the Curriculum

Science Have students do research to find out more about the rain forest ecosystem that Yossi encountered during his ordeal. Suggest they look for answers to questions like these: What is the average temperature? What is the average daily rainfall? What is the terrain like? What kinds of animals live in this type of rain forest?

YOSSI GHINSBERG

Yossi and Kevin have remained close friends, their ordeal creating a unique bond between them. Yossi also didn't give up the search for Marcus and Karl, presumed dead by the Bolivian authorities. After he was rescued, Yossi met Marcus's mother, who insisted her son was still alive. Partly at her urging, he followed a few faint leads that he had about the two men, including a supposed sighting of Karl in a remote Peruvian village. Unfortunately, their fate still remains a mystery.

Multimodal Learning

ALTERNATIVE ACTIVITIES

1. With a partner, create a **map** of Yossi's harrowing journey on the river. Review the story for details about the locations where events take place. You may also invent details if needed.
2. Present an **oral reading** of an excerpt from the selection. Let the expression in your voice capture the excitement of Yossi's adventure and his changing emotions as the selection unfolds.

CRITIC'S CORNER

A reviewer once described *Back from Tuichi* as "no ordinary autobiographical travel book" and further observed, "The need for loyalty and the extremes of physical and emotional limits are vividly portrayed." Do you think this assessment applies to the excerpt you just read of *Back from Tuichi*? Cite details to support your opinion.

YOSSI GHINSBERG

Born and raised in Israel, Yossi Ghinsberg grew up devouring classic adventure novels. His appetite for adventure was further whetted during his years in the Israeli navy, when he visited the Red Sea and the Sinai Desert. The spirit of adventure then took him to Europe and the Americas, where his temporary jobs included employment as a construction worker in Norway, a fisherman in Alaska, and a cook in New York City.

1959–

Yossi Ghinsberg's travels in South America almost claimed his life. After he was separated from Kevin on the Tuichi River, he spent 20 days struggling to survive in the rain forest with almost no food, supplies, or protection against the elements. The obstacles he encountered included incessant rain, termites, leeches, snakes, and jaguars. Luckily, Kevin found his way back to civilization and formed a rescue party that saved Yossi's life in the nick of time. Karl and Marcus were not so lucky; they vanished without a trace. *Back from Tuichi*, which was published in Israel in 1985, proved so popular that it was translated into several languages.

Although Ghinsberg returned to Israel to study at Tel Aviv University, he was drawn back to the South American rain forest. There he helped establish the Chalalan Project, an environmental organization that seeks to preserve the Tuichi valley economy without endangering its ecosystem. He also founded a pharmaceutical company that works hand in hand with the native people of the rain forest.

Alternative Activities

1. Remind students to include a map key, scale, and compass rose, if possible. Students may also wish to consult maps of Bolivia or of the Amazon basin.
2. Encourage students to vary their inflection and tone to help capture the excitement of their excerpt. Some students may wish to choose music to use as background accompaniment while they read.

PREVIEWING

DRAMA

The Ring of General Macías (mä-sē′äs)

Josephina Niggli Mexico / United States

Activating Prior Knowledge
PERSONAL CONNECTION

What does honor mean to you? Discuss the concept of honor with a small group of your classmates. Use a spider map like the one shown to explore the concept from different angles. Then compare your group's diagram to those produced by other groups.

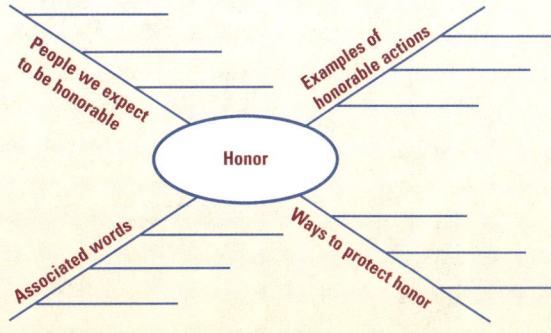

Building Background
HISTORICAL CONNECTION

Honor is central to the play you are about to read, which takes place during the Mexican Revolution (1910–1917). The Revolution began as a revolt by impoverished peasants against wealthy landowners. It called for an end to oppression suffered under the dictatorship of Porfirio Díaz (pôr-fēr′yô dē′äs) and the formation of a new government that would redistribute land so that everyone would have a fair share. A group called the Federalists opposed the uprising and fought to protect Mexico's existing government and way of life.

Detail of *The People in Arms*, 1957, David Alfáro Siqueiros, fresco, Museo Nacional de Historia, Mexico City (INAH).

Setting a Purpose
READING CONNECTION

Visualizing Drama Every drama is a story that is meant to be performed in front of a live audience. As you read *The Ring of General Macías*, which focuses on the concept of honor, try to visualize the play in performance in order to fully appreciate the story. Pay careful attention to the description of the setting and the stage directions, noting any indications of stage props or scenery. Imagine the kinds of actors needed for the characters' roles; decide how the actors might be dressed and what facial expressions, gestures, and movements they might use to portray the characters effectively.

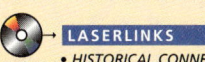

LASERLINKS
• HISTORICAL CONNECTION

869

OVERVIEW

Objectives
- To understand and appreciate a drama that explores different ideas of love, strength, and courage
- To understand and appreciate the use of a foil
- To express understanding of the drama through a choice of writing forms, including a letter, a psychological profile, and a speech
- To extend understanding of the drama through a variety of multimodal and cross-curricular activities

Skills

LITERARY CONCEPTS
- Foil
- Stage directions
- Character

READING SKILLS/STRATEGIES
- Visualizing drama

GENRE STUDY
- Drama: one-act play

GRAMMAR
- Sentence fragments

SPEAKING, LISTENING, AND VIEWING
- Speech
- Group discussion

HISTORICAL CONNECTION
The Mexican Revolution From 1910 to 1917, Mexican peasants fought to end the oppression they suffered under Mexico's wealthy landowners. These rare photographs of battles, encampments, and rebel and government leaders during the Mexican Revolution will provide students with historical context for understanding the characters and events in *The Ring of General Macías*.

Side A, Frame 49694

CUSTOMIZING FOR
Students Acquiring English

- Use **ACCESS FOR STUDENTS ACQUIRING ENGLISH**, *Reading Support*.
- The dialogue in this play contains only a few challenging words. Students may enjoy reading aloud the words of one of the characters with a partner taking the other role. Help them choose appropriate passages and provide encouragement and feedback as needed.
- As you guide students through the selection, you may want to use the suggestions in these boxes as well as the suggestions under Strategic Reading for Less-Proficient Readers.

PRINT AND MEDIA RESOURCES

UNIT SIX RESOURCE BOOK
Strategic Reading: Literature, p. 25
Vocabulary SkillBuilder, p. 26

GRAMMAR MINI-LESSONS
Transparencies, p. 1
Copymasters, p. 1

WRITING MINI-LESSONS
Transparencies, p. 56

ACCESS FOR STUDENTS ACQUIRING ENGLISH
Selection Summaries
Reading Support

FORMAL ASSESSMENT
Selection Test, p. 173
 Test Generator

 AUDIO LIBRARY
See Reference Card

 LASERLINKS
Historical Connection
Art Gallery

The Ring of General Macías

Josephina Niggli

SUMMARY

As this play opens, Raquel Rivera de Macías, wife of General Macías of the Mexican federal army, takes a bottle of poison away from her recently widowed sister-in-law, Marica, who is contemplating suicide. Presently, two revolutionaries appear at the patio door and demand sanctuary. They display the general's wedding ring and say that if they die, the general will be killed too. When federal soldiers arrive, Raquel cleverly protects the revolutionaries for the sake of her husband. Then she learns that he willingly gave up his ring to save his own life, even though he knew his actions would help the enemy gain important information. When the revolutionaries are not looking, Raquel poisons the wine and offers it to the revolutionaries. The two men drink the poisoned wine and die.

Thematic Link: *A Strength from Within*
A woman must find the strength to condemn her beloved husband to death for the sake of a worthy cause.

STRATEGIC READING FOR
Less-Proficient Readers

Set a Purpose Have students read to find out about the difficulties that Rachel and Marica are facing.

Use **UNIT SIX RESOURCE BOOK,** p. 25, for guidance in reading the selection.

Literary Concept:
STAGE DIRECTIONS

Ⓐ Ask students what the description of General Macías' home suggests about his status. (*Possible responses: He is wealthy; he is formal and educated; he is cultured.*)

CAST OF CHARACTERS

Marica (mä-rē′kä), the sister of General Macías
Raquel (rä-kĕl′), the wife of General Macías
Andrés de la O (än-drĕs′ dĕ-lä-ô′), a captain in the revolutionary army
Cleto (clĕ′tô), a private in the revolutionary army
Basilio Flores (bä-sē′lē-ô flô′rĕs), a captain in the federal army

Place: Just outside Mexico City
Time: A night in April, 1912.

The living room of General Macías' home is luxuriously furnished in the gold and ornate style of Louis XVI. In the right wall are French windows leading into the patio. Flanking these windows are low bookcases. In the back wall is, right, a closet door; and, center, a table holding a wine decanter and glasses. The left wall has a door upstage, and downstage a writing desk with a straight chair in front of it. Near the desk is an armchair. Down right is a small sofa with a table holding a lamp at the upstage end of it. There are pictures on the walls. The room looks rather stuffy and unlived in.

870 UNIT SIX PART 1: A STRENGTH FROM WITHIN

WORDS TO KNOW

farce (färs) *n.* a ludicrous, empty show; a mockery (p. 875)
ostentatiously (ŏs′tĕn-tā′shəs-lē) *adv.* in a showy manner that is meant to impress others (p. 874)
regally (rē′gəl-ē) *adv.* in a splendid or stately manner, as befitting a king or queen (p. 874)

sanctuary (săngk′chōō-ĕr′ē) *n.* a place of refuge, protection, and safety (p. 875)
stealthily (stĕl′thə-lē) *adv.* in a quiet, cautious, or secretive manner intended to avoid notice (p. 872)

Self-Portrait (1926), Frida Kahlo. Oil on canvas, 31″ × 23″, private collection, Mexico City.

CUSTOMIZING FOR
Gifted and Talented Students

As students read the selection, have them think about what the ring of the title might symbolize. *(Possible responses: love, honor, courage)*

Art Note

***Self-Portrait* by Frida Kahlo** Growing up in Mexico City during the Mexican Revolution, Kahlo suffered a terrible accident at the age of 18 that crippled her and left her in pain for most of her life. Her marriage to fellow-painter Diego Rivera was legendary for its passion and obsessive jealousy. This 1926 portrait is the first of Kahlo's self-portraits. This one, painted in an attempt to win back a lover, foreshadows the emotional tension that would become typical of her style.

Reading the Art *What is your impression of the subject of this painting? Why?*

Linking to History

The Mexican Revolution was not the first time that Mexicans took up arms to defend their rights. The history of Mexico is marked by battles against the imperial rule of Spain. Mexico was under Spanish rule from the early 16th century until the rebellion that lasted from 1810 to 1821. When independence was finally declared, Mexicans established their own empire, but a period of strife lasted for the next several decades. In 1857, a constitutional democracy was created; except for a three-year period from 1864 to 1867, Mexico was ruled by two presidents: Benito Juarez and Porfirio Diaz. During Diaz's presidency, from 1876 to 1910, conditions deteriorated, culminating in the Mexican Revolution.

CUSTOMIZING FOR
Students Acquiring English

1 If you have any Spanish speakers in the class, ask them to pronounce aloud the names of the characters appearing in or mentioned in the play.

Critical Thinking:
COMPARING/ CONTRASTING

B Contrast the views of war expressed by Marica and Raquel. Which views do you agree with more? *(Students should give reasons for their opinions.)*

When the curtains part, the stage is in darkness save for the moonlight that comes through the French windows. Then the house door opens, and a young girl in negligee enters stealthily. *She is carrying a lighted candle. She stands at the door a moment listening for possible pursuit, then moves quickly across to the bookcase down right. She puts the candle on top of the bookcase and begins searching behind the books. She finally finds what she wants: a small bottle. While she is searching, the house door opens silently and a woman, also in negligee, enters. (These negligees are in the latest Parisian style.) She moves silently across the room to the table by the sofa, and as the girl turns with the bottle, the woman switches on the light. The girl gives a half-scream and draws back, frightened. The light reveals her to be quite young—no more than twenty—a timid, dovelike creature. The woman has a queenly air, and whether she is actually beautiful or not, people think she is. She is about thirty-two.*

1 Marica (*trying to hide the bottle behind her*). Raquel! What are you doing here?

Raquel. What did you have hidden behind the books, Marica?

Marica (*attempting a forced laugh*). I? Nothing. Why do you think I have anything?

Raquel (*taking a step toward her*). Give it to me.

Marica (*backing away from her*). No. No, I won't.

Raquel (*stretching out her hand*). I demand that you give it to me.

Marica. You have no right to order me about. I'm a married woman. I . . . I . . . (*She begins to sob and flings herself down on the sofa.*)

Raquel (*much gentler*). You shouldn't be up. The doctor told you to stay in bed. (*She bends over Marica and gently takes the bottle out of the girl's hand.*) It was poison. I thought so.

Marica (*frightened*). You won't tell the priest, will you?

Raquel. Suicide is a sin, Marica. A sin against God.

Marica. I know. I . . . (*She catches* Raquel's *hand.*) Oh, Raquel, why do we have to have wars? Why do men have to go to war and be killed?

Raquel. Men must fight for what they believe is right. It is an honorable thing to die for your country as a soldier.

Marica. How can you say that with Domingo out there fighting, too? And fighting what? Men who aren't even men. Peasants. Ranch slaves. Men who shouldn't be allowed to fight.

Raquel. Peasants are men, Marica. Not animals.

Marica. Men. It's always men. But how about the women? What becomes of us?

Raquel. We can pray.

Marica (*bitterly*). Yes, we can pray. And then comes the terrible news, and it's no use praying anymore. All the reason for our praying is dead. Why should I go on living with Tomás dead?

Raquel. Living is a duty.

Marica. How can you be so cold, so hard? You are a cold and hard woman, Raquel. My brother worships you. He has never even looked at another woman since the first day he saw you. Does he know how cold and hard you are?

Raquel. Domingo is my—honored husband.

Marica. You've been married for ten years. And I've been married for three months. If Domingo is killed, it won't be the same for you. You've had ten years. (*She is crying wildly.*) I haven't anything . . . anything at all.

Raquel. You've had three months—three months of laughter. And now you have tears. How lucky you are. You have tears. Perhaps five months of tears. Not more. You're only twenty. In five months Tomás will become just a lovely memory.

Marica. I'll remember Tomás all my life.

Raquel. Of course. But he'll be distant and far

B

WORDS TO KNOW

stealthily (stĕl′thə-lē) *adv.* in a quiet, cautious, or secretive manner intended to avoid notice

872

Mini-Lesson   Grammar

SENTENCE FRAGMENTS Sentence fragments are groups of words that don't express complete thoughts and therefore don't make up complete sentences. Although as a rule they should be avoided in essays, they are often used in dialogue to make characters' speech sound realistic. Point out the sentence fragment Raquel uses in response to Marica's remark about peasants, where she says "Peasants are men, Marica. Not animals." The first part of her statement is both a complete thought and a complete sentence. The second part, however, is not a complete thought but an addition to the thought she has just stated. It is a sentence fragment.

Application Invite students to use complete sentences and sentence fragments to create dialogues that might take place between Raquel and General Macías if they met one last time.

Reteaching/Reinforcement
- Grammar Handbook, anthology p. 1058
- *Grammar Mini-Lessons* copymasters p. 1, transparencies p. 1

Sentence Fragments, pp. 631–636

872 THE LANGUAGE OF LITERATURE   TEACHER'S EDITION

away. But you're young . . . and the young need laughter. The young can't live on tears. And one day in Paris, or Rome, or even Mexico City, you'll meet another man. You'll marry again. There will be children in your house. How lucky you are.

Marica. I'll never marry again.

Raquel. You're only twenty. You'll think differently when you're twenty-eight, or nine, or thirty.

Marica. What will you do if Domingo is killed?

Raquel. I shall be very proud that he died in all his courage . . . in all the greatness of a hero.

Marica. But you'd not weep, would you? Not you! I don't think there are any tears in you.

Raquel. No, I'd not weep. I'd sit here in this empty house and wait.

Marica. Wait for what?

Raquel. For the jingle of his spurs as he walks across the tiled hall. For the sound of his laughter in the patio. For the echo of his voice as he shouts to the groom to put away his horse. For the feel of his hand . . .

Marica (*screams*). Stop it!

Raquel. I'm sorry.

Marica. You do love him, don't you?

Raquel. I don't think even he knows how much.

Marica. I thought that after ten years people slid away from love. But you and Domingo—why, you're all he thinks about. When he's away from you he talks about you all the time. I heard him say once that when you were out of his sight he was like a man without eyes or ears or hands.

Raquel. I know. I, too, know that feeling.

Marica. Then how could you let him go to war? Perhaps to be killed? How could you?

Raquel (*sharply*). Marica, you are of the family Macías. Your family is a family of great warriors. A Macías man was with Ferdinand when the Moors[1] were driven out of Spain. A Macías man was with Cortés when the Aztecans[2] surrendered. Your grandfather fought in the War of Independence.[3] Your own father was executed not twenty miles from this house by the French. Shall his son be any less brave because he loves a woman?

Marica. But Domingo loved you enough to forget that. If you had asked him, he wouldn't have gone to war. He would have stayed here with you.

Raquel. No, he would not have stayed. Your brother is a man of honor, not a whining, creeping coward.

Marica (*beginning to cry again*). I begged Tomás not to go. I begged him.

Raquel. Would you have loved him if he had stayed?

Marica. I don't know. I don't know.

Raquel. There is your answer. You'd have despised him. Loved and despised him. Now come, Marica, it's time for you to go to bed.

Marica. You won't tell the priest—about the poison, I mean?

Raquel. No. I won't tell him.

Marica. Thank you, Raquel. How good you are. How kind and good.

Raquel. A moment ago I was hard and cruel. What a baby you are. Now, off to bed with you.

Marica. Aren't you coming upstairs, too?

Raquel. No . . . I haven't been sleeping very well lately. I think I'll read for a little while.

Marica. Good night, Raquel. And thank you.

---

1. **Moors:** Moslem people from northwest Africa whose kingdom in Spain was defeated by Ferdinand of Aragon in 1492.
2. **Aztecans** (ăz'tĕk'ənz): people who lived in central Mexico and had an advanced civilization before the conquest of Mexico by Cortés in 1519.
3. **War of Independence:** the revolution (1810–1821) in which Mexico gained its independence from Spain.

STRATEGIC READING FOR
Less-Proficient Readers

E Make sure that students understand the situations that Rachel and Marica are in.

- Why does Marica want to kill herself? *(Her new husband has been killed in the war.)* **Clarifying**

- What kind of relationship does Raquel have with her husband? *(loving, passionate)* **Noting Relevant Details**

- Why did Raquel let her husband go off to war if she loved him so much? *(She knew that fighting was the honorable thing to do; she knew she could not have respected him if he didn't fight.)* **Clarifying**

Set a Purpose Have students read to find out what happens after Marica goes to bed.

Literary Concept:
STAGE DIRECTIONS

F Ask students what this stage direction shows about Raquel's character. *(Possible responses: She has enormous self-control; she is brave; she is used to giving orders.)*

Literary Concept: DIALOGUE

G Ask students what they think the conversation between Andrés and Raquel reveals about the problem between the classes. *(Possible responses: The classes have contempt for one another; the rift between the classes is very large.)*

E **Raquel.** Good night, little one.

(*Marica goes out through the house door left, taking her candle with her.* Raquel *stares down at the bottle of poison in her hand, then puts it away in one of the small drawers of the desk. She next selects a book from the downstage case and sits on the sofa to read it, but feeling chilly, she rises and goes to the closet, back right, and takes out an afghan.*[4] *Coming back to the sofa, she makes herself comfortable, with the afghan across her knees. Suddenly she hears a noise in the patio. She listens, then, convinced it is nothing, returns to her reading. But she hears the noise again. She goes to the patio door and peers out.*)

Raquel (*calling softly*). Who's there? Who's out there? Oh! (*She gasps and backs into the room. Two men—or rather a man and a young boy—dressed in the white pajama suits of the Mexican peasants, with their sombreros*[5] *tipped low over their faces, come into the room.* Raquel *draws herself up* regally. *Her voice is cold and commanding.*) **F** Who are you, and what do you want here?

Andrés. We are hunting for the wife of General Macías.

Raquel. I am Raquel Rivera de Macías.

Andrés. Cleto, stand guard in the patio. If you hear any suspicious noise, warn me at once.

Cleto. Yes, my captain. (*The boy returns to the patio.*)

(*The man, hooking his thumbs in his belt, strolls around the room, looking it over. When he reaches the table at the back he sees the wine. With a small bow to* Raquel *he pours himself a glass of wine and drains it. He wipes his mouth with the back of his hand.*)

Raquel. How very interesting.

Andrés (*startled*). What?

Raquel. To be able to drink wine with that hat on.

Andrés. The hat? Oh, forgive me, señora. (*He flicks the brim with his fingers so that it drops off his head and dangles down his back from the neck cord.*) In a military camp one forgets one's polite manners. Would you care to join me in another glass?

Raquel (*sitting on the sofa*). Why not? It's my wine.

Andrés. And very excellent wine. (*He pours two glasses and gives her one while he is talking.*) I would say amontillado of the vintage of '87.[6]

Raquel. Did you learn that in a military camp?

Andrés. I used to sell wines . . . among other things.

Raquel (ostentatiously *hiding a yawn*). I am devastated.

Andrés (*pulls over the armchair and makes himself comfortable in it*). You don't mind, do you?

Raquel. Would it make any difference if I did?

Andrés. No. The Federals are searching the streets for us, and we have to stay somewhere. But women of your class seem to expect that senseless sort of question. **G**

Raquel. Of course I suppose I could scream.

Andrés. Naturally.

Raquel. My sister-in-law is upstairs asleep. And there are several servants in the back of the house. Mostly men servants. Very big men.

Andrés. Very interesting. (*He is drinking the wine in small sips with much enjoyment.*)

Raquel. What would you do if I screamed?

Andrés (*considering the request as though it were another glass of wine*). Nothing.

Raquel. I am afraid you are lying to me.

Andrés. Women of your class seem to expect polite little lies.

---

4. **afghan** (ăf´găn): a crocheted or knitted blanket.
5. **sombreros** (sŏm-brâr´ōz): broad-brimmed, high-crowned straw or felt hats, traditionally worn by peasants in Mexico.
6. **amontillado** (ə-mŏn´tl-ä´dō) . . . '87: a pale, dry sherry bottled in 1887.

> **WORDS TO KNOW**
> **regally** (rē´gəl-ē) *adv.* in a splendid or stately manner, as befitting a king or queen
> **ostentatiously** (ŏs´tĕn-tā´shəs-lē) *adv.* in a showy manner that is meant to impress others

874

Mini-Lesson   Literary Concepts

REVIEWING STAGE DIRECTIONS Remind students that stage directions are instructions included in the scripts of plays that describe how actors should move and speak. They also describe the setting, or stage set, and any props that are necessary to the play. Some stage directions also include instructions for lighting, music, and sound effects.

Application Have students look back through the play and compile a list of the information about characters and setting that the reader gets from the stage directions. Then have them discuss whether such information could have been communicated in other ways.

874 THE LANGUAGE OF LITERATURE **TEACHER'S EDITION**

Raquel. Stop calling me "woman of your class."

Andrés. Forgive me.

Raquel. You are one of the fighting peasants, aren't you?

Andrés. I am a captain in the revolutionary army.

Raquel. This house is completely loyal to the federal government.

Andrés. I know. That's why I'm here.

Raquel. And now that you are here, just what do you expect me to do?

Andrés. I expect you to offer <u>sanctuary</u> to myself and to Cleto.

Raquel. Cleto? (*She looks toward the patio and adds sarcastically.*) Oh, your army.

Cleto (*appearing in the doorway*). I'm sorry, my captain. I just heard a noise. (Raquel *stands.* Andrés *moves quickly to her and puts his hands on her arms from the back.* Cleto *has turned and is peering into the patio. Then the boy relaxes.*) We are still safe, my captain. It was only a rabbit. (*He goes back into the patio.* Raquel *pulls away from* Andrés *and goes to the desk.*)

Raquel. What a magnificent army you have. So clever. I'm sure you must win many victories.

Andrés. We do. And we will win the greatest victory, remember that.

Raquel. This <u>farce</u> has gone on long enough. Will you please take your army and climb over the patio wall with it?

Andrés. I told you that we came here so that you could give us sanctuary.

Raquel. My dear captain—captain without a name . . .

Andrés. Andrés de la O, your servant. (*He makes a bow.*)

Raquel (*startled*). Andrés de la O!

Andrés. I am flattered. You have heard of me.

Raquel. Naturally. Everyone in the city has heard of you. You have a reputation for politeness—especially to women.

Andrés. I see that the tales about me have lost nothing in the telling.

Raquel. I can't say. I'm not interested in gossip about your type of soldier.

Andrés. Then let me give you something to heighten your interest. (*He suddenly takes her in his arms and kisses her. She stiffens for a moment, then remains perfectly still. He steps away from her.*)

Raquel (*rage forcing her to whisper*). Get out of here—at once!

Andrés (*staring at her in admiration*). I can understand why Macías loves you. I couldn't before, but now I can understand it.

Raquel. Get out of my house.

Andrés. (*Sits on the sofa and pulls a small leather pouch out of his shirt. He pours its contents into his hand.*) So cruel, señora, and I with a present for you? Here is a holy medal. My mother gave me this medal. She died when I was ten. She was a street beggar. She died of starvation. But I wasn't there. I was in jail. I had been sentenced to five years in prison for stealing five oranges. The judge thought it was a great joke. One year for each orange. He laughed. He had a very loud laugh. (*pause*) I killed him two months ago. I hanged him to the telephone pole in front of his house. And I laughed. (*pause*) I also have a very loud laugh. (Raquel *abruptly turns her back on him.*) I told that story to a girl the other night, and she thought it very funny. But of course she was a peasant girl—a girl who could neither read nor write. She hadn't been born in a great house in Tabasco. She didn't have an English governess. She didn't go to school to the nuns in Paris. She didn't marry one of the richest young men in the republic. But she thought

> **WORDS TO KNOW**
> **sanctuary** (săngk'chōō-ĕr'ē) *n.* a place of refuge, protection, and safety
> **farce** (färs) *n.* a ludicrous, empty show; a mockery

Multicultural Perspectives

THE PEOPLE OF MEXICO Most of the peasants fighting the federalists in the Mexican Revolution were the descendants of Mayan and Aztec Indians whose civilizations flourished in the area that is now Mexico before the arrival of the Spanish. The Spanish enslaved many of these Indians, and even after Mexico's independence, a feudal and prejudiced class system that exploited the Indians continued to survive. Today in Mexican states such as Chiapas and Oaxaca, traditional languages and cultures continue to flourish. In fact, many Mexican holidays and fiestas, such as The Day of the Dead, in which people celebrate their deceased ancestors, are based on ancient Indian traditions.

Literary Concept: CONFLICT

J Ask students to explain the choice that Andrés forces Raquel to make. *(Possible response: between turning the men in and her husband's life; between love and honor or loyalty to a cause)*

Literary Concept: CHARACTER

K Have students explain what Andrés's treatment of Cleto reveals about his character. *(Possible responses: He puts the safety of those who depend on him ahead of his own; he is very brave; he is very authoritative.)*

---

my story very funny. Of course she could understand it. Her brother had been whipped to death because he had run away from the plantation that owned him. (*He pauses and looks at her. She does not move.*) Are you still angry with me? Even though I have brought you a present? (*He holds out his hand.*) A very nice present—from your husband.

Raquel (*turns and stares at him in amazement*). A present! From Domingo?

Andrés. I don't know him that well. I call him the general Macías.

Raquel (*excitedly*). Is he well? How does he look? (*with horrified comprehension*) He's a prisoner . . . your prisoner!

Andrés. Naturally. That's why I know so much about you. He talks about you constantly.

Raquel. You know nothing about him. You're lying to me. (*Cleto comes to the window.*)

Andrés. I assure you, señora . . .

Cleto (*interrupting*). My captain . . .

Andrés. What is it Cleto? Another rabbit?

Cleto. No, my captain. There are soldiers at the end of the street. They are searching all the houses. They will be here soon.

Andrés. Don't worry. We are quite safe here. Stay in the patio until I call you.

Cleto. Yes, my captain. (*He returns to the patio.*)

Raquel. You are not safe here. When those soldiers come I shall turn you over to them.

Andrés. I think not.

Raquel. You can't escape from them. And they are not kind to you peasant prisoners. They have good reason not to be.

Andrés. Look at this ring. (*He holds his hand out, with the ring on his palm.*)

Raquel. Why, it's—a wedding ring.

Andrés. Read the inscription inside of it. (*As she hesitates, he adds sharply.*) Read it!

Raquel (*Slowly takes the ring. While she is reading, her voice fades to a whisper.*) "D.M.—R.R.—June 2, 1902." Where did you get this?

Andrés. General Macías gave it to me.

Raquel (*firmly and clearly*). Not this ring. He'd never give you this ring. (*with dawning horror*) He's dead. You stole it from his dead finger. He's dead.

Andrés. Not yet. But he will be dead if I don't return to camp safely by sunset tomorrow.

Raquel. I don't believe you. I don't believe you. You're lying to me.

Andrés. This house is famous for its loyalty to the federal government. You will hide me until those soldiers get out of this district. When it is safe enough, Cleto and I will leave. But if you betray me to them, your husband will be shot tomorrow evening at sunset. Do you understand? (*He shakes her arm.* Raquel *looks dazedly at him.* Cleto *comes to the window.*)

Cleto. The soldiers are coming closer, my captain. They are at the next house.

Andrés (*to* Raquel). Where shall we hide? (Raquel *is still dazed. He gives her another little shake.*) Think, woman! If you love your husband at all—think!

Raquel. I don't know. Marica upstairs—the servants in the rest of the house—I don't know.

Andrés. The general has bragged to us about you. He says you are braver than most men. He says you are very clever. This is a time to be both brave and clever.

Cleto (*pointing to the closet*). What door is that?

Raquel. It's a closet . . . a storage closet.

Andrés. We'll hide in there.

Raquel. It's very small. It's not big enough for both of you.

Andrés. Cleto, hide yourself in there.

Cleto. But, my captain . . .

Andrés. That's an order! Hide yourself.

Cleto. Yes, sir. (*He steps inside the closet.*)

Formation of Revolutionary Leadership (1926–1927), Diego Rivera. Fresco, 354 cm × 555 cm, Universidad Autónoma de Chapingo (Mexico), Chapel. Photo Copyright © 1995 Dirk Bakker / The Detroit Institute of Arts.

Andrés. And now, señora, where are you going to hide me?

Raquel. How did you persuade my husband to give you his ring?

Andrés. That's a very long story, señora, for which we have no time just now. (*He puts the ring and medal back in the pouch and thrusts it inside his shirt.*) Later I will be glad to give you all the details. But at present it is only necessary for you to remember that his life depends upon mine.

Raquel. Yes—yes, of course. (*She loses her dazed expression and seems to grow more queenly as she takes command of the situation.*) Give me your hat. (*Andrés shrugs and passes it over to her. She takes it to the closet and hands it to Cleto.*) There is a smoking jacket[7] hanging up in there. Hand it to me. (*Cleto hands her a man's velvet smoking jacket. She brings it to Andrés.*) Put this on.

Andrés (*puts it on and looks down at himself*). Such a pity my shoes are not comfortable slippers.

Raquel. Sit in that chair. (*She points to the armchair.*)

Andrés. My dear lady . . .

Raquel. If I must save your life, allow me to do it in my own way. Sit down. (*Andrés sits. She picks up the afghan from the couch and throws it over his feet and legs, carefully tucking it in so that his body is covered to the waist.*) If anyone speaks to you, don't answer. Don't turn your head. As far as you are concerned, there is no one in this room—not even me. Just look straight ahead of you and . . .

Andrés (*as she pauses*). And what?

Raquel. I started to say "and pray," but since you're a member of the revolutionary army, I don't suppose you believe in God and prayer.

Andrés. My mother left me a holy medal.

Raquel. Oh, yes, I remember. A very amusing story. (*There is the sound of men's voices in*

---

7. **smoking jacket:** a man's evening jacket, often made of fine fabric, and usually worn at home.

THE RING OF GENERAL MACÍAS **877**

Mini-Lesson The Writer's Style

USING DIALOGUE TO REVEAL CHARACTER Point out that dialogue is a playwright's main tool for characterization. Unlike novels and short stories, which can have an unlimited amount of omniscient description, plays can only give this information in the stage directions. Therefore, characters must be revealed through what they say and through what others say about them. In the scene described on page 877, for instance, once Raquel decides to hide the two men, her statements become very businesslike. She reveals the commanding aspect of her character through her dialogue with Andrés here.

Application Have students write brief dialogues to describe how Marica might have responded to the intruders. Advise students that her response should reveal aspects of her character.

Reteaching/Reinforcement
- *Writing Mini-Lessons* transparencies, p. 56

Using Dialogue, p. 453

Literary Concept: CHARACTER

 Ask students what Raquel's strategy for concealing Andrés's true identity reveals about her. *(Possible responses: She is very clever and brave, hiding him under the noses of the soldiers; she is a good bluffer; she is a good actress.)*

Critical Thinking: MAKING INFERENCES

 Ask students why they think Raquel is so desperate to keep Marica out of the room. *(Possible responses: Marica will become hysterical; Marica will expose Andrés.)*

---

the patio.) The federal soldiers are here. If you can pray, ask God to keep Marica upstairs. She is very young and very stupid. She'll betray you before I can shut her mouth.

Andrés. I'll . . .

Raquel. Silence! Stare straight ahead of you and pray. (*She goes to the French window and speaks loudly to the soldiers.*) Really! What is the meaning of this uproar?

Flores (*off*). Do not alarm yourself, señora. (*He comes into the room. He wears the uniform of a federal officer.*) I am Captain Basilio Flores, at your service, señora.

Raquel. What do you mean, invading my house and making so much noise at this hour of the night?

Flores. We are hunting for two spies. One of them is the notorious Andrés de la O. You may have heard of him, señora.

Raquel (*looking at* Andrés). Considering what he did to my cousin—yes, I've heard of him.

Flores. Your cousin, señora?

Raquel. (*Comes to* Andrés *and puts her hand on his shoulder. He stares woodenly in front of him.*) Felipe was his prisoner before the poor boy managed to escape.

Flores. Is it possible? (*He crosses to* Andrés.) Captain Basilio Flores, at your service. (*He salutes.*)

Raquel. Felipe doesn't hear you. He doesn't even know you are in the room.

Flores. Eh, it is a sad thing.

Raquel. Must your men make so much noise?

Flores. The hunt must be thorough, señora. And now if some of my men can go through here to the rest of the house . . .

Raquel. Why?

Flores. But I told you, señora. We are hunting for two spies . . .

Raquel (*speaking quickly from controlled nervousness*). And do you think I have them hidden someplace, and I the wife of General Macías?

Flores. General Macías! But I didn't know . . .

Raquel. Now that you do know, I suggest you remove your men and their noise at once.

Flores. But, señora, I regret—I still have to search this house.

Raquel. I can assure you, captain, that I have been sitting here all evening, and no peasant spy has passed me and gone into the rest of the house.

Flores. Several rooms open off the patio, señora. They needn't have come through here.

Raquel. So . . . you do think I conceal spies in this house. Then search it by all means. Look under the sofa . . . under the table. In the drawers of the desk. And don't miss that closet, captain. Inside that closet is hidden a very fierce and wicked spy.

Flores. Please, señora . . .

Raquel (*goes to the closet door*). Or do you prefer me to open it for you?

Flores. I am only doing my duty, señora. You are making it very difficult.

Raquel (*relaxing against the door*). I'm sorry. My sister-in-law is upstairs. She has just received word that her husband has been killed. They were married three months ago. She's only twenty. I didn't want . . .

Marica (*calling off*). Raquel, what is all that noise downstairs?

Raquel (*goes to the house door and calls*). It is nothing. Go back to bed.

Marica. But I can hear men's voices in the patio.

Raquel. It is only some federal soldiers hunting for two peasant spies. (*She turns and speaks rapidly to* Flores.) If she comes down here, she must not see my cousin. Felipe escaped, but her husband was killed. The doctor thinks the sight of my poor cousin might affect her mind. You understand?

Flores. Certainly, señora. What a sad thing.

Marica (*still off*). Raquel, I'm afraid! (*She tries to*

878 UNIT SIX PART 1: A STRENGTH FROM WITHIN

Mini-Lesson Literary Concepts

REVIEWING CHARACTER Remind students that a character is a person, an animal, or an imaginary creature who takes part in the action of a work of literature. Generally the plot of a work of literature focuses on one or more main characters, those who are the most important. Less important characters are known as minor characters. Both main and minor characters help to move the plot along.

Application Have students discuss and decide who the major and minor characters are in "The Ring of General Macías." How does each character, major and minor, help to move the plot along? Who do students think is the most important character in the play?

push past Raquel *into the room.* Raquel *and* Flores *stand between her and* Andrés.) Spies! In this house. Oh, Raquel!

Raquel. The doctor will be very angry if you don't return to bed at once.

Marica. But those terrible men will kill us. What is the matter with you two? Why are you standing there like that? (*She tries to see past them, but they both move so that she can't see* Andrés.)

Flores. It is better that you go back to your room, señora.

Marica. But why? Upstairs I am alone. Those terrible men will kill me. I know they will.

Flores. Don't be afraid, señora. There are no spies in this house.

Marica. Are you sure?

Raquel. Captain Flores means that no spy would dare to take refuge in the house of General Macías. Isn't that right, captain?

Flores (*laughing*). Of course. All the world knows of the brave General Macías.

Raquel. Now go back to bed, Marica. Please, for my sake.

Marica. You are both acting very strangely. I think you have something hidden in this room you don't want me to see.

Raquel (*sharply*). You are quite right. Captain Flores has captured one of the spies. He is sitting in the chair behind me. He is dead. Now will you please go upstairs!

Marica (*gives a stifled sob*). Oh! That such a terrible thing could happen in this house. (*She runs out of the room, still sobbing.*)

Flores (*worried*). Was it wise to tell her such a story, señora?

Raquel (*tense with repressed relief*). Better that than the truth. Good night, captain, and thank you.

Flores. Good night, señora. And don't worry. Those spies won't bother you. If they were anywhere in this district, my men would have found them.

Raquel. I'm sure of it.

(*The* Captain *salutes her, looks toward* Andrés, *and salutes him, then goes into the patio. He can be heard calling his men. Neither* Andrés *nor* Raquel *moves until the voices outside go away. Then* Raquel *staggers and nearly falls, but* Andrés *catches her in time.*)

Andrés (*calling softly*). They've gone, Cleto. (Andrés *carries* Raquel *to the sofa as* Cleto *comes out of the closet.*) Bring a glass of wine. Quickly.

Cleto (*as he gets the wine*). What happened?

Andrés. It's nothing. Just a faint. (*He holds the wine to her lips.*)

Cleto. She's a great lady, that one. When she wanted to open the closet door, my knees were trembling, I can tell you.

Andrés. My own bones were playing a pretty tune.

Cleto. Why do you think she married Macías?

Andrés. Love is a peculiar thing, Cleto.

Cleto. I don't understand it.

Raquel (*moans and sits up*). Are they—are they gone?

Andrés. Yes, they're gone. (*He kisses her hand.*) I've never known a braver lady.

Raquel (*pulling her hand away*). Will you go now, please?

Andrés. We'll have to wait until the district is free of them—but if you'd like to write a letter to your husband while we're waiting . . .

Raquel (*surprised at his kindness*). You'd take it to him? You'd really give it to him?

Andrés. Of course.

Raquel. Thank you. (*She goes to the writing desk and sits down.*)

Andrés (*to* Cleto, *who has been staring steadily at* Raquel *all the while*). You stay here with the señora. I'm going to find out how much of the district has been cleared.

Cleto (*still staring at* Raquel). Yes, my captain.

Critical Thinking: ANALYZING

R Ask students what it is that Cleto does not understand. *(Possible responses: he doesn't understand how someone as brave as Raquel could love General Macías; he doesn't understand why the general would choose love over the federalist cause.)*

Literary Concept: PLOT

S Ask students why Raquel wants to know the answer to this question. *(Possible responses: If it's true, then her husband sacrificed the federalist cause to save his own life; if it's true, she will have to reconsider her decision to hide Andrés and Cleto.)*

(Andrés *leaves by the French windows. Cleto keeps on staring at* Raquel *as she starts to write. After a moment she turns to him.*)

Raquel (*irritated*). Why do you keep staring at me?

Cleto. Why did you marry a man like that one, señora?

Raquel. You're very impertinent.[8]

Cleto (*shyly*). I'm sorry, señora.

Raquel (*after a brief pause*). What do you mean: "a man like that one"?

Cleto. Well, you're very brave, señora.

Raquel (*lightly*). And don't you think the general is very brave?

Cleto. No, señora. Not very.

Raquel (*staring at him with bewilderment*). What are you trying to tell me?

Cleto. Nothing, señora. It is none of my affair.

Raquel. Come here. (*He comes slowly up to her.*) Tell me what is in your mind.

Cleto. I don't know, señora. I don't understand it. The captain says love is a peculiar thing, but I don't understand it.

Raquel. Cleto, did the general willingly give that ring to your captain?

Cleto. Yes, señora.

Raquel. Why?

Cleto. The general wanted to save his own life. He said he loved you and he wanted to save his life.

Raquel. How would giving that ring to your captain save the general's life?

Cleto. The general's supposed to be shot tomorrow afternoon. But he's talked about you a lot, and when my captain knew we had to come into the city, he thought perhaps we might take refuge here if the Federals got on our trail. So he went to the general and said that if he fixed it so we'd be safe here, my captain would save him from the firing squad.

Raquel. Was your trip here to the city very important—to your cause, I mean?

Cleto. Indeed yes, señora. The captain got a lot of fine information. It means we'll win the next big battle. My captain is a very clever man, señora.

Raquel. Did the general know about this information when he gave his ring to your captain?

Cleto. I don't see how he could help knowing it, señora. He heard us talking about it enough.

Raquel. Who knows about that bargain to save the general's life beside you and your captain?

Cleto. No one, señora. The captain isn't one to talk, and I didn't have time to.

Raquel (*While the boy has been talking, the life seems to have drained completely out of her*). How old are you, Cleto?

Cleto. I don't know, señora. I think I'm twenty, but I don't know.

Raquel (*speaking more to herself than to him*). Tomás was twenty.

Cleto. Who is Tomás?

Raquel. He was married to my sister-in-law. Cleto, you think my husband is a coward, don't you?

Cleto (*with embarrassment*). Yes, señora.

Raquel. You don't think any woman is worth it, do you? Worth the price of a great battle, I mean?

Cleto. No, señora. But as the captain says, love is a very peculiar thing.

Raquel. If your captain loved a woman as much as the general loves me, would he have given an enemy his ring?

Cleto. Ah, but the captain is a great man, señora.

Raquel. And so is my husband a great man. He is of the family Macías. All of that family have been great men. All of them—brave and honorable men. They have always held their honor to be greater than their lives. That is a tradition of their family.

Cleto. Perhaps none of them loved a woman like you, señora.

---

8. **impertinent** (ĭm-pûr′tn-ənt): improperly bold or forward.

880 UNIT SIX PART 1: A STRENGTH FROM WITHIN

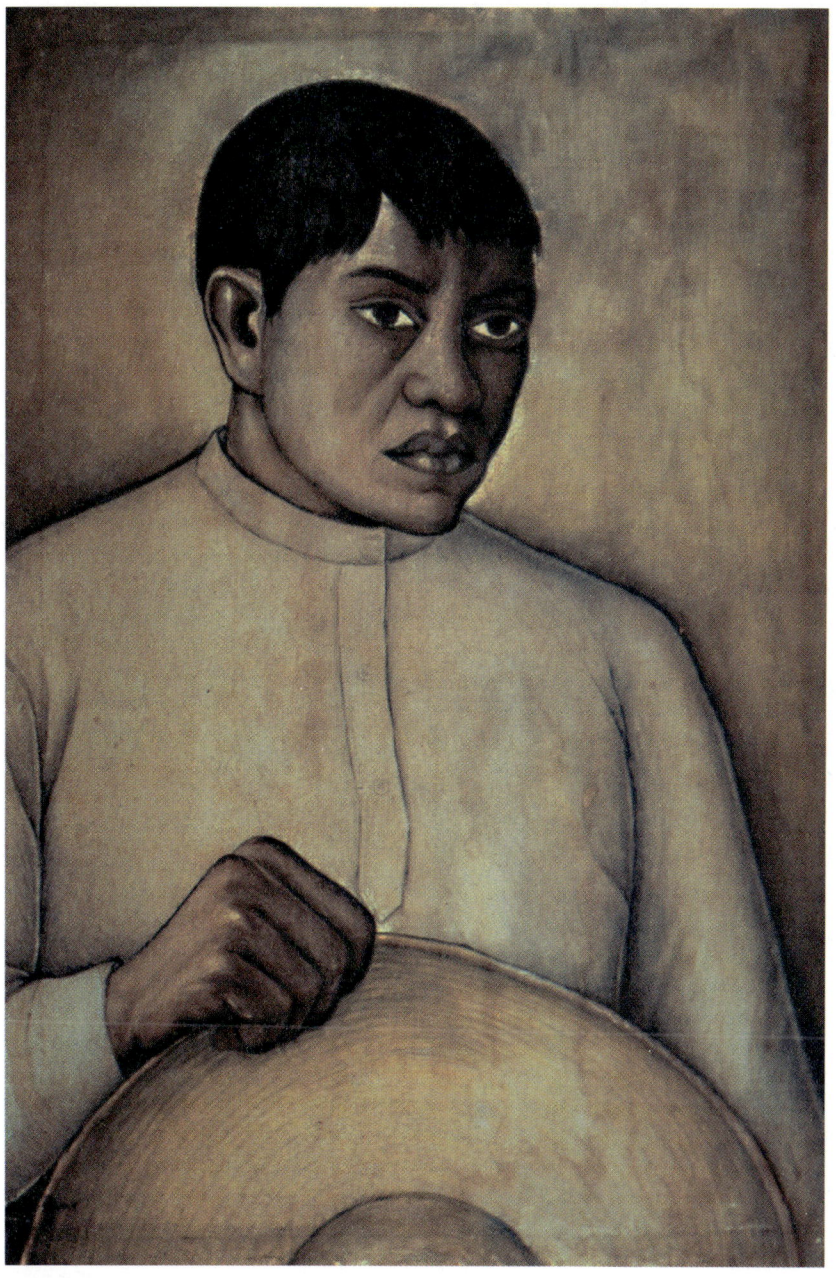

Peasant with Sombrero (1926), Diego Rivera.

Art Note

***Peasant With Sombrero* by Diego Rivera** Rivera spent the year 1920 in Italy, studying 14th-century Italian frescoes. On his return to Mexico in 1921, it became clear that this year had had a decisive influence on his style. He completely abandoned the Cubism of his early years, and adapted the realism of the early Italian Renaissance to fit his own highly original style and subject matter. This portrait shows the combination of Italian influence with his own Mexican voice.

Reading the Art *What mood does this painting convey to you? Use details from the painting to support your opinion.*

Critical Thinking:
MAKING JUDGMENTS

T Ask students to evaluate Cleto's statement. Do they think Cleto is making the right choice in risking his life fighting for a cause? Are there better ways to bring about social change? *(Accept all reasonable, well-supported responses.)*

CUSTOMIZING FOR
Gifted and Talented Students

Suggest that students read Mariano Azuela's classic novel about the Mexican Revolution, *The Underdogs*. Ask them to compare and contrast Niggli's and Azuela's views of the Mexican Revolution as they read.

Raquel. How strange you are. I saved you from the Federals because I want to save my husband's life. You call me brave, and yet you call him a coward. There is no difference in what we have done.

Cleto. But you are a woman, señora.

Raquel. Has a woman less honor than a man, then?

Cleto. No, señora. Please, I don't know how to say it. The general is a soldier. He has a duty to his own cause. You are a woman. You have a duty to your husband. It is right that you should try to save him. It is not right that he should try to save himself.

Raquel (*dully*). Yes, of course. It is right that I should save him. (*becoming practical again*) Your captain has been gone some time, Cleto. You'd better find out if he is still safe.

Cleto. Yes, señora. (*As he reaches the French windows, she stops him.*)

Raquel. Wait, Cleto. Have you a mother—or a wife, perhaps?

Cleto. Oh, no, señora. I haven't anyone but the captain.

Raquel. But the captain is a soldier. What would you do if he should be killed?

Cleto. It is very simple, señora. I should be killed, too.

Raquel. You speak about death so calmly. Aren't you afraid of it, Cleto?

Cleto. No, señora. It's like the captain says . . . dying for what you believe in—that's the finest death of all.

Raquel. And you believe in the revolutionary cause?

T **Cleto.** Yes, señora. I am a poor peasant, that's true. But still I have a right to live like a man, with my own ground, and my own family, and my own future. (*He stops speaking abruptly.*) I'm sorry, señora. You are a fine lady. You don't understand these things. I must go and find my captain. (*He goes out.*)

Raquel (*rests her face against her hand*). He's so young. But Tomás was no older. And he's not afraid. He said so. Oh, Domingo—Domingo! (*She straightens abruptly, takes the bottle of poison from the desk drawer and stares at it. Then she crosses to the decanter and laces the wine with the poison. She hurries back to the desk and is busy writing when* Andrés *and* Cleto *return.*)

Andrés. You'll have to hurry that letter. The district is clear now.

Raquel. I'll be through in just a moment. You might as well finish the wine while you're waiting.

Andrés. Thank you. A most excellent idea. (*He pours himself a glass of wine. As he lifts it to his lips, she speaks.*)

Raquel. Why don't you give some to—Cleto?

Andrés. This is too fine a wine to waste on that boy.

Raquel. He'll probably never have another chance to taste such wine.

Andrés. Very well. Pour yourself a glass, Cleto.

Cleto. Thank you. (*He pours it.*) Your health, my captain.

Raquel (*quickly*). Drink it outside, Cleto. I want to speak to your captain. (*The boy looks at* Andrés, *who jerks his head toward the patio.* Cleto *nods and goes out.*) I want you to give my husband a message for me. I can't write it. You'll have to remember it. But first, give me a glass of wine, too.

Andrés (*pouring the wine*). It might be easier for him if you wrote it.

Raquel. I think not. (*She takes the glass.*) I want you to tell him that I never knew how much I loved him until tonight.

Andrés. Is that all?

Raquel. Yes. Tell me, captain, do you think it possible to love a person too much?

Andrés. Yes, señora. I do.

Raquel. So do I. Let us drink a

882 UNIT SIX PART 1: A STRENGTH FROM WITHIN

Mini-Lesson   Genre Study

DRAMA Explain that a **one-act play** is a type of play that only has one act instead of several acts. One-act plays are usually shorter than plays with several acts. Although there may be several scenes, most one-act plays have only one setting. Many playwrights start out writing one-act plays, just as many novelists start out writing short stories.

Application Have students work in small groups to identify ways that this play could be expanded into a longer work with multiple acts. They might ask questions like the following:
- What settings might be added?
- What characters could be added?
- What other conflicts might be introduced?
- What new scenes could take place?

Each group can create an outline or plot synopsis for their expanded play.

toast, captain—to honor. To bright and shining honor.

Andrés (*raises his glass*). To honor. (*He drains his glass. She lifts hers almost to her lips and then puts it down. From the patio comes a faint cry.*)

Cleto (*calling faintly in a cry that fades into silence*). Captain. Captain.

(*Andrés sways, his hand trying to brush across his face as though trying to brush sense into his head. When he hears Cleto he tries to stagger toward the window but stumbles and can't quite make it. Hanging on to the table by the sofa he looks accusingly at her. She shrinks back against her chair.*)

Andrés (*his voice weak from the poison*). Why?

Raquel. Because I love him. Can you understand that?

Andrés. We'll win. The revolution will win. You can't stop that.

Raquel. Yes, you'll win. I know that now.

Andrés. That girl—she thought my story was funny—about the hanging. But you didn't . . .

Raquel. I'm glad you hanged him. I'm glad.

(*Andrés looks at her and tries to smile. He manages to pull the pouch from his shirt and extend it to her. But it drops from his hand.*)

Raquel (*runs to French window and calls*). Cleto. Cleto! (*She buries her face in her hands for a moment, then comes back to Andrés. She kneels beside him and picks up the leather pouch. She opens it and, taking the ring, puts it on her finger. Then she sees the medal. She rises, and, pulling out the chain from her own throat, she slides the medal on to the chain. Then she walks to the sofa and sinks down on it.*)

Marica (*calling off*). Raquel! Raquel! (*Raquel snaps off the lamp, leaving the room in darkness. Marica opens the house door. She is carrying a candle which she shades with her hand. The light is too dim to reveal the dead Andrés.*) What are you doing down here in the dark? Why don't you come to bed?

Raquel (*making an effort to speak*). I'll come in just a moment.

Marica. But what are you doing, Raquel?

Raquel. Nothing. Just listening . . . listening to an empty house.

(*Quick curtain*)

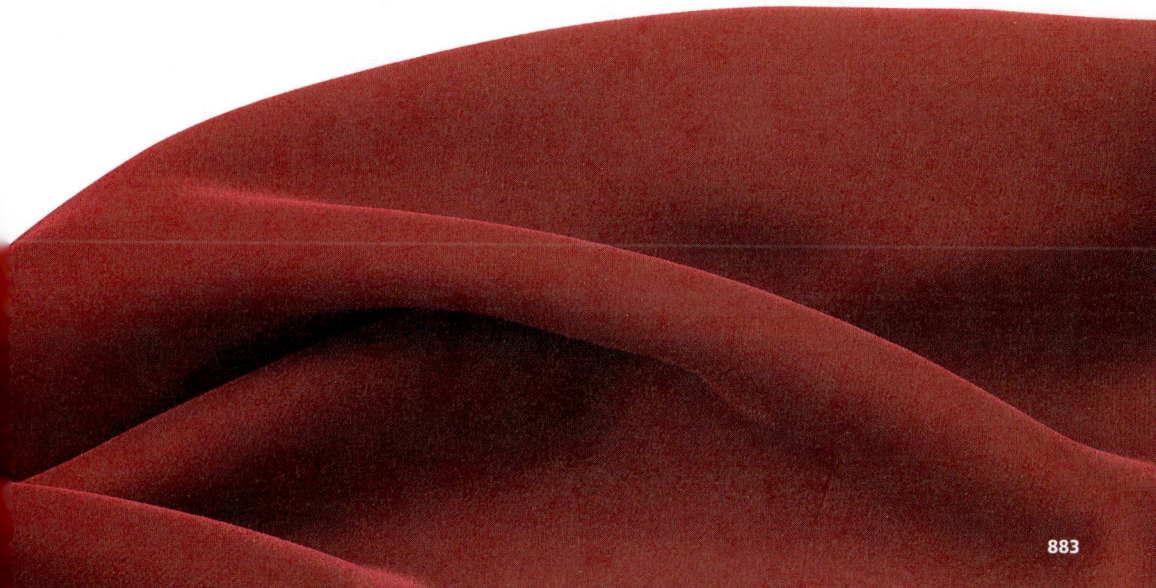

From Personal Response to Critical Analysis

1. Accept all reasonable responses.
2. Possible responses: She does not want her husband to live without honor; she cannot live with him again in honor.
3. Possible responses: She knows that the present form of government is corrupt and unjust; she knows that the peasants will fight to the death, so there is no way to defeat them.
4. Possible responses: They are both high-ranking, distinguished military men; they are around the same age; Macías is rich and educated, while Andrés is poor and uneducated; Andrés has honor and is willing to die for his cause, while Macías was willing to give up his cause in exchange for his life.
5. Possible responses: Raquel, Andrés, and Cleto all live—and die—with honor, while general Macías does not; Marica does not live with honor because she tries to kill herself; Flores is honorable because he works for his cause and respects the wishes of a lady.
6. Accept all reasonable, well-supported responses.
7. Accept all reasonable, well-supported responses.

Another Pathway

Cooperative Learning A summarizer can restate the group's conclusions about each character, while recorders can write down the director's notes. An extender can help the group delve further into a character's motivation and feelings.

Rubric
3 Full Accomplishment The director's notes contain substantial and accurate information on each character.
2 Substantial Accomplishment The director's notes are not informative enough about every character.
1 Little or Partial Accomplishment Students have trouble working together and their final set of notes are sketchy.

RESPONDING OPTIONS

FROM PERSONAL RESPONSE TO CRITICAL ANALYSIS

REFLECT
1. What was your response to Raquel's final act? Share your response with a classmate.

RETHINK
2. Why do you think Raquel poisons Andrés and Cleto, even though she knows that her husband will die if they do not return?
   Consider
   - how her actions will affect the war
   - Raquel's conversation with Cleto on page 880
   - General Macías's bargain and who knows about it
   - Raquel's feelings about her husband and about honor

Close Textual Reading

3. Why do you think Raquel agrees with Andrés that "the revolution will win"?
   Consider
   - her conversation with Marica on pages 872–873
   - what she learns about Andrés and Cleto
   - what she realizes about the two sides in the war

4. What do Andrés and General Macías have in common, and what sets them apart? Use details from the play to support your opinion.

Close Textual Reading

5. Which characters in the play live—or die—with honor? You might find it helpful to review the spider map you created for the Personal Connection on page 869.

6. In your opinion, who is the most admirable character in the play? Explain your views.

RELATE
7. Do you think people today are still willing to die for an honorable cause? Share your ideas, using examples.

Multimodal Learning
ANOTHER PATHWAY
Cooperative Learning
Imagine that your class is staging this play. With a group of classmates, create a set of director's notes for each character in the play. Provide information that will help the actors understand their characters and what motivates them to speak and act as they do.

QUICKWRITES

1. Raquel started a letter to her husband near the end of the play. Write the complete **letter** she might have written if she had had the time to finish it.
2. Write a **psychological profile** of one of the characters on the basis of information presented in the play.
3. Write the **speech** Andrés might give to the Mexican people urging their involvement in the Revolution.

📁 **PORTFOLIO** *Save your writing. You may want to use it later as a springboard to a piece for your portfolio.*

UNIT SIX PART 1: A STRENGTH FROM WITHIN

QuickWrites

1. Suggest that students look back through the play at Raquel's dialogue to get a sense of what her voice might be like in a letter.
2. Psychological profiles should include information about a character's intelligence, emotions, and motivation.
3. Encourage students to use the details that Andrés mentions and the story he tells Raquel in their speeches.

The Writer's Craft
Persuasive Speech, pp. 222–227

LITERARY CONCEPTS

A **foil** is a minor character who provides a striking contrast to a main character. A writer might use a foil to emphasize certain traits possessed by a main character or simply to set off or enhance the main character through contrast. What do you think Niggli emphasizes about Raquel by presenting Marica as her foil?

CONCEPT REVIEW: Verbal Irony Verbal irony occurs when a character says one thing and means another. Find examples of verbal irony in the play.

Multimodal Learning
ACROSS THE CURRICULUM

Film To learn more about the peasant uprising in the Mexican Revolution, watch a videocassette recording of the 1952 film *Viva Zapata!*

WORDS TO KNOW

Review the Words to Know at the bottom of the selection pages. Then write the word that best completes each sentence.

1. After entering Raquel's house, Andrés offends Raquel by acting _____; he drinks her wine and even kisses her, as if boasting of his charms.
2. Even though she knows the revolutionary soldiers threaten her entire way of life, she reacts as if they are absurd and their revolution is a _____.
3. Her lifestyle, her way of carrying herself, and her attitude all indicate that she is used to ruling her home _____ and will tolerate no insult.
4. She is quite open, at first, about her refusal to allow the revolutionaries to use her home as a _____ to escape the federalists.
5. In the end, it is not what she does obviously but what she does _____ that causes their downfall.

Multimodal Learning
ALTERNATIVE ACTIVITIES

1. Make **sketches** of costumes or of a set design to be used in a production of the play.
2. Create a **poster** to advertise a production of the play.

LITERARY LINKS

Do you think that *The Ring of General Macías* and "Two Friends" (page 567) present similar views of honor? Why or why not?

JOSEPHINA NIGGLI

Josephina Niggli (1910–1983) was born in the city of Monterrey in northeastern Mexico and lived there for several years before moving with her family to San Antonio, Texas. Fluent in both Spanish and English, Niggli was educated at home until she reached high school age. After obtaining her bachelor's degree, she studied drama in graduate school, where she wrote and saw produced two of her full-length plays as well as a number of the one-act plays for which she is now better known. She acted in several of the productions herself and even directed a few.

Josephina Niggli also published books about how to write stage and radio plays. She spent two years in Hollywood as a screenwriter for MGM Studios. Her plays, stories, and novels, which were written in English, have won praise for their memorable characters and vivid portrayals of Mexican history and village life.

OTHER WORKS *Mexican Silhouettes; Mexican Folk Plays; Mexican Village; Step Down, Elder Brother; A Miracle for Mexico*

Extended Reading

• ART GALLERY

THE RING OF GENERAL MACÍAS   **885**

Words to Know
1. ostentatiously
2. farce
3. regally
4. sanctuary
5. stealthily

Reteaching/Reinforcement
• *Unit Six Resource Book*, p. 26.

Across the Curriculum

Film Have students form discussion groups after viewing, where they can discuss and present their views about the film. Then have each group draft a cooperative review of the film, based on discussions.

Literary Links

Possible responses: Yes, they both present the view that dying for honor is admirable; no, "Two Friends" presents killing as dishonorable, while in this play it is an honorable thing to do.

ART GALLERY
Art of Mexican History and Revolution These paintings by famous Mexican artists convey the political struggles and the revolutionary spirit that have characterized Mexican history.

Side A, Frame 49703

Literary Concepts

Students might suggest that Niggli emphasizes Raquel's courage, strength, self-possession, and determination by having the cowardly, weak-willed, easily led Marica as a foil.

Verbal Irony Students may cite such examples as when Raquel tells Andrés she is devastated, when she refers to him as "my dear captain," or when she tells him that she thinks his story is funny.

Alternative Activities

1. Have students present their sketches to the class, explaining the reasons behind their choices.
2. Students can choose an aspect of the play to emphasize on their posters. They may wish to display posters in the classroom.

THE LANGUAGE OF LITERATURE TEACHER'S EDITION **885**

ON YOUR OWN

Gift from

OBJECTIVES
- To promote independent active reading
- To practice and apply skills learned in previous lessons
- To provide an opportunity to assess students' performance through an alternative assessment instrument

Reading Pathways
- As students read the selection, have them write down their thoughts about both Eric and his mother. Do their opinions change over the course of the essay?
- Have students read the selection in small groups. Suggest that they take turns reading sections aloud. After each section is read, students should pause to discuss it.
- Evaluate how well students can read, interpret, discuss, and write about the selection on their own by using the Alternative Assessment booklet. The assessment for this unit covers both On Your Own selections, "Gift from a Son Who Died" and "Old Song." Administer the assessment at the end of the unit after students have read all the selections and completed all the writing that they have been assigned.

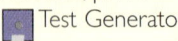
Eric Lund at age 18, 1968. Courtesy of Doris Lund.

PRINT AND MEDIA RESOURCES

UNIT SIX RESOURCE BOOK
Strategic Reading: Literature, p. 29

ACCESS FOR STUDENTS ACQUIRING ENGLISH
Selection Summaries

FORMAL ASSESSMENT
Selection Test, p. 175
Part Test, p. 177
Test Generator

ALTERNATIVE ASSESSMENT
Unit 6 Integrated Assessment, pp. 31-36

AUDIO LIBRARY
See Reference Card

886 THE LANGUAGE OF LITERATURE TEACHER'S EDITION

a Son Who Died

Doris Herold Lund
United States

> **SUMMARY**
>
> Doris Herold Lund describes the death of her son, Eric, from leukemia at the age of 22, after a 4½-year battle against the disease. Eric had suddenly become ill, just before his freshman year in college. To help her son both live and die as a man, Mrs. Lund tried to appear calm in the face of fear. Throughout the ordeal, his spirit remained strong. Eric bravely fought his illness, managing to complete two years of college, making the soccer team, and befriending other cancer patients. His mother took his humor and his ability to dare life as gifts. Because his final gift was to accept his death with dignity, his mother is left with a deep feeling of love and gratitude.
>
> **Thematic Link:** *A Strength from Within*
> In this essay, two people must find strength from within: a boy who fights death and then faces it with dignity, and a mother who conquers her own fear and sorrow in order to help her son.

At 17, Eric Lund was stricken with leukemia, a form of cancer in which white blood cells, which defend the body against infection, grow in an uncontrolled manner. Although leukemia can sometimes be successfully treated with drug therapy, in Eric's case the disease proved fatal. In this essay, Eric's mother describes her son's four-and-a-half-year battle with the disease and his eventual acceptance of his fate.

It's not the way I thought it would be. I thought the sun and the moon would go out. I thought joy itself would die when Eric died. He had given so much to all of us—his family, friends, the girl he loved. And yet his death is not the end of joy after all. It's somehow another beginning. . . .

Eric died at 22, after a four-and-a-half-year struggle with leukemia. While he left us with the deep bruises of grief, he left us so much more. So much to celebrate! There's a victory here that I'm still trying to understand. Why do I, even in loss, feel stronger? Why does life on this untidy, dangerous planet seem more wonderfully precious? I am conscious now of the value of each good moment, the importance of wasting nothing.

These things are Eric's gifts to me. They weren't easily bought or quickly accepted. And not all came tied with ribbons; many were delivered with blows. In addition to leukemia,

Linking To Science

In the more than 20 years since Eric was first diagnosed with leukemia, treatment for this cancer has come a long way. Acute lymphocytic leukemia once killed more than 90 percent of its victims within 6 months. Today, however, more than half the patients diagnosed with this disease are treated with drug therapies that allow them to remain free of leukemia for over 5 years. After 5 years, they are considered cured.

Eric was suffering from adolescence. And there were times when this condition took more out of us than his other one. A 17-year-old boy who may not live to become a man is suddenly in a great hurry. Like a militant new nation, he wants instant independence and no compromises. After the first few weeks Eric quickly took charge of his illness. I was no longer to talk to the doctors. In fact—the message came through clearly—I was no longer to talk at all unless I could avoid sounding like a worried mother.

Perhaps it would have been different if we'd had a chance to prepare for what was coming, but there was no beginning. It was a thunderbolt from a cloudless sky.

We live in a small Connecticut town, just a block from the beach. This had been a summer like many others. The front hall was, as usual, full of sand and kicked-off sneakers, mysterious towels that didn't belong to us, an assortment of swimming fins and soccer balls. By September, I, like many mothers, was half longing for school to start and half dreading it. Our 20-year-old daughter had married, and now Eric was packed and ready to go off for his freshman year at the University of Connecticut. But ten-year-old Lisa and 14-year-old Mark would still be at home. I kept telling myself how lucky I'd be to have less laundry and fewer cookie crumbs to contend with. But I didn't exactly believe it.

One afternoon Eric and I both wanted the car at the same moment. "I've *got* to run at the track, Mom." He was wearing his soccer shorts and running shoes. "I've only got two more days before school starts, and I'm not in shape."

I knew how much he wanted to make the freshman soccer team when he got to college, but I had work to do. "I have to go to the printer," I said. "But I'll drop you off at the field and pick you up later."

"Okay." He scowled a bit at the compromise. As we drove off together with the top down, the late summer sun poured over our shoulders, turning Eric's hair to yellow curly flames. His eyebrows were sunburned almost white, and the hairs on his powerful legs gleamed gold against deep tan. Then I noticed something on his leg—an ugly red sore, big and round as a silver dollar. There was another farther down. And another on his other leg.

"Eric! What have you got on your legs?"

"Dunno. Little infection maybe."

"It doesn't look little to me," I protested. "Impetigo[1] is what it looks like. We'd better go right over to the doctor's office."

"Mom! For God's sake!" He was furious.

"Eric," I said. "Impetigo spreads like mad. If that's what it is, they aren't even going to let you into the locker room. We've got two days before you go. Let's get the doctor to clear it up now."

"All right," he said dully.

The sores did not look like impetigo to our doctor. He told his secretary to call the hospital and arrange to have Eric admitted next morning for tests. "Be there at eight, Eric," he said. My son nodded and swung through the waiting room, full of mothers and toddlers, slamming the door behind him.

"What tests?" I turned to the doctor. Eric had had a complete physical, required of all freshmen, only 12 days before. Blood tests, too. He'd passed with flying colors.

"I want them to rerun some of the blood tests," said the doctor. "I've also ordered a bone marrow—"[2]

I blanked out the words "bone marrow" as if I'd never heard them. After all, I thought as we drove home, he'd just had that perfect physical. . . .

---

1. **impetigo** (ĭm′pĭ-tī′gō): a contagious skin infection.
2. **a bone marrow**: The doctor is referring to a test of the soft tissue that produces red blood cells and is found in the center of bones.

Yet the next afternoon when the phone rang and the doctor was saying, "I'd like to talk to you and your husband together—" I knew at once. "You don't have to tell me," I said. "I know. Eric has leukemia."

I was once in a house struck by lightning. The sensation, the scene, even the strange electrical smell returned at that moment. A powerful bolt seemed to enter the top of my skull as I got the message . . . Eric had leukemia. It was happening this minute in his bones. We'd been struck.

He'd always been a fine athlete, a competitor, a runner. Now fate had tripped him; he stumbled and fell. Yet how quickly he tried to get up and join the race again! Left at home that fall, very ill, with his friends scattering to schools and jobs, he still was determined to go to college later, study hard, make the soccer team, eventually make all-American. To these goals he soon added one more—to stay alive.

We both knew that tremendous ordeals lay ahead. Leukemia, cancer of the blood, had always been a swift killer. When Eric developed the disease in 1968, doctors had just found ways to slow it down by using powerful drugs to suppress symptoms and produce periods of remission.[3] They did not know how to cure it.

There was hope, though, in the fact that Eric had a type of childhood leukemia (acute lymphocytic[4]) that was especially responsive to drug therapy. (By now, a few youngsters are actually being cured of it.) But Eric, at 17, was beyond the age of most effective treatment. Soon we discovered that his body overreacted to many of the best drugs and that the recommended high dosage, needed to destroy diseased cells, tended too quickly to wipe out healthy ones.

There were times during those first months when I saw him shaken, fighting for control. After all, it hadn't been too long since he was a small boy who could throw himself in my arms for comfort. Part of him must have been crying, "Please save me! Don't let me die!" I couldn't save him, but I could show him my own best courage. I learned to hide my concern, my tenderness, and I saw he was strengthened by my calm. He had to run free to be a man. I wanted that. If there were to be no other alternative, eventually I would help him die like a man.

We learned to be casual with danger, to live with death just around the corner. Whenever Eric was discharged from the hospital after transfusions (first they would give him two, then five, then seven), he would fly down the steps swinging a duffel bag, as if he were just back from a great weekend. I'd hand him the keys to the car, slide over, and he would pick up his life as if nothing had happened. But there were always drugs, always bouts of nausea.

I remember once starting up the stairs to bring him a cup of weak tea. He passed me on the way down wearing his swim trunks and carrying a spear gun. Ignoring the tea, he said, "Maybe I'll get you a fish for supper." He played pick-up soccer, weekend football and basketball with a hemoglobin[5] so low it left him short of breath, occasionally faint. On the basketball court, his teammates, galloping for a

---

3. **remission:** the period during which the symptoms of a disease lessen or subside.
4. **acute lymphocytic** (lĭm′fə-sĭt′ĭk).
5. **a hemoglobin** (hē′mə-glō′bĭn): a count of the red blood cells, which carry oxygen from the lungs to other body tissues and carbon dioxide from the tissues to the lungs.

> A powerful bolt seemed to enter the top of my skull as I got the message . . . Eric had leukemia.

Linking To Science

There are three main types of leukemia: acute, chronic myeloid, and chronic lymphatic. The first type, most commonly found in children, is the form that Eric had. People with acute leukemia often experience a fever, a sore throat, joint pain, and bruising. Chronic myeloid, in contrast, afflicts those in middle age. The diagnosis is made on the basis of abdominal discomfort, fever, a general feeling of ill-health, and an elevated white blood cell count. Chronic lymphatic leukemia usually strikes middle-aged and elderly people. These patients show an enlargement of the lymph glands, general malaise, and fever. The causes of leukemia are unknown, although some researchers believe it can be caused by exposure to high doses of radiation.

A member of the University of Connecticut soccer team, Eric trained during periods of remission. Courtesy of Doris Lund.

goal at the other end of the gym, would shout, "Just stay there, Eric—we'll be right back."

It was always more than a game he played. His life was on the line. "Exercise, Attitude, Desire" were the chalked words on his blackboard. These three words would bring him through. "You don't die of leuk, you know," he said once to me. "Something else goes. Your heart. Or your kidneys. I'm going to be ready for it when it comes for me. I'm going to win."

But he was not confused about the nature of his enemy—at least not by the time he'd spent some weeks on the eighth floor of Memorial Hospital's Ewing Pavilion in New York. Ewing Eight has faces, bodies you might see in pictures of the inmates of Dachau or Auschwitz.[6] Worse. Ewing patients talk a lot about remissions, of

---

6. **Dachau** (dä′kou) or **Auschwitz** (oush′vĭts): World War II Nazi concentration camps. Prisoners were skeletally thin from starvation.

course. "Remission"—that seductive word! Hope, with the end to hope implied. Eric's remissions encouraged us to think that justice would triumph, the devil relent. Once he got an 11-month stay of execution with the drug Methotrexate. I remember looking at him that summer as he ran the beach with friends. All of them tan, glowing, happy, all with the same powerful shoulders, the same strong, brown legs. What could there be in the bones of one that differed from the others? I relaxed, reassured. He must be safe at last. The next day Memorial phoned. Eric's most recent tests had shown that his remission was at an end. Even as I watched him, wild cells had been springing up in his marrow like dragon's teeth.[7] More and then more. Always more than could be slain.

Eric endured and survived many crises. He learned to live on the edge of the ledge and not look down. Whenever he had to be in the hospital, Memorial's doctors gave him passes to escape the horror. He'd slip off his hospital bracelet (which was forbidden) and rush out to plunge into the life of the city. Crowds, shop windows, cut-rate records. Restaurants in Chinatown. Concerts in the park. Summer parties on rooftops. Dark, crazy bars. He liked the music, the talk and, when he could take it, the beer. He listened a lot but never told his own story. "Where you from?" His answer was always, "I've got my own pad on First Avenue, between 67th and 68th. Nice neighborhood—handy to everything." (Some way to describe your bed on Ewing Eight!)

Even more than exploring the city, he loved working out, trying to get back his strength on these brief passes. A pretty Memorial technician called his doctor in terror one afternoon. "I've got a date with Eric in a few minutes. What'll I do if he wants to run?" "Sit down and wait for him," came the reply. Once he went out waving good-bye to less fortunate inmates on the floor, only to return an hour later waving from the ambulance stretcher. There was no living without risks, and so he took them. (This is one of his special gifts to me. Dare! Take life, dangers and all.)

The disease gained on him. To prevent infection he was finally put in a windowless, isolated chamber, the laminar-airflow room. Sterile air, sterile everything, sterile masks, caps, gowns, gloves for anyone entering his room. He joked, played to the eager audience peering through his glass-windowed door. And then sudden severe hemorrhages.[8] Six days of unconsciousness, soaring fevers. His white count was dangerously low. Platelet count[9] zero! Hemoglobin hardly worth mentioning. Surely, I thought, this is the end. But friends came, literally by busloads, to give blood for transfusions. During that crisis, it took more than 32 blood donors a day just to keep him alive.

I watched the doctors and nurses jabbing for veins, taping both needled arms to boards, packing the hemorrhages, shaking him to rouse him from stupor, and I thought: Enough! Let him die in peace! Why bring him back for more? He's proved himself—and beyond. He's had two good years of college. He made the soccer team in spite of your wretched drugs which are only poisons in disguise. He even made the dean's list. No more! Let him go!

But I had more to learn about my son's strength and resources. There was still much good life to be lived at the edge of the dark place. Eric came back—it seemed to me "from the unknown bourne."[10] He had to remain in the laminar-

---

7. **springing . . . dragon's teeth:** In Greek mythology, a prince sowed the teeth of a dragon he had killed, and fierce armed men sprang from the ground.
8. **hemorrhages** (hĕm'ər-ĭj-ĭz): heavy discharges of blood, often internal.
9. **white count . . . platelet** (plāt'lĭt) **count:** counts of the white blood cells and the platelets, the cells necessary for clotting.
10. **"from the unknown bourne** (bôrn)**":** A *bourne* (or *bourn*) is an ultimate limit, destination, or goal. This quotation may be a reference to a speech in Shakespeare's *Hamlet* in which Hamlet describes "something after death" as "The undiscovered country from whose bourn / No traveler returns."

OPTION 1

Individual Activity
CREATE A COMIC STRIP

Have students create a comic strip that, like Eric's *Adventures of Ewing 8*, portrays some of the events described in this story. Remind students that animals are sometimes used in comics to represent people. Eric, for example, used Ralph the Camel to represent himself in *The Adventures of Ewing 8*.

Teacher's Role Help students create their comic strips by suggesting that first they look back through the essay and choose the events they want to depict. Then, before they begin the actual drawing, they should plan out and sketch the whole strip. Encourage students to display their finished comic strips in the classroom.

Rubric

3 Full Accomplishment Comic strips accurately portray events from the story and capture the character of Eric.

2 Substantial Accomplishment Comic strips are slightly inaccurate or show a slight lack of understanding of the essay's main points.

1 Little or Partial Accomplishment Comic strips are incomplete or lack characters. The subject matter indicates a misunderstanding of the essay's theme.

OPTION 2

Cooperative Learning
CREATE A CHARACTER WEB

Have students work together in cooperative groups to create detailed character webs of Eric, based on the details provided in this essay. Groups should review the selection to create a comprehensive account of Eric's character.

Teacher's Role Encourage students to make inferences about Eric's character based on details in the essay.

Rubric

3 Full Accomplishment Webs provide a comprehensive description of Eric based upon essay details.

2 Substantial Accomplishment Webs leave some story details unaccounted for or provide only a partial account of Eric's character.

1 Little or Partial Accomplishment Students have difficulty working together or transforming essay details into character traits for their webs.

---

airflow room, off and on, for nearly four months. The picture on page 890 was taken two days after his release. Within weeks he was running from 12 to 15 miles a day. That spring, he didn't get back to college, but in his absence they named him captain of the varsity soccer team; he received the award for the Most Improved Player and finally was listed among the All-New England All-Stars. Proud honors, justly won. And there were others. We have a bookcase full of plaques and medals.

But I treasure even more the things they don't give medals for: his irreverent[11] humor; the warmth and love and consideration he gave his friends, especially his comrades in the War on the Eighth Floor. For these last he was a jaunty[12] hero, survivor of epic battles. Yet he was always one of them; hopefully, the Golden Warrior who would lead them all to victory—or at least escape.

(He and a fellow inmate almost managed it once. Hiding themselves in laundry carts under dirty linen, they rode down nine floors on the service elevator and out to the sidewalk. Just short of being loaded with the laundry on a truck, they decided to give themselves up and go back to bone marrow, intravenous bottles, and the rest of it. There was, after all, no real way out.)

As a variation on the theme of escape, Eric invented Ralph the Camel, a melancholy dromedary who, although hospitalized for "humpomeia," somehow managed to survive all the witless treatments his doctors could devise, including daily injections of pineapple juice. Ralph starred in a series of underground comic books known as *The Adventures of Ewing 8*, which featured Memorial's top doctors, nurses, technicians, and other notables, all drawn by Eric in merciless caricature. As Dr. Bayard Clarkson put it, "Eric

> "We are all in the same boat in a stormy sea and we owe each other a terrible loyalty."

spared no one, but we could hardly wait for the next *Adventure*." When they asked for more, his price was simple: "Get me in remission."

One of his exploits became a legend. Ten important doctors made Grand Rounds together every week. This particular Monday they stopped by the bed of their liveliest patient, to find him huddled under blankets looking unusually bleak.

"Eric! How do you feel?" asked Dr. Dowling, concerned.

"Scaly," was the mumbled reply.

Only then was the doctor's eye caught by the live goldfish swimming around in Eric's intravenous bottle. The plastic tube running down under the covers wasn't, of course, hooked up, but it looked convincing. The doctors broke up. The ward cheered! For the moment, humor had death on the run.

The eighth floor was a bad place to make friends. As one crusty old patient put it, "Make 'em and you'll lose 'em." But for Eric, there was no way to stay uninvolved. In the beginning he looked for the secrets of survival in the most spirited people around him. "That Eileen is so great," he told me. "She's beaten this thing for five years!" Or, "Look at that old guy, Mr. Miller. They just took out his spleen,[13] but he's hanging in there!"

Then, as the months of his treatments lengthened into years, he began to see them go. The good, the brave, the beautiful, the weak, the whining, the passive. They were all going the same way . . . Eileen, Mr. Miller, and

---

11. **irreverent** (ĭ-rĕv′ər-ənt): satirical; critical of what is generally accepted or respected.
12. **jaunty:** having an easy confidence; happy and carefree.
13. **spleen:** an organ that has various functions in modifying the blood as it circulates through the body.

so many more. When he was at home during one of his last remissions, he chalked up new words on his blackboard. "We are all in the same boat in a stormy sea and we owe each other a terrible loyalty" (G. K. Chesterton). Eric would not desert or fault his companions. He would play his heart out while the game might still be won, but he was beginning to think of the unthinkable. The casualty lists on the eighth floor were long. . . .

At the end, Eric finally accepted his own death. This acceptance was his last, most precious gift to me—what made my own acceptance possible. There was no bitterness. He said, simply, "There comes a time when you say: 'Well, that's it. We gave it a helluva try.'"

I remember one afternoon in Memorial a few days before he died. He wanted to talk of all the good things: the way he felt about his sisters . . . the wild, wonderful times he'd had with his brother, Mark. Suddenly he closed his eyes and said, "Running! That was so great—running on a beach for miles and miles!" He smiled, eyes still closed. "And snow! Snow was fun—" He was summing it up, living it, feeling it all again while there was still time.

He talked on quietly, gently, in the past tense, telling me, without telling me, to be ready, to be strong.

Once, thinking the light was hurting his eyes, I started to lower the window blind. "No, no!" he stopped me. "I want all the sky." He couldn't move (too many tubes), but he looked at that bright blue square with such love. "The sun," he said. "It was so good—"

It grew dark. He grew tired. Then he whispered, "Do something for me? Leave a little early tonight. Don't run for the bus. Walk a few blocks and look at the sky. Walk in the world for me. . . ."

And so I do, and so I will. Loving life that much, Eric gave it to me—new, strong, beautiful!—even as he was dying. That was his victory. In a way it is also mine. And I think perhaps it is a victory for all of us everywhere when human beings succeed in giving such gifts to each other. ❖

DORIS HEROLD LUND

1919–

A native of Indianapolis, Indiana, Doris Herold Lund worked as an advertising copywriter before becoming a freelance writer, illustrator, and cartoonist. She has written and illustrated a number of books for children, and her verse collection, *The Attic of the Wind,* has been made into an animated movie. She is best known, however, for her 1974 book *Eric,* a longer and more detailed version of the story she tells in the essay "Gift from a Son Who Died." For Eric and his family, the physical struggle with leukemia was compounded by the emotional struggles that come with adolescence. As Lund said, "While Eric demanded his independence, even though he was ill, I had to overcome my need to mother him too much—to let him go even though he might be dying. In other words we *both* grew up—in different ways." She added, "It seems my whole life has been one long struggle to develop the kind of courage that I needed every minute during Eric's losing battle." *Eric* has been translated into 15 languages and was made into a Hallmark Hall of Fame television movie in 1975.

OTHER WORKS *Hello, Baby!; The Paint-Box Sea; Patchwork Clan: How the Sweeney Family Grew*

OPTION 3

Class Discussion
SHARING IDEAS

Teacher's Role After students have read the selection, engage them in a whole-class discussion using the following questions.

1. What do you think are the "gifts" that Eric gives his mother? *(Possible responses: he made her aware of "the value of each good moment"; he taught her about "the importance of wasting nothing"; he taught her to be strong in the face of adversity and grief.)*

2. When Eric realizes he is about to die, how does he respond? What do you think this says about Eric and his approach to life? *(Possible responses: Eric responds by focusing on all the good times he has had in his life; he focuses on what he loved about life; this shows that Eric's approach to life was optimistic and upbeat; he didn't want to let death rob him of his enjoyment of life.)*

3. What do you think is the theme of this essay? *(Possible responses: Death can be a positive as well as a negative experience; people have a lot to learn from those who are dying; life should be lived to the fullest, no matter how long or short it is.)*

4. Compare Eric to some of the characters you have read about in this part of the unit. Who do you think he is most like? Why? *(Possible responses: He is like "the man in the water," losing his battle with nature but maintaining dignity; he is like Azucena, beset by a fatal misfortune at a young age, and his mother is like Rolf Carlé; he is like Mrs. Bamjee, determined to beat something he feels is unjust; he is like Yossi Ghinsberg, struggling to survive against terrible odds.)*

OVERVIEW

In the Guided Assignment for this section, students will write an essay evaluating ideas and issues in a literary selection. Through analysis of the literature, they will see some of the techniques writers use to convey ideas and attitudes. The Writer's Style demonstrates how writers use elaboration to develop and support ideas. In Reading the World, students will question and evaluate subjective opinions expressed to advance a controversial idea.

Objectives

- To recognize how authors use elaboration to support and develop ideas
- To provide additional details though the use of adjective clauses
- To write a critical essay evaluating ideas and issues expressed in literature
- To evaluate controversial real-world issues

Skills

LITERATURE
- Identifying facts that support ideas

GRAMMAR AND USAGE
- Using adjective clauses
- Using adverbs
- Positioning adverbs correctly

MEDIA LITERACY
- Developing informed opinions

SPEAKING, LISTENING, AND VIEWING
- Peer response
- Discussing opinions

CRITICAL THINKING
- Establishing criteria for evaluation

Teaching Strategy: MODELING
In the following models, ideas are developed and attitudes are conveyed through the use of examples and sensory details.

A Gordimer Possible response: The husband is both proud and suspicious; the visitors are prominent community members and business men; the husband feels flattered and suspicious at the same time.

B Erdrich Possible response: hearing and touch; words and phrases such as *curled, roared, bounced, felt the brush of her lips, heard the beat of her heart, loud as thunder, long as the roll of drums*

WRITING ABOUT LITERATURE

A Critical View

As you read the literature in Unit Six, you may have thought about the ideas presented. A selection may have addressed a universal problem, told something of human nature, or reflected a set of beliefs. Did you question these ideas or simply accept them? On the next several pages, you will

- study how writers use elaboration to develop ideas
- express your opinion about the ideas in a selection
- use your skills to evaluate a real-world issue

Writer's Style: Elaboration Writers use elaboration—facts, sensory details, anecdotes, specific examples, quotations, or opinions—to support and develop their ideas.

Read the Literature

How do the writers of the following excerpts support their ideas?

Literature Models

Specific Examples
What is the main idea being presented here? What specific examples does the writer give to support that idea?

> He was used to coming home and finding his wife sitting at the table deep in discussion with strangers or people whose names were familiar by repute. Some were prominent Indians, like the lawyer, Dr. Abdul Mohammed Khan, or the big businessman, Mr. Moonsamy Patel, and he was flattered, in a suspicious way, to meet them in his house. As he came home from work next day, he met Dr. Khan coming out of the house, and Dr. Khan—a highly educated man—said to him, "A wonderful woman."
>
> Nadine Gordimer, from "A Chip of Glass Ruby"

Sensory Details
Which senses does the writer appeal to in this paragraph? Which words appeal to those senses?

> Curled as I was, against her stomach, I was not startled by the cries of the crowd or the looming faces. The wind roared and beat its hot breath at our back; the flames whistled. I slowly wondered what would happen if we missed the circle or bounced out of it. Then I wrapped my hands around my mother's hands. I felt the brush of her lips and heard the beat of her heart in my ears, loud as thunder, long as the roll of drums.
>
> Louise Erdrich, from "The Leap"

894 UNIT SIX: THE MAKING OF HEROES

PRINT AND MEDIA RESOURCES

UNIT SIX RESOURCE BOOK
Prewriting, p. 34
Elaboration, p. 35
Peer Response Guide, pp. 36–37
Revising and Proofreading, p. 38
Student Model, pp. 39–40
Rubric, p. 41

FORMAL ASSESSMENT
Guidelines for Writing Assignment

GRAMMAR MINI–LESSONS
Transparencies, pp. 2, 22, 26
Copymasters, pp. 2–3, 24–27

WRITING MINI–LESSONS
Transparencies, pp. 35, 42, 46

Connect to Life

Facts are statements that can be proved. Statistics are facts stated with numbers. Ideas supported by facts and statistics seem credible and authoritative. Credibility is particularly important in nonfiction writing. Notice the factual support in the following excerpt from a magazine article.

Magazine Article

On August 6, 1973, Clemente entered the hallowed Baseball Hall of Fame, alongside such other greats as Babe Ruth, Lou Gehrig, Ted Williams and Joe DiMaggio. His Hall of Fame plaque reads: Member of exclusive 3,000 hit club. Led National League in batting four times. Had four seasons with 200 or more hits while posting lifetime average of .317 and 240 home runs. Won most valuable player award in 1966. Rifle-armed defensive star. Set N.L. mark by pacing outfielders in assists five years. Batted .362 in two World Series, hitting in all 14 games.

John S. Babbitt,
from "Roberto Clemente—A Sports Legend,"
Stamps

Facts and Statistics
What general idea do these facts and statistics support?

Try Your Hand: Elaboration

1. **Elaborate on an Idea** Use sensory details to elaborate on ideas about a special party, a home-cooked meal, the first day of spring, or any other topic of your choosing.

2. **A QuickWrite Check** Check your portfolio for a QuickWrite or paragraph, and revise the piece, using elaboration to support one of its ideas.

3. **Work Together** With a partner, use elaboration to support or develop the following idea or an idea of your own choosing. Decide on the most effective type of elaboration to use.

   The weather can affect the way people think and act.

SkillBuilder

GRAMMAR FROM WRITING

Using Adjective Clauses

One way to elaborate is to provide additional detail through the use of adjective clauses. An adjective clause is a subordinate clause that modifies a noun or a pronoun. It tells *what kind* or *which one* and is usually placed after the word the clause modifies.

Adjective clauses often begin with a relative pronoun: *who, whom, whose, that, which*. This relative pronoun relates the adjective clause to the word it modifies. Look at the example below from "And of Clay Are We Created."

He filmed the volunteers who discovered her, and the first persons who tried to reach her.

In the example above, the adjective clause *who discovered her* modifies the word *volunteers*. *Who tried to reach her* modifies the word *persons*.

APPLYING WHAT YOU'VE LEARNED
Combine each of the following sentence pairs into one sentence with an adjective clause. Use the relative pronoun in parentheses.

1. Rolf Carlé found Azucena in a mud pit. The mud pit killed many people. (that)
2. The mud held her. It would not let her go. (that)
3. The girl remained brave. She did not cry and accepted her death. (who)

WRITING ABOUT LITERATURE **895**

Teaching Strategy: MODELING

C Babbitt Possible response: The details about Clemente's performance suggest that he was an extraordinary baseball player who earned his membership in the Baseball Hall of Fame.

Try Your Hand

1. Responses will vary. Sentences should use specific sensory details, as in the following example:
   - Jose's mouth watered as he prepared to savor the crimson richness of his father's raspberry pie.

2. If necessary, assist students in choosing a selection that lends itself to elaboration. Begin by asking a student volunteer to write a short paragraph on the chalkboard. Then encourage the entire class to work together to provide elaboration. Finally, ask students to elaborate on the work they have selected from their portfolios.

3. Responses will vary. Elaboration should emphasize sensory details, as in this example:
   - A stormy night can inspire children to imagine monsters under the bed and ghosts groaning outside the bedroom door.

SkillBuilder GRAMMAR FROM WRITING

USING ADJECTIVE CLAUSES Remind students that although adjective clauses add descriptive details to sentences, they are not necessary to the minimal subject-predicate structure of the sentence. Read aloud the sample sentence without the adjective phrases: "He filmed the volunteers and the first persons." Point out that although the sentence is complete, it lacks interest and raises the question "Which ones?"

Applying What You've Learned Answers:

1. Rolf Carlé found Azucena in the mud pit *that* killed many people.
2. The mud *that* held her would not let her go.
3. The girl, *who* remained brave, did not cry and accepted her death.

Additional Suggestions Have students write a paragraph describing either a heroic act or a great moment in sports history. They should use the relative pronouns *that, which,* and *who* in adjective clauses that describe the event.

Reteaching/Reinforcement
- *Grammar Mini-Lessons* transparencies, p. 50

The Writer's Craft
Adjective Clauses, pp. 607–608

Critical Thinking:
MAKING JUDGMENTS

D Remind students that making judgments requires analysis and evaluation. Invite them to use the prewriting notes on this page as a guide to selecting points to judge.

Teaching Strategy:
USING THE SKILLBUILDER

E You can help students understand the importance of being specific by teaching the SkillBuilder on Types of Peer Responses at this time. It will help students see that specific questions designed to evoke helpful answers usually produce the desired results.

WRITING ABOUT LITERATURE

Criticism

Writing a critical essay can help you understand and judge a literary work. You can then share your opinion with others, helping them understand why you evaluated the selection the way you did.

D **GUIDED ASSIGNMENT**
Write a Critical Essay On the next few pages, you'll identify selections from Unit Six that present ideas that interest you. Then you'll choose one of these selections and evaluate the ideas and values it contains.

1 Prewrite and Explore

Reflect on the selections you have read in Unit Six. Which present ideas that really catch your interest? Create a list of possible selections.

FINDING A FOCUS

Choosing a Selection As you reread one or more selections, jot down any questions, comments, or reactions that you have. Which selection seems most interesting to you?

E **Deciding on an Idea** What key ideas are presented? Which are striking or significant?

Focusing Your Position Think about the important ideas and how you feel about them. The notes at the right include questions you might ask yourself.

Decision Point Now make a decision on what idea you will evaluate.

LOOKING FOR EVIDENCE

Now that you know the selection and the idea you want to focus on, look for evidence of the idea in the selection. Ask yourself

- What passages or examples from the text reflect the ideas or values I want to write about?
- Do I agree with these ideas or values? Why or why not?

Student's Prewriting Notes

Notes on "A Chip of Glass Ruby"

What universal problem or experience does the text address?
—inequality and racism
—lack of freedom and voice

What lesson does it seem to teach?
—the importance of personal inner strength
—that human beings can overcome hardships

What does it show about human nature or relationships?
—human beings are reluctant to help others who are different from themselves
—people sometimes make judgments out of fear

How does the literature represent a particular set of beliefs or ideas?
—two sets of ideas: one of sympathy and commitment, one of criticism and selfishness

896 UNIT SIX: THE MAKING OF HEROES

Assessment Option

SELF-ASSESSMENT After students have answered the Looking for Support questions, ask them to decide whether they agree or disagree with the author. As they make their determinations, students should consider the following questions:
- *If I had the authority to require the author to make revisions, what would I ask him or her to change?*
- *When the author made a good case, what persuasive technique did he or she use effectively? Did the author use examples? Sensory description? Why did the technique appeal to me?*

2 Write and Analyze a Draft

When you begin writing, remember that your draft should briefly summarize the selection, explain the idea you will be writing about, and state your criticism of it. Don't forget to include a thesis statement and a clear summary of your position.

Check the draft and self-stick notes below to see how one student evaluated an idea from "A Chip of Glass Ruby."

Student's Draft

Have I made my thesis statement clear?

I will include ideas about social commitment in the body of my essay

> "A Chip of Glass Ruby" tells the story of an Indian woman who lives in South Africa. Her decision to reach out to the natives affects her family, but Zanip Bamjee takes chances anyway. In this story, Nadine Gordimer raises an important question about a moral problem: Who is responsible for helping others who are less fortunate than ourselves? Should we be compassionate or selfish? The story encourages the reader to decide which response is more appropriate. Since most human beings don't sympathize with others' problems, Mrs. Bamjee's answer to the problem of social responsibility is a good one.

3 Share Your Draft

Before you share your draft, read it over and ask yourself the following questions.

- What idea is the focus of this essay?
- What additional support for my position might I include?

Share the draft and ask a peer to consider these questions.

- In your own words, restate my opinion of this idea.
- How is my main point stated and supported?
- How do I use elaboration to bring out my ideas?

SkillBuilder

 SPEAKING & LISTENING

Types of Peer Responses

Giving helpful responses to a classmate's writing is not always easy. Consider some of the following techniques as you give and receive peer responses.

Pointing Ask your readers what they like best in your piece of writing. Request that they be specific and avoid comments such as "It's good" or "I liked it."

Summarizing Ask readers what they hear as the main message in your writing. They don't need to evaluate the writing at this time.

Responding to Specific Features Ask for feedback on qualities such as support of ideas and unity in a paragraph. Ask them to respond to specific questions such as, "Do I explore my reactions in depth?" "Is there anything in my paper that confuses you?"

Replying Discuss the ideas in your paper with your readers. Ask their opinions on your topic. Talk about what you have said, not how you have said it.

APPLYING WHAT YOU'VE LEARNED
Consider these techniques as you ask for and give peer responses to your critical essays.

WRITING HANDBOOK

For information on using peer response, see page 1020 of the Writing Handbook.

WRITING ABOUT LITERATURE **897**

Writing Skill: ELABORATION

F The Discovery Draft provides an opportunity for students to sort out the information they've gathered and to think through their ideas. They should ask themselves whether they have clearly stated their theses in their opening paragraphs. Remind students to use examples to support their critical positions.

CUSTOMIZING FOR
Less-Proficient Writers

G Ask students to write their thesis in one simple sentence and then to list the examples that support it. Encourage students to make sure they have provided ample support by using two or more examples.

SkillBuilder SPEAKING & LISTENING

TYPES OF PEER RESPONSES Explain that by asking specific questions about content—the ideas expressed and the position taken in the essay—writers should receive specific peer responses that will help their writing.

Applying What You've Learned Students can work in pairs to critique each other's critical essays. Responses will vary, but might resemble the following sample:
- I like the part of your essay that describes the student's sense of shame about cheating [Pointing], and I think you make it really clear that deception always leads to trouble [Summarizing]. The section telling that the student got caught confuses me [Responding to Specific Features], and I'd like to know what the teachers were like in that school [Replying].

Additional Suggestions Have students apply the response technique described in this SkillBuilder in the following way. One student will pretend to be the author of one of the selections in Unit Six, and the other student will act as the critic in the feedback process.

Critical Thinking: ANALYZING

 Explain that as they write a critical analysis, students must support their opinions with specific examples just as a prosecutor tries to get a conviction with abundant evidence. To revise and edit their essays, students should
- look for adequate elaboration through examples and details
- look for places to make the elaboration more vivid through the use of adjective clauses
- check the placement of adverbs to see that they modify details effectively

Teaching Strategy: MODELING

Discuss how the sample meets the Standards for Evaluation on this page. The writer states what Mrs. Bamjee is like and describes her behavior to provide support for the evaluation of her character. The writer also integrates quotes, and organizes the information well.

 Possible Responses:
- The single idea is that Mrs. Bamjee is an inspiring character who cares about other people. The writer calls her stance "correct" and "hopeful" expressing absolute agreement with her position.
- The author portrays Zanip as a strong and confident person by quoting her as she sticks up for her beliefs and stands up to her husband.

WRITING ABOUT LITERATURE

❹ Revise and Edit

Will your reader understand your opinion of the idea? When you revise, make sure that you have stated your topic and your position clearly. Reflect on your essay and make sure you have supported critical statements with specific examples or details.

Student's Final Draft

Since most human beings rarely sympathize with others' problems, Mrs. Bamjee's answer to the problem of social responsibility is correct and hopeful.

From the first scene in the story, Zanip accepts social responsibility. She is portrayed as gentle, confident, and strong. Unselfishly, she ignores her own problems and cares for others who are less fortunate and different from her. Some people, including her husband, might say that she is extremely irresponsible for neglecting her own family; however, I believe that she is acting very courageously. Few people can commit to solving major social problems with such intensity. She is truly driven to make a change. For example, her husband scolds her for helping the natives instead of attending to the Indians' own problems. She replies confidently, "What's the difference, Yusuf? We've all got the same troubles."

Zanip and her husband seem to be separated by two ideas that conflict. While she represents sympathy and understanding, Mr. Bamjee represents a harsh, judgmental, selfish point of view. Like most human beings, he does not want to become involved in others' problems. As he resists her efforts to help the natives, he seems fearful too. The government has been jailing protesters.

What single idea is being discussed? What is the writer's opinion of it?

How does the writer elaborate on the idea that Zanip is a confident, strong person?

Standards for Evaluation

A critical essay
- chooses a single idea to investigate
- presents evidence from the text to support critical, evaluative, and interpretive statements
- integrates appropriate quotations smoothly
- is organized clearly and logically

898 UNIT SIX: THE MAKING OF HEROES

Assessment Option

SELF-ASSESSMENT To help students assess their own writing, have them ask themselves the following questions:
- Have I written about a value or an idea that truly matters to me? If not, is there an issue closer to my heart that I can address?
- What do I expect my readers to know about me and my opinions after reading my essay?
- Did I support my opinions adequately, as if I were a skilled prosecutor presenting ample evidence?

898 THE LANGUAGE OF LITERATURE **TEACHER'S EDITION**

Grammar in Context

Using Adverbs Adverbs can help you elaborate on ideas by answering the questions *Where? When? How? To what extent?* They modify different parts of speech and therefore add detail to sentences.

An adverb can modify a verb.

> She replies, *confidently* "What's the difference, Yusuf? We've all got the same troubles."

An adverb can modify an adjective.

> Some people, including her husband, might say that she is *extremely* irresponsible for neglecting her own family.

An adverb can modify another adverb.

> I believe that she is acting *very* courageously.

Try Your Hand: Using Adverbs

Fill in adverbs in the paragraph below. Then compare your new version with a classmate's paragraph. How does the meaning of the paragraph change with your adverb choices?

"A Chip of Glass Ruby" is a story about an Indian woman who takes responsibility for the problems of others. Her actions raise important questions and teach that a person's spirit cannot be dampened. Even when she faces hardship, Mrs. Bamjee maintains her spirit and influences the people she touches.

SkillBuilder

GRAMMAR FROM WRITING

Positioning Adverbs Correctly

The placement of adverbs can alter the meaning or intensity of a sentence. Adverbs usually follow the verbs they modify. Look at the following examples from *Back from Tuichi* by Yossi Ghinsberg.

I was rowing desperately with all my strength.

Sometimes, though, adverbs can also come before the verb.

He carefully, wordlessly placed the wallet into the metal box.

Intensifiers, such as *very* and *extremely*, usually come before the adjective or adverb they modify.

We must be really close to the island.

APPLYING WHAT YOU'VE LEARNED

You can change the position of some adverbs to create sentence variety or a different emphasis. Experiment with the placement of the adverbs in parentheses.

1. We arrived at the river. (today)
2. Since we hurried into the raft, we did not realize our gear was still on the bank. (just)
3. Reaching for the gear, I slipped and became wet! (really)

GRAMMAR HANDBOOK

For more information on adverbs, see page 1076 of the Grammar Handbook.

WRITING ABOUT LITERATURE **899**

READING THE WORLD

This unit has helped students make thoughtful evaluations of literature and express their opinions by using elaborative techniques. They should also be aware of the need to evaluate real-world issues. In this lesson, students will practice developing informed opinions about controversial issues.

Critical Thinking: EXAMINING

L Students may notice the uniforms worn by the young people in the picture. They may note that there are both girls and boys in the group and that the setting suggests a school.

Media Literacy: INTERPRETING A CONDITION

M Students may assert that the girls and boys are wearing uniforms because they attend a private school. The reasoning behind wearing uniforms is to establish "uniformity" in the student population; for example, there may be a code of behavior that all students are required to follow. Also, uniforms allow students to be identified as belonging to a particular school.

Speaking and Listening: GROUP DISCUSSION

N Encourage students to be respectful of one another as they express diverse opinions. Evaluating complex ideas requires gathering as much information as possible about the topic. Therefore, listening to and discussing divergent viewpoints will improve one's understanding of the controversial issue.

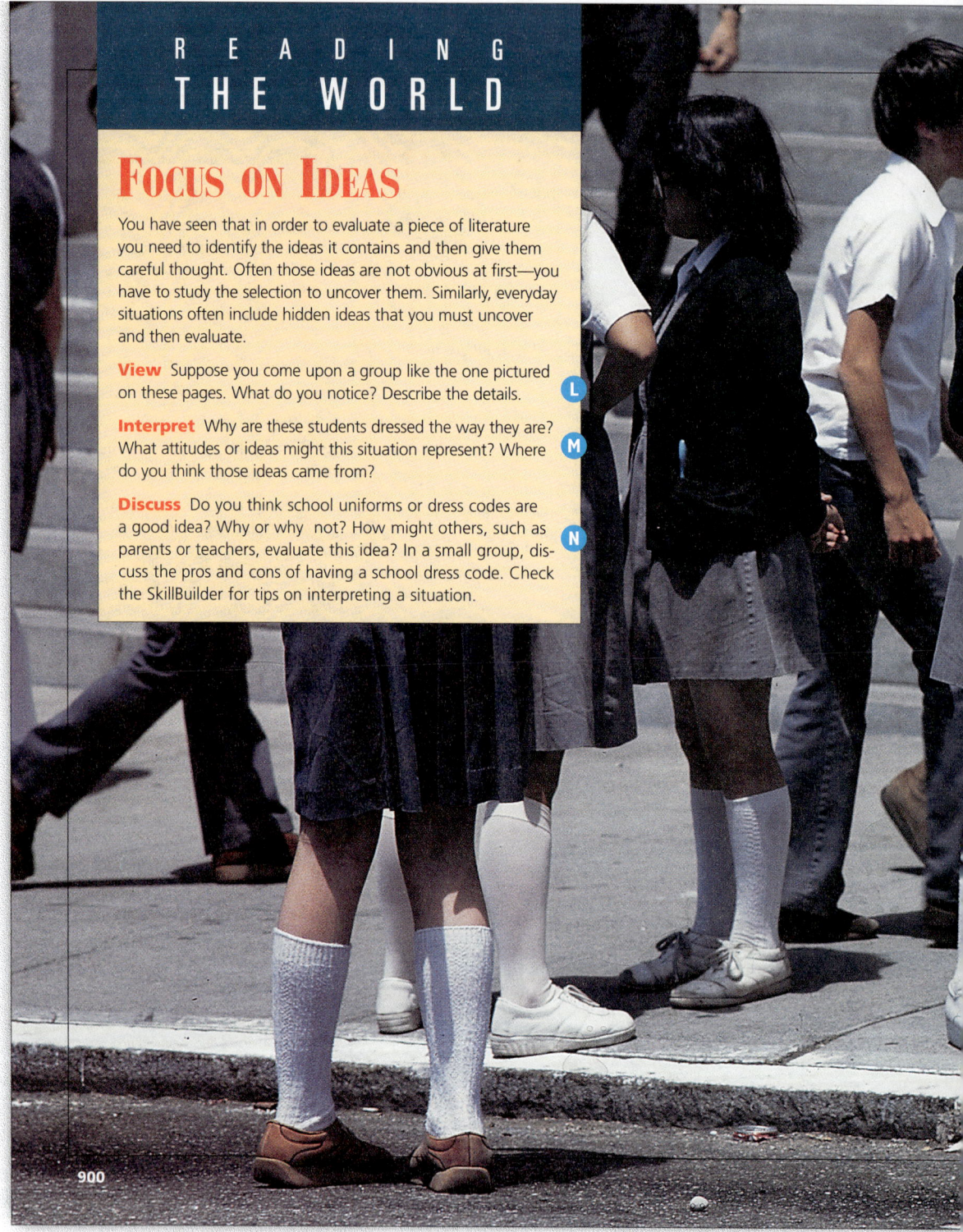

READING THE WORLD

FOCUS ON IDEAS

You have seen that in order to evaluate a piece of literature you need to identify the ideas it contains and then give them careful thought. Often those ideas are not obvious at first—you have to study the selection to uncover them. Similarly, everyday situations often include hidden ideas that you must uncover and then evaluate.

View Suppose you come upon a group like the one pictured on these pages. What do you notice? Describe the details.

Interpret Why are these students dressed the way they are? What attitudes or ideas might this situation represent? Where do you think those ideas came from?

Discuss Do you think school uniforms or dress codes are a good idea? Why or why not? How might others, such as parents or teachers, evaluate this idea? In a small group, discuss the pros and cons of having a school dress code. Check the SkillBuilder for tips on interpreting a situation.

900 THE LANGUAGE OF LITERATURE TEACHER'S EDITION

SkillBuilder

 CRITICAL THINKING

Interpreting a Situation

If you just witness a situation or an event and don't think any more about what you've seen, you could miss something fairly important or significant.

Asking questions such as the following can help you interpret and evaluate the ideas that may be hidden within a situation. You may even become a more careful observer in the process!

- What am I really seeing here? Notice what you notice—the big picture and the details.
- What does this mean? What is the hidden idea?
- Do I agree with the idea as I understand it? Why or why not?

By asking thoughtful questions, you will be less likely to miss important events or details. You will be more likely to understand and learn from what you see.

APPLYING WHAT YOU'VE LEARNED

In a small group, brainstorm a list of intriguing events or situations you have witnessed. Discuss and evaluate the hidden ideas in each. Record details and observations that lead to your interpretation and evaluation.

READING THE WORLD   901

SkillBuilder CRITICAL THINKING

ESTABLISHING CRITERIA FOR EVALUATION Subjecting strong personal opinions to sound evaluation is very challenging. The guiding questions provided in this SkillBuilder will help students be objective as they evaluate both their own opinions and the opinions of others with whom they disagree.

Applying What You've Learned Student questions may address the following topics:
- the effects of violence on different age groups; the various degrees of violence portrayed on networks; how often violence is presented during daytime viewing hours; the existence and implementation of a television code
- the problems that can be attributed to irresponsible parents; data about cases in which parents were made to take responsibility for their children's actions
- statistics about the lives of high school dropouts; information about various programs aimed at arresting the dropout rate and about the success rates of those programs

UNIT SIX
Part 2 Lesson Planner

TIME ALLOTMENTS SHOWN ARE APPROXIMATE. DEPENDING ON YOUR GOALS AND THE NEEDS OF YOUR STUDENTS, YOU MAY WISH TO ALLOW MORE OR LESS TIME FOR CERTAIN PORTIONS OF THE LESSON.

Table of Contents	Discussion	Previewing the Selection	Reading the Selection
PART OPENER **The Heroic Tradition** page 902	**20 MINUTES** • Reflect on the part theme		
SELECTIONS from **Le Morte d'Arthur:** **The Crowning of Arthur** **Sir Launcelot du Lake** page 905 AVERAGE		**20 MINUTES** • PERSONAL CONNECTION • LITERARY CONNECTION • WRITING CONNECTION	**90 MINUTES** • Introduce vocabulary • Read pp. 905–919 (15 pp.)
SELECTION from **The Acts of King Arthur and His Noble Knights** page 924 AVERAGE		**20 MINUTES** • PERSONAL CONNECTION • LITERARY CONNECTION • READING CONNECTION: Making inferences/Using your reading log	**60 MINUTES** • Read pp. 924–932 (9 pp.)
SELECTION **Antigone** page 938		**20 MINUTES** • PERSONAL CONNECTION • LITERARY CONNECTION • READING CONNECTION: Understanding classical drama	**150 MINUTES** • Read pp. 938–978 (41 pp.)
POETRY ON YOUR OWN **Old Song** page 982 AVERAGE			**20 MINUTES** • Read pp. 982–983 (2 pp.)
Writing	Exploring Topics	Prewriting	Drafting and Revising
WRITING FROM EXPERIENCE **Report**	**25 MINUTES**	**30 MINUTES**	**70 MINUTES**

Time estimates assume in-class work. You may wish to assign some of these stages as homework.

Responding to the Selection

FROM PERSONAL RESPONSE TO CRITICAL ANALYSIS	OR	ANOTHER PATHWAY	LITERARY CONCEPTS	QUICKWRITES
50 MINUTES				
• Discussion questions	OR	• Guidebook	• Romance	• Plot synopsis • Magazine article • Editorial
50 MINUTES				
• Discussion questions	OR	• Storyboard	• Style	• Feature article • Interview • Advice column • Soap-opera scene
50 MINUTES				
• Discussion questions	OR	• Flow chart	• Dramatic irony	• Letter • Diary entry • Lecture

Extension Activities

ALTERNATIVE ACTIVITIES	LITERARY LINKS	CRITIC'S CORNER	THE WRITER'S STYLE	ACROSS THE CURRICULUM	ART CONNECTION	WORDS TO KNOW	BIOGRAPHY
50 MINUTES							
✔	✔			HISTORY SPORTS	✔	✔	✔
50 MINUTES							
✔	✔	✔		HISTORY SPORTS		✔	✔
50 MINUTES							
✔		✔	✔	HISTORY		✔	✔

Publishing and Reflecting

25 MINUTES

PART 2

REFLECTING ON THEME

As a class, list some well-known stories in the heroic tradition, including popular legends, myths, and folk tales. Explore what elements these stories have in common, such as *conflicts* between good and evil and *characters* with great physical and mental strength. Then ask students to discuss any cultural influences they find in these heroic stories.

What Do You Think?

First have students brainstorm a list of heroic traits, such as bravery, intelligence, strength, and values. Then remind students that they can draw childhood heroes from life as well as from literature, movies, and television. Students will return to this activity on pages 922, 935, and 981.

UNIT SIX **PART 2**

THE HEROIC TRADITION

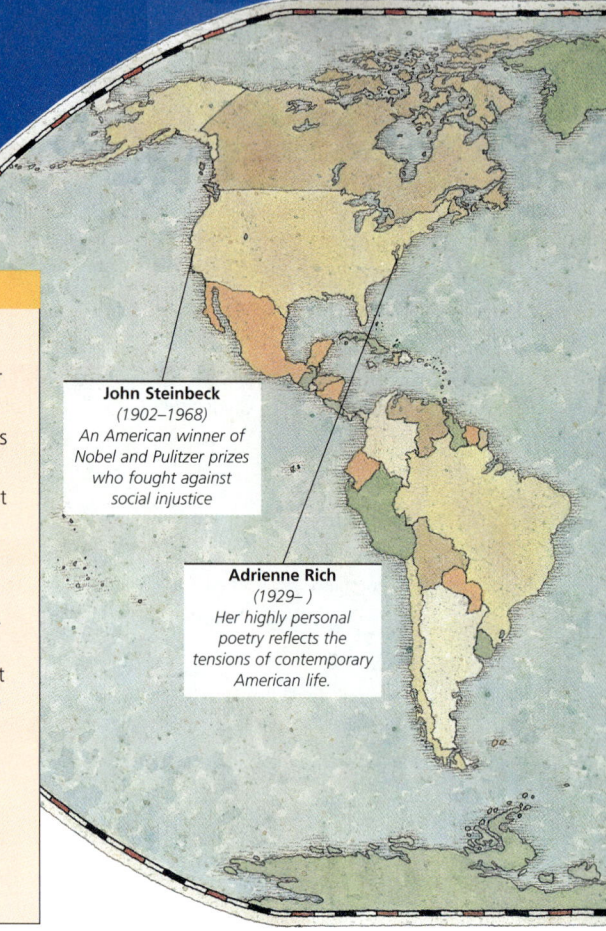

John Steinbeck
(1902–1968)
An American winner of Nobel and Pulitzer prizes who fought against social injustice

Adrienne Rich
(1929–)
Her highly personal poetry reflects the tensions of contemporary American life.

REFLECTING ON THEME

Can a hero exist without someone to tell his or her story? When you think about it, heroes and storytelling go hand and hand. From ancient times to the present, people have shared stories about great deeds, and each new generation learns about the heroes of old. Often, these heroes represent qualities or character traits that are valued by entire cultures. As you will see in this part of Unit Six, stories of heroes can be kept alive for centuries.

What Do You Think? In your notebook, create a list of your own childhood heroes. Then describe one of those heroes to a small group of classmates, explaining what you found admirable or interesting about him or her. After every person in the group has described a hero, discuss how the heroes reflect qualities and character traits that are valued by cultures.

Sir Thomas Malory	*from* **Le Morte d'Arthur**	904
	The Crowning of Arthur	
	A child conceived in mystery and destined for glory	
	Sir Launcelot du Lake	912
	The greatest knight of all	
John Steinbeck	*from* **The Acts of King Arthur and His Noble Knights**	923
	Fame and forbidden passion in Arthur's court	

902 THE LANGUAGE OF LITERATURE TEACHER'S EDITION

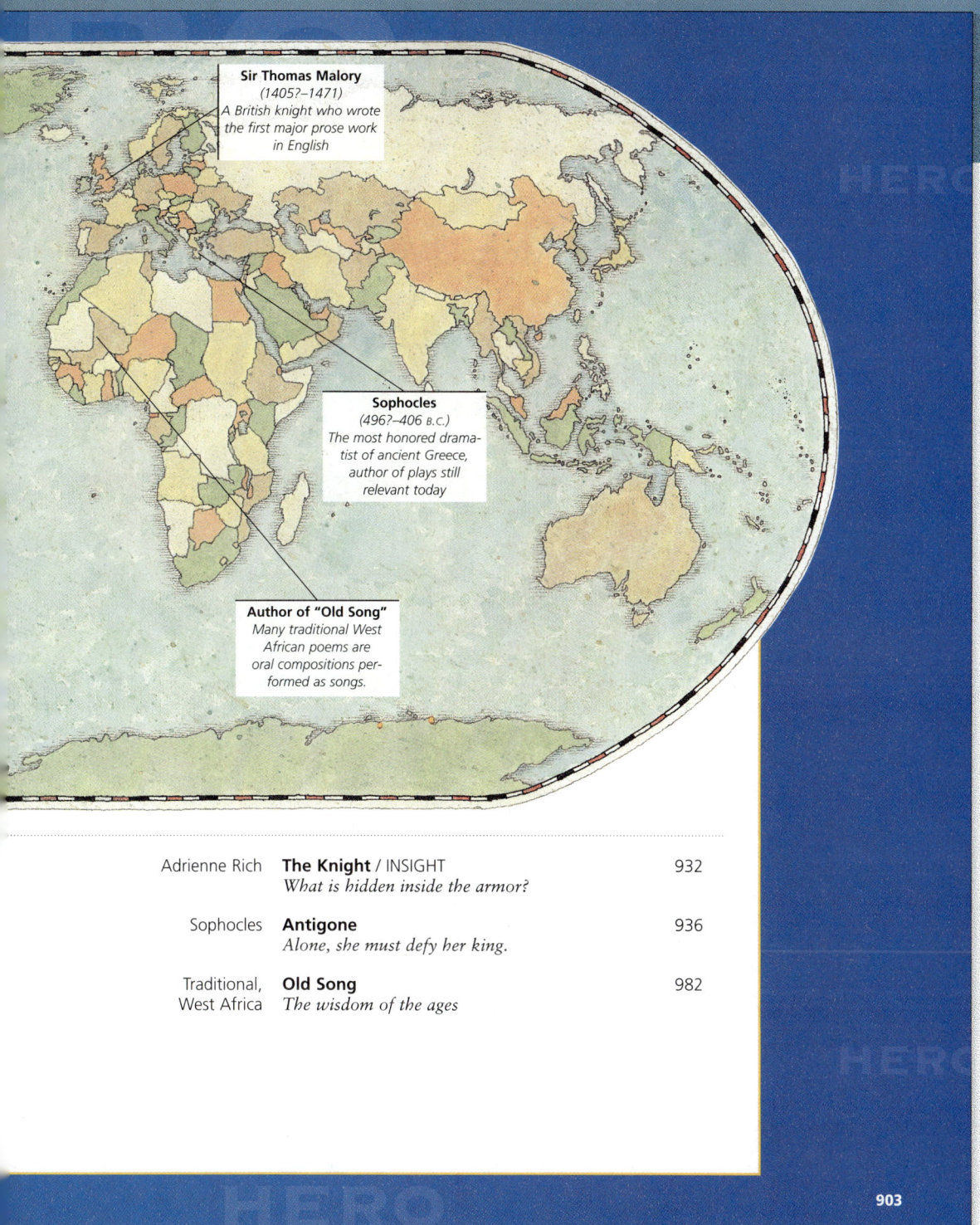

Sir Thomas Malory
(1405?–1471)
A British knight who wrote the first major prose work in English

Sophocles
(496?–406 B.C.)
The most honored dramatist of ancient Greece, author of plays still relevant today

Author of "Old Song"
Many traditional West African poems are oral compositions performed as songs.

Adrienne Rich	**The Knight** / INSIGHT *What is hidden inside the armor?*	932
Sophocles	**Antigone** *Alone, she must defy her king.*	936
Traditional, West Africa	**Old Song** *The wisdom of the ages*	982

Map Note

The purpose of this map is to identify the various cultures from which the authors in this section came. You may want to ask students one or more of the following questions:

- What countries and cultures are represented in this unit?
- Which of these authors wrote in a language other than English?
- What kinds of heroes do you think these authors might have written about?
- Why do you think some of these ancient stories about heroes are still enjoyed today?

OVERVIEW

Objectives

- To understand and appreciate excerpts from a classic romance that explore the heroic tradition
- To analyze the elements of medieval romance
- To express understanding of the story through a choice of writing forms, including a plot synopsis, a magazine article, and an editorial
- To extend understanding of the story through a variety of multi-modal and cross-curricular activities

Skills

LITERARY CONCEPTS
- Romance
- Plot

THE WRITER'S STYLE
- Diction

GRAMMAR
- Commas in a series

SPEAKING, LISTENING, AND VIEWING
- Dramatic reading
- Group discussion
- Oral presentation

CUSTOMIZING FOR Students Acquiring English

- Use **ACCESS FOR STUDENTS ACQUIRING ENGLISH**, *Reading Support*.
- To help clarify the rank of the characters in these stories, list these various titles on the board and discuss what each term means: *king, queen, duke, duchess, knight, archbishop*. Point out that important men and women are addressed using the term *Sir* or *Lady* before their names.
- In addition to these boxes, you may want to use the suggestions under Strategic Reading for Less-Proficient Readers.

PREVIEWING

ROMANCE

from Le Morte d'Arthur
The Crowning of Arthur
Sir Launcelot du Lake

Sir Thomas Malory Great Britain

Retold by Keith Baines

Activating Prior Knowledge
PERSONAL CONNECTION

In a small-group discussion, share what you know about the legend of King Arthur and his knights of the Round Table. What types of actions do you associate with Arthurian knights? What do you know about their ideals and motives? What personal qualities do they exhibit? Use a chart, like the one shown, to organize your information. Then share your group's results with the rest of the class.

Arthur and His Knights	
Name of Heroes	Ideals / Motives
Action	Personal Qualities

Building Background
LITERARY CONNECTION

In literature, great heroes rarely spring from humble origins. Legendary heroes are usually the sons of kings or even the sons of gods, whose births are foretold and heralded by miraculous signs. They are "chosen ones" fated to rule or inspire others, though in youth they may be unaware of their destined role. And so it is with King Arthur, the heroic ruler in one of the most popular and enduring legends in Europe and North America. According to legend, Arthur became king of England and established his court at Camelot. He then gathered the best knights of the realm to join with him in the fellowship of the Round Table. These knights lived according to a specific code of behavior—the chivalric code—which stressed, among other things, loyalty to the king, courage, personal honor, and defending those who could not defend themselves. The most famous model of chivalry was Sir Launcelot, Arthur's friend and the greatest knight of the Round Table.

The earliest tales of Arthur come from Welsh literature of the 6th through 12th centuries. Most English-speaking readers know of the Arthurian legend through Sir Thomas Malory's *Le Morte d'Arthur* ("The Death of Arthur"), completed about 1470, or one of its many adaptations. The excerpts you are about to read are from Keith Baines's modern retelling of *Le Morte d'Arthur*.

Setting a Purpose
WRITING CONNECTION

What makes a hero? Is it destiny? noble birth? Or is there some inner quality that motivates someone to act heroically? In your notebook, write down your own thoughts about what makes a hero. Keep these thoughts in mind as you read about the legendary Arthur and Sir Launcelot.

LASERLINKS
- CULTURAL CONNECTION

904   UNIT SIX PART 2: THE HEROIC TRADITION

PRINT AND MEDIA RESOURCES

UNIT SIX RESOURCE BOOK
Strategic Reading: Literature, p. 45
Vocabulary SkillBuilder, p. 46

GRAMMAR MINI-LESSONS
Transparencies, pp. 42–43
Copymasters, p. 43

WRITING MINI-LESSONS
Transparencies, p. 44

ACCESS FOR STUDENTS ACQUIRING ENGLISH
Selection Summaries
Reading Support

FORMAL ASSESSMENT
Selection Test, p. 179
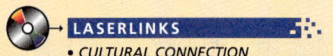 Test Generator

 **AUDIO LIBRARY**
See Reference Card

 **LASERLINKS**
Art Gallery

INTERNET RESOURCES
McDougal Littell Literature Center at http://www.hmco.com/mcdougal/lit

The Crowning of Arthur

from *Le Morte d'Arthur*
Sir Thomas Malory

King Uther Pendragon,[1] ruler of all Britain, had been at war for many years with the Duke of Tintagil in Cornwall when he was told of the beauty of Lady Igraine,[2] the duke's wife. Thereupon he called a truce and invited the duke and Igraine to his court, where he prepared a feast for them, and where, as soon as they arrived, he was formally reconciled to the duke through the good offices[3] of his courtiers.

In the course of the feast, King Uther grew passionately desirous of Igraine and, when it was over, begged her to become his paramour.[4] Igraine, however, being as naturally loyal as she was beautiful, refused him.

---

1. **Uther Pendragon** (ōō'thər pĕn-drăg'ən): *Pendragon* was a title used in ancient Britain to refer to a supreme chief or leader.
2. **Igraine** (ē-grān').
3. **offices:** services.
4. **paramour** (păr'ə-mŏŏr'): lover or mistress.

WORDS TO KNOW

adversary (ăd'vər-sĕr'ē) *n.* an opponent; enemy (p. 916)

champion (chăm'pē-ən) *v.* to fight for; defend (p. 915)

fidelity (fĭ-dĕl'ĭ-tē) *n.* faithfulness to duties and obligations; devotion; loyalty (p. 913)

prowess (prou'ĭs) *n.* superior strength, courage, or daring, especially in battle (p. 913)

recompense (rĕk'əm-pĕns') *n.* amends made, as for damage or loss; payment in return for something, such as a service (p. 916)

Art Note

***King Arthur Drawing Forth the Sword* by Howard Pyle** Howard Pyle (1853–1911) was born in Wilmington, Delaware. He gained renown first as a magazine illustrator, then as an author and illustrator of children's books. His style is noted for its clear, firm lines and careful composition.

Reading the Art *What details of this image show the solemnity and importance of this occasion?*

CUSTOMIZING FOR
Gifted and Talented Students

Have students form small discussion groups to discuss the following questions as they read the selection:

- What values does the author seem to be espousing?
- How are these values different from values in our society today?
- What deeds described in these two stories seem to you to be heroic?
- Would these deeds be considered heroic today?

Literary Note

The term *romance* has also been applied to other types of literature influenced by romances such as Malory's: romantic epics of the Renaissance period (the 14th through the 16th centuries) and romantic tales of the early 19th century. Romantic elements persist in modern literature.

The Granger Collection, New York.

906 UNIT SIX PART 2: THE HEROIC TRADITION

"I suppose," said Igraine to her husband, the duke, when this had happened, "that the king arranged this truce only because he wanted to make me his mistress. I suggest that we leave at once, without warning, and ride overnight to our castle." The duke agreed with her, and they left the court secretly.

The king was enraged by Igraine's flight and summoned his privy council.[5] They advised him to command the fugitives' return under threat of renewing the war; but when this was done, the duke and Igraine defied his summons. He then warned them that they could expect to be dragged from their castle within six weeks.

The duke manned and provisioned[6] his two strongest castles: Tintagil for Igraine, and Terrabyl, which was useful for its many sally ports,[7] for himself. Soon King Uther arrived with a huge army and laid siege to Terrabyl; but despite the ferocity of the fighting, and the numerous casualties suffered by both sides, neither was able to gain a decisive victory.

Still enraged, and now despairing, King Uther fell sick. His friend Sir Ulfius came to him and asked what the trouble was. "Igraine has broken my heart," the king replied, "and unless I can win her, I shall never recover."

"Sire," said Sir Ulfius, "surely Merlin the Prophet could find some means to help you? I will go in search of him."

Sir Ulfius had not ridden far when he was accosted by a hideous beggar. "For whom are you searching?" asked the beggar; but Sir Ulfius ignored him.

"Very well," said the beggar, "I will tell you: you are searching for Merlin, and you need look no further, for I am he. Now go to King Uther and tell him that I will make Igraine his if he will reward me as I ask; and even that will be more to his benefit than to mine."

"I am sure," said Sir Ulfius, "that the king will refuse you nothing reasonable."

"Then go, and I shall follow you," said Merlin. Well pleased, Sir Ulfius galloped back to the king and delivered Merlin's message, which he had hardly completed when Merlin himself appeared at the entrance to the pavilion. The king bade him welcome.

"Sire," said Merlin, "I know that you are in love with Igraine; will you swear, as an anointed[8] king, to give into my care the child that she bears you, if I make her yours?"

The king swore on the gospel that he would do so, and Merlin continued: "Tonight you shall appear before Igraine at Tintagil in the likeness of her husband, the duke. Sir Ulfius and I will appear as two of the duke's knights: Sir Brastius and Sir Jordanus. Do not question either Igraine or her men, but say that you are sick and retire to bed. I will fetch you early in the morning, and do not rise until I come; fortunately Tintagil is only ten miles from here."

The plan succeeded: Igraine was completely deceived by the king's impersonation of the duke, and gave herself to him, and conceived Arthur. The king left her at dawn as soon as Merlin appeared, after giving her a farewell kiss. But the duke had seen King Uther ride out from the siege on the previous night and, in the course of making a surprise attack on the king's army, had been killed. When Igraine realized that the duke had died three hours before he had appeared to her, she was greatly disturbed in mind; however, she confided in no one.

Once it was known that the duke was dead, the king's nobles urged him to be reconciled to Igraine, and this task the king gladly entrusted to Sir Ulfius, by whose eloquence it was soon accomplished. "And now," said Sir Ulfius to his fellow nobles, "why should not the king marry the beautiful Igraine? Surely it would be as well for us all."

---

5. **privy** (prĭv′ē) **council:** a group of advisors who serve a ruler.
6. **provisioned:** supplied.
7. **sally ports:** gates or passages in the walls of fortifications, from which troops can make a sudden attack.
8. **anointed:** chosen as if by divine intervention.

THE CROWNING OF ARTHUR 907

Mini-Lesson Study Skills

INFERRING WORD MEANINGS FROM CONTEXT Remind students that they can find the meaning of a word by thinking about its context, the sentence or group of sentences in which the word appears. There are also several types of context clues, often signaled by key words, that can help determine the meaning of a word: definition and restatement (*that is, or*); example (*like, such as, for instance*); comparison (*similar to, also, like*); contrast (*unlike, however*); cause and effect (*because, since, therefore*).

Application Have students write a separate sentence for each of the following six terms. Besides including the word, each sentence should include context clues and key words to signal the context clues. (Students may first use the dictionary to check the meaning of each word.)

martial

scabbard

gauntlet

knight errant

siege

quixotic

Cultural Note

C In the Middle Ages, women had little choice about whom they would marry, and women of high rank were often offered in marriage as a way of forging political alliances. Going into a convent was one of the few attractive alternatives to marriage. Within a convent, a woman had a job to do, a certain amount of independence, and encouragement to read, write, and study. An abbess or a mother superior, the head of a convent, was a woman with a great deal of power within her domain.

Critical Thinking: MAKING JUDGMENTS

D Point out that women in the Middle Ages were relatively powerless. Ask students to keep this in mind and explain why or why not they think Igraine's reaction is appropriate. *(Accept all reasonable responses.)*

Literary Concept: ROMANCE

E Point out that this is another example of hidden identity. Ask students why Merlin wants to keep the child's identity a secret. *(Possible responses: He may think the child, as heir to the throne, would be in danger or that others might exert undesirable influence on the child; he may want the child to grow up humble.)*

Critical Thinking: SPECULATING

F Ask students what motives Merlin might have for his intervention in the lives of King Uther, Igraine, and Arthur. *(Possible responses: He thinks of himself as an instrument of fate that helps the characters attain their destiny; he hopes to gain favor, and thus power, with the king and the future king.)*

C The marriage of King Uther and Igraine was celebrated joyously thirteen days later; and then, at the king's request, Igraine's sisters were also married: Margawse, who later bore Sir Gawain, to King Lot of Lowthean and Orkney; Elayne, to King Nentres of Garlot. Igraine's daughter, Morgan le Fay, was put to school in a nunnery; in after years she was to become a witch, and to be married to King Uryens of Gore, and give birth to Sir Uwayne of the Fair Hands.

A few months later it was seen that Igraine was with child, and one night, as she lay in bed with King Uther, he asked her who the father might be. Igraine was greatly abashed.

"Do not look so dismayed," said the king, "but tell me the truth, and I swear I shall love you the better for it."

"The truth is," said Igraine, "that the night the duke died, about three hours after his death, a man appeared in my castle—the exact image of the duke. With him came two others who appeared to be Sir Brastius and Sir Jordanus. Naturally I gave myself to this man as I would have to the duke, and that night, I swear, this child was conceived."

"Well spoken," said the king; "it was I who impersonated the duke, so the child is mine." He then told Igraine the story of how Merlin had arranged it, and Igraine was overjoyed to **D** discover that the father of her child was now her husband.

Sometime later, Merlin appeared before the king. "Sire," he said, "you know that you must provide for the upbringing of your child?"

"I will do as you advise," the king replied.

"That is good," said Merlin, "because it is my reward for having arranged your impersonation of the duke. Your child is destined for glory, and I want him brought to me for his baptism. I shall **E** then give him into the care of foster parents who can be trusted not to reveal his identity before the proper time. Sir Ector would be suitable: he is extremely loyal, owns good estates, and his wife has just borne him a child. She could give her child into the care of another woman, and herself look after yours."

Sir Ector was summoned and gladly agreed to the king's request, who then rewarded him handsomely. When the child was born, he was at once wrapped in a gold cloth and taken by two knights and two ladies to Merlin, who stood waiting at the rear entrance to the castle in his beggar's disguise. Merlin took the child to a priest, who baptized him with the name of Arthur, and thence to Sir Ector, whose wife fed him at her breast.

Two years later King Uther fell sick, and his enemies once more overran his kingdom, inflicting heavy losses on him as they advanced. Merlin prophesied that they could be checked only by the presence of the king himself on the battlefield, and suggested that he should be conveyed there on a horse litter.[9] King Uther's army met the invader on the plain at St. Albans, and the king duly appeared on the horse litter. Inspired by his presence, and by the lively leadership of Sir Brastius and Sir Jordanus, his army quickly defeated the enemy, and the battle **F** finished in a rout. The king returned to London to celebrate the victory.

But his sickness grew worse, and after he had lain speechless for three days and three nights, Merlin summoned the nobles to attend the king in his chamber on the following morning. "By the grace of God," he said, "I hope to make him speak."

In the morning, when all the nobles were assembled, Merlin addressed the king: "Sire, is it your will that Arthur shall succeed to the throne, together with all its prerogatives?"[10]

The king stirred in his bed and then spoke so that all could hear: "I bestow on Arthur God's blessing and my own, and Arthur shall succeed to the throne on pain of forfeiting my blessing."

---

9. **horse litter:** a stretcher fastened to a horse.
10. **prerogatives:** rights or privileges held by a person or group.

908 UNIT SIX PART 2: THE HEROIC TRADITION

 Mini-Lesson Grammar

COMMAS IN A SERIES Remind students to use a comma after every item in a series except the last one as illustrated by the  example above. A series consists of three or more items of the same kind, whether words, phrases, or clauses.

Application Have students insert commas where needed in the following sentences.

1. The rain came early in the day(,) grew heavy in the afternoon(,) and continued through the night.
2. Sir Kay was angry(,) frustrated(,) disappointed(,) and frightened.
3. Merlin planned to have Arthur baptized(,) send him to foster parents(,) and hide his identity.
4. Although Morgan Le Fay was beautiful and charming, she was cold(,) calculating(,) and selfish.

Reteaching/Reinforcement

- *Grammar Handbook,* anthology pp. 1090–1091
- *Grammar Mini-Lessons* copymasters p. 43, transparencies pp. 42–43

The Writer's Craft

Commas in a Series, p. 785

908 THE LANGUAGE OF LITERATURE TEACHER'S EDITION

Then King Uther gave up the ghost. He was buried and mourned the next day, as befitted his rank, by Igraine and the nobility of Britain.

During the years that followed the death of King Uther, while Arthur was still a child, the ambitious barons fought one another for the throne, and the whole of Britain stood in jeopardy. Finally the day came when the Archbishop of Canterbury, on the advice of Merlin, summoned the nobility to London for Christmas morning. In his message the archbishop promised that the true succession to the British throne would be miraculously revealed. Many of the nobles purified themselves during their journey, in the hope that it would be to them that the succession would fall.

The archbishop held his service in the city's greatest church (St. Paul's), and when matins[11] were done, the congregation filed out to the yard. They were confronted by a marble block into which had been thrust a beautiful sword. The block was four feet square, and the sword passed through a steel anvil which had been struck in the stone, and which projected a foot from it. The anvil had been inscribed with letters of gold:

WHOSO PULLETH OUTE THIS SWERD OF THIS STONE AND ANVYLD IS RIGHTWYS KYNGE BORNE OF ALL BRYTAYGNE

The congregation was awed by this miraculous sight, but the archbishop forbade anyone to touch the sword before mass had been heard. After mass, many of the nobles tried to pull the sword out of the stone, but none was able to, so a watch of ten knights was set over the sword, and a tournament proclaimed for New Year's Day, to provide men of noble blood with the opportunity of proving their right to the succession.

> WHOSO PULLETH OUTE THIS SWERD OF THIS STONE AND ANVYLD IS RIGHTWYS KYNGE BORNE OF ALL BRYTAYGNE

Sir Ector, who had been living on an estate near London, rode to the tournament with Arthur and his own son Sir Kay, who had been recently knighted. When they arrived at the tournament, Sir Kay found to his annoyance that his sword was missing from its sheath, so he begged Arthur to ride back and fetch it from their lodging.

Arthur found the door of the lodging locked and bolted, the landlord and his wife having left for the tournament. In order not to disappoint his brother, he rode on to St. Paul's, determined to get for him the sword which was lodged in the stone. The yard was empty, the guard also having slipped off to see the tournament, so Arthur strode up to the sword, and, without troubling to read the inscription, tugged it free. He then rode straight back to Sir Kay and presented him with it.

Sir Kay recognized the sword and, taking it to Sir Ector, said, "Father, the succession falls to me, for I have here the sword that was lodged in the stone." But Sir Ector insisted that they should all ride to the churchyard, and once there bound Sir Kay by oath to tell how he had come by the sword. Sir Kay then admitted that Arthur had given it to him. Sir Ector turned to Arthur and said, "Was the sword not guarded?"

"It was not," Arthur replied.

"Would you please thrust it into the stone again?" said Sir Ector. Arthur did so, and first Sir Ector and then Sir Kay tried to remove it, but both were unable to. Then Arthur, for the second time, pulled it out. Sir Ector and Sir Kay both knelt before him.

"Why," said Arthur, "do you both kneel before me?"

"My lord," Sir Ector replied, "there is only

---

11. **matins** (măt'nz): morning prayers.

Art Note

Arthur as King by Howard Pyle This portrait of Arthur is another illustration from Pyle's four-volume retelling of the Arthurian legends.

Reading the Art What details indicate royalty? How would you describe the attitude of the king in this image?

COMPREHENSION CHECK
1. Who is Uther Pendragon? *(King of Britain, father of Arthur)*
2. Who is Merlin? *(a prophet with magical powers)*
3. How does Igraine come to marry King Uther? *(because her husband dies)*
4. How is Arthur raised? *(He is raised by Sir Ector and his wife, and his identity remains a secret.)*
5. How does Arthur become king? *(He removes the sword from the stone, which only the rightful heir to the throne can do.)*

The Granger Collection, New York.

one man living who can draw the sword from the stone, and he is the true-born King of Britain." Sir Ector then told Arthur the story of his birth and upbringing.

"My dear father," said Arthur, "for so I shall always think of you—if, as you say, I am to be king, please know that any request you have to make is already granted."

Sir Ector asked that Sir Kay should be made Royal Seneschal,[12] and Arthur declared that while they both lived it should be so. Then the three of them visited the archbishop and told him what had taken place.

All those dukes and barons with ambitions to rule were present at the tournament on New Year's Day. But when all of them had failed, and Arthur alone had succeeded in drawing the sword from the stone, they protested against one so young, and of ignoble[13] blood, succeeding to the throne.

The secret of Arthur's birth was known only to a few of the nobles surviving from the days of King Uther. The archbishop urged them to make Arthur's cause their own; but their support proved ineffective. The tournament was repeated at Candlemas and at Easter, and with the same outcome as before.

Finally at Pentecost, when once more Arthur alone had been able to remove the sword, the commoners arose with a tumultuous cry and demanded that Arthur should at once be made king. The nobles, knowing in their hearts that the commoners were right, all knelt before Arthur and begged forgiveness for having delayed his succession for so long. Arthur forgave them and then, offering his sword at the high altar, was dubbed first knight of the realm. The coronation took place a few days later, when Arthur swore to rule justly, and the nobles swore him their allegiance. ❖

---

12. **Royal Seneschal** (sĕn′ə-shəl): the representative of a king in judicial and domestic matters.
13. **ignoble:** not noble; common.

FROM PERSONAL RESPONSE TO CRITICAL ANALYSIS

REFLECT 1. In your notebook, jot down your reaction to the events that occur in "The Crowning of Arthur." Then share your thoughts with a partner.

RETHINK 2. How much control would you say the characters have over their lives?
Consider
- Uther's passion for Igraine and the way he makes her his wife
- what happens to Igraine's sisters and daughter after her wedding
- Merlin's comment that Arthur is "destined for glory" and the instructions he gives for Arthur's care
- Arthur's discovery that he is heir to the throne

3. In your opinion, does Arthur deserve to be king?
Consider
- the sacrifices other people must make to bring him to power
- the support he receives from the common people
- the kind of person he seems to be

4. What do you think it would be like to live in the world depicted in this selection? Explain your views.

From Personal Response to Critical Analysis

1. Accept all responses.
2. Possible responses: The characters seem controlled by fate and their own passions. Uther wages war because he is so taken by Igraine's beauty. Arthur's entire life seems dictated by Merlin's prophecy. The women especially seem to have little control over their lives but are dependent on the will of men. These characters are not realistic; they live in a kind of magical world so it is not surprising that they do not seem in control of their lives.
3. Possible responses: Arthur seems worthy to be king. He is beloved by the commoners, loyal to Sir Ector, and kind. Arthur is the rightful king simply because he has pulled the stone out of the rock; fate has decreed him king.
4. Accept all reasonable responses.

Mini-Lesson: Speaking, Listening, and Viewing

DRAMATIC READING Use the chalkboard shown here as you explain how to plan and give an effective dramatic reading.
- Become thoroughly familiar with the entire passage, not just your part, making sure you understand all the vocabulary and the concepts.
- Do not try to memorize your passage, but practice aloud before a mirror until you are comfortable with your part.
- Try to imagine yourself as being your character, thinking about what he or she feels and thinks, and projecting his or her personality.
- Read slowly, clearly, and with expression. Is your character angry, sad, excited? Make sure your voice expresses that emotion.

Application Have students work in small groups to choose an episode from "Launcelot" or "The Crowning of Arthur" to present a dramatic reading. Allow students class time to practice their reading, and then have them present the reading to the class.

Know the entire passage
Practice by reading aloud
Become the character
Read with expression

Art Note

The Reign of Chivalry from *Guiron le Courtois* **by unknown artist** This is an illustration from a medieval French manuscript. Manuscripts with these elaborate illustrations and decorations are called "illuminated," because of the gold leaf which is one element of their decoration. Tell students that the text in Gothic lettering is in old French, and that the title of the manuscript means "Guiron the Courtier."

Reading the Art *What do the spears laying on the ground and the group of mounted knights observing the contest indicate?*

Tournament in King Arthur's court. MS Douce 383, fol. 16r. The Bodleian Library, Oxford, England.

912 UNIT SIX PART 2: THE HEROIC TRADITION

Multicultural Perspectives

Certain modern fraternal organizations have patterned themselves after knightly orders. They may limit their membership to men, conduct ceremonies, and require various initiation rites. The Knights of Pythias, for example, is an organization that performs charitable work and emphasizes high moral standards in its members. In the Knights of Pythias there are three ranks, or degrees, of knighthood: page, esquire, and knight. The members pledge to obey rules and to help fellow knights in distress.

Sir Launcelot du Lake

from Le Morte d'Arthur
Sir Thomas Malory

SUMMARY

Sir Launcelot, the finest knight of the Round Table, sets out in search of adventure with his nephew Sir Lyonel. Launcelot grows sleepy and rests beneath an apple tree. Meanwhile, Lyonel challenges the powerful Sir Tarquine, but is defeated and imprisoned. Sir Ector, who is following Launcelot, also fights Tarquine, loses, and is taken captive. Four queens discover the sleeping Launcelot, and one of them, Morgan le Fay, casts a spell on him and takes him to her castle. The queens demand that Launcelot choose one of them to love; if he refuses, he will die. Launcelot chooses death, but a noblewoman promises to help Launcelot escape if he agrees to champion her father, King Bagdemagus, at a tournament. Launcelot agrees, and he wins the contest for Bagdemagus. Launcelot then travels to Tarquine's castle, where he kills Tarquine and in a bloody fight releases the prisoners.

When King Arthur returned from Rome, he settled his court at Camelot, and there gathered about him his knights of the Round Table, who diverted themselves with jousting and tournaments. Of all his knights one was supreme, both in prowess at arms and in nobility of bearing, and this was Sir Launcelot, who was also the favorite of Queen Gwynevere, to whom he had sworn oaths of fidelity.

One day Sir Launcelot, feeling weary of his life at the court, and of only playing at arms, decided to set forth in search of adventure. He asked his nephew Sir Lyonel to accompany him, and when both were suitably armed and mounted, they rode off together through the forest.

At noon they started across a plain, but the intensity of the sun made Sir Launcelot feel sleepy, so Sir Lyonel suggested that they should rest

Literary Note

I After Arthur became king, Merlin became his guide and counselor, helping him put down a rebellion of princes. Arthur married the beautiful Gwynevere and held court at the castle Camelot in southern England. Arthur established the Knights of the Round Table, a brotherhood of knights selected for their bravery, skill, and moral purity.

Cultural Note

J Launcelot's relationship to Queen Gwynevere is governed by courtly love, a medieval concept of love with a demanding set of rules. A knight chose one lady to serve faithfully, performing noble deeds for her sake. Ideal courtly love was chaste, and a knight's chosen lady was often married and therefore unattainable.

WORDS TO KNOW
prowess (prou′ĭs) *n.* superior strength, courage, or daring, especially in battle
fidelity (fĭ-dĕl′ĭ-tē) *n.* faithfulness to duties and obligations; devotion; loyalty

913

Assessment Option

INFORMAL ASSESSMENT You can informally assess your students' understanding of the events up to this point by having them create a log of the significant events in the lives of Arthur and Launcelot. Have them add to the log as they read the story of Launcelot's exploits.

Rubric

3 Full Accomplishment Logs are complete and include all significant events in the lives of the characters in correct chronological order.

2 Substantial Accomplishment Logs contain most of the significant events, although they may not all be in correct order.

1 Little or Partial Accomplishment Logs may be incomplete or contain irrelevant details and may not be in chronological order.

THE LANGUAGE OF LITERATURE TEACHER'S EDITION **913**

CUSTOMIZING FOR
Students Acquiring English

6 Students may not be familiar with terms relating to horsemanship. Explain that to dismount is to get down from a horse and that to tether a horse is to tie it up.

Literary Concept: PLOT

K Point out that the plot of a romance contains many episodes. Ask students to identify two episodes on this page. *(Possible responses: three knights and Sir Lyonel are defeated and imprisoned by Sir Tarquine; Sir Ector seeks out Sir Tarquine and is defeated and imprisoned by him.)*

CUSTOMIZING FOR
Multiple Learning Styles

L **Spatial or Graphic Learners** Have interested students work in pairs or small groups to design a diorama of the castle, the tree with shields, and the caldron. Have them include a paragraph explaining the items. Display their work in the classroom.

Literary Concept: ROMANCE

M Ask students what seems to motivate the actions of Sir Ector and the other knights who have been introduced. *(Possible responses: a desire for adventure; a desire to prove their skill and win fame and glory)*

---

beneath the shade of an apple tree that grew by a hedge not far from the road. They dismounted, tethered their horses, and settled down.

"Not for seven years have I felt so sleepy," said Sir Launcelot, and with that fell fast asleep, while Sir Lyonel watched over him.

Soon three knights came galloping past, and Sir Lyonel noticed that they were being pursued by a fourth knight, who was one of the most powerful he had yet seen. The pursuing knight overtook each of the others in turn and, as he did so, knocked each off his horse with a thrust of his spear. When all three lay stunned, he dismounted, bound them securely to their horses with the reins, and led them away.

Without waking Sir Launcelot, Sir Lyonel mounted his horse and rode after the knight and, as soon as he had drawn close enough, shouted his challenge. The knight turned about, and they charged at each other, with the result that Sir Lyonel was likewise flung from his horse, bound, and led away a prisoner.

The victorious knight, whose name was Sir Tarquine,[1] led his prisoners to his castle and there threw them on the ground, stripped them naked, and beat them with thorn twigs. After that he locked them in a dungeon where many other prisoners, who had received like treatment, were complaining dismally.

Meanwhile, Sir Ector de Marys,[2] who liked to accompany Sir Launcelot on his adventures, and finding him gone, decided to ride after him. Before long he came upon a forester.

"My good fellow, if you know the forest hereabouts, could you tell me in which direction I am most likely to meet with adventure?"

"Sir, I can tell you: less than a mile from here stands a well-moated castle. On the left of the entrance you will find a ford where you can water your horse, and across from the ford a large tree from which hang the shields of many famous knights. Below the shields hangs a caldron, of copper and brass: strike it three times with your spear, and then surely you will meet with adventure—such, indeed, that if you survive it, you will prove yourself the foremost knight in these parts for many years."

"May God reward you!" Sir Ector replied.

The castle was exactly as the forester had described it, and among the shields Sir Ector recognized several as belonging to knights of the Round Table. After watering his horse, he knocked on the caldron, and Sir Tarquine, whose castle it was, appeared.

They jousted, and at the first encounter Sir Ector sent his opponent's horse spinning twice about before he could recover.

"That was a fine stroke; now let us try again," said Sir Tarquine.

This time Sir Tarquine caught Sir Ector just below the right arm and, having impaled him on his spear, lifted him clean out of the saddle and rode with him into the castle, where he threw him on the ground.

"Sir," said Sir Tarquine, "you have fought better than any knight I have encountered in the last twelve years; therefore, if you wish, I will demand no more of you than your parole[3] as my prisoner."

"Sir, that I will never give."

"Then I am sorry for you," said Sir Tarquine, and with that he stripped and beat him and locked him in the dungeon with the other prisoners. There Sir Ector saw Sir Lyonel.

"Alas, Sir Lyonel, we are in a sorry plight. But tell me, what has happened to Sir Launcelot? for he surely is the one knight who could save us."

"I left him sleeping beneath an apple tree, and what has befallen him since I do not know," Sir Lyonel replied; and then all the unhappy prisoners once more bewailed their lot.

While Sir Launcelot still slept beneath the

---
1. **Tarquine** (tär′kwĭn).
2. **Sir Ector de Marys** (măr′əs): brother of Launcelot.
3. **parole**: the promise of a prisoner to abide by certain conditions in exchange for full or partial freedom.

914 UNIT SIX PART 2: THE HEROIC TRADITION

Mini-Lesson Literary Concepts

REVIEWING PLOT The sequence of actions and events in a drama or work of fiction is called the plot. Almost all plots center on at least one conflict or problem, which the characters struggle to resolve. Some works have episodic plots consisting of loosely connected incidents or episodes. Episodic plots are common in medieval romances such as *Le Morte d'Arthur.*

Application Have students identify the conflict and the resolution for each of the episodic plots from "The Crowning of Arthur" and "Sir Launcelot du Lake." Then have them work in pairs to write a brief episode to add to one of the two stories, taking care to make sure the episode fits the overall structure of "The Crowning of Arthur" or of "Sir Launcelot."

apple tree, four queens started across the plain. They were riding white mules and accompanied by four knights who held above them, at the tips of their spears, a green silk canopy, to protect them from the sun. The party was startled by the neighing of Sir Launcelot's horse and, changing direction, rode up to the apple tree, where they discovered the sleeping knight. And as each of the queens gazed at the handsome Sir Launcelot, so each wanted him for her own.

"Let us not quarrel," said Morgan le Fay. "Instead, I will cast a spell over him so that he remains asleep while we take him to my castle and make him our prisoner. We can then oblige him to choose one of us for his paramour."

Sir Launcelot was laid on his shield and borne by two of the knights to the Castle Charyot, which was Morgan le Fay's stronghold. He awoke to find himself in a cold cell, where a young noblewoman was serving him supper.

"What cheer?"[4] she asked.

"My lady, I hardly know, except that I must have been brought here by means of an enchantment."

"Sir, if you are the knight you appear to be, you will learn your fate at dawn tomorrow." And with that the young noblewoman left him. Sir Launcelot spent an uncomfortable night, but at dawn the four queens presented themselves and Morgan le Fay spoke to him:

"Sir Launcelot, I know that Queen Gwynevere loves you, and you her. But now you are my prisoner, and you will have to choose: either to take one of us for your paramour, or to die miserably in this cell—just as you please. Now I will tell you who we are: I am Morgan le Fay, Queen of Gore; my companions are the queens of North Galys, of Estelonde, and of the Outer Isles. So make your choice."

"A hard choice! Understand that I choose none of you, lewd sorceresses that you are; rather will I die in this cell. But were I free, I would take pleasure in proving it against any who would champion you that Queen Gwynevere is the finest lady of this land."

"So, you refuse us?" asked Morgan le Fay.

"On my life, I do," Sir Launcelot said finally, and so the queens departed.

Sometime later, the young noblewoman who had served Sir Launcelot's supper reappeared.

"What news?" she asked.

"It is the end," Sir Launcelot replied.

"Sir Launcelot, I know that you have refused the four queens, and that they wish to kill you out of spite. But if you will be ruled by me, I can save you. I ask that you will champion my father at a tournament next Tuesday, when he has to combat the King of North Galys, and three knights of the Round Table, who last Tuesday defeated him ignominiously."

"My lady, pray tell me, what is your father's name?"

"King Bagdemagus."[5]

"Excellent, my lady; I know him for a good king and a true knight, so I shall be happy to serve him."

"May God reward you! And tomorrow at dawn I will release you and direct you to an abbey which is ten miles from here, and where the good monks will care for you while I fetch my father."

"I am at your service, my lady."

As promised, the young noblewoman released Sir Launcelot at dawn. When she had led him through the twelve doors to the castle entrance, she gave him his horse and armor, and directions for finding the abbey.

"God bless you, my lady; and when the time comes, I promise I shall not fail you."

Sir Launcelot rode through the forest in search of the abbey but at dusk had still failed to find it

---

4. **What cheer?:** How are you?
5. **Bagdemagus** (băg′də-măg′əs).

WORDS TO KNOW

champion (chăm′pē-ən) *v.* to fight for; defend

Art Note

Lancelot rescuing Guinevere by crossing the sword bridge from *Le Roman de Lancelot du Lac* by unknown artist
This illustration is from a French collection of tales about Launcelot, published around 1300. Note that the illustration contains more than one scene.

Reading the Art *What element of magic can you see in this illustration? Do you think this illustration captures the heroic spirit of Launcelot? Why or why not?*

CUSTOMIZING FOR
Students Acquiring English

⑧ Write the titles *my lord, man-at-arms,* and *sovereign* on the board and ask students to notice how each one is used in this sentence and to define each in their own words. Contrast the modern religious usage of the word *Lord* with the much older title which was used to honor an earthly ruler.

Literary Note

Ⓡ King Arthur established the Round Table at the feast of Pentecost. At Pentecost every year thereafter he accepted new knights and required both new and old knights to swear an oath to fight only in just causes, to be merciful, and to put the service of ladies foremost.

---

and, coming upon a red silk pavilion, apparently unoccupied, decided to rest there overnight and continue his search in the morning.

He had not been asleep for more than an hour, however, when the knight who owned the pavilion returned and got straight into bed with him. Having made an assignation[6] with his paramour, the knight supposed at first that Sir Launcelot was she and, taking him into his arms, started kissing him. Sir Launcelot awoke with a start and, seizing his sword, leaped out of bed and out of the pavilion, pursued closely by the other knight. Once in the open they set to with their swords, and before long Sir Launcelot had wounded his unknown <u>adversary</u> so seriously that he was obliged to yield.

The knight, whose name was Sir Belleus, now asked Sir Launcelot how he came to be sleeping in his bed and then explained how he had an assignation with his lover, adding:

"But now I am so sorely wounded that I shall consider myself fortunate to escape with my life."

"Sir, please forgive me for wounding you; but lately I escaped from an enchantment, and I was afraid that once more I had been betrayed. Let us go into the pavilion, and I will staunch your wound."

Sir Launcelot had just finished binding the wound when the young noblewoman who was Sir Belleus's paramour arrived and, seeing the wound, at once rounded in fury on Sir Launcelot.

"Peace, my love," said Sir Belleus. "This is a noble knight, and as soon as I yielded to him, he treated my wound with the greatest care." Sir Belleus then described the events which had led up to the duel.

"Sir, pray tell me your name, and whose knight you are," the young noblewoman asked Sir Launcelot.

"My lady, I am called Sir Launcelot du Lake."

"As I guessed, both from your appearance and from your speech; and indeed I know you

Lancelot rescuing Guinevere by crossing the sword bridge (about 1300). From *Le Roman de Lancelot du Lac*, M. 806, f. 166, The Pierpont Morgan Library, New York/Art Resource, New York.

better than you realize. But I ask you, in <u>recompense</u> for the injury you have done my lord, and out of the courtesy for which you are famous, to recommend Sir Belleus to King Arthur, and suggest that he be made one of the knights of the Round Table. I can assure you that my lord deserves it, being only less than yourself as a man-at-arms, and sovereign of many of the Outer Isles."

"My lady, let Sir Belleus come to Arthur's court at the next Pentecost. Make sure that you come

---

6. **assignation** (ăs′ĭg-nā′shən): an appointment for a meeting between lovers.

| WORDS TO KNOW | **adversary** (ăd′vər-sĕr′ē) *n.* an opponent; enemy
recompense (rĕk′əm-pĕns′) *n.* amends made, as for damage or loss; payment in return for something, such as a service |

916

Mini-Lesson The Writer's Style

DICTION Remind students that a writer's diction, or word choice, can be generally concrete or abstract, formal or informal. Concrete words name or describe things that you can see, hear, smell, touch, or taste. Abstract words name things that cannot be perceived through the senses. Formal diction is dignified and often serious. Informal diction is casual and conversational. Refer students to the conversation among Launcelot, Sir Belleus, and his lady on this page. Point out phrases such as *staunch your wound* and *pray tell me your name* on page 916. Ask students whether they would describe the diction as formal or informal. *(formal)*

Application Have students choose a passage from these stories that contains dialogue and rewrite it replacing formal diction with casual, informal diction.

Reteaching/Reinforcement
• *Writing Mini-Lessons,* p. 44

📁 **The Writer's Craft**
Diction, p. 421

---

916 THE LANGUAGE OF LITERATURE **Teacher's Edition**

with him, and I promise I will do what I can for him; and if he is as good a man-at-arms as you say he is, I am sure Arthur will accept him."

As soon as it was daylight, Sir Launcelot armed, mounted, and rode away in search of the abbey, which he found in less than two hours. King Bagdemagus's daughter was waiting for him and, as soon as she heard his horse's footsteps in the yard, ran to the window and, seeing that it was Sir Launcelot, herself ordered the servants to stable his horse. She then led him to her chamber, disarmed him, and gave him a long gown to wear, welcoming him warmly as she did so.

King Bagdemagus's castle was twelve miles away, and his daughter sent for him as soon as she had settled Sir Launcelot. The king arrived with his retinue[7] and embraced Sir Launcelot, who then described his recent enchantment, and the great obligation he was under to his daughter for releasing him.

"Sir, you will fight for me on Tuesday next?"

"Sire, I shall not fail you; but please tell me the names of the three Round Table knights whom I shall be fighting."

"Sir Modred, Sir Madore de la Porte, and Sir Gahalantyne. I must admit that last Tuesday they defeated me and my knights completely."

"Sire, I hear that the tournament is to be fought within three miles of the abbey. Could you send me three of your most trustworthy knights, clad in plain armor, and with no device,[8] and a fourth suit of armor which I

---

7. **retinue** (rĕt′n-o͞o): attendants.
8. **device:** a design, often a motto, on a coat of arms.

SIR LAUNCELOT DU LAKE **917**

Critical Thinking:
HYPOTHESIZING

V Ask students to discuss why Launcelot does not want to wear his own armor. *(Possible responses: He wants to surprise his opponents; he does not want his fellow Round Table knights to recognize him.)*

Critical Thinking:
MAKING JUDGMENTS

W Ask students to compare Launcelot's courteous behavior to ladies and to other knights with his violent behavior in the tournament. Have them give their opinions of Launcelot's code of conduct. *(Accept all reasonable responses.)*

---

myself shall wear? We will take up our position just outside the tournament field and watch while you and the King of North Galys enter into combat with your followers; and then, as soon as you are in difficulties, we will come to your rescue and show your opponents what kind of knights you command."

This was arranged on Sunday, and on the following Tuesday Sir Launcelot and the three knights of King Bagdemagus waited in a copse,[9] not far from the pavilion which had been erected for the lords and ladies who were to judge the tournament and award the prizes.

The King of North Galys was the first on the field, with a company of ninescore knights; he was followed by King Bagdemagus with fourscore[10] knights, and then by the three knights of the Round Table, who remained apart from both companies. At the first encounter King Bagdemagus lost twelve knights, all killed, and the King of North Galys six.

With that, Sir Launcelot galloped on to the field, and with his first spear unhorsed five of the King of North Galys's knights, breaking the backs of four of them. With his next spear he charged the king and wounded him deeply in the thigh.

"That was a shrewd blow," commented Sir Madore and galloped onto the field to challenge Sir Launcelot. But he too was tumbled from his horse, and with such violence that his shoulder was broken.

Sir Modred was the next to challenge Sir Launcelot, and he was sent spinning over his horse's tail. He landed headfirst, his helmet became buried in the soil, and he nearly broke his neck, and for a long time lay stunned.

Finally Sir Gahalantyne tried; at the first encounter both he and Sir Launcelot broke their spears, so both drew their swords and hacked vehemently at each other. But Sir Launcelot, with mounting wrath, soon struck his opponent a blow on the helmet which brought the blood streaming from eyes, ears, and mouth. Sir Gahalantyne slumped forward in the saddle, his horse panicked, and he was thrown to the ground, useless for further combat.

Sir Launcelot took another spear and unhorsed sixteen more of the King of North Galys's knights and, with his next, unhorsed another twelve; and in each case with such violence that none of the knights ever fully recovered. The King of North Galys was forced to admit defeat, and the prize was awarded to King Bagdemagus.

That night Sir Launcelot was entertained as the guest of honor by King Bagdemagus and his daughter at their castle and before leaving was loaded with gifts.

"My lady, please, if ever again you should need my services, remember that I shall not fail you."

The next day Sir Launcelot rode once more through the forest and by chance came to the apple tree where he had previously slept. This time he met a young noblewoman riding a white palfrey.[11]

"My lady, I am riding in search of adventure; pray tell me if you know of any I might find hereabouts."

"Sir, there are adventures hereabouts if you believe that you are equal to them; but please tell me, what is your name?"

"Sir Launcelot du Lake."

"Very well, Sir Launcelot, you appear to be a sturdy enough knight, so I will tell you. Not far away stands the castle of Sir Tarquine, a knight who in fair combat has overcome more than sixty opponents whom he now holds prisoner. Many are from the court of King Arthur, and if you can rescue them, I will then ask you to deliver me and my companions from a knight who distresses us daily, either by robbery or by other kinds of outrage."

"My lady, please first lead me to Sir

---

9. **copse** (kŏps): a thicket of small trees.
10. **ninescore . . . fourscore:** a score is a set of 20; thus, ninescore is 180 and fourscore is 80.
11. **palfrey:** a gentle riding-horse.

Critic's Corner

"Their style is hard, their adventures are incredible, their love affairs lewd, their compliments absurd, their battles long-winded, their speeches stupid, their travels preposterous, and lastly, they are devoid of all art and sense, and therefore deserve to be banished from a Christian commonwealth, as a useless tribe."

Miguel de Cervantes
writing about the knights of medieval romance

Ask students whether they agree with this assessment.

Tarquine; then I will most happily challenge this miscreant knight of yours."

When they arrived at the castle, Sir Launcelot watered his horse at the ford and then beat the caldron until the bottom fell out. However, none came to answer the challenge, so they waited by the castle gate for half an hour or so. Then Sir Tarquine appeared, riding toward the castle with a wounded prisoner slung over his horse, whom Sir Launcelot recognized as Sir Gaheris, Sir Gawain's brother and a knight of the Round Table.

"Good knight," said Sir Launcelot, "it is known to me that you have put to shame many of the knights of the Round Table. Pray allow your prisoner, who I see is wounded, to recover, while I vindicate the honor of the knights whom you have defeated."

"I defy you, and all your fellowship of the Round Table," Sir Tarquine replied.

"You boast!" said Sir Launcelot.

At the first charge the backs of the horses were broken and both knights stunned. But they soon recovered and set to with their swords, and both struck so lustily that neither shield nor armor could resist, and within two hours they were cutting each other's flesh, from which the blood flowed liberally. Finally they paused for a moment, resting on their shields.

"Worthy knight," said Sir Tarquine, "pray hold your hand for a while and, if you will, answer my question."

"Sir, speak on."

"You are the most powerful knight I have fought yet, but I fear you may be the one whom in the whole world I most hate. If you are not, for the love of you I will release all my prisoners and swear eternal friendship."

"What is the name of the knight you hate above all others?"

"Sir Launcelot du Lake; for it was he who slew my brother, Sir Carados of the Dolorous Tower, and it is because of him that I have killed a hundred knights and maimed as many more, apart from the sixty-four I still hold prisoner. And so, if you are Sir Launcelot, speak up, for we must then fight to the death."

"Sir, I see now that I might go in peace and good fellowship or otherwise fight to the death; but being the knight I am, I must tell you: I am Sir Launcelot du Lake, son of King Ban of Benwick, of Arthur's court, and a knight of the Round Table. So defend yourself!"

"Ah! this is most welcome."

Now the two knights hurled themselves at each other like two wild bulls; swords and shields clashed together, and often their swords drove into the flesh. Then sometimes one, sometimes the other, would stagger and fall, only to recover immediately and resume the contest. At last, however, Sir Tarquine grew faint and unwittingly lowered his shield. Sir Launcelot was swift to follow up his advantage and, dragging the other down to his knees, unlaced his helmet and beheaded him.

Sir Launcelot then strode over to the young noblewoman: "My lady, now I am at your service, but first I must find a horse."

Then the wounded Sir Gaheris spoke up: "Sir, please take my horse. Today you have overcome the most formidable knight, excepting only yourself, and by so doing have saved us all. But before leaving, please tell me your name."

"Sir Launcelot du Lake. Today I have fought to vindicate the honor of the knights of the Round Table, and I know that among Sir Tarquine's prisoners are two of my brethren, Sir Lyonel and Sir Ector, also your own brother, Sir Gawain. According to the shields there are also Sir Brandiles, Sir Galyhuddis,[12] Sir Kay, Sir Alydukis,[13] Sir Marhaus, and many others. Please release the prisoners and ask them to help themselves to the castle treasure. Give them all my greetings and say I will see them at the next Pentecost. And please request Sir Ector and Sir Lyonel to go straight to the court and await me there." ❖

---

12. **Galyhuddis** (găl′ĭ-hood′əs).
13. **Alydukis** (ăl′ĭ-doo′kəs).

From Personal Response to Critical Analysis

1. Accept all reasonable responses.
2. Possible responses: The code requires a knight to be skilled in arms, to champion the cause of a lady, to be honorable, chaste, truthful, courageous, and loyal, and to be courteous to one's opponents.
3. Possible responses: yes, because he champions the cause of those in need, he refuses to take one of the four queens paramour even when threatened that he will be killed, he is courteous and kind to Sir Belleus, he is truthful to Sir Tarquine, he risks his life to free his fellow knights; no, because he seems to revel in killing and slaughter
4. Possible responses: They are either evil and lewd, like the four queens, or they are unnamed and take little part in the story; they are the catalyst for the adventures.
5. Accept all reasonable, well-supported responses.
6. Accept all reasonable responses.

Another Pathway

Cooperative Learning Suggest that groups divide the task, assigning members to do graphics, others to write the material, and others to edit and compile the guidebook.

Rubric

3 Full Accomplishment The guidebook is entertaining, accurate and informative.

2 Substantial Accomplishment The guidebook is generally accurate and informative, though it could be more detailed.

1 Little or Partial Accomplishment The guidebook is inaccurate and uninformative.

Literary Links

Accept all reasonbable, well-supported responses.

RESPONDING OPTIONS

FROM PERSONAL RESPONSE TO CRITICAL ANALYSIS

REFLECT
1. What did you find to be the strongest image in "Sir Launcelot du Lake"? Draw a quick sketch of this image.

RETHINK
2. Judging from the behavior of Sir Launcelot and the other knights in this selection, how would you describe the chivalric code that they live by?

Close Textual Reading

Consider
- the reasons the knights fight
- Sir Launcelot's reaction to the four queens' proposal
- Sir Tarquine's reaction to the fighting skills of Sir Ector and Sir Launcelot
- Sir Launcelot's answer to Sir Tarquine's question about his identity

3. Do you think that Sir Launcelot is totally honorable and heroic?
Support your opinion with details from the selection.

4. What is your opinion of the female characters in this story? Use details from the story to support your answer.

RELATE
5. Do you think leaders and heroes with qualities like those of Uther, Arthur, and Launcelot still exist in today's world? Explain your opinion.

Thematic Link

6. Review the chart you created for the Personal Connection on page 904. Were your views or images of Arthur, Launcelot, and their world changed as a result of reading these two tales?

LITERARY LINKS

Think about the way Uther Pendragon, Launcelot, and other characters in these excerpts view war and fighting. What differences do you see between their views and those expressed by the characters in "On the Rainy River" (page 266), "Thoughts of Hanoi" (page 754), and other selections in this book?

920 UNIT SIX PART 2: THE HEROIC TRADITION

Multimodal Learning
ANOTHER PATHWAY

Cooperative Learning
With a small group of classmates, prepare a guidebook for tourists visiting the Arthurian world. Include descriptions and pictures of the people, their residences, and their activities, noting the distinctive features of life in this world. Also offer advice about how to behave. Share your guidebook with the class.

QUICKWRITES

1. Write a **plot synopsis** for a newspaper TV listing, adapting one of these tales to fit a contemporary genre, such as a police drama or a futuristic adventure. For example, you might summarize an episode of *Starbase Camelot*.

2. Write a **magazine article** about a typical day in the life of Sir Launcelot. Incorporate details about his habitual fighting, his relationships with women, and his friendships and rivalries with other knights.

3. In an **editorial**, persuade fellow students that society would either improve or worsen if people tried to live up to chivalric ideals as presented in these selections.

📁 **PORTFOLIO** Save your writing. You may want to use it later as a springboard to a piece for your portfolio.

QuickWrites

1. Have students work in small groups to brainstorm ideas for the plot, and then write their synopses individually.
2. Suggest that students outline the main ideas of the article before they begin writing, giving specific examples under each main idea.
3. Encourage students to list the chivalric ideals one by one and to think about how each would translate into action in today's world.

Editorial, pp. 228–232

LITERARY CONCEPTS

The term **romance** refers to any imaginative story concerned with noble heroes, chivalric codes of honor, passionate love, daring deeds, and supernatural events. Writers of romances tend to idealize their heroes as well as the eras in which the heroes live. Medieval romances, such as *Le Morte d'Arthur,* are stories of kings, knights, and ladies, who are motivated by love, religious faith, or simply a desire for adventure. Such romances are comparatively lighthearted in tone and loose in structure, containing many episodes. Usually the main character has a series of adventures while on a quest to accomplish some goal.

With your classmates, talk about the ways in which these excerpts from *Le Morte d'Arthur* illustrate the characteristics of a romance. Then discuss romantic elements in modern forms of entertainment, such as soap operas, romance novels, Westerns, and adventure films.

Multimodal Learning
ALTERNATIVE ACTIVITIES

1. Watch a videotape of *Camelot* or another film about the legend of Arthur. In an **oral movie review,** compare the view of the Arthurian world shown in the movie with the impression you get from these selections.

2. Create a **drawing** or **painting** of your favorite scenes or characters from these selections. For inspiration, examine some of the artwork in this part of the unit or in illustrated volumes of Arthurian legends.

3. With a partner, create a **television commercial** for a new movie or television series about Launcelot's glorious deeds. You may wish to include a dramatization, a catchy theme song, or an interview with the leading man.

Jousting at the court of Caerleon (1468). From *Les Chroniques de Hainaut,* MS 9243, f. 45, Bibliothèque Royale Albert I, Brussels, Belgium / Art Resource, New York.

ART CONNECTION

How does the picture *King Arthur Drawing Forth the Sword* (page 906) affect your view of the young Arthur and his suitability for kingship?

The Granger Collection, New York.

Multimodal Learning
ACROSS THE CURRICULUM

History/Sports Research medieval tournaments—their purpose, the equipment used, the participants, the contests or events held, and the way winners were determined. Then create a program for such a tournament, describing the events in which the knights of the Round Table might have participated.

THE CROWNING OF ARTHUR / SIR LAUNCELOT DU LAKE   921

Across the Curriculum

History/Sports Point out that early medieval tournaments were less structured and formal than later medieval tournaments, which were stylized combat. Encourage students to be aware of the time period they are researching. Suggest that students illustrate their programs with color copies of medieval artwork or with their own drawings and designs.

Literary Concepts

Initiate student discussion of the characteristics of romance in *Le Morte d'Arthur* by posing the following questions:
- What noble and heroic qualities do you see in Arthur and in Sir Launcelot?
- What supernatural elements do you see in the two stories?
- What do you think motivates Sir Launcelot?
- What scenes in these two stories seem lighthearted in tone?

Alternative Activities

1. Encourage students to pick several points for comparison before viewing the movie, such as portrayal of the hero, treatment of women, battle or tournament scenes, and so on.

2. If students do not wish to imitate the style of medieval illustration, suggest that they use a contemporary style to illustrate their chosen scenes.

3. If possible, show video recordings of television commercials for movies to give students ideas of how to begin.

THE LANGUAGE OF LITERATURE TEACHER'S EDITION   **921**

Words to Know

1. d
2. b
3. a
4. a
5. c

Reteaching/Reinforcement
- *Unit Six Resource Book*, p. 46.

SIR THOMAS MALORY

Malory composed eight separate tales that chronicle the rise and fall of Arthur's kingdom. He originally called his work *The Whole Book of Arthur and of his Noble Knights of the Round Table*. "Le Morte d'Arthur" (The Death of Arthur) is the title of the last tale, but it is by this title that the entire book has been known since it was first printed in 1485.

ART GALLERY
Art of the Arthurian Legends
The legendary exploits of King Arthur and his Knights of the Round Table have been a favorite subject of painters as well as writers. These paintings of famous characters and battles from the Arthurian legends will enhance students' understanding of this selection.

Side A, Frame 49720

WORDS TO KNOW

Write the letter of the word pair that best expresses a relationship similar to that of the first pair.

1. TIP : RECOMPENSE :: (a) arm : body, (b) prediction : recollection, (c) disk : computer, (d) memo : correspondence
2. DOG : FIDELITY :: (a) chicken : egg, (b) fox : cleverness, (c) wolf : timidity, (d) whale : mammal
3. PROWESS : GLADIATOR :: (a) tact : diplomat, (b) honesty : thief, (c) wisdom : fool, (d) humility : actor
4. CHAMPION : PROTECTOR :: (a) teach : instructor, (b) cure : patient, (c) referee : competitor, (d) arrest : judge
5. ADVERSARY : FRIEND :: (a) cat : pet, (b) hunter : trapper, (c) servant : ruler, (d) member : club

SIR THOMAS MALORY

The man who wrote *Le Morte d'Arthur* called himself "Syr Thomas Maleore, knyght." He also indicated that he completed this work in the ninth year of Edward IV's reign (1469 or 1470), and he added a prayer that he be safely delivered from prison. Although his precise identity remains uncertain, most scholars feel that he is the same person as Sir Thomas Malory (1405?–1471), a knight from the English county of Warwickshire who led a life of adventure at the end of the Middle Ages.

As a youth, Malory served bravely in battle under the Earl of Warwick, fighting for England during the final years of the Hundred Years' War with France. He inherited his father's estates in 1433 or 1434 and about a decade later represented Warwickshire in Parliament. In 1451, however, he was arrested and jailed for violently entering and robbing an abbey. Malory was imprisoned several more times in the next decade, accused of crimes such as cattle theft, highway robbery, and attempted murder, though the charges may have been politically motivated. Twice he escaped from prison but was recaptured. In 1462 he joined rebels opposing King Edward IV in the civil war known as the Wars of the Roses. Imprisoned for treason in 1468, he was specifically excluded from the pardons Edward granted to many of the other rebels. He spent the remainder of his life in London's Newgate Prison, where he apparently occupied his time by writing *Le Morte d'Arthur*. The work was published in 1485, 14 years after his death.

While legends of King Arthur were originally preserved in Wales, by Malory's day the French versions of the legends were better known than their Welsh sources. Malory based *Le Morte d'Arthur* on these French versions, although his efforts were far more creative than mere translation. His gracefully written romance is considered the first major prose work in the English language.

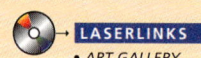

LASERLINKS
- ART GALLERY

922 UNIT SIX PART 2: THE HEROIC TRADITION

REFLECTING ON THEME
What Do You Think?

Ask students to compare the heroes of Malory's work with the heroes that they listed for the activity on page 902. Have them consider whether their own views of heroism might have been influenced by medieval ideals of chivalry.

PREVIEWING

ROMANCE

from The Acts of King Arthur and His Noble Knights

John Steinbeck United States

PERSONAL CONNECTION Activating Prior Knowledge/Setting a Purpose

Think of a famous person you admire. In your notebook, make notes on what it would be like to live the life of this person for one day, including both positive and negative aspects. Then discuss your ideas with classmates, comparing your views of fame with theirs.

Building Background

LITERARY CONNECTION

In this selection, modern novelist John Steinbeck portrays what it might be like to be Lancelot (also spelled *Launcelot*), the most famous knight of the Round Table. From childhood, Steinbeck was fascinated by the Arthurian legend, and as an adult he attempted to set it down in "plain, present-day speech" for his sons. He researched the legend in England and Italy, studying rare manuscripts, and wrote in a room he named Joyous Garde, after Lancelot's castle. Unfortunately, Steinbeck never completed his version of the legend; in 1976, several years after his death, his unfinished work was published as *The Acts of King Arthur and His Noble Knights*. The excerpt you are about to read offers a new perspective on some of the events from Malory's tale of Sir Launcelot.

Active Reading

READING CONNECTION

Inferences About Lancelot		
	Clues	Inferences
His Attitude Toward His Fame		
His Feelings About Guinevere		
Other Aspects of His Life		

Making Inferences To get the most out of this story, which presents a day in the life of the famed Lancelot, you will need to make **inferences,** or logical guesses, about Lancelot's feelings and behavior. For example, when Queen Guinevere (Gwynevere) asks Lancelot whether he has really encountered fair queen enchantresses, he looks away nervously and does not answer her directly. The reader can infer that he did meet such women and that he does not want to tell Guinevere about his encounters. As you read, look for other clues to help you understand Lancelot. In your notebook, keep track of your inferences by making a chart like the one shown.

Using Your Reading Log Use your reading log to record your responses to the questions inserted throughout the selection. Also jot down other thoughts and feelings that come to you as you read.

• HISTORICAL CONNECTION

OVERVIEW

Objectives

- To understand and appreciate a modern retelling of a medieval romance that explores the heroic tradition
- To enrich reading by using active reading strategies
- To identify and understand style
- To express understanding of the selection through a choice of writing forms, including a feature article, an interview, an advice column, and a soap-opera scene
- To extend understanding of the selection through a variety of multimodal and cross-curricular activities

Skills

LITERARY CONCEPTS
- Style
- Plot

READING SKILLS/ STRATEGIES
- Evaluating
- Questioning

THE WRITER'S STYLE
- Elaboration

GENRE STUDY
- Romance

GRAMMAR
- Subordinating conjunctions

SPEAKING, LISTENING, AND VIEWING
- Group discussion
- Dramatization

CULTURAL CONNECTION

Castle Life Steinbeck portrays castle life as rich and active, not a cold existence as it is sometimes portrayed. These paintings convey a similar impression. The images will help students visualize the setting of *The Acts of King Arthur and His Noble Knights.*

Side A, Frame 49737

PRINT AND MEDIA RESOURCES

UNIT SIX RESOURCE BOOK
Strategic Reading: Literature, p. 49
Vocabulary SkillBuilder, p. 50

GRAMMAR MINI-LESSONS
Transparencies, p. 50
Copymasters, p. 41

WRITING MINI-LESSONS
Transparencies, p. 42

ACCESS FOR STUDENTS ACQUIRING ENGLISH
Selection Summaries, Reading Support

FORMAL ASSESSMENT
Selection Test, p. 183
 Test Generator

 AUDIO LIBRARY
See Reference Card

 LASERLINKS
Cultural Connection
Author Background
Historical Connection

INTERNET RESOURCES
McDougal Littell Literature Center at http://www.hmco.com/mcdougal/lit

SUMMARY

At the Whitsun banquet and festivities held at King Arthur's Court, Sir Lancelot's victorious deeds are praised to the point of exaggeration. Embarrassed by the recitation of his exploits and preoccupied with his own thoughts, Lancelot asks Arthur for permission to leave. Arthur invites Lancelot to the tower room, where the two men and Guinevere recall the evening's events. Lancelot confesses that he does not remember doing the deeds that people claim he has done. Guinevere inquires about his rescue of damsels, but Lancelot assures the queen that he has kept his oath of chivalrous devotion to her. Soon after Guinevere leaves them, Lancelot bids Arthur good night. On the way to his room, he meets Guinevere on the stairs. She pulls him into her room, closes the door behind him, and they embrace passionately. Lancelot breaks free and leaves the room, weeping bitterly.

Thematic Link: *The Heroic Tradition*
Lancelot's heroism is tested by his passionate love for his best friend's wife

from THE ACTS of KING ARTHUR and HIS NOBLE KNIGHTS

JOHN STEINBECK

WORDS TO KNOW

carriage (kăr′ĭj) *n.* manner of moving one's body (p. 927)

decorous (dĕk′ər-əs) *adj.* behaving in a manner appropriate to the occasion; proper (p. 925)

disparagement (dĭ-spăr′ĭj-mənt) *n.* belittlement (p. 925)

exalt (ĭg-zôlt′) *v.* to glorify, praise, or honor (p. 925)

fallible (făl′ə-bəl) *adj.* capable of being wrong or mistaken (p. 931)

haggard (hăg′ərd) *adj.* appearing worn and exhausted (p. 931)

intemperate (ĭn-tĕm′pər-ĭt) *adj.* extreme (p. 931)

penitence (pĕn′ĭ-təns) *n.* expression of regret for sins or wrongdoing (p. 925)

reprisal (rĭ-prī′zəl) *n.* retaliation in the form of harm or injury similar to that received; revenge (p. 925)

vagrant (vā′grənt) *adj.* wandering (p. 927)

King Arthur held Whitsun[1] court at Winchester, that ancient royal town favored by God and His clergy as well as the seat and tomb of many kings. The roads were clogged with eager people, knights returning to stamp in court the record of their deeds, of bishops, clergy, monks, of the defeated fettered to their paroles,[2] the prisoners of honor. And on Itchen water, pathway from Solent[3] and the sea, the little ships brought succulents, lampreys, eels and oysters, plaice and sea trout, while barges loaded with casks of whale oil and casks of wine came tide borne. Bellowing oxen walked to the spits on their own four hooves, while geese and swans, sheep and swine, waited their turn in hurdle pens. Every householder with a strip of colored cloth, a ribbon, any textile gaiety, hung it from a window to flap its small festival, and those in lack tied boughs of pine and laurel over their doors.

In the great hall of the castle on the hill the king sat high, and next below the fair elite company of the Round Table, noble and <u>decorous</u> as kings themselves, while at the long trestle boards the people were as fitted as toes in a tight shoe.

Then while the glistening meat dripped down the tables, it was the custom for the defeated to celebrate the deeds of those who had overcome them, while the victor dipped his head in <u>disparagement</u> of his greatness and fended off the compliments with small defensive gestures of his hands. And as at public <u>penitence</u> sins are given stature they do not deserve, little sins grow up and baby sins are born, so those knights who lately claimed mercy perchance might raise the exploits of the brave and merciful beyond reasonable gratitude for their lives and in anticipation of some small notice of value.

This no one said of Lancelot, sitting with bowed head in his golden-lettered seat at the Round Table. Some said he nodded and perhaps dozed, for the testimony to his greatness was long and the monotony of his victories continued for many hours. Lancelot's immaculate fame had grown so great that men took pride in being unhorsed by him—even this notice was an honor. And since he had won many victories, it is possible that knights he had never seen claimed to have been overthrown by him. It was a way to claim attention for a moment. And as he dozed and wished to be otherwise, he heard his deeds <u>exalted</u> beyond his recognition, and some mighty exploits once attributed to other men were brought bright-painted out and laid on the shining pile of his achievements. There is a seat of worth beyond the reach of envy whose occupant ceases to be a man and becomes the receptacle of the wishful longings of the world, a seat most often reserved for the dead, from whom neither <u>reprisal</u> nor reward may be expected, but at this time Sir Lancelot was its unchallenged tenant. And he vaguely heard his strength favorably compared with elephants, his ferocity with lions, his agility with deer, his cleverness with foxes, his beauty with the stars, his justice with Solon,[4] his stern probity[5] with St. Michael, his humility with newborn lambs; his military

---

1. **Whitsun:** another name for Pentecost, a Christian festival celebrated on the seventh Sunday after Easter.
2. **fettered to their paroles:** bound by their word of honor to lay down arms.
3. **Itchen . . . Solent:** waterways in southern England.
4. **Solon:** Athenian statesman and lawgiver who lived in the sixth century B.C.
5. **probity:** uprightness; honesty.

WORDS TO KNOW
decorous (dĕk'ər-əs) *adj.* behaving in a manner appropriate to the occasion; proper
disparagement (dĭ-spăr'ĭj-mənt) *n.* belittlement
penitence (pĕn'ĭ-təns) *n.* expression of regret for sins or wrongdoing
exalt (ĭg-zôlt') *v.* to glorify, praise, or honor
reprisal (rĭ-prī'zəl) *n.* retaliation in the form of harm or injury similar to that received; revenge

---

CUSTOMIZING FOR
Students Acquiring English

- Use **ACCESS FOR STUDENTS ACQUIRING ENGLISH,** *Reading Support,* p. 44.
- Steinbeck's elevated diction and rich style may be challenging for students. You may wish to preteach all the Words to Know, located on the bottom of page 924. To familiarize students with Steinbeck's sentence style, you can also use the Grammar Mini-lesson on Subordinating Conjunctions, located on the bottom of this page.
- In addition to these boxes, you may wish to use the suggestions under Strategic Reading for Less-Proficient Readers.

STRATEGIC READING FOR
Less-Proficient Readers

Set a Purpose Ask students to read to find out how Lancelot and Queen Guinevere feel about each other.

Use **UNIT SIX RESOURCE BOOK,** p. 49, for guidance in reading the selection.

CUSTOMIZING FOR
Gifted and Talented Students

In his introduction to *The Acts of King Arthur,* Steinbeck writes: "In no sense do I wish to rewrite Malory, or reduce him, or change him, or soften or sentimentalize him." Have students work in pairs to analyze Lancelot's personality in episodes of Malory's account and to decide whether Steinbeck has softened or sentimentalized Malory's portrayal of Lancelot.

Mini-Lesson Grammar

SUBORDINATING CONJUNCTIONS Have students identify the subordinating conjunction in the highlighted sentence *(while)* and the subordinate clause *(while geese . . . pens).* Explain that a subordinating conjunction introduces subordinate clauses. Point out that an independent clause can stand by itself while a subordinate clause cannot.

Application Invite students to use subordinate conjunctions to combine these independent clauses into complex sentences:
1. Arthur held Whitsun court at Winchester. It was an ancient, royal town. *(because)*
2. The roads were clogged with eager people. The court was a hive of activity. *(while)*
3. The knights spoke of Lancelot. They recounted his great deeds. *(When)*

Reteaching/Reinforcement
- Grammar Handbook, anthology p. 1091
- *Grammar Mini-Lessons* copymasters p. 41, transparencies p. 50

 **The Writer's Craft**

Subordinating Conjunctions, pp. 445–446

Art Note

***Study for Lancelot* by Sir Edward Burne-Jones** Edward Burne-Jones was the professional name of Edward Coley Jones (1833–98), an English painter and designer. Born in Birmingham, Burne-Jones received his early art training at the University of Oxford. Burne-Jones subsequently studied with the Pre-Raphaelite painter Dante Gabriel Rosetti. This study of Lancelot, as with most of Burne-Jones' paintings, is noted for its dreamlike, sentimental style.

Reading the Art This is how painter Burne-Jones imagined Lancelot. Do you envision Lancelot the same way? Why or why not? Review page 925 for details to support your opinion.

Literary Note

The earliest references to King Arthur come from 9th- and 10th-century Welsh sources. These stories, written in Latin, were collected around 1100 in a volume called *The Mabinogion*. Lancelot was first introduced in the oldest of the French Arthurian romances, a series of 12th-century poems by Chrétien de Troyes.

Study for Lancelot (1893), Sir Edward Burne-Jones. From *Drawings of Sir Edward Burne-Jones*, published by Charles Scribner's Sons, New York. Photo by Hollyer.

Multicultural Perspectives

Steinbeck is not alone in his fascination with the Arthurian legend; many writers, musicians, and artists have adapted the stories of Arthur and his knights to the needs of their own culture and heritage. For example, the 16th-century English poet Edmund Spenser used Arthur to represent the perfect knight in his epic allegory of Elizabethan society, *The Faerie Queene*. In 1889, American humorist Mark Twain used the legend to contrast New England progress with medieval society in *A Connecticut Yankee in King Arthur's Court*. Among the most widely read contemporary versions of the legend is T.H. White's *The Once and Future King*. In music, the Arthurian legend forms the basis of Richard Wagner's *Parsifal* (1882) and *Tristan and Isolde*, as well as Alan Jay Lerner and Frederick Loewe's Broadway hit *Camelot* (1960).

niche would have caused the Archangel Gabriel[6] to raise his head. Sometimes the guests paused in their chewing the better to hear, and a man who slopped his metheglin[7] drew frowns.

EVALUATE

A Why do you think the knights are so extravagant in their praise of Lancelot?

Arthur on his dais[8] sat very still and did not fiddle with his bread, and beside him sat lovely Guinevere, still as a painted statue of herself. Only her inward eyes confessed her vagrant thoughts. And Lancelot studied the open pages of his hands—not large hands, but delicate where they were not knobby and scarred with old wounds. His hands were fine-textured—soft of skin and very white, protected by the pliant leather lining of his gauntlets.

The great hall was not still, not all upturned listening. Everywhere was movement as people came and went, some serving huge planks of meat and baskets of bread, round and flat like a plate. And there were restless ones who could not sit still, while everyone under burden of half-chewed meat and the floods and freshets of mead and beer found necessity for repeated departures and returns.

Lancelot exhausted the theme of his hands and squinted down the long hall and watched the movement with eyes so nearly closed that he could not see faces. And he thought how he knew everyone by carriage. The knights in long full floor-brushing robes walked lightly or thought their feet barely touched the ground because their bodies were released from their crushing boxes of iron. Their feet were long and slender because, being horsemen, they had never widened and flattened their feet with walking. The ladies, full-skirted, moved like water, but this was schooled and designed, taught to little girls with the help of whips on raw ankles, while their shoulders were bound back with nail-studded harnesses and their heads held high and rigid by painful collars of woven willow or, for the forgetful, by supports of painted wire, for to learn the high proud head on a swan's neck, to learn to flow like water, is not easy for a little girl as she becomes a gentlewoman. But knights and ladies both matched their movements to their garments; the sweep and rhythm of a long gown informs the manner of its moving. It is not necessary to inspect a serf or a slave, his shoulder wide and sloping from burdens, legs short and thick and crooked, feet splayed and widespread, the whole frame slowly crushed by weights. In the great hall the serving people walked under burdens with the slow weight of oxen and scuttled like crabs, crooked and nervous when the weight was gone.

A pause in the recital of his virtues drew Lancelot's attention. The knight who had tried to kill him in a tree had finished, and among the benches Sir Kay was rising to his feet. Lancelot could hear his voice before he spoke, reciting deeds like leaves and bags and barrels. Before his friend could reach the center of the hall, Sir Lancelot wriggled to his feet and approached the dais. "My lord king," he said, "forgive me if I ask leave to go. An old wound has broken open."

Arthur smiled down on him. "I have the same old wound," he said. "We'll go together. Perhaps you will come to the tower room when we have attended to our wounds." And he signed the trumpets to end the gathering, and the bodyguards to clear the hall.

QUESTION

Why do Lancelot and Arthur suddenly leave the hall?

---

6. **St. Michael . . . Archangel Gabriel:** In several religious traditions, Michael and Gabriel are archangels, the chief messengers of God. Both are celebrated as warriors against evil.
7. **metheglin** (mə-thĕg′lĭn): a liquor made from honey.
8. **dais** (dā′ĭs): a raised platform used for a seat of honor.

WORDS TO KNOW
vagrant (vā′grənt) *adj.* wandering
carriage (kăr′ĭj) *n.* manner of moving one's body

Active Reading: EVALUATE

A Possible responses: The knights sincerely admire Lancelot and his bravery; Lancelot has become a mythic hero, even in his own day.

Critical Thinking: SPECULATING

B Invite students to speculate what Guinevere's "vagrant thoughts" might be. Guide students to make inferences from context clues and prior knowledge. *(Possible responses: She is bored by the excessive praise and wishes to be elsewhere; she is dreaming of Lancelot.)*

Literary Concept: DESCRIPTION

C Guide students to analyze the details in this passage to explain what they reveal about medieval society. *(Possible responses: It is a highly ordered society bound by strict rules and codes of conduct. There is a great division between the nobility and the commoners. The "painted wire" reveals that it can also be a cruel, confining world where transgressions are harshly punished.)*

CUSTOMIZING FOR Multiple Learning Styles

D **Bodily-Kinesthetic Learners** Students might enjoy pantomiming Lancelot's body language during the long recitations of his virtues.

Active Reading: QUESTION

E Possible responses: They are embarrassed by the excessive praise; they have old physical wounds that need attention; they are tired.

Mini-Lesson   Genre Study

ROMANCE Draw the web shown here on the chalkboard. Use the web to discuss the characteristics of **romance**.

Application Lead a discussion on how Steinbeck's selection illustrates the characteristics of a romance. Then invite students to name contemporary examples of stories or films that have some of these characteristics. Discuss why romances continue to appeal to audiences today.

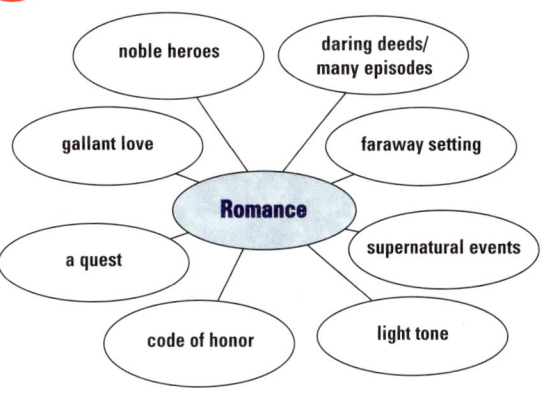

Art Note

Study on Brown Paper by Sir Edward Burne-Jones This study exemplifies the Pre-Raphaelites' concern for purity of form, stylization, and high moral tone, qualities they saw in medieval painting and design. Burne-Jones was a key figure in the revival of medieval arts led by his Oxford friend William Morris, a noted poet and artist. Burne-Jones designed stained-glass windows, tapestries, and mosaics in the medieval mode.

Reading the Art *What similarities and differences do you see between this picture and Burne-Jones's study of Lancelot on page 926? How do these contrasts affect your perception of the main characters in this selection?*

Study on Brown Paper (1895), Sir Edward Burne-Jones. From *Drawings of Sir Edward Burne-Jones*, published by Charles Scribner's Sons, New York. Photo by Hollyer.

Mini-Lesson  Study Skills

NOTE TAKING Explore with students how taking good notes helps them remember what they heard in class and what they read. Emphasize that there are many effective ways of taking notes; as a result, students should select the one that works best for them. Share these guidelines with the class:

1. *Keep your notes in one place.* Encourage students to use a separate folder or notebook for each subject.
2. *Jot down notes in outline form.* Show students how to jot down main ideas and write related ideas underneath each idea.
3. *Look for key words.* These include names, important facts, and crucial ideas.
4. *Use abbreviations and symbols.*

Application Have students work on their own to take notes on this selection, answering a single question such as *What does this selection reveal about life at court?* or *What makes Lancelot such a distinguished knight?* After reading, students can compare their notes.

F The stone stairway to the king's room was in the thickness of the wall of the round tower of the keep. At short intervals a deep embrasure[9] and a long, beveled[10] arrow slit commanded some aspect of the town below.

No armed men guarded this stairway. They were below and had passed Sir Lancelot in. The king's room was round, a horizontal slice of the tower, windowless save for the arrow slits, entered by a narrow arched door. It was a sparsely furnished room, carpeted with rushes. A wide bed, and at its foot a carved oaken chest, a bench before the fireplace, and several stools completed the furnishing. But the raw stone of the tower was plastered over and painted with solemn figures of men and angels walking hand in hand. Two candles and the reeky fire gave the only light.

When Lancelot entered, the queen stood up from the bench before the fire, saying, "I will retire, my lords."

"No, stay," said Arthur.

"Stay," said Lancelot.

The king was stretched comfortably in the bed. His bare feet projecting from his long saffron[11] robe caressed each other, the toes curled downward.

The queen was lovely in the firelight, all lean, down-flowing lines of green samite.[12] She wore her little mouth-corner smile of concealed amusement, and her bold golden eyes were the same color as her hair, and odd it was that her lashes and slender brows were dark, an oddity contrived with kohl[13] brought in a small enameled pot from an outland by a far-wandering knight.

"How are you holding up?" Arthur asked.

"Not well, my lord. It's harder than the quest."

"Did you really do all the things they said you did?"

G Lancelot chuckled. "Truthfully, I don't know. It sounds different when they tell about it. And most of them feel it necessary to add a little. When I remember leaping eight feet, they tell it at fifty, and frankly I don't recall several of those giants at all."

The queen made room for him on the fire bench, and he took his seat, back to the fire.

Guinevere said, "The damsel—what's her name—talked about fair queen enchantresses,[14] but she was so excited that her words tumbled over each other. I couldn't make out what happened."

Lancelot looked nervously away. "You know how excitable young girls are," he said. "A little back-country necromancy[15] in a pasture."

"But she spoke particularly of queens."

"My lady, I think everyone is a queen to her. It's like the giants—makes the story richer."

"Then they were not queens?"

"Well, for that matter, when you get into the field of enchantment, everyone is a queen, or thinks she is. Next time she tells it, the little damsel will be a queen. I do think, my lord, there's too much of that kind of thing going on. It's a bad sign, a kind of restlessness, when people go in for fortunetelling and all such things. Maybe there should be a law about it."

"There is," said Arthur. "But it's not in secular hands. The Church is supposed to take care of that."

"Yes, but some of the nunneries are going in for it."

"Well, I'll put a bug in the archbishop's ear."

The queen observed, "I gather you rescued damsels by the dozen." She put her fingers on

---

9. **embrasure** (ĕm-brā′zhər): opening in a wall, through which cannons are fired.
10. **beveled**: having a sloping edge.
11. **saffron**: golden yellow, named for the spice that has that color.
12. **samite**: a heavy silk fabric.
13. **kohl**: a cosmetic preparation used as eye makeup.
14. **fair queen enchantresses**: Morgan le Fay and three other queens, the four of whom, as related in "Sir Launcelot du Lake," imprisoned Lancelot, demanding that he take one of them as his lover.
15. **necromancy**: magic.

THE ACTS OF KING ARTHUR AND HIS NOBLE KNIGHTS   **929**

Literary Concept: SYMBOL

F Explain that the *keep* is the strongest, most secure part of a medieval castle. Point out that King Arthur takes Lancelot to the keep, and ask students what this reveals about the relationship between the king and his knight. *(Possible response: Welcoming Lancelot into the keep—the heart of his home—reveals that the king trusts Lancelot with his life. The keep symbolizes Arthur's trust.)*

Literary Concept: STYLE

G Call attention to the use of dialogue in this passage. Invite volunteers to analyze the diction, sentence structure, and tone to discover what they reveal about Lancelot. Then ask students if this is how they would expect Lancelot to speak. *(Possible responses: The commonplace words, simple sentences, and humble tone reveal a modest, self-effacing man—the ideal heroic character. Students may or may not have expected Lancelot to speak this way.)*

Mini-Lesson Literary Concepts

REVIEWING PLOT Remind students that *plot* refers to the actions and events in a literary work. Explore with the class how the plot progresses because of a *conflict*, or struggle between opposing forces, that is usually resolved by the work's end. Describe how some plots are episodic, consisting of a series of episodes or incidents that are only partly related to each other. Episodic plots are common in medieval romances such as *The Acts of King Arthur and His Noble Knights*.

Application Arrange students in teams to review the plots of popular adventure movies that have qualities of a romance, such as the Indiana Jones movies. Invite groups to discuss the episodic qualities of such movies and what they may owe to medieval romances.

Cultural Note

H *Courtly love* originated in Provence in the 11th century. It is a code of conduct for use between lovers, which requires that the man serves his lady and that all his daring exploits be performed for her sake. Generally, courtly love is unconsummated—a knight adores his lady chastely and wears her colors in tournaments.

Active Reading: CLARIFY

I Possible response: Lancelot loves Guinevere deeply and passionately.

Critical Thinking: HYPOTHESIZING

J Have students infer the duties of a knight and the rules of chivalry based on Lancelot's comments here. (*Possible response: The knight must be loyal to his lord, fulfill his duties to his vassals, respect Christianity, and protect and serve all women.*)

Literary Note

K According to Malory, the jealous husband, Pedivere, did indeed take his wife's body to the Pope. The Pope buried the wife and ordered Sir Pedivere to return to Queen Guinevere. He then repented his crime and became a hermit and a holy man.

---

his arm and a searing shock ran through his body, and his mouth opened in amazement at a hollow ache that pressed upward against his ribs and shortened his breath.

After a moment she said, "How many damsels did you rescue?"

His mouth was dry. "Of course there were a few, madame. There always are."

"And all of them made love to you?"

"That they did not, madame. There you protect me."

"I?"

H "Yes. Since with my lord's permission I swore to serve you all my life and gave my knightly courtly love to you, I am sheltered from damsels by your name."

"And do you want to be sheltered?"

CLARIFY

I How does Lancelot feel about Guinevere?

"Yes, my lady. I am a fighting man. I have neither time nor inclination for any other kind of love. I hope this pleases you, my lady. I sent many prisoners to ask your mercy."

"I never saw such a crop of them," Arthur said. "You must have swept some counties clean."

Guinevere touched him on the arm again and with side-glancing golden eyes saw the spasm that shook him. "While we are on this subject, I want to mention one lady you did not save. When I saw her, she was a headless corpse and not in good condition, and the man who brought her in was half crazed."[16]

J "I am ashamed of that," said Lancelot. "She was under my protection, and I failed her. I suppose it was my shame that made me force the man to do it. I'm sorry. I hope you released him from the burden."

"Not at all," she said. "I wanted him away before the feast reeked up the heavens. I sent him with his burden to the Pope. His friend will not improve on the way. And if his loss of interest in ladies continues, he may turn out to be a very holy man, a hermit or something of that nature, if he isn't a maniac first."

K The king rose on his elbow. "We will have to work out some system," he said. "The rules of errantry[17] are too loose, and the quests overlap. Besides, I wonder how long we can leave justice in the hands of men who are themselves unstable. I don't mean you, my friend. But there may come a time when order and organization from the crown will be necessary."

The queen stood up. "My lords, will you grant me permission to leave you now? I know you will wish to speak of great things foreign and perhaps tiresome to a lady's ears."

The king said, "Surely, my lady. Go to your rest."

"No, sire—not rest. If I do not lay out the designs for the needlepoint, my ladies will have no work tomorrow."

"But these are feast days, my dear."

"I like to give them something every day, my lord. They're lazy things and some of them so woolly in the mind that they forget how to thread a needle from day to day. Forgive me, my lords."

She swept from the room with proud and powerful steps, and the little breeze she made in the still air carried a strange scent to Lancelot, a perfume which sent a shivering excitement coursing through his body. It was an odor he did not, could not, know, for it was the smell of Guinevere distilled by her own skin. And as she passed through the door and descended the steps, he saw himself leap up and follow her, although he did not move. And when she was gone, the room was bleak, and the glory was gone from it, and Sir Lancelot was dog-weary, tired almost to weeping.

"What a queen she is," said King Arthur softly.

---

16. **When I saw her . . . half crazed:** Guinevere is referring to a woman Lancelot was unable to save—a woman who was beheaded by her jealous husband. As punishment, Lancelot commanded the husband to take the woman's body to Guinevere and to throw himself on her mercy.

17. **errantry** (ĕr′ən-trē): the knightly pursuit of adventure.

930 UNIT SIX PART 2: THE HEROIC TRADITION

Mini-Lesson The Writer's Style

ELABORATION Remind students that *elaboration* is the use of details to support ideas. Use the chart shown here to discuss types of elaboration.

Application Invite small groups of students to find the different types of elaboration Steinbeck uses on this page.

Reteaching/Reinforcement
• *Writing Handbook*, anthology pp. 1029–1030
• *Writing Mini-Lessons* transparencies, p. 42

Elaborate on Ideas, pp. 213–214

facts	statements that can be proved
statistics	facts that involve numbers
sensory details	details that tap one or more of the five senses
incidents	happenings or occurrences
examples	instances of something
quotation	a speaker's exact words

"And what a woman equally. Merlin was with me when I chose her. He tried to dissuade me with his usual doomful prophecies. That was one of the few times I differed with him. Well, my choice has proved him fallible. She has shown the world what a queen should be. All other women lose their sheen when she is present."

Lancelot said, "Yes, my lord," and for no reason he knew, except perhaps the intemperate dullness of the feast, he felt lost, and a cold knife of loneliness pressed against his heart.

The king was chuckling. "It is the device of ladies that their lords have great matters to discuss, when if the truth were told, we bore them. And I hope the truth is never told. Why, you look haggard, my friend. Are you feverish? Did you mean that about an old wound opening?"

"No. The wound was what you thought it was, my lord. But it is true that I can fight, travel, live on berries, fight again, go without sleeping, and come out fresh and fierce, but sitting still at Whitsun feast has wearied me to death."

Arthur said, "I can see it. We'll discuss the realm's health another time. Go to your bed now. Have you your old quarters?"

"No—better ones. Sir Kay has cleared five knights from the lovely lordly rooms over the north gate. He did it in memory of an adventure which we, God help us, will have to listen to tomorrow. I accept your dismissal, my lord."

And Lancelot knelt down and took the king's beloved hand in both of his and kissed it. "Good night, my liege[18] lord, my liege friend," he said and then stumbled blindly from the room and felt his way down the curving stone steps past the arrow slits.

As he came to the level of the next landing, Guinevere issued silently from a darkened entrance. He could see her in the thin light from the arrow slit. She took his arm and led him to her dark chamber and closed the oaken door.

"A strange thing happened," she said softly. "When I left you, I thought you followed me. I was so sure of it I did not even look around to verify it. You were there behind me. And when I came to my own door, I said good night to you, so certain I was that you were there."

He could see her outline in the dark and smell the scent which was herself. "My lady," he said, "when you left the room, I saw myself follow you as though I were another person looking on."

Their bodies locked together as though a trap had sprung. Their mouths met, and each devoured the other. Each frantic heartbeat at the walls of ribs trying to get to the other until their held breaths burst out and Lancelot, dizzied, found the door and blundered down the stairs. And he was weeping bitterly. ❖

---

18. **liege** (lēj): under feudal law, entitled to the service or allegiance of subjects.

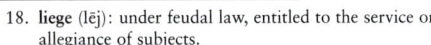

WORDS TO KNOW	**fallible** (făl′ə-bəl) *adj.* capable of being wrong or mistaken
	intemperate (ĭn-těm′pər-ĭt) *adj.* extreme
	haggard (hăg′ərd) *adj.* appearing worn and exhausted

Art Note

Millefleurs tapestry with horseman and arms of Jean de Daillon by unknown Flemish artist The nobility of the 14th and 15th centuries often commissioned tapestries to decorate walls. These heavy woolen tapestries helped block out the wind that leaked through the cold stone walls of their huge castles. Since the tapestries were easy to carry, kings were able to take them along to beautify temporary homes when traveling to battle, collect tithes, or oversee their lands. This particular tapestry shows a knight on horseback. The word "chivalry" comes from the old French word *chevalerie*, meaning "horse soldiery."

Reading the Art What can you infer about the way knights were regarded from the ornate work on this tapestry?

INSIGHT

THE KNIGHT
ADRIENNE RICH

Millefleurs tapestry with horseman and arms of Jean de Daillon (late 1400s), unknown Flemish artist. National Trust Photographic Library.

A knight rides into the noon,
and his helmet points to the sun,
and a thousand splintered suns
are the gaiety of his mail.
5 The soles of his feet glitter
and his palms flash in reply,
and under his crackling banner
he rides like a ship in sail.

A knight rides into the noon,
10 and only his eye is living,
a lump of bitter jelly
set in a metal mask,
betraying rags and tatters
that cling to the flesh beneath
15 and wear his nerves to ribbons
under the radiant casque.

Who will unhorse this rider
and free him from between
the walls of iron, the emblems
20 crushing his chest with their weight?
Will they defeat him gently,
or leave him hurled on the green,
his rags and wounds still hidden
under the great breastplate?

RESPONDING OPTIONS

FROM PERSONAL RESPONSE TO CRITICAL ANALYSIS

REFLECT 1. What were your feelings toward Lancelot as you read this selection? Describe them in your notebook.

RETHINK 2. What inferences did you make about Lancelot as you were reading? Make use of your reading log and the chart that you created for the Reading Connection on page 923.

3. The knights' tributes to Lancelot imply that he is a "winner." Do you think Lancelot would agree?

Close Textual Reading
Consider
- his fame and his achievements
- his relationships with Arthur and Guinevere
- why Lancelot weeps as he goes down the stairs

4. How does the view of fame presented in this selection compare with the views about fame expressed in your discussion for the Personal Connection on page 923?

5. Do you think the amount of detail Steinbeck includes adds to or detracts from the story? Explain your opinion.
Consider
- the description of the town and of Arthur's great hall during the feast
- Lancelot's observations about the carriage of different groups in society
- the physical descriptions of Lancelot, Arthur, and Guinevere

RELATE 6. Consider this statement in Steinbeck's tale: "There is a seat of worth beyond the reach of envy whose occupant ceases to be a man and becomes the receptacle of the wishful longings of the world." What modern-day figures, male or female, might you apply this statement to?

Thematic Link

Multimodal Learning
ANOTHER PATHWAY
Cooperative Learning
In a small group, choose a scene from the selection and create a storyboard for it that indicates not only what the characters say but also what they feel and think. If you prepare your storyboard on a computer, you could use different fonts or colors to distinguish between the characters' thoughts and words.

QUICKWRITES

1. Pretend you are a society reporter covering the feast at the castle. Write a brief **feature article** describing the event.

2. In an **interview** to be published in a celebrity magazine, have Lancelot discuss his views about fame.

3. Write an **advice column** in which you analyze Lancelot's dilemma regarding Guinevere and present possible options to him.

4. Write a **soap-opera scene** in which Guinevere discusses her plight with one of her ladies-in-waiting.

📁 **PORTFOLIO** Save your writing. You may want to use it later as a springboard to a piece for your portfolio.

THE ACTS OF KING ARTHUR AND HIS NOBLE KNIGHTS

From Personal Response to Critical Analysis

1. Accept all reasonable responses.
2. Possible responses: He is embarrassed at the way his fame has been exaggerated; he is passionately in love with Guinevere but feels guilty about betraying the king; he is a courageous, skilled, and compassionate knight.
3. Accept all reasonable, well-supported responses.
4. Responses will vary.
5. Possible responses: Some students may say that the details help them more sharply visualize the characters and actions; others, in contrast, may argue that the details slow down the narrative.
6. Accept all reasonable, well-supported responses

Another Pathway

Cooperative Learning All students can contribute to this activity. Some can draw pictures, some can write captions, and some can contribute to layout.

Rubric

3 Full Accomplishment The storyboard shows what the characters say, think, and feel in great detail.

2 Substantial Accomplishment The storyboard reveals the characters' dialogue and thoughts but could include more details.

1 Little or Partial Accomplishment The storyboard is inaccurate or incomplete.

QuickWrites

1. Point out to students that society news is written as much to entertain as to inform.
2. Remind students to use a question-and-answer format, revealing character through dialogue.
3. Have students use correct letter format in their columns.
4. Guide students to include a clear introduction, body, and conclusion in the scene.

Interviews, pp. 72–76
Observing Situations and Settings, pp. 58–71

Across the Curriculum

History Cooperative Learning Arrange students in small groups to complete their research. You may want to have group members divide the reference material to make the task more efficient.

Sports Students can consult an almanac or book of records to find the statistics on record-breaking jumps. Remind students to check two reliable sources to ensure accuracy.

ADDITIONAL SUGGESTION

Geography Students can find out what Winchester is like today. Possible research topics include population, major industries, and cultural attractions.

Critic's Corner

Have students work in teams to debate the issue and consider all sides of the topic. Guide students to cite details from the selection to support their opinion as they debate and share their conclusions.

Literary Links

Accept any reasonable response, but encourage students to provide specific reasons for their opinions.

LITERARY CONCEPTS

Style is the particular way in which a piece of literature is written. Style refers not so much to what is said but to how it is said. Use of descriptive detail, use of dialogue, depth of characterization, diction (word choice), and tone all contribute to a writer's style. Though both Steinbeck and Baines (writer of "The Crowning of Arthur" and "Sir Launcelot du Lake" on page 904) relied on the same sources for their versions of the Arthurian legend, each writer retold the legend in his own distinctive style. Baines, for instance, in trying to render Malory's work, included much less descriptive detail than Steinbeck did.

In a chart, compare the styles of Baines and Steinbeck. Create a separate column for each of the five elements of style mentioned in the previous paragraph and for any other elements you wish to analyze. After completing your chart, write a sentence for each writer, summing up key features of his style.

CRITIC'S CORNER

The noted critic Alfred Kazin praised Steinbeck for his "moving approach to human life" but also criticized his specific characterizations. "Nothing in his books is so dim," Kazin felt, ". . . as the human beings who live in them, and few of them are intensely imagined as human beings at all." On the basis of this selection, do you agree with Kazin's comments? Why or why not?

LITERARY LINKS

What do you think Guinevere and Lancelot, as portrayed in Steinbeck's story, would say to the speakers of the poems "Love Without Love" (page 371) and "The Taxi" (page 372)?

Multimodal Learning

ALTERNATIVE ACTIVITIES

1. **Cooperative Learning** Imagine that a foreign visitor has come to Winchester to interview Arthur, Guinevere, and Lancelot about their values and ideals. In a small group, create a **dramatization** of that interview.

2. Lancelot believes he can identify people by their gait, or way of walking. Reread the description of the gaits of knights, ladies, and serfs, beginning on page 923. With two classmates, present a **demonstration** of each gait for the class.

3. Review the selection for details about the kinds of food served at the Whitsun feast. With a partner, do research to find out more about the offerings at a medieval feast and how much food might have been required. Develop a **menu** for such a feast and share it with the class.

ACROSS THE CURRICULUM

Sports Lancelot admits to leaping eight feet. Is that possible? What is the highest a person has actually leaped—both with and without a pole? Create a poster that compares Lancelot's leap with these actual record-breaking jumps.

History Research the design and construction of medieval English castles. Then create a model or a diagram of Arthur's castle, using the information that you find as well as details from the selection.

View of medieval castle surrounded by moat. J. Allan Cash Photolibrary.

934 UNIT ONE PART 1: LASTING IMPRESSIONS

Literary Concepts

Students should note that Baines uses limited description and characterization. He recreates the era through the characters' speech and the grand scale of the events presented. Steinbeck uses detailed description, fuller characterization, and realistic dialogue to create an easily visualized world inhabited by people with familiar desires.

Alternative Activities

1. **Cooperative Learning** One student can serve as the recorder to write down the script; another can be the explainer of ideas to facilitate sharing ideas and opinions. Encourage students to perform their dramatization for the class.

2. Students should note specific words and phrases that suggest the kinds of body movements they will imitate.

3. Suggest that pairs find out what foods were commonly eaten by the royalty, the ways in which they were prepared, and what they might cost in today's dollars.

WORDS TO KNOW

EXERCISE A Review the Words to Know at the bottom of the selection pages. Then fill in each blank with the vocabulary word that best completes the sentence.

1. Although medieval romances often _____ knights and their gallantry, nonfiction accounts of the times are generally more critical.
2. Most people were poor, had inadequate diets, worked constantly, and slept on thin straw mats, leaving them _____ and in poor health.
3. Even nobles were uncomfortable, for castles were freezing cold in the winter, hot and stuffy in the summer—in short, miserable places in any _____ weather.
4. The ladies who walked so elegantly learned that graceful _____ through harsh, even cruel, training in their youth.
5. Most knights served a single lord; some, however, lived a more _____ life, moving from place to place, serving one lord and then another.
6. Good manners were critical for a knight, for _____ behavior was important to the upper class.
7. However, acts of cruelty toward women and peasants were common, and because such behavior was not considered wicked, it required no _____.
8. Knights expected great praise for their bravery and reacted negatively to insults or any form of _____.
9. Because tempers were short and law enforcement was lacking, insults or injuries were likely to be met by acts of _____.
10. Legal disputes were often decided by combat because people believed that while humans were _____ and might misjudge a situation, God would cause the guilty party to be defeated.

EXERCISE B With a partner, try using a minimal number of gestures or actions to communicate five of the Words to Know.

JOHN STEINBECK

1902–1968

One of 20th-century America's most famous authors, John Steinbeck is best known for novels that honor working people and point out social injustice. Steinbeck was born in the Salinas Valley in northern California, the setting of much of his fiction. He attended Stanford University on and off for several years but never earned a college degree. Instead, he worked at a series of odd jobs—fruit picker, house painter, caretaker, lab assistant—before becoming a writer.

During the 1930s, Steinbeck won fame for novels that sympathetically portrayed the economic hardships of the Great Depression. The best known of these, his Pulitzer Prize-winning *The Grapes of Wrath* (1939), depicts the plight of an Oklahoma farm family forced to turn to migrant work in California. During World War II, Steinbeck worked overseas as a newspaper war correspondent and also wrote training manuals for the U.S. Army. Two decades later, he wrote political speeches for President Lyndon B. Johnson and traveled to Vietnam to report on the war there for *Newsday*.

During his long writing career, Steinbeck also produced short stories, travel books, and several plays for stage and screen, including an award-winning stage adaptation of his 1937 novel *Of Mice and Men*. In 1962 he won the Nobel Prize in literature.

OTHER WORKS *The Red Pony, The Pearl, Travels with Charley in Search of America*

Extended Reading

• AUTHOR BACKGROUND

Words to Know

Exercise A
1. exalt
2. haggard
3. intemperate
4. carriage
5. vagrant
6. decorous
7. penitence
8. disparagement
9. reprisal
10. fallible

Exercise B
Accept all reasonable responses.

Reteaching/Reinforcement
• *Unit Six Resource Book*, p. 50

HISTORICAL CONNECTION
The Castles of England Castles were built in Europe from the 9th century through the 15th century; the strongly fortified residences provided a measure of security in a chaotic age. These photographs of English castles reflect the magnificence of these structures. Use the images to enhance a lesson about the Arthurian legends and the medieval world.

Side A, Frame 49765

AUTHOR BACKGROUND
John Steinbeck A Nobel-Prize-winning author, John Steinbeck is considered one of America's finest novelists. These pictures of Steinbeck and of several of his novels will supplement the biographical information in the student anthology.

Side A, Frame 49758

REFLECTING ON THEME
What Do You Think?

Ask students to think about the list of childhood heroes that they created for the activity on page 902. Do students think that the characters from Arthurian legend are suitable heroes for the children of today? Have them explain their reasoning.

OVERVIEW

Objectives

- To understand and appreciate a classical Greek tragedy that explores the heroic tradition and the conflict between contradictory principles
- To enrich reading by using active reading strategies
- To identify and understand irony
- To appreciate and understand allusions
- To express understanding of the drama through a choice of writing forms, including a letter, a diary entry, and a lecture
- To extend understanding of the drama through a variety of multimodal and cross-curricular activities

Skills

LITERARY CONCEPTS
- Irony
- Characterization

READING SKILLS/STRATEGIES
- Understanding classical drama

THE WRITER'S STYLE
- Dialogue in plays

GENRE STUDY
- Drama: tragedy

GRAMMAR
- Parallel structure

SPEAKING, LISTENING, AND VIEWING
- Film
- Press conference

READING CONNECTION
Classical Drama Originating in the sixth century B.C., classical drama developed a rich tradition in ancient Greece and Rome. These pictures of classical theaters, playwrights, and actors will enhance students' reading of Understanding Classical Drama on page 937.

Side A, Frame 49772

PREVIEWING

DRAMA

Antigone (ăn-tĭg′ə-nē)
Sophocles (sŏf′ə-klēz′) Ancient Greece
Translated by Dudley Fitts and Robert Fitzgerald

Activating Prior Knowledge
PERSONAL CONNECTION

Consider the principles listed on the right, and in your notebook, rank them in the order of their importance to you. Discuss your ranking and your reasoning with the class. Which of the principles might you be willing to fight for—or willing to uphold if it meant making a sacrifice?

- ☐ loyalty or obligation to family
- ☐ obedience to civil law
- ☐ observance of religious law
- ☐ protection of personal dignity
- ☐ freedom
- ☐ protection of community or nation

Building Background
LITERARY CONNECTION

Sophocles was one of the great dramatists of ancient Greece, and his play *Antigone* is regarded as one of the finest examples of classical Greek tragedy. The main characters in this play come into conflict because they stand firmly behind their principles—principles that are contradictory.

Most Greek tragedies are based on legends or myths that the audience of ancient Greece was very familiar with. *Antigone* is based on the legend of the family of Oedipus (ĕd′ə-pəs), the doomed king of Thebes. As the play begins, Antigone and her sister, Ismene (ĭs-mē′nē), recall their dead father, Oedipus, who unknowingly killed his father and then married his own mother. Upon discovering the truth, Oedipus blinded himself and went into exile, where he was cared for by his two daughters until his death. After his death, his sons, Eteocles (ē-tē′ə-klēz′) and Polyneices (pŏl′ĭ-nī′sēz), agreed to share the kingship of Thebes, ruling in alternate years. However, when Eteocles had served his first term as king, he banished Polyneices from Thebes and refused to relinquish the throne to him, claiming that Polyneices was unfit to rule. Polyneices then enlisted an army from Argos, a powerful city-state and a long-standing enemy of Thebes, to fight his brother. In the course of battle, the brothers killed each other. Their uncle, Creon, has become king and faces the task of restoring order in Thebes. As the new king, he plans to honor one corpse and insult the other.

Detail of bowl fragment, actor with mask (about 350 B.C.), unknown Sicilian artist. Terra cotta, 7⅞″, Martin von Wagner Museum, Würzburg, Germany.

936   UNIT SIX   PART 2: THE HEROIC TRADITION

• READING CONNECTION

PRINT AND MEDIA RESOURCES

UNIT SIX RESOURCE BOOK
Strategic Reading: Literature, p. 53
Vocabulary SkillBuilder, p. 54

GRAMMAR MINI-LESSONS
Transparencies, p. 42
Copymasters, p. 43

ACCESS FOR STUDENTS ACQUIRING ENGLISH
Selection Summaries
Reading Support

FORMAL ASSESSMENT
Selection Test, pp. 185–186
Test Generator

 **AUDIO LIBRARY**
See Reference Card

 **LASERLINKS**
Reading Connection
Cultural Connection

INTERNET RESOURCES
McDougal Littell Literature Center at http://www.hmco.com/mcdougal/lit

936   THE LANGUAGE OF LITERATURE   TEACHER'S EDITION

Active Reading
READING CONNECTION

Understanding Classical Drama

Classical drama arose in Athens, Greece, from religious celebrations in honor of Dionysus (dī'ə-nī'səs), the god of wine and fertility. These celebrations included ritual chants and songs performed by a group called a chorus. Drama evolved from these celebrations during the sixth century B.C., when individual actors began entering into dialogue with the chorus to tell a story.

The Theater Greek drama was filled with the spectacle and pageantry of a religious festival. Attended by thousands, plays were performed during the day in an outdoor theater with seats built into a hillside. The action of each play was presented at the foot of the hill, often on a raised platform. A long building, called the **skene,** served as a backdrop for the action and as a dressing room. A spacious circular floor, the **orchestra,** was located between the skene and the audience.

Actors and Chorus The actors—all men—wore elegant robes, huge masks, and often elevated shoes, all of which added to the grandeur of the spectacle. Sophocles used three actors in his plays; between scenes, they changed costumes and masks when they needed to portray different characters. The **chorus**—a group of about 15—commented on the action, and the leader of the chorus, the **choragus** (kə-rā'gəs), participated in the dialogue. Between scenes, the chorus sang and danced to musical accompaniment in the orchestra, giving insights into the message of the play. The chorus is often considered a kind of ideal spectator, representing the response of ordinary citizens to the tragic events unfolding in the play.

Tragedy and the Tragic Hero During Sophocles' lifetime, three playwrights were chosen each year to enter a theatrical competition in the festival of Dionysus. Each playwright would produce three tragedies, along with a satyr (sā'tər) play, a short comic interlude. A **tragedy** is a drama that recounts the downfall of a dignified, superior character who is involved in historically or socially significant events. The **protagonist,** or **tragic hero,** of the work is in conflict with an opposing character or force, the **antagonist.** The action builds from one event to the next and finally to a **catastrophe** that leads to a disastrous conclusion. Twists of fate play a key role in the hero's destruction.

According to the Greek philosopher Aristotle, a tragic hero possesses a defect, or **tragic flaw,** that brings about or contributes to his or her downfall. This flaw may be poor judgment, pride, weakness, or an excess of an admirable quality. The tragic hero, noted Aristotle, recognizes his or her flaw and its consequences, but only after it is too late to change the course of events.

Strategies for Reading Classical Drama

- Imagine the spectacle of the play as staged, visualizing as you read.
- Try to understand the hero's motivations and the qualities that make him or her a noble figure.
- Pay close attention to the causes of the conflict between the hero and his or her antagonist.
- Determine the circumstances or flaws that lead to the hero's downfall.
- Consider how the words and actions of minor characters help you to understand the main characters.
- Notice how the comments of the chorus interpret the action and point to universal themes.

SUMMARY

In the battle for the throne of Thebes, Antigone's brother Eteocles has died defending the city, while her brother Polyneices has died attacking it. Creon, the king of Thebes, has sworn that although Eteocles has been given a soldier's funeral, Polyneices' body will remain unburied. Antigone defies the decree and buries her brother, even though her sister, Ismene, refuses to help her. Creon then condemns both Antigone and Ismene to death. He changes his mind about Ismene, but locks Antigone away in a stone vault. Later, after the blind prophet Teiresias predicts doom, Creon decides to free Antigone, only to find that she has committed suicide. Antigone's death leads to the suicide of Creon's son, Haemon, who was betrothed to her, and then to the suicide of Creon's wife, Eurydice.

Thematic Link: The Heroic Tradition The tragic clash between moral and civil law forms the basis of this heroic tragedy.

WORDS TO KNOW

auspicious (ô-spĭsh'əs) *adj.* promising success; favorable (p. 944)

compulsive (kəm-pŭl'sĭv) *adj.* having the ability to compel, or force; having an irresistible, irrational impulse to do something (p. 958)

defile (dĭ-fīl') *v.* to make foul, dirty, unclean, or impure (p. 972)

dirge (dûrj) *n.* a slow, mournful piece of music; a funeral hymn (p. 968)

edict (ē'dĭkt') *n.* an order put out by a person in authority (p. 953)

lamentation (lăm'ən-tā'shən) *n.* an expression of grief (p. 968)

lithe (līth) *adj.* limber; physically flexible (p. 949)

perverse (pər-vûrs') *adj.* willfully determined to go against what is expected or desired (p. 963)

sated (sā'tĭd) *adj.* satisfied fully; **sate** *v.* (p. 942)

transgress (trăns-grĕs') *v.* to violate or break a law, command, or moral code (p. 968)

CUSTOMIZING FOR
Students Acquiring English

- Use **ACCESS FOR STUDENTS ACQUIRING ENGLISH,** *Reading Support.*

- Explain to students that classical drama was written as poetry. Most likely, students will find the long speeches and the choral odes the most difficult to read. Ask students to pay special attention to the punctuation marks—commas, periods, colons, semicolons, and so forth—as guides for reading. They should also make use of the annotations at the side of the text.

- As you guide students through the selection, you may want to use the suggestions in these boxes as well as the suggestions under Strategic Reading for Less-Proficient Readers.

ANTIGONE

Multicultural Perspectives

Sophocles' tragedy of *Antigone* has influenced playwrights as well as readers around the world. One of the most famous dramatic adaptations of the play came from 20th-century French playwright Jean Anouilh. In 1942, during the German occupation of France in World War II, Anouilh wrote his adaptation of the Greek legend of the daughter of Oedipus. His *Antigone* provides a forceful condemnation of the abuse of state power; audiences rightly interpreted the play as a veiled attack on the Nazis.

CAST OF CHARACTERS

Antigone } daughters of Oedipus, former king
Ismene } of Thebes

Creon (krē′ŏn′), king of Thebes, uncle of Antigone and Ismene

Haemon (hē′mŏn′), Creon's son, engaged to Antigone

Eurydice (yŏŏ-rĭd′ĭ-sē), wife of Creon

Teiresias (tī-rē′sē-əs), a blind prophet

Chorus, made up of about 15 elders of Thebes

Choragus, leader of the chorus

a Sentry

a Messenger

Bust of Sophocles. Museo Lateranense, Vatican Museums, Vatican City, Alinari / Art Resource, New York.

Antigone contemplates her fate. Culver Pictures.

Ruins of ancient theater at Epidaurus, Greece. Copyright © 1993 Barbara Ries / Photo Researchers, Inc.

Sophocles

Scene: Before the palace of Creon, king of Thebes. A central double door, and two doors at the side. A platform extends the length of the stage, and from this platform three steps lead down into the orchestra, or chorus ground.

Time: Dawn of the day after the repulse of the Argive army from the assault on Thebes

PROLOGUE

(*Antigone and Ismene enter from the central door of the palace.*)

Antigone. Ismene, dear sister,
You would think that we had already suffered enough
For the curse on Oedipus:
I cannot imagine any grief
5 That you and I have not gone through. And now—
Have they told you the new decree of our king Creon?

Ismene. I have heard nothing: I know
That two sisters lost two brothers, a double death
In a single hour; and I know that the Argive army
10 Fled in the night; but beyond this, nothing.

Antigone. I thought so. And that is why I wanted you
To come out here with me. There is something we must do.

Ismene. Why do you speak so strangely?

Antigone. Listen, Ismene:
15 Creon buried our brother Eteocles
With military honors, gave him a soldier's funeral,
And it was right that he should; but Polyneices,
Who fought as bravely and died as miserably—
They say that Creon has sworn
20 No one shall bury him, no one mourn for him,
But his body must lie in the fields, a sweet treasure
For carrion birds to find as they search for food.
That is what they say, and our good Creon is coming here
To announce it publicly; and the penalty—
25 Stoning to death in the public square!
                                  There it is,
And now you can prove what you are:
A true sister, or a traitor to your family.

Ismene. Antigone, you are mad! What could I possibly do?

Antigone. You must decide whether you will help me or not.

30 **Ismene.** I do not understand you. Help you in what?

Antigone. Ismene, I am going to bury him. Will you come?

GUIDE FOR READING

repulse: an act of turning away or beating back.

9 Argive: of Argos.

20–22 The obligation to bury the dead with appropriate burial rites was considered a sacred law among the ancient Greeks. They believed that the soul of someone left unburied would never find peace.

28–35 What contrast between Antigone and Ismene is suggested by the conversation between them?

Ismene. Bury him! You have just said the new law forbids it.

Antigone. He is my brother. And he is your brother, too.

Ismene. But think of the danger! Think what Creon will do!

35 **Antigone.** Creon is not strong enough to stand in my way.

Ismene. Ah sister!
Oedipus died, everyone hating him
For what his own search brought to light, his eyes
Ripped out by his own hand; and Jocasta died,
40 His mother and wife at once: she twisted the cords
That strangled her life; and our two brothers died,
Each killed by the other's sword. And we are left:
But oh, Antigone,
Think how much more terrible than these
45 Our own death would be if we should go against Creon
And do what he has forbidden! We are only women;
We cannot fight with men, Antigone!
The law is strong, we must give in to the law
In this thing, and in worse. I beg the dead
50 To forgive me, but I am helpless: I must yield
To those in authority. And I think it is dangerous business
To be always meddling.

Antigone.   If that is what you think,
I should not want you, even if you asked to come.
You have made your choice; you can be what you want to be.
55 But I will bury him; and if I must die,
I say that this crime is holy: I shall lie down
With him in death, and I shall be as dear
To him as he to me.
          It is the dead,
Not the living, who make the longest demands:
60 We die forever. . . .
          You may do as you like,
Since apparently the laws of the gods mean nothing to you.

Ismene. They mean a great deal to me; but I have no strength
To break laws that were made for the public good.

Antigone. That must be your excuse, I suppose. But as for me,
65 I will bury the brother I love.

Ismene.   Antigone,
I am so afraid for you!

Antigone.   You need not be:
You have yourself to consider, after all.

39 Jocasta, the mother of Antigone and Ismene, hanged herself when she realized the truth about her relationship with Oedipus.

55–61 What do these lines reveal about Antigone's feelings for her brother and the gods' laws?

Critical Thinking:
MAKING JUDGMENTS

E Ask students whether they agree with Antigone or Ismene. Would they break the law to bury a loved one or would they obey the law and leave their family member unburied? *(Possible responses: Moral law supersedes civil law; civil law is supreme because it protects everyone against anarchy.)*

Cultural Note

F Point out that Ismene's comment that she and Antigone are "only women" reflects the secondary role of women in ancient Greece. For example, married women were not even allowed to watch—let alone compete—in the ancient Olympics. The penalty for breaking the rule was to be thrown from a nearby cliff. Only one woman was known to have watched the games and lived, a widow named Callipateira. She dressed up as a male judge to watch her son compete. When he won, she was so overjoyed that she threw off her robes, revealing her gender. She escaped death because her father, brothers, and sons had all performed gloriously in successive Olympics.

GUIDE FOR READING

G Possible response: Antigone loved her brother very deeply and is willing to die to uphold the gods' law.

Mini-Lesson Genre Study

DRAMA Draw the web shown here on the chalkboard. Use the web to discuss the qualities of **tragedy**. Explain that a tragedy has the following elements:

- recounts the downfall of a dignified character involved in major events
- has a main character called a tragic hero who may possess a tragic flaw that brings about his own downfall
- evokes pity and fear in the audience
- often involves unexpected twists of fate
- ends disastrously, usually with the hero's death

Application Have students copy the web into their notebooks. Direct them to rewrite it with specific examples as they read *Antigone*.

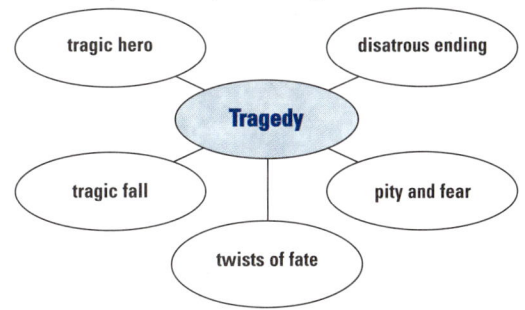

Literary Concept:
STAGE DIRECTIONS

H In Greek tragedy and other ancient dramas, the stage directions are typically implied by the characters' speeches. Have students find the implied stage directions here and explain what they reveal about Antigone's feelings. *(Possible response: Ismene's phrase "So fiery!" implies that Antigone is furious about Ismene's response to her request. Antigone's fierce emotions are also suggested by her use of exclamatory sentences.)*

CUSTOMIZING FOR
Multiple Learning Styles

I **Linguistic Learners** Have students debate the issue Ismene raises here: Should impossible things be tried?

Linking to History

J Thebes was one of the most celebrated cities in ancient Greece. Among its myths are stories of the twin brothers Amphion and Zethus, said to have ruled Thebes and built its walls; the tragic fate of King Oedipus and his sons; the return of the nature god Dionysus; and the birth and exploits of the famous hero Hercules.

Ismene. But no one must hear of this; you must tell no one!
I will keep it a secret, I promise!

Antigone. Oh tell it! Tell everyone!
70 Think how they'll hate you when it all comes out
If they learn that you knew about it all the time!

Ismene. So fiery! You should be cold with fear.

Antigone. Perhaps. But I am doing only what I must.

Ismene. But can you do it? I say that you cannot.

75 **Antigone.** Very well: when my strength gives out, I shall do no more.

Ismene. Impossible things should not be tried at all.

Antigone. Go away, Ismene:
I shall be hating you soon, and the dead will too,
For your words are hateful. Leave me my foolish plan:
80 I am not afraid of the danger; if it means death,
It will not be the worst of deaths—death without honor.

Ismene. Go then, if you feel that you must.
You are unwise,
But a loyal friend indeed to those who love you.

(*Exit into the palace.* Antigone *goes off, left. Enters the* Chorus, *with* Choragus.)

PARODOS

Chorus. Now the long blade of the sun, lying
Level east to west, touches with glory
Thebes of the Seven Gates. Open, unlidded
Eye of golden day! O marching light
5 Across the eddy and rush of Dirce's stream,
Striking the white shields of the enemy
Thrown headlong backward from the blaze of morning!

Choragus. Polyneices their commander
Roused them with windy phrases,
10 He the wild eagle screaming
Insults above our land,
His wings their shields of snow,
His crest their marshaled helms.

Chorus. Against our seven gates in a yawning ring
15 The famished spears came onward in the night;
But before his jaws were <u>sated</u> with our blood,

PARADOS: The parodos is a song that marks the entry of the chorus, which represents the leading citizens of Thebes.

5 Dirce's (dûr'sēz) **stream:** a stream flowing past Thebes. The stream is named after a murdered queen who was thrown into it.

14–15 Thebes had seven gates, which the Argives attacked all at once.

WORDS TO KNOW
sated (sā'tĭd) *adj.* satisfied fully **sate** *v.*

Or pine fire took the garland of our towers,
He was thrown back; and as he turned, great Thebes—
No tender victim for his noisy power—
20 Rose like a dragon behind him, shouting war.

Choragus. For God hates utterly
The bray of bragging tongues;
And when he beheld their smiling,
Their swagger of golden helms,
25 The frown of his thunder blasted
Their first man from our walls.

Chorus. We heard his shout of triumph high in the air
Turn to a scream; far out in a flaming arc
He fell with his windy torch, and the earth struck him.
30 And others storming in fury no less than his
Found shock of death in the dusty joy of battle.

Choragus. Seven captains at seven gates
Yielded their clanging arms to the god
That bends the battle line and breaks it.
35 These two only, brothers in blood,
Face to face in matchless rage,
Mirroring each the other's death,
Clashed in long combat.

Chorus. But now in the beautiful morning of victory
40 Let Thebes of the many chariots sing for joy!
With hearts for dancing we'll take leave of war:
Our temples shall be sweet with hymns of praise,
And the long night shall echo with our chorus.

 21–26 Zeus, the king of the gods, threw a thunderbolt, which killed the first Argive attacker. **What type of conduct was Zeus punishing?**

32–34 When the seven captains were killed, their armor was offered as a sacrifice to Ares (âr´ēz), the god of war.

DESIGN NOTE

The photograph shows a contemporary rendition of a Greek drama. Note that the masks worn by the chorus all reflect the same fixed expression.

Reading the Art *What emotion or emotions are conveyed by these masks? How do you think such masks would affect the audience?*

Literary Concept: IRONY

M Remind students that irony is a contrast between what is believed or expected and what actually exists or happens. Have students predict how these lines about Creon's reign might be ironic. *(Possible response: Right now, Creon is seen as a hero for restoring order and peace to Thebes; perhaps as the play unfolds he will suffer a fall.)*

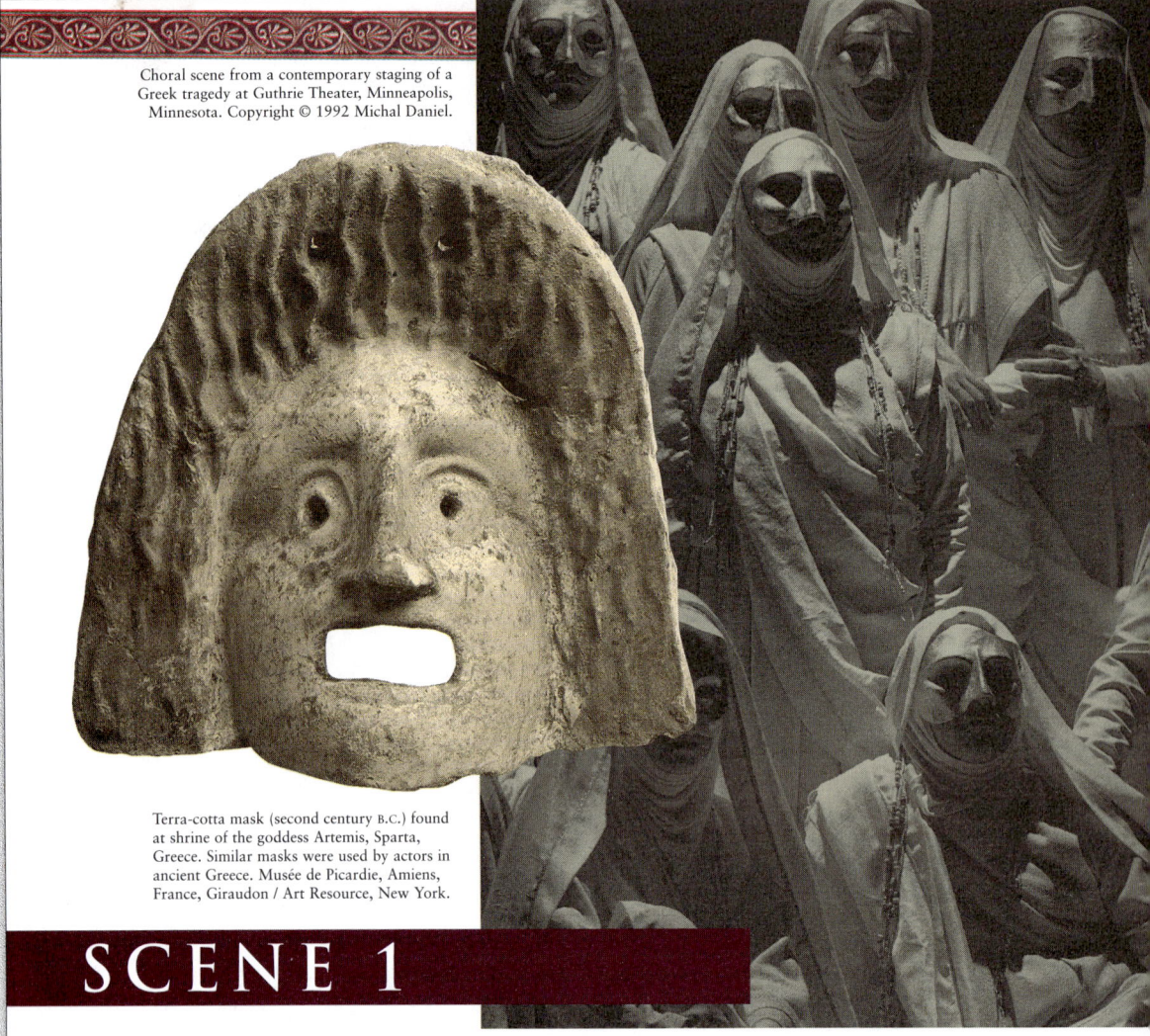

Choral scene from a contemporary staging of a Greek tragedy at Guthrie Theater, Minneapolis, Minnesota. Copyright © 1992 Michal Daniel.

Terra-cotta mask (second century B.C.) found at shrine of the goddess Artemis, Sparta, Greece. Similar masks were used by actors in ancient Greece. Musée de Picardie, Amiens, France, Giraudon / Art Resource, New York.

SCENE 1

M **Choragus.** But now at last our new king is coming:
Creon of Thebes, Menoeceus' son.
In this <u>auspicious</u> dawn of his reign
What are the new complexities
5   That shifting Fate has woven for him?
What is his counsel? Why has he summoned
The old men to hear him?

(*Enter* Creon *from the palace. He addresses the* Chorus *from the top step.*)

2 **Menoeceus** (mə-nē′syŏŏs).

5 The Greeks believed that human destiny was controlled by three sisters called the Fates: Clotho (klō′thō), who spun the thread of human life; Lachesis (lăk′ĭ-sĭs), who determined its length; and Atropos (ăt′rə-pŏs′), who cut the thread.

WORDS TO KNOW
auspicious (ô-spĭsh′əs) *adj.* promising success; favorable

944 THE LANGUAGE OF LITERATURE TEACHER'S EDITION

Creon. Gentlemen: I have the honor to inform you that our ship of
state, which recent storms have threatened to destroy, has come
safely to harbor at last, guided by the merciful wisdom of heaven.
I have summoned you here this morning because I know that I
can depend upon you: your devotion to King Laius was absolute;
you never hesitated in your duty to our late ruler Oedipus; and
when Oedipus died, your loyalty was transferred to his children.
Unfortunately, as you know, his two sons, the princes Eteocles and
Polyneices, have killed each other in battle; and I, as the next in
blood, have succeeded to the full power of the throne.

    I am aware, of course, that no ruler can expect complete loy-
alty from his subjects until he has been tested in office. Nevertheless, I say to you at the very outset that I have nothing but
contempt for the kind of governor who is afraid, for whatever
reason, to follow the course that he knows is best for the state;
and as for the man who sets private friendship above the public welfare—I have no use for him, either. I call God to witness
that if I saw my country headed for ruin, I should not be afraid
to speak out plainly; and I need hardly remind you that I would
never have any dealings with an enemy of the people. No one
values friendship more highly than I; but we must remember
that friends made at the risk of wrecking our ship are not real
friends at all.

    These are my principles, at any rate, and that is why I have
made the following decision concerning the sons of Oedipus:
Eteocles, who died as a man should die, fighting for his country, is to be buried with full military honors, with all the ceremony that is usual when the greatest heroes die; but his brother
Polyneices, who broke his exile to come back with fire and
sword against his native city and the shrines of his fathers'
gods, whose one idea was to spill the blood of his blood and
sell his own people into slavery—Polyneices, I say, is to have no
burial: no man is to touch him or say the least prayer for him;
he shall lie on the plain, unburied; and the birds and the scav-
enging dogs can do with him whatever they like.

    This is my command, and you can see the wisdom behind it.
As long as I am king, no traitor is going to be honored with the
loyal man. But whoever shows by word and deed that he is on
the side of the state—he shall have my respect while he is living, and my reverence when he is dead.

Choragus. If that is your will, Creon son of Menoeceus,
    You have the right to enforce it: we are yours.

Creon. That is my will. Take care that you do your part.

12 **Laius** (lā′əs): father of Oedipus.

18–30 According to Creon, what deserves the highest loyalty? How do you feel about Creon's principles?

31–42 Do you think Creon is justified in treating Polyneices' corpse in this way? What do you think his motive is?

Literary Concept: METAPHOR

Ask students to explain the meaning of the metaphor here. (*Possible response:* The metaphor compares the government to a ship that has successfully navigated dangerous waters.)

GUIDE FOR READING

Possible response: Creon feels that allegiance to the state deserves the highest loyalty. Students who place the public good above private needs will agree; those who place the private over the public will disagree.

Critical Thinking: SPECULATING

Ask students what they can predict about Creon's future actions as ruler from his words here. (*Possible response:* He will be inflexible and exceedingly rigid, which will cause his downfall.)

GUIDE FOR READING

Possible response: Students who place moral law above civil law will disagree with Creon's ruling; other students will support him. He seeks to assert his leadership and establish his power.

CUSTOMIZING FOR
Students Acquiring English

Have students use context clues to infer what *broke his exile* means. ("came back from abroad") What does Creon say Polyneices did after he returned to Thebes? (*He waged war against his own people.*)

ANTIGONE 945

Mini-Lesson — Grammar

PARALLEL STRUCTURE Explain that writers usually should construct sentences so that ideas of the same rank are in the same grammatical structure. Parallel grammatical structures include matching nouns, adjectives, prepositional phrases, and so on. Explain the following example of parallel infinitives from page 945:

"I have the honor *to inform* you that our ship of state, which recent storms have threatened *to destroy*, has come safely *to harbor*. . . ."

Application Invite students to correct each of these errors in parallel structure:
1. To Creon, the stability of the state requires loyalty and being obedient. (*obedience*)
2. Leaders should rule tolerantly and treat people with fairness. (*fairly*)

Reteaching/Reinforcement
- *Grammar Mini-Lessons* copymasters p. 43, transparencies p. 42

The Writer's Craft
Making Sentence Parts Parallel, pp. 415–416

THE LANGUAGE OF LITERATURE TEACHER'S EDITION **945**

Critical Thinking:
HYPOTHESIZING

 Have students hypothesize why the choragus suggests that the younger men carry out Creon's decree. *(Possible responses: They do not agree with his dictate; they fear retribution from the people because the rule is unfair.)*

Literary Concept:
CHARACTERIZATION

S Ask students to explain what the sentry's behavior suggests about Creon's reputation. *(Possible responses: From the sentry's terror, we can infer that Creon is greatly feared; he expects his orders to be carried out completely.)*

CUSTOMIZING FOR
Students Acquiring English

 Ask students to paraphrase Creon's speech in simple, everyday English. *(You are doing a good job of excusing yourself, but it would help if I knew what you were talking about.)*

Literary Concept:
RISING ACTION

T Ask students what the sentry has discovered. *(Someone has buried Polyneice's body, defying Creon's decree.)* How does this heighten the conflict? *(Creon will be looking for the rebel.)*

Choragus. We are old men: let the younger ones carry it out.
Creon. I do not mean that: the sentries have been appointed.
Choragus. Then what is it that you would have us do?
Creon. You will give no support to whoever breaks this law.
55 **Choragus.** Only a crazy man is in love with death!
Creon. And death it is; yet money talks, and the wisest
   Have sometimes been known to count a few coins too many.

(*Enter* Sentry.)

Sentry. I'll not say that I'm out of breath from running, King, because
60   every time I stopped to think about what I have to tell you, I felt
   like going back. And all the time a voice kept saying, "You fool,
   don't you know you're walking straight into trouble?"; and then
   another voice: "Yes, but if you let somebody else get the news to
   Creon first, it will be even worse than that for you!" But good sense
65   won out, at least I hope it was good sense, and here I am with a
   story that makes no sense at all; but I'll tell it anyhow, because, as
   they say, what's going to happen's going to happen, and—

Creon. Come to the point. What have you to say?
Sentry. I did not do it. I did not see who did it. You must not punish me for what someone else has done.
70 **Creon.** A comprehensive defense! More effective, perhaps,
   If I knew its purpose. Come: what is it?
Sentry. A dreadful thing . . . I don't know how to put it—
Creon. Out with it!
Sentry.   Well, then;
   The dead man—
                Polyneices—

(*Pause. The* Sentry *is overcome, fumbles for words.*
Creon *waits impassively.*)

                        out there—
                                someone—
75   New dust on the slimy flesh!

(*Pause. No sign from* Creon.)

   Someone has given it burial that way, and
   Gone. . . .

(*Long pause.* Creon *finally speaks with deadly control.*)

Creon. And the man who dared do this?
Sentry.   I swear I
   Do not know! You must believe me!

78 Note that Creon assumes it is a man who has tried to bury the body.

946   UNIT SIX   PART 2: THE HEROIC TRADITION

Listen:
80 The ground was dry, not a sign of digging, no,
Not a wheel track in the dust, no trace of anyone.
It was when they relieved us this morning: and one of them,
The corporal, pointed to it.
                    There it was,
The strangest—
            Look:
85 The body, just mounded over with light dust: you see?
Not buried really, but as if they'd covered it
Just enough for the ghost's peace. And no sign
Of dogs or any wild animal that had been there.

And then what a scene there was! Every man of us
90 Accusing the other: we all proved the other man did it;
We all had proof that we could not have done it.
We were ready to take hot iron in our hands,
Walk through fire, swear by all the gods,
It was not I!
95 *I do not know who it was, but it was not I!*

(*Creon's rage has been mounting steadily, but the Sentry is too intent upon his story to notice it.*)

And then, when this came to nothing, someone said
A thing that silenced us and made us stare
Down at the ground: you had to be told the news,
And one of us had to do it! We threw the dice,
100 And the bad luck fell to me. So here I am,
No happier to be here than you are to have me:
Nobody likes the man who brings bad news.

Choragus. I have been wondering, King: can it be that the gods
    have done this?

Creon (*furiously*). Stop!
105 Must you doddering wrecks
Go out of your heads entirely? "The gods!"
Intolerable!
The gods favor this corpse? Why? How had he served them?
Tried to loot their temples, burn their images,
110 Yes, and the whole state, and its laws with it!
Is it your senile opinion that the gods love to honor bad men?
A pious thought!—
            No, from the very beginning
There have been those who have whispered together,
Stiff-necked anarchists, putting their heads together,

85–88 Notice that the burial of Polyneices is symbolic and ritualistic rather than actual.

104–109 Note how quickly Creon rejects a reasonable question posed by the choragus. Creon is convinced that he knows how the gods think.

114 anarchists (ăn′ər-kĭsts): persons favoring the overthrow of government.

GUIDE FOR READING

 Possible response: He assumes that the people who buried Polyneices have defied him for money.

Literary Concept:
CHARACTERIZATION

 Have students explain what we learn about Creon's character here. Are these positive or negative qualities? *(Possible response: Creon is quick to jump to conclusions and seek revenge. He assumes that the sentry is part of a conspiracy, though he has no proof. These are undesirable qualities in a leader.)*

Critical Thinking: SPECULATING

 Ask students how they think they would act if they were in the sentry's position. You may wish to use the following model to demonstrate how to make a personal response to the text:

Think-Aloud Model: *No one could make me ever see King Creon again! I'd run away from the palace or move to another city. On second thought, perhaps I'd try to get a reward and win back Creon's favor.*

---

115   Scheming against me in alleys. These are the men,
      And they have bribed my own guard to do this thing.
      (*sententiously*) Money!
      There's nothing in the world so demoralizing as money.
      Down go your cities,
120   Homes gone, men gone, honest hearts corrupted,
      Crookedness of all kinds, and all for money!
                                    (*to* Sentry) But you—!
      I swear by God and by the throne of God,
      The man who has done this thing shall pay for it!
      Find that man; bring him here to me, or your death
125   Will be the least of your problems: I'll string you up
      Alive, and there will be certain ways to make you
      Discover your employer before you die;
      And the process may teach you a lesson you seem to have missed:
      The dearest profit is sometimes all too dear.
130   That depends on the source. Do you understand me?
      A fortune won is often misfortune.

Sentry. King, may I speak?

Creon.   Your very voice distresses me.

Sentry. Are you sure that it is my voice, and not your conscience?

Creon. By God, he wants to analyze me now!

135 **Sentry.** It is not what I say, but what has been done, that hurts you.

Creon. You talk too much.

Sentry.   Maybe; but I've done nothing.

Creon. Sold your soul for some silver: that's all you've done.

Sentry. How dreadful it is when the right judge judges wrong!

Creon. Your figures of speech
140   May entertain you now; but unless you bring me the man,
    You will get little profit from them in the end.

(*Exit* Creon *into the palace.*)

Sentry. "Bring me the man"—!
    I'd like nothing better than bringing him the man!
    But bring him or not, you have seen the last of me here.
145   At any rate, I am safe!

(*Exit* Sentry.)

---

117 sententiously (sĕn-tĕn'shəs-lē): in a pompous, moralizing manner.

117–122 What does Creon assume about the motives of those who have disobeyed him?

ODE 1

Chorus. Numberless are the world's wonders, but none
More wonderful than man; the storm-grey sea
Yields to his prows; the huge crests bear him high;
Earth, holy and inexhaustible, is graven
5 With shining furrows where his plows have gone
Year after year, the timeless labor of stallions.

The light-boned birds and beasts that cling to cover,
The lithe fish lighting their reaches of dim water,
All are taken, tamed in the net of his mind;
10 The lion on the hill, the wild horse windy-maned,
Resign to him; and his blunt yoke has broken
The sultry shoulders of the mountain bull.

Words also, and thought as rapid as air,
He fashions to his good use; statecraft is his,
15 And his the skill that deflects the arrows of snow,
The spears of winter rain: from every wind
He has made himself secure—from all but one:
In the late wind of death he cannot stand.

O clear intelligence, force beyond all measure!
20 O fate of man, working both good and evil!
When the laws are kept, how proudly his city stands!
When the laws are broken, what of his city then?
Never may the anarchic man find rest at my hearth,
Never be it said that my thoughts are his thoughts.

ODE: An ode is a song chanted by the chorus.

4 graven: carved; engraved.

24 What does this ode convey about human greatness and tragic limitation?

WORDS TO KNOW
lithe (līth) *adj.* limber; physically flexible

Literary Concept: FIGURATIVE LANGUAGE

Invite volunteers to point out the figures of speech in this passage and evaluate their effectiveness. *(Possible responses: Metaphor and personification are used throughout the lyrical hymn to illustrate man's power over nature.)*

GUIDE FOR READING

Possible response: The ode reveals that humans have the potential for enormous greatness as well as tragedy. Humans can achieve greatness when they stay within the laws; humans can suffer tragedy when they transgress those laws.

STRATEGIC READING FOR Less-Proficient Readers

Who has defied Creon and buried Polyneices? *(Antigone)* **Making Inferences**

- What principles does Creon live by? *(He sets public interest above private concerns.)* **Summarizing**

- What is the sentry's attitude toward Creon? *(He fears Creon greatly.)* **Drawing Conclusions**

- What does Creon ask the sentry to do? *(to bring him the man who has buried Polyneices)* **Noting Relevant Details**

Set a Purpose Invite students to read Scene 2 to find out if Creon captures Antigone.

Mini-Lesson: Speaking, Listening, and Viewing

FILM There are two versions of *Antigone* available for classroom use. The first is the well-known 1962 production starring the famous Greek actress Irene Pappas (see the photographs throughout the selection) and directed by George Tzavellas.

In 1991, the tragedy was reworked by director Amy Greenfield. Entitled *Antigone: Rites of Passage,* this 85-minute video retells the story of Antigone through action, dance, and rock-video techniques. This version stars Amy Greenfield, Bertram Ross, and Janet Eilber.

Application If possible, screen one film version of the play for the class and have students compare and contrast it to Sophocles' version. Students should consider what new perceptions of the tragedy they gained from watching the video.

DESIGN NOTE

Permanent stone theaters like the one shown in this photograph were not built until the 4th century B.C., after the classical period of playwriting. The open-air theaters had a flat circular area (the *orchestra*) used for choral dances, a raised stage for the actors, and a semicircular seating area built in a hillside around the perimeter. The theaters seated between 15,000 and 20,000 people. As the actors became more important and the chorus less so, the stage became higher.

Reading the Art *Study the design of the ancient Greek theater shown in this photograph. What might be some of the advantages and disadvantages of this theater design?*

Critical Thinking: SPECULATING

Ⓐ Invite students to predict how they think Creon will punish Antigone for defying his edict and burying Polyneices. *(Possible responses: He will have her exiled; he will have her executed.)*

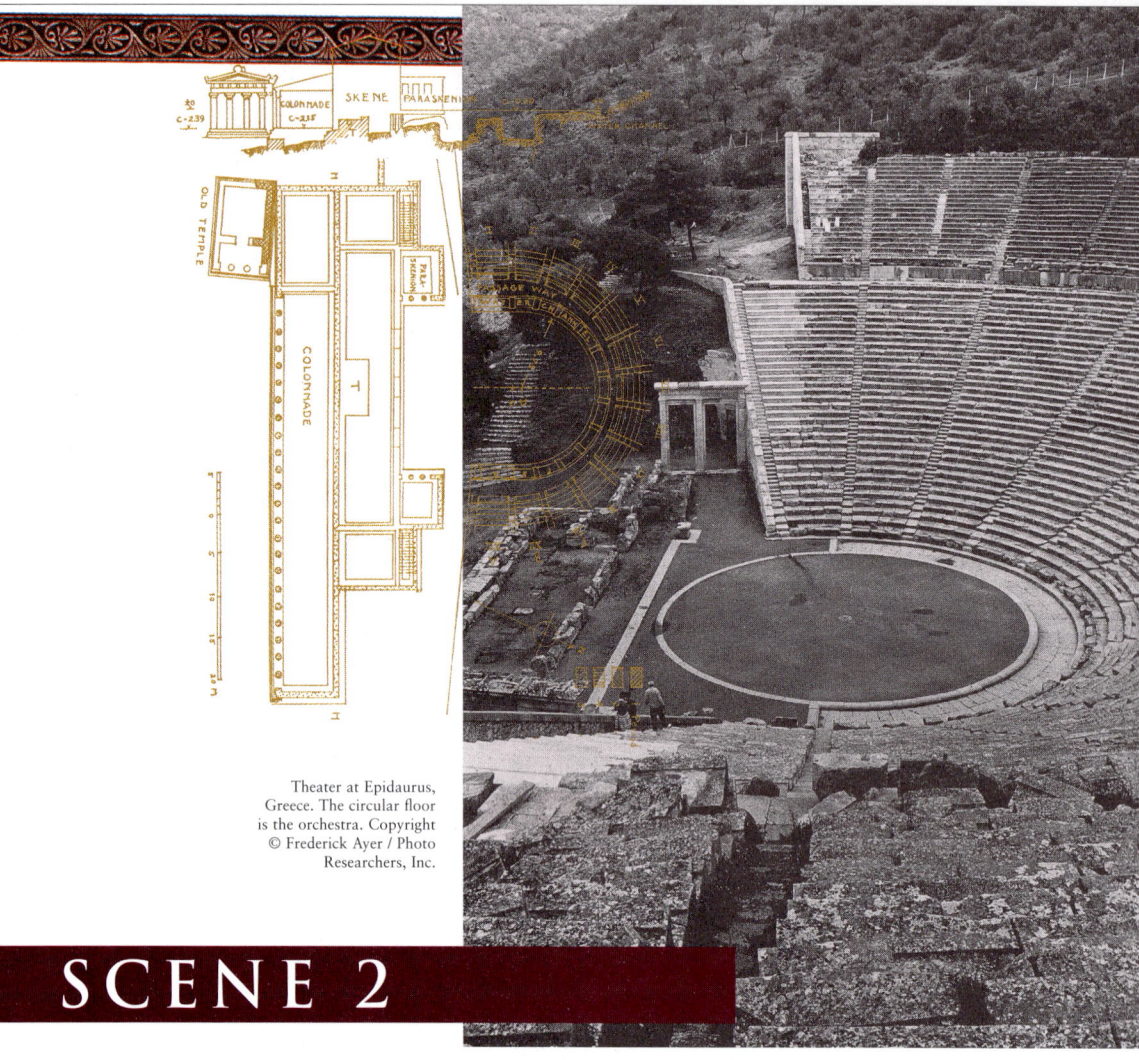

Theater at Epidaurus, Greece. The circular floor is the orchestra. Copyright © Frederick Ayer / Photo Researchers, Inc.

SCENE 2

(*Reenter* Sentry *leading* Antigone.)

Choragus. What does this mean? Surely this captive woman
    Is the princess, Antigone. Why should she be taken?

Sentry. Here is the one who did it! We caught her
    In the very act of burying him. Where is Creon?

5 **Choragus.** Just coming from the house.

(*Enter* Creon, *center.*)

Creon.   What has happened?
    Why have you come back so soon?

950   UNIT SIX   PART 2: THE HEROIC TRADITION

Sentry (*expansively*).   O King,
    A man should never be too sure of anything:
    I would have sworn
    That you'd not see me here again: your anger
10   Frightened me so, and the things you threatened me with;
    But how could I tell then
    That I'd be able to solve the case so soon?

    No dice throwing this time: I was only too glad to come!

    Here is this woman. She is the guilty one:
15   We found her trying to bury him.

    Take her, then; question her; judge her as you will.
    I am through with the whole thing now, and glad of it.

Creon. But this is Antigone! Why have you brought her here?

Sentry. She was burying him, I tell you!

Creon (*severely*).   Is this the truth?

20 **Sentry.** I saw her with my own eyes. Can I say more?

Creon. The details: come, tell me quickly!

Sentry.   It was like this:
    After those terrible threats of yours, King,
    We went back and brushed the dust away from the body.
    The flesh was soft by now, and stinking,
25   So we sat on a hill to windward and kept guard.
    No napping this time! We kept each other awake.
    But nothing happened until the white round sun
    Whirled in the center of the round sky over us:
    Then, suddenly,
30   A storm of dust roared up from the earth, and the sky
    Went out, the plain vanished with all its trees
    In the stinging dark. We closed our eyes and endured it.
    The whirlwind lasted a long time, but it passed;
    And then we looked, and there was Antigone!
35   I have seen
    A mother bird come back to a stripped nest, heard
    Her crying bitterly a broken note or two
    For the young ones stolen. Just so, when this girl
    Found the bare corpse, and all her love's work wasted,
40   She wept, and cried on heaven to damn the hands
    That had done this thing.
                            And then she brought more dust
    And sprinkled wine three times for her brother's ghost.

    We ran and took her at once. She was not afraid,

ANTIGONE   **951**

DESIGN NOTE

Reading the Art *What does the arrangement of figures in the film still suggest about the power of the state in this play?*

Not even when we charged her with what she had done.
45 She denied nothing.
　　　　　　　And this was a comfort to me,
And some uneasiness: for it is a good thing
To escape from death, but it is no great pleasure
To bring death to a friend.
　　　　　　　Yet I always say
There is nothing so comfortable as your own safe skin!

50 **Creon** (*slowly, dangerously*). And you, Antigone,
You with your head hanging—do you confess this thing?

Antigone. I do. I deny nothing.

Creon (*to Sentry*).　　　You may go.

(*Exit* Sentry.)

(*to* Antigone) Tell me, tell me briefly:
Had you heard my proclamation touching this matter?

55 **Antigone.** It was public. Could I help hearing it?

Creon. And yet you dared defy the law.

Antigone.　　　　　　　　I dared.
It was not God's proclamation. That final Justice
That rules the world below makes no such laws.

Your edict, King, was strong,
60 But all your strength is weakness itself against
The immortal unrecorded laws of God.
They are not merely now: they were, and shall be,
Operative forever, beyond man utterly.

I knew I must die, even without your decree:
65 I am only mortal. And if I must die
Now, before it is my time to die,
Surely this is no hardship: can anyone
Living, as I live, with evil all about me,
Think Death less than a friend? This death of mine
70 Is of no importance; but if I had left my brother
Lying in death unburied, I should have suffered.
Now I do not.

57–63 What law does Antigone recognize as the supreme one?

64–70 What is Antigone's attitude toward death?

Film still from the 1960 movie *Antigone*. Antigone is about to be taken prisoner after sprinkling dust and wine over her brother's corpse. Culver Pictures.

WORDS TO KNOW
edict (ē′dĭkt′) *n.* an order put out by a person in authority

953

Literary Concept: CHARACTERIZATION

E Ask students what the sentry's actions and comments reveal about his character. Then guide students to explore how the sentry might be a *foil*—a striking contrast—for Antigone. (*Possible response:* The sentry acknowledges that "it is no great pleasure/To bring death to a friend," but he freely places his own self-interest above her life. He is a foil for Antigone because his self-serving actions reinforce the heroism of her sacrifice.)

GUIDE FOR READING

F Possible response: Antigone recognizes God's law as the supreme one.

GUIDE FOR READING

G Possible response: She calmly accepts death as inevitable. She does not fear death.

Linking to Social Studies

H Honoring the dead through proper burial is important across cultures. Christians, Jews, and Muslims traditionally bury the bodies of their dead, while Hindus and Buddhists commonly burn the dead on funeral pyres. Eastern followers of the ancient Persian religion of Zoroastrianism place the corpses of their dead on high, exposed platforms known as Towers of Silence. The bodies are quickly eaten by vultures.

Mini-Lesson　Literary Concepts

REVIEWING CHARACTERIZATION
Remind students that **characterization** refers to the methods a writer uses to create and develop character. There are four basic methods of characterization: 1) physical description of the character; 2) the character's own speech, thoughts, feelings, or actions; 3) the speech, thoughts, feelings, or actions of other characters; 4) a narrator's direct comments about the character's nature. The fourth method is more common in fiction than drama, which usually does not have a narrator.

Application Invite students to complete the following chart to analyze how Sophocles develops some of the important characters in *Antigone*:

Character	Trait	Methods of Characterization
Antigone		
Creon		
Ismene		

THE LANGUAGE OF LITERATURE TEACHER'S EDITION　**953**

Literary Concept: IRONY

I Ask students to explain the irony in the comments the Choragus and Creon make. Then explore with the class how the irony in this scene adds to the tragedy. *(Possible response: The dual comments about stubbornness apply to Creon as much as they do to Antigone. Creon's lack of self-knowledge helps the play build to its climax and reinforces the inevitability of the tragedy.)*

Critical Thinking: MAKING JUDGMENTS

J Invite students to evaluate Creon's actions here. Do students agree that Ismene should be arrested and punished, too? *(Possible responses: Some students will say that Ismene should not be arrested because she is innocent; others might agree that she should be arrested because she must have known about Antigone's actions.)*

GUIDE FOR READING

K Possible response: Antigone assumes that the chorus agrees with her but they are too afraid of Creon to voice their true feelings. She is probably right.

You smile at me. Ah Creon,
Think me a fool, if you like; but it may well be
That a fool convicts me of folly.

75 **Choragus.** Like father, like daughter: both headstrong, deaf to
reason!
She has never learned to yield.

Creon. She has much to learn.
The inflexible heart breaks first, the toughest iron
Cracks first, and the wildest horses bend their necks
At the pull of the smallest curb.
Pride? In a slave?
80 This girl is guilty of a double insolence,
Breaking the given laws and boasting of it.
Who is the man here,
She or I, if this crime goes unpunished?
Sister's child, or more than sister's child,
85 Or closer yet in blood—she and her sister
Win bitter death for this!
(*to servants*) Go, some of you,
Arrest Ismene. I accuse her equally.
Bring her: you will find her sniffling in the house there.

Her mind's a traitor: crimes kept in the dark
90 Cry for light, and the guardian brain shudders;
But how much worse than this
Is brazen boasting of barefaced anarchy!

Antigone. Creon, what more do you want than my death?

Creon. Nothing.
That gives me everything.

Antigone. Then I beg you: kill me.
95 This talking is a great weariness: your words
Are distasteful to me, and I am sure that mine
Seem so to you. And yet they should not seem so:
I should have praise and honor for what I have done.
All these men here would praise me
100 Were their lips not frozen shut with fear of you.
(*bitterly*) Ah the good fortune of kings,
Licensed to say and do whatever they please!

Creon. You are alone here in that opinion.

Antigone. No, they are with me. But they keep their tongues in leash.

105 **Creon.** Maybe. But you are guilty, and they are not.

Antigone. There is no guilt in reverence for the dead.

82–83 Think about how Creon's perception of Antigone as a threat to his manhood heightens the conflict.

99–104 What does Antigone assume about the attitude of the chorus? Do you think she is right?

Confrontation between Antigone and Creon in the 1960 film. Photofest.

DESIGN NOTE

Reading the Art How does this picture suggest that Creon has much greater power than Antigone? Study the building, the arrangement of figures, and the characters' costumes and props for hints.

Literary Concept:
FIGURATIVE LANGUAGE

L Have students identify and explain the metaphors and personification in this passage. Then explore with the class how the figurative language helps readers visualize the characters and understand their motivation. *(Possible responses: "the cloud/That shadows her eyes rains down gentle sorrow" is a metaphor comparing tears to rain. It is also personification, giving human qualities to rain. The phrase "snake in my ordered house, sucking my blood" is a metaphor, comparing Ismene's supposed betrayal to a snake's treachery. The first figure of speech portrays Ismene as compassionate and helpless; the second shows Creon as irrationally suspicious.)*

GUIDE FOR READING

M Possible response: Some students may agree that it is justified; others may argue that Antigone is too harsh on Ismene.

Creon. But Eteocles—was he not your brother too?

Antigone. My brother too.

Creon. And you insult his memory?

Antigone (*softly*). The dead man would not say that I insult it.

110 **Creon.** He would: for you honor a traitor as much as him.

Antigone. His own brother, traitor or not, and equal in blood.

Creon. He made war on his country. Eteocles defended it.

Antigone. Nevertheless, there are honors due all the dead.

Creon. But not the same for the wicked as for the just.

115 **Antigone.** Ah Creon, Creon,
   Which of us can say what the gods hold wicked?

Creon. An enemy is an enemy, even dead.

Antigone. It is my nature to join in love, not hate.

Creon (*finally losing patience*). Go join them, then; if you must have
   your love,
120 Find it in hell!

Choragus. But see, Ismene comes:

(*Enter* Ismene, *guarded.*)

   Those tears are sisterly; the cloud
   That shadows her eyes rains down gentle sorrow.

Creon. You too, Ismene,
125 Snake in my ordered house, sucking my blood
   Stealthily—and all the time I never knew
   That these two sisters were aiming at my throne!

                                            Ismene,
   Do you confess your share in this crime or deny it?
   Answer me.

130 **Ismene.** Yes, if she will let me say so. I am guilty.

Antigone (*coldly*). No, Ismene. You have no right to say so.
   You would not help me, and I will not have you help me.

Ismene. But now I know what you meant; and I am here
   To join you, to take my share of punishment.

135 **Antigone.** The dead man and the gods who rule the dead
   Know whose act this was. Words are not friends.

Ismene. Do you refuse me, Antigone? I want to die with you:
   I too have a duty that I must discharge to the dead.

Antigone. You shall not lessen my death by sharing it.

140 **Ismene.** What do I care for life when you are dead?

Antigone. Ask Creon. You're always hanging on his opinions.

115–116 Unlike Creon, Antigone holds that humans cannot understand the thinking of the gods.

131–143 What do you think of Antigone's treatment of her sister?

Ismene. You are laughing at me. Why, Antigone?

Antigone. It's a joyless laughter, Ismene.

Ismene.   But can I do nothing?

Antigone. Yes. Save yourself. I shall not envy you.
145   There are those who will praise you; I shall have honor, too.

Ismene. But we are equally guilty!

Antigone.   No, more, Ismene.
   You are alive, but I belong to Death.

Creon (*to the* Chorus). Gentlemen, I beg you to observe these girls:
   One has just now lost her mind; the other,
150   It seems, has never had a mind at all.

Ismene. Grief teaches the steadiest minds to waver, King.

Creon. Yours certainly did, when you assumed guilt with the guilty!

Ismene. But how could I go on living without her?

Creon.   You are.
   She is already dead.

Ismene.   But your own son's bride!

155 **Creon.** There are places enough for him to push his plow.
   I want no wicked women for my sons!

Ismene. O dearest Haemon, how your father wrongs you!

Creon. I've had enough of your childish talk of marriage!

Choragus. Do you really intend to steal this girl from your son?

160 **Creon.** No; Death will do that for me.

Choragus.   Then she must die?

Creon. You dazzle me.
   —But enough of this talk!
   (*to guards*) You, there, take them away and guard them well:
   For they are but women, and even brave men run
   When they see Death coming.

(*Exeunt* Ismene, Antigone, *and guards.*)

ODE 2

Chorus. Fortunate is the man who has never tasted God's vengeance!
   Where once the anger of heaven has struck, that house is shaken
   Forever: damnation rises behind each child
   Like a wave cresting out of the black northeast,
5   When the long darkness under sea roars up
   And bursts drumming death upon the wind-whipped sand.

I have seen this gathering sorrow from time long past
Loom upon Oedipus' children: generation from generation
Takes the compulsive rage of the enemy god.
10   So lately this last flower of Oedipus' line
Drank the sunlight! but now a passionate word
And a handful of dust have closed up all its beauty.

    What mortal arrogance
    Transcends the wrath of Zeus?
15   Sleep cannot lull him, nor the effortless long months
Of the timeless gods: but he is young forever,
And his house is the shining day of high Olympus.
    All that is and shall be,
    And all the past, is his.
20   No pride on earth is free of the curse of heaven.

    The straying dreams of men
    May bring them ghosts of joy:
But as they drowse, the waking embers burn them;
Or they walk with fixed eyes, as blind men walk.
25   But the ancient wisdom speaks for our own time:
    Fate works most for woe
    With Folly's fairest show.
Man's little pleasure is the spring of sorrow.

17 Olympus: a mountain in northern Greece, home of the gods and goddesses.

28 Do you think this line could apply to Creon?

WORDS TO KNOW

compulsive (kəm-pŭl'sĭv) *adj.* having the ability to compel, or force resulting from an irresistible, irrational impulse

Painting on wine cup, showing the god Dionysus, the patron of theater, in his ship (540 B.C.), Exekias. Greek pottery often featured scenes from mythology. Antikensammlung, Munich, Germany. Photo Copyright © Erich Lessing / Art Resource, New York.

Theatrical masks on a fragment of a Greek bowl, about 410 B.C. The Granger Collection, New York.

SCENE 3

Choragus. But here is Haemon, King, the last of all your sons.
  Is it grief for Antigone that brings him here,
  And bitterness at being robbed of his bride?

(*Enter* Haemon.)

Creon. We shall soon see, and no need of diviners.
                                                    —Son,
5 You have heard my final judgment on that girl:
  Have you come here hating me, or have you come
  With deference and with love, whatever I do?

Haemon. I am your son, Father. You are my guide.
  You make things clear for me, and I obey you.

4 **diviners:** those who predict the future.

GUIDE FOR READING

B Possible response: Creon's words suggest that he sees his son as subservient, existing only to honor and serve his father.

GUIDE FOR READING

C Possible response: Creon sees government as controlling every aspect of his subject's lives. To Creon, kings must be obeyed without question—no matter how unjust their rules may appear.

Critical Thinking:
MAKING JUDGMENTS

D Ask students if they agree with Creon's view of leadership. Should rulers have absolute authority or are governments more effective when the ruled have greater input? *(Possible responses: Absolute authority may be necessary for order in some cases, such as war; governments exist to serve the people, not the rulers.)*

Linking to Government

Given Creon's method of ruling, it is ironic that the Greeks gave democracy to the world. *Demo-cracy* comes from the Greek word *demos*, "people," and *kratos*, "rule." Democracy evolved from the Greek city-states around the 7th-century B.C. The leading democracy was Athens, which overthrew its aristocracy in the 6th century and established a constitution that gave supreme power to the *ecclesia*, a citizens' assembly. Only freeborn male citizens—about 40,000 out of 400,000—could vote. Women, slaves, and immigrants were excluded. Sophocles served in government as president of the *Hellenotamiae*, the treasury board that managed tribute payments.

---

10 No marriage means more to me than your continuing wisdom.

  Creon. Good. That is the way to behave: subordinate
  Everything else, my son, to your father's will.
  This is what a man prays for, that he may get
  Sons attentive and dutiful in his house,
15 Each one hating his father's enemies,
  Honoring his father's friends. But if his sons
  Fail him, if they turn out unprofitably,
  What has he fathered but trouble for himself
  And amusement for the malicious?
                    So you are right
20 Not to lose your head over this woman.
  Your pleasure with her would soon grow cold, Haemon,
  And then you'd have a hellcat in bed and elsewhere.
  Let her find her husband in hell!
  Of all the people in this city, only she
25 Has had contempt for my law and broken it.

  Do you want me to show myself weak before the people?
  Or to break my sworn word? No, and I will not.
  The woman dies.

  I suppose she'll plead "family ties." Well, let her.
30 If I permit my own family to rebel,
  How shall I earn the world's obedience?
  Show me the man who keeps his house in hand,
  He's fit for public authority.
                    I'll have no dealings
  With lawbreakers, critics of the government:
35 Whoever is chosen to govern should be obeyed—
  Must be obeyed, in all things, great and small,
  Just and unjust! O Haemon,
  The man who knows how to obey, and that man only,
  Knows how to give commands when the time comes.
40 You can depend on him, no matter how fast
  The spears come: he's a good soldier; he'll stick it out.

  Anarchy, anarchy! Show me a greater evil!
  This is why cities tumble and the great houses rain down;
  This is what scatters armies!

45 No, no: good lives are made so by discipline.
  We keep the laws then, and the lawmakers,
  And no woman shall seduce us. If we must lose,
  Let's lose to a man, at least! Is a woman stronger than we?

  Choragus. Unless time has rusted my wits,

11–19 What do Creon's words suggest about his relationship with his son? **B**

26–44 What do Creon's words tell you about his views of government and his role as king? **C**

47–48 Again Creon hints that he feels his manhood is threatened.

960 UNIT SIX PART 2: THE HEROIC TRADITION

50 What you say, King, is said with point and dignity.

Haemon (*boyishly earnest*). Father:
Reason is God's crowning gift to man, and you are right
To warn me against losing mine. I cannot say—
I hope that I shall never want to say!—that you
55 Have reasoned badly. Yet there are other men
Who can reason, too; and their opinions might be helpful.
You are not in a position to know everything
That people say or do, or what they feel:
Your temper terrifies them—everyone
60 Will tell you only what you like to hear.
But I, at any rate, can listen; and I have heard them
Muttering and whispering in the dark about this girl.
They say no woman has ever, so unreasonably,
Died so shameful a death for a generous act:
65 "She covered her brother's body. Is this indecent?
She kept him from dogs and vultures. Is this a crime?
Death? She should have all the honor that we can give her!"

This is the way they talk out there in the city.

You must believe me:
70 Nothing is closer to me than your happiness.
What could be closer? Must not any son
Value his father's fortune as his father does his?
I beg you, do not be unchangeable:
Do not believe that you alone can be right.
75 The man who thinks that,
The man who maintains that only he has the power
To reason correctly, the gift to speak, the soul—
A man like that, when you know him, turns out empty.

It is not reason never to yield to reason!

80 In flood time you can see how some trees bend,
And because they bend, even their twigs are safe,
While stubborn trees are torn up, roots and all.
And the same thing happens in sailing:
Make your sheet fast, never slacken—and over you go,
85 Head over heels and under: and there's your voyage.
Forget you are angry! Let yourself be moved!
I know I am young; but please let me say this:
The ideal condition
Would be, I admit, that men should be right by instinct;
90 But since we are all too likely to go astray,
The reasonable thing is to learn from those who can teach.

51–60 In what ways does Haemon's speech reflect the ideals of democracy?

61–68 Haemon suggests that Creon is causing the very thing he most wants to prevent—anarchy.

79–85 Compare Haemon's words to Creon with Creon's words to Antigone in Scene 2, beginning "The inflexible heart breaks first . . ." (line 77, page 954).

ANTIGONE 961

Critical Thinking:
MAKING GENERALIZATIONS

H Ask students how the conflict between Haemon and Creon illustrates a typical conflict between a parent and a child. *(Possible responses: Creon wants his son to defer to his age, experience, and authority; Haemon does not want to be treated like a child; he wants his father to listen to his reasons.)*

Critical Thinking: ANALYZING

I Have students explain what Haemon means by this comment. *(Possible responses: The state needs to listen to its citizens; too-rigid governmental control can be destructive.)*

Literary Concept: MOTIVATION

J Ask students whether they agree with Creon that Haemon is motivated only by a desire to save Antigone. Be sure that students support their opinion with specific examples from the text. *(Possible responses: Yes, everything that Haemon says is directed towards saving Antigone; no, Haemon is also concerned with the welfare of the entire city; he knows that Creon's inflexibility invites disaster.)*

Choragus. You will do well to listen to him, King,
   If what he says is sensible. And you, Haemon,
   Must listen to your father. Both speak well.

95 **Creon.** You consider it right for a man of my years and experience
   To go to school to a boy?

Haemon.   It is not right
   If I am wrong. But if I am young, and right,
   What does my age matter?

Creon. You think it right to stand up for an anarchist?

100 **Haemon.** Not at all. I pay no respect to criminals.

Creon. Then she is not a criminal?

Haemon. The city would deny it, to a man.

Creon. And the city proposes to teach me how to rule?

Haemon. Ah. Who is it that's talking like a boy now?

105 **Creon.** My voice is the one voice giving orders in this city!

Haemon. It is no city if it takes orders from one voice.

Creon. The state is the king!

Haemon.   Yes, if the state is a desert.

(*Pause*)

Creon. This boy, it seems, has sold out to a woman.

Haemon. If you are a woman: my concern is only for you.

110 **Creon.** So? Your "concern"! In a public brawl with your father!

Haemon. How about you, in a public brawl with justice?

Creon. With justice, when all that I do is within my rights?

Haemon. You have no right to trample on God's right.

Creon (*completely out of control*). Fool, adolescent fool! Taken in
   by a woman!

115 **Haemon.** You'll never see me taken in by anything vile.

Creon. Every word you say is for her!

Haemon (*quietly, darkly*).   And for you.
   And for me. And for the gods under the earth.

Creon. You'll never marry her while she lives.

Haemon. Then she must die. But her death will cause another.

120 **Creon.** Another?
   Have you lost your senses? Is this an open threat?

Haemon. There is no threat in speaking to emptiness.

Creon. I swear you'll regret this superior tone of yours!

You are the empty one!

Haemon. If you were not my father,
125 I'd say you were perverse.

Creon. You girl-struck fool, don't play at words with me!

Haemon. I am sorry. You prefer silence.

Creon. Now, by God—!
I swear, by all the gods in heaven above us,
You'll watch it; I swear you shall!
(*to the servants*) Bring her out!
130 Bring the woman out! Let her die before his eyes,
Here, this instant, with her bridegroom beside her!

Haemon. Not here, no; she will not die here, King.
And you will never see my face again.
Go on raving as long as you've a friend to endure you.

(*Exit* Haemon.)

135 **Choragus.** Gone, gone.
Creon, a young man in a rage is dangerous!

Creon. Let him do, or dream to do, more than a man can.
He shall not save these girls from death.

Choragus. These girls?
You have sentenced them both?

Creon. No, you are right.
140 I will not kill the one whose hands are clean.

Choragus. But Antigone?

Creon (*somberly*). I will carry her far away,
Out there in the wilderness, and lock her
Living in a vault of stone. She shall have food,
As the custom is, to absolve the state of her death.
145 And there let her pray to the gods of hell:
They are her only gods:
Perhaps they will show her an escape from death,
Or she may learn,
though late,
That piety shown the dead is pity in vain.

(*Exit* Creon.)

WORDS TO KNOW

perverse (pər-vûrs′) *adj.* willfully determined to go against what is expected or desired

Critical Thinking: ANALYZING

N Ask students what the chorus believes has prompted the confrontation between Haemon and Creon. *(Possible response: The chorus blames everything on the power of Haemon's love for Antigone; the chorus blames Aphrodite, the goddess of love.)*

STRATEGIC READING FOR
Less-Proficient Readers

O What does Haemon want Creon to do in this scene? *(Haemon wants Creon to spare Antigone's life and to reconsider his approach to government.)* **Summarizing**

- What is Haemon's attitude toward his father at the beginning of their meeting? *(Haemon is respectful and polite.)* **Making Judgments**

- What reasons does Creon give for condemning Antigone to death? *(Creon says she deserves death because she broke the law; not to kill her would show he is weak and cannot keep his word.)* **Noting Relevant Details**

- How are Creon and Haemon the same? How are they different? *(Possible response: Both are intelligent, strong men. Creon is despotic and inflexible; Haemon is democratic and reasonable.)* **Comparing/Contrasting**

- What do you think Haemon might do next? *(Possible responses: try to help Antigone escape; try to get Antigone to placate Creon)* **Predicting**

Set a Purpose As students read Scene 4, direct them to see how Antigone faces the prospect of death.

ODE 3

Chorus. Love, unconquerable
  Waster of rich men, keeper
  Of warm lights and all-night vigil
  In the soft face of a girl:
5 Sea wanderer, forest visitor!
  Even the pure immortals cannot escape you,
  And mortal man, in his one day's dusk,
  Trembles before your glory.

  Surely you swerve upon ruin
10 The just man's consenting heart,
  As here you have made bright anger
  Strike between father and son—
  And none has conquered but Love!
  A girl's glance working the will of heaven:
15 Pleasure to her alone who mocks us,
  Merciless Aphrodite.

16 Aphrodite (ăf′rə-dī′tē): goddess of love and beauty.

Linking to Math

A Around 2000 B.C., metal had become a means of exchange in the Middle East. By the 7th century B.C., bronze was being cast in China into knives or spades, each assigned a fixed weight. The forerunner of modern coins first appeared around 650 B.C., in Lydia (eastern Turkey).

Critical Thinking: HYPOTHESIZING

B Ask students how the chorus's attitude toward Antigone here might affect the audience. *(Possible response: The chorus feels great sympathy for Antigone and her unjust plight. This makes the audience feel even greater sorrow and pity, building toward the tragic climax.)*

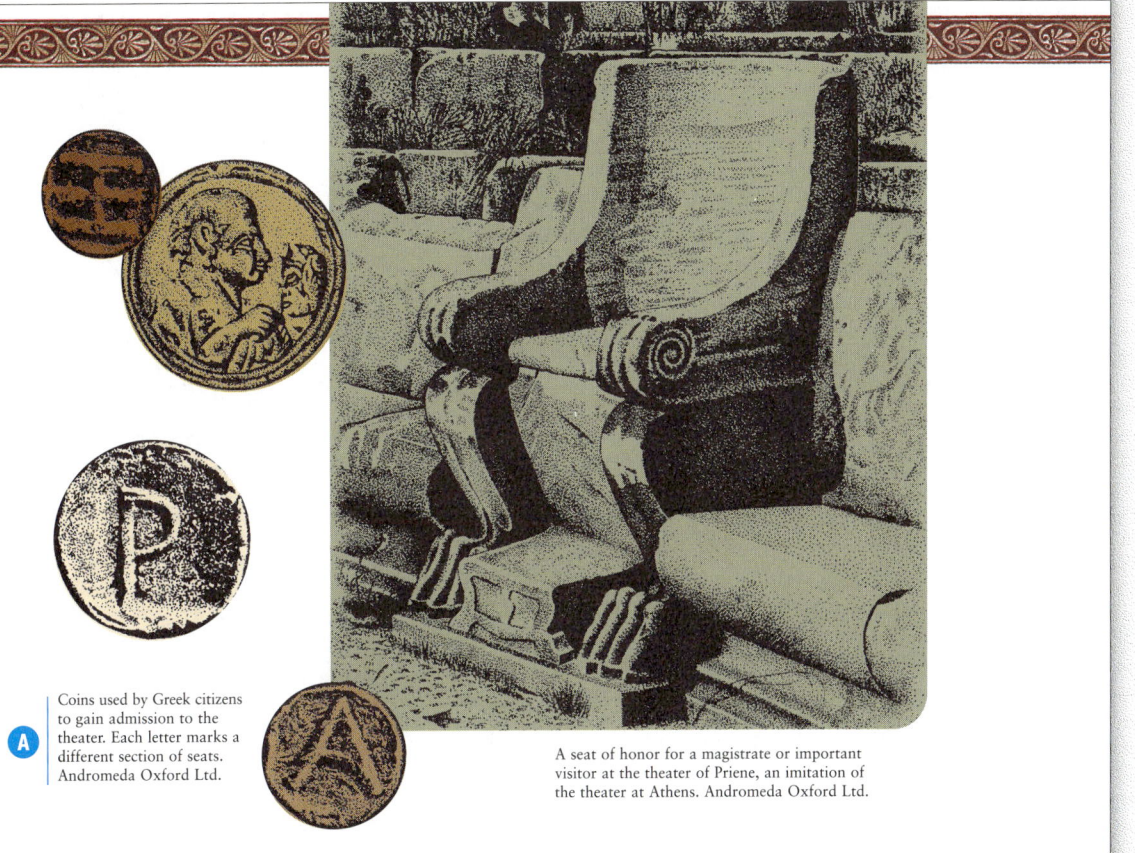

A Coins used by Greek citizens to gain admission to the theater. Each letter marks a different section of seats. Andromeda Oxford Ltd.

A seat of honor for a magistrate or important visitor at the theater of Priene, an imitation of the theater at Athens. Andromeda Oxford Ltd.

SCENE 4

Choragus (*as Antigone enters, guarded*). But I can no longer stand
    in awe of this,
B Nor, seeing what I see, keep back my tears.
Here is Antigone, passing to that chamber
Where all find sleep at last.

5 **Antigone.** Look upon me, friends, and pity me
Turning back at the night's edge to say
Good-bye to the sun that shines for me no longer;
Now sleepy Death
Summons me down to Acheron, that cold shore:

9 Acheron (ăk′ə-rŏn′): in Greek mythology, one of the rivers bordering the underworld, the place inhabited by the souls of the dead.

ANTIGONE **965**

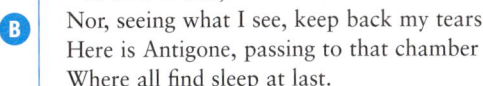 Mini-Lesson: Speaking, Listening, and Viewing

PRESS CONFERENCE Explain to students that a press conference conveys information about an individual or an organization to the media. Usually, a press conference consists of a prepared statement followed by a question-and-answer session. Sometimes, an official speaker at a press conference attempts to recast embarrassing incidents in a more flattering light. Reporters, in contrast, usually try to ask questions that reveal the unvarnished truth about the incident.

Application Invite students to work in small groups to hold a press conference explaining Creon's decision to sentence Antigone to death. Half the students in each group should be Creon's representatives; the rest, reporters asking questions. Guide the court representatives to recast Creon's decision in the best possible light; encourage reporters to press for the full story. You may wish to videotape the press conferences.

GUIDE FOR READING

C Possible response: The stone that entombs Antigone reminds her of Niobe. Both women feel enormous sadness and loneliness, having lost loved ones to a cruel fate.

Critical Thinking:
MAKING JUDGMENTS

D Ask students if they agree with Antigone's belief that she has been "unjustly judged." You can divide the class in half and have students debate the issue. (Possible response: no, because she did break the civil law of the land; yes, because she obeyed a higher law, the moral law of the gods)

Literary Concept:
CHARACTERIZATION

E Ask students whether they think Antigone has gone too far in following her own sense of duty. (Possible responses: Yes, in her way Antigone is just as inflexible as Creon; her unbending allegiance to the gods and her brother has led to her own downfall. No, Antigone is an innocent victim who is merely doing her duty in the face of an unreasonable tyrant.)

---

10   There is no bride song there, nor any music.

Chorus. Yet not unpraised, not without a kind of honor,
    You walk at last into the underworld;
    Untouched by sickness, broken by no sword.
    What woman has ever found your way to death?

15 **Antigone.** How often I have heard the story of Niobe,
    Tantalus' wretched daughter, how the stone
    Clung fast about her, ivy-close: and they say
    The rain falls endlessly
    And sifting soft snow; her tears are never done.
20   I feel the loneliness of her death in mine.

Chorus. But she was born of heaven, and you
    Are woman, woman-born. If her death is yours,
    A mortal woman's, is this not for you
    Glory in our world and in the world beyond?

25 **Antigone.** You laugh at me. Ah, friends, friends,
    Can you not wait until I am dead? O Thebes,
    O men many-charioted, in love with Fortune,
    Dear springs of Dirce, sacred Theban grove,
    Be witnesses for me, denied all pity,
30   Unjustly judged! and think a word of love
    For her whose path turns
    Under dark earth, where there are no more tears.

Chorus. You have passed beyond human daring and come at last
    Into a place of stone where Justice sits.
35   I cannot tell
    What shape of your father's guilt appears in this.

Antigone. You have touched it at last: that bridal bed
    Unspeakable, horror of son and mother mingling:
    Their crime, infection of all our family!
40   O Oedipus, father and brother!
    Your marriage strikes from the grave to murder mine.
    I have been a stranger here in my own land:
    All my life
    The blasphemy of my birth has followed me.

45 **Chorus.** Reverence is a virtue, but strength
    Lives in established law: that must prevail.
    You have made your choice;
    Your death is the doing of your conscious hand.

Antigone. Then let me go, since all your words are bitter,
50   And the very light of the sun is cold to me.

15–20 Niobe (nī′ə-bē) was a queen of Thebes whose children were killed by the gods because she had boasted that she was greater than a goddess. After their deaths, she was turned to stone but continued to shed tears. *Why might Antigone compare herself to Niobe?*

44 blasphemy of my birth: Antigone is referring to her father's marriage to his own mother, an incestuous relationship that resulted in her birth. This type of relationship was considered a sin against the gods.

Irene Papas playing the title role in the 1960 movie. Culver Pictures.

DESIGN NOTE

Reading the Art *Do you think this photograph portrays Antigone as courageous and proud or stubborn and arrogant?*

Lead me to my vigil, where I must have
Neither love nor lamentation; no song, but silence.

(Creon *interrupts impatiently.*)

Creon. If dirges and planned lamentations could put off death,
Men would be singing forever.
                (*to the servants*) Take her, go!
55 You know your orders: take her to the vault
And leave her alone there. And if she lives or dies,
That's her affair, not ours: our hands are clean.

Antigone. O tomb, vaulted bride-bed in eternal rock,
Soon I shall be with my own again
60 Where Persephone welcomes the thin ghosts underground: **60 Persephone** (pər-sĕf′ə-nē): wife
And I shall see my father again, and you, Mother,   of Hades (hā′dēz) and queen of the
And dearest Polyneices—   underworld.
                dearest indeed
To me, since it was my hand
That washed him clean and poured the ritual wine:
65 And my reward is death before my time!
And yet, as men's hearts know, I have done no wrong;
I have not sinned before God. Or if I have,
I shall know the truth in death. But if the guilt
Lies upon Creon who judged me, then, I pray,
70 May his punishment equal my own.

Choragus.   O passionate heart,
Unyielding, tormented still by the same winds!

Creon. Her guards shall have good cause to regret their delaying.

Antigone. Ah! That voice is like the voice of death!

Creon. I can give you no reason to think you are mistaken.

75 **Antigone.** Thebes, and you my fathers' gods,   **75–80** What do these lines suggest
And rulers of Thebes, you see me now, the last   about what Antigone values most?
Unhappy daughter of a line of kings,
Your kings, led away to death. You will remember
What things I suffer, and at what men's hands,
80 Because I would not transgress the laws of heaven.
(*to the guards, simply*) Come: let us wait no longer.

(*Exit* Antigone, *left, guarded.*)

WORDS TO KNOW	
lamentation (lăm′ən-tā′shən)	*n.* an expression of grief
dirge (dûrj)	*n.* a slow, mournful piece of music; a funeral hymn
transgress (trăns-grĕs′)	*v.* to violate or break a law, command, or moral code

ODE 4

Chorus. All Danae's beauty was locked away
In a brazen cell where the sunlight could not come:
A small room, still as any grave, enclosed her.
Yet she was a princess too,
5 And Zeus in a rain of gold poured love upon her.
O child, child,
No power in wealth or war
Or tough sea-blackened ships
Can prevail against untiring Destiny!

10 And Dryas' son also, that furious king,
Bore the god's prisoning anger for his pride:
Sealed up by Dionysus in deaf stone,
His madness died among echoes.
So at the last he learned what dreadful power
15 His tongue had mocked:
For he had profaned the revels
And fired the wrath of the nine
Implacable sisters that love the sound of the flute.

And old men tell a half-remembered tale
20 Of horror done where a dark ledge splits the sea
And a double surf beats on the grey shores:
How a king's new woman, sick
With hatred for the queen he had imprisoned,
Ripped out his two sons' eyes with her bloody hands
25 While grinning Ares watched the shuttle plunge
Four times: four blind wounds crying for revenge,

Crying, tears and blood mingled. Piteously born,
Those sons whose mother was of heavenly birth!
Her father was the god of the north wind,
30 And she was cradled by gales;
She raced with young colts on the glittering hills
And walked untrammeled in the open light:
But in her marriage deathless Fate found means
To build a tomb like yours for all her joy.

1–5 Danae (dăn′ə-ē′) was a princess who was imprisoned by her father because it had been predicted that her son would one day kill him. After Zeus visited Danae in the form of a shower of gold, she gave birth to his son Perseus, who eventually did kill his grandfather.

10–18 King Lycurgus (lĭ-kûr′gəs), son of Dryas (drī′əs), was driven mad and imprisoned in stone for objecting to the worship of Dionysus. The nine implacable sisters are the Muses, the goddesses who presided over literature, the arts, and the sciences. Once offended, they were impossible to appease.

19–34 These lines refer to the myth of King Phineus (fĭn′yōōs), who imprisoned his first wife, the daughter of the north wind, and allowed his new wife to blind his sons from his first marriage.

ANTIGONE **969**

Art Note

Sophocles, unknown artist During the classical period, Greek sculptors most often carved figures out of marble and other stone. Faces often showed expression and emotion. This statue of Sophocles is representative of the sculpture of the early Greek classical period. It displays the strength, simplicity, and seriousness characteristic of the sculpture of this age. Though many of the statues of this era have not survived, a number of Roman copies of the Greek originals exist.

Reading the Art *What qualities of Sophocles do you think are expressed by the statue?*

Critical Thinking: SPECULATING

A Direct students to read the side note on lines 1–7. Then invite students to predict what they think Teiresias will say to Creon. *(Possible response: The prophet will warn Creon about the consequences of his actions.)*

Two views of Sophocles, who was regarded by his Greek admirers as "the perfect man." *Left,* Museo Gregoriano Profano, Vatican Museums, Vatican State, Alinari / Art Resource, New York. *Right,* Museo Lateranense, Vatican Museums, Vatican City, Alinari / Art Resource, New York.

SCENE 5

(*Enter blind* Teiresias, *led by a boy. The opening speeches of* Teiresias *should be in singsong contrast to the realistic lines of* Creon.)

Teiresias. This is the way the blind man comes, princes, princes,
  Lock step, two heads lit by the eyes of one.
Creon. What new thing have you to tell us, old Teiresias?
Teiresias. I have much to tell you: listen to the prophet, Creon.
5 **Creon.** I am not aware that I have ever failed to listen.
Teiresias. Then you have done wisely, King, and ruled well.
Creon. I admit my debt to you. But what have you to say?

1–7 The blind Teiresias is physically blind but spiritually sighted. As a prophet, he is an agent of the gods in their dealings with humans. His revelation of the truth to Oedipus led Oedipus to leave Thebes, which indirectly helped Creon to become king.

970 UNIT SIX PART 2: THE HEROIC TRADITION

Mini-Lesson Study Skills

TAKING TESTS: PLANNING YOUR TIME
Remind students that they need not go into a test situation unprepared. They can maximize their chances for success if they use their time wisely to prepare. Present students with these guidelines:
1. *Know what to study.* Find out what the test will cover well ahead of time.
2. *Organize your time.* Make a study plan to avoid last-minute cramming and panic.
3. *Review all the material.* Study any relevant class notes and portion of the textbook.
4. *Memorize important facts.* Use mnemonics (memory aids) to help you remember names, dates, events, and vocabulary words.
5. *Take care of yourself.* Be sure to get enough sleep the night before the test and eat before the test.

Application Have students work in pairs to make a study plan they might use for a test on *Antigone.* Students should follow the steps outlined above.

Teiresias. This, Creon: you stand once more on the edge of fate.

Creon. What do you mean? Your words are a kind of dread.

10 **Teiresias.** Listen, Creon:
   I was sitting in my chair of augury, at the place
   Where the birds gather about me. They were all a-chatter,
   As is their habit, when suddenly I heard
   A strange note in their jangling, a scream, a
15 Whirring fury; I knew that they were fighting,
   Tearing each other, dying
   In a whirlwind of wings clashing. And I was afraid.
   I began the rites of burnt offering at the altar,
   But Hephaestus failed me: instead of bright flame,
20 There was only the sputtering slime of the fat thigh-flesh
   Melting: the entrails dissolved in grey smoke;
   The bare bone burst from the welter. And no blaze!

   This was a sign from heaven. My boy described it,
   Seeing for me as I see for others.

25 I tell you, Creon, you yourself have brought
   This new calamity upon us. Our hearths and altars
   Are stained with the corruption of dogs and carrion birds
   That glut themselves on the corpse of Oedipus' son.
   The gods are deaf when we pray to them; their fire
30 Recoils from our offering; their birds of omen
   Have no cry of comfort, for they are gorged
   With the thick blood of the dead.
                                        O my son,
   These are no trifles! Think: all men make mistakes,
   But a good man yields when he knows his course is wrong,
35 And repairs the evil. The only crime is pride.

   Give in to the dead man, then: do not fight with a corpse—
   What glory is it to kill a man who is dead?
   Think, I beg you:
   It is for your own good that I speak as I do.
40 You should be able to yield for your own good.

Creon. It seems that prophets have made me their especial province.
   All my life long
   I have been a kind of butt for the dull arrows
   Of doddering fortunetellers!
                              No, Teiresias:
45 If your birds—if the great eagles of God himself—
   Should carry him stinking bit by bit to heaven,
   I would not yield. I am not afraid of pollution:

11–17 The chair of augury is the place where Teiresias sits to hear the birds, whose sounds reveal the future to him. The fighting among the birds suggests that the anarchy infecting Thebes has spread even to the world of nature.

19 **Hephaestus** (hĭ-fĕs′təs): god of fire.

18–32 According to Teiresias, the birds and dogs that have eaten the corpse of Polyneices have become corrupt causing the gods to reject the Thebans' offerings and prayers. What do these lines suggest about how the gods view Creon's refusal to allow Polyneices to be buried?

44–48 What do these lines suggest about Creon's view of himself and the gods?

GUIDE FOR READING

E Possible response: Creon assumes that Teiresias is motivated by a desire for personal profit.

Literary Concept: APHORISM

F Explain that an aphorism is a brief statement that expresses a general observation about life in a witty, pointed way. Unlike proverbs, which may stem from an oral folk tradition, aphorisms originate with specific authors. An example would be Samuel Johnson's aphorism "A blighted spring makes a barren year." Invite students to write aphorisms that Teiresias might offer Creon to sum up his feelings about Creon's bitter misconception.

Literary Concept: IRONY

G Invite students to explain the irony in Teiresias' comment to Creon about the cost of Teiresias' words. (*Possible response: Teiresias' words do not cost money, but the truth will be costly for Creon because it will cause him great anguish.*)

GUIDE FOR READING

H Possible response: Creon will end up being punished by the Furies.

No man can <u>defile</u> the gods.
                        Do what you will;
Go into business, make money, speculate
50 In India gold or that synthetic gold from Sardis,
Get rich otherwise than by my consent to bury him.
Teiresias, it is a sorry thing when a wise man
Sells his wisdom, lets out his words for hire!

Teiresias. Ah Creon! Is there no man left in the world—

55 **Creon.** To do what? Come, let's have the aphorism!

Teiresias. No man who knows that wisdom outweighs any wealth?

Creon. As surely as bribes are baser than any baseness.

Teiresias. You are sick, Creon! You are deathly sick!

Creon. As you say: it is not my place to challenge a prophet.

60 **Teiresias.** Yet you have said my prophecy is for sale.

Creon. The generation of prophets has always loved gold.

Teiresias. The generation of kings has always loved brass.

Creon. You forget yourself! You are speaking to your king.

Teiresias. I know it. You are a king because of me.

65 **Creon.** You have a certain skill; but you have sold out.

Teiresias. King, you will drive me to words that—

Creon.   Say them, say them!
    Only remember: I will not pay you for them.

Teiresias. No, you will find them too costly.

Creon.   No doubt. Speak:
    Whatever you say, you will not change my will.

70 **Teiresias.** Then take this, and take it to heart!
The time is not far off when you shall pay back
Corpse for corpse, flesh of your own flesh.
You have thrust the child of this world into living night;
You have kept from the gods below the child that is theirs:
75 The one in a grave before her death, the other,
Dead, denied the grave. This is your crime:
And the Furies and the dark gods of hell
Are swift with terrible punishment for you.
Do you want to buy me now, Creon?
                              Not many days,
80 And your house will be full of men and women weeping,
And curses will be hurled at you from far

49–53 What does Creon assume is the motive behind Teiresias' prophecies?

50 Sardis (sär′dĭs): the capital of ancient Lydia, where metal coins were first produced.

77–78 Furies: three goddesses who avenge crimes, especially those that violate family ties. How might this prophecy be fulfilled?

WORDS TO KNOW

defile (dĭ-fīl′) *v.* to make foul, dirty, unclean, or impure

Cities grieving for sons unburied, left to rot before the walls of
  Thebes.
These are my arrows, Creon: they are all for you.
(*to boy*) But come, child: lead me home.
85 Let him waste his fine anger upon younger men.
Maybe he will learn at last
To control a wiser tongue in a better head.

(*Exit* Teiresias.)

Choragus. The old man has gone, King, but his words
  Remain to plague us. I am old, too,
90 But I cannot remember that he was ever false.

Creon. That is true. . . . It troubles me.
  Oh it is hard to give in! but it is worse
  To risk everything for stubborn pride.

Choragus. Creon: take my advice.

Creon.   What shall I do?

95 **Choragus.** Go quickly: free Antigone from her vault
  And build a tomb for the body of Polyneices.

Creon. You would have me do this?

Choragus.   Creon, yes!
  And it must be done at once: God moves
  Swiftly to cancel the folly of stubborn men.

100 **Creon.** It is hard to deny the heart! But I
  Will do it: I will not fight with destiny.

Choragus. You must go yourself; you cannot leave it to others.

Creon. I will go.
        —Bring axes, servants:
  Come with me to the tomb. I buried her; I
105 Will set her free.
          Oh quickly!
  My mind misgives—
  The laws of the gods are mighty, and a man must serve them
  To the last day of his life!

(*Exit* Creon.)

CUSTOMIZING FOR
Multiple Learning Styles

K **Musical and Bodily-Kinesthetic Learners** Choose one student to play the part of the choragus; the rest of the class can be divided into two sections. Explain to students that the Greek chorus often broke into two groups while dancing and singing. Then help the students prepare a choral reading of the paean. The first section of students can read the first and third choral parts of the paean; the second section of students can read the second and fourth parts of the paean. Have students chant their lines and accompany them with simple movements.

Literary Concept: ALLUSION

L Have students analyze the allusions in this paean to explain what they add to its main idea and impact. *(Possible response: The allusions show the power of Dionysus and his special relationship to Thebes. The chorus is desperately calling for divine intervention, realizing that humans cannot resolve this dilemma.)*

PAEAN

   Choragus. God of many names

   Chorus.   O Iacchus

                                            son

   of Cadmean Semele

                            O born of the thunder!

   guardian of the West

                              regent

   of Eleusis' plain

                         O prince of maenad Thebes

5   and the Dragon Field by rippling Ismenus:

   Choragus. God of many names

   Chorus.   the flame of torches

   flares on our hills

                       the nymphs of Iacchus

   dance at the spring of Castalia:

   from the vine-close mountain

                            come ah come in ivy:

10 *Evohé evohé!* sings through the streets of Thebes

   Choragus. God of many names

   Chorus.   Iacchus of Thebes

   heavenly child

                   of Semele bride of the Thunderer!

   The shadow of plague is upon us:

                           come

   with clement feet

                     oh come from Parnassus

15 down the long slopes

                      across the lamenting water

   Choragus. Io Fire! Chorister of the throbbing stars!
   O purest among the voices of the night!
   Thou son of God, blaze for us!

   Chorus. Come with choric rapture of circling Maenads
20 Who cry *Io Iacche!*

                    God of many names!

PAEAN: A paean (pē'ən) is a hymn appealing to the gods for assistance. In this paean, the chorus praises Dionysus, or Iacchus (yä'kəs), and calls on him to come to Thebes to show mercy and drive out evil.

2 Cadmus was the legendary founder of Thebes. Dionysus was the son of Cadmus' daughter Semele (sə-mē'lē) and Zeus, who is referred to here as thunder.

4–5 These lines name locations near Athens and Thebes. The maenads (mē'nădz') were priestesses of Dionysus.

8–9 The spring of Castalia is on the sacred mountain Parnassus. Grape vines and ivy were symbols of Dionysus.

10 evohé: hallelujah.

974   UNIT SIX   PART 2: THE HEROIC TRADITION

EXODOS

(*Enter* Messenger.)

Messenger. Men of the line of Cadmus, you who live
Near Amphion's citadel:
I cannot say
Of any condition of human life, "This is fixed,
This is clearly good, or bad." Fate raises up,
5   And Fate casts down the happy and unhappy alike:
No man can foretell his fate.
Take the case of Creon:
Creon was happy once, as I count happiness:
Victorious in battle, sole governor of the land,
Fortunate father of children nobly born.
10 And now it has all gone from him! Who can say
That a man is still alive when his life's joy fails?
He is a walking dead man. Grant him rich;
Let him live like a king in his great house:
If his pleasure is gone, I would not give
15 So much as the shadow of smoke for all he owns.

Choragus. Your words hint at sorrow: what is your news for us?

Messenger. They are dead. The living are guilty of their death.

Choragus. Who is guilty? Who is dead? Speak!

Messenger.   Haemon.
Haemon is dead; and the hand that killed him
20 Is his own hand.

Choragus.   His father's? or his own?

Messenger. His own, driven mad by the murder his father had done.

Choragus. Teiresias, Teiresias, how clearly you saw it all!

Messenger. This is my news: you must draw what conclusions you
can from it.

Choragus. But look: Eurydice, our queen:
25 Has she overheard us?

(*Enter* Eurydice *from the palace, center.*)

Eurydice. I have heard something, friends:
As I was unlocking the gate of Pallas' shrine,
For I needed her help today, I heard a voice
Telling of some new sorrow. And I fainted
30 There at the temple with all my maidens about me.
But speak again: whatever it is, I can bear it:
Grief and I are no strangers.

EXODOS: The exodos is the last episode in the play. It is followed by a final speech made by the choragus and addressed directly to the audience.

2 Amphion: Niobe's husband, who built a wall around Thebes by charming the stones into place with music.

15 How does the messenger compare with the sentry who appeared in Scenes 1 and 2?

27 Pallas: Athena, the goddess of wisdom.

32 Megareus (mə-găr'ē-əs), the older son of Eurydice and Creon, had died in the battle for Thebes.

ANTIGONE **975**

Critical Thinking:
SYNTHESIZING

P Ask students why they think Creon decided to give the remains of Polyneices' body a proper burial. *(Possible responses: Creon realized that he had been wrong in refusing Antigone's request, and he wanted to make amends for his error; Creon was afraid of displeasing the gods.)*

Literary Concept:
CHARACTERIZATION

Q Have students explain why they think Antigone killed herself. Explore with the class what this action reveals about Antigone's character. *(Possible responses: Antigone believed that she would not be rescued and wanted to die an honorable death, by her own hand; she had lost all hope and succumbed to despair.)*

Critical Thinking:
MAKING JUDGMENTS

R Ask students if they think Haemon's act of spitting in his father's face was justified or not. *(Possible responses: Some students will say that Haemon's action was justified because Creon is responsible for the chain of events that led to this tragedy; others will say that Haemon's anger was misplaced because Antigone's death was a result of fate, not of man.)*

Messenger. Dearest lady,
I will tell you plainly all that I have seen.
I shall not try to comfort you: what is the use,
35 Since comfort could lie only in what is not true?
The truth is always best.
           I went with Creon
To the outer plain where Polyneices was lying,
No friend to pity him, his body shredded by dogs.
We made our prayers in that place to Hecate
40 And Pluto, that they would be merciful. And we bathed
The corpse with holy water, and we brought
Fresh-broken branches to burn what was left of it,
And upon the urn we heaped up a towering barrow
Of the earth of his own land.
                     When we were done, we ran
45 To the vault where Antigone lay on her couch of stone.
One of the servants had gone ahead,
And while he was yet far off he heard a voice
Grieving within the chamber, and he came back
And told Creon. And as the king went closer,
50 The air was full of wailing, the words lost,
And he begged us to make all haste. "Am I a prophet?"
He said, weeping. "And must I walk this road,
The saddest of all that I have gone before?
My son's voice calls me on. Oh quickly, quickly!
55 Look through the crevice there, and tell me
If it is Haemon, or some deception of the gods!"

We obeyed; and in the cavern's farthest corner
We saw her lying:
She had made a noose of her fine linen veil
60 And hanged herself. Haemon lay beside her,
His arms about her waist, lamenting her,
His love lost underground, crying out
That his father had stolen her away from him.
When Creon saw him, the tears rushed to his eyes,
65 And he called to him: "What have you done, child? Speak to me.
What are you thinking that makes your eyes so strange?
O my son, my son, I come to you on my knees!"
But Haemon spat in his face. He said not a word,
Staring—
           and suddenly drew his sword
70 And lunged. Creon shrank back; the blade missed, and the boy,
Desperate against himself, drove it half its length

39–40 Hecate (hĕk'ə-tē) **and Pluto:** other names for Persephone and Hades, the goddess and god of the underworld.

43–44 Note the contrast between the barrow, or burial mound, erected by Creon and the handful of dirt used by Antigone to cover her brother.

60 Note that this is the same way in which Jocasta, Antigone's mother, killed herself.

Into his own side and fell. And as he died,
He gathered Antigone close in his arms again,
Choking, his blood bright red on her white cheek.
75 And now he lies dead with the dead, and she is his
At last, his bride in the houses of the dead.

(*Exit* Eurydice *into the palace.*)

Choragus. She has left us without a word. What can this mean?

Messenger. It troubles me, too; yet she knows what is best;
Her grief is too great for public lamentation,
80 And doubtless she has gone to her chamber to weep
For her dead son, leading her maidens in his dirge.

Choragus. It may be so: but I fear this deep silence.

(*Pause*)

Messenger. I will see what she is doing. I will go in.

(*Exit* Messenger *into the palace. Enter* Creon *with attendants, bearing* Haemon's *body.*)

Choragus. But here is the king himself: oh look at him,
85 Bearing his own damnation in his arms.

Creon. Nothing you say can touch me any more.
My own blind heart has brought me
From darkness to final darkness. Here you see
The father murdering, the murdered son—
90 And all my civic wisdom!
Haemon my son, so young, so young to die,
I was the fool, not you; and you died for me.

Choragus. That is the truth; but you were late in learning it.

Creon. This truth is hard to bear. Surely a god
95 Has crushed me beneath the hugest weight of heaven,
And driven me headlong a barbaric way
To trample out the thing I held most dear.
The pains that men will take to come to pain!

(*Enter* Messenger *from the palace.*)

Messenger. The burden you carry in your hands is heavy,
100 But it is not all: you will find more in your house.

Creon. What burden worse than this shall I find there?

Messenger. The queen is dead.

Creon. O port of death, deaf world,
Is there no pity for me? And you, angel of evil,
105 I was dead, and your words are death again.

Literary Concept: PLOT

V Remind students that a plot's climax is the turning point of the action, the moment when interest and intensity reach their peak. Have students identify the climax of this play. *(Possible response: The climax occurs here, when Creon realizes that he has lost everything that matters to him.)*

Critical Thinking: ANALYZING

W Ask students why they think Sophocles ends the play with Creon's comments. *(Possible responses: Creon's self-knowledge reinforces the tragedy, the senseless waste of human potential and life.)*

CUSTOMIZING FOR
Gifted and Talented Students

X Ask students to explain the moral of this play. *(Possible response: True wisdom comes in submitting to the gods; pride goeth before a fall.)*

STRATEGIC READING FOR
Less-Proficient Readers

Y What happens in this scene? *(Antigone hangs herself; Haemon and his mother Eurydice stab themselves to death.)* Summarizing

- At the beginning of the scene, why does Teiresias come to see Creon? *(The prophet comes to warn Creon that his own actions will bring tragedy to his land.)* Finding the Main Idea

- How does Creon treat Teiresias? *(with contempt; accusing the prophet of selling out)* Drawing Conclusions

COMPREHENSION CHECK

1. Why does Creon forbid Antigone to bury her brother Polyneices? *(because Polyneices came back from exile to attack Thebes)*
2. Who does Antigone want to help her bury Polyneices? *(Ismene, her sister)*
3. Who discovered that Antigone had buried Polyneices? *(a sentry)*
4. How does Creon punish Antigone for disobeying him? *(She is entombed alive.)*
5. What happens to Antigone? *(She hangs herself in her tomb.)*

Is it true, boy? Can it be true?
Is my wife dead? Has death bred death?

Messenger. You can see for yourself.

(*The doors are opened, and the body of* Eurydice *is disclosed within.*)

Creon. Oh pity!
110   All true, all true, and more than I can bear!
O my wife, my son!

Messenger. She stood before the altar, and her heart
Welcomed the knife her own hand guided,
And a great cry burst from her lips for Megareus dead,
115   And for Haemon dead, her sons; and her last breath
Was a curse for their father, the murderer of her sons.
And she fell, and the dark flowed in through her closing eyes.

Creon. O God, I am sick with fear.
Are there no swords here? Has no one a blow for me?

120   **Messenger.** Her curse is upon you for the deaths of both.

Creon. It is right that it should be. I alone am guilty.
I know it, and I say it. Lead me in,
Quickly, friends.
I have neither life nor substance. Lead me in.

125   **Choragus.** You are right, if there can be right in so much wrong.
The briefest way is best in a world of sorrow.

Creon. Let it come;
Let death come quickly and be kind to me.
I would not ever see the sun again.

130   **Choragus.** All that will come when it will; but we, meanwhile,
Have much to do. Leave the future to itself.

Creon. All my heart was in that prayer!

Choragus. Then do not pray any more: the sky is deaf.

Creon. Lead me away. I have been rash and foolish.
135   I have killed my son and my wife.
I look for comfort; my comfort lies here dead.
Whatever my hands have touched has come to nothing.
Fate has brought all my pride to a thought of dust.

(*As* Creon *is being led into the house, the* Choragus *advances and speaks directly to the audience.*)

Choragus. There is no happiness where there is no wisdom;
140   No wisdom but in submission to the gods.
Big words are always punished,
And proud men in old age learn to be wise.

SELF-ASSESSMENT To help students assess their understanding of *Antigone*, you may wish to have them respond to the following questions in writing or as brief oral reports.

1. Which character do you admire the most in the play? Why?
2. If you were Antigone, what would you have done in this situation? Why?
3. This play was written centuries ago. What do you think it can teach people about life today? Explain your answer.

RESPONDING OPTIONS

FROM PERSONAL RESPONSE TO CRITICAL ANALYSIS

REFLECT
1. How did you react to what happens at the end of this play? Jot down your impressions in your notebook.

RETHINK
2. How much do you think Creon is to blame for the suicides of Antigone, Haemon, and Eurydice?

Close Textual Reading

Consider
- Creon's judgment of himself at the end of the play
- how Haemon and Eurydice feel about Creon at the moment of death
- Creon's failed effort to rescue Antigone
- whether someone can be held accountable for another's suicide

3. What do you think is the main reason that Creon and Antigone cannot resolve their conflict?

Consider

Close Textual Reading
- what Polyneices means to each character
- the principles that motivate each character
- the attitude of each character toward the gods
- any flaws or defects exhibited by each character

4. Review the definition of a tragic hero on page 937. Who do you think best fits the definition, Antigone or Creon? Explain your response.

5. Who do you think suffers the most in this play and why?

6. How do other characters—such as Ismene, Teiresias, Haemon, and Eurydice—help you to understand and evaluate the actions of Antigone and Creon?

7. What effect did the choragus and the chorus have on your interpretation of the events in this play? Support your analysis with evidence from the play.

RELATE
8. Which of the messages conveyed by Sophocles do you think is most relevant for people today?

Thematic Link

Multimodal Learning
ANOTHER PATHWAY

With a partner, create a flow chart of the plot of Antigone, showing the cause-and-effect relationships between events. Mark the steps that you think are especially instrumental in leading to the tragic conclusion. Share your flow chart by posting it on a class bulletin board.

QUICKWRITES

1. Compare the way you ranked the principles listed in the Personal Connection on page 936 with the way you think Antigone, Creon, or some other character in the play would rank them. Then write a **letter** to that character, either in support of or in opposition to his or her decisions and behavior.

2. Think about how one of the less important characters—such as Ismene, the sentry, or Teiresias—might have viewed what happened to Antigone. Write a **diary entry** expressing the thoughts and feelings of this character.

3. Imagine that you have been asked to address a group on the topic "Women of Courage in Classic Literature." Write the portion of your **lecture** that concerns Antigone.

📁 **PORTFOLIO** Save your writing. You may want to use it later as a springboard to a piece for your portfolio.

ANTIGONE 979

From Personal Response to Critical Analysis

1. Accept all reasonable responses.
2. Possible responses: Creon is completely to blame because he passed the decree that placed civil above moral law; Creon is only partially to blame because the fate of people is determined by the gods.
3. Possible responses: Each is motivated by very different principles; each suffers from a tragic flaw, excessive pride.
4. Possible responses: Creon, because his fall comes from the greatest height; he realizes his flaw only after it is too late to change the course of events; Antigone, because her actions are the most important in the play
5. Accept all reasonable, well-supported responses.
6. Possible responses: Each of these characters reinforces an important trait in one of the main characters; they all comment on the action.
7. Possible responses: The choragus and the chorus provided another view of events, such as the death of Antigone, Haemon, and Eurydice.
8. Accept all reasonable, well-supported responses.

Another Pathway
To help students collaborate, assign one partner as recorder to write down the flow chart.

Rubric
3 Full Accomplishment Students have located the key events and traced the cause-and-effect relationships between them.
2 Substantial Accomplishment Students find most key events and causes and effects.
1 Little or Partial Accomplishment Students have difficulty finding key events and causes and effects.

QuickWrites
1. Tell students to decide whether their letters will be formal or informal, and to pay attention to their diction accordingly.
2. Guide students to write their diary entry from the first person, capturing the voice of their character. Also remind students to include sufficient details and examples to express the character's thoughts and feelings completely.
3. Encourage students to include a clear introduction, body, and conclusion in their lecture.

 **The Writer's Craft**

Varieties of Language, pp. 428–429

Literary Concepts

Students can record their responses on a list or chart. Appoint a clarifier/paraphraser in each group to restate points and to clarify the discussion. Possible examples of irony include Creon's optimistic speech, which foreshadows disaster rather than triumph (p. 944); the comments the Choragus and Creon make about stubbornness (p. 954); and Creon's comment "our hands are clean" (p. 968).

Critic's Corner

Encourage students to work in teams to debate the issue before they begin to write. Students can also consult additional critical sources for information to back up their assertions.

Across the Curriculum

History Cooperative Learning
Arrange students in small groups to complete their research. You may want to have group members divide up the reference material, with each student checking one source.

LITERARY CONCEPTS

Irony is a contrast between what is believed or expected and what actually exists or happens. **Dramatic irony** is a type of irony that occurs when readers or viewers are aware of information that a character is unaware of. For example, Creon tells Antigone, "That [her death] gives me everything." Once you know the outcome of the play, you realize that Antigone's death will not give Creon everything. On the contrary, it will take from Creon all that is meaningful in his life. This contrast between Creon's limited knowledge and your fuller understanding generates dramatic irony.

With a small group of classmates, find other examples of dramatic irony in *Antigone*. List each example and write a brief explanation of why you think it is ironic. After you have completed your list, share your findings with another group and speculate about why Sophocles used this technique.

Multimodal Learning
ALTERNATIVE ACTIVITIES

1. **Cooperative Learning** With a group of classmates, perform a **Readers Theater production** of a scene from this play. Sit in chairs at the front of the classroom and take turns reading the parts. Choose whether you want to present the scene in the formal manner of the ancient Greek theater or in a more contemporary style.
2. Create a **mask** to be worn in a production of *Antigone*. You may research the masks worn in ancient Greek productions or create your own original version.
3. In Scene 2 of the play, the choragus says of Antigone, "Like father, like daughter: both headstrong, deaf to reason!" Read Sophocles' play *Oedipus the King* to get a sense of Oedipus' character. Then create a **chart** that compares father and daughter.
4. Create a **model** of the Theater of Dionysus in Athens, where this play was first performed.

980 UNIT SIX PART 2: THE HEROIC TRADITION

CRITIC'S CORNER

According to the literary scholar David Grene, "the dilemma of Creon in . . . *Antigone* is incidental to the main emphasis of the play, which is on Antigone." Do you agree with this assessment? Cite details from the play to support your opinion.

THE WRITER'S STYLE

Throughout *Antigone*, Sophocles makes **allusions** to myths that his original audience would have been familiar with. With a partner, research the full story of one of these myths. Then write an explanation of how the myth relates to the story of Antigone and why you think Sophocles included the allusion.

ACROSS THE CURRICULUM

History At various times in *Antigone*, Creon's remarks show his attitude toward having his authority challenged by a woman. With a partner, research the typical role of noblewomen during the fifth century B.C. Then create a Venn diagram in which you compare and contrast Antigone's character with that of a typical noblewoman of the time. Does your diagram shed any light on Creon's behavior?

Marble head of woman from ancient Greek civilization. Published by permission of the Director of Antiquities and the Cyprus Museum, Nicosia, Cyprus.

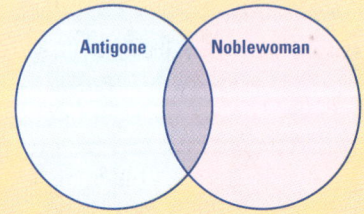

The Writer's Style

Guide students to use a standard book of myths, such as *The Age of Fable* by Bullfinch. Students may also want to include original illustrations to draw further parallels between *Antigone* and the original myth.

Alternative Activities

1. Explain to students that in a Readers Theater, actors and actresses stand on a bare stage and hold scripts. They do not use props, scenery, or costumes.
2. Suggest that students use quick-drying plaster or papier-mâché for their masks.
3. Students can also use a Venn diagram to compare father and daughter.
4. Suggest that students create their model with objects such as sugar cubes, small blocks, or plaster.

WORDS TO KNOW

Answer the questions that follow.

1. Is a **dirge** a piece of music that is sad, joyful, or complicated?
2. Are people who **transgress** a law those who make it, break it, or enforce it?
3. Would a person's appetite be **sated** by the smell of food, a light snack, or a large meal?
4. Is an **edict** a request, a command, or a question?
5. Would **lamentation** be most expected after a tragedy, a dinner party, or a graduation?
6. Does a person **defile** a lake by photographing it, polluting it, or stocking it with fish?
7. When is it most important to be **lithe**—while competing in a spelling bee, lifting weights, or performing gymnastics?
8. If people demonstrate **compulsive** behavior, is what they do rude, sympathetic, or beyond their control?
9. Is a person most likely to respond to **auspicious** events by feeling encouraged, frightened, or exhausted?
10. If a child was described to you as being **perverse**, would you expect the child to be angelic, disobedient, or shy?

SOPHOCLES

Born near Athens in the village of Colonus, Sophocles was the son of a wealthy manufacturer of armor. In his youth, he received a fine education and was said to be skilled in wrestling, dancing, and playing the lyre. These skills and a handsome appearance apparently resulted in his being chosen, as a youth, to lead a chorus in a celebration of the Greek victory over the Persians at the Battle of Salamis.

In 468 B.C., Sophocles defeated his teacher, the great playwright Aeschylus (ĕs′kə-ləs), in the Dionysian dramatic festival, an annual competition. That first-place award was followed by as many as 23 other victories, more than any other Greek playwright. Sophocles also was active in the political life of Athens. He was elected several times to the body of high executives commanding the military and was one of ten commissioners in charge of helping Athens recover after a severe military defeat in Sicily. In 406 B.C., the year of his death, he led a chorus of public mourners in honor of Euripides (yŏŏ-rĭp′ĭ-dēz′), a younger playwright who had often been his rival at the annual drama festivals.

Sophocles wrote more than 100 plays, although only 7 of them survive today. These include *Ajax, Oedipus the King* (sometimes called *Oedipus Rex*), *Electra,* and *Oedipus at Colonus. Antigone,* which rivals *Oedipus the King* as his best-known play, was probably first performed in 442 or 441 B.C. *Oedipus at Colonus,* which shows the playwright's affection for his native village, was written when Sophocles was around 90.

OTHER WORKS *Trachinian Women, Philoctetes*

496?–406 B.C.

Extended Reading

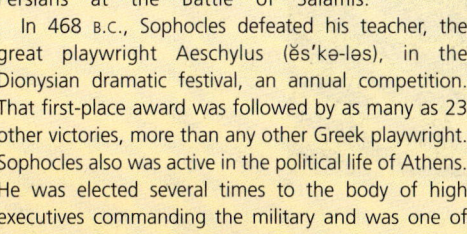
• CULTURAL CONNECTION

ANTIGONE **981**

Words to Know
1. sad
2. break it
3. large meal
4. command
5. tragedy
6. polluting it
7. performing gymnastics
8. beyond their control
9. encouraged
10. disobedient

Reteaching/Reinforcement
• *Unit Six Resource Book,* p. 54

SOPHOCLES

The English writer Matthew Arnold said that Sophocles "saw life steadily and saw it whole." Not only was Sophocles the most acclaimed playwright of his era, he was widely popular for his personal qualities as well.

CULTURAL CONNECTION
The World of Sophocles

Sophocles lived during the 5th century B.C., a period considered to be the golden age of ancient Athens. These pictures of Greek architecture and sculpture from the fifth century B.C. will help students visualize the great playwright's world.

Side A, Frame 49784

REFLECTING ON THEME
What Do You Think?

Ask students to review the list of their childhood heroes that they generated for the activity on p. 902. Ask students to compare Antigone and Creon to the heroes on their lists, and to consider whether their own views of heroism have been affected by reading *Antigone.*

OBJECTIVES

- To promote independent active reading
- To practice and apply skills learned in previous selections
- To provide an opportunity to assess students' performance through an alternative assessment instrument

Reading Pathways

- Invite students to read this poem silently. Have them take notes in a double-entry journal to clarify their responses to the poem and its relevance to this part of the unit.
- Invite students to read the poem aloud as a chorus, emphasizing its moral message.
- Suggest that students work in pairs to paraphrase the meaning of the poem.
- Evaluate how well students can read, interpret, discuss, and write about the selection on their own by using the Integrated Assessment for Unit Six, located in the Alternative Assessment booklet. The assessment for this unit covers both On Your Own selections, "Gift from a Son Who Died" and "Old Song." Administer the assessment at the end of the unit after students have read all the selections and completed all the writing they have been assigned.

Thematic Link: *The Heroic Tradition*
This poem offers advice on the right way to lead a heroic life.

Art Note

***Ere alaafin Shangó* [Shangó, Oyo-Ilé warrior-king], Oyé-Shangó artist** This statue of the thunder god Shangó as a mounted warrior King was made in the early 19th century.

Reading the Art What can you tell from this statue about the values or life of the people of West Africa?

ON YOUR OWN — REFLECT & ASSESS

OLD SONG

Traditional, West Africa

Ere alaafin Shangó [Shangó, Oyo-Ilé warrior-king] (early 1800s), Oyo-Shangó artist. Collection of the Nigerian Museum, Lagos. Photo by Robert Farris Thompson, 1962.

UNIT SIX PART 2: THE HEROIC TRADITION

PRINT AND MEDIA RESOURCES

UNIT SIX RESOURCE BOOK
Strategic Reading: Literature, p. 57

FORMAL ASSESSMENT
Selection Test, p. 187
Part Test, pp. 189–190
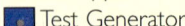 Test Generator

ALTERNATIVE ASSESSMENT
- Unit Six Integrated Assessment, pp. 31–36

Traditional African poetry was composed and then passed down orally from generation to generation, most often as songs or chants. The poetry includes myths, epics, religious chants, and magical formulas and touches on just about every aspect of daily African life. The selection you are about to read contains a series of proverbs. Highly creative and often humorous, African proverbs reinforce social behavior and express the collective wisdom of a people.

Do not seek too much fame,

but do not seek obscurity.

Be proud.

But do not remind the world of your deeds.

5 Excel when you must,

but do not excel the world.

Many heroes are not yet born,

many have already died.

To be alive to hear this song is a victory.

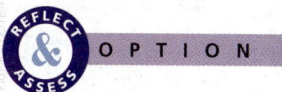

Class Discussion
SHARING IDEAS

Teacher's Role After students have read the poem, engage them in a whole-class discussion, using the following questions as prompts:

1. According to this song, how do you think the traditional people of West Africa might define a hero? *(Possible response: A hero would be a victor in battle who does not boast about his deeds; someone who accomplishes many deeds yet does not feel superior to others; someone who does his best but remains modest.)*

2. What modern-day people do you think would be heroes to the people who wrote and sang this song? *(Accept all reasonable responses.)*

3. How do you think Creon would react to the advice given in this poem at the beginning of Antigone and at the end of the play? Explain your opinion. *(Possible responses: At the beginning of the play, he would disagree with the poem because he sought fame; at the end, he would agree with it because he saw the results of excessive pride.)*

4. Which of the values in this poem are important in your own life? Why? *(Possible responses: pride and excellence because these values let a person achieve his or her personal best.)*

ORAL REPORTS

Teacher's Role Have students prepare oral presentations that illustrate each piece of advice offered by the poem through the use of examples. For instance, they can name someone who "does not seek too much fame" but who also does "not seek obscurity." Besides choosing examples, students need to explain how each example illustrates the advice offered by the poem.

OVERVIEW

To develop a deeper understanding of the literature they have read in this unit, students will explore the traits of a hero and then write a biographical research paper.

Objectives

- To plan a biographical research paper by defining heroism and using appropriate resources
- To draft a biographical research paper and solicit a response
- To revise, edit, and publish a biographical research paper
- To reflect on the process of writing a biographical research paper

Skills

WRITING AND LANGUAGE
- Using a thesis statement to unify the paper
- Developing an effective outline
- Crediting sources

GRAMMAR AND USAGE
- Using ellipses and brackets

MEDIA LITERACY
- Interpreting a political cartoon

- Understanding a magazine article

SPEAKING, LISTENING, AND VIEWING
- Discussing
- Conferencing

CRITICAL THINKING
- Evaluating sources

RESEARCH SKILLS
- Making source cards
- Making note cards
- Finding reference sources

Teaching Strategy: MODELING

A Have students consider how the clippings shown on page 984 demonstrate how Buzz Aldrin and Elizabeth Cady Stanton became known as heroes. Aldrin was famed for the physical courage that enabled him to walk on the moon. Stanton was known for her moral courage, which drove her to stand up for women's rights in a hostile era.

Teaching Strategy: STUMBLING BLOCK

B As students participate in this group discussion, they will probably voice differences of opinion about who is or is not a hero. Encourage them to be open-minded and tolerant of divergent viewpoints. Guide them to recognize that heroism is not restricted to those who have achieved fame. Ask them to think of local heroes, for example, firefighters.

WRITING FROM EXPERIENCE

WRITING A REPORT

In Unit Six, "The Making of Heroes," you read the legends of King Arthur and Sir Launcelot, heroes chosen by people searching for leadership or inspiration. Every age has its heroes. Who are some heroes of our time?

GUIDED ASSIGNMENT
Write a Biographical Research Paper A biographical research paper tells a person's life story, focusing on what made that life significant. Writing this kind of paper will help you learn more about a person you consider heroic. The following pages will help you research and write your report.

Photograph

Buzz Aldrin was one of the first astronauts to walk on the moon.

Historical Source

On September 10, 1855, Elizabeth Cady Stanton wrote this letter to her friend Susan B. Anthony, the women's rights activist:

> Peterboro, September 10, 1855
>
> Dear Susan,
> I wish that I were as free as you and I would stump the state in a twinkling. But I am not, and what is more, I passed through a terrible scourging when last at my father's. I cannot tell you how deep the iron entered my soul. I never felt more keenly the degradation of my sex. To think that all in me of which my father would have felt a proper pride had I been a man, is deeply mortifying to him because I am a woman. That thought has stung me to a fierce decision—to speak as soon as I can do myself credit.

She sounds really hurt and angry! Maybe these feelings made her such a passionate reformer.

When I read this I was really struck by her need to prove her work

① Read About Heroes

What do you know about the persons identified here? What is each known for? What qualities does each represent? Do you agree that each is a hero? Why or why not?

② Think About Heroes

With a group, discuss what makes someone a hero. Then brainstorm a list of heroes. Did all of you choose the same kind of person? Which qualities does each of you feel are important? What does this discussion show you about different ideas of what is heroic?

③ QuickWrite

Choose two or three people whom you consider heroic, and spend a few minutes writing about them. What makes each person heroic? Why does each interest you? What would you want to find out about each person?

Decision Point Choose the hero who interests you most. Write a statement of controlling purpose telling what your report will explain about this person. You can revise this statement as you find more information.

984 UNIT SIX: THE MAKING OF HEROES

PRINT AND MEDIA RESOURCES

UNIT SIX RESOURCE BOOK
Prewriting, p. 61
Elaboration, p. 62
Peer Response Guide, pp. 63–64
Revising and Proofreading, p. 65
Student Model, pp. 66–70
Rubric, p. 71

FORMAL ASSESSMENT
Guidelines for Writing Assignment

GRAMMAR MINI-LESSONS
Transparencies, p. 44
Copymasters, pp. 45–46

WRITING MINI-LESSONS
Transparencies, pp. 38, 60–62, 65, 67–69

 WRITING COACH

 LASERLINKS
Writing Springboard

Political Cartoon
Nelson Mandela was imprisoned for his work against apartheid, a policy of legalized discrimination in South Africa. He was later elected president.

PRISONER, 1963–1990   PRESIDENT, 1994–

Copyright © 1995 elDani (Aguila), *Filipino Reporter*, New York. Reprinted by permission.

Magazine Article

The former U.S. president slept in a room at a dormitory at Wilfrid Laurier University in Waterloo, Ont. By 7 a.m. last Tuesday, Jimmy Carter and his wife Rosalynn had eaten breakfast in the cafeteria and were aboard a bus full of volunteer home builders bound for a construction site five km away. Once the most powerful man in the world, Carter spent the day working with his wife and a group of unpaid laborers, installing windows, drywall, and vinyl siding on a small three-bedroom bungalow. The Carters were part of an army of 1,100 volunteers who, in just five days last week, built 40 homes for low-income families in 10 communities across

Former President Jimmy Carter with his wife, Rosalynn

Canada. The nonprofit, Georgia-based organization Habitat for Humanity International sponsored the event as part of its program to provide affordable housing for poor families around the world.

D'Arcy Jenish, from "Carter the Carpenter," *Maclean's*

What kind of information is provided by each of these sources?

- LASERLINKS
  - WRITING SPRINGBOARD
- WRITING COACH

WRITING FROM EXPERIENCE   985

CUSTOMIZING FOR
Less-Proficient Writers

C The term "apartheid" may be unfamiliar to some students. Explain that this word derives from the Afrikaans word for "apartness." It refers to the policy of strict racial segregation that codified discrimination against people of color in South Africa.

Media Literacy: GATHERING FACTS

D Have students look at the political cartoon and the news article on this page. Point out that the cartoon uses contrasting visual images to convey information about Nelson Mandela's heroism, whereas the article on Jimmy Carter uses plain facts to suggest his heroic qualities.

Teaching Strategy: MODELING

E Encourage students to be specific as they detail the information that they have gleaned from the cartoon and the article. Possible response:
- The Mandela cartoon depicts his transformation from a powerless prisoner to a victorious president. He heroically endured his harsh treatment in his fight against apartheid, and he continues to be heroic as he works with his former enemies to reform South Africa. The article on Carter demonstrates his humility and commitment to helping impoverished families.

WRITING SPRINGBOARD
Confrontation in Tiananmen Square This film shows the clashes between the Chinese military and the pro-democracy demonstrators in Beijing's Tiananmen Square in June 1989. The film includes the dramatic footage of a student's defiance of armored tanks. The images may help to generate a discussion about the nature of heroism.

Side B, Frame 33236

Writing Prompt Gather information about a group or person you consider to be heroic. Write a research paper about this person or group, explaining the heroic activities.

THE LANGUAGE OF LITERATURE **Teacher's Edition** 985

Speaking and Listening: GROUP DISCUSSION

F To help students understand how questions guide the research process, ask them to develop research questions about heroes Martin Luther King, Jr., and Amelia Earhart. List the questions on the board, and point out how the information gathered will depend on the questions asked. For example: a question about King's motivations will yield information about his values; a question about the obstacles Earhart faced will produce information about the role of women in the pre–World War II period.

Teaching Strategy: MODELING

G Ask students to consider the meanings of the words *primary* and *secondary*. Emphasizing that primary means "first" will assist them in making the distinction between primary and secondary sources. A primary (first) source gives "firsthand" information.
- Both the photo of Aldrin and Stanton's letter are primary sources. They are personal artifacts that yield information about both individuals. The Mandela cartoon and the article on Carter are secondary sources; each presents a third party's version of biographical information.
- Answers will vary. Possible responses: Primary sources include diaries, letters, account books, speeches; secondary sources include magazine articles, documentaries, biographies.

PREWRITING

Researching Your Hero

A Search for Sources Now that you have a subject, it's time to plan your research and start digging for information. The steps below can help you decide what information you need, where to look for it, and how to keep track of it all.

1 Ask Questions

To write a biographical report that is rich in detail, you need more than just facts. To guide your research, develop questions like these.

F
- What motivated my hero to succeed?
- What obstacles did he or she overcome?
- Who influenced my hero? How?

2 Search for Sources

You will want to use a variety of primary and secondary sources in writing your report. Primary sources come directly from the person you are writing about or from people who knew him or her. Secondary sources present ideas about a person or subject based on evidence from primary sources.

G
- Look at the sources on pages 984 and 985. Which are primary? Which are secondary?
- List some types of primary and secondary sources that might provide information on your subject.

3 Gather Information

Keep the following ideas in mind as you choose your sources and gather information from them.

Remember Your Purpose Refer to the statement of controlling purpose you wrote when you chose your topic. It can help you keep your research, and later your writing, on track.

Evaluate Your Sources As you gather secondary sources, consider whether each source contains up-to-date information and whether the author is a respected authority on your subject. See the SkillBuilder on page 989 for more information.

Journal Article

Student's Source Cards

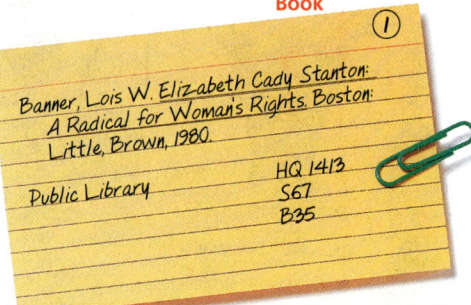

Book

Banner, Lois W. *Elizabeth Cady Stanton: A Radical for Woman's Rights*. Boston: Little, Brown, 1980.

Public Library   HQ 1413
                  S67
                  B35

Encyclopedia Entry

Sochen, June. "Stanton, Elizabeth Cady." *The World Book Encyclopedia*. 1995 ed.

School Library

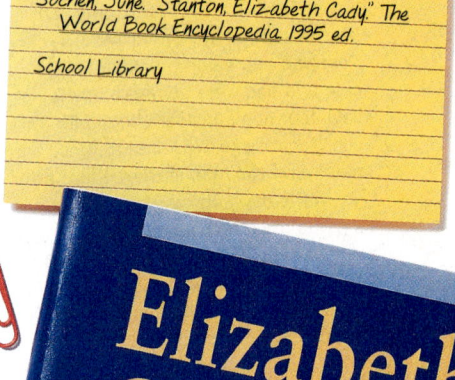

Welter, Barbara. "The Cult of True Womanhood, 1820–1860." *American Quarterly* 18 (1966): 151–174.

Public Library

986 UNIT SIX: THE MAKING OF HEROES

 SkillBuilder   **RESEARCH SKILLS**

CONSIDERING SOURCES An excellent way to help students understand the difference between primary and secondary sources and the information yielded by each kind of source is to ask them to apply the concepts to their own lives.

Application Ask students to make a list of primary sources that would reveal information about their own lives and then to make another list of real or imaginary secondary sources that could provide more information. To help students get started, present the following examples on the chalkboard:

Primary Sources—graded papers, family photo albums
Secondary Sources—newspaper articles, television documentaries about their families

Look for Variety Your report will be livelier if you include anecdotes and quotes from your subject as well as from critics and admirers.

4 Make Source Cards and Note Cards

Keep track of your sources on three-by-five-inch index cards. The models on the left show source cards for a book, an encyclopedia entry, and a journal article. In the upper right corner of each card, number the card so that you can easily identify the source when you take notes.

Take notes for your report on four-by-six-inch index cards, writing only one main idea per card. Label each card and note the source card number of the source from which the information is taken. For a source you intend to quote, copy the writer's sentences word for word and enclose them within quotation marks. Otherwise, paraphrase information by rewriting it in your own words. Write the page number from which the information is taken, and note whether the information is a quote or a paraphrase. For more information on making source cards and note cards, see page 1045 of the Writing Handbook.

Student's Note Card

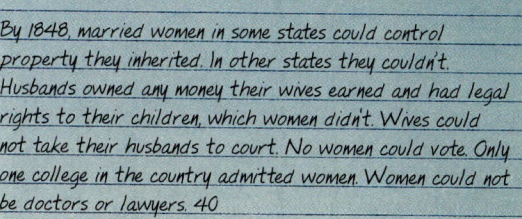

5 Write a Thesis Statement

A thesis statement is one or two sentences that tell briefly and clearly what you intend your report to show about your subject. Revise your statement of controlling purpose to reflect your point of view and to emphasize the main ideas of your report. Use your thesis statement to focus and organize your thoughts as you get ready to draft your report.

SkillBuilder

RESEARCH SKILLS

Finding Reference Sources
Your library's reference section is a good place to begin researching. A reference librarian can help you find some of the sources below.

- Sources for biographical information include *Webster's Biographical Dictionary*, *Who Was Who*, *Notable American Women*, *Dictionary of American Biography*, *World Authors*, and *Dictionary of Scientific Biography*.
- Indexes exist for most major newspapers. Newspapers that are more than a few months old are usually stored on microfilm or microfiche. Don't neglect newspaper indexes because your subject is a historical figure—the index for *The New York Times* goes back to 1851.

Secondary sources may direct you to primary sources or may include quotations from them.

THINK & PLAN

Looking at What You've Found

1. What information do you need to fill in the gaps in your report? Where could you look for it?
2. What ideas seem most important to include? Which facts, quotes, and anecdotes will support these ideas?

WRITING FROM EXPERIENCE **987**

Teaching Strategy: MODELING

H Review the model note cards on page 986. Identify the information listed for each kind of source. For example, the book note card specifies author, title, copyright date, publishing company, and place of publication. Remind students that encyclopedia articles usually do not list the authors of the entries, and so the reference should begin with the name caption of the encyclopedia entry. Point out that the journal note card also contains the volume number and the pages on which the article appears.

Teaching Strategy: COLLABORATIVE OPPORTUNITY

I Give students the opportunity to practice paraphrasing information and quoting information. Have pairs of students select facts about a person in the encyclopedia. One partner should paraphrase a fact, and the other should write a sentence that quotes the same information directly from the encyclopedia. Students can then compare their efforts, find new facts, and switch roles. Remind them of the necessity to use quotation marks for cited information.

SkillBuilder — CRITICAL THINKING

FINDING REFERENCE SOURCES Arrange to take the class to the library for a tour of its reference resources. Ask the school librarian to assist you in showing students available resources, including such computer access as is available.

Applying What You've Learned Encourage students to enrich their biographical reports through a multimedia approach. Biographical information might be available on videotapes, audiocassettes, or photographs. Guide students as they examine various resources in the library to gather biographical information. For example, a student researching Gandhi should be encouraged to use the *New York Times Index* and to view the 1982 film *Gandhi*. Caution students, however, that some films about real-life heroes may not be entirely factual.

Reteaching/Reinforcement
- *Writing Mini-lessons* transparencies, pp. 60–63

The Writer's Craft
The Library and Other Informational Sources, pp. 486–496

THE LANGUAGE OF LITERATURE TEACHER'S EDITION **987**

Writing Skill:
USING THE COMPUTER

J Students may find it useful to use a computer to write their drafts. Encourage them to use The Writing Coach as they organize their outlines. Recommend that they save data frequently, in order to avoid losing an evening's work to a single system error.

Teaching Strategy: MODELING

K Have students examine the sample outline. Point out that the paper begins with an interesting story about Stanton. Biographical details such as her birth date and place of birth are relegated to Part III of the paper.

Teaching Strategy: MODELING

L Draw students' attention to the close organization of the first paragraph of the sample paper. All three points under Part I of the outline are included in this opening paragraph. The second and third paragraphs of the sample follow Part II of the outline.

DRAFTING

Drafting Your Report

Ready to Write Your research is complete and you're ready to write—almost. Outlining your ideas first will help make the writing go more smoothly. An outline is your plan, and it is one you can change at any stage of the writing process.

Student's Outline and Rough Draft

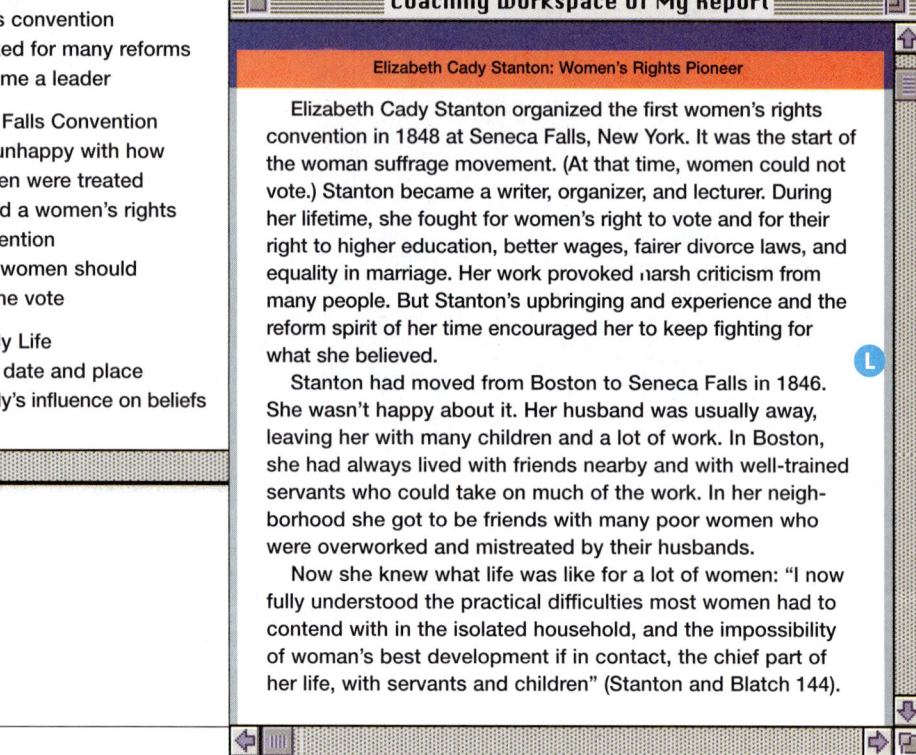

❶ Outline

Follow these steps as you outline:

- Group note cards by subject or idea.
- Write your thesis statement at the top of your outline.
- Using your note cards, list the main ideas in a logical order. Biographies often follow a chronological order.
- Instead of beginning with your hero's date of birth, show your readers why this person is important. Describe a dramatic moment or an achievement.
- Use main ideas as outline headings and supporting ideas as subheadings.

WRITING SPRINGBOARD
Eleanor Roosevelt This film montage focuses on the life of one of the most admired women in the 20th century, Eleanor Roosevelt. Use the film to help students think of topics for a research paper about a hero.

Side B, Frame 36480

Writing Prompt Gather information about a person who, like Eleanor Roosevelt, made a positive contribution to American society. Write a research paper about this person's life and contributions.

988 THE LANGUAGE OF LITERATURE TEACHER'S EDITION

2 Write a Rough Draft

For each heading in the outline, write at least one paragraph.

- Keep your thesis statement in mind as you write.
- Draft your report from beginning to end or concentrate on the parts of the topic you understand best.
- Credit your sources as you use them. Write the author's last name—or the title of the work if no author is given—and the page number of the source in parentheses following the quotation or information from that source. It is not necessary to credit information that is considered general knowledge—widely known facts that can be found in several sources.

3 Analyze Your Draft

Read your draft to see how well it meets each of following criteria. Where your draft needs improvement, mark it or make a note on how you can rework it. Your report should be

Structured The introduction includes a thesis statement explaining why your subject is a hero; the body provides details in well-organized paragraphs, and the conclusion ties your main points together.

Accurate Facts are correct and sources are credited.

Thorough Your report covers major events in your subject's life at least briefly and focuses on the most significant.

Clear Ideas are clearly expressed and flow logically.

Interesting You make your account of your subject's life interesting by including colorful facts, quotes, and anecdotes.

4 Rework and Share

Rework your draft, making the changes you marked.

PEER RESPONSE

Share your draft with a friend and ask the following.

- How could I make my thesis statement clearer?
- Does the way I organized my report make sense? If not, how could I better order my main points?
- What facts, quotes, or anecdotes did you find interesting?
- Have I focused on the parts of my subject's life that seem most important? If not, which parts seem more important?

SkillBuilder

CRITICAL THINKING

Evaluating Sources
In writing a report, you must decide which sources provide the most accurate and interesting facts and which facts are most important.

If sources disagree, think about why. One source may be more up-to-date or more respected than another. One source may conceal information because the author wants readers to have a certain idea of the subject. For example, an autobiography, or a biography by a close friend of the subject, may leave out embarrassing information about the subject.

APPLYING WHAT YOU'VE LEARNED
Review your draft, adding information important to support your thesis statement and deleting unimportant information.

WRITING HANDBOOK

For more information on evaluating sources, see page 1045 of the Writing Handbook.

RETHINK & EVALUATE

Preparing to Revise

1. How could you make your introduction more engaging?
2. How do your facts, quotes, and anecdotes support your thesis?
3. How effectively have you handled sources that disagree?

WRITING FROM EXPERIENCE 989

Critical Thinking: CLASSIFYING

M Some students may find it difficult to make the distinction between general knowledge and information that must be documented. To help them make this distinction, ask them what they know about Abraham Lincoln. List their information on the chalkboard. Point out that Lincoln's position as president of the United States is common knowledge, whereas the fact that his mother, Nancy, died of a mysterious disease called the milk sickness is not common knowledge.

Writing Skill: ELABORATION

N Ask students to consider whether they have provided enough details about the most significant event in their subject's life. Remind them that effective elaborative techniques include quoting the subject, providing detailed background information on the important event, and using descriptive language.

Critical Thinking: MAKING INFERENCES

O Ask pairs of students to use the questions under Peer Response as a guide to review each other's drafts. Then ask them to consider the following questions: What does the author admire most about the hero? Why do I get that impression? Possible response: George admires Stanton's perseverance. I get this impression from his description of her fighting spirit.

 CRITICAL THINKING

EVALUATING SOURCES As students gather information from research sources, they should consider the nature of each source. Some information may be factual and objective whereas other sources may be biased. Encourage students to question their sources and double-check surprising or contradictory information.

Applying What You've Learned Ask students to underline their thesis statements and then to scrutinize their papers to determine whether they have provided adequate support. For example, if a student's thesis statement reads, "Gandhi was a hero because he sacrificed his own comfort for his beliefs," then several accounts of his self-sacrificing behavior must be supplied.

THE LANGUAGE OF LITERATURE TEACHER'S EDITION 989

Critical Thinking: ANALYZING

P Invite students to analyze how the writer of the sample essay organized information about Stanton. They should note that the essay begins with an interesting fact that demonstrates Stanton's daring initiative. The opening tells the reader who Stanton was, and the next section provides both relevant biographical information about her and insight into her motivation to become an advocate of women's rights.

Teaching Strategy: STUMBLING BLOCK

Q Students writing research papers often place a low priority on making their papers interesting because they are so absorbed in gathering facts. Ask students to switch papers with a classmate and to read each other's papers carefully. Then encourage each student to give his or her partner feedback on the draft. Students should use the questions under Revise and Edit to guide the feedback process.

REVISING & PUBLISHING

The Finishing Touches

Your Final Product Your report is nearly complete. Look over your draft. Which parts are most interesting? Which are still unclear? Pay attention to peer responses and the Standards for Evaluation on the next page as you revise and edit to make your report clear and interesting from start to finish.

Student's Final Report

Sheila Wong
Ms. Flores
Sophomore English
24 April 1997

Elizabeth Cady Stanton: Women's Rights Pioneer

In 1848, when Elizabeth Cady Stanton organized the first women's rights convention, the idea of women voting in government elections was so shocking it had never been discussed in public. The convention marked the beginning of the woman suffrage movement and of Stanton's long career as a writer, organizer, and lecturer for the rights of women. During her 87 years, she fought for women's right to vote and for their right to higher education, to better wages, to fairer divorce laws, and to equality in marriage. Her work provoked harsh criticism from the press, from friends, and even from her husband and her father. Despite criticism and frustration with the slow progress of reform, Stanton persevered. Her unique upbringing and personal experiences and the 19th-century reform spirit all motivated her to become a leader in the movement for women's rights.

The Movement Begins

For the first several years of her marriage, Stanton was fairly content with her life. She had a successful husband, three healthy children, a comfortable home in Boston, excellent servants, and interesting friends.

---

① Revise and Edit

Read over your report.

- Does it hold your interest all the way through?
- Is any important information missing? What details, quotes, or anecdotes could help?
- Is your thesis statement clear?
- Does your report give a clear impression of your subject's personality?

② Polish It

Turn your rough draft into a finished piece.

- Credit your sources correctly.
- Refer to the SkillBuilder on the next page for help in using brackets and ellipses within text.
- Create a Works Cited list like the one on the next page. Pay close attention to punctuation. For more information on creating a Works Cited list, see page 1044 of the Writing Handbook.

The student explains the subject's importance in a brief introduction.

The student tells how changes in the subject's life influenced her ideas.

Wong 2

When Stanton moved to Seneca Falls in 1846, the change was not a happy one. Her husband, an aspiring politician, was often away, leaving her with a houseful of children and an endless round of chores. In her new neighborhood she came to know many poor women who were overworked and mistreated by their husbands. She later said of that time, "I now fully understood the practical difficulties most women had to contend with in the isolated household" (Stanton and Blatch 144).

Wong 7

Works Cited

Banner, Lois W. *Elizabeth Cady Stanton: A Radical for Women's Rights.* Boston: Little, Brown 1980.

DuBois, Ellen Carol, ed. *Elizabeth Cady Stanton, Susan B. Anthony: Correspondence, Writings, Speeches.* New York: Schocken Books, 1981.

Griffith, Elisabeth. *In Her Own Right: The Life of Elizabeth Cady Stanton.* New York: Oxford University Press, 1984.

Sochen, June. "Stanton, Elizabeth Cady." *The World Book Encyclopedia.* 1995 ed.

Stanton, Theodore, and Harriot Stanton Blatch, eds. *Elizabeth Cady Stanton, As Revealed in Her Letters, Diary, and Reminiscences.* New York: Harper & Brothers, 1922.

Standards for Evaluation

A biographical research report
- begins with a vivid introduction that reveals why the person is significant and makes the reader want to know more
- covers the most important parts of the subject's life in a clear and logical order
- contains accurate facts from a variety of sources
- uses quotes and anecdotes that convey important information about the subject's life or personality
- has a strong conclusion

SkillBuilder

GRAMMAR FROM WRITING

Using Ellipses and Brackets

When quoting sources, you need not always include every word. When you leave out words within a quote, use ellipsis points to replace the words you leave out. Three dots (. . .) indicate an omission within a sentence. Four dots (. . . .) indicate an omission between sentences. When you replace an author's word with another word or when you add words to explain something within a quote, use brackets [ ] to enclose words not in the original.

GRAMMAR HANDBOOK

For more information on punctuating quotations, see page 1096 of the Grammar Handbook.

Editing Checklist Use the following editing tips as you revise.
- Are sources quoted and cited correctly?
- Are names spelled correctly?

REFLECT & ASSESS

Evaluating the Experience

1. What did you learn about your subject in writing this report?
2. How did your concept of heroism grow or change?

   PORTFOLIO How well did you communicate your ideas about your subject? Put this evaluation in your portfolio.

WRITING FROM EXPERIENCE 991

Writing Skill: ELABORATION

Read aloud Stanton's words in the sample essay to underscore the way primary sources can enrich biographical reports. Ask students what they have learned about Stanton through hearing her own words. Students may observe that she became concerned with the general problems of women through her own experiences. Students might also point out that using quotations is an effective means of elaboration.

CUSTOMIZING FOR
Less-Proficient Writers

Have students look carefully at the Works Cited list. Point out that the references have been organized alphabetically, and list the kinds of information presented: author, title(s), date, and, if the source is a book, the publisher and place of publication.

PORTFOLIO

Encourage students to prepare honest evaluations of their reports for inclusion in their portfolios.

Standards for Evaluation

Have students review their reports for the following:

Ideas and Content
- includes an introduction that reveals why the person is significant
- covers the most important parts of the subject's life
- conveys important information about the subject's life or personality through facts, quotes, and anecdotes
- has a strong conclusion

Structure and Form
- presents information and ideas in a logical sequence
- gives credit for ideas and statements of others
- includes properly formatted Works Cited list

Grammar, Usage, and Mechanics
- contains no more than two or three minor errors in grammar and usage
- contains no more than two or three minor errors in spelling, capitalization, and punctuation

---

SkillBuilder GRAMMAR FROM WRITING

USING ELLIPSES AND BRACKETS Explain that a sentence or passage may be much too long or too detailed to include in a quote. Suggest that the use of ellipses may solve the problem. Also explain the functional use of brackets: They clarify or provide pertinent information about quoted information.

Applying What You've Learned Give students the opportunity to use ellipses and brackets. Suggest that they record a conversation between their peers, perhaps in the lunchroom or en route to the next class. Ask them to transcribe the core of the conversation, using ellipses to mark places where material has been omitted, and inserting bracketed material to clarify the content. To get them started, write the following example on the chalkboard: John said, "I can't believe how much work I had to do this weekend. [My mother] asked me to rake the yard and . . . basically do two months' work in two days."

THE LANGUAGE OF LITERATURE Teacher's Edition 991

UNIT REVIEW

This page has been designed to help students assess what they have learned in Unit Six. It also provides opportunities for them to evaluate the theme and to test their understanding of specific literary concepts. As students complete at least one of the optional activities for each section, you may want to conduct your own informal assessment of their performance, including their speaking and listening skills and their ability to engage in cooperative work.

Objectives

- To allow students to reflect on and assess their understanding of theme
- To allow students to reflect on and assess their understanding of literary concepts such as classical drama and the relationship between fact and fiction
- To give students the opportunity to assess and build their portfolios

REFLECTING ON THEME

OPTION 1

As you discuss this activity, remind students that heroic achievements are not always public and dramatic. Help them focus on everyday accomplishments that are heroic. Cite examples such as the mother who raises a family on her own; the senior citizen who runs a soup kitchen; or the person who puts himself or herself through college. Encourage students to think of those kinds of achievements as they consider the heroic possibilities in their own lives.

OPTION 2

You might ask each pair of students to read aloud selection passages that illustrate the leadership qualities of their choices.

 Self-Assessment Ask students to skim all the selections again before they choose those that gave them the deepest insights into heroism.

REFLECT & ASSESS

UNIT SIX: THE MAKING OF HEROES

How have your thoughts and feelings about heroism been affected by the selections in this unit? At this stage of the school year, how do you rate yourself as a reader and as a writer? Explore these questions by completing one or more of the options in each of the following sections.

REFLECTING ON THEME

OPTION 1 **Assessing Heroism** In Charles Dickens's novel *David Copperfield,* the narrator begins his life's story by wondering "whether I shall turn out to be the hero of my life." What qualities and accomplishments would you need in order to consider yourself a hero? Review the selections in this unit, and make a list of the heroic qualities and accomplishments they present that you would value in your own life.

OPTION 2 **Identifying Qualities of Leadership** Heroes often find themselves in positions of leadership. Review this unit's selections, identifying characters and authors who you believe possess strong leadership abilities, even if they are not in positions of authority. Then work with a partner to create a checklist that identifies the distinctive characteristics of a successful leader. Choose the individual from the unit who best represents those characteristics, and present your choice to your classmates.

Self-Assessment: Which of the selections in this unit gave you the deepest insights into the concept of heroism? Write a short paragraph in which you explain your choice.

REVIEWING LITERARY CONCEPTS

OPTION 1 **Understanding Classical Drama** Review the information about classical drama on page 937 and in the Literary Concepts feature on page 980. Then, in your own words, write definitions of the terms *chorus, tragedy, tragic hero, tragic flaw,* and *dramatic irony.* In each definition, include an example that illustrates the meaning of the term.

chorus:
tragedy:
tragic hero:
tragic flaw:
dramatic irony:

OPTION 2 **Separating Fact from Fiction** As you know, a fictional work can have a factual basis. Review five of the fictional narratives and dramas in this unit, jotting down aspects of plot, character, and setting that you think might have some basis in fact. Compile your results in a chart like the one shown. Then, with a small group of classmates, compare charts and discuss your views on the relationship between facts and imagination in works of literature.

992 UNIT SIX

Title	Factual Basis of Plot / Character	Factual Basis of Setting
from *The Acts of King Arthur and His Noble Knights*	• Knights engaged in fighting and boasting. • Ideals of chivalry influenced knights' conduct. • Court celebrations were common.	• Actual places in England are referred to by name. • Castles like the one described existed. • Descriptions of customs and clothing may be accurate.

Self-Assessment: On a sheet of paper, copy the following literary terms: characterization through dialogue, tone in nonfiction, conflict, foil, flashback, true-life adventure, romance, *and* style. *For each term, find an example from outside this unit that illustrates its meaning. To illustrate the concept of tone in nonfiction, for example, you might write a brief description of the tone of an essay in a previous unit. For examples of romance and true-life adventure, you will need to go outside this textbook. Use the Handbook of Literary Terms on page 1000 to refresh your memory about any terms you are not sure of.*

PORTFOLIO BUILDING

- **QuickWrites** Good writers know how to use language economically, without waste or needless repetition. Review the QuickWrites that you completed during this unit, and choose one or two that could profit from trimming and tightening. Revise them, attach the revisions to the originals, and add both versions to your portfolio, along with a note that explains the reasoning behind your revisions.

- **Writing About Literature** Earlier, you wrote a critical essay about one of the selections in this unit. How does it sound to you now? Write a brief note explaining how you chose a selection to write about and how successfully you think you evaluated it. Decide whether to include your note in your portfolio.

- **Writing from Experience** You may have just finished your biographical research paper. If you could ask your hero three questions, what would they be? Jot them down. Then decide how successfully you could tell someone else about your subject's life and why he or she is important to you.

- **Personal Choice** Sometimes our own mistakes provide valuable lessons. Look back through your records and evaluations of all the activities and writing that you completed in this unit, including any work that you did on your own. Which work do you regard as your least successful? Write a note in which you identify that activity or piece of writing and explain what you have learned from working on it. Add the note, along with your work (or evaluations of it), to your portfolio.

Self-Assessment: At this stage, your writing portfolio should represent the work of an entire year. Review the pieces in your portfolio and choose three of your best works—one done in the fall, one in the winter, and one in the spring. Write a note explaining what these works reveal about your progress and abilities as a writer.

SETTING GOALS

Reflect on all the goals that you set for yourself during the course of the year. Which goals did you reach? Which goals seem nearly within your reach? Which seem as far away as ever? Write an evaluation of your progress this year, and identify three goals for the next school year.

REFLECT & ASSESS **993**

REVIEWING LITERARY CONCEPTS

OPTION 1

Many students will choose examples from *Antigone* to illustrate the concepts. For example, the chorus in *Antigone* comments on the action, the play is a tragedy because a king's deadly decision causes his son and his wife to kill themselves, Creon is a tragic hero because he falls from a great height, Creon's tragic flaw is his overreaching pride in the correctness of his decision, and one dramatic irony is that Creon's law violates the law of the gods.

OPTION 2

When students form groups to compare their charts, you may wish to assign key roles such as "turn-taking monitor," who will invite everyone to participate, and a "direction giver," who will review the instructions, outline the parameters of the discussion, and make sure that the group focuses on illuminating the relationship between facts and imagination in works of literature.

Self-Assessment To make it easier for students to complete the assignment and to encourage extensive reading, you may wish to arrange a class library visit. Just before the visit, review the requirements of the activity, and invite students to share any ideas that they have begun to explore.

SETTING GOALS

Students may find it helpful to review the work that is in their portfolio. Encourage students to be realistic in assessing thier progress during the school year. You may find it useful to discuss students' goals with the class as a whole.

PORTFOLIO BUILDING

Encourage students to include drafts as well as final revisions so that they can reflect on and assess their development and progress. If students choose to complete the Personal Choice option, be sure that they understand that writers often learn the most from their least successful work.

**Self-Assessment** Students may benefit from developing a checklist as a way of judging the progress that they have made throughout the year. Encourage them to examine global concerns, such as the clear organization of ideas and effective word choice, as well as mechanical aspects of their writing, such as spelling, punctuation, and grammar.

THE LANGUAGE OF LITERATURE **Teacher's Edition** 993

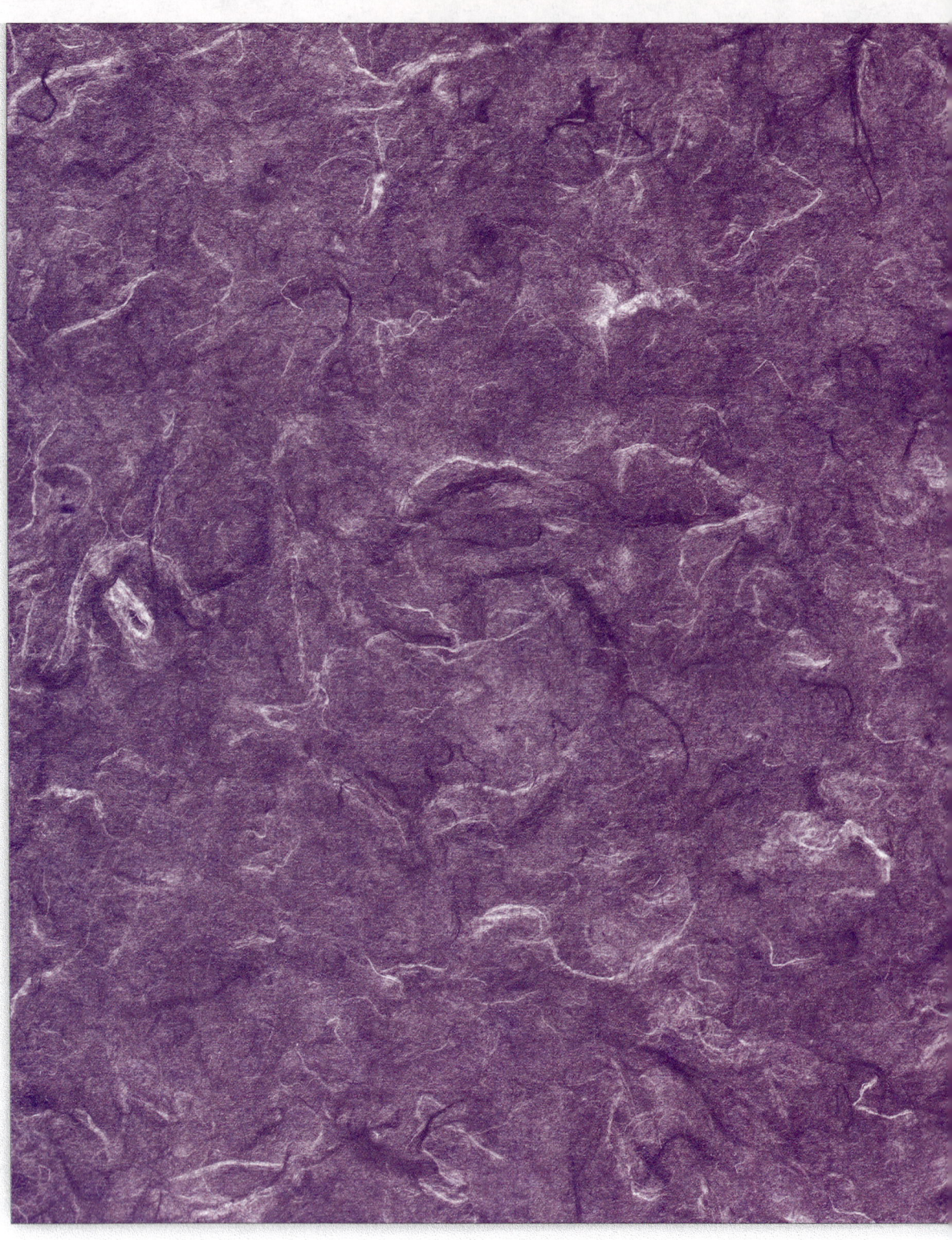

Student Resource Bank

Words to Know: Access Guide 996

Handbook of Literary Terms 1000

Writing Handbook
1 The Writing Process 1018
2 Building Blocks of Good Writing 1024
3 Narrative Writing 1034
4 Explanatory Writing 1036
5 Persuasive Writing 1042
6 Research Report Writing 1044

Multimedia Handbook
1 Getting Information Electronically 1048
2 Word Processing 1050
3 Using Visuals 1053
4 Creating a Multimedia Presentation 1055

Grammar Handbook
1 Writing Complete Sentences 1058
2 Making Subjects and Verbs Agree 1061
3 Using Nouns and Pronouns 1068
4 Using Modifiers Effectively 1076
5 Using Verbs Correctly 1081
6 Correcting Capitalization 1085
7 Correcting Punctuation 1089
8 Grammar Glossary 1098

Index of Fine Art 1104

Index of Skills 1108

Index of Titles and Authors 1119

Words to Know: Access Guide

A
abeyance, 41
abiding, 826
abstain, 142
acclimatized, 190
accost, 75
acquiescence, 271
acute, 237
adamant, 384
adversary, 916
affable, 206
affluent, 298
ambiguous, 287
amicable, 530
anathema, 185
anecdote, 749
animosity, 540
annihilate, 685
annul, 750
anonymity, 825
antiquated, 213
appallingly, 250
appraise, 563
apprehension, 41
apt, 465
archetype, 517
ardent, 401
arid, 547
assiduously, 527
atonement, 400
atrocity, 571
augment, 564
auspicious, 944
austere, 73
authoritarian, 85
averse, 528
aversion, 398
avid, 299

B
balmy, 432
bedlam, 235
beneficent, 391
benign, 367
bereft, 356
betrayal, 28
biased, 156
boding, 436
brooding, 153
brusquely, 327

C
cajole, 535
caliber, 194
callousness, 383
captivate, 69
carriage, 927
catalyst, 89
censure, 407
chagrin, 61
champion, 915
chaos, 235
chaotic, 824
chide, 564
churlish, 527
coalesce, 640
coercion, 228
coherently, 226
cohort, 204
commiserate, 784
commodity, 238
commune, 323
complacently, 157
composure, 625
compulsive, 958
congenial, 300
conniving, 245
consensus, 268
constricting, 850
contemplate, 202
contemptuously, 159
convalescence, 384
conversely, 251
conviction, 237
coquettishly, 391
cosmopolitan, 781
cower, 234
coyness, 399
credence, 75
cultivate, 527
cursory, 300

D
dastardly, 526
decipher, 361
decorous, 925
deduce, 192
deference, 785
defile, 972
deft, 467
defunct, 549
degrading, 222
deliberately, 113
deplorable, 453
derision, 42
desolation, 433
destined, 848
detestable, 55
devastate, 26
devoid, 228
dexterity, 323
diligent, 142
din, 313
diplomacy, 250
direst, 462
dirge, 968
disarm, 814
discern, 462
discordant, 24
discreetly, 598
disparagement, 925
dissuasion, 783
distasteful, 749
divulge, 206
doctrine, 117

E
edict, 953
efficacy, 747
elicit, 299
elusive, 600
emaciated, 311
emancipation, 480
embellish, 454
embody, 835
eminently, 453
empathy, 142
emphatically, 89
enigmatically, 642
enmity, 361
entail, 251
equanimity, 832
errant, 299
essence, 609
ethereal, 55
euphemism, 625
exacerbated, 518
exalt, 925
exaltation, 229

exasperated, 154
expendable, 685
exposé, 225
extricating, 849

F

fallible, 931
fanatical, 570
farce, 875
fastidious, 288
fathom, 269
fettered, 626
fiasco, 26
fidelity, 913
flail, 825
flair, 846
flout, 214
forlorn, 218
formidable, 85
forsaken, 785
fortitude, 832
fray, 549
furtive, 115; 434
futile, 481

G

grizzled, 432

H

haggard, 931
haunt, 705
heretic, 407
homily, 783
hone, 86

I

ignominy, 552
illicit, 456
immaculate, 206
imminent, 207
impassive, 280
impeccably, 362
impending, 624
imperative, 268
imperceptibly, 130
imperiously, 640
impertinent, 161
impetuous, 290
implacable, 826
implement, 193
implicitly, 285
imploring, 436
imposing, 56
impotently, 538
inauspicious, 285
incensed, 287
incessantly, 610
incipient, 517
inconsolable, 648
incredulously, 156
indelible, 707
indifferently, 750
indignation, 383; 643
indignity, 20
indomitable, 679
inexplicable, 184
infamy, 290
infatuated, 528
infernal, 527
infinitesimally, 686
ingratiating, 455
inkling, 74
inscrutable, 73

insolence, 540
intemperate, 931
interminable, 311
intervene, 625
irate, 60
irrelevant, 237
irreparably, 834
irreproachable, 243

J

judicious, 624

L

lament, 25
lamentation, 968
languidly, 710
languish, 480
lenient, 143
liberty, 480
lithe, 949
ludicrous, 356

M

maelstrom, 125
maim, 251
majestic, 54
makeshift, 251
malevolence, 640
malicious, 289
maliciously, 61
meager, 213
majestic, 54
makeshift, 251
malevolence, 640
malicious, 289
maliciously, 61
meager, 213
melancholy, 547
mentor, 85
methodically, 206
militant, 228

mirage, 127
miscreant, 193
morose, 814
mortify, 87
muse, 85
mystic, 385

N

naiveté, 399
notorious, 311

O

obscure, 323
obscurity, 41
omen, 674
oppress, 116
oppression, 228
ordained, 153
ostentatiously, 874

P

pallid, 468
pandemonium, 834
paradoxically, 74
parry, 399
patronize, 814
penitence, 925
pensive, 571
perfunctorily, 785
perilous, 250
perpetrate, 235
perpetually, 850
perpetuation, 228
persevere, 785
perspicacity, 55

WORDS TO KNOW: ACCESS GUIDE

pervade, 627
perverse, 963
petrified, 127
petulant, 708
pittance, 465
placidly, 391
platitude, 271
ponderous, 603
prattle, 623
precarious, 624
predecessor, 432
preoccupied, 273
preside, 213
presumption, 813
pretense, 277
pretext, 78
primeval, 691
proclaiming, 251
prodigy, 20
profuse, 465
protracted, 640
prowess, 913
prudence, 285
pulsate, 130
pummel, 60
purge, 251

Q

quaint, 624
quell, 528

R

rabid, 126
radiant, 224
rampant, 204
rank, 386
rapt, 130
ream, 23
rebuke, 453
recede, 564
recompense, 916
recrimination, 640
refined, 457
regally, 874
rejuvenated, 570
remorse, 785
renounce, 402
replete, 323
repressive, 185
reprieve, 41
reprisal, 925
reproach, 20
repugnant, 466
resignation, 357
resilient, 688
respite, 574
reticence, 274
retrospect, 300
reverie, 24
revoke, 691
ruefully, 235

S

sallow, 814
sanctuary, 875
sated, 942
saucy, 157
scruple, 294
scrutinize, 456
secular, 250
sedate, 435
seethe, 468
self-righteous, 643
serene, 130
sever, 432
sheathed, 688
shirk, 609
sidle, 113
silhouetted, 129
skulk, 206
slaking, 551
sniveling, 478
solace, 299

speculation, 185
squalor, 598
staidness, 244
stature, 310
stealthily, 872
stifle, 547
stridently, 547
stupefied, 610
stupor, 837
subliminal, 692
subtle, 245
subversive, 245
superciliously, 548
supple, 143
supplicating, 435
surreptitious, 201

T

tact, 87
taint, 692
taut, 299
temerity, 549
tempering, 609
tenacity, 832
tentatively, 706
tepid, 454
testily, 192
theological, 784
tirade, 237
transcend, 384
transgress, 968
traverse, 600
trepidation, 357
tribulation, 838

U

unassuming, 56
unavailing, 674
uncanny, 154
undulate, 689
unfathomable, 539
unnervingly, 364
unsolicited, 72
unwieldy, 298
utilitarian, 73
utterance, 563

V

vacillating, 361
vagrant, 927
vehemently, 468
versed, 515
vice, 129
vigil, 277
vile, 457
vindicate, 531
visceral, 837
void, 88
voluble, 677
vulnerable, 839

W

wanly, 646
wary, 518
wistful, 399
withered, 674

Pronunciation Key

Symbol	Examples	Symbol	Examples	Symbol	Examples
ă	at, gas	m	man, seem	v	van, save
ā	ape, day	n	night, mitten	w	web, twice
ä	father, barn	ng	sing, anger	y	yard, lawyer
âr	fair, dare	ŏ	odd, not	z	zoo, reason
b	bell, table	ō	open, road, grow	zh	treasure, garage
ch	chin, lunch	ô	awful, bought, horse	ə	awake, even, pencil, pilot, focus
d	dig, bored	oi	coin, boy		
ĕ	egg, ten	ŏŏ	look, full	ər	perform, letter
ē	evil, see, meal	ōō	root, glue, through		
f	fall, laugh, phrase	ou	out, cow		**Sounds in Foreign Words**
g	gold, big	p	pig, cap	KH	German *ich, auch;* Scottish *loch*
h	hit, inhale	r	rose, star		
hw	white, everywhere	s	sit, face	N	French *entre, bon, fin*
ĭ	inch, fit	sh	she, mash	œ	French *feu, cœur;* German *schön*
ī	idle, my, tried	t	tap, hopped		
îr	dear, here	th	thing, with	ü	French *utile, rue;* German *grün*
j	jar, gem, badge	*th*	then, other		
k	keep, cat, luck	ŭ	up, nut		
l	load, rattle	ûr	fur, earn, bird, worm		

Stress Marks

′ This mark indicates that the preceding syllable receives the primary stress. For example, in the word *language,* the first syllable is stressed: lăng′gwĭj.

′ This mark is used only in words in which more than one syllable is stressed. It indicates that the preceding syllable is stressed, but somewhat more weakly than the syllable receiving the primary stress. In the word *literature,* for example, the first syllable receives the primary stress, and the last syllable receives a weaker stress: lĭt′ər-ə-chŏŏr′.

Adapted from *The American Heritage Dictionary of the English Language, Third Edition;* Copyright © 1992 by Houghton Mifflin Company. Used with the permission of Houghton Mifflin Company.

Handbook of Literary Terms

Act An act is a major unit of action in a play. Acts are sometimes divided into scenes; each scene is limited to a single time and place. Shakespeare's plays all have five acts. Contemporary plays usually have two or three acts, although some only have one act. Josephine Tey's *The Pen of My Aunt* and Anton Chekhov's *The Bear* are examples of one-act plays.

Alliteration Alliteration is the repetition of initial consonant sounds. Alliteration occurs in everyday speech and in all forms of literature. Poets, in particular, use alliteration to emphasize certain words, to create mood, to underscore meaning, and to enhance rhythm. Note how D. H. Lawrence makes use of a repeated *s* sound in the following stanza of "Piano." Such repetition helps contribute to the quiet, pensive mood of the poem.

> Softly, in the dusk, a woman is
>   singing to me;
>
> Taking me back down the vista of
>   years, till I see
>
> A child sitting under the piano, in
>   the boom of the tingling strings
>
> And pressing the small, poised feet
>   of a mother who smiles as she
>   sings.

See *Assonance, Consonance.*

Allusion An allusion is a reference to a historical or literary person, place, thing, or event with which the reader is assumed to be familiar. In Bernard Malamud's story "The First Seven Years," the title is an allusion to a story from the Book of Genesis in the Bible. According to the biblical narrative, Jacob agreed to work for Laban for seven years in return for Laban's beautiful daughter Rachel's hand in marriage. Similarly, the title of Stephen Vincent Benét's "By the Waters of Babylon" is an allusion to the beginning of Psalm 137 in the Bible: "By the rivers of Babylon, there we sat down, yea, we wept, when we remembered Zion."

Antagonist The antagonist in a work of literature is the character or force against which the main character, or protagonist, is pitted. The antagonist may be another character, something in nature or society, or even an internal force within the protagonist. In Josephine Tey's *The Pen of My Aunt,* the antagonist is the German soldier who detains the aunt's "nephew"; in Isabel Allende's "And of Clay Are We Created," the destructive force unleashed by the volcano may be considered an antagonist.

See *Conflict, Protagonist.*

Aside In drama, an aside is a remark spoken in an undertone by one character either to the audience or to another character, which the remaining characters supposedly do not hear. The aside is a traditional dramatic convention, a device that the audience accepts even though it is obviously unrealistic. The aside can be used to express a character's feelings, opinions, and reactions, and thus functions as a method of characterization. In the following example from Anton Chekhov's *The Bear*, the aside shows Luke's growing antagonism towards Smirnov.

> **Luke** (*aside*). Now we'll never get rid of him, botheration take it! It's an ill wind brought him along.

Assonance Assonance is the repetition of a vowel sound within nonrhyming words. *Helter-skelter, sweet dreams,* and *high and mighty* are examples of assonance. Writers of both poetry and prose use assonance to give their work a musical quality and unify stanzas and passages. Notice the assonance of the long *a* sounds in the following lines from Robert Hayden's "Those Winter Sundays."

> then with cracked hands that a̱ched
> from la̱bor in the weekday weather ma̱de
> banked fires bla̱ze. . . .

See *Alliteration, Consonance.*

Author's Purpose Authors write for one or more of the following purposes: to inform, to express an opinion, to entertain, or to persuade. For example, the purpose of a news report is to inform; the purpose of an editorial is to persuade the readers or audience to do or believe something. Elie Wiesel wrote *Night* to inform readers about the horrors of concentration camps and to persuade them to resist the evil that made these horrors possible.

Autobiography An autobiography is the story of a person's life written by that person. Yevgeny Yevtushenko's *A Precocious Autobiography,* Mark Mathabane's *Kaffir Boy,* and Le Ly Hayslip's *When Heaven and Earth Changed Places* are all examples of autobiographies. Autobiographies are almost always written in the first person, and they typically focus on events and people that are particularly significant in the author's life.

Ballad A ballad is a narrative poem that was originally meant to be sung. Ballads usually begin abruptly, focus on a single tragic incident, contain dialogue and repetition, and imply more than they actually tell. Traditional ballads are written in four-line stanzas with regular rhythm and rhyme. The rhythm often alternates between four-stress and three-stress lines, and the rhyme scheme usually is *a b c b* or *a a b b*.

Folk ballads were composed orally and handed down by word of mouth. These ballads usually tell about ordinary people who have had unusual adventures or have performed daring deeds. The literary ballad is a poem written by a poet who imitates the form and content of the folk ballad.

The following anonymous ballad was popular during the Civil War. Each line has four stresses and the rhyme scheme is *a b c b*.

> "Mother, is the battle over?
>   Thousands have been slain, they say.
> Is my father come? and tell me,
>   Has the army gained the day?
>
> "Is he well, or is he wounded?
>   Mother, do you think he's slain?
> If he is, pray will you tell me.
>   Will my father come again?
>
> "Mother, I see you always sighing
>   Since that paper last you read;
> Tell me why you are crying:
>   Is my dearest father dead?"
>
> "Yes, my boy, your noble father
>   Is one numbered with the slain;
> Though he loves me very dearly,
>   Ne'er on earth we'll meet again."

See *Meter, Narrative Poem, Rhyme.*

Biography A biography is an account of a person's life written by another person. The writer of a biography, or biographer, often researches his or her subject in order to present accurate information. A biographer may also draw upon personal knowledge of his or her subject. For example, Coretta Scott King's *My*

Life with Martin Luther King, Jr., is based on the author's intimate knowledge of her subject. Although biographies are usually book length, there are also shorter forms of biographical writing, such as the excerpt from Colette's *Earthly Paradise,* which is a biographical sketch of the writer's mother, and Doris Herold Lund's "Gift from a Son Who Died," which focuses on the life of Lund's son. Although a biographer—by necessity and by inclination—presents a subject from a certain point of view, a skilled biographer strives for a balanced treatment, highlighting weaknesses as well as strengths, failures as well as achievements.

Blank Verse Blank verse is unrhymed poetry written in iambic pentameter. Each line has five metrical feet, and each foot has an unstressed syllable followed by a stressed syllable.

The "Passing of Arthur," by the English poet Alfred, Lord Tennyson, is written in blank verse. The following lines from the poem describe the famous scene in which, at King Arthur's request, his sword Excalibur is thrown into the water. Note the iambic pentameter and the lack of end rhyme.

So flash'd / and fell / the brand / Excal / i bur:
But ere / he dipt / the sur / face, rose /
   an arm
Clothed in / white sam / site, mys / tic,
   won / derful.
And caught / him by / the hilt / and
   bran / dish'd him
Three times, / and drew / him un / der in /
   the mere.

See *Meter, Rhythm.*

Character Characters are the individuals who participate in the action of a literary work. The most important characters are called **main characters.** Less prominent characters are known as **minor characters.** In Rabindranath Tagore's "The Cabulliwallah," the father, his daughter Mini, and the Cabulliwallah are main characters, while the mother is a minor character.

Whereas some characters are two-dimensional, with only one or two dominant traits, a fully developed character possesses many traits, mirroring the psychological complexity of a real person. In longer works of fiction, main characters often undergo change as the plot unfolds. Such characters are called **dynamic characters,** as opposed to **static characters,** who remain the same. In Amy Tan's "Two Kinds," the narrator is a dynamic character because her perception of her childhood and of her mother changes dramatically during the course of the story; on the other hand, the mother is a static character who remains essentially the same.

See *Antagonist, Characterization, Foil, Plot, Protagonist.*

Characterization Characterization refers to the techniques employed by writers to develop characters. There are four basic methods of characterization.

1. The writer may use physical description. In Nadine Gordimer's "A Chip of Glass Ruby," Mrs. Bamjee is described as follows: "She still wore the traditional dress of a Muslim woman, and her body, which was scraggy and unimportant as a dress on a peg when it was not host to a child, was wrapped in the trailing rags of a cheap sari, and her thin black hair was greased."

2. The character's own speech, thoughts, feelings, or actions may be presented. In Gordimer's story, the reader learns of Mrs. Bamjee's reaction to the arrival of the police: "Although she was not surprised, her hands shook like a very old person's as she undid the locks and the complicated catch on the wire burglarproofing."

3. The speech, thoughts, feelings, or actions of other characters provide another means of developing a character. Dr. Khan, in Gordimer's story, tells Bamjee that his wife is a "wonderful woman." After Mrs. Bamjee's arrest, one of the neighbors says in sympathy, "Poor Mrs. Bamjee, such a kind lady."

4. The narrator's own direct comments also serve to develop a character. The narrator says of Mrs. Bamjee, "She always treated Bamjee as if it were only a mannerism that made him appear uninterested in politics, the way some woman will persist in interpreting her husband's bad temper as an endearing gruffness hiding boundless goodwill. . . ."

See *Character, Narrator, Point of View.*

Chorus In the theater of ancient Greece, the chorus was a group of actors who commented on the action of the play. Between scenes the chorus sang and danced to musical accompaniment in the orchestra—the semicircular floor between the stage and the audience—giving insights into the message of the play. The chorus is often considered a kind of ideal spectator, representing the response of ordinary citizens to the tragic events unfolding in the play. In Sophocles' *Antigone,* the chorus represents the leading citizens of Thebes.

Climax In dramatic or narrative literature, the climax is the moment when the reader's interest and emotional intensity reach their highest point. This moment is also called the **turning point,** since it usually determines how the conflict of the story will be resolved. In Stephen Vincent Benét's "By the Waters of Babylon," John's discovery of the dead "god" is the climax of the story. As a result of his discovery, John realizes the truth about the past and the destruction of its way of life.

See *Falling Action, Plot, Rising Action.*

Comedy A comedy is a dramatic work that is light and often humorous in tone, usually ending happily with a peaceful resolution of the main conflict. *The Pen of My Aunt* is a comedy. A comedy differs from farce by having a more believable plot, more realistic characters, and less boisterous behavior.

See *Drama, Farce.*

Conflict Conflict is the struggle between opposing forces and is the basis of plot in dramatic and narrative literature. **External conflict** occurs when a character is pitted against an outside force, such as another character, a physical obstacle, or an aspect of nature or society. **Internal conflict** occurs when the struggle takes place within a character. In Abioseh Nicol's "As the Night the Day," the main character Kojo experiences internal conflict when he feels guilty about his actions and external conflict when his plan to confess his misdeeds is opposed by his classmate Bandele.

See *Antagonist, Plot, Rising Action.*

Connotation Connotation is the emotional response evoked by a word, in contrast to its **denotation,** which is its literal or dictionary meaning. *Kitten,* for example, is defined as a "young cat." However, the word also suggests, or connotes, images of softness, warmth, and playfulness. In W. P. Kinsella's "The Thrill of the Grass," the narrator describes baseball players who "recall sprawling in the lush outfields of childhood." The word *sprawling* connotes the joy and ease of childhood.

Consonance Consonance is the repetition of consonant sounds within and at the ends of words. "Last but not least" and a "stroke of luck" contain examples of consonance. Consonance, assonance, alliteration, and rhyme give writing a musical quality and may be used to unify poems and passages of prose writing. Notice the repetition of internal and final consonant s sounds in the following lines from Cathy Song's "Lost Sister."

> But in another wilderness,
> the possibilities,
> the loneliness,
> can strangulate like jungle vines.

See *Alliteration, Assonance.*

Couplet See *Sonnet*.

Denotation See *Connotation*.

Dénouement See *Falling Action*.

Description Description is writing that appeals to the senses. Good descriptive writing helps the reader to see, hear, smell, taste, or feel the subject that is described and usually relies on precise adjectives, adverbs, nouns, and verbs, as well as on vivid, original phrases. Figurative language, such as simile, metaphor, and personification, is also an important tool in description. The following passage from Tom Whitecloud's "Blue Winds Dancing" illustrates the use of vivid descriptive language.

> In my Wisconsin, the leaves change before the snows come. In the air there is the smell of wild rice and venison cooking; and when the winds come whispering through the forests, they carry the smell of rotting leaves. In the evenings, the loon calls, lonely; and the birds sing their last songs before leaving. Bears dig roots and eat late fall berries, fattening for their long winter sleep.

See *Connotation, Imagery, Style*.

Dialect A dialect is the particular variety of language spoken in a definite place by a distinct group of people. Dialects vary in pronunciation, vocabulary, colloquial expressions, sentence structure, and grammatical constructions. Writers use dialogue to establish setting, to provide local color, and to develop characters.

The following selection is from *The Adventures of Tom Sawyer* by Mark Twain. Twain effectively reproduces a dialect spoken in the Mississippi River town of Hannibal, Missouri, in about the middle of the 19th century.

> Hang the boy, can't I never learn anything? Ain't he played me tricks enough like that for me to be looking out for him by this time? But old fools is the biggest fools there is. Can't learn an old dog new tricks, as the saying is.

Dialect also plays an important role in Samuel Selvon's "When Greek Meets Greek." The main character, Ram, speaks a dialect of Caribbean English, except when he tries to convince his landlord that he is from India.

Dialogue Dialogue is written conversation between two or more characters. Dialogue is used in most forms of prose writing and also in narrative poetry. In drama the dialogue carries the story line. Realistic, well-placed dialogue enlivens narrative, descriptive, and expository prose and provides the reader with insights into characters' personalities and relationships with one another. The dialogue can also reflect the time and place in which the action takes place, giving a richness and believability to the literary work.

See *Characterization, Drama*.

Diction Diction is a writer's choice of words. Diction encompasses both vocabulary (individual words) and syntax (the order or arrangement of words). Diction can be described in terms such as formal or informal, technical or common, abstract or concrete, literal or figurative.

The writer of a scientific essay on thunderstorms, for example, would use formal, technical, and abstract words with precise denotative meanings. The essayist E. B. White, however, uses a more informal language in "Once More to the Lake," relying on words that are common and concrete, as shown by the following figurative description of a thunderstorm at a lake.

> Then the kettledrum, the snare, then the bass drum and cymbals, then crackling light against the dark, and the gods grinning and licking their chops in the hills. Afterward the calm, the rain steadily rustling in the calm lake. . . .

Drama Drama is literature that develops plot

and character through dialogue and action; in other words, drama is literature in play form. Dramas are meant to be performed by actors and actresses who appear on a stage, before radio microphones, or in front of television or movie cameras.

Unlike other forms of literature, such as fiction and poetry, a work of drama requires the collaboration of many people in order to come to life. In an important sense, a drama in printed form is an incomplete work of art. It is a skeleton that must be fleshed out by a director, actors, set designers, and others who interpret the work and stage a performance. When an audience becomes caught up in a drama and forgets to a degree the artificiality of a play, the process is called the "suspension of disbelief."

Most plays are divided into acts, with each act having an emotional peak, or climax, of its own. The acts sometimes are divided into scenes; each scene is limited to a single time and place. Shakespeare's plays all have five acts. Contemporary plays usually have two or three acts, although some have only one act. Josephine Tey's *The Pen of My Aunt* and Anton Chekhov's *The Bear* are examples of one-act plays.

See *Act, Dialogue, Props, Scene.*

Dramatic Irony See *Irony.*

Dramatic Monologue A dramatic monologue is a lyric poem in which a speaker addresses a silent or absent listener in a moment of high intensity or deep emotion, as if engaged in private conversation. To increase the dramatic impact of the poem, the poet often reveals the motivations as well as the feelings, personality, and circumstances of the speaker. "Thoughts of Hanoi" by Nguyen Thi Vinh is a dramatic monologue.

Essay An essay is a brief nonfiction composition on a single subject, usually presenting the personal views of the writer. An essay may seek to persuade, as does E. M. Forster's "Tolerance." An essay may offer a reflection on an episode in the writer's life, in the manner of E. B. White's "Once More to the Lake." Other essays, such as Roger Rosenblatt's "The Man in the Water" and Brent Staples's "Black Men and Public Space," are reflections on current events or social problems.

Some essays are formal and impersonal, and the major argument is developed systematically. Other essays are informal, personal, and less rigidly organized. The informal essay often includes anecdotes and humor.

Exposition Exposition is the part of a literary work that provides the background information necessary to understand characters and their actions. Exposition typically occurs at the beginning of a work and introduces the characters, describes the setting, and summarizes significant events that took place before the action begins. The exposition in Joan Aiken's "Searching for Summer" introduces the main characters Lily and Tom on their wedding day, tells about the bombs that had permanently darkened the sky, and announces the newlyweds' intention to find the sun.

See *Plot, Rising Action.*

Extended Metaphor In an extended metaphor two unlike things are compared in several ways. Sometimes the comparison is carried throughout a paragraph, a stanza, or an entire selection. William Shakespeare compares the world to a theatrical stage in a famous extended metaphor that begins as follows.

All the world's a stage,

And all the men and women merely players:

They have their exits and their entrances;

And one man in his time plays many parts. . . .

See *Figurative Language, Metaphor, Simile.*

External Conflict See *Conflict.*

Falling Action In a dramatic or narrative work, the falling action occurs after the climax, or high point of intensity or interest. The falling action shows the results of the major events and resolves loose ends in the plot. In Abioseh Nicol's "As the Night the Day," the falling action occurs after the main character Kojo decides to confess that he broke a laboratory thermometer—not Basu, who had been falsely blamed. We learn that Kojo's truthful account is not believed and that the innocent Basu had already confessed to the act. The final resolution or clarification of the plot is sometimes called the **dénouement.**

See *Rising Action, Climax, Plot.*

Fantasy The term *fantasy* is applied to a work of fiction characterized by extravagant imagination and disregard for the restraints of reality. The aim of a fantasy may be purely to delight or may be to make a serious comment on reality. One type of fantasy is represented by *Alice's Adventures in Wonderland* in which Lewis Carroll creates a nonexistent, unreal, imaginary world. A less extreme form of fantasy, such as Joan Aiken's "Searching for Summer," portrays characters who, within a realistic world, marginally overstep the bounds of reality. Finally, science fiction is a form of fantasy, for it extends scientific principles to new realms of time or place. An example is Ray Bradbury's "A Sound of Thunder," which is set in both the distant future and the distant past.

See *Science Fiction.*

Farce A farce is a play that prompts laughter through ridiculous situations, exaggerated behavior and language, and physical comedy. Characters are often stereotypes; that is, they conform to a fixed pattern or are defined by a single trait. In Anton Chekhov's *The Bear,* for example, Luke might be seen as a stereotype of a loyal but critical servant who tells the lady of the house more than she wants to hear.

See *Comedy, Stereotype.*

Fiction A work of fiction is a narrative that springs from the imagination of the writer, though it may be based on actual events and real people. The writer shapes his or her narrative to capture the reader's interest and to achieve desired effects. The two major types of fiction are novels and short stories. The basic elements of fiction are character, setting, plot, and theme.

See *Novel, Short Story.*

Figurative Language Figurative language is language that communicates ideas beyond the literal meanings of the words. Although what is said is not literally true, it stimulates vivid pictures or concepts in the mind of the reader. For example, the narrator in Alice Walker's "Everyday Use" says that Dee's hair "stands up straight like the wool on a sheep. It is black as night and around the edges are two long pigtails that rope about like small lizards disappearing behind her eyes." Obviously, Dee's pigtails do not literally move like lizards, but the passage vividly suggests the look of Dee's hair.

Figurative language appears in poetry and prose as well as in spoken language. The general term *figurative language* includes specific figures of speech, such as simile, metaphor, personification, and hyperbole.

See *Hyperbole, Metaphor, Personification, Simile, Understatement.*

First-Person Point of View
See *Point of View.*

Flashback A flashback is an account of a conversation, an episode, or an event that happened before the beginning of a story. Often a flashback interrupts the chronological flow of a story to give information that can help readers to understand a character's present situation. Tolstoy's "After the Ball" is a story told almost entirely in flashback. The events that happened to the main character Ivan as a young man help readers to understand his present situation and beliefs. Similarly, flashbacks play a vital role in Louise Erdrich's "The Leap," in which the narrator recounts her memories of her mother.

Foil A foil is a character who provides a striking contrast to another character. By using a foil, a writer calls attention to certain traits possessed by a main character or simply enhances a character by contrast. In Anton Chekhov's *The Bear*, for example, the dutiful servant Luke is a foil for Smirnov, the loud, rude, and quarrelsome visitor. In *The Ring of General Macías*, the unsophisticated Cleto is a foil for the suave and refined Andrés, the captain of the revolutionary soldiers.

Foreshadowing Foreshadowing is a writer's use of hints or clues to indicate events that will occur later in a narrative. This technique often creates suspense and prepares the reader for what is to come. Mark Twain's "The Californian's Tale" and Guy de Maupassant's "Two Friends" both contain elements of foreshadowing.

Form At its simplest, the word *form* refers to the physical arrangement of words in a poem—the length and placement of the lines and the grouping of lines into stanzas. The term can also be used to refer to other types of patterning in poetry, anything from rhythm and other sound patterns to the design of a traditional poetic type, such as a sonnet or dramatic monologue. Finally, *form* can be used as a synonym for *genre*, which refers to literary categories ranging from the broad (short story, novel) to the narrowly defined (sonnet, dramatic monologue).

Frame Story A frame story exists when a story is told within a narrative setting or frame—hence, there is a story within a story. This storytelling technique has been used for over one thousand years and has employed in famous works such as *One Thousand and One Arabian Nights* and Geoffrey Chaucer's *The Canterbury Tales*. In Rachel de Queiroz's "Metonymy" the narrator tells a story within a story in order to illustrate the meaning of the title.

Free Verse Free verse is poetry that does not contain regular patterns of rhyme and meter. The lines in free verse often flow more naturally than do rhymed, metrical lines and thus achieve a rhythm more like everyday human speech. Much of the poetry written in the 20th century is free verse.

An example of free verse is the following poem by Walt Whitman, the 19th-century poet generally credited with originating this type of poetry. The poem was written as a tribute to Abraham Lincoln.

> This dust was once the man,
> Gentle, plain, just and resolute, under
>   whose cautious hand,
> Against the foulest crime in history known
>   in any land or age,
> Was saved the Union of these States.

Hero The word *hero* has come to mean the main character in a literary work. A traditional hero possesses "good" qualities that enable him or her to triumph over an antagonist who is "bad."

The term *tragic hero,* first used by the Greek philosopher Aristotle, refers to a central character in a drama who is dignified or noble. According to Aristotle, a tragic hero possesses a defect, or **tragic flaw,** that brings about or contributes to his or her downfall. This flaw may be poor judgment, pride, weakness, or an excess of an admirable quality. The tragic hero, noted Aristotle, recognizes his or her own flaw and its consequences but only after it is too late to change the course of events. Creon in *Antigone* may be considered as a tragic hero, though some critics also apply the term to Antigone as well.

The term *cultural hero* refers to a hero who represents the values or his or her culture. King Arthur, for example, represents the physical courage, moral leadership, and loyalty that were valued in Anglo-Saxon society. Antigone can also be considered a cultural hero because her sense of duty to family and the gods, as well as her courage, reflect the values of ancient Greece.

See *Tragedy.*

Humor In literature there are three basic types of humor, all of which may involve exaggeration or irony. **Humor of situation** is derived from the plot of a work. It usually involves exaggerated events or situational irony, which occurs when something happens that is different from what is expected. **Humor of character** is often based on exaggerated personalities or on characters who fail to recognize their own flaws, a form of dramatic irony. **Humor of language** may include sarcasm, exaggeration, puns, or verbal irony, which occurs when what is said is not what is meant. Samuel Selvon's "When Greek Meets Greek" contains all three types of humor, as does Anton Chekhov's *The Bear*.

Hyperbole Hyperbole is a figure of speech in which the truth is exaggerated for emphasis or for humorous effect. The expression "I'm so hungry I could eat a horse" is an example of hyperbole. The following excerpt from John Steinbeck's *The Acts of King Arthur and His Noble Knights* also illustrates hyperbole. In this scene the knights of the Round Table are taking turns praising Lancelot, who is bored by their extravagant claims: "And he [Lancelot] vaguely heard his strength favorably compared with elephants, his ferocity with lions, his agility with deer, his cleverness with foxes, his beauty with the stars. . . ."

Iambic Pentameter See *Meter*.

Imagery Imagery describes words and phrases that re-create vivid sensory experiences for the reader. Because sight is the most highly developed sense, the majority of images are visual. Imagery may also appeal to the senses of smell, hearing, taste, and touch. Effective writers of both prose and poetry frequently use imagery that appeals to more than one sense simultaneously. In D. H. Lawrence's "Piano," the phrase "the boom of the tingling strings" appeals to the senses of hearing and touch, while "pressing the small, poised feet" appeals to the senses of sight and touch. The following lines from Nguyen Thi Vinh's "Thoughts of Hanoi" appeal to the senses of sight and hearing.

> Stainless blue sky,
> jubilant voices of children
> stumbling through the alphabet,
> village greybeards strolling to the temple. . . .

Internal Conflict See *Conflict*.

Irony Irony is a contrast between what is expected and what actually exists or happens. There are three basic types of irony.

Situational irony occurs when a character or the reader expects one thing to happen but something entirely different occurs. In Amy Tan's "Two Kinds," the narrator expects to play the piano like a prodigy at the talent show. In actuality, however, she performs dismally and embarrasses her family.

Verbal irony occurs when someone says one thing but means another. In *The Ring of General Macías*, Raquel insults the two peasant soldiers by saying, "What a magnificent army you have. So clever. I'm sure you must win many victories." Raquel's comment belittles their response to the noise of a scurrying rabbit, which they mistake for enemy soldiers.

Dramatic irony refers to the contrast between what a character knows and what the reader or audience knows. For example, the German soldier in *The Pen of My Aunt* comes to believe that he has mistakenly detained the nephew of the influential Madame. The audience learns, however, that the soldier has apprehended—and released—a member of the resistance.

See *Hyperbole, Understatement*.

Legend A legend is a story handed down from the past, especially one that is popularly believed to be based on historical events. The story of the rise and fall of King Arthur is a famous example of a legend. Though legends often incorporate supernatural elements and magical deeds, they claim to be the story of a real human being and are often set in a particular time and place. These characteristics separate a legend from a myth.

See *Myth*.

Lyric In ancient Greece, the lyre was a musical instrument, and the lyric became the name for a song accompanied by music. In ordinary speech the words of songs are still called lyrics.

In literature, a lyric is any short poem that presents a single speaker who expresses his or her innermost thoughts and feelings. In a love lyric, such as Amy Lowell's "Taxi" or Aleksandr Pushkin's "To," the speaker expresses romantic love. In other lyrics a speaker may meditate on nature or explore personal issues, such as those addressed by Juan Ramón Jiménez's "I Am Not I" and José Martí's *Simple Poetry*.

Magical Realism Magical realism refers to a style of writing that often includes exaggeration, unusual humor, magical and bizarre events, dreams that come true, and superstitions that prove warranted. Magical realism differs from pure fantasy in combining fantastic elements with realistic elements such as recognizable characters, believable dialogue, a true-to-life setting, a matter-of-fact tone, and a plot that sometimes contains historic events. Julio Cortázar's "House Taken Over" and Jorges Borges "The Meeting" are examples of magical realism.

Metaphor A metaphor is a form of figurative language that makes a comparison between two things that have something in common. Unlike a simile, a metaphor does not use the words *like* or *as;* instead the comparison is suggested rather than directly expressed.

In the following lines from Sonnet 73 by William Shakespeare, the poet draws a comparison between old age and approaching winter.

> That time of year thou mayst in me behold
> When yellow leaves, or none, or few, do hang
> Upon those boughs which shake against
>   the cold,

This metaphor helps the reader to perceive the similarity between a person approaching the cold of death and a tree enduring the cold of winter.

See *Extended Metaphor, Figurative Language, Simile*.

Meter Meter is the repetition of a regular rhythmic unit in a line of poetry. The meter of a poem is like the beat of a song; it establishes a predictable means of emphasis.

Each unit of meter is known as a **foot,** with each foot having one stressed and one or two unstressed syllables. The four basic types of metrical feet are the **iamb,** an unstressed syllable followed by a stressed syllable (˘ ´); the **trochee,** a stressed syllable followed by an unstressed syllable (´ ˘); the **anapest,** two unstressed syllables followed by a stressed syllable (˘ ˘ ´); and the **dactyl,** a stressed syllable followed by two unstressed syllables (´ ˘ ˘).

A line of poetry is named not only for the type of meter but also for the number of feet in the line. The most common metrical names are **trimeter,** a three-foot line; **tetrameter,** a four-foot line; **pentameter,** a five-foot line; and **hexameter,** a six-foot line.

These lines from Edna St. Vincent Millay's "Sonnet 30" illustrate **iambic pentameter,** the most common form of meter in the English language.

> Nŏr yét / ă flóat / ĭng spár / tŏ mén / thăt sínk
> Ănd rĭse / ănd sínk / ănd rĭse / ănd sínk / ăgaín;

Minor Characters See *Character*.

Monologue See *Soliloquy*.

Mood Mood is the feeling, or atmosphere, that a writer creates for the reader. The writer's use of connotation, imagery, and figurative language, as well as sound and rhythm, develop the mood of a selection. Notice how Tom Whitecloud makes use of all of these techniques in this passage from "Blue Winds Dancing" to create a peaceful, joyous mood.

> I walk along the trail to the lodge, watching the northern lights forming in the heavens. White waving ribbons that seem to pulsate with the rhythm of the drums. Clean snow creaks beneath my feet, and a soft wind sighs through the trees, singing to me. Everything seems to say, "Be happy! You are home now—you are free.

See *Connotation, Diction, Imagery, Figurative Language, Style.*

Myth A myth is a traditional story, usually concerning some superhuman being or unlikely event, that was once widely believed to be true. Frequently, myths attempt to explain natural phenomena, such as solar and lunar eclipses and the cycle of the seasons. For some peoples, myths were both a kind of science and a religion. In addition, myths served as literature and entertainment, just as they do for modern-day audiences.

The most famous myths, such as the stories of Theseus and Hercules, originated among the ancient Greeks and Romans. Norse mythology, consisting of myths from Scandinavia and Germany, is also important classical literature. Indian peoples throughout North America have produced fascinating myths of various kinds, as have the peoples of Africa and Latin America.

See *Legend.*

Narrative A narrative is any type of writing that is primarily concerned with relating an event or a series of events. A narrative can be imaginary, as is a short story and novel, or it can be factual, as is a newspaper account or a work of history.

See *Fiction, Nonfiction, Novel, Plot, Short Story.*

Narrative Poem A narrative poem tells a story. Like a short story, a narrative poem has characters, a setting, a plot, and a point of view, all of which combine to develop a theme. Epics, such as Homer's *Iliad* and Virgil's *Aeneid,* are narrative poems, as are ballads.

Nonfiction Nonfiction is prose writing that is about real people, places, and events. Unlike fiction, nonfiction is largely concerned with factual information, although the writer shapes the information according to his or her purpose and viewpoint. Nonfiction includes an amazingly diverse range of writing; newspaper articles, cookbooks, letters, movie reviews, editorials, speeches, true-life adventure stories—all are considered nonfiction.

See *Autobiography, Biography, Essay, Fiction.*

Novel The novel is an extended work of fiction. Like a short story, a novel is essentially the product of a writer's imagination. The most obvious difference between a novel and a short story is length. Because the novel is considerably longer, a novelist can develop a wider range of characters and a more complex plot.

Onomatopoeia The word *onomatopoeia* literally means "name-making." It is the process of creating or using words that imitate sounds. The *buzz* of the bee, the *honk* of the car horn, the *peep* of the chick are all onomatopoetic, or echoic, words.

Onomatopoeia as a literary technique goes beyond the use of simple echoic words. Writers, particularly poets, choose words whose sounds suggest their denotative and connotative meanings: for example, *whisper, kick, gargle, gnash,* and *clatter.*

Paradox A paradox is a seemingly contradictory or absurd statement that may nonetheless suggest an important truth. Shakespeare employed a paradox in *Julius Caesar.*

Cowards die many times before their deaths;
The valiant never taste of death but once.

The statement suggests that cowards' fearful and constant anticipation of death is worse than death itself. Juan Ramón Jiménez's poem "I Am Not I" reflects upon the paradox expressed in the title, which suggests that the speaker feels separated from himself.

Parody A parody imitates or mocks another serious work or type of literature. Like caricature in art, parody in literature mimics a subject or a style. The purpose of a parody may be to ridicule through broad humor. On the other hand, a parody may broaden understanding or add insight to the original work. Some parodies are even written in tribute to a work of literature.

Personification Personification is a figure of speech in which human qualities are attributed to an object, animal, or idea. Writers use personification to make images and feelings concrete for the reader. In Dahlia Ravikovitch's "Pride," human physical attributes are given to rocks in the phrases "they lie on their backs" and "the rock has an open wound."

See *Figurative Language, Imagery, Metaphor, Simile.*

Plot The word *plot* refers to the chain of related events that take place in a story. The plot is the writer's blueprint for what happens, when it happens, and to whom it happens. Usually, the events of a plot progress because of a **conflict,** or struggle between opposing forces.

Although there are many types of plots, most include the following stages.

- **Exposition** The exposition lays the groundwork for the plot and provides the reader with essential background information. Characters are introduced, the setting is described, and the plot begins to unfold. Although the exposition generally appears at the opening of a story, it may also occur later in the narrative.

- **Rising Action** As the story progresses, complications usually arise, causing difficulties for the main characters and making the conflict more difficult to resolve. As the characters struggle to find solutions to the conflict, suspense builds.

- **Climax** The climax is the turning point of the action, the moment when interest and intensity reach their peak. The climax of a story usually involves an important event, decision, or discovery that affects the final outcome.

- **Falling Action** The falling action consists of the events that occur after the climax. Often, the conflict is resolved, and the intensity of the action subsides. Sometimes this phase of the plot is called the **dénouement** (dā′nōō-mäN′), from a French word that means "untying." In the dénouement, also known as the resolution, the tangles of the plot are untied and mysteries are solved.

See *Climax, Conflict, Falling Action, Rising Action.*

Poetry Poetry is language arranged in lines. Like other forms of literature, poetry attempts to re-create emotions and experiences. Poetry, however, is usually more condensed and suggestive than prose. Because poetry frequently does not include the kind of detail and explanation found in prose, poetry tends to leave more to the reader's imagination. Poetry also may require more work on the reader's part to unlock meaning.

Poems often are divided into stanzas, or groups of lines. The stanzas in a poem may contain the same number of lines or they may vary in length. Some poems have definite patterns of meter and rhyme. Others rely more on the sounds of words and less on fixed rhythms and rhyme schemes. The use of figurative language is also common in poetry.

See *Form, Meter, Repetition, Rhyme, Rhythm.*

Point of View Point of view refers to the narrative method used in a short story, novel, or nonfiction selection. The two basic points of view are first-person and third-person.

When a character within a selection describes the action as a participant, in his or her own words, the writer is using the **first-person point of view.** A first-person narrator tends to involve the reader in the story and to communicate a sense of immediacy and personal concern. Tim O'Brien's "On the Rainy River" and Alice Walker's "Everyday Use" are examples of the first-person point of view.

Third-person point of view occurs when a narrator outside the action describes events and characters. In **third-person omniscient point of view,** the narrator is omniscient, or all-knowing, and can see into the minds of more than one character. The use of a third-person narrator gives the writer tremendous flexibility and provides the reader with access to all the characters and to events that may be occurring simultaneously. Yukio Mishima's "The Pearl" is told from a third-person omniscient point of view. In this story, the reader not only sees how the different characters react to the loss of the pearl but have access to their thoughts and feelings. The narrator also shows what each character does after Mrs. Sasaki's party, even though these events take place in different places and occur at approximately the same time.

In the **third-person limited point of view** events are related through the eyes of one character. The narrator describes only that character's feelings and events that he or she witnesses. Bernard Malamud's "The First Seven Years" and R. K. Narayan's "Like the Sun" are examples of the third-person limited point of view. In the Malamud story, the reader sees all events through the eyes of Feld the shoemaker, while in the Narayan story, everything is filtered through the perspective of the main character, Sekhar.

Props The word *prop*, an abbreviation of *property*, refers to the physical objects that are used in a stage production. In Josephina Niggli's *The Ring of General Macías,* the props include furniture, a wine decanter and glasses, and a bottle of poison. Props help to establish the setting for a play.

See *Drama*.

Protagonist The central character in a story or play is called the protagonist. The protagonist is always involved in the central conflict of the plot and often changes during the course of the work. Sometimes more than one character can be the protagonist of a story. The protagonist in R. K. Narayan's "Like the Sun" is the character Sekhar, who encounters problems while seeking to tell the absolute truth. The protagonist in Doris Lessing's "No Witchcraft for Sale" is Gideon, the servant who displays his knowledge of medicinal herbs.

See *Antagonist*.

Quatrain A quatrain is a four-line stanza, or unit of poetry. The most common stanza in English poetry, the quatrain can display a variety of meters and rhyme schemes. The following quatrain by English poet William Savage Landor follows a typical *a b a b* rhyme scheme.

I strove with none; for none was worth my strife, *a*
Nature I loved, and, next to Nature, Art; *b*
I warmed both hands before the fire of life; *a*
It sinks, and I am ready to depart. *b*

See *Meter, Poetry, Rhyme, Sonnet, Stanza*.

Realism In literature, realism has both a general meaning and a special meaning. As a general term, realism refers to any effort to offer an accurate and detailed portrayal of actual life. Thus, critics talk about Shakespeare's realistic portrayals of his characters and praise the medieval poet Chaucer for his realistic descriptions of people from different social classes.

More specifically, realism also refers to a

literary method developed in the 19th century. The realists based their writing on careful observations of their contemporary life, often focusing on the middle or lower classes. They attempted to present life objectively and honestly, without the sentimentality or idealism that had characterized earlier literature. Typically, realists developed their settings in great detail in an effort to re-create a specific time and place for the reader. Guy de Maupassant, Leo Tolstoy, and Mark Twain, and Sarah Orne Jewett are all considered realists.

Repetition Repetition is a literary technique in which a sound, word, phrase, or line is repeated for emphasis. Note the use of repetition in the following lines from Edna St. Vincent Millay's "Sonnet 30."

> Love is not all; it is not meat nor drink
> Nor slumber nor a roof against the rain;
> Nor yet a floating spar to men that sink
> And rise and sink and rise and sink again;

Resolution See *Falling Action.*

Rhyme Words rhyme when the sound of their accented vowels and all succeeding sounds are identical, as in *tether* and *together.* For **true rhyme,** the consonants that precede the vowels must be different, as in Shakespeare's rhyming of *day* and *May* in "Sonnet 18." Rhyme that occurs at the ends of lines of poetry is called **end rhyme.** End rhyme that is not exact but approximate is called **off rhyme,** as in *other* and *bother.* Rhyme that occurs within a single line, as in the following example from "The Raven" by Edgar Allan Poe, is called **internal rhyme.**

> Once upon a midnight dreary, while a pondered weak and weary,
> Over many a quaint and curious volume of forgotten lore,
> While I nodded, nearly napping, suddenly there came a tapping,
> As of someone gently rapping, rapping at my chamber door.

A **rhyme scheme** is the pattern of end rhyme in a poem. The pattern is charted by assigning a letter of the alphabet, beginning with the letter *a,* to each line. Lines that rhyme are given the same letter. The following example from Shakespeare's "Sonnet 18" has an *a b a b* rhyme scheme.

> But thy eternal summer shall not fade,   a
> Nor lose possession of that fair thou owest;   b
> Nor shall Death brag thou wander'st in his shade,   a
> When in eternal lines to time thou growest: b

Rhythm Rhythm refers to the pattern or beat of stressed and unstressed syllables in a line of poetry. Poets use rhythm to bring out the musical quality of language, to emphasize ideas, to create mood, and to reinforce subject matter.
See *Meter.*

Rising Action Rising action refers to the part of the plot in which complications develop and the conflict intensifies, building to the climax, or highest point of interest and intensity in the plot. The rising action in Anton Chekhov's *The Bear* describes the growing conflict between Smirnov and Mrs. Popov.
See *Climax, Falling Action, Plot.*

Romance A romance refers to any imaginative story concerned with noble heroes, chivalric codes of honor, passionate love, daring deeds, and supernatural events. Writers of romances tend to idealize their heroes as well as the eras in which the heroes live. Medieval romances, such as Malory's *Le Morte d'Arthur,* are stories of kings, knights, and ladies who are motivated by love, religious faith, or simply a desire for adventure. Such romances are comparatively lighthearted in tone and loose in structure, containing many episodes. Usually the main character has a series of adventures while on a quest to accomplish some goal.

Satire Satire is a literary technique in which ideas, customs, behaviors, or institutions are

HANDBOOK OF LITERARY TERMS

ridiculed for the purpose of improving society. Satire may be gently witty, mildly abrasive, or bitterly critical, and it often uses exaggeration to force readers to see something in a more critical light. Luisa Valenzuela's "The Censors" is a satire that criticizes not only censorship but government oppression and the citizens who cooperate with such practices.

Scene A scene is a subdivision of an act in drama. Each scene usually establishes a different time or place. In Shakespeare's *Julius Caesar,* for example, the first scene of Act One takes place at a public celebration on a street in Rome. The last scene in Act Five takes place on a battlefield.

Science Fiction Science fiction is prose writing that presents the possibilities of the future, using known scientific data and theories as well as the creative imagination of the writer. Most science fiction comments on present-day society through the writer's fictional conception of a future society. Stephen Vincent Benét's "By the Waters of Babylon," for example, warns about the danger of modern warfare and the potential for the destruction of our entire civilization. Ray Bradbury's "A Sound of Thunder" shows how all aspects of nature are interrelated and that human interference with the ecological cycle can lead to disaster.

Setting Setting is the time and place of the action of a story. In many stories, setting plays an important role. The prison setting of Bessie Head's "The Prisoner Who Wore Glasses" reflects the racial injustices of South African society, while the desolate frontier setting of Mark Twain's "The Californian's Tale" enables the reader to understand the loneliness of the characters and their need for companionship.

Shakespearean Sonnet See *Sonnet.*

Short Story A short story is a work of fiction that can be read in one sitting. Generally, a short story develops one major conflict. The four basic elements of a short story are setting, character, plot, and theme.

A short story must be unified; all the elements must work together to produce a total effect. This unity of effect is reinforced through an appropriate title and through the use of other literary devices, such as symbolism and irony.

See *Character, Conflict, Plot, Setting, Theme.*

Simile A simile is a stated comparison between two things that are actually unlike but that have something in common. Like metaphors, similes are figures of speech, but whereas a metaphor implies a comparison, a simile expresses the comparison clearly by the use of the words *like* or *as*. In W. P. Kinsella's "The Thrill of the Grass" the narrator describes his shadow as being "black as an umbrella." This simile links the shadow and the umbrella by their common color.

See *Figurative Language, Metaphor.*

Situational Irony See *Irony.*

Soliloquy In a dramatic work, soliloquy is a speech in which a character speaks his or her private thoughts aloud. The character is almost always on stage alone and generally appears to be unaware of the presence of an audience. The plays of William Shakespeare frequently include soliloquies.

Sonnet A sonnet is a lyric poem of 14 lines, commonly written in iambic pentameter. For centuries the sonnet has been a popular form, for it is long enough to permit development of a complex idea yet short and structured enough to challenge any poet's artistic skills.

The Shakespearean, or English, sonnet is sometimes also called the Elizabethan sonnet. It consists of three quatrains, or four-line units, and a final **couplet,** or two-line unit, which reflect the logical organization of the poem. The typical rhyme scheme is *a b a b c d c d e f e f g g.* In the English sonnet, the rhymed couplet at the end of the sonnet provides a final commentary on the subject developed in the preceding three quatrains. The poems by William Shakespeare and Edna St. Vincent Millay included in this text are sonnets.

Some poets have written a series of related sonnets that have the same subject. These are called sonnet sequences, or sonnet cycles. Toward the end of the 15th century, writing sonnets became fashionable, with a common subject being love for a beautiful but unattainable woman. Shakespeare's sonnets are the most famous of all sonnet sequences.

See *Meter, Quatrain, Rhythm, Rhyme, Poetry.*

Speaker The speaker in a poem is the voice that "talks" to the reader, similar to the narrator in fiction. Speaker and poet are not necessarily synonymous. Often a poet creates a speaker with a distinct identity in order to achieve a particular effect. In Nguyen Thi Vinh's "Thoughts of Hanoi," the speaker is a male Vietnamese soldier fighting in a civil war, while the poet is female.

Stage Directions The stage directions in a dramatic script serve as a kind of instructional manual for the director, actors, and stage crew as well as the general reader. Often the stage directions are printed in italic type, and they may be enclosed in parentheses or brackets.

Stage directions serve a number of important functions. They may describe the scenery, or setting. For example, in *The Pen of My Aunt,* the stage directions identify the country house where events unfold and the historical era, the Nazi occupation of France. Directions may also describe the props that are used during a performance. Stage directions may describe lighting, costumes, music, sound effects, or, in the case of film productions, camera angles and shots. Most important, the stage directions usually provide hints to the performers on how the characters look, move, and speak.

Stanza A stanza is a group of lines that form a unit of poetry. The stanza is roughly comparable to the paragraph in prose. In traditional poems, the stanzas usually have the same number of lines and often have the same rhyme scheme and meter as well. In the 20th century, poets have experimented more freely with stanza form than did earlier poets, sometimes writing poems that have no stanza breaks at all.

Stereotype In literature, simplified or stock characters who conform to a fixed pattern or are defined by a single trait are called stereotypes. Such characters do not usually demonstrate the complexities of real people. Familiar stereotypes in popular literature include the absent-minded professor, the dumb athlete, and the busybody. In Chekhov's *The Bear,* the servant Luke might be seen as a stereotype of a loyal but critical servant who tells the lady of the house more than she wants to hear.

See *Farce.*

Structure Structure is the way in which the parts of a work of literature are put together. In poetry, structure refers to the arrangement of words and lines to produce a desired effect. A common structural unit in poetry is the stanza, of which there are numerous types. In prose, structure is the arrangement of larger units or parts of a selection. Paragraphs, for example, are a basic unit in prose, as are chapters in novels and acts in plays. The structure of a poem, short story, novel, play, or nonfiction selection usually emphasizes certain important aspects of content.

Style Style is the way in which a piece of literature is written. Style refers not to what is said but to how it is said. Elements such as word choice, sentence length, tone, imagery, and use of dialogue contribute to a writer's personal style. Sarah Orne Jewett's style in "A White Heron," for example, might be described as a blend of the poetic and realistic. Through her use of sensory details, regional dialect, and a sensitive narrator, she creates both an accurate and an admiring picture of the main character and her world. Frank O'Connor's style in "The Study of History" might be described as matter-of-fact and humorously understated, reflecting the engaging personality of its youthful narrator.

Surprise Ending A surprise ending is an unexpected twist in plot at the conclusion of a story. The conclusion of Guy de Maupassant's "Two Friends" surprises the reader because earlier events in the story had suggested a different outcome.

Suspense Suspense is the tension or excitement felt by the reader as he or she becomes involved in a story and eager to know the outcome of the conflict. In Stephen Vincent Benét's "By the Waters of Babylon," the reader wants to know if John will survive his journey, what he will discover, and what understandings he will gain from his experiences.

Symbol A symbol is a person, place, or object that represents something beyond itself. For instance, a star on a door represents fame; a star pinned to the shirt of a sheriff stands for authority and power. Symbols can succinctly communicate complicated, emotionally rich ideas. A flag, for example, can symbolize patriotism and a national heritage. The cranes in Hwang Sunwŏn's story of the same name symbolize the childhood friendship of the two main characters, as well as peace and tranquillity. The medicinal plant in Doris Lessing's "No Witchcraft for Sale" symbolizes native African culture.

Theme The theme is the central idea or message in a work of literature. Theme should not be confused with subject, or what the work is about. Rather, theme is a perception about life or human nature shared with the reader. Sometimes the theme is directly stated within a work; at other times it is implied, and the reader must infer the theme.

One way to discover the theme of a work of literature is to think about what happens to the central characters. The importance of those events, stated in terms that apply to all human beings, is often the theme. In several selections throughout this book, for example, the theme involves the need for people to accept one another despite differences in culture.

Third-Person Narration See *Point of View*.

Title The title of a literary work often reflects the meaning of the work. For example, the title of Nadine Gordimer's "A Chip of Glass Ruby" refers to a traditional Indian adornment. When Mrs. Bamjee was a girl, her mother had fixed a glass ruby in her daughter's nostril, "but she [Mrs. Bamjee] had abandoned that adornment . . . long ago." On one hand, the title suggests her rejection of a narrowly defined traditional role. On the other hand, the title suggests the husband's frustrated desire for a wife solely focused on traditional duties.

Tone Tone is the attitude a writer takes toward a subject. The language and details a writer chooses help to create the tone, which might be playful, serious, bitter, angry, or detached, among other possibilities. To identify the tone of a work of literature, you might find it helpful to read the work aloud, as if giving a dramatic reading before an audience. The emotions that you convey in reading should give you hints as to the tone of the work.

Unlike mood, which refers to the emotional response of the reader to a work, tone reflects the feelings of the writer. For example, Roger Rosenblatt's "The Man in the Water" exhibits a philosophic, somber tone, reflecting the writer's efforts to draw a lesson from a tragic yet heroic event. Luisa Valenzuela's "The Censors" has an ironic, amusing tone, showing the writer's disapproval of censorship and governmental oppression.

See *Connotation, Diction, Mood, Style*.

Tragedy In broad terms tragedy is literature, especially drama, in which actions and events turn out disastrously for the main character or characters. In tragedy the main characters, and sometimes other involved characters and innocent bystanders as well, are destroyed. Usually the destruction is death, as in Shakespeare's *Julius Caesar* or Sophocles' *Antigone*. Some tragedies, however, end with the main characters alive but in a devastated condition. Tragic heroes evoke both pity and fear in readers or viewers—pity because they feel sorry for the characters and fear because they realize that the problems and struggles faced by the characters are perhaps a necessary part of human life. At the end of a tragedy, a reader or viewer generally feels a sense of waste, because humans who were in some way superior have been destroyed.

See *Hero*.

Tragic Flaw See *Hero*.

Tragic Hero See *Hero*.

True-Life Adventure A true-life adventure is a nonfiction account of heroic deeds or exciting excursions, usually organized chronologically. Often, a true-life adventure is narrated from the first-person point of view, presenting the experience as it happened to the writer, as illustrated by Yossi Ghinsberg's *Back from Tuichi*. A true-life adventure may also be written from a third-person point of view, as reported to the writer.

Turning Point See *Climax*.

Understatement Understatement is the technique of creating emphasis by saying less than is actually or literally true. As such, it is the opposite of exaggeration, or hyperbole. Understatement can be a biting form of sarcasm or verbal irony. Jonathan Swift, the 18th-century English writer best known for *Gulliver's Travels*, often used understatement as a satiric weapon. For example, Swift wrote, "Last week I saw a woman flayed [skinned alive], and you will hardly believe how much it altered her appearance for the worse."

See *Hyperbole, Irony*.

Verbal Irony See *Irony*.

Voice The term *voice* refers to a writer's unique use of language that allows a reader to "hear" a human personality in his or her writing. The elements of style that determine a writer's voice include sentence structure, diction, and tone. For example, some writers are noted for their reliance on short, simple sentences, while others make use of long, complicated ones. Certain writers use concrete words, such as *lake* or *cold*, which name things that you can see, hear, feel, taste, or smell. Others prefer abstract terms like *memory*, which name things that cannot be perceived with the senses. A writer's tone also leaves its imprint on his or her personal voice.

The term can be applied to the narrator of a selection, as well as the writer. For example, in Alice Walker's "Everyday Use" the narrator establishes her personality through her manner of narration. She emerges as a strong, down-to-earth character with a gift for descriptive language, as shown by her following account of her daughter exiting from a car.

> Dee next. A dress down to the ground, in this hot weather. A dress so loud it hurts my eyes. There are yellows and oranges enough to throw back the light of the sun. I feel my whole face warming from the heat waves it throws out. Earrings gold, too, and hanging down to her shoulders. Bracelets dangling and making noises when she moves her arm up to shake the folds of the dress out of her armpits. The dress is loose and flows, and as she walks closer, I like it. . . .

1 The Writing Process

The writing process consists of four stages: prewriting, drafting, revising and editing, and publishing and reflecting. As the graphic to the right shows, these stages are not steps that you must complete in a set order. Rather, you may return to any one at any time in your writing process, using feedback from your readers along the way.

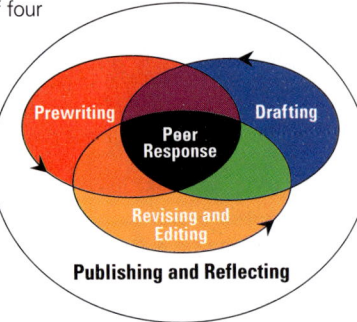

1.1 Prewriting

In the prewriting stage, you explore your ideas and discover what you want to write about.

Finding Ideas for Writing

Ideas for writing can come from just about anywhere: experiences, memories, conversations, dreams, or imaginings. Try one or more of the following techniques to help you find and explore a writing topic.

Personal Techniques
Practice imaging, or trying to remember mainly sensory details about a subject—its look, sound, feel, taste, and smell.
Complete a knowledge inventory to discover what you already know about a subject.
Browse through magazines, newspapers, and on-line bulletin boards for ideas.
Start a clip file of articles that you want to save for future reference. Be sure to label each clip with source information.

Sharing Techniques
With a group, brainstorm a topic by trying to come up with as many ideas as you can without stopping to critique or examine them.
Interview someone who knows a great deal about your topic.

1018 WRITING HANDBOOK

Writing Techniques
After freewriting on a topic, try looping, or choosing your best idea for more freewriting. Repeat the loop at least once.
Make a list to help you organize ideas, examine them, or identify areas for further research.

Graphic Techniques
Create a pro-and-con chart to compare the positive and negative aspects of an idea or course of action.
Use a cluster map or tree diagram to explore subordinate ideas that relate to your general topic or central idea.

Determining Your Purpose

At some time during your writing process, you need to consider your purpose, or general reason, for writing. For example, your purpose may be one of the following: to express yourself, to entertain, to inform, to describe, to analyze, or to persuade. To clarify your purpose, ask yourself questions like these:

- Why did I choose to write about my topic?
- What aspects of the topic mean the most to me?
- What do I want others to think or feel after they read my writing?

Identifying Your Audience

Knowing who will read your writing can help you clarify your purpose, focus your topic, and choose the details and tone that will best communicate your ideas. As you think about your readers, ask yourself questions like these:

- What does my audience already know about my topic?
- What will they be most interested in?
- What language is most appropriate for this audience?

1.2 Drafting

In the drafting stage, you put your ideas on paper and allow them to develop and change as you write.

There's no right or wrong way to draft. Sometimes you might be adventuresome and dive right into your writing. At other times, you might draft slowly, planning carefully beforehand. You can combine aspects of these approaches to suit yourself and your writing projects.

 LINK TO LITERATURE

Personal experiences are often the richest source of ideas for writing. Elie Wiesel's painful memories of his time in a Nazi concentration camp during World War II informed the world about one of the darkest periods in history. In the excerpt from *Night,* page 308, notice how details add a sense of "you are there" immediacy to the account of endurance during the Holocaust.

LINK TO LITERATURE

Alice Walker, author of "Everyday Use," page 110, realizes the importance of both Standard English and African-American dialect. "I use them both naturally," Walker has said. "In speaking to you, I speak in the language we both understand, and it's perfectly easy to do. But when I'm speaking to my mother, it's in black folk English. . . . It's very cozy; it immediately creates a world."

Discovery drafting is a good approach when you've gathered some information on your topic or have a rough idea for writing but are not quite sure how you feel about your subject or what exactly you want to say. You just plunge into your draft and let your ideas lead you where they will. After finishing a discovery draft, you may decide to start another draft, do more prewriting, or revise your first draft.

Planned drafting may work better for research reports, critical reviews, and other kinds of formal writing. Try thinking through a writing plan or making an outline before you begin drafting. Then, as you write, you can develop your ideas and fill in the details.

1.3 Using Peer Response

The suggestions and comments your peers or classmates make about your writing are called peer response.

Talking with peers about your writing can help you discover what you want to say or how well you have communicated your ideas. You can ask a peer reader for help at any point in the writing process. For example, your peers can help you develop a topic, narrow your focus, discover confusing passages, or organize your writing.

Questions for Your Peer Readers

You can help your peer readers provide you with the most useful kinds of feedback by following these guidelines:

- Tell readers where you are in the writing process. Are you still trying out ideas, or have you completed a draft?
- Ask questions that will help you get specific information about your writing. Open-ended questions that require more than yes-or-no answers are more likely to give you information you can use as you revise.
- Give your readers plenty of time to respond thoughtfully to your writing.
- Encourage your readers to be honest when they respond to your work. It's OK if you don't agree with them—you always get to decide which changes to make.

The chart on the following page explains different peer-response techniques you might use when you're ready to share your work with others.

Technique	When to Use It	Questions to Ask
Sharing	Use this when you are just exploring ideas or when you want to celebrate the completion of a piece of writing.	Will you please read or listen to my writing without criticizing or making suggestions afterward?
Summarizing	Use this when you want to know if your main idea or goals are clear.	What do you think I'm saying? What's my main idea or message?
Replying	Use this strategy when you want to make your writing richer by adding new ideas.	What are your ideas about my topic? What do you think about what I have said in my piece?
Responding to Specific Features	Use this when you want a quick overview of the strengths and weaknesses of your writing.	Are the ideas supported with enough examples? Did I persuade you? Is the organization clear enough so you could follow the ideas?
Telling	Use this to find out which parts of your writing are affecting readers the way you want and which parts are confusing.	What did you think or feel as you read my words? Would you show me which passage you were reading when you had that response?

Tips for Being a Peer Reader

Follow these guidelines when you respond to someone else's work:

- Respect the writer's feelings.
- Make sure you understand what kind of feedback the writer is looking for, and then respond accordingly.
- Use "I" statements, such as "I like . . .," "I think . . .," or "It would help me if. . . ." Remember that your impressions and opinions may not be the same as someone else's.

1.4 Revising and Editing

In the revising and editing stage you improve your draft, choose the words that best express your ideas, and proofread for mistakes in spelling, grammar, usage, and punctuation.

The changes you make in your writing during this stage usually fall into three categories: revising for content, revising for structure, and editing to correct mistakes in mechanics. Use the questions and suggestions that follow to help you assess problems in your draft and determine what kinds of changes would improve it.

WRITING TIP

Writers are more likely to accept criticism of their work if they first receive positive feedback. When you act as a peer reader, try to start your review by telling something you like about the piece.

WRITING HANDBOOK **1021**

WRITING TIP

Be sure to consider the needs of your audience as you answer the questions under Revising for Content. For example, before you can determine whether any of your material is unnecessary or irrelevant, you need to identify what your audience already knows.

WRITING TIP

For help identifying and correcting problems that are listed in the Proofreading Checklist, see the Grammar Handbook, pages 1058–1097.

Revising for Content

- Does my writing have a main idea or central focus? Is my thesis clear?
- Have I incorporated adequate detail? Where might I include a telling detail, revealing statistic, or vivid example?
- Is any material unnecessary, irrelevant, or confusing?

Revising for Structure

- Is my writing unified? Do all ideas and supporting details pertain to my main idea or advance my thesis?
- Is my writing clear and coherent? Is the flow of sentences and paragraphs smooth and logical?
- Do I need to add transitional words, phrases, or sentences to make the relationships among ideas clearer?
- Are my sentences well constructed? What sentences might I combine to improve the grace and rhythm of my writing?

Editing to Correct Mistakes in Mechanics

When you are satisfied with your draft, proofread and edit it, correcting any mistakes you might have made in spelling, grammar, usage, and punctuation. You may want to proofread your writing several times, looking for different types of mistakes each time. The following checklist may help you proofread your work.

Proofreading Checklist	
Sentence Structure and Agreement	Are there any run-on sentences or sentence fragments? Do all verbs agree with their subjects? Do all pronouns agree with their antecedents? Are verb tenses correct and consistent?
Forms of Words	Do adverbs and adjectives modify the appropriate words? Are all forms of *be* and other irregular verbs used correctly? Are pronouns used correctly? Are comparative and superlative forms of adjectives correct?
Capitalization, Punctuation, and Spelling	Is any punctuation mark missing or not needed? Are all words spelled correctly? Are all proper nouns and all proper adjectives capitalized?

If you have a printout of your draft or a handwritten copy, mark changes on it by using the proofreading symbols shown in the chart on the next page. The Grammar Handbook, starting on page 1058, includes models for using these symbols.

Proofreading Symbols	
∧ Add letters or words.	/ Make a capital letter lowercase.
⊙ Add a period.	¶ Begin a new paragraph.
≡ Capitalize a letter.	— or ⌐ Delete letters or words.
⌒ Close up space.	∾ Switch the positions of letters or words.
∧ Add a comma.	

1.5 Publishing and Reflecting

After you've completed a writing project, consider sharing it with a wider audience—even when you've produced it for a class assignment. Reflecting on your writing process is another good way to bring closure to a writing project.

Creative Publishing Ideas

Following are some ideas for publishing and sharing your writing.

- Post your writing on an electronic bulletin board or send it to others via e-mail.
- Create a multimedia presentation and share it with classmates.
- Publish your writing in a school newspaper or literary magazine.
- Present your work orally in a report, a speech, a reading, or a dramatic performance.
- Submit your writing to a local newspaper or a magazine that publishes student writing.
- Form a writing exchange group with other students.

Reflecting on Your Writing

Think about your writing process and consider whether you'd like to add your writing to your portfolio. You might attach to your work a note in which you answer questions like these:

- What did I learn about myself and my subject through this writing project?
- Which parts of the writing process did I most and least enjoy?
- As I wrote, what was my biggest problem? How did I solve it?
- What did I learn that I can use the next time I write?

WRITING TIP

You might work with other students to publish an anthology of class writing. Then exchange your anthology with another class or another school. Reading the work of other student writers will help you get ideas for new writing projects and for ways to improve your work.

WRITING HANDBOOK **1023**

Building Blocks of Good Writing

2.1 Introductions

A good introduction catches your reader's interest and often presents the main idea of your writing. To introduce your writing effectively, try one of the following methods.

Make a Surprising Statement

Beginning with a startling or interesting fact can capture your reader's curiosity about the subject, as in the example below.

> The Star of Africa, a diamond that is part of the British Crown Jewels, is roughly the size of a golf ball. It is only one of hundreds of jewels, crowns, and scepters on display at the Tower of London. These treasures not only are impressive but also tell much of the history of the British Empire.

Provide a Description

A vivid description sets a mood and brings a scene to life for your reader. The following description introduces a travel article about Greenland.

> The glowing orb hovered on the horizon, its brilliant rays reflected in the powdery, crystalline snow that blanketed everything. This breathtaking sight was my first impression of Greenland.

Pose a Question

Beginning with a question can make your readers want to read on to find out the answer. The following introduction asks readers to think about something they may not have thought about before.

LINK TO LITERATURE

A vivid description is a good way to introduce readers to the characters or setting of a narrative. A description that sets a mood is an effective way to draw the reader into the setting for a narrative. Kay Boyle conveys the mood of a dark and lonely New York apartment in her opening for "Winter Night," page 40.

> Why does a paperback printed ten years ago fall apart, while a book published centuries ago remains intact? The answer can be found by exploring the different materials used in bookmaking throughout history.

Relate an Anecdote

Beginning with a brief anecdote, or story, can hook readers and help you make a point in a dramatic way. The following anecdote sets the scene for a discussion of class distinctions in Britain.

> Young Winston Churchill was once stopped on his way up the stairs by a member of parliament from an opposing political party. "Stand back," the man said brusquely. "I don't make way for fools." Stepping well back to give the man a wide berth, Churchill replied, "*I do.*"

WRITING TIP

Dialogue can enhance an introduction. The comments by Winston Churchill and his fellow member of parliament make the anecdote at the left more vivid and realistic.

Address the Reader Directly

Speaking directly to readers in your introduction establishes a friendly, informal tone and involves them in your topic.

> *Masterpiece Theatre* has been praised for bringing great works to the screen; however, you may recall a few of the "masterpieces" that have been downright clunkers.

Begin with a Thesis Statement

A thesis statement expressing a paper's main idea may be woven into both the beginning and the end of a piece of nonfiction. The following is a thesis statement that introduces a literary analysis.

> By telling the story "After the Ball" almost entirely through the words of one character, Tolstoy provides little interpretation. With this technique, the author allows readers to experience for themselves the intertwining of good and evil.

2.2 Paragraphs

A paragraph is made up of sentences that work together to develop an idea or accomplish a purpose. Whether or not it contains a topic sentence stating the main idea, a good paragraph must have both unity and coherence.

Unity

A paragraph has unity when all the sentences support and develop one stated or implied idea. Use the following techniques to create unity in your paragraphs.

Write a Topic Sentence A topic sentence states the main idea of the paragraph; all the other sentences in the paragraph provide supporting details. A topic sentence is often the first sentence in a paragraph, as shown in the model below. However, it may also appear later in the paragraph or at the end, to summarize or reinforce the main idea.

> *Extrasensory perception (ESP) is the term for awareness or communication by means other than the known physical senses.* ESP includes clairvoyance and telepathy—knowledge of facts and of another's thoughts gained without using ordinary sensory processes. People have believed in such phenomena for thousands of years, but only since the late 1800s have scientists explored ESP.

Relate All Sentences to an Implied Main Idea A paragraph can be unified without a topic sentence as long as every sentence supports the implied, or unstated, main idea. In the example below, all the sentences work together to create a unified impression of a cool spring morning.

> Budding leaves formed a pale green veil over the gray trees. The fragrance of the damp earth, as the last traces of snow melted into it, was invigorating. People on the street greeted one another familiarly, as if they were fellow inmates jointly released from winter's prison. None of this stirred Kim, however. Her somber mood remained untouched by spring.

WRITING TIP

The same techniques that create unity in paragraphs can be used to create unity in an entire paper. Be sure that all of your paragraphs support the thesis statement or the implied main idea of your paper. If a paragraph includes information irrelevant to the main idea, you should delete it or revise it to establish a clear connection.

Coherence

A paragraph is coherent when all its sentences are related to one another and flow logically from one to the next. The following techniques will help you achieve coherence in paragraphs.

- Present your ideas in the most logical order.
- Use pronouns, synonyms, and repeated words to connect ideas.
- Use transitional devices to show the relationships among ideas.

In the example below, the italicized words show how the writer used some of these techniques to create a unified paragraph.

> Most comets "die" by being flung out of the solar system. In 1994, *however*, scientists videotaped the unusual *death* of Comet Shoemaker-Levy 9. *It* passed close enough to Jupiter for *the planet's* gravitational pull to rip *the comet* apart. Even if *it* had passed Jupiter safely, *it* would have died, eventually, perhaps by crashing into the sun. We probably wouldn't have known about *its death*, *though*, since *that event* might not have occurred for a few hundred thousand more years.

WRITING TIP

You can use the techniques at the left to create coherence in an entire paper. Be sure that paragraphs flow logically from one to the next.

2.3 Transitions

Transitions are words and phrases that show the connections between details, such as relationships in time and space, order of importance, causes and effects, and similarities or differences.

Time or Sequence

Some transitions help to clarify the sequence of events over time. When you are telling a story or describing a process, you can connect ideas with such transitional words as *first, second, always, then, next, later, soon, before, finally, after, earlier, afterward,* and *tomorrow.*

> *First* I had to determine where I was. The sun high above told me that it was noon, but I could not tell which way was east. *Then* I hit on the idea of heading left until I could see which way the building numbers ran. *Finally*, after walking many blocks, I got my bearings and was on my way.

LINK TO LITERATURE

In "Like the Sun," page 608, notice how author R. K. Narayan begins his story in the morning and marks the sequence of the day throughout the narrative with transitional phrases, such as "the very first test," "his next trial," and "during the last period."

Spatial Relationships

Transitional words and phrases such as *in front, behind, next to, along, nearest, lowest, above, below, underneath, on the left,* and *in the middle* can help readers visualize a scene.

> Ben surveyed the great room. *The middle* of the room was dominated by a huge stone fireplace. *To his left* were a large brown sofa and two easy chairs. Dark wooden bookcases covered the entire wall *to his right.* A colorful oil painting hung *above* the fireplace, and as Ben crossed the room, he felt the rough plank floor *underneath* his feet.

Degree

Transitions of degree, such as *mainly, strongest, weakest, first, second, most important, least important, worst,* and *best,* may be used to rank ideas or to show degree of importance, as in the model below.

> *At worst,* Margot would have to repeat a grade. *At best* she would barely pass and move on to 11th grade.

Compare and Contrast

Words and phrases such as *similarly, likewise, also, like, as, neither . . . nor,* and *either . . . or* show similarity between details. *However, by contrast, yet, but, unlike, instead, whereas,* and *while* show difference. Note the use of both types of transitions in the model below.

> At first glance the couple seemed ideally suited. *Each* was tall and fit. *Each* was articulate and social. *On the other hand,* she thrived on competition, *but* he shrank from it.

Cause and Effect

When you are writing about a cause-and-effect relationship, use transitional words and phrases such as *since, because, thus, therefore, so, due to, for this reason,* and *as a result* to help clarify that relationship and to make your writing coherent.

LINK TO LITERATURE

Note the use of transitions that show degree in "Montgomery Boycott," page 221. In the introduction, Coretta Scott King uses words such as *most* and *worse* to describe how African Americans in the South were treated when they used public transportation.

> *Because* so many early chess players were Persian, historians long thought that the game began in Persia in about A.D. 590. Ivory chess pieces, recently discovered in Russia, date to the second century A.D., however, *so* historians are reconsidering.

2.4 Elaboration

Elaboration is the process of developing a writing idea by providing specific supporting details that are appropriate for the purpose and form of your writing.

Facts and Statistics

A fact is a statement that can be verified, while a statistic is a fact stated in numbers. As in the model below, the facts and statistics you use should strongly support the statements you make.

> Cats are often kept inside for their own safety, but this practice is also safer for other animals as well. A recent study shows that the average city cat kills about 28 birds per year.

WRITING TIP

Facts and statistics can be used to explain more than one idea, depending on how you interpret the information for the reader. Be certain that you clearly and logically establish how the facts you have chosen support your writing.

Sensory Details

Details that show how something looks, sounds, tastes, smells, or feels can enliven a description. Which senses does the writer appeal to in the following paragraph?

> She ran her hand over the many fabrics displayed on the counter—sliding over the smooth Connaught satin, moving the crisp silk organza between her fingers, judging the heft of the resisting brocade. What a gown this would be—if she could only make up her mind!

Incidents

One way to illustrate a point is to relate an incident or tell a story, as in the example on the following page.

> Eva had expected courtesy and dignity—but not warmth—from the people of this land of bracing winds, barren moors, and stone walls. Now here was this stranger saying, "You must be Laura's mother. Do join us for tea." Her image of reserved Britons did an about-face.

Examples

An example can help make an abstract or complex idea concrete for the reader.

> The fast-food eating habits of Americans create large amounts of waste. For example, one takeout cup of coffee can create several waste items: a cup, a wooden stir stick, a plastic lid, plastic cream containers, and paper sugar packets.

LINK TO LITERATURE

Note Rachel de Queiroz's use of examples in "Metonymy, or the Husband's Revenge," on page 452. When she introduces the term *applied metonymy,* she uses an example to demonstrate the abstract idea.

Quotations

Choose quotations that clearly support your points and be sure that you copy each quotation word for word. Remember always to credit the source.

> Tolerance may be the most necessary virtue for ensuring peace, because the practice of tolerance requires us to think carefully before we react and before we judge others. In his essay "Tolerance," E. M. Forster says that tolerance "entails imagination. For you have all the time to be putting yourself in someone else's place."

2.5 Description

A good description contains carefully chosen details that create a unified impression for the reader.

Description is an important part of most writing genres—essays, stories, biography, and poetry, for example. Effective description can help readers to recognize the significance of an issue, to visualize a scene, or to understand a character.

Use a Variety of Details

If you include plenty of sensory details, the reader can better imagine the scene you are describing. In the example below, the sensory details help capture the character's mood.

> Phil dragged the worn canvas backpack from the dark recesses of the closet. The musty odor rekindled memories of his many trips with Joe. Hastily he rolled up a new bar of yellow soap and his toothbrush in the soft gray sweatshirts he would be living in for days. The prospect of camping with his brother transported him back in time.

LINK TO LITERATURE

E. B. White uses a variety of sensory details in his essay "Once More to the Lake." In his description of the lake on page 707, he writes, "In the shallows, the dark, water-soaked sticks and twigs, smooth and old, were undulating in clusters on the bottom against the clean ribbed sand."

Show, Don't Tell

Simply telling your readers about an event or an idea in a general way does not give them a clear impression. Showing your readers the specific details, however, helps them develop a better sense of your subject. The following example only tells you about the character.

> Warren had the best time at Mona's party.

The paragraph below uses descriptive details to show how he enjoyed the evening's activities.

> Warren had looked at his watch soon after arriving at Mona's party, but it was four hours later when he thought to check the time again. After all, the music was just his style, and the food was delicious. What's more, his wit did not fail him. He was the life of the party.

Use Figurative Language

Figurative language is descriptive writing that evokes associations beyond the literal meaning of words. The following types of figurative language can make your descriptions clear and fresh.

WRITING HANDBOOK **1031**

- A **simile** is a figure of speech comparing two essentially unlike things, signaling the comparison with a word such as *like* or *as*.
- A **metaphor** is a figure of speech describing something by speaking of it as if it were something else, without using a word such as *like* or *as* to signal the comparison.

The example below uses a simile to describe a cat.

> The cat perched on the armoire, wound up and poised for action like a spring.

WRITING TIP

Be careful not use two or more comparisons that create a confusing image. *The football player was a bowling ball, rolling through the defensive line and flattening his opponents like a bulldozer.*

Organize Your Details

Organize descriptions carefully to create a clear image for your reader. Descriptive details may be organized chronologically, spatially, by order of importance, or by order of impression.

> Rung by rung she ascended, remembering her father's advice not to look down. To distract her from an acute awareness of the swaying of the ladder, she focused on her goal. "Once I reach the window, the rest will be easy," she said to herself. "If only I hadn't forgotten my key."

WRITING TIP

Clarify your descriptive writing by choosing precise words. For example, you can replace general nouns (*instrument*) with more specific nouns (*scalpel*).

2.6 Conclusions

A conclusion should leave readers with a strong final impression. Try any of these approaches for concluding your writing.

Restate Your Thesis

A good way to conclude an essay is by restating your thesis, or main idea, in different words. The conclusion below restates the thesis introduced in an example on page 1025.

> By allowing one of the characters to tell his own story in "After the Ball," Tolstoy lures readers in and invites them to experience and to interpret the events for themselves. Therefore, it is Tolstoy's narrative technique—not the events of the story—that makes readers feel the intertwining of good and evil so acutely.

Ask a Question

Try asking a question that sums up what you have said and gives readers something new to think about. The question below concludes a persuasive argument for eating healthier food.

> The next time you want to grab a quick snack, ask yourself, Do I really need these french fries? or Can my body afford to eat these chips?

Make a Recommendation

When you are persuading your audience to take a position on an issue, you can conclude by recommending a specific course of action.

> To learn firsthand about campaigns and the election process, you should participate in the high school's mock presidential election.

Make a Prediction

Readers are concerned about matters that may affect them and therefore are moved by a conclusion that predicts the future.

> The mild winter and light snows of recent years will leave people unprepared for the bitter winter that has been forecast for the city this year.

Summarize Your Information

Summarizing reinforces your main ideas, leaving a strong, lasting impression. The model below concludes with a statement that summarizes an analysis of Winslow Homer's art.

> Winslow Homer's art captured a range of 19th-century American experiences—from events as significant as the Civil War to lighthearted scenes of children at play.

LINK TO LITERATURE

In the last two paragraphs of his essay "Black Men and Public Space," on page 297, Brent Staples summarizes what he has learned to do over the years in response to people's fearful reactions to him.

3 Narrative Writing

Narrative writing tells a story. If you write a story from your imagination, it is called a fictional narrative. A true story about actual events is called a nonfictional narrative.

Writing Standards

Good narrative writing
- includes descriptive details and dialogue to develop the characters, setting, and plot
- has a clear beginning, middle, and end
- has a logical organization with clues and transitions to help the reader understand the order of events
- maintains a consistent tone and point of view
- uses language that is appropriate for the audience
- demonstrates the significance of events or ideas

Key Techniques of Narrative Writing

Depict Characters Vividly
Use vivid details to show your readers what your characters look like, what they say, and what they think.

Example
"Sit!" she ordered. I was surprised to hear such anger in my aunt's voice. All I had done was skip school.

Clearly Organize the Events
Choose the important events and explain them in an order that is easy to understand. In a fictional narrative, this series of events is the story's plot.

Example
- Kelly moves from a city to a small town.
- She meets new friends; her aunt warns her about getting into trouble.
- Kelly and friends are caught skipping school.
- Kelly admits that she was acting foolishly and tries to make up for her mistake.

Describe the Conflict
The conflict of a narrative is the problem that the main character faces. In the example below, the conflict is between the main character, Kelly, and her aunt.

Example
After my friends left, my aunt followed me to my room. She said, "Those kids are trouble, and trouble's the last thing you need to be messing with at your new school."

1034 WRITING HANDBOOK

Organizing Narrative Writing

One way to organize a piece of narrative writing is to arrange the events in chronological order, as shown in Option 1 below.

Option 1

Focus on Events
- Introduce characters and setting
- Show event 1
- Show event 2
- End, perhaps showing the significance of the events

Example

Kelly moves from the city to a small town to live with her aunt.

When Kelly brings her new friends home, her aunt says, "Those kids are trouble."

Kelly is caught skipping school with her friends, and her aunt grounds her for a week.

Kelly admits that she was acting foolishly and offers to clean her aunt's basement to make up for the trouble she caused her.

When the telling of a fictional narrative focuses on a central conflict, the story's plot may follow the model shown in Option 2. It is also possible in narrative writing to arrange the order of events by starting *in medias res,* or in the middle of things (Option 3).

Option 2

Focus on Conflict
- Describe the main characters and setting
- Present the conflict
- Relate the events that make the conflict complex and cause the characters to change
- Present the resolution, or outcome of the conflict

Option 3

Flashback
- Begin with the conflict
- Present the events leading up to the conflict
- Present the resolution, or outcome of the conflict

Remember: Good narrative writing shows action rather than telling about it.

WRITING TIP

Introductions Try to hook your reader's interest by opening your story with an exciting event or some attention-grabbing dialogue.

WRITING TIP

As the writer, you decide what your characters say. You can make every word count by using dialogue for any of the following purposes: to reveal character, to highlight the relationship between characters, or to move the action along.

WRITING HANDBOOK **1035**

 Explanatory Writing

Explanatory writing is writing that informs and explains. For example, you can use it to evaluate the effects of a new law, to compare two movie reviews, or to analyze a narrative.

 LINK TO LITERATURE

Explanatory writing provides many opportunities to explore issues presented in literature. The examples on the following pages examine the excerpt from Le Ly Hayslip's nonfictional narrative *When Heaven and Earth Changed Places* and Hwang Sunwŏn's fictional narrative "Cranes."

Types of Explanatory Writing

Compare and Contrast

Compare-and-contrast writing explores the similarities and differences between two or more subjects.

Example
Le Ly Hayslip and the character Sŏngsam in "Cranes" may not seem to have much in common. However, both choose to follow personal values rather than acting the part of warriors.

Cause and Effect

Cause-and-effect writing explains why something happened, why certain conditions exist, or what resulted from an action or a condition.

Example
The war in Vietnam causes dramatic changes in Le Ly Hayslip's family life.

Analysis

Analysis explains how something works, how it is defined, or what its parts are.

Example
Le Ly Hayslip's father defined his daughter's job as follows: "to stay alive, to find a husband and have babies," and "to live in peace."

Problem-Solution

Problem-solution writing identifies a problem, analyzes the problem, and proposes a solution to it.

Example
Le Ly's father faces the problem of protecting his family's farm from enemy soldiers by hiding and keeping watch.

1036 WRITING HANDBOOK

4.1 Compare and Contrast

Compare-and-contrast writing explores the similarities and differences between two or more subjects.

Organizing Compare-and-Contrast Writing

Compare-and-contrast writing can be organized in different ways. The examples below demonstrate feature-by-feature organization and subject-by-subject organization.

Option 1

Feature by Feature
- Feature 1
  - Subject A
  - Subject B
- Feature 2
  - Subject A
  - Subject B

Example
- Le Ly Hayslip and the character Sŏngsam both learn the value of acting peacefully during wartime.
- Le Ly learns that she should live in peace and tend the shrines of her ancestors.
- Sŏngsam realizes that his friend's life is more important than the duty of being a soldier.
- Le Ly Hayslip and Sŏngsam learn this value from two different sources.

Option 2

Subject by Subject
- Subject A
  - Feature 1
  - Feature 2
- Subject B
  - Feature 1
  - Feature 2

Example
- Le Ly learns an important lesson during a time of war.
- She learns that she should live in peace and tend the shrines of her ancestors.
- She learns this from the example of her father, who devoted himself to his family and farm.
- The character Sŏngsam learns an important lesson during a time of war.
- He realizes that his friend's life is more important than the duty of being a soldier.
- He learns this value by recollecting their shared childhood experiences.

Writing Standards

Good compare-and-contrast writing
- clearly identifies the subjects that are being compared and contrasted
- includes specific, relevant details
- follows a clear plan of organization dealing with the same features of both subjects under discussion
- uses language and details appropriate to the audience
- uses transitional words and phrases to clarify similarities and differences

WRITING TIP

Remember your purpose for comparing the items you are writing about and support your purpose with expressive language and specific details.

WRITING HANDBOOK **1037**

Writing Standards
Good cause-and-effect writing
▶ clearly states the cause-and-effect relationship being examined
▶ shows clear connections between causes and effects
▶ presents causes and effects in a logical order and uses transitions effectively
▶ uses facts, examples, and other details to illustrate each cause and effect
▶ uses language and details appropriate to the audience

WRITING TIP

Possible topics for cause-and-effect writing include important historical events that had an impact on society. For example, what effect did the invention of the cotton gin have on the Southern economy and society? You can explore current events and their potential outcomes as well.

4.2 Cause and Effect

Cause-and-effect writing explains why something happened, why certain conditions exist, or what resulted from an action or a condition.

Organizing Cause-and-Effect Writing

Your organization will depend on your topic and purpose for writing. If your focus is on explaining the effects of an event such as the passage of a law, you might first state the cause and then explain the effects (Option 2). If you want to explain the causes of an event such as the closing of a factory, you can first state the effect and then examine its causes (Option 3). Sometimes you'll want to describe a chain of cause-and-effect relationships (Option 1) to explore a topic such as the disappearance of tropical rain forests or the development of home computers.

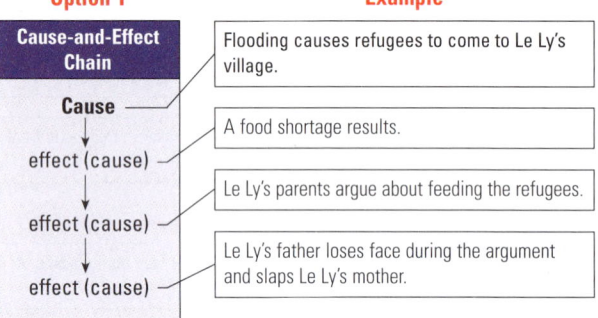

Option 2		Option 3	
Cause to Effect		**Effect to Cause**	
Cause		Effect	
• Effect 1		• Cause 1	
• Effect 2		• Cause 2	
• Effect 3		• Cause 3	

Remember: You cannot assume that a cause-and-effect relationship exists simply because one event follows another. Be sure your facts indicate that the effect could not have happened without the cause.

4.3 Problem-Solution

Problem-solution writing clearly states a problem, analyzes the problem, and proposes a solution to the problem.

Organizing Problem-Solution Writing

Your organization will depend on the goal of your problem-solution piece, your intended audience, and the specific problem you choose to address. The organizational methods outlined below are effective for different kinds of problem-solution writing.

Writing Standards

Good problem-solution writing
- identifies the problem and helps the reader understand the issues involved
- analyzes the causes and effects of the problem
- integrates quotes, facts, and statistics into the text
- explores potential solutions to the problem and recommends the best one(s)
- uses language, tone, and details appropriate to the audience

Option 1

Simple Problem-Solution
- Description of problem and why it needs to be solved
- Recommended solution
- Explanation of solution
- Conclusion

Example
- Should you endanger yourself to protect something you value? In *When Heaven and Earth Changed Places*, Le Ly's father risks capture to protect his family's farm from enemy troops.
- I wouldn't endanger myself to protect a possession, but I would take risks to protect my family.
- Even though I know it is dangerous, I would risk my own safety to protect my family from a dangerous situation such as a fire.
- Taking risks to protect something I value could be dangerous, but I would do it for my family.

Option 2

Deciding Between Solutions
- Description of Problem
- Solution A
  - Pros
  - Cons
- Solution B
  - Pros
  - Cons
- Recommendation

Example
- What would you do if invading troops threatened to destroy your city or town?
- You could pack some of your possessions and go somewhere that isn't being threatened.
- You and your family would be in a safe place to wait until your town is out of danger.
- Your home and possessions could be destroyed while you are away seeking safety.
- You could stay near your home and try to protect your possessions and property.

WRITING TIP

Ask a classmate to read and respond to your problem-solution writing. Here are some questions for your peer reader to respond to: Is my language clear? Is the writing organized in a way that is easy to follow? Do the proposed solutions seem logical?

Writing Standards

A good analysis

▶ hooks the reader's attention with a strong introduction

▶ clearly states the subject and its individual parts

▶ uses a specific organizing structure to provide a logical flow of information

▶ shows connections among facts and ideas through subordinate clauses and transitional words and phrases

▶ uses language and details appropriate for the audience

WRITING TIP

Introductions To capture the reader's attention, you may want to begin your analysis with a vivid description of the subject. For example, a description of the father's efforts to protect his farm and family during the war could introduce an analysis of the excerpt from *When Heaven and Earth Changed Places*.

4.4 Analysis

In an analysis you try to help your readers understand a subject by explaining how it works, how it is defined, or what its parts are.

The details you include will depend upon the kind of analysis you're writing.

- A **process analysis** should provide background information—such as definitions of terms and a list of needed equipment—and then explain each important step or stage in the process. For example, you might explain the steps to program a VCR or the stages in a plant's growth cycle.
- A **definition** should include the most important characteristics of the subject. To define a quality, such as honesty, you might include the characteristic of telling the truth.
- A **parts analysis** should describe each of the parts, groups, or types that make up the subject. For example, you might analyze the human brain by looking at its parts, or a new law by looking at how different groups are affected by it, or jazz music by describing the different styles of jazz.

Organizing Your Analysis

Organize your details in a logical order appropriate for the kind of analysis you're writing. A process analysis is usually organized chronologically, with steps or stages in the order they occur.

Option 1	Example
Process Analysis	
Introduce topic	The war in Vietnam involved many warring factions and different countries over many years.
Background information	Vietnam is a tropical country in Southeast Asia. Most of the people of Vietnam are farmers. Vietnam was at war—with other countries and internally—roughly from 1946 until 1975.
Explain steps	
• Step 1	Some Vietnamese began fighting French rule in 1946.
• Step 2	In 1954 a United Nations peace treaty divided Vietnam into two parts, North and South.
• Step 3	Despite many years of support from the United States, in 1975 the South Vietnamese government was toppled by North Vietnam.

WRITING HANDBOOK

You can organize the details in a definition or parts analysis in order of importance or impression.

Option 2

Definition	Example
Introduce term	*When Heaven and Earth Changed Places* shows what survival means to Le Ly and her family during the Vietnam War.
General definition	Survival takes on new meaning during wartime since people are required to behave in uncommon ways.
Explain qualities	
• Quality 1	Survival requires taking extraordinary action to keep the family safe.
• Quality 2	Survival can require dividing the family for safety's sake.
• Quality 3	Survival requires self-sacrifice for the sake of others.

In the following parts analysis, the challenges of surviving during wartime are broken down into three different aspects.

Option 3

Parts Analysis	Example
Introduce subject	Survival during wartime can be as difficult for civilians as it is for soldiers.
Explain parts	Le Ly's family members choose different ways to adapt to wartime in order to survive.
• Part 1	Le Ly's father adapts to wartime by singing comical songs about the soldiers who are nearby.
• Part 2	Le Ly's mother adapts by taking a serious outlook on the war and protecting her children.
• Part 3	As a child, Le Ly views the war as part of everyday life. She spends time with her father learning about family traditions and ancestors.

WRITING TIP

Conclusions Since analytical writing often deals with numerous details, it will help your readers if your conclusion summarizes the main points.

WRITING HANDBOOK **1041**

5 Persuasive Writing

Persuasive writing allows you to use the power of language to inform and influence others.

Key Techniques of Persuasive Writing

Writing Standards

Good persuasive writing

- clearly states the issue and the writer's position
- gives opinions and supports them with facts or reasons
- has a reasonable and respectful tone
- takes into account and answers opposing views
- uses sound logic and effective language
- concludes by summing up reasons or calling for action

State Your Opinion

Taking a stand on an issue and clearly stating your opinion are essential to every piece of persuasive writing you do.

Example
If you liked the story "The Witness for the Prosecution" by Agatha Christie, you should see the movie of the same name.

Know Your Audience

Knowing who will read your writing will help you decide what information you need to share and what tone you should use to communicate your message. In the example below, the writer has chosen an informal tone appropriate for a review to be presented to fellow students.

Example
Like many other Agatha Christie mysteries, "The Witness for the Prosecution" now has quite a following.

Support Your Opinion

Using reasons, examples, facts, statistics, and anecdotes to support your opinion will show your audience why you feel the way you do. Below, the writer gives a reason to support her opinion.

Example
In both the movie and the story, unfolding events hook the audience into discovering who the real villain is, step by step.

1042 WRITING HANDBOOK

Organizing Persuasive Writing

In persuasive writing, you need to gather information to support your opinions. Here are some ways you can organize that material to persuade your audience.

Option 1

Reasons for Your Opinion

Your opinion
- Reason 1
- Reason 2
- Reason 3

Example

If you liked the story "The Witness for the Prosecution" by Agatha Christie, you should see the movie of the same name.

As in the story, the fascinating characters and exciting courtroom drama capture the audience's attention.

Like the defense attorney in the story, the audience becomes involved in solving the crime.

The unexpected final twist stuns the audience.

Depending on the purpose and form of your writing, you may want to show the weaknesses of other opinions as you explain the strength of your own. Two options for persuasive writing that include opposing viewpoints are shown below.

Option 2

Why Your Opinion Is Stronger

Your opinion
- your reasons

Other opinion
- evidence refuting reasons for other opinion and showing strengths of your opinion

Option 3

Why Another Opinion Is Weaker

Other opinion
- reasons

Your opinion
- reasons supporting your opinion and pointing out the weaknesses of the other side

Remember: Effective persuasion often uses deductive reasoning—arguing from a general statement to specific points. Keep this in mind as you organize the reasons supporting your opinion.

WRITING TIP

Introductions Capture your readers' attention in the introduction to your piece. Try opening with a quote, a statistic, or an anecdote that shows the importance of your topic.

WRITING TIP

Conclusions Writing persuasively means convincing the reader to feel the way you do about something. Your conclusion might summarize your opinion, make a final appeal, or urge your readers to take action.

Research Report Writing

A research report explores a topic in depth, incorporating information from a variety of sources.

Writing Standards

Good research report writing
- clearly states purpose of the report in a thesis statement
- uses evidence and details from a variety of sources to support the thesis
- contains only accurate and relevant information
- documents sources correctly
- develops the topic logically and includes appropriate transitions
- includes a properly formatted Works Cited list

Key Techniques of Research Report Writing

Clarify Your Thesis
A thesis statement is one or two sentences clearly stating the main idea that you will develop in your report. A thesis may also indicate the organizational pattern you will follow and reflect your tone and point of view.

Example
Although H. G. Wells's predictions about space travel were mostly inaccurate scientifically, he did successfully predict the impact such developments would have on society.

Support Your Ideas
You should support your ideas with relevant evidence—facts, anecdotes, and statistics—from reliable sources. In the following example, the writer supports a claim about the accuracy of H. G. Wells's predictions of the future.

Example
Most of Wells's predictions were scientifically inaccurate, but sometimes he got things right. Although Wells wrote *The First Men in the Moon* 60 years before the first crewed space flight, he accurately described the effects of weightlessness in space (McConnell 155).

Document Your Sources
You need to document, or credit, the sources you use in your writing. In the example below, the writer uses a quotation as a supporting detail and documents the source.

Example
Jonathan Rose claims that "futurology is more than just predicting new gadgetry. It is far more important to foresee the impact that future technology will have on everyday life" (20).

1044 WRITING HANDBOOK

Evaluating Sources

To help you determine whether your sources are reliable and contain useful and accurate information, use the following checklist.

Checklist for Evaluating Your Sources	
Authoritative	Someone who has written several books or articles on your subject or whose work has been published in a well-respected newspaper or journal may be considered an authority.
Up-to-date	Check the publication dates to see whether the source reflects the most current research on your subject.
Respected	In general, tabloid newspapers and popular-interest magazines are not reliable sources. If you have questions about whether you are using a respected source, ask your librarian.

WRITING TIP

For additional help, see the research report about Elizabeth Cady Stanton on page 991 or McDougal Littell's *Writing Research Papers*.

Making Source Cards

For each source you find, record the bibliographic information on a separate index card. You will need this information to give credit to the sources you use in your paper. The samples at the right show how to make source cards for magazine articles, on-line articles, and books. You will use the source number on each card to identify the notes you take during your research.

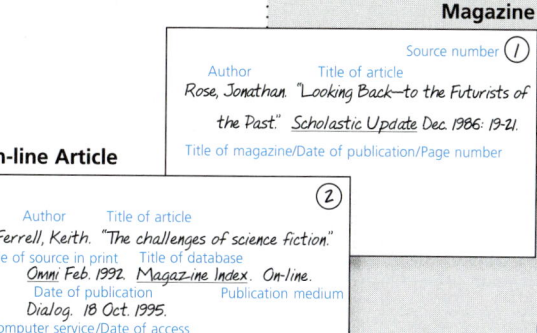

Taking Notes

As you read your sources, record on note cards information that is relevant to the purpose of your research. You will probably use all three of the following note-taking methods.

- **Paraphrase,** or restate in your own words, the main ideas and supporting details from a passage.
- **Summarize,** or rephrase the original material in fewer words, trying to capture the key ideas.
- **Quote,** or copy the original text word for word, if you think the author's own words best clarify a particular point. Use quotation marks to signal the beginning and the end of the quotation.

WRITING HANDBOOK 1045

Organizing Your Research Report

Making an outline can help guide the drafting process. Begin by reading over your note cards and sorting them into groups. The main-idea headings may help you find connections among the notes. Then arrange the groups of related note cards so that the ideas flow logically from one group to the next.

Note the format for a topic outline shown below. Remember that in a topic outline, items of the same degree of importance should be parallel in form. For instance, if A is a noun, then B and C should also be nouns. Subtopics need not be parallel with main topics.

```
            Predicting the Future in The First Men in the Moon
Introduction—Predictions in Wells's science fiction
   I. Predictions about science and technology
      A. Accurate predictions
      B. Inaccurate predictions
         1. Design of space ships
         2. Life on the moon
   II. Predictions about society
```

WRITING TIP

Plagiarism Presenting someone else's writing or ideas as your own is plagiarism. To avoid plagiarism, you need to credit sources as noted at the right. However, if a piece of information is common knowledge—information available in several sources—you do not need to credit a source. To see an example of parenthetical documentation, see the essay on page 991.

Documenting Your Sources

When you quote, paraphrase, or summarize information from one of your sources, you need to credit that source, using parenthetical documentation.

Guidelines for Parenthetical Documentation	
Work by One Author	Put the author's last name and the page reference in parentheses: (McConnell 152). If you mention the author's name in the sentence, put only the page reference in parentheses: (152).
Work by Two or Three Authors	Put the authors' last names and the page reference in parentheses: (Philmus and Hughes 34).
Work by More than Three Authors	Give the first author's last name followed by *et al.* and the page reference: (Schreck et al. 212).
Work with No Author Given	Give the title or a shortened version and the page reference: ("Science Fiction" 574).
One of Two or More Works by Same Author	Give the author's last name, the title or a shortened version, and the page reference: (Rose, "Looking Back" 19).

1046 WRITING HANDBOOK

Following MLA Manuscript Guidelines

The final copy of your report should follow the Modern Language Association guidelines for manuscript preparation.

- The heading in the upper left-hand corner of the first page should include your name, your teacher's name, the course name, and the date, each on a separate line.
- Below the heading, center the title on the page.
- Number all the pages consecutively in the upper right-hand corner, one-half inch from the top. Also, include your last name before the page number.
- Double-space the entire paper.
- Except for the margins above the page numbers, leave one-inch margins on all sides of every page.

The Works Cited list at the end of your paper is an alphabetized list of the sources you have used and documented in your report. The additional line of each entry is indented one-half inch.

WRITING TIP

When your report includes a quotation that is longer than four lines, set it off from the rest of the text by indenting the entire quotation one inch from the left margin. In this case, you should not use quotation marks.

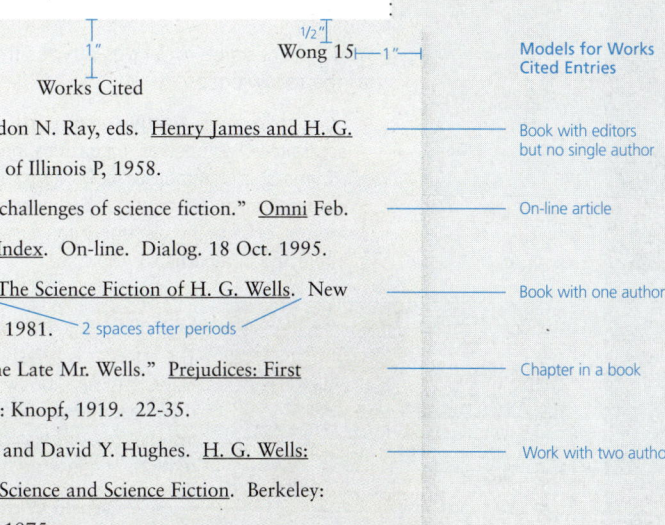

Wong 15

Works Cited

Edel, Leon, and Gordon N. Ray, eds. <u>Henry James and H. G. Wells</u>. Urbana: U of Illinois P, 1958.

Ferrell, Keith. "The challenges of science fiction." <u>Omni</u> Feb. 1992. <u>Magazine Index</u>. On-line. Dialog. 18 Oct. 1995.

McConnell, Frank. <u>The Science Fiction of H. G. Wells</u>. New York: Oxford UP, 1981.

Mencken, H. L. "The Late Mr. Wells." <u>Prejudices: First Series</u>. New York: Knopf, 1919. 22-35.

Philmus, Robert M., and David Y. Hughes. <u>H. G. Wells: Early Writings in Science and Science Fiction</u>. Berkeley: U of California P, 1975.

Rose, Jonathan. "Looking Back—to the Futurists of the Past." <u>Scholastic Update</u> Dec. 1986: 19-21.

Schorer, Mark. "Technique as Discovery." <u>The Hudson Review</u> 1 (1948): 67-87.

Models for Works Cited Entries

- Book with editors but no single author
- On-line article
- Book with one author
- Chapter in a book
- Work with two authors
- Article in magazine
- Article in scholarly journal

WRITING HANDBOOK **1047**

MULTIMEDIA HANDBOOK

1 Getting Information Electronically

Electronic resources provide you with a convenient and efficient way to gather information.

1.1 On-line Resources

When you use your computer to communicate with another computer or with another person using a computer, you are working "on-line." On-line resources include commercial information services and information available on the Internet.

Commercial Information Services

You can subscribe to various services that offer information such as the following:

- up-to-date news, weather, and sports reports
- access to encyclopedias, magazines, newspapers, dictionaries, almanacs, and databases (collections of information)
- electronic mail (e-mail) to and from other users
- forums, or ongoing electronic conversations among users interested in a particular topic

Internet

The Internet is a vast network of computers. News services, libraries, universities, researchers, organizations, and government agencies use the Internet to communicate and to distribute information. The Internet includes two key features:

- **World Wide Web,** which provides you with information on particular subjects and links you to related topics and resources (such as the linked Web pages shown at the left)
- **Electronic mail** (e-mail), which allows you to communicate with other e-mail users worldwide

1048 MULTIMEDIA HANDBOOK

1.2 CD-ROM

A CD-ROM (compact disc–read-only memory) stores data that may include text, sound, photographs, and video.

Almost any kind of information can be found on CD-ROMs, which you can use at the library or purchase, including

- encyclopedias, almanacs, and indexes
- other reference books on a variety of subjects
- news reports from newspapers, magazines, television, or radio
- museum art collections
- back issues of magazines
- literature collections

WHAT YOU'LL NEED

- To access on-line resources, you need a computer with a modem linked to a telephone line. Your school computer lab or resource center may be linked to the Internet or to a commercial information service.
- To use CD-ROMs, you need a computer system with a CD-ROM player.

1.3 Library Computer Services

Many libraries offer computerized catalogs and a variety of other electronic resources.

Computerized Catalogs

You may search for a book in a library by typing the title, author, subject, or key words into a computer terminal. If you enter the title of a book, the screen will display the bibliographic information and the current availability of the book. When a particular work is not available, you may be able to search the catalogs of other libraries.

Other Electronic Resources

In addition to computerized catalogs, many libraries offer electronic versions of books or other reference materials. They may also have a variety of indexes on CD-ROM, which allow you to search for magazine or newspaper articles on any topic you choose. When you have found an article on the topic you want, the screen will display the kind of information shown at the right.

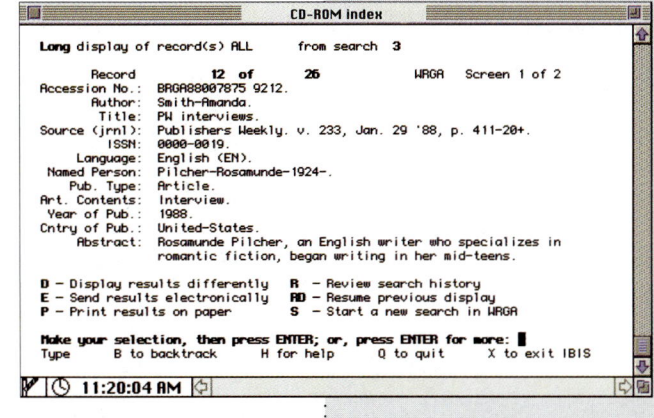

MULTIMEDIA HANDBOOK **1049**

② Word Processing

WHAT YOU'LL NEED

- Computer
- Word-processing program
- Printer

Word-processing programs allow you to draft, revise, edit, and format your writing and to produce neat, professional-looking papers. They also allow you to share your writing with others.

2.1 Revising and Editing

Improving the quality of your writing becomes easier when you use a word-processing program to revise and edit.

Revising a Document

Most word-processing programs allow you to make the following kinds of changes:

- add or delete words
- move text from one location in your document to another
- undo a change you have made in the text
- save a document with a new name, allowing you to keep old drafts for reference
- view more than one document at a time, so you can copy text from one document and add it to another

Editing a Document

Many word-processing programs have the following features to help you catch errors and polish your writing:

- The **spell checker** automatically finds misspelled words and suggests possible corrections.
- The **grammar checker** spots possible grammatical errors and suggests ways you might correct them.
- The **thesaurus** suggests synonyms for a word you want to replace.
- The **dictionary** will give you the definitions of words so you can be sure you have used words correctly.
- The **search and replace** feature searches your whole document and corrects every occurrence of something you want to change, such as a misspelled name.

WRITING TIP

Spell checkers and grammar checkers offer suggestions for corrections, but you must carefully assess these suggestions before picking the right one. Making such an assessment involves looking at the suggested change in the context of your writing.

2.2 Formatting Your Work

Format is the layout and appearance of your writing on the page. You may choose your formatting options before or after you write.

Formatting Type

You may want to make changes in the typeface, type size, and type style of the words in your document. For each of these, your word-processing program will most likely have several options to choose from. These options allow you to

- change the typeface to create a different look for the words in your document
- change the type size of the entire document or of just the headings of sections in the paper
- change the type style when necessary; for example, use italics or underline for the titles of books and magazines

Typeface	Size	Style
Geneva	7-point Times	*Italic*
Times	10-point Times	**Bold**
Chicago	12-point Times	Underline
Courier	14-point Times	

Formatting Pages

Not only can you change the way individual words look; you can also change the way they are arranged on the page. Some of the formatting decisions you make will depend on how you plan to use a printout of a draft or on the guidelines of an assignment.

- Set the line spacing, or the amount of space you need between lines of text. Double spacing is commonly used for final drafts.
- Set the margins, or the amount of white space around the edges of your text. A one-inch margin on all sides is commonly used for final drafts.
- Create a header for the top of the page or a footer for the bottom if you want to include such information as your name, the date, or the page number on every page.
- Determine the alignment of your text. The screen at the left shows your options.

Announcement!

The results of the East High School fundraising drive are posted below. The money that was raised will be added to other donations to repair the speaker system in the gym.

```
9th grade ............ $48.00
10th grade .......... $62.00
11th grade .......... $54.60
12th grade .......... $56.22
Total ............. $220.82
```

Centered · Left-aligned · Right-aligned

WRITING TIP

Keep your format simple. Your goal is to create not only an attractive document but also one that is easy to read. Your readers will have difficulty if you change the type formatting frequently.

TECHNOLOGY TIP

Some word-processing programs or other software packages provide preset templates, or patterns, for writing outlines, memos, letters, newsletters, or invitations. If you use one of these templates, you will not need to adjust the formatting.

2.3 Working Collaboratively

Computers allow you to share your writing electronically. Send a copy of your work to someone via e-mail or put it in someone's drop box if your computer is linked to other computers on a network. Then use the feedback of your peers to help you improve the quality of your writing.

Peer Editing on a Computer

The writer and the reader can both benefit from the convenience of peer editing "on screen," or at the computer.

- Be sure to save your current draft and then make a copy of it for each of your peer readers.
- You might have each peer reader use a different typeface or type style for making comments, as shown in the example below.
- Ask each of your readers to include his or her initials in the file name.

TECHNOLOGY TIP

Some word-processing programs, such as the Writing Coach software referred to in this book, allow you to leave notes for your peer readers in the side column or in a separate text box. If you wish, leave those areas blank so your readers can write comments or questions.

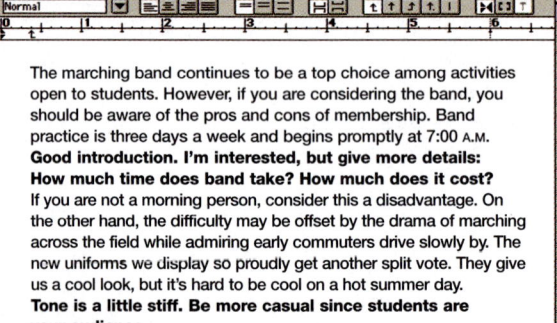

- If your computer allows you to open more than one file at a time, open each reviewer's file and refer to the files as you revise your draft.

Peer Editing on a Printout

Some peer readers prefer to respond to a draft on paper rather than on the computer.

- Double-space or triple-space your document so that your peer editor can make suggestions between the lines.
- Leave extra-wide margins to give your readers room to note their reactions and questions as they read.
- Print out your draft and photocopy it if you want to share it with more than one reader.

Using Visuals

Tables, graphs, diagrams, and pictures often communicate information more effectively than words alone do. Many computer programs allow you to create visuals to use with your written text.

3.1 When to Use Visuals

Use visuals in your work to illustrate complex concepts and processes or to make a page look more interesting.

Although you should not expect a visual to do all the work of written text, combining words and pictures or graphics can increase the understanding and enjoyment of your writing. Many computer programs allow you to create and insert graphs, tables, time lines, diagrams, and flow charts into your document. An art program allows you to create border designs for a title page or to draw an unusual character or setting for narrative or descriptive writing. You may also be able to add clip art, or premade pictures, to your document. Clip art can be used to illustrate an idea or concept or to make your writing more appealing for young readers.

WHAT YOU'LL NEED

- A graphics program to create visuals
- Access to clip-art files from a CD-ROM, a computer disk, or an on-line service

3.2 Kinds of Visuals

The visuals you choose will depend on the type of information you want to present to your readers.

Tables

Tables allow you to arrange facts or numbers into rows and columns so that your reader can compare information more easily. In many word-processing programs, you can create a table by choosing the number of vertical columns and horizontal rows you need and then entering information in each box, as the illustration shows.

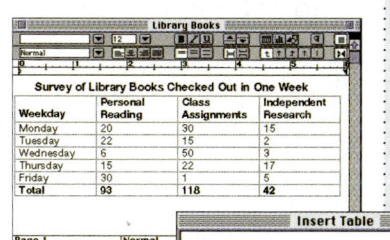

TECHNOLOGY TIP

A spreadsheet program provides you with a preset table for your statistics and performs any necessary calculations.

TECHNOLOGY TIP

To help your readers easily understand the different parts of a pie chart or bar graph, use a different color or shade of gray for each section.

Graphs and Charts

You can sometimes use a graph or chart to help communicate complex information in a clear visual image. For example, you could use a line graph to show how a trend changes over time, a bar graph such as the one at the right to compare statistics from different years, or a pie chart to compare percentages. You might want to explore ways of displaying data in more than one visual format before deciding which will work best for you.

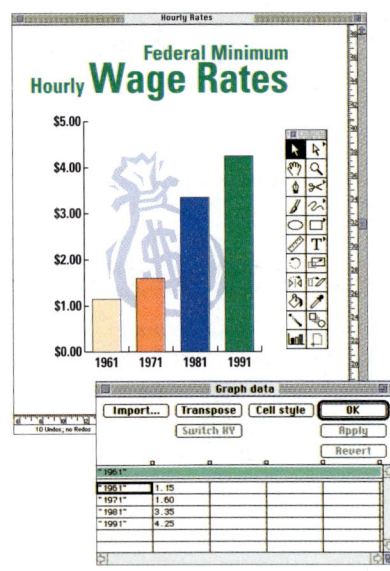

Other Visuals

Art and design programs allow you to create visuals for your writing. Many programs include the following features:

- drawing tools that allow you to draw, color, and shade pictures
- clip art that you can copy or change with drawing tools

- page borders that you can use to decorate title pages, invitations, or brochures
- text options that allow you to combine words with your illustrations, as shown at the left
- tools for making geometric shapes in flow charts, time lines, and diagrams that show a process or sequence of events

Creating a Multimedia Presentation

A multimedia presentation is a combination of text, sound, and visuals such as photographs, videos, and animation. Your audience reads, hears, and sees your presentation at a computer, following different "paths" you create to lead the user through the information you have gathered.

4.1 Features of Multimedia Programs

To start planning your multimedia presentation, you need to know what options are available to you. You can combine sound, photos, videos, and animation to enhance any text you write about your topic.

Sound

Including sound in your presentation can help your audience understand information in your written text. For example, the user may be able to listen and learn from

- the pronunciation of an unfamiliar or foreign word
- a speech
- a recorded interview
- a musical selection
- a dramatic reading of a work of literature

Photos and Videos

Photographs and live-action videos can make your subject come alive for the user. Here are some examples:

- videotaped news coverage of a historical event
- videos of music, dance, or theater performances
- charts and diagrams
- photos of an artist's work
- photos or video of a geographical setting that is important to the written text

WHAT YOU'LL NEED

- Individual programs to create and edit the text, graphics, sound, and videos you will use
- A multimedia authoring program that allows you to combine these elements and create links between the screens

Animation

Many graphics programs allow you to add animation, or movement, to the visuals in your presentation. Animated figures add to the user's enjoyment and understanding of what you present. You can use animation to illustrate

- what happens in a story
- the steps in a process
- changes in a chart, graph, or diagram
- how your user can explore information in your presentation

4.2 Planning Your Presentation

To create a multimedia presentation, first choose your topic and decide what you want to include. Then plan how you want the user to move through your presentation.

Imagine that you are creating a multimedia presentation exploring the differences between old and new architecture by focusing on a historic old house in your community. You decide to include the following items:

- a photo of the old house
- text about the history and construction of the house
- a blueprint of the old house
- an interview with an architect comparing old and new architecture and building techniques
- photos of architectural details in a house
- a video tour of an old house
- photos of new houses
- text describing how quickly new houses are built

You can choose one of the following ways to organize your presentation:

- step by step with only one path, or order, in which the user can see and hear the information
- a branching path that allows users to make some choices about what they will see and hear, and in what order

A flow chart can help you figure out the path a user can take through your presentation. Each box in the flow chart on the following page represents something about the house for the user to read, see, or hear. The arrows on the flow chart show a branching path the user can follow.

> **TECHNOLOGY TIP**
>
> You can download photos, sound, and video from Internet sources onto your computer. This process allows you to add elements to your multimedia presentation that would usually require complex editing equipment.

> **TECHNOLOGY TIP**
>
> You can now find CD-ROMs with videos of things like wildlife, weather, street scenes, and events, and other CD-ROMs with recordings of famous speeches, musical selections, and dramatic readings.

Whenever boxes branch in more than one direction, it means that the user can choose which item to see or hear first.

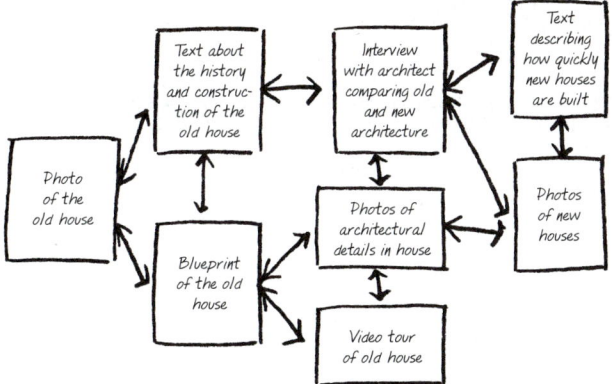

WRITING TIP

You usually need permission from the person or organization that owns the copyright on materials if you want to copy them. You do not need permission, however, if you are not making money from your presentation, if you use it only for educational purposes, and if you use only a small percentage of the original material.

4.3 Guiding Your User

Your user will need directions to follow the path you have planned for your multimedia presentation.

Most multimedia authoring programs allow you to create screens that include text or audio directions that guide the user from one part of your presentation to the next. In the example below, the user can choose between several paths, and directions on the screen explain how to make the choice.

If you need help creating your multimedia presentation, ask your school's technology adviser. You may also be able to get help from your classmates or your software manual.

The user clicks on a button to select any of these options.

Navigational buttons take the user back and forth, one screen at a time.

This screen shows a photo of architectural details.

1 Writing Complete Sentences

1.1 Sentence Fragments

A sentence fragment is a group of words that does not express a complete thought. Sentence fragments may be missing a subject, a predicate, or both.

Completing an Incomplete Thought

You can correct a sentence fragment by adding the missing subject or predicate to complete the thought.

> In "Two Kinds," a story about mother-daughter conflict, ^*the mother* wants desperately to make her daughter a prodigy. The independent and unwilling daughter ^*refuses*.

When the fragment is a subordinate clause, you can join the fragment to an existing sentence and change the punctuation or you can rewrite the clause so it can stand alone.

> When the mother pushes her daughter to perform publicly on the piano, ^the girl rebels. While refusing *She refuses* to practice diligently or correct her mistakes.

Correcting Punctuation

When the fragment is a phrase, it can be connected to a complete sentence. Simply change the punctuation.

> By the time of the recital, ^the girl has actually convinced herself that she can play well.

GRAMMAR HANDBOOK

APPLY WHAT YOU'VE LEARNED

Rewrite this paragraph, correcting the sentence fragments.

¹"Two Kinds" explores the world of a would-be musical child prodigy. ²In this selection from *The Joy Luck Club,* the mother tries to turn her daughter into a prodigy. ³But is not successful. ⁴In the case of Sarah Chang, on the other hand, was different. ⁵She was a natural musician. ⁶Who at the age of 12 was already performing on television with symphony orchestras. ⁷Most of the great violinists of the first half of this century. ⁸Came from Russia and Eastern Europe. ⁹Recently, gifted Asians have appeared. ¹⁰And have been making musical news. ¹¹Both of Chang's parents. ¹²Musicians who emigrated from Korea in 1979. ¹³Other former child prodigies. ¹⁴Tell funny or painful stories. ¹⁵About their childhood experiences. ¹⁶Itzhak Perlman, who inherited the mantle of Jascha Heifetz.

1.2 Run-On Sentences

A run-on sentence consists of two or more sentences incorrectly written as one. It is unclear where one idea ends and the next begins.

Forming Separate Sentences

One way to correct a run-on sentence is to form two separate sentences. Use a period or other end punctuation after the first complete thought and capitalize the first letter of the next sentence.

> Many of us remember teachers who influenced our lives positively, one good example is Marjorie Hurd in "The Teacher Who Changed My Life."

Sometimes a writer mistakenly uses a comma instead of a period to separate two complete thoughts. You can correct this kind of mistake, called a comma splice, by changing the comma to a period and capitalizing the first letter of the second sentence.

> The author had endured horrible experiences by age nine, one teacher helped him use his experiences in his writing.

 REVISING TIP

To correct run-on sentences, read them to yourself, noticing where you naturally pause between ideas. The pause usually indicates where you should place end punctuation.

1.1 Sentence Fragments

Answers will vary. See typical answers below.

1 "Two Kinds" explores the world of a would-be musical child prodigy. **2-3** In this selection from *The Joy Luck Club,* the mother tries to turn her daughter into a prodigy but is not successful. **4** In the case of Sarah Chang, on the other hand, the outcome was different. **5-6** She was a natural musician who at the age of 12 was already performing on television with symphony orchestras. **7-8** Most of the great violinists of the first half of this century came from Russia and Eastern Europe. **9-10** Recently, gifted Asians have appeared and have been making musical news. **11-12** Both of Chang's parents are musicians who emigrated from Korea in 1979. **13-15** Other former child prodigies tell funny or painful stories about their childhood experiences. **16** One example is Itzhak Perlman, who inherited the mantle of Jascha Heifetz

Joining Sentences

If the ideas expressed in a run-on sentence are closely related, you may wish to join them to form a compound sentence. One way to do this is to use a comma and a coordinating conjunction to join the main clauses.

> The heroic stand of Nicholas Gage's mother resulted in her death**,** **but** she arranged her children's escape to freedom in the United States.

Use a semicolon alone, or with a conjunctive adverb, to join main clauses having closely related ideas.

Some commonly used conjunctive adverbs are *however, therefore, nevertheless,* and *besides.*

> The young Greek boy learned to love English as an ordinary means of expression**;** **besides,** it helped him communicate intense feelings in writing.

APPLY WHAT YOU'VE LEARNED

Rewrite this paragraph, correcting the run-on sentences.

¹In recent history Turkey, Yugoslavia, and the United States have all been involved in fighting or providing aid to Greece, during World War II the Communists in Greece engaged in antiroyalist activities. ²In 1946 the Communists resumed guerrilla warfare there was full-scale war on the northern frontier. ³Nicholas Gage writes about this period from his childhood memories liberal, conservative, and coalition governments supplanted each other. ⁴Violence became part of daily life women and even children participated actively. ⁵Gage's mother, Eleni Gatzoyiannis, was one of the patriots not until 1956 did women win the vote in Greece. ⁶Following a coup in 1967, a military government took over the country, in 1974 parliamentary government was restored. ⁷Instability has gradually yielded to a more stable government in recent years in 1981 Greece joined the European Economic Community. ⁸Today the country enjoys defense and economic agreements with the United States, possession of the island of Cyprus is still a bone of contention in some quarters.

1.2 Run-On Sentences

Answers will vary. See typical answers below.

1 In recent history Turkey, Yugoslavia, and the United States have all been involved in fighting or providing aid to Greece. During World War II the Communists in Greece engaged in antiroyalist activities. **2** In 1946 the Communists resumed guerrilla warfare, and there was full-scale war on the northern frontier. **3** Nicholas Gage writes about this period from his childhood memories. Liberal, conservative, and coalition governments supplanted each other. **4** Violence became part of daily life; women and even children participated actively. **5** Gage's mother, Eleni Gatzoyiannis, was one of the patriots; however, not until 1956 did women win the vote in Greece. **6** Following a coup in 1967, a military government took over the country, but in 1974 parliamentary government was restored. **7** Instability has gradually yielded to a more stable government in recent years, and in 1981 Greece joined the European Economic Community. **8** Today the country enjoys defense and economic agreements with the United States; nevertheless, possession of the island of Cyprus is still a bone of contention in some quarters.

Making Subjects and Verbs Agree   ②

2.1 Simple and Compound Subjects

A verb must agree in number with its subject. The word *number* refers to whether a word is singular or plural. When a word refers to one thing, it is singular. When it refers to more than one thing, it is plural.

Agreement with Simple Subjects

Use a singular verb with a singular subject.

When the subject is a singular noun, you use the singular form of the verb. The present-tense third-person singular form of a regular verb usually ends in *-s* or *-es*.

> In "On the Rainy River" the narrator confess^(es) what to him is a shameful secret.

Use a plural verb with a plural subject.

> Many people remembers̸ the period during the Vietnam War about which Tim O'Brien writes.

Agreement with Compound Subjects

Use a plural verb with a compound subject whose parts are joined by *and*, regardless of the number of each part.

> In the story the river and the wilderness helps̸ the narrator work through his problems.

> **REVISING TIP**
>
> To find the subject of a sentence, first find the verb. Then ask *who* or *what* is being spoken about. Say the subject and the verb together to see whether they agree.

When the parts of a compound subject are joined by *or* or *nor,* make the verb agree in number with the part that is closer to it.

Neither the young man nor the older one talk[s] about the problem.

APPLY WHAT YOU'VE LEARNED

Write the correct form of the verb.

¹In "On the Rainy River" the narrator's internal conflict reflect that of the Vietnam War itself. ²Americans is still divided about whether American involvement in the war was right. ³Some people feels that the war divided not only Vietnam but the United States as well. ⁴Other people sees U.S. participation as having been the only defense against encroaching communism. ⁵Conscience or the laws involves principle. ⁶Sometimes neither logical reasons nor patriotism supply simple, clear-cut answers. ⁷Often a decision and an action causes far-reaching results. ⁸Both a hawk and a dove finds their place in Vietnam. ⁹Some war resisters opts for prison. ¹⁰Emigration or illegal entry into Canada offer another option. ¹¹Going underground and changing one's identity provides a solution for war resisters. ¹²Returning home or contacting one's family result in prosecution. ¹³Today many Vietnam War resisters still resides in Canada.

2.2 Pronoun Subjects

When a pronoun is used as a subject, the verb must agree with it in number.

Agreement with Personal Pronouns

When the subject is a singular personal pronoun, use a singular verb. When the subject is plural, use a plural verb.

Singular pronouns are *I, you, he, she,* and *it.* Plural pronouns are *we, you,* and *they.*

In *Earthly Paradise* the author remembers her mother. She look[s] back fondly on her mother's independence, for example. As we read[s], we think[s] of our own mothers.

1062 GRAMMAR HANDBOOK

2.1 Simple and Compound Subjects

1. reflects
2. are
3. feel
4. see
5. involve
6. supplies
7. cause
8. find
9. opt
10. offers
11. provide
12. results
13. reside

When *he, she,* or *it* is the part of the subject closer to the verb in a compound subject containing *or* or *nor,* use a singular verb. When a pronoun is part of a compound subject containing *and,* use a plural verb.

> Colette and she shares a sense of determination. Neither another reader nor she appreciate their similarities fully.

Agreement with Indefinite Pronouns

When the subject is a singular indefinite pronoun, use the singular form of the verb.

The following are singular indefinite pronouns: *another, either, nobody, anybody, everybody, somebody, no one, anyone, everyone, someone, one, anything, everything, something, nothing, each,* and *neither.*

> Perhaps everyone like a garden, but Sido values gardens as much as she does people. Almost no one deserve one of her roses, she feels.

When the subject is a plural indefinite pronoun, use the plural form of the verb.

The following are plural indefinite pronouns: *both, few, many,* and *several.*

> Many considers their mothers special, but few expresses their feelings as well as Colette. The mother and daughter may at times exasperate each other. Both, however, respects individual differences.

GRAMMAR HANDBOOK 1063

2.2 Pronoun Subjects

1. relate
2. have
3. refuse; is
4. feels
5. owe
6. was
7. has
8. are
9. appear
10. rush
11. reveal

 REVISING TIP

In many sentences the indefinite pronouns listed at the right will be followed by a prepositional phrase that might help you determine whether the subject is singular or plural. Remember, however, that the object of the preposition is not the subject of the sentence.

The indefinite pronouns *some, all, any, none,* and *most* can be either singular or plural. When the pronoun refers to one thing, use a singular verb. When the pronoun refers to more than one thing, use a plural verb.

> Some of Sido's strength diminish^(es) with age, but most of her views remains as strong as ever. Many of the duties in her day becomes too hard for her to handle alone, but most of her determination stay^(s) intact to the end.

APPLY WHAT YOU'VE LEARNED

In each sentence, write the correct form of the verb.

¹Few (relate, relates) to their gardens as closely as Colette's mother, Sido, of whom the author speaks in *Earthly Paradise.* ²The French artist Claude Monet and she (has, have) this trait in common. ³We discover that both (refuse, refuses) to live in Paris, where it (is, are) difficult to find space for a garden. ⁴Each (feel, feels) an intense attachment to nature, especially flowers. ⁵"I (owe, owes) having become a painter to flowers," Monet once said. ⁶In his opinion his garden took priority over his paintings; he said that it (was, were) his greatest work of art. ⁷Almost everyone (has, have) seen prints of Monet's blue-and-lavender water-lily paintings. ⁸They (is, are) among his most loved works. ⁹Some (appear, appears) in almost every showing of impressionistic art. ¹⁰My friends and I (rush, rushes) to see displays of Monet's art. ¹¹All of them (reveal, reveals) his perception of people and nature.

 LINK TO LITERATURE

Note how subjects and verbs agree throughout W. P. Kinsella's "The Thrill of the Grass." Kinsella increases sentence variety by using interrupting words and phrases, as well as inverted sentences. With them he holds the reader's interest and builds tension.

2.3 Common Agreement Problems

Several other situations can cause problems in subject-verb agreement.

Interrupting Words and Phrases

Be sure the verb agrees with its subject when words or phrases come between them.

The subject of the verb is never found in a prepositional phrase or an appositive, which may follow the subject and come before the verb. Other phrases can also separate the subject and verb.

In "The Thrill of the Grass" the narrator, one of many disgruntled baseball fans, plan[s] simply to replace one square of artificial turf with another of sod.

Phrases beginning with *including*, *as well as*, *along with*, *such as*, and *in addition to* are not part of the subject.

The fan, as well as many of his friends, protest[s] the modernization of the grand old game of baseball. Even families of fans, including a great grandfather past 80, joins in the revolt.

Inverted Sentences

When the simple subject comes after the verb, be sure the verb agrees with the subject in number.

A sentence in which the subject follows the verb is called an inverted sentence. Questions are usually in inverted form, as are sentences beginning with *Here* and *There*. (*Where is the turf? Here come the fans.*)

Where is [are] the workers? Here comes [come] the laborers, and before them lie[s] the field of artificial turf, ready for them to harvest. Before long there are [is] a whole new field of real grass to replace the offensive artificial turf.

REVISING TIP

The forms of *do*, *be*, and *have* can be main verbs or helping verbs. They can also be part of contractions with *not* (*doesn't/don't*, *isn't/aren't*, *hasn't/haven't*). In every case the verb should agree in number with its subject.

REVISING TIP

To check subject-verb agreement in inverted sentences, place the subject before the verb. For example, change *There is the grass* to *The grass is there*.

GRAMMAR HANDBOOK **1065**

REVISING TIP

To find the subject, look carefully at words that come before the verb. Remember that the subject may not be the noun or pronoun closest to the verb.

Singular Nouns with Plural Forms

Be sure to use a singular verb when the subject is a noun that is singular in meaning but appears to be plural.

Words such as *rickets, measles,* and *series* appear to be plural because they end in *s*. However, these words are singular in meaning. Words ending in *ics* that refer to sciences or branches of study (*economics, civics, politics, semantics*) are also singular.

> The mathematics of the plan create̸ ^s only minor problems.
> A series of events follow̸ ^s because the motivation to make a statement is so strong.

Collective Nouns

Use a singular verb when the subject is a collective noun—such as *group, audience,* or *congregation*—that refers to a group acting as a unit. Use a plural verb when the collective noun refers to members of a group acting individually.

> The group continue̸ ^s to work together night after night.
> The team ha̸s ^have various reasons for doing what they do.

Nouns of Time, Weight, Measure, Number

Use a singular verb with a subject that identifies a period of time, a weight, a measure, or a number.

> Two months or so transform̸ ^s the stadium from artificial to natural. Perhaps a hundred thousand square feet of grass appear̸ ^s before the season has passed.

1066 GRAMMAR HANDBOOK

Titles

Use a singular verb when the subject is the title of a work of art, literature, or music, even though the title may contain plural words.

"Field of Dreams" ~~take~~ *takes* the characters and plot from the book *Shoeless Joe*, a work by W. P. Kinsella.

 REVISING TIP

The fact that a title is set off with quotation marks, italics, or underscoring helps to remind you it is singular and takes a singular verb.

Predicate Nominatives

Use a verb that agrees with the subject, not with the predicate nominative, when the subject is different in number from the predicate nominative.

When the workers finish their job, their feeling ~~are~~ *is* triumph and pride in a job well done.

APPLY WHAT YOU'VE LEARNED

Write the correct form of each verb.

1. W. P. Kinsella's novel *Shoeless Joe*, like his short story "The Thrill of the Grass," (deal, deals) with baseball.
2. *Shoeless Joe*, made into the highly successful movie *Field of Dreams*, (involve, involves) baseball fans.
3. Where (do, does) the author's ideas come from?
4. (Has, Have) he played baseball himself?
5. Unlike his ball-playing dad, he feels "there (was, were) essentially no place on the field it was safe for me to be."
6. A team sometimes (has, have) differences among themselves.
7. Kinsella, like some other writers, (has been, have been) a clerk and a cab driver.
8. His other jobs—including ad salesman, pizza-parlor owner, and college professor—(seem, seems) less interesting than those of his characters.
9. However, a million dollars (is, are) not enough to pay for experiences like his.
10. Most successful of all his enterprises (has, have) been his writing about baseball.
11. Someday a world series for baseball writers (is, are) likely to include Kinsella.

2.3 Common Agreement Problems

1. deals
2. involves
3. do
4. Has
5. was
6. have
7. has been
8. seem
9. is
10. has
11. is

3 Using Nouns and Pronouns

3.1 Plural and Possessive Nouns

Nouns refer to people, places, things, and ideas. A noun is plural when it refers to more than one person, place, thing, or idea. A possessive noun shows who or what owns something.

Plural Nouns

Follow these guidelines to form noun plurals.

- For most nouns, add -s (*bill—bills, date—dates*).
- For nouns ending in *s, sh, ch, x,* or *z,* add -es (*church—churches, fox—foxes*).
- For nouns ending in a consonant and *y,* change *y* to *i* and add -es (*lady—ladies, baby—babies*).
- For most nouns that end in a consonant and *o,* add -es (*hero—heroes, tomato—tomatoes*).
- For many nouns that end in *f* or *fe,* change *f* to *v* and add -s or -es (*knife—knives, loaf—loaves*).

Some nouns have the same spelling in both the singular and the plural: *moose, deer, salmon.* Some noun plurals have irregular forms that don't follow any rule: *teeth, geese.*

> There are interesting echos in this excerpt from "Tolerance," one of E. M. Forster's essayes. He argues for tolerance between nationes. People can love, in his view; countrys cannot.

Possessive Nouns

Follow these guidelines to form possessive nouns.

- Add an apostrophe and -s to form the possessive of a singular noun or a plural noun that does not end in -s (*father—father's, women—women's*).
- Add only an apostrophe to plural nouns that end in -s (*bottles—bottles', favorites—favorites'*).

REVISING TIP

A dictionary usually lists the plural form of a noun if the plural is formed irregularly or if it might be formed in more than one way. For example, the plural of *index* is given as both *indexes* and *indices.* Dictionary listings are especially helpful for nouns that end in *o, f,* and *fe.*

One human beings‸ attitude toward another is personal, he says. When nations‸ attempts to love one another fail, people abandon hope and cease trying to cooperate.

APPLY WHAT YOU'VE LEARNED

Write the correct plural or possessive.

¹E. M. Forsters "Tolerance" is only one of his many essay's. ²He also wrote short storys, a documentary, a biography, and a guidebook. ³Forsters' fame, however, rests mainly on his noveles. ⁴Some of these have been made into movies', including *A Passage to India*. ⁵His various work's themes include the virtues of truthfulness and kindness. ⁶The everyday values' of common sense, goodwill, and respect for others' feelings pervade his work. ⁷Each characters' experiences reflect his or her attitudes. ⁸The "good" one's commune with nature on an almost spiritual level. ⁹They rise above crass monetary concerns, to focus on the essentials of life. ¹⁰Throughout his writing's he urges liberality. ¹¹In *A Passage to India,* for example, a womans overreaction to fear of a dark cave results in a false accusation. ¹²In *A Room with a View* peoples' values create conflict.

3.1 Plural and Possessive Nouns

1. Forster's; essays
2. stories
3. Forster's; novels
4. movies
5. works'
6. values
7. character's
8. ones
9. concerns
10. writings
11. woman's
12. people's

3.2 Pronoun Forms

A personal pronoun is a pronoun that can be used in the first, second, or third person. A personal pronoun has three cases or forms: the subject form, the object form, and the possessive form.

Subject Pronouns

Use the subject form of a pronoun when it is the subject of a sentence or the subject of a clause. *I, you, he, she, it, we,* and *they* are subject pronouns.

Problems usually arise when a noun and a pronoun or two pronouns are used in a compound subject or compound object. To see whether you are using the correct form, read the sentence as if it contained just one pronoun.

LINK TO LITERATURE

Notice how Alice Walker uses pronouns to avoid repetition of the nouns and to create an informal effect throughout "Everyday Use," page 110.

"Everyday Use" reminds me of a discussion I had about a week ago. My mother and me‸ think that things were made to be used, not saved.

GRAMMAR HANDBOOK **1069**

REVISING TIP

To check for the right pronoun, see if the sentence still makes sense when the subject and pronoun are reversed. (*It was he. He was it.*)

Use the subject form of a pronoun when it is a predicate pronoun following a linking verb.

You often hear the object form used in casual conversation (*It is him*). However, the subject form is preferred for more formal writing.

> Many people save dishes and linens to use for special company. We should remember that special company can also be you or me. [*I*]

Object Pronouns

Use the object form of a pronoun when it is the object of a verb or verbal, or the object of a preposition. *Me, you, him, her, it, us,* and *them* are object pronouns.

> Maggie knew that her sister Dee looked down on her mother and she. [*her*] The mother, however, had always treated Dee and she [*her*] the same.

Possessive Pronouns

Never use an apostrophe in a possessive pronoun. *My, mine, your, yours, his, her, hers, its, our, ours, their,* and *theirs* are possessive pronouns.

> Perhaps you know people like Dee. They might think that they're [*their*] sense of what's appropriate is better than your's.

1070 GRAMMAR HANDBOOK

APPLY WHAT YOU'VE LEARNED

Write the following sentences, correcting the pronouns.

¹In "Everyday Use" Alice Walker introduces two sisters and they're mother. ²One sister, who has left home, thinks of some of the antiques as her's. ³She especially wants her mother to give some handmade quilts to her friend and she. ⁴Dee feels that the rightful inheritor of the quilts is her. ⁵Mrs. Johnson has earmarked the quilts for Maggie's intended husband and she. ⁶Quilts were made for daily use, but them are also works of art. ⁷During the Civil War, soldiers' families sometimes gave the soldiers small quilts for they're cots. ⁸Recently, my friends and me have heard about quilts used in protest movements.

3.3 Pronoun Antecedents

An antecedent is the noun or pronoun to which a personal pronoun refers. The antecedent usually precedes the pronoun.

Pronoun and Antecedent Agreement

The pronoun must agree with its antecedent in number, person, and gender.

Use a singular pronoun to refer to a singular antecedent; use a plural pronoun to refer to a plural antecedent.

Do not allow interrupting words to determine the number of the personal pronoun.

> In this excerpt from *Farewell to Manzanar*, Jeanne Wakatsuki Houston recounts the indignities of internment in a relocation center and tells how it haunts her still.
> *they*

If the antecedent is a noun that could refer to either a male or a female, use *he or she (him or her, his or her)* or reword the sentence to avoid the singular pronoun.

> Each person in camp had to deal with the humiliation and discomfort in their own way.
> *his or her*

LINK TO LITERATURE

Notice the care that Jeanne Wakatsuki Houston and James D. Houston take to ensure that pronouns agree with their antecedents in the excerpt from *Farewell to Manzanar*, on page 330. Readers have no trouble understanding the events and relationships described in the story, which records a dark time in modern American history.

REVISING TIP

You could also revise the example at the left this way: *All of the people* in camp had to deal with the humiliation and discomfort in their own way.

3.2 Pronoun Forms

1 In "Everyday Use" Alice Walker introduces two sisters and their mother. 2 One sister, who has left home, thinks of some of the antiques as hers. 3 She especially wants her mother to give some handmade quilts to her friend and her. 4 Dee feels that the rightful inheritor of the quilts is she. 5 Mrs. Johnson has earmarked the quilts for Maggie's intended husband and her. 6 Quilts were made for daily use, but they are also works of art. 7 During the Civil War, soldiers' families sometimes gave the soldiers small quilts for their cots. 8 Recently, my friends and I have heard about quilts used in protest movements.

 **REVISING TIP**

To avoid vague pronoun reference, do not use *this* or *that* alone to start a clause. Instead, include a word stating the thing or idea to which *this* or *that* refers—*this alternative, this concept, that theory.*

Be sure that the antecedent of a pronoun is clear.

In most cases do not use a pronoun to refer to an entire idea or clause. Writing is much clearer if you give the exact idea.

> A new teacher's hostility contrasted starkly with a former-teacher's warmth. That hurt the young girl.
> (^experience after "That")

Unclear Antecedents

Make sure that each personal pronoun has a clear reference.

Clarify unidentified references.

The words *it, they, this, which,* and *that* can create problems when there is no clear antecedent to which they refer.

> In *Farewell to Manzanar* it shows the reader how irrationally people behave during wartime.

Clarify ambiguous references.

Ambiguous means "having two or more possible meanings." A pronoun reference is ambiguous if the pronoun may refer to more than one antecedent.

> An old woman was as modest as the author's mother. She (The woman) allowed her (the mother) to use her (the) makeshift screen.

Compound Antecedents Using *Or* or *Nor*

When two or more singular antecedents are joined by *or* or *nor,* use a singular pronoun. When two or more plural antecedents are joined by *or* or *nor,* use a plural pronoun.

> Neither the mother nor her daughter had a bed of their (her) own in the tiny camp unit.

When one singular and one plural antecedent are joined by *or* or *nor,* use the noun or pronoun nearer the verb to determine whether the pronoun should be singular or plural.

> Too excited to be tired, neither the mother nor the girls found ~~her~~ *their* trip exhausting.

REVISING TIP

Be careful with the indefinite use of *you* and *they*.

> ~~You~~ *One* should always try to make the best of ~~it when they~~ *being* put ~~you~~ in a situation such as this.

Indefinite Pronouns as Antecedents

When a singular indefinite pronoun is the antecedent, use *he or she (him or her, his or her),* or rewrite the sentence.

> Everyone ran around to see if ~~their~~ *his or her* friends were there.

APPLY WHAT YOU'VE LEARNED

Correct the pronouns to clarify antecedents.

¹In *Farewell to Manzanar* you did not have to commit a crime to be relocated. ²The U.S. government and society discriminated against Americans of Japanese descent; it was unfair. ³Canada did not have internment camps, but they too relocated West Coast citizens of Japanese heritage. ⁴All family members or a single Japanese Canadian had to move to a place new to them. ⁵Canada might assign one of these citizens, regardless of their level of education or skill, to work in the fields. ⁶Everyone was in the same situation, so they made the best of it. ⁷A doctor or a farmer—each had their individual experiences. ⁸The author kept her mother's spirits up, but she often felt bad.

3.4 Pronoun Usage

The form that a pronoun takes is always determined by its function within its own clause or sentence.

Who and Whom

Use *who* or *whoever* as the subject of a clause or a sentence.

> "The Pearl" leaves readers wondering not ~~whom~~ *who* stole a missing pearl but why everybody lied about it.

REVISING TIP

In the example at the left, *who* is the subject of the clause *who stole a missing pearl.*

GRAMMAR HANDBOOK 1073

REVISING TIP

Whom should replace *who* in each sentence of the example at the right:
Whom (she disliked)—direct object of the verb *disliked*
(To) whom—object of the preposition *to*

Use *whom* as the direct or indirect object of a verb or verbal and as the object of a preposition.

People often use *who* for *whom* when speaking informally. However, in written English the pronouns should be used correctly.

> One made up a story to place another, who [m] she disliked, in an uncomfortable position. Who [m] did she tell the story to that day?

In trying to determine the correct pronoun form, ignore interrupters that come between the subject and the verb.

In the example that follows, *who* should replace *whom* because the pronoun is the subject of the clause *who would actually steal*.

> Whom [who] of the women do you think would actually steal?

Pronouns in Contractions

Do not confuse these contractions—*it's, they're, who's,* and *you're*—with possessive pronouns that sound the same—*its, their, whose,* and *your*.

> It's [Its] not hard to imagine being in a situation similar to that of the birthday guests. They're [Their] responses seem excessive, however. Who's [Whose] pride requires such extreme measures as these?

Pronouns with Nouns

Determine the correct pronoun form in phrases such as *we students* by imagining what the sentence would look like if the pronoun appeared without the noun.

> The foibles of others may seem funny to we [us] readers, but what if the same thing happened to you or I [me]?

1074   GRAMMAR HANDBOOK

Pronouns in Comparisons

Be sure you use the correct form of a pronoun in a comparison.

Than or *as* often begins an elliptical clause, one in which some words have been left out. To decide which form of the pronoun to use, fill in the missing words.

> Author Yukio Mishima writes with more subtlety than ~~me~~ I [do].
> Few writers can show as effectively as ~~him~~ he [does] how a small occurrence can trigger a chain of events.

Shifts in Person

Be sure that a pronoun agrees with its antecedent in person.

One, everyone, and *everybody* are in the third person. They should be referred to by the third-person pronouns.

> Everyone should try to consider the feelings of others. ~~You~~ One cannot go wrong using this approach.

APPLY WHAT YOU'VE LEARNED

Rewrite the sentences correctly.

1 Reading "The Pearl," one can laugh at several minor deceptions; you are surprised at the suspicion that prompts them. **2** When one reads Guy de Maupassant's "The Necklace," we do not laugh at a deception. **3** The event changes the life of the woman, whom the reader discovers has lost only fake jewels. **4** She spends years working to repay the friend from who she borrowed the necklace. **5** Us readers are astounded when we learn that her sacrifice was needless. **6** Its sad to see the woman age prematurely. **7** The youth of her husband and her might have been more carefree than they were. **8** In this story, deceiving the woman who she asked for the necklace is not unkind. **9** The women in "The Pearl" were less considerate than her. **10** Who do you have more sympathy for?

3.4 Pronoun Usage

Answers will vary. See typical answers below.

1 Reading "The Pearl," one can laugh at several minor deceptions; one is surprised at the suspicion that prompts them. **2** When one reads Guy de Maupassant's "The Necklace," one does not laugh at a deception. **3** The event changes the life of the woman, who the reader discovers has lost only fake jewels. **4** She spends years working to repay the friend from whom she borrowed the necklace. **5** We readers are astounded when we learn that her sacrifice was needless. **6** It's sad to see the woman age prematurely. **7** The youth of her husband and her might have been more carefree than it was. **8** In this story, deceiving the woman whom she asked for the necklace is not unkind. **9** The women in "The Pearl" were less considerate than she. **10** Whom do you have more sympathy for?

4 Using Modifiers Effectively

4.1 Adjective or Adverb?

Use an adjective to modify a noun or a pronoun. Use an adverb to modify a verb, an adjective, or another adverb.

> The hero of "The Man in the Water" kept his mind on his chosen duty amazing^ly. Risking his own life, he careful^ly worked to save plane crash survivors from drowning.

REVISING TIP

Always determine first which word is being modified. In the first sentence of the example at the right, *kept* is the word being modified. Because *kept* is a verb, its modifier must be an adverb.

Use an adjective after a linking verb to describe the subject.

In addition to forms of the verb *be*, the following are linking verbs: *become, seem, appear, look, sound, feel, taste, grow,* and *smell*.

> Perhaps he'd never seemed heroically before, but he appeared quite courageously during his struggle to save lives.

APPLY WHAT YOU'VE LEARNED

Rewrite these sentences, selecting the correct modifier in each pair.

1. In "The Man in the Water" a passenger (heroic, heroically) saved some survivors of a plane crash.
2. After his death (busy, busily) investigators identified him as Arland D. Williams of South Carolina.
3. Not long after the tragedy, (grateful, gratefully) Washington, D.C., officials named part of a bridge after him.
4. Many have looked as (brave, bravely) as he.
5. In 1989 in the United Airlines crash at Sioux City, Iowa, a very (brave, bravely) passenger ran back into the burning plane.
6. That person rescued a baby who was tossed (high, highly) into a baggage compartment during the crash.
7. Some crash survivors cannot remember (easy, easily) the crash itself or the (intense, intensely) moments leading up to it.

4.1 Adjective or Adverb?

1. heroically
2. busy
3. grateful
4. brave
5. brave
6. high
7. easily; intense

4.2 Comparisons and Negatives

Comparative and Superlative Modifiers

Use the comparative form of an adjective or adverb to compare two things or actions. Use the superlative form to compare more than two things or actions.

Form the comparative by adding *-er* to short modifiers or by using the word *more* with longer modifiers. Form the superlative by adding *-est* or by adding the word *most*.

> In "A White Heron" Sylvia, a far more ~~quieter~~ person than the hunter, works ~~eagerlier~~ *more eagerly* to please him than he knows. Her ~~bestest~~ *best* efforts include climbing the ~~most tall~~ *tallest* tree to find the heron's home.

Illogical Comparisons

Avoid comparisons that don't make sense because of missing words or illogical construction.

> Sylvia feels more sympathy for the heron than the hunter *feels*. He was more eager to find the bird than any visitor *had been*.

Double Negatives

To avoid double negatives in comparisons, use only one negative word in a clause.

Besides *not* and *no*, the following are negative words: *never, nobody, none, no one, nothing, nowhere, hardly,* and *scarcely*.

> Sylvia had never been ~~nowhere~~ *anywhere* as high as the top of the majestic old pine tree, which towered above the other trees.

REVISING TIP

Without the added words, the comparisons in the second example are hard to understand. In the first sentence, the reader might conclude that Sylvia feels more sympathy for the heron than for the hunter. Similar logic applies to the second sentence.

4.2 Comparisons and Negatives

Answers will vary. See typical answers below.

1. In "A White Heron" Sylvia must decide between saving the largest bird in the woods—a heron—and winning the gratitude of the friendliest hunter she's ever met.
2. Sylvia's actions prove puzzling, and the people around her can hardly understand why she acts in such a manner.
3. The hunter has been trying to create the largest collection of stuffed birds that he can.
4. Sylvia can't understand why he has to kill the birds.
5. Sylvia's final decision about the heron was wiser than any other decision she had made.
6. The hunter's motives were more selfish than Sylvia's.
7. He could have killed the birds more quickly than they could reproduce.
8. Some herons form part of one of the most productive ecosystems, the salt marsh.
9. Long legs and huge bills help them hunt frogs and fishes best in shallow water.
10. Without herons as predators, populations of small aquatic animals would increase faster than their food supply.

APPLY WHAT YOU'VE LEARNED

Rewrite these sentences, correcting mistakes in modifiers.

1. In "A White Heron" Sylvia must decide between saving the most large bird in the woods—a heron—and winning the gratitude of the friendlier hunter she's ever met.
2. Sylvia's actions prove puzzling, and the people around her can't hardly understand why she acts in such a manner.
3. The hunter has been trying to create the most largest collection of stuffed birds that he can.
4. Sylvia can't scarcely understand why he has to kill the birds.
5. Sylvia's final decision about the heron was wiser than any decision she had made.
6. The hunter's motives were more selfish than Sylvia.
7. He could have killed the birds quicklier than they could reproduce.
8. Some herons form part of one of the productivest ecosystems, the salt marsh.
9. Long legs and huge bills help them hunt frogs and fishes most well in shallow water.
10. Without herons as predators, populations of small aquatic animals would increase more faster than their food supply.

REVISING TIP

Misplaced modifiers cause confusion. Without the change shown in the example at the right, the reader momentarily wonders how a man can be an actress.

4.3 Misplaced or Dangling Modifiers

A misplaced modifier is separated from the word it modifies. It may appear to modify the wrong word and can confuse the reader. A dangling modifier seems unrelated to any word in the sentence. Misplaced or dangling modifiers are usually phrases or clauses.

Misplaced Modifier

Place a modifier near the word it modifies.

In "The Witness for the Prosecution" the accused man, ~~an actress,~~ says that his girlfriend, *an actress,* can verify his alibi for the night of the murder.

Dangling Modifier

Be sure a modifier describes a particular word in the sentence.

Discovering a flaw in one witness's testimony, *the lawyer found* ~~was found~~ the truth too late to serve justice.

APPLY WHAT YOU'VE LEARNED

Rewrite these sentences, correcting misplaced and dangling modifiers.

1. In "The Witness for the Prosecution" the murderer of a clever scheme risks discovery.
2. The accused man and his girlfriend wait impatiently for the jury, probably hoping for the inheritance money, to announce its verdict.
3. The twists and turns of this story's plot in real life seldom are duplicated.
4. Although sometimes expedient, the risk of a liar's being discovered increases with the complexity of the lie.
5. "Witness" resembles the 1924 crime committed by Leopold and Loeb, as an intellectual exercise, who killed Robert Franks.
6. They escaped execution only through a resounding speech by their lawyer against capital punishment, Clarence Darrow.

4.4 Special Problems with Modifiers

The following terms are frequently misused in spoken English. Be careful to use them correctly in written English.

Bad and *Badly*

Always use *bad* as an adjective, whether before a noun or after a linking verb. *Badly* should generally be used to modify an action verb.

> "The Californian's Tale" shows how bad**ly** a husband can miss his wife.

This, That, These, Those, and *Them*

Whether used as adjectives or pronouns, *this* and *these* refer to people and things that are nearby, and *that* and *those* refer to people and things that are farther away.

Them is a pronoun; it never modifies a noun. *Those* may be a pronoun or an adjective.

> His wife had left home to visit ~~them~~ relatives, long delayed in her return, and the widower had a hard time dealing with ~~this~~ *that* devastating event.

REVISING TIP

Avoid the use of *here* with *this* and *these*; also, do not use *there* with *that* and *those*.

What else could the widower do when those ~~there~~ sad memories tormented him?

4.3 Misplaced or Dangling Modifiers

Answers will vary. See typical answers below.

1. In "The Witness for the Prosecution" the murderer risks discovery of a clever scheme.
2. The accused man and his girlfriend, probably hoping for the inheritance money, wait impatiently for the jury to announce its verdict.
3. The twists and turns of this story's plot are seldom duplicated in real life.
4. Although a lie is sometimes expedient, the risk of a liar's being discovered increases with the complexity of the lie.
5. "Witness" resembles the 1924 crime committed by Leopold and Loeb, who killed Robert Franks as an intellectual exercise.
6. They escaped execution only through a resounding speech against capital punishment by their lawyer, Clarence Darrow.

Few, Fewer, Fewest and Little, Less, Least

Few, fewer, and **fewest** refer to numbers of things that can be counted. **Little, less,** and **least** refer to amounts or quantities.

> Each year, ~~less~~ *fewer* miners remained in the territory. When the visitor arrived, he realized that some miners had ~~fewer~~ *less* hope than others in their chances for success.

Misplacement of Only

For clarity, *only* should be positioned before the word or words it modifies.

The misplacement of *only* can alter, and sometimes confuse, the meaning of a sentence. Notice in the example below the difference in meaning when *only* is moved.

> *Only* The old miners ~~only~~ knew the whole truth about the story of their friend's sweet young wife.

APPLY WHAT YOU'VE LEARNED

Rewrite these sentences, correcting the errors in modifiers.

1. In "The Californian's Tale" Henry had few pleasure to look forward to.
2. His cottage was thickly covered by these vines and roses that the narrator had seen elsewhere in this region.
3. Many like him went to California in 1849 and afterward for the gold rush. They wanted gold very bad.
4. They only thought they would be happy if they had this precious metal.
5. However, less newcomers did well than you might think.
6. Henry's home furnishings imply that he made a fair amount of money during them boom years.
7. Of the forty-niners, little could have afforded this varnished furniture, these framed pictures, or them china vases.
8. Yet he certainly wasn't rich, except perhaps in this fantasy that his wife was still alive.
9. Most of them prospectors and miners spent their earnings on overpriced essentials and made the shopkeepers only rich.
10. That there makes me wonder whether Henry had kept a general store before the gold ran out.

4.4 Special Problems with Modifiers

1. In "The Californian's Tale" Henry had little pleasure to look forward to.
2. His cottage was thickly covered by those vines and roses that the narrator had seen elsewhere in that region.
3. Many like him went to California in 1849 and afterward for the gold rush. They wanted gold very badly.
4. They thought they would be happy only if they had that precious metal.
5. However, fewer newcomers did well than you might think.
6. Henry's home furnishings imply that he made a fair amount of money during those boom years.
7. Of the forty-niners, few could have afforded that varnished furniture, those framed pictures, or those china vases.
8. Yet he certainly wasn't rich, except perhaps in that fantasy that his wife was still alive.
9. Most of those prospectors and miners spent their earnings on overpriced essentials and made only the shopkeepers rich.
10. That makes me wonder whether Henry had kept a general store before the gold ran out.

Using Verbs Correctly 5

5.1 Verb Tenses and Forms

Verb tense shows the time of an action or a condition. Writers sometimes cause confusion when they use different verb tenses in describing actions that occur at the same time.

Consistent Use of Tenses

When two or more actions occur at the same time or in sequence, use the same verb tense to describe the actions.

> In "And of Clay Are We Created," when Rolf Carlé arrives at the scene of a disaster, he embarked (s/embarks) on a demanding journey within himself.

A shift in tense is necessary when two events occur at different times or out of sequence. The tenses of the verbs should clearly indicate that one action precedes the other.

> Carlé confronted (p) the fears he buries (d/buried) in childhood, as he will offer (p/offers) human closeness to a trapped child.

Tense	Verb Form
Present	dream/dreams
Past	dreamed
Future	will/shall dream
Present perfect	has/have dreamed
Past perfect	had dreamed
Future perfect	will/shall have dreamed

LINK TO LITERATURE

In "And of Clay Are We Created" Isabel Allende has her narrator use the past tense and past perfect tense to describe what happened to Rolf Carlé during the disaster. On page 839, however, the narrator moves into the present tense to describe the continuing impact of that time on Carlé. The shift emphasizes the profound change in him.

REVISING TIP

In telling a story, be careful not to shift tenses so often that the reader finds the sequence of events unclear.

Past Tense and Past Participle

The simple past form of a verb can always stand alone. The past participle of the following irregular verbs should always be used with a helping verb.

Present Tense	Past Tense	Past Participle
know	knew	(have, had) known
lay	laid	(have, had) laid
lie	lay	(have, had) lain
ride	rode	(have, had) ridden
rise	rose	(have, had) risen
run	ran	(have, had) run
say	said	(have, had) said
see	saw	(have, had) seen
sing	sang	(have, had) sung
sit	sat	(have, had) sat
speak	spoke	(have, had) spoken
steal	stole	(have, had) stolen
swim	swam	(have, had) swum
take	took	(have, had) taken
teach	taught	(have, had) taught

> **REVISING TIP**
>
> The past tense and past participle of regular verbs have the same spelling. Both forms end in -d or -ed. However, you usually double the final consonant before adding -ed when a short-vowel sound precedes the consonant (*slip—slipped, knit—knitted, rot—rotted, pat—patted, stub—stubbed*).

During her ordeal the child ^*had* known strength beyond her years. Her courage and wisdom ^*had* given Carlé consolation.

APPLY WHAT YOU'VE LEARNED

Write the correct verb form or tense in the parentheses.

1. In "And of Clay Are We Created" a volcano (causes, will cause) the vast tide of mud that (buried, buries) several villages.
2. The volcanic disaster described in the story closely (resembles, will resemble) that of Nevado del Ruiz, which killed 22,000 people in 1985 in the Colombian town of Armero.
3. This actual eruption, like the fictional one, (occurs, occurred) in November.
4. Because the eruption (throws, had thrown) hot rock fragments on the mountain's ice cap, mudflows (had begun, began).
5. They unlocked water that had long (laid, lain) frozen.
6. In the past, overpopulation (has led, leads) to the construction of towns too close to volcanoes.
7. People should (have known, know) better.
8. In 1845 Nevado del Ruiz killed a thousand people with a mudflow over territory that later (became, becomes) Armero.

1082 GRAMMAR HANDBOOK

5.1 Verb Tenses and Forms

1. causes; buries
2. resembles
3. occurred
4. had thrown; began
5. lain
6. has led
7. have known
8. became

5.2 Commonly Confused Verbs

The following verb pairs are often confused.

Affect and Effect

Affect means "to influence." **Effect** means "to cause."

> In *The Ring of General Macías* the general's wife attempts to ~~effect~~ *affect* future events. Killing de la O might ~~affect~~ *effect* a change in history.

Lie and Lay, Sit and Set

Lie means "to rest in a flat position" or "to be in a certain place"; **lay** means "to put or place." **Sit** means "to be in a seated position"; **set** means "to put or place."

> Raquel forces the intruder, de la O, to ~~set~~ *sit*, staring into space; meanwhile, the poison ~~lays~~ *lies* in a desk drawer.

 REVISING TIP

If you're uncertain about which verb to use, check to see whether the verb has an object. The verbs *lie* and *sit* never have objects—and they both refer to position. The verbs *lay* and *set* both have objects—and they have the same meaning.

Rise and Raise

Rise means "to move upward." **Raise** means "to move something upward."

> De la O ~~rises~~ *raises* the poisoned wine to his lips, then Raquel ~~raises~~ *rises* and runs to call Cleto.

Learn and Teach

Learn means "to gain knowledge or skill." **Teach** means "to help someone learn."

> The rebel leader attempted to ~~learn~~ *teach* Raquel that his people would win.

Bring and Take

Bring refers to movement toward or with the speaker or writer.
Take refers to movement away from the speaker or writer.

> Raquel wondered what had taken [brought] de la O to her door. Eventually he offers to bring [take] a letter to her prisoner husband.

> **REVISING TIP**
> When no movement is implied, *bring* may be used to mean "produce a result."

Present Tense	Past Tense	Past Participle
affect	affected	(have, had) affected
effect	effected	(have, had) effected
lie	lay	(have, had) lain
lay	laid	(have, had) laid
sit	sat	(have, had) sat
set	set	(have, had) set
rise	rose	(have, had) risen
raise	raised	(have, had) raised
learn	learned	(have, had) learned
teach	taught	(have, had) taught
bring	brought	(have, had) brought
take	took	(have, had) taken

APPLY WHAT YOU'VE LEARNED

Choose the correct verb from each pair in parentheses.

1. *The Ring of General Macías* explores incidents near Mexico City that (sit, set) a course for change in April of 1912.
2. The revolution (affected, effected) great tumult during those days.
3. Frequent betrayal by their leaders (learned, taught) landless peasants to (raise, rise) up repeatedly against wealthy landowners.
4. Some rebels attempted to (take, bring) justice to Mexico by violent means.
5. They approached the problem in extreme ways because reasonable approaches hadn't (learned, taught) the powerful people anything.
6. The rebels realized that leaders can't just (lay, lie) around and hope for the best.
7. Leaders must skillfully (effect, affect) the course of events.

5.2 Commonly Confused Verbs

1. set
2. effected
3. taught; rise
4. bring
5. taught
6. lie
7. affect

Correcting Capitalization

6.1 Proper Nouns and Adjectives

A common noun names a class of persons, places, things, or ideas. A proper noun names a particular person, place, thing, or idea. A proper adjective is an adjective formed from a proper noun. Capitalize all proper nouns and proper adjectives.

Names and Titles

Capitalize the name of a person and the initials that stand for the name of a person.

> In "The Meeting" maneco uriarte challenges duncan to a duel at a country house outside Buenos Aires, Argentina.

Capitalize a title used before a name or an abbreviation for the title. In general, do not capitalize either a title that follows a name or a title that stands alone.

> In 1910—about the same year as the duel—the leadership of Argentina shifted from president alcorta to roque sáenz peña, his successor as President.

Capitalize a title indicating a family relationship when it is used before or as someone's name *(Aunt Vera, Grandpa)* **but not when used simply to identify a person** *(Marco's uncle).*

> The narrator was only nine or ten years old, and cousin lafinur took him to a barbecue. The Cousin was older.

LINK TO LITERATURE

In "The Meeting" on page 514, notice how Jorge Luis Borges refers to specific places, people, and things. These precise names help you visualize scenes. More general words probably would not help you see the story or believe it as well.

REVISING TIP

Prefixes and suffixes such as *ex-* and *-elect* are not capitalized when used with a title. (*On the morning after Election Day in 1988, President-elect George Bush began to assemble a transition team.*)

Languages, Nationalities, Religious Terms

Capitalize languages and nationalities, as well as religious names and terms. Do not capitalize the words *god* and *goddess* when they refer to mythological deities.

Capitalize languages and nationalities, such as *Norwegian, Bengali, Hebrew, Japanese, Louisiana French,* and *Turkish*. Capitalize religious names and terms, such as *God, Buddha,* the *Bible,* and the *Koran*.

> Even back then, many argentineans celebrated their gaucho heritage in ballads. Many of these ballads originated in uruguay.

> **REVISING TIP**
> Do not capitalize pronouns that refer to a deity. (*The earth goddess Gaia in **her** joy nurtures you.*)

School Subjects

Capitalize the name of a specific school course (*Astronomy I, Ancient History*). Do not capitalize a general reference to a school subject (*physical education, computer science*).

> The narrator was never a student in literature 101, but his experiences would have given him much to say in a Writing class.

Organizations, Institutions

Capitalize the important words in the official names of organizations and institutions (*Congress, Kendall College*).

Do not capitalize words that represent kinds of organizations or institutions (*school, church, university*) or words that refer to a specific organization when they are not part of its official name (*at the university*).

> By 1910 the national autonomist party, a conservative group, had begun to lose control of Argentina. In 1912 sáenz peña used the congress to confirm radical power.

> **REVISING TIP**
> Do not capitalize minor words in a proper noun that is made up of several words. (*the Department **of** Agriculture*)

1086 GRAMMAR HANDBOOK

Geographical Names, Events, Time Periods

Capitalize geographical names—as well as the names of events, historical periods and documents, holidays, months, and days—but not the names of seasons.

Names	Examples
Continents	South America, Europe, Antarctica
Bodies of water	Atlantic Ocean, Iguaçu Falls, Strait of Magellan
Political units	Argentina, Brazil, Montevideo, Bahía Blanca
Areas of a country	the Pampa, Patagonia, the Gran Chaco
Public areas	Columbus Park, Don Torcuato Airport
Roads and structures	Casa Rosada, Rodeo Drive
Events	Congress of Tucumán, the Mexican Revolution
Documents	Treaty of Paris, the Constitution of 1853
Periods of history	the Great Depression, the Enlightenment
Holidays	Cinco de Mayo, Veterans Day
Months and days	November, Monday
Seasons	summer, fall
Directions	south, northeast

 REVISING TIP

Do not capitalize a reference that does not use the full name of a place, an event, or a period. (*The night of the tragedy, Lafinur sang a ballad about a knife fight in Jun'in Street. That **street** had seen much violence.*)

> The duel took place at Señor Acevedo's country house, the laurels, north of buenos aires and near the paraná river. It happened late on a warm Summer evening, perhaps in february of 1910.

APPLY WHAT YOU'VE LEARNED

Rewrite the following sentences, correcting errors in capitalization.

1. In "The Meeting" a group of argentinean men and a boy, the narrator, see a fatal duel.
2. The narrator sets the time of the duel by the appearance of halley's comet in 1910.
3. In 1910 in argentina, the constitution of 1853 structured political life.
4. general urquiza helped finalize the document on may 25, 1853.
5. The argentinean congress dates from that time.
6. Later on, buenos aires gained a University and the national historical museum.
7. Three decades before the 1910 duel, general julio roca fought the last of the indian wars.
8. In 1929 the narrator talks with josé olave, a retired police Captain, about the duel.
9. The Captain tells stories about the tough neighborhood called the retiro.
10. Finally, olave recalls that one of the knives used in the duel belonged to an outlaw, juan almada from tapalquén.

GRAMMAR HANDBOOK **1087**

6.1 Proper Nouns and Adjectives

1. In "The Meeting" a group of Argentinean men and a boy, the narrator, see a fatal duel.
2. The narrator sets the time of the duel by the appearance of Halley's Comet in 1910.
3. In 1910 in Argentina, the Constitution of 1853 structured political life.
4. General Urquiza helped finalize the document on May 25, 1853.
5. The Argentinean Congress dates from that time.
6. Later on, Buenos Aires gained a university and the National Historical Museum.
7. Three decades before the 1910 duel, General Julio Roca fought the last of the Indian wars.
8. In 1929 the narrator talks with José Olave, a retired police captain, about the duel.
9. The captain tells stories about the tough neighborhood called the Retiro.
10. Finally, Olave recalls that one of the knives used in the duel belonged to an outlaw, Juan Almada from Tapalquén.

6.2 Titles of Created Works

The titles of published material follow certain capitalization rules.

Books, Plays, Magazines, Newspapers, Films

Capitalize the first word, the last word, and all other important words in the title of a book, play, periodical, newspaper, or film. Underline or italicize the title to set it off.

Within a title, do not capitalize articles, conjunctions, and prepositions of fewer than five letters unless they appear at the beginning or the end of the title.

> D. H. Lawrence's novel sons and lovers describes his boyhood as the son of a coal miner. His first published story appeared in the nottinghamshire guardian, and his first novel, the white peacock, was published in 1911.

Poems, Stories, Articles

Capitalize the first word, last word, and all other important words in the title of a poem, a short story, or an article. Enclose the title in quotation marks.

> Students often read his short stories, such as the prussian officer, or the poem called piano.

APPLY WHAT YOU'VE LEARNED

Rewrite the sentences, correcting the punctuation and capitalization of titles.

1. Three of Lawrence's poems about animals are fish, snake, and mountain lion. They appear in his book called birds, beasts, and flowers.
2. Many readers enjoy his travel books, including sea and sardinia and a later volume, mornings in mexico.
3. His interest in Mexico can also be seen in his novel the plumed serpent.
4. Lawrence's story the horse dealer's daughter is in the collection england, my england and other stories.
5. He also wrote a brilliant but eccentric book about American writers, called studies in classic american literature.

6.2 Titles of Created Works

1. Three of Lawrence's poems about animals are "Fish," "Snake," and "Mountain Lion." They appear in his book called *Birds, Beasts, and Flowers*.
2. Many readers enjoy his travel books, including *Sea and Sardinia* and a later volume, *Mornings in Mexico*.
3. His interest in Mexico can also be seen in his novel *The Plumed Serpent*.
4. Lawrence's story "The Horse Dealer's Daughter" is in the collection *England, My England and Other Stories*.
5. He also wrote a brilliant but eccentric book about American writers, called *Studies in Classic American Literature*.

Correcting Punctuation

7.1 Punctuating Compound Sentences

Punctuation helps organize sentences that have more than one clause.

Commas in Compound Sentences

Use a comma before the conjunction that joins the clauses of a compound sentence.

Do not use a comma before the conjunction that joins a compound subject or a compound predicate.

> In "By the Waters of Babylon" Stephen Vincent Benét tells a story in the first person‸and this focus proves to be very effective.

Semicolons in Compound Sentences

Use a semicolon between the clauses of a compound sentence when no conjunction is used. Use a semicolon before a conjunctive adverb that joins the clauses of a compound sentence.

Conjunctive adverbs include *therefore, however, consequently, nevertheless,* and *besides.* You should place a comma after a conjunctive adverb in a compound sentence.

> The reader identifies with the boy who is telling about his adventure‸however‸few readers will ever have an adventure like John's.

 REVISING TIP

Even when clauses are connected by a coordinating conjunction, you should use a semicolon between them if one or both clauses contain a comma. *(The hero of Benét's story, a boy named John, visits the Dead Places; and during his journey he discovers a great truth.)*

7.1 Punctuating Compound Sentences

1 In "By the Waters of Babylon" John, the son of a priest, undergoes a rite of passage to prove his manhood, and he passes the test. **2** Most societies observe specific rites of passage; in modern times, the most formalized of these rites, such as Christian confirmation and Jewish bar mitzvah, celebrate spiritual passages. **3** Most rites help people understand their new roles in society, but they also help others to recognize the people in their new roles. **4** Rites of passage have three stages; in the first, a participant is temporarily separated from the rest of society. **5** The second, or transitional stage, is a time of instruction; the participant learns about his or her new position. **6** The final stage involves the acknowledgment by the community of the new status of the individual; therefore, a celebration often marks the individual's achievement of this status.

APPLY WHAT YOU'VE LEARNED

Rewrite this paragraph, correcting problems with commas or semicolons.

1In "By the Waters of Babylon" John, the son of a priest, undergoes a rite of passage to prove his manhood and he passes the test. **2**Most societies observe specific rites of passage in modern times, the most formalized of these rites, such as Christian confirmation and Jewish bar mitzvah, celebrate spiritual passages. **3**Most rites help people understand their new roles in society but they also help others to recognize the people in their new roles. **4**Rites of passage have three stages in the first, a participant is temporarily separated from the rest of society. **5**The second, or transitional stage, is a time of instruction the participant learns about his or her new position. **6**The final stage involves the acknowledgment by the community of the new status of the individual therefore a celebration often marks the individual's achievement of this status.

7.2 Setting Off Elements in a Sentence

Most elements that are not essential to a sentence are set off by commas or by other punctuation marks to highlight the main idea of the sentence. A nonessential element merely adds information to an already complete sentence. An essential element is necessary to convey the accurate meaning of the sentence; without it, the meaning is unclear.

Commas

You should often use a comma to separate an introductory word or phrase from the rest of the sentence.

An introductory prepositional phrase usually need not be set off with a comma. However, you should use a comma for two or more prepositional phrases or for a phrase that includes a verb or a verbal.

> In the play *The Pen of My Aunt* by Josephine Tey‸ the setting is rural France during World War II. Known as the Occupation‸ that time saw much intrigue as spies and members of the resistance came and went.

1090 GRAMMAR HANDBOOK

In a complex sentence, set off an introductory subordinate clause with a comma.

> As the play opens, a Nazi corporal brings in a stranger who was found wandering in Madame's woods.

Use commas to set off a word or group of words that interrupt the flow of a sentence. When a subordinate clause interrupts the main clause, set off the subordinate clause with commas only if it is not essential.

> Madame and her servant Simone, thinking very quickly, scramble to support the stranger's claim that he's Madame's nephew. The stranger, who also thinks quickly, has no papers with him.

The words shown in the chart below are commonly used to begin a subordinate clause. When such words appear with introductory or interrupting clauses, they usually signal the need for one or more commas.

Words Often Used to Introduce Subordinate Clauses				
Subordinating Conjunctions	after although as as if as long as as though as much as	because before even if even though if in order that provided	since so that than though till unless until	whatever when whenever where wherever while
Relative Pronouns	which	who	whom	whose

REVISING TIP

Try saying the sentence without the interrupter; if the basic meaning doesn't change, you should use punctuation (commas, dashes, or parentheses) to set off the interrupter.

 REVISING TIP

A colon often follows a word or phrase such as *these* or *the following items*. Never use a colon after a preposition or after a verb when the items listed are essential to the clause.

Parentheses

Use parentheses to set off material that is only incidentally connected to the main idea of a sentence.

The Nazi corporal(who is negligent and easily fooled)tries unsuccessfully to see the stranger's papers.

Dashes

Use dashes to set off a word, or a group of words, that abruptly interrupts the flow of a sentence.

Simone almost throws away the stranger's freedom by speaking too soon. Luckily—through some clever wrangling—the damage is reversed.

Colons

Use a colon to introduce a list of items or a long quotation.

The stranger is told to seek help in these places: Forty Avenue in Crest, the pot boy at Mans, and Denis at Laloupe.

Use a colon between two sentences when the second explains or summarizes the first.

The stranger escapes in extraordinary company: the Nazi corporal drives him to the crossroads.

1092 GRAMMAR HANDBOOK

For Clarity

Use commas to prevent misreading or misunderstanding.

> A short time before, the Nazi corporal had planned to apprehend the stranger.

 REVISING TIP

Sometimes when a comma is missing, parts of a sentence can be grouped in more than one way by a reader. A comma separates the parts so they can be read in only one way.

APPLY WHAT YOU'VE LEARNED

Rewrite these sentences. Add commas, parentheses, dashes, and colons where necessary.

¹The stranger in *The Pen of My Aunt* is a member of the resistance a network of civilians working to defeat the Nazis. ²Participants included two groups civilians and armed guerrillas most likely accompanied by faithful animal companions. ³Their activities were legion they included printing secret newspapers and helping to rescue Allied pilots from enemy territory. ⁴Surprise attacks on German patrols a challenging way to start the day were part of the resistance's duties. ⁵Although all resistance groups had the same goals they didn't necessarily work together effectively. ⁶In spite of the unbelievable threat however much progress was made. ⁷In the play both Madame and the stranger are most likely Communists the Communists dominated the resistance in occupied France.

7.3 Elements in a Series

Use commas to separate three or more elements in a series and to separate multiple adjectives preceding a noun.

Subjects, Verbs, Objects, and Other Elements

Use a comma after every item except the last in a series of three or more items.

The three or more items can be nouns, verbs, adjectives, adverbs, phrases, independent clauses, or other parts of a sentence.

> In "The Balek Scales" the family picks herbs such as woodruff, thyme, mint, hayflowers, and foxgloves.

 REVISING TIP

Note in the example that a comma followed by a conjunction precedes the last element in the series. That comma is always used.

7.2 Setting Off Elements in a Sentence

Answers will vary. See typical answers below.

1 The stranger in *The Pen of My Aunt* is a member of the resistance, a network of civilians working to defeat the Nazis. **2** Participants included two groups: civilians and armed guerrillas—most likely accompanied by faithful animal companions. **3** Their activities were legion: they included printing secret newspapers and helping to rescue Allied pilots from enemy territory. **4** Surprise attacks on German patrols—a challenging way to start the day—were part of the resistance's duties. **5** Although all resistance groups had the same goals, they didn't necessarily work together effectively. **6** In spite of the unbelievable threat, however, much progress was made. **7** In the play both Madame and the stranger are most likely Communists (the Communists dominated the resistance in occupied France).

Two or More Adjectives

When more than one adjective precedes a noun, in most cases use a comma after each adjective except the last one.

If you can't reverse the order of adjectives without changing the meaning or if you can't use the word *and* between them, do not separate them with a comma.

> I consider the Baleks to have been arrogant˄ despotic˄ dishonest people. The narrator came from a good⸝ old family.

APPLY WHAT YOU'VE LEARNED

Rewrite the paragraph, correcting the comma errors.

¹"The Balek Scales" is set in a hilly wooded region whose borders have been changing for generations. ²Germany Czechoslovakia and now the Czech Republic have claimed these lands. ³Prague today is one of the most beautiful cosmopolitan and colorful cities in all of Europe. ⁴Its charm and its museums churches bridges and city square attract tourists from all over the world. ⁵The original settlements that merged into present-day Prague spanned hills river valleys and riverside terraces. ⁶Prague is famed for its exquisite crystal garnets and china. ⁷The Czechs call this historic, old-world city by its original name—Praha.

7.4 Dates, Addresses, and Letters

Punctuation in addresses, dates, and letters makes information easy to understand.

Dates

Use a comma after the day and the year to set off the date from the rest of the sentence.

> "Searching for Summer" might have been written about a wedding taking place November 21˄ 2088˄ somewhere in England.

REVISING TIP

In dates that include only the month and the year, do not use a comma after the month. (*Lily and Tom married in November 2088 not far from Inverness.*)

7.3 Elements in a Series

1 "The Balek Scales" is set in a hilly, wooded region whose borders have been changing for generations. **2** Germany, Czechoslovakia, and now the Czech Republic have claimed these lands. **3** Prague today is one of the most beautiful, cosmopolitan, and colorful cities in all of Europe. **4** Its charm and its museums, churches, bridges, and city square attract tourists from all over the world. **5** The original settlements that merged into present-day Prague spanned hills, river valleys, and riverside terraces. **6** Prague is famed for its exquisite crystal, garnets, and china. **7** The Czechs call this historic old-world city by its original name—Praha.

1094 GRAMMAR HANDBOOK

Addresses

In an address with more than one part, use a comma after each part to set it off from the rest of the sentence.

In what might as well be Brigadoon▲Scotland▲the young couple in the story find a bit of sunshine to make their joy complete.

REVISING TIP

In an address that includes the ZIP code, do not use a comma between the state abbreviation and the ZIP code.

Parts of a Letter

Use a comma after the greeting and after the closing of a letter.

Dear Mrs. Hatching▲

How can we ever thank you for our honeymoon—the kind that dreams are made of!

                         Gratefully▲
                         Lily and Tom

APPLY WHAT YOU'VE LEARNED

Rewrite the following paragraph, correcting the comma errors.

¹In "Searching for Summer" the skies above Bournemouth England are virtually always overcast. ²A weather forecaster might report information such as the following:

Dear Pat
   Please warn our listeners! Cumulus-shaped clouds suggest thunderstorms in the Antioch Illinois region. If they become cumulonimbus clouds, we are in for a tornado.
                With concern
                Jack

³In November, 1998, we might distinguish among numerous kinds of clouds. ⁴However, a different April 8 2088 radio announcement would be more usual in the world of "Searching for Summer." ⁵The "lowering" sky near Molesworth England would likely be stratus or stratocumulus clouds.

7.5 Quotations

Quotation marks tell readers who said what. Incorrectly placed or missing quotation marks lead to misunderstanding.

Direct Quotation from a Source

Use quotation marks at the beginning and the end of a direct quotation from source material and to set off the title of a short work. Do not use quotation marks to set off an indirect quotation.

> In ˅The First Seven Years˅ Malamud explores the struggles of a father, Feld, who wants the best for his child. Feld says he wants "to snare Max, the college boy, for his daughter Miriam."

Introducing a Quotation

Introduce a short direct quotation with a comma. Use a colon for a long quotation. Capitalize the first word in a direct quotation but not in an indirect one.

> Max says to Feld ˄"And is she sensible—not the flighty kind?"
> Feld replies˄ "She is very sensible."

End Punctuation

Place periods inside quotation marks. Place question marks and exclamation points inside quotation marks if they belong to the quotation; place them outside if they do not belong to the quotation. Place semicolons outside quotation marks.

> Max asks about her age, "Did you say nineteen"?
> Feld replies, "Yes;" then Max says, "Would it be all right to inquire if you have a picture of her"?

 REVISING TIP

If quoted words are from a written source and are not complete sentences, begin the quote with a lowercase letter. (*Bernard Malamud wrote that one's fantasy "goes for a walk and returns with a bride."*)

 REVISING TIP

Use a colon to introduce a long quotation. (*Anne Frank said: "Whoever is happy will make others happy too. He who has courage and faith will never perish in misery!"*)

1096 GRAMMAR HANDBOOK

Use a comma to end a quotation that is a complete sentence followed by explanatory words.

"Call her up. She comes home from work six o'clock" says Feld to Max.

Divided Quotations

Capitalize the first word of the second part of a direct quotation if it begins a new sentence.

"He has no soul," says Miriam. "he's only interested in things."

> **REVISING TIP**
>
> Should the first word of the second part of a divided quotation be capitalized? Imagine the quotation without the explanatory words. If a capital letter would not be used, then do not use one in the divided quotation.

Do not capitalize the first word of the second part of a divided quotation if it does not begin a new sentence.

"So how," Feld sighed after a sip, "Did you enjoy?"

APPLY WHAT YOU'VE LEARNED

Rewrite the sentences, inserting quotation marks and other appropriate punctuation.

1. In The First Seven Years Sobel, the shoemaker's assistant, is revealed as a Holocaust survivor.
2. An actual Holocaust survivor, author Cynthia Ozick, said the whole world wants us dead.
3. "The world has always wanted" she said "To wipe us out."
4. Rabbi Harold Schulweis asked if he must be like Yudka, in the short story The Sermon.
5. Yudka told a kibbutz meeting that "if it were up to him, he would simply forbid teaching Jewish history"
6. Yet Rabbi Schulweis says that "The survivors place a mirror to his soul."
7. In the article Half a Million Schindlers the author says "all of us, Jews and non-Jews, may find it hard to believe—evil has become more credible than good."
8. The people quoted in the article agree that "Jews need Christian heroes." and "Christians need Jewish heroes."

7.5 Quotations

1. In "The First Seven Years" Sobel, the shoemaker's assistant, is revealed as a Holocaust survivor.
2. An actual Holocaust survivor, Cynthia Ozick, said, "The whole world wants us dead."
3. "The world has always wanted," she said, "to wipe us out."
4. Rabbi Harold Schulweis asked if he must be like Yudka, in the short story "The Sermon."
5. Yudka told a kibbutz meeting that if it were up to him, he would simply forbid teaching Jewish history.
6. Yet Rabbi Schulweis says that the survivors place a mirror to his soul.
7. In the article "Half a Million Schindlers" the author says, "All of us, Jews and non-Jews, may find it hard to believe—evil has become more credible than good."
8. The people quoted in the article agree that Jews need Christian heroes and Christians need Jewish heroes.

8 Grammar Glossary

This glossary contains various terms you need to understand when you use the Grammar Handbook. Used as a reference source, this glossary will help you explore grammar concepts and how they relate to one another.

A

Abbreviation An abbreviation is a shortened form of a word or word group; it is often made up of initials. (*B.C., Lt., YWHA*)

Active voice. *See* **Voice.**

Adjective An adjective modifies, or describes, a noun or pronoun. (*strange* order, *happy* you)

A **predicate adjective** follows a linking verb and describes the subject. (The teacher seemed *energetic*.)

A **proper adjective** is formed from a proper noun. (*Egyptian* pyramids, *Irish* stew)

The **comparative** form of an adjective compares two items. (*more ambitious, kinder*)

The **superlative** form of an adjective compares more than two things. (*most certain, driest*)

What Adjectives Tell	Examples
How many	*some* oranges *most* explorers
What kind	*faint* outline *tighter* schedule
Which one(s)	*this* class *those* games

Adjective phrase. *See* **Phrase.**

Adverb An adverb modifies a verb, an adjective, or another adverb. (Ilya skates *gracefully*.)

The **comparative** form of an adverb compares two actions. (*more swiftly*)

The **superlative** form of an adverb compares more than two actions. (*most frankly*)

What Adverbs Tell	Examples
How	speak *softly* chew *thoroughly*
When	followed *after* *later* in the day
Where	traveled *there* fell *down*
To what extent	*too* angry *really* hurt

Adverb, conjunctive. *See* **Conjunctive adverb.**

Adverb phrase. *See* **Phrase.**

Agreement Sentence parts that correspond with one another are said to be in agreement.

In **pronoun-antecedent agreement,** a pronoun and the word it refers to are the same in number, gender, and person. (*Sue* caught the bus. *She* arrived on time.)

In **subject-verb agreement**, the subject and verb in a sentence are the same in number. (*I play* chess. *He plays* chess.)

Ambiguous reference An ambiguous reference occurs when a pronoun may refer to more than one word. (Arturo told Ramon that *he* had to leave.)

Antecedent An antecedent is the noun or the pronoun to which a pronoun refers. (*Dee* helps *her* friend.)

Appositive An appositive is a word or phrase that explains one or more words in a sentence. (Joe, *a drummer*, plays in the band.)

An **essential appositive** is needed to make the sense of a sentence complete. (My friend *Dom* went camping last week.)

A **nonessential appositive** is one that adds information to a sentence but is not necessary to its sense. (Will Rogers, *the noted humorist,* entertained them.)

Article Articles are the special adjectives *a, an,* and *the*. (*the* box, *a* poem)

The **definite article** (the word *the*) refers to a specific thing. (*the* cat)

An **indefinite article** indicates that a noun is not unique but is one of many of its kind. (*a* glove, *an* anchor)

Auxiliary verb. *See* **Verb.**

1098 GRAMMAR HANDBOOK

Clause A clause is a group of words that contains a verb and its subject. (*They help*)

An *adjective clause* is a subordinate clause that modifies a noun or pronoun in the main clause of a sentence. (She wrote the poem *that we recited.*)

An *adverb clause* is a subordinate clause used as an adverb to modify a verb, an adjective, or an adverb. (I can't remember *when she arrived.*)

A *noun clause* is a subordinate clause that is used as a noun. (*What I should eat for lunch* is my main concern right now.)

An *elliptical clause* is a clause from which a word or words have been omitted. (John writes better *than I.*)

A *main (independent) clause* can stand by itself as a sentence. (*a car sped by*)

A *subordinate (dependent) clause* does not express a complete thought and cannot stand by itself. (*when a stranger appeared at the door*)

Clause	Example
Main (independent)	The telephone rang shrilly
Subordinate (dependent)	after we had gone to bed.

Collective noun. See **Noun.**

Comma splice A comma splice is an error caused when two sentences are separated with a comma instead of a correct end mark. (*The music started, the flag was raised.*)

Common noun. See **Noun.**

Comparative. See **Adjective; Adverb.**

Complement A complement is a word or group of words that completes the meaning of the verb. (Rain ruined the *float.*) See also **Direct object; Indirect object.**

An *objective complement* is a word or a group of words that follows a direct object and renames or describes that object. (The parents considered their son a *genius.*)

A *subject complement* follows a linking verb and renames or describes the subject. (The vote was *unanimous.*) See **Noun, predicate; Adjective, predicate.**

Complete predicate The complete predicate of a sentence consists of the main verb plus any words that modify or complete the verb's meaning. (The circus *came to town.*)

Complete subject The complete subject in a sentence consists of the simple subject plus any words that modify or describe the simple subject. (*Several athletes from our school* entered the competition.)

Sentence Part	Example
Complete subject	The tall ship in the distance
Complete predicate	headed for the harbor.

Compound sentence part A sentence element that consists of two or more subjects, predicates, objects, or other parts is compound. (*Jay* and *Art* paint. Diane *sews* and *embroiders.* Pat speaks *English* and *Spanish.*)

Conjunction A conjunction is a word or group of words that links other words or groups of words.

A *coordinating conjunction* connects related words, groups of words, or sentences. (*and, but, or*)

A *correlative conjunction* is one of a pair of conjunctions that work together to connect sentence parts. (*either . . . or, neither . . . nor, not only . . . but also, both . . . and*)

A *subordinating conjunction* introduces a subordinate clause. (*after, although, as, as if, as long as, as though, because, before, if, in order that, provided, since, so that, than, though, till, unless, until, whatever, when, whenever, where, wherever, while*)

Conjunctive adverb A conjunctive adverb joins the clauses of a compound sentence. (*however, therefore, besides*)

Contraction A contraction is formed by joining two words and substituting an apostrophe for a letter or letters left out of one of the words. (*I've, shouldn't*)

Coordinating conjunction. See **Conjunction.**

Correlative conjunction. See **Conjunction.**

Dangling modifier A dangling modifier is a modifier that does not clearly modify any word in the sentence. (*Running to catch a train,* the newspaper headlines caught my attention.)

Demonstrative pronoun. See **Pronoun.**

Dependent clause. See **Clause.**

Direct object A direct object receives the action of a verb. Direct objects follow transitive verbs. (Rita knew the *answer.*)

Direct quotation. See **Quotation.**

Divided quotation. See **Quotation.**

Double negative A double negative is an incorrect use of two negative words when only one is needed. (*I won't never* finish this!)

End mark An end mark is one of several punctuation marks that can end a sentence. See the punctuation chart on page 1102.

Fragment. See **Sentence fragment.**

Future tense. See **Verb tense.**

Gender The gender of a personal pronoun indicates whether the person or thing referred to is male, female, or neuter. (Duke is a great watch dog; *he* won't let any strangers enter the house.)

Gerund A gerund is a verbal that ends in *-ing* and functions as a noun. (I've always enjoyed *swimming*.)

Helping verb. See **Verb, auxiliary.**

Illogical comparison An illogical comparison is a comparison that does not make sense because words are missing or illogical. (Ken likes basketball *more than any sport.*)

Indefinite pronoun. See **Pronoun.**

Indefinite reference Indefinite reference occurs when a pronoun refers to an idea that is vaguely expressed. (We addressed all the envelopes, and *it* was time consuming.)

Independent clause. See **Clause.**

Indirect object An indirect object tells to whom or for whom (sometimes to what or for what) something is done. (Vi gave *me* a book.)

Indirect question An indirect question tells what someone asked without using the person's exact words. (Al asked me what I wanted.)

Indirect quotation. See **Quotation.**

Infinitive An infinitive is a verbal beginning with *to* that functions as an adjective, an adverb, or a noun. (I want *to go*.)

Intensive pronoun. See **Pronoun.**

Interjection An interjection is a word or phrase used to express strong feeling. (*No! Good grief!*)

Interrogative pronoun. See **Pronoun.**

Intransitive verb. See **Verb.**

Inverted sentence An inverted sentence is one in which the subject comes after the verb. (*There goes my last chance. Where are the notes for the history exam?*)

Irregular verb. See **Verb.**

Linking verb. See **Verb.**

Main clause. See **Clause.**

Main verb. See **Verb.**

Modifier A modifier makes another word more precise. Modifiers most often are adjectives or adverbs; they may also be phrases, verbals, or clauses that function as adjectives or adverbs. (*bright* coin, laughed *gaily*, boy *in gym clothes*, *crying* baby)

An **essential modifier** is one that is necessary to the meaning of a sentence. (Everybody *who rides a bicycle* should wear a helmet.)

A **nonessential modifier** is one that merely adds more information to a sentence that is clear without the addition. (Mark Twain, *coming from Missouri*, represented middle America.)

Noun A noun names a person, a place, a thing, or an idea. (*Heidi, garden, box, unity*)

An **abstract noun** names an idea, a quality, or a feeling. (*faith, liberty*)

A **collective noun** names a group of things. (*committee, flock, class*)

A **common noun** is a general name of a person, a place, a thing, or an idea. (*waiter, pond, dress, happiness*)

A **compound noun** contains two or more words. (*mother-in-law, sidewalk, home run*)

A **noun of direct address** is the name of a person being directly spoken to. (*Gene*, will you teach me to dance? Slow down, *Mandy*, or you'll hurt yourself.)

A **possessive noun** shows who or what owns something. (*Wayne's* tie, *Jill's* flute)

A **predicate noun** follows a linking verb and renames the subject. (Rosa is my *assistant*.)

A **proper noun** names a particular person, place, or thing. (*Ann Smith, Westminster Abbey, Vienna Boys Choir*)

Number A word is **singular** in number if it refers to just one person, place, thing, idea, or action and **plural** in number if it refers to more than one person, place, thing, idea, or action. (The words *it, boy,* and *skips* are singular. The words *them, boys,* and *skip* are plural.)

Object of a preposition The object of a preposition is the noun or pronoun that follows a preposition. (We waited for the *train*. I took a message to *him*.)

Object of a verb The object of a verb receives the action of a verb. (Tim collects *stamps*.)

Participle A participle is often used as part of a verb phrase. (had *noticed*) It can also be used as a verbal that functions as an adjective. (the *flaming* arrows, the dog *brought* to the veterinarian)

The **present participle** is formed by adding -*ing* to the present tense of a verb. (*Finding* a dry area, we camped for the night.)

The **past participle** of a regular verb is formed by adding -*d* or -*ed* to the present tense. The past participle of irregular verbs does not follow this pattern. (*Polished* silver gleamed in the jeweler's window. My favorite vase was *broken*.)

Passive voice *See* **Voice.**

Past tense. *See* **Verb tense.**

Perfect tenses. *See* **Verb tense.**

Person The person of pronouns is a means of classifying them.

A **first-person** pronoun refers to the person speaking. (*I* danced.)

A **second-person** pronoun refers to the person spoken to. (*You* ate.)

A **third-person** pronoun refers to some other person(s) or thing(s) being spoken of. (*They* clapped.)

Personal pronoun. *See* **Pronoun.**

Phrase A phrase is a group of related words that lacks both a subject and a verb. (*in a short time, holding a long-stemmed rose*)

An **adjective phrase** modifies a noun or a pronoun. (A part *of the answer* appears.)

An **adverb phrase** modifies a verb, an adjective, or an adverb. (Bob knocked *on the door*.)

An **appositive phrase** explains one or more words in a sentence. (Model-airplane builders often work with balsa, *a lightweight wood*.)

A **gerund phrase** consists of a gerund and its modifiers and complements. (She disliked *taking care of her younger brothers*.)

An **infinitive phrase** consists of an infinitive, its modifiers, and its complements. (The boy tried *to stop the leak in the dike*.)

A **participial phrase** consists of a participle and its modifiers and complements. (*Coming to a complete stop*, the freight train blocked traffic.)

A **prepositional phrase** consists of a preposition, its object, and the object's modifiers. (Homes near the river banks were swept away *by the floodwater's force*.)

A **verb phrase** consists of a main verb and one or more helping verbs. (*might have listened, should be coming*)

Possessive A noun or pronoun that is possessive shows ownership. (*Mary's* brother, *our* parents)

Possessive noun. *See* **Noun.**

Possessive pronoun. *See* **Pronoun.**

Predicate The predicate of a sentence tells what the subject is or does. (The horse *bucked the inexperienced rider*. Joan *is a good friend*.) *See* **Complete predicate; simple predicate.**

Predicate adjective. *See* **Adjective.**

Predicate nominative A predicate nominative is a noun or pronoun that follows a linking verb and renames or explains the subject. (The twins are *cheerleaders*. The leader was *he*.)

Predicate pronoun. *See* **Pronoun.**

Preposition A preposition is a word that relates its object to another part of the sentence or to the sentence as a whole. (I wrote a letter *to* my pen pal.)

Prepositional phrase. *See* **Phrase.**

Present tense. *See* **Verb tense.**

Progressive form. *See* **Verb.**

Pronoun A pronoun replaces a noun or another pronoun. (*Jim* and *she* carried *their* own bags.) Some pronouns allow a writer or speaker to avoid repeating a proper noun. Other pronouns let a writer show a situation in which some information is not known.

A **demonstrative pronoun** singles out one or more persons or things. (*This* is my hat.)

An **indefinite pronoun** refers to an unidentified person or thing. (*Someone* should have seen the car. Is *anybody* there?)

An **intensive pronoun** emphasizes a noun or pronoun. (The teacher *herself* told me.)

An **interrogative pronoun** asks a question. (*What* happened here?)

A **personal pronoun** refers to first, second, or third person. (*I* swim. *You* go. *She* eats.)

A **possessive pronoun** shows ownership. (*My* work is finished. Where is *yours*?)

A **predicate pronoun** follows a linking verb and renames the subject. (A reliable helper is *she*.)

A **reflexive pronoun** reflects an action back on the subject of the sentence. (Jetaun taught *herself*.)

A **relative pronoun** relates a subordinate clause to the word it modifies in the main clause. (The courses *that* we took in summer school were interesting.)

Pronoun-antecedent agreement. *See* **Agreement.**

Pronoun forms

The *subject form of a pronoun* is used when the pronoun is the subject of a sentence or follows a linking verb as a predicate pronoun. (*She* knows Ed. Bob is *he*.)

The *object form of a pronoun* is used when the pronoun is the direct or indirect object of a verb or a verbal or the object of a preposition. (Jo gave *her* a shawl. Ben will stay with *them*.)

Proper adjective. *See* **Adjective.**

Proper noun. *See* **Noun.**

Punctuation Punctuation clarifies the structure of sentences. See the punctuation chart below.

Quotation A quotation consists of words from another speaker or writer.

A *direct quotation* is the exact words of a speaker or writer. (May said, *"I can't finish this job tonight."*)

A *divided quotation* is a quotation separated by words that identify the speaker. (*"I can't,"* said May, *"finish this job tonight."*)

An *indirect quotation* repeats what a person said without using the exact words. (*May said that she couldn't finish the job tonight.*)

Reflexive pronoun. *See* **Pronoun.**

Regular verb. *See* **Verb.**

Relative pronoun. *See* **Pronoun.**

Run-on sentence A run-on sentence consists of two or more sentences written incorrectly as one. (*No one answered the phone it kept ringing and ringing.*)

Sentence A sentence expresses a complete thought. The chart at the top of the next page shows the four kinds of sentences.

A *complex sentence* contains one main clause and one or more subordinate clauses. (*If I call, please come right away. The dog barks when I whistle.*)

A *compound sentence* is made up of two or more main clauses combined with a comma and a conjunction or a semicolon. (*The baby let his balloon escape, and Jim could not get it back.*)

A *simple sentence* consists of only one main clause. (*Our soccer team won the series. Jane and Andy arrived late.*)

Sentence fragment A sentence fragment is a group of words that is only part of a sentence. (*While we spoke. Rowing swiftly.*)

Simple predicate The simple predicate is the verb in the predicate. (*Jim always knows the answer.*)

Simple subject The simple subject is the key noun or pronoun in the subject. (*The heavy bag fell to the floor.*)

Punctuation	Uses	Examples
Apostrophe (')	Shows possession Forms a contraction	Al's radio boys' coach I'll stay. He's tried hard.
Colon (:)	Introduces a list or long quotation Divides some compound sentences	the following games: baseball, football, and tennis Time was short: he had one hour to do a two-hour job.
Comma (,)	Separates ideas Separates modifiers Separates items in series	The day was hot, and the clothes dried quickly. The cute, playful puppy jumped onto my lap. We'll need plates, cups, and saucers.
Exclamation point (!)	Ends an exclamatory sentence	I had a wonderful time!
Hyphen (-)	Joins words in some compound nouns	son-in-law, great-grandchild
Period (.)	Ends a declarative sentence Indicates most abbreviations	Everyone helped with the dishes. gal. pt. Rd. Sr. Nov.
Question mark (?)	Ends an interrogative sentence	Who was on the phone?
Semicolon (;)	Divides some compound sentences Separates items in series that contain commas	Linda will be late; she missed her train. The student council elected Brigid, a freshman; Juan, a sophomore; and Leo, a senior.

Kind of Sentence	Example
Declarative (statement)	I received a letter.
Exclamatory (strong feeling)	You're here!
Imperative (request, command)	Hold the door.
Interrogative (question)	Who can help?

Split infinitive A split infinitive occurs when a modifier is placed between the word *to* and the verb in an infinitive. (*to gladly give*)

Subject The subject is the part of a sentence that tells whom or what the sentence is about. (*Penny* sang.) See **Complete subject; Simple subject.**

Subject-verb agreement. See **Agreement.**

Subordinate clause. See **Clause.**

Superlative. See **Adjective; Adverb.**

Transitive verb. See **Verb.**

Unidentified reference An unidentified reference often occurs when the word *it, they, this, which,* or *that* is used. (In Louisiana *they* observe Mardi Gras as a holiday.)

Verb A verb expresses an action, a condition, or a state of being.

An **action verb** tells what the subject does, has done, or will do. The action may be physical or mental. (Abdul *shouted*.)

An **auxiliary verb** is added to a main verb to express tense, add emphasis, or otherwise affect the meaning of the verb. Together the auxiliary and main verb make up a verb phrase. (*do* believe, *has* seen, *will* forget)

A **linking verb** expresses a state of being or connects the subject with a word or words that describe the subject. (The soup *tastes* wonderful.) Linking verbs include *appear, be (am, are, is, was, were, been, being), become, feel, grow, look, remain, seem, smell, sound, taste.*

A **main verb** describes action or state of being; it may have one or more auxiliaries. (may be *chosen*)

The **progressive form** of a verb shows continuing action. (Kites *are flying*.)

The past tense and past participle of a **regular verb** are formed by adding *-d* or *-ed*. (*charge, charged*) An **irregular verb** does not follow a predictable pattern in its formation. (*sink, sank, sunk; teach, taught, taught; forget, forgot, forgotten*)

The action of a **transitive verb** is directed toward someone or something, called the object of the verb. (Ralph *takes* lessons in scuba diving.) An **intransitive verb** has no object. (Geraldo *swims* well.)

Verb phrase. See **Phrase.**

Verb tense Verb tense shows the time of an action or the time of a state of being.

The **present tense** places an action or condition in the present. (Sarah *enjoys* hiking.)

The **past tense** places an action or condition in the past. (We *stayed*.)

The **future tense** places an action or condition in the future. (She *will forget*.)

The **present perfect tense** describes an action in an indefinite past time or an action that began in the past and continues in the present. (*has carried, have seen*)

The **past perfect tense** describes one action that happened before another action in the past. (*had remained, had allowed*)

The **future perfect tense** describes an event that will be finished before another future action begins. (*will have agreed, shall have completed*)

Verbal A verbal is formed from a verb and acts as a noun, an adjective, or an adverb.

Verbal	Example
Gerund (used as a noun)	*Writing* essays takes time.
Infinitive (used as an adjective, an adverb, or a noun)	Try *to finish* the job tonight.
Participle (used as an adjective)	The hikers, *helped* by the guide, reached camp.

Voice The voice of a verb depends on whether the subject performs or receives the action of the verb.

In the **active voice** the subject of the sentence performs the action. (Melissa *cooked* dinner. Everyone *will enjoy* it.)

In the **passive voice** the subject of the sentence receives the action of the verb. (The jewels *were kept* in the safe. The game *will be played* rain or shine.)

Index of Fine Art

xi, 137	*Sunday Morning Breakfast* (1943), Horace Pippin.
xiii, 298	*Homage to Sterling Brown* (1972), Charles White.
xv, 455	*Le coeur* [The heart] (1947), Henri Matisse.
xvi, 563	*Cosmos Dog* (1989), George Rodrigue.
xix, 748	*The Ukimwi Road* (1994), John Harris.
xxi, 916–917	Lancelot rescuing Guinevere by crossing the sword bridge, (about 1300). From *Le Roman de Lancelot du Lac*.
3	*Self-Portrait* (1986), Chuck Close.
11	*Border Patrol* (1951), Andrew Wyeth.
22	*Laundryman's Daughter* (1988), Tomie Arai.
27	*The Stairway* (1970), Will Barnet.
30	*Comadre Rafaelita* (1934), Emil J. Bisttram.
37	Yi Dynasty rank badge (about 1600–1700).
45	*Elizabeth in a Red Chair* (1961), Fairfield Porter.
52	*The Reception* (about 1883–1885), James Tissot.
57	*Self-Portrait* (about 1865), James Tissot.
60	*The Monument to Peter I on Senate Square in Petersburg* (1870), Vasilii Ivanovich Surikov.
93	*Old House and Garden, East Hampton, Long Island* (1898), Frederick Childe Hassam.
111	*Working Woman* (1947), Elizabeth Catlett.
114	*Nia: Purpose* (1991), Varnette Honeywood.
127	*Descending Stars*, Zoltan Szabo.
155	*Jimmy O'D* (about 1925), Robert Henri.
158	*Spring in St. John's Wood* (1933), Dame Laura Knight.
164	Haitian drum (1940s), unknown artist.
176–177	*Central America: Children in Transition* (1982), Betty LaDuke.
186	*The Suitor* (1893), Édouard Vuillard.
191	*L'Arlésienne: Madame Joseph-Michel Ginoux (Marie Julien, 1848–1911)* (1888), Vincent van Gogh.
200–201	*Busch Stadium* (1982), Jim Dow.
205	*Michael W. Straus* (1961), Fairfield Porter.
208	*Stretching at First* (about 1976), John Dobbs.
212	*Scales* (about 1968–1977), Mitsumasa Anno.
217	*Une Battue en Campine* [Beating the bushes in Campine] (about 1882–1885), Théodor Verstraete.
233	*Chain Gang* (1939–1940), William H. Johnson.
236	*Le nègre Scipion* [Black Scipio] (about 1866–1868), Paul Cézanne.
239	*Hombre y su sombra* [Man and his shadow] (1971), Rufino Tamayo.
249	*Italian Landscape II: Europa* (1944), Ben Shahn.
267	*Portrait of Donald Schrader* (1962), Fairfield Porter.
275	*Sea Air* (1987), Douglas Brega.
278	*Atascadero Dusk* (about 1990), Robert Reynolds.
286	*Firescreen* (1935), Vanessa Bell.
305	*Shaded Lives* (1988), Phoebe Beasley.

318	*Never Ending Work* (1990), Lelde Vinters-Ore.
325	*El novio* [The groom] (1974), Jacobo Borges.
326	*That Which I Should Have Done I Did Not Do* (1931–1941), Ivan Le Lorraine Albright.
350–351	*The Lovers (Somali Friends)* (1950), Lois Mailou Jones.
355	*Portrait of Amber* (1991), Charles Warren Mundy.
360	*First Sail* (1993), Charles Warren Mundy.
366	*The Cove* (1964), Fairfield Porter.
372	*Times Square, New York City No. 2* (1990), Robert Gniewek.
378	*Lovers III* (1990), Eng Tay.
382	*Golden Retriever* (1972), Fairfield Porter.
387	*Old Farmhouse* (1872), Edward Henry Fahey.
390	*Portrait of Fridel Battenberg* (1920), Max Beckmann.
393	*Still Life with Three Puppies* (1888), Paul Gauguin.
397	*Red Peonies* (1929), Ch'i Pai-Shih.
401	*Forbidden Fruit,* Simon Ng.
405	Painting in the class-education exhibition, Niutung People's Commune No. 4 (about 1970), Niutung People's Commune Spare-Time Art Group.
408	*New Look of a Village* (about 1970), Niutung People's Commune Spare-Time Art Group.
413	*Rebecca* (about 1947), Raphael Soyer.
416	*Fire and Water* (1927), Winifred Nicholson.
431	*Old-Time Cabin,* Maynard Dixon.
434	*Into the Past* (1941), Hananiah Harari.
438	Chinese equestrienne (about 700–750, Tang Dynasty).
443	*Corn Maiden* (1982), David Dawangyumptewa.
448	*Portrait of the Princess Saltikova, 1802–1863* (1837), Karl Pavlovitch Briullov.
449	*Couple Above St. Paul* (1970–1971), Marc Chagall.
461	*Les souliers* [A pair of boots] (1887), Vincent van Gogh.
464	*Girl with a Book* (1927), Matej Sternen.
475	*Portrait of the Pianist, Conductor, and Composer A. G. Rubinstein* (1881), Ilya Efimovich Repin.
479	*A Room in the Brasovo Estate* (1916), Stanislav Iulianovich Zhukovskii.
482	*Portrait of M. K. Oliv* (1895), Valentin Aleksandrovich Serov.
488–489	*The Bride Wore Red* (about 1988–1989), Yang Hsien Min.
493	Painted clay figure of a woman (China, Han Dynasty, 206 B.C.–A.D. 200).
510–511	*The Flooded Field* (1992), Claire B. Cotts.
516	*Niño en azul* [Boy in blue] (1928), Rufino Tamayo.
519	*The Dream* (1986), Arnaldo Roche Rabell.
524	*Portrait of Count Fürstenberg-Herdringen* (1924), Tamara de Lempicka.
533	*Portrait de Madame M.,* Tamara de Lempicka.
537	*Der Rote Turm in Halle II* [The red tower in Halle II] (1930), Lyonel Feininger.
546	*In a Past Life* (1993), John Harris.
550	*Los Chicos* [The boys] (1957), Fletcher Martin.

556	*The Endless Enigma* (1938), Salvador Dali.
559	*La reproduction interdite (Portrait d'Edward James)* [Not to be reproduced (Portrait of Edward James)] (1937), René Magritte.
568	*Portrait of André Derain* (1905), Henri Matisse.
573	*The Talisman* (1888), Paul Serusier.
575	*Green Fish* (about 1928), Selden Gile.
577	*Carving the Spirit of the Flesh* (1980), Arnaldo Roche Rabell.
581	*Welcome to My Ghetto Land* (1986), Jean Lacy.
597	*Springtime* (1885), Lionel Percy Smythe.
601	*Cosmos* (1908–1909), Marsden Hartley.
606	*Approaching Storm* (1886), Edward Mitchell Bannister.
609	Suria Pragnapti, detail of Jain ceremonial scroll.
611	Detail of *The Dance of Krishna* (about 1650, Mewar, Rajasthan, India).
612	*June '70* (1970), Biren De.
616	Ijo mask.
619	*Elena in the Kitchen* (1991), Richard Maury.
623	*The Charpoi*, Robert Wade.
634–635	*Tidal Flats, Deer Isle, Sunset* (1978), A. Robert Birmelin.
653	*Before the Game* (1983), Claudio Bravo.
656	*Portrait of B. Amanov, People's Artist of the USSR* (1969), Aman Amangheldyev.
668–669	*La región más transparente* [Where the air is clear] (1989), Ismael Vargas.
673	*The Mysterious Bird* (1917), Charles Burchfield.
678	*Embrace II* (1981), George Tooker.
706	*Morning of Life* (1907), David Ericson.
709	From the Potomac River Series (1991), Diana Suttenfield.
714	*Starburst*, Colin Hay.
716	*Hills* (1914), Man Ray.
721	*Toto* (1988), Jimmy Lee Sudduth.
745	*Conjur Woman* (1975), Romare Bearden.
762–763	*The Grey House* (1917), Marc Chagall.
766	*Le juif en vert* [Jew in green] (1914), Marc Chagall.
783	*Wooing* (1984), Varnette Honeywood.
790	*Portrait of Miss Jen Sun-ch'ang* (1934), William McGregor Paxton.
806–807	*Still Life #31* (1993), Tom Wesselmann.
813	*News from the Gulf* (about 1991), Robert A. Wade.
817	*Light in the Souk* (about 1991), Robert A. Wade.
833	*The Volcanos* (1950), Dr. Atl (Gerardo Murillo).
840	*Nocturnal Landscape* (1947), Diego Rivera.
869	Detail of *The People in Arms* (1957), David Alfáro Siquieros.
871	*Self-Portrait* (1926), Frida Kahlo.
877	*Formation of Revolutionary Leadership* (1926–1927), Diego Rivera.
881	*Peasant with Sombrero* (1926), Diego Rivera.
912	Tournament in King Arthur's court.
921	Jousting at the court of Caerleon (1468). From *Les Chroniques de Hainaut*.
926	*Study for Lancelot* (1893), Sir Edward Burne-Jones.
928	*Study on Brown Paper* (1895), Sir Edward Burne-Jones.
932	Millefleurs tapestry with horseman and arms of Jean de Daillon (late 1400s), unknown Flemish artist.

936	Detail of bowl fragment, actor with mask (about 350 B.C.), unknown Sicilian artist.
938 *left*	Bust of Sophocles.
944 *left*	Terra-cotta mask (second century B.C.) found at the shrine of Artemis, Sparta, Greece.
959 *top*	Painting on wine cup, showing the god Dionysus, the patron of theater, in his ship (540 B.C.), Exekias.
959 *bottom*	Theatrical masks on a fragment of a Greek bowl (about 410 B.C.).
970	Two statues of Sophocles.
980	Marble head of woman from ancient Greek civilization.
982	*Ere alaafin Shangó* [Shangó, Oyo-Ilé warrior-king] (early 1800s), Oyo-Shangó artist.

Index of Skills

Literary Terms

Act, 1000
Alliteration, 133, 560, 1000
Allusion, 471, 650, 713, 1000
Antagonist, 180, 578, 937, 1000
Aside, 1000
Assonance, 133, 1001
Author's purpose, 230, 1001
Autobiography, 65, 149, 1001
    diaries, 65
    journals, 65
    letters, 65
Ballad, 1001
Biography, 65, 1001
Blank verse, 1002
Catastrophe, 937
Characterization, 162, 630, 1002
    interpreting, 744
Characters, 16, 49, 180, 622, 992, 1002. *See also* Characterization.
    comparing, 622
    in drama, 180, 181, 486, 992
    dynamic, 16, 180, 1002
    evaluating, 51
    in fiction, 16, 49, 622
    flat, 180
    main, 16, 1002
    minor, 16, 1002
    round, 180
    static, 16, 180, 1002
Chorus, 937, 1003
Climax, 17, 752, 1003
Conflict, 16, 31, 1003
    external, 31, 181, 842
    internal, 31, 181, 650, 842
    understanding, 174
Connotation and denotation, 1003
Consonance, 133, 1003
Couplet, 376
Denouement, 17
Description, 131, 1004
Descriptive language, 821
Dialect, 1004
Dialogue, 80, 100, 101, 181, 821, 1004
Diction, 554, 557, 712, 1004
Drama, 180, 486, 1004
    antagonist in, 937, 1000
    asides in, 181, 1000
    catastrophe in, 937
    characters in, 180, 181, 486, 992
    chorus in, 937, 1003
    classical, 937, 992
    conflict in, 181
    dialogue in, 181
    farce, 486, 1006
    monologue in, 181
    plot in, 180, 196
    props, 181, 1012
    protagonist in, 937, 1012
    scenes in, 180
    setting and, 181
    soliloquy, 1014
    stage directions in, 181, 196, 1015
    tragedy, 937, 1017
    tragic flaw and, 937
    tragic hero in, 937
    visualizing, 869
Dramatic monologue, 759, 1005
Essay, 66, 90, 1005
    personal, 703, 804–805
    purposes of, 90
    reflective, 565
Exposition, 16–17, 368, 394, 1005
Falling action, 16, 1005
Fantasy, 321, 328, 672, 1006
Farce, 486, 1006
Fiction, 16–17, 1006
    characters in, 16, 49, 622
    climax in, 17, 752
    conflict in, 16, 31, 174, 650, 842
    elements of, 16–17
    exposition in, 16–17, 368, 394
    fact and, 830, 993
    figures of speech in, 209, 421
    flashback in, 63, 396, 844, 853
    imagery in, 138, 171, 666, 680, 694
    magical realism in, 328, 521
    narrator in, 521, 606, 725, 842
    novel, 16, 1010
    plot in, 16–17, 38, 175, 180, 196, 394, 752, 992
    point of view in, 240, 282, 349, 354, 542, 606, 630, 725, 786
    reading, strategies for, 17
    setting in, 16, 38, 132, 240, 258, 262, 263, 328, 430, 565, 786, 992
    short story, 16, 1014
    theme in, 16, 174, 252, 348, 409, 804, 992, 1016
    tone in, 220, 252, 295, 585, 712, 804, 821, 1016
Figurative language, 122, 134, 446, 557, 694, 1006
Figures of speech, 421
    metaphor, 373, 421, 427, 441, 446, 1009
    personification, 421, 441, 446, 1011
    simile, 209, 373, 420, 421, 441, 446, 1014

Flashback, 63, 396, 844, 853, 1006
Foil, 885, 1007
Foreshadowing, 439, 471, 853, 1007
Form, 1007
Frame story, 458, 1007
Free verse, 557, 620, 1007
Hero, 1007
Humor, 32, 1008
    of character, 613, 1008
    of language, 613, 1008
    of situation, 613, 1008
Hyperbole, 1008
Imagery, 50, 134, 135, 138, 171, 557, 632, 666, 680, 694, 1008
    in poetry, 319, 370, 441, 700
Imagism, 370
Inferences, 33, 303, 594, 923
Irony, 246, 348, 725, 1008
    dramatic, 246, 980, 1008
    situational, 246, 578, 770, 1008
    verbal, 246, 885, 1008
Legend, 1008
Lyric, 1009
Magical realism, 328, 521, 1009
Meaning
    literal, 557
    symbolic, 557
Metaphor, 134, 373, 421, 427, 441, 446, 1009
    extended, 1005
    mood and, 508
Meter, 379, 450, 1009
Metonymy, 458
Mood, 40, 50, 132, 508, 700, 1009
Myth, 1010
Narrative, 394, 1010
Narrator, 521, 606, 842
    informed, 725
    naive, 725
Nonfiction, 65–66, 394, 1010
    autobiography, 65, 149, 1001
    biography, 65, 1001
    essay, 66, 90, 565, 703, 804–805, 1005
    true-life adventure, 66
Novel, 16, 1010
Onomatopoeia, 133, 1010
Paradox, 1010
Parody, 1011
Personification, 134, 421, 441, 446, 636, 1011
Plot, 16–17, 38, 175, 180, 196, 992, 1011
    climax and, 17, 752, 180
    conflict and, 16
    denouement and, 17, 180
    diagram of, 394, 752
    in drama, 180, 196
    exposition in, 16–17, 180, 394
    falling action and, 17, 180
    rising action and, 17, 180, 394
Poetry, 133, 1011. *See also* Free verse; Sonnet.
    climax and, 752
    figures of speech in, 373, 420, 441, 446
    form in, 133
    free verse, 620, 1007
    imagery in, 319, 370, 441, 700
    metaphor in, 134, 373, 421, 441, 446
    modern, 557, 667
    mood in, 508
    personification in, 134, 441, 636
    repetition in, 134, 446, 560
    rhyme in, 133, 450, 1013
    rhyme scheme and, 376, 450, 1013
    rhythm and, 134, 379, 450, 636, 694, 1013
    simile in, 134, 373, 420, 441, 446
    sound in, 133
    stanzas in, 319
    theme in, 306
    tone in, 584
    traditional African, 983
Point of view, 240, 349, 354, 542, 630, 725, 786, 1012
    first-person, 240, 282, 725, 1012
    naive narrator and, 725
    omniscient, 606, 1012
    third-person, 240, 606, 1012
Protagonist, 180, 578, 937, 1012
Quatrain, 376, 1012
Realism, 1012
Repetition, 694, 1013
    in poetry, 134, 446, 560
Rhyme, 133, 450, 1013
    end rhyme, 450, 1013
    internal rhyme, 1013
    off rhyme, 450, 1013
Rhyme scheme, 376, 450, 1013
Rhythm, 134, 379, 450, 636, 694, 1013
Rising action, 16, 394, 1013
Romance, 904, 921, 1013
Satire, 295, 1013
Scene, 180, 1014
Science fiction, 693, 1014
Setting, 16, 38, 132, 240, 258, 262, 263, 328, 565, 786, 992, 1014
    cultural, 786
    in drama, 181
    visualizing, 810
Short story, 16, 1014
Simile, 209, 373, 420, 441, 446, 1014
Sonnet, 375, 376, 509, 1014
Sound devices in poetry, 133. *See also* Alliteration; Assonance; Consonance; Onomatopoeia; Rhyme.
Speaker, in poetry, 306, 1015
Stage directions, 181, 196, 1015
Stanzas, 319, 1015
Stereotypes, 486, 1015
Structure, 301, 1015
Style, 315, 693, 712, 804, 821, 934, 1015
Surprise ending, 1016
Suspense, 542, 867, 1016

Symbol, 712, 793, 805, 1016
    cultural, 793
    literary, 793
Theme, 16, 174, 252, 306, 348, 409, 804, 992, 1016
Title, 779, 1016
Tone, 220, 252, 295, 584, 585, 617, 696, 712, 804, 821, 827, 1016
Tragedy, 937, 1017
Tragic flaw, 937
Tragic hero, 937
True-life adventure, 66, 867, 1017
Understatement, 1017
Viewpoint, 744
Voice, 712, 770, 1017

Reading and Critical Thinking Skills

Analysis, 31, 38, 49, 62, 80, 90, 121, 131, 151, 162, 209, 219, 219, 246, 281, 282, 295, 301, 306, 315, 319, 328, 373, 394, 439, 446, 450, 458, 470, 486, 542, 553, 558, 560, 565, 578, 605, 613, 620, 629, 649, 680, 693, 700, 711, 724, 752, 759, 769, 778, 786, 820, 827, 841, 852, 867, 884, 979
Brainstorming, 168
Cause and effect, 83, 90, 209, 230, 514, 521, 884, 979
Chart. *See* Graphic organizers.
Chronological order, 448
Clarifying, 17, 77, 216, 248, 290, 400, 404, 520, 598, 710, 812, 930
Classical drama, strategies for reading, 937
Clues, finding, 523
Compare and contrast, 31, 62, 80, 91, 122, 123, 138, 149, 163, 219, 231, 240, 241, 319, 320, 328, 373, 379, 394, 410, 439, 441, 447, 450, 522, 542, 567, 605, 613, 620, 621, 622, 633, 629, 636, 693, 694, 700, 724, 741, 769, 842, 867, 933, 979
Concepts, clarifying, 248
Conflicts, searching for, 181
Connecting, 18, 33, 38, 40, 49, 51, 62, 67, 80, 83, 87, 110, 121, 124, 135, 138, 140, 149, 151, 182, 195, 198, 209, 211, 219, 221, 232, 242, 246, 248, 266, 284, 297, 303, 304, 308, 317, 321, 354, 370, 375, 381, 396, 430, 441, 446, 452, 460, 473, 514, 523, 545, 556, 567, 578, 594, 608, 615, 622, 632, 633, 638, 668, 672, 682, 696, 713, 724, 754, 761, 769, 780, 789, 810, 823, 829, 841, 844, 855, 869, 904, 923
Context clues. *See entry in the* Vocabulary Skills *index.*
Contrasts. *See* Compare and contrast.
Cooperative learning. *See* Working in groups *in the* Speaking, Listening, and Viewing *index.*
Drama
    strategies for reading, 181
    understanding classical, 937
Drawing conclusions, 31, 38, 49, 62, 110, 138, 149, 252, 266, 315, 759, 820
Evaluating, 17, 38, 49, 74, 80, 112, 113, 121, 140, 149, 246, 252, 281, 295, 306, 315, 368, 373, 407, 450, 458, 467, 470, 521, 553, 560, 600, 747, 778, 816, 867, 927, 930
    characters, 51, 121
    images, 107
    sources, 343, 989
Facts, 66, 830. *See also* Fiction; Opinion.
Fantasy, recognizing, 321
Fiction
    fact and, 830
    strategies for reading, 17
Flashbacks, understanding, 396
Graphic organizers, 737
    brainstorming web, 168
    charts and graphs, 18, 38, 51, 110, 135, 149, 196, 248, 266, 284, 303, 317, 328, 348, 370, 31, 441, 508, 514, 523, 554, 562, 586, 594, 615, 622, 649, 650, 659, 660, 666, 696, 713, 754, 779, 780, 804, 810, 841, 867, 904, 923, 992, 1054
    cluster maps, 772
    diagrams, 83, 163, 211, 221, 321, 342, 394, 448, 545, 672, 744, 821, 855, 869
    lists, 246, 315, 348, 542, 786, 936
    maps, 132, 140, 196, 308, 354, 430, 554, 567, 622, 638
    pie graph, 219
    time line, 396, 693
    Venn diagram, 379, 460, 503, 737, 786, 980
    word pyramid, 241
    word web, 242, 632, 737
Ideas, identifying, 900
Inferring, 31, 33, 80, 131, 162, 209, 219, 230, 281, 295, 303, 304, 306, 315, 328, 379, 409, 439, 458, 521, 558, 560, 594, 613, 617, 620, 636, 711, 769, 778, 841, 920, 933, 979
Judging, 38, 49, 131, 149, 162, 195, 240, 252, 281, 379, 394, 486, 553, 558, 560, 578, 605, 613, 649, 724, 752, 778, 786, 820, 841, 920
Main idea, 565
Modern poetry, strategies for reading, 557
Mood, identifying, 40, 49
Motivation, interpreting, 460
Multiple effects, identifying, 221
Nonfiction, strategies for reading, 66
Observing, 17, 427, 591
Opinion, 62, 66, 80, 90, 121, 131, 138, 149, 162, 195, 209, 209, 131, 219, 230, 240, 246, 252, 281, 295, 301, 306, 315, 328, 373, 379, 394, 409, 439, 446, 450, 458, 470, 486, 521, 542, 560, 565, 578, 605, 629, 636, 649, 680, 693, 700, 711, 724, 752, 759, 769, 786, 820, 827, 841, 852, 867, 884, 920, 933, 979
Oral reading, 630, 868. *See also* Dramatic reading *and* Public speaking *in the* Speaking, Listening, and Viewing *index.*
Peer interaction, 103, 171, 181, 259, 345, 423, 505, 587, 663, 737, 801, 897, 989, 1020–1021. *See also* Working in groups in the Speaking, Listening, and Viewing index.
Personal response, 31, 38, 62, 80, 90, 121, 131, 138, 149, 162, 219, 230, 240, 246, 252, 281, 295, 301, 315, 319, 328, 368, 379, 394, 409, 439, 446, 450, 458, 470, 486, 521, 542, 553, 560, 565, 578, 605, 613, 620, 629, 636,

649, 680, 693, 700, 724, 752, 778, 786, 820, 827, 841, 867, 884, 933, 979
Persuasion, 1043. *See also* Persuasive writing *in the* Writing Skills, Modes, and Formats *index.*
Poetry, strategies for reading, 134
Predicting, 17, 49, 70, 162, 211, 214, 219, 292, 295, 319, 328, 373, 409, 518, 605, 693, 751, 761, 841
Previewing, 17, 66
Problems/Solutions, 284
Questioning, 17, 119, 287, 465, 706, 814, 927
Reading log, 67, 110, 211, 284, 396, 460, 702, 744, 810, 923
Recalling prior experience, 31, 138, 306, 680, 759
Recalling prior knowledge, 62, 542, 578, 752, 778, 786
Reflecting, 17
Rereading, 131, 131
Setting
    analyzing components of, 263
    impact of, 262
Setting a purpose, 66, 169, 343, 345, 1019
Situations, interpreting, 901
Strategies
    for classical drama, 937
    for drama, 181
    for fiction, 17
    for modern poetry, 557
Summarizing, 66
Supporting details, 1029, 1030, 1031
Symbols, interpreting, 605
Venn diagram. *See* Graphic organizers.
Visualizing, 17, 134, 135, 181, 195, 304, 306, 558, 711, 759, 920
Word web. *See* Graphic organizers.

Grammar, Usage, and Mechanics

Addresses, commas in, 1095
Adjectives
    or adverbs, 1076
        comparative form of, 1077
        multiple, commas and, 1093
        proper, 1085
        superlative form of, 1077
Adverbs
    or adjectives, 1076
    comparative form of, 1077
    conjunctive, 1060
    positioning of, 899
affect and *effect,* 1083
Agreement
    in person, 1075
        predicate nominative and, 1067
        pronoun-antecedent, 105, 1071
        subject-verb, 261, 1061–1067
and, 1061
Antecedents, indefinite pronouns as, 1073
Antecedents, of pronouns, 105, 1071–1073, 1075

    compound, 1072–1073
    unclear, 1072
Apostrophes, 1070
    possessives formed with, 1068
Appositives, 1064
Articles
    capitalization and, 1088
Article titles, 589
bad and *badly,* 1079
Book titles, 589
    capitalization of, 1088
Brackets, 991
bring and *take,* 1084
Capitalization
    of articles, 1088
    of conjunctions, 1088
    deities and, 1086
    in divided quotations, 1097
    of events, 1087
    of geographical names, 1087
    of institutions, 1086
    of languages, 1086
    of names, 1085
    of nationalities, 1086
    of organizations, 1086
    in personal titles, 1085
    in poems, 1088
    of prepositions, 1088
    of proper adjectives, 1085
    of proper nouns, 1085
    quotations and, 1096
    of religious terms, 1086
    of school subjects, 1086
    in stories, 1088
    of time periods, 1087
    of titles of created works, 1088
Clauses
    adjective, 895
    in compound sentences, 1089
    independent, 665
    main, 1060
    subject of, 1069, 1073
    subordinate, 665, 895, 1058, 1091
    subordinating conjunctions and, 1091
Collective nouns, 1066
Colons, 425, 1092
    quotations and, 1096
Commas
    in addresses, 1095
    adjectives and, 1093, 1094
    for clarity, 1093
    in compound sentences, 1060, 1089
    in dates, 1094
    introductory clauses and, 1091
    introductory words or phrases and, 1090
    in letters, 1095
    with quotations, 1096, 1097
    run-on sentences and, 1059

    in series, 1093
    subordinate clauses and, 1091
Comma splice, 1059
Comparative forms, 1077
Comparisons
    double, 507
    double negatives in, 1077
    illogical, 1077
    pronouns in, 1075
Complex sentences, 1091
Compound predicates, 735, 1089
Compound sentences, 1060
    commas in, 1089
    semicolons in, 1089
Compound subject, 735, 1061, 1089
Conjunctions, 735
    capitalization and, 1088
    commas used with, 1060, 1089
    compound sentences and, 1089
    coordinating, 1060
    subordinating, 665, 1091
Conjunctive adverb, 1060
    semicolon and, 1089
Contractions, 1065
    pronouns in, 1074
Dangling modifiers, 1078
Dashes, 1092
Dates, commas in, 1094
Dialogue, 173
Direct object, 1074
Direct quotations, 1096
Double comparisons, avoiding, 507
Double negatives, avoiding, 1077
Ellipses, 991
End punctuation, 1096–1097
Essay titles, 589
Events, capitalization of, 1087
Exclamation point, with quotation marks, 1096
few, fewer, fewest, 1080
Film titles. *See* Movie titles.
Fragments, 665, 1058–1059
Gender, 1071
Geographical names, capitalization of, 1087
Helping verbs, 1065, 1082
Indirect object, 1074
Intensifiers, 899
Institutions, capitalization of names of, 1086
Inverted sentences, 1065
Italics
    for titles, 589
Languages, capitalization of, 1086
learn and *teach,* 1083
Letters, commas in, 1095
lie and *lay,* 1083
Linking verbs, 1070, 1076
little, less, least, 1080
Magazine titles, 589
    capitalization of, 1088

Measure, nouns of, 1066
Misplaced modifiers, 1078
Modifiers
    adjectives as, 1076
    adverbs as, 1076
    comparative, 1077
    dangling, 1078
    misplaced, 1078
    special problems with, 1079–1080
    superlative, 1077
Movie titles, 589
    capitalization of, 1088
Musical compositions, titles of, 589
Nationalities, capitalization of, 1086
Newspaper titles, 589
    capitalization of, 1088
Nouns, 895, 1068, 1071, 1079. *See also* Plural nouns; Possessive nouns.
    collective, 1066
    common, 1085
    pronouns with, 1074
    proper, 1085
    singular in meaning, 1066
Number
    pronoun-antecedent agreement in, 1071
    subject-verb agreement in, 1061–1067
Numbers, 1066
Objects
    direct, 1074
    indirect, 1074
    personal pronouns as, 1070
    of prepositions, 1074
    pronouns as, 1070
    of verbs, 1074
only, misplacement of, 1080
or and *nor,* 1062, 1063
Organizations, capitalization of names of, 1086
Parentheses, 1092
Participles
    past, 739
Past participle, 1082
    helping verbs and, 1082
Past perfect tense of verbs, 739
Past tense of verbs, 1082
Period, 1059
    with quotation marks, 1096
Person, 1071
    shifts in, 1075
Phrases
    interrupting, 1064–1065
    introductory, 1090
    prepositional, 261, 1090
Play titles, 589
    capitalization of, 1088
Plural nouns, 1061, 1068
    forming, 1068
Poem titles, 589
Possessive nouns, 1068

apostrophe and, 1068
   forming, 1068
Possessive pronouns, 1070, 1074
Predicate nominative, 1067
Predicate pronouns, 1070
Predicates, 1058
   compound, 735
Prepositional phrases, 261
   subject-verb agreement and, 261, 1064
Prepositions, 1070
   capitalization of, 1088
   objects of, 1074
Pronouns, 105, 895, 1079
   agreement with antecedent, 1071, 1075
   agreement with verb, 1062, 1063, 1064
   antecedents of, 105, 1071–1073
   in comparisons, 1075
   in contractions, 1074
   indefinite, 1063, 1064, 1073
   nouns with, 1074
   object, 1070
   personal, 347, 1062, 1071, 1073
   possessive, 1070, 1074
   predicate, 1070
   relative, 895
   as subjects, 1062–1064, 1069
   usage of, 1073–1075
Punctuation
   colons, 425, 1092, 1096
   correcting, 1089
   commas, 1059–1060, 1090–1091, 1093–1097
   of dialogue, 173
   periods, 1059
   in poetry, 425
   semicolons, 1060, 1089, 1096
   sentence fragments and, 1058
   of titles, 589, 1088
Question marks, with quotation marks, 1096
Questions, 1065
Quotation marks
   with dialogue, 173
   with direct quotations, 1096
   exclamation point with, 1096
   period with, 1096
   question mark with, 1096
   semicolons and, 1096
   titles and, 589, 1088, 1096
Quotations
   brackets in, 991
   capitalization and, 1096
   colon and, 1092
   direct, 1096, 1097
   divided, 1097
   ellipses in, 991
   indirect, 173
   introducing, 1096
Religious terms, capitalization of, 1086
rise and *raise*, 1083

Run-on sentences, 1059–1060
Semicolons
   in compound sentences, 1089
   conjunctive adverbs and, 1060
   main clauses joined by, 1060
   quotation marks and, 1096
Sentences
   clauses and, 665
   complex, 1091
   compound, 1060, 1089
   compound parts of, 735
   fragments of, 665, 1058–1059
   inverted, 1065
   run-on, 1059–1060
   subject of, 1073
Series, commas in, 1093
Short story titles, 589
Singular nouns, 1061
sit and *set*, 1083
Subjects, 1058
   agreement with verb, 261, 1061–1067
   of clauses, 1069
   compound, 735, 1061, 1062, 1063
   finding, 1066
   pronouns as, 1062–1064, 1069, 1073
   simple, 1061, 1065
Subordinating conjunctions, 665, 1091
Superlative forms, 1077
Tenses of verbs, 739
   consistent use of, 1081
   past tense, 1082
   shift in, 1081
that, 1079
them, 1079
these, 1079
this, 1079
those, 1079
Time, nouns of, 1066
Time periods, capitalization of, 1087
Titles of created works
   capitalization and, 1088
   italics and, 589, 1067
   quotation marks and, 589, 1067
   singular verb and, 1067
   underscoring and, 1067
Verbals, 1074, 1090
Verbs, 735, 1065, 1066, 1090
   adverbs and, 899, 1076
   agreement with subject, 261, 1061–1067
   helping, 1065
   irregular, 739
   linking, 1070
   number and, 1061–1064
   objects of, 1074
   pronouns and, 1062
   regular, 739
   tenses of, 739, 1061, 1081–1082
   using, 1081–1084

Weight, nouns of, 1066
who and *whom*, 1073–1074

Writing Skills, Modes, and Formats

Allusions, 980
Analysis, 486. *See also* Explanatory writing.
    critical, 252
    literary, 439, 613, 820
    of setting, 258
    of title, 852
Assonance, 423
Audience, 169, 170, 343, 799
    defining, 503
    identifying, 661, 1019
Bias, 340
Cause and effect, 1038
Classificatory writing
    chart, 18, 38, 149, 754, 841
    list of pros and cons, 368
    note taking, 458, 724
    time line, 693
Clichés, avoiding, 421
Coherence in writing, 663, 1027
Conclusions, 1032–1033
Conflict, 796
    through dialogue, 800
    understanding, 174
Connotation, 585
Consonance, 423
Criticism, 894–898
Description, 102, 1024, 1030–1032
    of action, 209
    of characters, 301
    of physical appearance, 121
    of setting, 257, 700
Descriptive writing, 259, 395
Details, 1029, 1030, 1031
    organizing, 257, 1032
    related, 735
    sensory, 894
Dialogue, 101
    writing, 100, 102
Drafting, 103, 170–171, 259, 344–345, 423, 504–505, 587, 662–663, 737, 800–801, 897, 988–989, 1019–1020
    audience and, 170
Editing, 104, 172, 173, 260, 346, 347, 424, 506, 507, 588, 664, 738, 802, 803, 898, 991, 1021, 1022
Elaboration, 103, 894, 895, 1029
Emotions, comparing, 508
Emphasis, creating, 345
Evaluation, 171, 345, 505, 801
    standards for, 104, 173, 260, 347, 424, 507, 588, 665, 738, 898, 991
Examples, 103, 894, 1030
Explanatory writing, 500–507, 658–665
    analysis, 1040–1041
    cause-and-effect, 658–665, 1038
    compare-and-contrast, 501–507, 1037
    problem-solution, 1039
    types of, 1036
Expressive and personal writing
    advice column, 149, 409, 933
    autobiographical essay, 149
    autobiographical incident, 162, 166
    biographical research paper, 984–991
    biographical sketch, 470
    diary entry, 31, 230, 394, 629, 786, 820, 979
    essay, 90, 121, 240, 252, 281, 328, 565, 759, 820, 827, 852
    eulogy, 80, 138
    eyewitness account, 315, 565
    first-person narrative, 553
    horoscope, 560
    journal entry, 219, 348, 373, 724
    letter, 240, 246, 281, 319, 458, 979
    log entry, 195
    love letter, 162, 841
    opinion column, 778
    personal narrative, 301
    tribute, 827
Facts, 1029
    fiction and, 830
    statistics and, 895
Figurative language, 420, 694
Figures of speech, using, 421, 1031–1032
    metaphor, 421
    personification, 420
    simile, 420
Formal language, 171
Freewriting, 348, 423, 659, 797
Images, 50, 171, 373, 694
Incidents, 1029
Informal language, 171
Informative writing, 500–507
    article, 209, 542, 553, 769, 827, 852, 920, 933
    book jacket copy, 867
    book report, 867
    brochure, 521, 693
    compare-and-contrast essay, 500–501
    interview, 933
    job evaluation, 649
    newspaper column, 62
    personality profile, 31, 379
    police report, 521
    press release, 700
    public-service announcement, 80, 470
    rules, list of, 246
    thesaurus entry, 636
    travel brochure, 605
    true-life adventure, 867
    wedding announcement, 470
Interpretation, 586–588
Introductions, 1024–1025

Journal writing, 219, 373, 724
Language, levels of, 171
List, 808, 902
Letters, 38, 62, 162, 240, 246, 281, 319, 439, 458, 578, 620, 629, 786, 792, 841, 884, 979
Main idea, 1026
    implied, 734
    stated, 734
Manuscripts, MLA guidelines for, 1047
Mood, creating, 259
Narrative and imaginative writing, 1034–1035
    afterward, 752
    alternative ending, 281, 578
    alternative title, 792
    anecdote, 1025
    ballad, 521
    character analysis, 565
    character sketch, 90, 295, 769
    children's book, 605
    comic scene, 439
    definition, extended, 450, 759
    description in, 121, 209, 301, 395, 700, 1024
    dialogue, 80, 100, 101, 295, 649, 680, 752
    dramatic monologue, 759
    dramatic scene, 62, 195, 246, 301, 486, 796–801, 820
    epilogue, 605
    fable, 252
    fairy tale, 629
    firsthand, 166–171, 175
    haiku, 605
    legend, 131
    letter, 38, 62, 439, 578, 620, 786, 792, 884
    memo, 121
    monologue, 195, 409, 446, 841
    nonfiction narrative, 394
    parable, 252
    poem, 138, 306, 319, 373, 379, 446, 450, 560, 636, 700
    satiric story, 295
    science fiction, 693
    script, 368, 542
    sequel, 121
    soap-opera scene, 933
    song lyric, 149, 450
    sonnet, 379
    story, 328
    story opening, 680
Note taking, 987
Observation, 658
Order. *See also* Details.
    combined, 257
    of impression, 256
    spatial, 256, 257
Organization. *See also* Graphic organizers *in the* Reading and Critical Thinking Skills *index*.
    of details, 257
    of narrative writing, 1035
    order of impression, 256
    of persuasive writing, 1043
    of research report, 1046
    spatial order, 256, 257
Outlining, 988
Paragraphs
    coherence in, 663, 1027
    unity in, 734, 735, 1026
Parallel structure, 505
Peer readers. *See* Peer response.
Peer response, 103, 171, 259, 345, 423, 505, 587, 663, 737, 801, 897, 989, 1020–1021
Personal response, 102–104
Persuasive writing, 340–347, 1042–1043
    advertisement, 711
    editorial, 49, 219, 301, 394, 711, 920
    essay, 340
    letter to the editor, 629
    proposal, 62, 368
    sermon, 219
    speech, 131, 319, 884
    television commercial, 209
Plot, 175
Portfolios, 175, 349, 509, 805, 993
Portrayal, discussing, 100, 102
Prewriting, 102, 168–169, 258, 342, 422, 502–503, 586, 660, 736, 798, 896, 986
    audience and, 169
    brainstorming, 168
    finding ideas, 1018–1019
    note taking, 102
    purpose and, 169
Proofreading, 1022–1023
Publishing/presenting, 173, 347, 507, 1023
Purpose, 169, 343, 345, 1019
Quotations, 103, 1030
    from literary texts, 589
Reflecting on your writing, 169, 173, 347, 507, 803, 991
Reports, 984–990
    research, 1044–1047
Revising, 171, 172, 260, 346, 424, 506, 588, 664, 738, 802, 990, 1021–1022
    dialogue, 101
Sound devices, 423
Source cards, 987, 1045
Sources
    documenting, 1046
    evaluating, 986
    locating, 169, 986, 987
Spatial relationships, 257. *See also* Order.
Statistics, 895, 1029
Style, 307, 821
    allusions, 980
    description, 395
    diction and, 187
    elaboration, 894, 895
    figurative language, 420, 694
    formal, 296
    humor, 32, 196
    images, 50, 373, 694

    magical realism, 328
    mood, 132
    paragraph coherence, 256
    realism, 579, 606
    sentence length and, 253
    setting, 132
    tone, 584
Thesis
    in research report, 1044
    restating, 1032
    statement of, 587, 987, 1025
Tone, 584, 585
Topic sentence, 1026
Transitional words and phrases, 171, 257, 663, 1027–1028
Writing about literature. *See also* Criticism.
    analyzing setting, 258–260
    capturing a moment, 420–421
    changing elements, 734–738
    character evaluation, 409
    criticism, 894–898, 993
    meaning, searching for, 584–588
    personal response, 102, 175
    plot summary, 240
    plot synopsis, 920
    poems, 422–424, 509
    portrayal, discussing, 100–104
    psychological profile, 884
    report card, 306
    review, 31, 195, 486, 769
    settings, 256–257, 258
Writing process. *See also* Drafting; Editing; Prewriting; Publishing/presenting; Revising.
    brainstorming, 168
    coherence in, 663, 1027
    conclusions, 1032–1033
    details in, 257, 735, 894, 1029–1032
    elaboration in, 103, 894, 895, 1029
    main idea in, 734, 1026
    organization, 256, 257, 737, 1035, 1042, 1046
    paragraphs in, 663, 734, 735, 1026, 1027
    stages of, 1018
    topic sentence in, 1026

Vocabulary Skills

Analogies, 64, 197, 410, 566, 922
Antonyms, 91, 163, 231, 296, 302, 395, 631, 788, 843
Charades, 459
Clichés, avoiding, 421
Connotations, 585
Context clues, 50, 82, 123, 150, 220, 247, 283, 316, 329, 487, 522, 579, 607, 753, 788, 822, 828, 885, 935, 981
    definition and restatement, 64, 614, 651
Dictionary, 1068
    meanings in, 585
Idioms, 631, 681

Illustrating words, 302, 607
Language, levels of, 171
Pantomime, 788
Restatement clues. *See* Context clues.
Spatial relationships, words for, 257
Synonyms, 32, 132, 210, 231, 253, 296, 369, 395, 440, 459, 472, 544, 555, 695, 712, 843, 854
Word pyramid, 241
Word web, 242, 632

Research and Study Skills

Almanacs, 1048, 1049
Books
    bibliographies in, 503
Card catalogs, 503
    computerized, 503, 1049
Databases, 1048
Dictionaries, 1048, 1068
Dictionary of American Biography, 987
Dictionary of Scientific Biography, 987
Encyclopedias, 410, 1048, 1049
Interview, 14, 395
Library, 503, 987
    computer services, 1049
Magazine articles, 501, 503, 659, 735, 895, 985, 1048
New York Times index, 987
News reports, 1048, 1049
Notable American Women, 987
Note cards. *See* Source cards.
Note taking, 422, 458, 503, 724, 987
    paraphrase in, 1045
    quotes in, 987, 1045
    summarizing in, 1045
Outlining, 988
Readers' Guide to Periodical Literature, 503
Research activities
    apartheid, 81, 821
    Black Muslim movement, 122
    castles, 934
    civil rights movement, 231
    Chekhov, 487
    Chinese culture, 793
    circuses, 853
    Cultural Revolution in China, 410
    evidence-gathering techniques, 543
    Greek noblewomen, 980
    Hindu marriage customs, 630
    Ice Age, 566
    Jewish Sabbath, 770
    immigrants, 32
    medicinal plants, 753
    medieval tournaments, 921
    news stories, 742
    name changes, 779
    nonviolent resistance, 63

purpose for, 660
repression, 842
sharecropping system, 122
street crime, 302
Vietnamese culture, 149
Vietnam War, 150, 282, 760
volcanic eruption, 841
Yiddish, 770
Source cards, 987, 1045
Sources
documenting, 1046–1047
evaluating, 343, 989
locating, 169, 986, 987
notes from, 503
primary, 986, 987
secondary, 986, 987
Webster's Biographical Dictionary, 987
Who Was Who, 987
Word processors, 1050
dictionary in, 1050
formatting and, 1051
grammar checker in, 1050
revising and editing with, 1050–1052
search and replace feature, 1050
spell checker in, 1050
thesaurus in, 1050
World Authors, 987

Speaking, Listening, and Viewing

Audio recordings
making, 329, 374, 701
playing, 231, 282, 636
CD-ROM, 1049, 1056
Computers. *See* Computer visuals; CD-ROM; On-line resources.
Computer visuals
art and design programs, 1054
clip art, 1054
graphics programs, 1053
graphs and charts, 1054
tables, 1053
using, 1053
Cooperative learning. *See* Working in groups.
Dramatic reading
choral reading, 138
dramatic monologue, 91, 821
improvisation, 650, 787
interview, 934
oral reading, 630, 868
oral tale, 753
radio commercial, 681
readers theater, 195, 980
poems, 306, 320
skits, 150, 296
speeches, 316, 606

stories, 50
television commercial, 921
"weather report," 380
Electronic resources for information, 1048–1049
Emotions, visual representations of, 450
Films
storyboards for, 162, 933
viewing, 210
LaserLinks videodisc
18, 33, 51, 64, 67, 83, 110, 123, 124, 140, 151, 182, 198, 211, 221, 230, 266, 307, 308, 329, 354, 380, 381, 396, 430, 440, 451, 460, 473, 487, 514, 522, 545, 555, 561, 567, 594, 608, 621, 622, 638, 672, 695, 701, 713, 744, 753, 761, 772, 780, 788, 810, 822, 823, 829, 854, 869, 885, 904, 922, 923, 935, 936, 981
Multimedia presentations, 579, 630
animation, 1056
directions in, 1057
photos and videos, 1055, 1056
planning, 1056
sound, 1055
Music. *See also* Audio recording.
composing, 842
performing, 380
playing, 139
On-line resources
commercial information services, 1048
electronic mail, 1048
Internet, 1048, 1056
World Wide Web, 1048
Photographs
album, 681
display, 701, 787
Photocopying, 39
Photographic essay, 374
Political cartoon, 821
Public speaking
debates, 150
eulogy, 409
mock trial, 209
newscast, 459
oral commentary, 694
oral monologue, 554
oral movie review, 922
oral reports, 91, 316, 395
speeches, 241, 253
television report, 828
wedding toast, 471
Retelling stories, 231
Videos
creating, 542
viewing, 91, 694
Word processors, 1050–1052
Working in groups, 31, 38, 49, 62, 80, 90, 131, 149, 230, 240, 252, 295, 296, 306, 315, 319, 368, 409, 439, 486, 605, 620, 636, 649, 680, 693, 700, 711, 724, 769, 778, 827, 867, 884, 902, 920
dramatic monologues, 821

group discussions, 560
illustrations, 668
panel discussions, 281, 629
pamphlets, 394
partners, 14, 246, 320, 379, 542, 554, 561, 617, 742, 759, 979
role-playing, 32, 39, 121, 471, 542, 621
storyboard, 933
tall tales, 522
television newscast, 521
television talk show, 373, 853
visual representations of emotions, 450

Index of Titles and Authors

Page numbers that appear in italics refer to biographical information.

A

Achebe, Chinua, 780, *788*
Acosta, Teresa Paloma, 120
Acts of King Arthur and His Noble Knights, The, from, 923
Afro-American Fragment, 164
After the Ball, 51
Aiken, Joan, 672, *681*
Allende, Isabel, 829, *843*
And of Clay Are We Created, 829
Antigone, 936
As the Night the Day, 638

B

Back from Tuichi, from, 855
Balek Scales, The, 211
Bear, The, 473
Benét, Stephen Vincent, 713, *726*
Black Men and Public Space, 297
Blue Winds Dancing, 124
Bo, Li. *See* Li Bo
Böll, Heinrich, 211, *220*
Bora Ring, 794
Borges, Jorge Luis, 514, *522*
Boyle, Kay, 40, *50*
Bradbury, Ray, 682, *695*
Brigid, 411
Brooks, Gwendolyn, 303, *307*
By Any Other Name, 772
By the Waters of Babylon, 713

C

Cabuliwallah, The, 622
Californian's Tale, The, 430
Case of Cruelty, A, 381
Castellanos, Rosario, 840
Catacalos, Rosemary, 30
Censors, The, 242
Chekhov, Anton, 473, *487*
Chip of Glass Ruby, A, 810
Christie, Agatha, 523, *544*
Clifton, Lucille, 303, *307*
Colette, 92, *99*
Cortázar, Julio, 321, *329*
Cranes, 33
Crowning of Arthur, The, from *Le Morte d'Arthur,* 904

D

Desai, Anita, 545, *555*
Dickinson, Emily, 612
Dimitrova, Blaga, 317, *320*

E

Earthly Paradise, from, 92
Eight Puppies, 392
Eiseley, Loren, 562, *566*
Erdrich, Louise, 844, *854*
Everyday Use, 110

F

Farewell to Manzanar, from, 330
Fighting South of the Ramparts, 254
First Seven Years, The, 460
For the New Year, 1981, 632
Forster, E. M., 248, *253*

G

Gage, Nicholas, 83, *91*
Games at Twilight, 545
Ghinsberg, Yossi, 855, *868*
Gift from a Son Who Died, 886
Gordimer, Nadine, 810, *822*
Grudnow, 768

H

Hayden, Robert, 135, *139*
Hayslip, Le Ly, 140, *150*
Head, Bessie, 232, *241*
Herriot, James, 381, *395*
House Taken Over, 321
Houston, James D., 330, *339*
Houston, Jeanne Wakatsuki, 330, *339*
Hughes, Langston, 164, *165*

I

I Am Not I, 556

J

Jewett, Sarah Orne, 594, *607*
Jie, Zhang. *See* Zhang Jie
Jiménez, Juan Ramón, 556, *561*

K

Kaffir Boy, from, 67
King, Coretta Scott, 221, *231*
Kinsella, W.P., 198, *210*
Kitchenette Building, 303
Knight, The, 932
Kumin, Maxine, 615, *621*

L

La Calle, 556
La Casa, 30
Lady Who Was a Beggar, The, 488
Lalla, 354
Lavin, Mary, 411, *419*
Lawrence, D.H., 135, *139*
Le Morte d'Arthur, from, 904, *912*
Leap, The, 844
Lem, Stanislaw, 727, *733*
Lessing, Doris, 744, *753*
Levertov, Denise, 632, *637*
Li Bo, 254
Like the Sun, 608
Lost Sister, 789
Love Must Not Be Forgotten, 396
Love Without Love, 370
Lowell, Amy, 370, *374*
Lund, Doris Herold, 886, *893*

M

Making the Jam Without You, 615
Malamud, Bernard, 460, *472*
Malory, Sir Thomas, 904, *922*
Man in the Water, The, 823
Marriage Is a Private Affair, 780
Martí, José, 577
Mathabane, Mark, 67, *82*
Maupassant, Guy de, 567, *579*
Meeting, The, 514
Metonymy, or The Husband's Revenge, 452

Millay, Edna St. Vincent, 375, *380*
Mishima, Yukio, 284, *296*
Miss Rosie, 303
Mistral, Gabriela, 392
Momaday, N. Scott, 441, *447*
Montgomery Boycott, 221
My Mother Pieced Quilts, 120

N

Narayan, R.K., 608, *614*
Neruda, Pablo, 441, *447*
Nguyen Thi Vinh, 754, *760*
Nicol, Abioseh, 638, *651*
Niggli, Josephina, 869, *885*
Night, from, 308
No Han Podido, 239
No Witchcraft for Sale, 744
Nobel Prize Acceptance Speech, The, from, 314
Nocturne, 840

O

O'Brien, Tim, 266, *283*
Ocho Perritos, 392
O'Connor, Frank, 151, *163*
Okara, Gabriel, 615, *621*
Old Song, 982
Oliver, Mary, 696, *701*
On the Rainy River, 266
Once More to the Lake, 702
Once upon a Time, 615

P

Pastan, Linda, 768
Paz, Octavio, 556, *561*
Pearl, The, 284
Pen of My Aunt, The, 182
Piano, 135
Pilcher, Rosamunde, 354, *369*
Po, Su Dong. *See* Su Dong Po
Poem on Returning to Dwell in the Country, 696
Precocious Autobiography, A, from, 652
Pride, 632
Prisoner Who Wore Glasses, The, 232
Puedo Escribir Los Versos . . . , 441
Pushkin, Aleksandr, 448, *451*

Q

Qian, Tao. *See* Tao Qian
Queiroz, Rachel de, 452, *459*

R

Rau, Santha Rama, 772, *779*
Ravikovitch, Dahlia, 632, *637*
Rich, Adrienne, 932
Ring of General Macías, The, 869
Rosenblatt, Roger, 823, *828*

S

Searching for Summer, 672
Selvon, Samuel, 580, *583*
Shakespeare, William, 375, *380*
Simile, 441
Simple Poetry, from, 577
Singer, Isaac Bashevis, 761, *771*
Sir Launcelot du Lake, from *Le Morte d'Arthur,* 912
Sit-Ins, 229
Son from America, The, 761
Song, Cathy, 789, *793*
Sonnet 18 (Shakespeare), 375
Sonnet 30 (Millay), 375
Sophocles, 936, *981*
Sound of Thunder, A, 682
Staples, Brent, 297, *302*
Steinbeck, John, 923, *935*
Street, The, 556
Study of History, The, 151
Su Dong Po, 438
Sun, The, 696
Sunwŏn, Hwang, 33, *39*

T

Tagore, Rabindranath, 622, *631*
Tan, Amy, 18, *32*
Tao Qian, 696, *701*
Taxi, The, 370
Teacher Who Changed My Life, The, 83
Teasdale, Sara, 723
Tell all the Truth but tell it slant—, 612
Tey, Josephine, 182, *197*
There Will Come Soft Rains, 723
They Have Not Been Able, 239
Those Winter Sundays, 135
Thoughts of Hanoi, 754
Thrill of the Grass, The, 198
To . . . , 448
To a Traveler, 438
Tolerance, 248
Tolstoy, Leo, 51, *64*
Tonight I Can Write . . . , 441
Torres, Luis Lloréns, 370, *374*
Trurl's Machine, 727
Twain, Mark, 430, *440*
Two Friends, 567
Two Kinds, 18

U

Unexpected Universe, The, from, 562

V

Valenzuela, Luisa, 242, *247*
Valladares, Armando, 239
Versos Sencillos, from, 577
Vinh, Nguyen Thi. *See* Nguyen Thi Vinh.

W

Walker, Alice, 110, *123*
Walker, Margaret, 229
When Greek Meets Greek, 580
When Heaven and Earth Changed Places, from, 140
White, E. B., 702, *712*
White Heron, A, 594
Whitecloud, Tom, 124, *132*
Wiesel, Elie, 308, 314, *316*
Winter Night, 40
Witness for the Prosecution, The, 523
Women Who Are Poets in My Land, The, 317
Wright, Judith, 794, *795*

Y

Yevtushenko, Yevgeny, 652, *657*
Yo No Soy Yo, 556

Z

Zhang Jie, 396, *410*

Acknowledgments *(continued)*

Nicholas Gage and Parade Magazine: "The Teacher Who Changed My Life," from *Parade Magazine* by Nicholas Gage; Copyright © 1989 by Nicholas Gage. By permission of the author and Parade Magazine. All rights reserved.

Farrar, Straus & Giroux, Inc.: Excerpts from *Earthly Paradise* by Colette, edited by Robert Phelps; Copyright © 1966 by Farrar, Straus & Giroux, Inc. By permission of Farrar, Straus & Giroux, Inc.

Harcourt Brace & Company: "Everyday Use," from *In Love and Trouble: Stories of Black Women* by Alice Walker; Copyright © 1973 by Alice Walker. Reprinted by permission of Harcourt Brace & Company.

El Centro Chicano: "My Mother Pieced Quilts" by Teresa Paloma Acosta, from *Festival de Flor y Canto: An Anthology of Chicano Literature*, published by the University of Southern California Press. By permission of El Centro Chicano (University of Southern California) and Teresa Paloma Acosta.

Simon & Schuster: "Blue Winds Dancing" by Tom Whitecloud, from *Scribner's Magazine*, February 1938; Copyright 1938 by Charles Scribner's Sons, renewed © 1966. Reprinted with the permission of Scribner, an imprint of Simon & Schuster.

Viking Penguin: "The Piano," from *The Complete Poems of D. H. Lawrence* by D. H. Lawrence, Edited by V. de Sola Pinto and F. W. Roberts; Copyright © 1964, 1971, by Angelo Ravagli and C. M. Weekley, Executors of the Estate of Frieda Lawrence Ravagli. By permission of Viking Penguin, a division of Penguin Books USA Inc.

Liveright Publishing Corporation: "Those Winter Sundays," from *Angle of Ascent: New and Selected Poems* by Robert Hayden; Copyright © 1975, 1972, 1970, 1966 by Robert Hayden. By permission of Liveright Publishing Corporation.

Doubleday: Excerpt from *When Heaven and Earth Changed Places* by Le Ly Hayslip: Copyright © 1989 by Le Ly Hayslip and Charles Jay Wurts. By permission of Doubleday, a division of Bantam Doubleday Dell Publishing Group, Inc.

Alfred A. Knopf, Inc., and Joan Daves Agency: "The Study of History," from *Collected Stories of Frank O'Connor* by Frank O'Connor; Copyright 1957 by Frank O'Connor. Reprinted by permission of Alfred A. Knopf, Inc., and Joan Daves Agency.

Alfred A. Knopf, Inc.: "Afro-American Fragment," from *Selected Poems of Langston Hughes* by Langston Hughes; Copyright © 1959 by Langston Hughes. By permission of Alfred A. Knopf, Inc.

Unit Two

David Higham Associates Ltd.: *The Pen of My Aunt* by Gordon Daviot (also known as Josephine Tey) from *Plays by Gordon Daviot*.

Viking Penguin: "The Thrill of the Grass," from *The Thrill of the Grass* by W. P. Kinsella; Copyright © 1984 by W. P. Kinsella. Used by permission of Viking Penguin, a division of Penguin Books USA Inc., and Penguin Ltd., Toronto.

Joan Daves Agency & Leila Vennewitz: "The Balek Scales," from *18 Stories* by Heinrich Böll; Copyright © 1966 by Heinrich Böll. By permission of Verlag Kiepenheuer & Wirsch c/o Joan Daves and Leila Vennewitz.

Henry Holt & Company, Inc.: "Montgomery Boycott," from *My Life with Martin Luther King, Jr.* by Coretta Scott King; Copyright © 1969 by Coretta Scott King. By permission of Henry Holt & Company, Inc.

University of Georgia Press: "Sit-Ins," from *This Is My Century: New and Collected Poems* by Margaret Walker; Copyright © 1989 by Margaret Walker

Alexander. Reprinted by permission of The University of Georgia, Athens, Georgia.

John Johnson Limited: "The Prisoner Who Wore Glasses," from *Tales of Tenderness and Power* by Bessie Head, Heinemann Educational Books, African Writers Series. Reprinted by permission of John Johnson, Ltd., London. Copyright © 1989 by the Estate of Bessie Head.

Rowan Tree Press: "They Have Not Been Able / No Han Podido" from *Landscape and Exile* by Armando Valladares and edited by Marguerite Bouvard; Copyright © 1985. Reprinted with permission from Rowan Tree Press.

Rosario Santos Literary and Cultural Services, Inc.: "The Censors," from *Open Door* by Luisa Valenzuela; Copyright © 1976, renewed 1988 by Luisa Valenzuela. By permission of Rosario Santos Literary and Cultural Services, Inc.

Harcourt Brace & Company and The Society of Authors: Excerpt from "Tolerance," from *Two Cheers for Democracy* by E. M. Forster; Copyright 1951 by E. M. Forster and renewed © 1979 by Donald Parry, reprinted by permission of the publisher and The Society of Authors as the literary representatives of the E. M. Forster Estate.

HarperCollins Publishers, Limited: "Fighting South of the Ramparts," from *The Poetry and Career of Li Po* by Li Po, translated by Arthur Walley; Copyright 1950. By permission of HarperCollins Publishers, Limited, London.

Houghton Mifflin Company: "On the Rainy River," from *The Things They Carried* by Tim O'Brien; Copyright © 1990 by Tim O'Brien. By permission of Houghton Mifflin Company / Seymour Lawrence. All rights reserved.

Excerpt from *Farewell to Manzanar*, by James D. and Jeanne Wakatsuki Houston; Copyright © 1973 by James D. Houston. Reprinted by permission of Houghton Mifflin Company. All rights reserved.

New Directions Publishing Corporation: "The Pearl," from *Death in Midsummer* by Yukio Mishima and translated by Geoffrey W. Sargent; Copyright © 1966 by New Directions Publishing Corp. Reprinted by permission of New Directions Publishing Corporation.

Brent Staples: "Black Men and Public Space" from *Life Studies: A Thematic Reader* by Brent Staples and edited by David Cavitch; Copyright © 1989. Mr. Staples is a member of the *New York Times* editorial board, where he writes on politics and culture.

BOA Editions: "Miss Rosie," from *Good Woman: Poems and a Memoir 1969–1980* by Lucille Clifton; Copyright © 1987 by Lucille Clifton. Reprinted with the permission of BOA Editions, Ltd., 92 Park Ave., Brockport, NY 14420.

Gwendolyn Brooks: "Kitchenette Building," from her book *Blacks*, published by Third World Press, Chicago, © 1991. By permission of the author.

Farrar, Straus & Giroux, Inc.: Excerpt from *Night* by Elie Wiesel, translated by Stella Rodway; Copyright © 1960 by MacGibbon & Kee. Copyright renewed © 1988 by the Collins Publishing Group. By permission of Farrar, Straus & Giroux, Inc.

The Nobel Foundation: Excerpt from Elie Wiesel's Noble Prize acceptance speech; Copyright © 1986 by the Nobel Foundation. By permission of the Nobel Foundation.

University Press of New England: "The Women Who Are Poets in My Land," from *Because the Sea Is Black* (Wesleyan University Press) by Blaga Dimitrova; Copyright © 1989 by Blaga Dimitrova. By permission of University Press of New England.

Random House, Inc.: "House Taken Over," from *End of the Game and Other Stories* by Julio Cortázar; Copyright © 1967 by Random House, Inc. By permission of Random House, Inc.

Tribune Media Services: Excerpt from "Fed Up with Custody Shuffle," from *Chicago Tribune*, April 22, 1992. Excerpt from "Richard, a Baby No More," from *Chicago Tribune*, March 16, 1995. Reprinted by permission of Tribune Media Services.

Unit Three

Felicity Bryan, Ltd.: "Lalla," from *Love Stories* by Rosamunde Pilcher; copyright © Rosamunde Pilcher. By permission of Felicity Bryan, Ltd., Oxford, England.

Editorial Cordillera: "Amor sin amor / Love Without Love" by Luis Lloréns Torres; Copyright © 1967 by Editorial Cordillera. By permission of Editorial Cordillera, Hato Rey, Puerto Rico.

Elizabeth Barnett, literary executor: "Sonnet XXX," from *Fatal Interview* by Edna St. Vincent Millay. From *Collected Poems*, HarperCollins. Copyright 1931, © 1958 by Edna St. Vincent Millay and Norma Millay Ellis. Reprinted by permission of Elizabeth Barnett, literary executor.

St. Martin's Press, Inc., & Harold Ober Associates, Inc.: "A Case of Cruelty" from *All Things Bright and Beautiful* by James Herriot. Copyright © 1973, 1974 by James Herriot. By permission of St. Martin's Press, Inc., New York, NY, and Harold Ober Associates, Inc.

Joan Daves Agency: "Eight Puppies" by Gabriela Mistral, translated by Doris Dana. Copyright © 1972 by Doris Dana. Reprinted by arrangement with Doris Dana, c/o Joan Daves Agency as agent for the proprietor.

Chinese Literature Press: "Love Must Not Be Forgotten" by Zhang Jie from *Seven Contemporary Chinese Women Writers*.

Mary Lavin: "Brigid," from *Collected Stories* by Mary Lavin; Copyright © 1971 Houghton Mifflin Company, renewed by Mary Lavin. By permission of Mary Lavin.

New Directions Publishing Corporation: "To a Traveler" from *One Hundred Poems from the Chinese* by Su Tung P'o (Su Dong Po), edited by Kenneth Rexroth; Copyright © 1971 by Kenneth Rexroth. By permission of New Directions Publishing Corp.

N. Scott Momaday: "Simile," from *Angle of Geese and Other Poems* by N. Scott Momaday. By permission of the author.

Random House UK, Limited: "Tonight I Can Write," from *Selected Poems* by Pablo Neruda. By permission of Jonathan Cape, publisher, at Random House UK, Limited.

Ardis Publishers: "To . . . ," from *Collected Narrative and Lyrical Poetry* by Alexander Pushkin. By permission of ARDIS Publishers, Inc.

University of California Press: "Metonymy, or The Husband's Revenge," by Rachel de Queiroz from *Modern Brazilian Short Stories*. Reprinted by permission of University of California Press.

Farrar, Straus & Giroux, Inc.: "The First Seven Years," from *The Magic Barrel* by Bernard Malamud; Copyright 1950, renewed © 1977, 1986 by Bernard Malamud. By permission of Farrar, Straus & Giroux, Inc.

Sterling Lord Literistic, Inc.: *The Bear* by Anton Chekhov and adapted by Ronald Hingley; Copyright © 1968 by Ronald Hingley. By permission of Sterling Lord Literistic, Inc.

Indiana University Press: "The Lady Who Was a Beggar," from *Stories from a Ming Collection* translated by Cyril Birch; Copyright © 1958. By permission of Indiana University Press, Bloomington, Indiana.

Warner Bros. Publications: Excerpt from the song "New Year" by Kim Deal from the album *Last Splash* by The Breeders; Copyright © 1993 Period Music (Administered by Zomba Songs Inc.). All rights reserved. Used by permission of Warner Bros. Publications U.S. Inc., Miami, FL 33014.

Northern Lights: Excerpt from "I Love Words," from *Louis Ginsberg: Collected Poems* by Louis Ginsberg. Reprinted by permission of Northern Lights.

Cambridge University Press: Excerpt from "Hindu Rites of Passage," from *The Cambridge Encyclopedia of India, Pakistan, Bangladesh, Sri Lanka, Nepal, Bhutan and the Maldives,* edited by Francis Robinson. Copyright © 1989 by the Cambridge University Press. Reprinted by permission of Cambridge University Press.

Seventeen Magazine: Excerpt from "Dating Through the Decades," from *Seventeen Magazine,* October, 1994. Reprinted by permission of Seventeen Magazine.

The Roper Center for Public Opinion Research: Survey entitled "If you could change any one of the following about your family, which would it be?" from *Women's Day,* August 12–18, 1993. Survey by Yankelovich Partners, Inc. Reprinted by permission of Roper Center for Public Opinion Research, University of Connecticut, Storrs.

Unit Four

Dutton Signet: "The Meeting" by Jorge Luis Borges, translated by Norman Thomas di Giovanni, copyright © 1968, 1969, 1970 by Emece Editores, SA, and Norman Thomas di Giovanni.

Excerpt from *A Precocious Autobiography* by Yevgeny Yevtushenko, translated by Andrew R. MacAndrew; Copyright © 1963 by Yevgeny Yevtushenko, renewed 1991 by Yevgeny Yevtushenko. Translation copyright © 1963 by E. P. Dutton, renewed 1991 by Penguin USA.
Reprinted by permission of Dutton Signet, a division of Penguin Books USA, Inc.

The Putnam Publishing Group: "The Witness for the Prosecution" from *The Witness for the Prosecution and Other Stories* by Agatha Christie; Copyright 1924 by Agatha Christie Ltd., renewed 1954, © 1982. Reprinted by permission of The Putnam Publishing Group.

HarperCollins Publishers, Inc.: "Games at Twilight" by Anita Desai from *Games at Twilight and Other Stories.* Copyright © 1978 by Anita Desai. Reprinted by permission of HarperCollins Publishers, Inc.

New Directions Publishing Corporation: "The Street," from *Selected Poems of Octavio Paz* by Octavio Paz; Copyright © 1973 by Octavio Paz and Muriel Rukeyser. By permission of New Directions Publishing Corp.

Robert Bly: "I Am Not I," from *Lorca and Jiménez: Selected Poems* (Beacon Press, 1973), edited and translated by Robert Bly; Copyright © 1973 by Robert Bly. Reprinted with his permission.

Harcourt Brace & Company: Excerpt from "The Angry Winter" from *The Unexpected Universe,* copyright © 1968 by Loren Eiseley, reprinted by permission of Harcourt Brace & Company.

Carroll & Graf Publishers, Inc.: "Two Friends," from *The Dark Side of Guy de Maupassant* by Guy de Maupassant and adapted by Arnold Kellett. By permission of Carroll & Graf Publishers, Inc.

Holmes & Meier Publishers, Inc.: Poem XXIII from *Jose Martí: Major Poems,* bilingual edition by Jose Martí, translated by Elinor Randall, edited by Phillip S. Foner; Copyright © 1982 Holmes and Meier Publishers, Inc. By permission of Holmes & Meier Publishers, Inc.

Althea N. Selvon: "When Greek Meets Greek" from *Island Voices: Stories from* *the West Indies* by Samuel Selvon. Reprinted by permission of Althea N. Selvon, Executor.

Viking Penguin: "Like the Sun" from *Under the Banyan Tree* by R. K. Narayan; Copyright © 1985 by R. K. Narayan. By permission of Viking Penguin, a division of Penguin Books USA Inc.

Gabriel Okara: "Once upon a Time," from *Poems from Black Africa* by Gabriel Okara. By permission of the author.

Viking Penguin: "Making the Jam Without You," from *Our Ground Time Here Will Be Brief* by Maxine Kumin. Copyright © 1970 by Maxine Kumin. Used by permission of Viking Penguin, a division of Penguin Books USA, Inc.

Simon & Schuster, Inc.: "The Cabuliwallah," from *A Tagore Reader* by Rabindranath Tagore, edited by Amiya Chakravarty; Copyright © 1961 Macmillan Publishers, Inc. By permission of Simon & Schuster, Inc.

Sheep Meadow Press: "Pride" from *The Window: New and Selected Poems* by Dahlia Ravikovitch; Copyright © 1989 The Sheep Meadow Press. By permission of The Sheep Meadow Press.

New Directions Publishing Corporation: "For the New Year, 1981," from *Candles in Babylon* by Denise Levertov; Copyright © 1981 by Denise Levertov. Reprinted by permission of New Directions Publishing Corp.

David Higham Associates Limited: "As the Night the Day" from *Modern African Prose* by Abioseh Nicol. Reprinted by permission of David Higham Associates, Limited.

Unit Five

Brandt & Brandt Literary Agents, Inc.: "Searching for Summer," from *The Green Flash and Other Stories of Horror, Suspense, and Fantasy* by Joan Aiken; Copyright 1957, © 1958, 1959, 1960, 1965, 1968, 1969, 1971 by Joan Aiken Enterprises.

"By the Waters of Babylon" by Stephen Vincent Benét; Copyright 1937 by Stephen Vincent Benét. Copyright renewed © 1965 Thomas C. Benét, Stephanie B. Mahin, Rachel Benét Lewis.
Reprinted by permission of Brandt & Brandt Literary Agents, Inc.

Don Congdon Associates, Inc.: "A Sound of Thunder," from *R Is for Rocket* by Ray Bradbury; Copyright 1952, renewed © 1980 by Ray Bradbury. By permission of Don Congdon Associates, Inc.

Grove / Atlantic, Inc.: "Poem on Returning to Dwell in the Country" by T'ao Ch'ien (Tao Qian), from *Anthology of Chinese Literature*, edited by Cyril Birch; Copyright © 1965 by Grove Press, Inc. By permission of Grove / Atlantic, Inc.

Beacon Press: "The Sun," from *New and Selected Poems by Mary Oliver;* Copyright © 1992 by Mary Oliver. Reprinted by permission of Beacon Press.

HarperCollins Publishers: "Once More to the Lake," from *One Man's Meat* by E. B. White; Copyright 1941 by E. B. White.

"By Any Other Name," from *Gifts of Passage* by Santha Rama Rau; Copyright 1951 by Vasanthi Rama Rau Bowers, Copyright renewed.
Reprinted by permission of HarperCollins Publishers, Inc.

Macmillan Publishing Group, Inc.: "There Will Come Soft Rains," from *Collected Poems of Sara Teasdale* by Sara Teasdale; Copyright 1920 by Macmillan Publishing Company, renewed 1948 by Mamie T. Whaless.

The Continuum Publishing Company: "Trurl's Machine," from *The Cyberiad: Fables for the Cybernetic Age* by Stanislaw Lem: Copyright © 1974. Reprinted by permission of The Continuum Publishing Company.

Simon & Schuster, Inc.: "No Witchcraft for Sale," from *African Stories* by Doris Lessing. Copyright 1951, 1953, 1954, 1957, © 1958, 1962, 1963, 1964, 1965, by Doris Lessing. Reprinted by permission of Simon & Schuster, Inc.

Nguyen Ngoc Bich: "Thoughts of Hanoi," from *A Thousand Years of Vietnamese Poetry* by Nguyen Thi Vinh, translated by Nguyen Ngoc Bich. Copyright © 1962, 1967, 1968, 1969, 1970, 1971, 1974 by the Asia Society and Nguyen Ngoc Bich.

Farrar, Straus & Giroux, Inc.: "The Son from America," from *A Crown of Feathers* by Isaac Bashevis Singer; Copyright © 1973 by Isaac Bashevis Singer. By permission of Farrar, Straus & Giroux, Inc.

W. W. Norton & Company, Inc.: "Grudnow," from *The Imperfect Paradise: Poems* by Linda Pastan; Copyright © 1988 by Linda Pastan. By permission of W. W. Norton & Company, Inc.

Doubleday: "Marriage Is a Private Affair," from *Girls at War and Other Stories* by Chinua Achebe; Copyright © 1972, 1973 by Chinua Achebe. By permission of Doubleday, a division of Bantam Doubleday Dell Publishing Group, Inc.

Yale University Press: "Lost Sister," from *Picture Bride* by Cathy Song; Copyright © 1983 by Cathy Song. Reprinted by permission of Yale University Press.

Carcanet Press Limited: "Bora Ring" by Judith Wright from *Collected Poems, 1942–1985*, p. 8. Copyright © 1994.

Unit Six

Viking Penguin: "A Chip of Glass Ruby" by Nadine Gordimer from *Selected Stories*. Copyright © 1961 by Nadine Gordimer, renewed 1980. Reprinted by permission of Viking Penguin, a division of Penguin Books USA, Inc.

Time Picture Syndication: "The Man in the Water" by Roger Rosenblatt, from *Time*, January 26, 1982; Copyright © 1982 by Time, Inc. By permission of Time, Inc.

Scribner: "And of Clay Are We Created," from *The Stories of Eva Luna* by Isabel Allende, translated by Margaret Sayers Peden; Copyright © 1989 by Isabel Allende. English translation Copyright © 1991 by Macmillan Publishing Company. Reprinted by permission of Scribner, an imprint of Simon and Schuster, Inc.

Graywolf Press: "Nocturne" from *The Selected Poems of Rosario Castellanos* by Rosario Castellanos; Copyright © 1988 by the Estate of Rosario Castellanos. Translation copyright © 1988 by Magda Bogin. By permission of the Graywolf Press, St. Paul, Minnesota.

Harper's Magazine: "The Leap," from *Harper's Magazine* by Louise Erdrich; Copyright © 1990. All rights reserved. Reproduced from the March 1990 issue by special permission of Harper's Magazine.

Random House, Inc., and Yossi Ghinsberg: Excerpt from *Back from Tuichi* by Yossi Ghinsberg; Copyright © 1993 by Yossi Ghinsberg. By permission of Random House, Inc., and Yossi Ghinsberg.

HarperCollins Publishers, Inc.: Excerpt from "Gift from a Son Who Died" by Doris Lund, as it appeared in the April 1973 issue of *Good Housekeeping Magazine*; Copyright © 1974 by Doris Lund. Reprinted by permission of HarperCollins Publishers, Inc.

Random House, Inc.: "The Crowning of Arthur" and "Sir Launcelot du Lake" from *Le Morte D'Arthur* by Sir Thomas Malory, translated by Keith Baines; Copyright © 1962 by Keith Baines, renewed © 1990 by Francesca Evans. Reprinted by permission of Crown Publishers and Penguin Books, USA.

Farrar, Straus & Giroux, Inc.: Excerpt from *The Acts of King Arthur and His Noble Knights* by John Steinbeck; Copyright © 1976 by Elaine Steinbeck. By permission of Farrar, Straus & Giroux, Inc.

214–215 Rebecca McClellan. 106, 107, 167 *bottom*, 172, 258 *bottom*, 340, 341, 345, 420, 421, 422 *top*, 424–425 *bottom*, 426, 427, 504–506, 586–587 *bottom*, 658–661, 664, 665, 798, 898 *top*, 987, 991 Allan Landau. 199, 203 Maryann Thomas. 285 Leslie Wu. 427 Josh Neufeld. 444–445, 845, 848 Sarah Figlio. 856–865 Clinton Meyer.

Maps on all Previewing pages and Responding pages: Robert Voights.

Miscellaneous Art Credits
xi *Sunday Morning Breakfast* (1943), Horace Pippin. Private collection, courtesy of Galerie St. Etienne, New York. **xiii** *Homage to Sterling Brown* (1972), Charles White. Collection of Dr. Edmund Gordon, courtesy of the Heritage Gallery, Los Angeles. **xv, 455** *Le coeur* [The heart] (1947), Henri Matisse. Plate 7 from *Jazz*, published by Tériade, Paris. The Metropolitan Museum of Art, New York, gift of Lila Acheson Wallace, 1983 (1983.1009). Copyright © 1995 Succession H. Matisse, Paris / Artists Rights Society (ARS), New York. Photo Copyright © 1985 The Metropolitan Museum of Art, all rights reserved. **xvi** *Cosmos Dog* (1989), George Rodrigue. Oil on canvas, courtesy of The Rodrigue Gallery of New Orleans. Copyright © 1989 George Rodrigue. **xix** *The Ukimwi Road* (1994), John Harris. **xxi** Lancelot rescuing Guinevere by crossing the sword bridge (about 1300). From *Le Roman de Lancelot du Lac*, M. 806, f. 166, The Pierpont Morgan Library, New York / Art Resource, New York. **xxvi–1** Detail of *Self-Portrait* (1986), Chuck Close. Oil on canvas, 54½″ × 42¼″, courtesy of The Pace Gallery, New York. Photo by John Back. **2** *bottom left* Copyright © A. Giampiccolo / FPG International Corp.; *bottom right* Copyright © Arthur Tilley / FPG International Corp. **3** *top* The Bettmann Archive; *center* Copyright © Koji Yamashita / Panoramic Images; *bottom left* Copyright © Carole Elies / Tony Stone Images; *bottom right*, *Self-Portrait* (1986), Chuck Close. Oil on canvas, 54½″ × 42¼″, courtesy of The Pace Gallery, New York. Photo by John Back. **12–13** The Granger Collection, New York. **27** *The Stairway* (1970), Will Barnet. Photo courtesy of Terry Dintenfass Gallery, New York. Copyright © 1995 Will Barnet / Licensed by VAGA, New York. **40** Archive Photos / Lambert. **63** Photo by Malcolm Varon. **76** Copyright © Louise Gubb / JB Pictures Ltd. **106–107** Reprinted courtesy of 'TEEN Magazine. **110** Copyright © Mike Mitchell / Photo Researchers, Inc. **115–116** Detail of *Nia: Purpose* (1991), Varnette Honeywood. Monoprint, collection of Karen Kennedy. Copyright © 1991 Varnette P. Honeywood. **122** Copyright © Mitch Reardon / Photo Researchers, Inc. **135** *bottom right and left* Copyright © Ron Chapple / FPG International Corp.; *top right* Copyright © Bruce Ayres / Tony Stone Images. **140** *left* Le Ly Hayslip's parents. Photos from *When Heaven and Earth Changed Places* by Le Ly Hayslip. Copyright © 1989 by Le Ly Hayslip and Charles Jay Wurts. Used by permission of Doubleday, a division of Bantam Doubleday Dell Publishing Group, Inc. **141, 144, 148** Copyright © Warner Brothers / Regency Enterprises / Le Studio Canal. Photo courtesy of Photofest. **158** *Spring in St. John's Wood* (1933), Dame Laura Knight. Oil on canvas, 51¾″ × 45½″, Board of Trustees of the National Museums and Galleries on Merseyside, Walker Art Gallery, Liverpool, Great Britain. Copyright © Dame Laura Knight, reproduced by permission of Curtis Brown Group, Ltd., London. **167** *center* 1982 *The Far Side* cartoon by Gary Larson is reprinted by permission of Chronicle Features, San Francisco. All rights reserved. **172** *bottom* Courtesy of Laurie Duncan. **182** Courtesy of the French Embassy–Photo department. **198** *top* Courtesy of The Topps Company, Inc. **205** *Michael W. Straus* (1961), Fairfield Porter. Oil on canvas, 45 3/16″ × 39½″, Hirschl & Adler Modern, New York.

211 Copyright © Charlie Waite / Tony Stone Images. **212** *Scales* (about 1972), Mitsumasa Anno. From *The Unique World of Mitsumasa Anno*, published by Kodansha Ltd., Tokyo. **231** UPI / Bettmann. **247, 314, 376** The Bettmann Archive. **254** Robert Harding Picture Library. **255** Copyright © Lawrence Migdale / Photo Researchers, Inc. **262–263** Copyright © 1993 Jay Ullah / Stern / Black Star. **282** *top* Detail of *Portrait of Donald Schrader* (1962), Fairfield Porter. The Metropolitan Museum of Art, bequest of Arthur M. Bullowa, 1993 (1993.406.12). Photo Copyright © 1995 The Metropolitan Museum of Art; *bottom* Copyright © David R. Frazier / Photo Researchers, Inc. **322** *foreground* Copyright © Hidenori Kataoka / Photonica; *background* Copyright © Shunsuke Yamamoto / Photonica. **323–327** Copyright © Shunsuke Yamamoto / Photonica. **330** *left* Library of Congress. **371** *dove* Copyright © Uniphoto, Inc.; *background* Copyright © David Rigg / Tony Stone Images. **340–341** Courtesy of Hayun Cho. **347** *inset* Copyright © Chicago Tribune / Mazzenga / The Gamma Liaison Network. **377** Copyright © Eiji Vanagi / Photonica. **382–383** Copyright © Masakazu Kure / Photonica. **397** *Red Peonies* (1929), Ch'i Pai-Shih. Ink and colors on paper, 53½" × 12⅞", courtesy of the Arthur M. Sackler Museum, Harvard University Art Museums, loan from the family of F. Y. Chang (321.1985). Copyright © President and Fellows, Harvard College, Harvard University Art Museums. **420–421, 422** *top*, **424–425** *top, bottom* Copyright © Steve McCurry / Leo de Wys, Inc. **431–432, 436** Courtesy of the Economics and Public Affairs Section, The New York Public Library, Astor, Lenox, and Tilden Foundations. **433** Courtesy of Carmine Fantasia. **438** Chinese equestrienne tomb figure (about 700–750, Tang Dynasty). Buff earthenware with traces of polychromy, 56.2 × 48.2 cm, The Art Institute of Chicago, gift of Mrs. Pauline Palmer Wood (1970.1073). Photo by Robert Hashimoto. Photo Copyright © 1994 The Art Institute of Chicago, all rights reserved. **442** Detail of *Corn Maiden* (1982), David Dawangyumptewa. Photo Copyright © 1987 by Jerry Jacka. **459** H. Armstrong Roberts. **490, 497** The Granger Collection, New York. **493** Painted clay figure of a woman (China, Han dynasty, 206 B.C.–A.D. 220. Collection of Mr. & Mrs. Ezekiel Schloss. Photo by Wan-go Weng. **500** *bottom* From *Folk and Festival Costume of the World* by R. Turner Wilcox. Copyright © 1965 R. Turner Wilcox. Reprinted with the permission of Scribner, a division of Simon & Schuster Inc. **502** *bottom* Courtesy of *Elegant Bride*. **506** *top inset* Copyright © Sheila Nardulli / Gamma Liaison. *bottom inset* Courtesy of Karen Sapp-Crowe. **507** *inset* Courtesy of Karen Sapp-Crowe. **523** Photofest. **524** *Portrait of Count Fürstenberg-Herdringen* (1924), Tamara de Lempicka. Oil on canvas, 16⅛" × 10¾", courtesy of Barry Friedman Ltd., New York. Copyright © 1996 Artists Rights Society (ARS), New York / SPADEM, Paris. **533** *Portrait de Madame M.*, Tamara de Lempicka (1898–1980). Oil on canvas, 99 cm × 65 cm, private collection, Paris. Copyright © 1996 Artists Rights Society (ARS), New York / SPADEM, Paris. **543** Detail of *Portrait de Madame M.*, Tamara de Lempicka (1898–1980). Oil on canvas, 99 cm × 65 cm, private collection, Paris. Copyright © 1996 Artists Rights Society (ARS), New York / SPADEM, Paris. **590–591** Copyright © The Walt Disney Company. **609** Suria Pragnapti, detail of Jain ceremonial scroll. Spencer Collection, The New York Public Library, Astor, Lenox and Tilden Foundations (Indian MS. 69). **615** Copyright © Stephanie Rausser / FPG International Corp. **623** *background*, **624, 626–627** Copyright © Antonio Martinelli, Milan, Italy. **637** Sheet music courtesy of Marianna Ryan. **652** Detail of *Portrait of B. Amanov, People's Artist of the USSR* (1969), Aman Amangheldyev. Oil on canvas, 145 cm × 170 cm, Union of Artists of the Russian Federation, Moscow. **683, 685, 690** Image Copyright © 1995 PhotoDisc, Inc. **696** Copyright © D. Muench/H. Armstrong Roberts. **697–698**

Copyright © M. Miller / H. Armstrong Roberts. **699** Copyright © R. Fukuhara / Westlight. **702** *top,* **726, 753** H. Armstrong Roberts. **704** *background,* **705–708, 709** *background* Illustration by Gary Head. **740–741** *label insets* Images Copyright © 1995 PhotoDisc, Inc. **760** *left* Copyright © Dirck Halstead / Gamma-Liaison; *right* Copyright © R. Vogel / Gamma-Liaison. **779** List of passengers on ship that carried immigrants from Great Britain to the United States, 1867. Copyright © Temple University–Balch Institute Center for Immigration Research, Balch Institute for Ethnic Studies Library. **787** *right* Village on the Niger River, Nigeria. Copyright © M. and E. Bernheim / Woodfin Camp. **794, 795** *background* Copyright © H. Franca / Superstock. **796** *inset* Copyright © C. Niklas Hill / Gamma Liaison. **823** Copyright © 1982 The New York Times. Reprinted by permission. **831** Reuters / Bettmann. **845, 853** Detail Copyright © 1989 Michelle Barnes / The Image Bank. **858** James P. Blair / National Geographic Image Collection. **868** Cover from *Back from Tuichi* by Yossi Ghinsberg. Copyright © 1993 Yossi Ghinsberg. Published by Random House, New York. Jacket photo: Telegraph Colour Library / FPG International Corp. **887** *center* Eric Lund at age 18, 1968. Courtesy of Doris Lund. **894** *inset* Copyright © Jacques Jangoux / Tony Stone Images. **900–901** Copyright © Costa Manos / Magnum Photos Inc. **984** *top* NASA. **985** *bottom inset* UPI / Bettmann. **1034** Copyright © Penny Tweedie / Tony Stone Images. **1036, 1044** UPI / Bettmann. **1042** Photofest. **1048** Netscape, Netscape Navigator and the Netscape Communications Corporation Logo are trademarks of Netscape Communications Corporation; *center* Courtesy of Internet Direct, Inc. **1051–1053** Screen shots reprinted with permission from Microsoft Corporation. **1054** Used with express permission. Adobe and Adobe Illustrator are trademarks of Adobe Systems Incorporated. **1055** Copyright © Ed Malitsky / Gamma Liaison. **1057** Copyright © Andrea Sperling / FPG International Corp.

Teacher Review Panels *(continued)*

Eileen Jones, English Department Chairperson, Spanish River High School, Palm Beach County School District

Jan McClure, Winter Park High School Orange County School District

Wanza Murray, English Department Chairperson (retired), Vero Beach Senior High School, Indian River City School District

Shirley Nichols, Language Arts Curriculum Specialist Supervisor, Marion County School District

Debbie Nostro, Ocoee Middle School, Orange County School District

Barbara Quinaz, Assistant Principal, Horace Mann Middle School, Dade County School District

OHIO

Joseph Bako, English Department Chairperson, Carl Shuler Middle School, Cleveland City School District

Deb Delisle, Language Arts Department Chairperson, Ballard Brady Middle School, Orange School District

Ellen Geisler, English/Language Arts Department Chairperson, Mentor Senior High School, Mentor School District

Dr. Mary Gove, English Department Chairperson, Shaw High School, East Cleveland School District

Loraine Hammack, Executive Teacher of the English Department, Beachwood High School, Beachwood City School District

Sue Nelson, Shaw High School, East Cleveland School District

Mary Jane Reed, English Department Chairperson, Solon High School, Solon City School District

Nancy Strauch, English Department Chairperson, Nordonia High School, Nordonia Hills City School Dictrict

Ruth Vukovich, Hubbard High School, Hubbard Exempted Village School District

TEXAS

Anita Arnold, English Department Chairperson, Thomas Jefferson High School, San Antonio Independent School District

Gilbert Barraza, J.M. Hanks High School, Ysleta School District

Sandi Capps, Dwight D. Eisenhower High School, Alding Independent School District

Judy Chapman, English Department Chairperson, Lawrence D. Bell High School, Hurst-Euless-Bedford School District

Pat Fox, Grapevine High School, Grapevine-Colley School District

LaVerne Johnson, McAllen Memorial High School, McAllen Independent School District

Donna Matsumura, W.H. Adamson High School, Dallas Independent School District

Ruby Mayes, Waltrip High School, Houston Independent School District

Mary McFarland, Amarillo High School, Amarillo Independent School District

Adrienne Thrasher, A.N. McCallum High School, Austin Independent School District

CALIFORNIA

Steve Bass, 8th Grade Team Leader, Meadowbrook Middle School, Ponway Unified School District

Cynthia Brickey, 8th Grade Academic Block Teacher, Kastner Intermediate School, Clovis Unified School District

Karen Buxton, English Department Chairperson, Winston Churchill Middle School, San Juan School District

Bonnie Garrett, Davis Middle School, Compton School District

Sally Jackson, Madrona Middle School, Torrance Unified School District

Sharon Kerson, Los Angeles Center for Enriched Studies, Los Angeles Unified School District

Gail Kidd, Center Middle School, Azusa School District

Corey Lay, ESL Department Chairperson, Chester Nimitz Middle School, Los Angeles Unified School District

Myra LeBendig, Forshay Learning Center, Los Angeles Unified School District

Dan Manske, Elmhurst Middle School, Oakland Unified School District

Joe Olague, Language Arts Department Chairperson, Alder Middle School, Fontana School District

Pat Salo, 6th Grade Village Leader, Hidden Valley Middle School, Escondido Elementary School District

Manuscript Reviewers *(continued)*

Beverly Ann Barge, Wasilla High School, Wasilla, Alaska

Louann Bohman, Wilbur Cross High School, New Haven, Connecticut

Rose Mary Bolden, J. F. Kimball High School, Dallas, Texas

Angela Boyd, Andrews High School, Andrews, Texas

Judith H. Briant, Armwood High School, Seffner, Florida

Hugh Delle Broadway, McCullough High School, The Woodlands, Texas

Stephan P. Clarke, Spencerport High School, Spencerport, New York

Dr. Shawn Eric DeNight, Miami Edison Senior High School, Miami, Florida

JoAnna R. Exacoustas, La Serna High School, Whittier, California

Linda Ferguson, English Department Head, Tyee High School, Seattle, Washington

Ellen Geisler, Mentor Senior High School, Mentor, Ohio

Ricardo Godoy, English Department Chairman, Moody High School, Corpus Christi, Texas

Robert Henderson, West Muskingum High School, Zanesville, Ohio

Martha Watt Hosenfeld, English Department Chairperson, Churchville-Chili High School, Churchville, New York

Janice M. Johnson, Assistant Principal, Union High School, Grand Rapids, Michigan

Eileen S. Jones, English Department Chair, Spanish River Community High School, Boca Raton, Florida

Paula S. L'Homme, West Orange High School, Winter Garden, Florida

Bonnie J. Mansell, Downey Adult School, Downey, California

Ruth McClain, Paint Valley High School, Bainbridge, Ohio

Rebecca Miller, Taft High School, San Antonio, Texas

Deborah Lynn Moeller, Western High School, Fort Lauderdale High School

Bobbi Darrell Montgomery, Batavia High School, Batavia, Ohio

Wanza Murray, Vero Beach High School, Vero Beach, Florida

Marjorie M. Nolan, Language Arts Department Head, William M. Raines Sr. High School, Jacksonville, Florida

Julia Pferdehirt, free-lance writer, former Special Education teacher, Middleton, Wisconsin

Pauline Sahakian, English Department Chairperson, San Marcos High School, San Marcos, Texas

Jacqueline Y. Schmidt, Department Chairperson and Coordinator of English, San Marcos High School, San Marcos, Texas

John Sferro, Butler High School, Vandalia, Ohio

Faye S. Spangler, Versailles High School, Versailles, Ohio

Milinda Schwab, Judson High School, Converse, Texas

Rita Stecich, Evergreen Park Community High School, Evergreen Park, Illinois

GayleAnn Turnage, Abeline High School, Abeline, Texas

Ruth Vukovich, Hubbard High School, Hubbard, Ohio

Charlotte Washington, Westwood Middle School, Grand Rapids, Michigan

Tom Watson, Westbridge Academy, Grand Rapids, Michigan